The Watchtower

Announcing Jehovah's Kingdom

January 1, 1987

PROCLAIM LIBERTY!

January 1, 1987
Vol. 108, No. 1

The Watchtower®

Announcing Jehovah's Kingdom

THE PURPOSE OF "THE WATCHTOWER" is
to exalt Jehovah God as the Sovereign of the
universe. It keeps watch on world events as
they fulfill Bible prophecy. It comforts all peoples with the good news that God's Kingdom
will soon destroy those who oppress their
fellowmen and that it will turn the earth into a
paradise. It encourages faith in the now-
reigning King, Jesus Christ, whose shed blood
opens the way for mankind to gain eternal life.
"The Watchtower," published by Jehovah's
Witnesses continuously since 1879, is nonpolitical. It adheres to the Bible as its authority.

"WATCHTOWER" STUDIES FOR THE WEEKS

February 8: Jehovah's Jubilee—Time for Us to
Rejoice. Page 18. Songs to Be Used: 105, 205.

February 15: The Christian Jubilee Climaxes in the
Millennium. Page 23. Songs to Be Used: 7, 142.

Average Printing Each Issue: 12,315,000

Now Published in 103 Languages

SEMIMONTHLY LANGUAGES AVAILABLE BY MAIL
Afrikaans, Arabic, Cebuano, Chichewa, Chinese, Cibemba,
Danish,* Dutch,* Efik, English,* Finnish, French,* German,*
Greek,* Hiligaynon, Igbo, Iloko, Italian,* Japanese,* Korean,*
Lingala, Malagasy, Maltese, Norwegian, Portuguese,* Russian,
Sepedi, Sesotho, Shona, Spanish,* Swahili, Swedish, Tagalog,
Thai, Tsonga, Tswana, Xhosa, Yoruba, Zulu

MONTHLY LANGUAGES AVAILABLE BY MAIL
Armenian, Bengali, Bicol, Bulgarian, Croatian, Czech, Ewe, Fijian,
Ga, Greenlandic, Gujarati, Gun, Hausa, Hebrew, Hindi, Hiri Motu,
Hungarian, Icelandic, Kannada, Malayalam, Marathi, New Guinea
Pidgin, Pangasinan, Papiamento, Polish, Rarotongan, Romanian,
Samar-Leyte, Samoan, Sango, Serbian, Silozi, Sinhalese, Slo-
venian, Solomon Islands-Pidgin, Tahitian, Tamil, Telugu, Tongan,
Tshiluba, Turkish, Twi, Ukrainian, Urdu, Venda, Vietnamese
* Study articles also available in large-print edition.

	Yearly subscription for the above:	
	Semimonthly	Monthly
Watch Tower Society offices	Languages	Languages
America, U.S., Watchtower, Wallkill, N.Y. 12589	$4.00	$2.00
Australia, Box 280, Ingleburn, N.S.W. 2565	A$7.00	A$3.50
Canada, Box 4100, Halton Hills, Ontario L7G 4Y4	$5.20	$2.60
England, The Ridgeway, London NW7 1RN	£5.00	£2.50
Ireland, 29A Jamestown Road, Finglas, Dublin 11	IR£6.00	IR£3.00
New Zealand, P.O. Box 142, Manurewa	NZ$15.00	NZ$7.50
Nigeria, PMB 001, Shomolu, Lagos State	₦7.50	₦3.80
Philippines, P.O. Box 2044, Manila 2800	₱50.00	₱25.00
South Africa, Private Bag 2067, Krugersdorp, 1740	R6,50	R3,25

Remittances should be sent to the office in your country or to
Watchtower, Wallkill, N.Y. 12589, U.S.A.

Changes of address should reach us 30 days before your
moving date. Give us your old and new address (if possible,
your old address label).

20 cents (U.S.) a copy

The Bible translation used is the "New World Translation of the
Holy Scriptures," unless otherwise indicated.

The Watchtower (ISSN 0043-1087) is published semimonthly
for $4.00 (U.S.) per year by Watch Tower Bible and Tract Society
of Pennsylvania, 25 Columbia Heights, Brooklyn, N.Y. 11201.
Second-class postage paid at Brooklyn, N.Y., and at additional
mailing offices.

Postmaster: Send address changes to Watchtower,
Wallkill, N.Y. 12589.

Published by
**Watch Tower Bible and Tract Society
of Pennsylvania**
25 Columbia Heights, Brooklyn, N.Y. 11201, U.S.A.
Frederick W. Franz, President

PROCLAIM LIBERTY!

THE FIVE BILLIONTH person on earth is said to have been born on July 7, 1986. What kind of future must this five billionth human, and indeed all humans, face? Is there any possibility that billions of mankind may someday enjoy true liberty? Confidently, we say yes. But what are we to understand by "liberty"? Does it mean license to do anything that one pleases? No, for as the 19th-century English novelist Charles Kingsley wrote: "There are two freedoms, the false where one is free to do what he likes, and the true where he is free to do what he ought."

Man will gain true liberty only by doing "what he ought." And what ought he to do? When Jesus was here on earth, he stated simply that there are two great commandments —the first, to love God with all one's heart, soul, mind, and strength, and the second, to love one's neighbor as oneself. (Mark 12:29-31) Real liberty is to be attained only by those who in truth demonstrate such genuine love—love of God and of fellow humans.—John 8:31, 32.

Does the world today display that kind of love? Sadly, no. Without love, the false kind of liberty prevails. It breathes a selfish, independent spirit. It insists on 'doing its own thing,' with no regard for God or neighbor. This spirit extends beyond the individual to communities, races, and nations. While the me-first attitude persists, the foundation for any liberty, any peace, any happiness on this earth, must be a shaky one. Remember, Jesus said, "You must love your neighbor *as yourself*." Such neighbor love is essential to the enjoyment of true liberty.

The United Nations organization was formed to liberate mankind by replacing the scourge of war with "peace and security." On its 40th anniversary, the UN proclaimed 1986 to be the International Year of Peace. But has this amounted to a proclamation of liberty with sure guarantees of peace? Have the appalling expenditures on armaments (amounting now to more than $1,000 billion a year) been curtailed? Have terrorism and car bombings decreased? Have the religion-based slaughters in Northern Ireland, the Middle East, and Asia abated? Religious leaders are getting into politics and talking much about peace. But the dove of true peace appears to have flown far out of reach of the UN and the world's religions.

Is there any group today that has renounced the violent, me-first ways of the world? Yes, there is! The foretold "Prince of Peace," Jesus Christ, has gathered lovers of peace 'out of all tribes, tongues, peoples, and nations.' (Isaiah 2: 3, 4; 9:6, 7; Revelation 5:9; 7:9) They rejoice that God's Kingdom by Christ is about to wipe out all wickedness and bring in an earth-wide paradise of peace, where true liberty will prevail. This group is known as Jehovah's Witnesses. (Daniel 2: 31-35, 44; Isaiah 43:10, 12; 65:17-25) Unitedly, these Christians share in a jubilant proclamation foreshadowed by features of the Jubilee arrangement in ancient Israel. In each of 200 and more lands around the globe, they joyfully obey God's command: "Proclaim liberty in the land to all its inhabitants." (Leviticus 25:10) Have you heard and heeded that jubilant shout?

JUBILATION
Among God's People

THE words of King David, recorded at Psalm 68, verses 2-4, include a warm invitation to all lovers of true liberty: "Sing you to God, make melody to his name; raise up a song to the One riding through the desert plains as Jah, which is his name; and jubilate before him." What greater privilege could there be than to jubilate before our God? (Isaiah 12:2, 3) Throughout the year 1986, Jehovah has sustained his witnesses marvelously as they have continued to proclaim liberty to the peoples of earth.

The following pages give a summary of the worldwide activity of Jehovah's Witnesses during 1986. What reason for jubilation! As the figures show, the peak number of active Witnesses in the 208 lands reporting has risen to 3,229,022, a 6.8-percent increase during the year. The number baptized was 225,868.

Memorializing Jesus' Death

Attendance at the principal meeting of the year, the Memorial of Jesus' death, rose to at least 8,160,597, though some reports were not received because of worsening world conditions. The number partaking of the Memorial emblems fell to 8,927 as older anointed ones completed their earthly service.—Revelation 2:10.

Many of those who assembled in obedience to Jesus' command showed exemplary courage. (1 Corinthians 11:23-26; John 16:33) In an African land where Jehovah's work is banned, the congregation had gathered at a sister's home to celebrate the Memorial. Just eight minutes into the talk, local authorities showed up to arrest the brothers. They ordered them to stop the meeting. The brothers kindly but firmly insisted that they must honor this Memorial to Jesus' sacrificial death. After reasoning and pleading with the police, they were allowed to continue in the hearing of the officers. The meeting was concluded in peace, and all were then arrested. After a period of interrogation, five were detained. They remained in prison for a time but were then released, happy that they had been able to observe the Lord's Evening Meal!—1 John 5:3, 4.

Nigeria, where the number of Witnesses has increased to 128,461, had a Memorial attendance of 394,370—the highest ever. One Memorial meeting was held at the construction site of the new Bethel complex at Igieduma, and over 700—almost the entire local village—were there!

From Mexico comes the report: "Everywhere we go in the country, the publishers are just bubbling over with enthusiasm, and the whole country seems to be on fire with the truth. The truth envelops the brothers, and their lives revolve around the truth. Whole families are coming into the truth. A good percentage of the people that study start to attend meetings at the same time. This helps them to make rapid progress." Mexico reported a Memorial attendance of 838,467. In August the 198,003 Kingdom publishers in that land were conducting 327,664 Bible studies in the homes of the people. What a potential they have for continued increase!

Further Global Expansion

From the heart of Christendom come similar reports of expansion. Italy reached a new peak of 139,570 publishers in August, and 301,009 were present for the celebration of the Lord's Evening Meal. Jehovah's Witnesses are indeed 'letting their light shine before men.' (Matthew 5:16) For example: "A sister was putting money into a ticket machine on a bus when an acquaintance told her that there was no need to pay for a ticket as the ride was so short. The sister explained that it was right to pay the ticket, even for just one stop. After that, her friend got off the bus. At that, the bus driver turned to her and said: 'Are you one of Jehovah's Witnesses?' 'Yes,' replied the sister, 'what made you ask?' 'I heard your conversation about paying the bus ticket, and I know that Jehovah's Witnesses are among the very few people who do so and are honest in all things.' A few months later, a man approached the sister at a meeting and said, 'Do you know me? I'm the bus driver who talked to you about paying for the ticket. Observing your conduct, I decided to begin studying the Bible with Jehovah's Witnesses.'"

Britain had a peak of 107,767 Kingdom publishers, including this newly baptized brother: "George is now 84 years of age. After 50 years as a lay preacher in the local church, he came to a knowledge of the truth. Initially, when he would finish his home Bible study, he would hasten into another room to smoke a cigarette. He had been a regular smoker for 70 years. But after studying chapter 26 of the book *You Can Live Forever in Paradise on Earth,* he has never smoked again. George has now been baptized for over a year and is very zealous in field service, telling others of the blessings Jehovah will bring in His new system of things."

The Federal Republic of Germany reports a peak of 118,645 publishers. There are also thousands of faithful Witnesses 'letting their light shine' in the neighboring German Democratic Republic. In Germany faithful oldsters refuse to lay down "the sword of the spirit." (Ephesians 6: 16, 17) A congregation reports: "We have a sister who is 103 years old and still lives alone. The elders arranged for a group of seven to eight sisters to take turns in caring for her each week. They have been doing this now for the past three to four years. Social workers, who are paid by the community, come to care for the bathing and changing. But when they are ill or on vacation, our sisters take over the work. This evidence of Christian love and sacrifice has served as a good witness to outsiders. Our 103-year-old sister is mentally alert and considers the social workers to be her 'territory.' She preaches zealously to them while they are bathing her and gives them literature." Truly, "grayheadedness is a crown of beauty when it is found in the way of righteousness." —Proverbs 16:31.

However, the invitation to praise Jehovah goes out to people of all ages—"you young men and also you virgins, you old men together with boys." Many young people are 'remembering their Grand Creator in the days of their young manhood.' (Psalm 148:12; Ecclesiastes 12:1) In Brazil, where there was a splendid new peak of 196,948 publishers, the Watch Tower Society received a letter from an out-of-the-way town where two young brothers witnessed for some months. It read in part: "I would like to commend you for the fine young people you have in your religion. I am a schoolteacher and deal with youth, and I know they are not what they used to be. Your youths are really an example. They respect their elders, are polite and modestly dressed. And how they know their Bibles! That truly is religion! It's a pity they have to leave."

Families of our brothers are now moving permanently into some of these isolated areas to take care of the interest.

What progress is the truth making in non-Christian areas? *The Wall Street Journal* of July 9, 1986, published a lengthy article under the headline *"Barren Ground*—Christian Missionaries Sow the Seed in Japan But Find Little Grows." A missionary of the United Church of Christ was reported as saying, "There is no way that Christianity will ever really take root in Japan," and a Franciscan priest as stating, "The day of the foreign missionary in Japan is finished." Both had labored in vain for more than 30 years. The article said: "Less than 1% of the population is Christian, and despite all the missionary work, the percentage is dropping." So much for Christendom's religions! But what of Jehovah's Witnesses, who teach the pure Christianity in that land? For the past 92 months in a row, they have increased their number of active ministers to a peak of 113,062 (including an average of 46,390 pioneers each month). In Japan 146,316 home Bible studies are being conducted with newly interested people. This is surely a harbinger of further grand increase. Here, we see a living fulfillment of Isaiah 65:13, 14.

The Field of Pioneering

What about the hub of all this dynamic activity—the United States of America? There, 744,919 Kingdom publishers were in the field as a peak. But are such 'home missionaries' really needed? Truly they are, as crime, drugs, immorality, disease, and corruption escalate to a far worse degree than in most so-called pagan lands. People who desire better things need comfort and hope, and Jehovah's Witnesses have such a message. (Isaiah 61:1, 2; Matthew 24:14) In the United States, during 1986, these ministers devoted 146,673,490 hours to declaring the good news of the Kingdom. That amounts to a 12.6-percent increase, or 16,449,229 more hours than last year. That time was profitably spent, as 6,138,938 books were distributed, which is a 23.2-percent improvement over the last year. In April alone, the total was over 1,000,000 books explaining the true hope for peace and security.

One of the most exciting features of the United States report is the expansion of pioneer service. In April there was a peak of 45,786 regular pioneers, an increase of 23 percent over last year. When you combine that figure with the average of 43,369 auxiliary pioneers and the average of 279 special pioneers, it means that each month nearly 90,000 were declaring abroad the Kingdom of God in the pioneer work. These are young people and older folk, too, who are wisely making use of their time in praising Jehovah.

Giving a Thorough Witness

In teaching publicly and from house to house, the apostle Paul "thoroughly bore witness" to the good news. (Acts 20: 20, 21) A similar witness is being given in many territories today. For example, this report comes from Guadeloupe: "By the end of the service year, we had one publisher for 72 people. Needless to say, we

In Our Next Issue

■ **The Social Gospel—What Has It Accomplished?**

■ **So Great a Cloud of Witnesses!**

■ **Earthquakes —Distress Upon Distress**

are more than well known throughout the country! In fact, in many places, we go into the same territory each week. Some could say that certainly people are tired of seeing us, or that it is a source of discouragement to be in the same territory week after week. But on the contrary, the more we work the territory, the more interest is aroused. And the proof? Well, it is the peak last April of 7,136 home Bible studies conducted by our 4,558 publishers! Recently a magazine carried a headline: 'Jehovah's Witnesses—Kings From Door to Door'! We consider that an honor. During the service year, 458 new brothers and sisters were baptized." Steadfastness and joy displayed in working our territory over and over, getting to know and befriend the people, lovingly breaking down their prejudices—this can lead to finding many sheeplike ones.

Jehovah is richly blessing his servants in an African country where the work is banned and civil war rages. In that land many of our brothers suffer in prisons, and some youthful Witnesses have been executed. Yet, April had an outstanding report, with ten all-time peaks. The new publisher figure is an increase of 29 percent over last year. What zeal these dear brothers manifest! Average hours in April were over 18 per publisher, and home Bible studies were 2.6 per publisher.

A cryptic message received by the branch office caring for this territory is sufficient to convey some idea of existing conditions. It reads: "The heat continues to beat down on us. The effort required to move around and see someone is proof we are having a heat wave. But we know we are made in such a way as to adapt to any temperature and any environment. In spite of everything, we persevere and trust we will survive." Such integrity!

Individual integrity keepers make an integrity-keeping organization. The global organization of 3,229,022 witnesses of Jehovah is just that! They look forward to surviving the coming "great tribulation" and to sharing, under Christ's Kingdom, in the grand work of transforming earth into a paradise. (Revelation 7:14; 21:3, 4; Isaiah 65:17, 21-23, 25) They are jubilant about the way Jehovah is even now blessing their zealous activity, whether they are preaching the word "in favorable season" or "in troublesome season." (2 Timothy 4:2) The following pages show how they have obeyed the theme of their 1986 yeartext: "Go . . . , declare abroad the kingdom of God."—Luke 9:60.

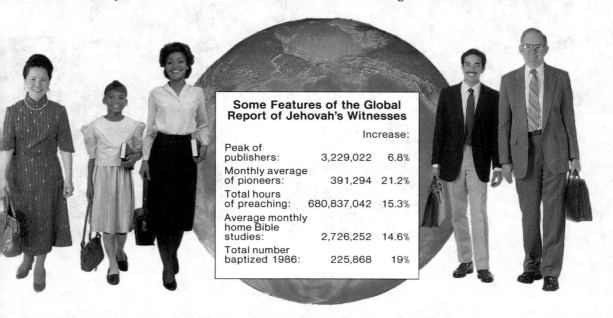

Some Features of the Global Report of Jehovah's Witnesses

		Increase:
Peak of publishers:	3,229,022	6.8%
Monthly average of pioneers:	391,294	21.2%
Total hours of preaching:	680,837,042	15.3%
Average monthly home Bible studies:	2,726,252	14.6%
Total number baptized 1986:	225,868	19%

WITNESSING "PUBLICLY AND FROM HOUSE TO HOUSE"

Davao
Philippines

Venice
Italy

Castle Combe
England

Kowloon
Hong Kong

Gålå
Norway

Taipei
Taiwan

Queenstown
New Zealand

Bolgatanga
Ghana

Paris
France

Quetzaltenango
Guatemala

Kerala
India

Banff
Canada

"TO THE MOST DISTANT PART OF THE EARTH"

1986 SERVICE YEAR REPORT OF JEHOVAH'S WITNESSES WORLDWIDE

Country or Territory	Population	1986 Peak Pubs.	Ratio, One Publisher to:	1986 Av. Pubs.	% Inc. Over 1985	1985 Av. Pubs.	1986 No. Bptzd.	Av. Pio. Pubs.	No. of Congs.	Total Hours	Av. Bible Studies	Memorial Attendance
Alaska	529,200	2,018	262	1,868	5	1,777	132	243	26	382,729	1,143	4,610
Algeria	22,000,000	43	511,628	37	9	34	2		3	2,217	38	84
American Samoa	35,600	88	405	77	-4*	80	12	10	1	18,386	98	340
Andorra	44,596	108	413	98	14	86	3	5	1	14,620	59	239
Anguilla	6,524	18	362	16		16		2	1	4,312	9	52
Antigua	70,794	225	315	212	7	198	21	28	4	49,072	222	656
Argentina	30,000,000	61,373	489	59,348	11	53,395	5,587	7,823	877	14,151,278	75,111	149,905
Aruba	66,200	369	179	345	15	300	43	36	5	75,666	355	1,063
Australia	15,851,800	44,362	357	42,998	4	41,299	2,206	4,550	599	8,776,738	21,530	83,976
Austria	7,557,676	16,515	458	16,185	3	15,738	804	1,233	235	2,938,026	8,157	28,247
Azores	261,300	353	740	331	14	291	17	39	12	75,879	329	1,001
Bahamas	209,505	848	247	791	15	686	109	145	14	231,924	1,314	2,616
Bangladesh	100,000,000	22	4,545,455	19	12	17	3	4	1	6,335	39	98
Barbados	265,000	1,553	171	1,501	6	1,411	99	169	16	304,489	1,621	4,102
Belau	13,000	61	213	46	10	42	4	12	1	16,698	103	210
Belgium	9,788,895	22,202	441	21,343	2	20,838	1,180	1,740	302	3,973,912	9,638	42,960
Belize	145,000	730	199	695	1	690	60	94	17	176,092	916	3,299
Benin	3,792,000	1,758	2,157	1,491	8	1,386	50	64	64	222,954	1,460	8,383
Bermuda	57,000	349	163	330	7	309	30	50	4	80,198	292	745
Bolivia	6,500,000	4,928	1,319	4,467	11	4,017	642	895	86	1,490,388	7,433	21,674
Bonaire	10,340	57	181	49	11	44	4	4	1	9,473	68	178
Botswana	1,224,056	464	2,638	430	10	392	46	56	18	108,028	537	1,656
Brazil	138,403,000	196,948	703	185,126	11	166,925	19,878	17,298	3,055	33,768,325	199,169	533,400
Britain	55,060,000	107,767	511	101,863	5	97,370	6,197	10,835	1,213	20,070,729	52,423	198,693
Brunei	225,000	6	37,500	5	-17*	6	1			351	8	38
Burkina Faso	7,318,695	324	22,589	288	17	247	38	76	14	120,692	619	1,235
Burma	35,000,000	1,447	24,188	1,342	5	1,284	88	226	72	378,186	1,051	4,001
Burundi	4,800,000	572	8,392	457	34	340	115	104	12	156,242	889	1,338
Canada	25,123,600	88,130	285	84,343	5	80,614	4,431	8,881	1,189	16,175,023	42,875	161,820
Cape Verde Islands	310,000	231	1,342	212	10	193	23	27	7	54,667	370	872
Cayman Islands	16,821	67	251	54	-2*	55		6	1	11,569	61	140
Central Afr. Rep.	2,740,000	1,280	2,141	1,170	-6*	1,244	40	143	40	280,610	1,274	2,898
Chad	4,000,000	188	21,277	172	29	133	6	50	9	80,189	353	1,486
Chile	12,271,173	29,340	418	27,585	12	24,691	3,052	3,347	316	6,492,235	42,913	90,290
Colombia	27,867,326	29,235	953	27,587	12	24,669	3,831	3,392	365	6,523,366	41,501	121,358
Congo	1,700,000	1,219	1,395	1,084	5	1,029	39	79	40	218,189	1,542	4,414
Cook Islands	17,000	89	191	79	18	67	11	14		19,124	82	265
Costa Rica	2,579,503	10,012	258	9,433	10	8,578	641	792	178	1,806,195	11,418	25,990
Curaçao	171,088	1,293	132	1,265	12	1,130	116	157	13	305,131	1,890	3,862
Cyprus	600,000	1,112	540	1,096	3	1,068	62	113	15	211,224	526	2,282

Country												
Denmark	5,116,273	15,186	337	14,796	2	14,453	481	1,030	240	2,153,524	5,139	23,956
Djibouti	400,000	8	50,000	5	-44*	9	13	1	1	1,132	7	15
Dominica	81,000	233	348	222	8	205		29	7	56,088	196	994
Dominican Rep.	5,647,977	9,687	583	9,307	8	8,596	718	1,316	143	2,329,616	16,358	35,374
Ecuador	9,100,000	10,527	864	10,013	13	8,846	1,011	1,406	147	2,649,519	17,476	49,967
El Salvador	5,244,000	15,119	347	14,546	7	13,640	1,363	2,115	281	3,859,728	21,444	51,151
Equatorial Guinea	312,120	158	1,975	143	16	123	13	38	4	58,287	352	352
Falkland Islands	1,900	4	475			4			1	127	3	6
Faeroe Islands	45,754	91	503	85	-3*	88	2	19	4	23,502	54	156
Fiji	700,125	1,159	604	1,098	12	981	122	228	24	353,137	1,336	4,360
Finland	4,910,712	16,346	300	15,533	3	15,033	681	1,807	261	2,956,180	7,609	26,022
France	55,282,000	92,397	598	89,785	6	84,925	6,302	7,440	1,261	18,186,752	54,377	183,225
French Guiana	84,177	427	197	400	13	355	34	47	5	103,769	786	1,592
Gabon	1,000,000	539	1,855	499	8	464	33	36	13	103,553	926	1,942
Gambia	700,000	20	35,000	18	6	17	2	6	1	9,552	41	66
Germany, F. R.; W. Berlin	61,020,500	118,645	514	116,152	2	114,188	4,954	7,572	1,609	19,715,174	49,405	199,863
Ghana	12,848,514	32,211	399	28,635	9	26,388	1,522	4,226	523	7,541,196	46,906	122,936
Gibraltar	28,843	129	224	124	13	119	6	9	1	20,478	44	181
Greece	9,740,417	23,162	421	22,815	8	22,240	708	2,253	340	4,406,110	8,767	40,391
Greenland	53,406	90	593	85	-6*	90	2	15	7	23,084	63	172
Grenada	112,000	358	313	340	3	331	22	51	7	78,926	383	1,224
Guadeloupe	328,000	4,576	72	4,397	15	3,828	458	283	48	870,264	6,397	12,553
Guam	118,338	254	466	243	8	224	20	56	2	79,197	420	939
Guatemala	7,750,000	8,941	867	8,401	8	7,787	811	828	130	1,812,752	9,765	29,720
Guinea	5,143,284	218	23,593	151	-1*	153	4	31	11	53,947	202	725
Guinea-Bissau	600,000	4	150,000	2	-33*	3			1	222	3	25
Guyana	842,000	1,368	615	1,346	5	1,281	66	249	29	340,685	1,597	4,899
Haiti	6,000,000	4,443	1,350	4,220	8	3,922	699	456	79	1,008,109	7,106	22,530
Hawaii	1,053,900	5,467	193	5,353	5	5,117	322	851	68	1,336,645	4,610	14,659
Honduras	4,385,108	4,436	989	4,161	10	3,799	370	562	73	1,097,086	6,941	20,080
Hong Kong	5,300,000	1,416	3,743	1,360	9	1,248	96	337	16	516,437	2,163	3,070
Iceland	242,089	180	1,345	173	15	151	5	20	3	36,016	122	356
India	800,000,000	7,551	105,946	7,184	1	6,805	556	743	278	1,451,088	4,345	21,018
Ireland	5,099,352	2,520	2,024	2,472	6	2,403	136	472	80	746,339	1,290	5,129
Israel	5,560,000	338	16,450	316	3	303	13	30	6	67,093	252	694
Italy	56,556,911	139,570	405	134,677	9	123,253	11,714	22,138	2,102	37,291,922	95,109	301,009
Ivory Coast	9,273,167	2,340	3,963	2,207	7	2,056	343	396	58	708,591	3,945	8,953
Jamaica	2,300,000	8,104	284	7,620	3	7,375	525	847	170	1,475,270	7,878	24,844
Japan	120,720,542	113,062	1,068	108,702	11	97,823	10,900	46,390	1,809	53,608,147	146,316	263,302
Kenya	20,525,000	3,885	5,283	3,686	8	3,422	406	844	102	1,388,095	5,895	13,067
Kiribati	63,843	13	4,911	12	-20*	15	2	3	1	4,733	34	113
Korea, Republic of	41,569,000	44,291	939	41,751	12	37,263	4,805	14,807	715	17,252,462	49,498	95,738
Kosrae	6,005	26	231	24	4	23		4	1	4,722	41	176
Lebanon	3,000,000	2,344	1,280	2,230	7	2,087	158	192	52	449,982	1,624	4,972
Lesotho	1,577,000	870	1,813	791	6	746	58	95	42	180,573	774	3,597
Liberia	1,800,000	1,405	1,281	1,318	9	1,211	114	250	32	430,532	2,386	7,839
Libya	3,356,000	14	239,714	5	-44*	9		4		541	4	16
Liechtenstein	27,076	46	589	43		43			1	7,184	29	82

Country or Territory	Population	1986 Peak Pubs.	Ratio, One Publisher to:	1986 Av. Pubs.	% Inc. Over 1985	1985 Av. Pubs.	1986 No. Bptzd.	Av. Pio. Pubs.	No. of Congs.	Total Hours	Av. Bible Studies	Memorial Attendance
Luxembourg	431,200	1,284	336	1,246	6	1,178	41	104	21	242,777	858	2,818
Macao	400,000	22	18,182	19	19	16		6	1	10,594	36	63
Madagascar	10,063,435	2,265	4,443	2,146	14	1,884	226	234	36	502,124	4,434	10,952
Madeira	266,800	506	527	483	6	456	47	35	11	87,409	457	1,375
Malaysia	15,880,000	824	19,272	790	9	725	53	129	19	235,722	1,297	2,026
Mali	7,000,000	55	127,273	50	4	48	1	28	1	43,773	221	296
Malta	380,000	320	1,188	297	8	276	27	32	4	66,277	213	574
Marshall Islands	31,042	178	174	150	-4*	156	3	45	2	48,240	371	997
Martinique	328,566	2,117	155	2,005	14	1,757	205	235	24	472,628	2,606	5,696
Mauritius	998,471	780	1,280	759	8	706	48	80	9	166,786	794	1,854
Mayotte	67,167	20	3,358	18	13	16	2	7		11,016	48	56
Mexico	79,754,346	198,003	403	186,291	15	162,130	22,054	26,859	5,878	47,468,565	300,473	838,467
Montserrat	13,076	35	374	32	45	22	1	3	1	5,289	20	128
Morocco	22,500,000	81	277,778	71	-15*	84	3	9	3	18,373	51	163
Nauru	6,000	8	750	6	20	5	1	1		451	5	27
Nepal	16,000,000	41	390,244	39	11	35		4	1	8,068	30	119
Netherlands	14,529,430	29,507	492	28,367	2	27,745	1,102	2,230	310	4,644,903	8,947	48,039
Nevis	15,482	39	397	36	6	34		7	1	12,530	64	134
New Caledonia	155,000	889	174	789	16	683	107	88	8	189,034	954	2,145
New Zealand	3,307,084	9,546	346	9,165	6	8,621	651	1,018	136	1,836,709	5,633	19,933
Niger	6,083,000	81	75,099	71	-1*	72	7	16	5	32,388	108	297
Nigeria	102,900,000	128,461	801	121,670	6	115,074	4,828	12,712	2,391	25,585,712	132,220	394,370
Niue	2,500	18	139	15	7	14		2	1	2,361	17	82
Norway	4,167,163	8,189	509	7,929	3	7,684	390	462	172	1,064,444	2,826	14,960
Pakistan	97,000,000	252	384,921	231	3	225	23	43	6	71,186	340	733
Panama	2,227,254	4,811	463	4,480	6	4,207	384	527	96	1,019,007	6,980	17,466
Papua New Guinea	3,006,799	1,827	1,646	1,732	5	1,644	125	185	88	388,459	2,121	8,684
Paraguay	3,366,467	2,401	1,402	2,251	8	2,092	157	358	35	556,734	2,644	5,696
Peru	20,000,000	23,021	869	21,471	9	19,638	2,580	4,380	432	7,015,335	34,296	95,062
Philippines	56,000,000	95,746	585	88,174	12	78,867	9,070	16,919	2,540	22,963,383	64,641	274,565
Ponape	28,000	74	378	62	-10*	69	2	24	1	28,275	156	505
Portugal	9,654,000	30,505	316	29,617	7	27,751	2,124	2,296	425	5,003,720	21,842	76,212
Puerto Rico	3,350,000	21,943	153	21,231	7	19,891	1,681	1,988	258	4,181,925	17,959	57,328
Réunion	550,500	1,172	470	1,093	17	938	141	117	14	268,572	1,101	3,062
Rodrigues	35,284	25	1,411	23	15	20	1	4	1	8,727	41	77
Rota	1,274	8	159	7	-30*	10	1	4		4,925	22	49
Rwanda	6,125,000	483	12,681	435	3	424	48	56	14	142,691	798	1,102
Saba	972	4	243	4	New			4		3,146	20	22
St. Eustatius	1,335	6	223	6	200	2	2	1		759	4	34
St. Helena	6,000	107	56	97		97		4	2	12,241	42	240
St. Kitts	36,538	150	244	142	8	132	18	20	2	35,566	185	370
St. Lucia	120,000	314	382	302	6	285	16	46	5	71,062	349	1,179
St. Maarten	15,926	89	179	80	3	78	1	7	1	14,516	74	343
St. Pierre & Miquelon	6,041	10	604	9	-25*	12		1	1	971	3	17

Country												
St. Vincent	110,000	161	683	152	17	130	14	20	4	38,672	149	436
Saipan	20,350	39	522	32	14	28	7	14	1	20,035	109	173
San Marino	21,240	87	244	86	1	85		8	1	19,403	49	188
São Tomé	100,000	15	6,667	13	44	9	4		1	3,008	57	79
Senegal	6,600,000	476	13,866	451	7	423	35	103	10	185,468	840	1,166
Seychelles	70,000	62	1,129	57	24	46	4	5	1	14,665	82	188
Sierra Leone	3,517,530	682	5,158	635		637	29	131	29	209,446	957	3,266
Solomon Islands	271,259	681	398	649	5	619	34	85	30	149,808	631	3,160
South Africa	32,435,207	40,800	795	38,291	8	35,326	3,045	4,761	972	8,984,082	37,641	101,797
South-West Africa	1,033,196	428	2,414	368	12	328	27	40	11	84,758	385	1,069
Spain	38,818,355	65,680	591	63,453	7	59,514	4,801	8,132	938	14,943,952	44,191	142,751
Sri Lanka	15,900,000	996	15,964	924	10	842	91	165	28	287,729	1,148	3,473
Sudan	23,000,000	256	89,844	240	26	191	47	56	4	99,420	732	763
Suriname	350,000	1,236	283	1,167	10	1,063	87	154	19	275,324	1,362	3,888
Swaziland	669,734	960	698	860	13	761	77	190	44	318,700	1,152	2,499
Sweden	8,368,954	20,877	401	20,350	4	19,612	932	2,319	323	3,825,743	10,230	35,416
Switzerland	6,484,800	13,659	475	13,373	5	12,785	773	801	250	2,332,171	8,057	25,616
Tahiti	176,516	720	245	683	15	596	92	75	10	165,114	985	1,977
Taiwan	19,500,000	1,199	16,264	1,121	7	1,050	116	258	21	376,037	1,369	3,343
Tanzania	21,700,000	2,500	8,680	2,425		2,420	134	385	83	686,333	2,196	6,966
Thailand	52,800,000	914	57,768	883	5	841	83	166	29	257,328	874	2,128
Togo	2,948,753	3,024	975	2,822	12	2,517		248	64	598,545	5,275	8,825
Tokelau Islands	1,703	6	284	4	33	3			1	348	2	36
Tonga	98,540	53	1,859	39	11	35	5	9	2	14,929	55	171
Trinidad	1,162,458	4,558	255	4,335	10	3,948	364	753	50	1,120,992	5,881	13,961
Truk	38,650	41	943	36	-5*	38		13	2	19,778	144	400
Tunisia	7,300,000	60	121,667	45	7	42		2	1	4,952	20	86
Turkey	50,000,000	830	60,241	795	4	768	35	57	10	153,214	503	1,393
Turks & Caicos Isls.	8,000	38	211	33	10	30	8	7	1	13,518	83	131
Tuvalu	8,582	26	330	23		23	1	5	1	4,815	32	69
Uganda	15,500,000	328	47,256	310	4	297	37	64	11	109,593	729	1,402
U.S. of America	237,166,000	744,919	318	710,344	5	678,510	41,697	88,312	8,336	146,673,490	486,426	1,691,297
Uruguay	2,921,000	5,862	498	5,596	11	5,033	654	797	92	1,355,961	3,104	16,828
Vanuatu	140,000	90	1,556	84	20	70	3	12	2	24,364	191	583
Venezuela	18,500,000	35,248	525	31,691	15	27,528	4,008	4,884	307	8,920,847	52,451	128,627
Virgin Isls. (Brit.)	12,000	96	125	90	5	86	5	9	3	19,777	144	399
Virgin Isls. (U.S.)	96,000	488	197	464	2	454	12	50	8	94,507	487	1,748
Wallis & Futuna Isls.	14,000	2	7,000	2	New			1		228		
Western Samoa	165,000	166	994	148		148	15	26	3	43,551	139	436
Yap	9,320	36	259	27	-27*	37	1	8	1	10,047	65	154
Zaire	32,000,000	38,572	830	35,680	4	34,207	3,191	6,883	1,034	10,638,058	58,552	93,581
Zambia	6,776,232	64,881	104	57,624	5	55,007	4,834	5,384	1,622	11,078,133	76,530	329,766
Zimbabwe	8,241,545	15,790	522	14,557	10	13,236	963	1,372	512	2,878,422	12,633	41,334
175 Countries		2,955,641		2,808,141	7.1	2,621,260	212,629	381,368	47,449	648,232,167	2,552,797	7,674,412
# 33 Other Countries		273,381		255,148	4.6	243,923	13,239	9,926	4,728	32,604,875	173,455	486,185
GRAND TOTAL (208 countries)		3,229,022		3,063,289	6.9	2,865,183	225,868	391,294	52,177	680,837,042	2,726,252	8,160,597

During the 1986 service year the Watch Tower Society spent $23,545,801.70 in caring for special pioneers, missionaries, and traveling overseers in their field service assignments.

MEMORIAL PARTAKERS WORLDWIDE: 8,927
* Percentage of decrease
# Work banned and reports are incomplete

"THEY WILL BE CERTAIN TO FIGHT AGAINST YOU,

THE Sovereign Lord Jehovah told youthful Jeremiah that He would make him "a fortified city and an iron pillar and copper walls" against any who might seek his destruction. In modern times, we as Jehovah's Witnesses have like assurance from our God. Yes, under Satan's influence, 'they will be certain to fight against us,' but they will not prevail. "For 'I am with you,' is the utterance of Jehovah, 'to deliver you.'"—Jeremiah 1:18, 19.

In outlying villages of the Solomon Islands, strangers enter at the risk of their lives, especially if they bring a new religion. That was the experience of two special pioneers of Jehovah's Witnesses. Fierce-looking villagers trained bows and arrows on them. They had orders to shoot! As the situation became tense, an old man suddenly intervened, saying: "These are my visitors. Don't harm them." To the dismay of the villagers, he led them to his home. This man had heard of the Witnesses; now he obtained the book *You Can Live Forever in Paradise on Earth,* and a Bible study was started. He immediately began to travel to the meetings. Today the brothers can witness freely in that area, thankful for Jehovah's initial deliverance.

Deliverance has often come through being identified as one of Jehovah's Witnesses. Because of the house-to-house preaching, people get to know who the Witnesses are and what their position is on issues of the day. In a small village in Peru, terrorists accused the villagers of having betrayed them. They rounded up the men of the town and put them in a line to be shot. (In similar situations entire villages had been wiped out.) But at this point, one of the terrorists recognized a brother and said to the executioners: "That man is not one of them. I know him to be a Jehovah's Witness, and they don't meddle in politics." The brother was released. Certainly, Jehovah protects his own!

The island territory of Cyprus reports that the Greek Orthodox Church has been very active in trying to undermine the work of Jehovah's Witnesses. The church distributes leaflets accusing the Witnesses of many things and discourages its people from having any discussions with the Witnesses. Some theologians have even organized themselves to visit people who have been studying with Jehovah's Witnesses, trying to discourage them. Characteristic is what happened in Paphos, where Paul and Barnabas once overcame similar opposition. (Acts 13:6-12) A priest-theologian tried to convince three different persons to stop examining the Bible with Jehovah's Witnesses. They, in turn and separately from one another, arranged for a brother to join them in a discussion with this theologian. As a result, all three are now actively associated with the Witnesses. The priest commented, 'I will never have another discussion with Jehovah's Witnesses.'

Some priests went so far as to hit the Witnesses while these were doing house-to-house work in one of the villages. Strangely enough, a few days later, a whirlwind struck the village, destroying the roofs of many houses. Some villagers commented: 'This is a punishment from God for what the priests did to Jehovah's Witnesses.' In this village, honesthearted persons are still accepting our brothers at their homes. In one instance, while a brother was presenting the current magazines to an interested person, one of the priests who had hit the brothers happened to pass by and told the brother to leave 'his flock' alone. The interested person said to the priest, 'I am old enough to know what I am doing.' So the clergy do not prevail against Jehovah's Witnesses; their efforts backfire on them, and more people take their stand for Jehovah.

In a war-torn country in Central Africa, a circuit overseer was stopped for a routine check by soldiers. They objected to something in a letter that he was carrying and

BUT THEY WILL NOT PREVAIL AGAINST YOU"

took him to police headquarters, where he was whipped and tortured by three soldiers. Although no charge was made against him and no trial was held, he was put in detention for one year. For six months he was kept in an overcrowded cell with 40 other prisoners. Because of the cramped quarters, they had to take turns sleeping, three hours at a time. The rest of the time, they had to remain standing. While our brother was there, 137 prisoners died, and he was given the work of putting their bodies in sacks for burial.

This circuit overseer kept up his spiritual strength by spending much time witnessing to fellow prisoners. His reports show over 30 hours a month spent in preaching; he conducted four Bible studies while in prison. One of his students even started witnessing to others. Through all his trials, Jehovah cared for this brother, who gives this advice to others: "When in prison, just leave everything in Jehovah's hands. Wait on him. Trust in him. Don't worry too much. Be faithful."

In one area in Zimbabwe, children of Jehovah's Witnesses were expelled from school for not participating in political exercises. Not satisfied with this, local gangs even burned down the homes of the parents and destroyed their crops. Witness families were forced to flee for their lives, leaving behind cattle and other possessions. However, the matter was taken to higher governmental authorities who kindly arranged for the families to return to their homes. Their cattle were restored, and the government has taken steps to reimburse the brothers for their losses. Jehovah's Witnesses truly appreciate it when "superior authorities" thus show themselves to be 'God's ministers for good.' (Romans 13:1-4) Through it all, a fine witness was given, and local people are now showing much interest in the Kingdom message. As one of the brothers put it, 'We know that Jehovah can make such situations work out as a witness to his name.'

The past service year saw Jehovah's blessing on the work in Malawi. It was only in areas where local villagers harbor hatred that the Witnesses experienced harassment. The following report testifies to this: "In many parts of the field, the situation is quiet. But in one congregation, two Witness families were badly molested by the youth leagues. The head of one of these families was so severely beaten that he was unconscious for four hours. Thereafter, he was taken to the police station, where the policeman on duty also continued to beat him and the others that were taken in with him. Later, however, a different policeman came on duty. This one was kind. He released the brothers and sent them back home, and they thanked Jehovah for this unexpected deliverance. It was later found that the cause of this incident was personal hatred by close relatives. Our Memorial attendance this year was encouraging. We had 23,476. This shows that there are still sheeplike persons who must be helped to become disciples of Jesus Christ here in Malawi."

A country in Eastern Europe sent this message of appreciation: "We are thankful for the close contact we are experiencing with the Governing Body through all the channels of Jehovah's earthly organization. By this we are allowed to see how our heavenly Father is gathering, through his Son and all the angels, his sheep today, and how we may have a small share in it. What a privilege this is! Our Father has blessed our efforts with increase. More time spent in the field, more auxiliary pioneers zealously preaching the good news, and the highest number of bound books ever loaned or placed in the field are the results of this blessing."

The modern-day Jubilee horn has sounded loud and clear. The preceding tabulated report shows how Jehovah's Witnesses in all parts of the earth are answering that call.

Did John Lack Faith?

JOHN the Baptizer, who has been in prison about a year now, receives the report about the resurrection of the widow's son at Nain. But John wants to hear directly from Jesus regarding the significance of this, so he sends two of his disciples to inquire: "Are you the Coming One or are we to expect a different one?"

That may seem a strange question, especially since John saw God's spirit descend upon Jesus and heard God's voice of approval when baptizing him nearly two years before. John's question may cause some to conclude that his faith has grown weak. But this is not so. Jesus would not speak so highly of John, which he does on this occasion, if John has begun to doubt. Why, then, does John ask this question?

John may simply want a verification from Jesus that He is the Messiah. This would be very strengthening to John as he languishes in prison. But apparently there is more to John's question than that. He evidently wants to know if there is to be another one coming, a successor, as it were, who will complete the fulfillment of all the things that were foretold to be accomplished by the Messiah.

According to Bible prophecies with which John is acquainted, God's anointed One is to be a king, a deliverer. Yet John is still being held prisoner, even many months after Jesus was baptized. So John evidently is asking Jesus: 'Are you the one to establish the Kingdom of God in outward power, or is there a different one, a successor, for whom we should wait to fulfill all the prophecies relating to the Messiah's glory?'

Instead of telling John's disciples, 'Of course I am the one who was to come!' Jesus in that very hour puts on a remarkable display by healing many people of all kinds of diseases and ailments. Then he tells the disciples: "Go your way, report to John what you saw and heard: the blind are receiving sight, the lame are walking, the lepers are being cleansed and the deaf are hearing, the dead are being raised up, the poor are being told the good news. And happy is he who has not stumbled over me."

In other words, since John's question may imply an expectation of Jesus' doing more than he is doing, such as freeing John himself, Jesus is telling John not to expect more than all of this.

When John's disciples leave, Jesus turns to the crowds and tells them that John is the "messenger" of Jehovah foretold in Malachi 3:1 and is also the prophet Elijah foretold in Malachi 4:5, 6. He thus extols John as being the equal of any prophet who lived before him, explaining:

"Truly I say to you people, Among those born of women there has not been raised up a greater than John the Baptist; but a person that is a lesser one in the kingdom of the heavens is greater than he is. But from the days of John the Baptist until now the kingdom of the heavens is the goal toward which

men press, and those pressing forward are seizing it."

Jesus is here showing that John will not be in the heavenly Kingdom, since a lesser one there is greater than John. John prepared the way for Jesus, but his death occurs before Christ sealed the covenant, or agreement, with his disciples to be corulers with him in his Kingdom. That is why Jesus says that John will not be in the heavenly Kingdom. John will instead be an earthly subject of God's Kingdom.

Luke 7:18-30; Matthew 11:2-15.

♦ Why does John ask whether Jesus is the Coming One or whether a different one should be expected?

♦ What prophecies does Jesus say that John fulfilled?

♦ Why will John the Baptizer not be in heaven with Jesus?

Jehovah's Jubilee
—*Time for Us to Rejoice*

"And you must sanctify the fiftieth year and proclaim liberty in the land to all its inhabitants. It will become a Jubilee for you . . . It should become something holy to you . . . Then you will certainly dwell on the land in security."
—LEVITICUS 25:10-12, 18.

WHEREVER you live, you may have heard of the famous Liberty Bell, located in Philadelphia, Pennsylvania, U.S.A. *The World Book Encyclopedia* says that this bell "was rung July 8, 1776, with other church bells, to announce the adoption of the Declaration of Independence. Its inscription, 'Proclaim Liberty throughout all the land unto all the inhabitants thereof,' is from the Bible (Leviticus 25:10)."

² Liberty continues to have great appeal, does it not? Likely you would rejoice at the prospect of genuine liberty—from false concepts, from political pressure or oppression, from the debilitating effects of old age and sickness, resulting in death. If so, there is good reason for you to rejoice, and there will be greater reason soon. 'How can that be so?' you may ask, since no government has yet provided full freedom, and neither scientists nor doctors can prevent aging, sickness, and eventual death. But, we repeat, there *is* a basis for you to rejoice over true liberty. To understand how, consider important background information that can involve you —now and in the future.

³ The above-cited passage uses the word "Jubilee." The Jubilee was a yearlong Sabbath-keeping period for the land of

---

1. What inscription appears on the Liberty Bell, and from where are the words taken?
2. How do you feel about the prospect of liberty, but what problems may come up about it?

3. What was the Jubilee, and what happened during that year?

"The path of the righteous ones is like the bright light that is getting lighter and lighter until the day is firmly established." (Proverbs 4:18) In line with that principle, this article and the following one present an updated and amplified explanation of the Jubilee.

Israel. It followed a series of seven agricultural Sabbath years that altogether covered 49 years. The 50th year, the Jubilee, was the culmination of this series of Sabbath observances for the land that Jehovah had given his people, fulfilling the promise made to their forefather Abraham, "Jehovah's friend." (James 2:23; Isaiah 41:8) On the occasion of the Jubilee, liberty was proclaimed throughout the land. This meant freedom for all Israelites who had sold themselves into servitude because of debt. Another feature of the Jubilee was that all hereditary land possessions that had been sold (likely because of financial reverses) were returned.—Leviticus 25:1-54.

⁴ With that background, you can appreciate why the Jubilee was a festive year of liberty. It was announced by sounding a horn on the Day of Atonement.* As Moses wrote in Leviticus 25:9, 10: "You must cause the horn of loud tone to sound in the seventh month on the tenth of the month; on the day of atonement you people should cause the horn to sound in all your land. And you must sanctify the fiftieth year and proclaim liberty in the land to all its inhabitants. It will become a Jubilee for you, and you must return each one to his possession and you should return each one to his family." In 1473 B.C.E., Joshua led the Israelites across the Jordan River into the Promised Land, where they were to observe the Jubilee.

An Initial Freedom Proclaimed

⁵ The foregoing might seem to be ancient history having little bearing on our

---

* The annual Day of Atonement was held on the 10th of Tishri, a month in the Hebrew calendar, corresponding to our September-October period.

---

4. When was the Jubilee announced, and how?
5. What aspects of liberation and Jubilee will we consider?

lives, especially if we are not of Jewish descent. However, Jesus Christ gave us valid reason to expect a grander Jubilee. It is this that constitutes the basis for our rejoicing over liberty, or freedom. In order to appreciate why, we need to see how Jesus in two ways provided for liberation in the first century. Then we will consider how those correspond to two liberations in our lifetime, but liberations on a much grander scale and providing us with much greater reason for rejoicing.

⁶ Though not speaking directly of the ancient Jubilee year, a prophetic reference to a coming type of liberation was made at Isaiah 61:1-7: "The spirit of the Sovereign Lord Jehovah is upon me, for the reason that Jehovah has anointed me to tell good news to the meek ones. He has sent me to bind up the brokenhearted, *to proclaim liberty to those taken captive* and the wide opening of the eyes even to the prisoners; to proclaim the year of goodwill on the part of Jehovah and the day of vengeance on the part of our God; to comfort all the mourning ones . . . Rejoicing to time indefinite is what will come to be theirs." But how and when would that prophecy find fulfillment?

⁷ After the celebration of the Passover in the year 30 C.E., Jesus Christ went into a synagogue on the Sabbath day. He there read part of Isaiah's prophecy and applied it to himself. Luke 4:16-21 says, in part: "He opened the scroll and found the place where it was written: 'Jehovah's spirit is upon me, because he anointed me to declare good news to the poor, he sent me forth to preach a release to the captives and a recovery of sight to the blind, to send the crushed ones away with a release, to preach Jehovah's acceptable year' . . .

6, 7. (a) Isaiah 61:1-7 foretold what wonderful developments? (b) How did Jesus indicate that Isaiah's prophecy was being fulfilled?

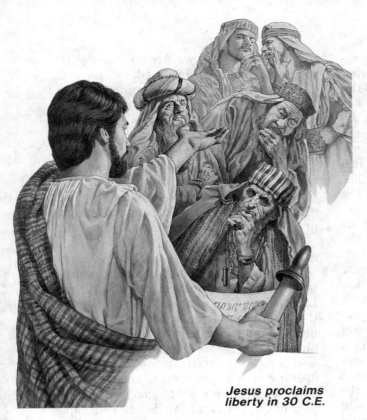

Jesus proclaims liberty in 30 C.E.

Then he started to say to them: 'Today this scripture that you just heard is fulfilled.'"

⁸ The good news that Jesus declared provided spiritual liberation for Jews accepting it. By having their eyes opened to what true worship really meant and required, they were freed from many mistaken notions. (Matthew 5:21-48) This freedom had greater value than physical cures that Jesus performed. Hence, though Jesus opened the eyes of a man born blind, more lasting good resulted to the man from his recognizing Jesus as a prophet from God. That man's new freedom contrasted with the condition of religious leaders who were enslaved to their traditions and mistaken beliefs. (John 9:

1-34; Deuteronomy 18:18; Matthew 15:1-20) Yet this was just an initial or preliminary freedom. Even in the first century, Jesus was to assist with another sort of liberation that paralleled the Jubilee in ancient Israel. Why is it reasonable to conclude that?

⁹ Jesus said to the formerly blind man: "For this judgment I came into this world: that those not seeing might see and those seeing might become blind." Then he told the Pharisees: "If you were blind, you would have no sin. But now you say, 'We see.' Your sin remains." (John 9: 35-41) Yes, sin leading to death was still a major problem, even as it is now. (Romans 5:12) The Jews, including the apostles, who benefited from the initial liberation, the spiritual liberation that Jesus provided, remained imperfect humans. They continued enslaved to sin and resulting death. Could Jesus change that? Would he? And if so, when?

¹⁰ Earlier, Jesus had said: "If you remain in my word, you are really my disciples, and *you will know the truth, and the truth will set you free.*" His Jewish listeners replied: "We are Abraham's offspring and never have we been slaves to anybody. How is it you say, 'You will become free'?" Jesus answered: "Most truly I say to you, Every doer of sin is a slave of sin. Moreover, the slave does not remain in the household forever; the son remains forever." (John 8:31-36) Therefore, fleshly descent from Abraham could not liberate the Jews from slavery to sin. Jesus made this historical declaration regarding freedom to call attention to something that was

8. (a) What preliminary liberation did Jesus provide? (b) How is this illustrated at John 9: 1-34?

9. Even for those spiritually liberated, what form of enslavement remained?
10. Jesus promised that he would provide what additional freedom?

coming and that would be greater than what Israelites experienced in any Jubilee.

The Christian Jubilee Begins

[11] The Jews did not see that the Jubilee of the Mosaic Law covenant was typical of a greater Jubilee. (Colossians 2:17; Ephesians 2:14, 15) This Jubilee for Christians involves "the truth" that can set humans free—that truth centering on the Son, Jesus Christ. (John 1:17) When did this greater Jubilee that could bring freedom even from sin and its effects begin to be celebrated? It was in the spring of 33 C.E., on the day of Pentecost. This was ten days after Jesus' ascension to heaven to present the merit of his sacrifice to Jehovah God.—Hebrews 9:24-28.

[12] Before Jesus, no human creature had been resurrected from the dead to continue living forever. (Romans 6:9-11) Rather, all fell asleep in death and would continue sleeping until the time was due for the resurrection of the human family. By his resurrection through the power of God, Jesus Christ became what the inspired Scriptures call him, "the firstfruits of those who have fallen asleep in death." —1 Corinthians 15:20.

[13] Fifty days after his resurrection, there was evidence that the resurrected Jesus Christ had ascended into the heavens and had entered into the presence of Jehovah God with the value of his perfect human sacrifice and had applied it in behalf of mankind. This was on the day of Pentecost 33 C.E. In obedience to instructions from Jesus, about 120 disciples met together in Jerusalem. Then Christ poured out holy spirit on these disciples, in fulfillment of Joel 2:28, 29. Tongues as

if of fire hovered above their heads, and they began to speak in languages foreign to them. (Acts 2:16-21, 33) This was proof that the resurrected Jesus Christ had ascended into the heavens and had entered into the presence of God with the value of a perfect human sacrifice to apply in behalf of mankind.

[14] What were the consequences for those disciples? For one thing, they were set free from the Mosaic Law covenant, which God had made with the nation of natural Israel but which he had now canceled, nailing it to Jesus' torture stake. (Colossians 2:13, 14; Galatians 3:13) That covenant was superseded by a new covenant made, not with the nation of natural Israel, but with the new "nation" of spiritual Israel. (Hebrews 8:6-13; Galatians 6:16) This new covenant, foretold at Jeremiah 31:31-34, was arranged through a mediator greater than the ancient prophet Moses. Out of interest in liberation, we should especially note one feature of the new covenant. The apostle Paul called attention to this, writing: " 'This is the covenant that I shall covenant toward them after those days, . . . I shall by no means call their sins and their lawless deeds to mind anymore.' Now where there is forgiveness of these, there is no longer an offering for sin."—Hebrews 10:16-18.

[15] Jesus was pointing to this liberation from sin when he said: "If the Son sets you free, you will be actually free." (John 8:36) Imagine—freedom from sin made possible on the basis of Christ's sacrifice! Starting on the day of Pentecost, God declared believing ones righteous and then adopted them as spiritual sons having the

---

11. Why does our interest in the Christian Jubilee focus on the year 33 C.E.?
12, 13. What happened after Jesus' death that soon brought a unique experience to his disciples?

14. (a) What was the situation of Christ's disciples as regards covenants? (b) The new covenant involved what outstanding blessing?
15. Why can we say that at Pentecost 33 C.E. the Christian Jubilee began for anointed ones? (Romans 6:6, 16-18)

prospect of reigning with Christ in heaven. Paul explains: "For you did not receive a spirit of slavery causing fear again, but you received a spirit of adoption as sons . . . If, then, we are children, we are also heirs: heirs indeed of God, but joint heirs with Christ." (Romans 8:15-17) Unquestionably, the Christian Jubilee had begun for anointed Christians.

16 So on that day of Pentecost in the year 33 C.E., the new nation of spiritual Israel came into existence. It was made up of humans whose sins had been forgiven on the basis of Christ's sacrificial blood. (Romans 5:1, 2; Ephesians 1:7) Who of us could deny that those first members of spiritual Israel taken into the new covenant experienced a marvelous liberation by having their sins forgiven? They were made by God into "'a chosen race, a royal priesthood, a holy nation, a people for special possession, that [they] should declare abroad the excellencies' of the one that called [them] out of darkness into his wonderful light." (1 Peter 2:9) True, their fleshly bodies were still imperfect and they would die in time. Yet, now that God had declared them righteous and had adopted them as spiritual sons, their fleshly death was just a "releasing" that allowed for their resurrection to Christ's "heavenly kingdom."—2 Timothy 4:6, 18.

17 The initial or preliminary step of freeing believing Jews from mistaken notions and practices had much value. However, we have seen that Jesus went beyond that spiritual liberation. From Pentecost 33 C.E. onward, he liberated believing humans from "the law of sin and of death." (Romans 8:1, 2) Thus began the Christian

16. What additional blessings and prospects were involved for those celebrating the Christian Jubilee?
17, 18. Why was the liberation of the Christian Jubilee more valuable than the preliminary freedom that Jesus proclaimed?

Jubilee for anointed Christians. This truly was a much more valuable liberation, for it included the prospect of life in heaven as joint heirs with Christ.

18 We have so far considered two aspects of Christian freedom in the first century, which undeniably were a basis for rejoicing. And the first-century believers did rejoice. (Acts 13:44-52; 16:34; 1 Corinthians 13:6; Philippians 4:4) That was especially true regarding their share in the Christian Jubilee, which opened the way for them to receive everlasting blessings in the heavens.—1 Peter 1:3-6; 4: 13, 14.

19 Where, though, do most true Christians today fit into this picture, since they have not been declared righteous for life and anointed with holy spirit? There is Scriptural reason to look for a large-scale liberation in their behalf as part of the Christian Jubilee. Call to mind Acts 3: 20, 21: "Jesus, whom heaven, indeed, must hold within itself until the times of restoration of *all things* of which God

19. What questions remain for Christians who are not spirit begotten, and what indicates that they will have a part in divinely provided liberation?

What Are Your Thoughts?
□ What were the benefits of the Jubilee in ancient Israel?
□ How did Jesus proclaim an initial liberation, and what did it involve?
□ When did the Christian Jubilee begin, and what is the basis for concluding that?
□ Why do we have reason to look forward to liberation involving the millions of Christians who are not spirit anointed?

spoke through the mouth of his holy prophets of old time." (Compare Acts 17: 31.) In the same vein, John, an anointed apostle who was already enjoying the Christian Jubilee, wrote about Jesus Christ: "He is a propitiatory sacrifice for our sins, yet not for ours only but also for the whole world's." (1 John 2:2) Does that mean that the many loyal Christians today who do not have the heavenly hope can rejoice in Christian freedom? Is that just in the future, or do we already have reason to rejoice? We can find that out by examining the aspects of Christian liberation and the Jubilee that have special meaning for true worshipers today.

The Christian Jubilee
Climaxes in the Millennium

EVEN in the Republic of Israel (founded in 1948), the many Jews who consider themselves to be under the Mosaic Law have not reinstituted the celebrating of the Jubilee year. And there would be many complications if they tried. Massive economic problems would result, for property rights are involved. The Republic of Israel does not occupy all the land inhabited by the ancient 12 tribes. There is also no temple with a high priest of the tribe of Levi, tribal identities of the people having been lost.

[2] Where does that leave us, though, as to the blessings of a Jubilee celebration?

---

1. What have the Jews in the Republic of Israel made no effort to reinstitute, and why?

2. How have some Christians already begun to celebrate a Jubilee foreshadowed by that of ancient Israel?

We recall that the ancient Jubilee was a festival year of liberty—Israelites who had sold themselves into slavery were freed and hereditary lands were returned. (Leviticus 25:8-54) In the previous article, we saw that this arrangement ended with the Mosaic Law covenant in 33 C.E. (Romans 7:4, 6; 10:4) Then a new covenant was put in force whereby God could forgive believers' sins, anoint them with holy spirit, and adopt them as sons to be taken to heaven. (Hebrews 10:15-18) Yet those thus benefiting from this new covenant arrangement are a "little flock" of 144,000 "who have been bought from the earth." So how can the millions of other loyal Christians obtain liberation foreshadowed by the Jubilee?—Luke 12:32; Revelation 14:1-4.

A Sacrifice for *All!*

3 In pre-Christian times, the benefits of the annual Day of Atonement lasted for only one year. The benefits of the Lord Jesus Christ's ransom sacrifice are continuous, perpetual. Thus the antitypical High Priest, Jesus, does not have to become a man again, sacrifice himself, and then return to heaven to present the value of that sacrifice year after year in the Most Holy of Jehovah God. As the Scriptures state: "Christ, now that he has been raised up from the dead, dies no more; death is master over him no more."—Romans 6:9; Hebrews 9:28.

4 Hence, in the years since Pentecost 33 C.E., as believers have become spirit-begotten disciples of the glorified Lord Jesus, they have begun celebrating the Christian Jubilee. Once 'set free from the law of sin and of death,' they have enjoyed

invigorating freedom. (Romans 8:1, 2) They have also proclaimed the Christian message so that yet others can have their sins forgiven, be anointed, and become spiritual sons of God. Does this mean, though, that if one is not of that group limited to 144,000, he cannot experience joyful liberation now?

5 Significant in this connection are the apostle Paul's words at Romans 8:19-21: "The eager expectation of the creation is waiting for the revealing of the sons of God. For the creation was subjected to futility [being sinful and unable to eliminate sin]." Paul then stressed that there is "hope that the creation itself also will be set free from enslavement to corruption and have the glorious freedom of the children of God." Such freedom, therefore, is not limited to those becoming "children of God" in heaven. The familiar words at John 3:16 confirm that. And, as mentioned, the anointed apostle John said that Christ died "for our sins, yet not for ours only but *also for the whole world's.*" —1 John 2:2.

1919—An Initial Liberation

6 In modern times the anointed who are celebrating the Christian Jubilee have been declaring liberating good news, especially since 1919. 'Why from that time?' you may wonder if you have been born more recently. Let us see, keeping in mind that your enjoyment of liberation is involved.

7 For decades before that date, Jehovah's anointed ones published Biblical truths, such as in the famous series *Studies in the Scriptures* (1886-1917). They also distributed many informative booklets and tracts. During World War I, there came opposition, testing and sifting, and

---

3. How effective and lasting is Jesus' sacrifice?
4, 5. (a) What has been the result of the application of Jesus' sacrifice from Pentecost 33 C.E.? (b) We have what indication that his sacrifice is going to be applied more widely?

6, 7. Since 1919, what sort of liberation has been proclaimed, and why especially since then?

Liberty proclaimed at Cedar Point, 1919

a slackening of their activities. But in 1919 the anointed remnant went forth with renewed zeal to proclaim Bible truths. As Jesus in 30 C.E. could say that he was anointed to preach "a release to the captives and a recovery of sight to the blind," so could these modern-day anointed ones. After a thrilling convention September 1-7, 1919,* they vigorously surged ahead in preaching truths that liberated countless people.—Luke 4:18.

⁸ Consider, for example, the Bible study aid *The Harp of God* (1921), which presented vital truths as if they were ten strings on a harp. The book acknowledged that "many have been frightened away from studying the Bible" by the doctrine that "the punishment for the wicked . . . is everlasting torment or torture in a hell burning with unquenchable fire and brimstone." Readers of the nearly 6,000,000 copies of this book learned that this doctrine could "not be true for at least four separate and distinct reasons: (1) because it is unreasonable; (2) because it is repugnant to justice; (3) because it is contrary to the principle of love; and (4) because it is entirely unscriptural." You can imagine how liberating that was for people who had grown up in fear of eternal torment in hell or of agony in purgatory!

⁹ Yes, the zealous preaching of Bible truth by these anointed ones freed people around the globe who had been enslaved to false teachings, superstitions, and unscriptural practices (such as ancestor wor-

ship, fear of ghosts or evil spirits, and financial exploitation by the clergy). The very titles of some Bible study aids reflect the liberating influence they had on millions.* Thus Jesus' words have proved true, when he said that his disciples 'would do works greater' than he did. (John 14:12) Compared with the preliminary spiritual liberating work that Jesus did in preaching "a release to the captives," God's modern-day servants have done far more—reaching many millions around the globe.

¹⁰ Call to mind, however, that in the first century a further liberating began at Pentecost 33 C.E. There the Christian Jubilee began for the "little flock" who would have their sins forgiven, leading to their becoming "sons of God" in heaven. What about in our time? Could the millions of other devoted Christians be released from bondage to sin and thus celebrate a grand

---

* A new magazine was there released that was to be "like a voice in the wilderness of confusion, its mission [being] to announce the incoming of the Golden Age." Today this magazine is called *Awake!*

8, 9. In what sense have many been set free, and what aids have been used in proclaiming such liberation?

---

* *Millions Now Living Will Never Die* (1920); *Deliverance* (1926); *Freedom for the Peoples* (1927); *Liberty* (1932); *"The Truth Shall Make You Free"* (1943); *What Do the Scriptures Say About "Survival After Death"?* (1955); *Life Everlasting—In Freedom of the Sons of God* (1966); *The Truth That Leads to Eternal Life* (1968); *The Path of Divine Truth Leading to Liberation* (1980).

10. Why can we expect that an additional and greater liberation will be experienced?

*"Other sheep" share in the
Millennial Jubilee*

Jubilee? Yes, and the apostle Peter indicated this when he spoke of "the times of restoration of all things of which God spoke through the mouth of his holy prophets of old time."—Acts 3:21.

A Jubilee for Millions

11 It is noteworthy that twice in Leviticus chapter 25 the Israelites were reminded that from Jehovah's standpoint they were his "slaves" whom he had liberated out of Egypt. (Verses 42 and 55) This Jubilee chapter also mentions the "settlers" and the 'aliens in their midst.' Such ones find a parallel today in the "great crowd" who are sharing with the spiritual Israelites in proclaiming the Christian good news.

12 Since 1935 the "fine shepherd" Jesus Christ has brought into active association with the anointed remnant those whom he referred to as "other sheep." These he had to "bring," and they were to form "one

flock" under "one shepherd." (John 10:16) The "other sheep" now number in the millions. If you are of that happy multitude, you are already counted righteous as a friend of God, and as part of human creation, you are looking forward to being "set free from enslavement to corruption" during the coming "times of restoration of all things" on earth. This is no misplaced hope.—Romans 8:19-21; Acts 3:20, 21.

13 After the apostle John saw 144,000 who enjoy the Christian Jubilee with a heavenly destiny, he described a "great crowd," saying: "These are the ones *that come out of the great tribulation, and they have washed their robes and made them white in the blood of the Lamb.* That is why they are before the throne of God; and they are rendering him sacred service day and night in his temple."—Revelation 7: 14, 15.

14 Even now, before the great tribulation, these are exercising faith in Christ's shed blood and thus benefit from his sac-

---

11. How does Leviticus chapter 25 suggest that we can look for a liberation that extends beyond spiritual Israel?
12. Since 1935, what happy development has been in progress?

13. What blessing in particular should we note as occurring after the "great tribulation"?
14, 15. Why do those of the "great crowd" have special reason to rejoice now?

rificial death. They also rejoice at being liberated from Babylon the Great, at having a good conscience before Jehovah God, and in their privilege of sharing in the fulfillment of Matthew 24:14 by preaching the good news of the Kingdom before the end comes.

15 However, what of the prospect of the great crowd's being liberated from inborn sin and imperfection? Is that time near? We have good reason to hold that there are still with us some of the generation of mankind that Jesus Christ foretold was not to pass away until all the things predicted would be fulfilled. (Matthew 24:34) Hence, the grand finale of "the conclusion of the system of things" should be very close at hand.—Matthew 24:3.

Crowning Features of the Christian Jubilee

16 "The war of the great day of God the Almighty" comes on apace, and the remnant of the "little flock," as well as the "great crowd" of their faithful, loyal companions will keep integrity toward Jehovah God and look forward to having divine protection. They eagerly anticipate Jehovah's crushing defeat of all the enemy forces, to the vindication of him as the Universal Sovereign. What a crowning feature this will be to their enjoyment of Christian freedom!—Revelation 16:14; 19:19-21; Habakkuk 2:3.

17 The reign of the victorious King Jesus Christ over the cleansed earth will follow, with Jehovah's universal sovereignty reaffirmed, and with Jesus Christ in full control of the earth as King of kings and Lord of lords. Then he will directly apply the merit of his sacrifice to the millions of humans, including the resurrected dead,

who exercise faith and who willingly accept the forgiveness of sins that God will provide through Christ. This will be evidenced by God's wiping out "every tear from their eyes, and death will be no more, neither will mourning nor outcry nor pain be anymore." (Revelation 21:3, 4) If that is not true liberation, what is?

18 Moreover, the earth will no longer be controlled, polluted, and ruined by greedy individuals, corporations, and human governments. (Revelation 11:18) Rather, it will be returned to true worshipers. They will be charged with the delightful task of sharing in a literal fulfillment of Isaiah's prophecy: "They will certainly build houses and have occupancy; and they will certainly plant vineyards and eat their fruitage. They will not build and someone else have occupancy; they will not plant and someone else do the eating . . . They will not toil for nothing, nor will they bring to birth for disturbance; because they are the offspring made up of the blessed ones of Jehovah." (Isaiah 65:21-25) By the end of the Millennial Reign, all traces of inherited sin and imperfection will have been wiped out and God's loyal ones on earth will be celebrating the full climax with which the Jubilee terminates. So the liberation foreshadowed by the Jubilee will have been accomplished.—Ephesians 1:10.

After the Millennial Climax of the Jubilee

19 Revelation 20:1-3 foretells that Satan the Devil, ruler of demon hordes, will be off the scene for the thousand years of Christ's reign over mankind. When, at the end of the Millennium, the Devil and his

---

16. Where do we stand in the outworking of God's purpose, and what lies ahead?
17. How will millions yet receive liberation in a grand Jubilee?

18. Comparable to a feature of the ancient Jubilee, what will occur with the earth in the new system?
19, 20. How will Satan and the demons try to interfere with the blessings resulting from the Millennial Jubilee, but with what outcome?

demons will be allowed briefly to come forth, these wicked spirits will see the earth, not in the condition in which they left it, but as an indescribably beautiful, global paradise. They will see the earth occupied by the faithful "great crowd" and by the billions of resurrected human dead for whom Jesus Christ died as a ransom sacrifice. By the end of the Millennium, the Christian Jubilee will have achieved its purpose of fully releasing mankind from the effects of sin. (Romans 8:21) How diabolically disgraceful it would be for anyone to try to ruin that fine situation! But by almighty God's permission, the Devil will make a last attempt to do this, and in desperate bitterness he will strike. To this effect it is written at Revelation 20:7-10, 14:

20 "Now as soon as the thousand years have been ended, Satan will be let loose out of his prison, and he will go out to mislead those nations in the four corners of the earth, Gog and Magog, to gather them together for the war. The number of these is as the sand of the sea. And they advanced over the breadth of the earth and encircled the camp of the holy ones and the beloved city. But fire came down out of heaven and devoured them. And the Devil who was misleading them was hurled into the lake of fire and sulphur."

21 True liberty, brought about by the Jubilee arrangement, will continue to be enjoyed everywhere; all creatures will be free and will be honoring the One who alone bears the name Jehovah. (Psalm 83:18) That will be true as Jehovah continues to carry out his purposes in all the universe. At the creation of the earth, before mankind was placed upon it, "the morning stars joyfully cried out together, and all

21. After the Christian Jubilee ends with the Millennium, what response by the heavenly sons of God will be reminiscent of Job 38:7?

the sons of God began shouting in applause" at the beautiful sight. (Job 38:7) How much more will they do so at seeing earth populated by men and women who have demonstrated and proved their total dedication and integrity to almighty God.

22 All things being taken into account in the light of the dazzling brilliance being shed upon the Scriptures, we cannot do otherwise than spontaneously jubilate with the heavens and say, Hallelujah! This is the exhortation to us with which the book of Psalms closes: "Hallelujah. Praise God in His sanctuary; praise Him in the sky, His stronghold. Praise Him for His mighty acts; praise Him for His exceeding greatness. Praise Him with blasts of the horn; praise Him with harp and lyre. Praise Him with timbrel and dance; praise Him with lute and pipe. Praise Him with resounding cymbals; praise Him with loud-clashing cymbals. Let all that breathes praise the LORD. Hallelujah." —Psalm 150:1-6, *Tanakh Bible* (1985), Jewish Publication Society of America.

22. What should be our attitude, in harmony with the exhortation found at Psalm 150:1-6?

How Would You Answer?

☐ From what were Jesus' disciples released at Pentecost 33 C.E., marking the start of what for them?

☐ Why is there reason to expect greater liberation than occurred in the first century?

☐ What sort of liberating has been going on since 1919?

☐ How and when will the "other sheep" benefit from a grand Jubilee?

☐ After the climax of the Jubilee, what will the earth be like?

Kingdom Proclaimers Report

"AMAZING DISTRICT CONVENTION"

THIS was the headline of a newspaper in Martinez de la Torre, Veracruz, Mexico, about a convention of Jehovah's Witnesses held in that city. The newspaper commented: "The large attendance at the district convention of [Jehovah's Witnesses] held at the local Exposition Grounds is the most eloquent demonstration of an outstanding happening all over the world in our days: the increasing distrust people have in the doctrines of the so-called 'Christian' churches and the firm conviction that the magnitude of the problems alarmingly transcends the power of governments to solve them.

"Never has a political meeting or social event gathered such a crowd displaying such order and cleanliness. It was simply amazing to see 5,000 people carefully following a program built exclusively around information from the Bible and dealing with aspects of daily life from raising children and living together as a family to morality and spiritual health, along with Bible story dramatization and its application in modern times."

After commenting on the "overwhelming demonstration of coordinated efficiency and organization," the news report observed: "The importance of the activity carried out by the local Jehovah's Witnesses can be measured by the results that have been obtained in just a few years. Today it is an association that grows by leaps and bounds, that worries not at all about the negative comments that usually surround them. Whatever negative thing that could be attributed to them becomes nonexistent when one observes their stand on the things that surround them, the orderly way in which they expand, their respect for authority, and the great appreciation they have for cleanliness and good speech.

"These Bible students are made up almost 100 percent of former activists of different religions, mostly Catholics, that have noticed religion's drifting toward politics and its acceptance and approval of un-Biblical practices like interfaith, immorality, and violence. It has been a source of satisfaction for them to conform to Scriptural principles of conduct without resorting to idolatry or traditions of obscure origin. This has given them a praiseworthy unity of faith that seems to distinguish them wherever they are found."

These comments remind us of the principle that Jesus stated: "By their fruits you will recognize them." (Matthew 7:16) Many honesthearted ones in Mexico are recognizing the Scripturalness of the teachings of Jehovah's Witnesses, are associating with them, and are being richly blessed spiritually by Jehovah God.

A typical convention scene in Mexico

Questions From Readers

■ In ancient Israel a cycle of 49 years was followed by a Jubilee year (50th year). Does that Jubilee correspond to the period following God's creative week of 49,000 years?

Because the number 49 occurs in both cases, it might seem that the Jubilee would foreshadow the time *following* the end of a creative week of 49,000 years. But for mankind in general who receive God's approval, what occurred during Israel's Jubilee corresponds more with what will occur *during* the Millennium, the last thousand years of such creative week, not what follows after that week. Consider the basis for this:

First, the Mosaic Law required that every seventh year be a sabbath for the land; crops were not to be sown, cultivated, or harvested. After the seventh Sabbath year (the 49th year), there came a special Jubilee year, the 50th year. It was a sabbath during which the land was again to rest. More importantly, liberty was proclaimed. Hebrews who had sold themselves into slavery were freed from indebtedness and servitude. Also, hereditary land was returned to families who had been forced to sell it. So the Jubilee was a time of release and restoration for the Israelites.—Leviticus 25:1-46.

Second, a study of the fulfillment of Bible prophecy and of our location in the stream of time strongly indicate that each of the creative days (Genesis, chapter 1) is 7,000 years long. It is understood that Christ's reign of a thousand years will bring to a close God's 7,000-year 'rest day,' the last 'day' of the creative week. (Revelation 20:6; Genesis 2:2, 3) Based on this reasoning, the entire creative week would be 49,000 years long.

Noting the similarity in numbers, some have compared the 49 years of the ancient Jubilee cycle to such 49,000 years of the creative week. Reasoning this way, they have thought that Israel's *Jubilee* (50th) year should prefigure, or foreshadow, what will come *after* the end of the creative week.

However, bear in mind that the Jubilee was particularly a year of release and restoration for people. The creative week largely relates to the planet Earth and its development. But with regard to the outworking of God's purpose for man on earth, the globe itself has *not* been sold into slavery and thus is not in need of liberation. It is mankind that needs that, and humans have existed, not for 49,000 years, but for about 6,000 years. The Bible shows that some time after Adam and Eve were created, they rebelled against God, thus coming into captivity to sin, imperfection, and death. According to Romans 8:20, 21, Jehovah God purposes to liberate believing mankind from this slavery. As a result, true worshipers on earth "will be set free from enslavement to corruption and have the glorious freedom of the children of God."—See also Romans 6:23.

While the small group selected to be taken to heaven have had their sins forgiven from Pentecost 33 C.E. onward and thus already enjoy the Jubilee, the Scriptures show that the liberation for believing mankind will occur *during* Christ's Millennial Reign. That will be when he applies to mankind the benefits of his ransom sacrifice. By the end of the Millennium, mankind will have been raised to human perfection, completely free from inherited sin and death. Having thus brought to an end the last enemy (death passed on from Adam), Christ will hand the Kingdom back to his Father at the end of the 49,000-year creative week.—1 Corinthians 15:24-26.

Consequently, for believing mankind with earthly prospects, the liberation and restoration that marked the Jubilee year in ancient Israel will find a fitting parallel *during* the coming Millennial Sabbath. Then liberation and restoration will be experienced. That will be under Christ's rulership, "for Lord of the sabbath is what the Son of man is."—Matthew 12:8.

"Gather Yourselves Together"

JEREMIAH spoke the above words as calamity threatened ancient Jerusalem and Judah. It was urgent that repentant, true worshipers of Jehovah be gathered for salvation. Likewise today, apostate Christendom is about to perish in "a great crash," along with the entire world empire of false religion. Though the years have stretched out since 1914, when the clergy of Christendom gave full support to the bloodbath of World War I, "the burning anger of Jehovah has not turned back"

any more than it did during the comparable time period that spanned the reigns of Judah's kings from bloodguilty Manasseh to faithless Zedekiah. The meek of the earth must now seek Jehovah in order to survive.—Jeremiah 4:5-8; 2 Kings 24:3, 4; Zephaniah 2:2, 3.

How has the modern-day warning been given? The magazine that you are now reading has been one effective instrument. Continuously since 1879, this journal, like a watchman on his watchtower, has called attention to the impending fall of false religion, as typified by Babylon, and the peaceful Millennial Reign of Christ that will follow. (Isaiah 21:6-12; Revelation 20:2, 3; 21:1-4) From its initial issue of 6,000 copies in English, it has expanded until *The Watchtower—Announcing Jehovah's Kingdom* today enjoys a global circulation of 12,315,000 copies in 103 languages. Moreover, its format has been enhanced over the years. It is now printed in four colors in 21 languages, but other editions also appear in attractive form, as befits the magazine's vital mission.

With the increase in production, it has become necessary to decentralize the printing, so that this is now handled by Society-operated factories in 35 branches outside the United States. Further, from January 1987, editions of our companion magazine *Awake!* printed in the United

States, Brazil, Britain, Canada, Denmark, Finland, Germany, Italy, and Japan will be in four colors. In the United States this has been made possible by the installation of three MAN-Roland high-speed rotary magazine presses at the Watchtower Farms factory at Wallkill, New York.

The Society's branch in Japan is also using three high-speed presses to produce Bibles, books, and magazines in a number of Asiatic languages. Moreover, this branch has given generous support to the Australian, Korean, and South African branches in equipping them with four-color presses, so that these three branches are now moving into four-color magazine printing.

Over the years, there has been a sharing of resources among the Society's branches, with the headquarters organization setting the lead. Thus many have been assisted according to the need, whether it has been in constructing or extending branch buildings, equipping these, or in financing the all-important preaching work in the field. This "equalizing" process, made possible by the generous contributions of Jehovah's Witnesses throughout the earth, has been richly blessed by Jehovah.—2 Corinthians 8:12-15.

Examples That Encourage Faithfulness

Do day-to-day responsibilities of life ever wear on you, robbing you of joy and causing you to lose perspective? They can. What is a solution? A woman from Kentucky, U.S.A., writes:

"I had been so depressed, worrying about so many little things. After I read the *Yearbook,* I felt so guilty. All those Christian brothers and sisters went through so much more and remained faithful. It has helped me so much. Thank you, again!"

Now the *1987 Yearbook of Jehovah's Witnesses* is available with its many thrilling accounts of Christians maintaining faithfulness to God—in Switzerland, Liechtenstein, Trinidad, Tobago, Puerto Rico, the Virgin Islands, and other lands around the globe. Don't miss reading it!

The Watchtower

Announcing Jehovah's Kingdom

January 15, 1987

THE SOCIAL GOSPEL

What Has It Accomplished?

January 15, 1987
Vol. 108, No. 2

The Watchtower

Announcing Jehovah's Kingdom

THE PURPOSE OF "THE WATCHTOWER" is to exalt Jehovah God as the Sovereign of the universe. It keeps watch on world events as they fulfill Bible prophecy. It comforts all peoples with the good news that God's Kingdom will soon destroy those who oppress their fellowmen and that it will turn the earth into a paradise. It encourages faith in the now-reigning King, Jesus Christ, whose shed blood opens the way for mankind to gain eternal life. "The Watchtower," published by Jehovah's Witnesses continuously since 1879, is nonpolitical. It adheres to the Bible as its authority.

"WATCHTOWER" STUDIES FOR THE WEEKS

February 22: So Great a Cloud of Witnesses!
Page 10. Songs to Be Used: 64, 215.

March 1: The World Was Not Worthy of Them.
Page 15. Songs to Be Used: 70, 174.

Average Printing Each Issue: 12,315,000

Now Published in 103 Languages

SEMIMONTHLY LANGUAGES AVAILABLE BY MAIL
Afrikaans, Arabic, Cebuano, Chichewa, Chinese, Cibemba, Danish,* Dutch,* Efik, English,* Finnish, French,* German,* Greek,* Hiligaynon, Igbo, Iloko, Italian,* Japanese,* Korean, Lingala, Malagasy, Maltese, Norwegian, Portuguese,* Russian, Sepedi, Sesotho, Shona, Spanish,* Swahili, Swedish, Tagalog, Thai, Tsonga, Tswana, Xhosa, Yoruba, Zulu

MONTHLY LANGUAGES AVAILABLE BY MAIL
Armenian, Bengali, Bicol, Bulgarian, Croatian, Czech, Ewe, Fijian, Ga, Greenlandic, Gujarati, Gun, Hausa, Hebrew, Hindi, Hiri Motu, Hungarian, Icelandic, Kannada, Malayalam, Marathi, New Guinea Pidgin, Pangasinan, Papiamento, Polish, Rarotongan, Romanian, Samar-Leyte, Samoan, Sango, Serbian, Silozi, Sinhalese, Slovenian, Solomon Islands-Pidgin, Tahitian, Tamil, Telugu, Tongan, Tshiluba, Turkish, Twi, Ukrainian, Urdu, Venda, Vietnamese
* Study articles also available in large-print edition.

Watch Tower Society offices	Yearly subscription for the above: Semimonthly Languages	Monthly Languages
America, U.S., Watchtower, Wallkill, N.Y. 12589	$4.00	$2.00
Australia, Box 280, Ingleburn, N.S.W. 2565	A$7.00	A$3.50
Canada, Box 4100, Halton Hills, Ontario L7G 4Y4	$5.20	$2.60
England, The Ridgeway, London NW7 1RN	£5.00	£2.50
Ireland, 29A Jamestown Road, Finglas, Dublin 11	IR£6.00	IR£3.00
New Zealand, P.O. Box 142, Manurewa	NZ$15.00	NZ$7.50
Nigeria, PMB 001, Shomolu, Lagos State	₦8.00	₦4.00
Philippines, P.O. Box 2044, Manila 2800	₱60.00	₱30.00
South Africa, Private Bag 2067, Krugersdorp, 1740	R6,50	R3,25

Remittances should be sent to the office in your country or to Watchtower, Wallkill, N.Y. 12589, U.S.A.

Changes of address should reach us 30 days before your moving date. Give us your old and new address (if possible, your old address label).

20 cents (U.S.) a copy

The Bible translation used is the "New World Translation of the Holy Scriptures," unless otherwise indicated.

The Watchtower (ISSN 0043-1087) is published semimonthly for $4.00 (U.S.) per year by Watch Tower Bible and Tract Society of Pennsylvania, 25 Columbia Heights, Brooklyn, N.Y. 11201. Second-class postage paid at Brooklyn, N.Y., and at additional mailing offices.

Postmaster: Send address changes to Watchtower, **Wallkill, N.Y. 12589.**

Published by
**Watch Tower Bible and Tract Society
of Pennsylvania**
25 Columbia Heights, Brooklyn, N.Y. 11201, U.S.A.
Frederick W. Franz, President

'Preaching the Gospel'
Through Social Work

KUO TUNG, a young Buddhist man from Hong Kong, received a college education. Hsiu Ying, a mother in Taiwan, found much-needed treatment for her son's critical illness. What do these two seemingly unrelated events have in common?

A college education would normally have been out of the question for Kuo Tung. But through the church to which he belongs, doors were opened for him. Similarly, the complicated medical procedure needed by Hsiu Ying's son was available only at the church-owned hospital in her area. Again, through connections with the church, the problem was solved.

The stories of Kuo Tung and Hsiu Ying are by no means unusual. Thousands of people in developing countries have been drawn to schools, hospitals, orphanages, and other social institutions operated by churches. In this way they have gained considerable material benefit for themselves. And in the process, by joining the church many of them have helped to swell the church membership rolls.

A Practice With a Long History

Church schools and hospitals, of course, are not new. In fact, from the early days when missionaries were sent forth to what some have called hostile heathen lands, schools and hospitals have been looked upon as the most effective means of opening up new territories and gaining the trust and friendship of the local populace.

For example, in describing the situation in India in the early 19th century, the book *Nineteen Centuries of Missions* (1899) says: "The missionaries are not only earnestly engaged in *evangelistic* work, but they also labor with marked success in *educational, medical* and *zenana* work." The result? "Each mission has its *day* schools, *industrial* and *boarding* schools, a high school or *college,* and in nearly every case, a *theological seminary.*"

Commenting on the role of medical work in the "missionary enterprise," the book continues: "The physician is always welcome, and the relief given from physical suffering not only inspires confidence in the physician, but is often followed by faith in the religion which he teaches. Whole villages are often led as an outcome of medical treatment, to renounce idolatry and receive Christian instruction."

What was true in India also became true in other countries in the Far East, South America, and Africa. The idea of preaching the gospel through social means had caught on. European and American missionary societies, both Catholic and Protestant, sent forth workers into these areas and established their missions along with their schools, hospitals, and other institutions. Much of this proved so successful in attracting the local people that such social work soon became an integral part of the overseas missionary work sponsored by the churches.

Over the years these church-run establishments have grown to occupy a very important place in the local communities. Their schools and universities often are the most prestigious and sought-after institutions of higher learning. Generally, their hospitals are the best equipped and most up-to-date. And, in many areas, where governments are hard pressed by overwhelming social problems, they are welcomed, if not also honored.

There is no question that the services provided through such a program have resulted in much good for the communities thus served. Church-run schools and universities have provided literally thousands of students with an education that they might have been denied otherwise. Such hospitals and health services have brought relief to countless numbers of people in remote and backward areas. The humanitarian work of Albert Schweitzer and "Mother" Teresa, for example, are well known internationally and both of them have won the Nobel peace prize.

On the other hand, one must ask: Has the social gospel really achieved its aim? Has it made real Christians of those who have benefited from the charitable works? Has it given the people true faith and hope? Even more importantly, we must ask: Is this what Jesus had in mind when he commissioned his followers to 'preach the gospel in all the world'?—Matthew 24: 14, *King James Version.*

Social Ministry
—*How It Affects People*

STARTING with only five barley loaves and two small fishes, Jesus Christ miraculously fed over 5,000 men, women, and children about the time of the Passover (March-April) in 32 C.E. (Matthew 14:14-21; John 6:1-13) Recognizing the tremendous potential Jesus held, the people wanted to make him their king. Possibly they felt that he would deliver them from the Roman yoke and improve their lot in life. What was Jesus' response?

Instead of submitting to the popular demand, Jesus "withdrew again into the mountain all alone." (John 6:15) But the crowd did not give up easily. They came to him again the next day. Detecting their ulterior motive, Jesus said to them: "You are looking for me, not because you saw signs, but because you ate from the loaves and were satisfied." Then he added: "Work, not for the food that perishes, but for the food that remains for life everlasting."—John 6:25-27.

What can we learn from this account? Among other things, it clearly shows that with material benefits it is relatively easy to attract people. However, building genuine appreciation for spiritual things —things of lasting value—is an entirely different matter. Today, the tendency to look at things from a purely materialistic point of view is even greater.

Strong Appeal of Social Ministry

In the eyes of the people of the developing countries, the advanced Western nations represent all the opportunities and material benefits that one could want —opportunities that are unavailable in their own country. The prosperity is envied, the life-style emulated. The opportunity for higher education is set in front of virtually every student as a passport to advancement and success. Against such a background it is not hard to understand why the social programs of the foreign churches have had such a strong appeal in these countries. But what are the results?

In the Orient, for example, the willingness of the people to do just about anything the churches require in order to qualify for the gifts or handouts has given rise to the contemptuous label "rice Christians." The saddest part, of course, is that

when such relief or support stops, so does the interest of the people. Many of the rice Christians simply vanish from the scene. Thus, among the Cantonese, there is a popular saying that translates into something like this: "God loves the world, but the world loves powdered milk."

Although most church groups no longer operate relief programs, except perhaps during times of disaster, what happened in the past has left its mark. To many Orientals, churches are synonymous with charitable organizations, and the only reason to go to church is to get, not to give. They see no need to make any personal sacrifice for the church. This attitude is shown, for example, in their reluctance to contribute for Bible literature because, in their minds, something produced by a church should be free.

Using the church as a means to an end is most readily seen in the field of education. In many developing countries, to gain a Western-style education is viewed as a sure way to fame and success. According to one source, at the time of India's gaining independence from Britain, 85 percent of that nation's members of parliament had attended "Christian schools." And, according to Confucian ideals, in the Far East, to be well educated is one of the highest goals in life. Naturally, many look to the church schools, which generally use Western methods and standards, as a means for self-advancement. And, hoping to get their children into one of the church-run schools and perhaps overseas later, many Oriental parents who normally follow the traditional religions happily go to church themselves and urge their children to do the same.

What Is the Fruitage?

Compared with the churches back home, the mission churches are usually well attended. Many people are thus introduced to church teachings and to some concept of Christianity. But has this exposure helped them to understand the Bible and its message? Has it really made them Christians, that is, followers of Jesus Christ?

Take, for instance, Kuo Tung, the young man mentioned earlier. When asked whether he now believed in God after having attended church for some time, he replied: "No. Proof that God exists was never discussed." In fact, he admitted that he was not sure if any of his friends believed in a personal God, even though they had been attending church with him. They went along merely for the opportunity to learn English, he said.

Another young man came home for vacation from college in the United States. When one of Jehovah's Witnesses called on him, he asked if the Witnesses hold their meetings in English. Why? "So I can keep up with my English," he said. When he was told that the meetings were held in the local language so that all could benefit spiritually, the young man said he would go where English meetings were held twice a week.

Even those who have become church members and have been baptized show little change in their outlook. Many of them still cling to their former beliefs or practices, often with the approval, if not also the blessing, of their church. In China, for example, Roman Catholics are allowed to continue their ancestor worship, although this is forbidden elsewhere. Plaques beseeching the blessing of the door god are often seen around doorways of "Christian" homes. And in Okinawa, animal depictions of native gods are put on roof corners to protect the family.

What about those who have benefited from the church programs? In their new-found financial and material security, it is not uncommon to hear them say that the answer to today's problems is to rely on oneself. The result is that many of them have either totally separated themselves from any church involvement or, at best, kept themselves at a respectable distance.

Missionaries of the churches have had many fine opportunities to instruct the people in what the Bible teaches. But rather than teaching them to follow Jesus' admonition to "keep on, then, seeking first the kingdom and his righteousness, and all these other things will be added to you," they have placed the emphasis on the "other things." (Matthew 6:33) Through their social programs, they have done much to help people physically, medically, and educationally, but the benefits are primarily of a temporal kind. Without providing a spiritual outlook, frequently such programs only become an incentive to strive for more temporal, or worldly, advantages.

The churches set out to preach the gospel. But what has resulted, in many instances, is the promotion of the Western, materialistic way of life. Yes, they have gained many converts. But as we have seen, many of these have turned out to be more worldly and materially inclined than ever. In Jesus' day, he said of religious leaders: "You traverse sea and dry land to make one proselyte, and when he becomes one you make him a subject for Gehenna twice as much so as yourselves." (Matthew 23:15) In this sense, Christendom's effort in preaching the gospel through social means has backfired. It has fallen far short of the great commission given by Jesus Christ: "Go therefore and make disciples of people of all the nations, . . . teaching them to observe all the things I have commanded you."—Matthew 28:19, 20.

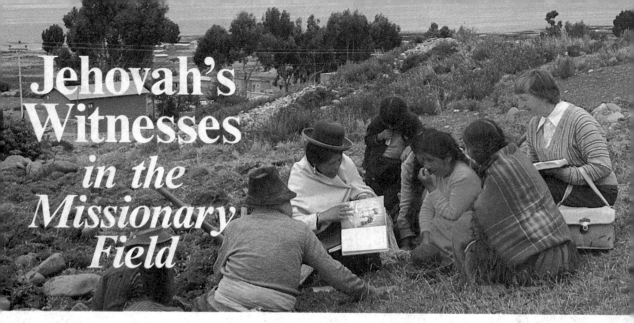

Jehovah's Witnesses in the Missionary Field

MISSIONARIES of Jehovah's Witnesses in Asia and elsewhere are often asked: "Why don't you have English classes like the other missionaries?" "Do you have schools that I can send my children to or hospitals for the sick?" The answer, of course, is no. But why not? In fact, what is the objective of the Witnesses? And what have they done for the people in these countries?

Contrast in Viewpoints

It is undeniable that the missionaries of Christendom have made many converts by the social services they provide. But because such works are directed mainly at satisfying the people's material needs rather than their spiritual ones, these missionaries have not been successful in making real disciples of Jesus Christ. (Matthew 7:22, 23; 28:19, 20) More importantly, they have not been able to point out any permanent solution to the social ills they are trying to overcome.

Jehovah's Witnesses, on the other hand, are concerned with the more important commission of preaching the good news of God's Kingdom. (Matthew 24:14) This is not because they are unaware of or unconcerned about all the human suffering and injustices they see. Rather, it is because they recognize that the only remedy for these serious problems lies, not in human hands, but in God's Kingdom.—Psalm 146:3-10.

That was precisely what Jesus and his disciples preached in the first century. "I must declare the good news of the kingdom of God," Jesus said, "because for this I was sent forth." (Luke 4:43) Jesus pointed to and preached about God's Kingdom as the only complete remedy, for he knew that the world's problems were too vast for man to cope with alone. Although Jesus performed many miraculous cures, he urged his disciples to "keep on, then, seeking first the kingdom and [God's] righteousness, and all these other things will be added to you."—Matthew 6:33.

Later, when Jesus sent out his disciples, he first told them: "As you go, preach, saying, 'The kingdom of the heavens has drawn near.'" Then he added: "Cure sick people, raise up dead persons, make lepers clean, expel demons." (Matthew 10:7, 8)

Solutions to Social Ills by God's Kingdom

Read in your own Bible the following scriptures and be comforted by seeing how God promises to do away with today's problems and social ills in the following areas:

Health
Isaiah 33:24;
35:5, 6;
Revelation 21:4

Education
Isaiah 11:9;
Habakkuk 2:14

That sets the priority for modern-day disciples of Jesus Christ. They, too, must put preaching the Kingdom good news as their primary objective, over and above performing humanitarian works. That is what missionaries of Jehovah's Witnesses endeavor to do.

Filling People's Spiritual Needs

As a group of Christians, Jehovah's Witnesses are engaged in a massive volunteer program of providing Bible education for the people. Being publishers of the good news, they are interested in helping others benefit from the Bible's wisdom and counsel, both now and in the future. (Psalm 68:11) Why is this so?

The Witnesses realize that when people are helped to understand and follow the Bible's counsel, they become better equipped to deal with the problems and pressures of life. On the one hand, they gain the moral fortitude needed to overcome enslaving and physically damaging habits such as smoking, overdrinking, misuse of drugs, poor hygiene, gambling, and sexual promiscuity. On the other hand, Bible truth helps them to make their minds over, bringing them a purpose in life and a realistic hope for the future.

Thus, by providing the highest form of education—that which comes from God's Word, the Bible—Jehovah's Witnesses are making a direct contribution toward raising the moral and physical health of the community in which they live and preach. Often this is noted by others who

Employment
Isaiah 65:21-23

Food
Psalm 67:6; 72:16;
Isaiah 25:6

Justice
Isaiah 11:3-5;
32:1, 2

have observed them objectively. For example, Dr. Bryan Wilson of Oxford University, who studied the activities of Jehovah's Witnesses in Africa, stated in a letter to the London *Times:*

"Jehovah's Witnesses are hard-working and often more conscientious and enterprising than the average among their fellow citizens. They are enjoined by their leaders to pay their taxes promptly, to refrain from violence, and to avoid giving offence. They are orderly, honest and sober. These values were of great importance in the economic and social development of Western society, and it would not be an exaggeration to say that Jehovah's Witnesses are among the most upright and diligent of the citizenry of African countries."

In similar words, another observer in South America stated this in a newspaper editorial:

"The Jehovah's Witnesses are hard-working, honest, God-fearing people. They are conservative and tradition-loving and their religion is based on the teachings of the Bible."

So while Jehovah's Witnesses do not put stress on what is commonly referred to as the social gospel, they actively contribute to community interests by helping others to bring their lives into harmony with the high standards of the Bible. (Romans 12:1, 2) Most importantly, they are also helping people everywhere to look beyond the injustices and inequalities of this rapidly deteriorating system of things to the new system of God's making, soon to come.—Revelation 21:5.

SO GREAT A CLOUD OF WITNESSES!

"Because we have so great a cloud of witnesses surrounding us, . . . let us run with endurance the race that is set before us."—HEBREWS 12:1.

PICTURE yourself as a runner in a stadium. You press onward, straining every muscle, your eyes fixed on the goal. But what about the observers? Why, all of them have been triumphant runners! They have been not mere spectators but active witnesses in both word and deed.

[2] The apostle Paul may have had such a figurative setting in mind when writing to Hebrew Christians (c. 61 C.E.). They needed firm faith. (Hebrews 10:32-39) Only by faith could they heed Jesus' warning to flee when Jerusalem was surrounded by encamped armies (in 66 C.E.) a few years before its destruction at Roman hands (in 70 C.E.). Faith would also sustain them when they were "persecuted for righteousness' sake."—Matthew 5:10; Luke 21:20-24.

[3] After reviewing pre-Christian acts of faith (in Hebrews, chapter 11), Paul urged: "Because we have so great a cloud of witnesses surrounding us, let us also put off every weight [that would encumber us spiritually] and the sin [lack of faith] that easily entangles us, and let us run with endurance the race [for life eternal] that is set before us." (Hebrews 12:1) Paul's review of faith in action highlights various aspects of it and will help us, whether we are anointed Christians running the race for immortality in heaven or we are part of the "great crowd" with the goal of endless life on a paradise earth. (Revelation 7:4-10; Luke 23:43; Romans 8:16, 17) But just what is faith? What are some facets of this spiritual gem? And how will we act if we have faith? As you seek answers to such questions, please read cited verses of He-

---

1, 2. (a) What figurative setting may Paul have had in mind when writing to Hebrew Christians? (b) Why did Hebrew fellow believers need firm faith?

---

3. At Hebrews 12:1, what is "the sin that easily entangles us," and Christians are urged to run what race with endurance?

brews chapters 11 and 12 during private and congregational study.

What Faith Is

[4] Paul first defined faith. (*Read Hebrews 11:1-3.*) In part, faith is "the assured expectation of things hoped for." The person having faith has a guarantee that everything God promises is as good as fulfilled. Faith is also "the evident demonstration of realities though not beheld." The convincing proof of unseen realities is so powerful that faith is said to be equivalent to that evidence.

[5] By means of faith "men of old times had witness borne to them" that they pleased God. Also, "by faith we perceive that the systems of things"—the earth, the sun, the moon, and the stars—"were put in order by God's word, so that what is beheld has come to be out of things that do not appear." We are convinced that Jehovah is the Creator of such things, although we cannot see him because he is an invisible Spirit.—Genesis 1:1; John 4:24; Romans 1:20.

Faith and the "Ancient World"

[6] One of the many facets of faith is appreciation for the need of a sacrifice for sins. (*Read Hebrews 11:4.*) In the "ancient world," faith in a blood sacrifice was shown by Abel, the second son of the first human pair, Adam and Eve. (2 Peter 2:5) Doubtless Abel discerned in himself the death-dealing effects of inherited sin. (Genesis 2:16, 17; 3:6, 7; Romans 5:12) Evidently he also noted the fulfillment of God's decree that brought laborious toil upon Adam and considerable pain during pregnancy to Eve. (Genesis 3:16-19) So

Abel had "the assured expectation" that other things spoken by Jehovah would come true. These included the prophetic words directed to the archdeceiver Satan when God said to the serpent: "I shall put enmity between you and the woman and between your seed and her seed. He will bruise you in the head and you will bruise him in the heel."—Genesis 3:15.

[7] Abel displayed faith in the promised Seed by presenting to God an animal sacrifice that could substitute pictorially for Abel's own life. But his faithless elder brother Cain offered bloodless vegetables. As a murderer, Cain thereafter spilled Abel's blood. (Genesis 4:1-8) Yet Abel died knowing that Jehovah considered him righteous, "God bearing witness respecting his gifts." How? By accepting Abel's sacrifice offered in faith. Because of his faith and divine approval, about which the Inspired Record continues to bear witness, 'although Abel died, he yet speaks.' He saw the need for a sacrifice for sins. Do you have faith in Jesus Christ's far more significant ransom sacrifice?—1 John 2: 1, 2; 3:23.

[8] Faith will move us to speak God's message with boldness. (*Read Hebrews 11: 5, 6.*) Jehovah's early witness Enoch courageously foretold divine execution of judgment upon the ungodly. (Jude 14, 15) Doubtless Enoch's foes sought to kill him, but God "took him" so that he did not suffer the pangs of death. (Genesis 5:24) First, however, "he had the witness that he had pleased God well." How so? "By faith Enoch was transferred so as not to see death." Similarly, Paul was transferred, or "caught away into paradise,"

4. What is faith?
5. By faith we perceive what?
6. Why did Abel have an "assured expectation" that Jehovah's prophetic words about the 'seed of the woman' would come true?

7. (a) How did Abel show appreciation for the need of a sacrifice for sins? (b) In what way did God 'bear witness respecting Abel's gifts'?
8. (a) What do we learn about faith from Enoch's courageous witnessing? (b) How was Enoch "transferred so as not to see death"?

evidently receiving a vision of the future spiritual paradise of the Christian congregation. (2 Corinthians 12:1-4) So Enoch apparently was enjoying a vision of the coming earthly Paradise when Jehovah put him to sleep in death, safe from enemy hands. To be pleasing to God we, like Enoch, must speak God's message with boldness. (Acts 4:29-31) We must also believe that God exists and "becomes the rewarder of those earnestly seeking him."

9 Following God's instructions closely is another facet of faith. (*Read Hebrews 11:7.*) Acting in faith, Noah did 'just as God commanded.' (Genesis 6:22; 7:16) Noah received "divine warning of things not yet beheld" and believed Jehovah's statement that an earth-wide flood would occur. In faith and with reverential fear of God, Noah "constructed an ark for the saving of his household." By obedience and righteous acts, he thus condemned the unbelieving world for its wicked works and showed that it deserved destruction. —Genesis 6:13-22.

10 Noah was also one of Jehovah's witnesses in that he was "a preacher of righteousness." (2 Peter 2:5) Although busy building the ark, he took time to preach, as Jehovah's Witnesses do today. Indeed, Noah spoke out boldly as a herald of God's warning to those antediluvians, but "they took no note until the flood came and swept them all away."—Matthew 24:36-39.

Faith Among Post-Flood Patriarchs

11 Faith includes complete confidence in Jehovah's promises. (*Read Hebrews 11:8-12.*) By faith Abraham (Abram) obeyed God's command and left Ur of the Chaldeans, a city with much to offer in a material way. He believed Jehovah's promise that "all the families of the ground" would bless themselves by means of him and that his seed would be given a land. (Genesis 12:1-9; 15:18-21) Abraham's son Isaac and grandson Jacob were "heirs with him of the very same promise." By faith Abraham "resided as an alien in the land of promise as in a foreign land." He looked forward to "the city having real foundations, the builder and maker of which city is God." Yes, Abraham awaited God's heavenly Kingdom under which he would be resurrected to life on earth. Does the Kingdom hold such an important place in your life? —Matthew 6:33.

12 The wives of the God-fearing patriarchs also had faith in Jehovah's promises. For instance, by faith Abraham's wife Sarah, though barren until about 90 years old and "past the age limit," was empowered "to conceive seed, . . . since she esteemed him [God] faithful who had promised." In time, Sarah bore Isaac. Thus from 100-year-old Abraham, "as good as dead" as regards reproduction, eventually "there were born children just as the stars of heaven for multitude." —Genesis 17:15-17; 18:11; 21:1-7.

13 Faith will keep us loyal to Jehovah even if we do not see the immediate fulfillment of his promises. (*Read Hebrews 11:13-16.*) The faithful patriarchs all died without seeing the complete fulfillment of

---

9. How did Noah's course show that following God's instructions closely is another facet of faith?
10. Although Noah was building the ark, he took time for what other activity?
11. (a) How did Abraham show that faith includes complete confidence in Jehovah's promises? (b) In faith, Abraham was awaiting what "city"?

12. What happened because Sarah had faith in Jehovah's promises?
13, 14. (a) Although Abraham, Isaac, and Jacob "did not get the fulfillment of the promises," how did they react? (b) How can we benefit from considering the patriarchs' loyalty to Jehovah even if we do not see the immediate fulfillment of his promises?

God's promises to them. But "they saw [the promised things] afar off and welcomed them and publicly declared that they were strangers and temporary residents in the land." Yes, they lived out their lives in faith, for generations passed before the Promised Land became the possession of Abraham's offspring.

14 The fact that they did not get the fulfillment of divine promises in their lifetime did not embitter Abraham, Isaac, and Jacob or cause them to become apostates. They did not abandon Jehovah and go back to Ur, becoming immersed in worldly activities. (Compare John 17:16; 2 Timothy 4:10; James 1:27; 1 John 2:15-17.) No, those patriarchs 'reached out' for a place far better than Ur, "that is, one belonging to heaven." So Jehovah 'is not ashamed to be called upon as their God.' They maintained faith in the Most High until death and will soon be resurrected to life on earth, part of the domain of the "city," the Messianic Kingdom God made ready for them. But what about you? Even if you have 'walked in the truth' for years, growing old in Jehovah's service, you must maintain your confidence in his promised new system. (3 John 4; 2 Peter 3:11-13) What a reward you and the faithful patriarchs will receive for such faith!

15 Unquestioning obedience to God is a vital facet of faith. (Read Hebrews 11: 17-19.) Because Abraham obeyed Jehovah without question, he "as good as offered up Isaac," his "only-begotten son"—the only one he ever had by Sarah. How could Abraham do this? Because "he reckoned that God was able to raise [Isaac] up even from the dead," if necessary, to fulfill the promise of offspring through him. In a

moment the knife in Abraham's hand would have ended Isaac's life, but an angel's voice prevented this. Hence, Abraham received Isaac out of death "in an illustrative way." We should likewise be moved to obey God in faith even if our life or that of our children is at stake. (1 John 5:3) It is noteworthy, too, that Abraham and Isaac then prophetically portrayed how Jehovah God would provide his only-begotten Son, Jesus Christ, as a ransom so that those exercising faith in him might have everlasting life.—Genesis 22: 1-19; John 3:16.

16 If we have faith, we will help our offspring to set their hope on what God promises for the future. (Read Hebrews 11:20-22.) So strong was the faith of the patriarchs that although Jehovah's promises to them were not completely fulfilled in their lifetime, they passed these on to their children as a cherished inheritance. Thus, "Isaac blessed Jacob and Esau concerning things to come," and dying Jacob pronounced blessings on Joseph's sons Ephraim and Manasseh. Because Joseph himself had strong faith that the Israelites would leave Egypt for the land of promise, he made his brothers swear to take his bones with them when departing. (Genesis 27:27-29, 38-40; 48:8-22; 50: 24-26) Are you helping your family to develop comparable faith in what Jehovah has promised?

Faith Makes Us Put God First

17 Faith motivates us to put Jehovah and his people ahead of anything this world has to offer. (Read Hebrews 11:23-26.) The Israelites were slaves needing deliverance from Egyptian bondage when Moses' parents acted in faith. 'They did not fear the

---

15. (a) What enabled Abraham virtually to offer Isaac as a sacrifice? (b) How should our faith be affected by the event involving Abraham and Isaac? (c) What was prophetically portrayed by that event?

16. With regard to our children and faith in God's promises, what example did the patriarchs furnish?
17. How did Moses' parents act in faith?

king's order' to kill Hebrew males at birth. Rather, they hid Moses for three months, finally placing him in a papyrus ark among the reeds by the bank of the Nile River. Found by Pharaoh's daughter, he was 'brought up as her own son.' First, however, Moses was nursed and spiritually trained in the home of his father and mother, Amram and Jochebed. Then, as a member of Pharaoh's household, he "was instructed in all the wisdom of the Egyptians" and became "powerful in his words and deeds," mighty in mental and physical capabilities.—Acts 7:20-22; Exodus 2: 1-10; 6:20.

¹⁸ Yet, Egyptian education and the material splendor of the royal house did not cause Moses to abandon Jehovah's worship and become an apostate. Rather, "by faith Moses, when grown up, refused to be called the son of the daughter of Pharaoh," a course implied when he defended a Hebrew brother. (Exodus 2:11, 12) Moses chose "to be ill-treated with the people of God [Israelite fellow worshipers of Jeho-

---

18. Because of his faith, what position did Moses take with regard to Jehovah's worship?

How Would You Answer?

□ What is faith?

□ Enoch's example teaches us what about faith?

□ How did God-fearing patriarchs show that faith includes complete confidence in Jehovah's promises?

□ What action by Abraham indicates that unquestioning obedience to God is a vital facet of faith?

□ What actions by Moses show that faith means putting Jehovah and His people ahead of anything the world has to offer?

vah] rather than to have the temporary enjoyment of sin." If you are a baptized servant of Jehovah who has a solid background of proper spiritual training, will you follow Moses' example and stand firm for true worship?

¹⁹ Moses threw in his lot with Jehovah's people "because he esteemed the reproach of the Christ as riches greater than the treasures of Egypt." Most likely Moses 'esteemed the reproach of being an ancient type of Christ, or God's Anointed One, as riches greater than Egypt's treasures.' As a member of the royal household, he could have enjoyed wealth and fame in Egypt. But he exercised faith and "looked intently toward the payment of the reward"—eternal life through resurrection on earth in God's promised new system.

²⁰ Faith makes us fearless because we are confident in Jehovah as a deliverer. (*Read Hebrews 11:27-29.*) After hearing that Moses had killed an Egyptian, Pharaoh sought his death. "But Moses ran away from Pharaoh that he might dwell in the land of Midian." (Exodus 2:11-15) So Paul seems to allude to the Hebrews' later Exodus from Egypt when he says: "By faith he [Moses] left Egypt, but not fearing the anger of the king [who threatened him with death for representing God in Israel's behalf], for he continued steadfast as seeing the One who is invisible." (Exodus 10:28, 29) Although Moses never actually saw God, Jehovah's dealings with him were so real that he acted as if he did see 'the invisible One.' (Exodus 33:20) Is your relationship with Jehovah that strong?—Psalm 37:5; Proverbs 16:3.

---

19. (a) How is it evident that Moses put Jehovah and His people first in life? (b) Moses looked toward the payment of what reward?
20. What is there about Moses' experience that shows that faith makes us fearless as Jehovah's servants?

21 Just before Israel's departure from Egypt, "by faith he [Moses] had celebrated the passover and the splashing of the blood, that the destroyer might not touch their [the Israelites'] firstborn ones." Yes, it took faith to hold the Passover with the conviction that Israel's firstborn sons would be spared while those of the Egyptians would die, and this faith was rewarded. (Exodus 12:1-39) Also "by faith they [the people of Israel] passed through the Red Sea as on dry land, but on venturing out upon it the Egyptians were swallowed up." What a marvelous deliverer God proved to be! And because of this deliverance, the Israelites "began to fear Jehovah and to put faith in Jehovah and in Moses his servant."—Exodus 14: 21-31.

22 The faith of Moses and the patriarchs is indeed a model for Jehovah's Witnesses today. But what happened when God dealt further with Abraham's descendants as a theocratically organized nation? What can we learn from further acts of faith in ancient times?

21. As regards Israel's departure from Egypt, what happened "by faith"?

22. Regarding faith, what questions remain for consideration?

THE WORLD WAS NOT WORTHY OF THEM

"They were stoned, they were tried, . . . and the world was not worthy of them."—HEBREWS 11:37, 38.

JEHOVAH'S WITNESSES of ancient times maintained integrity to God despite many tests brought upon them by unrighteous human society. For instance, God's servants were stoned and slaughtered with the sword. They suffered illtreatment and tribulation. Yet they did not waver in faith. Surely, then, as the apostle Paul said: "The world was not worthy of them."—Hebrews 11:37, 38.

2 The faith-inspiring acts of godly antediluvians, patriarchs, and Moses prompt Jehovah's modern-day witnesses to serve God in faith. But what about others mentioned in Hebrews chapters 11 and 12? How can we benefit from considering the facets of their faith?

Faith of Judges, Kings, and Prophets

3 Faith is not mere belief; it must be proved by works or actions. (Read Hebrews 11:30, 31.) After Moses' death, faith brought the Israelites one victory after another in Canaan, but this called for effort on their part. For instance, by the faith of Joshua and others "the walls of Jericho fell down after they had been encircled for seven days." But "by faith Rahab the harlot did not perish with those [faithless residents of Jericho] who acted

1, 2. Under what circumstances did Jehovah's witnesses of ancient times maintain integrity, and how do their acts affect God's servants today?

3. How do incidents involving Jericho and Rahab show that faith must be proved by works?

disobediently." Why? "Because she received the [Israelite] spies in a peaceable way," proving her faith by hiding them from the Canaanites. Rahab's faith had a solid basis in reports that "Jehovah dried up the waters of the Red Sea" from before the Israelites and granted them victory over Amorite kings Sihon and Og. Rahab made proper moral changes and was blessed for her active faith by being preserved along with her household when Jericho fell and by becoming an ancestress of Jesus Christ.—Joshua 2:1-11; 6:20-23; Matthew 1:1, 5; James 2:24-26.

⁴ Faith is shown by complete reliance upon Jehovah in the face of danger. (*Read Hebrews 11:32.*) Paul admitted that time would fail him if he went on to tell about "Gideon, Barak, Samson, Jephthah, David as well as Samuel and the other prophets," whose exploits gave abundant evidence of faith and reliance upon God in perilous situations. Thus, by faith and with a band of only 300 men, Judge Gideon was empowered by God to crush the military might of the oppressive Midianites. (Judges 7:1-25) Encouraged by the prophetess Deborah, Judge Barak and an infantry force of 10,000 poorly equipped men triumphed over King Jabin's far greater forces having 900 armored war chariots commanded by Sisera.—Judges 4:1–5:31.

⁵ Another example of faith from the days of Israel's judges was Samson, mighty enemy of the Philistines. True, he eventually became their blinded captive. But Samson brought death to many of them when he pulled down the pillars of the house in which they were presenting a

David showed faith by relying completely upon Jehovah. A fine example for Jehovah's people today!

great sacrifice to their false god Dagon. Yes, Samson died with those Philistines but not as a despairing suicide. In faith he relied upon Jehovah and prayed to him for the strength needed to wreak vengeance upon those foes of God and His people. (Judges 16:18-30) Jephthah, to whom Jehovah granted victory over the Ammonites, also displayed faith that gave evidence of his complete reliance upon Jehovah. Only with such faith could he have fulfilled his vow to God by devoting his daughter to Jehovah's service as a perpetual virgin.—Judges 11:29-40.

⁶ Also notable for his faith was David. He was only a young man when he fought the Philistine giant Goliath. 'You come to me with sword, spear, and javelin,' said David, 'but I come to you with the name of Jehovah of armies.' Yes, David relied upon God, killed the towering Philistine, and went on to become a valiant warrior-king fighting in the interests of God's people. And because of David's faith, he was a man agreeable to Jehovah's heart.

---

4. What do the experiences of Gideon and Barak emphasize as to showing faith in the face of danger?
5. In what ways did Samson and Jephthah display faith that gave evidence of complete reliance upon Jehovah?

6. How did David show his faith?

(1 Samuel 17:4, 45-51; Acts 13:22) Throughout life, Samuel and other prophets also displayed great faith and full dependence upon God. (1 Samuel 1:19-28; 7: 15-17) What fine examples for Jehovah's present-day servants, young and old!

7 By faith we can successfully meet every test of integrity and can accomplish anything harmonizing with the divine will. (*Read Hebrews 11:33, 34.*) In citing further acts of faith, apparently Paul had in mind Hebrew judges, kings, and prophets, for he had just named such men. "Through faith" such judges as Gideon and Jephthah "defeated kingdoms in conflict." So did King David, who subdued the Philistines, Moabites, Syrians, Edomites, and others. (2 Samuel 8:1-14) Also through faith, upright judges "effected righteousness," and the righteous counsel of Samuel and other prophets moved at least some to avoid or abandon wrongdoing.—1 Samuel 12:20-25; Isaiah 1:10-20.

7. (a) Who "through faith defeated kingdoms in conflict"? (b) Who "effected righteousness" through faith?

8 David was one who through faith "obtained promises." Jehovah promised him: "Your very throne will become one firmly established to time indefinite." (2 Samuel 7:11-16) And God kept that promise by establishing the Messianic Kingdom in 1914.—Isaiah 9:6, 7; Daniel 7:13, 14.

9 The prophet Daniel successfully met a test of integrity when he continued to pray to God according to his daily custom despite a royal interdict. With the faith of an integrity keeper, Daniel thus "stopped the mouths of lions" in that Jehovah preserved him alive in the lions' pit into which he was cast.—Daniel 6:4-23.

10 Daniel's integrity-keeping Hebrew associates Shadrach, Meshach, and Abednego in effect "stayed the force of fire." When threatened with death in a superheated furnace, they told King Nebuchadnezzar that, whether their God rescued them or not, they would not serve the Babylonian monarch's gods or worship the image he had set up. Jehovah did not put out the fire in that furnace, but he made sure that it did the three Hebrews no harm. (Daniel 3:1-30) Comparable faith enables us to maintain integrity to God to the point of possible death at enemy hands.—Revelation 2:10.

11 David "escaped the edge of the sword" of King Saul's men. (1 Samuel 19:9-17) The prophets Elijah and Elisha also escaped death by the sword. (1 Kings 19:1-3; 2 Kings 6:11-23) But who 'from a weak state were made powerful through faith'? Well, Gideon considered himself and his

8. What promise did David obtain, and to what did it lead?
9. Under what circumstances were 'the mouths of lions stopped through faith'?
10. Who "stayed the force of fire" through faith, and what will comparable faith enable us to do?
11. (a) Through faith, who "escaped the edge of the sword"? (b) Who were "made powerful" through faith? (c) Who "became valiant in war" and "routed the armies of foreigners"?

men too weak to save Israel from the Midianites. But he was "made powerful" by God, who gave him the victory—and that with only 300 men! (Judges 6:14-16; 7:2-7, 22) "From a weak state" when his hair was shorn, Samson was "made powerful" by Jehovah and brought death to many Philistines. (Judges 16:19-21, 28-30; compare Judges 15:13-19.) Paul may also have thought of King Hezekiah as one "made powerful" from a weak state militarily and even physically. (Isaiah 37:1–38:22) Among God's servants who "became valiant in war" were Judge Jephthah and King David. (Judges 11:32, 33; 2 Samuel 22:1, 2, 30-38) And those who "routed the armies of foreigners" included Judge Barak. (Judges 4:14-16) All these exploits should convince us that by faith we can successfully meet every test of our integrity and can accomplish anything that is in accord with Jehovah's will.

Others of Exemplary Faith

12 Faith includes belief in the resurrection, a hope that helps us to maintain integrity to God. (*Read Hebrews 11:35.*) Because of faith, "women received their dead by resurrection." By faith and God's power, Elijah resurrected a widow's son at Zarephath and Elisha raised to life the boy of a Shunammite woman. (1 Kings 17:17-24; 2 Kings 4:17-37) "But other men were tortured [literally, "beaten with sticks"] because they would not accept release by some ransom, in order that they might attain a better resurrection." Apparently these Scripturally unidentified witnesses of Jehovah were beaten to death, refusing to accept deliverance requiring that they compromise their faith. Their resurrection will be "better" because it will be without the unavoidable need to die again (as did

"Women received their dead by resurrection." Faith in the resurrection helps us to maintain integrity to Jehovah

those raised by Elijah and Elisha) and will occur under Kingdom rule by Jesus Christ, the "Eternal Father" whose ransom provides an opportunity for endless life on earth.—Isaiah 9:6; John 5:28, 29.

13 If we have faith, we will be able to endure persecution. (*Read Hebrews 11:36-38.*) When we are persecuted, it is helpful to remember the resurrection hope and to realize that God can sustain us as he did "others [who] received their trial [or, test of faith] by mockings and scourgings, indeed, more than that, by bonds and prisons." The Israelites "were continually . . . mocking at his prophets, until the rage of Jehovah came up against his people." (2 Chronicles 36:15, 16) By faith, Micaiah, Elisha, and other servants of God endured "mockings." (1 Kings 22:24; 2 Kings 2:23, 24; Psalm 42:3) "Scourgings" were known in the days of Israel's kings and prophets, and opponents "struck" Jeremiah, not merely slapping him as an insult. "Bonds and prisons" may remind us of his

12. (a) What "women received their dead by resurrection"? (b) In what way will the resurrection of certain men of faith be "better"?

13. (a) "Mockings and scourgings" were suffered by whom? (b) Who experienced "bonds and prisons"?

experiences as well as those of the prophets Micaiah and Hanani. (Jeremiah 20: 1, 2; 37:15; 1 Kings 12:11; 22:26, 27; 2 Chronicles 16:7, 10) Because of having similar faith, Jehovah's modern-day witnesses have been able to endure comparable sufferings "for the sake of righteousness."—1 Peter 3:14.

[14] "They were stoned," said Paul. One such man of faith was Zechariah, son of priest Jehoiada. Enveloped by God's spirit, he spoke out against Judah's apostates. The result? At the order of King Jehoash, conspirators pelted him to death with stones in the courtyard of Jehovah's house. (2 Chronicles 24:20-22; Matthew 23:33-35) Paul added: "They were tried, they were sawn asunder." He may have thought of the prophet Micaiah as one of those who "were tried," and uncertain Jewish tradition has it that Isaiah was sawed in two during King Manasseh's reign.—1 Kings 22:24-28.

[15] Others "died by slaughter with the sword," as, for example, Elijah's fellow prophets of God who were "killed with the sword" in the days of wicked King Ahab. (1 Kings 19:9, 10) Elijah and Elisha were among those with faith who "went about in sheepskins, in goatskins, while they were in want, in tribulation, under ill-treatment." (1 Kings 19:5-8, 19; 2 Kings 1:8; 2:13; compare Jeremiah 38:6.) Those who "wandered about in deserts and mountains and caves and dens of the earth" as objects of persecution must include not only Elijah and Elisha but also the 100 prophets that Obadiah hid by 50's in a cave, supplying them with bread and water when idolatrous Queen Jezebel started to "cut off Jehovah's prophets." (1 Kings 18:4, 13; 2 Kings 2:13; 6:13, 30, 31) What integrity keepers! No wonder Paul said: "The world [unrighteous human society] was not worthy of them"!

[16] Faith gives us the conviction that in God's due time all who love him will "get the fulfillment of the promise." (Read Hebrews 11:39, 40.) Pre-Christian integrity keepers "had witness borne to them through their faith," now a matter of Scriptural record. But they have not yet received "the fulfillment of the promise" of God by an earthly resurrection with the prospect of eternal life under Kingdom rule. Why? "In order that they might not be made perfect apart from" Jesus' anointed followers, for whom "God foresaw something better"—immortal heavenly life and privileges of corulership with Christ Jesus. By their resurrection, beginning after the Kingdom's establishment in 1914, anointed Christians are "made perfect" in the heavens before Jehovah's witnesses of pre-Christian times are resurrected on earth. (1 Corinthians 15:50-57; Revelation 12:1-5) For those earlier witnesses, being "made perfect" must relate to their earthly resurrection, their eventually being "set free from enslavement to corruption," and their attaining human perfection through the services of the High Priest Jesus Christ and his 144,000 heavenly underpriests during his Millennial Reign.—Romans 8:20, 21; Hebrews 7:26; Revelation 14:1; 20:4-6.

Keep in View the Perfecter of Our Faith

[17] Having discussed the acts of pre-Christian witnesses of Jehovah, Paul

---

14. (a) Who was among those "stoned"? (b) Who may have been "sawn asunder"?
15. Who suffered "ill-treatment" and "wandered about in deserts"?

16. (a) Why have pre-Christian witnesses of Jehovah not yet received "the fulfillment of the promise"? (b) For Jehovah's witnesses of pre-Christian times, being "made perfect" must relate to what?
17, 18. (a) To succeed in our race for eternal life, what must we do? (b) How is Jesus Christ the "Perfecter of our faith"?

pointed to the prime example of faith. (*Read Hebrews 12:1-3.*) What a source of encouragement to have 'so great a cloud of witness bearers surrounding us'! This prompts us to put off every weight that would impede our spiritual progress. It helps us to avoid the sin of loss or lack of faith and to run with endurance the Christian race for everlasting life. To reach our goal, however, we must do something more. But what is that?

¹⁸ If we are to succeed in our race for eternal life in God's new system, we need to "look intently at the Chief Agent [or, Chief Leader] and Perfecter of our faith, Jesus." The faith of Abraham and other integrity keepers living prior to Jesus Christ's earthly ministry was imperfect, incomplete, in that they did not understand then unfulfilled prophecies about the Messiah. (Compare 1 Peter 1: 10-12.) But by Jesus' birth, ministry, death, and resurrection, many Messianic prophecies were fulfilled. Thus faith in a perfected sense "arrived" through Jesus Christ. (Galatians 3:24, 25) Moreover, from his heavenly position Jesus continued to be the Perfecter of the faith of his followers, as when pouring out upon them the holy spirit at Pentecost of 33 C.E. and by revelations that progressively developed their faith. (Acts 2:32, 33; Romans 10:17; Revelation 1:1, 2; 22:16) How thankful we are for this "Faithful Witness," this "Chief Leader" of Jehovah's Witnesses!—Revelation 1:5; Matthew 23:10.

¹⁹ Since it is not easy to endure the reproaches of the faithless, Paul urged: "Consider closely the one [Jesus] who has endured such contrary talk by sinners against their own interests, that you may not get tired and give out in your souls." Indeed, if we keep our eyes fixed on "the

19. Why should Jesus be 'considered closely'?

Faithful Witness," Jesus Christ, we will never tire of doing the divine will.—John 4:34.

²⁰ From the 'great cloud of witnesses' we learn much about the facets of faith. For instance, faith like that of Abel enhances our appreciation for Jesus' sacrifice. True faith makes us courageous witnesses, even as Enoch boldly spoke Jehovah's message. As with Noah, our faith moves us to follow God's instructions closely and serve as preachers of righteousness. Abraham's faith impresses us with the need to obey God and trust in His promises, even though some of them have not yet been fulfilled. Moses' example shows that faith enables us to keep unspotted by this world and stand loyally by Jehovah's people. Exploits of Israel's judges, kings, and prophets prove that faith in God can sustain us amid persecution and trials. And how grateful we are that the superlative example of Jesus Christ makes our faith firm and unshakable! Therefore, with Jesus as our Leader and in the strength of our God, let us continue to manifest enduring faith as Jehovah's Witnesses.

20. What are some things you have learned about faith by considering Hebrews 11:1–12:3?

What Are Your Answers?

☐ What acts of pre-Christian witnesses of Jehovah prove that faith is shown by complete reliance upon God in the face of danger?

☐ Why can it be said that by faith we can successfully meet every test of our integrity?

☐ What proof is there that through faith we can endure persecution?

☐ Why is Jesus called the "Perfecter of our faith"?

☐ What are some of faith's many facets?

Earthquakes
—Distress Upon Distress

"IT was horrible. We were lost. It was like an ocean, an ocean, everything moving."

So said a survivor of one of the most lethal earthquakes on record. That devastating earthshock struck in 1976 in China, leveling the city of Tangshan and snuffing out some 800,000 lives. Amazingly, that escapee was able to struggle barefoot out of a hotel that, along with 20 square miles (52 sq km) of cityscape, had collapsed into rubble.

Such seismic events have affected more people in our time than during any other century on record, stimulating worldwide interest in earthquakes. Millions have suffered injury and loss, and millions more have been killed. Major quakes make headlines globally. The 1985 temblor that killed over 9,000 people in Mexico City shook the world emotionally, galvanizing nations to rush aid to the city.

Scientific study of earthquakes has intensified, employing modern technology. The magnitude of quakes is generally rated by the Richter scale, with larger values indicating greater release of energy. Yet, if you were caught in an earthquake, do you suppose you would be wondering about its Richter rating? Not likely. You would be worrying about staying alive. Knowing the Richter magnitude would not alter your personal experience.

Earthquakes in Bible Prophecy

In a prophecy having many features, Jesus Christ included earthquakes, saying: "There will be . . . earthquakes in one place after another." He also predicted: "There will be great earthquakes." Their significance was in their association with the other parts of his prophecy foretelling a generation marked by a unique combination of war, famine, pestilence, lawlessness, fear, and distress on a global scale. The fulfillment would form "the sign" of Jesus' enthronement as King of God's Kingdom and would mark the entry of the world system into its last days. "The sign," including its earthquake feature, has been evident since 1914.—Matthew 24:3, 7-12; Luke 21:11, 25, 26, 31, 32.

Many seismologists believe that earthquakes are no greater or more frequent now than they were in the past. Conversely, others conclude that our generation has experienced earthquakes more frequently than did previous ones. Based on available records, the 20th century does significantly overshadow the past in seismic activity. Publications of the Watch Tower Society have repeatedly called attention to this, highlighting the Biblical significance of earthquakes occurring since 1914.*

Records of earthquakes before 1914 are not complete, however. And earlier generations did not have scientific means of measurement that would permit us reliably to compare the magnitudes of earthquakes past and present. Does this mean that we cannot recognize the fulfillment of Jesus' prophecy?

No, not at all. Jesus apparently foresaw

* See "Earthquakes—A Sign of the End?" in *The Watchtower* of May 15, 1983.

that history would not record all pre-1914 quakes and that earlier generations would not have accurate seismological instruments, just as he foresaw the other circumstances of our time. Consequently, he did not word the prophecy in such a way that recognition of the fulfillment would require earthquake records from earlier centuries or instrument readings. Jesus did not say that the number of earthquakes in "the last days" would be X times greater than the number during some earlier period, nor did he state that we would see the greatest earthquakes ever. (2 Timothy 3:1) He did not speak as a seismologist.

Jesus focused on the human experience. Earthquakes were to be part of "a beginning of pangs of distress." (Matthew 24:8) Distress is not measured by instruments. The travail of people is the ultimate measure of a calamity, including an earthquake. For Jesus' prophecy to be fulfilled, distress caused by earthquakes would have to be present in a significant way. Recognition of the earthquake feature of the prophecy is thus not dependent on the vagaries of human record-keeping or upon scientific measurements of energy released. Today's reports of earthquakes graphically portray the dimensions of human distress resulting from seismic activity.

Why Earthquake Distress Has Increased

Jesus apparently knew that world population would "explode" and that man's practices would verge on "ruining the earth." (Revelation 11:18) In fact, world population has almost tripled since 1914. In prior centuries, an earthquake of a given magnitude usually affected fewer people than it would now.

Consider Tangshan. It was just a hamlet until the 1870's. If the 1976 quake had struck then, fatalities could not have exceeded the small number of residents. In 1879 industrial development began. By the 1970's the population had grown to over a million, setting the stage for grave disaster in 1976.

Furthermore, comparisons based simply on the Richter scale can be misleading. For example, the 1964 earthquake in Alaska killed 115 people and was 8.5 on the Richter scale. The Tangshan quake was rated lower at 8.2. Which one was truly greater? Measured by the human toll rather than by the Richter scale, the Tangshan event was clearly worse, the most severe of the 20th century. Instruments cannot measure the magnitude of human distress.

Relief From All Distress

Just as Jesus foretold, mankind's experience since 1914 has been one of "pangs of distress," with earthquakes contributing their share. He showed the significance, saying: "When you see these things occurring, know that the kingdom of God is near. Truly I say to you, This generation will by no means pass away until all things occur." What would that mean for Jesus' disciples? "As these things start to occur," he said, "raise yourselves erect and lift your heads up, because your deliverance is getting near."—Luke 21:28, 31, 32.

Soon now, no more will distress, including that caused by earthquakes, plague mankind. Under God's Kingdom, every tear of sorrow will be wiped away forever. That is the prospect for people of this generation. And that can be your hope if you respond to the fulfillment of another part of Jesus' prophecy, the message now being heralded worldwide by Jehovah's Witnesses: "This good news of the kingdom will be preached in all the inhabited earth for a witness to all the nations; and then the end will come."—Matthew 24:14; Revelation 21:3, 4.

Insight on the News

"A Bad Idea"

Increasing concern over contaminated blood is forcing medical professionals to take a second look at the advisability of transfusing blood. Henry B. Soloway, M.D., editor of the journal *Pathologist,* noted that from its inception the transfusing of blood has been plagued with problems. "Early on," he explains, "the transfusion of blood contaminated during collection and storage . . . caused numerous deaths from sepsis [infection] and endotoxic [poisonous] shock. The transmission of hepatitis B by blood and blood products caused considerable morbidity during World War II." Even with the advent of technical measures designed to ensure a "safe" blood supply, the transmission of such diseases as AIDS continues.

New concerns have now surfaced over the long-term survival of cancer patients following surgery during which blood transfusions were administered. Soloway says: "There is a significant survival disadvantage when . . . transfusions are given to patients undergoing surgery for cancer of the lung, breast, and colon." What, then, are the alternatives? Soloway concedes: "Jehovah's Witnesses have insisted . . . that transfusion is a bad idea. Perhaps one of these days they will be proved to be wrong. But in the meantime there is considerable evidence to support their contention, despite protestations from blood bankers to the contrary."

Actually, it is obedience to divine law that has kept Jehovah's Witnesses free of the many negative consequences of blood transfusions. Leviticus 17:14 says: "You must not eat the blood of any sort of flesh, because the soul of every sort of flesh is its blood." And Christians were told to 'abstain from blood.' (Acts 15: 28, 29) Clearly, God views taking blood *in any form* as "a bad idea."

"A Gap in Evolution"

"The wings of the insects did not evolve from any extremities or from anything else. They began as exceedingly small appendages sticking up from the back." So states the Swedish newspaper *Svenska Dagbladet,* reporting on recent research as to how insects got their wings. "According to one theory," the report says, "they could have used their prospective wings as a sort of flyswatter for catching insects, until they one day found that they could also fly and carry themselves up from the ground through the air or down from the trees."

The report also shows that biologists are discussing the idea that the "prospective wings," while too small for flying, could have served as solar receptors for warming up and energizing the body. What made them grow from miniature to full size? "Here is a gap in evolution that is hard to explain," admits the report.

The Bible, however, clearly indicates how insects got their wings. "God proceeded to create . . . every winged flying creature according to its kind," says Genesis 1:21. While years of scientific research have merely resulted in speculative theories and a "gap . . . that is hard to explain," the Bible's account fits the known facts. The marvelous design and function of insect wings give credit not to blind evolution but to an intelligent Creator.

Abuse of the Elderly

Older people are more and more becoming the victims of abuse and neglect. It is common nowadays to hear reports of the aged being mistreated, robbed, beaten, and murdered—even in lands where the elderly have traditionally been held in great esteem. In one Eastern country, "a social worker tells of an old woman chained up by her family for fourteen years and allowed only one bath a fortnight," reports *Asiaweek.* It adds that a 60-year-old woman in another Asiatic land "died recently in an old people's home. Her son and daughter-in-law didn't even turn up at her deathbed." The situation is no less true in Western lands. "About 1 in 25 elderly Americans is neglected or abused, either at home or in institutions," says *U.S.News & World Report.* "Neglect is the most common form of mistreatment . . . But both physical abuse and sexual abuse are on the rise."

Inhabitants of ancient Israel as well as members of the early Christian congregation were admonished to show respect, consideration, and honor for older ones. (Exodus 20:12; Leviticus 19:32; Ephesians 6:1, 2; 1 Timothy 5:1, 2) However, the apostle Paul foretold that in the last days we would come into "critical times" when people would move further and further away from God's direction. (2 Timothy 3:1) One of the characteristics Paul singled out was that people would be "utterly lacking in . . . normal human affections." (2 Timothy 3: 2, 3, *The New Testament in Modern English,* by J. B. Phillips) Who can doubt the truthfulness of his words?

The Proud and the Lowly

AFTER mentioning the virtues of John the Baptizer, Jesus turns attention to the proud, fickle people around him. "This generation," he declares, "is like young children sitting in the marketplaces who cry out to their playmates, saying, 'We played the flute for you, but you did not dance; we wailed, but you did not beat yourselves in grief.'"

What does Jesus mean? He explains: "John came neither eating nor drinking, yet people say, 'He has a demon'; the Son of man did come eating and drinking, still people say, 'Look! A man gluttonous and given to drinking wine, a friend of tax collectors and sinners.'"

It is impossible to satisfy the people. Nothing pleases them. John has lived an austere life of self-denial as a Nazirite, in keeping with the angel's declaration that "he must drink no wine and strong drink at all." And yet the people say he is demonized. On the other hand, Jesus lives like other men, not practicing any austerity, and he is accused of excesses.

How hard to please the people are! They are like playmates, some of whom refuse to respond with dancing when other children play the flute or with grief when their fellows wail. Nevertheless, Jesus says: "Wisdom is proved righteous by its works." Yes, the evidence —the works—make clear that the accusations against both John and Jesus are false.

Jesus goes on to single out for reproach the cities of Chorazin, Bethsaida, and Capernaum, where he

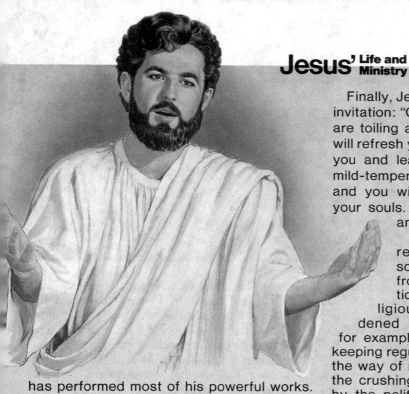

Finally, Jesus gives the appealing invitation: "Come to me, all you who are toiling and loaded down, and I will refresh you. Take my yoke upon you and learn from me, for I am mild-tempered and lowly in heart, and you will find refreshment for your souls. For my yoke is kindly and my load is light."

How does Jesus offer refreshment? He does so by providing freedom from the enslaving traditions with which the religious leaders have burdened the people, including, for example, restrictive Sabbath-keeping regulations. Also, he shows the way of relief to those who feel the crushing weight of domination by the political authorities and to those who feel the weight of their sins through an afflicted conscience. He reveals to such afflicted ones how their sins can be forgiven and how they can enjoy a precious relationship with God.

The kindly yoke Jesus offers is one of complete dedication to God, being able to serve our compassionate, merciful heavenly Father. And the light load Jesus offers to those who come to him is that of obeying God's requirements for life, His commandments, which are not at all burdensome. **Matthew 11: 16-30; Luke 1:15; 7:31-35; 1 John 5:3.**

♦ How is Jesus' generation like children?

♦ How will it be more endurable for Sodom than for Capernaum?

♦ In what ways are people burdened down, and what relief does Jesus offer?

has performed most of his powerful works. If he had done them in the Phoenician cities of Tyre and Sidon, Jesus says, these cities would have repented in sackcloth and ashes. Condemning Capernaum, which apparently has been his home base during his ministry, Jesus declares: "It will be more endurable for the land of Sodom on Judgment Day than for you."

What does Jesus mean by this? Evidently he is showing that, during Judgment Day when proud ones in Capernaum are resurrected, it will be more difficult for them to admit their mistakes and accept Christ than it will be for the resurrected ancient Sodomites to repent humbly and learn righteousness.

Jesus next publicly praises his heavenly Father. He is moved to do so because God conceals precious spiritual truths from wise and intellectual ones but reveals these marvelous things to lowly ones, to babes, as it were.

The "Divine Peace" District Convention
—Just What We Needed!

"**H**EARTS have been reached and attitudes affected." "Jehovah spread a banquet of many wonderful dishes." "The talks were straightforward and specific." "Just what we needed NOW!" "This is just what we needed!"

Such are typical of the many expressions of appreciation heard for the 1986 "Divine Peace" District Convention of Jehovah's Witnesses. All such expressions showed that those in attendance had heeded the fine counsel given both by the chairman and by the opening talk: "Listen and Get the Sense of It."

Since the theme of peace is made so prominent in God's Word, the term occurring more than 300 times in the Bible, it was most fitting that it should be made the theme of our 1986 district conventions. In fact, 18 of the inspired letters from Romans to Revelation begin with such statements as, "May undeserved kindness and peace be increased to you." Let it be noted that in the Hebrew Scriptures the word translated "peace" is *shalohm′*, which not only means the absence of war and strife but also implies health, prosperity, and welfare.—1 Peter 1:2.

Peace was highlighted time and again throughout the program. As the keynote speaker stressed, Jehovah is "the God of peace" and "the God who gives peace." His Son, the "Prince of Peace," promised his followers peace. (Philippians 4:9; Romans 16:20; Isaiah 9:6; John 14:27; 16:33) The keynote speaker showed that the peace that we Witnesses enjoy is unique in that it does not depend on outward circumstances. It is dependent on our respect for authority, which is the reason why the world is without peace—it has no respect for the greatest Authority, Jehovah God. Isaiah put it so well: "O if only you would actually pay attention to my commandments! Then your peace would become just like a river."—Isaiah 48:18.

Among the helpful suggestions given so that we might enjoy divine peace more fully was that we strive to take away from each meeting one practical point of counsel to work on. This talk showed that to be peacemakers it is not enough for us to be *peaceful;* we must work for peace, being willing to yield in the interest of peace.

Feet Shod With the Equipment of the Good News of Peace

Well is our message called "the good news of peace." (Ephesians 6:15) We received much fine counsel on how to bring this good news of peace to others. A three-part symposium on our ministry was very helpful toward this end. The first speaker showed how our house-to-house ministry has become a trademark of Jehovah's Witnesses. Since this work is not easy, we prove our love for God and man by engaging in it. To be truly effective, we must be conscientious and resourceful, keeping accurate records and calling at different times so as to reach all.

The second speaker explained that for us to make disciples we must keep on making return visits on interested persons, doing so with a positive attitude. We should take a personal interest in those we call on, having noted on the original call what interests the householder. Make sure that the householder learns something new on each return visit.

The third speaker pointed out that our Bible students will be helped to become Witnesses if we reach their hearts with viewpoint questions. We want to show genuine interest in them by directing them to God's organization, helping them get to meetings, visiting them at other times, and even inviting them to our homes. In the past 35 years, Bible studies have increased tenfold.

Following this symposium, we had stressed for us the need to manifest an eagerness to share the good news of peace wherever possible and under all circumstances. Age is no handicap. Young children and those in their 90's keep preaching. Some are pioneers, or full-time preachers, though totally blind. Others pioneer though deaf, still others though confined to wheelchairs. One pioneer couple has six young children accompanying them in field service.

Most fitting was the counsel "Do Your Utmost by Sharing in the Full-Time Ministry." Full-time service is the most satisfying, the most rewarding, way of life. Having started, pioneers were urged to do their utmost to remain in full-time service.

As at previous conventions, we heard from longtime proclaimers of the good news, some having served from 30 to as many as 70 years. They told of their joy in preaching the good news. It was indeed encouraging to hear how they overcame obstacles to continue in the ministry. For instance, one brother did not fail to participate in the field ministry a single month in 43 years of service.

Counsel for Family Members

The fine counsel for family members was greatly needed in view of the threat the wicked system of things poses to those in the Christian family. Youths were asked, "Are You Spiritually Progressive?" Today many are serving full-time as pioneers and in Bethel homes. But could more be doing so? To be spiritually progressive means to put God's will first in our lives. It also means having good study habits and sharing regularly in congregation activities and in the field service, as well as having good relations with older ones. And it means not finding pleasure in anything God's Word forbids.

Another three-part symposium began with the searching question, "Is Your Home a Place of Rest and Peace?" Basic to this is choosing as a mate a witness of Jehovah who puts Kingdom interests first and who manifests the fruitage of God's spirit. For a home to be a place of rest and peace, the husband must take the lead in spiritual things, and he ought to love his wife as his own body. The wife should be supportive and have deep respect for her husband. It is also essential to pray together and not to allow place for the Devil. Children can contribute to making a home a place of peace and rest by being submissive and cooperative. Family ties are strengthened when families study the Bible and Bible literature together. —Psalm 34:11.

Greatly needed was the talk that followed, "Is Separation a Way for Marital Peace?" The answer? Perhaps for worldlings but not for Witnesses! For them, separation is not an easy way out of a trialsome marriage. The entire tenor of God's counsel on marriage is that couples remain united. Separation almost invariably has a harmful effect on the children involved, and there is other bad fruitage. Bluntly put, separation is an admission that either one marriage mate or both of them are not manifesting the fruitage of the spirit.—Galatians 5:22, 23.

Fine counsel was given to single Christians in the talk "Should an Unmarried Person Feel Incomplete?" By no means! Since the ministry is the center of our lives, we can be complete whether single or married. In fact, as Paul shows, single Christians have certain advantages. By cultivating contentment, they can rejoice in the gift of singleness and make the most of it.—1 Corinthians 7:32-34.

Needed Counsel on Clean Living

The ever-worsening moral climate of this world has resulted in a number of Witnesses' getting reproved or even disfellowshipped for bad conduct. So how fitting was the straightforward counsel given on matters of conduct! To enjoy divine peace, we must watch our conduct at all times. This was made clear, for example, in the talk "Avoid the Snares of Social Entertainment." Parties can be a lot of fun, but if we are not careful, they can easily interfere with theocratic activities and lead to uncleanness. The imperfect human heart is deceitful and ready to take advantage of any opportunity for toying with immorality. Especially do large parties pose serious dangers, and so does debasing music.—1 Corinthians 15:33.

To preserve our divine peace, we must "Avoid This World's Death-Dealing 'Air.'"

Like the air we breathe, this selfish and disobedient spirit of the world is all around us. The talk dealt with nine manifestations of this death-dealing air, among which are toying with immorality, extremes in clothing and grooming, immoderate use of food and drink, addiction to sports, and pride of race. Keep breathing in this air and it will kill you spiritually.

This matter was driven home still further by the talk "Are You Remaining Clean in Every Respect?" Carelessness makes us guilty of hypocrisy. To have a good conscience, we must keep clean physically, mentally, morally, and spiritually. To that end we must "hate what is bad," "abhor what is wicked." This includes abhorring apostate propaganda.—Psalm 97: 10; Romans 12:9.

The fine talk "Jehovah's Discipline Yields Peaceable Fruit" was pertinent here. Jehovah is the Great Disciplinarian, and he disciplines us because he loves us. None of us are beyond the need for discipline. Even the Son of God was not! (Hebrews 5:8) Yes, discipline basically means training, not always chastisement, and to benefit from the many ways that God administers it, we must be honest with ourselves—and keep humble!

The talk "Keep Building One Another

In Our Next Issue

■ **Customs or Bible Principles —Which Govern *Your* Life?**

■ **Determination Helped Me Succeed**

■ **Do You Have an Inquiring Mind?**

Up" gave fine counsel as regards our speech. How much harm we can do by thoughtless, critical, or complaining talk! Truly, the tongue is hard to control. Fittingly, we were reminded that we should "quit speaking against one another." (James 4:11) Brotherly love will make us careful. And before we say something, it will make us ask: "Is it really true?" "Must I speak of it?" "Will it be upbuilding?"

Drawing On the Prophecies

Talk after talk drew on the inspired prophecies for reminders and admonition. Thus, in the talk "God's Judgments—Unpopular With the World," the speaker stressed that we not only have good news to preach about a paradise but also, like Jeremiah, proclamations to give about God's coming judgments. (Jeremiah, chapters 6 and 7) As Jeremiah boldly exposed the false teachings and corrupt practices of the religious leaders of his day, so we are admonished to do.

The talk "A Time of Testing and Sifting" showed the modern application of Malachi 3:1-3. Jehovah's people have, indeed, been cleansed from false Babylonian teachings and practices. The instituting of theocratic order and the realization that the house-to-house ministry is of prime importance were among the positive points the speaker made.

We also heard a fine talk in which the speaker discussed chapters 11 and 12 of Daniel. It was entitled "Sacred Secrets Unsealed Yield a Sure Hope for Peace." The rivalry between the king of the north and the king of the south keeps the world in turmoil. From Daniel's prophecy, we can see that these kings will never end their conflicts. Only Michael can bring lasting peace.

Another talk drawing on the inspired prophecies was "Worldwide Security Under the 'Prince of Peace.'" It dealt with

Isaiah 9:6, 7 and the context of those verses, showing how that prophecy fittingly applied to Jesus Christ. The speaker stated in his conclusion that Michael "will crown his brilliant career with the victory at Armageddon that will resound without fading at all to time eternal . . . So, then, onward to greater world prominence than ever before, all you witnesses of Jehovah, with complete trust in your God and his reigning King, the 'Prince of Peace'! Display outright fearlessness of the present world conspiracy . . . Be all of you for signs and miracles to the honor of Jehovah!" This really was one of the convention's most stirring talks.

Appreciate Those Taking the Lead

A two-part symposium entitled "Overseers Who Serve the Interests of Peace" truly helped us to appreciate those taking the lead. The first speaker considered the role of traveling overseers and showed that they are, indeed, worthy of double honor because of their many duties. These include giving talks, helping out with problems, training brothers in witnessing, and visiting the physically or spiritually sick. Truly, all traveling overseers deserve our full cooperation and Lydialike hospitality.—Acts 16:15.

The second speaker spelled out the duties of the elders and their role in promoting peace in the congregation. This they can do by preparing for and conducting meetings, making shepherding calls, handling judicial matters, taking the lead in field service, and setting a fine example in conduct and family life. Surely, all of us should want to show appreciation for the appointed elders by being obedient and submissive, as we are counseled at Hebrews 13:17.

"Reaching Out and Acquiring a Fine Standing" was a talk that drove home the need for qualified elders in view of the great increases in Witnesses. It showed all dedicated brothers who are not elders how they can reach out for greater privileges. Especially did the talk urge those who were qualified but did not see the need to serve to a greater extent to ask themselves, Why am I holding back?

Other Spiritual Treats

Much appreciated was the talk "Are You Satisfied With Jehovah's Provisions?" We heard Biblical examples of those who did appreciate the spiritual provisions God supplied and those who did not. To the extent that we are conscious of our spiritual need, we will be satisfied with Jehovah's provisions and will show it. How? By buying out time for personal Bible study and by disciplining ourselves while at the meetings so as to get the most out of them.

What might be said to have posed another challenge to our spirituality was

mentioned in the talk "How Meaningful Are Your Prayers?" It was suggested that we ask ourselves: Have I let my prayers become repetitious, stereotyped, or hurried, as though I am too busy to do justice to my talking with God? In prayer, we come to the greatest Personage in the universe. For our prayers to be meaningful, God must be very real to us. They must come from the heart and be specific, and we must give them thought.

Another treat was the baptism talk, "Gaining Peace With God Through Dedication and Baptism." The speaker showed that our baptism is at one and the same time a most serious and a most joyous occasion. By means of it, we gain peace with God and become ordained ministers of Jehovah's Witnesses. And our dedication is no mere commitment, for we can have and care for a number of commitments at the same time. Rather, to be dedicated means for us to be exclusively devoted to the Divine Being, Jehovah God.

The two Bible dramas were among the most popular convention features. *Preserving Life in Time of Famine* dealt with the touching story of Joseph and his brothers, which brought forth many a tear. Joseph's bighearted, forgiving spirit is a fine example for all of us to imitate. The account also has prophetic significance. The second drama, *Seek God's Righteousness for Survival,* gave forceful and dramatic counsel regarding the problems of our young people. It stressed the need to watch our conduct, put Kingdom interests first, and not be quick in judging the motives of others.

Right in line with the theme of the convention was the public talk, "Peace at Last!—When God Speaks." First, we heard exposed the folly of all the nuclear preparations and the hopelessness of the world situation from any human stand-

---

"Divine Peace" Convention Releases

First released was a revision of the booklet *"Look! I Am Making All Things New,"* at the conclusion of a talk on that subject. It is now a four-color brochure, printed in large type and containing additional information. It should be ideal for starting home Bible studies.

Jehovah's Witnesses—Unitedly Doing God's Will Worldwide, a four-color magazine-size brochure, was the second release. It is a fine instrument to acquaint others with our various activities and gives much historical information about Jehovah's Witnesses.

The third release was a 192-page Bible study aid for initial use at our Congregation Book Studies. It is entitled *Worldwide Security Under the "Prince of Peace."*

Kingdom Melodies No. 7 was the fourth release, an excerpt from which delighted all the conventioners.

When listening to the concluding remarks, all greatly rejoiced to hear that the *Watch Tower Publications Index* for 1930-1985 would be available by September 1. What a blessing to all earnest Bible students!

1. Joseph sold by his brothers in drama at a convention of Korean Witnesses in the United States
2. Watch Tower Society's president, F. W. Franz, addressing a convention audience
3. Part of attentive audience at Yankee Stadium, New York City
4. Thousands were baptized in symbol of their dedication to Jehovah God

point. Only God's Kingdom offers any real hope. What does it mean to listen when God speaks? It means not only that we listen carefully and understand what God is saying but also that we do something about what he says. Then we will not be deceived by the deceptive cry "Peace and security!"

The concluding talk, "Equipped by the God of Peace to Do His Will," sent all the conventioners home feeling good at heart for all the spiritual feasting they enjoyed during the four days. As never before, the convention truly has equipped us for the doing of God's will. So "let us go forward fully resolved to do what? To press ahead in the grand work of Kingdom preaching, truly appreciating our divine peace and all it means to us!"

In the United States, 135 conventions were held in 65 different locations and in 11 languages. The peak attendance was 1,276,578, with 12,603 baptized. The three conventions at Yankee Stadium in New York City had a peak attendance of 95,-091, with 1,110 baptized.

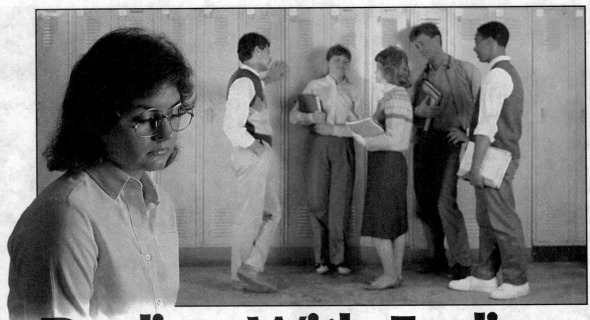

Dealing With Feelings

To deal with our feelings successfully is a real challenge. A youth tells her experience: "I was feeling happy, but the next minute I was in a deep depression. Sometimes I didn't even know what I was feeling. It was as if I was completely lost in the dark. I couldn't express myself and what my emotions were no matter who I talked to, not even to myself. I felt like I wasn't getting attention from people around me, especially my schoolmates, because I wasn't attractive enough. Eventually all these feelings were killing me inside, and I began hating myself and my personality."

The girl got a copy of the book *Your Youth—Getting the Best out of It.* "It was all very interesting," she writes, "so I wanted to read the chapter 'Moving into Womanhood.' I couldn't believe what I was reading because the chapter described exactly how I've felt lately, and it gave the answer. It was so encouraging to read that it was not so unusual to feel this way. I just have to know the *right* way to handle it."

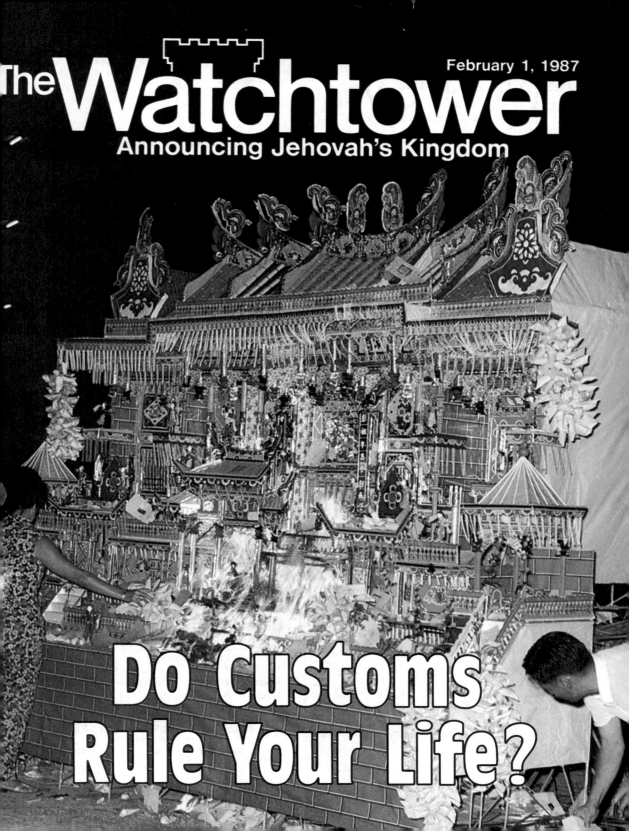

February 1, 1987

The Watchtower

Announcing Jehovah's Kingdom

Do Customs Rule Your Life?

February 1, 1987
Vol. 108, No. 3

The Watchtower®

Announcing Jehovah's Kingdom

In This Issue

THE PURPOSE OF "THE WATCHTOWER" is to exalt Jehovah God as the Sovereign of the universe. It keeps watch on world events as they fulfill Bible prophecy. It comforts all peoples with the good news that God's Kingdom will soon destroy those who oppress their fellowmen and that it will turn the earth into a paradise. It encourages faith in the now-reigning King, Jesus Christ, whose shed blood opens the way for mankind to gain eternal life. "The Watchtower," published by Jehovah's Witnesses continuously since 1879, is nonpolitical. It adheres to the Bible as its authority.

"WATCHTOWER" STUDIES FOR THE WEEKS

Average Printing Each Issue: 12,315,000

Now Published in 103 Languages

SEMIMONTHLY LANGUAGES AVAILABLE BY MAIL
Afrikaans, Arabic, Cebuano, Chichewa, Chinese, Cibemba, Danish,* Dutch,* Efik, English,* Finnish, French,* German,* Greek,* Hiligaynon, Igbo, Iloko, Italian,* Japanese,* Korean, Lingala, Malagasy, Maltese, Norwegian, Portuguese,* Russian, Sepedi, Sesotho, Shona, Spanish,* Swahili, Swedish, Tagalog, Thai, Tsonga, Tswana, Xhosa, Yoruba, Zulu

MONTHLY LANGUAGES AVAILABLE BY MAIL
Armenian, Bengali, Bicol, Bulgarian, Croatian, Czech, Ewe, Fijian, Ga, Greenlandic, Gujarati, Gun, Hausa, Hebrew, Hindi, Hiri Motu, Hungarian, Icelandic, Kannada, Malayalam, Marathi, New Guinea Pidgin, Pangasinan, Papiamento, Polish, Rarotongan, Romanian, Samar-Leyte, Samoan, Sango, Serbian, Silozi, Sinhalese, Slovenian, Solomon Islands-Pidgin, Tahitian, Tamil, Telugu, Tongan, Tshiluba, Turkish, Twi, Ukrainian, Urdu, Venda, Vietnamese

* Study articles also available in large-print edition.

Watch Tower Society offices	Yearly subscription for the above: Semimonthly Languages	Monthly Languages
America, U.S., Watchtower, Wallkill, N.Y. 12589	$4.00	$2.00
Australia, Box 280, Ingleburn, N.S.W. 2565	A$7.00	A$3.50
Canada, Box 4100, Halton Hills, Ontario L7G 4Y4	$5.20	$2.60
England, The Ridgeway, London NW7 1RN	£5.00	£2.50
Ireland, 29A Jamestown Road, Finglas, Dublin 11	IR£6.00	IR£3.00
New Zealand, P.O. Box 142, Manurewa	NZ$15.00	NZ$7.50
Nigeria, PMB 001, Shomolu, Lagos State	₦8.00	₦4.00
Philippines, P.O. Box 2044, Manila 2800	₱60.00	₱30.00
South Africa, Private Bag 2067, Krugersdorp, 1740	R6,50	R3,25

Remittances should be sent to the office in your country or to Watchtower, Wallkill, N.Y. 12589, U.S.A.

Changes of address should reach us 30 days before your moving date. Give us your old and new address (if possible, your old address label).

20 cents (U.S.) a copy

The Bible translation used is the "New World Translation of the Holy Scriptures," unless otherwise indicated.

The Watchtower (ISSN 0043-1087) is published semimonthly for $4.00 (U.S.) per year by Watch Tower Bible and Tract Society of Pennsylvania, 25 Columbia Heights, Brooklyn, N.Y. 11201. Second-class postage paid at Brooklyn, N.Y., and at additional mailing offices.

Postmaster: Send address changes to Watchtower, *Wallkill, N.Y. 12589.*

Published by
**Watch Tower Bible and Tract Society
of Pennsylvania**
25 Columbia Heights, Brooklyn, N.Y. 11201, U.S.A.
Frederick W. Franz, President

Customs or Bible Principles
—*Which Govern Your Life?*

THE Japanese man visiting another Asian land looked on in shocked disbelief. His host, using his own chopsticks, picked over the meat on the serving platter, selected a choice piece, and then placed it on the guest's bowl of rice! Back home in Japan, this would be regarded as bad manners. No one would use his own chopsticks to take food from the common dish unless the chopsticks were first reversed so that the end that is placed in the mouth did not contact the food. Yet his host was really seeking only to honor him, not to offend him. What was unthinkable in Japan was a gesture of respect in this land!

How customs vary! How inconsequential many customs are! And who can say which ones are best? However, some customs are based on superstitions or false teachings. For those whose consciences have been trained by the Bible, such customs are clearly to be avoided. What can help one who is desiring to please God to decide which customs can be observed and to what extent? Following Bible principles can, for a Christian accepts the Bible as his standard no matter where he lives.

Applying Bible Principles

That God's Word does have great power to work on a hum-

Burning models at a funeral

ble person's heart and to bring his life more and more into harmony with God's way has been amply demonstrated. The apostle Paul said that the Christians in Thessalonica received God's Word "just as it truthfully is, as the word of God, which is also at work in you believers." (1 Thessalonians 2:13) So powerful is that Word that, as 1 Corinthians 6:9-11 points out, it had caused many in ancient Corinth, noted for its licentiousness, to forsake their former course of thievery, fornication, drunkenness, and homosexuality. Is God's Word also at work in you? Do its principles govern your life to the fullest extent, enabling you to discern what to do when confronted with local customs?

At times it is obvious that a custom is directly in conflict with Bible principles. In such cases one knowing Jehovah's standards and desiring to be pleasing to him will avoid such customs. For example, the custom may be that of burning incense at a funeral to appease the deceased or his "departed soul" or to give him a good send-off and make his "soul" happy. Or it may be that models of houses, TV sets, cars, and so on, are burned with a view to providing him with enjoyment in the spirit realm. However, a Christian who believes the Bible's statement that the dead "are conscious of nothing at all" knows that such practices are based on false beliefs and thus avoids them.—Ecclesiastes 9:5, 10; Psalm 146:4.

However, when a custom does not directly violate Bible principles but simply makes it more difficult to serve Jehovah God fully, it is harder to draw the line and show that Bible principles govern your life. High regard for education and material success, lifelong subjection to parents, and parental choosing of marriage mates are among some widespread customs that can affect one's relationship with Jehovah. How can Bible principles be applied in situations such as these?

Following Bible Principles

—*The Superior Way*

"**K**UNGSHI, *kungshi fa tsai!*" (Congratulations, may you become rich!) This customary Chinese New Year's greeting puts the emphasis on material success that is so common worldwide. To enhance one's ability to become rich, education may be esteemed almost to the point of becoming an object of worship. In many Oriental countries, often the chief concern of parents is how to get their children into the best kindergarten so that they may then get into the best primary school and so on through college or university. Similarly, in Western lands many are preoccupied with the pursuit of affluence and its easy way of life.

How does such customary preoccupation with material pursuits compare with Bible principles? "Those who are determined to be rich fall into temptation and a snare and many senseless and hurtful desires, which plunge men into destruction and ruin," warns the apostle Paul. He goes on to say: "For the love of money is a root of all sorts of injurious things, and by reaching out for this love some have been led astray from the faith and have stabbed themselves all over with many pains." (1 Timothy 6:9, 10) Pointing up a fact so often evident when people make material goals their prime interest in life, Ecclesiastes 5:10 states: "A mere lover of silver will not be satisfied with silver, neither any lover of wealth with income. This too is vanity."

How often it happens that husband and wife both work hard to obtain all the luxuries of life, only to become so busy that they are never at home to enjoy their possessions! By contrast, before giving the above warning to Timothy, Paul stated:

"To be sure, it is a means of great gain, this godly devotion along with self-sufficiency. So, having sustenance and covering, we shall be content with these things." (1 Timothy 6:6, 8) And Proverbs 28:20 adds this thought: "A man of faithful acts will get many blessings, but he that is hastening to gain riches will not remain innocent." How tragic it is to see otherwise friendly, hospitable people sacrifice the high principles of honesty, dignity, and ethical behavior in their effort to amass ever greater riches!

Within the Family Circle

It is the custom among some tribes and peoples to expect their children—especially their daughters, who will eventually leave home to marry—to go off to work and send home a monthly remittance to demonstrate their filial piety and repay their parents for having raised them. For example, in one family of Jehovah's Witnesses, the daughter told her parents she would like to go to a city in order to become a pioneer (full-time minister). Imagine her dismay when her parents told her they wanted her to go to work so that she could send home a monthly remittance to help them! No, they were not in material need. So the principle of children caring for aged, sick, or needy parents did not apply in this case. (Matthew 15:4-6; 1 Timothy 5:8) It was simply a matter of custom among their tribe that the children should help lay up riches for the family. While often necessary because of a lack of social provisions, this custom was being followed only to save face in the community or because of being infected with the prevalent desire to *"fa tsai."*

When the father discussed this matter with a Christian elder, he was encouraged to consider a number of scriptures and then make his decision. Among the texts pointed out to him was 2 Corinthians 12:14 where Paul states this principle: "For the children ought not to lay up for their parents, but the parents for their children." After considering this and other Bible principles, the parents made their decision. How delighted the daughter was to receive permission—and even some financial help—to become a regular pioneer!

Subjection—How Far?

Another area in which local customs and prevailing attitudes often conflict with Bible principles is in the matter of subjection. In some lands it is the custom to require absolute subjection to parental and other authorities in all areas of life. It is not unusual in such lands for men of 40 or even more years of age to refuse to read any literature of a religion different from that of their parents or to make any major decision without first consulting them, for fear of displeasing the parents. Yet, in such lands it is becoming more common to find young people rebelling outright against their parents. The Bible with its balanced view of matters helps us to avoid both extremes. The principle of *relative* subjection to human authority is clearly stated in Acts 4:19 and 5:29. Also, note how Paul encourages children to be obedient to parents, and yet he shows that it is not without some limitations when he says: "Children, be obedient to your parents *in union with the Lord,* for this is righteous: 'Honor your father and your mother'; which is the first command with a promise."—Ephesians 6:1-3.

Another Bible principle that will affect the extent of one's subjection to parents is that of subjection of a wife to her husband. "Let wives be in subjection to their husbands as to the Lord, because a husband is head of his wife," wrote the apostle Paul. He then amplified that principle by recalling what Jehovah said after arranging the first human marriage: "For this reason a man will leave his father and his mother and he will stick to his wife, and the two will become one flesh."—Ephesians 5:22-31.

However, what about the situation that exists in many lands where the son continues to live in his parents' home following his marriage? The Bible indicates that, in pre-Christian times at least, worshipers of Jehovah often did this. Under such circumstances the father of the household remained the patriarchal head of the family, but wives were to be subject to their own husbands. In some lands, though, it often works out that the mother-in-law is the head of the daughter-in-law. This makes it more difficult for the son to apply fully the principle of husbandly headship and for his wife to be truly in subjection to her husband. Nevertheless, the son will have to balance respect for his parents with the necessity of being head of his own household if he is to have Jehovah as the third strand in the symbolic 'threefold cord that is not easily torn in two.'—Ecclesiastes 4:12.

In some lands an even more difficult situation presents itself when a man marries into a family in which there is no male heir. The following case typifies the plight of many such men when later in life they learn and try to apply Bible principles. A young Catholic man married into a Catholic family. Right from the start, he found he was looked down upon by the family and was little more than an unpaid worker who was expected to father children so that the family name would be kept alive. As is the custom in such an arrangement, he had to give up his own name, allowing his children to be considered the heirs to the family property. When he learned the principle of family headship and tried to apply it, his wife's response was like that of the whole family: 'You brought nothing

into this family, so you don't have any say in how things are to be done!'

While not all such marriage alliances are as extreme as this particular case, it can readily be seen that where such a custom is common and subjection on the part of the husband is expected, problems will arise in applying the Bible principles regarding headship. It becomes very difficult for a Christian husband to exercise his loving headship over his own family and equally difficult for the wife to be in subjection to her husband with "deep respect," rather than to her parents under whose roof they most likely continue to live.—Ephesians 5:33.

Another illustration of how Bible principles might conflict with local custom involves the matter of parents' arranging the marriages of their children. For Christian children with unbelieving parents, this often presents a real problem, as parents feel that they have failed if their children are not married off by a certain age. Thus, great pressure, including beatings, is applied to force the children, and especially girls, to marry. When there is a shortage of suitable Christian mates, the unbelieving parents will do almost anything to arrange a marriage, while the Christian will remember the principle of marrying "only in the Lord."—1 Corinthians 7:39; Deuteronomy 7:3, 4.

Benefit by Following Bible Principles

The outstanding beauty of Bible principles is that they can improve the life of anyone who wishes to apply them, no matter where he lives. They are consistent and draw families together. They make people more honest, make them better husbands and fathers, better wives and mothers, better children, better employees. They can overcome the problems caused by conflicting local customs and balance the application of those customs

Accept the Bible as "the word of God"

Allow that Word to be "at work in you"

Strive to learn what God's Word has to say for your benefit

that do not directly conflict with God's will for man but perhaps make conformity to that will more difficult. How can this be done?

First, just as the Christians in Thessalonica did, you must accept the fact that the Bible really is "the word of God." This means realizing that it truly is wisdom from the highest Source. Second, you must strive to learn what that "word of God" has to say for your benefit. Learn to isolate the principles and laws of God as you read and study the Bible. Then, as a third step, you must allow that word to be "at work in you." (1 Thessalonians 2:13) This involves close association with the congregations of God's people now located in over 200 lands and islands of the sea. It is this that has made the worldwide

brotherhood of Jehovah's Witnesses just that—a brotherhood in fact and not in name only.

First and foremost, Jehovah's people are interested in unity with God by allowing Bible principles to govern their lives. With what results? True and lasting unity with others who are also at unity with God, as well as peace of mind that sustains one through all situations existing in this present system of things. (Philippians 4: 6, 7) Such unity and close relationship with God and with one another is a positive aid in improving the quality of life now and holds the promise of everlasting life in God's righteous new system where all things will finally be brought fully into subjection to God's will.—1 Timothy 4:8; 1 Corinthians 15:28.

A Lesson in Mercy

JESUS may still be in Nain, where he recently resurrected a widow's son, or perhaps he is visiting a city nearby. A Pharisee named Simon desires a closer look at the one who is performing such remarkable works. So he invites Jesus to have a meal with him.

Viewing the occasion as an opportunity to minister to those present, Jesus accepts the invitation, even as he has accepted invitations to eat with tax collectors and sinners. Yet, when he enters Simon's house, Jesus does not receive the cordial attention usually accorded guests.

Sandal-clad feet become hot and dirty due to traveling dusty Galilean roads, and it is a customary act of hospitality to wash the feet of guests with cool water. But Jesus' feet are not washed when he arrives. Neither does he receive a welcoming kiss, which is common etiquette. And the customary oil of hospitality is not provided for his hair.

During the course of the meal, while the guests are reclining at the table, an

"I suppose," says Simon, perhaps with an air of indifference at the seeming irrelevance of the question, "it is the one to whom he freely forgave the more."

"You judged correctly," Jesus says. And then turning to the woman, he says to Simon: "Do you behold this woman? I entered into your house; you gave me no water for my feet. But this woman wet my feet with her tears and wiped them off with her hair. You gave me no kiss; but this woman, from the hour that I came in, did not leave off tenderly kissing my feet. You did not grease my head with oil; but this woman greased my feet with perfumed oil."

The woman has thus given evidence of heartfelt repentance for her immoral past. So Jesus concludes: "By virtue of this, I tell you, her sins, many though they are, are forgiven, because she loved much; but he who is forgiven little, loves little."

Jesus is in no way excusing or condoning immorality. Rather, this incident reveals his compassionate understanding of people who make mistakes in life but who then manifest that they are sorry for these and so come to Christ for relief. Providing true refreshment to the woman, Jesus says: "Your sins are forgiven. . . . Your faith has saved you; go your way in peace." **Luke 7:36-50; Matthew 11:28-30.**

♦ How is Jesus received by his host Simon?
♦ Who seeks Jesus out, and why?
♦ What illustration does Jesus provide, and how does he apply it?

uninvited woman quietly enters the room. She is known in the city to be living an immoral life. Likely she has heard Jesus' teachings, including his invitation for 'all those who are loaded down to come to him for refreshment.' And being deeply moved by what she has seen and heard, she has now sought out Jesus.

The woman comes up behind Jesus at the table and kneels at his feet. As her tears fall on his feet, she wipes them off with her hair. She also takes perfumed oil from her flask, and as she tenderly kisses his feet, she pours the oil on them. Simon watches with disapproval. "This man, if he were a prophet," he reasons, "would know who and what kind of woman it is that is touching him, that she is a sinner."

Perceiving his thinking, Jesus says: "Simon, I have something to say to you."

"Teacher, say it!" he responds.

"Two men were debtors to a certain lender," Jesus begins. "The one was in debt for five hundred denarii, but the other for fifty. When they did not have anything with which to pay back, he freely forgave them both. Therefore, which of them will love him the more?"

Manifest an Eagerness
to Declare the Good News

"There is eagerness on my part to declare the good news also to you."—ROMANS 1:15.

"THEY came from all over . . . hundreds of volunteers pouring into the bi-county area, arriving with truckloads of food and clothing, setting up evacuation shelters, some working 18 to 20 hours a day, some getting no sleep in the first days after the terrifying levee break."

² That was how the people reacted when a flash flood hit a central California community last spring, causing some 24,000 people to flee for safety. Yes, when disasters—from local floods to earthquakes to nuclear accidents—strike, people often respond voluntarily and pitch in to help. They roll up their sleeves, so to speak, brave many dangers and inconveniences, and eagerly come to the aid of others —even total strangers.

A Time of Urgency

³ Today, mankind is face-to-face with

1, 2. How do people often react in an emergency?

3. What extreme emergency is mankind facing today?

the greatest disaster in history. It is not because of the damage man is doing to the environment, the threat of nuclear war, or the increase of crime and violence, as serious as these things are. Rather, mankind is facing what Jesus Christ called a "great tribulation such as has not occurred since the world's beginning until now, no, nor will occur again." To show how devastating the "great tribulation" will be, Jesus went on to say: "In fact, unless those days were cut short, no flesh would be saved."—Matthew 24:21, 22.

⁴ How would you react if you knew that many people, including some who were close to you, would soon perish in that tribulation? Would you be eager to help? Recall Ezekiel's prophetic vision of the man with the secretary's inkhorn. He was told that only those who had received the symbolic mark on their forehead would survive the destruction of Jerusalem, and he was the one to administer that lifesaving mark. How did he respond? "I have done just as you have commanded me," he reported.—Ezekiel 9:1-11.

⁵ Are you manifesting the same willingness and eagerness as the man clothed with linen, doing just as Jehovah has commanded? What has Jehovah commanded? Through his Son, Jesus Christ, he has given the order: "Go therefore and make disciples of people of all the nations, . . . teaching them to observe all the things I have commanded you." (Matthew 28: 19, 20) This is as much a lifesaving work as the symbolic marking of the foreheads in Ezekiel's day. Anyone who does not respond and become a disciple of Jesus Christ will suffer destruction at the hand of God's Chief Executioner. (2 Thessalonians 1:6-8) Do you sense the urgency? Do

you show it by manifesting an eagerness to declare the good news?

Eagerness—How Manifested?

⁶ Jehovah's people, on the whole, do sense the urgency of the time. All of us are eager to see as many people as possible saved from the impending "great tribulation." Eagerness, according to one dictionary, is a "keen or vehement desire in the pursuit or for the attainment of something." One who is eager about something directs both thought and action toward attaining it. He will do everything within his power to overcome any obstacle and hindrance, and he will persist in doing so until he reaches his goal. That was how the apostle Paul felt about his ministry, and we do well to imitate him.—1 Corinthians 4:16.

⁷ Consider, for example, Paul's words to the Christians in Rome, at Romans 1: 13-16. "I many times purposed to come to you," he told them. Why? "In order that I might acquire some fruitage also among you," he explained. By this, did Paul simply have in mind visiting the brothers in Rome and perhaps encouraging them to develop more fully "the fruitage of the spirit," as some commentators claim? (Galatians 5:22, 23) No, for his added words "even as among the rest of the nations" make it clear that he was intent on gaining *Kingdom* fruitage among the non-Christian community there in Rome. He wanted to bring the good news to Rome and perhaps from there to places beyond. —Romans 15:23, 24.

⁸ "But I have been hindered until now," Paul said. Hindered by what? Was he too busy with personal matters to reach out? Well, Paul was a busy man but not with

---

4. In the face of such emergency, how should we react?
5. What work are we under command to do, and how urgent is it?

6. What is meant by "eagerness"?
7. Why did Paul want to go to Rome?
8. How had Paul "been hindered" from going to Rome?

personal interests. By the time he wrote to the Romans (about 56 C.E.), he had already completed two extensive missionary journeys and was busily engaged in his third. Often, on these journeys he was directed by holy spirit to specific assignments. (See Acts 16:6-9.) Even as he wrote his letter, plans were already made for him to go to Jerusalem "to minister to the holy ones" there. (Romans 15:25, 26) And he had also experienced numerous other 'hindrances' of this sort.—See 2 Corinthians 11:23-28.

⁹ Even so, Paul did not feel that he had enough to do, nor did he reason that he had his assignment and that was plenty. He wanted to do more. In fact, he said: "There is eagerness on my part to declare the good news also to you there in Rome." That is what eagerness is all about! Fittingly, Professor F. F. Bruce in his book *The Epistle of Paul to the Romans* said this of the apostle: "The preaching of the gospel is in his blood, and he cannot refrain from it; he is never 'off duty' but must constantly be at it, discharging a little more of that debt which he owes to all mankind—a debt which he will never fully discharge so long as he lives." Is that how you view the ministry?

¹⁰ Today, all of Jehovah's people are busy with many responsibilities. Some have families to care for. Some have obligations in other areas. Others are limited in what they can do because of age or poor health. And still others have weighty assignments in the Christian congregation. Yet, we also realize that time is running out for the present system of things, and the Kingdom witness must be given. (Mark 13:10) Thus, like Paul, we should

manifest an eagerness to reach out in the preaching work in spite of the 'hindrances' that may be in our way. We should not feel complacent, considering that we have enough to do as it is.—1 Corinthians 15:58.

"A Debtor" to All

¹¹ There was another motivating force behind Paul's tireless efforts in declaring the good news. "Both to Greeks and to Barbarians, both to wise and to senseless ones I am a debtor," Paul said. (Romans 1:14) In what way was Paul "a debtor"? Other translations render this expression as "I am under obligation" (*New English Bible*), "I have an obligation" (*Today's English Version*), or "I owe a duty" (*Jerusalem Bible*). Was he saying, then, that the preaching work was a burdensome duty or obligation that he had to discharge before God? It is easy to develop such an attitude if we lose sight of the urgency or are distracted by worldly attractions. But that was not what Paul had in mind.

¹² As God's "chosen vessel" and as "an apostle to the nations," Paul did have a very heavy responsibility before God. (Acts 9:15; Romans 11:13) Yet his sense of obligation was not just to God. He said he was "a debtor" to 'Greeks, Barbarians, wise and senseless ones.' For the mercy and privilege granted him, he felt it his duty to preach so that all people could hear the good news. He realized, too, that it is God's will that "all sorts of men should be saved and come to an accurate knowledge of truth." (1 Timothy 1:12-16; 2:3, 4) That was why he labored incessantly, not just to live up to his responsibility toward God but also to discharge his debt to his fellow humans. Do you feel such a personal debt

---

9. How did Paul manifest an eagerness to declare the good news?
10. What 'hindrances' may be in our way, but how should we deal with them?

11. What is meant by "I am a debtor"?
12. To whom was Paul "a debtor," and why?

toward the people in your territory? Do you feel you owe it to them to exert yourself to bring them the good news?

"Not Ashamed of the Good News"

[13] Paul was certainly an outstanding example in manifesting an eagerness to declare the good news. He deeply appreciated the undeserved kindness shown him by God, and he did not want it to be in vain. (1 Corinthians 15:9, 10) That is why he went on to say: "For I am not ashamed of the good news." (Romans 1:16) From a human point of view, the Christians were not only unpopular but also despised. "We have become as the refuse of the world, the offscouring of all things," Paul said. (1 Corinthians 4:13) Yet he was not ashamed to take the good news to Rome, the center of the learned world and the seat of the imperial Roman Empire. When faced with apathy, abuse, or even opposition in our preaching work, we can remember Paul's encouraging example.

[14] "Not ashamed of the good news" is really another way of saying "proud of the good news," and that is what we should be. Why? Because "it is, in fact, God's power for salvation to everyone having faith," Paul explained. He had ample personal experience to back up his statement. With the good news, Paul said, "we are overturning reasonings and every lofty thing raised up against the knowledge of God; and we are bringing every thought into captivity to make it obedient to the Christ." (2 Corinthians 10:5) Whether it was against the tradition of the Jews, the philosophy of the Greeks, or the might of the Romans, the good news proved triumphant.

[15] How fine it is that instead of feeling it a burden, Paul was 'eager' to fulfill his God-given responsibility! As he himself expressed it: "For necessity is laid upon me. Really, woe is me if I did not declare the good news!" (1 Corinthians 9:16) This eagerness helped him carry on for many years of tireless service, so that finally he could say: "I have fought the fine fight, I have run the course to the finish, I have observed the faith."—2 Timothy 4:7.

Effectiveness Adds to Results

[16] Like Paul, the man with the secretary's inkhorn in Ezekiel's vision was no doubt eager about his assignment. He brought back a good report: Mission accomplished! The account does not tell us how he went about finding all the ones "sighing and groaning over all the detestable things that are being done." (Ezekiel 9:4) Though nothing was said about how all this marking was accomplished, clearly it was not a simple task.

[17] Similarly today, our commission is not a simple one. The question, therefore, is: How effective are we at this lifesaving task? To make disciples of as many people as possible, we must engage in this work regularly and systematically, not passing up any opportunity to share the good news. Like us, the people in our community are busy; they may seldom be at home when we call, and even if they are, they are often preoccupied. What can we do? Well, we need to keep accurate records and return at different times, over and over again, hoping that we will find

---

13. What was Paul's estimation of the good news?
14. Why was Paul "not ashamed of the good news"?
15. How was eagerness a motivating force in Paul's life?
16. What possible challenges do you think faced the man with the secretary's inkhorn in Ezekiel's vision?
17. (a) What challenges do you face in the disciple-making work, and how do you deal with them? (b) Are the needed efforts worth it?

someone to talk to. Are such efforts worth it? Let the following brief notes from two householders give the reply:

"I would like to express my appreciation to the Jehovah's Witnesses for their many visitations to my house. I know at times your mission is not viewed by those outside of your church with the enthusiasm it richly deserves. So I thought I'd share my experiences with you and say thank you!"

"There are so many of us hungering for the truth, so many of us believing that all roads lead to salvation. You who dare to keep searching for someone to minister to, don't give up on us! We are not awful people, though we insult you, embarrass you, and reject you. Do not give up, because we have been taught many lies, told many horrible stories, and educated to hate you to keep the message of Jehovah's Kingdom from us."

¹⁸ To reach the heart of individuals and help them get the sense of the good news takes more than superficial contact, delivering a prepared message, or leaving some Bible literature. We must endeavor to discern their needs and concerns, likes and dislikes, fears and prejudices. All of this

---

18. (a) How can you help others to get the sense of the good news? (b) How did one publisher overcome apparent apathy?

Consider Paul's Example According to Romans 1:13-16—

☐ Why was he eager to go to Rome?

☐ What hindered him from going? But how did he react?

☐ To whom and why was he "a debtor"?

☐ How did he feel about the good news? Why?

☐ Like Paul, what can we do to be effective in declaring the good news?

---

takes a great deal of thought and effort —and eagerness on our part. Consider the following experience:

A publisher talked to a woman at an apartment door but did not get much response. Noticing there were several children around, she asked how many children the woman had. She replied that these were not her children but belonged to her brother-in-law, who had just immigrated from another country. The conversation soon came to the topic of inadequate housing. The publisher agreed that reasonable housing was hard to find in big cities, as she also had relatives coming soon, and she offered to help. The lady was elated and called her brother-in-law to the door. The discussion continued, and they exchanged phone numbers. Not forgetting the purpose of the call, the publisher tactfully opened to page 157 in the *Live Forever* book and explained that in the promised new system, problems in housing and employment will be gone. The man was very impressed and readily accepted the book. Later, the publisher returned with word about a rental apartment; she also renewed their Bible discussion.

¹⁹ The time for preaching the good news is fast running out. How much longer the "four angels" will go on "holding tight the four winds of the earth" we do not know. (Revelation 7:1) In any case, the "great tribulation" is still ahead, and people of honest heart are being gathered. Indeed, the "fields" are "white for harvesting." (Matthew 24:21, 22; John 4:35) Now is the time for us to exert ourselves vigorously in this never-to-be-repeated work. How can we make best use of the remaining time? What can we do to have a fuller share in this lifesaving work? And what can help us to continue manifesting an eagerness to declare the good news? These questions will be discussed in the next article.

---

19. It is now time for us to do what? And what do we need to discuss further?

Doing Our Utmost
to Declare the Good News

"Do your utmost to present yourself approved to God, a workman with nothing to be ashamed of."
—2 TIMOTHY 2:15.

"A FEW years ago, many of us thought that only those with special circumstances could pioneer," wrote a pioneer, or full-time minister, in Japan. "It seems we were wrong. We are learning that only those with special circumstances *cannot* pioneer."

[2] That positive outlook has resulted in one of the most phenomenal growths in the ranks of full-time ministers among Jehovah's Witnesses in recent years. Today in Japan, two out of every five Kingdom publishers are engaged in some form of full-time ministry. But this zealous spirit is not limited to Japan. In the last service year, the number of publishers around the world grew by 5 percent, whereas the number of full-time ministers increased by 22 percent. Clearly, Jehovah's people have taken to heart the apostle Paul's words: "Do your utmost to present yourself approved to God, a workman with nothing to be ashamed

---

1, 2. What growth in the ranks of full-time ministers have you observed? What has contributed to it?

of." (2 Timothy 2:15) Is this the case with you?

"This Is What the Love of God Means"

³ When pioneers are asked why they have taken up the full-time ministry, invariably their answer is that it is because of their love for Jehovah God. (Matthew 22:37, 38) This, of course, is as it should be, for without love as the proper motive, any amount of effort would be in vain. (1 Corinthians 13:1-3) It is truly commendable that so many of our fellow Christians—in fact, an average of more than seven publishers in every congregation around the world—have made room in their lives to demonstrate their love for God in this way.

⁴ Of course, all of us who have dedicated our lives to Jehovah did so because we love him. When we learned of the love that Jehovah and his Son, Jesus Christ, have for us, and of the marvelous blessings his Kingdom will bring, our hearts were moved to respond with love for him. This is how the apostle John put it: "We love, because he first loved us." (1 John 4:19) We respond naturally in that way because that is how we are made. But is that warm feeling in our hearts all that love of God involves?

⁵ No, love of God means more. The apostle John tells us: "This is what the love of God means, that we observe his commandments; and yet his commandments are not burdensome." (1 John 5:3) Yes, true love, like true faith, is expressed by action. (Compare 2 Corinthi-

ans 8:24.) It wants to please and gain the approval of the one loved. What an excellent way those in the full-time ministry have chosen to demonstrate their love for Jehovah and Jesus Christ!

⁶ Individual circumstances do vary, and they must be taken into consideration. Yet when we look at those who are in the full-time ministry, we find that they include people in every possible situation—young and old, single and married, having good and poor health, with and without family responsibilities, and so on. The difference is that, rather than allowing these factors to become roadblocks, they, like the apostle Paul, have learned to work around them or to live with them. (2 Corinthians 11:29, 30; 12:7) Consider, for instance, a typical family.

Eiji is an elder in his congregation. He and his wife have been pioneering together for 12 years while bringing up three children. How did they do it? "We had to live more simply," says Eiji. Even the children had to learn to accept a no for many of the things they wanted. "Though we've had some difficult times, Jehovah has always provided what we needed."

Have the sacrifices been worth it? "Every night before we turn out the lights, I watch my wife write out her preaching report for the day," says Eiji. "When I see my family putting spiritual interests first like this, I feel that everything is as it should be, and I have a sense of accomplishment. I can't imagine us not pioneering together." How does his wife feel about it? "Eiji has taken care of us very well," she says. "When I see him busy with spiritual matters, I feel a deep inner contentment. I hope we can continue."

With father and mother spending so much time in the preaching work every day, what has been the effect on the children? The older son is now working on a four-year construc-

---

3. What is the motivating force behind this growth?
4. How did we come to love God? (Romans 5:8)
5. What does the love of God involve? (1 John 2:5)

---

6. (a) What sort of persons have been able to pioneer? What made it possible for them to do so? (b) Do you know of any such examples?

tion project at the Watch Tower Society's branch. The daughter is a regular pioneer, and the school-age son is aiming to become a special pioneer. They are all glad that their parents are pioneers.

7 Families like this one can be found among Jehovah's Witnesses in many countries around the world. They put forth a real effort to make the best of their circumstances in order to enter and then remain in the full-time service. By their actions, they demonstrate what the love of God really means to them. Earnestly, they are heeding Paul's admonition: "Do your utmost to present yourself approved to God, a workman with nothing to be ashamed of."—2 Timothy 2:15.

"A Workman With Nothing to Be Ashamed Of"

8 When Paul wrote those words to Timothy, about 65 C.E., Timothy was already serving in a very responsible position in the Christian congregation. Paul called him "a fine soldier of Christ Jesus" and repeatedly reminded him of his responsibility in teaching and instructing others. (2 Timothy 2:3, 14, 25; 4:2) Yet, he urged Timothy: "Do your utmost to present yourself approved to God." The expression "do your utmost" is translated from a Greek term meaning "speed you up." (See Kingdom Interlinear Translation.) In other words, Paul was telling Timothy that in order to have God's approval he needed to step up his activity, even though he was already carrying a heavy load of responsibility.

Why? So that he could be "a workman with nothing to be ashamed of."

9 This latter phrase reminds us of the three slaves in Jesus' parable of the talents, as recorded at Matthew 25:14-30. Upon the master's return, it was time for them to submit their work to the master for his approval. The slaves given five and two talents were commended by the master for what they had done with the things entrusted to them. They were invited to 'enter into the joy of their master.' But the slave entrusted with one talent was found wanting. What he had was taken away, and to his shame, he was thrown out "into the darkness outside."

10 The first two slaves worked hard and multiplied their master's interests. They were truly workmen "with nothing to be ashamed of." But why was the third slave shamed and punished even though he did not lose what was given him? It was because he did nothing constructive with it. As the master pointed out, he could at least have deposited the money in the bank. But what was basically wrong was that he had no genuine love for his master. "I grew afraid and went off and hid your talent in the ground," he confessed to the master. (Matthew 25:25; compare 1 John 4:18.) He viewed his master as a harsh, "exacting man" and his assignment as a burden. He did the least possible in order to get by rather than doing his "utmost" to win the master's approval.

11 Today that parable is undergoing fulfillment. The Master, Jesus Christ,

_____

7. (a) Give examples regarding individuals you know who overcame obstacles to enter the full-time service. (b) What Bible counsel have they taken to heart?
8. Why did Paul urge Timothy to 'do his utmost' and what does that mean?

9. What parable of Jesus can help us to understand Paul's words about "a workman with nothing to be ashamed of"?
10. Why was the slave who was given one talent shamed and punished?
11. How does that parable concern us today?

'Throw the good-for-nothing
slave out'

has returned and is inspecting the work of his "slave" class, as well as that of their companions, the "great crowd" of sheeplike ones. (Matthew 24:45-47; Revelation 7:9, 15) What does the Master find? If we content ourselves with token service just to get by, then it could be that we will be found among those shamed and thrown "into the darkness outside." On the other hand, if we 'do our utmost,' that is, 'speed up' our work in response to the urgency of the time, we will be found approved as 'workmen with nothing to be ashamed of' and will share in the 'joy of our master.'

Discipline and Self-Sacrifice Needed

12 The continued expansion of the pioneer ranks in country after country around the world is clear evidence that Jehovah's people as a whole are 'doing their utmost' to prove themselves 'workmen with nothing to be ashamed of.' But have you ever wondered why in some countries the percentage of brothers able to enter the full-time service is so much greater than in other countries? This interesting question was put to some of

12. What factors have enabled a high percentage of the publishers in Japan to enter the full-time ministry?

the pioneers in Japan. Consider these answers:

"I don't think it means that the faith, or the love, of the Japanese Witnesses is greater than that of their brothers in other countries," said a Bethel worker who has been in full-time service for some 30 years. "But I believe that the Japanese personality probably has something to do with it. As a whole, the Japanese people are obedient; they respond readily to encouragement."

"Because there are so many pioneers in almost every congregation," an elder commented, "the general idea is that anyone can do it." The Japanese people do like to do things in groups. They have an excellent team spirit.

These are surely thought-provoking remarks, and if we are serious about improving our service to Jehovah, there are a number of salient points worthy of our careful consideration.

[13] First of all, there is the matter of being obedient and ready to respond to encouragement. When direction and encouragement come from the proper source, it is only right that we should respond readily. Thus, rather than viewing these qualities as mere national traits, we keep in mind Jesus' words: "My sheep listen to my voice, and I know them, and they follow me." (John 10:27) We also remember that one feature of "the wisdom from above" is being "ready to obey." (James 3:17) These are qualities that all Christians are encouraged to put on. Due to background and upbringing, some may be more given to independent thinking and self-will than others. Perhaps this is an area where we need to discipline ourselves and 'make our mind over' so that we can perceive more clearly what the "will of God" is.—Romans 12:2.

[14] As dedicated Christians, we have accepted Jesus' invitation: "If anyone wants to come after me, let him disown himself and pick up his torture stake and continually follow me." (Matthew 16:24) To "disown" oneself means literally 'to deny oneself utterly' and thereafter willingly to accept being owned by Jehovah God and Jesus Christ, letting them control our lives and tell us what we should and should not do. What better way is there to demonstrate that we have disowned ourselves than to follow Jesus' steps in the full-time ministry?

[15] Then there is the matter of being content with less materially. This clearly runs contrary to the general trend of the world, which promotes "the desire of the flesh and the desire of the eyes and the showy display of one's means of life." (1 John 2:16) But Jesus said emphatically: "You may be sure, none of you that does not say good-bye to all his belongings can be my disciple." (Luke 14:33) Why is this so? Because to be Jesus' disciple means more than just being a believer. When Jesus called Andrew, Peter, James, John, and the others to be his disciples in the second year of his ministry, he did not stop at asking them to believe in him as the Messiah. He later invited them to follow him and to do the work he was doing, that is, the full-time preaching work. What was their response? "At once they abandoned their nets and followed him." James and John even "left their father Zebedee in the boat with the hired men and went off after him." (Mark 1:16-20) They left behind their business and former associates and took up preaching full-time.

13. How can we benefit from the matter of being obedient and ready to respond to encouragement?

14. What invitation have all dedicated Christians accepted, and what is involved?
15. (a) How is being content with less materially connected with following Jesus? (b) How did the early disciples respond to Jesus' invitation to follow him?

¹⁶ It is easy to see, therefore, why being content with less is such an important factor in doing our utmost in Jehovah's service. If we are burdened down with many material things or obligations, we might become like the rich young ruler who turned down Jesus' invitation to be his follower, not because he could not do it, but because he was not willing to leave behind his "many possessions." (Matthew 19: 16-22; Luke 18:18-23) So rather than squandering our time and energy pursuing things that will soon 'pass away,' we want to invest these valuable assets for our lasting welfare.—1 John 2:16, 17.

¹⁷ Finally, there is the matter of team spirit. Andrew, Peter, James, and John undoubtedly influenced one another in their decision to accept Jesus' invitation to follow him. (John 1:40, 41) Similarly, the fact that so many of our brothers are able to make room in their busy lives to enter the full-time service should move us to consider our own case seriously. On the other hand, those among us who are already enjoying this privilege can share their happy experiences with others, thereby encouraging these also to join their ranks. And, of course, full-time ministers can help one another to the mutual benefit of all.—Romans 1:12.

¹⁸ Even those whose present circumstances do not permit them to take up the full-time ministry can do much to add to the pioneer spirit. How? By supporting and encouraging those who are pioneering, by showing an active interest in those who have the potential to do so, by arranging for at least one member of their family to pioneer, by engaging in the auxiliary pioneer work whenever possible, and by working toward entering the full-time service as soon as possible. Doing so, all of us can show that we are 'doing our utmost' to serve Jehovah whether we are presently enrolled in the full-time ministry or not.

Persevere in Doing Our Utmost

¹⁹ Indeed, as Jehovah is speeding up the work, it is now the time for us to 'do our utmost' in order to be 'workmen with nothing to be ashamed of.' As fine soldiers of Jesus Christ, we also need to put aside all unnecessary burdens so that we may serve effectively and gain his approval. (2 Timothy 2:3-5) As we work hard to expand our share in Kingdom service, we can be assured that our efforts will be richly rewarded. (Hebrews 6:10; 2 Corinthians 9:6) Thus, rather than standing on the sidelines, so to speak, let us persevere in doing our utmost to preach the good news, in answer to the psalmist's invitation: "Serve Jehovah with rejoicing. Come in before him with a joyful cry."—Psalm 100:2.

19. What should we resolve to do in view of the time?

<hr>

16. As dedicated Christians, in what should we invest our time and energy? (Proverbs 3:9)
17. To what extent can team spirit be a positive influence?
18. How can all of us contribute to the pioneer spirit?

Review Box

☐ What does love of God involve?

☐ What was the real problem with the third slave in Jesus' illustration of the talents?

☐ What does disowning ourselves mean?

☐ Why must followers of Jesus 'say good-bye to their material belongings'?

☐ How can all of us contribute to the pioneer spirit?

Kingdom Proclaimers Report

Honesty Brings Praise to Jehovah

JEHOVAH requires that his servants be honest, just, and trustworthy. For instance, Moses was advised to select as overseers those who were "capable men, fearing God, trustworthy men, hating unjust profit." (Exodus 18:21) Like those chosen men, Jehovah's Witnesses worldwide are known to be trustworthy, as the following experience shows.

□ A Witness who works at the Watch Tower Society's branch office in Ghana was mistakenly overpaid $3,630 by a bank cashier. The mistake was not noticed by the cashier or the brother at the time. Reaching home, however, the brother saw that he had been overpaid and immediately returned to the bank with the money. The cashier, catching sight of the brother,

exclaimed: "Here he is! He has truly returned! David, your man has brought the money!" The money was returned to the cashier. David, one of Jehovah's Witnesses who works at the same bank, had assured the cashier and others who knew of the mistake that the money would be returned as soon as the brother discovered the mistake.

"While this drama was going on," the report states, "all eyes" were upon the two brothers. The one who returned the money explained: "Well, I couldn't have kept this money with a good conscience before my God, Jehovah." This incident added to the respect the bank officials already have for the Watch Tower Society.

Honesty engenders respect,

especially in a world that is so dishonest. This brother knew that he was accountable to one higher than man, Jehovah God. Such honesty brings praise to Jehovah, as he is "a God of faithfulness, with whom there is no injustice."—Deuteronomy 32:4.

□ Being honest and maintaining a good conscience toward God is also noted in an experience of a young man in Thailand. He had subscribed for *The Watchtower* and *Awake!* and was starting to apply the Bible counsel he found in these journals. He was the chief accountant of the company he worked for, and his conscience began to bother him, since it was the custom for many businesses to keep two sets of books in order to evade taxes. When he approached the manager about this matter, the manager just laughed. Then came in one of the magazines another article stressing the need for honesty. With a troubled conscience, the accountant prayed to Jehovah to help him straighten out this tax matter with his manager. A large amount of money was involved. The next morning he asked the manager for permission to pay the taxes due, and to his surprise, the manager agreed without any further argument.

Now this man is happy as he leads an honest life before God and man. Such a wise course makes Jehovah happy, too, for as Proverbs 27:11 states: "Be wise, my son, and make my heart rejoice, that I may make a reply to him that is taunting me."

"I couldn't have kept this money with a good conscience"

Determination
Helped Me Succeed

As told by Joseph A. Oakley

WHAT a joy it was in 1950 to be among the 123,707 who attended the international convention of Jehovah's Witnesses at New York City's Yankee Stadium in the United States! And what a privilege afterward to attend the 16th class of the Gilead missionary school in upstate New York!

Upon graduation I was assigned, along with a group of fellow Australians, to the missionary work in far-off Pakistan. We arrived there in the summer of 1951. The first year especially brought severe tests.

One of these was the dry, dusty heat, so utterly different from the coolness of Australia's southern Victoria and Tasmania where I had lived. Then there were the typhoid, the jaundice, and other prolonged sicknesses from which most of us new arrivals suffered. One of our young classmates died that first year.

Another test was the poverty and different living conditions. Not long after arriving, I was assigned as a traveling minister, which required long, lonely trips on trains and sometimes involved sleeping on railway-station platforms.

Yet another test was the lack of response to our Kingdom message among the predominately Muslim population. And it was also a real trial trying to express this message in a difficult, new tongue, the Urdu language.

It would have been easy to give up and go home. To stay called for strong determination. I am glad that my earlier experiences helped me to meet the tests successfully.

Experiences That Shaped My Life

I was reared on a farm about 11 miles (18 km) outside of Geelong, a coastal city in the Australian state of Victoria. One April day in 1935, while visiting in town, a Miss Hudson engaged me in conversation and urged me to attend a Bible talk. I worried all week because I had promised this dear, sincere, and obviously dedicated old lady that I would attend. I really didn't want to go, but I didn't have the heart to disappoint her.

So when the time came, with some misgivings I kept my promise and went. To my surprise, I enjoyed the meeting so much that I began attending regularly. What I learned convinced me that I had found the truth, and I was baptized at an assembly held in Geelong that same year.

A few months later, two zealous pioneer girls walked more than a mile (1.6 km) over a plowed field to reach our farm. What impressed me about them was their faith and zeal. I remember asking them where they would be accommodated that night, for they mentioned they were en route to a new territory assignment in the small town of Bacchus Marsh, about 35 miles (56 km) away.

"We don't know yet, but we'll find some place before nightfall," they replied. "If not, we will pitch our tent."

It was already past four, and the days were short and cold. I thought to myself: 'This is really pioneering!' It also started me thinking to myself: 'What am I doing out here on the farm, tucked miles away

'You will bring disgrace on your family's religion.' 'You are joining an unknown and very unpopular group.' And, 'What guarantee will you have of financial support?'

This attempted persuasion—possibly quite well meant—went on for weeks. Strangely, however, the more they tried to dissuade me, the more determined I became to join the pioneer ranks.

June 30 arrived, cold and blustery! I packed all I had on my motorcycle and set off for Melbourne, about 40 miles (64 km) away. I had been invited to work with a group of pioneers there. A whole new purposeful life now opened up to me, but there were many trials.

Determinedly Facing Opposition

In those days a principal way of spreading the Kingdom message was by using sound cars to broadcast the recorded Bible talks of the president of the Watch Tower Society, J. F. Rutherford. For about five years, I operated one of these "cars," a well-equipped panel van known everywhere as the "Red Terror."

Brother Rutherford's rich, deep voice coming over the sound horn was to a few truth seekers "sweet," but to opposers of truth it was like poison. (Compare 2 Corinthians 2:14-16.) Occasionally, a garden hose would be turned on me, or stones would be pelted at the van.

Brother Rutherford's lectures exposing religious falsehood, on the other hand, really appealed to some. A well-to-do gentleman, for example, requested a copy of every one of Rutherford's recorded talks and every book he had written. When we visited his large home, I could hardly carry all those records and books. The man was delighted to get them, writing a check for £15 (then $70) right there on the spot. That was my biggest placement ever!

In 1938 Brother Rutherford was

from people? What prevents me from being a pioneer minister like these young women? I am young and healthy too. If they can do it, why can't I?' I determined right then that before long I would also become a pioneer.

Determined to Stick to My Decision

My father was very opposed to my leaving home and taking up the full-time preaching work with Jehovah's Witnesses. He had been a Sunday school superintendent for about 30 years and was prejudiced against the Witnesses. However, I had turned 21 years of age, and my mother had no real objection when I outlined my plans to her. So, finally, the date of June 30, 1936, was set as the day that I would leave home.

My father asked several prominent businessmen to talk me out of this "awful business" as he called it. These men tried hard to persuade me to stay at home, using all manner of arguments, such as:

Sound car used to advertise the Kingdom message in Sydney

scheduled to visit Australia and give a Bible lecture in the Sydney, New South Wales, Town Hall. I was among the ones to cover Sydney streets with a sound car, making spot announcements of the forthcoming visit. The "Red Terror" was specially outfitted for the six-week program with a large advertisement on both sides of the van. This "blitzkrieg" of activity brought quite a lot of opposition.

Because of strong religious pressure, the Sydney Town Hall booking was canceled. My assignment now was to use the sound car in getting petitions of protest signed. We visited large groups of workers during their meal breaks and, in spite of opposition in many places, succeeded in obtaining hundreds of signatures in favor of freedom of speech. Altogether tens of thousands of signatures were obtained throughout the country. But despite presenting this large petition to the Sydney councillors, use of the Town Hall was still denied.

Yet, as so often happens, this worked to the advantage of Jehovah's people. The Sydney Sports Grounds were then hired, and because of the great publicity afforded

by the opposition, the attendance at Brother Rutherford's talk swelled to some 12,000, according to police estimates. Since the Town Hall could seat only about 5,000, the opposition resulted in more than twice as many people hearing the talk!

Determination During Ban

With the outbreak of World War II in 1939, opposition grew. Then, in January 1941, the work of Jehovah's Witnesses was banned throughout Australia. I was pioneering in Melbourne at the time and living at the Society's literature depot.

One day six hefty Commonwealth policemen arrived there and confronted depot servant Jack Jones and me. I was given just five minutes to get out of my upstairs room. Have you ever tried to pack all your belongings in five minutes? I had nowhere near finished when the policemen stalked into the room and roughly threw all my remaining clothes and equipment out the window.

In Our Next Issue

- **Do You Worry About Your Children?**

- **The Two Greatest Expressions of Love Ever Made**

- **Is There Any Benefit in Suffering?**

However, the ban did not stop our activity. Using the Bible only, we continued to preach from house to house and to hold regular meetings in Melbourne. During 1942, the second year of the ban, I was called to Sydney again, this time to help in organizing the work in the seven congregations of Jehovah's Witnesses there.

The Bethel home in Sydney was at the time occupied by Commonwealth government officers. From a large two-story home just a few blocks away, we planned all organizational activity. My assignment was to visit each of the Sydney congregations and, using a motorcycle with sidecar, deliver the outlines for meetings and other things necessary for keeping the congregations organized and moving ahead.

Joe Oakley with the small congregation in Quetta, Pakistan, when a new Kingdom Hall was opened December 15, 1955

Serving in Tasmania

When the ban was lifted in June 1943, I was assigned to assist in getting the Melbourne literature depot set up again. Then, in 1946, I was appointed to serve as a traveling servant to the brethren (now, circuit overseer) in Australia's island state of Tasmania. Geographically, Tasmania is a beautiful, hilly island with many peaks, snowcapped most of the year.

When I served as traveling overseer, there were only seven congregations and several isolated groups on the entire island. Between visits to congregations, I pioneered at a small town named Mole Creek. Violent opposition toward the Witnesses had erupted there during the war.

But by this time it had died down, and a number of persons that I placed literature with eventually became dedicated Witnesses.

It was while in Tasmania, in 1950, that I received an invitation to attend the 16th class of Gilead. After graduation, as related earlier, I was assigned to Pakistan.

Marriage and Family

When I had been in Pakistan six years, I married Edna Marsh, who had been serving as a missionary in Japan. Edna joined me, and we opened up a new missionary home in Quetta, situated in the highlands region of Pakistan. We spent two years in Quetta, but then, with our first child on the way, we decided to return to Australia. What lay ahead of us now?

Where to settle and raise our family was never in doubt. I had promised that if ever I had to return from foreign service, I would come back to Tasmania. However, we were virtually penniless, and jobs for a 45-year-old were scarce. Yet we resolved not to let secular work keep us from congregation meetings and field service.

With the kindly help of spiritual brothers, I was able to set up my own window-cleaning business. For over 20 years, I did not miss a meeting or field service because of engaging in secular work, although at times it took determination to resist work offers and the extra money. Thus we were able to rear our two children in the way of the truth and to have a regular share in all Kingdom activities.

Our children are now grown and are no longer dependent on us. Both of them are firm in the truth, our daughter having enjoyed several years of pioneering before her marriage. Our son and his wife are now about to serve where the need is greater in the pioneer service.

A Rewarding Life

Recently we received a visit from an old friend who was the first person to take a stand for the truth in the town of Quetta in Pakistan. After a meeting at our Launceston Congregation here in Tasmania, she told the congregation that she had twice instructed her servant to tell me she was not at home when I called. Later, however, when I met her in the garden and she had no escape, she began to ask questions, finally accepting a Bible study. She related how grateful she is that I had demonstrated determination by persevering in that difficult foreign assignment of Pakistan.

A few years earlier, at a convention in Sydney, a young woman ran up to me and embraced me quite fervently. Surprised, I suggested that she had made a mistake. "No," she responded, "aren't you Joe Oakley? You and Alex Miller studied with our family in Lahore, Pakistan, and now my mother and sister and I are in the truth and are living in Sydney."

Experiences like these have indeed contributed to the satisfaction of having had a full share in the Kingdom proclamation. How fine it is to see God's blessing on the work! When I first served here in Tasmania in 1946, there were nine Kingdom publishers in the entire city of Launceston. Now there are three congregations, each with more than 90 publishers!

Truly, from the satisfying experiences of my more than 50 years of Christian service, I can say without any hesitation that *determination* has helped me make a success of it.

Polygamist and Witch Doctor Gets the Truth

AN African man called Isaac, along with several other men, broke away from the Apostolic Church of his village because it did not practice what it preached. Later all, including their wives, became Jehovah's Witnesses—except Isaac. They decided to visit him and tell him they had found the truth. Isaac, meanwhile, had become a successful witch doctor and had several wives. After studying the brochure *Enjoy Life on Earth Forever!* dealing with his life-style, Isaac gave up his witch-doctor practice, which was very lucrative, and also his wives except his senior one. He legalized his marriage to his senior wife, then 63 (he was 68). He says he feels "very happy and free, no longer in fear of the spirits."

Do You Have an Inquiring Mind?

CURIOSITY is a "desire to know." A strong curiosity makes a person eager to learn, to find out about things. Jehovah implanted this eagerness in us, so that almost from the moment of birth we are driven to explore the world about us. Our very existence is a never-ending learning process. If we are to become mature, well-adjusted adults, we need to gratify our curiosity, our desire to find things out.

This is especially true on a spiritual level. Our prospects for eternal life depend upon our learning about Jehovah God. (John 17:3) The Bible tells us that he wants us to inquire about him, to "grope for him and really find him." (Acts 17:23, 24, 27) If we suppress our curiosity or fail to allow it to develop, our advancement will be very slow. In fact, a lack of interest in spiritual things can be fatal. —Psalm 119:33, 34; Hosea 4:6.

Accordingly, Jehovah's people from ancient times have always had stressed to them the need for instruction and learning in order to satisfy a proper desire to learn. (Deuteronomy 6:6, 7; 31:12; 2 Chronicles 17:9) Jesus the Messiah was the greatest teacher ever on earth. (Matthew 9:35) His disciples followed his example. Even when facing opposition, they "continued without letup *teaching* and declaring the good news." (Acts 5:42) Such teaching stirred up interest in inquiring minds. Many were like the Beroeans, who responded with "the greatest eagerness of mind, carefully examining the Scriptures daily as to whether these things were so." —Acts 17:11.

Similarly, many of the activities of the modern Christian congregation are centered around teaching. Thus, the congregation fulfills a primary purpose for its existence, namely, to promote and satisfy a desire to learn about Jehovah and his purposes. This kind of curiosity is wholesome and beneficial.

Proper Limits to Curiosity

Sometimes, however, children have to be protected from their own curiosity. When a baby reaches out to touch something hot or inquisitively puts a glass object into his mouth to see how it tastes, he may be harmed. We are not hindering his growth when we discourage his curiosity in those directions.

When children get older, their curiosity may again lead them into trouble. Thus, a teenage boy may be very curious about what is in a pornographic magazine. Or a teenage girl may, out of curiosity, experiment with tobacco or other drugs. A group of youngsters may get together and drink a lot of beer—trying to get drunk just to see what it is like! Once again, we are not restricting a teenager's natural growth and development if we discourage this kind of curiosity.

Are there areas in which a mature Christian's curiosity may get him into trouble? Yes, indeed. Paul warned Timothy against those who may appeal to a Christian's curiosity in an effort to subvert his faith. "O Timothy," said Paul, "guard what is laid up in trust with you, turning away from the empty speeches that violate what is holy and from the contradictions of the falsely called 'knowledge.' For making a show of such knowledge some have deviated from the faith." —1 Timothy 6:20, 21.

In his second letter to Timothy, Paul gave a further warning: "These very men have deviated from the truth, saying that the resurrection has already occurred; and they are subverting the faith of some." (2 Timothy 2:18) Can you imagine how such speech must have provoked curiosity? Unwary persons may have wondered: 'What do these men mean? How can they say that the resurrection has already happened?' Intrigued, they may have listened. The result? The faith of some was subverted. Listening to such speech out of curiosity was dangerous in the same way that experimenting with drugs or pornography out of curiosity is dangerous.

Does this mean that Christians are narrow-minded, unwilling to listen to other people's opinions? No, that is not the point. Rather, they are counseled to avoid opening their minds to things that can cause them grief later. Just imagine how different history might have been if Eve had refused to indulge her curiosity

by listening to the deceitful words of Satan the Devil! (Genesis 3:1-6) The apostle Paul warned the Ephesian elders of "wolves" who, manifesting the same spirit that Satan had manifested toward Eve, "speak twisted things to draw away the disciples after themselves." (Acts 20: 29, 30) They use "counterfeit words" designed to "exploit" us. These words express thoughts that are poisonous to the spirituality of a Christian.—2 Peter 2:3.

If you knew that a certain drink was poisonous, would you drink it out of curiosity to see what it tasted like, or to see whether your body was strong enough to handle the poison? Of course not. Similarly, is it wise to open your mind to words that are *purposely designed* to deceive you and draw you away from the truth? Hardly!

Beware of Worldly Philosophies

Curiosity can harm us, too, if it leads us to investigate worldly philosophies. Philosophy is defined as "human endeavors to understand and interpret through reason and speculation the whole of human experience, the underlying causes and principles of reality." Ultimately, however, those proposing human philosophies turn out to be like those who are "always learning and yet never able to come to an accurate knowledge of truth." (2 Timothy 3:7) Their failure is due to one basic flaw: They rely on human wisdom rather than wisdom from God.

This flaw was frankly exposed by the apostle Paul. He spoke to the Corinthians about "the wisdom of this world," which is "foolishness with God." (1 Corinthians 3:19) And he warned the Romans against those who were "empty-headed in their reasonings." (Romans 1:21, 22) Jehovah is the source of all we have. Rightly, we look to him to provide "accurate knowledge and full discernment" and to reveal to us "the deep things of God." (Philippians 1:9; 1 Corinthians 2:10) The primary source of God's wisdom is his Word, the Bible.

Because human philosophies ignore God's Word, we should never underestimate the danger they present. Modern philosophical thinking has seduced many teachers of Christendom to accept the doctrine of evolution. They even abandon their belief in the inspiration of the Bible in favor of higher criticism in an effort to gain intellectual respectability. Political and social philosophies stressing personal freedom have led to an epidemic of abortions, widespread sexual immorality, drug abuse, and other destructive practices. Materialistic thinking leads most people today to measure happiness and success by their material possessions.

All these philosophies represent efforts to solve problems or seek happiness by human reasoning and without God's help. They all ignore the basic truth that Jeremiah recognized: "I well know, O Jehovah, that to earthling man his way does not belong. It does not belong to man who is walking even to direct his step." (Jeremiah 10:23) Our happiness and our salvation depend on our obedience to and reliance upon Jehovah. It is thus the course of wisdom to resist the temptation to give free rein to our curiosity, exposing our mind to human ideas that can corrupt our thinking and eventually leave us lost among those who have no hope.

Curiosity About the Approaching End

Since Jehovah's revelation in Eden that he had a purpose to remove the evil effects of Satan's rebellion, His faithful servants have always had a lively curiosity about the outworking of the divine purpose.

Why, even the angels have shown curiosity about this! (1 Peter 1:12) In Jesus' day, many were intensely interested in knowing the exact time when the Kingdom would come. However, Jesus repeatedly told them that it was not Jehovah's will for them to know. (Matthew 25:13; Mark 13:32; Acts 1:6, 7) Any attempt to fix a specific date would have been futile. Instead, he wisely urged them to pay attention to their Christian responsibilities, maintaining a sense of urgency every day. —Luke 21:34-36.

Today, world events provide overwhelming evidence that the end is near, and curiosity abounds about the date when it will occur. Certain developments may have convinced some that they had discovered the day and the hour. They experienced much anguish, perhaps even to the point of falling away from serving God, when their expectations were not realized. It is far better to leave the matter in Jehovah's hands, trusting that he will bring the end at just the right time. Everything we need in order to be in readiness has been provided.

The Need for Balance

So, like many other things in life, our curiosity can be a blessing or a curse. Properly directed, it can uncover priceless gems of knowledge that bring joy and refreshment. A healthy curiosity about our Creator, his will, and his purposes can be profoundly satisfying and beneficial. An unbridled, morbid curiosity can lure us into a morass of speculation and human theories wherein genuine faith and godly devotion cannot survive. Hence, when your curiosity threatens to lead you into something questionable, "be on your guard that you may not be led away . . . and fall from your own steadfastness." —2 Peter 3:17.

Attend the 1987
"Trust in Jehovah" District Convention

WHAT a fine theme we have for our 1987 district conventions: "Trust in Jehovah"! Surely our trusting in Jehovah sets us apart from the rest of the world. All others put their trust in such things as their riches, their wisdom, their might, or their political and religious rulers and leaders. Soon all such will come to bitter disappointment. —Psalm 146:3, 4.

What does it mean to put our trust in someone or something? According to lexicographers, "trust implies an absolute and assured resting on something or someone."* Yes, and that is the way we feel about it. We absolutely and assuredly rest our confidence in Jehovah.

The importance of trusting in Jehovah is called to our attention ever so often in God's Word. The psalmists repeatedly tell of their trusting in Jehovah: "But as for me, in Jehovah I do trust." "In you I have put my trust, O Jehovah." Their expressions call to mind the words of one of our Kingdom songs: "Jehovah is our refuge,/Our God in whom we trust . . . Jehovah is a stronghold,/A haven for all the just."—Psalm 31:6, 14.

The Scriptures time and again command us to put our trust in God: "Trust in Jehovah and do good." "Trust in Jehovah with all your heart and do not lean upon your own understanding." (Psalm 37:3; Proverbs 3:5) God's Word also tells us of Jehovah's faithful servants who were rewarded because they put their trust in him during times of great peril. Among such were King Hezekiah, Ebed-Melech, the three Hebrews, and Daniel.—2 Kings 18:5; Jeremiah 39:18; Daniel 3:28; 6:23.

How do we show that we trust in Jehovah? One way is by getting to know him and taking him at his Word. Jesus Christ gave us a very simple formula: "Keep on, then, seeking first the kingdom

* *Webster's New Dictionary of Synonyms.*

and his righteousness, and all these other things will be added to you." Yes, if we trust in Jehovah with all our heart, we will put the interests of his Kingdom first in our lives and follow a course of upright conduct.—Matthew 6:33.

Why does our trust in Jehovah need to be strong? Because of the pressures brought against us on every hand. For some it is outright persecution, for others temptations to wrongdoing. Still others have their trust tested by the requirement of endurance. Our coming district convention is among the many helps that Jehovah has provided in these last days.

This year the convention will be for three full days, Friday, Saturday, and Sunday. By adjustments in the length of the sessions, the program will virtually contain the same amount of material as last year. The purpose of all the features of the program, we may be sure, will be to strengthen our trust in Jehovah as well as in the visible organization he is using at the present time.

So let each Christian witness of Jehovah be resolved to attend at least one of these conventions. Bring your children. Be on hand for the opening song and prayer on Friday morning and remain until the closing song and prayer on Sunday afternoon. Come prepared with Bible, songbook, notebook, and pencil. Enter fully into the spirit of what is presented, including the songs and prayers. Pay close attention to what is being presented. And let us make certain that at all times our grooming and our conduct are above reproach.

The Scriptural principle 'sow bountifully, reap bountifully' applies to our attending the "Trust in Jehovah" District Convention. The more earnest we are in taking in the entire program, the more blessings we will carry away from the convention and the greater blessing we will be to others. —2 Corinthians 9:6.

Convention Locations

United States

June 12-14: **BIRMINGHAM, AL,** Civic Center Coliseum, One Civic Center Plaza. **CICERO, IL,** Hawthorne Race Course, 35th & Cicero Ave. **DAYTONA BEACH, FL,** The Ocean Center, 250 N. Beach St. **FT. WORTH, TX,** Will Rogers Memorial Coliseum, One Amon Carter Sq. **GREENVILLE, SC,** Greenville Memorial Auditorium, 300 E. North St. **MADISON, WI,** Dane County Memorial Coliseum, John Nolen Dr. **SAN DIEGO, CA,** Jack Murphy Stadium, 9449 Friars Rd. **WICHITA, KS,** Kansas Coliseum, I-135 at 85th St. N.

June 19-21: **DAYTONA BEACH, FL,** The Ocean Center, 250 N. Beach St. **DENVER, CO,** McNichols Sports Arena, 1635 Clay St. **FT. WORTH, TX** (Sign language also), Will Rogers Memorial Coliseum, One Amon Carter Sq.

GREENVILLE, SC, Greenville Memorial Auditorium, 300 E. North St. **HIALEAH, FL,** Hialeah Park Race Track, E. 32nd St. at E. 2nd Ave. **JACKSONVILLE, FL,** Memorial Coliseum, Gator Bowl Sports Complex. **LOS ANGELES, CA,** Dodger Stadium, 1000 Elysian Park Ave. **MACON, GA,** Macon Coliseum, 200 Coliseum Dr. **MADISON, WI,** Dane County Memorial Coliseum, John Nolen Dr. **NEW HAVEN, CT,** Veterans Memorial Coliseum, 275 S. Orange St. **NEW YORK, NY,** Yankee Stadium, 157th St. & River Ave. **OGDEN, UT,** Dee Events Center, 4600 South 1400 East. **PHILADELPHIA, PA,** Veterans Stadium, S. Broad & Pattison Ave. **PINE BLUFF, AR,** Convention Center Arena, 500 E. 8th Ave. **PONTIAC, MI,** Silverdome, 1200 Featherstone. **PROVIDENCE, RI,** Providence Civic Center, One LaSalle Sq. **ST. PETERSBURG, FL,** Bayfront Center, 400 1st St. S. **SAN FRANCISCO, CA,** Cow Palace, Geneva Ave.

June 26-28: **AMARILLO, TX**, Civic Center Coliseum, 3rd & Buchanan Sts. **CICERO, IL**, Hawthorne Race Course, 35th & Cicero Ave. **COLUMBIA, SC**, Carolina Coliseum, Assembly & Sweet Sts. **CORVALLIS, OR**, Gill Coliseum, 600 S.W. 26th St. **DENVER, CO** (Sign language also), McNichols Sports Arena, 1635 Clay St. **FT. WORTH, TX**, Will Rogers Memorial Coliseum, One Amon Carter Sq. **FRESNO, CA**, Convention Center, 700 "M" St. **GREENSBORO, NC**, Greensboro Coliseum, 1921 W. Lee St. **HIALEAH, FL**, Hialeah Park Race Track, E. 32nd St. at E. 2nd Ave. **KNOXVILLE, TN**, Civic Center Coliseum, 500 Church Ave. S.E. **MACON, GA**, Macon Coliseum, 200 Coliseum Dr. **MADISON, WI**, Dane County Memorial Coliseum, John Nolen Dr. **NEW HAVEN, CT**, Veterans Memorial Coliseum, 275 S. Orange St. **PHOENIX, AZ**, Veterans Memorial Coliseum, 1826 W. McDowell Rd. **PINE BLUFF, AR**, Convention Center Arena, 500 E. 8th Ave. **PROVIDENCE, RI**, Providence Civic Center, One LaSalle Sq. **ROCHESTER, NY**, Memorial Auditorium, 100 Exchange St. **ST. PETERSBURG, FL** (Sign language also), Bayfront Center, 400 1st St. S. **SAN FRANCISCO, CA** (Sign language also), Cow Palace, Geneva Ave. **SOUTH BEND, IN**, N.D.U. Athletic Center, Juniper Rd. **WILLOUGHBY, OH** (Greek only), Jehovah's Witnesses Assembly Hall, 38025 Vine St.

July 3-5: **CICERO, IL** (Sign language also), Hawthorne Race Course, 35th & Cicero Ave. **COLUMBIA, SC**, Carolina Coliseum, Assembly & Sweet Sts. **CORVALLIS, OR**, Gill Coliseum, 600 S.W. 26th St. **FRESNO, CA**, Convention Center, 700 "M" St. **GREENSBORO, NC**, Greensboro Coliseum, 1921 W. Lee St. **HIALEAH, FL** (Spanish only), Hialeah Park Race Track, E. 32nd St. at E. 2nd Ave. **HOUSTON, TX**, Astrodome, Loop 610 at Kirby Dr. **LINCOLN, NE**, Devaney Sports Center, 16th & Military. **LOS ANGELES, CA** (Japanese and sign language also), Dodger Stadium, 1000 Elysian Park Ave. **LOUISVILLE, KY**, Coliseum, Kentucky Fair & Exposition Center. **MACON, GA**, Macon Coliseum, 200 Coliseum Dr. **NASHVILLE, TN**, Municipal Auditorium, 417 4th Ave. **NEW ORLEANS, LA** (Sign language also), Superdome, Sugar Bowl Dr. **OKLAHOMA CITY, OK**, Myriad, One Myriad Gardens. **PINE BLUFF, AR**, Convention Center Arena, 500 E. 8th Ave. **PROVIDENCE, RI**, Providence Civic Center, One LaSalle Sq. **ROCHESTER, MN**, Mayo Civic Center Arena, 30 2nd Ave. S.E. **ROCHESTER, NY**, Memorial Auditorium, 100 Exchange St. **ST. LOUIS, MO**, The Arena, 5700 Oakland Ave. **ST. PETERSBURG, FL**, Bayfront Center, 400 1st St. S. **SAN ANTONIO, TX** (Spanish only), Convention Center Arena, S. Alamo & Market Sts. **SAN FRANCISCO, CA**, Cow Palace, Geneva Ave. **SOUTH BEND, IN**, N.D.U. Athletic Center, Juniper Rd. **TACOMA, WA**, Tacoma Dome, 2727 E. "D" St.

July 10-12: **ALBANY, GA**, Albany Civic Center, 100 West Oglethorpe Ave. **ANCHORAGE, AK**, Sullivan Arena, 1600 Gambell. **BILLINGS, MT**, Yellowstone Metra, Hwy. #10. **BISMARCK, ND**, Bismarck Civic Center Arena, 6th & Sweet Sts. **CICERO, IL**, Hawthorne Race Course, 35th & Cicero Ave. **CORVALLIS, OR**, Gill Coliseum, 600 S.W. 26th St. **FT. LAUDERDALE, FL** (French only), Jehovah's Witnesses Assembly Hall, 20850 Griffin Rd. **FRESNO, CA** (Spanish only), Convention Center, 700 "M" St. **HAMPTON, VA**, Hampton Coliseum, 1000 Coliseum Dr. **HIALEAH, FL** (Spanish only), Hialeah Park Race Track, E. 32nd St. at E. 2nd Ave. **LANDOVER, MD**, Capital Centre, Beltway Exit 15 E. or 17. **LINCOLN, NE** (Sign language also), Devaney Sports Center, 16th & Military. **LOS ANGELES, CA** (Korean only), Jehovah's Witnesses Assembly Hall, 4310 Degnan Blvd. **LOS ANGELES, CA** (Spanish only), Dodger Stadium, 1000 Elysian Park Ave. **LOUISVILLE, KY** (Sign language also), Coliseum, Kentucky Fair & Exposition Center. **NASHVILLE, TN**, Municipal Auditorium, 417 4th Ave. **ROANOKE, VA**, Civic Center, 710 Williamson Rd. N.E. **ROCHESTER, MN**, Mayo Civic Center Arena, 30 2nd Ave. S.E. **SACRAMENTO, CA**, ARCO Arena, 1515 Sports Dr. **ST. LOUIS, MO**, The Arena, 5700 Oakland Ave. **SAN ANTONIO, TX** (Spanish only), Convention Center Arena, S. Alamo & Market Sts. **TACOMA, WA** (Spanish and sign language also), Tacoma Dome, 2727 E. "D" St.

July 17-19: **ALBANY, GA** (Sign language also), Albany Civic Center, 100 West Oglethorpe Ave. **CHARLESTON, WV**, Charleston Civic Center Coliseum, 200 Civic Center Dr. **CICERO, IL**, Hawthorne Race Course, 35th & Cicero Ave. **CROWNSVILLE, MD** (Korean only), Jehovah's Witnesses Assembly Hall, Sunrise Beach Rd. **EL PASO, TX** (Spanish only), Special Events Center, Baltimore at Mesa. **FRESNO, CA** (Spanish only), Convention Center, 700 "M" St. **HAMPTON, VA**, Hampton Coliseum, 1000 Coliseum Dr. **HIALEAH, FL** (Spanish only), Hialeah Park Race Track, E. 32nd St. at E. 2nd Ave. **LANDOVER, MD** (Sign language also), Capital Centre, Beltway Exit 15 E. or 17. **LITTLE ROCK, AR**, Barton Coliseum, Roosevelt & Dennison St. **MIDLAND, TX**, Chaparral Center, Midland College, 3600 N. Garfield. **PITTSBURGH, PA** (Sign language also), Three Rivers Stadium, 420 Stadium Cir. **ROCHESTER, MN**, Mayo Civic Center Arena, 30 2nd Ave. S.E. **SACRAMENTO, CA**, ARCO Arena, 1515 Sports Dr. **SPRINGFIELD, MA**, Civic Center, 1277 Main St. **TUCSON, AZ** (Spanish only), Community Center, 260 S. Church.

July 24-26: **BROOKLYN, NY** (Italian only), Jehovah's Witnesses Assembly Hall, 973 Flatbush Ave. **JERSEY CITY, NJ** (French only), Jehovah's

Witnesses Assembly Hall, 2932 Kennedy Blvd. **LANDOVER, MD**, Capital Centre, Beltway Exit 15 E. or 17. **LITTLE ROCK, AR**, Barton Coliseum, Roosevelt & Dennison St. **MIDLAND, TX**, Chaparral Center, Midland College, 3600 N. Garfield. **NATICK, MA** (Portuguese only), Jehovah's Witnesses Assembly Hall, 85 Bacon St. **NEW YORK, NY** (Sign language also), Yankee Stadium, 157th St. & River Ave. **NIAGARA FALLS, NY**, International Convention Center, 305 4th St. **RENO, NV**, Centennial Coliseum, 4590 S. Virginia St. **ROCHESTER, MN**, Mayo Civic Center Arena, 30 2nd Ave. S.E. **SACRAMENTO, CA**, ARCO Arena, 1515 Sports Dr. **SPRINGFIELD, MA** (Sign language also), Civic Center, 1277 Main St.

July 31–August 2: **ABILENE, TX** (Spanish only), Taylor County Coliseum, E.S. 11th and Loop 322.

August 7-9: **NEW YORK, NY** (Spanish only), Yankee Stadium, 157th St. & River Ave.

Britain

June 12-14: **GUERNSEY, C.I.**, Beau Sejour Centre, Amherst, St. Peter Port.

June 26-28: **NOTTINGHAM**, Nottingham Forest Football Club, City Ground. **SOUTHAMPTON**, Southampton Football Club, The Dell, Milton Road.

July 3-5: **EDINBURGH**, Rugby Union Ground, Murrayfield. **MANCHESTER**, Manchester City Football Club, Maine Road, Moss Side. **PLYMOUTH**, Plymouth Argyle Football Club, Home Park. **LONDON** (Italian only), North London Assembly Hall, 174 Bowes Road.

July 10-12: **LEEDS**, Leeds United Football Club, Elland Road. **NORWICH**, Norwich City Football Club, Carrow Road. **BIRMINGHAM**, Aston Villa Football Club, Villa Park.

July 17-19: **CARDIFF**, Welsh National Rugby Ground, Cardiff Arms Park.

July 24-26: **LONDON** (Greek and Spanish sessions also), Rugby Union Ground, Whitton Road, Twickenham. **CRYSTAL PALACE**, National Sports Centre, Norwood.

Ireland

July 3-5: **NAVAN**, Navan Exhibition Centre, Trim Road.

July 10-12: **NAVAN**, Navan Exhibition Centre, Trim Road.

Canada

July 3-5: **BRAMPTON, ONT.** (Spanish only), Assembly Hall of Jehovah's Witnesses, Hwy. 7, 1 mile W. of Mississauga Rd., Norval, Ont. **EDMONTON, ALTA.** (Ukrainian sessions also), Edmonton Northlands Coliseum, 75th St. & 118th Ave. **KAMLOOPS, B.C.**, Kamloops Exhibition Association, 479 Chilcotin St. **LETHBRIDGE, ALTA.** (French and Spanish sessions also), The Sportsplex, 2510 Scenic Dr. **OTTAWA, ONT.**, Civic Centre Arena, Lansdowne Park, 1015 Bank St. **PRINCE GEORGE, B.C.**, Kin Centre, Arenas I & II, Ospika Blvd. & 18th Ave. **REGINA, SASK.**, The Agridome, Exhibition Park. **WINNIPEG, MAN.** (Ukrainian sessions also), Winnipeg Convention Centre, 375 York Ave.

July 10-12: **BRAMPTON, ONT.** (Portuguese only), Assembly Hall of Jehovah's Witnesses, Hwy. 7, 1 mile W. of Mississauga Rd., Norval, Ont. **CASTLEGAR, B.C.**, Castlegar & District Community Complex, 2101 6th Ave. **MONTREAL, QUE.** (French and Italian; Arabic sessions also), Olympic Stadium, Pie IX Blvd. & Sherbrooke St. **PRINCE GEORGE, B.C.**, Kin Centre, Arenas I & II, Ospika Blvd. & 18th Ave. **SAULT STE. MARIE, ONT.**, Sault Memorial Gardens, 269 Queen St. E. **SASKATOON, SASK.** (Ukrainian sessions also), Saskatoon Arena, 19th St. E. **SYDNEY, N.S.**, Sydney Centre, 200 George & Falmouth Sts. **VANCOUVER, B.C.** (Portuguese also), B.C. Place Stadium, 777 Pacific Blvd. S.

July 17-19: **BRAMPTON, ONT.** (Italian only), Assembly Hall of Jehovah's Witnesses, Hwy. 7, 1 mile W. of Mississauga Rd., Norval, Ont. **CORNER BROOK, NFLD.**, Humber Gardens, O'Connell Dr. **HAMILTON, ONT.** (Chinese and Hungarian sessions also), Copps Coliseum, 101 York Blvd. **LONDON, ONT.**, Grandstand Western Fairgrounds, Queen's Park, 900 King St. **QUEBEC CITY, QUE.** (French only), Colisée, Parc de l'Exposition, 2205, av. du Colisée. **SAINT JOHN, N.B.**, Lord Beaverbrook Rink, 536 Main St. **SUMMERLAND, B.C.**, Summerland Recreation Centre, 8820 Jubilee St.

July 24-26: **BRAMPTON, ONT.** (Italian only), Assembly Hall of Jehovah's Witnesses, Hwy. 7, 1 mile W. of Mississauga Rd., Norval, Ont. **HAMILTON, ONT.** (Korean and Ukrainian sessions also), Copps Coliseum, 101 York Blvd.

July 31–August 2: **BRAMPTON, ONT.** (Greek only), Assembly Hall of Jehovah's Witnesses, Hwy. 7, 1 mile W. of Mississauga Rd., Norval, Ont.

'To Wipe Away Her Loneliness'

A man on a work assignment in the Sultanate of Oman wrote the branch office of the Watch Tower Society in India. "A few days back," he said, "I happened to see the book *Happiness —How to Find It* in the house of one of my friends here. Needless to say the book as a whole is a real asset. To be frank, this small book influenced me a lot, and I want to present this very loving book to my wife as a wedding anniversary gift to wipe away her present loneliness. Kindly favour me by sending a copy of this book to my wife on my behalf as early as possible. Her address is given above."

The Watchtower

Announcing Jehovah's Kingdom

February 15, 1987

Do You Worry About Your Children?

The Watchtower®

Announcing Jehovah's Kingdom

February 15, 1987
Vol. 108, No. 4

In This Issue

THE PURPOSE OF "THE WATCHTOWER" is to exalt Jehovah God as the Sovereign of the universe. It keeps watch on world events as they fulfill Bible prophecy. It comforts all peoples with the good news that God's Kingdom will soon destroy those who oppress their fellowmen and that it will turn the earth into a paradise. It encourages faith in the now-reigning King, Jesus Christ, whose shed blood opens the way for mankind to gain eternal life. "The Watchtower," published by Jehovah's Witnesses continuously since 1879, is nonpolitical. It adheres to the Bible as its authority.

"WATCHTOWER" STUDIES FOR THE WEEKS

March 22: The Two Greatest Expressions of Love Ever Made. Page 10. Songs to Be Used: 114, 150.

March 29: Showing Appreciation for the Two Greatest Expressions of Love. Page 15. Songs to Be Used: 32, 156.

Average Printing Each Issue: 12,315,000

Now Published in 103 Languages

SEMIMONTHLY LANGUAGES AVAILABLE BY MAIL
Afrikaans, Arabic, Cebuano, Chichewa, Chinese, Cibemba, Danish,* Dutch,* Efik, English,* Finnish, French,* German,* Greek,* Hiligaynon, Igbo, Iloko, Italian,* Japanese,* Korean, Lingala, Malagasy, Maltese, Norwegian, Portuguese,* Russian, Sepedi, Sesotho, Shona, Spanish,* Swahili, Swedish, Tagalog, Thai, Tsonga, Tswana, Xhosa, Yoruba, Zulu

MONTHLY LANGUAGES AVAILABLE BY MAIL
Armenian, Bengali, Bicol, Bulgarian, Croatian, Czech, Ewe, Fijian, Ga, Greenlandic, Gujarati, Gun, Hausa, Hebrew, Hindi, Hiri Motu, Hungarian, Icelandic, Kannada, Malayalam, Marathi, New Guinea Pidgin, Pangasinan, Papiamento, Polish, Rarotongan, Romanian, Samar-Leyte, Samoan, Sango, Serbian, Silozi, Sinhalese, Slovenian, Solomon Islands-Pidgin, Tahitian, Tamil, Telugu, Tongan, Tshiluba, Turkish, Twi, Ukrainian, Urdu, Venda, Vietnamese

* Study articles also available in large-print edition.

	Yearly subscription for the above:	
Watch Tower Society offices	*Semimonthly Languages*	*Monthly Languages*
America, U.S., Watchtower, Wallkill, N.Y. 12589	$4.00	$2.00
Australia, Box 280, Ingleburn, N.S.W. 2565	A$7.00	A$3.50
Canada, Box 4100, Halton Hills, Ontario L7G 4Y4	$5.50	$2.75
England, The Ridgeway, London NW7 1RN	£5.00	£2.50
Ireland, 29A Jamestown Road, Finglas, Dublin 11	IR£6.00	IR£3.00
New Zealand, P.O. Box 142, Manurewa	NZ$15.00	NZ$7.50
Nigeria, PMB 001, Shomolu, Lagos State	₦8.00	₦4.00
Philippines, P.O. Box 2044, Manila 2800	₱60.00	₱30.00
South Africa, Private Bag 2067, Krugersdorp, 1740	R6.50	R3.25

Remittances should be sent to the office in your country or to Watchtower, Wallkill, N.Y. 12589, U.S.A.

Changes of address should reach us 30 days before your moving date. Give us your old and new address (if possible, your old address label).

20 cents (U.S.) a copy

The Bible translation used is the "New World Translation of the Holy Scriptures," unless otherwise indicated.

The Watchtower (ISSN 0043-1087) is published semimonthly for $4.00 (U.S.) per year by Watch Tower Bible and Tract Society of Pennsylvania, 25 Columbia Heights, Brooklyn, N.Y. 11201. Second-class postage paid at Brooklyn, N.Y., and at additional mailing offices.

Postmaster: Send address changes to Watchtower, *Wallkill, N.Y. 12589.*

Published by
Watch Tower Bible and Tract Society of Pennsylvania
25 Columbia Heights, Brooklyn, N.Y. 11201, U.S.A.
Frederick W. Franz, President

Do You Worry About Your Children?

OF COURSE you do! Disease, drug abuse, and delinquency are just three of the problems that you know endanger your children. It is normal for parents to be concerned about their children—even to worry about them.

That is how most parents have felt down through history, as the Bible shows. Remember that Jacob sent Joseph to check up on his brothers because Jacob was concerned about them. (Genesis 37:13, 14) Job, too, worried, even though his sons were grown-ups with families of their own. He thought: "Maybe my sons have sinned and have cursed God in their heart."—Job 1:4, 5.

Why, even Joseph and Mary were concerned about their perfect son Jesus! In fact, on one occasion when Jesus was 12 years old, they became particularly worried about him, for they found that he was missing. Nevertheless, their child Jesus was a credit to them, and they had no reason to reproach themselves. Let us see exactly what happened on that memorable occasion and consider what lessons modern parents can draw from it.

A Lost Son

If you are a parent, you can probably sympathize with Mary's feelings when she scoldingly said to Jesus: "Son, why have you done this to us? Your father and I have been terribly worried trying to find you." Joseph and Mary had been separated from Jesus for three days. You can appreciate why they were anxious as to the whereabouts of the 12-year-old boy. —Luke 2:48, *Today's English Version.*

Why did Joseph and Mary lose Jesus? A well-known commentator criticized them for this, writing: "Knowing what a treasure they possessed, how could they be so long without looking into it? Where were the bowels and tender solicitude of the mother?" But really, as we will see, close analysis of the account clears Joseph and Mary of serious blame.

The fact is that the Bible shows that Mary was a fine woman and a good mother. The angel Gabriel, when he came to foretell Jesus' birth, said that she had "found favor with God." (Luke 1:28, 30) She willingly accepted the assignment of giving birth to this special man-child, along with the weighty responsibility of raising and training him. She was a woman of humility and strong faith in God. After Jesus' birth, she did everything required by Jehovah's Law, "just as it is written."—Luke 1:38, 45-48; 2:21-23, 39.

Joseph, the man who married Mary and became the adoptive father of Jesus, was also a fine, righteous man who had had communication with Jehovah's angel on four occasions. (Matthew 1:19, 20; 2:13, 19, 22) Remember, Jehovah selected Joseph and Mary to rear His precious, only-begotten Son. Would God have done less than choose a couple who would do well in helping this son to grow in divine wisdom?

Of course, parents today likely worry about their children because of the dangerous and delinquent environment they have. And they know that their children are not perfect as was Jesus. Still, we can profit from the example of Joseph, Mary, and Jesus.

Helping a Child to Grow in Godly Wisdom

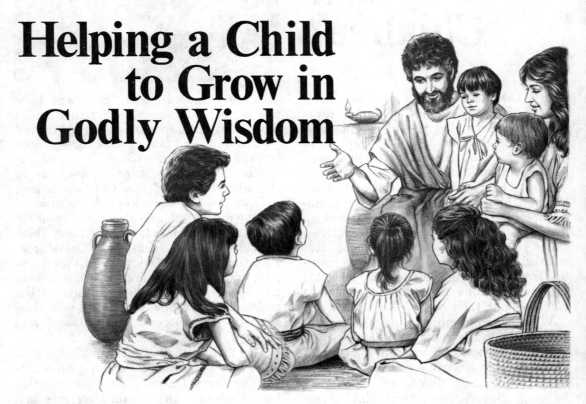

THINKING people of many nations and backgrounds acknowledge that Jesus was a marvelous teacher and moralist. But did certain things in his youthful training contribute to this? What lessons can today's parents learn from his family life and upbringing?

The Bible tells us very little about Jesus' childhood. Basically, his first 12 years are covered in two verses: "So when [Joseph and Mary] had carried out all the things according to the law of Jehovah, they went back into Galilee to their own city Nazareth. And the young child continued growing and getting strong, being filled with wisdom, and God's favor continued upon him." (Luke 2:39, 40) But there are lessons here for parents to learn.

The young child "continued growing and getting strong." Hence, his parents were caring for him physically. Also, he was continually "being filled with wisdom."* Whose responsibility was it to teach him the knowledge and understanding that would be the basis for such wisdom?

Under the Mosaic Law, his parents had that duty. The Law said to Israelite parents: "These words that I am commanding you today must prove to be on your heart; and you must inculcate them in your son and speak of them when you sit in your house and when you walk on the road and when you lie down and when you get up." (Deuteronomy 6:6, 7) The fact that Jesus continued "being filled with wisdom," and also that "God's favor continued upon him," indicates that Joseph and Mary were obeying this command.

Some may feel that since Jesus was a perfect child, his upbringing does not really provide a realistic pattern for the rearing of other children. However, Joseph and Mary were not perfect. Yet they evidently continued to supply his physical and spiritual needs, and they did so despite the pressures of an enlarging family. (Matthew 13:55, 56) Also, Jesus, even though perfect, still had to grow from babyhood through childhood and adolescence to adulthood. There was a lot of formative work for his parents to do, and they evidently did it well.

Jesus at Age 12

"Now his parents were accustomed to go from year to year to Jerusalem for the festival of the passover." (Luke 2:41) According to God's Law, every male was to appear in Jerusalem for the festivals. (Deuteronomy 16:16) But the record says

---

* The original Greek here carries the thought that Jesus' "being filled with wisdom" was a continuous, progressive process.

that "his parents were accustomed to go." Joseph took Mary, and likely the rest of the family, on that trek of more than 60 miles (100 km) to Jerusalem for the joyful occasion. (Deuteronomy 16:6, 11) It was their custom—a regular part of their lives. Also, they did not make just a token appearance; they remained for *all the days* of the festival.—Luke 2:42, 43.

This provides a useful lesson for parents today. These annual festivals in Jerusalem were times of solemn assembly as well as of rejoicing. (Leviticus 23:4, 36) They provided a spiritually uplifting experience for Joseph, Mary, and young Jesus. Today, parents do well to seek similar occasions for their young children to have an exciting change as well as to enjoy spiritual upbuilding. Parents who are Jehovah's Witnesses do this by taking their children to the assemblies and large conventions held at regular intervals during the year. Thus, children may have the exciting experience of traveling and being able to mix with hundreds or thousands of fellow believers for a few days. A father who successfully raised ten children attributes much of his success to the fact that since his baptism as a Christian 45 years ago, he has not missed one session of any assembly. And he has encouraged his family not to miss any.

An Oversight

When Jesus was younger, he doubtless stayed close to his parents during these annual trips to the big city of Jerusalem. However, as he got older he may have been given more latitude. When he was 12, he was about the age that the Jews view as an important milestone in the path toward manhood. Perhaps because of this normal and natural change, an oversight occurred when the time came for Joseph's family to leave Jerusalem and return home. The account reads: "But when they were

returning, the boy Jesus remained behind in Jerusalem, and his parents did not notice it. Assuming that he was in the company traveling together, they covered a day's distance and then began to hunt him up among the relatives and acquaintances."—Luke 2:43, 44.

There are features of this incident that both parents and youngsters will recognize. However, there is one difference: Jesus was perfect. Since he was obediently subject to Joseph and Mary, we cannot imagine that he failed to obey some arrangement that they made with him. (Luke 2:52) It is far more likely that there was a breakdown in communication. The parents *assumed* that Jesus was in the company of relatives and acquaintances. (Luke 2:44) It is easy to imagine that, in the bustle of leaving Jerusalem, they would give their first attention to their younger children and assume that their eldest son, Jesus, was coming along too.

However, Jesus evidently thought that his parents would know where he was. This is suggested by his later reply: "Why did you have to go looking for me? Did you not know that I must be in the house of my Father?" He was not being disrespectful. His words merely reveal his surprise at the fact that his parents did not know

where to find him. It was a typical case of misunderstanding that many parents of growing children can appreciate. —Luke 2:49.

Think of Joseph and Mary's concern at the end of that first day, when they found that Jesus was missing. And imagine their growing worry during the two days that they searched Jerusalem for him. However, it turned out that their training of Jesus paid off in this crisis. Jesus had not got into bad company. He was not bringing shame on his parents. When they found Jesus, he was "in the temple, sitting in the midst of the teachers and listening to them and questioning them. But all those listening to him were in constant amazement at his understanding and his answers."—Luke 2:46, 47.

The fact that he was spending his time in such a way, and his evident fine grasp of Scriptural principles, also speak well of Joseph and Mary's training of him up to that point. Nevertheless, Mary's reaction seems typical for a worried mother: first, relief at finding that her son was safe; then expressing her feelings of worry and frustration: "Child, why did you treat us this way? Here your father and I in mental distress have been looking for you." (Luke 2:48) It is not unexpected that Mary spoke before Joseph in expressing the concern of both parents. Many teenagers reading the account will likely say: "That is just like my mother!"

Lessons Learned

What lessons can we learn from this experience? Teenagers are prone to assume that their parents know what they are thinking. They are often heard to say: "But I thought you would know." Parents, if your teenager has ever said this when there was a misunderstanding, you are not the first to have the problem.

As children approach adolescence, they become less dependent on their parents. This change is natural, and parents need to make adjustments to allow for it. Yet even with the best of training, misunderstandings will arise and parents will have their share of worries. However, if they follow the fine example of Joseph and Mary, when crises do arise, the training given will stand their children in good stead.

Apparently Jesus' parents kept working with him through his teenage years. After the event just considered, he submissively "went down with them" to his hometown and "continued subject to them." With what result? "Jesus went on progressing in wisdom and in physical growth and in favor with God and men." So this episode had a happy ending. (Luke 2:51, 52) Parents who follow the example of Joseph and Mary, who help their children to grow in divine wisdom, who give them a good home atmosphere and expose them to the fine influences of godly association, increase the likelihood that something similar will happen to their offspring. Such children are more likely to enjoy a happy life as they grow to responsible, Christian adulthood.

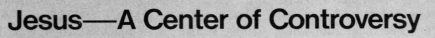

Jesus' Life and Ministry

Jesus—A Center of Controversy

SHORTLY after he is entertained at the home of Simon, Jesus begins a second preaching tour of Galilee. On his previous tour of the territory, he was accompanied by his first disciples, Peter, Andrew, James, and John. But now the 12 apostles accompany him, as well as certain women. These include Mary Magdalene, Susanna, and Joanna, whose husband is an officer of King Herod.

As the pace of Jesus' ministry intensifies, so does the controversy regarding his activity. A demon-possessed man, who is also blind and unable to speak, is brought to Jesus. When Jesus cures him, so that he is free of demon control and can both speak and see, the crowds are simply carried away. They begin to say: "May this not perhaps be the Son of David?"

Crowds gather in such numbers around the house where Jesus is staying that he and his disciples cannot even eat a meal. Besides those who consider that perhaps he is the promised "Son of David," there are scribes and Pharisees who have come all the way from Jerusalem to discredit him. When Jesus' relatives hear about the commotion revolving around Jesus, they come to lay hold of him. For what reason?

Well, Jesus' own brothers do not as yet believe that he is God's Son. Also, the public uproar and strife that he has created is totally uncharacteristic of the Jesus that they knew while he was growing up in Nazareth. Therefore they believe that something is seriously wrong with Jesus mentally. "He has gone out of his mind," they conclude, and they want to seize him and take him away.

Yet the evidence is clear that Jesus healed the demonized man. The scribes and Pharisees know that they cannot deny the actuality of this, as well as of other miracles of Jesus. So to discredit Jesus they tell the people: "This fellow does not expel the demons except by means of Beelzebub, the ruler of the demons."

Knowing their thinking, Jesus calls the scribes and Pharisees to him and says: "Every kingdom divided against itself comes to desolation, and every city or house divided against itself will not stand. In the same way, if Satan

expels Satan, he has become divided against himself; how, then, will his kingdom stand?"

What devastating logic! Since the Pharisees claim that persons from their own ranks have cast out demons, Jesus also asks: "If I expel the demons by means of Beelzebub, by means of whom do your sons expel them?" In other words, their charge against Jesus should just as well be applied to them as to him. Jesus then warns: "But if it is by means of God's spirit that I expel the demons, the kingdom of God has really overtaken you."

To illustrate that his casting out of demons is evidence of his power over Satan, Jesus says: "How can anyone invade the house of a strong man and seize his movable goods, unless first he binds the strong man? And then he will plunder his house. He that is not on my side is against me, and he that does not gather with me scatters." The Pharisees clearly are against Jesus, demonstrating themselves to be Satan's agents. They are scattering Israelites away from him.

Consequently, Jesus warns these satanic opposers that "the blasphemy against the spirit will not be forgiven." He explains: "Whoever speaks a word against the Son of man, it will be forgiven him; but whoever speaks against the holy spirit, it will not be forgiven him, no, not in this system of things nor in that to come." Those scribes and Pharisees have committed that unforgivable sin by maliciously attributing to Satan what is plainly a miraculous operation of God's holy spirit.   **Matthew 12:22-32; Mark 3:19-30; John 7:5.**

♦ How does Jesus' second tour of Galilee differ from the first?

♦ Why do Jesus' relatives attempt to lay hold of him?

♦ How do the Pharisees attempt to discredit Jesus' miracles, and how does Jesus refute them?

♦ Of what are those Pharisees guilty, and why?

"**G**OD is love." The apostle John made that statement twice. (1 John 4:8, 16) Yes, Jehovah God is loving not simply in the way that he is wise, just, and mighty; he IS love. He is the embodiment, the personification, of love. You might ask yourself: 'Do I know why that is the truth? Could I provide someone with a clear explanation, backed by evidence or examples proving that He is love? And what bearing does it have on my life and activities?'

[2] How much love Jehovah God has bestowed upon his human creatures on earth! Reflect on the complete beauty and function of our eyes, the marvel of our strong bones, the power of our muscles, and the sensitivity of our touch. We have reason to echo the sentiments of the psalmist: "I shall laud you because in a fear-inspiring way I am wonderfully made." Consider, too, the majestic mountains, the calm brooks of clear water, the fields of spring flowers, and the glorious

The Two Greatest Expressions of Love Ever Made

"God loved the world so much that he gave his only-begotten Son, in order that everyone exercising faith in him might . . . have everlasting life."—JOHN 3:16.

sunsets. "How many your works are, O Jehovah! All of them in wisdom you have made. The earth is full of your productions."—Psalm 139:14; 104:24.

[3] The expressions of God's love did not cease when his first human creatures rebelled. For example, Jehovah showed love by permitting that couple to produce offspring who might benefit by Jehovah's provision through his "seed" of promise. (Genesis 3:15) Later, he had Noah prepare an ark for the preservation of the human race and other earthly creatures. (Genesis 6:13-21) Then he showed great love for Abraham, who became known as Jehovah's friend. (Genesis 18:19; Isaiah 41:8) In rescuing Abraham's descendants from Egyptian bondage, God gave further expression of his love, as we read at Deuteronomy 7:8: "It was because of Jehovah's loving you . . . that Jehovah brought you out with a strong hand."

[4] Though the Israelites kept showing ingratitude and rebelled

---

1. What is meant by the statement "God is love"?
2. God has given what visible expressions of his love?

3, 4. What examples do the Hebrew Scriptures provide of God's expressions of love?

repeatedly, God did not cast them off at once. Rather, he lovingly pleaded with them: "Turn back from your bad ways, for why is it that you should die, O house of Israel?" (Ezekiel 33:11) However, even though Jehovah is the personification of love, he is also just and wise. The time thus came when his rebellious people reached the limit of his long-suffering! They went to the point that "there was no healing," so he let them go into Babylonian captivity. (2 Chronicles 36:15, 16) Even then God's love did not stop forever. He saw to it that after 70 years a remnant of them were allowed to return to their native land. Please read Psalm 126 and see from it how the returnees felt about it.

Preparing for His Greatest Expression of Love

5 Further down in history the time came for Jehovah to give the greatest expression of his love. It was a truly sacrificial love. Preparing for this, God had the life of his only-begotten Son transferred from spirit existence in heaven to the womb of the Jewish virgin Mary. (Matthew 1: 20-23; Luke 1:26-35) Imagine the special closeness that had existed between Jehovah and his Son. We read about Jesus' prehuman existence under the symbol of wisdom personified: "I came to be beside [God] as a master worker, and I came to be the one he was specially fond of day by day, I being glad before him all the time." (Proverbs 8:30, 31) So can you not agree that just having His only-begotten Son leave His presence was a sacrifice for Jehovah?

6 Without doubt, Jehovah watched with keen and great interest the development of his son from human conception onward.

God's holy spirit overshadowed Mary so that nothing could damage the growing embryo. Jehovah saw to it that Joseph and Mary went to Bethlehem for the census so that Jesus would be born there in fulfillment of Micah 5:2. Through an angel, God warned Joseph about King Herod's murderous scheme, causing Joseph and his family to flee to Egypt until Herod's death. (Matthew 2:13-15) God must have continued his interest in Jesus' progress. What a pleasure it was for God to watch 12-year-old Jesus amaze the teachers and others in the temple with questions and answers!—Luke 2:42-47.

7 Eighteen years later Jehovah was watching when Jesus came to John the Baptizer to be immersed. Then he joyfully sent his holy spirit upon Jesus and said: "This is my Son, the beloved, whom I have approved." (Matthew 3:17) Any Christian father can imagine how pleasant it would be for God to follow Jesus' ministry and to see the way he directed all praise to his heavenly Father. On one occasion Jesus took some apostles up on a lofty mountain. There Jehovah caused Christ to shine with a supernatural splendor, and the Father said: "This is my Son, the beloved, whom I have approved; listen to him." (Matthew 17:5) Jehovah had his voice heard a third time in answer to Jesus' petition for God to glorify his own name. Jehovah said: "I both glorified it and will glorify it again." Apparently this was said primarily for Jesus' benefit, for some with him thought an angel had spoken, whereas others thought it had thundered.—John 12: 28, 29.

8 What have you concluded from this brief review of God's actions toward his Son and his interest in him? It should be plain that Jehovah dearly loves his

---

5. Why can it be said that sending his Son to earth was an expression of God's love?
6. What paternal interest must Jehovah have had in Jesus' early life?

7. What three expressions evidenced God's interest in Jesus' ministry?
8. How do you feel about God's love?

only-begotten Son. With that in mind, and appreciating how almost any human parent would feel toward an only child, consider what next occurred—Jesus' sacrificial death.

The Greatest Expression of Love

9 The Bible shows that our heavenly Father has empathy. We read at Isaiah 63:9 regarding his people Israel: "During all their distress it was distressing to him. And his own personal messenger saved them. In his love and in his compassion he himself repurchased them, and he proceeded to lift them up and carry them all the days of long ago." How much more distressing it must have been for Jehovah to hear and see Jesus' "strong outcries and tears." (Hebrews 5:7) Jesus prayed in that way in the garden of Gethsemane. He was made a prisoner, faced a mock trial, was beaten and scourged, and had a crown of thorns pressed down upon his head. Remember, his loving Father was observing all of it. He also saw Jesus stumble under the weight of the execution stake and watched as his Son was finally impaled on that stake. Let us not forget that God could have prevented this suffering on the part of his beloved Son. Yet Jehovah allowed Jesus to suffer so much. Since God has feelings, for him to witness these events without a doubt caused the most pain he ever had or ever will have.

10 In view of all the foregoing, we can see how much meaning there is in Jesus' words to Nicodemus: "God loved the world so much that he gave his only-begotten Son, in order that everyone exercising faith in him might not be destroyed but have everlasting life." (John 3:16) Of similar import are the words of John, Jesus' dear apostle: "By this the love of God was made manifest in our case, because God sent forth his only-begotten Son into the world . . . as a propitiatory sacrifice for our sins."—1 John 4:9, 10.

11 You can, then, understand why the apostle Paul, at Romans 5:6-8, stressed Jehovah God's great love in the words: "Christ, while we were yet weak, died for ungodly men at the appointed time. For hardly will anyone die for a righteous man; indeed, for the good man, perhaps, someone even dares to die. But God recommends his own love to us in that, while we were yet sinners, Christ died for us." Certainly, in having his only-begotten Son come to earth, suffer, and die a most ignominious death, Jehovah God made the greatest expression of love.

The Second Greatest Expression

12 'What,' you may ask, 'was the next greatest expression of love?' Jesus Christ said: "No one has love greater than this, that someone should surrender his soul in behalf of his friends." (John 15:13) True, throughout mankind's history, there have been some who sacrificed their lives for others. But theirs was only a limited life; sooner or later they would have died anyway. Jesus Christ, however, was a perfect human with the right to life. He was not facing inherited death as were and are all the rest of mankind; nor could anyone have forcibly taken Jesus' life without his allowing it. (John 10:18; Hebrews 7:26) Recall his words: "Do you think that I cannot appeal to my Father to supply me at this moment more than twelve legions of angels?"—Matthew 26:53; John 10: 17, 18.

13 We can further appreciate the love

9, 10. What was God's greatest expression of love toward mankind, underscoring what Scriptural testimony?

11. How does the apostle Paul highlight God's greatest expression of love?

12, 13. (a) In what way was Jesus' expression of love unique? (b) How does Paul call attention to Jesus' great love?

involved in what Jesus did by looking at the following aspect: He had left a glorious existence as a spirit creature in the heavens where he had lived as the close companion and fellow worker of the universal Sovereign and King of eternity. Still, out of unselfish love, Jesus did as the apostle Paul tells us: "Although he was existing in God's form, [he] gave no consideration to a seizure, namely, that he should be equal to God. No, but he emptied himself and took a slave's form and came to be in the likeness of men. More than that, when he found himself in fashion as a man, he humbled himself and became obedient as far as death, yes, death on a torture stake."—Philippians 2:6-8.

¹⁴ Was that not an expression of love? It most certainly was—second only to that of Jehovah God, his heavenly Father. The prophetic words of Isaiah chapter 53 testify to all that Jesus endured: "He was despised and was avoided by men, a man meant for pains and for having acquaintance with sickness. . . . Truly our sicknesses were what he himself carried; and as for our pains, he bore them. But we ourselves accounted him as plagued, stricken by God and afflicted. But he was being pierced for our transgression; he was being crushed for our errors. . . . Because of his wounds there has been a healing for us. . . . He poured out his soul to the very death."—Isaiah 53:3-5, 12.

¹⁵ Because of all that was bound up with his death, Jesus prayed in the garden of Gethsemane: "My Father, if it is possible, let this cup pass away from me. Yet, not as I will, but as you will." (Matthew 26:39) What was Jesus asking for when he uttered those words? Was he wanting to beg off from being "the Lamb of God that takes away the sin of the world"? (John 1:29) It simply could not mean that, for all along Jesus had told his disciples that he would suffer and die, even indicating the kind of death he would die. (Matthew 16: 21; John 3:14) So Jesus must have had something else in mind when praying thus.

¹⁶ Without a doubt Jesus was concerned about the charge of blasphemy that he saw would be hurled against him, the worst crime a Jew could possibly be guilty of. Why be concerned about a false charge? Because his death under that circumstance would bring reproach upon his heavenly Father. Yes, the spotless Son of God, who so loved righteousness and hated lawlessness and who had come to earth to glorify his Father's name, was now to be put to death by God's own people as a blasphemer of Jehovah God.—Hebrews 1:9; John 17:4.

¹⁷ Earlier in his ministry Jesus had

14. How did the prophet Isaiah testify to the great expression of Jesus' love?
15, 16. That it was a sacrifice for Jesus can be seen from what words of his?

17. Why did the kind of death Jesus was facing prove to be such an ordeal to him?

stated: "Indeed, I have a baptism with which to be baptized, and how I am being distressed until it is finished!" (Luke 12:50) Now was the climax of this baptism. Evidently that is why his sweat became as drops of blood when he prayed. (Luke 22:44) Moreover, there was an enormous burden resting upon his shoulders that night, a burden beyond our ability to comprehend. He knew that he had to prove faithful because if he failed, what a slap in the face of Jehovah that would be! Satan would claim that he was right and Jehovah God was wrong. But what a slap in the face Satan the Devil got because Jesus proved faithful unto death! Thereby he proved Satan to be a base, gross, and monstrous liar.—Proverbs 27:11.

[18] Jehovah God had such confidence in his Son's loyalty that he foretold that Jesus would prove faithful. (Isaiah 53:9-12) Yet Jesus also knew that the burden of maintaining integrity rested upon him. He could have failed. He could have sinned. (Luke 12:50) His own eternal life and that of the entire human race hung in the balance that night. What a terrible

18. Why was Jesus under a terrible strain that night?

Do You Recall?

□ What expressions of God's love can all mankind see?

□ How can we know that Jehovah suffered when he saw his Son suffering?

□ How was Jesus' death in behalf of humans different from that of others who may have sacrificed their lives?

□ How should we be affected by the love shown us by Jehovah and Jesus?

strain that must have been! If Jesus had weakened and sinned, he could not have called for mercy on the basis of another's sacrifice, as we imperfect creatures can do.

[19] Certainly, Jesus' endurance on Nisan 14, 33 C.E., was the greatest expression of unselfish love ever made by any human, second only to that of Jehovah God. And what grand things he accomplished for us by his death! By his death he became "the Lamb of God that takes away the sin of the world." (John 1:29) He opened up the way for 144,000 of his footstep followers to be kings and priests and to reign with him for a thousand years. (Revelation 20:4, 6) In addition, the "great crowd" of "other sheep" today are benefiting from Christ's sacrifice and can hope to survive the end of this old system of things. These will be the first to enjoy the blessings of an earthly paradise. There will also doubtless be billions of humankind who will be resurrected as a result of what Jesus did. They, too, will have the opportunity to enjoy endless life in the earthly Paradise. (Revelation 7:9-14; John 10:16; 5:28, 29) Truly, "no matter how many the promises of God are, they have become Yes by means of him," that is, by means of Jesus Christ.—2 Corinthians 1:20.

[20] It is surely most fitting that we show appreciation for all that Jehovah God and Jesus Christ have done in our behalf by giving us these greatest of all expressions of love. We owe them such appreciation, and for us truly to benefit to the full, we must express such appreciation. The following article will show some of the very best ways that we can do this.

19. What did Jesus accomplish by his unselfish course?
20. How should we respond to the two greatest expressions of love on the part of Jehovah God and Jesus Christ?

Showing Appreciation for the Two Greatest Expressions of Love

"As for us, we love, because he first loved us."—1 JOHN 4:19.

HOW can we best show our appreciation for the great love that Jehovah God and Jesus Christ have expressed toward us? A primary way is by imitating Jesus, who tirelessly witnessed to his Father's name and Kingdom. (1 Peter 2:21) He did so in homes, in synagogues, in the temple, on mountainsides, and at the seashore. Let us consider nine distinct ways that may be open to us.

The House-to-House Activity

² The first, and perhaps most distinctive, way in which we can show our love and appreciation is by going from house to house with the good news of God's Kingdom. Doing so requires real freeness of speech because it continually involves direct confrontation with others, many of whom will view us as a bother. It takes genuine love for God and for neighbor to keep going from door to door, though we may meet up with indifference, annoyance, contempt, or direct opposition. —Compare Ezekiel 3:7-9.

³ The Gospel record of Jesus' instructions to his 12 apostles, and later to the 70 evangelists, clearly indicates that they were to go from house to house preaching the good news of God's Kingdom. (Matthew 10:5-14; Luke 10:1-7) At Acts 20:20 Paul tells of his going from house to house. Those words have been applied to his making shepherding calls, but verse 21 leaves no doubt as to the activity meant, for Paul adds: "I thoroughly bore witness both to Jews and to Greeks"—not to Christian brothers and sisters—"about repentance toward God and faith in our Lord Jesus." When making shepherding calls, an elder usually does not urge 'repentance toward God and faith in Jesus.' Rather, he encourages fellow Christians to have increased appreciation of meetings or the ministry, or he helps them with personal problems.

⁴ Not only is there sound Scriptural basis for our going from house to house but the fruits of that activity show that Jehovah's blessing is upon it. Yes, "wisdom is proved righteous by its works." (Matthew 11:19) Frequently, those going from house to house have seen evidence of angelic direction that leads them to those who are hungering and thirsting for righteousness. The householder has said that he or she had been praying for help and that the Witness' visit answered that prayer.

⁵ What great help for the field service we have in the book *Reasoning From the Scriptures!* It contains many appealing

---

1. What example did Jesus set for us?
2. How can you persevere in the house-to-house work?

3. What Scriptural basis do you have for the house-to-house activity?
4. What encourages us to share in preaching from house to house?
5. What fine aid do we have for our house-to-house ministry, and in what various ways can it help us?

introductions for Bible discussions as well as useful information on numerous Scriptural or religious subjects. So not only carry it but keep referring to it. The pioneers in particular have expressed great appreciation for this valuable field-service aid. Could you manifest your appreciation for God's love by using this book more fully and more effectively?

6 We should not overlook the fact that we personally stand to benefit greatly by sharing in the house-to-house ministry. As we Christians act on our faith, it becomes more firm; as we speak with conviction, it is strengthened. We cannot tell others about our hope without our own hope becoming brighter. There is nothing like participating regularly in the house-to-house ministry for cultivating the fruits of the spirit mentioned at Galatians 5:22, 23. It simply has to be that way, for the Bible assures us: "A generous man will prosper; he who refreshes others will himself be refreshed."—Proverbs 11:25, *New International Version*.

Making Return Visits

7 A second way for us to respond to the love that God and Christ have shown us is

by making return visits on persons who previously evinced an interest in the Kingdom message. Paul and Barnabas were concerned about those to whom they had preached. (Acts 15:36) In fact, consistency requires that we make return visits. While witnessing from door to door, informally, or on the streets, we are looking for those "conscious of their spiritual need." (Matthew 5:3) Obviously, giving them, as it were, one glass of spiritual water or one piece of spiritual bread is by no means enough. For them to get on the road to life, they need more help.

8 Our first efforts might be likened to planting seeds of truth. But as the apostle Paul indicated at 1 Corinthians 3:6, 7, more is needed. It was not enough that he planted. The seeds also required water, such as Apollos supplied. Then it could be expected that God would make it grow. This feature of the work is neglected by some, and yet many consider it to be really the easiest feature of the Christian ministry. Why? Because the people we call on have already shown some interest.

Conducting Home Bible Studies

9 When return visits are made regularly on persons who have shown an interest in the Kingdom message, the result often is

6. We stand to gain what personal benefit by going from house to house with the Kingdom message?
7, 8. For what logical and practical reasons should we make return visits?

9. Why should conducting a home Bible study be your goal?

a home Bible study—a third way in which we can show our appreciation. It really can be the most enjoyable and most rewarding feature of our ministry. Why? Well, what a joy it is to see people grow in knowledge and appreciation of Bible truths, to see them make changes in their lives, and to assist them until they dedicate themselves to do God's will and get baptized! Such ones can truly be viewed as our spiritual children and we as their spiritual parents.—Compare 1 Corinthians 4: 14, 15; 1 Peter 5:13.

¹⁰ Consider a typical example. A missionary going from house to house in a Caribbean island met a hippie couple whose home was anything but neat and orderly. Yet they expressed interest. A Bible study aid was placed, and a home Bible study was started with the couple, who were not married although they had several children. As the study progressed, the home began to look more presentable and so did the couple and their children. Before long the couple asked the missionary to marry them, opening the way to their getting baptized. Then one day the new brother happily displayed his auto driver's license, the first he had ever obtained. Yes, before he became one of Jehovah's Witnesses, he had not seen the need

to get either a marriage license or a driver's license, but now he was obeying both God's laws and those of caesar.

Street Witnessing

¹¹ A fourth way in which we can show our appreciation for what God and Christ have done for us is by street witnessing. When we take part, we are helping to fulfill Proverbs 1:20, 21 in a somewhat literal way: "True wisdom itself keeps crying aloud in the very street. In the public squares it keeps giving forth its voice. At the upper end of the noisy streets it calls out."

¹² There are ever so many good reasons for us to share regularly in this feature of Kingdom preaching. In many areas, it is more and more difficult to find people at home. They are either sharing in some form of recreation, shopping, or working. Also, many people live in exclusive apartment buildings or condominiums, not to mention those living in hotels. But usually there are people to be seen on the streets.

¹³ An elder in the United States currently conducts four home Bible studies with individuals whom he first contacted

10. What typical example shows the value of conducting home Bible studies?

11, 12. (a) We have what Scriptural encouragement to share in street witnessing? (b) What reasons are there for our doing so?
13. Street witnessing can have what results? Illustrate.

in the street witnessing activity. Of course, he does not simply stand mute (although in some lands that is all that the law permits). Rather, with a friendly smile and cheerful voice, he approaches people who are standing, waiting for a bus, or walking along leisurely. His 'utterances are with graciousness, seasoned with salt,' and he uses discernment as to how to approach each one. (Colossians 4: 5, 6; 1 Peter 3:15) Not only has he obtained home Bible studies by such street witnessing but he is also very successful in placing literature with many. Yes, by being neatly groomed and having a friendly smile together with freeness of speech, you can be very effective in street witnessing. In fact, five Witnesses recently placed more than 30 copies of the book *Life—How Did It Get Here? By Evolution or by Creation?* in public shopping areas. Many of the books were obtained by people sitting in their cars.

Informal Witnessing

14 A fifth way for us to show appreciation for the great love that God and Christ have expressed to us is by informal witnessing. How effective this has often been, both in finding persons hungering and thirsting for righteousness and in placing

literature! It certainly is one way by which we can heed the advice found at Ephesians 5:15, 16, 'to buy out the opportune time for ourselves.' A missionary struck up a conversation with a fellow passenger in a taxicab. The man showed interest. Return visits were made and a Bible study was started. Today that man is a Christian elder. Elsewhere an elder started a conversation with a woman who, it turned out, was changing her religion to marry a Jew. She wanted to know who came first, Moses, Noah, David, and so forth. He told her that what she needed was the *Bible Stories* book, which presents Bible events in chronological order. Although he was a perfect stranger to her, she readily gave him her name and address and the necessary contribution so that he could mail the book to her.

15 Sometimes, for fear we may get rebuffed, we may hesitate to start a conversation with someone traveling next to us. How often, though, we are richly rewarded if we summon up the courage to do so! Appreciation of God's goodness and people's need will help us to have the necessary courage. Yes, remember that "God did not give us a spirit of timidity, but a spirit of power, of love and of self-discipline."—2 Timothy 1:7, *NIV*.

14. How is the value of informal witnessing evident?

15. What will help us to be alert to opportunities for informal witnessing?

Welcoming Strangers

¹⁶ A sixth way in which we can show our gratitude to God and Christ is by welcoming strangers that show up at our Kingdom Hall. Love for neighbor should make us alert to notice any stranger that visits our place of worship. Let us strive to make him feel at ease, to feel that he is among friends who are sincerely interested in his spiritual well-being. Most likely, more than idle curiosity brought him there. He may truly be hungering and thirsting for righteousness. Our genuine concern for him may result in our starting a home Bible study, helping him on the road to life. (Matthew 5:3, 6; 7:13, 14) In fact, this very thing has happened often. A missionary from the first class of the Watchtower Bible School of Gilead noted that his two most promising Bible students were those whom he first met at the Kingdom Hall.

Witnessing by Writing Letters

¹⁷ A seventh way for us to witness, in response to the love God and Christ have shown us, is by writing letters. Often, those who use this form of witnessing get some very appreciative letters in reply. This is a method employed by some full-time ministers who may temporarily be unable to go from house to house because of physical infirmity. For example: There was a family with 12 children. One day the father came home to find five of them shot in cold blood by one of his daughter's suitors. In vain he looked for comfort from Christendom's clergy. Then one day he received a letter from a stranger, a Witness who had read in the press about his tragedy and who wanted to comfort him, enclosing a *Truth* book. This was just what the man was looking for. Today he, too, is a zealous Witness.*

Making Phone Calls

¹⁸ To mention an eighth avenue of witnessing, there is the opportunity to use the telephone in preaching the Kingdom good news. This increasingly is proving to be a pleasant and an effective form of witnessing. More and more Witnesses are becoming skilled in this feature of the ministry, which has much to recommend it. By it we reach some people whom we are unable to meet in the house-to-house activity. When phone witnessing is done discreetly, with kindness, tact, and skill, some have found even better response than from calling on such persons at their homes.

* For details, see *Awake!,* October 22, 1986, pages 12-16.

16. Why should we be alert to notice strangers visiting our Kingdom Hall?
17. Witnessing by writing letters can have what results?

18, 19. What other avenue for preaching the good news have some found effective, and why?

¹⁹ A Japanese congregation in an English-speaking country uses the telephone book as part of its territory. Publishers phone up Japanese names and arrange to make a personal call where they find interest. They have started literally dozens of studies by this means.

Witnessing by Good Conduct

²⁰ A ninth way in which we can bring praise to God is by our good conduct. A Russian journalist once stated that our fine conduct was our best sermon. In fact, repeatedly the press has commented on Jehovah's Witnesses' high morality. One reported: "Jehovah's Witnesses are recognizably the most honest people in the Federal Republic of Germany." At the beginning of her school term, a Witness girl brought the *School* brochure to her teacher. He bluntly rejected it, saying he wanted nothing to do with the Witnesses. However, in time her fine conduct won her his highest praise and caused an entire change of attitude on his part toward the Witnesses. Of similar import is the letter that Witness parents received from their children's schoolteacher: "The undeniable measure of the success of your beliefs is your children."

²¹ Those in the world cannot say good about Jehovah's Witnesses without bringing honor to God and Christ. That is the way it simply has to be. Did not Jesus say that we should let our light shine so that men might see our good works and give glory to our heavenly Father? (Matthew 5:16) Truly, by our fine conduct, we can adorn the truth. (Titus 2:10) Surely, the fact that our fine conduct brings praise to God and Christ and helps others get on the way to life is powerful reason for our being deeply concerned that our conduct at all times is above reproach.

20, 21. Our conduct can have what good effects? Illustrate.

²² As we have seen, there are many ways by which we can show our appreciation for all that Jehovah and Jesus Christ have done for us, particularly in their great expressions of love. In the process, we can prove our neighbor love.—Mark 12:30, 31.

²³ Finally, let us note that we can show our appreciation for the two greatest expressions of love by celebrating the Lord's Evening Meal. On his last night on earth as a human, Jesus instituted an annual commemorative meal consisting of bread and wine, representing his flesh and his blood. He commanded that this celebration be held in memory of him. (1 Corinthians 11:23-26) This year the Lord's Evening Meal falls on Sunday, April 12, after sundown. Throughout the earth, Jehovah's Witnesses will be coming together in obedience to Jesus' command. Do not miss it!

22. In which of the ways of showing appreciation will you be striving, and why?
23. In what final way can you show appreciation to God and Jesus?

Questions for Review

☐ How and where did Jesus witness?

☐ In what ways may we imitate Jesus in showing appreciation for God's great love?

Insight on the News

An "Offensive" Name?

Not speaking the divine name, transcribing it at most as JHWH, and pronouncing it as "Lord," is a recommendation that should be accepted, says the Catholic periodical *Com- nuovi tempi*. This was the reaction to a petition raised by the "Association for Jewish-Christian Friendship" of Rome and signed jointly by eminent Catholic and Jewish theologians and scholars. The petition requested that "publishing firms and the editorial staffs of news-papers and magazines" stop using the name "Jahweh" because it is "offensive to Jews, who consider the name of God to be unpronounceable." Their appeal, the Association says, is based on a "long-standing Jewish tradition" that "has been maintained without interruption" until today.

But should Christians be guided by Jewish traditions? Would it be right for them to put God's name aside and avoid pronouncing it? The Bible shows that God wants all to know that he, "whose name is Jehovah," is the Most High. (Psalm 83:18; Ezekiel 38:23; Malachi 3:16) Jesus set the example in this. Rather than following Jewish traditions that "made the word of God invalid," he taught his followers to pray: "Let your name be sanctified." (Matthew 6:9; 15:6) And only a few hours before his sacrificial death, he said in prayer: "I have made your name known to [the disciples] and will make it known."—John 17:26.

Engagement: A Contract?

The young Brazilian woman and her fiancé had just finished furnishing their new home. The invitations had been sent out, and everything seemed in order for their wedding, just three days away. Anticipating her new life, the bride had quit her job. Then, without any notice, the groom broke the engagement. Stunned and disappointed, the rejected bride sought legal recourse. Her lawyer argued that the 'marriage engagement is a preliminary contract, and if broken unjustifiably, the innocent party should be compensated for any damages suffered.' The court agreed and ordered the man to give to his ex-fiancée 'a dowry equal to a legally preset salary and to pay court costs and lawyers' fees.' Commenting on the decision, lawyer Nereu Mello, wrote in the São Paulo newspaper *Jornal da Lapa:* "The marriage engagement is a very serious contract and breaking it is not viewed with indifference before the Law."

This concept of the seriousness of the marriage engagement is not new. Under the Mosaic Law an engaged woman who committed fornication received the same punishment as did an adulterous married woman. She was thus treated differently from the single woman who fornicated. (Deuteronomy 22:23, 24, 28, 29) Back then the engagement was viewed as binding —as if the couple were already married. (Matthew 1:19) Christians today also recognize engagement as a serious step. They do not view it lightly. —Compare Matthew 5:37.

Adapted to Modern Technology

After Martin Luther railed against the *sale* of indulgences (exemption from certain forms of punishment for sin), the Roman Catholic Church outlawed the practice in 1562. But Vatican official Pedro Albellan stressed recently that the teaching on *granting* indulgences remains "unrenounceable and immutable." A revised Roman Catholic manual on indulgences shows that the Vatican has harnessed this ancient belief to modern technology. According to *The Times* of London, bishops can now "grant a full indulgence to their faithful by radio or television three times a year when they impart a blessing in the name of the Pope." However, there is a restriction. "It's got to be a live transmission," says Luigi De Magistris of the Vatican's Sacred Apostolic Penitentiary, the office that deals with indulgences. "Watching a replay is not sufficient."

But whether sold or given in person or by TV, are indulgences Scriptural? While Jesus, at times, freely forgave sins, he said nothing about the need of indulgences. Neither did the apostles. "The blood of Jesus [God's] Son cleanses us from *all* sin," the apostle John wrote. "If we confess our sins, he is faithful and righteous so as to forgive us our sins and to cleanse us from all unrighteousness." (1 John 1:7, 9) If *all* sins are thus forgiven, what is left to be paid for by punishment or covered by indulgences?—John 3:36; Romans 5:10.

Is There Any Benefit in Suffering?

WHEN faced with intense suffering, many people get bitter. Others going through the same or even worse experiences become more compassionate and tender in their feelings for fellow humans. Similarly, there are those who deny God's very existence when subjected to prolonged hardships, while others pass through severe trials with unwavering faith in the Almighty. Why is this?

Often people become bitter and lose faith because they consider themselves too important and fail to recognize that they are sinful humans living in a world that ignores God's law. They wrongly attribute to the Almighty the bad things for which men are to blame. Hence, they learn nothing beneficial from difficulties and, after experiencing relief, may show even more undesirable personality traits than they did formerly.

So that this does not happen to us, we should make it a point to profit from whatever may befall us. This requires having a right view toward human suffering. The Bible book of Lamentations is most helpful in putting this matter in the right perspective.

Maintain Hope

The book itself consists of five poems lamenting or mourning the terrible destruction that came upon Jerusalem at the hands of the Babylonians. In the third of these poems, the prophet Jeremiah, impelled by God's spirit, pours out his intense feelings, transferring them to the whole nation under the figure of an able-bodied man. (Lamentations 3:1) Though Jeremiah had suffered along with the entire nation, the experience did not embitter him. He looked hopefully to the time when God's favor would again be with His people and accepted what came upon the nation as a rightful execution of divine judgment.

The hope of future deliverance sustained Jeremiah. We read: "Without fail your soul [Jehovah himself] will remember and bow low over me. This is what I shall bring back to my heart. That is why I shall show a waiting attitude." (Lamentations 3:20, 21) There was no doubt in Jeremiah's mind that Jehovah would eventually look with favor upon His repentant people. True, they had been brought very low in utter defeat. But Jehovah would, as it were, stoop down from his heaven-high position, lifting them up from their debased state. With this thought, Jeremiah could comfort his heart and patiently wait until Jehovah would act in behalf of His repentant people.

So, when undergoing a distressing experience, we should not give up hope. We should call to mind the fact that trials have a beginning and also an end. Never will the Most High allow his faithful servants to suffer indefinitely along with those who are not his devoted people. That is why we should patiently wait until Jehovah brings certain relief.

The very fact that a person is still alive should give him reason for hope. Back in the time of Jeremiah, the city of Jerusalem and the land of Judah were desolated, and many Israelites perished. Still, there

Jeremiah, who composed Lamentations, could write from experience about suffering

were survivors. This gave assurance of God's continued mercy toward his people. We read: "It is the acts of loving-kindness of Jehovah that we have not come to our finish, because his mercies will certainly not come to an end. They are new each morning. Your faithfulness is abundant. 'Jehovah is my share,' my soul has said, 'that is why I shall show a waiting attitude for him.'"—Lamentations 3:22-24.

If it had not been for God's loving-kindness, his compassionate concern for his people, there would have been no survivors among the Israelites. But Jehovah God did show mercy. So his expressions of mercy would continue to flow toward his people, being renewed each morning. The fact that Jehovah's faithfulness is abundant made certain that his mercies could be depended upon. They would be con-

stant, never weak or ineffectual. Since the Most High remained the share, or inheritance, of his people, there was good reason for them to continue waiting for a reversal of the trying circumstances into which he had permitted them to come because of their unfaithfulness.

How to Wait Patiently

What should characterize such waiting? The book of Lamentations answers: "Good is Jehovah to the one hoping in him, to the soul that keeps seeking for him. Good it is that one should wait, even silently, for the salvation of Jehovah. Good it is for an able-bodied man that he should carry the yoke during his youth. Let him sit solitary and keep silent, because he has laid something upon him. Let him put his mouth in the very dust. Perhaps there exists a hope.

Let him give his cheek to the very one striking him. Let him have his sufficiency of reproach."—Lamentations 3:25-30.

Note that during such a time of affliction, one should continue looking hopefully to God for relief and draw closer to him. A person should want to be patient, waiting silently or without complaining until the Almighty has brought deliverance, or salvation. For a person to learn thus to bear a yoke of suffering in youth is most beneficial. Why? Because it makes it much easier for him to undergo such an experience later in life without losing hope. Knowing that he has passed through great hardships before, he has a basis for hope that he will be able to do so again.

Now, when a person has a yoke of affliction put upon him, he should not be running about voicing his complaints. No, he should sit solitary, as does a person in mourning, and remain silent. He should lie prostrate, with his mouth touching the very dust. This means that he should humbly submit to the trials that God is permitting him to bear, and he should look hopefully to the coming deliverance. He should not rise up in revolt against his persecutors but patiently put up with physical and verbal abuse. This reminds us of the way Jesus Christ conducted himself. The Bible record reports: "When he was being reviled, he did not go reviling in return. When he was suffering, he did not go threatening, but kept on committing himself to the one who judges righteously."—1 Peter 2:23.

Another vital point to remember when experiencing suffering is that God is not giving his approval to the hateful things that men may do. The Most High does, however, permit certain things to happen with a good purpose in view. This is nicely expressed in the following words from the book of Lamentations: "For not to time indefinite will Jehovah keep on casting off. For although he has caused grief, he will also certainly show mercy according to the abundance of his loving-kindness. For not out of his own heart has he afflicted or does he grieve the sons of men. For crushing beneath one's feet all the prisoners of the earth, for turning aside the judgment of an able-bodied man before the face of the Most High, for making a man crooked in his legal case, Jehovah himself has had no countenance."—Lamentations 3:31-36.

In the case of the unfaithful Israelites, Jehovah God permitted them to undergo a terrible experience at the hands of the Babylonians. He cast them off to the extent of allowing them to be taken into exile. Yet, this was with a good purpose in view, namely, to produce a repentant remnant among the survivors and their offspring. It was toward this remnant that Jehovah would show mercy. The Almighty had no pleasure in punishing the Israelites. It was not his heart's desire to cause them grief and affliction by giving them into the hands of their enemies. Jehovah did not countenance the terrible treatment these gave to his people. He did not look approvingly upon men who oppressed prisoners of war, those who denied a man his God-given rights, and those who refused to render justice in a legal case.

Accordingly, when we suffer at the hands of men, we should not blame God

In Our Next Issue

- Fortune-Telling—Still in Fashion

- 'Upon the Watchtower I Am Standing'

- Making All Things New

for the wrongs that men commit. The Most High does not approve of their oppression and violence. Eventually they will have to answer to him for their wrong deeds.

Then, again, people may bring suffering upon themselves. The faithless Israelites turned their backs on Jehovah God, rejecting his protective care. Rightly, then, he abandoned them to their enemies. So they had no basis for complaint regarding what had befallen them. This is stressed in the question: "How can a living man indulge in complaints, an able-bodied man on account of his sin?" (Lamentations 3:39) Instead of complaining, the Israelites should have repentantly returned to Jehovah, imploring him for mercy. We read: "Do let us search out our ways and explore them, and do let us return clear to Jehovah. Let us raise our heart along with our palms to God in the heavens: 'We ourselves have transgressed, and we have behaved rebelliously.'"—Lamentations 3: 40-42.

Yes, it was no time for grumbling and complaining. It was a time to look carefully at their ways, their course of life or conduct, and to consider what had been the result. Instead of continuing in their own ways to their hurt, they should return to Jehovah and conform to his commands. Outward expressions of repentance, the mere raising of the palms in prayer, were not enough. Heartfelt repentance over transgressions was needed.

So when undergoing suffering, we should look at our course of life. Have we brought troubles upon ourselves by ignoring God's law? If so, we have no basis for blaming the Most High. Rather, we should show that we have profited from the painful discipline by forsaking the wrong course and repentantly turning to God. If we have tried to lead an upright life and yet experience affliction, we should not forget that what wicked men may do to us is not what God approves. Meanwhile, we should humbly submit to our trials, waiting patiently and without complaint until Jehovah God brings relief. If we apply the counsel of God's Word when faced with suffering, we will benefit. We will learn patience, endurance, and total reliance on Jehovah. Never will we imitate the hateful ways of oppressive men, but we will continue to be kind and compassionate toward fellow humans.

"Honest With His Religion"

While government departments have been very helpful to the Watchtower Society's building project in Nigeria, some newspapers and religious leaders have tried to make trouble for Jehovah's Witnesses over the neutrality issue. Other newspaper reporters, however, have given commendation. One writer, a lawyer, asked whether Jehovah's Witnesses "portray themselves as really unpatriotic." Giving his own answer, he said:

"Witnesses are tax-paying and law-abiding citizens. Any . . . Witness who can be honest with his religion to the extent of obeying it at the risk of losing certain privileges will be equally honest in most other things . . . The reason he refuses to steal government money while his other colleagues . . . sing the national anthem and yet embezzle funds is because his Bible which asks him not to sing the national anthem also said he should not steal."

A Day in Calcutta
Reaching "People of All Sorts" With the Good News

CALCUTTA, India, is a city teeming with "people of all sorts." Among its more than ten million inhabitants, Jehovah's Witnesses are busy preaching the good news of God's Kingdom. It takes a great deal of ingenuity and endurance to reach all these people with their highly diversified racial, social, cultural, religious, and economic backgrounds. But like the Christian apostle Paul, whose missionary journeys took him to the far corners of the world of that time, Jehovah's Witnesses in Calcutta also "have become all things to people of all sorts" so that they might "by all means save some." —1 Corinthians 9:22; Colossians 1:23.

How do the Witnesses there go about their preaching work, and what kind of people and conditions do they meet in their ministry? Recently, as a visitor, I spent a day in Calcutta with a pioneer, or full-time preacher. Would you like a peek into that unique experience?

A Vast and Varied Field

Late in that busy and fascinating day of house-to-house preaching, my companion and I were ready to go home. As we were waiting for the bus, we began talking about the challenges that he and other pioneers face in this enormous city.

"Well," he commented, "ask anyone in

the full-time preaching work here if he would like to move to an easier assignment. I don't think he would be keen about it."

He was right. The pioneers in Calcutta view their work as one of the most interesting careers in the world. They have a vast and varied field in this city of great contrasts.

Though the Hindu religion dominates the city, churches and Muslim mosques are plentiful, and one finds a few Buddhist temples here and there. In some quarters, stately mansions house some of the world's richest people. Not so far away are the lean-to shacks of the migrant workers who can expect to earn as little as 150 rupees (about $12, U.S.) per month. Their customs, languages, and appearances are as varied as their religions and their living conditions.

In the midst of all of this flourishes one congregation of Jehovah's Witnesses with about a hundred active Kingdom proclaimers. Though the challenge is formidable, the Witnesses find special joy and satisfaction in being able to adapt themselves in order to respond to the needs of the people.

Just then, Bus No. 45 juddered to a halt in front of us. It was so packed that my immediate reaction was: "I can't possibly get on!" A friendly push came from behind, and soon both of us were swept along onto the bus by a wave of arms and bodies. At least ten more people got on after we did. They were riding on the footboard, hanging on like bees around the entrance. Inside the vehicle, designed to seat 46, I counted over a hundred heads before giving up the count to resume my conversation with my friend.

"Are the buses always like this?"

"They often are a little crowded," he explained, "but they are inexpensive, which means we can easily afford to ride even 6 to 9 miles (10 to 15 km) each day to some of the more distant parts of the city to preach."

"Wouldn't it be better to work in communities closer to home more often?"

"Yes, but some of us full-time workers have decided to make the effort to reach the people in other areas. Our records show that many neighborhoods of Calcutta have not been visited with the good news in the last 50 years!"

Yet reaching everyone in a given area is a real challenge due to the sheer quantity of people. A survey once put the density of the population in Calcutta at three times that of New York City at the time, and the number has increased in recent years.

At least one third of Calcutta's people live in overcrowded slums known locally as bustees. Typical bustees are rows upon rows of small huts, usually within arm's reach of one another. Each hut consists of a dirt floor and walls made of mud and cow dung smeared on wooden frames, all under the cover of a clay-tile roof. Each hut, with little or no ventilation, is the sleeping quarters of as many as seven or eight people. There is usually one water standpipe for about every 150 people, and in long-established bustees, the government provides a few community latrines.

As one starts to make calls in a bustee, it is not uncommon to be escorted by crowds of as many as a hundred curious onlookers, mostly children. One Witness, somewhat annoyed by a persistent youth who heralded his visit at each home, asked the young man if he would like to do the rest of the talking too. At this seeming invitation, the good-natured youth took the tract from the Witness and gave the presentation word for word, even offering the *Watchtower* and *Awake!* magazines.

Tackling the
Varied Religious Backgrounds

About half of the city's bustees are inhabited by followers of Islam. The tolerant attitude prevailing in the city, however, makes it possible to preach from house to house in such areas, a privilege not always enjoyed in other countries with large Muslim communities. I asked if the pioneers in Calcutta have a special approach with people of this background.

"Some use local problems to highlight man's inability to solve his woes," my friend replied, "while others try to overcome religious prejudice by discussing points held in common, such as belief in one God (not a trinity) or our common belief that the original Bible was inspired of God."

"And the results?" I wondered.

"Very few are interested enough to want a Bible study. Making a living and bettering their station in life seem to be the only things on their mind. That, coupled with minimal, if any, education, makes it very difficult for them to accept the good news."

Hindu views are most commonly encountered in the city. The Bengali people in particular are fond of quoting a saying of Ramakrishna, who lived and preached in the mid-19th century. *"Jotto moth, totto poth,"* means, when loosely translated, that all religions are but different roads leading to the same goal.

"Is this viewpoint difficult to overcome?" I asked.

"Not if the person is open to reason. We can tactfully explain some obvious differences, such as our Bible-based hope of living forever in human perfection on earth. Or we can point out that it is not possible for opposite views to be true at the same time. For example, either there is an immortal soul or there is not one."

"That's sound reasoning."

"Yes, but too often people refuse to take what we say seriously. They are sure that they know what we believe and that they believe the same thing. This attitude tends to foil any constructive discussion. So we try to leave some literature and move on to the next person."

"Have there been any from the Hindu community who seek a deeper knowledge of God and his purposes?"

"Yes, the pioneers contacted a young man who had been disillusioned by his association with the followers of Ramakrishna," my friend related. "He accepted the magazines and had read them by the time he was visited again two days later. After several discussions, he began to study the booklet *The Path of Divine Truth Leading to Liberation*. He would write out his answers and comments on the study questions in a notebook. Within five months, this man was baptized and serving as an auxiliary pioneer so that he could share his knowledge with many others."

"That's quite an experience! But what was the reaction of his family?"

"He was living with his widowed mother and grandmother, both devout Hindus. They, too, began to show interest and started to study the Bible. Soon the neighbors noticed the changes in the women, and three others became interested as a result. The mother has now been baptized, and granny, a little slower due to her 70 years, is hoping to be baptized soon."

From my friend's excitement in relating this story, I could see that such experiences are a real stimulus for the pioneers. Sometimes there may appear to be little progress, but then someone takes an exceptional interest. Thus the pioneers are encouraged to press on in their search for yet others who may be interested.

Hurdling the Language Barriers

The crowd on the bus had begun to thin a little, and I recognized some English. "Ticket, *apnar* ticket," cried a short, non-uniformed man, who had a colorful fan of bank notes in his right hand and a leather pouch of change on his side to show that he was the conductor. I offered to pay, but my friend's Indian hospitality would not hear of it. He thrust his briefcase into my hands and delved into his shirt pocket for change.

"Whatever have you got in here?" I exclaimed. "This must weigh a ton!"

"Well, the Indian language editions of the Bible are rather large. To be fully equipped in Calcutta, we really need to carry Bibles in three languages—Bengali, Hindi, and English—plus Bible literature, of course."

"Surely you could just take an English Bible and translate the verses."

"I suppose we could. However, many people who read only Bengali or Hindi have never seen a complete Bible in their own language. We feel especially good when we can show them a copy and read to them from it. It's well worth the extra effort and weight."

Adjusting to the needs of the different language groups here keeps the pioneers busy. Most of them teach themselves to witness effectively in the three main languages. Some with exceptional skill have learned to speak five or six languages. The local people appreciate the efforts of the visitors in trying to speak in the tongue of the community, and their attentive response can be reward enough for the long hours of language study.

Finding Joy in a Challenging Territory

Just then our bus again grated to a halt on brake linings that had long since worn out, and I was jostled outside.

"Why here?" I asked. "This is not where you live."

"No, it's a Punjabi area. These people make the best tea, you know. I thought you might like to try a cup."

The tea was excellent.

"How did you know about this place?" I queried.

"Working around each area, we pioneers get to know what the local specialties are and where the best and cheapest shops are. If your stomach is strong enough, we can go and sample some interesting foods tonight."

Remembering the advice of some of my more cautious friends, I declined the invitation. But I did enjoy the tea. I could see that the pioneers are balanced and have learned to make the best of their circumstances. Even things that at first seem to be obstacles can be overcome and enjoyed.

"Is there anything you don't enjoy about your work?" I finally asked.

My friend contemplated this question for a while. "I think the summer and monsoon weather is something we will never really get used to. Yet that is a problem you have whether you are pioneering or not. Heat and humidity get so high that perspiration often drips from the tip of your nose onto your Bible as you read from it. Still, we learn to put up with it. Why, in May, perhaps the hottest month of the year, we see the highest number of auxiliary pioneers joining us in the preaching work."

Looking back on the day and my conversation with my pioneer friend, I am impressed with the ability of Calcutta's pioneers to adapt to so many varied situations and peoples so that they can reach them with the good news. Of course, I realize that pioneers all over the world are doing just the same. They are truly happy 'to be all things to people of all sorts.' —*Contributed.*

Questions From Readers

■ Once someone has signed a Declaration Pledging Faithfulness, can that arrangement be terminated?

The question has to do with a provision that does not apply in most lands. So let us first see what that solemn interim arrangement is.

The Watchtower of March 15, 1977, discussed a problem existing in some lands. Though God permits divorce on Scriptural grounds, some governments have no divorce provision. (Matthew 19:9) Or the law may make it very hard to get a divorce, perhaps requiring many years. Hence, that magazine issue explained that Jehovah's Witnesses have a concession *applying only in such lands;* it involves a Declaration Pledging Faithfulness. Consider an example of the arrangement:

A woman comes to a knowledge of Christian truth while living with (and perhaps having children by) a man who has long been separated from his legal wife. The newly interested woman is faithful to him and wants to marry him, but that is impossible because the law does not permit him to divorce his legal wife. Hence, if the congregation elders are convinced that her relationship with this man would otherwise be accepted by God, they will allow her to sign a Declaration Pledging Faithfulness. She therein states that she has done all she can to legalize this relationship; that she acknowledges before God the binding nature of the Declaration; and that she promises to get legally married as soon as that is possible, thus terminating the Declaration that had enabled her to become part of the Christian congregation.

However, the question arises: Once she (or anyone in that situation) comes into the congregation under such a Declaration, is there any other way that it ends or could be ended?

The Declaration itself states that its signer 'recognizes his or her relationship as a binding tie before Jehovah God and before all persons, to be held to and honored in full accord with the principles of God's Word.' It thus is, from the congregation's standpoint, as morally binding as a legal marriage. However, death of a mate ends either a marriage or a union under such a Declaration. (Romans 7:2) The Bible also says that if one's marriage mate is guilty of *por·nei'a* (sexual immorality outside the union), the innocent partner can get a divorce. (Matthew 5:32; 19:9) Parallelwise, under a Declaration Pledging Faithfulness, immorality by a mate can be a basis for ending the union, if the innocent one so chooses. The innocent Christian would have to establish with the elders proof of the unfaithfulness. This would terminate the Declaration; thereafter the innocent one would be Scripturally free.

Recognizing that the congregation considers a Declaration Pledging Faithfulness as being as morally binding as a legal marriage raises a related issue. This comes about when the previous impediment to marriage is removed. For instance, in the example above, the man's legal wife might die or the government might legalize divorce, and he is willing to marry the Christian woman legally. In that case the sister cannot continue under the Declaration Pledging Faithfulness, even for reasons such as its being embarrassing to get legally married now or because she might lose some material advantage. In accord with her Declaration, she must now take steps to have their union legalized. Otherwise, the congregation would invalidate the Declaration, and she would have to separate from the man or be disfellowshipped.

What, though, if the unbeliever refuses to marry her? When she signed the Declaration, the congregation viewed the union as binding and moral. The fact that she is unable to force her unbelieving partner to legalize their union does not now make the union immoral. So she could continue to be a faithful mate, not needing to separate from the unbeliever, although she should persist in her efforts toward having the union legalized. (This adjusts the comment in "Questions From Readers" of November 1, 1985.)—Compare Judges 11:35; Luke 18:1-5.

Of course, the situation is different if *both* parties signed the Declaration and became baptized Christians. In this case, both solemnly committed themselves to enter into a legal marriage when the governmental impediment was removed, at which point the Declaration would be terminated. They are obliged to do this within a reasonable time, or else separate in order to remain in the congregation. (Compare "Questions From Readers" in *The Watchtower* of September 1, 1982.) If they do separate, the morally binding Declaration still applies, so neither is free to enter into a union with someone else.—Compare 1 Corinthians 7:10, 11.

Though the arrangement for a Declaration Pledging Faithfulness does not apply in most places, the above discussion centers on the Bible standard that applies everywhere: "Let marriage be honorable among all, and the marriage bed be without defilement, for God will judge fornicators and adulterers."—Hebrews 13:4.

It Points to a Bright Future

Gloom and doom are so often the forecasts as the world faces one crisis after another. What a contrasting message in the new book *Worldwide Security Under the "Prince of Peace"!* "Upon opening it, a look of sheer delight sprang to my eyes," writes one reader. "The illustrations are so beautifully thought-provoking, and how delightfully the final illustration depicts the entire universe at peace."

She continues: "My heart is so full of gladness over this book. I just could not help but excitedly read out loud portions of it to my husband, and now I cannot put the little book—with the big message—down, but keep drinking from it as often as possible during the day. It is more refreshing than the coolest mountain stream."

The Watchtower

Announcing Jehovah's Kingdom

March 1, 1987

Fortune-Telling
—Why So Popular?

March 1, 1987
Vol. 108, No. 5

The Watchtower®
Announcing Jehovah's Kingdom

In This Issue

THE PURPOSE OF "THE WATCHTOWER" is to exalt Jehovah God as the Sovereign of the universe. It keeps watch on world events as they fulfill Bible prophecy. It comforts all peoples with the good news that God's Kingdom will soon destroy those who oppress their fellowmen and that it will turn the earth into a paradise. It encourages faith in the now-reigning King, Jesus Christ, whose shed blood opens the way for mankind to gain eternal life. "The Watchtower," published by Jehovah's Witnesses continuously since 1879, is nonpolitical. It adheres to the Bible as its authority.

"WATCHTOWER" STUDIES FOR THE WEEKS

Average Printing Each Issue: 12,315,000

Now Published in 103 Languages

SEMIMONTHLY LANGUAGES AVAILABLE BY MAIL
Afrikaans, Arabic, Cebuano, Chichewa, Chinese, Cibemba, Danish,* Dutch,* Efik, English,* Finnish, French,* German,* Greek,* Hiligaynon, Igbo, Iloko, Italian,* Japanese,* Korean, Lingala, Malagasy, Maltese, Norwegian, Portuguese,* Russian, Sepedi, Sesotho, Shona, Spanish,* Swahili, Swedish, Tagalog, Thai, Tsonga, Tswana, Xhosa, Yoruba, Zulu

MONTHLY LANGUAGES AVAILABLE BY MAIL
Armenian, Bengali, Bicol, Bulgarian, Croatian, Czech, Ewe, Fijian, Ga, Greenlandic, Gujarati, Gun, Hausa, Hebrew, Hindi, Hiri Motu, Hungarian, Icelandic, Kannada, Malayalam, Marathi, New Guinea Pidgin, Pangasinan, Papiamento, Polish, Rarotongan, Romanian, Samar-Leyte, Samoan, Sango, Serbian, Silozi, Sinhalese, Slovenian, Solomon Islands-Pidgin, Tahitian, Tamil, Telugu, Tongan, Tshiluba, Turkish, Twi, Ukrainian, Urdu, Venda, Vietnamese

* Study articles also available in large-print edition.

| | Yearly subscription for the above: | |
| | Semimonthly | Monthly |
Watch Tower Society offices	Languages	Languages
America, U.S., Watchtower, Wallkill, N.Y. 12589	$4.00	$2.00
Australia, Box 280, Ingleburn, N.S.W. 2565	A$7.00	A$3.50
Canada, Box 4100, Halton Hills, Ontario L7G 4Y4	$5.50	$2.75
England, The Ridgeway, London NW7 1RN	£5.00	£2.50
Ireland, 29A Jamestown Road, Finglas, Dublin 11	IR£6.00	IR£3.00
New Zealand, P.O. Box 142, Manurewa	NZ$15.00	NZ$7.50
Nigeria, PMB 001, Shomolu, Lagos State	₦8.00	₦4.00
Philippines, P.O. Box 2044, Manila 2800	₱60.00	₱30.00
South Africa, Private Bag 2067, Krugersdorp, 1740	R6,50	R3,25

Remittances should be sent to the office in your country or to Watchtower, Wallkill, N.Y. 12589, U.S.A.

Changes of address should reach us 30 days before your moving date. Give us your old and new address (if possible, your old address label).

20 cents (U.S.) a copy

The Bible translation used is the "New World Translation of the Holy Scriptures," unless otherwise indicated.

Copyright © 1987 by Watch Tower Bible and Tract Society of Pennsylvania and International Bible Students Association. All rights reserved. Printed in U.S.A.

The Watchtower (ISSN 0043-1087) is published semimonthly for $4.00 (U.S.) per year by Watch Tower Bible and Tract Society of Pennsylvania, 25 Columbia Heights, Brooklyn, N.Y. 11201. Second-class postage paid at Brooklyn, N.Y., and at additional mailing offices.

Postmaster: Send address changes to Watchtower, *Wallkill, N.Y. 12589.*

Published by
Watch Tower Bible and Tract Society of Pennsylvania
25 Columbia Heights, Brooklyn, N.Y. 11201, U.S.A.

Frederick W. Franz, President

Fortune-Telling
—Still in Fashion

"**O**NE would imagine, in this day of widespread enlightenment and education, that it would be unnecessary to debunk beliefs based on magic and superstition." This was part of a statement signed by 186 eminent scientists, including 18 Nobel prize winners. What were they talking about? Astrology, a common form of fortune-telling using the stars that, according to them, "pervades modern society." Do you personally believe in some forms of fortune-telling? Or are you perhaps skeptical, or even strongly opposed, like these prominent scientists? Your view of this matter is important. Let us see why.

This practice is extremely widespread. According to the spokesman for a congress of fortune-tellers in Paris, "4 million French [people] go to psychics every six months." In the United States there are an estimated 175,000 part-time astrologers and 10,000 full-time. They are also numerous in Great Britain, where they have their own schools. And the French magazine *Ça m'intéresse* (That's Interesting) comments: "Everywhere, including in the most highly developed societies, we meet up with similar statistics. Psychics are flourishing at the close of our century."

Who Consults Them —And Why?

Some may believe that only poorly educated, lower-class people are interested in the occult "sciences," of which astrology is probably the most widespread. But Madame Soleil, a famous French astrologer, reveals: "They all come to me, whether rightist or leftist, politicians of all points of view, and foreign chiefs of state. I even have priests and communists." In harmony with this, when the magician Frédéric Dieudonné died, an article appearing in *Le Figaro,* a serious French daily newspaper, recalled that he attracted "a very large clientele of Parisian personalities, ministers, high officials, writers and actors."

Gamblers consult astrologers to learn how to place their bets. Businessmen go to them to find out how to invest their money. Astrologers are even willing to tell you when to leave on a trip or what to cook. And fortune-telling has invaded other fields too. Police departments in different countries resort to seers to search for criminals or missing persons. And according to the French weekly *Le Figaro Magazine*, "the Pentagon employs 34 persons gifted with second sight to supply information on what is going on in secret military bases in the U.S.S.R." The same magazine reports U.S. congressman Charles Rose as saying that the Russians also resort to psychic powers.

Why is astrology still so fashionable? Is it a harmless diversion or pastime? Is it the best way to find out what the future holds—or is there a better way? Let us see if we can find answers to these important questions.

Your Future

A Better Way to Learn About It

I N 1962 Indian astrologers predicted a worldwide catastrophe "because of a rare conjunction of eight planets in the sign of Capricorn." Nothing came of it, however. More recently, at the end of 1980, most French astrologers were of the opinion that then president of France, Giscard d'Estaing, would be reelected for a second term. But his opponent, François Mitterrand, won the election. Failures like these remind us that astrology provides no sure way to know the future.

Is there, then, another way? For example, will efforts of scientists to predict the future help you? Well, here is the prediction made by the McGraw Hill Institute (United States) in 1970 of what would happen by 1980: "Drugs to defeat cancer, manned spaceflights to Mars and Venus, a permanent lunar base, cars run on electricity, a generalization of home computers, the possibility of choosing your baby's sex, and three-dimensional television and cinema."

Back in 1970 the scientists of this institute stated: "This method [of predicting] aims at achieving a reliable forecast by the unanimous opinion of a group of experts."

But these experts' predictions have proved wrong in these fields and a number of others, such as politics and economics.

A Sure Source of Information

If astrologers and scientists cannot foresee with any certainty what is going to happen, does that mean that it is impossible to get reliable information about the future? Before giving up, we should check what the Bible says on the subject. Remember, Jehovah, the Author of the Bible, is described as "the One telling from the beginning the finale, and from long ago the things that have not been done."—Isaiah 46:10.

God's Word contains many prophecies. How do they differ from the predictions of astrologers? Following is the reply of a work entitled *The Great Ideas:* "But so far as the foreknowledge of mortal men is concerned, the Hebrew prophets seem to be unique. Unlike pagan diviners or soothsayers, . . . they do not have to employ arts or devices for penetrating divine secrets. . . . For the most part their prophetic speeches, unlike those of the oracles, seem to be unambiguous. At least the intention seems to be to reveal, not to conceal, God's plan on such matters as He Himself wishes men to foresee the course of providence."

As an example of this, much information about Jesus was recorded in the Bible many centuries before his birth. It was prophesied that he would be born in the town of Bethlehem and in the family line of Jesse, the father of King David. (Micah 5:2; Isaiah 11:1, 10) The Scriptures also foretold that he would be put to death on a stake but that none of his bones would be broken, as was the custom with such executions. These details proved true, and they are just a few examples of what one Bible scholar estimates to be more than 120 prophecies that were fulfilled in Jesus. —Psalm 22:16, 17; 34:20.

"And the Sign . . . Does Come True"

'What is wrong with going to a fortune-teller or reading your horoscope in a newspaper? Isn't this just harmless fun?'

The Bible does not treat the matter so lightly. In fact, it puts us on our guard against mediums and diviners. In the book of Deuteronomy, Jehovah gives the following warning: "In case a prophet or a dreamer of a dream . . . does give you a sign or a portent, and the sign or the portent does come true of which he spoke to you, saying, 'Let us walk after other gods,' . . . you must not listen to the words of that prophet or to the dreamer of that dream." —Deuteronomy 13:1-3.

Notice that the Scriptures do not question the fact that some of the predictions of mediums and astrologers may come true. Rather, the Bible warns us that, if these predictions are based on signs in the heavens or other methods of divination, they come from the demons, are deceiving, and may turn men away from the true God. —See Acts 16:16-18.

To pay attention to astrologers or to others who claim to predict the future is to run the risk of incurring serious spiritual problems and ending up a slave of "the wicked spirit forces in the heavenly places." (Ephesians 6:12) Thus, to consult such individuals is considered by God to be a serious sin; those who practice such things are detestable in his eyes and they will not inherit his Kingdom. —Revelation 22:15.

It is thus for our own good that the Bible puts us on guard against astrology and all other forms of divination.

THE BIBLE FORETOLD IN ADVANCE THAT:

◆ Jesus would be born in Bethlehem. —Micah 5:2

◆ He would be born in the family of Jesse, the father of King David. —Isaiah 11:1, 10

◆ He would be put to death on a stake.—Psalm 22:16, 17

◆ None of his bones would be broken.—Psalm 34:20

A Prophecy Fulfilled Today

Moreover, the Bible contains prophecies that focus on our day. Let us consider one of the most important of these. It describes a series of events that would mark the period immediately preceding a dramatic intervention of God's Kingdom in earthly affairs. These events include world wars, earthquakes, epidemics, famines, and increasing lawlessness. Has not the intensification of these things become prominent in world news during our 20th century?—Matthew 24:3, 7-14; Luke 21:7, 10, 11; 2 Timothy 3:1-5.

Jesus explained that the fulfillment of these prophecies would herald the arrival of his Kingdom just as surely as the appearing of buds on the trees announces the arrival of spring. He even specified that they would have to be fulfilled in just one generation. All the aspects of the sign, including the details mentioned above, have been fulfilled before our eyes since 1914.* We can therefore have complete confidence that the Kingdom will act very soon.—Luke 21:29-33.

Another feature prophesied for this

---

* For more details about the fulfillment of these prophecies since 1914, see chapter 7 of the book *True Peace and Security—How Can You Find It?* published by the Watchtower Bible and Tract Society of New York, Inc.

time was "anguish of nations, not knowing the way out." (Luke 21:25) Now, why is there such a fascination today with astrology and other forms of the occult? The French newspaper *Le Monde Dimanche* answers: "Faced with the crisis, people will stop at nothing to find reassurance. Parapsychology gives great comfort for little effort, and in this age of fear-inspiring scientific accomplishments such as nuclear feats and gene splicing, people are tempted to escape to the unknown and irrational, trying to rediscover a meaning to life." So we should not be surprised at the widespread interest in occult practices, such as astrology. It is one of the symptoms of the "anguish" that people are experiencing today in fulfillment of Jesus' prophecy.

'Lift Your Head Up'

What should Christians do when they see all these things? Give way to fear, like the people around them? Jesus offered the following counsel: "But as these things start to occur, *raise yourselves erect and lift your heads up,* because your deliverance is getting near."—Luke 21:28.

Would you like to know your future in more detail? Then take the time to examine the Bible in depth and "test the inspired expressions to see whether they originate with God." (1 John 4:1) You can do this with the help of the magazine *The Watchtower,* which regularly discusses Bible prophecies and explains their application to our day. Thus, as you become convinced that the end of the present troubled world is close, you, too, will be able to 'lift your head up.' You will also learn what you must do to enjoy the blessings of the Messianic Kingdom, which will soon intervene in world affairs for the benefit of all right-hearted people.

Kingdom Proclaimers Report

Expanded Facilities to Match Kingdom Increase

DEDICATION day for recently expanded branch facilities of Jehovah's Witnesses was a very happy day in the Caribbean island of Jamaica. This expansion had become necessary because of Jehovah's blessing on the faithful efforts of the brothers in preaching the good news in this beautiful tropical island.

A missionary home was established in Jamaica as early as 1946. With the missionaries spearheading the work, the increase in publishers was rapid, so that in just ten years the average number of Witnesses reporting monthly grew from 732 to 3,216. In order to care for the increase, it became necessary to arrange for new facilities.

In 1954 suitable land was obtained and construction began on a sturdy new two-story building in a quiet suburban area of Kingston. It was completed in May 1958. The number of publishers that year rose to a peak of 4,367.

The 'planting' and 'watering' continued and Jehovah "kept making it grow," so that by 1983 the number of publishers had grown to over 7,000, creating the need for further expansion. (1 Corinthians 3:6) The Branch Committee, with the approval of the Governing Body, decided to expand the present facilities. Over 250 brothers from all over the island came to help out. Skilled and unskilled workers volunteered their services as masons, carpenters, electricians, and plumbers. Their ages ranged from 10 to 86. Some contributed financially to the project, others contributed food

for the workers, and still others opened up their homes to provide accommodations for volunteers who came from far away. In one year the project, consisting of adding a third floor of five rooms and a recreational area, a room on the second floor, and 400 square feet (37 sq m) of storage space, was completed, ready for use by the 11 members of the Bethel family.

Milton Henschel, a member of the Governing Body of Jehovah's Witnesses, gave the dedication talk on February 22, 1986. He spoke on the theme "The Triumphal Procession." (2 Corinthians 2:14) Those listening to the dedication pro-

gram totaled 2,949. Of these, 380 were located in the Kingdom Hall and other parts of the building, and the others were tied in by telephone and radio to other Kingdom Halls in the city and to a school auditorium.

Most of those invited to the branch Kingdom Hall were brothers and sisters who had been in the truth for 30 years or more. Many expressions of appreciation were heard for the fine addition to the building. It is our hope that many more of the "great crowd" of "other sheep" will yet join the triumphal procession as the new branch facilities are used in caring for the Kingdom increase in Jamaica.

Jesus Rebukes the Pharisees

IF IT is by Satan's power that he expels demons, Jesus argues, then Satan is divided against himself. "Either you people make the tree fine and its fruit fine," he continues, "or make the tree rotten and its fruit rotten; for by its fruit the tree is known."

It is foolish to charge that the good fruit of casting out demons is due to Jesus' serving Satan. If the fruit is fine, the tree cannot be rotten. On the other hand, the Pharisees' rotten fruitage of absurd accusations and groundless opposition to Jesus is proof that they themselves are rotten. "Offspring of vipers," Jesus exclaims, "how can you speak good things, when you are wicked? For out of the abundance of the heart the mouth speaks."

Since our words reflect the condition of our hearts, what we say provides a basis for judgment. "I tell you," Jesus says, "that every unprofitable saying that men speak, they will render an account concerning it on Judgment Day; for by your words you will be declared righteous, and by your words you will be condemned."

Despite all Jesus' powerful works, the scribes and Pharisees request: "Teacher, we want to see a sign from you." Although these particular men from Jerusalem may not personally have seen his miracles, irrefutable eyewitness evidence regarding them exists. So Jesus tells the Jewish leaders: "A wicked and adulterous generation keeps on seeking for a sign, but no sign will be given it except the sign of Jonah the prophet."

Explaining what he means, Jesus continues: "Just as Jonah was in the belly of the huge fish three days and three nights, so the Son of man will be in the heart of the earth three days and three nights." After being swallowed by the fish, Jonah came out as if resurrected, so Jesus foretells that he will die and on the third day be raised alive. Yet the Jewish leaders, even when Jesus later is resurrected, reject "the sign of Jonah."

Thus Jesus says that the men of Nineveh who repented at the preaching of Jonah will rise up in the judgment to condemn the Jews who reject Jesus. Similarly, he draws a parallel with the queen of Sheba, who came from the ends of the earth to hear Solomon's wisdom and marveled at what she saw and heard. "But, look!" Jesus notes, "something more than Solomon is here."

Jesus then gives the illustration of a man from whom an unclean spirit comes out. The man, however, does not fill the void with good things and so becomes possessed by seven more wicked spirits. "That is how it will be also with this wicked generation," Jesus says. The Israelite nation had been cleansed and

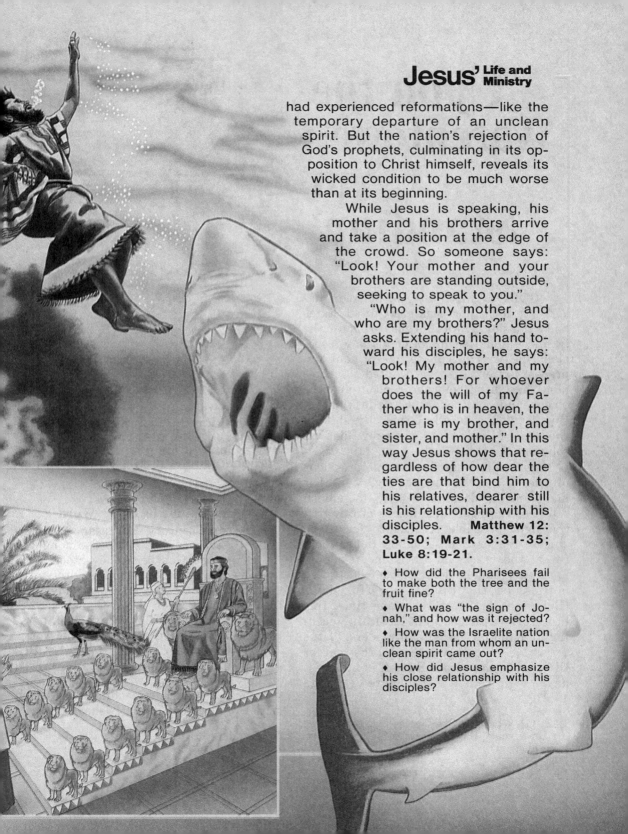

had experienced reformations—like the temporary departure of an unclean spirit. But the nation's rejection of God's prophets, culminating in its opposition to Christ himself, reveals its wicked condition to be much worse than at its beginning.

While Jesus is speaking, his mother and his brothers arrive and take a position at the edge of the crowd. So someone says: "Look! Your mother and your brothers are standing outside, seeking to speak to you."

"Who is my mother, and who are my brothers?" Jesus asks. Extending his hand toward his disciples, he says: "Look! My mother and my brothers! For whoever does the will of my Father who is in heaven, the same is my brother, and sister, and mother." In this way Jesus shows that regardless of how dear the ties are that bind him to his relatives, dearer still is his relationship with his disciples. **Matthew 12: 33-50; Mark 3:31-35; Luke 8:19-21.**

♦ How did the Pharisees fail to make both the tree and the fruit fine?

♦ What was "the sign of Jonah," and how was it rejected?

♦ How was the Israelite nation like the man from whom an unclean spirit came out?

♦ How did Jesus emphasize his close relationship with his disciples?

'Upon the Watchtower I Am Standing'

"And he proceeded to call out like a lion: 'Upon the watchtower, O Jehovah, I am standing constantly by day, and at my guardpost I am stationed all the nights.'"—ISAIAH 21:8.

A GOD-FEARING 21-year-old man living in the northeastern United States had a mission. It was his goal to expose the false religious teachings of his day, especially the doctrines of eternal torment and predestination. Also, he wanted to champion the truth about the ransom and the object and manner of Christ's coming. How would he do all of this? By shining the light of God's Word, the Holy Bible, on religious beliefs.—Psalm 43:3; 119:105.

[2] Charles T. Russell, the first president of the Watch Tower Society, was that man, and he decided in 1873 to publish religious literature as a means of bringing the light of Bible truth into focus. To sincere readers, those publications would reveal the cracks in Christendom's dogmas. Any hidden doctrinal defects would not escape the Bible's powerful light. (Ephesians 5:13) At the same time, this literature would spotlight 'healthful teaching' to build up the faith of readers. (Titus 1:9; 2:11; 2 Timothy 1:13) Did the zeal for Bible truth that drove Russell in his quest have a precedent?—Compare 2 Kings 19:31.

Early Christians: Champions of God's Word

[3] The first-century Christians championed the use of God's Word among the Jews and the Gentiles. They stood as if stationed on a watchtower, heralding forth the truth to all who would hear. (Matthew 10:27) Their Leader, Jesus Christ, set the pace. He said: "For this I have been born, and for this I have come into the world, that I should bear witness to the truth." (John 18:37) Although perfect, he refused to rely on his own wisdom or personal opinions. Rather, his teachings originated with his Superior Teacher, Jehovah God. "I

1, 2. (a) What goal did Charles T. Russell have? (b) How would Bible literature help to accomplish his goal?

3. How did Christ Jesus set the pace for championing the truth?

do nothing of my own initiative," he told a group of Jews. "But just as the Father taught me I speak these things." (John 8:28; see also John 7:14-18.) According to the Gospel accounts of his earthly ministry, Jesus quoted (or spoke parallel thoughts) from about one half of the books of the Hebrew Scriptures.—Luke 4:18, 19 (Isaiah 61:1, 2); Luke 23:46 (Psalm 31:5).

⁴ Even after his death and resurrection, Christ was still using God's Word to teach the truth. For example, when Cleopas and his companion were traveling from Jerusalem to Emmaus, Jesus helped those disciples reason on the Scriptures. The account states: "And commencing at Moses and all the Prophets he interpreted to them things pertaining to himself in all the Scriptures." (Luke 24:25-27) Later that same day, Jesus appeared to the 11 apostles and some of his disciples to build up their faith. How? By the skillful use of the Scriptures. Luke writes: "Then he [Jesus] opened up their minds fully to grasp the meaning of the Scriptures, and he said to them: 'In this way it is written that the Christ would suffer and rise from among the dead on the third day.'"—Luke 24:45, 46.

⁵ Following its Exemplar, in the year 33 C.E. the Christian congregation began its public ministry with the use of the Scriptures. The setting: an open area outside a house in Jerusalem. After hearing the sound of "a rushing stiff breeze" upon this house, a crowd of thousands of Jews of Jerusalem and Jewish pilgrims are drawn to this place and assembled. Peter steps forward—the 11 other apostles are around him—and with a powerful voice he begins to speak: "Men of Judea and all you inhabitants of Jerusalem, let this be known to you and give ear to my sayings."

Then pointing out "what was said through the prophet Joel" and what "David says," Peter explains the miracle that has just taken place and that "God made him both Lord and Christ, this Jesus whom you impaled."—Acts 2:2, 14, 16, 25, 36.

⁶ When the early Christians needed clarifying information on faith and conduct, the first-century governing body also made good use of the Scriptures. For example, at the meeting of the governing body in the year 49 C.E., the disciple James, acting as chairman, focuses their attention on a pertinent scripture found at Amos 9:11, 12. "Men, brothers, hear me," he says. "Symeon has related thoroughly how God for the first time turned his attention to the nations to take out of them a people for his name. And with this the words of the Prophets agree, just as it is written." (Acts 15:13-17) The entire body concurred with James' proposition and then put their scripturally based decision in written form so that it could be delivered to all the congregations and read by them. What were the results? The Christians "rejoiced over the encouragement," and "the congregations continued to be made firm in the faith and to increase in number from day to day." (Acts 15:22-31; 16:4, 5) Thus, the early Christian congregation became "a pillar and support of the truth." But what about modern history? Would C. T. Russell and his associate Bible students imitate this fine, first-century example? How would they champion the truth?—1 Timothy 3:15.

Magazines With a Far-Reaching View

⁷ July 1879 saw the birth of Russell's principal vehicle for Bible enlightenment

4. Give examples of how Jesus used God's Word to teach the truth.
5. At Pentecost 33 C.E., how did Peter follow the example of Christ in using the Scriptures?

6. (a) Explain what took place at a meeting of the first-century governing body. (b) How were the congregations informed of the governing body's decision, and with what benefit?
7. (a) What was the purpose of *Zion's Watch Tower*? (b) To whom did it look for support?

—*Zion's Watch Tower and Herald of Christ's Presence.* Its first issue laid out the magazine's noble purpose: "As its name indicates, it aims to be the lookout from whence matters of interest and profit may be announced to the 'little flock,' and as the *'Herald of Christ's Presence,'* to give the 'meat in due season' to the 'household of faith.'" Trust in almighty God was the magazine's cornerstone. Its second issue stated: "'Zion's Watch Tower' has, we believe, JEHOVAH for its backer, and while this is the case it will never *beg* nor *petition* men for support. When He who says: 'All the gold and silver of the mountains are mine,' fails to provide necessary funds, we will understand it to be time to suspend the publication."

8 *Zion's Watch Tower,* now *The Watchtower,* has been published continuously for more than 107 years. It has grown from a monthly magazine of 6,000 copies printed in one language to a semimonthly magazine of 12,315,000 copies available in 103 languages.—Compare Isaiah 60:22; Zechariah 4:10.

9 The title, *Watch Tower,* was an apt choice by Russell. The word usually used in the Hebrew Scriptures for "watchtower" means "lookout" or "observation point," from which a guard could easily spot an enemy in the distance and sound an advance warning of the approach of danger. Suitably, then, for its first 59 years of publication, the title page carried this challenging quotation from Isaiah 21:11, 12, *King James Version:* "Watchman, What of the Night?" "The Morning Cometh."

10 The posted watchman of Isaiah's prophecy was due to step forward shortly. Amid the earth's prevailing wicked state of gloom, Russell had gladly broadcast the good news of "the morning" to come. Jesus Christ's Millennial Reign of peace is the theme of a welcome bulletin. But before "the morning" arrives, the class serving as a watchman—the remnant of spiritual Israel today—boldly warns of the progress of "the night," which will reach its darkest point in "the war of the great day of God the Almighty" at Har-Magedon.—Revelation 16:14-16.

11 Earlier, in Isaiah 21:8, we are introduced to this faithful watchman with these words: "And he proceeded to call out like a lion: 'Upon the watchtower, O Jehovah, I am standing constantly by day, and at my guardpost I am stationed all the nights.'"

12 Picture in your mind a watchman stationed on a high tower, bending forward, scanning the horizon during the daylight, straining to pierce the darkness during the night—always on the alert. You now have the main idea conveyed by the Hebrew word for "watchtower" (*mitspeh'*) as used in Isaiah 21:8. Since the watchman is so vigilant, who in his right mind would doubt his ringing report? Likewise today, the watchman class has exerted itself by searching through the Scriptures to see what Jehovah has in store for this system of things. (James 1:25) This watchman then calls out that message loudly and fearlessly, principally through the pages of *The Watchtower.* (Compare Amos 3:4, 8.) This magazine

---

8. Explain *The Watchtower's* growth in light of Isaiah 60:22 and Zechariah 4:10.
9. How was the title *Watch Tower* an appropriate one?

10. Who serves as the watchman of Isaiah 21:11, and what message does he announce?
11, 12. (a) How do the words at Isaiah 21:8 show that the watchman class is faithful and alert? (b) By what agent does today's report come, and how is it principally spread?

will never shrink in fear from championing the truth!—Isaiah 43:9, 10.

[13] On October 1, 1919, a new magazine appeared on the world stage: *The Golden Age.** The watchman class would use this instrument as an associate to *The Watchtower.* Although its articles would not delve into Bible subjects as deeply as those in *The Watchtower,* it would alert mankind to false religious teachings, the coming destruction of the present wicked system of things, and the new earth of righteousness to follow. Yes, it too would champion the truth!

[14] Eighteen years later the name of *The Golden Age* was changed to *Consolation.* "The new name stands for truth," stated the issue of October 6, 1937. *Consolation* became *Awake!* with the August 22, 1946, issue. In that issue it pledged: "Integrity to the truth will be the highest aim of this magazine." To this day, it has not failed to keep that promise. Uniquely, *The Watchtower* and *Awake!* carry the banner of truth high for all to see. In so doing, the magazines follow the path blazed by the early Christian congregation.—3 John 3, 4, 8.

---

* Interestingly, some readers were at first disappointed with the cover design of *The Golden Age.* To them it appeared too commonplace. In response the Watch Tower Society's annual report said: "In this connection we would suggest that just at the time the publication of *The Golden Age* started there was a printers' strike in Greater New York. Only a few days before, a contract had been made for the publication of *The Golden Age* and the men who were operating the presses which take the kind of paper and cover used in it did not go on strike. It thus seemed providential that the character of cover and paper had been selected, for the reason that had any other been selected it would have been impossible to start the magazine at all. Thus the Lord seemed to favor the infant publication."

---

13. What associate journal appeared in 1919, and what similar purpose does it have?
14. What was the aim of *Consolation,* and later *Awake!?*

History-Making *Watchtower* Articles, Decade by Decade

1879:	"God Is Love"—championed Jesus' ransom sacrifice as the basis for mankind's redemption
1879:	"Why Evil Was Permitted"—explained why Jesus Christ's presence would be invisible
1880:	"One Body, One Spirit, One Hope"—pinpointed 1914 for the ending of the Gentile Times
1882:	"The Wages of Sin Is Death"—exposed the doctrine of eternal torment as a denial of God's love
1885:	"Evolution and the Brain Age"—exposed the evolution theory as false
1897:	"What Say the Scriptures About Spiritism?" —gave proof of spiritism's demonic origin
1902:	"God First—His Appointments"—emphasized obeying God's law in the family and in business dealings
1919:	"Blessed Are the Fearless"—brought new life to an awakening organization of fearless worshipers
1925:	"Birth of the Nation"—made plain the prophecies showing that God's Kingdom was born in 1914
1931:	"A New Name"—henceforth the name Jehovah's Witnesses would set true Christians apart from apostate Christendom
1935:	"The Great Multitude"—showed that gathering of those who would live forever on earth was under way
1938:	"Organization"—introduced a truly theocratic arrangement among Jehovah's Witnesses
1939:	"Neutrality"—fortified Jehovah's Witnesses worldwide to withstand the pressures of World War II
1942:	"The Only Light"—sounded a go-ahead signal for the courageous witness work to continue
1945:	"Immovable for the Right Worship"—showed that Christians must abstain from receiving blood transfusions
1952:	"Keeping the Organization Clean"—showed that disfellowshipping by congregations is Scriptural
1962:	"Subjection to 'Superior Authorities'—Why?"— offered reasons for relative subjection to human powers
1973:	"Keeping God's Congregation Clean in 'the Time of His Judgment'"—urged shunning tobacco use
1979:	"Zeal for Jehovah's House"—reiterated that house-to-house preaching follows the apostolic pattern
1982:	"Beloved Ones, . . . Keep Yourselves in God's Love"—alerted Christians to apostates' method of operation
1983:	"Walking With God in a Violent World" —confirmed that Christians must have no part with violence
1984:	"The Recent Pen for 'Other Sheep'"—clarified how this earthly class is brought into unity with those in the new covenant "fold"
1987:	"Christian Jubilee Climaxes in the Millennium" —showed how all loyal Christians gain liberty and life

The *Watchtower* and *Awake!*: Champions of Truth

[15] The "faithful and discreet slave" class, the "watchman," today uses the *Watchtower* magazine under the direction of the Governing Body of Jehovah's Witnesses as its main channel for dispensing spiritual "food at the proper time." (Matthew 24: 45) This follows the pattern of the first-century congregation, which put clarifying information on doctrine and morals into written form "to be read to all the brothers." (1 Thessalonians 5:27) Right from its start *The Watchtower* has been a Bible-using and Bible-teaching magazine. For example, the first issue of *Zion's Watch Tower* quoted or cited more than 200 texts from at least 30 Bible books. But more is needed than merely quoting Bible verses. People need help to understand them. *The Watchtower* has always advanced Bible comprehension. From 1892 to 1927 each issue contained weekly Bible readings and a discussion of a key text from each reading. For other examples, see the chart entitled "History-Making *Watchtower* Articles, Decade by Decade."

[16] How would *The Watchtower* maintain the purity of its printed message? The magazine's first editor, C. T. Russell, instituted safeguards to make certain that what was printed in *The Watchtower* was the truth as then understood. One of those safeguards is identified in his will made on June 27, 1907. (Russell died on October 31, 1916.) His will states:

"I direct that the entire editorial charge of *ZION'S WATCH TOWER* shall be in the hands of a committee of five brethren, whom I exhort to great carefulness and fidelity to the truth. All articles appearing in the columns of *ZION'S WATCH TOWER* shall have the unqualified approval of at least three of the committee of five, and I urge that if any matter approved by the three be known or supposed to be contrary to the views of one or both of the other members of the committee, such articles shall be held over for thought, prayer and discussion for three months before being published—that so far as possible the unity of the faith and the bonds of peace may be maintained in the editorial management of the journal."

[17] Each member of the Editorial Committee, according to Russell's will, had to be "thoroughly loyal to the doctrines of the Scriptures" and had to exhibit, as prominent characteristics, "purity of life, clearness in the truth, zeal for God, love for the brethren and faithfulness to the Redeemer." Also, Russell stipulated that "it shall not in any manner be indicated by whom the various articles appearing in the journal are written . . . that the truth may be recognized and appreciated for its own worth, and that the Lord may more particularly be recognized as the Head of the church and the Fountain of truth."

---

15. (a) What method of dispensing spiritual food today is similar to that in the early Christian congregation? (b) Besides quoting Bible verses, what else is needed? Give examples.

16, 17. What did *The Watchtower's* first editor do to ensure that this magazine would always champion Bible truth?

Do You Remember?

☐ Why did C. T. Russell begin publishing Bible literature?

☐ How did early Christians champion the truth?

☐ Why is the word "Watchtower" in the title of this magazine?

☐ Who is the modern-day watchman, and what instrument does he principally use to amplify his voice?

☐ How do *The Watchtower* and *Awake!* champion Bible truth?

¹⁸ To this day the Governing Body follows similar guidelines. Each article in both *The Watchtower* and *Awake!* and every page, including the artwork, is scrutinized by selected members of the Governing Body before it is printed. Furthermore, those who assist in writing articles for *The Watchtower* are Christian elders who appreciate the seriousness of their assignment. (Compare 2 Chronicles 19:7.) They spend many hours in researching the Bible and other reference material to make sure that what is written is the truth and that it faithfully follows the Scriptures.

18. Why can we read *The Watchtower* and *Awake!* with confidence?

(Ecclesiastes 12:9, 10; 2 Timothy 1:13) It is not unusual for one magazine article —that you may read in 15 minutes—to take from two weeks to over a month to prepare.

¹⁹ Therefore, you can read *The Watchtower* and *Awake!* with confidence. But you can do more. You can enthusiastically offer these magazines to others so that they also can learn the truth and benefit from hearing the messages of the 'watchman standing upon the watchtower.' (Isaiah 21:8) Yes, along with the modern-day watchman, you too can champion Bible truth.

19. What can you do to champion Bible truth?

'Riding in the Cause of Truth'

T HE poet-singer was eager to begin his song. Anticipation of the coming of a good government in the hands of an incorruptible, righteous ruler was too strong. He could not keep silent. No longer able to contain himself, the psalmist burst forth with these words: "My heart has become astir with a goodly matter. I am saying: 'My works are concerning a king.' May my tongue be the stylus of a skilled copyist." (Psalm 45:1) The original poet-singer is long dead. But his prophetic song still lives, and the force of it was never more

1, 2. (a) What message excited the psalmist? (b) Why should that same message stir us?

"And in your splendor go on to success; ride in the cause of truth and humility and righteousness, and your right hand will instruct you in fear-inspiring things."—PSALM 45:4.

powerful than now.—Compare Colossians 3:16.

² What has the "goodly matter" that stirred the psalmist's heart proved to be? It is related to the good news of God's Kingdom! So "goodly" is the Kingdom message that it deserves to "be preached in all the inhabited earth for a witness to all the nations" before "the end" of these nations comes. (Matthew 24:14) Today, has the "goodly" theme of God's Messianic Kingdom stirred your heart? It should. Why? Because the Hebrew verb translated "has become astir" (*ra·chash'*) signifies excited motion, like a bubbling, boiling liquid. The verb also connotes fullness. And remember, our Leader, Jesus Christ, said: "Out of the heart's abundance [the] mouth speaks." (Luke 6:45) Thus, do you, like the psalmist, have a heart overflowing with the "goodly matter"? If so, then nothing can stop you from singing out this superlative truth: Jesus Christ is ruling in God's Kingdom!

Spreading the Song of Truth

³ How can this regal song be spread? By means of holy spirit, the psalmist's tongue became a "stylus" in the hands of Jehovah. (Compare 2 Samuel 23:2.) His penned lyrics were sung for all of Jehovah's ancient worshipers to hear. We today can champion the truth of God's Kingdom in two similar ways. First, by our words heard in public preaching and, second, by our words read in our literature. Hence, when we distribute Bible-based literature, we are telling what the tongue of inspired holy men has already said. (2 Timothy 3:16; 2 Peter 1:20, 21) And today the printed Kingdom message is circulated in numbers and languages and at a speed beyond the imagination of the psalmist.

_____
3. What two main methods are used in spreading the Kingdom good news today?

Are you having a regular part in its dissemination, especially by the distribution of the *Watchtower* and *Awake!* journals?

⁴ The appearance of Jehovah's King stimulates the psalmist to write: "You are indeed more handsome than the sons of men. Charm has been poured out upon your lips. That is why God has blessed you to time indefinite." (Psalm 45:2) From the day of his anointing with the spirit of God, Jesus' lips persistently preached the Kingdom, until the human agents of Satan temporarily silenced them. Because of Jesus' loyalty, Jehovah then blessed him forever by resurrecting him from the dead and exalting him above all other creatures. (Philippians 2:8-11) Since Jesus' heavenly glorification, when he became 'the exact representation of God's very being,' he is more beauteous than the most exalted ruler, human or angelic. (Hebrews 1:3, 4) Now, as the enthroned King, Jesus empowers the lips of the anointed watchman class and their associates to sing out boldly the good news of the Kingdom. However, this is also a song of war.

⁵ The psalmist next calls out to the reigning King: "Gird your sword upon your thigh, O mighty one, with your dignity and your splendor. And in your splendor go on to success; ride in the cause of truth and humility and righteousness, and your right hand will instruct you in fear-inspiring things." (Psalm 45:3, 4) Since 1914 Christ has been riding a war steed, ready for action. (Revelation 6:1, 2) He is girded with a sword—the symbol of war and also of authority and power from God to execute opposing nations. Christ has

_____
4. (a) How has Christ Jesus become "more handsome than the sons of men"? (b) How does the anointed watchman class imitate the 'charm of Christ's lips'?
5, 6. (a) What does Christ's 'riding in the cause of truth' imply? (b) How does the watchman class use *The Watchtower* and *Awake!*?

already battled with Satan and his demons, pitching them down from the heavens and confining them to the vicinity of the earth.—Revelation 12:1-13.

⁶ However, before peace is restored, things more terrible than this will be wrought by the King's right hand when he 'rides in the cause of truth' at Armageddon to destroy all of God's enemies on earth. (Psalm 45:4; Revelation 16:14, 16; 19:17, 18) Christ has emboldened the anointed watchman class to sing out this warning too. What does the "watchman" use to amplify his voice? Principally the pages of the *Watchtower* magazine—the journal that is preeminent in announcing Jehovah's established Kingdom. The watchman class, like an army of stinging scorpion-locusts, is imbued with the same spirit that drives Christ to "ride in the cause of truth." (Revelation 9:7-11) Effectively, they use the magazines prepared under the direction of the "watchman" —*The Watchtower* and *Awake!*—"in the cause of truth."—Matthew 24:45; compare Revelation 9:16-19.

'Riding for Truth'

⁷ For more than one hundred years, *The Watchtower* has been championing 'the cause of Kingdom truth.' It skillfully uses God's Word as a sword in peeling away the layers of error wrapped around false religious teachings. (Compare Ephesians 6:17; Hebrews 4:12.) *Awake!* magazine also advocates the cause of truth. When it comes to current events, *Awake!* slices through the veil that enshrouds Bible-discrediting scientific theories and dangerous social and moral trends. What can we do to place these magazines in the hands of more people so that they can hear the life-saving Kingdom message?

---

7. In what aggressive way do the *Watchtower* and *Awake!* magazines promote Bible truth?

⁸ All who love truth should "become astir" with the message that the *Watchtower* and *Awake!* journals contain. (Psalm 45:1) How? Why not read them as soon as you receive them? 'I am not going to read a secular magazine or book until I have first read through our magazines,' Lillian said to herself ten years ago. She is still faithful to that resolve. (Matthew 6:33) What can you do after you read them? Talk about their contents with others—family and fellow congregation members. This should also fire you with zeal for witnessing with the magazines so that you may tell your neighbors about the good things you have read. No doubt you will *want* to share in magazine witnessing each week, taking them to neighbors' homes. This may be compared with the way that the apostle Paul "thoroughly bore witness."—Acts 20: 20, 21.

⁹ Peter and his wife Petra have been serving as missionaries in an African country for the past four years. The *Watchtower* and *Awake!* magazines are one of their chief sources of spiritual stamina. "*The Watchtower* helps us to keep spiritually alert in our territory," says Petra. "We derive encouragement and strength from each issue of *The Watchtower* and *Awake!*," Peter adds, "and every time the magazines arrive, it seems to us that we are receiving a letter from home." (Compare Psalm 46:1.) Do you have the same deep appreciation for our journals and are you as eager to read them as are Peter and Petra? That kind of spirit will prompt you to offer the magazines regularly to others too.

8, 9. How can applying the principle at Ephesians 5:16 to the reading of *The Watchtower* and *Awake!* help you "become astir" to share in magazine witnessing? Give examples.

¹⁰ Kingdom publishers should have a positive attitude toward magazine witnessing. People who are sincerely religious still welcome the Bible-based information contained in our journals. (Compare Acts 10:15, 30-33.) Why? Because they can get it from no other source. More than 45 years ago in Sweden, Lars got a stack of *Watchtower* magazines from an employee. "This makes sense," he told his wife after reading them. "What the Bible says, *The Watchtower* says." What Lars read moved him to baptism —March 1940. Consider another example. Two pioneer ministers from the southern United States said:

"A woman was contacted in the magazine work. She's the treasurer of a large Baptist church and a very serious Bible student too. When she read the series on the theme of Armageddon in the *Watchtower* issues of January 1 to February 15, 1985, she was delighted. Previously, she had spent hours researching that subject and came up with nothing except the scripture found at Revelation 16:16. She had asked her minister: 'What is Armageddon? Can you explain it?' He looked at her and said, 'That's a deep subject,' and then walked away. She remarked that *The Watchtower,* on the other hand, answered her every question and that this was the only source she had found with the needed scriptures on the subject of Armageddon."

¹¹ Can you schedule at least one day for magazine witnessing each week, making this part of your spiritual routine? (Compare Philippians 3:16.) "Publishers, and pioneers too, do not spend sufficient time in magazine work," observes the Watch Tower Society's Nigerian branch. But

PLACING MAGAZINES
Have You Tried?—
♦ House-to-house witnessing
♦ Street witnessing
♦ Business witnessing
♦ Magazine-route witnessing
♦ Evening witnessing
♦ When book offer is refused
♦ When making return visits
♦ Calling on former Bible students
♦ When traveling or shopping
♦ When talking to relatives, coworkers, neighbors, schoolmates, or teachers

10. What type of attitude is needed for effective magazine witnessing, and what benefits can it produce?
11. (a) Why schedule magazine witnessing, and how often? (b) Can magazine service be a help in the Bible study work? Explain. (c) How may you be able to place *The Watchtower* and *Awake!?* See box.

should magazine witnessing now overshadow the disciple-making work? On the contrary, reports from the Society's branches in Australia and Brazil show that placing magazines can be the initial step in starting many Bible studies. "From my initial magazine placements, three studies were started," says an Australian sister. How may you be able to place magazines that might lead to a Bible study? Look at the box entitled "Placing Magazines" for suggestions.

Have You Tried These Suggestions?

[12] *Our Kingdom Ministry* of March 1984 had a four-page insert on magazine witnessing. Have you tried the suggestions it offered? Kingdom publishers would do well to read that insert again and apply its advice in the field service. One sister from the United States did this; the results pleasantly surprised her. She writes:

"I've been putting into practice the points outlined in the March 1984 *Kingdom Ministry* insert about magazine placements, and it's working! At the end of 1983 I had only placed 36 magazines the whole year! I was unhappy, not so much because of the numbers on the report, but because I had failed to get this life-giving information into the hands of people who need it. I prayed to Jehovah about the matter and determined to make more of an effort to place *The Watchtower* and *Awake!* I put to use the suggestions about setting a personal goal for placements, using a *brief* presentation that highlights only one magazine, regularly going out in field service on magazine day, and having a positive attitude. Now when the householder rejects the regular offer, I say: 'Well, in that case I'll just leave you the latest issues of *The Watchtower* and *Awake!* for 40 cents.' These points really work. In the last four months, I've been able to average 14 magazines per month!"

[13] In the December 1888 issue of *Zion's Watch Tower,* under the heading "A Suggestion to the Reapers," this advice was given: "The greatest difficulty on the part of many seems to be, that their hearts are so full of the good tidings, that they are tempted to tell a little too much concerning the Plan of God." Is that advice still applicable? When asked what publishers can do to increase magazine placements, one circuit overseer from France answered: "Be brief. Get to the point."

[14] In many of the languages in which the magazines appear, attractive illustrations in four colors have added to the appeal of the Kingdom message as it reaches different types of people. With the January 8, 1987, issue, *Awake!* joined *The Watchtower* in being printed in four colors in most major languages. Have you used the illustrations and pictures in the magazines as talking points? Many have, with good results. Theresa, a missionary in the Far East since 1976, has. She distributes 260 magazines a month. "I use the pictures to highlight the main point of my presentation," she says. "Many times I just show the cover to the householder and mention the topic, and the magazine almost places itself."

[15] Kay, a missionary in the country of Suriname, has had a similar experience. She and her husband have been there for ten years, and they find the pictures to be effective when witnessing, especially to those of the Hindu faith. Why? Kay explains:

"The Hindu religion is a picture religion. At one door, I asked a woman: 'Please tell me the name of your gods on your pictures.'

"'This one is Shiva,' she answered.

"'Now, which one is the top god?' I next asked. No answer. 'Shall we read Jeremiah 10: 10-12? Which God can make the claim of being the Creator? Only Jehovah. We know you love pictures. Aren't these pictures in *The Watchtower* and *Awake!* beautiful and interesting? Wouldn't you like the joy of learning what they mean?'"

Why not try weaving the pictures into your conversation next time you are in magazine work?

---

12. What suggestions proved helpful to one publisher?
13. What advice published in 1888 is still practical today?

14, 15. How can the pictures in *The Watchtower* and *Awake!* be used in witnessing? Give examples.

¹⁶ While serving in Hong Kong, Gene averaged over 300 magazine placements per month. How did he do it? He explains:

"First, pray for Jehovah's blessing upon your magazine witnessing. Second, be positive, smiling, and friendly. Third, be adaptable and agreeable, and look for a common ground with the householder. Fourth, order enough magazines for the entire month. I have a large order, since this gives me extra motivation. Fifth, set aside one evening a week for magazine service, since more people are at home then and in a relaxed mood. Sixth, start a magazine route, even if it is a small one."

Starting a Magazine Route

¹⁷ "Keeping accurate records of where magazines have been placed and then calling back regularly is one way to increase magazine distribution," says Ollie, who has served in the African country of Burkina Faso. "I have had 15 people on my magazine route. Since Burkina Faso is not a printing branch and mail delivery is uncertain, the Witnesses often receive their magazines for distribution in bunches, maybe four or five issues at a time." Is that true of your country too? If so, what can be done to overcome this challenge to magazine placements? "You can hold copies of each issue in your hands, fan the magazines out, and invite the interested person to select which one he would like to read," suggests Ollie. "Usually, he will take all of them."

'Keep Astir With a Goodly Matter'

¹⁸ You publishers of the Kingdom have helped the number of subscriptions obtained for both magazines to rise dramatically. You are to be commended for your zeal in spreading the good news in this way. Also commendable is the rise in the total number of magazines placed. Perhaps, though, we can give more attention to our individual placements of the magazines. With more intensive territory coverage, magazine placements per publisher have declined. Since we are living deep in the time of the end, can we become even more 'astir with the goodly matter' of the Kingdom by means of magazine witnessing?—Psalm 45:1; 1 Peter 4:7.

¹⁹ Christ in Kingdom splendor is riding on to success in sanctifying his Father's holy name and vindicating His universal sovereignty. (Revelation 6:2) Let us use our tongues and the printed page to announce his arrival. May we loyally raise our voices with the anointed watchman class as it joins with Christ in championing the truth of God's established Messianic Kingdom. Yes, let us widely distribute *The Watchtower* and *Awake!* —magazines that fill a vital role as our King 'rides in the cause of truth.'—Psalm 45:4.

19. In what two ways can we champion Kingdom truth?

16. What suggestions from a publisher in Hong Kong may you find helpful?
17. (a) To what feature of our magazine witnessing can the principle at Acts 15:36 be applied? (b) In countries that have poor mail service, what is one way the publishers can place magazines?
18. What aspects of recent field-service reports are especially commendable, and to what could we give greater attention?

Do You Remember?

☐ What is the "goodly matter" that should stir your heart?

☐ Christ's 'riding in the cause of truth' brings what results?

☐ In what sense do *The Watchtower* and *Awake!* serve "in the cause of truth"?

☐ How can we give more attention to magazine witnessing?

Praise Be to God,
the Source of Life and Growth

As told by Eduard Warter

THE eyes feast on majestic mountain ridges interspersed with deep, narrow canyons and broad valleys. Torrents rush through gullies—watering gardens, vineyards, and fields on the fruitful plains. But does the onlooker consider the Source of life, who makes such growth possible, worthy of praise?—Psalm 36:9.

This sunny mountainous landscape is in the Kirghiz Republic—a populous Soviet republic in Central Asia. Tens of thousands of Soviet citizens of German origin live there. My family, too, lived in this fruitful place for a time, and we marveled at the God who brings about such wonderful growth. Yes, we praised him and talked openly to others about his grand deeds.

Obedient to the Source of Life

When I was born in 1901, my parents lived in Memelland (now Klaipėda), then part of East Prussia, on the Baltic coast, about ten kilometers (6 mi) from the Russian border. While I was going to school, the first world war broke out, and we became eyewitnesses to the horrors of mass murder. We German frontier dwellers had been on good terms with our Russian neighbors and wondered: 'Whose fault was it? Whose side was God on?' At school, however, slogans such as "For God, Emperor, and Country" stirred up patriotic feelings.

In time, after the war, I succumbed to this influence, volunteering for service in the frontier guard and later in the German Army in Königsberg, now Kaliningrad. Here I reached the conclusion that the ordinary soldier was simply a pawn, shunted around at the whim of others. Shortly after the annexation of Memelland by Lithuania in January 1923, my mother wrote to me: "You ought not to go to war, as the fifth commandment says, 'You must not kill.' The Bible Students [Jehovah's Witnesses] do not go to war either." I was puzzled. Who were these Bible Students? While home on leave, I learned of their basic Bible truths. It had a powerful effect on me—my whole religious and political outlook on life took a major turn.

Now I grasped that the end of the present wicked system of things was imminent, making way for God's Kingdom. Why spend more time trying to help get Germany back on its feet again? Without delay I made arrangements to leave the service, and I returned to my hometown to learn more about these truths. Baptism followed in 1924, and one thing I understood clearly: This step meant serving God, not until a certain date, but forever and in every situation. My heart was full of joy. The highest privilege possible for us feeble humans —serving the Most High and carrying his message to others—had been granted to me.

I was determined to prove myself worthy. We had a large rural area with many scattered settlements and farmhouses to cover. On Sundays it was therefore not unusual for us to walk for from 10 to 12 hours visiting people with the message. Fellow believers having spacious homes offered them for our Christian meetings. There was no journey too far, or stormy weather too bad, to keep us away from these valuable gatherings. They strengthened us for the trialsome times ahead.

Praising Him Even Under Adversity

The Kingdom work began to grow in the Baltic countries, and it now came under the supervision of the Northern European Office of the Watch Tower Society in Denmark. In 1928 I married, and my wife Ruth and I associated with the Hydekrug Congregation. While our brothers in Nazi Germany suffered cruel persecution, we were spared this—until 1939. Early on the morning of March 22, the news broke: "Memelland liberated! The Führer is coming!"

The ominous droning of numerous aircraft overhead filled our ears all morning. Hitler's occupation had begun. The very next day all of Jehovah's Witnesses had their homes searched, and some Witnesses were arrested. Our literature, even Bibles, was confiscated and burned publicly in the marketplace. No sooner were our activities banned than we began to work underground, circulating literature and visiting interested ones secretly.

At the outbreak of World War II, I was called up for military service. I consistently refused, and the Military Court of the Reich in Berlin imposed the death sentence on April 10, 1940. My wife was fetched from home to persuade me to join the military. She, too, remained unmoved and earned the respect of an elderly officer, who remarked: "I must admit, your attitude is quite right. War is inhuman." My wife was left without a breadwinner to support her, our four children, and her aging mother. Did Ruth ever complain? In the few letters she was allowed to write, she encouraged me to remain loyal and not to become weak because of the loved ones I was leaving behind.

In October 1940 my sentence was rescinded. However, I was still kept in custody in various detention centers, finally landing in the concentration camp at Stutthof, near Danzig (today Gdansk). Loyal Witnesses already in the camp, such as Joseph Scharner, Wilhelm Scheider, Herman Raböse, and Hermine Schmidt, were to become my close comrades, and they strengthened my faith.* There, in the midst of 30,000 internees, each doomed and robbed of hope, we were privileged to bring the comfort of Jehovah's Kingdom.

Grateful for Jehovah's Goodness

In January 1945, as war on the eastern front got nearer and nearer, the evacuation of the camp began. In Danzig harbor, the ship *Wilhelm Gustloff* was waiting to carry us westward. Arriving too late —our convoy had been bombarded by airplanes—we missed what turned out to be a voyage to disaster, as few survived the sinking of that ship.# We were then kept for a while in a fenced-in barn with about 200 other prisoners. Under unsanitary conditions, I contracted typhoid fever. Then came the order: "Return to the Stutthof camp!" Running a high temperature, I was hardly able to walk, and I made the long way back only with the help of a brother, Hans Deike. It took ten days in the camp's infirmary for the fever to subside.

April 25, 1945, saw us on our way back

In Our Next Issue

■ Women in the Workplace
  —Tests and Challenges

■ Divine Peace for Those Taught
  by Jehovah

■ Will You Cling to the Truth?

* See *The Watchtower*, March 15, 1968, pages 187-90.
# See *Awake!*, May 22, 1978, pages 16-20.

Eduard and Ruth Warter today

to the coast. I was still seriously ill, and the sisters had a struggle to keep me on my feet. Nevertheless, some of them were singing our songs. We were loaded onto a simple river barge to begin our perilous voyage. With over 400 people on board, the vessel was rocking severely. In order to keep the barge in trim, prisoners were beaten and forced into the lower cargo-hold. There, people were literally lying on top of one another. The dead were thrown overboard. It was a blessing that our small group of 12 Witnesses was allowed to stay on deck, and we thanked God for that.

Frozen stiff, we landed next morning at Sassnitz on the island of Rügen. Unwilling to receive us, the locals gave us only some fresh water. In the night of April 29/30, our barge grounded on one of the many underwater reefs near the island of Eulenbruch. The towboat had cast our vessel loose in an area infested with mines and had vanished. Was this a way to get rid of us? Hearing the underwater reefs scraping the barge hull, we trusted in God not to desert us.

The coast guard brought us to land in rubber dinghies. Our crew was forced at gunpoint to proceed with the journey on another vessel. All German ports were occupied by Allied troops, so we bypassed them and finally made land on the Danish island of Møn. Free at last, we asked the onlookers if there were any of Jehovah's Witnesses on the island. Within two hours we were being warmly embraced by two sisters. How the ones standing around were amazed. Once the Watch Tower Society's branch office heard of our arrival, Filip Hoffmann was dispatched to arrange for loving care and attention to be given us. How grateful we were to Jehovah!

God Gives Life and Growth

We quickly recovered from the ordeal and in September were delighted to attend an assembly of Jehovah's Witnesses in Copenhagen. Two young women, a Lett and a Ukrainian, who had learned the truth in the Stutthof camp were baptized. They both returned to the Soviet Union as our spiritual sisters. And God was to give us still further growth!

Memelland was now part of the Soviet Socialist Republic of Lithuania. Contrary to the urgings of Russian refugees, I made my way eastward in June 1946 to rejoin my family. I took with me a heavy bundle of Bible literature. When I crossed the border, the patrols ignored my bundle, paying more attention to the generous quantity of garlic I was carrying. How delighted the local brothers were to receive the precious spiritual food!

I was filled with gratitude to Jehovah for his wonderfully preserving my family through the war and the difficult times afterward so that we could continue our work. We have never ceased praising God!

A Crushing Blow

However, in September 1950 all Witnesses in our area were arrested and transported elsewhere. A number of us were sentenced to between 10 and 25 years in a labor

The group of Witnesses from Stutthof concentration camp after arrival in Denmark in 1945, with Eduard Warter on extreme left, being welcomed by a local brother

camp. All our family members were banished to Siberia for life.*

This was a crushing blow to us, but we quickly came to realize that the Kingdom message had to be spread in this huge country also. It was my privilege, along with about 30 other Witnesses, to preach to the 3,000 internees of the Vorkuta camp in the north of European Russia. Many accepted the truth, were baptized, and continued the work in virgin territories after their release.

After about five years, in the spring of 1957, I was granted permission to move to the Tomsk area, and this reunited our family. Our brothers in Siberia had to work from morning till evening, with no day off. Finally, almost all those banished ones were released, and a large southward migration of German nationals followed. As mentioned in the beginning, we settled in the Central Asian Republic of Kirghiz in

---

* See *The Watchtower,* April 15, 1956, pages 233-6.

1960. Here, in the town of Kant near Frunze, we found several families of Jehovah's Witnesses who had arrived ahead of us.

The first few years passed peacefully enough. As the waters of truth took effect, a spiritual paradise started to grow here and in other parts of the country. Our active praising of Jehovah, however, did not go unnoticed. The press published libelous articles about us. Leaders of officially registered religions forbade us to visit their "sheep," threatening to take action against us. In 1963 five brothers were suddenly grasped from our midst and sentenced to from seven to ten years in labor camps. The fearless and uncompromising stand of our brothers in court amazed the public. They saw that there were people who were determined to 'obey God rather than men.' —Acts 5:29.

When I reached the age of retirement, we were told that we would be allowed to emigrate to the Federal Republic of Germany. Before our departure, the brothers and sisters in Kirghiz and South Kazakhstan impressed upon us that we should pass on their tender love and greetings, with Job 32:19-22 and Jeremiah 20:9, 10, to all of Jehovah's Witnesses worldwide. Ruth and I have now lived in Bremerhaven since 1969. Despite advancing age, we continue to praise Jehovah, the Source of life and growth, for his goodness. We confidently look forward to the day when the whole earth will be a literal paradise, and every breathing thing will praise him!—Psalm 150:6.

Making All Things New

"The One seated on the throne said: 'Look! I am making all things new.' Also, he says: 'Write, because these words are faithful and true.'"—REVELATION 21:5.

"THERE is nothing new under the sun." Those are the words of wise King Solomon. Continuing, he asked: "Does anything exist of which one may say: 'See this; it is new'?" (Ecclesiastes 1:9, 10) How would we answer that question today?

[2] Have not science and technology brought forth many new things during this 20th century? Just look at the world of travel, with its jet airplanes, its high-powered automobiles, and its bullet trains. Then there are the astounding advances in telecommunications, the use of orbiting satellites, and the launching of spaceships that have actually landed men on the moon. And what of the modern kitchen appliances, refrigerators, and laundry machines that adorn so many homes? Some people may be inclined to say, 'Why, there is everything new under the sun!'

[3] But wait a moment! There is also something hideous, most disturbing,

---

1, 2. (a) What question did Solomon pose three millenniums ago? (b) What, today, seems to contradict Solomon's words?

3. What shocking situation has developed down here "under the sun"? (Luke 21: 25, 26; Psalm 53:1)

to be seen under the sun. What is that? Why, the earth has become an armed camp! This got started in 1914 when World War I erupted. For the first time, machine guns, airplanes, tanks, and submarines were used in warfare. In less than 30 years World War II followed. It was four times as destructive of life and property as was the first world war. It made appalling use of even more murderous devices—flamethrowers, napalm bombs, and finally the atom bomb—forerunner of the demonic nuclear devices that now threaten the very survival of mankind here on earth.

What a shocking commentary it is on so-called civilization that the world is now spending on armaments the colossal sum of 1.9 million dollars each minute! This is more than enough to feed, clothe, and shelter all those of the human race who are living in poverty today. On the other hand, the stockpile of megaton bombs could destroy *all humans on earth*—five billion of us—*12 times over*. Yet it is reported that half a million of the world's best brains are employed in developing even more devastating weapons of destruction.

U.S. Army photo

all-wise Creator arranged for this controlled, beneficial release of nuclear energy for our earth! (Psalm 104:24) Though ungodly men scheme to use nuclear devices for mass murder, happily God will "bring to ruin those ruining the earth."—Revelation 11:18.

⁵ Solomon was correct in saying: "There is nothing new under the sun." For there is nothing new about the materials, the energy sources, and the natural laws that form the basis for earth's physical system of things. These have long been part of God's creation. (Psalm 24:1; Revelation 4:11) There is nothing new in the rising and setting of the sun, in the weather patterns, and in the natural cycle for watering and renewing the earth. And as for the life-style of imperfect mortal man, there is nothing really new, despite changing fashions. Even in affluent societies, life for many becomes repetitious, and at length "wearisome." In some 70 or 80 years, sin-stained man 'walks to his long-lasting house'—the grave. As Solomon states it: "That which has come to be, that is what will come to be; and that which has been done, that is what will be done; and so there is nothing new under the sun."—Ecclesiastes 1:4-9; 12:5.

⁴ Can we truly say, then, that "there is nothing new under the sun"? Yes, we can, for all these productions come within the framework of the material world in which mankind has always lived. Even when man detonates hydrogen-fusion devices, it is nothing new. Hydrogen fusion has been going on within the sun for billions of years. This is the source of the constant blaze of energy that illuminates, warms, and enlivens our earth. Light from the sun also interacts with the chlorophyll in green plants, building the sugars and starches that are the basic food source for a numberless host of living things around us. How grateful we can be that earth's

4. (a) To what framework did Solomon refer in speaking of "nothing new"? (b) How are God's wisdom and love apparent in what he has done and will yet do "under the sun"?

5. (a) Why was Solomon correct in saying: "There is nothing new under the sun"? (b) How does the life-style of imperfect man bear out Solomon's words?

"A New Creation" Under the Sun

⁶ Truly, in a physical way "there is nothing new under the sun"; nor will Jehovah bring forth new material productions during the present 7,000-year day of resting from his works of creation. But something new *has* appeared under the sun. When? It was in the year 2 B.C.E. that Jehovah's angel appeared suddenly to humble shepherds near Bethlehem to make an astoundingly new announcement. He said: "Look! I am declaring to you good news of a great joy that all the people will have, because there was born to you today a Savior, who is Christ the Lord, in David's city." A multitude of holy angels then joined him in praising God and saying: "Glory in the heights above to God, and upon earth peace among men of goodwill." —Luke 2:8-14.

⁷ At 30 years of age, this Savior was baptized in Jordan's waters. Immediately, another new thing happened under the sun. Luke 3:21, 22 describes it in these words: "As [Jesus] was praying, the heaven was opened up and the holy spirit in bodily shape like a dove came down upon him, and a voice came out of heaven: 'You are my Son, the beloved; I have approved you.'" At that point Jesus became "a new creation," a spirit-begotten Son of God. (2 Corinthians 5:17) During the next three and a half years, Jesus gave a powerful witness to God's Kingdom, gathering his first disciples. Then, in 33 C.E., after his sacrificial death and his resurrection as a spirit, Jesus appeared "before the person of God" to open the way for further marvelous developments down here "un-

der the sun."—Hebrews 9:24; 1 Peter 3:18.

⁸ On the day of Pentecost in that year, Jesus began to pour out holy spirit upon his faithful disciples, indicating that they had been brought into union with him as sons of God. The apostle Paul speaks of this "new creation" at 2 Corinthians 5: 17, 18, saying: "If anyone is in union with Christ, he is a new creation; the old things passed away, look! new things have come into existence. But all things are from God, who reconciled us to himself through Christ and gave us the ministry of the reconciliation."

⁹ The apostle Peter addresses this "new creation," saying: "You are 'a chosen race, a royal priesthood, a holy nation, a people for special possession, that you should declare abroad the excellencies' of the one that called you out of darkness into his wonderful light." (1 Peter 2:9) While here on earth, the royal priesthood has zealously proclaimed "the magnificent things of God" related to his Kingdom purposes. Those of this "new creation" who finish their earthly course in integrity get resurrected after Jesus comes to Jehovah's temple.—Acts 2:11; Romans 8:14-17; Malachi 3:1, 2.

"The Re-Creation"

¹⁰ However, is this "new creation" starting with Jesus Christ the only "new" thing that appears "under the sun"? Not at all! While still here on earth, Jesus told his disciples: "Truly I say to you, In the re-creation, when the Son of man sits down upon his glorious throne, you who have followed me will also yourselves sit upon twelve thrones, judging the twelve

---

6. (a) Why are new material creations not to be expected in the near future? (b) How and when did Jehovah proceed to bring forth something "new under the sun"?
7. (a) What new thing happened at Jesus' baptism? (b) How did Jesus open the way for further developments?

8. How was "a new creation" brought forth?
9. What purpose does the "new creation" fulfill?
10. (a) What did Jesus say about a "re-creation"? (b) In what are those of the "new creation" invited to share?

tribes of Israel." (Matthew 19:28) The "little flock" of Jesus' tried and proved disciples—144,000 of them—are thus invited to share with Jesus in his Kingdom and "sit on thrones to judge the twelve tribes of Israel."—Luke 12:32; 22:28-30; Revelation 14:1-5.

¹¹ Who, then, are these "twelve tribes"? The arrangement that Jehovah made for the Atonement Day in ancient Israel provides a clue. Each year, on the tenth day of the seventh month, the high priest was required to sacrifice a bull as a sin-offering "in behalf of himself and his house." This pictured Jesus' sacrifice as applied to "his house" of underpriests. But what of other Israelites? The high priest next drew lots over two goats. One of these he slaughtered as "the goat of the sin offering, which is for the people." After confessing the people's sins over the second goat, he sent it away into the wilderness. The disposal of these two goats thus pictured Jesus' pouring out his lifeblood in sacrifice and his completely carrying away the sins of all mankind other than those of his priestly house. —Leviticus 16:6-10, 15.

¹² "The twelve tribes of Israel" have the same significance at Matthew 19:28. Here the application broadens out beyond Jesus' spirit-begotten underpriests to include all others of mankind. An Expository Dictionary of New Testament Words, by W. E. Vine, defines the Greek word here used for "re-creation," pa·lin·ge·ne·si′a, as "new birth . . . spiritual regeneration," and adds: "In Matt[hew] 19:28 the word is used, in the Lord's discourse, in the wider sense, of the 'restoration of all things' (Acts 3:21, R.V.), when, as a result of the Second Advent of Christ, Jehovah 'sets

His King upon His holy hill of Zion' (Ps. 2:6) . . . Thereby will be accomplished the deliverance of the world from the power and deception of Satan and from the despotic and antichristian rulers of the nations."

¹³ In line with this, Bible translations here render pa·lin·ge·ne·si′a variously as: regeneration, new world, new birth, world born anew, world that is to be, New Creation, new order of life, new age. Do you get the sense of that? "The twelve tribes of Israel," representing all the peoples of mankind, are to be judged by Christ and his loyal underpriests. This is to be in connection with a regeneration, a grand renewal of all that Jehovah has purposed for this earth, down here "under the sun."

"The Times of Restoration"

¹⁴ When does that regeneration take place? At Acts 3:20, 21, Peter speaks of "Jesus, whom heaven, indeed, must hold within itself until the times of restoration of all things of which God spoke through the mouth of his holy prophets of old time." This points to Jesus' waiting at God's right hand in the heavens until "the appointed times of the nations are fulfilled." (Luke 21:24; Psalm 110:1, 2) Then, in 1914, Jehovah does indeed 'install his king upon Zion, his holy mountain.' What restoration then takes place?—Psalm 2:6.

¹⁵ First, a new thing is seen under the sun, in that the remaining faithful underpriests of Christ—the last ones of the "new creation"—are gathered and set to work in 'preaching this good news of the

11. What two aspects of Jesus' sacrifice were pictured on Atonement Day, and how?
12. How does one dictionary elaborate on the meaning of "the re-creation"?

13. (a) What do various Bible versions indicate as to the meaning of pa·lin·ge·ne·si′a? (b) So, what is to happen "under the sun"?
14. (a) According to Acts 3:20, 21, for what must Jesus wait? (b) How and when is Jesus installed as King?
15. (a) What happened "under the sun" following Jesus' enthronement? (b) How have Matthew 25:31-34 and Isaiah 11:6-9 been fulfilled?

established Kingdom.' Next, a "great crowd" is assembled "out of all nations" for preservation through "the great tribulation." (Matthew 24:14; Revelation 7: 9, 14) At this present time the enthroned King, Jesus Christ, is separating people one from another, "just as a shepherd separates the sheep from the goats." "The sheep" are those who show themselves righteously disposed toward the King and his spirit-begotten brothers of the "new creation." These "sheep" are therefore invited to inherit everlasting life in the earthly realm of Jehovah's Kingdom. Already, they enjoy the spiritual paradise restored here on earth.—Matthew 25: 31-34, 46; Isaiah 11:6-9.

16 The judging of the nations and of "the sheep" at this time is as to worthiness for survival during the "great tribulation." (Matthew 24:21, 22) However, is this the judging referred to in Matthew 19:28? No, for further judging is to be carried out by Christ and his underpriests after that tribulation. It is the judging of the figurative "twelve tribes of Israel," peoples other than the royal priesthood. The number "twelve" indicates a completeness of those of mankind that will be judged. This includes the survivors of "the great tribulation," any offspring they may yet have, and the billions of mankind that will be brought forth on earth in the resurrection.

17 Concerning this, Paul states at Acts 17:31 that God "has set a day in which he purposes to judge the inhabited earth in righteousness by a man [Christ Jesus] whom he has appointed, and he has furnished a guarantee to all men in that he has resurrected him from the dead." The post-Armageddon "inhabited earth," made

up of all mankind then on earth, will not be judged according to past sins committed during the present system of things. Rather, they will be "judged individually according to their deeds" performed in the new earth as they avail themselves of Christ's ransom provision.—Revelation 20:13; Matthew 20:28; 1 John 2:2.

18 What magnificent things will appear under the sun at that time! The spiritual paradise will expand into a literal paradise, in fulfillment of Jehovah's original purpose toward this earth. Our God tells us that 'the earth is his footstool,' a sanctuary where he should be worshiped, and he also declares: "I shall glorify the very place of my feet." (Isaiah 66:1; 60:13) So here under the sun, earth is to be made a glorious paradise, a garden of delight, in which a perfect, peaceful, and united mankind will forever praise their God and Creator. "Faithful and true" are Jehovah's thrilling words of promise: "Look! I am making all things new"! (Revelation 21:5) And in the eternity ahead, what marvelous new creations may our loving God yet bring forth down here under the sun to delight his human family!

18. (a) As indicated by Isaiah, what will then appear "under the sun"? (b) What words of promise will thus be fulfilled, and what may we expect for the eternity ahead? (Romans 8:21)

16. (a) What judging is now proceeding? (b) What further judging takes place after Armageddon?
17. Who are then judged, and according to what "deeds"?

How Would You Answer as to Events "Under the Sun"?—

☐ In what sense is there "nothing new"?

☐ When and how did "a new creation" appear?

☐ What does "the re-creation" embrace?

☐ How do "the times of restoration" proceed, and with what grand result?

A Brochure With

THE information in the preceding article was presented earth wide during 1986 at the "Divine Peace" District Conventions of Jehovah's Witnesses. Herewith we summarize further interesting comments made by the speaker:

"Look! I Am Making All Things New." That was the title of a booklet published by the Watch Tower Society back in 1959. A booklet of this kind had been requested by missionaries in Japan. A need was felt there for a publication that would present the Kingdom message in a clear, simple manner for the benefit of people not well acquainted with the Bible itself. Under the supervision of the Watch Tower Society, more than 30 missionaries shared in compiling the booklet. Did this new booklet fill the need as it became the principal instrument for starting new studies in Japan?

The results speak for themselves. At the time of the release of the *"Look!"* booklet, there was a peak of 1,390 Kingdom publishers in Japan. Today, the peak is 114,480 publishers. Almost all of these were introduced to Bible study through the *"Look!"* booklet. During the past 27 years, more than 8,750,000 copies of this booklet have been distributed in the Japanese language alone. And in the past 20 years, Japan has reported a new peak of Kingdom publishers every month except two. Though there are no doubt other causes contributing to this fine increase, there is no question that using the *"Look!"* booklet to start Bible studies has been a big factor.

This booklet has now been updated, according to present needs, and was released at the "Divine Peace" conventions as a magazine-size brochure of 32 pages. A new section has been added on the topic "Bad Things—Why Does God Permit Them?" Further, the concluding paragraphs have been rewritten to give the student warm encouragement to associate with Jehovah's organization. Now the publication appears with large, readable type and a number of teaching illustrations. Its beautiful new four-color cover spread is depicted in reduced size on the opposite page.

Is this new brochure, *"Look! I Am Making All Things New!,"* to be used only in the Orient? It will no doubt be very effective there. However, it is believed that the *"Look!"* brochure will be useful also throughout the world field in starting Bible studies. Almost 30 years have passed since the original booklet was produced. During that time, knowledge of the Bible has sunk to a new low, even in lands that claim to be Christian. Instead of hearing from their parents the well-known stories from the Bible, a new generation has grown up with eyes and ears glued to television, absorbing whatever the world has to offer. This, together with other distractions of a pleasure-mad world, has crowded out precious hours that might have been used for spiritual development. The modern generation, whether in Christendom or elsewhere, knows very little about God's Word. It needs the 'milk of the Word,' as set forth plainly in the *"Look!"* brochure.—Hebrews 5:12.

Worldwide, there are people whose hearts are inclined toward righteousness and who will re-

a New Look

joice to learn how they may become identified with the "great crowd" that will survive Armageddon. (Revelation 7:9, 14) In our house-to-house service, we may find many who are impressed by the lovely picture-cover of the brochure and by the captivating description of Paradise in the opening paragraphs. On a return visit, we can use the array of scriptures cited in support of those paragraphs to show that this hope is much more than a dream. Then, through a regular Bible study, using the *"Look!"* brochure, we can help them get started on the way to life. As Jesus said in prayer to his Father: "This means everlasting life, their taking in knowledge of you, the only true God, and of the one whom you sent forth, Jesus Christ."—John 17:3.

May all of us make zealous use of the *"Look!"* brochure in beaming forth Kingdom truth, the "great crowd" joining with the remaining anointed ones of the royal priesthood in 'letting their light shine before men.' (Matthew 5:16) May the illustrious name of the Sovereign Lord Jehovah be fully sanctified. May it be demonstrated for all time that the promises of Jehovah God, Creator of heaven and earth, are ever "faithful and true." He it is who declares from his throne in heaven: "Look! I am making all things new."—Revelation 21:5.

A Catholic Enjoys It

One of Jehovah's Witnesses had a flat tire in a rural area of Virginia, U.S.A. A house was nearby, and she knocked on the door. The lady of the house let her in to call for road service. Later the Witness sent a thank-you note, enclosing a gift copy of the book *You Can Live Forever in Paradise on Earth.* The following, in part, is the reply she received:

"I shall be very frank and honest with you. I am a Roman Catholic. And whenever anyone comes to my door with Watchtower or any other tracts, I try not to accept them. If they are forced upon me, I throw them into the trash can. I have had Catholicism deeply engrained in me since I was a small child.

"However, I was attracted to your book because it had 'Paradise' within the title and because the reading was clear and easy. The questions at the foot of the pages encouraged reading, and the pictures were attractive to me. I particularly loved page 11 because I am trying to create such a paradise here for the birds and animals. I have deer, rabbits, chipmunks, squirrels, wild turkeys and birds of all kinds. . . .

"You really accomplished something by getting a Catholic to read a book in another religion. Ha! I doubt that I shall ever convert to another religion. But I read the book, and my husband is now reading it. Thanks again!"

March 15, 1987

The Watchtower

Announcing Jehovah's Kingdom

Women in the Workplace

—Tests and Challenges

The Watchtower

Announcing Jehovah's Kingdom

March 15, 1987
Vol. 108, No. 6

In This Issue

THE PURPOSE OF "THE WATCHTOWER" is to exalt Jehovah God as the Sovereign of the universe. It keeps watch on world events as they fulfill Bible prophecy. It comforts all peoples with the good news that God's Kingdom will soon destroy those who oppress their fellowmen and that it will turn the earth into a paradise. It encourages faith in the now-reigning King, Jesus Christ, whose shed blood opens the way for mankind to gain eternal life. "The Watchtower," published by Jehovah's Witnesses continuously since 1879, is nonpolitical. It adheres to the Bible as its authority.

"WATCHTOWER" STUDIES FOR THE WEEKS

April 26: Divine Peace for Those Taught by Jehovah. Page 10. Songs to Be Used: 155, 36.

May 3: How You Can Experience Divine Peace More Fully. Page 15. Songs to Be Used: 159, 213.

Average Printing Each Issue: 12,315,000

Now Published in 103 Languages

SEMIMONTHLY LANGUAGES AVAILABLE BY MAIL
Afrikaans, Arabic, Cebuano, Chichewa, Chinese, Cibemba, Danish,* Dutch,* Efik, English,* Finnish,* French,* German,* Greek,* Hiligaynon, Igbo, Iloko, Italian,* Japanese,* Korean, Lingala, Malagasy, Maltese, Norwegian, Portuguese,* Russian, Sepedi, Sesotho, Shona, Spanish,* Swahili, Swedish,* Tagalog, Thai, Tsonga, Tswana, Xhosa, Yoruba, Zulu

MONTHLY LANGUAGES AVAILABLE BY MAIL
Armenian, Bengali, Bicol, Bulgarian, Croatian, Czech, Ewe, Fijian, Ga, Greenlandic, Gujarati, Gun, Hausa, Hebrew, Hindi, Hiri Motu, Hungarian, Icelandic, Kannada, Malayalam, Marathi, New Guinea Pidgin, Pangasinan, Papiamento, Polish, Rarotongan, Romanian, Samar-Leyte, Samoan, Sango, Serbian, Silozi, Sinhalese, Slovenian, Solomon Islands-Pidgin, Tahitian, Tamil, Telugu, Tongan, Tshiluba, Turkish, Twi, Ukrainian, Urdu, Venda, Vietnamese

* Study articles also available in large-print edition.

	Yearly subscription for the above:	
Watch Tower Society offices	Semimonthly Languages	Monthly Languages
America, U.S., Watchtower, Wallkill, N.Y. 12589	$4.00	$2.00
Australia, Box 280, Ingleburn, N.S.W. 2565	A$7.00	A$3.50
Canada, Box 4100, Halton Hills, Ontario L7G 4Y4	$5.50	$2.75
England, The Ridgeway, London NW7 1RN	£5.00	£2.50
Ireland, 29A Jamestown Road, Finglas, Dublin 11	IR£6.00	IR£3.00
New Zealand, P.O. Box 142, Manurewa	NZ$15.00	NZ$7.50
Nigeria, PMB 001, Shomolu, Lagos State	₦8.00	₦4.00
Philippines, P.O. Box 2044, Manila 2800	₱60.00	₱30.00
South Africa, Private Bag 2067, Krugersdorp, 1740	R6.50	R3.25

Remittances should be sent to the office in your country or to Watchtower, Wallkill, N.Y. 12589, U.S.A.

Changes of address should reach us 30 days before your moving date. Give us your old and new address (if possible, your old address label).

20 cents (U.S.) a copy

The Bible translation used is the "New World Translation of the Holy Scriptures," unless otherwise indicated.

The Watchtower (ISSN 0043-1087) is published semimonthly for $4.00 (U.S.) per year by Watch Tower Bible and Tract Society of Pennsylvania, 25 Columbia Heights, Brooklyn, N.Y. 11201. Second-class postage paid at Brooklyn, N.Y., and at additional mailing offices.

Postmaster: Send address changes to Watchtower, ***Wallkill, N.Y. 12589.***

Published by
**Watch Tower Bible and Tract Society
of Pennsylvania**
25 Columbia Heights, Brooklyn, N.Y. 11201, U.S.A.
Frederick W. Franz, President

Women in the Workplace
—Tests and Challenges

"WOMEN have entered the formal labor force in unprecedented numbers during the past three decades." So reports the research organization Worldwatch Institute. "In both rich countries and poor," the report continued, "inflation encourages women to work for pay." Or as one Nigerian woman put it: "The economic pressure is such that I just have to go out and work."

Like the "capable wife" of Bible times, many women are happy to make a necessary economic contribution to the welfare of their families. (Proverbs 31:10, 16, 24) And some find having a job to be challenging and satisfying. But while secular work has its benefits, it may also have its drawbacks.

For example, one woman who is a store manager says: "I love my job. My boss is great, my office is beautiful. But I hate it when that job takes more of my time than I can give it, because afterward I've got another job waiting for me at home—as wife and mother." Still, many women care for job, home, and family quite ably, and for that they are to be warmly commended.*

Secular jobs, though, also expose women to a number of problems unique to the workplace. For many, the challenge is keeping a balanced attitude when forced to work in an atmosphere charged with fierce competition or thick with indifference. A desire to advance, to get ahead, has driven some women to make their jobs the main focus of their lives.

Sometimes the workplace is also a source of *moral* pressures. Exposure to daily doses of degrading talk is one common complaint of working women. Worse yet, some find themselves the victims of unrelenting sexual harassment. "When I first started working," recalls one Christian woman, "I was the only girl in the office. The men would make suggestive remarks, and it was really hard for me."

Such problems are a real concern to women who must daily face them, especially those who desire to maintain Christian standards. Happily, there is a source of real help for them.

---

* See the discussion "Working Couples—Facing the Challenges," in the February 8, 1985, issue of our companion magazine *Awake!*

Christian Women
—Maintaining Integrity in the Workplace

"SOMETIMES the tension at [work] is so thick you could cut it with a knife." So said one working woman.* Pressure to produce, backstabbing competition, demanding supervisors, monotony—these are just a few of the things that make many jobs a drudgery. Few jobs deliver the glamour and excitement promised by media propaganda. But if you are a working woman, you should strive to make a success of your job.

By this, however, we do not refer to monetary gain. The workplace is an arena in which your *Christian integrity* is put to the test! The way you perform at your job, fend off the spirit of cutthroat competition, and resist moral encroachments reveals the extent to which you are devoted to godly principles. To gain Jehovah God's favor, the working woman must be able to

---

* Here denoting a woman secularly employed. Of course, housewives, mothers, and other women also work.

say as did the psalmist: "I myself have walked in my own integrity."—Psalm 26:1.

The Bible helps you to do just that. For example, when urged to stoop to dog-eat-dog tactics or when tempted to let a job overshadow family responsibilities, Bible study, Christian meetings, and the ministry, you may well recall the words of King Solomon: "I myself have seen all the hard work and all the proficiency in work, that it means the rivalry of one toward another; this also is vanity and a striving after the wind." (Ecclesiastes 4:4) Viewing secular work this way prevents or cools burning ambition. It helps you to have the right perspective on a job, viewing it as secondary to spiritual matters.—Matthew 6:33.

But does this mean being indifferent toward secular work? Hardly, because the Bible condemns laziness. (Proverbs 19:15) It speaks of 'seeing good because of your *hard work.'* (Ecclesiastes 2:24) Further, providing for one's family is a God-given responsibility. (1 Timothy 5:8) So if meeting that obligation means doing secular work that is unpleasant, reflect upon the Bible's words at Colossians 3:23: "Whatever you are doing, work at it wholesouled as to Jehovah, and not to men." Viewing oneself as working "as to Jehovah" is a powerful motivation to be productive, far more so than a pay raise or the lure of a promotion.

"Hard to Please" Employers

A woman named Sally says: "I feel as if [my supervisor is] looking over my shoulder all the time. He never has a good word to say to anyone." Working under a boss who is "hard to please" or short-tempered can be equally frustrating, especially when one is new to the workplace.—1 Peter 2:18.

Quitting, though, may be economically out of the question. It may thus be best to follow the Bible's advice that workers —male and female—"be in subjection." (1 Peter 2:18) Rather than escalating a conflict with sarcasm or disrespect, try to "please [employers] well, not talking back." (Titus 2:9) Such self-control may even prevent you from losing your job. Said Solomon: "If the spirit of a ruler [someone in authority] should mount up against you, do not leave your own place, for calmness itself allays great sins."—Ecclesiastes 10:4.

A harsh taskmaster may even be shamed when his impatience is countered with mildness, his unreasonable demands with graciousness. (Proverbs 15:1; Colossians 4:6) And as you prove your competence and dependability, his attitude toward you may gradually improve. If not, you may have little choice but to "exercise patience," knowing that God is pleased with your Christian conduct.—James 5:7, 8.

Staying Morally Chaste

Integrity also involves Christian morals. An article in *Ladies' Home Journal* warned: "The office—where everyone is expected to dress up, behave well, spend time together and pursue common goals— has an atmosphere that can easily become sexually charged." Office affairs are commonplace. So it is wise to be cautious. Keep relationships with men on the job on a professional basis. Avoid conversations that could arouse romantic feelings. "For this is what God wills, . . . that you abstain from fornication."—1 Thessalonians 4:3, 4.

At times, though, women are victims of an age-old problem: sexual harassment. The Bible tells us that a man named Boaz ordered the young men in his employ "not to touch" Ruth, a woman working in his field. Bible scholar John P. Lange speaks of "the coarse jests with which such peasant laborers were perhaps in the habit of assailing women." (Ruth 2:9) And though certain present-day employers are trying to protect their female employees, some estimate that 40 to *85 percent* of working women (in the United States) have been exposed to some form of sexual harassment.

A young woman named Valerie, for example, worked as a secretary. From time to time, her boss—more than three times her age—would make suggestive remarks about her clothing. Once he tried to trick her into looking at pornographic pictures. Finally, he called her into his office and told her, "To keep your job, you will have to perform sexual favors for me." Of course, she refused to do so.

Such humiliating treatment takes many forms. Says the British magazine *New Statesman:* "It ranges from leering, pinching, unnecessary physical contact and verbal abuse." Often the pressure to engage in sexual immorality is as subtle as being called pet names (Honey, Sweetheart) or as overt as an open proposition. Some women tolerate the harassment out of fear of losing their jobs. And surveys show that a minority of women even seem flattered by the attention!

But while attention from the opposite sex may be flattering, overfamiliarity is often the opening move in the game of seduction. It is thus an assault on your integrity and an affront to your Christian dignity.—1 Corinthians 6:18.

Preventive Measures

"When wisdom enters into your heart . . . , thinking ability itself will keep guard over you, discernment itself will safeguard you." (Proverbs 2:10, 11) So how can you use practical wisdom and discernment to protect yourself? A working woman named Diane says: "I let it be known on the job that I am one of Jehovah's Witnesses." (Compare Matthew 5:16.) When men know you have high moral standards, often they are less prone to make advances.

A discerning woman named Betty takes yet another precaution. She says: "I'm very careful about associating with my coworkers because their morals are not the same as mine." (1 Corinthians 15:33) This does not mean being aloof or hostile to fellow workers. But when they insist on discussing matters offensive to a Christian, do not hesitate to excuse yourself. (Ephesians 5:3, 4) Your listening to such immoral talk could give men at work the impression that you would be receptive to their advances.

Maintaining a *professional bearing* can also discourage unwanted attention. Too, the Bible advises women "to adorn themselves in well-arranged dress, with modesty and soundness of mind." (1 Timothy 2:9; contrast Proverbs 7:10.) Says the book *Sexual Harassment on the Job:* "Pro-

vocative attire—that is, plunging necklines; sundresses; short, short skirts; and masses of glittery makeup—*do not* belong in the workplace. . . . Your chances of creating a professional image are vastly improved if you do choose to dress unspectacularly."

Finally, a discerning woman avoids *compromising situations.* An invitation to have an alcoholic drink or to remain at work after hours for no apparent reason may well be a trap. (Compare 2 Samuel 13: 1-14.) "Shrewd is the one that has seen the calamity and proceeds to conceal himself," says a wise proverb.—Proverbs 22:3.

Halting Harassment

Of course, it is not realistic to imagine that you can rearrange the thinking of all the men on the job or change long-ingrained behavior patterns. (Compare Jeremiah 13:23.) And it is not fair to conclude that all men who appear rather overfriendly have "eyes full of adultery." (2 Peter 2:14) So at times it is appropriate to extend the benefit of the doubt.

But when *obvious overfamiliarity* is involved, take a firm stand. When Solomon made unwanted overtures to a young maiden, she was not coy. She responded to his flattery with expressions of unswerving love for a modest shepherd boy. Since she had refused to yield to Solomon's advances, she could say, "I am a wall." —Song of Solomon 8:10.

Show the same firmness. Often advances can be nipped in the bud by saying: "No touching, please"; "Call me by my name"; or, "I don't appreciate that type of humor." One Christian woman has more than once simply said, "Cut it out!" At any rate, make it clear that your no means *no!* (Compare Matthew 5:37.) A weak or vague response may simply encourage a harasser to try harder.

If you are married, it would be good to

For Maintaining Integrity in the Workplace:

Be careful about socializing with coworkers

Adorn yourself with modest dress

Let it be known that you have high moral standards

share your feelings with your husband. He may have some practical ideas about how to handle the situation. If it seems best simply to change employment, remember God's promise: "I will by no means leave you nor by any means forsake you."—Hebrews 13:5.

Your Job and Your Integrity

So while a secular job is often necessary, it can in some cases present threats to your Christian integrity. Thus Jesus' words at Matthew 10:16 are quite apropos: "Prove yourselves cautious as serpents and yet innocent as doves."

Keeping Christian integrity in the workplace is not easy, but it can be done. Thousands of women among Jehovah's Witnesses are doing so by following the counsel of the Bible. They keep themselves spiritually strong by means of Bible study, prayer, Christian meetings, the Kingdom-preaching work, and other godly activities. As a result, they enjoy something no paycheck can give. It is the knowledge that they have the favor of Jehovah, the One whose Word promises: "He that is walking in integrity will walk in security."—Proverbs 10:9.

Teaching With Illustrations

JESUS is apparently in Capernaum when he rebukes the Pharisees. Later that day he leaves the house and walks to the nearby Sea of Galilee, where crowds of people gather. There he boards a boat, pulls away, and begins teaching the people on the shore about the Kingdom of the heavens. He does so by means of a series of parables, or illustrations, each with a setting familiar to the people.

First, Jesus tells of a sower who sows seed. Some seed falls on the roadside and is

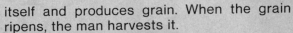

eaten by birds. Other seed falls on soil with an underlying rock-mass. Since the roots lack depth, the new plants wither under the scorching sun. Still other seed falls among thorns, which choke the plants when they come up. Finally, some seed falls on good soil and produces a hundredfold, some sixtyfold, and some thirtyfold.

In another illustration, Jesus says the Kingdom of God is as when a man sows seed. As the days go by, while the man sleeps and when he is awake, the seed grows. The man does not know how. It grows all by

itself and produces grain. When the grain ripens, the man harvests it.

Jesus tells a third illustration about a man who sows the right kind of seed, but while he is sleeping, an enemy comes and sows weeds in among the wheat. The man's servants ask if they should pull out the weeds. But he replies: 'No, you will uproot some of the wheat if you do. Let them both grow together until the harvest. Then I will tell the reapers to sort out the weeds and burn them and put the wheat in the barn.'

Continuing his speech to the crowds on the shore, Jesus provides two more illustrations. He explains that "the kingdom of the heavens" is like a mustard grain that a man plants. Though it is the tiniest of all seeds, he says, it grows into the largest of all vegetables. It becomes a tree to which birds come, finding shelter among its branches.

Some today object that there are tinier seeds than mustard seeds. But Jesus is not giving a lesson in botany. Of the seeds that Galileans of his day are familiar with, the mustard seed really is the tiniest. So they appreciate the matter of phenomenal growth that Jesus is illustrating.

Finally, Jesus compares "the kingdom of the heavens" to leaven that a woman takes and mixes into three large measures of flour. In time, he says, it permeates every part of the dough.

After giving these five illustrations, Jesus dismisses the crowds and returns to the house where he is staying. Soon his 12 apostles and others come to him there. **Matthew 13:1-9, 24-36; Mark 4:1-9, 26-32; Luke 8:1-8.**

♦ When and where did Jesus speak with illustrations to the crowds?
♦ What five illustrations did Jesus tell the crowds?
♦ Why did Jesus say the mustard seed is the tiniest of all seeds?

Divine Peace
for Those Taught by Jehovah

If that most important relationship is shattered, it is impossible to have true peace with God, with one's fellowman, or within oneself.—Isaiah 57:21.

"All your sons will be persons taught by Jehovah, and the peace of your sons will be abundant."—ISAIAH 54:13.

PEACE! How desirable it is! Yet the record of humankind has been anything but peaceful. Why is this so?

² The enjoyment of peace is closely connected with respect for authority. And who is the highest authority in the universe? The Creator, Jehovah God. An approved relationship with him is therefore essential to peace. (Psalm 29:11; 119:165)

1, 2. On what does the enjoyment of peace depend?

Why the World Does Not Have Peace

³ As we well know, it was shortly after the dawn of human history that a spirit son of God rebelled against Jehovah. Rebellion is a state of war. That peace wrecker, who came to be known as Satan the Devil, urged Eve not to let God's law stand in the way of her doing something if she felt it would be to her advantage. The Devil twisted the facts to make her think she was being deprived of something good by paying attention to God. The appeal was to selfishness, to a me-first attitude.

3. How was humankind's relationship with God spoiled?

Soon her husband joined her in lawless conduct, and as a result, all their offspring have been infected by that spirit.—Genesis 3:1-6, 23, 24; Romans 5:12.

⁴ It is not just a small segment of mankind that shoves aside divine law. The Scriptures tell us that Satan is "misleading the entire inhabited earth." (Revelation 12:9) Some people are grossly lawless, showing complete disregard for God and for their fellowman; others are less so. But so successful has Satan been in influencing the thinking of mankind that the apostle John could say: "The whole world is lying in the power of the wicked one." (1 John 5:19) Whether people profess to believe that the Devil exists or not, they do what he wants. They obey him, so he is their ruler. As a result, mankind is alienated from God, is at enmity with him. In such an environment, is it any wonder that human efforts to achieve peace have been frustrated?—Colossians 1:21.

⁵ Nevertheless, a growing number of people out of all nations are experiencing divine peace, peace that has its origin with God. How has this come about?

The Satisfying Peace That God Gives

⁶ At Romans 15:33 Jehovah is appropriately described as "the God who gives peace." From the very beginning, it has been God's purpose for all his creatures to enjoy peace. Over 300 times his inspired Word, the Bible, refers to peace. It makes clear that Jesus Christ is the "Prince of Peace." (Isaiah 9:6, 7) He is the one commissioned by God to break up the works of that foremost peace wrecker, Satan the

Devil. (1 John 3:8) And by means of the "Prince of Peace" it is possible for each one of us to enjoy the satisfying peace that God gives.

⁷ What a marvelous peace this is! It is more than the absence of war. The Hebrew word *sha·lohm′*, which is usually translated "peace," implies health, prosperity, and welfare. The peace of God that is the possession of true Christians is unique in that it does not depend upon their environment. This does not mean that unpleasant surroundings do not affect them. But they come to have an inner strength that enables them to avoid contributing to the turmoil by retaliating when it touches them. (Romans 12:17, 18) Though a person may be physically ill or have little materially, he can still be healthy and prosperous from a spiritual standpoint and thus enjoy the peace that God gives. Obviously, the peace that such ones experience will be enhanced when this selfish world is gone, and it will deepen when all mankind has attained perfection. But the divine peace that is possible right now is a calm condition of mind and heart, an inner state of quiet regardless of what may be taking place on the outside. (Psalm 4:8) It springs from an approved relationship with God. What a priceless possession!

Sons Taught by Jehovah

⁸ Who have such peace because of being taught by Jehovah and paying attention to his commandments? In reply, the Bible directs our attention first to those who make up spiritual Israel. They are spoken of at Galatians 6:16, where we read: "All

---

4, 5. (a) To what extent has Satan succeeded in influencing the thinking of mankind? (b) What effect has this had on man's efforts to achieve peace?
6. (a) What emphasis does the Bible place on peace? (b) By means of whom is it possible for us to enjoy the peace that God gives?

7. (a) What does God-given peace include? (b) Why is it not something that we must wait for until the old system is gone and we have finally attained perfection?
8. Who were the first to enjoy this peace with God through Jesus Christ?

those who will walk orderly by this rule of conduct, upon them be peace and mercy, even upon the Israel of God." These are the 144,000 who have been chosen by God to share heavenly life with Jesus Christ. —Revelation 14:1.

⁹ Back in the first century, those of spiritual Israel were learning a basic truth, a "rule of conduct," that was directly connected with their enjoyment of peace. It was vital that they grasp this rule of conduct. For over 15 centuries, Jehovah had used the Mosaic Law to set out shadows of good things to come. But after the sacrificial death of Jesus Christ, the requirements of the Mosaic Law were no longer binding. (Hebrews 10:1; Romans 6:14) This was manifested by the decision of the Christian governing body in Jerusalem on the issue of circumcision. (Acts 15:5, 28, 29) It was emphasized again in the inspired letter to the Galatians. The good things that the Mosaic Law foreshadowed had gone into effect. Patiently Jehovah was impressing on the minds and hearts of Christ's anointed followers the significance of His undeserved kindness expressed through Christ. By exercising faith in this provision, by conducting themselves in harmony with it, they could enjoy peace of a sort that had never before been possible for sinful humans.—Galatians 3:24, 25; 6:16, 18.

¹⁰ Those of spiritual Israel were experiencing fulfillment of the grand promise recorded at Isaiah 54:13. There God himself said to his wifelike organization of loyal spirit creatures: "All your sons will be persons taught by Jehovah, and *the peace of your sons will be abundant.*" Of

9. What was the "rule of conduct" associated with spiritual Israel's enjoyment of peace?
10. (a) Spiritual Israel was experiencing fulfillment of what promise recorded at Isaiah 54:13? (b) How has Jehovah's disciplining of them been a factor in their experiencing peace?

course, her principal Son is Jesus Christ himself, brought forth as the Messiah when he was anointed with holy spirit in 29 C.E. But Jehovah's heavenly "woman" has more sons—144,000 others who become the secondary part of the seed foretold at Genesis 3:15. Jehovah promised that he would be the Grand Instructor of all these sons. He has taught them the truth about himself and his purposes. He has told them how to serve him. At times, he has had to discipline them. This has been necessary when they have failed to heed his Word. Discipline can be hard to take. But they have humbly acknowledged their need of it and made the required changes, and that discipline has yielded good results—"peaceable fruit, namely, righteousness."—Hebrews 12:7, 11; Psalm 85:8.

"A Great Crowd" Instructed in God's Ways

¹¹ In our day, spiritual Israel is not the only group that Jehovah is teaching. During the past half century, attention has also been directed to others. Isaiah was inspired to write about them in chapter 2,

11. (a) Who else is being taught by Jehovah in our day? (b) How do they demonstrate that they fit the description found at Isaiah 2:2, 3, and with what effect on others?

In Our Next Issue

- God—Is He a Real Person?

- Worldwide Security Under the "Prince of Peace"

- Do You Always Get the Point?

verses 2 and 3: "It must occur in the final part of the days that the mountain of the house of Jehovah will become firmly established above the top of the mountains, and it will certainly be lifted up above the hills; and to it all the nations must stream." Yes, those who embrace the worship of the only true God give it the most highly exalted place in their lives. Thus it stands out as elevated above every other sort of worship in which they formerly engaged and in which the world around them continues to engage. People of all nations have observed this. They have seen that, regardless of demands made by worldly authorities or the prevalence of unchristian practices in the world, those who worship Jehovah put their relationship with him above everything else. Observers have also seen the fruitage that this produces in the lives of such worshipers, and many want to share in true worship. So upwards of three million people are now saying to others: "Come, you people, and let us go up to the mountain of Jehovah, to the house of the God of Jacob; and he will instruct us about his ways, and we will walk in his paths."—See also Zechariah 8:23.

¹² Just think what that means—having *God* as their Instructor! Those who receive such instruction and truly appreciate its source are not plagued by constant mental conflicts. They do not find themselves torn between two opinions or on the horns of a dilemma as to what is right. The truth from God's Word is crystal clear. And what does Isaiah 2:4 indicate would be an outstanding part of the instruction they receive? It involves how to enjoy peace in a strife-torn world. Thus, regardless of what others choose to do, those taught by

Jehovah take the initiative to beat their swords into plowshares and their spears into pruning shears. They learn war no more.

¹³ It is this same group that is depicted at Revelation 7:9, 10, 14 as survivors into God's peaceful new earth that follows the coming "great tribulation." The surviving "great crowd" come out of all ethnic groups, tribes, peoples, and tongues. Many of them formerly belonged to factions that were at war with one another. Others simply pursued a course of life that was basically selfish; yet, that too interfered with enjoyment of peace. But now these who have come out of all nations are a peace-loving, peace-promoting people. And what has made them that way? They have been taught by Jehovah.—Isaiah 11:9.

A Unique Kind of Peace

¹⁴ The peace with which Jehovah favors his people is truly unique. It is not the sort of thing that results when a shaky agreement is made between two parties that do not trust each other. It involves no compromises. It is based on righteousness. (Isaiah 32:17) But how can that be true of peace that involves imperfect humans? As sinners, what righteousness do any of us have? Well, by faith we can enjoy a righteousness that is made possible through the sin-atoning value of Jesus' sacrifice.

¹⁵ This helps us to appreciate what Jesus said as recorded at John 6:45-47. There he was speaking to Jews who were not drawn to him as the Messiah and so were murmuring against him. But it was with

12. How are those mentioned at Isaiah 2:2, 3 benefited by having God as their Instructor, and what is an outstanding part of the instruction he gives them?

13. From what backgrounds did the "great crowd" come, but what has made them the sort of people they are?
14. On what is the peace of Jehovah's people based, and how is this so?
15. During Jesus' earthly ministry, what was Jehovah teaching his prospective sons that was vital to peace?

reference to his disciples that he said: "It is written in the Prophets [specifically, at Isaiah 54:13], 'And they will all be taught by Jehovah.' *Everyone that has heard from the Father and has learned comes to me.* Not that any man has seen the Father, except he who is from God; this one has seen the Father. Most truly I say to you, He that believes has everlasting life." Those disciples accepted the instruction that Jehovah was giving them. They were drawn to Jesus. When others rejected the things he taught and forsook Jesus, his apostles stayed. As Peter said: "We have believed and come to know that you are the Holy One of God." (John 6:69) Because of their faith in Jesus Christ, it would be possible for them to come into a peaceful relationship with Jehovah God, a relationship that carries with it the assurance of everlasting life.

¹⁶ Starting at Pentecost 33 C.E., the benefits of Christ's sacrifice began to be applied to those faithful followers of Jesus. What Paul later wrote at Romans 5:1 came to be true of them: "Now that we have been declared righteous as a result of faith, let us enjoy peace with God through our Lord Jesus Christ." By birth all of these were descendants of Adam. As sin-

"Everyone that has heard from the Father and has learned comes to me"

ners, they were alienated from God. No good works that they might personally have done could have canceled out their inheritance of sin. But by His undeserved kindness, Jehovah accepted the sacrifice of Jesus' perfect human life in behalf of Adam's offspring. For those who exercised faith in this provision, it now became possible to have righteousness credited to them and for them to be adopted by God as sons with heavenly life in view. (Ephesians 1:5-7) But was more required on their part? Yes, they had to walk in Jehovah's ways. No longer were they to make a practice of sin. But they realize that whatever righteousness they have is a result of God's undeserved kindness expressed through Christ. As the scripture says, they 'enjoy peace with God through Jesus Christ.'

¹⁷ What about those to whom Jesus re-

16. (a) Starting at Pentecost 33 C.E., how did Jesus' followers benefit from the provision made through Christ? (b) Thereafter, what was required of them?

17, 18. (a) Do the "other sheep" enjoy such peace with God? (b) What further questions deserve consideration?

Review Questions

□ Why does the world not have peace?

□ What is the peace that God gives now?

□ Who can enjoy such peace?

□ How is righteousness a vital factor in this peace?

---

ferred as his "other sheep"? (John 10:16) Do they enjoy such peace with God? Not as sons of God, but Colossians 1:19, 20 does include them as recipients of divine peace. It says that God saw good through Christ "to reconcile again to himself all other things by making peace through the blood he [Jesus] shed on the torture stake, no matter whether they are the things upon the earth [that is, those who will be favored with eternal life on a paradise earth] or the things in the heavens."

These with earthly prospects are declared righteous and enjoy peace with God even now, not as sons, but as 'friends of God,' as was Abraham. What a favored position that is!—James 2:23.

18 Do you personally enjoy that peace? Are you experiencing it as fully as is possible for humans who are living during this most significant time in history? In the following article, we will consider some of the things that can help to make that possible.

How You Can Experience
Divine Peace
More Fully

"O if only you would actually pay attention to my commandments! Then your peace would become just like a river, and your righteousness like the waves of the sea."
—ISAIAH 48:18.

THOSE who share regularly in congregational study of the Bible with the help of this magazine recognize the value of the peace that God gives, and they want that peace. The majority undoubtedly do enjoy it. But not all experience it as fully as they might. Why is this? Regarding those who would have divine peace, Jehovah says: "I, Jehovah, am your God, the One teaching you to benefit yourself, the One causing you to tread in the way in which you should walk. *O if only you would actually pay attention to my commandments! Then your peace would become just*

like a river, and your righteousness like the waves of the sea."—Isaiah 48:17, 18.

2 Obviously, anyone can benefit from attending meetings where we discuss the Bible. But only those who *pay attention* to Jehovah's commandments, making personal application of them and conforming to them, truly enjoy divine peace. Are there areas in which you need to do this more fully? (2 Peter 1:2) It is not enough for us to heed a few of God's requirements but then sidestep those that we find inconvenient or more difficult. When the Devil tried to entice Jesus Christ over to his

---

1. What is needed if we are to experience peace as fully as we might?

2. (a) What is implied in the expression "pay attention"? (b) To how many of God's commandments must we pay attention? (1 John 5:3)

selfish way of thinking, Jesus firmly responded: "It is written, 'Man must live, not on bread alone, but on *every utterance coming forth through Jehovah's mouth.'*"—Matthew 4:4.

3 God's commandments touch every aspect of our lives. First of all, they involve our relationship with Jehovah. Then they affect our viewpoint toward his visible organization and the Christian ministry, the way we treat family members, and our dealings with people of the world. Those who earnestly pay attention to Jehovah's commandments in all these matters are the ones blessed with abundant peace. Let us consider a few things that can help us to experience that personally.

Do Any of These Matters Need Your Attention?

4 Have you recently begun studying the Bible with Jehovah's Witnesses? Or have you perhaps been associating with the local congregation for a number of months or even years? If so, you have undoubtedly found joy in having a knowledge of God's purposes open up before you. But the fact that a person enjoys a home Bible study or finds pleasure in going to the Kingdom Hall does not prove that he is at peace with God. We were all born in sin, and peace with God is possible for us only through Jesus Christ. (Isaiah 53:5; Acts 10:36) A mere passive belief in Jesus does not bring that peace. It is necessary to appreciate personally our need of the ransom, to exercise faith in the value of Jesus' sacrifice, and then to give evidence of that faith by obeying his commandments.

---

3. What aspects of our lives must be brought into harmony with Jehovah's ways if we truly are to have abundant peace?
4. (a) Why does having a home Bible study or going to the Kingdom Hall not guarantee that we are at peace with God? (b) What is included in exercising faith in Jesus Christ? (John 3:36)

Baptism

(James 2:26) One of the commands that Jesus gave while on earth was that those who would become his disciples should be baptized in water. (Matthew 28:19, 20) Have you been immersed in symbol of your dedication to Jehovah through Jesus Christ?

5 Is there anything in your life that disqualifies you for baptism? If you know that there is, or if during the course of your study you learn that this is the case, do not delay to set matters straight. Realize that any attitude or conduct that would disqualify a person for baptism is also an obstacle to his being at peace with God. Act with urgency while there is still the opportunity. As indicated at 1 Peter 3: 21, those who are granted a good conscience by Jehovah God first dedicate themselves to him on the basis of faith in the sacrifice of Christ, get baptized in symbol of that dedication, and do God's will. Then the peace that goes with a good conscience because of having an approved standing before God becomes theirs; it is

---

5. Why are dedication and baptism important to our being at peace with God?

possible in no other way. Of course, it is only a beginning.

⁶ Next, consider your regularity in attending congregation meetings and your participation in them as you are able. Do these meetings have a place in your life that you do not allow to be infringed on by the world or by other personal activities? Do you prepare for the meetings and count it a privilege to participate? These things, too, have a definite bearing on one's enjoyment of peace. Why? Because God's spirit is with his congregated people, and peace is a fruit of that spirit. (Galatians 5:22) It is at these meetings that we are helped to understand Jehovah's requirements, and we need this in order to do what is pleasing in his eyes. Here, too, we learn how to promote peace in our relations with fellow humans—in the congregation, at home, at school, and at our secular work. Our meetings are one of the principal ways in which we are taught by Jehovah, and as the Scriptures point out, it is those who are taught by Jehovah that enjoy abundant peace.—Isaiah 54:13.

6. Why does our attitude toward congregation meetings have a bearing on our enjoyment of peace?

⁷ A closely related point that deserves attention is the progressive application in our personal lives of what we learn. We do not want to be like those Israelites who Jehovah said would 'hear again and again but not understand.' (Isaiah 6:9) Moreover, do we want to be like those whom Jehovah described to Ezekiel—people who would listen to Jehovah's prophet but not do what he said because they chose to fulfill their unclean or materialistic desires? (Ezekiel 33:31, 32) In contrast, those who would gather at Jehovah's house in our day and would gain his approval are described as saying: "Let us go up to the mountain of Jehovah and to the house of the God of Jacob; and he will instruct us about his ways, and *we will walk in his paths.*" (Micah 4:2) If we truly take to heart the instruction that we receive at our meetings, if at each meeting we isolate at least one point that we personally need and then work on it, we are

7. What follow-through on the things discussed at our meetings is needed?

Applying what we learn

Sharing fully in the field ministry

⁹ Our heeding all this counsel, however, does not make us immune to the pressures of life in the present system of things. But regardless of how difficult situations may be, God assures us of his loving help if we will turn to him. (1 Peter 5:6, 7) Have we learned to seek Jehovah's help and direction in everything we do, freely turning to him in prayer and, after we have done what we can about difficult situations, throwing our burdens on Jehovah, confidently leaving them with him? (Proverbs 3:5, 6; Psalm 55:22) Warmly we are encouraged at Philippians 4:6, 7: "Do not be anxious over anything, but in everything by prayer and supplication along with thanksgiving let your petitions be made known to God; and the peace of God that excels all thought will guard your hearts and your mental powers by means of Christ Jesus." What a marvelous provision that is! Have you learned to benefit

9. What can help us to maintain our God-given peace even when we experience very severe difficulties?

going to reap peaceable fruitage. As Jesus said at Luke 11:28: "Happy are those hearing the word of God *and keeping it!*"

⁸ One of the things emphasized at our meetings is the importance of sharing fully in the proclaiming of God's Kingdom and in helping others to become disciples. (Matthew 24:14; 28:19) How prominent are these activities in your life? If we have truly paid attention to what Jehovah is saying to us through his Word and by means of his organization, we know that this is the most important work being done on earth today. (Revelation 14:6, 7) And it is a well-known fact that those who are in full-time service—as well as those who, though they cannot be pioneers, are truly zealous in the ministry—are the ones among us who are outstandingly happy. The peace they enjoy is not like a mere drop of water, but as Jehovah said, it becomes "just like a river." (Isaiah 48:18) Is that what you are experiencing? All of us can.

8. How can sharing in the field ministry to the fullest extent that our circumstances permit benefit us personally?

Throwing our burdens on Jehovah

fully from the peace of God that is thus made possible?

Continually Pursue Peace

¹⁰ Once we have such peace, we cannot afford to be careless about it. Diligent effort is required in order to maintain it. Thus 1 Peter 3:10, 11 says: "He that would love life and see good days, . . . let him seek peace and pursue it." Having sought a goal and attained it, a person would be foolish to treat that goal lightly. After seeking and attaining peace, we need to be on guard against things that could disrupt it. More than that, we should actively pursue those things that contribute to peace.

¹¹ If we have attained to peace with God through the means that he has provided, we need to be careful not to disrupt that relationship by returning to a practice of sin. Of course, since all of us are imperfect, all of us sin. But there is danger when a person justifies in himself attitudes and actions that God condemns. We cannot afford simply to shrug our shoulders and say, "That's just the way I am." (Romans 6:16, 17) We need to repent of wrongdoing instead of justifying it, and then we ought to beg God to forgive us on the basis of our faith in Jesus' sacrifice. We also need to learn to turn to God for help *before* we do wrong, instead of trying to fight the battle alone, finally giving in, and then begging for forgiveness. With God's help, we can succeed in putting on "the new personality which was created according to God's will in true righteousness and loyalty." —Ephesians 4:20-24.

10. After seeking peace, what is needed on our part?
11. (a) What attitude might endanger our relationship with Jehovah? (b) When should we really be asking for God's help with regard to temptations? (Matthew 6:13)

¹² Enjoyment of peace, of course, also involves relationships with other people. True Christians serve God as part of an organization; they are an "association of brothers." (1 Peter 2:17) As Jesus said would be true of his followers, they are outstanding in their love for one another. (John 13:35) But none of them are perfect. Because of our own imperfections and those of others, we may need to pray earnestly about certain situations and work hard to resolve problems. Hebrews 12:14 urges us: "Pursue peace with all people." And in our relations with our Christian brothers and sisters, there is a special obligation to persevere in pursuing peace. Pointedly, 1 Thessalonians 5:13 says: "Be peaceable with one another." That means not merely to refrain from retaliating but to be active peace promoters, taking the first step to restore peace and being willing to yield in the interest of peace.—Ephesians 4:1-3.

¹³ Outside the congregation, however, not everyone is willing to be peaceable. So, realistically, Romans 12:18 counsels: *"If possible, as far as it depends upon you,* be peaceable with all men." But our efforts to promote peace do not include compromising with regard to Jehovah's righteous requirements. We may adjust the times for doing certain things, but we know that it would be unwise to quit attending congregation meetings or to refrain from sharing in the field ministry in order to maintain peace with marriage mates or relatives. And we know that Jehovah would not approve our joining in ungodly practices with workmates or schoolmates

12. (a) To enjoy peace, what other relationships need attention? (b) What is required of us in this regard?
13. (a) In promoting peace with unbelievers, what might we do, but how do we demonstrate that peace with God comes first? (b) How is it possible for us to have peace when there is turmoil around us?

in order to have their approval. We recognize that real peace belongs only to those who first of all enjoy peace with God, to those who love Jehovah's law and walk in his ways. It is that peace that we prize above all else. (Psalm 119:165) True, around us there may be turmoil. Unbelievers may argue and fight with one another; they may even heap abuse upon us because of our faith. But we know how God's Word has taught us to conduct ourselves. By continuing to pursue a course that is in harmony with Jehovah's righteous ways, we are not deprived of the peace that counts most.—Compare Psalm 46:1, 2.

¹⁴ On the final night before his death, Jesus told his faithful apostles: "I have said these things to you that by means of me you may have peace. In the world you are having tribulation, but take courage! I have conquered the world." (John 16:33) Yes, we do experience tribulation. As Christians, we undergo persecution of various sorts. We may experience injustice, and many suffer severe illness. But divine peace sustains us through all of this. Because we have been taught by Jehovah, we know why Christians are persecuted. We are in no doubt as to why there is injustice and why we suffer illness. We also know what the future holds. We know that as a result of Jesus' faithful life course and his sacrificial death, deliverance is a certainty. Furthermore, we know that regardless of the problems that confront us now, we can turn to God in prayer with the confidence that he lovingly cares for us and will sustain us by means of his spirit.—Romans 8:38, 39.

¹⁵ Appropriately, Jesus said at John 14:27: "I leave you peace, I give you my peace.

14. Even though we personally experience tribulation, what makes it possible for us to continue to maintain inner calm and a bright outlook?
15. How is it true that the peace Christ makes possible is not like what the world offers?

I do not give it to you the way that the world gives it. Do not let your hearts be troubled nor let them shrink for fear." It certainly is true—the world has nothing like the peace that God gives through Jesus Christ. It enables us to be strong in the face of situations that would make others give up all hope.

¹⁶ What a marvelous future lies ahead for all who now embrace the peace that comes from God and who give it the prominence that it deserves in their lives! Soon the world that is at enmity with God will be gone. All creation will in time be fully united in peace by the righteous requirements of the Universal Sovereign. May our gratitude for this grand prospect move us to work in full harmony with it now. May all of us listen carefully to Jehovah's instruction and get his commandments firmly implanted in our heart so that we truly love his ways and do what he requires. As Proverbs 3:1, 2 states: "My son, my law do not forget, and my commandments may your heart observe, because length of days and years of life *and peace* will be added to you."

─────

16. (a) What prospect lies ahead for those who now truly treasure the peace that God gives? (b) How can we demonstrate that we do prize that peace?

─────

Review Questions

□ According to Isaiah 48:18, what is needed if we are to have abundant peace?

□ By doing what things may we experience divine peace more fully?

□ What is expected of us as to maintaining peace with our brothers and sisters?

□ How can we maintain peace even when surrounded by unbelievers?

A Joyful People
—Why?

TRUE Christians today are a joyful people. After all, we serve "the happy God," Jehovah. (1 Timothy 1:11) He supplies us with his spirit, and a fruit of that spirit is joy.—Galatians 5:22.

Such deep-seated joy is resilient and stands up to pressure. For example, Jesus Christ was subjected to the pain of impalement and the disgrace of being executed as a blasphemer. Yet, "for the joy that was set before him he endured a torture stake." (Hebrews 12:2) Jesus knew that ahead of him lay grand opportunities and privileges in connection with his service to Jehovah. Focusing on these future privileges helped him to maintain his joy in the midst of suffering.

Jesus wants his disciples to be joyful also. He said: "These things I have spoken to you, that my joy may be in you and your joy may be made full." (John 15:11) This has proved true of Jehovah's Witnesses today. Many are the reasons that we are a joyful people. We know the truth, which has freed us from the grip of superstition and false religious beliefs. (John 8:32) Then, too, we know where we are in the stream of time and rejoice in the soon-to-be-realized hope of salvation. (Luke 21:28) We are also protected from many of the problems—among them sexually transmitted diseases—faced by those who do not practice Bible-based morality. We enjoy the very finest of association with people interested in doing Jehovah's will. And, yes, we have the grand privilege of sharing in preaching the good news of the Kingdom and making disciples of sheeplike ones.—Matthew 24:14; 28:19, 20.

But while this is true of Jehovah's Witnesses as a whole, what about you as an individual? Why can it be said that you have reason to rejoice along with the rest of Jehovah's people?

Finding Joy in the Evangelizing Work

Some find it difficult to engage in the house-to-house preaching work. Perhaps they are uneasy about approaching strangers and striking up conversations. Or they may simply feel inadequate when it comes to teaching others. Do you feel that way at times? If so, how can you find joy in the evangelizing work?

First of all, keep a positive attitude. Many people would be thrilled to be employed by some celebrity or well-known politician. But what greater joy we should find in being used by "the King of eternity," Jehovah God himself!—1 Timothy 1:17.

Remember, too, that this is a never-to-be-repeated work. Just think! The angels themselves are guiding and directing Christians here on earth in their endeavors to locate sheeplike ones. (Revelation 14:6) Does this not bring joy to your heart?

Finding Joy in Kingdom Increase

Another reason to have a positive view of the preaching work is the fine effect it is having. The Bible foretold: "The little one himself will become a thousand, and the small one a mighty nation. I myself, Jehovah, shall speed it up in its own time." (Isaiah 60:22) This promise of

Jehovah has come true in recent times. For example, during the 1986 service year, 225,868 were baptized in symbol of their whole-souled dedication to Jehovah God. There was an increase of 6.9 percent in the average number sharing in spreading the Bible's truths to others.

No doubt this increase is evident in your own congregation or circuit. New ones are coming to meetings and making necessary changes in their lives so as to be able to serve God. Does this not point to the fact that the preaching work has Jehovah's blessing? Having a share in this increase can thus be a source of great joy to you. True, you may not have personally studied with an individual to the point of his getting baptized. But we cannot take credit for bringing someone into the truth anyway. 'God makes it grow,' said Paul. (1 Corinthians 3:6-9) All members of the congregation have a share in helping new ones. How? By being present at meetings, commenting, hospitably greeting new ones, and conducting themselves in a way that makes the truth appealing.

However, greater joy can be obtained if you have a more direct share in the house-to-house preaching activity and the home Bible study work. Last year, on the average, 2,726,252 weekly Bible studies were conducted. Why not make more of an effort to share in this joyous work? Offer a Bible study to someone you know, perhaps a neighbor or an individual with whom you have placed literature. Ask Jehovah for help in locating such a sheeplike person.

Overcoming Obstacles to Joy

Of course, if a person feels inadequate about teaching others, this can be a real obstacle to his finding joy in the field ministry. Remember, though, that "our being adequately qualified issues from God." (2 Corinthians 3:5) And through his organization Jehovah has provided many fine aids to help us qualify as effective ministers.

First of all, there are many among us who have been serving God for a long time and have much experience in the field ministry. We can join these experienced ministers in their activity and learn from them. Moreover, every month fine suggestions appear in *Our Kingdom Ministry.* Then there is the publication *Reasoning From the Scriptures,* which contains a wealth of information to sharpen our preaching skills. Utilize these tools and prepare more thoroughly for the field ministry. Think of new and interesting ways to introduce yourself at the door. Or consider different ways to draw householders into conversations. As you become more effective in the field, your enthusiasm and joy in preaching will doubtless increase.

The ministry is more enjoyable when we are able to talk to people. In some territories this admittedly is a problem. Can you arrange to share in the field service at a time when more people are at home, such as in the early evening? Many find doing so quite effective. You can also take the initiative and talk to people wherever they are to be found—on the streets, sitting on park benches, washing their cars. Remember that people need the truth and that lives are involved. This can help motivate you to overcome tendencies toward shyness. While it is true that the vast majority of people will not respond favorably, those who do so bring us much joy.

However, one of the greatest aids to our maintaining joy is prayer. Ask Jehovah for his spirit to strengthen and encourage you. Paul said: "For all things I have the strength by virtue of him who imparts power to me." (Philippians 4:13) We can feel that way, too, as we learn to rely more fully on Jehovah.

Enduring as a Joyful People

Many individuals do not appreciate our work. Jesus was aware that this would be the case. So when he sent his followers out to preach, he counseled them: "Wherever anyone does not take you in or listen to your words, on going out of that house or that city shake the dust off your feet. . . . Look! I am sending you forth as sheep amidst wolves; therefore prove yourselves cautious as serpents and yet innocent as doves." Jesus also said: "The very hairs of your head are all numbered. Therefore have no fear."—Matthew 10:11-16, 30, 31.

These words help us to endure joyfully. They help us to realize that when we meet people who do not appreciate our efforts on their behalf, we are still making Jehovah's name known; we are still praising him. (Psalm 100:4, 5) Interestingly, at times householders who refuse to open the door can be heard to say to others: "It was Jehovah's Witnesses." Yes, without our saying a word, Jehovah's name has been magnified, and people have received the opportunity to accept or reject the truth. (Matthew 25:31, 32) So even unresponsive territories can be endured joyfully.

Besides, we never know when such individuals may have a change of attitude. One day, a woman who had turned a Christian sister away from her door on a number of occasions asked the sister if she had any new literature. The sister was surprised and remarked that the woman had never accepted Bible literature before. The woman explained that her husband worked with a man who was studying the Bible with Jehovah's Witnesses. He had given her and her husband one of the Watch Tower Society's publications. Out

Our evangelizing work is a source of true joy —even when people do not respond to the Kingdom message

of curiosity, the woman had read it and had recognized the message as the truth. So she decided then and there that the next time a Witness called she would let him in. A home Bible study was started, and the woman later became a dedicated witness of Jehovah!

We thus have a grand privilege—a joyful privilege—of declaring the only message of hope in the world. And the preaching work is the assignment God has given us during these last days. It must be done before the end comes. (Matthew 24:14) How long will it be before the end of Satan's wicked system? We know the end will not come late. (Compare Habakkuk 2:3.) In the meantime, there is still time for others to learn the truth. Let us take advantage of this remaining time and zealously be at our preaching work. And let us have a positive attitude, working hard so as to 'save both ourselves and those who listen to us.' (1 Timothy 4:16) In doing so, we will remain a joyful people sharing in Kingdom increase.

Happy God, Happy People!

Happiness is a goal most people never attain. For a small group of others, though, happiness is a way of life. Their key to it? True worship! The Psalms convince us that Jehovah is a happy God, and therefore we can be happy by worshiping him. For evidence of this, let us look at Book Five of the Psalms, that is, Psalms 107 to 150.

Jehovah the Deliverer

Please read Psalms 107 to 119. The prayer of the Jews for deliverance from Babylonian captivity is answered, and "the reclaimed ones of Jehovah" celebrate the return in song. (Psalm 107) Upon being delivered earlier, David 'made melody' to God and declared His goodness and love. (Psalms 108, 109) With strength from Jehovah, David's Lord, who is Jesus Christ, was to subdue God's enemies. (Psalm 110) In addition to rescuing His people, Jehovah blesses the upright man fearing Him. (Psalms 111, 112) Following their deliverance from Babylon, the Jews sang the Hallel Psalms, or songs of praise, at the great annual feasts. (Psalms 113–118) The 119th Psalm is the longest, and all but 2 of its 176 verses refer to the word or law of God.

♦ 107:27—How did 'their wisdom prove confused'?

Like sailors caught in a destructive storm, the Jews' wisdom proved futile during their captive state in Babylon; all human means of delivering them had failed. But by turning to Jehovah in the midst of this stormy situation, deliverance had come. He caused the symbolic storm to abate and delivered them to a safe "haven"—the land of Judah.—Psalm 107:30.

♦ 110:3—What is the significance of having "young men just like dewdrops"?

Dew is associated with blessing, productivity, and abundance. (Genesis 27:28) Dewdrops are also gentle, refreshing, life-sustaining, and numerous. In the day of the Messianic King's military force, his subjects quickly, cheerfully offer themselves in numbers so great that they can be compared to dewdrops. Just like refreshing dewdrops, throughout Jehovah's organization today numerous young men and women render service to God and their fellow worshipers.

♦ 116:3—What are "the ropes of death"?

It seemed as if death had so tightly bound the psalmist with unbreakable ropes that escape was impossible. Ropes tied tightly about limbs produce sharp pains, or pangs, and the Greek *Septuagint* version renders the Hebrew word for "ropes" as "pangs." Hence, when Jesus Christ died, he was in the paralyzing grip, or pangs, of death. When Jehovah resurrected Jesus, therefore, He was "loosing the pangs of death."—Acts 2:24.

♦ 119:83—How was the psalmist "like a skin bottle"?

While waiting for Jehovah to comfort him, the psalmist had become like a skin bottle that would be hung up when not in use. Because of the smoke in a tent or a house lacking a chimney, this type of bottle would gradually darken, dry up, and shrivel. In effect, this is what happened to the psalmist at the hands of persecutors. (Verse 84) His distressed state was probably evident in his dismal countenance and lined face, and his entire body may have been so affected as to have lost some of its moisture. (Compare Psalm 32:4.) Thus he may have felt as worthless as a withered skin bottle that others cast aside as unsuitable to hold liquids. Yet he had not 'forgotten God's regulations.'

♦ 119:119—How does God make the wicked cease "as scummy dross"?

The scum that forms on molten metal or in the smelting furnace is a worthless waste product, something impure to be discarded. Thus a refiner separates such metal as gold or silver from the "scummy dross." Similarly, Jehovah considers the wicked ones fit only for the slag heap and makes them cease, separating them from those of value who have his favor.—Compare Ezekiel 22:17-22.

Lesson for Us: Like the Jews of old, Jehovah's Witnesses today await deliverance—this time through the storm of Armageddon. (Revelation 16:14, 16) At God's appointed time, this system of things will be swept away by this great war. Those who do not look to Jehovah for salvation will be utterly helpless as they are tossed about by the waves of this great destruction. The survivors, however, will "give thanks to Jehovah for his lovingkindness." Therefore, in these last days, both Jesus' anointed followers and the "great crowd" can put their full trust in Jehovah. —Psalm 107:31; Revelation 7:9.

'Songs of the Ascents'

Read Psalms 120 to 134. These 15 psalms are called songs "of the ascents." Scholars disagree as to the precise meaning of "ascents," but perhaps these psalms were sung by Israelites when they went up, or ascended, to the lofty city of Jerusalem for their three annual festivals.—Psalm 122:1.

♦ 120:4—What were these "sharpened arrows" and "burning coals"?

A slanderous tongue can be as destructive as a weapon or a fire. (Proverbs 12:18; James 3:6) In retribution, Jehovah sees to it that the slanderous tongue is silenced as by a warrior's arrows. Interestingly, charcoal made from the shrublike broom tree burns very intensely, pointing to the severity of the divine judgment upon "the tricky tongue." —Psalm 120:2, 3.

♦ 131:2—How does the soul become like a "weanling"?

Before being weaned, an infant longs for its mother to satisfy its desire to be fed. And a weanling in its mother's arms finds satisfaction, security, and solace. Content to pursue a humble course (verse 1), the psalmist felt "soothed and quieted," like a weanling in his mother's arms. Humbly waiting on Jehovah and doing his will bring security and rich blessings.

Lesson for Us: Although Jehovah can rescue his people from calamity, he does not shield them from all adversity. Indeed, adversities moved the composers to utter these psalms. However, God "will not let you be tempted beyond what you can bear" but "will also make the way out." (1 Corinthians 10:13) Jehovah does protect us from spiritual ruin. He can either maneuver events so as to eliminate the calamity itself or strengthen us so that we can withstand the pressure. To that end, very soothing and beneficial is the unity we enjoy at our Christian meetings. —Psalm 133:1-3.

The Praiseworthy God

Read Psalms 135 to 145. In contrast with idols whose makers become just like them, Jehovah is the praiseworthy God and Deliverer. (Psalms 135, 136) Even when his people were in Babylon, they did not forget "the songs of Zion." (Psalm 137) David says 'kings will laud Jehovah' and exults in how wonderfully he is made. (Psalms 138, 139) He prays for God's protection and extols His goodness, knowing that only a good relationship with Jehovah brings true happiness. —Psalms 140-145.

♦ 138:2—How did God magnify his saying above his name?

When Jehovah declares something on the basis of his name, we expect much in the way of fulfillment. However, he always exceeds our expectations, causing the realization to surpass by far our anticipation. God magnifies his "saying" by making its fulfillment grander than what we expect.

♦ 139:9—What is meant by "the wings of the dawn"?

This expression depicts the light of dawn, as if having wings, swiftly spreading over the sky from east to west. Were David to "take the wings of the dawn" and reach the remotest part of the west, there he would still be under Jehovah's care and control.—Psalm 139:10; compare Amos 9:2, 3.

♦ 141:3—Why did David want 'a watch over the door of his lips'?

David knew the damage the tongue can do and how imperfect men are tempted to speak rashly, especially when provoked. Moses was the meekest man on earth, yet he sinned with his tongue in connection with the waters of Meribah. (Numbers 12:3; 20:9-13) Control of the lips is necessary, then, to avoid injurious speech and preserve a good heart.—James 3:5-12.

♦ 142:7—Why did David think his soul was in a "dungeon"?

He felt all alone with his problems, as in a dark, dangerous dungeon, misunderstood and separated from all humans. When we have similar feelings and think that our "right hand" is open to attack, we can confidently call out to Jehovah for help.—Psalm 142:3-7.

Lesson for Us: In Psalm 139, David expressed delight in God's ability to 'search through' him and "know" him and his ways. Rather than seeking escape, David wanted to yield more fully to Jehovah's guidance and control. He knew that God always observed him. Such knowledge not only restrains one from wrongdoing but also provides one with the ut-

most comfort. The fact that Jehovah sees our deeds, understands our problems, and is always ready to help us produces a deep sense of security and peace, which is essential to our happiness.

Praise Jah!

Read Psalms 146 to 150. These psalms strike up the theme of the entire Book of Psalms—"Praise Jah, you people!" Each of them begins and ends with those glorious words. All of this rises to a grand crescendo in the 150th Psalm, which calls on all creation to "praise Jah"!

♦ Psalm 146:3—Why not put confidence in human leaders?

Human leaders are mortal. They can save neither themselves nor those trusting in them. Thus, confidence in human leadership is undermined by the eventuality of death. But "happy is the one . . . whose hope is in Jehovah his God." (Psalm 146:5, 6) The psalmist saw the need for guidance superior to what humans themselves can give.

♦ 148:4—What are the 'waters above the heavens'?

The psalmist apparently meant the water-carrying clouds above the earth that empty themselves from time to time in the form of rain, which eventually flows back into the oceans. This cycle is essential to life, and its very existence gives praise to the Creator. Since the atmospheric expanse between the earth and the clouds can be spoken of as heavens, the psalmist referred to the clouds as the 'waters above the heavens.'

___

The Psalms make this truth self-evident: To be truly happy, we need a good relationship with Jehovah. Thus, the whole aim of God's people and the purpose of our existence can be summed up in the psalmist's concluding call: "Every breathing thing—let it praise Jah. Praise Jah, you people!"—Psalm 150:6.

A Look at the Bahamas
—Through the Eyes of a Traveling Minister

THE Bahamas. There was a time when those words conjured up in me dreams of lying on beautiful sandy beaches beneath gently swaying coconut palms or swimming in crystal-clear turquoise waters. Indeed, to the thousands of vacationers who visit the Bahamas each month, such visions become a reality. And no wonder, for the climate on these tropical islands is enjoyable, with an average temperature of 70 degrees Fahrenheit (21° C.) in winter and 85 degrees Fahrenheit (29° C.) in summer!

Now, though, the Bahamas mean much more to me than just soaking up the warmth of the tropical sun as a vacationer. They have become my assignment as a traveling minister of Jehovah's Witnesses. Come with me and see the Bahamas through my eyes.

The Out Islands

Only about 20 of the 700 islands and cays are populated, and the majority of the Bahamians live in the capital city of Nassau on the island of New Providence. Nas-

sau is known as a port of call for ocean cruise ships and has a number of large hotels for vacationers. Maybe you have stayed at one of them. But have you toured the other islands?

A large number of Bahamians live on the Out Islands, which are also called Family Islands. These islands surround Nassau, the farthest one being over 300 miles (480 km) away. On a few of these Out Islands, you can enjoy all the modern conveniences of Nassau, but others are not as developed. For example, some do not have electricity or running water. On others, you can still see people cooking on wood fires in their thatched-roof kitchens or grinding corn in hand mills.

How I Travel

All the Out Islands can be reached from Nassau by boat or airplane, but their remote location may present a challenge to persons with a profession such as mine. In a procedure similar to that followed by first-century Christians, a traveling minister, or circuit overseer, will visit congregations and small groups of Jehovah's Witnesses to strengthen and encourage them spiritually.—Acts 15:36; 16:4, 5.

I remember a group of only three Witnesses that I was to visit on one of the Out Islands. This group had not been visited by a circuit overseer for over three years. I wrote to them from Nassau, notifying them of the dates for my visit. But when I arrived by boat, no Witness met me at the dock. So I asked if anybody could help me find one of the Witnesses. I was directed to a certain woman, and as I introduced myself as the circuit overseer, she got so excited that she ran off to tell the other Witnesses about my arrival. She left me standing there with my luggage. Those Witnesses had never received my letter, and they were surprised and delighted by my visit.

I became very nervous when I saw smoke fill the cockpit of the plane as it lifted off the ground

---

The return trip to Nassau was by means of a small freight-and-mail boat. The voyage took more than 30 hours through rough seas, but the time passed quickly, at least for me. I seized the opportunity to preach to some of the passengers. Sometime later, one of the crew members began studying the Bible and is now attending meetings at one of the congregations in Nassau.

Another way to visit the Out Islands is by airplane. However, only small planes can land on some of the island airstrips. These are usually quite safe, but sometimes there are frightening experiences. On one occasion, I became very nervous when I saw smoke fill the cockpit of the plane as it lifted off the ground. The plane quickly returned to the airstrip. The cause of the smoke? A rodent's nest built in the heating and ventilation air duct next to the engine!

What About the People?

While traveling in the Out Islands, I have found many persons who desire Bible literature. But for some of them, even the low cost of the literature is beyond their means. For example, on one extremely hot day, five of us were preaching on a remote island when I met a woman who showed keen interest in the publication *My Book of Bible Stories*. She did not have any money to contribute toward its cost, but what she did have in her refrigerator was just what we needed—five cans of a cool beverage. We traded the book for her cool drinks, which made everyone happy.

The Bahamians have a real love for the Bible. This makes it a joy to bring them the "good news" of Jehovah's Kingdom. (Matthew 24:14) Often when calling at a home, you will find the householder reading the Bible. At one home I visited, the mother proudly had her three-year-old daughter recite to me the names of all 66 books of the Bible in their proper order.

During the past few years, the Out Islanders have enjoyed seeing slide presentations on Bible subjects prepared by the Watch Tower Society. On one island, no hall was available, so we made arrangements to show the slides outside on a newly painted white wall next to a small food store. About 60 people gathered around—some standing, others sitting.

On another occasion, 120 people assembled. They relished the slide program so much that when the lights were turned on, no one left. I remembered that I had brought along another set of slides on a different Bible subject. So off went the lights again, and the second set was shown—to the delight of the crowd.

Sometimes problems can spring up. On one island a group of people gathered in the local schoolhouse to see our slide program. As I turned the projector on, the bulb burned out. I did not have an extra projector bulb, and one was not available on this Out Island. Needless to say, the crowd was disappointed. However, by quickly taking the projector apart and making a few adjustments, I was able to use an ordinary household bulb as a fair, but somewhat dimmer, substitute. The audience did not care. They enjoyed the program anyway.

Tarantulas, Mosquitoes, and "Fried Cats"

Making regular visits to the Out Islands calls for some adaptations to the tropical conditions. I remember the first time I saw a tarantula. The spider was crawling across the floor and seemed as big as my hand! I stood frozen—terrified. I am thankful that the householder came to my rescue. With one swift blow from his machete, the "enemy" was dispatched. The householder was an 82-year-old man. Formerly, he had bitterly opposed his wife's efforts to serve Jehovah. But in time he began attending the meetings at the Kingdom Hall and studying the Bible with her.

Because of the warm climate, mosquitoes may pose a problem. At times they are so numerous that, as you speak, one may fly right into your mouth. Of course, many other living things are a joy to behold, like the beautiful pink flamingos living in the midst of their natural habitat of lush tropical plants and fruit trees.

Learning about local foods can be quite a revelation. On one island, I spotted what looked like an orange tree full of that juicy fruit. I asked the lady of the house if I might pick one or two of her oranges. She cautioned me. They were not oranges but sours. Nevertheless, I could help myself, she said. Well, I figured that I knew an orange when I saw one. So I picked a nice fat one and took a bite. What a surprise! My mouth puckered. The fruit was extremely sour, like a lemon. The woman laughed, but I learned that although the fruit of the sour "orange" tree looks like an orange, it surely does not taste like one!

I thought I was adjusting to island life quite well until a trip to one of the islands not long ago. I was staying with an elderly widower as I served the congregation. Upon arising the first morning, he invited me to join him for breakfast. My mouth watered in anticipation—until he mentioned the menu. "Fried cats"! As I entered the kitchen and was about to decline the offer, I saw him flipping pancakes. "Where are the 'fried cats'?" I asked. He pointed to the pancakes. I heaved a big sigh of relief, and we both broke out laughing. He thought that I knew that pancakes were called fried cats on that island.

Rewards of Traveling

Because of the remote location of some of the islands, there is a great need for more ministers to help in spreading the good news of God's Kingdom. This need is not only to reach the English-speaking people of the Bahamas but also to contact the Haitian immigrants who speak French.

I asked him, "Where are the 'fried cats'?"

Being a traveling minister in the Bahamas is an exciting challenge that calls for some adjustments to the island way of living. But there are also great rewards. One is the inestimable joy of seeing people respond to the Bible's message. Another is the fine privilege of spiritually stimulating the scattered congregations and isolated groups.

We in the Bahamas delight in the beauty of beaches sparkling with pink sand and white sand and the enchanting coral reefs gorgeously arrayed with fish. But we are especially delighted with what is now taking place here and around the globe. As Jehovah's Witnesses, we see Psalm 97:1 being fulfilled. It says: "Jehovah himself has become king! Let the earth be joyful. Let the many *islands* rejoice."—*As told by Anthony Reed.*

Will You Cling to the Truth?

IF YOU have begun to study the Bible with Jehovah's Witnesses, the principal question you must answer to your own satisfaction is, Is this the truth? If you find that it is, will you cling to it? Similar questions confronted people in the days of Jesus Christ and his apostles.

When the apostles preached about Jesus, how did people react? Well, news regarding Christ's Kingdom, his miracles, his ransom sacrifice, his resurrection, and everlasting life sounded good, and many accepted what they heard as the truth. But the majority did not. In fact, the Christian organization of that time was "spoken against" everywhere. (Acts 28:22) So accepting the truths Jesus' disciples preached meant going against popular opinion and encountering opposition. Interested people therefore had to prove to their own satisfaction that Christian teachings were the truth. Only then could they take a firm stand.

When Paul and Barnabas visited Antioch in Asia Minor, many people listened to their message with keen interest. The Bible record says: "Now when they were going out, the people began entreating for these matters to be spoken to them on the following sabbath. The next sabbath nearly all the city gathered together to hear the word of Jehovah." (Acts 13: 42, 44) But this initial interest waned in a great number of the people when they heard emotional opposers speaking against the apostles.

Verse 45 of Acts chapter 13 says: "When the Jews got sight of the crowds, they were filled with jealousy and began blasphemously contradicting the things being spoken by Paul." Then verse 50 goes on to say: "But the Jews stirred up the reputable women who worshiped God and the principal men of the city, and they raised up a persecution against Paul and Barnabas and threw them outside their boundaries." Interested people had to decide whether to continue listening to Jesus' followers despite the opposition. They had either to accept what they heard as the truth or to close their ears to it.

Opposition Today

Even as Christians were opposed in the first century C.E., so there are present-day opposers who try to close the ears of interested people to the Scriptural truths Jehovah's Witnesses are teaching. Friends, relatives, and religious leaders often try desperately to discourage interested ones from studying the Bible with the Witnesses. Without Scriptural proof, the opposers contradict what is taught and make false accusations.

What should interested people do? Should they permit the words of opposers to close their minds and ears as some did in Antioch? Or should they prove to themselves from the Bible whether what they are studying is the truth or not?

The receptive people in the city of Beroea were commended because they examined the Scriptures to see if what Paul told them was the truth. Upon finding that he spoke the truth, they took a firm stand for it. We are told: "The [Beroeans] were more noble-minded than those in Thessalonica, for they received the word with the greatest eagerness of mind, carefully examining the Scriptures daily as to whether these things were so."—Acts 17: 10, 11.

The people of Beroea did not permit the statements of opposers to close their minds to the good news. Rather, they examined the Scriptures daily to confirm that the things they heard were truthful. They had found a valuable treasure and were not going to let opposers turn them away from it. Would this not be the reasonable course to take with regard to the same good news that Jehovah's Witnesses proclaim today?

Why Some Oppose

Sometimes opposers are well-meaning relatives that you love and respect, and you have every reason to believe that they are sincerely interested in your welfare. But you need to consider why they are opposed to your studying the Bible with Jehovah's Witnesses. Do they have firm Scriptural proof that what you are learning is not the truth? Or is their opposition due to what others have told them? Do they lack accurate knowledge about what the Witnesses teach? Many who opposed Jesus did so in ignorance of what he taught and because they believed the false accusations of opposers.

When Jesus was hanging on the torture stake, people passing by "would speak abusively to him, wagging their heads and saying: 'Bah! You would-be thrower-down of the temple and builder of it in three days' time, save yourself by coming down off the torture stake.' In like manner also the chief priests were making fun among themselves with the scribes and saying: 'Others he saved; himself he cannot save! Let the Christ the King of Israel now come down off the torture stake, that we may see and believe.'" (Mark 15:29-32) What was the reason for this bad attitude?

The people had permitted their opinion of Jesus to be shaped by the religious leaders who hated him because he had exposed them as false teachers whose actions were not in harmony with their claims of being representatives of the true God. With frankness, Jesus had said to them: "Why is it you also overstep the commandment of God because of your tradition? You hypocrites, Isaiah aptly prophesied about you, when he said, 'This people honors me with their lips, yet their heart is far removed from me. It is in vain that they keep worshiping me, because they teach commands of men as doctrines.'"—Matthew 15:3, 7-9.

So intensely did the religious leaders hate Jesus and the truths he taught that they conspired to kill him and made every effort to turn the people against him. Today, many religious leaders oppose Jehovah's Witnesses with the same intensity. And as was the case with the early Christians, the Witnesses are "spoken against" everywhere. But is it wise to permit this popular opposition to shape your thinking?

The same Scriptural truths about God's Kingdom that Jesus and his apostles preached are being proclaimed today by Jehovah's Witnesses. Hundreds of thousands of people all over the world are accepting this good news notwithstanding intense opposition by friends, relatives, and religious leaders. Those accepting the Kingdom message have proved to their satisfaction that it is the truth, and they are determined to hold on to it.

So why be like those of the first century who permitted others to turn them away from the life-giving Scriptural truths that came to them through the unpopular followers of Jesus Christ? Instead, continue studying the Bible with the Witnesses, using the written Word of God to prove to your own satisfaction that what you are learning is indeed the truth. (John 8:32) And with God's help cling to the truth.

Questions From Readers

■ What is meant at 2 Samuel 18:8, which says: "The forest did more in eating up the people than the sword did"?

King David's handsome son Absalom usurped the throne and forced his father to flee Jerusalem. Thereafter, in the forest of Ephraim (perhaps east of the Jordan River) a battle took place between Absalom's forces and those loyal to Jehovah's anointed king, David. The account at 2 Samuel 18:6, 7 reports that in the fierce battle David's men slaughtered 20,000 rebels. In part, the next verse adds: "Furthermore, the forest did more in eating up the people than the sword did in eating them up on that day."

Some have suggested that this refers to rebel soldiers' being devoured by wild beasts dwelling in the woods. (1 Samuel 17:36; 2 Kings 2:24) But such literal eating by animals need not be meant, any more than that "the sword" literally ate those slain in battle. Actually, the battle "got to be spread out over all the land that was in sight." So a more likely explanation is that Absalom's routed men, who were fleeing in panic through the rocky forest, perhaps fell into pits and hidden ravines, and became entangled in dense underbrush. Interestingly, the account goes on to relate that Absalom himself became a victim of the forest. Apparently because of his abundant hair, his head got caught in a big tree, leaving him helplessly exposed to a fatal attack by Joab and his men. Absalom's corpse was 'pitched in the forest into a big hollow, and a very big pile of stones was raised up over him.'—2 Samuel 18:9-17.

'It Exceeds All Expectations'

A man in the Netherlands employed as a scientific researcher writes: "It is not often that I take my pen to express my appreciation for things I have read. But the publication *Life—How Did It Get Here? By Evolution or by Creation?* really is a unique book."

The man explains that he comes in daily contact with biologists and that "it would take a miracle for such a one ever to be convinced of creation. But this book really does exceed all expectations. The logical buildup of the chapters and the illustrations are scientifically so up-to-date that you would have to be blind to raise any objections to them. . . . What more than anything else makes this book credible are the literature references, in which famous evolutionists are allowed to speak . . . I certainly intend to bring this book to the notice of some of my (former and future) colleagues."

April 1, 1987

The Watchtower

Announcing Jehovah's Kingdom

Is God a Real Person?

The Watchtower®

Announcing Jehovah's Kingdom

April 1, 1987
Vol. 108, No. 7

In This Issue

THE PURPOSE OF "THE WATCHTOWER" is to exalt Jehovah God as the Sovereign of the universe. It keeps watch on world events as they fulfill Bible prophecy. It comforts all peoples with the good news that God's Kingdom will soon destroy those who oppress their fellowmen and that it will turn the earth into a paradise. It encourages faith in the now-reigning King, Jesus Christ, whose shed blood opens the way for mankind to gain eternal life. "The Watchtower," published by Jehovah's Witnesses continuously since 1879, is nonpolitical. It adheres to the Bible as its authority.

"WATCHTOWER" STUDIES FOR THE WEEKS

May 10: Grandest Childbirth on Earth Preludes Worldwide Security. Page 10. Songs to Be Used: 21, 105.

May 17: Worldwide Security Under the "Prince of Peace." Page 15. Songs to Be Used: 168, 119.

Average Printing Each Issue: 12,315,000

Now Published in 103 Languages

SEMIMONTHLY LANGUAGES AVAILABLE BY MAIL
Afrikaans, Arabic, Cebuano, Chichewa, Chinese, Cibemba, Danish,* Dutch,* Efik, English,* Finnish,* French,* German,* Greek,* Hiligaynon, Igbo, Iloko, Italian,* Japanese,* Korean, Lingala, Malagasy, Maltese, Norwegian, Portuguese,* Russian, Sepedi, Sesotho, Shona, Spanish,* Swahili, Swedish,* Tagalog, Thai, Tsonga, Tswana, Xhosa, Yoruba, Zulu

MONTHLY LANGUAGES AVAILABLE BY MAIL
Armenian, Bengali, Bicol, Bulgarian, Croatian, Czech, Ewe, Fijian, Ga, Greenlandic, Gujarati, Gun, Hausa, Hebrew, Hindi, Hiri Motu, Hungarian, Icelandic, Kannada, Malayalam, Marathi, New Guinea Pidgin, Pangasinan, Papiamento, Polish, Rarotongan, Romanian, Samar-Leyte, Samoan, Sango, Serbian, Silozi, Sinhalese, Slovenian, Solomon Islands-Pidgin, Tahitian, Tamil, Telugu, Tongan, Tshiluba, Turkish, Twi, Ukrainian, Urdu, Venda, Vietnamese

* Study articles also available in large-print edition.

	Yearly subscription for the above:	
	Semimonthly	Monthly
Watch Tower Society offices	Languages	Languages
America, U.S., Watchtower, Wallkill, N.Y. 12589	$4.00	$2.00
Australia, Box 280, Ingleburn, N.S.W. 2565	A$7.00	A$3.50
Canada, Box 4100, Halton Hills, Ontario L7G 4Y4	$5.50	$2.75
England, The Ridgeway, London NW7 1RN	£5.00	£2.50
Ireland, 29A Jamestown Road, Finglas, Dublin 11	IR£6.00	IR£3.00
New Zealand, P.O. Box 142, Manurewa	NZ$15.00	NZ$7.50
Nigeria, PMB 001, Shomolu, Lagos State	₦8.00	₦4.00
Philippines, P.O. Box 2044, Manila 2800	₱60.00	₱30.00
South Africa, Private Bag 2067, Krugersdorp, 1740	R6,50	R3,25

Remittances should be sent to the office in your country or to Watchtower, Wallkill, N.Y. 12589, U.S.A.

Changes of address should reach us 30 days before your moving date. Give us your old and new address (if possible your old address label).

20 cents (U.S.) a copy

The Bible translation used is the "New World Translation of the Holy Scriptures," unless otherwise indicated.

The Watchtower (ISSN 0043-1087) is published semimonthly for $4.00 (U.S.) per year by Watch Tower Bible and Tract Society of Pennsylvania, 25 Columbia Heights, Brooklyn, N.Y. 11201. Second-class postage paid at Brooklyn, N.Y., and at additional mailing offices.

Postmaster: Send address changes to Watchtower, *Wallkill, N.Y. 12589.*

Published by
Watch Tower Bible and Tract Society of Pennsylvania

25 Columbia Heights, Brooklyn, N.Y. 11201, U.S.A.

Frederick W. Franz, President

GOD

Is He a Real Person?

"THERE *must* be a God" declared the August 14, 1981, issue of the *Daily Express*. The paper was reporting on the apparent conversion of two prominent scientists to a belief in God. Their newfound conviction emerged after they discovered the prodigious mathematical odds against life's appearing spontaneously. However, what did these two new believers mean when they said "God"? Reports the *Daily Express:* "God they suggest, IS the universe."

If you believe in God, what is *your* conception of him? Do you likewise view him as an indefinable intelligence, an abstract omnipresent force, a great "Something"? Or do you view him as a definable, intelligent Person?

Some find it hard to think of God as a Person. They may even feel that doing so reduces him to a mere humanlike being—as in the childish image of an old man in a hooded robe and with a long white beard, sitting on a cloud. Or as Michelangelo portrayed God in his famous Sistine-chapel ceiling fresco —a muscular, dynamic old man who floats in the air.

True, when we hear the word "person," we may automatically think of a human.

Webster's Third New International Dictionary, for example, defines "person" as "an individual human being." But it also defines "person" as "a being characterized by conscious apprehension, rationality, and a moral sense." Therefore, one can accurately think of God as a Person without depicting him as a human.

But some may object: 'What difference does it make whether you view God as an abstract force or as a Person?' Well, if God is merely a force, a "Something," does this not mean that human life is likewise purely mechanical? Man would thus be reduced to an "it," a cog in a big machine. But if God is an intelligent Person, would that not give life greater meaning? Indeed, it would open up the possibility of having a relationship with God—a relationship not between two "its" but between two persons.

Obviously, a person-to-person relationship with God would be most desirable. But in the first place, how do we know whether God is a Person or not? And, if he is, how can we have such a relationship? Let us look at what the Bible has to say on this matter.

How We Can Get To Know GOD

SOME people believe that God is everywhere, present in the stars and planets, in the rainbow, in a bird's wing, in a blade of grass. However, the Bible teaches that God, as a Person, has a definite location. Wise King Solomon said in a prayer to God: "You must also hear from the heavens, your established place of dwelling." And in the Bible book of Isaiah, God himself is quoted as saying: "The heavens are my throne."—1 Kings 8:49; Isaiah 66:1.

Though God himself is not present in his creation, his personality traits are reflected there. Said the apostle Paul at Romans 1:20: "His invisible qualities are clearly seen from the world's creation onward, because they are perceived by the things made, even his eternal power and Godship." The psalmist David similarly wrote: "The heavens are declaring the glory of God; and of the work of his hands the expanse is telling. One day after another day causes speech to bubble forth, and one night after another night shows forth knowledge."—Psalm 19:1, 2.

Yes, look out on a starry night and contemplate for a moment the enormous wisdom and power needed to create and maintain our universe! (Compare Isaiah 40:26.) Indeed, creation is an inexhaustible source of information about God's personality. And man can never fully perceive the enormous witness it sounds out regarding God's qualities and attributes. The book of Job reminds us: "Look! These are the fringes of his ways, and what a whisper of a matter has been heard of him!" (Job 26:14) There is an old Swedish saying:
'The master is greater than his works.' Accordingly, if creation is great, God must be greater; if creation displays wisdom, God must be wiser; if creation demonstrates power, God must be even more powerful!

The Bible—God's Book

Creation thus yields much information about God. However, can a study of creation tell you God's name? Will it reveal what is the purpose behind creation or why he permits wickedness? Answers to such questions require more than a study of God's material works. Fortunately, God has seen to it that such information about him is set out in the Bible.

There God is never presented as an abstract, indefinable intellect or an omnipresent force or power. At Acts 3:19 we read about "the *person* of Jehovah." When his Son, Jesus Christ, was raised from the dead, the Bible says that he entered into heaven itself to appear before "the *person* [literally, "face"] of God." (Hebrews 9:24, *Kingdom Interlinear*) Certainly, Jesus never called God a Great Force, Infinite Intellect, or any other abstract term when he talked about him or prayed to him. On the contrary, he often called him heavenly Father, a term revealing his deep intimacy with God.—Matthew 5:48; 6:14, 26, 32.

God is therefore not a nameless "Something" but rather a Person with a name. Says Psalm 83:18: "That people may know

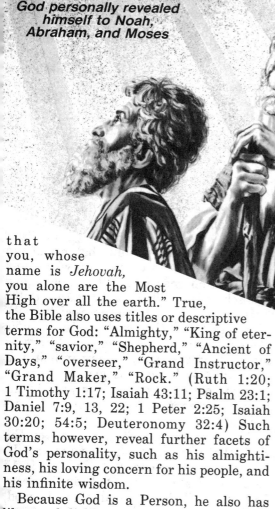

God personally revealed himself to Noah, Abraham, and Moses

that you, whose name is *Jehovah,* you alone are the Most High over all the earth." True, the Bible also uses titles or descriptive terms for God: "Almighty," "King of eternity," "savior," "Shepherd," "Ancient of Days," "overseer," "Grand Instructor," "Grand Maker," "Rock." (Ruth 1:20; 1 Timothy 1:17; Isaiah 43:11; Psalm 23:1; Daniel 7:9, 13, 22; 1 Peter 2:25; Isaiah 30:20; 54:5; Deuteronomy 32:4) Such terms, however, reveal further facets of God's personality, such as his almightiness, his loving concern for his people, and his infinite wisdom.

Because God is a Person, he also has likes and dislikes—even feelings. The Bible tells us that he loves his people (1 Kings 10:9), rejoices in his works (Psalm 104:31), hates idolatry (Deuteronomy 16:22), and feels hurt over wickedness. (Genesis 6:6) At 1 Timothy 1:11 he is even called "the happy God."

Knowing God Intimately

True, no human mind is roomy enough to hold the entire revelation of God's personality. "O the depth of God's riches and wisdom and knowledge! How unsearchable his judgments are and past tracing out his ways are! For 'who has come to know Jehovah's mind, or who has become his counselor?'" (Romans 11:33, 34) Nevertheless, for one with faith, God can be as real as any other person. The Bible tells us that "Noah walked with the true God," as if Jehovah were by his very side. (Genesis 6:9) God was also so real to Moses that it was as if he were "seeing the One who is invisible." (Hebrews 11:27) And of Abraham it was said that he was "Jehovah's friend."—James 2:23.

Of course, God personally revealed himself to Noah, Abraham, and Moses. 'Well, if God would reveal himself to *me* in such a personal way,' some might say, 'he would be real to me too.' Remember, though, Noah, Abraham, and Moses did not have the Bible. They did not know about Jesus Christ nor of all the dozens of prophecies he fulfilled. As a result, all that Jesus Christ revealed about God was unknown to them. Under such circumstances, it was necessary and appropriate for God to make such direct revelations of himself.

Today, however, we have both the Bible and the perspective of centuries of fulfillment of Bible prophecies. We have the Gospel records of the life, works, and words of Jesus Christ. And says Paul: "It is in him [Christ] that all the fullness of the divine quality dwells bodily." (Colossians 2:9) Yes, we are in a position to know God with an intimacy that was not possible in the days of the patriarchs. Does this not overwhelmingly compensate for the fact that he has not directly revealed himself to us?

Bible Reading Brings Us Close to God

We read at James 4:8: "Draw close to God, and he will draw close to you." By reading the Bible, we can draw close to God. But how? For one thing, by reading a portion of the Bible each day, you learn new characteristics and attributes of his personality. As you read, repeatedly stop and ask yourself: 'What did I learn about God in this verse or portion?' In addition, you can pray for God's spirit to act as a "helper" in your comprehension and in your drawing close to God.—John 14:26.

"I have appreciated getting a much better understanding of *Jehovah as a person*," declared one Christian woman who read the Bible from cover to cover. She was a student at the Watchtower Bible School of Gilead, which trains missionaries who are sent all over the world. What method of Bible study is used in this school? Explains one of the instructors: "We started on a project of studying the whole Bible as a group. We took 10 to 15 pages a day, with all . . . students doing research and contributing to our discussion. If we encountered a difficult verse, we considered (1) the context, (2) the circumstances at the time of writing, and (3) the meaning of key words in the text. We constantly asked, 'What does this tell us about Jehovah and his qualities?' We found it always told us something about him."

Although you may not have the privilege of studying the Bible formally at this school, some of these study methods may work well for you and your family. For example, among Jehovah's Witnesses it is the custom to study a few chapters of the Bible each week in connection with their congregation meetings. Why not follow this schedule of Bible reading as a family? Further, the Watch Tower Society publishes research helps, such as *Aid to Bible Understanding* and the *New World Translation Reference Bible,* which can help you with difficult Bible passages.* A regular program of Bible reading can greatly enhance your appreciation of Jehovah's personality.

You may also select a portion of the Bible that has particular appeal to you. If, for example, you choose to study the 17 verses in Psalm 86, you will find at least 15 traits in God's personality: He is good, ready to forgive, abundant in lovingkindness, willing to answer prayers, unequaled among the gods, unmatched as a creative worker, a sovereign ruler, a great doer of wondrous things, a deliverer from death, merciful, gracious, slow to anger, abundant in trueness, a helper, and a comforter. What better goal could you have than trying to learn about your Creator?

---

* The *Watch Tower Publications Index 1930-1985* will help you locate explanations and discussions of such passages in these research helps.

Creation is an inexhaustible source of information about God's personality

Great Benefits From Knowing God

Reaching our ultimate goal of everlasting life is just one benefit from knowing God. (John 17:3) Additionally, there is the benefit of having a daily companion who cares for you and is as stable as a rock. (Psalm 18:31) When King David felt surrounded by enemies and burdened down by problems, he found that God was the only real helper available. He therefore said: "Throw your burden upon Jehovah himself, and he himself will sustain you. Never will he allow the righteous one to totter."—Psalm 55:22.

You, too, can enjoy such a relationship with God, if you but take the time to come to know him. It is not too difficult. Put forth the effort to read his Word. Associate with those whose lives demonstrate that they know God, such as the ones who brought you this journal. Call upon Jehovah in prayer. For God is not some impersonal force that will be deaf to your outcries. He is a living God and a "Hearer of prayer." And "if you search for him, he will let himself be found by you."—Psalm 65:2; 1 Chronicles 28:9.

Benefiting From Jesus' Illustrations

WHEN the disciples come to Jesus after his speech to the crowds on the beach, they are curious about his new method of teaching. Oh, they have heard him use illustrations before but never so extensively. So they want to know: "Why is it you speak to them by the use of illustrations?"

One reason he does so is to fulfill the prophet's words: "I will open my mouth with illustrations, I will publish things hidden since the founding." But there is more to it than this. His use of illustrations serves the purpose of helping to reveal the heart attitude of people.

Actually, most people are interested in Jesus simply as a masterful storyteller and miracle worker, not as one to be served as Lord and to be unselfishly followed. They do not want to be disturbed in their view of things or their way of life. They do not want the message to penetrate to that extent. So Jesus says:

"This is why I speak to them by the use of illustrations, because, looking, they look in vain, and hearing, they hear in vain, neither do they get the sense of it; and toward them the prophecy of Isaiah is having fulfillment, which says, ' . . . For the heart of this people has grown unreceptive.'"

"However," Jesus continues, "happy are your eyes because they behold, and your ears because they hear. For I truly say to you, Many prophets and righteous men desired to see the things you are beholding and did not see them, and to hear the things you are hearing and did not hear them."

Yes, the 12 apostles and those with them have receptive hearts. Therefore Jesus says: "To you it is granted to understand the sacred secrets of the kingdom of the heavens, but to those people it is not granted." Because of their desire for understanding, Jesus provides his disciples an explanation of the illustration of the sower.

"The seed is the word of God," Jesus says, and the soil is the heart. Of the seed sown on the hard roadside surface, he explains: "The Devil comes and takes the word away from their hearts in order that they may not believe and be saved."

On the other hand, seed sown on soil with an underlying rock-mass refers to the hearts of people who receive the word with joy. However, because the word cannot take deep root in such hearts, these people fall away when a time of testing or persecution comes.

As for the seed that fell among the thorns, Jesus continues, this refers to people who have heard the word. These ones, however, are carried away by anxieties and riches and pleasures of this life, so they are completely choked and bring nothing to perfection.

Finally, as for the seed sown on fine soil, Jesus says, these are the ones who, after hearing the word with a fine and good heart, retain it and bear fruit with endurance.

How blessed are these disciples who have sought out Jesus to obtain an explanation of his teachings! Jesus intends that his illustrations be understood, to impart truth to others. "A lamp is not brought to be put under a measuring basket or under a bed, is it?" he asks. No, "it is brought to be put upon

a lampstand." Thus Jesus adds: "Therefore, pay attention to how you listen."   **Matthew 13:10-23, 34-36; Mark 4:10-25, 33, 34; Luke 8:9-18; Psalm 78:2; Isaiah 6:9, 10.**

• Why did Jesus speak in illustrations?
• How do Jesus' disciples show themselves to be different from the crowds?
• What explanation does Jesus provide of the illustration of the sower?

Grandest Childbirth on Earth Preludes Worldwide Security

"There has been a child born to us, there has been a son given to us; and the princely rule will come to be upon his shoulder. And his name will be called Wonderful Counselor, Mighty God, Eternal Father, Prince of Peace."—ISAIAH 9:6.

WORLDWIDE security! Under "the Prince of this world," Satan the Devil, it is an impossible dream. (John 12: 31, *The New English Bible*) But worldwide security under the "Prince of Peace," Jesus Christ, is an absolute certainty. Jehovah assures us of this in the prophecy about the birth and career of the "Prince of Peace." At Isaiah 9:6, 7, we read: "There has been a child born to us, there

has been a son given to us; and the princely rule will come to be upon his shoulder. And his name will be called Wonderful Counselor, Mighty God, Eternal Father, Prince of Peace. To the abundance of the princely rule and to peace there will be no end, upon the throne of David and upon his kingdom in order to establish it firmly and to sustain it by means of justice and by means of righteousness, from now on and to time indefinite. The very zeal of Jehovah of armies will do this."

---

1. Under whom is worldwide security a certainty, and how do we know this?

² What a marvelous prophecy! It will be thrilling to examine this prophecy about the grandest childbirth on earth. But before we can fully appreciate it, we need to focus on the circumstances under which the prophecy was given. It was a time of international conspiracies during the days of the kingdom of Judah under King Ahaz. Although unfaithful to Jehovah, that king was permitted to sit upon Jehovah's throne. This forbearance was shown to him because of the covenant that Jehovah made with David for an everlasting kingdom in his line of descent. Though David was denied the privilege of building a temple to Jehovah, God gave him an alternative blessing. This was set forth in the words of the prophet Nathan: "And Jehovah has told you that a house is what Jehovah will make for you. And your house and your kingdom will certainly be steadfast to time indefinite before you; your very throne will become one firmly established to time indefinite." (2 Samuel 7:11, 16) That divine promise proved to be so satisfying to King David that he looked forward to its glorious fulfillment.

³ That covenant with David finds its fulfillment in the great Son of David, Jesus Christ, the "Prince of Peace." No other royal house on the face of this earth has ever enjoyed such a covenant for a kingdom, with no end to the abundance of its princely rule, with no end of peace. But that Kingdom covenant held forth a challenge to all the kingdoms of the world of which Satan is prince, or ruler. So the Devil and his demons made it their goal to try to destroy the house of David and thereby eliminate the prospect of its having a permanent heir. Satan found ready instruments in King Rezin of Syria, in King Pekah of the ten-tribe kingdom of Israel, and in the king of Assyria.

Conspiracy Against the Kingdom Covenant

⁴ What was the Devil's scheme? His aim was to force King Ahaz of Judah, out of fear, into an improper alliance with the king of Assyria. How could the Devil do this? Well, he caused King Pekah of Israel and King Rezin of Syria to enter into a conspiracy against the house of David. They conspired to remove Ahaz from the throne of Judah in order to install their own man, the son of Tabeel, as puppet king. Who was this son of Tabeel? It is significant that he was not a descendant of David's house. Hence, he was not a man through whom God's covenant for the Kingdom could be passed along until it found its permanent Heir in the "Prince of Peace." He was to be *their* man, not God's man, on the throne of Judah. Thus the Bible exposes Satan's effort to stop the operation of Jehovah's Kingdom covenant that was made with David.

⁵ How did King Ahaz react to this threat? He and his people trembled with fear. So Jehovah gave him some encouraging information to turn him away from forming a protective alliance with the king of the rising world power, Assyria. Jehovah sent his prophet Isaiah to meet Ahaz and to deliver this message found at Isaiah 7:4-9:

⁶ "Do not be afraid . . . for the reason

---

2. (a) What were the circumstances under which the prophecy of Isaiah 9:6, 7 was given? (b) How do we know that Jehovah will unfailingly hold to the covenant he made with David for an everlasting kingdom in his line of descent?
3. (a) With whom does that covenant with David find fulfillment, and how was that covenant unique? (b) What did the Devil make his goal with regard to the Kingdom covenant?

---

4. How did the Devil proceed in his efforts to stop the operation of Jehovah's Kingdom covenant that was made with David?
5, 6. How did King Ahaz react to the conspiracy against the house of David, and what encouraging message did Jehovah give him?

that Syria with Ephraim [the leading member of the kingdom of Israel] and the son of Remaliah [Pekah] has advised what is bad against you, saying: 'Let us go up against Judah and tear it apart and by breakthroughs take it for ourselves; and let us make another king reign inside it, the son of Tabeel.' This is what the Sovereign Lord Jehovah has said: 'It will not stand, neither will it take place. . . . Unless you people have faith, you will in that case not be of long duration.'"

A Sign of the Conspiracy's Failure

7 Thus, Jehovah foretold the overthrow of the conspirators. At that moment came the time for a divine prophecy of world-rocking importance, for it pointed to the royal Heir of the Kingdom covenant with David. But what led up to that remarkable prophecy? Well, Jehovah was speaking to King Ahaz. He told Ahaz to ask for any miraculous sign that he could think of, and then Jehovah would perform it as an absolute guarantee that God would break up the conspiracy against the house of David. But Ahaz declined to ask for such a sign. What happened next? Isaiah 7:14 tells us: "Therefore Jehovah himself will give you men a sign: Look! The maiden herself will actually become pregnant, and she is giving birth to a son, and she will certainly call his name Immanuel." That name means "With Us Is God." Since Immanuel and Isaiah's two other sons were to serve as signs, the prophet said at Isaiah 8:18: "Look! I and the children whom Jehovah has given me are as signs and as miracles in Israel from Jehovah of armies." So the birth of Immanuel was a reliable sign that all the conspirators and their conspiracies against God's Kingdom

covenant and its Heir would come to nothing!

8 The Bible record does not say who gave birth to the son named Immanuel. It may have been a Jewish maiden who became the second wife of the prophet Isaiah. In any event, the prophecy went on to state that before the boy would grow old enough to distinguish between good and bad, the two kings conspiring against the house of David would come to a disastrous end. (Isaiah 7:15, 16) This proved true. The fact that the identity of Immanuel in the days of Isaiah remains uncertain to us may be in order not to distract the attention of later generations from the Greater Immanuel when he would appear as a miraculous sign from heaven.

9 Of course, in the days of Ahaz, there was only a miniature fulfillment of the sign and of the overthrow of the worldly conspiracy against God's Kingdom covenant. Yet that first fulfillment guaranteed that the sign and the overthrow of world conspiracy would be fulfilled in the major sense in our critical time. Today we are face to face with the greatest world conspiracy of all time. In what sense? In that the nations completely ignore Jehovah's arrangement for bringing in lasting peace, and they even oppose the representatives of the "Prince of Peace." The conspiracy is really against the Heir of the Kingdom covenant, the "Prince of Peace." What, now, about the complete fulfillment of the prophecy? If we discern the sign, then we will appreciate that the fate of

---

7. (a) What led up to the remarkable prophecy of Isaiah 7:14? (b) Of what was the birth of Immanuel a reliable sign, and as what were Isaiah's sons to serve?

8. (a) What did the prophecy at Isaiah 7:15, 16 state about the boy Immanuel, and what was the outcome? (b) Why might it be that the identity of Immanuel in the days of Isaiah remains uncertain?

9. (a) What did the fulfillment of the sign and the overthrow of the conspiracy against the Kingdom covenant guarantee? (b) What is the greatest world conspiracy of all time?

this world conspiracy is a foregone conclusion.

Birth of the "Prince of Peace"

[10] In the prophecy's complete fulfillment, the maiden who produced the child as the sign and Heir of the Kingdom covenant was Mary, a Jewish virgin descended from King David. The angel Gabriel told her that she would give birth to a son who would be named Jesus, that Jehovah God would "give him the throne of David his father," and that there would be "no end of his kingdom." (Luke 1:26-33) The inspired historian Matthew connects the sign of Immanuel with the house of David. We read at Matthew 1:20-23: "Jehovah's angel appeared to [Joseph] in a dream, saying: 'Joseph, son of David, do not be afraid to take Mary your wife home, for that which has been begotten in her is by holy spirit. She will give birth to a son, and you must call his name Jesus, for he will save his people from their sins.' All this actually came about for that to be fulfilled which was spoken by Jehovah through his prophet, saying: 'Look! The virgin will become pregnant and will give birth to a son, and they will call his name Immanuel,' which means, when translated, 'With Us Is God.'"

[11] When and where did this foretold birth of Immanuel take place? All Jewish eyes were turned in the right direction by the words of Micah 5:2, quoted at Matthew 2:6: "And you, O Bethlehem of the land of Judah, are by no means the most insignificant city among the governors of Judah; for out of you will come forth a governing one, who will shepherd my people, Israel." It was in the year 2 B.C.E. in the city of Bethlehem that the "Prince of Peace" was born, and the thrilling prophecy of Isaiah 9:6, 7 began to be fulfilled.

[12] Who of us would not consider it an honor and a joy to become the parent of the one who was to have the title "Prince of Peace"? It therefore brought great glory to the kingly Father of this Prince. In fact, never, no never before, has a human birth been attended by such glorious and dazzling features.

[13] Jehovah's radiant angel appeared to shepherds watching over their flocks by night in the fields outside Bethlehem, and "Jehovah's glory gleamed around them." The angel then announced the birth in fulfillment of divine prophecy, saying: "There was born to you today a Savior, who is Christ the Lord, in David's city." As if that were not glorious enough, there appeared in the skies above a multitude of angels praising the Father of the newborn child and saying as with one voice: "Glory in the heights above to God, and upon earth peace among men of goodwill." How appropriate for the angels to announce at the birth of the destined "Prince of Peace" that there would be divine peace for all men who have God's goodwill!—Luke 2: 8-14.

[14] Long before the birth of the one to be "Prince of Peace," the angels had praised God on a special occasion. That was when, at creation, he founded the earth. (Job 38:4) Have you seen pictures of our earth taken by astronauts from outer space? Then you saw what only the angels had

10. (a) In the complete fulfillment of Isaiah 7: 14, who produced the child as the sign and Heir of the Kingdom covenant? (b) How does the historian Matthew connect the sign of Immanuel with the house of David?
11. When and where did the foretold birth of Immanuel take place?

12, 13. To whom did the birth of the "Prince of Peace" bring great honor, and what glorious and dazzling features attended this birth?
14, 15. (a) Over what events did the heavenly sons of God praise Jehovah? (b) Why could no other childbirth in all human history compare with this one?

seen up until recent times. And how did the angels respond then? Job 38:7 tells us: "The morning stars joyfully cried out together, and all the sons of God began shouting in applause."

15 The grandest birth ever to honor the earth would be no less an event over which the sons of God would unite their melodious voices in a song of praise. Just as an earthly father is congratulated at the birth of his firstborn son, so the celestial Father responsible for this grandest birth ever to take place on earth deserves to be magnified in song by members of his heavenly family. How that exquisitely beautiful concert must have been enjoyed by the divine Being on his becoming for the first time a father in an absolutely new set of circumstances! Never before in all universal history had there been a childbirth to compare with that of the destined "Prince of Peace."

"A Great Light" Shines

16 When Jesus began his public ministry, there was further fulfillment of Isaiah chapter 9. This pertained to its first two verses, which foretold that "a great light" would shine on people "walking in the darkness." The fulfillment of those verses

16. When and how was there further fulfillment of Isaiah chapter 9?

Do You Recall—

☐ What conspiracy developed in the days of King Ahaz?

☐ What was the miniature fulfillment of the sign of Isaiah 7:14?

☐ What was the complete fulfillment of that sign?

☐ Why was the birth of the "Prince of Peace" the grandest childbirth on earth?

---

is explained for us by the inspired historian Matthew at chapter 4, verses 13 through 17: "Further, after leaving Nazareth, [Jesus] came and took up residence in Capernaum beside the sea in the districts of Zebulun and Naphtali, that there might be fulfilled what was spoken through Isaiah the prophet, saying: 'O land of Zebulun and land of Naphtali, along the road of the sea, on the other side of the Jordan, Galilee of the nations! the people sitting in darkness saw a great light, and as for those sitting in a region of deathly shadow, light rose upon them.' From that time on Jesus commenced preaching and saying: 'Repent, you people, for the kingdom of the heavens has drawn near.'"

17 Zebulun and Naphtali lay in the northern extremity of Israel and included the district of Galilee. Naphtali bordered the entire western shore of the Sea of Galilee. So it was by preaching the good news of God's Kingdom in those areas that Jesus, along with his disciples, caused the light to shine to the people there who had so long been sitting in darkness. Jesus said at John 8:12: "I am the light of the world. He that follows me will by no means walk in darkness, but will possess the light of life." Thus, by means of Jesus "those sitting in a region of deathly shadow" were enabled to possess "the light of life" because he gave his life "a ransom in exchange for many." He is the one Jehovah used to shed light on the means whereby men could gain life. —Matthew 4:23; 20:28.

18 This "great light" promising deliverance from death and oppression was not

17. Why could Jesus cause light to shine on the people in Zebulun and Naphtali, and what would this light mean for those sitting in darkness?
18. (a) Why was this "great light" not to be restricted to people of Galilee? (b) What will be considered in the next article?

restricted to men of Galilee. Had not Isaiah foretold that the government's abundance would be without end? And had not Isaiah foretold that the role of the "Prince of Peace" would be a tremendous one? Yes, for Isaiah 9:6, 7 says: "His name will be called Wonderful Counselor, Mighty God, Eternal Father, Prince of Peace. To the abundance of the princely rule and to peace there will be no end." In the following article, we will consider the role of Jesus Christ as "Wonderful Counselor, Mighty God, Eternal Father," as well as "Prince of Peace."

Worldwide Security Under the "Prince of Peace"

"To the abundance of the princely rule and to peace there will be no end, upon the throne of David and upon his kingdom in order to establish it firmly and to sustain it by means of justice and by means of righteousness, from now on and to time indefinite. The very zeal of Jehovah of armies will do this."—ISAIAH 9:7.

JUST as the birth of Jesus, the perfect man-child, was an occasion of extraordinary joy, so the birth of his long-promised Kingdom would be an occasion of immense joy. (Psalm 96:10-12) According to the facts of modern history, that government was placed upon the shoulder of the glorified Jesus in 1914. The existence of the United Nations organization today does not belie that fact. None of the rulers of the 159 members of the UN are of the house of David. Nevertheless, the charter of that world conspiracy assigns to *them* the task of achieving worldwide peace and security for mankind.

2 But Jehovah's covenant for the Kingdom has never been canceled. At Isaiah 9:7 the expression "upon the throne of David" confirms the covenant that God made with David for an endless kingdom. Moreover,

Jehovah has sworn to its successful completion. That Jehovah will hold to this covenant is made clear at Psalm 89:3, 4, 35, 36: "I have concluded a covenant toward my chosen one; I have sworn to David my servant, 'Even to time indefinite I shall firmly establish your seed, and I will build your throne to generation after generation.' Once I have sworn in my holiness, to David I will not tell lies. His seed itself will prove to be even to time indefinite, and his throne as the sun in front of me." That covenant, as well as the title "Prince of Peace," assigns to Jesus Christ the task of bringing in worldwide security.

3 However, the time for Jehovah God to put the government upon the shoulder of his Crown Prince was not to be a year of peace either in heaven above or on earth down below. According to Revelation chapter 12, the birth of his Kingdom would be followed by war in heaven. Satan the Devil and his demons fought against the newly

---

1, 2. (a) The birth of God's Kingdom would be an occasion for what, and when did this birth take place? (b) What does the charter of the United Nations assign to that organization, but what has the Kingdom covenant assigned to Jesus Christ? (c) How do we know that Jehovah will unfailingly hold to the Kingdom covenant?

3. Why was the time for the "Prince of Peace" to begin his rule not a time of peace for heaven or for the earth?

established government, and the newly enthroned King with his holy angels fought those demonic forces. The result was that Satan and his demons were hurled out of the heavens and down to the vicinity of our earth. Consequently, the cry rang out: "Woe for the earth and for the sea, because the Devil has come down to you, having great anger, knowing he has a short period of time." (Revelation 12:12) Since the Devil's debasement, our earth has sadly become the site of unparalleled violence and warfare. How mankind needs the rule of the "Prince of Peace," for it will result in worldwide security!

⁴ According to Isaiah 9:6, other titles, in addition to "Prince of Peace," were to be added to the glorious name of Jesus Christ. One of these titles was to be "Mighty God." He was not to be called almighty God, as though he were a coequal member of a trinity of gods. Even on his resurrection day, he let it be known that he was still inferior to Jehovah. He made an appearance to Mary Magdalene and sent her to inform his anxious disciples that he was returning to their Father and his Father and to their God and his God. (John 20:17) Down to this very day, he continues to lead all creation in the worship of the "God of gods," Jehovah. (Daniel 11:36) Ah, yes, Jesus Christ has a

God and that God is not Jesus himself but is the heavenly Father Jehovah. How grandly the "Prince of Peace" serves as the precursor of universal lasting peace and security!

⁵ For all eternity, the glorified Son of God will continue to lead all intelligent creatures in the worship of this one and true living Deity, Jehovah. The exalted Son of God is eminently qualified for this. Of all creatures in heaven and on earth, the glorified Son of God is the one who has known Jehovah for the longest period of time and that most intimately. At 1 Corinthians 2:11 the apostle Paul says: "For who among men knows the things of a man except the spirit of man that is in him?" So it is in the case of Jesus Christ. Although he was used by

4. Why should the title "Mighty God" not be confused with almighty God?

5. Why is Jesus Christ the most qualified one to lead all intelligent creatures in the worship of the true and living God, Jehovah?

The entire universe will be united in peaceful worship of the Universal Sovereign

kind as "Wonderful Counselor." (Isaiah 9:6) His counsel is always wise, perfect, and infallible. As the Mediator between Jehovah God and those who have been taken into the new covenant, he has been serving indeed as a wonderful counselor for these past 19 centuries. Now, since 1935, "a great crowd" of his "other sheep" has been taking in his wonderful counsel and is getting the finest instruction and guidance. (Revelation 7: 9-17; John 10:16) As an agency for this counseling work, he has in this "conclusion of the system of things" raised up the promised "faithful and discreet slave" class and set it up over all his earthly goods, or royal interests. (Matthew 24:3, 45-47; Luke 12:42-44) The "great crowd" is now receiving spiritual counsel that is indeed wonderful and trustworthy because it is based upon the revealed Word of God.

Jehovah God in the creation of man, it was another thing for him actually to become a man himself, to be surrounded by all the earthly circumstances and experience the feelings of a man firsthand. Thus it is written that "although he was a Son, he learned obedience from the things he suffered" as a man down here on earth. (Hebrews 5:8) He indeed proved worthy to be safely entrusted with 'all authority in heaven and on the earth' and to bear the title "Mighty God." —Matthew 28:18; compare Philippians 2: 5-11.

"Wonderful Counselor" and "Eternal Father"

⁶ For all these potent reasons, God's heavenly Prince is fully able to serve man-

⁷ As a result of their responding to that counsel, Satan the Devil, "the god of this system of things," is no longer a mighty god to us as Jehovah's people. (2 Corinthians 4:4) We have obediently come out of Babylon the Great, the world empire of false religion, and we no longer share in her vicious sins. We have taken our stand immovably upon the side of the One upon

---

6. How has Jesus Christ been serving as "Wonderful Counselor," and how has the "great crowd" benefited from his wonderful counsel?

7. Why is Satan the Devil no longer a mighty god to Jehovah's people?

whose shoulder Jehovah God has laid His government.

8 The title "Eternal Father" is an endearing one. The "great crowd" of the "other sheep" especially appreciate this term. The fatherhood of Satan the Devil has not appealed to them. They shudder as they recall the Jewish religious leaders who opposed Jesus and to whom he said: "You are from your father the Devil, and you wish to do the desires of your father. That one was a manslayer when he began, and he did not stand fast in the truth, because truth is not in him. When he speaks the lie, he speaks according to his own disposition, because he is a liar and the father of the lie." (John 8:44) The "great crowd" has got out from among those spiritual children of Satan the Devil, whose fatherhood over fallen mankind will not be everlasting. Those who allow him to be their spiritual father will perish with him. Utter destruction, symbolized by "the everlasting fire" of Matthew 25:41, awaits the Devil and all humans who do not escape from under his fatherhood. —Matthew 25:41-46.

9 On the other hand, the "great crowd" is getting a foretaste of the fatherhood of the "Eternal Father."* How? By listening to his voice and becoming his "other sheep" and by associating with the remnant of spiritual Israel. This warm family relationship bespeaks peace. Writing under inspiration, the apostle Paul referred to Jehovah at Romans 16:20 as "the God who gives peace." How appropriate, then, that his only-begotten Son should be called "Prince of Peace"! By restoring peace to the entire universe, the "Prince of Peace" will without fail live up to the significance of his great title.

The Royal Government of the "Prince of Peace"

10 After Isaiah foretold the grandest childbirth ever—yes, that of the Son of God who would be honored with the title "Prince of Peace"—the prophet was borne along by Jehovah's spirit to say: "To the abundance of the princely rule and to peace there will be no end . . . The very zeal of Jehovah of armies will do this." —Isaiah 9:7.

11 In saying "the abundance of the princely rule," the prophecy shows that the realm of the "Prince of Peace" will not end short of embracing the entire earth. There will be no boundaries on earth that will limit his domain. It will cover the entire globe. Furthermore, in the Paradise earth to come, there will be no end of peace. Never will there be disorders anywhere. Peace will extend all over the earth and always abound. (Psalm 72:7) Peace in this case means more than the absence of violence and war. It includes justice and righteousness, for Isaiah said that the princely rule would be sustained "by means of justice and by means of righteousness, from now on and to time indefinite." There will be a plentitude of blessings for mankind. And the indefatigable zeal of Jehovah God will accomplish it within our time.

---

* For a detailed discussion of the role of Jesus Christ as the "Eternal Father," see chapter 20 of the book *Worldwide Security Under the "Prince of Peace,"* published by the Watchtower Bible and Tract Society of New York, Inc.

---

8. (a) Why is the title "Eternal Father" especially appealing to the "great crowd"? (b) What will happen to those who allow Satan the Devil to be their spiritual father?
9. How is the "great crowd" getting a foretaste of the fatherhood of the "Eternal Father"?

10, 11. After foretelling the grandest childbirth ever, what did Isaiah go on to say, and what do his words mean?

¹² Even now, this government on the shoulder of the "Prince of Peace" is being represented throughout the earth. The acceptance of his royal heavenly government is spreading rapidly. The remnant of the spirit-begotten disciples of Jesus Christ has been fully gathered out from among the nations. In addition, the "great crowd" is being gathered out from over 200 different lands. There are now 3,229,022 witnesses of Jehovah, and the joyful work of ingathering is not yet completed. This "great crowd" acclaims the government that is upon the shoulder of the "Prince of Peace." Its members are most thankful to be subject to that government and to be envoys of it throughout the whole earth, in association with the "ambassadors substituting for Christ," the anointed remnant.—2 Corinthians 5:20.

Modern-Day Conspiracy to Be Shattered

¹³ The Kingdom envoys also keep peace among themselves. They 'earnestly endeavor to observe the oneness of the spirit in the uniting bond of peace.' (Ephesians 4:3) They do this despite all the turmoil that now rages throughout the earth. National entities inside and outside the United Nations are in reality lined up against the government of the "Prince of Peace." As God views it, the United Nations is a colossal world conspiracy. Why? Because it declares itself set to gain the objectives that God has laid only upon his "Prince of Peace" to gain. And it calls upon the peoples of all nations to support it in establishing worldwide security by man's ef-

forts. It even proclaimed 1986 to be the "International Year of Peace." It thus proves itself to be a conspiracy against the "Prince of Peace" and against Jehovah's covenant with him for the everlasting Kingdom.

¹⁴ For a reason like that, the prophet Isaiah warned King Ahaz and his subjects back there against seeking peace and security by entering into an alliance with the Assyrian World Power. The warning is found at Isaiah 8:9, 10. In poetic grandeur, the prophet warns all of those in opposition to Jehovah and his Kingdom covenant: "Be injurious, O you peoples, and be shattered to pieces; and give ear, all you in distant parts of the earth! Gird yourselves, and be shattered to pieces! Gird yourselves, and be shattered to pieces! Plan out a scheme, and it will be broken up! Speak any word, and it will not stand, for God is with us!"

¹⁵ So let the nations under the prince of this world, Satan the Devil, conspire against the Kingdom covenant and its princely Heir and Ruler. The conspiracy will be shattered to pieces, just as was the conspiracy in the days of King Ahaz. King Rezin of Syria and King Pekah of Israel did not fear Jehovah of armies but conspired against his covenant for the Kingdom. Well, their conspiracy was broken to pieces. Likewise, King Ahaz of Judah did not fear Jehovah but entered into conspiracy with the world power of Assyria. This did not really help Ahaz and bring him peace and security. It brought distress and bondage. Worst of all, it put Ahaz out of favor with Jehovah.

---

12. How is the government that is on the shoulder of the "Prince of Peace" being represented throughout the earth?
13. (a) What do the Kingdom envoys endeavor to do among themselves? (b) How does God view the United Nations?

14. How did the prophet Isaiah warn all those in opposition to Jehovah and his Kingdom covenant?
15. What will happen to the conspiracy against the Kingdom covenant today, as demonstrated by the conspiracy in the days of King Ahaz?

¹⁶ After the death of Ahaz and in the days of his son Hezekiah, Jehovah of armies broke the Assyrian conspiracy against the Kingdom covenant. The king of Assyria was forced to retreat from the land of Judah after Jehovah's angel annihilated 185,000 of his soldiers. The enemy did not get to shoot even one arrow against the city of Jerusalem. (Isaiah 37: 33-36) A like defeat of the present-day world conspiracy against Jehovah's Kingdom covenant and "Prince of Peace" is a certainty, for God is with his Prince Immanuel and with all who acclaim him!

Standing Fearlessly for Jehovah's Universal Sovereignty

¹⁷ The political elements will soon direct their efforts not just against Christendom but against all of Babylon the Great, the entire world empire of false religion, to wipe it out of existence. At that critical juncture, divine protection of Jehovah's people will have to come into play to an extraordinary degree. Egged on by the gory victory over Babylon the Great, the atheistic rulers will viciously turn against those who are on the side of God's government by Jesus Christ. Then Jehovah will use his "Prince of Peace" to fight "the war of the great day of God the Almighty." (Revelation 16:14) Jesus Christ will prove to be an unconquerable Warrior whose government is to experience no decrease. He will prove to be the "Mighty God" under the triumphant almighty God, Jehovah. This "Mighty God" will crown his brilliant career with the victory at Arma-

geddon that will resound without fading at all to time eternal. All hail to that peerless victory!

¹⁸ So, then, onward to greater world prominence than ever before, all you witnesses of Jehovah, with complete trust in your God and his reigning King, the "Prince of Peace"! Display outright fearlessness of the present world conspiracy. By your proclamation everywhere of the message of the Kingdom and its coming victory over the world conspiracy at Armageddon, be all of you for signs and miracles to the honor of Jehovah. When the Devil turns the worldly rulers against us, remember, the victory will be with those who stand true and faithful for the Kingdom of Immanuel, the "Prince of Peace," for "With Us Is God"! (Matthew 1:23; compare Isaiah 8:10.) And let all the angels of heaven and all integrity-keeping mankind on earth say "Amen" to the vindication of Jehovah's sovereignty over all created things in heaven and on earth, with a security never to end!

---

16. How did Jehovah break the Assyrian conspiracy against the Kingdom covenant, and what did this foreshadow for our day?
17. (a) What will the political elements shortly do to Babylon the Great, and what will Jehovah's people need and receive? (b) After disposing of Babylon the Great, what will the atheistic rulers now do, prompting Jehovah to take what action?

18. In the face of the modern-day conspiracy against the Kingdom covenant, what are Jehovah's Witnesses determined to do, and with what outcome?

Questions in Summary

□ How does the title "Mighty God" apply to Jesus Christ?

□ How has Jesus been serving as "Wonderful Counselor"?

□ Whose fatherhood should we seek, and whose should we reject?

□ What in reality is the United Nations?

□ What will happen to today's conspiracy against the Kingdom covenant and its Heir, the "Prince of Peace"?

Kingdom Proclaimers Report

"You Must Be Holy"

GOD'S direction to Christians is to "quit being fashioned according to the desires you formerly had in your ignorance, but, in accord with the Holy One who called you, do you also become holy yourselves in all your conduct, because it is written: 'You must be holy, because I am holy.'" (1 Peter 1:14-16) Such holy conduct often is a good witness to others. (1 Peter 2:12) All over the earth, as the following experiences show, sincere persons are making the necessary changes to bring their conduct into harmony with this counsel.

□ In Ecuador a man stopped his Bible study when the Witness who studied with him was disfellowshipped for immorality.

"For I am Jehovah your God; and you must sanctify yourselves and you must prove yourselves holy, because I am holy."
—Leviticus 11:44.

His spiritual need led him to investigate other religions. He settled for the Evangelist religion and advanced to the point of becoming a pastor of his own church. However, his conscience bothered him, as he was not married to the woman with whom he was living. When he consulted with pastors of other churches, they assured him that this was no problem. However, he felt that this was not right, as the very Witness who studied with him was disfellowshipped for immorality. He could not understand why he was not reproved by his own church. Later, his live-in companion came in contact with Jehovah's Witnesses and began to study with them. The man began to study along with her. Both of them are now attending the meetings, progressing in knowledge of Bible principles, and taking steps to get married so they can serve Jehovah in a clean and acceptable way.

□ In another experience from Ecuador, a Witness relates: "In February 1984, a middle-aged lady asked us to study with her." What motivated this request? This lady's brother had become one of Jehovah's Witnesses, and she had been very impressed by his fine conduct. During the second Bible study, they touched on the subject of smoking, which was one of the lady's problems. However, at the next study a week later she proudly announced that since learning the Bible's viewpoint on smoking she had not touched a cigarette! She had another problem—her house was full of religious images. But on reading Deuteronomy 7:26, which says: "And you must not bring a detestable thing into your house . . . It is something devoted to destruction," she proceeded to burn all of them.

From that time forward, she began attending meetings and has not missed one since. Shortly after that, she was able to overcome her most difficult obstacle—she broke off an immoral relationship with a married man. Now, for the first time in her life, she was able to experience genuine happiness, as she was now able to serve Jehovah with a clean conscience. She was baptized in April 1985 and at the time was conducting four Bible studies with others. Her next goal is to become a pioneer, as she feels this is the

---

"Let us cleanse ourselves of every defilement of flesh and spirit."
—2 Corinthians 7:1.

---

best way that she can show her appreciation to Jehovah, who has liberated her from "a vain and immoral life."

□ The fine results of godly conduct were seen in a girls' boarding school in Kenya, where the good conduct of a Witness became noticeable in an outstanding way. Nine male teachers were hired by the school, including one of Jehovah's Witnesses. But one by one they had to be dismissed for sexual immorality with the students. After a while, only one out of the nine was left—the teacher who was one of Jehovah's Witnesses!

Indeed, it is possible for people who have lived immoral lives to change. When we become 'holy in all our conduct,' we not only provide a fine witness to others but also make Jehovah's heart glad. Thus, we put ourselves in line for everlasting life. —Proverbs 27:11.

Jehovah Is Guarding Us

WHACK! Down came the book on my head. This was my first contact with the Bible, and it was at the hand of a Catholic priest. Why? Because of a question I had asked.

The priest was teaching catechism and religion and was trying to encourage us boys to take up the priesthood. In his effort to do this, he used the scripture at 1 Thessalonians 4:17, where it speaks of those 'being caught away in the clouds to meet the Lord in the air.'

I was always full of questions, so I asked: "Why do you say priests go straight to heaven, when, as the Creed says, Jesus had to go to hell?" (Acts 2:31) That was when the Bible came down on my head.

A Desire to Know

But I sincerely wanted answers. I was very much inclined to worship God, even as a young boy. I used to enter to pray in almost every church I passed. Yet I wasn't satisfied. Somehow I always got angry at things I saw, such as the gross idolatry of some of the people or the behavior of some priests.

When I was only about eight years old, I read my first book. It was entitled *The Christianization of Brazil*. I was shocked. To me it seemed like a murder story, the murder of Indians in the name of religion. Learning about such things was enough to change my mind about a lot of things.

This all happened back in the 1920's. I was born in Vienna, Austria, August 19, 1919, the only child of my parents. When I was about six, my father, an electrical engineer, accepted a job in northern Czechoslovakia, in the German-speaking section of Sudetenland. So my family moved there, and finally to a small town called Warnsdorf.

I became very disillusioned with the Catholic Church. One day, quite bitter because of the punishment I had again received from the priest, I cried on the way home from school. While walking through some fields, I thought that it was not possible that there was a God, in view of the many crooked things I had seen and had been taught.

Then the song of birds came through, and I noticed the flowers, the butterflies, and all the beauty of creation. And it dawned on me that there must be a loving God but that the so-called men of God maybe were not such at all. And perhaps God had given up on humanity. That was when I said my first real, conscious prayer, asking God to help me to get to know him if he ever again would become interested in man. That was in 1928.

About a month later my mother traveled to a family reunion in Vienna; it was her mother's 60th birthday. There my mother saw her brother, Richard Tautz, who at the time lived in Maribor, Yugoslavia. He had recently become one of the Bible Students, as Jehovah's Witnesses were then called. Mother returned home all excited with the new Bible truths she had learned. What she related made sense to me. It seemed that Jehovah's hand was at work. —Psalm 121:5.

Practicing What I Had Learned

Later, Bible Students came over from Germany, and the preaching got under

As related by Erich Kattner

...vay in our area. Some months later, regular meetings began to be held in a neighboring town in Germany, and we walked the few miles across the border to attend them. It was at this time that I met Otto Estelmann, with whom I worked closely in later years.

In 1932 our family moved to Bratislava, the capital of Slovakia, about 45 miles (72 km) from Vienna. There were no other Witnesses there at that time. I decided I had to get active in the preaching work. So I chose what I thought was the toughest territory, an apartment-house project occupied mostly by families of government officials. Four languages were then spoken in Bratislava: Slovak, Czech, German, and Hungarian.

Carrying cards that had a little sermon printed on them in four languages, I went alone ringing bells on the apartment doors. Sometimes my father, who had not as yet become a Witness, would stand on the other side of the street, watching me and shaking his head. Shortly afterward he also took a firm stand for Jehovah.

On February 15, 1935, at a special meeting with a traveling overseer in our home, I, along with others, was baptized in a bathtub. I graduated from business school that year and was given an attractive job offer, but at the same time I was invited to work at the Watch Tower Society's branch office in Prague, Czechoslovakia. After a serious talk with my parents, we took the matter to Jehovah in prayer. So, shortly before turning 16, I entered the full-time service on June 1, 1935.

Serving in Difficult Times

At the Society's office in Prague, I learned to operate the typesetting machines and to compose type into pages. We produced tracts for our brothers in Germany, who were under ban by Hitler, and also produced *The Watchtower* in several languages. However, these were difficult times for our work in Europe, and finally the authorities closed our branch in December 1938.

I returned home to Bratislava, where the government had passed into the hands of Nazi sympathizers, and I worked unobtrusively for two months doing house-to-house preaching. About this time the Central European Office of the Watch Tower Society in Bern, Switzerland, wrote me that if I was willing to serve as a pioneer anywhere in the world, I should come to Bern.

I accepted the invitation and left home. It was the last time I saw my father, and it would be 30 years before I would see my mother again. But Jehovah guarded all three of us through the many difficulties that followed. For example, I learned later that the infamous Hlinka Guarda (a kind of Slovakian SS) was after me the day I left Bratislava. And on the trip, when Nazi agents learned that I was one of Jehovah's Witnesses, they tried to get me arrested at the borders of Yugoslavia and Italy. But Jehovah kept guarding me. —Psalm 48:14; 61:3.

In Bern I learned that I would be sent to Shanghai, China, but later this assignment was changed to Brazil. I worked at the branch in Bern until I received my visa for Brazil. By this time troubles in Europe were increasing. Borders were being closed, so in August 1939 the Society urged me to get into France. The Brazilian merchant ship *Siqueira Campos* was leaving from Le Havre, France, August 31, and I was to be on it. Just four hours before World War II broke out, the ship sailed.

The dozen or so passengers I traveled with in the second-class cabin section, I later learned, were all Nazi agents. They did not like my preaching at all. Several times they tried to get me off the ship. In Vigo, Spain, the friendly captain warned me not to go ashore while there. In Lisbon, Portugal, the Nazi agents falsified the departure time of the ship on the notice board so that I would be stranded there. But again Jehovah was guarding me. (Psalm 121:3) I arrived in Santos, Brazil, on the evening of September 24, 1939. The next day I traveled up to São Paulo, where the Society's office was located.

Serving in Brazil

In September 1939 there were only 127 Witnesses in Brazil, which then had a population of about 41 million people. After about a week in São Paulo, I left for my pioneer assignment in the southernmost state, Rio Grande do Sul. I was to stay with some German-speaking Witnesses of Polish descent who lived in a remote jungle area.

The train trip took four days. The end of the line was Giruá, which resembled a wild West town of the early days of North America. From Giruá I still had some 20 miles (32 km) to go into the jungle to get to where the Witnesses lived. A delivery truck gave me a ride, leaving me off on a dirt road. Traveling on by foot for about a mile through virgin forest and wading through a small stream, I finally arrived.

Because of the remoteness of the area my pioneer service was restricted to times when someone could take me along on a small horsedrawn wagon. Reaching people involved traveling for days, sleeping on dirt roads to avoid snakes or under the wagon when it rained. We also preached in such towns as Cruz Alta.

In 1940 the Society reassigned me to Pôrto Alegre, the capital of the state of Rio Grande do Sul. There I joined my childhood friend Otto Estelmann, who had also been assigned to Brazil. The authorities there seemed to be Nazi sympathizers. We were arrested and given the choice of signing a paper renouncing our faith or leaving on the evening train for confinement at the Uruguayan border. We were on the train that evening.

Under Restriction

There on the border we spent close to two years under house arrest. But again Jehovah came to our aid. Some Jewish businessmen offered their help. As a result, instead of being kept in jail, I was permitted to do secular work, but we were kept under close surveillance. We were not able to make contact with the Society's branch office.

However, one day on the street we met a pioneer brother from Europe who had been assigned to Uruguay. He just happened to be visiting the border. What a reunion! He gave us a German Bible and an English *Watchtower*. That is when I really started studying English.

Then, on August 22, 1942, Brazil declared war on Germany and Italy, which meant a change in our situation. We were brought back to Pôrto Alegre, and after some questioning, I was released. Afterward, I met some young Witnesses whom I had known earlier in the jungle area where I had first been assigned. So I was able to make contact with the branch office, and I again began pioneering. Four of these youths joined me in the pioneer work, and we found people who accepted the Kingdom message, some of whom are still preaching.

The new authorities were favorable toward us, so in 1943 we arranged for the first small assembly in Pôrto Alegre. The total attendance was 50, almost half of them plainclothes policemen. A year later, in 1944, we arranged for another assembly. After that I was called to serve at the Society's branch office, which had been moved from São Paulo to Rio de Janeiro.

N. H. Knorr speaking, with Erich Kattner interpreting, in São Paulo, Brazil, 1945

Gilead and Afterward

In 1950 I was invited to attend the 16th class of the Watchtower Bible School of Gilead at South Lansing, New York. After graduation in February 1951, I received a temporary special pioneer assignment with the South Bronx, New York, Congregation, but later I returned to Brazil.

For about a year and a half I served as a traveling representative of the Society, both as a district overseer and as a circuit overseer. Then, in February 1953, I was called back to the branch office in Rio de Janeiro and assigned to do translation work. Later, from September 1961 to September 1963, I had the privilege of working on a special translation assignment at the Society's headquarters in Brooklyn, New York. While there, I contacted a couple whom I had known in Brazil. The husband agreed to study with me in the hotel where they were staying and became convinced of the truth.

A few months later, when we were back in Brazil, I contacted him again. But he was somewhat complacent. So I told him:

"I'm telling you that unless you act on what you know, you're in trouble"

"Look, Paul, you are a civil engineer. But suppose I were the civil engineer and told you that the roof was ready to fall in on you. What would you do? Well, as a Bible 'engineer,' I am telling you that unless you act on what you know, you're in trouble."

In a short time he was baptized and has been serving as a Christian elder for some years. He was also very instrumental in the construction of the large new branch facilities in Cesário Lange, São Paulo, where 480 of us now work to serve the spiritual needs of the growing number of Witnesses in Brazil.

Continued Increases

In 1945 we had the first visit of the Watch Tower Society's president, Nathan H. Knorr, and also of the then vice president, Frederick Franz. A convention was arranged in the Pacaembu gymnasium in São Paulo City, and I served as translator for the visiting brothers. Our peak attendance was 765.

I remember Brother Knorr looking at the big adjoining stadium and wondering if we would ever fill it. Well, we did in December 1973, when 94,586 packed out Pacaembu Stadium at the "Divine Victory" Convention. This was topped in August 1985 at the "Integrity Keepers" Convention in the Morumbi Stadium, São Paulo City, where 162,941 were present. And simultaneously, another 86,410 were in attendance at a stadium in Rio de Janeiro. Later, 23 additional gatherings raised the total attendance for the "Integrity Keepers" Conventions in Brazil to 389,387!

Over the years, I have been privileged to translate for visiting speakers from the Brooklyn, New York, headquarters. Recently one of them, while he was walking along with me and noting the many persons with whom I had studied over the years coming up to greet me, jokingly said: "I never saw a single man with so many children."

Real highlights in my life have also been the international conventions that I have been able to attend in other countries. At the Nuremberg convention in 1969, I saw my mother for the first time in 30 years. She died faithful in 1973. Father was not allowed to travel out of the country for the convention, and I never did see him again after leaving home. In 1978 I had the privilege of giving the public talk at the international convention in Vienna, Austria, the first big convention I attended in the city of my birth.

During these many years in Brazil, I have witnessed that Jehovah is the One "who makes it grow." (1 Corinthians 3:7) In 1948 we passed the 1,000-publisher mark. After that, the number of publishers jumped to 12,992 in 1958 and to 60,139 in 1970. Instead of the 127 Kingdom publishers we had in September 1939, there were 196,948 in August 1986. Certainly, the 'small one has become a mighty nation' also in this country.—Isaiah 60:22.

But the population of Brazil has also increased, from 41 million in 1939 to more than 135 million now. So we still have a vast field for activity. It has been my joy personally to have been involved in the marvelous increases Jehovah has given, and how thrilling it has been! So I can recommend to anyone who wants to serve Jehovah full-time: Go ahead! Don't be afraid of what might come up, for "Jehovah himself will guard your going out and your coming in."—Psalm 121:7, 8.

Do You Always Get the Point?

THE older brother was furiously angry. The object of his rage was his younger brother. And its cause? His brother had been accorded recognition that he himself had been denied. As his anger grew, a wise acquaintance counseled him to control his hurt feelings. Otherwise something bad would happen. But the man ignored the good advice. Instead, tragically, he killed his younger brother.

That man was Cain, eldest son of our first parents, Adam and Eve. Cain killed his younger brother Abel when Jehovah accepted Abel's sacrifice and rejected Cain's. The wise acquaintance was none other than Jehovah God, who offered the loving counsel that Cain rejected. As a result, murder invaded the fledgling human family, and Cain was sentenced to live the rest of his long life as a rejected outcast. What a sad result from failing to get the point of counsel!—Genesis 4: 3-16.

Many centuries after Cain, King David of Israel committed adultery with Bathsheba, the wife of Uriah the Hittite, and the woman came to be pregnant. David tried to handle the problem by urging Uriah to go in to his wife. When he refused, David arranged for Uriah to die on the battlefield and then married Bathsheba to prevent her having to die as an adulteress. A prophet of God came to David and brought to his attention the seriousness of what he had done. David soon grasped the point of the counsel. Thus, although for the rest of his life he suffered the consequences of that crime, Jehovah accepted his heartfelt repentance. —2 Samuel 11:1–12:14.

These two historical examples show the importance of listening to counsel. It can make the difference between success and failure, happiness and sorrow, even life and death. No wonder the Bible says: "The way of the foolish one is right in his own eyes, but the one listening to counsel is wise." (Proverbs 12:15) Yet it is not easy to listen to counsel. Why is this? How can we develop the good attitude of King David in this regard and avoid the bad example of Cain?

Humility Helps

Quite often people find it hard to listen to counsel because they cannot accept the fact that they need help. Or if they do, they cannot see why they should accept counsel from *this* person. Really, this is pride, and a little reasoning can help to overcome it. For example, Paul said: "All have sinned and fall short of the glory of God." (Romans 3:23) That tells us that everyone needs counsel from time to time. It also tells us that even the ones who offer us counsel have shortcomings. No one is exempt. So do not let another person's perceived shortcomings prevent you from accepting any help that he may be in a position to give.

Jesus stressed the need to fight pride when he told his followers: "Unless you turn around and become as young children, you will by no means enter into the kingdom of the heavens." (Matthew 18:3) Young children get a sense of security when their parents counsel and guide them. Do you feel the same way when someone counsels you, realizing that such counsel proves that one's love and concern for you? (Hebrews 12:6) King David, whose humble willingness to accept counsel opened the way for Jehovah to accept his repentance, was moved to write: "Should the righteous one strike me, it would be a loving-kindness; and should he reprove me, it would be oil upon the head." —Psalm 141:5.

Such a meek attitude can help us when the counsel we receive touches those areas where there are no set rules. For example, if we are counseled that our grooming or manner of dress is stumbling some in the congregation, it may take real humility to get the point. Nevertheless, doing so would be following the apostle Paul's admonition: "Let each one keep seeking, not his own advantage, but that of the other person."—1 Corinthians 10:24.

Happily, Jehovah has provided the Bible, which abounds with the finest of counsel. In fact, the word "counsel" in its various forms is found therein more than 170 times. Also, he provides loving shepherds to assist us in applying this counsel. The family arrangement is another provision from Jehovah to render loving assistance by means of counsel from parents who are aware of their responsibilities. Let us always humbly listen to such counsel.

"Be Swift About Hearing"

James 1:19 advises: "Every man must be swift about hearing, slow about speaking, slow about wrath." This is particularly true when we are receiving counsel. Why? For one thing, is it not true that we are often aware of our own shortcomings, and it does not come as a complete surprise when a concerned friend points them out and offers counsel? It surely makes it easier for all concerned if we quickly discern what he is trying to say and humbly accept the loving help.

When a friend approaches us with counsel, we should remember that he or she may be quite nervous. It is not easy to give counsel. Perhaps the would-be counselor has given much thought to the words or approach to be used. An elder may begin the conversation by commending us for

In Our Next Issue

- God's Wisdom —Can You See It?

- Increase Your Peace Through Accurate Knowledge

- Traditional Medicine in Africa —Compatible With Christianity?

some area of Christian service in which we have been doing well. But that should not cause us to question his motives when he goes on to offer counsel. The one offering counsel may speak in an indirect way at first, trying not to be tactless or blunt. Our being discerning enough to get the point quickly will help the counselor in his task and perhaps spare us hurt feelings.

Sometimes the counselor may use an example or an illustration to help us get the point. One young man had not yet become a serious wrongdoer, but he was on an errant course. In reasoning with him, an older Christian man picked up a ruler that was lying on the desk. Flexing the ruler in his hands, he asked: "If I bend a ruler like this, can I still measure a straight line with it?" The young man got the point. He had been trying to bend the rules to fit his own desires. The illustration helped him to follow the wise advice of Proverbs 19:20: "Listen to counsel and accept discipline."

Recognize Indirect Counsel

Such discernment may help us to benefit from indirect counsel, even without the intervention of someone else. This happened in the case of a young man in Portugal. He was studying the Bible and obtained a copy of the book *Your Youth —Getting the Best out of It.* Just a few days later, he revealed that he had already read the book three times and been helped by it. In what way? Here is what the youth said:

"I had no real hope for the future, but chapter 2 ["Why You Can Look to the Future With Confidence"] has given my life meaning. Also, I have masturbated for some years now; no one ever told me this was displeasing to God as well as harmful to me. After reading chapter 5 ["Masturbation and Homosexuality"], I made a decision to discontinue this practice. Chap-

ter 7 ["Your Clothes and Appearance Talk —About *You*"] helped me to value my personal appearance, and as you can see, I've already had a haircut."

He continued: "For years I've smoked. Chapter 15 ["Drugs—Key to Real Living?"] straightened me out on that score. I have prayed to Jehovah, and since Sunday I've not smoked another cigarette. You know, for some time I have been having sexual relations with my girlfriend, but chapter 18 ["Does Sexual Morality Make Sense?"] brought to my attention God's point of view on this subject. I already spoke with her about this matter, and she decided to end our relationship."

What a joy it is to see such changes in so short a time in the life of a young person! What made it possible? The fact that he was able to recognize what he read as counsel that applied to him personally.

Heeding Counsel Brings Benefits

Counsel—whether it comes to us indirectly through the Bible or Bible literature, or directly from a friend—can be beneficial. This is seen in the experience of a father who sought help from spiritually older men in his congregation because his 18-year-old son was not responding to his disciplinary efforts. The Christian elders lovingly reasoned with the father, who had a zeal for serving God but apparently needed more balance in dealing with his family.

Paul's words were read to him: "And you, fathers, do not be irritating your children, but go on bringing them up in the discipline and mental-regulating of Jehovah." (Ephesians 6:4) The father was asked to reflect: Had the way he had tried to encourage his son, even though he was well meaning, actually been irritating the boy? Had it been a case of expecting the son to fall in line with the father's own zeal for Christian meetings and service without trying to implant a love of such things in his heart? Had he helped his son to 'learn to fear Jehovah his God'?—Deuteronomy 31:12, 13.

The father listened to the counsel and applied it. The result? His 18-year-old son is now attending Christian meetings, and the father is conducting a weekly Bible study with him. And as the father commented, "We now have a much better father-son relationship." Yes, both father and son got the point of the counsel.

There is no doubt that we all make mistakes and need counsel from time to time. (Proverbs 24:6) If we get the point and heed wise counsel, we will enjoy many blessings. Among them will be the most precious blessing of all: cultivating and maintaining a meaningful, personal relationship with our loving heavenly Father, Jehovah. Thus, we will echo the words of King David: "I shall bless Jehovah, who has given me advice."—Psalm 16:7.

A "Very Rich Encounter"

DURING the summer of 1984, Gerard, a young man from France, set out on a six-month adventure—a bicycle tour through the United States and Canada. The majestic Rocky Mountains thrilled him, the peaceful parks calmed him, but the scene he saw in Montmagny, Quebec, Canada, impressed him the most; it changed the course of his life.

On Sunday, September 16, Gerard was peddling through Montmagny when he noticed a long line of cars parked alongside the road. Next, he saw hundreds of people milling around a construction site. "What's happening here?" he asked one of the workers who was directing the traffic. Although the man was busy, he took time out to explain to Gerard that all these workers were Jehovah's Witnesses using their weekend to build a hall for their religious meetings. Unknown to Gerard, he had arrived during the final hectic hours of a two-day Kingdom Hall project. He was impressed by all he saw and heard. That night he wrote in his diary: "In the evening I met Jehovah's Witnesses. They have built a house in two days. There were more than 1,000 of them. Very rich encounter."

Shortly thereafter Gerard returned to France. Two years later, on July 26,

1986, he mailed a letter to the Kingdom Hall of Jehovah's Witnesses in Montmagny. He wrote:

'Do you still remember talking to a cyclist from France during the second day of your Kingdom Hall building project? That day the traffic controller sowed a seed. Some months later the Witnesses visited me in France, and I accepted the offer to study the Bible with them. Since I'm from a staunch Catholic family, the study was not easy. But Jehovah made the seed grow. Two weeks ago I was baptized at a convention in Nantes. I thank Jehovah for allowing me to find the truth, and I am grateful for all that the brother taught me that Sunday, September 16, 1984. Brotherly greetings from an adventurer converted to the truth.'

What joy the congregation in Montmagny felt after hearing Gerard's letter read in their Kingdom Hall! All those who helped in building the hall experienced the truthfulness of Solomon's words: "Send out your bread upon the surface of the waters, for in the course of many days you will find it again." (Ecclesiastes 11:1) Yes, the good effects of Kingdom Hall projects are long lasting and far reaching in many ways.

Questions From Readers

■ Is it fitting for a Christian to permit an autopsy on a relative?

The Bible does not directly comment on autopsy, but there are some relevant Biblical thoughts that a Christian can consider. Then a personal decision can be made in the light of such texts and the particulars of the given situation.

An autopsy is a surgical (dissection) examination of a corpse in order to determine the cause of death. It can also provide information about the effects or mechanism of disease. Some religions' view of autopsies has been affected by unscriptural teachings. For example, a Catholic encyclopedia states: "The body of the deceased should be treated reverently as the former abode of his soul . . . It is destined to rise with its soul, during the general resurrection, into eternal life . . . There may be an interval between medical death and the soul's departure." However, the Bible shows that when a person (a living soul) dies, he becomes a dead soul. (Genesis 2:7; 7: 21-23; Leviticus 21:1, 11) What about his body? Regarding both "the sons of mankind" and the "beasts," we read: "They have all come to be from the dust, and they are all returning to the dust." (Ecclesiastes 3:18-20) In the resurrection, God will not raise the body that has long since become mere dust, but he will provide a body as it pleases him. —See 1 Corinthians 15:38, 47, 48.

Another aspect of the Biblical view of the dead can be considered in connection with autopsy. God commanded Israel: "You must not make cuts in your flesh for a deceased soul, and you must not put tattoo marking upon yourselves. I am Jehovah." (Leviticus 19:28; Deuteronomy 14:1, 2; Jeremiah 47:5; Micah 5:1) Yes, God's people were not to imitate surrounding nations in mutilating their flesh as a sign of grief over the dead nor for other false religious reasons. This command must also have encouraged the Israelites to manifest respect for their bodies as God's creations.—Psalm 100:3; 139: 14; Job 10:8.

Christians likewise should have due respect for their lives and bodies, which they have dedicated to God. (Romans 12:1) Some have concluded that this respectful view of the body should shape their thinking about autopsies. They have felt that unless there was some compelling reason otherwise, they would prefer that the body of a beloved relative not be subjected to a postmortem dissection. They may know that in some places blood taken from cadavers has been used for transfusions or other purposes, of which they would want no part.*

Why, then, have some Christians permitted autopsies? They realize that the Bible does not pointedly comment on this medical procedure. They may also have noted that the Israelites in Egypt permitted the Egyptian physicians to embalm Jacob and Joseph, which likely involved surgical steps to remove internal organs. (Genesis 50:2, 3, 26) In certain cases today, the law of the land requires that an autopsy be performed. For example, if a young, healthy person dies of no apparent cause, a postmortem may be mandatory. Obviously, when the law demands an autopsy, Christians bear in mind the counsel to "be in subjection to the superior authorities."—Romans 13:1, 7; Matthew 22:21.

Even in the case of a person who had been under a doctor's care, and thus the likely cause of death is known, an autopsy may provide helpful information. Surviving children may want to know the precise cause so as to increase information about their family's medical history. Such information could affect their own future life pattern or treatment. There are other reasons, too, why some have permitted an autopsy. A postmortem report documented by tissue studies might enable a family to qualify for survivors' benefits, such as by providing proof of black-lung disease associated with coal mining. Some have even felt that an autopsy could increase their peace of mind by helping them understand what did or did not cause a loved one's death. Persons outside the family might also be involved. The relatives might sincerely feel that permitting an autopsy might help a physician to understand the course of a disease, and thus he might be better equipped to treat others.

Consequently, it is appropriate for Christians to manifest respect for their bodies, but there are other factors that they can consider in deciding whether to permit an autopsy in a particular situation.

---

* Concerning possible use of human body parts for transplant purposes, see The Watchtower of March 15, 1980, page 31.

APRIL 12 MEMORIAL

"Also, he took a loaf, gave thanks, broke it, and gave it to them, saying: 'This means my body which is to be given in your behalf. Keep doing this in remembrance of me.' Also, the cup in the same way after they had the evening meal, he saying: 'This cup means the new covenant by virtue of my blood, which is to be poured out in your behalf.'"—Luke 22:19, 20.

Jehovah's Witnesses invite you to be present for the observation of this very important Memorial celebration. This year the date on our calendar that corresponds to the day Jesus died is Sunday, April 12, after sunset. You can attend on that evening at the Kingdom Hall nearest your home. Check with Jehovah's Witnesses locally for the exact time.

April 15, 1987

The Watchtower

Announcing Jehovah's Kingdom

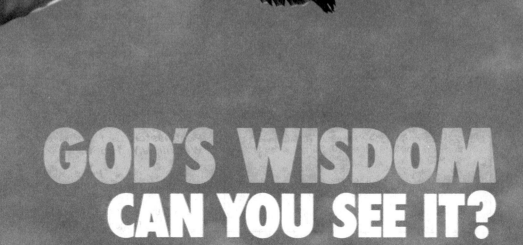

GOD'S WISDOM
CAN YOU SEE IT?

April 15, 1987
Vol. 108, No. 8

In This Issue

THE PURPOSE OF "THE WATCHTOWER" is to exalt Jehovah God as the Sovereign of the universe. It keeps watch on world events as they fulfill Bible prophecy. It comforts all peoples with the good news that God's Kingdom will soon destroy those who oppress their fellowmen and that it will turn the earth into a paradise. It encourages faith in the now-reigning King, Jesus Christ, whose shed blood opens the way for mankind to gain eternal life. "The Watchtower," published by Jehovah's Witnesses continuously since 1879, is nonpolitical. It adheres to the Bible as its authority.

"WATCHTOWER" STUDIES FOR THE WEEKS

May 24: Gaining Peace With God Through Dedication and Baptism. Page 10. Songs to Be Used: 13, 202.

May 31: Increase Your Peace Through Accurate Knowledge. Page 15. Songs to Be Used: 135, 91.

Average Printing Each Issue: 12,315,000

Now Published in 103 Languages

SEMIMONTHLY LANGUAGES AVAILABLE BY MAIL
Afrikaans, Arabic, Cebuano, Chichewa, Chinese, Cibemba, Danish,* Dutch,* Efik, English,* Finnish,* French,* German,* Greek,* Hiligaynon, Igbo, Iloko, Italian,* Japanese,* Korean, Lingala, Malagasy, Maltese, Norwegian, Portuguese,* Russian, Sepedi, Sesotho, Shona, Spanish,* Swahili, Swedish,* Tagalog, Thai, Tsonga, Tswana, Xhosa, Yoruba, Zulu

MONTHLY LANGUAGES AVAILABLE BY MAIL
Armenian, Bengali, Bicol, Bulgarian, Croatian, Czech, Ewe, Fijian, Ga, Greenlandic, Gujarati, Gun, Hausa, Hebrew, Hindi, Hiri Motu, Hungarian, Icelandic, Kannada, Malayalam, Marathi, New Guinea Pidgin, Pangasinan, Papiamento, Polish, Rarotongan, Romanian, Samar-Leyte, Samoan, Sango, Serbian, Silozi, Sinhalese, Slovenian, Solomon Islands-Pidgin, Tahitian, Tamil, Telugu, Tongan, Tshiluba, Turkish, Twi, Ukrainian, Urdu, Venda, Vietnamese

* Study articles also available in large-print edition.

Watch Tower Society offices	Yearly subscription for the above.	
	Semimonthly Languages	Monthly Languages
America, U.S., Watchtower, Wallkill, N.Y. 12589	$4.00	$2.00
Australia, Box 280, Ingleburn, N.S.W. 2565	A$7.00	A$3.50
Canada, Box 4100, Halton Hills, Ontario L7G 4Y4	$5.50	$2.75
England, The Ridgeway, London NW7 1RN	£5.00	£2.50
Ireland, 29A Jamestown Road, Finglas, Dublin 11	IRE6.00	IRE3.00
New Zealand, P.O. Box 142, Manurewa	NZ$15.00	NZ$7.50
Nigeria, PMB 001, Shomolu, Lagos State	N8.00	N4.00
Philippines, P.O. Box 2044, Manila 2800	₱60.00	₱30.00
South Africa, Private Bag 2067, Krugersdorp, 1740	R6,50	R3,25

Remittances should be sent to the office in your country or to Watchtower, Wallkill, N.Y. 12589, U.S.A.

Changes of address should reach us 30 days before your moving date. Give us your old and new address (if possible, your old address label).

20 cents (U.S.) a copy

The Bible translation used is the "New World Translation of the Holy Scriptures," unless otherwise indicated.

The Watchtower (ISSN 0043-1087) is published semimonthly for $4.00 (U.S.) per year by Watch Tower Bible and Tract Society of Pennsylvania, 25 Columbia Heights, Brooklyn, N.Y. 11201. Second-class postage paid at Brooklyn, N.Y., and at additional mailing offices.

Postmaster: Send address changes to Watchtower, **Wallkill, N.Y. 12589.**

Published by
**Watch Tower Bible and Tract Society
of Pennsylvania**

25 Columbia Heights, Brooklyn, N.Y. 11201, U.S.A.

Frederick W. Franz, President

God's Wisdom
Can You See It?

VISUALIZE the court of an ancient king. There, arrayed in royal robes, the monarch sits on a throne of splendor as he presides. He is renowned not only for his wealth but also for his wisdom. His court attendants are organized to perfection. The scene of magnificence is breathtaking. Behold: King Solomon! —1 Kings 10:1-9, 18-20.

Listen, now, to the man recognized as the Great Teacher, Jesus Christ: "On the matter of clothing, why are you anxious? Take a lesson from the lilies of the field, how they are growing; they do not toil, nor do they spin; but I say to you that not even Solomon in all his glory was arrayed as one of these."—Matthew 6:28, 29.

What did Jesus mean by that? Well, he was certainly giving counsel about not being materialistic. But could his words about Solomon be literally true? Remember, Jesus used true-to-life illustrations. So Solomon's designers and craftsmen, though competent, could not equal the designs, the blending of colors, the symmetry of "the lilies of the field" framed in their natural surroundings.

Jehovah's Wisdom Made Manifest

Even a casual examination of flowers may cause you to endorse Jesus' statement. We do not know just what variety of lily Jesus may have had in mind, but flowers abound in most parts of the earth. Look carefully at a flower, any flower: a lily, a rose, an orchid. What delicate shades of color and intricate designs you see, a blending of the sepals, the leaves, and other parts of the flower's body. Can you see the silent but strong proof that a Great Designer of infinite wisdom and imagination is behind this beautiful handiwork? Not only do our eyes revel in their beauty but our nostrils take in their fragrant perfumes in the air we breathe.

The apostle Paul observed that Jehovah God's "invisible qualities are clearly seen from the world's creation onward, because they are perceived by the things made." (Romans 1:20) However, God created more than flowers to robe the earth; he made countless shrubs and trees, all of which form a practical, yet handsomely verdant, kingdom. If you could visit the Humboldt National Forest in California, U.S.A., you would find a giant redwood that is believed to be the tallest tree in the world. If you could stand at its foot and gaze up at its height of over 360 feet (110 m), would you not silently praise the One who knew how to make such a tree?

The Instinctive Wisdom of Animals

On land and sea there are animals, small and great, that impress us with God's wisdom. Apparently each serves some purpose of the Creator. Wise King Solomon counseled: "Go to the ant, you lazy one; see its ways and become wise." (Proverbs 6:6) Those who have observed the ant marvel at its organizing ability. Ants are not isolationists; they live in communities. Some are farmers and harvest seeds. In the tropics you see some ants busily nipping off pieces of leaves to carry to their nests. How do they know to do this? Agur, one of the writers of the book of Proverbs, answers that the ant is "instinctively wise." Who made it that way? Jehovah, the Producer of heaven and earth. —Proverbs 30:24, 25.

Yes, the animal creation has instinctive wisdom. It is very apparent in the migration of birds. You may have heard about the migration of the Capistrano swallows. At a certain time each year, they travel thousands of miles from their wintering grounds in South America to a mission at San Juan Capistrano, California, U.S.A. Instinctively and unerringly they come to the same place at the same time in March.

As to the vast sea, the psalmist states: "How many your works are, O Jehovah! All of them in wisdom you have made. The earth is full of your productions. As for the sea so great and wide, there there are moving things without number." (Psalm 104:24, 25) From the tiny minnows to the great whales, divine wisdom is seen in their form and function.

God's crowning creation on earth was man himself. Here was a creature that did not act just by built-in, or instinctive, wisdom. He had the capability of being like God in many ways. How true of him that "in a fear-inspiring way" he is wonderfully made! Even if we are not medical scientists, we can read their findings and draw the same conclusions as the inspired writer. The Creator's works evident in the human body are wonderful.—Psalm 139:14.

Jehovah's Heavenly Wisdom

Psalm 19:1 states that the heavens declare the glory of God. How very true! The psalmist David had no telescopes or electronic instruments, but he had reverential appreciation for what he could see. Today, the average person knows much more than David did about our solar system and our great galaxy, the Milky Way. He also knows that there are countless other great galaxies in the limitless reaches of space. How do you feel as you contemplate the wisdom of the great and matchless Designer? Can you say with reverential voice: 'Jehovah, you are "doing great things unsearchable, and wonderful things without number"'? You should. —Job 9:10.

In the untold past aeons, Jehovah proceeded with his acts of creation, first his only begotten Son, then the rest of his spirit creation. This was followed by the material universe. All was serene and orderly. Why, the angelic sons of God actually shouted their appreciation in applause at the founding of the earth! (Job 38:4-7) Man and woman were created and placed in a perfect garden, but then a shocking thing occurred. A voice out of the invisible, speaking through a serpent, slandered the Grand Creator. It charged that Jehovah was misusing his sovereignty; it called God a liar. Hence, the owner of the voice gained unsavory names that identify him, such as Devil, Serpent, and Satan. What now would the All-Wise One do? What could he do? A new dimension of wisdom would be required that would eclipse designs that already outshone Solomon's glory.—Genesis 3:1-5.

A New Dimension of
Divine Wisdom

"AT THIS God said to Moses: 'I SHALL PROVE TO BE WHAT I SHALL PROVE TO BE.' And he added: 'This is what you are to say to the sons of Israel, "I SHALL PROVE TO BE has sent me to you."'" (Exodus 3:14) Jehovah explained to Moses that before this even His servants did not understand the full significance of His name. He is the God of purpose and always fulfills his will. If circumstances require, he can alter his method to achieve his purpose. He is that wise!

Satan himself did not appreciate what God's name implied. Likely, he did know of the tree of life in the garden of Eden. If he had led Adam and Eve to it, that might have seemed to put Jehovah on the horns of a dilemma: either to keep his word that sin would mean their death or to keep his word as to the tree of life. (Genesis 2:9; 3: 1-6) In any event, Satan was in for a disappointment.

God now began to demonstrate a wisdom unanticipated by his spirit sons and previously unrevealed to them. (Compare Ephesians 3:10.) He began to inaugurate a series of pronouncements and events that over a long period of time would marvelously demonstrate his great wisdom and his ability to fulfill his eternal purpose, which was to have the earth full of happy, loyal humans who could live forever in Paradise. (Genesis 1:27, 28) Time and again God would thwart Satan's efforts to interfere.

The Sacred Secret Unfolds

Immediately after the first rebellion, God acted. He held court for the guilty couple and upheld his sanction of death for disobedience. What about Adam and Eve's eating from the tree of life? "Jehovah God went on to say: 'Here the man has become like one of us in knowing good and bad, and now in order that he may not put his hand out and actually take fruit also from the tree of life and eat and live to time indefinite,—' With that Jehovah God put him out of the garden of Eden."—Genesis 3:17-23.

At this time God also undertook the role of Evangelizer, or Proclaimer of good news. He uttered the first prophecy: "Jehovah God proceeded to say to the serpent: . . . 'I shall put enmity between you and the woman and between your seed and her seed. He will bruise you in the head and you will bruise him in the heel.'" (Genesis 3:14, 15) Centuries later the apostle Paul explained: "For the [human] creation was subjected to futility, not by its own will but through him that subjected it, on the basis of hope."—Romans 8:20.

Yes, man thereafter would be helplessly shackled to death inherited from Adam, but God was declaring his purpose to rescue Adam's obedient offspring. Yet, what was "the basis of hope"? How could he rescue humans and still uphold his sentence of death for sin? This was to be God's hidden wisdom; it involved "the sacred secret that was hidden from the past systems of things and from the past generations." (Colossians 1:26; 1 Corinthians 2:7, 8) Although faithful ones of old did not understand the secret, they did have a hope that somehow God would rescue them. Why, even the angels were eager to learn how Jehovah would fulfill his purpose! (1 Peter 1:10-12) Do you understand this sacred secret?

Redeemed by Ransom

Gradually over the centuries, Jehovah added information to his original promise. To faithful Abraham he promised a seed through whom blessings for all obedient humans would come. (Genesis 22:15-18) Through Jacob he revealed that the seed would be a king from the tribe of Judah. (Genesis 49:10) By this time godly men believed in a resurrection of the dead, although they could not fully understand how this was to be. (Job 14:14, 15; Hebrews 11:19) Finally, God promised David that the coming King, or Messiah, would be a descendant of David and would reign to time indefinite.—2 Samuel 7:16.

All the prophets added bits of understanding to the sacred secret, but men could not see the complete picture. Eventually, the time for the appearance of the Messiah arrived, and then, at long last, this greatly diversified wisdom of God became much clearer. It centered around Jesus Christ and the provision of his perfect human life as a corresponding ransom for mankind. With that as a basis, the rest of the glorious purpose of Jehovah through the Kingdom would proceed. Do you understand the ransom?

In Romans chapters 5 and 6, Paul gives a fine explanation of it. At Romans 5:12 he explains our inherited sin and death. He goes on to show how the effect of just one sin by perfect Adam and the forfeiture of life for his offspring could be balanced by another perfect human life. That proved to be the life of the "man Jesus Christ." (Verses 15-21; see also 1 Timothy 2:5, 6.) Why could Jesus provide this ransom? Because he was the Son of God, Jesus was "loyal, guileless, undefiled, sep-

arated from the sinners." (Hebrews 7:26; Luke 1:32, 33) We need not attempt to explain the details of the genetics of Jesus' birth. The angel Gabriel assured Jesus' mother, Mary, and us, that nothing is impossible with God. (Luke 1:37) So Jesus, although born out of a female descendant of Adam, was the Son of God—actually a perfect man. His blood, or life, was worth far more than the blood of countless animals that had been sacrificed by the Aaronic priests of Israel at the temple in Jerusalem. He was "the Lamb of God that takes away the sin of the world."—John 1:29; 3:16.

Could God make this arrangement through Jesus and still be just? If God raised his Son to life on the third day, what happened to the ransom? Paul assures us that God *is* just. Follow his reasoning: "But by his mercy they are made upright for nothing [it being free], by the deliverance secured through Christ Jesus. For God showed him publicly dying as a sacrifice of reconciliation to be taken advantage of through faith. This was to vindicate his own justice (for in his forbearance, God passed over men's former sins —to vindicate his justice at the present time, and show that he is upright himself and that he makes those who have faith in Jesus upright also." (Romans 3:24-26, *An American Translation*) Now, what does this mean? Simply that Jesus, as a perfect, flesh-and-blood man, actually died as a man and remains dead as a man forever. He died "once for all time when he offered himself up." (Hebrews 7:27) So the ransom is valid. Jesus died in the flesh; on the third day he was "made alive in the spirit."—1 Peter 3:18.

The New Covenant and the New Creation

Now we see the crowning part of the sacred secret. Jesus' being faithful to

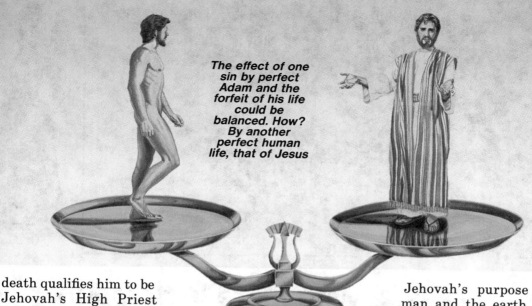

The effect of one sin by perfect Adam and the forfeit of his life could be balanced. How? By another perfect human life, that of Jesus

death qualifies him to be Jehovah's High Priest and King. With his shed blood he validates a new covenant. This new covenant is to produce heavenly associates who will rule with Jesus as kings and priests. (Revelation 5: 9, 10; 20:4, 6) They constitute a new nation, "a new creation," and that certainly is something!—Galatians 6:15, 16.

Consider: God through Christ Jesus chooses a representative number out of mankind, both men and women. He can legally declare them righteous and call them to be spiritual sons. In God's due season after their death, he resurrects them to heaven and grants them immortality, even as he rewarded Jesus. (1 Peter 1:3, 4) What confidence he has in his "new creation" and their loyalty to him! What an answer to the one who has falsely accused them before Jehovah! (Revelation 12:10) Although immortal with Jesus Christ, they will *never* be disloyal to Jehovah. But that is not all.

The Paradise Earth

Christ Jesus, with his associate heavenly kings and priests, will see to it that Jehovah's purpose for man and the earth will be fully carried out during his Millennial Reign. Applying the benefits of the ransom, Jesus will resurrect the dead and will bring to human perfection the faithful ones among them and the survivors of the end of this wicked system. At the same time, the earth will be made a paradise. All who then reject Satan's final effort to corrupt them will be granted perfect human life forever. Satan and all his evil crowd will be destroyed forever. Peace and unity will prevail in all creation, fully vindicating Jehovah's sovereignty and his rule by love. Both angels and men will have demonstrated loyal love for their Creator and God.—Revelation, chapter 20.

Now we can better understand the sacred secret. Now we see Jehovah's wisdom that excels even his creative designs in the plant and animal worlds. We have good reason to exclaim: "O the depth of God's riches and wisdom and knowledge! How unsearchable his judgments are . . . Because from him and by him and for him are all things. To him be the glory forever. Amen."—Romans 11:33-36.

Blessed With More Instruction

THE disciples have just received an explanation of the illustration of the sower. But now they want to learn more. "Explain to us," they request, "the illustration of the weeds in the field."

How different the attitude of the disciples from that of the rest of the crowd on the beach! Those people lack an earnest desire to learn the meaning behind the illustrations, being satisfied with merely the outline of things set out in them. Contrasting that seaside audience with his inquisitive disciples, Jesus says:

"With the measure that you are measuring out, you will have it measured out to you, yes, you will have more added to you." The disciples are measuring out to Jesus earnest interest and attention and so are blessed with receiving more instruction. Thus, in answer to his disciples' inquiry, Jesus explains:

"The sower of the fine seed is the Son of man; the field is the world; as for the fine seed, these are the sons of the kingdom; but the weeds are the sons of the wicked one, and the enemy that sowed them is the Devil. The harvest is a conclusion of a system of things, and the reapers are angels."

After identifying each feature of his illustration, Jesus describes the outcome. At the conclusion of the system of things, he says, "the reapers," or angels, will separate weedlike imitation Christians from the true "sons of the kingdom." "The sons of the wicked one" will then be marked for destruction, but the sons of God's Kingdom, "the righteous ones," will shine brilliantly in the Kingdom of their Father.

Jesus next blesses his inquisitive disciples with three more illustrations. First, he says: "The kingdom of the heavens is like a treasure hidden in the field, which a man found and hid; and for the joy he has he goes and sells what things he has and buys that field."

"Again," he continues, "the kingdom of the heavens is like a traveling merchant seeking fine pearls. Upon finding one pearl of high value, away he went and

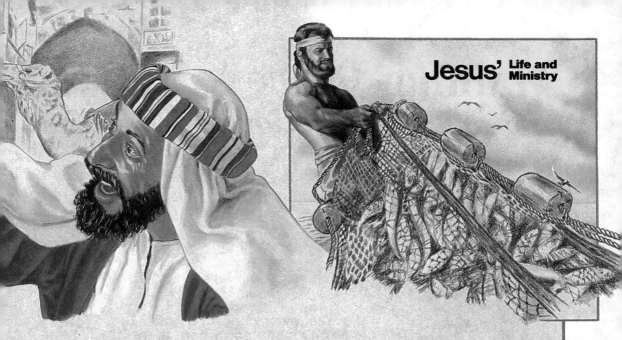

promptly sold all the things he had and bought it."

Jesus himself is like the man who discovers a hidden treasure and like the merchant who finds a pearl of high value. He sold everything, as it were, giving up an honored position in heaven to become a lowly human. Then, as a man on earth, he suffers reproach and hateful persecution, proving worthy of becoming the Ruler of God's Kingdom.

The challenge is placed before Jesus' followers also to sell everything in order to obtain the grand reward of being either a coruler with Christ or an earthly Kingdom subject. Will we consider having a share in God's Kingdom as something more valuable than anything else in life, as a priceless treasure or a precious pearl?

Finally, Jesus likens "the kingdom of the heavens" to a dragnet that gathers up fish of every kind. When the fish are separated, the unsuitable are thrown away but the good are kept. So, Jesus says, it will be in the conclusion of the system of things; the angels will separate the wicked from the righteous, reserving the wicked for annihilation.

Jesus himself begins this fishing project, calling his first disciples to be "fishers of men." Under angelic surveillance, the fishing work continues down through the centuries. At last the time comes to haul in the "dragnet," which symbolizes the organizations on earth professing to be Christian.

Although the unsuitable fish are cast into destruction, thankfully we can be counted among the 'good fish' that are kept. By exhibiting the same earnest desire as Jesus' disciples did for more knowledge and understanding, we will be blessed not only with more instruction but with God's blessing of eternal life. **Matthew 13:36-52; 4:19; Mark 4: 24, 25.**

♦ How do the disciples differ from the crowds on the beach?

♦ Who or what is represented by the sower, the field, the fine seed, the enemy, the harvest, and the reapers?

♦ What three additional illustrations did Jesus provide, and what can we learn from them?

Gaining Peace With God
Through Dedication and Baptism

"Jehovah went on to say: ' . . .
Any man upon whom there is
the mark do not go near.'"
—EZEKIEL 9:4, 6.

GAINING peace with God? But why? Few persons consider themselves in conflict with God. Is it possible, however, to be an actual enemy of God and not be aware of it? The apostle Paul explained to Christians in the first century: "We all at one time conducted ourselves in harmony with the desires of our flesh, doing the things willed by the flesh and the thoughts, and we were naturally *children of wrath* even as the rest."—Ephesians 2:3.

² Likewise today, though you may be

interested in pleasing God, sin inherited from Adam affects your outlook and can cause you to pursue "the things willed by the flesh." Even if you are a person studying the Bible with Jehovah's Witnesses or an unbaptized youth whose parents are Witnesses, a self-centered do-as-I-please attitude may characterize much of your life and continue to alienate you from God. A person who maintains such a course is 'storing up wrath for himself.' (Romans 2:5; Colossians 1:21; 3:5-8) God will express his anger completely during the fast-approaching "day of wrath and of the revealing of God's righteous judgment." (Romans 1:28–2:6) How can you gain

---

1, 2. (a) Why are people in general not at peace with God? (b) Why is it vital for all to gain such peace?

peace with God and survive this "day of wrath"?

The Foundation for Peace

[3] Jehovah took the initiative to help. "He loved us and sent forth his Son as a propitiatory sacrifice for our sins." (1 John 4:10) Jesus' sacrificial death propitiates, that is, appeases or satisfies Jehovah's justice. This provides a legal basis for the forgiveness of sins and, eventually, for the complete removal of the enmity between God and man. Yes, it is possible to become "reconciled to God through the death of his Son," as the apostle Paul wrote.—Romans 5:8-10.

[4] But to benefit personally from Christ's sacrifice, we must take certain steps. These are indicated in a dramatic vision given to the prophet Ezekiel, a vision that is fulfilled during our time when God's "day of wrath" is imminent. God's executional forces are pictured in the vision by six armed men. Before these express God's wrath, a seventh man, carrying a secretary's inkhorn, is told: " 'Pass through the midst of the city, . . . and you must put a mark on the foreheads of the men that are sighing and groaning over all the detestable things that are being done in the midst of it.' And to [the six armed men] he said in my ears: 'Pass through the city after him and strike. . . . But to any man upon whom there is the mark do not go near.' "—Ezekiel 9:1-6.

[5] These protectively 'marked' ones were sickened because persons claiming to worship the true God had 'filled the land with violence' and had engaged in sexual immorality, idolatry, and all manner of other wrong conduct. (Ezekiel 8:5-18; Jeremiah

7:9) Likewise today, those who would be 'marked' must first learn, through a study of the Bible, to value God's standards and become grieved at heart, yes, to 'sigh and groan,' over teachings and practices that dishonor him. Perhaps because of ignorance some engaged in wrongdoing or consented to such by giving their support. Yet, now they begin to view such activities as God views them—with disgust! (Romans 1:24-32; Isaiah 2:4; Revelation 18:4; John 15:19) This increased appreciation leads to one of the first steps to gain peace with God: repentance. The apostle Peter urged: "Repent, therefore, and turn around so as to get your sins blotted out, that seasons of refreshing [rather than wrath] may come from the person of Jehovah." (Acts 3:19) How refreshing such forgiveness is!

Getting the "Mark"

[6] To be spared from God's wrath, those who 'sighed and groaned' had to be marked on their forehead. (Ezekiel 9:4) In ancient times slaves were often marked on the forehead to be clearly identified. Distinctive marks on the forehead and elsewhere might also show that a person worshiped a certain deity.* (Compare Isaiah 44:5.) So, in our day, what is the distinctive, lifesaving mark that clearly identifies its bearers as true worshipers and slaves of Jehovah?

[7] The symbolic mark is the evidence, as if displayed on your uncovered forehead, (1) that you are a dedicated, baptized

* About 150 years after Ezekiel's vision, the Greek historian Herodotus, noting that the marks on devotees of the god Hercules afforded them protection, wrote: "If the slave of any person whatsoever takes refuge [in Hercules' temple], and has sacred marks impressed on him, so devoting himself to the god, it is not lawful to lay hands on him."

3. How did God provide the basis for reconciliation?
4. What relevant vision was given to Ezekiel, and why is it of importance to us?
5. What leads to repentance?

6. For what reasons were some people marked during ancient times?
7. What is the symbolic mark?

disciple of Jesus Christ and (2) that you have put on the Christlike new personality. (Ephesians 4:20-24) Since those thus 'marked' must first make a dedication, we need to know what this involves. Jesus explains: "If anyone wants to come after me, let him disown himself and pick up his torture stake and follow me continually." —Mark 8:34.

[8] The Greek word translated "disown" means "to deny utterly" or "renounce." Therefore, to 'disown yourself' means more than denying yourself a certain pleasure or indulgence now and then. Rather, it means being willing to say no to yourself when it comes to letting your life be dominated by your personal desires and ambitions. We are helped to see the scope of Jesus' words by noting how this concept is translated into different languages: "To stop doing what one's own heart wants" (Tzeltal, Mexico), "to not belong to oneself any longer" (K'anjobal, Guatemala), and "to turn his back on himself" (Javanese, Indonesia). Yes, this means an exclusive dedication, not just a commitment that could be made to a number of things.

[9] A Christian named Susan, who formerly was quite independent, explains what dedication meant to her: "I was surrendering my whole self to someone else. Jehovah now determines my course, tells me what to do, and sets my priorities." Are you willing to make the same exclusive dedication to Jehovah God? Remember, the symbolic mark identifies you as 'belonging' to God, as a happy slave to his Master. —Compare Exodus 21:5, 6; Romans 14:8.

[10] "Who of you that wants to build a tower does not first sit down and calculate the expense, to see if he has enough to complete it?" asked Jesus. (Luke 14:28) So are you willing to: Attend Christian meetings regularly? (Hebrews 10:25) Maintain the high moral standard set by God for his servants? (1 Thessalonians 4:3, 4, 7) Have as full a share in the Kingdom preaching work as you can? Put God's will first when choosing a career or setting goals in life? (Matthew 6:33; Ecclesiastes 12:1) Care for your family obligations? (Ephesians 5:22-6:4; 1 Timothy 5:8) Once you have made a personal dedication in prayer, a further step lets others know this officially.

Baptism—For Whom?

[11] Jesus commanded that his followers be baptized. (Matthew 28:19, 20) They were to be totally immersed in water and raised out of it. Like a burial and a resurrection, this well pictures a person's dying to a self-centered way of life and being made alive to do God's will. By baptism you identify yourself as one of Jehovah's Witnesses in association with God's worldwide congregation.* Baptism validates a solemn agreement made with God. (Compare Exodus 19:3-8.) Your life must be in harmony with his laws. (Psalm 15; 1 Corinthians 6:9-11) Baptism, which ordains you as a minister of God, reflects also a "request made to God for a good conscience" because you know that you are at peace with God.—1 Peter 3:21.

[12] Should even youths consider baptism? Well, recall that Jehovah told the six armed men in the vision: "Old man, young

---

* Recently the two questions addressed to baptismal candidates were simplified so that candidates could answer with full comprehension of what is involved in coming into intimate relationship with God and his earthly organization.

8, 9. (a) What does it mean to 'disown yourself'? (b) How can what dedication requires be illustrated?
10. What matters should one consider before making a dedication?
11. What does baptism symbolize, and what is accomplished by it?
12. When are children protected by their parent's "mark"?

man and virgin and little child and women you should kill off—to a ruination. But to any man upon whom there is the mark do not go near." (Ezekiel 9:6) Of course, children too young to make a dedication would be protected by a parent's "mark" if that parent is striving to bring the children up to love Jehovah and if they are obediently responding. (1 Corinthians 7:14) Yet, if a child is intelligent enough to make a personal decision and has reached the point where he "knows how to do what is right," do not presume that he will continue indefinitely under the merit of his parent's "mark."—James 4:17.

¹³ Before making a dedication, a youth should have adequate knowledge to comprehend what is involved and should be seeking a personal relationship with God. He should understand and be adhering to Bible principles, knowing that he will be held accountable for any infraction thereof. He should also have sufficient experience in sharing his faith with others and know that this is a vital part of true worship; he should truly want to serve God. Naturally, he would not be expected to show the maturity of an adult, but his spiritual progress should be reasonably steady.

---

13. What are some considerations in determining a youth's readiness for baptism?

¹⁴ If one has 'counted the cost,' it places one at no disadvantage to make a dedication as a youth. With almost all new Christians, after baptism appreciation deepens. "Getting baptized as a youngster was a protection for me," explained David. "As I got older, I noticed how some unbaptized teenagers in the congregation felt free of the authority of the elders and as a consequence veered into bad conduct. But I always remembered that I had dedicated my life to God. My life was already taken, so I could not follow such teenagers."

¹⁵ 'What, though, if my son or daughter gets baptized when young and then cools off?' some parents wonder. Certainly, a youth should not get baptized just to please a parent or because some friends do. Yet Joseph, Samuel, King Josiah, and Jesus when teenagers all had a serious view of the worship of God and held to it. (Genesis 37:2; 39:1-3; 1 Samuel 1:24-28; 2: 18-21; 2 Chronicles 34:3; Luke 2:42-49) In modern times, a Christian named Jean was baptized when she was only ten years old. When asked years later if she really understood the step, Jean replied: "I knew I loved Jehovah, I appreciated what Jesus

---

14. Why did one youngster consider his baptism a protection?
15. (a) How do we know that it is possible for youths to maintain a serious view of true worship? (b) How can parents best assist?

Immersion or Sprinkling?

The account of Jesus' baptism mentions his "coming up out of the water." (Mark 1:10) That Jesus was immersed is consistent with the meaning of the Greek word translated baptism (ba·ptiˑsma). This comes from the word ba·ptiˊzo, which means "dip, immerse." It was sometimes used to describe the sinking of a ship. The second-century writer Lucian uses a related word to describe one person's drowning another: "Plunging him down so deep [ba·ptiˊzonˑta] that he cannot come up again." *The New International Dictionary of New Testament Theology* concludes: "Despite assertions to the contrary, it seems that baptizō, both in Jewish and Christian contexts, normally meant 'immerse', and that even when it became a technical term for baptism, the thought of immersion remains."

did for us, and I wanted to serve Jehovah." She has served faithfully for some 40 years since her baptism. Each youth is an individual; no one can set a standard age limit. Parents should strive to reach their child's heart, helping him or her to develop godly devotion.* They should not only keep before their children the privilege of dedication and baptism but also fortify them to be steadfast worshipers.

Overcoming Obstacles

16 While Bible knowledge is essential, the "mark" involves more than head knowledge. For instance, in the vision given to Ezekiel, likely the elders executed for offering up incense to false gods had extensive knowledge of Jehovah's written Word. But their behavior behind closed doors showed that they were not true worshipers. (Ezekiel 8:7-12; 9:6) So, to be 'marked' for survival requires putting on "the new personality which was created according to God's will in true righteousness and loyalty."—Ephesians 4:22-24.

17 A formidable obstacle is the influence

---

* See "Train Your Child to Develop Godly Devotion" in our issue of August 15, 1985.

---

16. Why is more than head knowledge required?
17. (a) What obstacle holds some back from baptism? (b) How can the counsel of James 4:8 be applied?

Points for Review

□ How does God help us to gain peace with him?

□ What is the symbolic lifesaving mark?

□ What is the significance of dedication and baptism?

□ What sort of obstacles must be faced, and how can these be overcome?

---

of your sinful flesh. (Romans 8:7, 8) Some even hold back from baptism because o[f] not controlling some serious fleshly weakness or because of wanting to indulge i[n] illicit worldly pleasures. (James 4:1, 4[)] Such ones are missing a precious relation[-] ship. God's Word advises: "Draw close t[o] God, and he will draw close to you. Cleans[e] your hands, you sinners, and purify you[r] hearts, you indecisive ones." (James 4:8[)] Decisive action is required. As an example[,] one man who began to study the Bible ha[d] abused alcohol and drugs for 16 years an[d] was deathly sick of this. Wit[h] determination he overcame these bad hab[-] its. "But just as I was progressing towar[d] dedication, a woman began begging me t[o] have an affair with her. It was a rea[l] temptation," he admitted. "Though th[e] woman thought I was crazy, I told her: 'I'[m] studying the Bible with Jehovah's Wit[-] nesses, and I cannot.'" What prompted hi[s] response? "I had seen what Jehovah did fo[r] my life by helping me to get off the alcohol[.] He helped me in other ways too. This kep[t] drawing me closer to him. I could no[t] disappoint him." This man had grow[n] close to God.

18 What counts is not how much yo[u] know but how much you love what yo[u] know. Psalm 119:165 says: "Abundan[t] peace belongs to those loving [not jus[t] knowing] your law, and for them there i[s] no stumbling block." The key is lovin[g] God's law, deeply appreciating its value i[n] your life.—Isaiah 48:17, 18.

19 Of course, other obstacles or stum[-] bling blocks may arise. "The hardest on[e] for me," said the brother mentioned above[,] "was fear of men. I had some worldl[y] 'friends' that I used to drink with. It wa[s]

---

18. What is a key to overcoming obstacles?
19, 20. (a) What obstacles must be overcome[,] and what assurance do we have? (b) Successfull[y] overcoming all obstacles will result in what?

he most difficult thing for me to tell them that I was cutting off my association because I was going to dedicate my life to God." (Proverbs 29:25) Others have faced the scorn of family members. One newly baptized Witness, who overcame her husband's opposition, observed: "Rather than one major hurdle, there were a lot of little hurdles I had to get over one at a time." Faithfully overcoming each obstacle as it comes will fortify your heart. Be assured that there is no obstacle that cannot be overcome by those loving God's law! —Luke 16:10.

[20] As you prevail over each stumbling block, you will gain "abundant peace." (Psalm 119:165) Yes, "you will walk in security on your way . . . Your sleep must be pleasurable. You will not need to be afraid of any sudden dreadful thing, nor of the storm upon the wicked ones, because it is coming. For Jehovah himself will prove to be, in effect, your confidence."—Proverbs 3:23-26.

Increase Your Peace
Through Accurate Knowledge

"May undeserved kindness and peace be increased to you by an accurate knowledge of God and of Jesus our Lord."—2 PETER 1:2.

THE peaceful relationship established with Jehovah God at your baptism is, in some respects, like a marriage. Although the wedding day is delightful, it is only the start of a precious relationship. With effort, time, and experience, a marriage relationship will grow even dearer, becoming a haven during times of distress. So, too, by diligence and with Jehovah's help, you can increase your peace with him.

[2] The apostle Peter explained how those who had "obtained a faith" could strengthen their peace with God. He wrote: "May undeserved kindness and peace be increased to you by an accurate knowledge of God and of Jesus our Lord."—2 Peter 1: 1, 2.

"Accurate Knowledge of God"

[3] The Greek word for "accurate knowledge" (e·pi'gno·sis) used in this context means a deeper, more intimate knowledge. The verb form can refer to knowledge gained by personal experience and is rendered "know fully" at Luke 1:4. Greek scholar Culverwel explains that to him the word implies becoming "better acquainted with a thing I knew before; a more exact viewing of an object that I saw before afar off." Gaining such "accurate knowledge" involves getting to know Jehovah and Jesus more intimately as persons, becoming better acquainted with their qualities.

[4] Two ways to gain this knowledge are through good personal study habits and

1, 2. (a) Why can a peaceful relationship with God be compared to a marriage? (b) How can we strengthen our peace with God?

3. Having accurate knowledge of Jehovah and Jesus means what?
4. How can we increase our knowledge of God, and why does this improve our peace with him?

regular attendance at meetings of God's people. In these ways you will learn more clearly how God conducts himself and what he thinks. You will form a more distinct mental image of his personality. But knowing God intimately means to imitate and reflect this image. For instance, Jehovah described a person who reflected godlike unselfishness, and then He said: "Was not that a case of *knowing* me?" (Jeremiah 22:15, 16; Ephesians 5:1) Imitating God more closely increases your peace with him because you improve in putting on the new personality, "which through accurate knowledge is being made new according to the image of the One who created it." You become more pleasing to God.—Colossians 3:10.

5 One Christian woman named Lynn found it hard to be forgiving because of a misunderstanding with a fellow Christian. But Lynn's careful personal study caused her to examine her attitude. "I recalled the type of God Jehovah is, how he does not hold a grudge," she admitted. "I thought of all the little things we do to Jehovah every day, yet he does not keep account of them. This matter with my Christian sister was so small by comparison. So whenever I saw her, I said to myself, 'Jehovah loves her just as he loves me.' This helped me to get over the problem." Do you see areas where you also need to imitate Jehovah more closely?—Psalm 18:35; 103:8, 9; Luke 6:36; Acts 10:34, 35; 1 Peter 1:15, 16.

Accurate Knowledge of Christ

6 Having accurate knowledge of Jesus requires having "the mind of Christ" and imitating him. (1 Corinthians 2:16) Jesus was an enthusiastic proclaimer of truth.

(John 18:37) His intense evangelizing spirit was not shackled by community prejudices. Though other Jews hated Samaritans, he witnessed to a Samaritan woman at a well. Why, even talking at length in public with any woman may have been frowned upon!* But Jesus did not allow community feelings to stop him from giving a witness. God's work was refreshing. He said: "My food is for me to do the will of him that sent me and to finish his work." The joy of seeing the response of people, like the Samaritan woman and many of the townspeople, sustained Jesus like food.—John 4:4-42; 8:48.

7 Do you feel as did Jesus? Granted, starting up a conversation about the Bible with a stranger is hard for many and is often frowned upon by others in the community. Yet, to have the same mental attitude as Jesus had, we cannot escape this fact: We must witness. Of course, not all can do the same amount of preaching. This varies according to our abilities and circumstances. So do not feel that God is never satisfied with your sacred service. Our knowledge of Jesus, however, should spur us to do our best. Jesus commended whole-souled service.—Matthew 13:18-23; 22:37.

The Need to Hate Wickedness

8 Accurate knowledge also helps us to appreciate what things are hated by Jesus and by Jehovah. (Hebrews 1:9; Isaiah 61:8) "There are six things that Jehovah does hate; yes, seven are things detestable to

---

* According to the Talmud, ancient rabbis advised that a scholar "should not converse with a woman in the street." If this custom prevailed in Jesus' day, it may be why his disciples "began to wonder because he was speaking with a woman."—John 4:27.

---

5. (a) How did accurate knowledge help one Christian woman? (b) In what ways can we more closely imitate Jehovah?
6. How did Jesus Christ show that the preaching work was of foremost importance to him?

7. (a) Knowledge of Jesus should motivate us to do what? (b) Does God expect all of his servants to do the same amount of preaching? Explain.
8, 9. What are some things that God hates, and how can we reflect the same hatred?

Jesus refused to allow community prejudices to hinder his giving a witness. Do you imitate his zeal for preaching?

his soul: lofty eyes, a false tongue, and hands that are shedding innocent blood, a heart fabricating hurtful schemes, feet that are in a hurry to run to badness, a false witness that launches forth lies, and anyone sending forth contentions among brothers." (Proverbs 6:16-19) These attitudes and forms of conduct are "detestable to his soul." The Hebrew word here rendered "detestable" comes from a word meaning "to loathe, nauseate," "to be averse to, as to that which is offensive to all the senses; to detest, hate with indignation." So to be at peace with God, we must develop a similar aversion.

⁹ For instance, shun "lofty eyes" and any show of pride. After baptism some have felt that they were no longer in need of the regular assistance of those who taught them. But new Christians should humbly accept help as they become well grounded in the truth. (Galatians 6:6) Also, avoid gossiping, which can easily cause "contentions among brothers." By spreading unkind hearsay, unjustifiable criticism, or lies, we may not be "shedding innocent blood," but we surely can destroy another person's good reputation. We cannot be at peace with God if we are not at peace with our brothers. (Proverbs 17:9; Matthew 5:23, 24) God also says in his Word that "he has hated a divorcing."

(Malachi 2:14, 16) If married, do you, therefore, work to keep your marriage strong? Are flirting and taking undue liberties with another's mate disgusting to you? Do you, like Jehovah, abhor sexual immorality? (Deuteronomy 23:17, 18) Hating such practices is not easy, since these may appeal to our sinful flesh, and they are smiled upon by the world.

¹⁰ As an aid to cultivating a hatred for wickedness, avoid being entertained by movies, TV programs, or literature featuring spiritism, immorality, or violence.

---

10. How can we cultivate a hatred for wickedness?

When faced with a serious problem, David supplicated Jehovah . . .

. . . and disguised his sanity to plan an escape. Jehovah heard David's prayer

(Deuteronomy 18:10-12; Psalm 11:5) By making wrongdoing seem 'not that bad' or even humorous, such entertainment undercuts efforts to develop godly hatred of it. On the other hand, earnest prayer will help, for Jesus said: "Pray continually, that you may not enter into temptation. The spirit, of course, is eager, but the flesh is weak." (Matthew 26:41) Regarding being faced with a strong fleshly desire, one Christian said: "I make myself pray. Sometimes I feel unworthy to approach Jehovah, but by making myself do it, by appealing to him, I get the strength I need." You will better understand why Jehovah detests wrongdoing if you review in your mind its painful consequences.—2 Peter 2:12, 13.

[11] Despite having peace with God, you will at times be troubled by everyday pressures and temptations and even by your own weaknesses. Remember, you have made yourself a special target of Satan. He wars against those who keep God's commandments and are Jehovah's Witnesses! (Revelation 12:17) How, then, can your inner peace be maintained?

Coping With Peace-Disturbing Calamities

[12] "Many are the calamities of the righteous one," wrote David at Psalm 34:19.

---

11. What things may trouble us at times?
12. (a) What is the background of Psalm 34? (b) How do the Scriptures describe David's feelings during this experience?

According to the superscription of this psalm, David penned it following a close encounter with death. Fleeing from King Saul, David sought refuge with Achish, the Philistine king of Gath. That king's servants recognized David and, recalling his previous military exploits for Israel, complained to Achish. When David overheard the conversation, he "began to take these words to his heart, and he became very much afraid on account of Achish the king of Gath." (1 Samuel 21:10-12) After all, this was the hometown of Goliath, and David had killed their hero—he was even carrying the giant's sword! Would they now use this huge sword to cut off *his* head? What could David do?—1 Samuel 17:4; 21:9.

¹³ David supplicated God with intense cries for help. "This afflicted one called, and Jehovah himself heard. And out of all his distresses He saved him," said David. He also said: "Out of all my frights he delivered me." (Psalm 34:4, 6, 15, 17) Have you also learned to supplicate Jehovah, pouring out your heart during times of anxiety? (Ephesians 6:18; Psalm 62:8) Though your particular distress may not be as dramatic as David's, still you will find that God will give you help at the right time. (Hebrews 4:16) But David did more than pray.

¹⁴ "He [David] disguised his sanity under their eyes and began acting insane. . . . Finally Achish said to his servants: 'Here you see a man behaving crazy. Why should you bring him to me?'" (1 Samuel 21: 13-15) David thought out a strategy by which he escaped. Jehovah blessed his efforts. Likewise, when we are confronted with knotty problems, Jehovah expects us to use our mental faculties and not simply

to expect him to work them out for us. He has given us his inspired Word, which will "give to the inexperienced ones shrewdness, . . . knowledge and thinking ability." (Proverbs 1:4; 2 Timothy 3:16, 17) God has also provided congregation elders, who can help us to know how to maintain God's standards. (1 Thessalonians 4:1, 2) Oftentimes, these men can assist you in researching the publications of the Watch Tower Society for help in making a right decision or coping with a problem.

¹⁵ Even when our heart pains us because of our own weaknesses or failures, if we have the right attitude, we can maintain our peace with God. David wrote at Psalm 34:18: "Jehovah is near to those that are broken at heart; and those who are crushed in spirit he saves." If we ask for forgiveness and take any necessary steps to correct matters (especially in cases of serious transgression), Jehovah will stay close to us, supporting us emotionally. —Proverbs 28:13; Isaiah 55:7; 2 Corinthians 7:9-11.

Personal Knowledge Gives Peace

¹⁶ Another way in which we gain accurate knowledge of God, besides taking in spiritual information, is through our personally experiencing his loving help. (Psalm 41:10, 11) Being delivered out of distress does not always mean the immediate or complete end of a problem; you may have to continue to endure it. (1 Corinthians 10:13) Though David's life was spared at Gath, he remained a fugitive for several years, facing one danger after another. Through it all, David sensed Jehovah's care and support. He had pursued and found peace with God, and he learned that those who do so "will not lack

---

13. What did David do during this calamity, and how can we follow his example?
14. How did David use "thinking ability," and what has God provided to help us do the same?

15. Why is Psalm 34:18 comforting?
16. (a) What is another way in which we gain accurate knowledge of God? (b) Explain David's statement: "Taste and see that Jehovah is good."

anything good." Realizing by personal experience how Jehovah supported him during calamity, David could say: "Taste and see that Jehovah is good, O you people; happy is the able-bodied man that takes refuge in him."—Psalm 34:8-10, 14, 15.

[17] Taking refuge in Jehovah during difficulties will also enable you to "taste and see that Jehovah is good." Because of an accident, a Christian in the midwestern United States lost the well-paying job that he had had for 14 years. Since they had no income, he and his family supplicated God. At the same time, though, they cut down on expenses, gleaned in nearby fields, and fished for food. With help from some in the congregation and by taking part-time work when available, this family of four managed. A year after the accident, the mother reflected: "We can fool ourselves into thinking that we are relying upon Jehovah, when we are really relying upon our own abilities, our mate, or our job. We, though, really learned to trust just Him. These other things can be taken away, but Jehovah never left us—not for one moment. Though we have just the bare necessities, our relationship with Jehovah as a family is much closer."

[18] Yes, a financial hardship may persist. Or one may be plagued with a chronic physical illness; a personality conflict with another; an emotional disorder, such as depression; or one of a host of other problems. Yet, by truly knowing God, you will have faith in his support. (Isaiah 43:10) This unbreakable trust will help you to endure and to have "the peace of God that excels all thought."—Philippians 4:7.

[19] When going through a troubling experience, never forget that Jehovah knows what you are suffering. In a psalm that was also composed when he reflected on his experience at Gath, David entreated Jehovah: "Do put my tears in your skin bottle. Are they not in your book?" (Psalm 56:8) Certainly, God listened to David's request. How consoling to know that God would gather up such tears caused by affliction and anxiety and put these, as it were, in his skin bottle, just as one would pour into such a container precious wine or drinking water! Such tears would always be remembered, yes, written down in God's book. How tender is Jehovah's regard!

[20] So your baptism is just the beginning of a peaceful relationship with God. By becoming better acquainted with the personal qualities of God and Jesus, and personally experiencing Jehovah's support during trials, you will increase your peace with God. Not only will you have a relationship with Jehovah that becomes a haven of security now but you will also have the precious hope of living forever in Paradise, where you will find "exquisite delight in the abundance of peace."—Psalm 37:11, 29.

17. During a calamity, what effect did taking refuge in Jehovah have on one family?
18. What will enable you to endure even persistent problems?
19. How do we know that Jehovah does not take our sufferings lightly?
20. How can we increase our peace with God?

Do You Recall?

□ In what ways can we gain accurate knowledge of God and Jesus?

□ Imitating God and Jesus will cause us to do what?

□ How do we imitate God's hatred for evil?

□ How can we maintain peace despite difficulties?

Insight on the News

Catholic-Marxist Dialogue

In Budapest, Hungary, in October 1986, 15 Catholic theologians and philosophers met with 15 Marxist intellectuals. The meeting was convened by the Vatican Secretariat for Unbelievers and the Hungarian Academy of Science to discuss the evolution of moral values.

Among the Catholics present were French Cardinal Poupard, chairman of the Secretariat for Unbelievers, and Austrian Cardinal Koenig, a specialist on the Catholic Church's relations with communist nations. The Marxists included the heads of the Hungarian Institute of Philosophy and of the Soviet Institute of Scientific Atheism.

The French daily *Le Monde* reported: "Marxist intellectuals recognize that they are faced with a crisis of moral values, the seriousness of which they measure by the number of suicides, the use of drugs, and the consumption of alcohol. According to the Catholic delegation, in their search for a solution they [the Marxists] are counting on the cooperation of the Christian churches. On the Roman [Catholic] side, the twofold purpose was to evaluate better how man and morals fit into a Marxist society and to 'examine the moral basis for concrete coexistence between Christians in the Eastern [communist] countries and Marxists.'"

The true solution to the moral problems of the day will not be found in conferences between conflicting ideologies. Rather, it will be found when Jehovah's Kingdom in the hands of his Son, Jesus, overturns the present system of things, building in its place a new world under that heavenly Kingdom.—Daniel 2:44; Revelation 21:4, 5.

True Liberation?

Liberation theology—a movement that condones violence as a way to "liberate the poor and oppressed," especially in the Third World, is becoming more popular. This was the topic of discussion at the Second International Assembly of the Ecumenical Association of Third World Theologians held in Oaxtepec, Mexico, December 8-13, 1986. Why are these religious scholars more determined as to their goals for social change than ever before?

Although in 1985 the Vatican released an instruction condemning liberation theology, the *Instruction on Christian Freedom and Liberation* sent out in 1986 stated that it is "perfectly legitimate that those who suffer oppression on the part of the wealthy or politically powerful take action." "Armed struggle" is now approved of as a "last resort."

However, while on earth, did Jesus Christ get involved in the world's social movements? No, on the contrary, when the apostle Peter resorted to "the sword" to defend God's Son, Jesus rebuked him by saying: "Return your sword to its place, for all those who take the sword will perish by the sword." (Matthew 26:52) The Bible promises that true liberation will come through divine intervention when God rids the world not only of poverty, international strife, racial discrimination, and oppression but also of tears, pain, sorrow, and death. (Revelation 21:4) Surely, this will be true liberation!

Baptism of Children Refused

A German Protestant minister from Frankfurt recently informed church authorities that he henceforth would refuse "to baptize unaware children of his parish." Explaining why his own baptism as an infant was not worthy of the name baptism, 58-year-old Klaus Hoffmann said: "It neither fulfilled the prerequisite of a Biblical baptism, that is faith, nor had the right symbol, namely immersion." In support of his view, he chose to be rebaptized and thus "underwent the Biblical baptism of immersion," reports the German newspaper *Frankfurter Allgemeine Zeitung*.

At first, church officials suspended Hoffmann from all duties, but the judgment was commuted to "a leave of three months for research purposes." With what results? The newspaper reports that his further research on the matter only confirmed "that within the Bible there is no support for infant baptism. Also, writings of the first Christians are silent as to the introduction of this act until the third century."

Not surprisingly, religious authorities cite tradition as the basis for this act. However, in spite of these facts, infant baptism continues to be practiced throughout much of Christendom. Does such clerical support make it right? Jesus instructed his followers to baptize, not babies, but believers who were taught to keep all his commandments. He himself was not a baby but "about thirty years old" when he was immersed in the waters of the Jordan River.—Luke 3:21-23; Matthew 28:19, 20.

Proving "Zealous for Fine Works" in Kenya

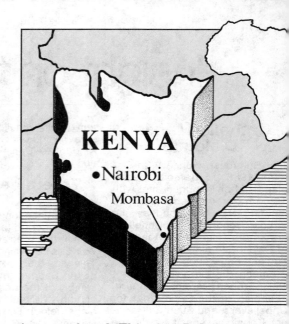

KENYA
•Nairobi
Mombasa

"THIS is what I have been looking for all my life!" exclaimed a man of Hindu background after having attended a recent convention of Jehovah's Witnesses in Kenya, Africa. "This is something special."

What was it that moved him to say that? "People of so many colors, backgrounds, and countries—all mixing freely with evident affection for one another," he said. But how was this possible in a world so full of disunity and racial prejudice? What led to such unity and spiritual harmony in Kenya?

Early Pioneers Pave the Way

Back in 1931, Frank and Gray Smith sailed from South Africa to Mombasa with 40 cartons of books. From there they made an exhausting and hazardous journey to Nairobi, where they distributed their entire supply of literature in about a month. Both contracted malaria, and Frank died —faithful to the end. Later the same year, Robert Nisbet and David Norman followed up on a similar expedition, distributing 200 cartons of publications in East Africa. Thus were the first seeds of truth sown in Kenya.

Then in 1935, Gray Smith and his wife, together with Robert Nisbet and his brother George, set out to follow up the

interest found. This time Robert contracted typhoid fever. The others were afflicted with malaria and blackwater fever. Opposition and deportation orders by the colonial government added to the hardships. Despite all of this, however, these early zealous pioneers distributed a tremendous amount of literature, laying a foundation for growth. For instance, about 30 years later, a Witness working remote rural territory in Kenya was surprised to find a man who had a copy of the book *Reconciliation*. His brother had obtained it in 1935. This man progressed and is now one of Jehovah's Witnesses.

Further Growth

It was not until 1949 that the first Witness, Mary Whittington, came to reside in Nairobi, the capital of Kenya. She had been baptized in England only one year earlier. Little did she know of the isolation, hindrances, and opposition she was about to face. Yet, she had the joy of seeing the 'little one become a thousand.' (Isaiah 60:22) Today, at the age of 73, she is still serving as a regular pioneer.

Bill and Muriel Nisbet, the first grad-

...uates of the Watchtower Bible School of Gilead to be assigned to Kenya, arrived in 1956. At the time, racial segregation was prevalent, and the colonial administration had laws that restricted the preaching activity and limited the size of meetings to no more than nine people. So the work of the Nisbets was confined to only the European field and informal discussions with the African people. Nevertheless, growth came.

In 1962 the work of Jehovah's Witnesses was legally recognized. Shortly thereafter, in 1963, colonial rule ended, thus opening the door to further expansion of our Christian work. Now publications could be printed in the Swahili language, and elders of Jehovah's Witnesses were authorized by the government to officiate at weddings. Since that time, Jehovah's Witnesses have been instrumental in helping almost 2,000 couples to register their marriage legally.

By 1972 a fine new branch office building, conveniently located in Nairobi, was dedicated. (It has since been expanded.) Kenya was now better equipped to oversee the Kingdom work in the ten East African countries under its care and to fill the need for publications in the various native languages.

Fine Examples of Zeal

The proclaimers of the good news in Kenya manifest the same 'zeal for fine works' that was noticeable among the first-century Christians. (Titus 2:14) They do not allow hardships to deter them from helping others to gain an accurate knowledge of the Bible.

In one instance, a Witness received a request from the branch office to call on an interested blind man, who lived 16 miles (26 km) away. The Witness regularly made the journey by bicycle to conduct a Bible study with him. Although this man went through stages of negative thinking and depression, now he is a Witness himself, zealously telling others about God's promise of Paradise restored when even the eyes of the blind will be opened.—Isaiah 35:5.

In some areas, great efforts have to be made to attend Christian meetings. A 70-year-old woman regularly walks about six miles (10 km) to get to the weekly meetings. On the way, she wades through one of Kenya's biggest rivers, even though crocodiles are lurking nearby. At times the current becomes so strong that it almost sweeps her away. Yet, she considers the spiritual feast well worth the effort. What an outstanding example of zeal!

Another fine example of zeal and appreciation was provided by a Witness who walked nine hours to attend the circuit

Bible dramas
presented in Swahili
and English edified
the audience

assembly. Why did he do so, even though he had enough money for bus fare? Motivated by love, he gave his funds to his Bible student so that he, too, could enjoy the assembly program! Yes, love and 'zeal for fine works,' based on accurate Bible knowledge, are clearly seen in Kenya.

Pioneer Spirit

This zeal has been displayed in the full-time pioneer ministry in an outstanding way. Many have found joy in this service in spite of difficult circumstances. One young regular pioneer serves in the hot and humid port city of Mombasa. Some years ago both his legs had to be amputated because of a truck accident. While in the hospital, he contemplated suicide and begged the nurse to give him a lethal injection, which she refused to do. After his release, he found the Witnesses and began studying the Bible with them. This led to his baptism and a new life in the full-time service. He overflows with zeal and gratitude.

A large number of mothers with family responsibilities have also become regular pioneers. Among them is one with three children. She has severe high blood pressure and a speech impediment. She has to work full-time, and her husband is not a Witness. Yet, she is a happy pioneer. Of course, not only mothers share in the regular pioneer service; recently, a father who has eight children to look after and a job that involves shift work also took up this privilege of service.

Many who are not able to be regular pioneers glow with the pioneer spirit. They look for opportunities to share in the full-time ministry as auxiliary pioneers, spending 60 hours in the preaching work each month.

In April 1984, as well as in 1985, more than a third of all the publishers in Kenya participated in some form of full-time service. One congregation had 73 publishers enrolled as auxiliary pioneers that month, working along with the five regular pioneers. The other 28 members of the congregation averaged 64.6 hours, even though many of them were not baptized. As a result, a total of 233 Bible studies were conducted!

Age does not prove to be a barrier. A 99-year-old grandmother took up the auxiliary pioneer ministry. Despite her physical limitations, she lets her light shine courageously toward young and old. (Matthew 5:16) Through her efforts, a number of others have been helped to become Kingdom proclaimers, and they fondly remember the devotion and pioneer spirit of this grandma. Yes, such 'zeal for fine works' has led many to cultivate the pioneer spirit.

The public baptism gave evidence of Jehovah's blessing

Praise—Out of the Mouths of "Babes"

Young ones, too, though not yet baptized, happily and eagerly accompany their parents in bringing good news from the true God to other people. (Matthew 21:16) During a special campaign, a four-and-a-half-year-old girl worked with her parents in isolated territory. She spent 160 hours in the field ministry that month, placing 27 books, 66 booklets, and 47 magazines with people who were interested in the Bible!

This 'zeal for fine works' is manifest in the schools as well. In a rural area outside Nairobi, a primary-school boy, whose mother was studying the Bible with Jehovah's Witnesses, was able to help his teacher on the road to eternal life. In class, when the teacher brought up the subject of life after death, this young boy politely mentioned that his mother had taught him something different, based on the Bible. This aroused the teacher's curiosity. She contacted the boy's mother, who directed her to a more experienced Witness. Now the teacher herself is spreading Bible truth to others, thanks to the courage of this young one. What a fine example of the zeal that exists among Christian children today!

More Growth Expected

Over half of Kenya's population have yet to hear the good news of the Kingdom. Because of distance, some isolated territories can be covered only once a year. Upon arriving in such areas, it is common for Witnesses to be greeted with the words: "Where have you been? We have been missing you." Then, after witnessing there for a few days or weeks and the time comes to leave, one is touched to hear expressions like: "Now are you going to leave us again? How are we going to progress?" Happily, arrangements have been made to call back on most of these spiritually hungry individuals.

Today, there are 3,686 Kingdom ministers in Kenya. At the 1986 Memorial celebration of Christ's death, 13,067 were in attendance. That was almost four times the number of Witnesses! Former alcoholics, brawlers, gang leaders, extortioners, spiritists, and others have made great changes in their lives and now walk in the pathways of truth. What does this tell us about the future?

Obviously, more growth is to be expected. Yes, people in Kenya are responding favorably to the "good news of the kingdom." (Matthew 24:14) Many have joined the ranks of Jehovah's Witnesses—a people "zealous for fine works." Because of these works, they stand out as a unique people, free from racial barriers and other hindrances to true unity. Truly, "this is something special."

Traditional Medicine in Africa
—Compatible With Christianity?

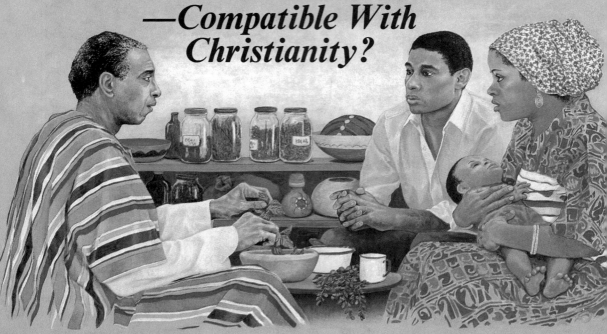

For millions of Africans, traditional healers are their only contact with medicine of any kind. Particularly is this true in rural areas where hospitals are few and doctors are rare. Traditional medicine, however, usually has strong roots in superstition and spiritualism. What should a Christian do under these circumstances?

"'THIS "agbo" will in all probability kill him off and put an end to all his misery and ours.' And so, on the assumption that the new remedy was going to result in good riddance of me, the concoction was poured down my throat."

This was written by a medical doctor in a Lagos, Nigeria, *Sunday Times* article entitled "Don't Despise the Traditional Healer." He was describing how his parents had given up hope of his recovery from a critical illness when he was only one year old. The medicine, sent to them by a traditional healer, was credited with saving his life.

Many Africans who favor traditional medicine tell of surprising cures that have been effected in cases where hospital treatment had failed. Others condemn it as unhygienic, superstitious quackery. On the middle ground are those who call for scientific research into the local herbal remedies and for greater recognition and acceptance of traditional healers. Many would like to see a blending of traditional and modern medicine, citing the cooperation between practitioners of both groups in China and India.

Even if you do not live in Africa, you may be interested in knowing if African folk medicine is really effective and beneficial. What about the ritual element so common among Africans? Is the supernatural an essential ingredient or a harmful feature that should be rejected? What should be the Christian's position toward such traditional African medicine?

Herbal Medicines

Vegetation, of course, is our main source of food and is essential to our existence. There are also plants that yield drugs or poisons that have destroyed countless numbers of people who have misused them. But did you know that some of these same drugs are used in modern medicines? Scientists discovered some of these drugs by investigating plants that were being used in folk medicine or in the concoctions of medicine men. They collected samples, analyzed them chemically, and tested their effects on the body and on microorganisms that cause disease. The result has been the production of some important medical drugs, such as quinine, reserpine, digitalis, and codeine.

People of ancient times discovered many herbal remedies accidentally, by trial and error, or by observing what happened to animals when they ate certain plants. Often those who made such discoveries and who became healers kept the art in their families. The knowledge of herbs thus came to be passed on from father to son or to other persons selected as apprentices. Most traditional healers still tend to be very secretive, often very reluctant to reveal from which plants they make their medicines. But more is involved in African traditional medicines than just herbal remedies.

The Strong Influence of Spiritism

Much of African traditional healing has been closely associated with the supernatural. Many believe that plants possess feelings, powers of communication, and extrasensory perception. Some healers claim to understand the language of plants and to be able to communicate with them. Others do not see the communication as coming from the plants, for they claim that unseen spirits have directed them to herbs that have healing properties.

Spiritism has thus played a prominent role in traditional medicine in Africa. Many Nigerians, for instance, believe that diseases and deaths are caused either by offended gods (or ancestral spirits) or by enemies who employ witchcraft. So sacrifices of appeasement are made, and spiritistic rituals and methods are employed.

Asuquo, a Nigerian healer, is one who strongly believed this. He says: "I learned herbal medicine from my father and used to sacrifice to the gods and to the spirits of our forefathers in preparing my concoctions. I believed that they produced the cures and that failure to sacrifice to them would bring sickness and death."

In actuality, it often works the other way around. Such beliefs have subjected millions of people to superstitious fears and enslavement to unseen spirit forces. Many have suffered spiritistic obsession and harassment. This alone is strong reason to reject any cure that includes sacrifices or other spiritistic rituals. And spirits that would obsess and harass people or deceive them into thinking that their ancestors are still alive or that plants can communicate are obviously deceptive and evil. The Bible warns: "The things which the nations sacrifice they sacrifice to demons, and not to God; and I do not want you to become sharers with the demons." —1 Corinthians 10:20.

The demons, disobedient angels condemned by God to future destruction, are bent on diverting people from worshiping the true God, Jehovah. (2 Peter 2:4; Jude 6) They pretend in some cases that they themselves are benevolent gods. (2 Corinthians 11:14) Carrying their deception further, they impersonate the dead and lead people to think that their ancestors are still alive in a spirit world. However, the Bible clearly says: "The dead . . . are conscious of nothing at all, . . . for there is no work nor devising nor knowledge nor wisdom in Sheol, the place to which you are going."—Ecclesiastes 9: 5, 10.

So it would be wrong for worshipers of the true God to accept from herbalists any cures that involve spiritistic practices. Likewise, herbalists who desire to render acceptable worship to God must discontinue every form of spiritistic practice. Truly, those who resort to spiritism forfeit Jehovah's favor and protection and have no place in the Christian congregation. (Galatians 5:19-21; Revelation 21:8) There are many who have rejected spiritism, and they have found that some herbal cures can be quite effective without the spiritistic practices.

The Change to Christianity

Speaking of his personal experiences, Erhabor, an officially recognized physician who operates an herbal hospital, says: "Formerly I believed that sacrifices had to be included with the medicine in order to combat the spirit behind the disease. But after I studied the Bible with Jehovah's Witnesses and became a Christian, I discarded these practices and now conform to Bible principles. I have found that the healing properties are in the plants themselves."

Similarly, Asuquo says: "Things I learned about Jehovah brought new meaning to my life. My fear about ancestors was removed, and I got to know the true God. I also got to see that sacrifices were not necessary and that it is the juice of barks and leaves that heals people. Many people now come to me for treatment because I do not exploit their superstitions by asking for sacrifices. My treatment does not cost them as much as when they go to the juju healers."

Because Okon, who also practices herbal medicine, does not use incantations or sacrifices in his practice, he is accused by other herbalists of "spoiling their practice." "Some of my patients," he says, "came as spies to prove that I still use sacrifices secretly. After being successfully treated for two weeks, they admitted that I do not use any form of juju. They also benefited from the Scriptural discussions I had with them. I was surprised to see four former patients at the 'Divine Love' Convention of Jehovah's Witnesses in December 1980. They embraced me and said: 'We came to you for physical healing. You also gave us spiritual healing.'"

Christians like these have had to resist those who desire that they return to spiritistic practices. They know that if they combined their healing methods with any form of spiritism, they would no longer be fit to remain in the Christian congregation. So they do not offer sacrifices or use incantations. They do not make lying claims that they can cure every kind of

In Our Next Issue

■ **Do All Prophecies Come From God?**

■ **Death-Dealing Famine in a Time of Plenty**

■ **Looking Back Over 93 Years of Living**

illness, nor do they try to give the impression of having special powers. They avoid even the appearance of spiritism.

True Healing From God

In many developing nations, the majority of the inhabitants depend on the treatment given by traditional healers, in whom most have great confidence. Besides, hospitals and medical doctors are too few to meet the demands for treatment. Hence, most people in these lands likely will continue to consult healers, many of whom use spiritistic methods. But what will you do?

"The truth," said Jesus, "will set you free." (John 8:32) Knowing that the Bible condemns such practices, the Christian would refuse to become disloyal to God by consulting oracles or by seeking from an herbalist a cure involving divination. (Deuteronomy 18:10-13; compare Numbers 23:21, 23.) And if ill, neither would it be wise for a Christian to assume that the problems stem from a spiritistic spell. One need not have fear of being made ill by witchcraft when remaining firmly on God's side by rejecting anything connected with spiritism. If, because of the imperfection that all of us have, illness is experienced, then a personal decision must be made concerning types of treatment.*

The ransom sacrifice offered by Jesus is the only means of deliverance from sin and the resultant sickness and death. (John 3:16; Acts 4:12) It alone opens the way for faithful persons to gain everlasting life on a paradise earth where "no resident will say: 'I am sick.'"—Isaiah 33:24.

Until that happy day, the almighty God assures us that he will protect those who trust him. So all Christians need to rely on Jehovah, keeping close to him in prayer and supplication. This will result in a healthier life now, and it will ensure our receiving perfect life in the promised Paradise earth.—2 Peter 3:10-14; 1 John 2:17.

* See *The Watchtower* of June 15, 1982, pages 22-9.

"Treasures by a False Tongue . . . an Exhalation"

THESE days, lying and cheating are often viewed as legitimate—and eminently successful—business tactics. This was true in Bible times. The psalmist Asaph wrote of those who "have increased their means of maintenance," evidently by fraudulent schemes. Such ones can appear to be "at ease indefinitely" because of the wealth their treachery has brought them. —Psalm 73:8, 12.

Christians today, however, must avoid 'loving dishonest gain' and resorting to shady or dishonest business maneuvers. (1 Peter 5:2) Warns Proverbs 21:6: "The getting of treasures by a false tongue is an exhalation driven away, in the case of those seeking death." Yes, any "treasures" obtained by lying and fraud are bound to be as temporary as "an exhalation," as evanescent as a vapor. "The treasures of the wicked one will be of no benefit" in the long run. (Proverbs 10:2) Really, the lying one is "seeking death" by pursuing a death-dealing course. His life could be cut short prematurely as his lying schemes backfire. (Compare Esther 7:10.) Or at the very latest, his life will be terminated on God's day of judgment.

Do You Remember?

Have you given careful thought to recent issues of *The Watchtower*? If so, you will likely be able to recall the following:

□ **Why should a Christian not celebrate Christmas?**

One reason is that the festival of Christmas originated in the pagan celebration of Saturnalia, the Roman festival of the agricultural god Saturn. God's Word says: "Do not become unevenly yoked with unbelievers." (2 Corinthians 6:14-17) A Christian cannot be separated from unbelievers while he is still celebrating a festival of pagan origin.—12/15, page 6.

□ **What is the Christian Jubilee?**

It is a liberation involving "the truth" that can set humans free from "the law of sin and of death." This truth is centered on "the Son," Jesus Christ. (John 8: 31-36; Romans 8:1, 2, 21)—1/1, page 21.

□ **When is the Christian Jubilee celebrated?**

On Pentecost 33 C.E., the Christian Jubilee began to be celebrated by those destined for life in heaven. For believing mankind who will enjoy everlasting life on earth, a grand Christian Jubilee will be experienced during the Millennium, as all traces of inherited sin and imperfection are wiped out.—1/1, pages 21, 22, 27.

□ **Why do Jehovah's Witnesses not operate schools for children in Asia and elsewhere?**

Because of what the Bible says, Jehovah's Witnesses must be principally concerned with their commission to preach the vital message about God's Kingdom. (Matthew 24:14; 28:19, 20) They are not unaware of human suffering and injustices in the present system, and they help as they can. Yet they recognize that the true remedy lies, not in human hands, but in the deliverance that God's Kingdom will soon bring. (Psalm 146:3-10)—1/15, page 7.

□ **What facets of faith can we learn from the examples of Abel, Enoch, Noah, Abraham, and Moses?**

Faith like Abel's enhances our appreciation for Jesus' sacrifice. True faith helps us to be courageous, like Enoch. As with Noah, faith moves us to follow God's instructions. Abraham's faith impresses us with the need to obey God and to trust in his promises. We should remain unspotted from the world and stand loyally by God's people, as Moses exemplified.—1/15, page 20.

□ **In what way can curiosity be either a blessing or a curse?**

A healthy curiosity about our Creator, his will, and his purposes can be very satisfying and beneficial, bringing joy and refreshment into our life. On the other hand, an unbridled curiosity can lead us into a morass of speculation and human theories, undermining genuine faith and godly devotion.—2/1, page 29.

□ **What did Jesus mean when he prayed: "My Father, if it is possible, let this cup pass away from me"? (Matthew 26:39)**

Jesus was concerned about the charge of blasphemy that he saw would be hurled against him. This was the worst crime of which a Jew could be guilty. His death under that circumstance might seem, therefore, to bring reproach upon his heavenly Father. —2/15, page 13.

□ **If a person has to endure suffering or affliction, what is the wise course for him to take?**

It is best for him to be patient, looking hopefully to God for relief, and to draw closer to Him. This will make it easier for the person to undergo other similar experiences in life without losing hope. (Lamentations 3:25-31)—2/15, page 24.

□ **Who are "the twelve tribes of Israel" spoken of by Jesus at Luke 22:28-30?**

These represent all the peoples of mankind who are to be judged by Christ and his 144,000 underpriests in connection with a regeneration of all that Jehovah has purposed for this earth. (Matthew 19:28)—3/1, page 28.

□ **What is meant by divine peace, and how can it be attained?**

Divine peace is a calm condition of mind and heart, an inner state of quiet, regardless of what may be taking place. (Psalm 4:8) It can only come about from an approved relationship with God, made possible by the ransom sacrifice of Christ Jesus. (Colossians 1:19, 20)—3/15, pages 11, 14, 15.

□ **What provisions do we have today to help us get to know God intimately?**

We have both the Bible and the perspective of centuries of fulfilled Bible prophecies. Also, we have the Gospel records of the life, works, and words of Jesus Christ, concerning whom Paul wrote: "It is in him [Christ] that all the fullness of the divine quality dwells bodily." (Colossians 2:9) —4/1, page 6.

Questions From Readers

■ **May a person making a dedication of his life to Jehovah God rightly speak of it as a *vow*?**

Humans who come to love the true God and who determine to serve him completely should dedicate their lives to Jehovah and then be baptized. While the Bible does not use the word "vow" regarding Christian dedication, doing so does not seem to be objectionable.

Aid to Bible Understanding explains that Scripturally a vow is "a solemn promise to perform some act, make some offering or gift, or enter some service or condition; a pledge, either positive or negative." Some vows of Biblical record involved a pledge to follow a stated course *if* God first did something. For example, Numbers 21:2 relates: "Consequently Israel made a vow to Jehovah and said: 'If you will without fail give this people into my hand, I shall also certainly devote their cities to destruction.'" (Genesis 28:20-22; Judges 11: 30-39) A Christian's dedication of his life to God is certainly not such a conditional vow. He does not say, as it were: 'If you, Jehovah, make me happy and prosperous now and guarantee me everlasting life in the new system of things, I promise to serve you all my life.'

The Bible presents some vows as being unrequested and unsolicited. *Wilson's Old Testament Word Studies* says of the Hebrew word involved: "[*na·darʹ*] to vow, *i.e.* to promise voluntarily to give or do something; the primary idea is that of setting apart." So a person *voluntarily* makes a vow to God. May it thus be reasoned that a person's becoming a dedicated, baptized disciple of Jesus would not constitute a vow because God now *requires* dedication of all who want His approval?*

However, the fact that Jehovah has certain requirements in order for an individual to be his friend does not mean that no personal choice is involved. Moses told the Israelites: "I have put life and death before you, the blessing and the malediction; and you must choose life in order that you may keep alive, you and your offspring." (Deuteronomy 30:19, 20; Psalm 15: 1-5; compare Joshua 24:15; 1 Kings 18:21.) Recall Jesus' words: "Come to me, all you who are toiling and loaded down, and I will refresh you. Take my yoke upon you and learn from me, for I am mild-tempered and lowly in heart, and you will find refreshment for your souls." (Matthew 11:28, 29) Is that an arbitrary requirement, a demand? Or is it an invitation allowing for voluntary response?

Jesus was born into a nation dedicated to God; many aspects of his life and death were predetermined in prophecy; and God prepared a body for Jesus to sacrifice. Still, Christ's voluntary decision in presenting himself for special service is reflected in his words: "Then I said, 'Look! I am come (in the roll of the book it is written about me) to do your will, O God.'" (Hebrews 10:5-10) In a similar way, each individual has to determine personally to become a dedicated, baptized Christian.

Furthermore, Christians today realize that usage of a word such as "vow" is not limited just to how it was employed in the Bible. Jehovah's Witnesses have long used "marriage vows" in weddings solemnized at their Kingdom Halls.* This accords with the general meaning of "vow," as in the definition: "a solemn promise or undertaking, especially in the form of an oath to God."—*Oxford American Dictionary,* 1980, page 778.

Consequently, it does not seem necessary to limit the use of the word "vow." A person who decides to serve God may feel that, for him, his unreserved dedication amounts to a personal vow—a vow of dedication. He 'solemnly promises or undertakes to do something,' which is what a vow is. In this case, it is to use his life to serve Jehovah, doing His will faithfully. Such an individual should feel seriously about this. It should be as with the psalmist, who, referring to things that he had vowed, said: "What shall I repay to Jehovah for all his benefits to me? The cup of grand salvation I shall take up, and on the name of Jehovah I shall call. My vows I shall pay to Jehovah."—Psalm 116:12-14; see also Psalm 50:14.

---

* This was the position taken in *The Watchtower* of October 1, 1973, page 607.

* During a wedding, the bride and groom make a vow to one another, but they are also doing so before witnesses and in God's sight.

'Helped to understand Someone I never thought I could'

In the following letter to the Watch Tower Society, a person describes where she received such help.

"Dear Sirs:

"I would like to let you know how much your books are helping me to understand Someone I never thought I could. The Bible is now the most fascinating book I've ever read because of the help you have given me through your books.

"Could you please send me a list of all the books you publish, if possible?

"Enclosed is $2.50 for two copies of *Reasoning From the Scriptures* . . . I must share this great 'little helper.'"

the Watchtower

May 1, 1987

Announcing Jehovah's Kingdom

O ALL
ROPHECIES
OME FROM
OD?

May 1, 1987
Vol. 108, No. 9

The Watchtower®
Announcing Jehovah's Kingdom

THE PURPOSE OF "THE WATCHTOWER" is to exalt Jehovah God as the Sovereign of the universe. It keeps watch on world events as they fulfill Bible prophecy. It comforts all peoples with the good news that God's Kingdom will soon destroy those who oppress their fellowmen and that it will turn the earth into a paradise. It encourages faith in the now-reigning King, Jesus Christ, whose shed blood opens the way for mankind to gain eternal life. "The Watchtower," published by Jehovah's Witnesses continuously since 1879, is nonpolitical. It adheres to the Bible as its authority.

"WATCHTOWER" STUDIES FOR THE WEEKS

June 7: Death-Dealing Famine in a Time of Plenty.
  Page 10. Songs to Be Used: 49, 151.

June 14: Preserving Life in Time of Famine.
  Page 15. Songs to Be Used: 143, 42.

Average Printing Each Issue: 12,315,000

Now Published in 103 Languages

SEMIMONTHLY LANGUAGES AVAILABLE BY MAIL
Afrikaans, Arabic, Cebuano, Chichewa, Chinese, Cibemba, Danish,* Dutch,* Efik, English,* Finnish,* French,* German,* Greek,* Hiligaynon, Igbo, Iloko, Italian,* Japanese,* Korean, Lingala, Malagasy, Maltese, Norwegian, Portuguese,* Russian, Sepedi, Sesotho, Shona, Spanish,* Swahili, Swedish,* Tagalog, Thai, Tsonga, Tswana, Xhosa, Yoruba, Zulu

MONTHLY LANGUAGES AVAILABLE BY MAIL
Armenian, Bengali, Bicol, Bulgarian, Croatian, Czech, Ewe, Fijian, Ga, Greenlandic, Gujarati, Gun, Hausa, Hebrew, Hindi, Hiri Motu, Hungarian, Icelandic, Kannada, Malayalam, Marathi, New Guinea Pidgin, Pangasinan, Papiamento, Polish, Rarotongan, Romanian, Samar-Leyte, Samoan, Sango, Serbian, Silozi, Sinhalese, Slovenian, Solomon Islands-Pidgin, Tahitian, Tamil, Telugu, Tongan, Tshiluba, Turkish, Twi, Ukrainian, Urdu, Venda, Vietnamese

* Study articles also available in large-print edition.

Watch Tower Society offices	Yearly subscription for the above: Semimonthly Languages	Monthly Languages
America, U.S., Watchtower, Wallkill, N.Y. 12589	$4.00	$2.00
Australia, Box 280, Ingleburn, N.S.W. 2565	A$7.00	A$3.50
Canada, Box 4100, Halton Hills, Ontario L7G 4Y4	$5.50	$2.75
England, The Ridgeway, London NW7 1RN	£5.00	£2.50
Ireland, 29A Jamestown Road, Finglas, Dublin 11	IR£6.00	IR£3.00
New Zealand, P.O. Box 142, Manurewa	NZ$15.00	NZ$7.50
Nigeria, PMB 001, Shomolu, Lagos State	₦8.00	₦4.00
Philippines, P.O. Box 2044, Manila 2800	₱60.00	₱30.00
South Africa, Private Bag 2067, Krugersdorp, 1740	R6,50	R3,25

Remittances should be sent to the office in your country or to Watchtower, Wallkill, N.Y. 12589, U.S.A.

Changes of address should reach us 30 days before your moving date. Give us your old and new address (if possible, your old address label).

20 cents (U.S.) a copy

The Bible translation used is the "New World Translation of the Holy Scriptures," unless otherwise indicated.

The Watchtower (ISSN 0043-1087) is published semimonthly for $4.00 (U.S.) per year by Watch Tower Bible and Tract Society of Pennsylvania, 25 Columbia Heights, Brooklyn, N.Y. 11201. Second-class postage paid at Brooklyn, N.Y., and at additional mailing offices.

Postmaster: Send address changes to Watchtower, **Wallkill, N.Y. 12589.**

Published by
**Watch Tower Bible and Tract Society
of Pennsylvania**
25 Columbia Heights, Brooklyn, N.Y. 11201, U.S.A.
Frederick W. Franz, President

DO ALL PROPHECIES COME FROM GOD?

"**G**OD . . . must be conceived of as being too large and too universal to confine Himself to just one religion, one path or, for that matter, just one people." So wrote a philosopher in *The Guardian,* a Nigerian newspaper. He holds that African traditional religions were revealed by God for the African situation and suggests that other great religions were conceived to fit local circumstances.

Traditionalists see Christianity as a European religion and traditional soothsayers as genuine agents of prophecy. A letter to the Nigerian *Daily Times* said: "Almighty God manifests himself at different times to different peoples . . . The wise men of the world murmur that the Supreme Being is currently manifesting Himself in Africa." Some even hope for an African prophet, similar to Jesus and, some say, Muhammad.

These views give rise to such questions as these: Do all prophecies come from God? Did he reveal the different religious concepts that divide the world? Does he have different religious requirements for different races? Or are there true and false prophets, and true and false religions? What really is true prophecy, and what is the purpose of it?

What Is Prophecy?

Webster's Ninth New Collegiate Dictionary defines prophecy as "the inspired declaration of divine will and purpose **2:** an inspired utterance of a prophet **3:** a prediction of something to come." This suggests that there can be various sources of prophecies.

In defending traditional religions, a university professor of religious studies, E. Bolaji Idowu, speaks of "the multi-sided concept of God in Africa." His book *African Traditional Religion* explains that this "usually takes its emphasis and complexion from the sociological structure and climate." For example, he says that "whereas in most of Africa, God is conceived in masculine terms, there are localities [particularly in matriarchal communities] where he is regarded as feminine." Could such localized and contradictory notions be inspired by God? Professor Idowu acknowledges that "there is nothing to prevent . . . any . . . race in Africa from developing its own concept of God." This suggests that such religious concepts spring from human ideas and observation rather than from divine revelation. —Compare Romans 1:19-23.

Traditional soothsayers and oracles do not reveal the true God's personality or his will and purpose. They deal with the taboos and rituals demanded by a variety of local "gods." Their predictions are based on mystic knowledge and divination. Therefore, such prophecies are not inspired declarations of the divine will. Almighty God, who inspires true prophecy, is not their source.—2 Peter 1:20, 21; Deuteronomy 13:1-5; 18:20-22.

What, then, is the source of such predictions? Please read the next article for the answer to this question and the others raised earlier in this discussion.

WHAT IS THE PURPOSE OF PROPHECY?

THOSE who claim that their various forms of worship are revelations from superhuman sources also acknowledge that there are good and bad supernatural powers. This acknowledgment raises these questions: Was each of these forms of worship revealed from a good source? Or do they have a bad source? Which one is inspired by the true God?

The First Religion

Mankind is recognized as being one family, and this agrees with the Bible's account of one original human pair, Adam and Eve. Jehovah, the Creator, made himself known to them. He revealed to Adam and Eve their role in his purpose and their true relationship to him. God made Adam his first prophet, responsible to pass divine revelations on to his wife and eventually to their offspring, that is, all mankind. —Genesis 1:27-30; 2:15-17.

This was the only religion, the one form of worship revealed by Jehovah God. It was expressed by obedience to God's will. No rituals, sacrifices, shrines, or oracles were required.

False Religion Appears

The first opposing "revelation" came from an angel who wanted to be worshiped. He offered an alternative to true religion and induced Adam and Eve to join him in rebellion against their Creator. This made him Satan, Jehovah's op-

poser. His "prophecy" pretended to offer self-determination and independence from God. Instead, it caused enslavement to Satan and to sin, bringing death.—Genesis 3:1-19; Matthew 4:8-10; Romans 5:12.

Satan was eventually joined by other rebellious angels, or demons. No doubt these spawned false religious concepts that contributed to the corrupting of mankind. In the days of Adam's grandson Enosh, "a start was made of calling on the name of Jehovah." According to the *Targum of Palestine,* this was done profanely as part of the idolatrous worship of that time.—Genesis 4:26; 6:1-8; 1 Peter 3:19, 20; 2 Peter 2:1-4.

False religion was wiped out in the Flood of Noah's day, leaving just the true form of worship practiced by Jehovah's prophet, Noah. (Genesis 6:5-9, 13; 7:23; 2 Peter 2:5) The demons remained, though, and reintroduced counterfeit prophecies and religious concepts. They caused Noah's descendants to offend Jehovah by building the city of Babel as a center of false worship. But God confused their language and

"scattered them from there over all the surface of the earth."—Genesis 11:1-9.

What does all of this tell us? We are all descendants of Noah and Adam. So all cultures have a common origin and have retained some concept of God as a vestige of knowledge that has survived from Noah's day. But this basic concept is corrupted by false religious ideas inherited from those forefathers who scattered from Babel (later restored as Babylon) to all parts of the earth. This is seen in common superstitions about spirits of the dead, in ancestor worship, and in the practice of astrology, divination, and witchcraft.—Daniel 2:1, 2.

The Purpose of Prophecy

Does this mean that present-day religions are based only on concepts inherited from that ancient past? No. Satan and the demons still inspire false prophecy to deceive and divide mankind, confuse true revelations about God, and establish false ideas and religions. (1 Timothy 4:1; 1 John 4:1-3; Revelation 16:13-16) The Bible says: "There also came to be false prophets among the people, as there will also be false teachers among you. These very ones will quietly bring in destructive sects." —2 Peter 2:1.

On the other hand, Jehovah has preserved the true religion given in Eden. He has added information to enhance our knowledge of him and of our responsibility in the outworking of his purpose. So true prophecies make known the truth about God, his will, and his moral standards. They clarify man's relationship to him so as to bring mankind back into harmony with his purpose, leading up to its full accomplishment.—Isaiah 1:18-20; 2:1-5; 55:8-11.

At the start of man's rebellion, Jehovah spoke a prophecy that gave hope to the offspring of Adam and Eve. He revealed that there would be a deliverer, a "seed," who would destroy Satan and his progeny. (Genesis 3:15) Later prophecies helped to identify this promised "seed," or God's "anointed one," and revealed that he would play the principal role in the fulfillment of God's purposes.—Psalm 2:2; 45:7; Isaiah 61:1.

Thus a primary intent of prophecy was to make known God's purposes and the "anointed one," or "Christ," through whom they would be fulfilled. Since this chosen one proved to be Jesus, Jehovah's angel said: "Worship God; for the bearing witness to Jesus is what inspires [or, is the spirit of] prophesying." (Revelation 19:10) Two facts are made clear by this declaration. First, no agent of true prophecy will demand to be worshiped because true worship belongs only to Jehovah God. (Matthew 4:4; John 4:23, 24) Second, the ultimate aim of all true prophecy must be to reveal events and facts relating to Jesus. This recognizes the key role Jehovah assigned him in the outworking of His purpose to sanctify His name and restore earth to its proper place in His arrangement of things.—John 14:6; Colossians 1: 19, 20.

For this reason, inspired messages from God pointed primarily toward Jesus. The entire spirit, or intent and purpose, of such true prophecy was to bear witness to him. Furthermore, the realization of the prophecies in Jesus marks them all as true. This is why the Bible says that "the truth came to be through Jesus Christ." "For no matter how many the promises of God are, they have become Yes by means of him."—John 1:17; 2 Corinthians 1:20; Acts 10:43; 28:23.

Why to the Israelites?

Jehovah started off his "witness to Jesus" by his prophecy regarding the promised "seed." God later revealed the earthly lineage of the "seed" as being through

Noah, Shem, Abraham, Isaac (not *Ishmael*), and *Jacob*. These men remained loyal to the true religion, proving themselves faithful prophets of Jehovah while all the nations were corrupted by the worship of false gods. (Genesis 6:9; 22:15-18; Hebrews 11:8-10, 16) The lineage continued through descendants of these men—the *nation of Israel* and particularly the family of *David,* Israel's most prominent king. —2 Samuel 7:12-16.

Showing why he chose Israel, Jehovah said: "It was not because of your being the most populous of all the peoples . . . [but] because of his keeping the sworn statement . . . to your forefathers," Abraham, Isaac, and Jacob. (Deuteronomy 7:6-8; 29:13) Obviously, only one nation could provide the lineage for the promised "seed." However, true religion was not limited to the Israelites. While revelations of truth were not given to other nations, individuals from among them could join Israel in worship, and some of these were even included in the lineage of the "seed." (Numbers 9:14; Ruth 4:10-22; Matthew 1:5, 6) Separate revelations given along national or racial lines would only have caused greater religious division, whereas it is Jehovah's will to reunite mankind in one worship.—Genesis 22:18; Ephesians 1:8-10; 2:11-16.

God's requirements are the same for all races. Since he is unchangeable in his moral standards and purpose, his dealings with Israel showed how he will deal with similar situations at any given time. (Malachi 3:6) So Israel served as a model for all nations. Through it God demonstrated the benefits of true worship and the folly of false cults. While the Israelites remained faithful to him, he protected and blessed them. When they turned to false gods of other nations, they fell under oppression by those nations, just as Jehovah had warned them.—Deuteronomy 30:15-20; Daniel 9:2-14.

Israel also served as a prophetic model, and David became a prophetic figure of Jesus, who inherited God's Kingdom covenant with David. (1 Chronicles 17:11, 14; Luke 1:32) The Law given to Israel, with its sacrifices and priesthood, foreshadowed the sacrifice of Jesus and pointed to his heavenly Kingdom and priesthood. The Law thus became a "tutor leading to Christ."—Galatians 3:19, 24; Acts 2:25-36; Hebrews 10:1-10; Revelation 20:4-6.

The Book of True Prophecy

This vital information could not be accurately preserved by oral tradition or by separate revelations to various nations. The best avenue of preservation and of transmission to all nations is a written record. And the Bible fills this role. It alone contains God's inspired revelations and preserves the historical and prophetic account of his dealings with humans. It alone points to *Jesus Christ* as God's Agent for salvation and contains the final prophecies regarding the future accomplishment of his Messianic assignment. This is thus the complete inspired written Word of God.—Romans 15:4; 1 Corinthians 10:11; 2 Peter 1:20, 21.

Since the completing of the Bible, those who have introduced new "prophecies," religions, and sects could not be inspired by God. True prophecies were not given to reveal new religions. They kept the one true religion current and made known the future outworking of Jehovah's purpose. Their fulfillment gives proof of his unique Godship and power, showing that he alone can foretell events centuries in advance and unerringly bring them to pass.—Isaiah 41:21-26; 46:9-11.

So all who desire to be acquainted with true prophecy and to practice true religion need to turn to the Bible. It is God's book of prophecy—his complete message to mankind.—2 Timothy 3:16, 17.

Lineage of the promised "seed"

Shem

Noah

Abraham

Isaac

Jacob

David

Jesus

Silencing a Terrifying Storm

JESUS' day has been filled with activity, including teaching the crowds on the beach and afterward explaining the illustrations privately to his disciples. When evening comes, he says: "Let us cross to the other shore."

Over on the eastern shore of the Sea of Galilee is the region called the Decapolis, from the Greek de´ka, meaning "ten," and po´lis, meaning "city." The cities of the Decapolis are a center of Greek culture, although doubtless they are also the home of many Jews. Jesus' activity in the region, however, is very limited. Even on this visit, as we will see later, he is prevented from staying long.

When Jesus requests that they leave for the other shore, the disciples take him in the boat. Their departure, however, does not go unnoticed. Soon others board their boats to accompany them. It is not very far across. Actually, the Sea of Galilee is just a large lake about 13 miles (21 km) long and a maximum of 7 1/2 miles (12 km) wide.

Jesus is understandably tired. So, soon after they shove off, he lies down in the back of the boat, puts his head on a pillow, and falls fast asleep. Several of the apostles are experienced sailors, having fished extensively on the Sea of Galilee. So they take charge of sailing the boat.

But this is not to be an easy trip. Because of the warmer temperature at the lake's surface, which is about 700 feet (210 m) below sea level, and the colder air in the nearby mountains, strong winds at times sweep down and create sudden violent windstorms on the lake. This is what now occurs. Soon the waves are dashing against the boat and splashing into it, so that it is close to being swamped. Yet, Jesus continues to sleep!

The experienced seamen work frantically to steer the boat. No doubt they have maneuvered through storms before. But this time they are at the end of their resources. Fearing for their lives, they wake Jesus up. 'Master, do you not care? We are sinking!' they exclaim. 'Save us, we are going to drown!'

Rousing himself, Jesus commands the wind and the sea: 'Hush! be quiet!' And the raging wind stops and the sea becomes calm. Turning to his disciples, he asks: 'Why are you so fearful? Do you not yet have any faith?'

At that, an unusual fear grips the disciples. 'Who really is this man?' they ask one another. 'For he orders even the winds and the water, and they obey him.'

What power Jesus displays! How reassuring it is to know that our King has power over the natural elements and that when his full attention is directed toward our earth during his Kingdom rule, all will dwell in security from terrifying natural calamities!

Sometime after the storm subsides, Jesus and his disciples arrive safely on the eastern shore. Perhaps the other boats were spared the intensity of the storm and safely returned home. **Mark 4:35–5:2; Matthew 8:18, 23-28; Luke 8: 22-27.**

♦ What is the Decapolis, and where is it located?

♦ What physical features are responsible for violent storms on the Sea of Galilee?

♦ When their sailing skills cannot save them, what do the disciples do?

Death-Dealing Famine
in a Time of Plenty

"My own servants will eat, but you yourselves will go hungry."—ISAIAH 65:13.

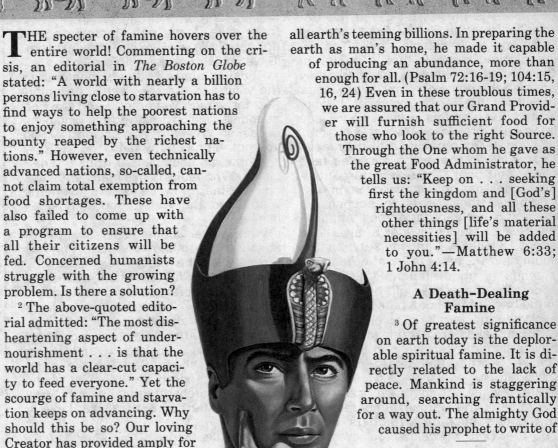

THE specter of famine hovers over the entire world! Commenting on the crisis, an editorial in *The Boston Globe* stated: "A world with nearly a billion persons living close to starvation has to find ways to help the poorest nations to enjoy something approaching the bounty reaped by the richest nations." However, even technically advanced nations, so-called, cannot claim total exemption from food shortages. These have also failed to come up with a program to ensure that all their citizens will be fed. Concerned humanists struggle with the growing problem. Is there a solution?

² The above-quoted editorial admitted: "The most disheartening aspect of undernourishment . . . is that the world has a clear-cut capacity to feed everyone." Yet the scourge of famine and starvation keeps on advancing. Why should this be so? Our loving Creator has provided amply for

all earth's teeming billions. In preparing the earth as man's home, he made it capable of producing an abundance, more than enough for all. (Psalm 72:16-19; 104:15, 16, 24) Even in these troublous times, we are assured that our Grand Provider will furnish sufficient food for those who look to the right Source. Through the One whom he gave as the great Food Administrator, he tells us: "Keep on . . . seeking first the kingdom and [God's] righteousness, and all these other things [life's material necessities] will be added to you."—Matthew 6:33; 1 John 4:14.

A Death-Dealing Famine

³ Of greatest significance on earth today is the deplorable spiritual famine. It is directly related to the lack of peace. Mankind is staggering around, searching frantically for a way out. The almighty God caused his prophet to write of

1, 2. (a) With what problem do the nations struggle in vain? (b) To what realistic hope does the Bible point?

3. What is the famine of greatest significance, and how was it foretold?

this situation many centuries ago, saying: "'Look! There are days coming,' is the utterance of the Sovereign Lord Jehovah, 'and I will send a famine into the land, a famine, not for bread, and a thirst, not for water, but for hearing the words of Jehovah. And they will certainly stagger from sea all the way to sea, and from north even to the sunrise. They will keep roving about while searching for the word of Jehovah, but they will not find it.'"—Amos 8:11, 12.

⁴ However, is there a way out of the impasse? The apostle Paul answers yes, encouraging us with the words: "The God that made the world . . . decreed the appointed times and the set limits of the dwelling of men, for them to seek God, if they might grope for him and really find him, although, in fact, he is not far off from each one of us." —Acts 17:24-27.

⁵ If God is "not far off from each one of us," why is it that many grope for him, yet do not find him? It is because they are searching for him in the wrong places. How many who call themselves Christians personally consult the basic textbook of Christianity, the Holy Bible? How many so-called "shepherds" use God's Word to teach the "sheep"? (Compare Ezekiel 34:10.) Jesus told the proud religious leaders of his day that they knew "neither the Scriptures nor the power of God." (Matthew 22:29; John 5:44) However, Jesus both knew the Scriptures and taught them to the people, for whom he felt pity "because they were skinned and thrown about like sheep without a shepherd."—Matthew 9:36.

How a Time of Plenty?

⁶ Jehovah reassures and encourages those sincerely seeking to know him. In reproving false religious shepherds, he says through his prophet Isaiah: "Look! My own servants will eat, but you yourselves will go hungry. Look! My own servants will drink, but you yourselves will go thirsty. Look! My own servants will rejoice, but you yourselves will suffer shame." (Isaiah 65:13, 14) But how does God provide plenty for his own servants? What must we do to share with joy in his provision for the preservation of life, despite today's spiritual famine?

⁷ Since survival depends so completely on our knowing God's requirements and acting in faith on them, we should gladly go to God's Word, seeking to know his will for us and to discern his manner of dealing with us. (John 17:3) To this end, we will now consider a Biblical drama that parallels what is happening today. The central character in this drama is the patriarch Joseph. As Jehovah made wise provision for His people through Joseph, so He lovingly leads those who search for Him today.—Compare Romans 15:4; 1 Corinthians 10:11, *Reference Bible* footnote (*); Galatians 4:24.

Joseph, Preserver of Life

⁸ As a preserver of life, Joseph the son of Jacob played a striking role. Does this depict something in later times? Well, consider Joseph's endurance of undeserved treatment by his brothers, his coping with tests and trials in a foreign land, his unshakable faith, his maintaining integrity, and his being exalted to the position of wise administrator in a time of catastrophic famine. (Genesis 39:1-3, 7-9; 41:38-41) Do we not see a parallel in the life course of Jesus?

⁹ It was through adversity that Jesus became the Bread of Life amid a world that

4, 5. (a) Why do some not find God though they search for him? (b) How did Jesus contrast with the religious leaders of his day? (Matthew 15: 1-14)
6. As to spiritual plenty, how does Jehovah reassure his servants?

7. What ancient drama was lovingly provided for our encouragement today?
8, 9. (a) What parallels do we find in later times for Joseph and for Jacob and Pharaoh? (b) How may we ourselves be involved in the fulfillment?

is starved "for hearing the words of Jehovah." (Amos 8:11; Hebrews 5:8, 9; John 6:35) In their relations with Joseph, both Jacob and Pharaoh remind us of Jehovah and what he accomplishes through his Son. (John 3:17, 34; 20:17; Romans 8:15, 16; Luke 4:18) There were others also who shared in acting out this real-life drama, and we will consider their parts with interest. We will no doubt be reminded of our own dependency upon the Greater Joseph, Christ Jesus. How thankful we are that he preserves us from death-dealing famine during these worsening "last days"! —2 Timothy 3:1, 13.

The Drama Unfolds

10 In Joseph's day, no human could have known in advance what Jehovah had in store for His people. But by the time Joseph was called on to fulfill his vital role, Jehovah had already trained and perfected him as to his qualifications. With regard to his early life, the account reads: "Joseph, when seventeen years old, happened to be tending sheep with his brothers among the flock, and, being but a boy, he was with the sons of Bilhah and the sons of Zilpah, the wives of his father. So Joseph brought a bad report about them to their father." (Genesis 37:2) He showed loyalty to his father's interests even as Jesus was unswervingly loyal in tending his Father's flock amid a "faithless and twisted generation."—Matthew 17:17, 22, 23.

11 Joseph's father, Israel, came to love him more than all his brothers and favored him by having a long, striped shirtlike garment made for him. Because of this, Joseph's half brothers "began to hate him, and they were not able to speak peacefully to

him." They found further reason to hate him when he had two dreams that they interpreted to mean he would dominate over them. In like manner, the leaders among the Jews came to hate Jesus because of his loyalty, his persuasive teaching, and Jehovah's obvious blessing upon him. —Genesis 37:3-11; John 7:46; 8:40.

12 In time, Joseph's brothers were tending sheep near Shechem. Joseph's father was properly concerned because it was there that Shechem had defiled Dinah, so that Simeon and Levi, with their brothers, had killed the men of that city. Jacob asked Joseph to go and see about their welfare and report back to him. Despite his brothers' animosity toward him, Joseph immediately set out to find them. In like fashion, Jesus gladly accepted Jehovah's assignment here on earth, even though it would mean great suffering during his perfecting as the Chief Agent of salvation. In his endurance, what a fine exemplar Jesus became for all of us!—Genesis 34:25-27; 37:12-17; Hebrews 2:10; 12:1, 2.

13 Joseph's ten half brothers saw him coming at a distance. Immediately their anger flared up against him, and they schemed to get rid of him. At first they planned to kill him. But Reuben, out of fear for his responsibility as firstborn, prevailed upon them to pitch Joseph into a dry waterpit, expecting to return later and free him. Meantime, however, Judah persuaded his brothers to sell him as a slave to some Ishmaelites whose caravan was passing. The brothers then took Joseph's long garment and dipped it into the blood of a male goat and sent it to their father. When Jacob examined it, he exclaimed: "It is my son's

---

10. (a) How was Joseph prepared for the responsible role he was to play? (b) What qualities did he display early in life?
11. (a) Why did Joseph's half brothers come to hate him? (b) What similar situation involved Jesus?

12. (a) Why was Jacob concerned about the welfare of his sons? (b) What parallel do we find between Joseph's course and that of Jesus?
13. (a) How did Joseph's half brothers vent their hatred? (b) To what may Jacob's sorrow be compared?

long garment! A vicious wild beast must have devoured him! Joseph is surely torn to pieces!" Jehovah must have felt similar grief over Jesus' suffering as he fulfilled his assignment on earth.—Genesis 37:18-35; 1 John 4:9, 10.

Joseph in Egypt

14 We must not conclude that the fulfillments of the dramatic events involving Joseph take place in exact chronological sequence. Rather, we find back there a series of patterns that are for our instruction and encouragement today. As the apostle Paul states: "All the things that were written aforetime were written for our instruction, that through our endurance and through the comfort from the Scriptures we might have hope. Now may the God who supplies endurance and comfort grant you to have among yourselves the same mental attitude that Christ Jesus had, that with one accord you may with one mouth glorify the God and Father of our Lord Jesus Christ."—Romans 15:4-6.

15 Joseph was taken to Egypt, and there he was sold to an Egyptian named Potiphar, the chief of Pharaoh's bodyguard. Jehovah proved to be with Joseph, who continued to live by the fine principles that his father had instilled in him, even though he was far away from his father's house. Joseph did not abandon Jehovah's worship. His master, Potiphar, got to appreciate Joseph's outstanding qualities and placed him over

his entire household. Jehovah kept blessing the house of Potiphar because of Joseph. —Genesis 37:36; 39:1-6.

16 It was there that the wife of Potiphar tried to seduce Joseph. He kept refusing her. One day she grabbed hold of his garment, but he fled, leaving it in her hand. Before Potiphar, she accused Joseph of making immoral advances, and Potiphar had Joseph thrown into prison. For a time he was put in fetters of iron. But throughout the adversities of his prison experience, Joseph continued to prove that he was a man of integrity. Thus, the keeper of the prison placed him in charge of all the prisoners.—Genesis 39:7-23; Psalm 105:17, 18.

17 In the course of time, Pharaoh's chief cupbearer and chief baker displeased him and were imprisoned. Joseph was assigned to minister to them. Again, Jehovah maneuvered matters. The two court officials had dreams that perplexed them. After emphasizing that "interpretations belong to God," Joseph told them what the dreams meant. And just as Joseph had indicated, three days later (on Pharaoh's birthday) the cupbearer was restored to his position, but the chief baker was hanged.—Genesis 40:1-22.

18 Though Joseph had implored the cupbearer to speak to Pharaoh in his behalf, two years passed before the man remembered Joseph. Even then, this was only

14. How may this ancient drama benefit us today?
15. Why did Joseph and the house of Potiphar prosper?

16, 17. (a) How did Joseph meet a further test of integrity? (b) Joseph's experience in prison shows what direction of matters?
18. (a) How did Joseph come to be remembered? (b) What was the substance of Pharaoh's dreams?

A columnist in **The Sunday Star** (*Toronto, March 30, 1986*) *said of the so-called mainline churches: "Where they are failing badly is in making contact with the deep spiritual hunger of today's men, women and young people"*

because of Pharaoh's twice having perplexing dreams in one night. When none of the king's magic-practicing priests could unravel their meaning, the cupbearer told Pharaoh that Joseph could interpret dreams. So Pharaoh sent for Joseph, who humbly pointed to the Source of true interpretations, saying: "God will announce welfare to Pharaoh." Egypt's ruler then related the dreams to Joseph, as follows:

"Here I was standing on the bank of the river Nile. And here ascending out of the river Nile were seven cows fat-fleshed and beautiful in form, and they began to feed among the Nile grass. And here there were seven other cows ascending after them, poor and very bad in form and thin-fleshed. For badness I have not seen the like of them in all the land of Egypt. And the skinny and bad cows began to eat up the first seven fat cows. So these came into their bellies, and yet it could not be known that they had come into their bellies, as their appearance was bad just as at the start. . . .

"After that I saw in my dream and here there were seven ears of grain coming up on one stalk, full and good. And here there were seven ears of grain shriveled, thin, scorched by the east wind, growing up after them. And the thin ears of grain began to swallow up the seven good ears of grain. So I stated it to the

---

How Do You Answer?

☐ In what twofold way is famine a menace today?

☐ What fine qualities did Joseph cultivate while with his half brothers?

☐ What can we learn from Joseph's early experiences in Egypt?

☐ Jehovah's concern for Joseph and the famine-stricken people assures us of what?

---

magic-practicing priests, but there was none telling me."—Genesis 40:23–41:24.

[19] What strange dreams! How could anyone explain them? Joseph did, but not for his own self-glory. He said: "The dream of Pharaoh is but one. What the true God is doing . . . he has caused Pharaoh to see." Then Joseph went on to reveal the powerful prophetic message of those dreams, saying:

"Here there are seven years coming with great plenty in all the land of Egypt. But seven years of famine will certainly arise after them, and all the plenty in the land of Egypt will certainly be forgotten and the famine will simply consume the land. . . . And the fact that the dream was repeated to Pharaoh twice means that the thing is firmly established on the part of the true God, and the true God is speeding to do it."—Genesis 41:25-32.

[20] What could Pharaoh do about this impending famine? Joseph recommended that Pharaoh make preparation by setting a discreet and wise man over the land to store the surplus harvest of the good years. By now Pharaoh had recognized Joseph's outstanding qualities. Removing his signet ring from his own hand and putting it upon the hand of Joseph, Pharaoh thus appointed him over all the land of Egypt.—Genesis 41: 33-46.

[21] Joseph was 30 years old when he stood before Pharaoh, the same age as Jesus Christ when he was baptized and began his life-giving ministry. The article that follows will show how Joseph was used by Jehovah in foreshadowing Jehovah's "Chief Agent and Savior" in time of spiritual famine with special reference to our own day. —Acts 3:15; 5:31.

---

19. (a) How did Joseph show humility? (b) What message was conveyed by the interpretation of the dreams?
20, 21. (a) How did Pharaoh react to the warning? (b) At this point, how may Joseph and Jesus be compared?

Preserving Life
in Time of Famine

IMMEDIATELY after his appointment as food administrator, Joseph toured the land of Egypt. He had matters well organized by the time the years of plenty began. Now the land yielded its produce by the handfuls! Joseph kept collecting the foodstuffs from the field around each city, storing it up in the city. He kept "piling up grain in very great quantity, like the sand of the sea, until finally they gave up counting it, because it was without number."—Genesis 41:46-49.

2 The seven years of plenty ended, and the famine began as Jehovah had foretold —a famine not just in Egypt but "over all the surface of the earth." When the famished people in Egypt began to cry out to Pharaoh for bread, Pharaoh told them: "Go to Joseph. Whatever he says to you, you are to do." Joseph sold grain to the Egyptians until their money ran out. Then he accepted their livestock in payment. Finally, the people came to Joseph, saying: "Buy us and our land for bread, and we together with our land will become slaves to Pharaoh." So Joseph bought all the land of the Egyptians for Pharaoh.—Genesis 41:53-57; 47:13-20.

Provision for Spiritual Feeding

3 Just as the grain distributed by Joseph meant life to the Egyptians, so true spiritual food is essential for sustaining Christians who become slaves of Jehovah by their dedication to Him through the Greater Joseph, Jesus Christ. During his earthly ministry, Jesus foretold that his anointed footstep followers would bear the responsibility of dispensing these provisions. He asked: "Who really is the faithful and discreet slave whom his master appointed over his domestics, to give them their food at the proper time? Happy is that slave if his master on arriving finds him doing so."—Matthew 24:45, 46.

4 The faithful remnant of this "discreet slave" class today go to any Scriptural lengths to see that Jehovah's dedicated witnesses, as well as interested people out in the world, receive life-sustaining spiritual food. This trust is recognized as a sacred duty and is performed as a sacred service to Jehovah. Moreover, the "slave" has organized congregations and supplied these with Bible literature in such quantity that they have ample Kingdom "seed" for scattering publicly in their assigned fields. This corresponds to Joseph's day, when he gathered the people into cities and provided them with grain not only for sustenance but also for sowing with a later harvest in view.—Genesis 47:21-25; Mark 4:14, 20; Matthew 28:19, 20.

5 Even when the public preaching work

---

1. What wise action did Joseph take during the years of plenty, and with what result?
2. At what personal sacrifice were the people able to obtain sustenance?
3. What agency did Jesus foretell for providing food at the proper time?

4. How does the provision made by the "slave" class today correspond with what was organized in Joseph's day?
5. (a) What special attention does the "slave" pay to household needs in time of crisis? (b) How does the "overflow" of spiritual provisions in 1986 compare with supplies back in Joseph's time?

is under ban and Jehovah's Witnesses are persecuted, the 'faithful slave' views this providing of spiritual food as a sacred trust. (Acts 5:29, 41, 42; 14:19-22) When disaster strikes, such as by storms, floods, and earthquakes, the "slave" sees to it that both the physical and the spiritual needs of God's household are supplied. Even those in concentration camps have been reached regularly with the printed word. National boundaries are not permitted to stop the flow of spiritual food to those needing it. Keeping up the supply requires courage, faith in Jehovah, and often considerable ingenuity. Worldwide during 1986 alone, the "slave" produced an overflow of 43,-958,303 Bibles and hardcovered books, as well as 550,216,455 magazines—truly a "very great quantity, like the sand of the sea."

Retaliation, Punishment, or Mercy?

⁶ Eventually the famine came to the land of

6, 7. (a) How did the famine result in the ten half brothers' prostrating themselves before Joseph? (b) In what ways was Joseph himself now on trial?

Canaan. Jacob sent the ten half brothers of Joseph down to Egypt to buy grain. But he did not send Benjamin, Joseph's only full brother, for fear, as he said, that "a fatal accident may befall him." Since Joseph was the one who did the selling, his brothers came to him and prostrated themselves before him. Though they did not recognize their brother, Joseph knew them.—Genesis 42:1-7.

⁷ Joseph now remembered his earlier dreams concerning them. But what was he to do? Should he retaliate? In their time of great need, should he forgive the treatment he had received at their hands? What of his father's ago-

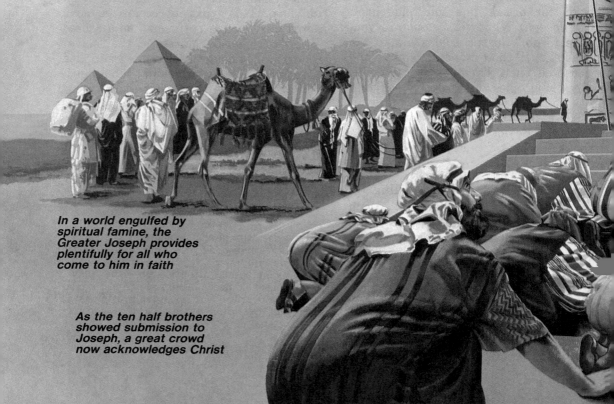

In a world engulfed by spiritual famine, the Greater Joseph provides plentifully for all who come to him in faith

As the ten half brothers showed submission to Joseph, a great crowd now acknowledges Christ

nizing grief? Should this be forgotten? How did his brothers now feel about the great wrong they had committed? Joseph, too, was on trial in this matter. Would his actions be in line with the attitude that the Greater Joseph, Jesus Christ, would show later, as described at 1 Peter 2:22, 23: "He committed no sin, nor was deception found in his mouth. When he was being reviled, he did not go reviling in return. When he was suffering, he did not go threatening, but kept on committing himself to the one who judges righteously."

8 Since Joseph could see Jehovah's hand in the outworking of events, he would be careful to observe God's laws and principles. In the same way, Jesus was always eager to 'do the will of his Father' as he dispensed everlasting life to 'everyone exercising faith in him.' (John 6:37-40) As "ambassadors substituting for Christ," his anointed disciples also fulfill their sacred trust in "speaking to the people all the sayings about this life." —2 Corinthians 5:20; Acts 5:20.

9 Joseph did not reveal himself to his brothers right away. Instead, he spoke to them harshly through an interpreter, saying: "You are spies!" Since they had mentioned a younger brother, Joseph demanded that they prove their truthfulness by bringing this one down to Egypt. Joseph overheard them saying repentantly to one another that this turn of events must be in recompense for their

---

8. By what would Joseph be guided, illustrating what with regard to Jesus and His disciples?
9, 10. (a) What course did Joseph now take, and why? (b) How did Joseph show compassion comparable to what Jesus would show?

Like the 70 souls of Jacob's household, the complete number of Jehovah's "sheep" arrive in a good "land" —the spiritual paradise we now enjoy

selling him, Joseph, into slavery. Turning aside, Joseph wept. Nevertheless, he had Simeon bound as hostage until they returned with Benjamin.—Genesis 42:9-24.

¹⁰ Joseph was not retaliating for the wrong done to him. He wanted to determine whether their repentance was genuine, from the depths of their hearts, so that they might be shown mercy. (Malachi 3:7; James 4:8) With a compassionate attitude, comparable to the one Jesus would display, Joseph not only filled their sacks with grain but also returned their money to them in the mouth of each one's sack. Additionally, he gave them provisions for their journey.—Genesis 42:25-35; compare Matthew 11:28-30.

¹¹ In time, they finished the food they had bought in Egypt. Jacob asked the nine sons to return and buy more. Previously, he had pleaded with regard to Benjamin, saying: "My son will not go down with you men, because his brother is dead and he has been left by himself. If a fatal accident should befall him on the way on which you would go, then you would certainly bring down my gray hairs with grief to Sheol." However, after much persuasion and Judah's offer to become personally responsible for Benjamin, Jacob reluctantly agrees to allow them to take the boy with them. —Genesis 42:36–43:14.

¹² When Joseph saw that Benjamin had come with the brothers, he invited them to his house, where he spread a feast. For Benjamin he provided a portion five times that of the portion for each of the others.

The modern-day Benjamin class have been specially favored by Christ, receiving an abundance of "food at the proper time"

Then Joseph made a final test of his brothers. Again, he returned all their money in their individual sacks, but his own special silver cup was placed in the mouth of Benjamin's sack. After their departure, Joseph sent his house manager to accuse them of theft and to search their sacks for his cup. When it was found in Benjamin's sack, the brothers ripped their mantles apart. They were led back to face Joseph. Judah made an impassioned plea for mercy, offering to become a slave in Benjamin's place so that the boy could be returned to his father.—Genesis 43: 15-44:34.

¹³ Convinced now of his brothers' change of heart, Joseph could no longer control his emotions. After ordering everyone else to go out from him, Joseph declared: "I am Joseph your brother, whom you sold into Egypt. But now do not feel hurt and do not be angry with yourselves because you sold me here; be-

---

11. (a) In time, what was Jacob forced to do, and why did he finally agree? (b) How do Romans 8:32 and 1 John 4:10 likewise assure us of God's love?

12, 13. (a) How did Joseph impose a test to reveal the heart attitude of his brothers? (b) How did the result give Joseph a basis for showing mercy?

cause for the preservation of life God has sent me ahead of you . . . in order to place a remnant for you men in the earth and to keep you alive by a great escape." He then said to his brothers: "Go up quickly to my father, and you must say to him, ' . . . Come down to me. Do not delay. And you must dwell in the land of Goshen, and . . . I will supply you with food there, for there are yet five years of famine; for fear you and your house and everything you have may come to poverty.' "—Genesis 45:4-15.

¹⁴ When Pharaoh heard the news about Joseph's brothers, he told Joseph to have wagons taken from the land of Egypt to bring his father and all of his family to Egypt because the best of the land was to be theirs. Hearing all that had happened, Jacob was revived in spirit and exclaimed: "It is enough! Joseph my son is still alive! Ah, let me go and see him before I die!" —Genesis 45:16-28.

Spiritual Food Aplenty

¹⁵ What does all of this mean for us today? Ever conscious of our spiritual need, we look to One far greater than the kindly Pharaoh of Joseph's time. It is the Sovereign Lord Jehovah who provides sustenance and guidance through these dark days of a world starved for Bible truth. We have exerted ourselves in the interests of his Kingdom, bringing our tithes, as it were, into his storehouse. How generously he has opened to us "the floodgates of the heavens," pouring out a blessing "until there is no more want"!—Malachi 3:10.

¹⁶ At Jehovah's right hand is his Food

Administrator, now the enthroned King, the glorified Jesus. (Acts 2:34-36) As the people had to sell themselves as slaves to keep alive, so all today who want to keep living must come to Jesus, becoming his followers dedicated to God. (Luke 9:23, 24) As Jacob directed his sons to go to Joseph for food, so Jehovah guides repentant humans to his beloved Son, Jesus Christ. (John 6:44, 48-51) Jesus gathers his followers into citylike congregations—more than 52,000 strong throughout the world today—where they are fed from a bounty of spiritual food and are supplied with an overflow of "grain," as "seed" for sowing in the field. (Genesis 47:23, 24; Matthew 13:4-9, 18-23) Willing workers are these witnesses of Jehovah! More and more of them are volunteering for full-time pioneer service, with as many as 595,896 of them sharing, as a peak, in this privileged work in one month last year. That averages out at more than 11 pioneers in each congregation!

¹⁷ It is noteworthy that all ten of Joseph's half brothers, now repentant of former attitudes and actions, were united with him down in Egypt, which, along with Sodom, typifies the world in which Jesus was impaled. (Revelation 11:8) This reminds us of Zechariah 8:20-23, which climaxes with a description of "ten men" who say, "We will go with you people," that is, with Jehovah's anointed people, of whom a remnant still serve here on earth.

¹⁸ However, what of Joseph's one full brother, Benjamin, whose hard birth cost the life of Jacob's beloved wife Rachel? Benjamin was specially favored by Joseph, who no doubt felt a closer intimacy with this son of his own mother. This most

---

14. What joyful news was conveyed to Jacob?
15. To whom do we now look for spiritual sustenance, and how may we be assured of an abundance?
16. (a) Where only is life-preserving "food" to be found today? (b) How has the sowing of "grain" in behalf of famished mankind been expanded?

17. What other prophetic account has a similarity to the uniting of the ten half brothers with Joseph?
18. The special favor shown to Benjamin resembles what in modern times?

likely accounts for Benjamin's receiving the fivefold portion when all 12 brothers were first reunited at the feast in Joseph's house. Does not Benjamin well portray the remnant of anointed Witnesses today, most of those who survive having been gathered to the Lord's side since 1919? This "Benjamin" class have indeed received a special portion from Jehovah, as his 'spirit bears witness with their spirit.' (Romans 8:16) These, too, have been tested as to their integrity while the Lord's "sheep" have ministered to them.—Matthew 25:34-40.

[19] It is of interest that, when Pharaoh arranged to transport Jacob and his households to Egypt, all the male "souls" who settled there numbered 70, a multiple of 7 and 10. (Genesis 46:26, 27) These two numbers are used significantly throughout the Scriptures, "7" often indicating heavenly and "10" earthly completeness. (Revelation 1:4, 12, 16; 2:10; 17:12) This parallels the situation today, when we may expect that Jehovah will gather into his "land," the spiritual paradise in which we now rejoice, every last one of his family of Witnesses. (Compare Ephesians 1:10.) "Jehovah knows those who belong to him," and even now he is settling them in "the very best of the land," as was Goshen back in Pharaoh's domain.—Genesis 47:5, 6; 2 Timothy 2:19.

[20] In Joseph's day, the years of famine followed the years of plenty. Today, they run concurrently. In contrast with the spiritual famine in the land outside of Jehovah's favor, there is an abundance of spiritual food in Jehovah's place of worship. (Isaiah 25:6-9; Revelation 7:16, 17) Yes, although there is a famine for hearing the words of Jehovah in Christendom, as Amos foretold, the word of Jehovah does go forth out of heavenly Jerusalem. How that makes us rejoice!—Amos 8:11; Isaiah 2:2, 3; 65:17, 18.

[21] Today, under the direction of the Greater Joseph, Jesus Christ, we have the great privilege to be gathered into citylike congregations. There we can feast on an abundance of rich spiritual food and also sow seeds of truth and spread the good news that spiritual food is available. This we do for the benefit of all who accept the terms and provisions lovingly arranged for by the Sovereign Ruler, Jehovah. How grateful we can be to our God for the gift of his Son, the Greater Joseph, who serves as the wise Administrator of spiritual food! It is he who has been delegated by Jehovah to act as the Preserver of life in this time of spiritual famine. May each one of us show diligence in rendering sacred service after his example and under his leadership!

---

19. What parallel is to be observed between the moving of the households of Israel to Goshen and the gathering of God's people today?
20. Despite the spiritual famine today, why must we rejoice?

21. (a) What great privilege do we enjoy today? (b) For what should we be grateful, and how may we express our thanks?

Do You See the Parallel?

□ How did Joseph resemble Jesus as Food Administrator?

□ What in the Joseph drama compares with becoming slaves to God through dedication?

□ What quality was shown by Joseph and by Jesus as an example for us today?

□ As in Joseph's time, what thorough arrangement for food distribution exists today?

□ What should our consideration of this drama impel us to do?

Kingdom Proclaimers Report

A Reward for Faithfulness

IT WAS in Italy that, 15 years ago, Mrs. B——, then 15 years old, got to know the truth. However, she did not progress, and so she married an unbeliever. The seeds of truth remained in her heart, though, and about a year ago she accepted a Bible study with one of Jehovah's Witnesses and began to attend meetings. Her husband was violently opposed and threatened to make her leave home. He would hit her so severely that she needed medical attention. One evening he burst into the Kingdom Hall during a meeting, hit a brother, broke the glass in the door, and shouted with rage.

When she returned home, she found that her husband had locked her out of the house. Without losing her courage, she went to the carabinieri (police) station to inform them of what had happened and then went to sleep at an aunt's house. After two days her husband allowed her to come home.

The husband is very well known in the town. He began denouncing Jehovah's Witnesses publicly, saying that they had ruined his family. In this anti-Witness campaign, he was backed up by the clergy. A priest had adhesive stickers stamped with the following words: "JEHOVAH'S WITNESSES: Do not disturb the peace of this family. THANK YOU!" He had these stickers put on doors in the town. Everyone was talking about Jehovah's Witnesses and making them the butt of their mockery and scorn. In spite of this, the brothers took courage and went forth in their ministry with more zeal than before. Most families had not wanted the stickers on their doors. Some boys, sent by the priest, were given 100 lire for sticking them on the doors, it was reported.

In the meantime, Mr. B—— informed his wife that she would have to leave home, as he had already taken steps for a legal separation. But things were beginning to change in this town. A local radio station presented a program, and the reporter described the case as "a maneuver of doubtful taste, of base manners." During the program, our brothers explained that many

families had the stickers imposed on them. This was proved by the fact that they were placed during the night even on some doors of Jehovah's Witnesses and families that were welcoming their visits. The radio reporter praised Jehovah's Witnesses and said that they are people "with an exquisite politeness, and they behave with the utmost kindness."

Finally, the time came for the couple to appear before the judge to begin the legal separation that the husband had requested. The judge praised Mrs. B—— for her desire not to separate, and while she was waiting for the lawsuit, he granted her custody of the children. They could continue living in their home, and her husband would have to give her 250,-000 lire per month. The husband objected, saying: "The house is my mother's property, and my wife cannot stay there." The judge answered: "You want to be husband and boss. Your wife must always say yes, and for once she said no. So you send the whole town into chaos. If your wife had been unfaithful to you, I could understand, but the fact that she follows one faith instead of another is none of your business."

Mrs. B—— is now happily serving Jehovah. (Matthew 5:10) The people of the town have changed their attitude, and wonderful Bible discussions are taking place. They agree that it is not Jehovah's Witnesses that disturb family peace. If there are still stickers on the doors, they no longer have any meaning.

Looking Back Over 93 Years of Living

As told by Frederick W. Franz

ON September 12, 1893, a baby boy was born in Covington, Kentucky, which is on the south side of the river opposite Cincinnati, Ohio. His happy father, Edward Frederick Franz, and delighted mother, Ida Louise née Krueger, named this son of theirs Frederick William Franz.

That was the start of my 93 years of living. My father, who was born in Germany, professed to be of the Lutheran Church and so had me baptized by the clergyman's laying of his moistened hand upon my forehead. A baptismal certificate was filled out, and it was framed and hung on the wall of our home, along with the baptismal certificates of my two older brothers, Albert Edward and Herman Frederick. Only 20 years later did I learn how unscriptural such a religious formality is.

It was when we had moved to Greenup Street that I saw for the first time a horseless carriage, a two-seater open automobile, being driven up the street. Years later I would first see an airplane. We then lived next to Krieger's Bakery, where my father worked nights as a baker. He would come home in the morning and go to sleep. Then in the afternoon he would be free to spend some time with us boys.

When I became of school age, I was sent first to the parochial school and religious services of St. Joseph's Roman Catholic Church, since it was nearby at 12th and Greenup streets. I can still recall the school classroom. On one occasion the religious "brother" acting as teacher had me come to the front of the class and stretch out my open palm to receive several whacks with a 12-inch ruler because of a misdemeanor on my part.

I also recall going into the church's unlighted confession box, speaking to the confessor behind the partition, and saying a memorized prayer and confessing how bad a boy I was. After that, I went down to the altar rail and kneeled there as a priest put a piece of bread in my mouth, thus serving me Communion as taught by the church, while reserving the wine for himself to drink later. This was the start of my formal religious training and my respect for God that would grow in the years to come.

After my completing a year in the parochial school in 1899, my family moved across the Ohio River to Cincinnati, to 17 Mary Street (now called East 15th Street). This time I was sent to the public school and put in the third grade. I proved to be an inattentive student, and I recall that, on one occasion, the student at the desk to my right and I were sent to the principal's office because of our misconduct. There Principal Fitzsimmons had both of us bend over and touch the tip of our shoes with our fingers while he administered a number of strokes with a rattan switch on our rear end. As you might expect, I flunked.

But my father was unwilling that I should spend two years in the same grade. So when the next school term began, he took me to the Liberty Street school, to the office of the school principal, Mr. Logan. He asked Mr. Logan to enroll me in the fourth grade. Mr. Logan was kindly disposed toward me, and he said: "Well, let's see what the young man knows." After I answered a number of probing questions to his evident satisfaction, he stated: "Well, it seems that he qualifies for the fourth grade." In this way, he personally promoted me to the grade higher than the one that I had flunked. From then on I settled down and applied myself seriously to my schoolwork, and never again did I flunk.

The religious aspects of my young life also changed. Somehow, representatives of the Second Presbyterian Church of Cincinnati got in touch with my mother, and she decided to send Albert, Herman, and me to the Sunday school of that church. At that time, Mr. Fisher was the superintendent of the Sunday school, and young Bessie O'Barr became my Sunday-school teacher. In this way, I became acquainted with the inspired Holy Bible. How grateful I was when my Sunday-school teacher conferred upon me a personal copy of the Holy Bible as a Christmas gift!

I determined to make it a must in my life to read a portion of the Bible each and every day. This resulted in my becoming very well acquainted with that holy book. And its wholesome influence kept me from becoming involved with the immoral speech and conduct of my classmates. It was no wonder that they looked upon me as being different.

High School and College

After I graduated from the third intermediate school in 1907, my parents permitted me to continue my education and enter Woodward High School, where Albert, my oldest brother, had attended for one year. Like him, I decided to take up the classical course. So I took up the study of Latin—a study that I pursued for the next seven years.

Then came the time of graduation in the spring of the year 1911. I was selected to be the valedictorian for Woodward High School at the graduation exercises that were to be held in Cincinnati's largest auditorium, the Music Hall.

At the time, all three of Cincinnati's high schools—Woodward High School, Hughes High School, and Walnut Hills High School—met together for graduation exercises. The high-school seniors sat on the large platform facing a packed auditorium. The opening speech was assigned to the valedictorian for Woodward High School. The subject that I chose for the occasion was "School and Citizenship." All three speakers were given a handsome round of applause. I was now in my 18th year of life.

My parents allowed me to go on with my educational career, so I entered the University of Cincinnati, taking the liberal arts course. I had now decided that I was going to become a Presbyterian preacher.

To the continued study of Latin, I now added the study of Greek. What a blessing it was to study Bible Greek under Professor Arthur Kinsella! Under Dr. Joseph Harry, an author of some Greek works, I also studied the classical Greek. I knew that if I wanted to become a Presbyterian clergyman, I had to have a command of Bible Greek. So I furiously applied myself and got passing grades.

In addition to studying Greek and Latin at school, I got interested in learning Spanish, which I found to be quite similar to Latin. Little did I realize at the time how much I would be able to use Spanish in my Christian ministry.

In lower center with fellow Bethel workers 1920

A high point in my academic life was when Dr. Lyon, the university's president, announced to an assembly of students in the auditorium that I had been chosen to go to Ohio State University to take competitive examinations with others to win the prize of the Cecil Rhodes Scholarship, qualifying me for admission to Oxford University in England. One of the contestants outranked me with regard to field athletics, but because of my comparable grades, they wanted to send me, along with him, to Oxford University. I appreciated that I had measured up to the requirements for gaining the scholarship, and, normally, this would have been very gratifying.

"This Is the Truth!"
We recall that on one occasion Jesus Christ said to his disciples: "You will know the truth, and the truth will set you free." (John 8:32) The year previous, 1913, my brother Albert got "the truth" in Chicago. How did Albert get "the truth"?

One Saturday night in the spring of 1913, Albert had gone to bed early in the dormitory of the YMCA, where he was living while working in Chicago. Later, his roommate burst into the room to explain a difficulty. He was invited that night to the home of a Mr. and Mrs. Hindman, and their daughter Nora was to have a girlfriend there at the house. Two girls would be too much for Albert's roommate to handle by himself. With alacrity, Albert rose to the occasion. During the course of the evening, Albert's roommate was getting along quite famously with the two young ladies. But Mr. and Mrs. Hindman concentrated on Albert, introducing to him the teachings of the Watch Tower Bible and Tract Society.

Albert then sent me a booklet entitled *Where Are the Dead?* written by a Scottish doctor, John Edgar, a member of the Glasgow Congregation of the International Bible Students. At first, I laid the booklet aside. Then one evening, having a little time on my hands before going to choir practice, I began to read it. So interesting did I find it that I could not lay it down. I kept on reading it as I walked about a mile to the Presbyterian church. Since the church door was still locked, I sat on the cold stone steps and kept on reading. The organist came along and, noting how absorbed I was in what I was reading, said: "That must be something interesting." I replied: "It sure is!"

Since I so enjoyed the new truths I was learning, the thought occurred to me to ask the preacher, Dr. Watson, what he thought of this booklet. So that very evening, I handed him the booklet and asked: "Dr. Watson, what do you know about this?"

He took the booklet, opened it up, and then sneered: "Oh, that must be some of that Russell stuff. What does he know about eschatology?" I was really taken aback by his contemptuous attitude. As I took the booklet back and turned away, I thought to myself: "I don't care what he thinks about it. This is the TRUTH!"

Before long, on one of his visits back home, Albert brought me the first three volumes of *Studies in the Scriptures,* written by Charles Taze Russell. Albert also got me acquainted with the local congregation of Bible Students, which happened to meet right next door to the Presbyterian church. I was delighted with what I was learning and soon decided that the time had come for me to sever my connection with the Presbyterian Church.

So later, when Albert again was visiting us, we went to one of Dr. Watson's Sunday night lectures. Afterward, Albert

With N. H. Knorr 1961

and I walked down to where he was shaking hands with the departing parishioners. I said to him: "Dr. Watson, I'm leaving the church."

He said: "I knew it! I knew it! Just as soon as I saw you reading that Russell stuff. That man, Russell, I wouldn't allow him to step inside my door!" He then added: "Fred, don't you think we had better step up to my vestry and have prayer together?" I told him: "No, Dr. Watson, I've made up my mind."

With that, Albert and I walked out of the church. What a glorious feeling it was to be free from bondage to a religious system that was teaching falsehoods! How good it was to be taken into the congregation of the International Bible Students, who were so loyal to God's Word! On April 5, 1914, in Chicago, Illinois, I symbolized my consecration—as we used to call dedication—by water baptism.

I have never regretted that, shortly before the announcements by the educational authorities regarding the outcome of the examinations for the Cecil Rhodes Scholarship, I wrote a letter to the authorities and advised them that I had lost interest in the Oxford University scholarship and that they should drop me from the list of contestants. This I did even though my professor in Greek at the university, Dr. Joseph Harry, informed me that I had been chosen to receive it.

Two months later, or on June 28, 1914, the murder of Archduke Ferdinand of Austria-Hungary and his wife took place at Sarajevo in Bosnia. On that very same date, the International Bible Students were having the third day of their general convention at Memorial Hall, Columbus, Ohio. Just one month later, or on July 28, 1914, the first world war of all human history broke out. We Bible Students were expecting the end of the Gentile Times of 2,520 years by October 1 of that year.

With my father's permission, I had left the University of Cincinnati in May 1914, just a couple of weeks before the end of my third term there as a junior classman. I immediately arranged with the Watch Tower Bible and Tract Society to become a colporteur, or pioneer, as such a full-time minister is called today. By then I had become actively associated with the Cincinnati Congregation of the International Bible Students.

Later I became an elder of the Cincinnati Congregation. So when the United States of America got involved in World War I on the side of the Allies, and the young men were drafted for the army, I was exempted as a minister of the gospel.

Addressing a convention in Japan 1978

Getting to Know Brother Russell

Among the incidents in my life that I look back on with fondness were the times I had the joy of meeting the Society's first president, Charles Taze Russell. I first became personally acquainted with him the day before the premiere exhibition of the *Photo-Drama of Creation* at the Music Hall on Sunday, January 4, 1914. That Saturday an elder of the Cincinnati Congregation met me outside the Music Hall and said: "Say, Brother Russell is in there, and

if you go backstage you can see him." Very eagerly I went in and subsequently found myself speaking to him face-to-face. He had come to inspect arrangements for that initial presentation of the *Photo-Drama of Creation*.

Then in 1916 he happened to be making a train connection in Cincinnati and had several hours' layover. A sister and I, being told about it, hastened to the railroad station, where we found him along with his secretary. He had brought his lunch along with him, and when lunchtime came, he shared it with us.

Upon finishing lunch, he asked if anyone had a Bible question. I asked about the likelihood of Adam's being resurrected in view of the fact that he was an unrepentant, willful sinner. With a twinkle in his eye, he replied: "Brother, you are asking a question and answering it at the same time. Now, just what was your question?"

"The Finished Mystery"

On Tuesday, October 31, 1916, Charles Taze Russell died, without having produced the seventh volume to his series of *Studies in the Scriptures*. When on his deathbed, aboard a train returning from California, he was asked by his secretary about the seventh volume, he replied: "Someone else will have to write that."

In the following year, 1917, the seventh volume did appear as a commentary on the prophetic books of Ezekiel and Revelation, together with a lovely explanation of the Bible book The Song of Solomon. The Society planned a tremendous circulation of the new book. Accordingly, they sent cartons of this seventh volume to certain ones in the congregations throughout the United States. Many cartons were sent to my home at 1810 Baymiller Street, Cincinnati, Ohio, and stored while we awaited further instructions as to how the contents were to be distributed.

There were eight pages of *The Finished Mystery* that contained quotations of what prominent figures had adversely declared regarding warfare. Under incitement by the religious organizations of Christendom, Catholic and Protestant, the United States government raised objections, so pages 247-54 were cut out. Thereafter, when *The Finished Mystery* was offered to the people, an explanation was made to them as to why these pages were missing. The United States government did not remain satisfied with this move, and under further incitement by the religious organizations of the land, it banned the entire seventh volume of *Studies in the Scriptures*.

I recall that on one Sunday morning I was working at the rear door of our house. Men came walking down the walkway alongside the house, and the leader pulled back his coat lapel, showed me his metallic badge and demanded entrance into the house. So I was obliged to take them inside and show them the cartons containing copies of *The Finished Mystery*. After a few days, they sent a truck and took them all away.

Later we learned that Joseph F. Rutherford, the Watch Tower Society's second president, and six of his associates serving at the Brooklyn headquarters were erroneously convicted of interfering with the war effort of the United States. They were sentenced to serve 20 years at the Atlanta Federal Penitentiary on each of four counts, the sentences, however, to run concurrently. The war ended on November 11, 1918, and then on March 25, 1919, Brother Rutherford and his associates were released on bail. They were later completely exonerated. The book *The Finished Mystery* was also removed from under ban and authorized to be circulated freely once again.

How reviving it was to our spirits when the Society arranged for our first postwar convention at Cedar Point, situated on the tip of a resort peninsula near Sandusky, Ohio, for September 1-8, 1919! It was a most joyous privilege for me to attend that convention.

Invited to Bethel

In the following year of 1920, President Rutherford accepted an invitation to address a public audience in Cincinnati, Ohio. I was doing colporteur work at the time, and Brother Rutherford invited me to write him a letter applying for service at the Brooklyn Bethel headquarters.

I sent the letter, and after receiving a favorable reply, I entrained for New York City. On Tuesday night, June 1, 1920, I arrived there and was met by Leo Pelle, an old friend from Louisville, Kentucky, and he conducted me to the Bethel home. The next day, Wednesday, I was formally assigned to room with Hugo Riemer and Clarence Beatty in an attic room, becoming number 102 of the Brooklyn Bethel family.

The Society had established its first printing plant at 35 Myrtle Avenue, in the basement of which was installed our first rotary printing press, which we called the Battleship because of its size. We were turning out the Society's new magazine entitled *The Golden Age*—later named *Consolation* and now *Awake!* As the magazines came up through a slot in the floor and were conveyed on a wire system over a sloping board, I gathered them up, jogging them and stacking them for later trimming and handling.

On Saturday morning, when the printing press was not turning out magazines, a number of us brothers would wrap up the magazines in brown folder sheets containing the names and addresses of subscribers. Then we would seal them for handling by the post office. I continued doing this work for a number of months until Donald Haslett, who was serving on the Colporteur Desk, left to marry Mabel Catel. Then I was transferred from 35 Myrtle Avenue to the Society's office at 124 Columbia Heights to serve at the Colporteur Desk.

Also, as a member of the New York Congregation, I was assigned to conduct a book study at the home of the Afterman family in the Ridgewood area of Brooklyn.

Radio and Convention Privileges

I continued serving at the Colporteur Desk until 1926. In the meantime, the Watch Tower Bible and Tract Society had established on Staten Island its first radio station, WBBR. That was in 1924. I had the joyous privilege of serving on the Society's programs, not only delivering speeches but also rendering tenor solos, and even playing the mandolin to piano accompaniment. Further, I sang second tenor in our WBBR male quartet. Of course, Brother Rutherford, as the president of the Society, was the featured speaker over WBBR and had a vast listening audience.

It was in the year 1922 that a general convention of the Watch Tower Bible and Tract Society was held for the second time at Cedar Point, Ohio. Here we were most powerfully exhorted by Brother Rutherford to "advertise, advertise, advertise, the King and his kingdom."

One of my highly prized privileges in the '20's was serving with Brother Rutherford at the international convention in London, England, in 1926. There he delivered his public talk in the Royal Albert Hall of London before a large audience after I had sung a tenor solo to the accompaniment of the hall's famous organ.

The following night he spoke to a Jewish audience on "Palestine for the Jews —Why?" and I sang a solo from Handel's *Messiah,* "Comfort Ye, My People." Some thousands of Jews attended that special service. At the time, we were mistakenly applying prophecies from the Hebrew Scriptures to the fleshly, circumcised Jews. But in 1932 Jehovah opened our eyes to see that those prophecies applied to spiritual Israel.

And how thrilling it was for me to be at the Columbus, Ohio, convention in 1931 when Brother Rutherford submitted the 'new name' Jehovah's Witnesses, and all of us adopted it enthusiastically! Immediately afterward, all the congregations of Jehovah's people around the globe adopted that 'new name.'—Compare Isaiah 62:2.

Friday, May 31, 1935, found me serving as the orchestra conductor in the pit right underneath the podium of the platform from which Brother Rutherford gave his epoch-making discourse on Revelation 7: 9-17, correctly identifying for us the membership of the "great multitude" there depicted. The so-called Jonadab class was especially invited to be present, and the reason therefor became apparent when Brother Rutherford showed that the "great multitude" (*King James Version*),

---

In Our Next Issue

- **What Has God Done for You?**

- **Peace at Last!—When God Speaks**

- **"Treasures of the Holy Land"**

or "great crowd," was to be made up of the "other sheep" of "the good shepherd" Jesus Christ. (John 10:14, 16, *KJ*) It was a thrilling occasion. How heart stirring it was to me when the next day, Saturday, June 1, 840 conventioners got immersed in water to symbolize their dedication to God through Christ with an earthly paradise outlook in view! From then on, the number of Christ's "other sheep" went on to outnumber, by far, the dwindling membership of the "little flock" of spirit-begotten sheeplike disciples of the Fine Shepherd, Jesus Christ.—Luke 12:32.

However, when World War II broke out in 1939, it seemed as if this meant the end of the gathering of the "great crowd." I recall Brother Rutherford's saying to me one day: "Well, Fred, it looks as if the 'great multitude' is not going to be so great after all." Little did we realize the great ingathering that was yet ahead.

The Society introduced the portable phonograph in 1934, and recordings of President Rutherford's lectures were used to introduce the Bible literature. When his recordings, translated into Spanish, came out, I concentrated on using them in reaching Spanish-speaking people in the neighborhood of our factory at 117 Adams Street. Then, by return visits, I helped interested persons to learn Bible truths, and by this means I was eventually privileged to organize the first Spanish-speaking congregation in Brooklyn. I have belonged to the Brooklyn Spanish Congregation, number one, ever since it was formed.

Changes in the Society's Presidency

At Brother Rutherford's death on January 8, 1942, Nathan H. Knorr succeeded him to the presidency of the Society. Despite the raging second world war, his public address in the summer of 1942 on the subject "Peace—Can It Last?" reversed our outlook for the immediate future. Shortly thereafter, Brother Knorr opened up the Watchtower Bible School of Gilead at Kingdom Farm on Monday, February 1, 1943, with a hundred students composing the first class. I had the privilege of serving on the program for the inaugural occasion. Brothers Eduardo Keller, Maxwell G. Friend, Victor Blackwell, and Albert D. Schroeder served as teachers.

In his opening address, Brother Knorr advised us that the Society had enough money to keep the school running for five years. But lo and behold, today Jehovah God Almighty has kept the school operating for nine times that length of time!

It was a tremendous privilege to be associated with Nathan H. Knorr. Little did I realize when he got immersed after the discourse that I gave to the baptismal candidates on July 4, 1923, alongside the Little Lehigh River outside his hometown of Allentown, Pennsylvania, that he would become the third president of the Watch Tower Bible and Tract Society.

Under Brother Knorr's presidency, I traveled extensively, speaking to large gatherings of the brothers around the world—including Latin America and Australia—encouraging them to remain faithful. On one such occasion, in 1955, when there was a ban on the work of Jehovah's Witnesses in Spain, I served a secret assembly in the woods outside Barcelona. Our gathering of Spanish brothers was surrounded by armed secret policemen, and the men were taken in trucks to the police headquarters. There we were detained and interrogated. As I was an American citizen, I pretended not to know Spanish. Also, two sisters had escaped and informed the American Consulate about my arrest, and they, in turn, got in touch with the police. Wishing to avoid an international incident and adverse publicity, they finally dismissed us foreigners and, later, the other brothers. Afterward, a number of us gathered together at the home of the Serrano brothers and rejoiced greatly over Jehovah's deliverance of his people. In 1970 Spain granted legal recognition to Jehovah's Witnesses. Today we have a branch office near Madrid, and this past year the organization in Spain included over 65,000 Kingdom publishers, with congregations throughout the land.

On June 8, 1977, Nathan H. Knorr passed away, finishing his earthly course, and I succeeded him to the office of president of the Society. Brother Knorr had served for more than 35 years in the presidency, longer than either of the two preceding presidents of the Society, Russell and Rutherford. As a member of the Governing Body of Jehovah's Witnesses, I have been assigned to serve on the Publishing Committee and on the Writing Committee of the Governing Body.

It is a great privilege and pleasure indeed to continue on serving in the Society's offices at 25 Columbia Heights. This calls for a regular workday walk between the general offices and the Bethel home —an excellent physical exercise for the aging body. Although I am 93 years of age and my eyesight is failing, I am very happy that Jehovah has blessed me with good health, so that I have not missed a day of work because of sickness for 66 years at Bethel, and I am still able to serve full-time. It has indeed been a divine favor for me to be here since the year 1920 and see the growth and expansion of the organization at Brooklyn headquarters and around the world.

With full confidence in the Universal Sovereign, Jehovah God, and his Field Marshal, Jesus Christ, who is over the innumerable hosts of seraphs, cherubs, and holy angels of heaven, I look forward, at this writing, along with millions of fellow Witnesses, to what the Bible shows still lies ahead: the destruction of Babylon the Great, the world empire of false religion, and the war of the great day of God the Almighty at Armageddon, culminating in the victory of victories on the part of the Universal Sovereign, Jehovah God, who is "from eternity to eternity." Hallelujah!—Psalm 90:2, *Byington.*

Questions From Readers

■ Is it fitting to speak of a coming "new world"?

This question may properly be asked, since the Greek word often translated "world," ko'smos, basically means *mankind,* and God is not going to make a new race of mankind. Moreover, in the Bible we do not find the expression kai·nos' ko'smos (literally, "new world").

But the Biblical use of ko'smos allows for a Christian to speak of a "new world" when referring to the coming Paradise restored on earth. *The New International Dictionary of New Testament Theology* explains: 'The noun kosmos denoted originally building, but more especially it denotes order.' This dictionary adds that the word also has specific senses, such as "ornament and adornment," "the regulation of life in human society," and "the inhabitants of the earth, humanity."

In the Christian Greek Scriptures, ko'smos is often used in the sense of the entire human family. We thus read that "all have sinned [that is, *all* Adam's imperfect descendants] and fall short of the glory of God." (Romans 3:19, 23) On the other hand, "God loved the world [ko'smos] so much that he gave his only-begotten Son, in order that *everyone* exercising faith in him might . . . have everlasting life." (John 3:16) Yes, Christ's sacrifice is available to everyone in the human family who exercises faith.

Righteous mankind will restore Paradise in the new world

If that were the only Biblical use of *ko´smos*, it would be incorrect to speak of an approaching "new world." Why? Because some of mankind will survive the coming great tribulation. These ones will then have the opportunity to live in the restored Paradise. So God will not create a new race of humans, a new mankind, a new world of people. However, the Bible does not use *ko´smos* only to mean all mankind.

For instance, sometimes the Greek word signifies all humans who are alienated from God. Hebrews 11:7 says that "by faith Noah . . . condemned the world [*ko´smos*]." He obviously did not condemn every last person, all of mankind; Noah and seven of his family survived the Flood. Similarly, Jesus prayed: "I make request, not concerning the world [*ko´smos*], but concerning those you have given me . . . The world has hated them, because they are no part of the world, just as I am no part of the world."—John 17: 9, 14; compare 2 Peter 2:5; 3:6.

Let us, though, focus on still *another* sense in which the Bible uses *ko´smos*. This is to signify the framework, order, or sphere of human life.* We encounter such a use in Jesus' comment: "What benefit will it be to a man if he gains the whole world [*ko´smos*] but forfeits his soul?" (Matthew 16:26) Clearly, Christ was not referring to a person's 'gaining the whole world of mankind,' nor to 'the whole world of people alienated from God.' It was not humanity that a materialistic person might gain, but it was what people have, do, or arrange. This was true also of the apostle Paul's observations about a married person's 'being anxious for the things of the world.' Likewise, a Christian should not be 'using the world to the full.'—1 Corinthians 7:31-33.

In this sense, *ko´smos* has a meaning similar to that of the Greek word *ai·on´*, which can be rendered "system of things" or "age." (See *Aid to Bible Understanding*, pages 1671-4.) We find in some cases that the two words can almost be interchanged. Consider two examples of similarity between *ko´smos* and *ai·on´*: (1) Paul wrote that he was forsak-

---

* The above-quoted dictionary points out that even in ancient, non-Biblical Greek *"kosmos* is the basic term for the world-order, the world-system."

en by Demas, who "loved the present system of things [*ai·on´*]." But the apostle John counseled against 'loving the world [*ko´smos*],' from which originate "the desire of the flesh and the desire of the eyes and the showy display of one's means of life." (2 Timothy 4:10; 1 John 2:15-17) (2) John 12:31 speaks of "the ruler of this world [*ko´smos*]," who is identified at 2 Corinthians 4:4 as "the god of this system of things [*ai·on´*]."

Consequently, *ko´smos*, or "world," can be used regarding all mankind as well as the framework of the human sphere. For this reason, we can fittingly and with equal correctness speak of the coming of a "new system of things" or of a "new world." This will be a new framework, world order, or sphere of human life. Most inhabiting the restored earthly Paradise will have lived in the old system of things. Yet they will have survived it or have been resurrected. So they will be the same humanity. In the absence, however, of the world of mankind alienated from God, and with a new arrangement, or order, based on God's revealed will prevailing, that restored Paradise will be a new world.

Did You Miss Them?

- **Are the Dead Alive?**
- **The Global Power Struggle —Who Will Win?**
- **Are We Living in the "Time of the End"?**
- **AIDS—Who Are at Risk? How Can You Protect Yourself?**
- **Terrorism—Is Anyone Safe?**
- **Drinking and Driving**

The above are just a few of the subjects covered in *The Watchtower* and its companion magazine *Awake!* during the past year, and they represent the type of subjects planned for you in the months ahead.

Illustrating the value of *Awake!,* when a driver's education supervisor obtained a copy of the issue "Drinking and Driving," he ordered more than 400 copies for use in their driver's education program.

DON'T MISS THE NEXT 12 MONTHS

the **Watchtower**

Announcing Jehovah's Kingdom

May 15, 1987

WHAT HAS GOD DONE FOR YOU?

May 15, 1987
Vol. 108, No. 10

The Watchtower®

Announcing Jehovah's Kingdom

In This Issue

THE PURPOSE OF "THE WATCHTOWER" is to exalt Jehovah God as the Sovereign of the universe. It keeps watch on world events as they fulfill Bible prophecy. It comforts all peoples with the good news that God's Kingdom will soon destroy those who oppress their fellowmen and that it will turn the earth into a paradise. It encourages faith in the now-reigning King, Jesus Christ, whose shed blood opens the way for mankind to gain eternal life. "The Watchtower," published by Jehovah's Witnesses continuously since 1879, is nonpolitical. It adheres to the Bible as its authority.

"WATCHTOWER" STUDIES FOR THE WEEKS

June 21: Peace at Last!—When God Speaks. Page 10. Songs to Be Used: 95, 60.

June 28: Listening to Jehovah as the End Draws Near. Page 15. Songs to Be Used: 139, 59.

Average Printing Each Issue: 12,315,000

Now Published in 103 Languages

SEMIMONTHLY LANGUAGES AVAILABLE BY MAIL
Afrikaans, Arabic, Cebuano, Chichewa, Chinese, Cibemba, Danish,* Dutch,* Efik, English,* Finnish,* French,* German,* Greek,* Hiligaynon, Igbo, Iloko, Italian,* Japanese,* Korean, Lingala, Malagasy, Maltese, Norwegian,* Portuguese,* Russian, Sepedi, Sesotho, Shona, Spanish,* Swahili, Swedish,* Tagalog, Thai, Tsonga, Tswana, Xhosa, Yoruba, Zulu

MONTHLY LANGUAGES AVAILABLE BY MAIL
Armenian, Bengali, Bicol, Bulgarian, Croatian, Czech, Ewe, Fijian, Ga, Greenlandic, Gujarati, Gun, Hausa, Hebrew, Hindi, Hiri Motu, Hungarian, Icelandic, Kannada, Malayalam, Marathi, New Guinea Pidgin, Pangasinan, Papiamento, Polish, Rarotongan, Romanian, Samar-Leyte, Samoan, Sango, Serbian, Silozi, Sinhalese, Slovenian, Solomon Islands-Pidgin, Tahitian, Tamil, Telugu, Tongan, Tshiluba, Turkish, Twi, Ukrainian, Urdu, Venda, Vietnamese

* Study articles also available in large-print edition.

Watch Tower Society offices	Yearly subscription for the above:	
	Semimonthly Languages	Monthly Languages
America, U.S., Watchtower, Wallkill, N.Y. 12589	$4.00	$2.00
Australia, Box 280, Ingleburn, N.S.W. 2565	A$7.00	A$3.50
Canada, Box 4100, Halton Hills, Ontario L7G 4Y4	$5.50	$2.75
England, The Ridgeway, London NW7 1RN	£5.00	£2.50
Ireland, 29A Jamestown Road, Finglas, Dublin 11	IR£6.00	IR£3.00
New Zealand, P.O. Box 142, Manurewa	NZ$15.00	NZ$7.50
Nigeria, PMB 001, Shomolu, Lagos State	₦8.00	₦4.00
Philippines, P.O. Box 2044, Manila 2800	₱60.00	₱30.00
South Africa, Private Bag 2067, Krugersdorp, 1740	R6.50	R3.25

Remittances should be sent to the office in your country or to Watchtower, Wallkill, N.Y. 12589, U.S.A.

Changes of address should reach us 30 days before your moving date. Give us your old and new address (if possible, your old address label).

20 cents (U.S.) a copy

The Bible translation used is the "New World Translation of the Holy Scriptures," unless otherwise indicated.

The Watchtower (ISSN 0043-1087) is published semimonthly for $4.00 (U.S.) per year by Watch Tower Bible and Tract Society of Pennsylvania, 25 Columbia Heights, Brooklyn, N.Y. 11201. Second-class postage paid at Brooklyn, N.Y., and at additional mailing offices.

Postmaster: Send address changes to Watchtower, **Wallkill, N.Y. 12589.**

Published by
Watch Tower Bible and Tract Society of Pennsylvania
25 Columbia Heights, Brooklyn, N.Y. 11201, U.S.A.
Frederick W. Franz, President

What Has God Done for You?

'**N**OTHING!**'** some might reply. 'I have to work hard and look after myself.' If that is how you feel, just reflect for a moment. How did you come to be?

Some nine months before you were born, two minute organisms met inside your mother. Together they formed a new, unique organism.

The larger of the two organisms was an ovum, or egg, supplied by your mother. The smaller organism was a sperm from your father—so minute that, according to Sheila Kitzinger's book *The Experience of Childbirth,* if all the sperm that produced all the people in the world were laid side by side, they would "cover little more than one inch [2.5 cm]." But once your father's sperm penetrated your mother's ovum, your genetic code was established and you were conceived!

Highly complex processes of development then began. They were "so intricate that, after more than a century of study, scientists aren't even close to deciphering them," wrote Andrea Dorfman in *Science Digest.*

As an example of growth processes that puzzle scientists, the same writer comments: "Growth control is an equally complex issue. Left and right arms, for example, develop completely independently from millimeter-long buds of tissue, yet they end up equal lengths. How do the cells know when to stop multiplying? . . . Each organ seems to have an internal means of growth control." Are we not happy that this is so?

What causes and controls growth in all living organisms? A mindless force called nature? A hit-and-miss process called evolution? Is it not obvious that the astoundingly complex, tremendously varied, and superbly beautiful forms of life on this enchanting planet can only be the work of an almighty Creator? That being so, should we not feel deeply grateful for what he has done for us?

Infinite Evidence of Creative Marvels

Every day—even hourly—we benefit from creative marvels. For example, what happens when we sleep? Mental and muscular activities slow down automatically. This is not by our own volition, for we often fall asleep without realizing it. And how refreshing a good sleep is! Some can go for weeks with no food, but those who go for more than three days without sleeping have great difficulty thinking, seeing, and hearing.

After you awake in the morning, maybe someone brings you sweetened coffee. Sugar, once rare and expensive, is now so abundant that we seldom give it a thought. But how is it made? It is formed in plants by the process of photosynthesis —the reaction of sunlight with water and carbon dioxide. At the same time oxygen, vital to all living creatures on earth, is released. Photosynthesis is a highly complex process that is still not fully understood by scientists. "How . . . is photosynthesis itself achieved?" asks the book *The Plants.* (Life Nature Library) "This is like asking how life begins—we just do not know."

Perhaps as you drink your coffee, you recall a television program of the previous evening. In your mind's eye you can see those interesting scenes again. How were they transmitted to your brain, stored there like a roll of film, then played back so that you can describe them to others? Marvelous, is it not? How did man get the intelligence to do the amazing things he accomplishes? Certainly not from animals. Is not the human brain awesome?

The day has hardly begun. Yet what a lot we already have to thank the Creator for! But there is so much more.

What Other Benefits Flow From God?

DO YOU enjoy beautiful flowers, the perfume of roses, the song of birds? Were you thrilled by your baby's first smile? Do you not appreciate appetizing aromas? And who does not admire a rainbow, a glorious sunset, or the stars on a clear night? God's marvelous provisions are endless, are they not?

Yet there is so much misery. In spite of earth's ability to produce plenty for all, millions are underfed. Millions more are poisoned by pollution. And billions today are affected by crime, greed, selfishness, and fear of what the future will bring.

Since the Creator has been so bountiful, why is there so much unhappiness? This planet is a marvelous place, made for us to enjoy. But the world—mankind—is in a pitiful state. For the majority of earth's inhabitants, the outlook is dark, frightening. Why? What went wrong? Did God make man and then abandon him? Is there any light on this puzzling situation? Do we have any hope for the future?

A Source of Light and Hope

Nearly 2,000 years ago a unique baby boy was born—unique because his mother, Mary, was human, and his father was God himself! 'Impossible!' do some say? No, not for the Originator of conception, the Maker of all the complex forms of life. That little boy grew up to be the perfect "man, Christ Jesus."—1 Timothy 2:5; Matthew 1:18-25.

It was an epoch-making birth. In fact, most nations acknowledge this by dating historical events before his day as B.C. —before Christ. And yet his early years were spent quietly as an assistant carpenter at his adoptive father's home in Nazareth. Thirty years passed. Then, at the Jordan River, Jesus presented himself to do God's will and was baptized, and Jehovah God's holy spirit descended upon him. (Matthew 3:13-17) Jesus then began a dynamic campaign of preaching and teaching. As prophesied by Isaiah, "the people sitting in darkness saw a great light."—Matthew 4:14-17; Isaiah 9:2.

Jesus became the most famous and widely respected Teacher of all time. No other human teacher has exerted such a powerful influence on mankind or provided so much spiritual light and hope. What was his textbook? The Bible, as it was then—the Hebrew Scriptures, or "Old Testament." Jesus made them come alive. Many ancient prophecies were fulfilled in him. (Compare Micah 5:2 with Matthew 2: 3-6.) He confirmed the account of Genesis regarding man's origin. (Genesis 2:24; Matthew 19:3-6) Jesus took up, amplified, and broadcast far and wide the main theme of the Bible—the vindication of Jehovah by means of the Kingdom of God. (Matthew 4:23; 6:10) Moreover, accounts of Jesus Christ's life and works are prominent portions of the Christian Greek Scriptures, or "New Testament." Yes, the Bible is a marvelous gift from God, a gleaming light in a dim, sad world. —Psalm 119:105.

Why Is Mankind in a Mess?

Does the Bible answer that question? Yes. It shows that it was not a case of God's abandoning man but, rather, of

JESUS CHRIST—

♦ Fulfilled many ancient prophecies, for instance, Micah 5:2; Matthew 2:3-6

♦ Confirmed the Genesis account of man's origin—Matthew 19:3-6

♦ Amplified and broadcast the Bible's main theme, Jehovah's vindication by means of the Kingdom—Matthew 4:23; 6:9, 10; Luke 8:1

♦ Paid back what Adam lost, a perfect human life, thereby enabling those exercising faith in Him to gain everlasting life—John 3:16

man's abandoning God. Too, the basic principle of freedom of choice was involved. Humans were not created as robots, programmed to obey. We can choose to obey or to disobey.

When God created the first human pair in the beautiful Paradise of Eden, how happy and carefree they must have been! No sickness, no fear, no worries. Delightful birds and animals were present, and there was delicious food in abundance. (Genesis 1:26; 2:7-9) In time, however, an invisible enemy came on the scene. A powerful spirit creature became ambitious, coveting control of the future human family. By telling the first lie, he seduced Eve, and Adam was persuaded to disobey God's command not to partake of the forbidden fruit. (Genesis 3:1-7) Like so many today, the first humans thought they would 'do their own thing.' But thereby they actually put themselves under the control of Satan, the god of the present evil system of things.—2 Corinthians 4:4.

This raised a tremendous and vital issue: Could man successfully rule himself without God? It would require much time to resolve this question satisfactorily. Meanwhile, Adam and Eve had to pay the penalty God had prescribed—death. And since they had become decadent sinners, neither they nor their offspring had any prospect of everlasting life independent of God.—Romans 5:12; 1 Corinthians 15: 21, 22.

A Glorious Future

Since Adam's day many generations have come and gone. And in the ever-changing scene of men's affairs, many types of human governments have been tried—autocracy, democracy, socialism, communism, and others. But all have failed. Political, social, and international problems proliferate; so do ghastly weapons of mass destruction that threaten world suicide. During World War II, Western politicians promised that victory would bring freedom from want and fear, but both are increasing.

What is the solution? A massive problem needs a colossal remedy—nothing less than a global cleanup and the bringing in of a new world. Who can accomplish that? Certainly not the United Nations or any other combination of political powers that often break peace agreements almost before the signatures have dried! They are mere helpless pawns in the grip of Satanic power. (1 John 5:19) Only Jehovah, the Almighty, can get rid of Satan and his demons, put an end to the present corrupt world, and bring about a glorious new one under the heavenly Kingdom with his Son, Jesus Christ, as the King of kings. —Matthew 6:9, 10; Daniel 2:44; Revelation 20:1-3.

What will this Kingdom accomplish? Who will survive the devastating global cleanup, or Armageddon? A very interesting fact that more and more people are coming to realize is that this heavenly government is already operating and preparing people to survive Armageddon! (Revelation 16:14-16) What kind of people must they be? Jesus Christ said: "Happy are the mild-tempered ones [the meek], since they will inherit the earth." (Matthew 5:5) He thereby confirmed this ancient prophecy: "Before there comes upon you the day of Jehovah's anger, seek Jehovah, all you meek ones of the earth, who have practiced His own judicial decision. Seek righteousness, seek meekness. Probably you may be concealed in the day of Jehovah's anger."—Zephaniah 2:2, 3.

Meek ones not only will survive Armageddon but, by remaining faithful to God, will also inherit everlasting life. How? As already mentioned, Adam's vast family of descendants lost the prospect of everlasting life through his sinful disobedience. Death came upon the whole human race through Adam. Since he was a perfect man, another perfect man was needed to ransom, or buy back, what Adam lost. Jesus Christ filled that need and gave his life "in order that everyone exercising faith in him might not be destroyed but have everlasting life."—John 3:16.

This ransom provision is God's greatest gift to man. It will apply not only to those who survive to enter the new world but also to those who come back from the dead. Does that sound too marvelous? Said Jesus: "Do not marvel at this, because the hour is coming in which all those in the memorial tombs will hear his voice and come out, those who did good things to a resurrection of life, those who practiced vile things to a resurrection of judgment." What a thrill! How joyful for Armageddon survivors, who will be able to welcome their loved ones back from the dead! —John 5:28, 29.

What a glorious prospect and hope! And all of this is provided by a loving Creator, Jehovah, through his beloved Son, Jesus. Although today the outlook is so dark and alarming, the future is full of light and hope for those who study the Bible and act on its heartening message. We live in

'What will you repay Jehovah for all his benefits?'

thrilling times. The Kingdom of God is at hand. (Matthew 24:33, 34) Praise Jehovah, the Giver of "every good gift and every perfect present"!—James 1:17.

As you meditate on the many ways in which we benefit from God's provisions and purposes, you may feel a deep sense of gratitude and a desire to express it in some way. But if you are just beginning to understand and accept the real hope for the future, you may feel the need to delve a bit deeper. We encourage you to do just that. Continue studying God's Word along with publications like this one that can help you to increase your knowledge and appreciation for God's glorious purposes.

Those already having a clear conviction that God's Kingdom is the only solution to mankind's woes may feel like the inspired psalmist who said: "What shall I repay to Jehovah for all his benefits to me?" (Psalm 116:12) Such individuals will find that telling others about what God has done for us and the glorious future he holds out to those who love and serve him brings deep satisfaction and real joy. Why? Because, as Jesus said: "There is more happiness in giving than there is in receiving."—Acts 20:35.

An Unlikely Disciple

WHAT a frightening sight as Jesus steps ashore! Two unusually fierce men come out from the nearby cemetery and run toward him. They are demon possessed. Since one of them is possibly more violent than the other and has suffered much longer under demon control, he becomes the focus of attention.

For a long time this pitiful man has been living naked among the tombs. Continually, day and night, he cries out and slashes himself with stones. He is so violent that nobody has the courage to pass that way on the road. Attempts have been made to bind him, but he tears the chains apart and breaks the irons off his feet. Nobody has the strength to subdue him.

As the man approaches Jesus and falls at his feet, the demons controlling him make him scream: "What have I to do with you, Jesus, Son of the Most High God? I put you under oath by God not to torment me."

"Come out of the man, you unclean spirit," Jesus keeps saying. But then Jesus asks: "What is your name?"

"My name is Legion, because there are many of us," is the reply. The demons revel in seeing the sufferings of those they are able to possess, apparently taking delight in ganging up on them in a cowardly mob spirit. But confronted with Jesus, they beg not to be sent into the abyss. We again see the great power Jesus had to conquer even vicious demons. This also reveals that the demons are aware that an abyssing along with their leader, Satan the Devil, is God's eventual judgment for them.

A herd of about 2,000 swine are grazing nearby on the mountain. So the demons say: "Send us into the swine, that we may enter into them." Evidently the demons get some sort of unnatural, sadistic pleasure from invading the bodies

Jesus' Life and Ministry

of fleshly creatures. When Jesus permits them to enter the swine, all 2,000 of them stampede over the cliff and drown in the sea.

When those taking care of the swine see this, they rush to report the news in the city and the countryside. At that, the people come out to see what has happened. When they arrive, why, there is the man from whom the demons came out, clothed and in his sound mind, sitting at the feet of Jesus!

Eyewitnesses report to the people how the man had been made well. They also tell about the bizarre death of the swine. When hearing this, great fear grips the people, and they earnestly urge Jesus to leave their territory. So he complies and boards the boat. The former demoniac begs Jesus to allow him to come along. But Jesus tells him: "Go home to your relatives, and report to them all the things Jehovah has done for you and the mercy he had on you."

Jesus usually instructs those whom he heals not to tell anyone, since he does not want to have people reach conclusions on the basis of sensational reports. But this exception is appropriate because the former demoniac will be witnessing among people that Jesus now will probably not have opportunity to reach. Moreover, the man's presence will provide testimony about Jesus' power to work good, counteracting any unfavorable report that might be circulated over the loss of the swine.

In keeping with Jesus' instruction, the former demoniac goes away. He starts proclaiming throughout the Decapolis all the things Jesus did for him, and the people are simply amazed. **Matthew 8:28-34; Mark 5:1-20; Luke 8:26-39; Revelation 20:1-3.**

♦ Why, perhaps, is attention focused on one demoniac when two were present?
♦ What shows that the demons know about a future abyssing?
♦ Why, apparently, do demons like to possess humans and animals?
♦ Why does Jesus make an exception with the former demoniac, instructing him to tell others about what He did for him?

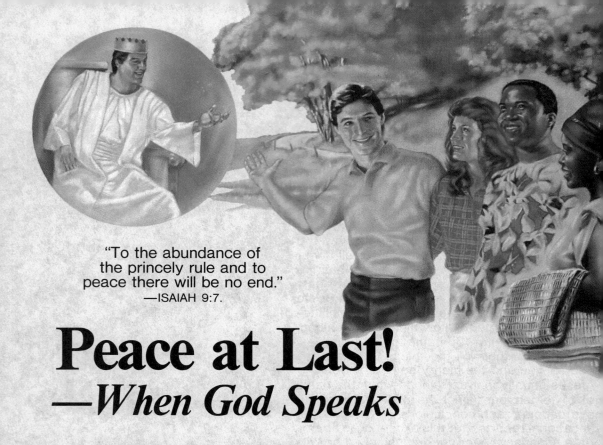

"To the abundance of the princely rule and to peace there will be no end."
—ISAIAH 9:7.

Peace at Last!
—When God Speaks

WORLD leaders constantly speak about peace, and people in general say that they desire it. Yet, the situation today reminds us of what the prophet Jeremiah said: "There was a hoping for peace, but no good came; for a time of healing, but, look! terror!" (Jeremiah 8:15) Actually, ever since Cain killed Abel, the world has not had real peace but has been plagued by violence. And our 20th century has been the most violent age of all, with wars accounting for about a hundred million deaths. In our time, 97 percent of the world's population has been involved in at least one war. So while world leaders speak about peace, they have led their people into one catastrophe after another.

2 To all that violence must be added the daily toll of violent crime. For example, in the United States, every year about 20,-000 people are murdered. Over 80,000 women are raped, with many more rapes not reported. Nearly two million women are severely battered by the man with whom they live. And about one fourth of all households are victimized by some type of crime. A report concludes: "We have become a terribly violent society." The situation is similar in most other lands.

3 However, all of that is as nothing compared with the violence that could be done

___

1. While world leaders constantly speak about peace, what has happened throughout human history?
2. What toll of additional violence is noted in all nations?
3. What even greater violence could be done to the human family now?

by today's nuclear weapons. There are enough of them to kill every inhabitant on earth 12 times over! A doctor said: "Modern medicine will have nothing to offer the victims of a nuclear conflict." Why not? Another answered: "Most doctors, nurses and technicians would be killed . . . Hospitals would be destroyed. So there would be few left with enough knowledge and equipment to save anybody."

[4] Regarding the lack of peace in our time, the main article of a recent *Encyclopædia Britannica* yearbook was entitled: "Our Disintegrating World—The Menace of Global Anarchy." It stated: "After 1945 the ideas that 'progress' was somehow inevitable and that the future of the modern world would be one basically of cohesion and coherence were assumed." But those assumptions, it said, "have proved to be totally misguided," adding: "What has happened instead . . . is that the world is quietly but relentlessly being rent by a slow-motion disintegration. Many countries whose structural and spiritual cohesion was taken for granted have been breaking apart . . . [into] tribes, clans, religious [sects], . . . city gangs, death squads, terrorist movements, guerrilla movements, and narrow and rabid self-interest groups."

[5] Similarly, a former high government official in the United States said: "The factors that make for international instability are gaining the historical upper hand over the forces that work for more organized cooperation. The unavoidable conclusion of any detached analysis of global trends is that social turmoil, political unrest, economic crisis, and international friction are likely to become more widespread during the remainder of this century." He concluded: "The menace confronting humanity, in brief, is . . . global anarchy."

'Visitors From Space'

[6] In view of all of this, an editor wrote in a Cleveland newspaper: "If visitors arrived next week from some distant galaxy, could we tell them we had to kill ourselves in order to establish the superiority of communism or capitalism? Could we explain that we were a species that divided itself into nations, and that those nations were sworn to murder each other in periodic orgies of blood lust? How would we explain that we let some of our species starve and others wallow in degradation and ignorance because the invention of mass death had a greater priority for us? The visitors from that distant galaxy would certainly describe us back home as barbarians. . . . We might protest that we also made great art and believed in justice. They would smile sadly and leave before the explosions."

[7] 'Of course,' some may say, 'there are no "visitors from space" making any such inspection.' No, not from physical space. But for some years now, very powerful, highly intelligent visitors have been making a thorough inspection of what mankind has been doing to itself and to the earth. In addition, they are seeing to it that a clear message is being delivered "before the explosions."

[8] Who are those powerful visitors who have been making an inspection of mankind? God's Word tells us that they are God's representatives in the spirit realm, faithful angels, whom he has dispatched to

4, 5. (a) What comment did one publication make about the lack of peace in our time? (b) How did a former government official similarly comment?

6. How did a newspaper editor describe observations that visitors from space might make about the world today?

7, 8. (a) What powerful visitors are now making an inspection of mankind? (b) Why are they here?

earth to inspect it. Of these spirit creatures, Psalm 103:20 says: "Bless Jehovah, O you angels of his, mighty in power, carrying out his word, by listening to the voice of his word." These powerful angels are often mentioned in the Bible. For example, at Matthew chapter 25 the prophecy about our time says in verses 31 and 32: "When the Son of man arrives in his glory, and all the angels with him, then he will sit down on his glorious throne. And all the nations will be gathered before him, and he will separate people one from another, just as a shepherd separates the sheep from the goats."

⁹ This "Son of man" is God's chief representative, Jesus Christ. After his resurrection to heaven, he waited for Jehovah to give him this special assignment. As Psalm 110:1 described it, Jehovah said to him: "Sit at my right hand until I place your enemies as a stool for your feet." The fulfillment of Bible prophecy shows that the time for God to send this powerful spirit creature into action came in the year 1914.

¹⁰ But he would not come alone, for Matthew 25:31 said that "all the angels" would be with him. How many might that be? Revelation 5:11 says: "I saw, and I heard a voice of many angels around the throne [of God] . . . and the number of them was myriads of myriads." A myriad is 10,000. One myriad times one myriad is 10,000 times 10,000, a total of 100 million angels! Yet, Revelation speaks in the plural, of "myriads of myriads" of angels serving God. That is hundreds of millions, perhaps billions or more. Under Christ's direction, these spirit creatures are assisting God's representatives on earth in separating mankind into two groups, one for

"everlasting cutting-off," the other for "everlasting life."—Matthew 25:46; see also Matthew 13:41, 42.

"Everlasting Good News"

¹¹ What is the central message that these angelic visitors are supporting on earth at this time? Revelation 14:6 informs us: "I saw another angel flying in midheaven, and he had everlasting good news to declare as glad tidings to those who dwell on the earth, and to every nation and tribe and tongue and people." What is this "everlasting good news"? It has to do with what Jesus said would be one of the many evidences that we are living in the last days. At Matthew 24:14 he declared: "And this *good news of the kingdom* will be preached in all the inhabited earth for a witness to all the nations; and then the end will come."

¹² God's Kingdom is the heavenly government that will rule over the earth after present human rule is eliminated. (Daniel 2:44; Matthew 6:9, 10) Its King is Christ Jesus, and he has associate rulers with him. (Revelation 14:1-4; 20:4) That Kingdom is the one spoken of at Daniel 7:14 in these terms: "To him there were given rulership and dignity and kingdom, that the peoples, national groups and languages should all serve even him. His rulership is an indefinitely lasting rulership that will not pass away, and his kingdom one that will not be brought to ruin."

¹³ Why is the message about Kingdom rule such good news, the very best of news? Because it will bring in a new world, a new framework of human society. Under God's Kingdom mankind will receive blessings so marvelous that Psalm 37:11 says of those who will live then:

---

9. What part does Christ Jesus play during this inspection of mankind?
10. How many angels could be with Christ as they assist in the separating work?

11. What is the "everlasting good news" that angelic forces are supporting at this time?
12, 13. (a) What is Kingdom rule? (b) Why is the Kingdom message the very best of news?

"The meek ones themselves will possess the earth, and they will indeed find their *exquisite delight in the abundance of peace.*" Yes, "Jehovah himself will bless his people with peace." (Psalm 29:11) Today, before the Kingdom takes full control of all earth's affairs, the good news of its permanent, peaceful rule in the hands of the "Prince of Peace" is being preached in all nations. This is being done by God's earthly servants under the guidance of Christ and the angels.—Isaiah 9:6, 7.

¹⁴ Who are these earthly servants of God? Well, who are the only ones that regularly call on people with the Kingdom good news? Even opposers recognize them as Jehovah's Witnesses. Now more than three million strong, the ranks of these Kingdom proclaimers are rapidly increasing. Last year, 225,868 new ministers of the good news were ordained. And in that one year, 2,461 new congregations of Jehovah's Witnesses were established earth wide, an average of over 6 each day, making a total of 52,177 congregations in 208 lands. Truly, the prophecy of Isaiah 60:22 is having its fulfillment: Jehovah is speeding up his preaching and ingathering work "in its own time." And now is that time!

¹⁵ How people react to the news of Kingdom rule is the basis for determining

The work of Jehovah's Witnesses is backed by angelic forces

whether they will be separated for "everlasting cutting-off" or for "everlasting life" in the new world. Many react as did those described at 2 Chronicles 36:15, 16: "Jehovah . . . kept sending against them by means of his messengers, sending again and again, because he felt compassion . . . But they were continually making jest at the messengers of the true God and despising his words and mocking at his prophets, until the rage of Jehovah came up." But others react favorably and come under Jehovah's protection. "As for the one *listening* to me [true wisdom], he will reside in security and be undisturbed from dread of calamity."—Proverbs 1:20, 33; Matthew 25:34-46.

---

14. (a) What is one way in which we can positively identify God's earthly servants? (b) How has God's evident blessing been upon them?
15. What is the basis for judging people today?

Heavenly Armies Into Action

16 Before long, the preaching work of Jehovah's servants will be completed to the extent that he has determined. God's patience with disobedient mankind will come to its end. The peaceful message that he has been speaking to mankind in this generation will change. Instead, "at that time he will speak to them in his anger and in his hot displeasure he will disturb them." (Psalm 2:5) As Jehovah himself declares: "In my ardor, in the fire of my fury, I shall have to speak." (Ezekiel 38:19) Then he will give Jesus Christ the signal to move his heavenly armies into action against this rebellious and lawless world.

17 What those armies will accomplish can be seen by what happened to Assyria when God's time came to act against it. Second Kings 19:35 says: "It came about on that night that the angel of Jehovah proceeded to go out and strike down a hundred and eighty-five thousand in the camp of the Assyrians. . . . All of them were dead carcasses." That is what *just one angel* did! What myriads of myriads of

16. How will God soon speak to disobedient mankind?
17. How was the power of just one angel demonstrated?

them will accomplish shortly will be awesome.

18 Jeremiah 25:31-33 describes what will happen in these words: "'There is a controversy that Jehovah has with the nations. He must personally put himself in judgment with all flesh. As regards the wicked ones, he must give them to the sword,' is the utterance of Jehovah. This is what Jehovah of armies has said, 'Look! A calamity is going forth from nation to nation, and a great tempest itself will be roused up from the remotest parts of the earth. And those slain by Jehovah will certainly come to be in that day from one end of the earth clear to the other end of the earth. They will not be bewailed, neither will they be gathered up or be buried. As manure on the surface of the ground they will become.'"

19 Revelation chapter 19 describes how Jehovah will accomplish all of this. It is by having his King Jesus Christ go into action with, as verse 14 says, "the armies that were in heaven" following him. Then verses 17 and 18 say: "I saw also an angel standing in the sun, and he cried out with a loud voice and said to all the birds that fly in midheaven: 'Come here, be gathered together to the great evening meal of God, that you may eat the fleshy parts of kings and the fleshy parts of military commanders and the fleshy parts of strong men and the fleshy parts of horses and of those seated upon them, and the fleshy parts of all, of freemen as well as of slaves and of small ones and great." And verses 19 to 21 describe the destruction of all human institutions because they refused to listen when God spoke through his earthly messengers.

18. How thorough will the destruction be at this system's end?
19. What further details does Revelation chapter 19 add?

What Are Your Answers?

☐ How has the lack of peace been evident, especially in our time?

☐ How are angelic forces involved in separating mankind today?

☐ Why is the Kingdom message "everlasting good news"?

☐ On what basis will people be judged for life or for death?

---

[20] Thus, the time is soon coming for God to bring an end to this violent, disintegrating world system. But that end will not be self-destruction through nuclear warfare among nations. If that happened, the righteous would be annihilated along with the wicked. However, God's "explosions" against this world will not be like that but will be selective. There will be survivors into the new world. As Proverbs 2:21, 22 says: "The upright are the ones that will reside in the earth, and the blameless are the ones that will be left over in it. As regards the wicked, they will be cut off from the very earth; and as for the treacherous, they will be torn away from it."

[21] Why has this world come to the state where such an earth-wide destruction is imminent? Is it not possible that the current peace efforts of world leaders will bear fruit, so that this system can be saved? And if we want to be included among "the upright" and "the blameless" who will survive into the new world and keep living, how should we conduct ourselves at this most important time in all human history? Our next article will consider these questions.

---

20. Why could this world not end in a nuclear catastrophe?

21. What further questions will be considered in our next article?

Listening to Jehovah
as the End Draws Near

"Happy is the man that is listening to me . . . For the one finding me will certainly find life."—PROVERBS 8:34, 35.

DESPITE the lack of peace throughout history, especially in this 20th century, some say that the nations are taking steps to resolve their difficulties. They point to the fact that world leaders hold summit meetings to talk about peace and sign various agreements. Why, the United Nations even declared last year to be the "International Year of Peace"! It was hoped that this would see the beginning of an extra effort by the nations to promote peace, with possible success in the near future.

[2] However, in all history, have similar efforts ever brought permanent peace? If that were humanly possible, there should have been peace long ago—long before there were five billion people split into more than 160 nations, with countless varieties of political, economic, and religious philosophies. But there has never been peace; nor will peace ever result from the efforts of this world's leaders. Why not? For one reason, because mankind's problems are now so serious that they are unsolvable by human efforts alone. As Jeremiah 10:23 so correctly says: "It does not belong to man who is walking even to direct his step."

1, 2. (a) Despite the lack of peace throughout man's history, what do some now say? (b) Why is true peace through human efforts impossible?

Why Human Efforts Cannot Succeed

³ There is another reason why the efforts of men and nations can never bring true peace. The Bible refers to it at 1 John 5:19, saying: "The whole world is lying in the power of the wicked one." Revelation 12:9 indicates that "the wicked one" is "the one called Devil and Satan, who is misleading the entire inhabited earth." Second Corinthians 4:4 calls him "the god of this system of things." Thus, the entire present system of political, economic, and religious rule that has produced so much violence is the product of Satan's rule, not of God's rule. That is why, when speaking of the wisdom that comes from God, 1 Corinthians 2:8 says: "This wisdom not one of the rulers of this system of things came to know."—Luke 4:5, 6.

⁴ When Satan rebelled against God, he induced our first parents to listen to him instead of listening to God. As a result, they deviated from obedience to God and brought upon the human family some 6,000 years of agony. The Bible clearly tells us that Satan induced humans to believe that they would do better by not listening to their Creator. (Genesis 3:1-5) In his wisdom, Jehovah has let the world of mankind in general proceed on its own, without his guidance, up to the present time. And surely, in all these centuries, it has been amply demonstrated that human rule has been a failure.—Deuteronomy 32:5; Ecclesiastes 8:9.

⁵ Moreover, when Adam and Eve stopped listening to Jehovah, the Source of perfect life, they became imperfect and eventually died. Thus, all their descendants were born imperfect. Sickness, old age, and death became mankind's lot. (Romans 5:12) Therefore, even if humans could succeed in bringing peace, they still could not cure inherited imperfection. We would still get sick, grow old, and die. Since Satan was responsible for this, Jesus said of him: "That one was a manslayer [a murderer] when he began, and he did not stand fast in the truth." (John 8:44) Really, when you think about the billions who have lived and died in the past, it is as if Satan murdered all of them.

⁶ Satan also induced other spirit creatures to join him in rebellion, and all these wicked ones refused to listen when Jehovah spoke. So it is Satan, his demons, and rebellious humans who have brought this world to its present condition. They must all be put out of the way, ending this disastrous 6,000-year experiment in independence from God. "The God who gives peace," assures Romans 16:20, "will crush Satan . . . shortly," as well as his demons and all humans who refuse to listen when God speaks.—Matthew 25:41.

Greater Need to Listen Now

⁷ We are now very deep into the final part of these "last days." (2 Timothy 3: 1-5) As a result, there is an ever-greater need to listen to what Jehovah is saying to us. There is a corresponding need to intensify our willingness to make sacrifices to serve him. Why intensify our efforts? Because Satan knows that he has only "a short period of time" left. (Revelation 12:12) So he will surely intensify his efforts to corrupt and destroy.

⁸ Satan would especially like to stop Jeho-

---

3. For what other reason will men and nations never bring true peace?
4. What resulted after our first parents stopped listening to Jehovah?
5. Even if peace could be brought about by human efforts, what would still be with us?

6. Who are the peace wreckers, and what must happen to them?
7. Why should we intensify our efforts to serve Jehovah now?
8. (a) Why can the preaching work not be stopped by its enemies? (b) What must we do to keep divine backing?

vah's Witnesses from preaching the Kingdom good news. But he cannot, for Jehovah has promised them: "Any weapon whatever that will be formed against you will have no success." (Isaiah 54:17) Those who oppose his servants will "be found fighters actually against God." (Acts 5:38, 39) So, with the powerful backing of Jehovah's spirit, Christ Jesus, and multitudes of angelic forces, the work of Kingdom proclamation grows in intensity each year. To keep that divine backing, Jehovah's servants are careful to obey the counsel at James 4:7, 8: "Subject yourselves, therefore, to God; but oppose the Devil, and he will flee from you. Draw close to God, and he will draw close to you."

⁹ Do not underestimate Satan's capacity for deception and harm. God's Word warns: "Keep your senses, be watchful. Your adversary, the Devil, walks about like a roaring lion, seeking to devour someone. But take your stand against him, solid in the faith." (1 Peter 5:8, 9) If you knew that a crazed lion was on the loose in your neighborhood, you would take precautions to protect yourself and your family. Where Satan is concerned, we must be even more alert, as he can do us everlasting harm. Sadly, most people are defenseless because they do not even know that Satan exists. Why so? Because they choose not to listen to Jehovah's Word. And what will result from that bad choice? "Whatever a man is sowing, this he will also reap."—Galatians 6:7.

When They Cry "Peace and Security!"

¹⁰ Do not be caught off guard by any

---

9. Why should we not underestimate Satan?
10, 11. (a) What should we bear in mind regarding any success the nations may have in bringing peace? (b) What Bible prophecy bears on the search for peace by the nations in our time? (c) How lasting will any such peace be?

Like a roaring lion, Satan is intensifying his efforts to corrupt and destroy

*When this system is crushed
like grapes in a winepress, "Jehovah will be a refuge for his people"*

success that the nations may have in bringing peace. Always keep in mind that Jehovah is not using any of this world's agencies toward that end. Jehovah has his own way of bringing true peace, and that is only by means of his Kingdom under Christ. So whatever success the nations may have in establishing peace, it will be brief and only a veneer. Nothing will really have changed. Crime, violence, war, hunger, poverty, family breakdown, immorality, sickness, death, and Satan and his demons will still be with us until Jehovah eliminates all of them. "Unless Jehovah himself builds the house, it is to no avail that its builders have worked hard on it."—Psalm 127:1.

¹¹ Bible prophecy does show that the nations would make a concerted effort toward peace in our time. It states: "You yourselves know quite well that Jehovah's day is coming exactly as a thief in the night. Whenever it is that they are saying: 'Peace and security!' then sudden destruction is to be instantly upon them just as the pang of distress upon a pregnant woman; and they will by no means escape." (1 Thessalonians 5:2, 3) That cry of "Peace and security!" will not mean that the decay of this world has been reversed. Second Timothy 3:13 says that "wicked men and impostors will advance from bad to worse." The reality will still be as the head of an environmental organization said: "The central problem facing society is that it has become ungovernable."

¹² Many in the world will be deluded by vain hopes during the coming cry of "Peace and security!" But Jehovah's servants will not be, for they listen when God speaks. Thus they know from his Word that such a declaration will not bring true peace and security. Instead, it will in reality be the final signal that "sudden destruction is to be instantly upon them." It will herald the imminent beginning of the "great tribulation" that Jesus foretold for our time. He said: "For then there will be great tribulation such as has not occurred since the world's beginning until now, no, nor will occur again."—Matthew 24:21.

¹³ During the "great tribulation," human rule will be brought to an end. Psalm 2:2-6 says: "The kings of earth take their stand and high officials themselves have massed together as one against Jehovah and against his anointed one, saying: 'Let us tear their bands apart and cast their cords away from us!' The very One sitting in the heavens will laugh; Jehovah himself will hold them in derision. At that time he will speak to them in his anger and in his hot displeasure he will disturb them, saying: 'I, even I, have installed my king upon [heavenly] Zion, my holy mountain.'" Psalm 110:5, 6 adds: "Jehovah himself . . . will certainly break kings to pieces on the day of his anger. He will execute judgment among the nations." All political schemes will end, for Isaiah 8:9, 10 declares: "Gird yourselves, and be shattered to pieces! Gird yourselves, and be shattered to pieces! Plan out a scheme, and it will be broken up! Speak any word, and it will not stand, for God is with us!"

Confident of Survival

¹⁴ We are confident that Jehovah will keep his people well informed so that they can take proper steps for surviving the coming "great tribulation." How can we be so certain? Because the prophecy at Revelation 7:9, 14 shows that "a great crowd" does indeed survive. Why? Because of listening when Jehovah speaks and being properly instructed. In this way those of the "great crowd" are able to do what Revelation 7:15 says: "They are rendering him sacred service day and night." Thus they do God's will, meet his approval, and are protected to survive this world's end. —1 John 2:15-17.

¹⁵ Joel 3:13-16 also refers to the survival of God's servants when this system is crushed like grapes in a wine press. It states: "Thrust in a sickle, for harvest has grown ripe. . . . The press vats actually overflow; for their badness has become abundant. Crowds, crowds are in the low plain of the decision, for the day of Jehovah is near in the low plain of the decision. Sun and moon themselves will certainly become dark, and the very stars will actually withdraw their brightness. And out of [heavenly] Zion Jehovah himself will roar . . . Heaven and earth certainly will rock; but Jehovah will be a refuge for his people."

¹⁶ Similarly, at Isaiah 26:20, 21, Jehovah says of that coming time: "Go, my people, enter into your interior rooms, and shut your doors behind you. Hide yourself for but a moment until the denunciation passes over. For, look! Jehovah is coming forth from his place to call to account the error of the inhabitant of the land against him." Therefore, Zephaniah 2:2, 3 urges: "Before there comes upon you the day of

---

12. What do Jehovah's servants know about the real significance of the coming 'peace and security' cry?
13. How does the Bible describe the end of human rulerships?
14. Why are we confident that there will be survivors of this world's end?

15. How does Joel describe the crushing of this system, and what will be the result for God's servants?
16. What other prophecies show that Jehovah will preserve his people through world destruction?

Jehovah's anger, seek Jehovah, all you meek ones of the earth, who have practiced His own judicial decision. Seek righteousness, seek meekness. Probably you may be concealed in the day of Jehovah's anger."

'Running' to Jehovah

[17] Proverbs 18:10 states: "The name of Jehovah is a strong tower. Into it the righteous runs and is given protection." Are you 'running' to Jehovah? Remember what Jesus said about people in Noah's day. They were "eating and drinking, men marrying and women being given in marriage, until the day that Noah entered into the ark; and *they took no note* until the flood came and swept them all away." (Matthew 24:38, 39) What was wrong was their preoccupation with everything else to the exclusion of listening to God when he spoke through his servant Noah, "a preacher of righteousness." (2 Peter 2:5) Because they did not listen, when the Flood came it "swept them all away" into destruction.

[18] Many of those who died in the Flood no doubt considered themselves "nice" people, not being involved in the violence that filled society in those days. But just being "nice" did not save them. By their apathy they condoned the evil of their day. The crucial thing was that they did not 'run' to Jehovah; they did not listen when God's servant spoke. So they did not take the proper steps for survival. On the other hand, those who did listen survived.

[19] Today God is speaking peace to those who listen to him. With what result to them? Isaiah 54:13 states: "All your sons will be persons taught by Jehovah, and the peace of your sons will be abundant." Yes, "Jehovah himself will bless his people with peace." (Psalm 29:11) Thus, in the midst of this violent world, Jehovah's Witnesses have true, unbreakable peace among themselves. They have a loving international brotherhood that world leaders, their nations, and their religions cannot duplicate. Why not? Because these do not really listen when God speaks. So they do not act on what he says. But Jehovah's Witnesses do listen to God. They take seriously the words at Ecclesiastes 12:13: "Fear the true God and keep his commandments. For this is the whole obligation of man."

[20] That is what every person—yes, all who want to live in God's new world—must do. They must 'run' to Jehovah without delay. Indeed, they must be guided by God-given wisdom that is represented as saying: "Listen to me; yes, happy are the ones that keep my very ways. Listen to discipline and become wise, and do not show any neglect. Happy is the man that is listening to me . . . For the one finding me will certainly find life."—Proverbs 8:32-35.

---

17. (a) What must be done to get Jehovah's protection? (b) What did people in the pre-Flood world do wrong?
18. Why did their just being "nice" people not save those who were destroyed in the Flood?
19. What marvelous benefit do Jehovah's servants reap even now, and why?

20. What must every person do to survive into God's new world?

How Would You Respond?

□ Why will human efforts never succeed in bringing peace?

□ Why is there now a greater need to listen to Jehovah?

□ What will the coming cry of "Peace and security!" really mean?

□ What must we do if we want to survive into God's new system?

Help in Making Wise Decisions

ALICE made an unwise decision that turned out disastrously. "I disassociated myself from Jehovah and from his organization," she admits. Although she finally returned, it took her over 13 years to do so—"miserable years" she calls them.

A Christian should not underestimate the danger of making unwise decisions in connection with his service to God. It is not that wrong decisions are deliberately made after a consideration of relevant facts. Sometimes they are made simply on the basis of instinctive reactions. Once emotions succeed in beclouding the issue and an imperfect heart exerts undue influence on thinking ability, all manner of harm and grief can result.

Indeed, "the heart is more treacherous than anything else." (Jeremiah 17:9) The Bible, however, tells us how to protect ourselves. "When wisdom enters into your heart," it says, "discernment itself will safeguard you." (Proverbs 2:10, 11) But how do we get wisdom to enter into our heart?

Learn From the Past

Try this. Put yourself in the position of earlier servants of God who faced trialsome situations similar to yours. Suppose, for example, that a situation inside the local Christian congregation is causing you concern. Try to think of a parallel situation mentioned in the Bible.

What about the first-century Christian congregation at Corinth? Imagine that you are a member of the Corinth congregation. You have been a Christian for two or three years. What a joy it was to come to a knowledge of the truth during Paul's 18-month stay there! But now, things are looking bad.

A tendency to form cliques and factions is causing dissension in the congregation, threatening its unity. (1 Corinthians 1:10, 11) A toleration of immoral conduct is endangering its spirit. (1 Corinthians 5:1-5) A public airing of differences between the congregation's members before worldly courts of law is damaging its fine reputation.—1 Corinthians 6:1-8.

Still imagining yourself in ancient Corinth, you are concerned that some members of the congregation are always wrangling over matters that are really of only minor importance. (Compare 1 Corinthians 8:1-13.) You are saddened by the strife, jealousy, anger, and disorder you see. (2 Corinthians 12:20) Indeed, you are disturbed by an arrogant few who are making Christian living unduly difficult. (1 Corinthians 4:6-8) You are pained to hear that some are even questioning the apostle Paul's position and authority, making unjust accusations, and deriding him for his lack of eloquence as a speaker. (2 Corinthians 10:10; 12:16) You are worried lest those who openly promote personal opinions should undermine the congregation's faith in basic doctrine. —1 Corinthians 15:12.

Faced With a Decision

'This just should not be,' you sigh. 'Why do the elders not correct matters? Something is terribly wrong.'

Will you leave the congregation in Corinth, concluding that you will be better off serving God elsewhere? Or will you possibly even decide that it is best to stop associating with fellow Christians altogether? Will you allow these problems to dampen your joy and your confidence that

Jehovah God and Jesus Christ are in charge of things? Are you going to develop a critical, complaining spirit, causing you to question the motives of fellow Christians? Will you slow down in the preaching work, reasoning that there is little point in directing interested ones to such a congregation?

Viewing the situation dispassionately from today's vantage point, you may find it easy to say that your decision would have been loyally to stay close to God's congregation, despite its imperfections. But if faced with a similar situation today, would you be able to maintain a clear mind and a calm heart? Would you decide *today* as you think you would have decided if you had lived *then?*

Benefiting From Wise Counsel

The Corinthian Christians who made a wise decision were those who stayed close to the congregation. They felt as Peter had years earlier. When some of the disciples left off associating with Jesus, Peter said: "Lord, whom shall we go away to? You have sayings of everlasting life; and we have believed and come to know that you are the Holy One of God." (John 6:68, 69) Obviously, only by staying close to God's organization can we benefit from its counsel.

In new congregations, like the one back in Corinth, it is not unusual for human imperfection to cause a problem that may require the giving of strong counsel. But in giving counsel to the Corinthian Christians, Paul remembered that by far the majority of them were still "beloved ones." (1 Corinthians 10:14; 2 Corinthians 7:1; 12:19) He did not forget that Jehovah extends undeserved kindness and forgiveness to those responding to His direction. —Psalm 130:3, 4.

Of course, since the Christian congregation attracts all kinds of people, some take longer to respond to this direction than do others. This is true for a variety of reasons. Some changes are more difficult to make than are others. Also, every individual differs in physical and mental makeup, environment, background, and circumstances. So how wise it is to avoid becoming overly critical and to remember that "love covers a multitude of sins"! (1 Peter 4:8) After all, if Jehovah and his Son are willing to put up with human imperfection and immaturity in *their* congregation, should we not manifest the same spirit?—1 Corinthians 13:4-8; Ephesians 4:1, 2.

If you had been in the congregation in ancient Corinth, listening to Paul's loving but firm counsel would have reminded you that Christ, as head of the Christian congregation, is keenly interested in its welfare. (Matthew 28:20) It would have built up your confidence in Jesus' promise to keep his followers unified as they responded to help provided through "the faithful and discreet slave." (Matthew 24:45-47; Ephesians 4:11-16) Yes, and Paul's words would have helped you to maintain joy and stability even under trying circumstances. You would have been confident that God would give you strength to cope with any difficulty he might temporarily allow to exist.

This is not to say that a Christian should do nothing if a bad condition devel-

---

In Our Next Issue

- **Who Will Care for the Elderly?**

- **'My Cup Has Been Full'**

- **A New School to Open!**

ops in a congregation. Back in Corinth, mature men like Stephanas, Fortunatus, Achaicus, and some from the household of Chloe, acted. They evidently advised Paul of the situation. (1 Corinthians 1:11; 5:1; 16:17) But once they had done so, they confidently left matters in his hands. Zeal for righteousness did not cause them to lose confidence in Christ's headship or to become "enraged against Jehovah." —Proverbs 19:3.

Our zeal for righteousness today will prevent us from even considering the option of slowing down in our God-given assignment to preach the good news. To do so would manifest a lack of concern for the welfare of others and would be a failure to do what Christ wants us to do. "Consequently, my beloved brothers," Paul counseled, "become steadfast, unmovable, always having plenty to do in the work of the Lord, knowing that your labor is not in vain in connection with the Lord."—1 Corinthians 15:58.

Do Not Be Ignorant of Satan's Designs

Congregation difficulties like those that existed in Corinth can sometimes be more difficult to handle than outright persecution. Satan exploits such situations in an attempt to cause us to make wrong decisions that will draw us away from Jehovah. But 'we are not ignorant of Satan's designs.'—2 Corinthians 2:11.

Paul told the Corinthian Christians that they could benefit from examining the record of earlier servants of God. "Now these things went on befalling them as examples," he said of the Israelites, "and they were written for a warning to us upon whom the ends of the systems of things have arrived." (1 Corinthians 10:11) Likewise, we today can benefit from carefully examining the early Christian record. For example, we can consider what took place in Corinth. Meditating about how we would have made right decisions *then* will help us avoid making wrong decisions *now*.

After 13 "miserable years" of absence, Alice says of her first meeting in the Kingdom Hall: "I was afraid to talk lest I should cry. I was home—really home. I couldn't believe it." So be determined, despite problems that may arise, to hold to your wise decision never to leave Jehovah's organization! Your blessings in association with God's people will be many. And they will be without end.—Proverbs 2:10-15, 20, 21.

"Praise the Name of Jehovah"

On September 2, 1986, the German Democratic Republic (East Germany) released a series of stamps depicting historical German coins. The first in the series is shown below. The coin depicted is dated 1633. However, of particular interest are the four radiant Hebrew characters shown imprinted on the coin. What do they mean? Briefmarkenwelt, a German magazine on philately, gives this explanation: "Two angels, suspended over the town profile, are carrying between them the name Jehovah."

During the 16th and 17th centuries, it was very common to mint such coins in Europe. A German encyclopedia dated 1838 remarks: "The term Jehovah-coins includes all coins and medals that depict the word יהוה, Jehovah, as radiating, either alone or together with the word Jesus, . . . often with the motto in reference thereto; since this is primarily found on many Talers [silver coins issued by various German states between the 15th and 19th centuries], they have been classed together under the name Jehovah-talers."

Likely, most people using the stamps do not know that the Hebrew letters represent the name of God. But Jehovah's Witnesses are happy to point out this feature on the stamp and to explain the meaning and importance of Jehovah's name. Thus, from an unexpected quarter they are helped to "praise the name of Jehovah."—Psalm 135:1.

"Treasures of the Holy Land"

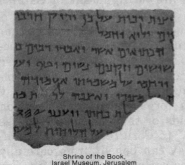

Shrine of the Book,
Israel Museum, Jerusalem

The Habakkuk Commentary

Israel Museum, Jerusalem

"House of God" ostracon

Israel Museum, Jerusalem

Pontius Pilate inscription

BUSTLING Manhattan is an unusual setting for a collection of art that corroborates Bible history. Yet, in New York City's Central Park sits The Metropolitan Museum of Art, which recently hosted "Treasures of the Holy Land: Ancient Art From the Israel Museum." This exhibition consisted of almost 200 objects on loan from the Israel Museum in Jerusalem.

The ancient dwellers of the land of the Bible tell their story through these works of art. Come, let us look, listen, and learn. First, though, you must climb the 28 steps leading to the Metropolitan Museum's columned entrance. Once inside, you are ready to begin your walking tour among several thousand years of Bible history. The following is what you will see:

The Habakkuk Commentary—an almost five-foot-long (1.5 m) parchment scroll, in which the divine name appears several times. This scroll is one of the first discovered and the best preserved of the Dead Sea Scrolls, which have been called "the greatest archaeological discovery of this century." (The scrolls contain parts of every book of the Hebrew Scriptures except Esther and date back into the second century B.C.E. Thus, except for manuscript fragments, they predate by a millennium the oldest-known Biblical copies.) The Habakkuk Commentary contains nearly two thirds of the book of Habakkuk (1:4–2:20), was copied in Aramaic block script at the end of the first century B.C.E., and was interwoven with commentary. "But the four-letter name of Jehovah, tetragrammaton, is everywhere written in archaic Hebrew script," states the museum's information card. Yes, you could plainly see the Tetragrammaton!

"House of God" Ostracon—a pottery fragment on which the divine name appears twice in Tetragrammaton form. This potsherd found in southern Israel was a letter addressed to a man named Eliashib and dates back to the second half of the seventh century B.C.E. "To my lord Eliashib: May Jehovah ask for your peace," the letter begins. It ends: "He dwells in the house of Jehovah."—See page 12 of the brochure *The Divine Name That Will Endure Forever*, published by the Watchtower Bible and Tract Society of New York, Inc.

Pontius Pilate Inscription—a unique historical document from the first century, discovered in Caesarea. Prior to 1961 the only mention of Pontius Pilate was in the pages of the Bible and the first-century writings of Roman and Jewish historians. Now, though, you can see written in fragmentary Latin on a limestone block the words "Pontius Pilate Prefect of Judea." This corroborates the existence of the man who authorized the execution of Jesus Christ.

"Place of Trumpeting" Inscription—once part of the

Israel Museum, Jerusalem

"Place of Trumpeting" inscription

Israel Museum, Jerusalem

Funerary inscription of Uzziah

Israel Museum, Jerusalem

Cult stand with musicians

southwest parapet of the temple enclosure in Jerusalem. When the temple was destroyed in 70 C.E., this piece of stone fell to the street below. The words "to the place of trumpeting" are inscribed in Hebrew on this roughly rectangular, three-foot-long (1 m) stone and refer to the place where a trumpeter stood, perhaps when marking the start and the close of the Sabbath with his trumpet blasts. Of the buildings that were situated on the temple grounds, this inscription is the only significant item remaining, thus confirming the fulfillment of Jesus' prophecy at Matthew 24:1, 2.

Funerary Inscription of Uzziah, King of Judah—a one-foot-square (0.3 m) stone tablet bearing the Aramaic inscription: "Hither were brought the bones of Uzziah King of Judah. Do not open." The warning may allude to his leprosy, or it may refer to a general prohibition against opening tombs. (2 Chronicles 26:16-23) This tablet, dating from around the first century B.C.E., was found near Jerusalem and marked the reinterment of the king's bones centuries after his death, since he was not originally interred in the royal burial field of that city.

Cult Stand With Musicians—an unusual pottery stand about one foot (0.3 m) tall vividly illustrating Philistine cultic ceremonies. The pedestal has five musicians, each playing a musical instrument—cymbals, double pipes, a stringed instrument, and a tambourine. This stand was found in Ashdod and dates from late 11th to early 10th century B.C.E.

Canaanite Cult Stand—a hollow, square stand of clay decorated with human and animal figures. It includes the major Canaanite deities Asherah, personified in the form of a sacred tree or pole, and Baal, in calf form surmounted by a winged sun disk. (Exodus 34:12-14; 2 Kings 23:4, 5) The nearly two-foot-tall (0.6 m) stand, probably intended for offerings or libations, was found near Megiddo and dates from the late 10th century B.C.E.—Compare 2 Chronicles 34:4.

Ivories From Samaria—carvings from Samaria dating from the 9th to the 8th century B.C.E. They remind one of "the house of ivory" Ahab built at Samaria or of the trimmings of the "couches of ivory" characteristic of the spoiled life-style spoken against by the prophet Amos. (1 Kings 22:39; Amos 3:15; 6:4) Since Phoenician artisans specialized in ivory, some of these art miniatures echo the pagan cult of Baal, perhaps introduced by Ahab's Phoenician wife, Jezebel.

Many of the exhibited objects are beautiful in form and color. But some of them, such as the fertility-goddess statues, illustrate the debased religious practices of the land. Others illuminate how foreign influences shaped its character. The exhibition "Treasures of the Holy Land" and others like it add to one's understanding of the people, politics, religion, and art of the land of the Bible.

'Buying Out Time' in Italy

'**B**UY out the opportune time,' the apostle Paul twice urged fellow Christians while he was in Rome, Italy. (Ephesians 5:15, 16; Colossians 4:5) His readers in the first century responded well. They looked for opportune times to spread the "good news" and help others to become worshipers of the true God.—Matthew 24:14.

Modern-day servants of Jehovah in Italy, where Paul wrote those letters, are still responding well to his advice. Like the early Christians, they look for ways to increase their share in the Kingdom-preaching work. How do they find "the opportune time"?

Benefits of Identification

Giuseppe, an elderly full-time minister of Jehovah's Witnesses in Rome, recalls the time that he held a secular job. He had made sure that all his colleagues knew that he was one of Jehovah's Witnesses. This identification led to an "opportune" time for sharing Bible truths. One day he was assigned to train a man named Gianni. Right away the other workers told

Gianni that his teacher was one of Jehovah's Witnesses. As soon as the worker was alone with Giuseppe, he told Giuseppe: "Now we talk about our job, but at lunchtime I want to learn something about Jehovah."

During lunchtimes, they had several discussions. Giuseppe taught Gianni that God has a name, Jehovah. He also explained God's purpose for the earth. What happened, though, when the training period was over? "I gave him my phone number and some Bible literature," says Giuseppe. "He accepted the literature but said: 'If I find something in these publications that is not in harmony with Bible truth, I will come back here and prove you wrong in front of all your colleagues.'"

Months passed by. No word from Gianni. "But then," continues Giuseppe, "one day he called me and said that he wanted to see me. We met, and he had a list of questions. We talked for ten hours! He accepted my offer to study the Bible regularly." What was the result? Giuseppe says: "The favorable changes he made impressed his wife and his mother so much that they, too, began to show interest in the Bible study. Today Gianni, his wife, and his mother are all faithful servants of Jehovah."

Forced to Burn His Bible

Fine Christian conduct also leads to 'opportune times' for sharing Bible truths with others. As the apostle Paul says, good conduct can "adorn the teaching of our Savior, God, in all things."—Titus 2:10.

Pietro, now a Witness in his late 20's, was attracted to such "teaching" by the Christian conduct of a classmate. "I was in the fifth grade," recalls Pietro, "but I still remember that boy's conduct. He was the only one who refused to stay in class during religious instruction."

One day Pietro asked the boy why he always left. The boy explained that he was exempted from class because he was one of Jehovah's Witnesses. Pietro's interest was aroused. He asked the boy to bring him a Bible. After reading some parts of the Bible, "I understood that it contained the truth," says Pietro. "I decided that I wanted to follow it from then on. I took the Bible to school with me and told everybody that I was one of Jehovah's Witnesses. I was only ten years old."

Troubles began. Pietro continues: "The priest who conducted the religious classes at school told my parents that I was using the Bible at school, and he advised them to destroy it. When I came home, my mother tried to grab my Bible, but I held it as tightly as I could. Then Mother began to hit me and tore it out of my hands. After that she forced me to burn my own Bible." Pietro lost his Bible but not his faith. He thought: 'As soon as I grow up, I'll buy a new Bible and go out to others to share its message.'

Two years went by. Then Pietro learned that a Bible study was conducted in the house of one of his friends. He secretly attended the study. "One day," says Pietro, "I told my parents, 'I have decided to become one of Jehovah's Witnesses. This time nothing will change my mind!'" Seeing the determination of their 12-year-old son, the parents gave in. Pietro began attending meetings at the Kingdom Hall right away. Four years later he was baptized as one of Jehovah's Witnesses. Today, 18 years after he first learned the truth from the Bible because of the faithful conduct of his classmate, Pietro is "buying out the opportune time" by serving as a full-time minister in Italy.

Zealous at 70 Years of Age

Mafalda, a Christian woman from Livorno, is another of the more than 22,000 zealous pioneers, or full-time ministers, in Italy. She began working as a pioneer at age 56. "Pioneer work," she explains, "requires that at least 1,000 hours a year are dedicated to the preaching work. But since this is an important message, I spend 2,000 hours each year as a pioneer worker." Mafalda is now 70 years old. What are her plans? "Among the first-century Christians, there were hardworking housewives who shared in the ministry," she says. "Like them, I want to continue announcing God's Kingdom. That's the goal in my life."

Indeed, from the snow-tipped mountain peaks in the alpine north to the Mediterranean island of Sicily in the south, modern-day witnesses of Jehovah in Italy reflect the zeal of their first-century counterparts. Each day of the year they spend, on an average, over 100,000 hours in the Kingdom-preaching work. The result? Last year alone, almost 12,000 persons were baptized and became ordained ministers of Jehovah. Now they, together with the 131,000 other witnesses of Jehovah, are "buying out the opportune time" in Italy.

Fear Jehovah and You Will Be Happy

"The fear of Jehovah is the start of wisdom." (9:10) How well this is shown in Proverbs! This Bible book, completed about 716 B.C.E., helps us to display wisdom, applying knowledge aright. Heed these wise sayings and you will be happy.

Listen to Wisdom

Read Proverbs 1:1–2:22. "The fear of Jehovah" is the very essence of knowledge. If we accept discipline, we will not join sinners in wrongdoing. To those fearing Jehovah, he gives wisdom that safeguards them against wrongdoers.

♦ 1:7—What is "the fear of Jehovah"?

It is awe, profound reverence, and a wholesome dread of displeasing him because we appreciate his loving-kindness and goodness. "Fear of Jehovah" means acknowledging that he is the Supreme Judge and the Almighty, with the right and power to bring punishment or death upon those disobeying him. It also means serving God faithfully, trusting in him completely, and hating what is bad in his sight.—Psalm 2:11; 115:11; Proverbs 8:13.

♦ 2:7—What is integrity?

Hebrew terms relating to integrity have the root meaning of that which is "whole" or "complete." They often signify moral soundness and uprightness. "Those walking in integrity" are unswerving in devotion to Jehovah. For such "upright ones" he is a protective "shield" because they manifest true wisdom and conform to his righteous standards.

Lesson for Us: If we fear Jehovah, we will accept the discipline he provides through his Word and organization. Failure to do so would class us with "fools," ungodly sinners. So let us accept his loving discipline. —Proverbs 1:7; Hebrews 12:6.

Prize Wisdom

Read Proverbs 3:1–4:27. To have good insight, "trust in Jehovah with all your heart." Happiness is enjoyed by those esteeming wisdom highly. Their path is like an ever-brightening light, but they need to safeguard the heart.

♦ 4:18—How does 'the path of the righteous' get lighter?

The sun's light gets brighter from dawn until "the day is firmly established." Similarly, spiritual light gets brighter for Jehovah's people as time goes on. As we draw much closer to events, our understanding of the outworking of Jehovah's purposes becomes clearer. Divine prophecies open up to us as God's holy spirit sheds light upon them, and as they are fulfilled in world events or in the experiences of Jehovah's people. Thus their 'path gets lighter and lighter.'

Lesson for Us: Displaying true wisdom and complying with divine commands will safeguard us against pursuing a foolish course that may lead to an early death. For instance, those ignoring Jehovah's commands against sexual immorality may contract sexually transmitted diseases that could result in premature death. So let us act in harmony with God's requirements, for then wisdom will be "a tree of life" in our case. —Proverbs 3:18.

Ways to Display Wisdom

Read Proverbs 5:1–9:18. It is a display of wisdom to avoid immorality and "rejoice with the wife of your youth." Seven things detestable to Jehovah are cited, and warnings are given against the seductions of a harlot. Wisdom personified is God's "master worker." And "fear of Jehovah is the start of wisdom."

♦ 6:1-5—Is this counsel contrary to the spirit of generosity?

This proverb does not discourage generosity, though it does counsel against getting involved in the business dealings of others, especially strangers. The Israelites were to help their brother who had 'grown poor.' (Leviticus 25:35-38) But some got involved in speculative business ventures and obtained financial backing by convincing others to 'go surety' for them, promising to pay their creditors if necessary. If a person got into such a predicament, perhaps through bragging, the wise advice was to deliver himself from it without delay.—Proverbs 11:15.

♦ 8:22-31—Is this merely a description of wisdom?

No, for wisdom has always existed as an attribute of the eternal God. (Job 12:13) Here, though, it is said that wisdom was "produced" and was "beside [Jehovah]" as a master worker" during earth's creation. Identifying wisdom personified as God's Son fits the fact that "carefully concealed in him are all the treasures of wisdom and of knowledge."—Colossians 1: 15, 16; 2:3.

Lesson for Us: By mentioning her "communion sacrifices" and "vows," the immoral woman of Proverbs chapter 7 may have been hinting that she did not lack spirituality. Communion sacrifices consisted of meat, flour, oil, and wine. (Leviticus 19:5, 6; 22:21; Numbers 15: 8-10) So she was indicating that there was plenty to eat and drink at her house, and the "young man in want of heart" would have a good time there. This is typical of how a wrongly motivated person is led into immorality. How important to heed this warning and avoid such sin against God!—Genesis 39: 7-12.

Thought-Provoking Contrasts

Read Proverbs 10:1–15:33. Solomon's proverbs begin largely with contrasting maxims. "The fear of Jehovah" is stressed.—10:27; 14:26, 27; 15:16, 33.

♦ 10:25—Why is reference made to a "storm wind"?

Lacking a foundation in righteous principles, the wicked are like unstable buildings that collapse in violent storms. But the righteous are stable because their thinking is solidly founded upon godly principles. Like a structure having a good foundation, they do not cave in under pressure.—Matthew 7: 24-27.

♦ 11:22—How could a woman be like a nose ring in a pig's snout?

A gold nose ring inserted through a side of the nose or the partition separating the nostrils suggested that the wearer was a cultured person. But the Israelites considered swine unclean and loathsome. So a pretty but senseless woman is like an inappropriate gold nose ring in a pig's snout.

♦ 14:14—How is a faithless one satisfied?

"One faithless at heart" is satisfied with his materialistic life-style. (Psalm 144:11-15a) Doing what is right in God's eyes is of no consequence to him, and he does not think about having to render an account to Jehovah. (1 Peter 4:3-5)

But "the good man" rejects the practices of faithless ones and is satisfied "with the results of his dealings." He keeps spiritual interests first, adheres to God's standards, has the supreme joy of serving Him, and is satisfied with divine blessings.—Psalm 144:15b.

♦ 15:23—How can we 'rejoice in the answer of our mouth'?

This can happen if our counsel is heeded and produces good results. But to assist someone, we must listen carefully, weigh the factors contributing to his problem, and base our counsel on the Bible. Such "a word at its right time is O how good!'

Lesson for Us: "A foolish person" angrily responds to an insult or "dishonor" quickly, "in the same day." But "the shrewd one"—a prudent individual—prays for God's spirit so as to exercise self-control and follow His Word. (Proverbs 12:16) By doing this, we can avoid further contention that could result in emotional or physical harm to ourselves or others.

Proverbs With Parallels

Read Proverbs 16:1–24:34. These wise sayings of Solomon give guidance mostly through parallel thoughts. Stressed again is "fear of Jehovah."—16:6; 19:23; 22:4; 23:17; 24:21.

♦ 17:19—What is wrong with a high entryway?

Those who did not make the doors to their houses and courts low risked having men on horseback ride in and take their goods. This proverb could also allude to the mouth as an entryway raised high by arrogant speech and boasting. Such talk fosters strife and eventually leads to disaster.

♦ 19:17—Why is helping the lowly like lending to Jehovah?

Lowly ones belong to God, and what we do to them is counted as

done to him. (Proverbs 14:31) If love and generosity prompt us to show favor to the lowly or give gifts to the poor, expecting no return from them, Jehovah considers such giving as loans to him that he repays with favor and blessings. —Luke 14:12-14.

♦ 20:1—How is wine "a ridiculer"?

Wine can cause one overindulging in it to act in a ridiculous and boisterous way. Since heavy drinking produces such bad effects, Christians must avoid it.—1 Timothy 3:2, 3, 8; 1 Corinthians 6:9, 10; Proverbs 23:20, 21.

♦ 23:27—How is a prostitute a "pit" and a "well"?

As animals were caught in 'deep pits' dug by hunters, so the patrons of a prostitute are trapped in immorality. "A foreign woman" denotes a harlot, doubtless because most prostitutes in Israel were foreigners. Getting water from "a narrow well" involves difficulties because earthenware jars easily break on its sides. Similarly, those having dealings with harlots may experience emotional and physical calamities.—Proverbs 7:21-27.

Lesson for Us: "A lying witness" shows disrespect for God and could be put to death under the Law. Thus he could "perish" at the hands of men or Jehovah. (Proverbs 21:28; Deuteronomy 5:20; 19:16-21; compare Acts 5:1-11.) But 'the man listening' attentively spoke only when sure of what he had heard. His testimony stood "forever," not later being rejected as falsehood. Moreover, he was not executed as a false witness. Those testifying at judicial hearings among Jehovah's Witnesses should have listened carefully so as to be able to provide accurate information, for inaccurate or false testimony can be spiritually damaging.

Helpful Comparisons

Read Proverbs 25:1–29:27. Solomon's proverbs transcribed by King Hezekiah's men teach largely by comparison. Among other things, dependence on Jehovah is encouraged.

♦ 26:6—Why is a comparison drawn with 'mutilating one's feet'?

A person mutilating his feet would cripple himself, even as an individual employing "someone stupid" is doing crippling violence to his own interests. A project entrusted to a stupid person will fail. How wise, then, to 'test men for fitness' before recommending them for congregational responsibility! —1 Timothy 3:10.

♦ 27:17—How is a face 'sharpened'?

As a piece of iron can be used to sharpen a blade made of the same metal, one person may succeed in sharpening the intellectual and spiritual state of another. If disappointments and contact with uncongenial individuals depress us, a fellow believer's sympathetic look and Scriptural encouragement can be very uplifting. Our sad countenance changes for the better, and we are enlivened with fresh hope for renewed action.—Proverbs 13:12.

♦ 28:5—What does "everything" include?

Those practicing what is bad are blind spiritually. (Proverbs 4:14-17; 2 Corinthians 4:4) They do not "understand judgment" or what is right according to God's standards. Thus they cannot judge matters correctly and make proper decisions. But those "seeking Jehovah" by prayer and study of his Word "understand everything" needed to serve him acceptably.—Ephesians 5:15-17.

♦ 29:8—How do boastful talkers "inflame a town"?

Boasters who disrespect authority speak brashly. They thus fuel the fires of dispute and fan the flames so much that residents of an entire town are inflamed. But wise persons "turn back anger," speaking mildly and sensibly, dousing flames of wrath and promoting peace.—Proverbs 15:1.

Lesson for Us: If we are proud, haughtiness will result in our being humbled. (Proverbs 29:23) A haughty person is likely to be presumptuous, and this can lead to dishonor, stumbling, and a crash. (Proverbs 11:2; 16:18; 18:12) God may see to it that a proud individual is humbled, brought low in some way, perhaps to the point of destruction. Such a man craves glory, but people find his ways abhorrent. However, a person "humble in spirit will [eventually] take hold of glory."

'Weighty Messages'

Read Proverbs 30:1–31:31. Agur's "weighty message" acknowledges that "every saying of God is refined." Also cited are things too wonderful to comprehend, and so forth. (30:1-33) "The weighty message" Lemuel received from his mother warns that drinking intoxicants can pervert judgment, urges one to judge righteously, and describes a good wife.—31:1-31.

♦ 30:15, 16—What is the point of these examples?

They illustrate the insatiableness of greed. Leeches gorge themselves with blood, even as greedy persons always demand more money or power. Likewise, Sheol is never satisfied but remains open to receive more victims of death. A barren womb 'cries out' for children. (Genesis 30:1) Drought-stricken land drinks up rainwater and soon appears dry again. And a fire that has consumed things thrown into it sends out flames that lick up other combustibles in reach. So it is with greedy persons. But those guided by godly wisdom are not endlessly goaded on by such selfishness.

♦ 31:6, 7—Why give wine to those "bitter of soul"?

Intoxicating liquor and wine are sedatives. So they would be given to "one about to perish," or die, or to 'those bitter of soul' to make them less conscious of their pain and hardships. The ancient custom of giving criminals drugged wine to blunt the pain of execution may explain why Roman soldiers offered it to Jesus Christ at the time of his impalement. He refused such wine because he wanted to be in full possession of his faculties at that trying time and thus maintain integrity to God.—Mark 15:22-24.

♦ 31:15—Who are these "young women"?

Household maidservants are meant here. They had no reason to complain for want of food or assigned work. The industrious wife gave food to her household and also saw to it that these women had something to eat and duties to perform.

Lesson for Us: Being imperfect, at times we may senselessly 'lift ourselves up,' making efforts at self-exaltation. If we do this or speak angrily, we should "put the hand to the mouth," refraining from additional words that would further provoke the one we offended. As milk must be churned to make butter and a nosebleed usually requires the squeezing of the nose, a quarrel occurs when people give free rein to anger. (Proverbs 30:32, 33) In such cases, how wise it is to be silent and prevent more trouble!

What benefits we can derive from the book of Proverbs! Let us cherish these wise sayings that promote reverential fear of Jehovah. Applying them will surely make us happy.

"The Damage Done Will Be Very Considerable"

WORLD WAR I took an enormous toll in human lives and property. Less well known, however, is the damage that the war did to the image of Christendom's missionaries in Africa. According to Catholic missionary Francis Schimlek in his book *Medicine Versus Witchcraft,* news of this global conflagration "was like an earthquake, the tremor of which was felt as far as the last mission station in the African bush.... The messengers of Christ were embarrassed, and the Native Christians puzzled."

Why so? Schimlek quotes missionary Albert Schweitzer as explaining: "We are, all of us, conscious that many Natives are puzzling over the question how it can be possible that the whites, who brought the Gospel of Love, are now murdering each other, and throwing to the winds the commands of the Lord Jesus. When they put the question to us we are helpless.... I fear that the damage done will be very considerable."

Questions From Readers

■ Moses told the Israelites that "the things revealed belong to us and to our sons to time indefinite." (Deuteronomy 29:29) Have these "things revealed" come to include the light that has been shed on God's Word during these last days?

No, it would not be correct to put the understanding of prophecies that we have been granted during these last days on the same level as "the things revealed" that Moses was discussing.

According to the context of Moses' words, "the things revealed" that he was talking about had to do with the Law covenant. (Deuteronomy 29:25) Moses showed that these "things revealed" carried responsibilities. Failure to live up to these responsibilities would cause Jehovah to discipline his people.

The Law covenant, of course, was a revelation from Jehovah God. It was preceded by other revelations to the patriarchs, to Noah, and going all the way back to Adam. Moses was used to put into writing the things revealed up to his time, and they have been preserved for us in the first five books of the Bible. Later, as the article "The Things Revealed Belong to Us" (*The Watchtower,* May 15, 1986) explained, these "things revealed" came to include all the information recorded in the Bible.—2 Timothy 3:16.

Thus, the Bible contains "the sacred pronouncements of God," the things revealed by him. (Romans 3:2) When the natural Jews proved unfaithful, anointed Christians became the stewards of these "things revealed," and the Christian congregation became "a pillar and support" for them. (1 Timothy 3:15; 1 Corinthians 4:1) Hence, members of that congregation today can properly echo Moses' words, that "the things revealed belong to us."

Today, Jehovah has shed much light on these "things revealed." As prophesied by Daniel, Jehovah's people have 'roved about' in the inspired Word, and 'true knowledge has become abundant.' (Daniel 12:4) Thus, we now know the identity of the "other sheep." (John 10:16) We recognize the "great crowd." (Revelation 7:9-17) We see the fulfillment of the parable of the sheep and the goats. (Matthew 25:31-46) Such things have been disclosed, or made known, to us but not in the sense of "the things revealed" as recorded in Jehovah's inspired Word.

Therefore, it would not be correct to put such advances in understanding on the same level as the inspired revelations that make up "the things revealed" recorded in the Bible. Rather, through an intensive study of the Bible, Jehovah's people have prayerfully sought a correct understanding of those "things revealed." Jehovah, by means of holy spirit, has given that understanding in his own due time.

The Bible tells us that "the path of the righteous ones is like the bright light that is getting lighter and lighter until the day is firmly established." (Proverbs 4:18) The increasing light that Jehovah has shed on "the things revealed" shows that that "day" is getting closer and proves that his blessing is on the Christian congregation today.

He Ordered 50 Copies!

When the book *Life—How Did It Get Here? By Evolution or by Creation?* was released about two years ago, a woman in England thought it would be an ideal gift for her uncle, an influential 84-year-old businessman in the Yorkshire area. So she gave him a copy.

Within a week he called her and said: "Marvelous, that book is just marvelous! Can you get me some more copies? I would like to give them as gifts to my business colleagues."

Only 25 were immediately available, and he quickly distributed these among his associates. But he wanted 25 more. These were soon obtained, and he gave these to his colleagues as well—50 in all!

The Watchtower
Announcing Jehovah's Kingdom
June 1, 1987

Who Will Care for the Elderly?

The Watchtower®

Announcing Jehovah's Kingdom

June 1, 1987
Vol. 108, No. 11

In This Issue

THE PURPOSE OF "THE WATCHTOWER" is to exalt Jehovah God as the Sovereign of the universe. It keeps watch on world events as they fulfill Bible prophecy. It comforts all peoples with the good news that God's Kingdom will soon destroy those who oppress their fellowmen and that it will turn the earth into a paradise. It encourages faith in the now-reigning King, Jesus Christ, whose shed blood opens the way for mankind to gain eternal life. "The Watchtower," published by Jehovah's Witnesses continuously since 1879, is nonpolitical. It adheres to the Bible as its authority.

"WATCHTOWER" STUDIES FOR THE WEEKS

July 5: Keeping An Eye On the Interests of the Elderly. Page 8. Songs to Be Used: 62, 66.

July 12: Practicing Godly Devotion Toward Elderly Parents. Page 13. Songs to Be Used: 95, 86.

Average Printing Each Issue: 12,315,000

Now Published in 103 Languages

SEMIMONTHLY LANGUAGES AVAILABLE BY MAIL
Afrikaans, Arabic, Cebuano, Chichewa, Chinese, Cibemba, Danish,* Dutch,* Efik, English,* Finnish,* French,* German,* Greek,* Hiligaynon, Igbo, Iloko, Italian,* Japanese,* Korean, Lingala, Malagasy, Maltese, Norwegian, Portuguese,* Russian, Sepedi, Sesotho, Shona, Spanish,* Swahili, Swedish,* Tagalog, Thai, Tsonga, Tswana, Xhosa, Yoruba, Zulu

MONTHLY LANGUAGES AVAILABLE BY MAIL
Armenian, Bengali, Bicol, Bislama, Bulgarian, Croatian, Czech, Ewe, Fijian, Ga, Greenlandic, Gujarati, Gun, Hausa, Hebrew, Hindi, Hiri Motu, Hungarian, Icelandic, Kannada, Malayalam, Marathi, New Guinea Pidgin, Pangasinan, Papiamento, Polish, Rarotongan, Romanian, Samar-Leyte, Samoan, Sango, Serbian, Silozi, Sinhalese, Slovenian, Solomon Islands-Pidgin, Tahitian, Tamil, Telugu, Tongan, Tshiluba, Turkish, Twi, Ukrainian, Urdu, Venda, Vietnamese

* Study articles also available in large-print edition.

Watch Tower Society offices	Yearly subscription for the above:	
	Semimonthly Languages	Monthly Languages
America, U.S., Watchtower, Wallkill, N.Y. 12589	$4.00	$2.00
Australia, Box 280, Ingleburn, N.S.W. 2565	A$7.00	A$3.50
Canada, Box 4100, Halton Hills, Ontario L7G 4Y4	$5.50	$2.75
England, The Ridgeway, London NW7 1RN	£5.00	£2.50
Ireland, 29A Jamestown Road, Finglas, Dublin 11	IR£6.00	IR£3.00
New Zealand, P.O. Box 142, Manurewa	NZ$15.00	NZ$7.50
Nigeria, PMB 001, Shomolu, Lagos State	₦8.00	₦4.00
Philippines, P.O. Box 2044, Manila 2800	₱60.00	₱30.00
South Africa, Private Bag 2067, Krugersdorp, 1740	R9,00	R4,50

Remittances should be sent to the office in your country or to Watchtower, Wallkill, N.Y. 12589, U.S.A.

Changes of address should reach us 30 days before your moving date. Give us your old and new address (if possible, your old address label).

20 cents (U.S.) a copy

The Bible translation used is the "New World Translation of the Holy Scriptures," unless otherwise indicated.

The Watchtower (ISSN 0043-1087) is published semimonthly for $4.00 (U.S.) per year by Watch Tower Bible and Tract Society of Pennsylvania, 25 Columbia Heights, Brooklyn, N.Y. 11201. Second-class postage paid at Brooklyn, N.Y., and at additional mailing offices.

Postmaster: Send address changes to Watchtower, **Wallkill, N.Y. 12589.**

Published by
**Watch Tower Bible and Tract Society
of Pennsylvania**
25 Columbia Heights, Brooklyn, N.Y. 11201, U.S.A.
Frederick W. Franz, President

Is the Future Bleak for the Elderly?

"A YOUNG man I used to be," said King David. "I have also grown old." (Psalm 37:25) In Bible times the old were an esteemed minority. If present trends continue, however, the old might soon be neither a minority nor esteemed.

In the United States alone, there are an estimated 26 million people over 65 years of age. By the year 2040 this number could almost triple! According to the magazine *Asiaweek,* some Asian nations "expect the numbers of their elderly to double in the coming decade." The prospect of the old nearly outnumbering the young, however, does not bode well for the elderly. Already, an alarming number find themselves destitute and homeless. Others are being left to wither away in hospitals or nursing homes—alone, unvisited, and uncared for. Shocking cases of neglect and abuse are reported even in countries where parents have customarily been revered.

Wrote G. M. Ssenkoloto for *World Health* magazine: "Traditionally in most African countries, and indeed in most of the Third World, every family looked after its old women. A woman who had no children to care for her was looked after by neighbours or by the village as a whole."

He reports, however: "Age-old values are changing. Adverse economic forces, the misallocation of resources, the yearning for material things, the struggle for self-esteem and status—all these factors are overtaking the traditional positive values as regards support for the elderly."

The words of the Bible writer Agur are thus proving true on a large scale: "There is a generation that calls down evil even upon its father and that does not bless even its mother." (Proverbs 30:11) Yes, the elderly are being toppled from the position of honor they enjoyed in times past. Many view them as social liabilities rather than assets. For the most part, their prospects look bleak.

How, though, do true Christians view the aged? Do they retain the "traditional positive values" regarding them?

True Christians Honor Older Ones!

"THE aged," says researcher Suzanne Steinmetz, "are at the end of their economically productive life, which is the basis on which our culture values individuals and provides them with deference, status, respect and rewards." Modern society's view of the elderly is thus a gloomy, negative one. Little wonder, then, that we often read of their being neglected and abused.

However, what view of the elderly does the Bible take? God's Word realistically acknowledges that growing old is not easy. Prayed the psalmist: "Do not throw me away in the time of old age; just when my power is failing, do not leave me." (Psalm 71:9) In his old age, he felt more need than ever of Jehovah's support. And the Bible's view is positive in showing that we, too, should give attention to the needs of the aged.

True, Solomon called old age "the calamitous days" in which one would "have

no delight." (Ecclesiastes 12:1-3) But "length of days and years of life" are also associated in the Bible with *blessings* from God. (Proverbs 3:1, 2) To illustrate, Jehovah promised Abraham: "As for you, . . . you will be buried at a good old age." (Genesis 15:15) Surely, God was not sentencing faithful Abraham to dismal, "calamitous days" in which he could "have no delight." Abraham found peace and serenity in his latter years, looking back with satisfaction on a life spent in service to Jehovah. He could also look forward to a "city having real foundations," God's Kingdom. (Hebrews 11:10) Thus he could die "old and satisfied."—Genesis 25:8.

Why, then, did Solomon call old age "the calamitous days"? Solomon referred to the unrelenting deterioration of health that occurs in old age. However, one who has failed to 'remember his Grand Creator in the days of his young manhood' finds his declining years particularly calamitous. (Ecclesiastes 12:1) Because he has wasted his life, such an old person 'has no delight' in his latter days of life. His godless life-style may even have resulted in physical problems that aggravate the discomforts of old age. (Compare Proverbs 5:3-11.) So when looking ahead, he sees no future but the grave. A person who has devoted his life to serving God also experiences "calamitous days" as his body weakens. But like Abraham, he can find joy and satisfaction in a life well spent and in using his remaining strength in God's service. "Gray-headedness is a crown of beauty when it is found in the way of righteousness," says the Bible. —Proverbs 16:31.

In fact, old age even has certain advantages. "Youth and the prime of life are vanity," says Solomon. While young people may enjoy vibrant health, they often lack experience and judgment. Old age, though, brings with it a lifetime of experience. The elderly one 'wards off calamity,' unlike the impulsive youth who often rushes headlong into it. (Ecclesiastes 11:10; 2 Timothy 2:22) Consequently, Solomon could say: "The splendor of old men is their gray-headedness."—Proverbs 20:29.

The Bible therefore honors the elderly. How does this affect the way in which Christians deal with them?

'Rising' Before Elderly Ones

God made respect for the aged a national policy in Israel. The Mosaic Law stated: "Before gray hair you should rise up, and you must show consideration for the person of an old man." (Leviticus 19:32) Jews in later years evidently took this law quite literally. Says Dr. Samuel Burder in his book *Oriental Customs:* "The Jewish writers say that the rule was, to rise up to them when they were at the distance of four cubits; and as soon as they were gone

by, to sit down again, that it might appear they rose purely out of respect to them." Such respect was not limited to men of prominence. "Respect even the old man who has lost his learning," declared the Talmud. One rabbi argued that this respect should also include an ignorant and unlettered old man. "The very fact that he has grown old," he reasoned, "must be due to some merit."—*The Jewish Encyclopedia.*

Christians today are no longer subject to the sanctions of the Mosaic Law. (Romans 7:6) But this does not mean that they are no longer obliged to show special regard for the elderly. This is evident from the instructions the apostle Paul gave the Christian overseer Timothy: "Do not severely criticize an older man. To the contrary, entreat him as a father, . . . older women as mothers." (1 Timothy 5:1, 2) Paul told young Timothy that he had authority to "command." (1 Timothy 1:3) Nevertheless, if someone older than he —especially one serving as an overseer— erred in judgment or made an incorrect statement, Timothy was not to "severely criticize" him as an inferior. Rather, he was respectfully to "entreat him as a father." Timothy was to show similar respect to older women in the congregation. Yes, he was still, in effect, to 'rise before gray hair.'

Christianity is thus a religion that respects the elderly. Ironically, though, much of the mistreatment of older ones takes place in nations professing to be Christian. There are, however, worshipers that still adhere to Bible standards. Jehovah's Witnesses, for example, enjoy the presence of many thousands of elderly ones in their midst; they do not view them as a burden or a liability. While fragile health may prevent such older ones from being as active as they once were, many have long records of faithful Christian service, and this encourages younger Witnesses to imitate their faith.—Compare Hebrews 13:7.

The elderly, however, are not expected to take a passive role in the congregation. They are urged to set fine examples in being "moderate in habits, serious, sound in mind, healthy in faith, . . . reverent in behavior," freely sharing their wisdom and experience with others. (Titus 2:2, 3) Joel prophesied that among those sharing in the proclaiming of the Bible message, would be "old men." (Joel 2:28) No doubt you have personally observed that many elderly Witnesses still delight to share actively in the door-to-door preaching activity.

Showing Them Honor "in Fuller Measure"

Jehovah's Witnesses endeavor to give older ones special consideration in many ways. At yearly religious conventions, for example, they often arrange for seats to be set aside for older ones. Consideration is also shown them on an individual basis. In Japan one Witness gives up his seat in the family car so that an 87-year-old woman can have a ride to congregation meetings. How does he get to the meetings himself? By bicycle. In Brazil there is a full-time evangelizer 92 years of age. Observers report that Witnesses there "treat him with respect, talk with him . . . He is a useful part of the congregation."

This does not mean that there is no room for improvement in honoring older ones. Paul wrote to Christians in Thessalonica: "However, with reference to brotherly love, . . . you are doing it to all the brothers in all of Macedonia. But we exhort you, brothers, to go on doing it in fuller measure." (1 Thessalonians 4:9, 10) Similar counsel is at times needed today when it comes to our treatment of older ones. One 85-year-old Christian, for example, was very disappointed when he did not receive a copy of a new Bible-based publication. The problem? He is nearly deaf and did not hear an announcement reminding everyone to order the book; nor did anyone in the congregation think of ordering it for him. The situation, of course, was quickly rectified. It nevertheless illustrates that there is a need to be especially conscious of the needs of older ones.

There are any number of ways in which God's people today can do this "in fuller measure." Christian meetings afford an opportunity to "incite" older ones "to love and fine works." (Hebrews 10:24, 25) And while young and old already mix freely at Kingdom Halls of Jehovah's Witnesses, perhaps even more effort can be made along those lines. For example, some parents encourage their children respectfully to approach and talk with senior members of the congregation.

Honor can also continue to be shown the elderly on an informal basis. In harmony with the principle Jesus set forth at Luke 14:12-14, more effort can be made to invite older ones to social gatherings. Even if they are unable to attend, they will certainly appreciate your remembering them. Christians are further exhorted to "follow the course of hospitality." (Romans 12:13) This need not call for something fancy or elaborate. Suggests one Witness from Germany: "Invite older ones over for a cup of tea, and let them tell their experiences from the past."

The apostle Paul said: "In showing honor to one another take the lead." (Romans 12:10) Among Jehovah's Witnesses, appointed congregation elders especially take the lead in showing honor to elderly Christians. Often the elders are able to assign older ones appropriate tasks to perform, such as training new ones as evan-

In congregations of Jehovah's Witnesses, older ones find much satisfying work to do

gelists or assisting with maintenance at Christian meeting places. Younger men serving as congregation elders show older overseers honor by humbly approaching them for advice, using discernment in getting their mature viewpoints. (Proverbs 20:5) At meetings of such elders, they follow the Biblical example of young Elihu and respectfully defer to older, more experienced men, giving them full opportunity to express themselves first.—Job 32:4.

Admittedly, it is easy to become impatient with elderly ones because they may not be able to move or think as fast as younger ones do. Dr. Robert N. Butler well describes some of the problems old age can bring: "One loses one's physical stamina,

one's ability to keep up, and that in itself can be extremely frightening. One may lose important sensory elements such as hearing or vision." Appreciating this, should not younger ones show fellow feeling and be compassionate?—1 Peter 3:8.

Yes, Christians today are obliged to show true love, concern, and respect for the older ones in their midst. And among Jehovah's Witnesses, this is being done in an exemplary way. What happens, though, when elderly Christians—or the parents of Christians—become ill or impoverished? Whose responsibility is it to render them care? The following articles will explore how the Bible answers these questions.

Keeping An Eye On
the Interests of
the Elderly

"Keeping an eye, not in personal interest upon just your own matters, but also in personal interest upon those of the others."
—PHILIPPIANS 2:4.

SHORTLY after Pentecost 33 C.E. "a murmuring arose [in the Christian congregation] on the part of the Greek-speaking Jews against the Hebrew-speaking Jews, because their widows were being overlooked in the daily distribution [of food to the needy]." No doubt a number of these widows were elderly and unable to fend for themselves. At any rate, the apostles themselves intervened, saying: "Search out for yourselves seven certified men from among you, full of spirit and wisdom, that we may appoint them over this necessary business."—Acts 6:1-3.

² Early Christians thus viewed caring for the needy as "necessary business." Years later the disciple James wrote: "The form of worship that is clean and undefiled from the standpoint of our God and Father is this: to look after orphans and widows in their tribulation." (James 1:27) Did this mean, then, that the all-important preaching work was neglected? No, for the account in Acts says that after the relief work for widows was properly organized, "the word of God went on growing, and the number of the disciples kept multiplying in Jerusalem very much."—Acts 6:7.

³ Today we face "critical times hard to deal with." (2 Timothy 3:1) Caring for the demands of family life and secular work may leave us little energy—or desire—to concern ourselves with the needs of the elderly. Appropriately, then, Philippians 2:4 urges us to be "keeping an eye, not in personal interest upon just [our] own matters, but also in personal interest upon those of the others." How can this be done in a balanced, practical way?

Rendering Honor to Widows

⁴ In 1 Timothy chapter 5, Paul shows how early Christians looked after elderly widows in the congregation. He urged Timothy: "Honor widows that are actually widows." (Verse 3) Elderly widows were singled out as particularly worthy of receiving honor in the form of regular financial support. Such ones were cut off from all visible means of support and could only 'put their hope in God and persist in supplications and prayers night and day.' (Verse 5) How were their prayers for sustenance answered? Through the congregation. In an organized manner, deserving widows were provided with a modest livelihood. Of course, if a widow had financial means, or relatives capable of supporting

---

1, 2. (a) How did the first-century governing body demonstrate an interest in the needs of the elderly? (b) What evidence is there that the preaching work was not neglected?

3. What encouragement is given at Philippians 2:4, and why is this particularly appropriate today?
4. (a) Why and how did the first-century congregation "honor" widows? (b) Were such provisions always necessary?

her, such provisions were unnecessary. —Verses 4, 16.

5 "But the [widow] that goes in for sensual gratification," cautioned Paul, "is [spiritually] dead though she is living." (Verse 6) Paul does not explain how some were, as the *Kingdom Interlinear* literally renders it, "behaving voluptuously." Some may have been fighting a battle with their "sexual impulses." (Verse 11) However, according to *Liddell & Scott's Greek-English Lexicon,* "behaving voluptuously" could also have involved 'living softly or in excessive comfort or indulgence.' Perhaps, then, some wanted the congregation to enrich them, to finance an extravagant, self-indulgent life of immoderation. Whatever the case, Paul indicates that such ones were disqualified from receiving congregation support.

6 Paul then said: "Let a widow be put on the list [of those receiving financial support] who has become not less than sixty years old." In Paul's day a woman over age 60 was evidently viewed as unable to support herself and unlikely to remarry.* "On the other hand," Paul said, "turn down younger widows [for enrollment], for when their sexual impulses have come between them and the Christ, they want to marry, having a judgment because they

have disregarded their first expression of faith."—Verses 9, 11, 12.

7 Had "the list" been open to younger widows, some might hastily have declared an intention to remain single. As time passed, though, they might have had difficulty controlling their "sexual impulses" and wanted to remarry, 'having a judgment for disregarding their first expression of faith' to remain single. (Compare Ecclesiastes 5:2-6.) Paul averted such problems, further declaring, "I desire the younger widows to marry, to bear children."—Verse 14.

8 The apostle also limited enrollment to those with long records of fine Christian works. (Verse 10) The congregation was thus not a "welfare state" for the lazy or the greedy. (2 Thessalonians 3:10, 11) But what of elderly men or younger widows? If such ones fell into need, the congregation would no doubt have cared for them on an individual basis.—Compare 1 John 3: 17, 18.

9 Such arrangements were likely quite adequate for the needs of first-century congregations. But as *The Expositor's Bible Commentary* observes: "Today, with insurance income, social security, and job opportunities, the situation is very different." As a result of a changed social and economic picture, rarely is it necessary for congregations today to maintain lists of elderly beneficiaries. Nevertheless, Paul's words to Timothy help us appreciate: (1) The problems of the elderly are of concern to the entire congregation—particularly the elders. (2) The care of the

---

* Leviticus 27:1-7 refers to the redemption of individuals 'offered' (by means of a vow) to the temple as laborers. The redemption price varied according to age. At age 60 this price fell precipitously, evidently because a person that old was felt to be unable to work as hard as a younger one. *The Encyclopædia Judaica* further says: "According to the Talmud, old age . . . begins at 60."

---

5. (a) How might some widows have 'gone in for sensual gratification'? (b) Was the congregation obligated to support such ones?
6, 7, and footnote. (a) What was "the list"? (b) Why were those under age 60 disqualified from receiving support? (c) How did Paul assist young widows from receiving an adverse "judgment"?

8. (a) How did Paul's guidelines protect the congregation? (b) Were needy younger widows or elderly men also cared for?
9. (a) Why would arrangements for the care of the elderly today differ from those made in the first century? (b) What does Paul's discussion of widows in 1 Timothy chapter 5 help us appreciate today?

elderly should be properly organized. (3) Such care is limited to those truly in need.

As Elders, Keeping An Eye On Their Interests

[10] How do overseers today take the lead in showing an interest in older ones? From time to time they can feature the needs of the elderly on the agenda of their meetings. When specific help is needed, they can arrange for it to be given. They may not personally render the care, inasmuch as there are often many willing ones—including youths—in the congregation who can help out. However, they can closely supervise such care, perhaps by assigning a brother to coordinate the care given to an individual.

[11] Solomon counseled: "You ought to know positively the appearance of your flock." (Proverbs 27:23) Overseers can thus personally visit the elderly so as to determine how best to "share . . . accord-

ing to their needs." (Romans 12:13) A traveling overseer put it this way: "Some elderly ones are very independent, and just asking them what needs to be done is no good. It is best to discern what needs to be done and get on with the job!" In Japan some overseers found that an 80-year-old sister needed much attention. They report: "We now see to it that someone has contact with her twice a day, morning and night, by visit or by telephone."—Compare Matthew 25:36.

[12] Overseers are also concerned that elderly ones get the benefit of congregation meetings. (Hebrews 10:24, 25) Do some need transportation? Are some simply unable to "listen and get the sense of" meetings because of hearing impairments?

10. How can elders today take the lead in showing an interest in older ones?
11. How can elders acquaint themselves with the needs of the elderly?

12. (a) How can elders see to it that elderly ones get the benefit of congregation meetings? (b) What good use can be made of tapes produced by the Society?

(Matthew 15:10) Perhaps it would be practical to install headphones for them. Similarly, a number of congregations now have meetings carried over the telephone lines so that infirm ones can listen in at home. Others record the meetings on tapes for those too sick to attend—in some cases purchasing the tape recorders for them. And speaking of tapes, an elder in Germany observed: "I have visited several elderly ones who just sat in front of the television and looked at programs that could hardly be described as being spiritually upbuilding." Why not encourage them to listen instead to tapes produced by the Society, such as those containing Kingdom melodies and Bible reading?

[13] Some senior members of the congregation have become irregular or inactive as preachers. Age, though, does not necessarily prevent one from proclaiming the "good news of the kingdom." (Matthew 24:14) Some might respond to a simple invitation to work with you in the field service. Perhaps you can rekindle their love for preaching by sharing field-service experiences with them. If walking up stairs is a problem, arrange for them to work apartments with elevators or residential areas without steps. Some publishers can also have elderly ones accompany them on Bible studies—or hold the study in the elderly one's home.

[14] 'Money is a protection.' (Ecclesiastes 7:12) Yet many an aged brother or sister is in dire financial straits and has no relatives willing to help out. Individuals in the congregation, though, are usually happy to assist when made aware of the need.

13. How can older ones be helped to stay active as Kingdom proclaimers?
14 and box. (a) What can the elders do if an elderly brother or sister falls into dire financial straits? (b) How have some congregations met the needs of elderly publishers?

(James 2:15-17) The elders can also look into what government or social services, insurance policies, pensions, and so forth, are available. In some lands, however, such services are hard to come by, and there may be no alternative but to follow the pattern at 1 Timothy chapter 5 and arrange for the congregation as a whole to

Helping the Elderly
—What Some Are Doing

A congregation in Brazil found a convenient way of caring for the physical needs of a brother who lives near their Kingdom Hall: The book study group assigned to clean the hall also cleans his home.

Another congregation there found a simple way to keep an infirm brother active in the Theocratic Ministry School. When his turn to give a talk comes up, a brother is assigned to take two or three publishers with him to visit the brother. A brief meeting is opened with prayer, and the brother delivers his assignment. Necessary counsel is given. What an encouragement this visit proves to be!

Traveling overseers have set a fine example in taking the lead. In one congregation an elderly brother who was confined to a wheelchair became quite irritable and as a result was seldom visited. A traveling overseer, however, arranged to give the brother a private viewing of his slide talk. The elderly brother was moved to tears by what he saw. Says the overseer: "I felt greatly rewarded to see how a little attention and love could bring such results."

Some elders in Nigeria made a shepherding call on an aged brother and discovered that he was seriously ill. He was immediately taken to the hospital. The aged brother was found to need extensive medical treatment, but he was unable to pay for it. When the congregation was informed of his need, the publishers came up with enough money to care for his expenses. Two elders took turns driving him back and forth to the hospital, although this required their taking time off from work. They had the joy, though, of seeing the brother recover from his illness and auxiliary pioneer until his death some four years later.

In the Philippines an elderly sister had no family. The congregation made arrangements for her care during three years of illness. They provided her with a small place to live, brought her meals each day, and cared for her hygiene.

provide relief. (See *Organized to Accomplish Our Ministry,* pages 122-3.)

Publishers in Nigeria regularly assisted an 82-year-old regular pioneer and his wife with material gifts. After the government scheduled for demolition the building they lived in, the congregation invited them to move into a room attached to the Kingdom Hall until other accommodations could be arranged.

In Brazil a congregation hired a nurse to care for an elderly couple. At the same time, a sister was assigned to keep the house clean, prepare their food, and care for other physical needs. Each month the congregation sets aside funds for their use.

[15] As in the first century, such provisions are for worthy ones who truly need them. Overseers are not obliged to meet extravagant requests or cater to unreasonable demands for attention. Elderly ones, too, must keep a 'simple eye.'—Luke 11:34.

As Individuals, Keeping An Eye On Their Interests

[16] Some time ago an elderly sister was admitted to a hospital. The diagnosis was malnutrition. "If more in the congregation had taken a personal interest in her," wrote an elder, "perhaps this would not have happened." Yes, elders are not the only ones who must take an interest in the elderly. Paul said: "We are members belonging to one another."—Ephesians 4:25.

[17] Doubtless some of you are already burdened with personal responsibilities. But 'keep an eye, not in personal interest upon just your own matters.' (Philippians 2:4) With proper personal organization, you can often 'buy out time.' (Ephesians 5:16) For example, could you visit an elderly one after field service? Weekdays are particularly lonely periods for some. Teenagers, too, can get involved in visiting the elderly and doing chores for them. Prayed one sister who was helped by a youth: "Thank you Jehovah for young Brother John. What a fine person he is."

[18] At meetings, do you simply give older ones a cursory greeting? Granted, it may not be easy conversing with someone who is hard of hearing or has difficulty expressing himself. And since failing health takes its toll, not all elderly ones have cheery dispositions. Nevertheless, "better is one who is patient." (Ecclesiastes 7:8) With a little effort, a real "interchange of encouragement" can ensue. (Romans 1:12) Try relating a field-service experience. Share a point you read in *The Watchtower* or *Awake!* Or better yet, listen. (Compare Job 32:7.) Older ones have much to share if you let them. Admitted one elder: "Visiting that elderly brother did me a lot of good."

---

18. (a) Why may conversation with an elderly one be difficult at times? (b) How can one make a visit or a conversation with an older person mutually upbuilding?

---

15. (a) Are there limitations on the help the congregation can provide? (b) How might the counsel at Luke 11:34 be appropriate for certain ones who become overly demanding?
16, 17. (a) Why is it important for others besides elders to take an interest in the elderly? (b) How can busy publishers 'buy out time' for the elderly?

Do You Remember?

☐ What provisions were made in the first century for elderly widows?

☐ How can overseers organize the care of older ones in the congregation?

☐ How can individuals in the congregation display an interest in elderly brothers and sisters?

☐ What can older ones do to assist those rendering them care?

[19] Should not your concern for the elderly also extend to the families caring for them? One couple looking after aging parents reported: "Rather than encouraging us, some in the congregation have become quite critical. One sister said: 'If you keep missing meetings, you'll get spiritually sick!' But she wasn't willing to do anything to help us get to more meetings." Equally discouraging are vague promises such as, If you ever need help, let me know. These often amount to little more than saying, "Keep warm and well fed." (James 2:16) How much better it is to let your concern translate into action! Reports one couple: "The friends have been wonderful and supportive! Some will take care of Mom for a couple of days at a time so that we can have an occasional break. Others take her on Bible studies. And it really encourages us when others inquire as to her welfare."

[20] By and large our older ones are well cared for. However, what can elderly Witnesses themselves do so that such work is done with joy and not with sighing? (Compare Hebrews 13:17.) Cooperate with the arrangements elders make for your care. Express thanks and appreciation for whatever deeds of kindness are performed, and avoid being overly demanding or overly critical. And though the aches and pains of old age are quite real, try to manifest a cheerful, positive attitude. —Proverbs 15:13.

[21] 'The brothers are wonderful. I do not know what I would do without them,' many older ones have been heard to say. Nevertheless, the prime responsibility of caring for the elderly rests upon their children. What does this involve, and how can this challenge best be met?

---

19. (a) Our concern for the elderly extends to whom? (b) What are some ways in which we can prove helpful to families caring for older parents?

20, 21. What can older ones do to assist those rendering them care?

Practicing Godly Devotion
Toward Elderly Parents

"Let [children or grandchildren] learn first to practice godly devotion in their own household and to keep paying a due compensation to their parents and grandparents, for this is acceptable in God's sight." —1 TIMOTHY 5:4.

AS A child, you were nurtured and protected by them. As an adult, you sought their advice and support. But now they have grown old and need someone to support them. Says the apostle Paul: "But if any widow has children or grandchildren, let these learn first to practice godly devotion in their own household and to keep paying a due compensation to their parents and grandparents, for this is acceptable in God's sight. Certainly if anyone does not provide for those who are his

---

1, 2. (a) Whom does the Bible hold responsible for the care of aging parents? (b) Why would it be a serious matter for a Christian to neglect this duty?

own, and especially for those who are members of his household, he has disowned the faith and is worse than a person without faith."—1 Timothy 5:4, 8.

2 Thousands of Jehovah's Witnesses today care for aging parents. They do so not merely out of "kindness" (*The Living Bible*) or "duty" (*The Jerusalem Bible*) but out of "godly devotion," that is, reverence for God. They recognize that to abandon one's parents at a time of need would be tantamount to 'disowning the [Christian] faith.'—Compare Titus 1:16.

'Carry Your Load' of Care

3 Looking after elderly parents has become a real challenge, especially in Western lands. Families are often scattered. Costs have risen out of control. Housewives frequently have secular jobs. Caring for an aging parent can thus be a huge undertaking, especially when the one who gives the care is no longer young himself. "We are now in our 50's, with grown children and grandchildren that also need help," says one sister struggling to care for her parent.

4 Paul indicated that the responsibility could be shared by the "children or grandchildren." (1 Timothy 5:4) Sometimes, though, siblings are unwilling to 'carry their load' of care. (Compare Galatians 6:5.) "My older sister has just washed her hands of the situation," complains one elder. But can such a course be pleasing to Jehovah? Recall what Jesus once told the Pharisees: "Moses said, 'Honor your father and your mother' . . . But you men say, 'If a man says to his father or his mother: "Whatever I have by which you may get benefit from me is corban, (that is, a gift dedicated to God,)"'—you men no longer let him do a single thing for his father or his mother, and thus you make the word of God invalid by your tradition."—Mark 7:10-13.

5 If a Jew did not care to assist his destitute parents, he needed only to declare his belongings "corban"—a gift set aside for temple use. (Compare Leviticus 27:1-24.) He was evidently under no immediate compulsion, however, to hand over this supposed gift. Thus he could hold onto (and no doubt use) his belongings indefinitely. But if his parents needed financial help, he could wriggle out of his duty by piously declaring that all he owned was "corban." Jesus condemned this fraud.

6 A Christian who uses empty excuses to evade his duty is thus not fooling God. (Jeremiah 17:9, 10) True, financial problems, failing health, or similar circumstances may greatly limit how much one can do for one's parents. But some may simply value assets, time, and privacy more than their parents' welfare. How hypocritical it would be, though, to preach the Word of God but make it "invalid" by our inaction toward parents!

Family Cooperation

7 Some experts recommend that when a crisis involving an aged parent develops, a family conference be called. One family member may have to shoulder the bulk of the responsibility. But by calmly and objectively engaging in "confidential talk," families can often work out ways to share

---

3. Why may the care of one's parents be a real challenge?
4, 5. (a) With whom does the Bible indicate that the load of care can often be shared? (b) How did some evade responsibility to their parents in Jesus' day?

6. What may motivate some today to evade their parental duties, and is this pleasing to God?
7. How can families cooperate in providing care for an aged parent?

A family conference can be held to discuss how the care of a parent can be shared

the work load. (Proverbs 15:22) Some living far away may be able to contribute financially and visit periodically. Others may be able to handle chores or provide transportation. Why, simply agreeing to visit the parents regularly may be a valuable contribution. Says one sister in her 80's regarding visits by her children, "It's like a tonic!"

⁸ Families may face a delicate problem, though, when a member is engaged in full-time service. Full-time ministers do not excuse themselves from such obligations, and many have made extraordinary efforts to render their parents care. Says a circuit overseer: "We never imagined how physically and emotionally taxing the caring for our parents could be, especially when at the same time trying to meet the demands of the full-time service. Indeed, we have been brought to the limits of our endurance and have felt the need for 'power beyond what is normal.'" (2 Corinthians 4:7) May Jehovah continue to sustain such ones.

⁹ At times, though, after exploring all other possibilities, a family member has no alternative but to leave full-time service. Understandably, such a one may have mixed feelings over relinquishing his service privileges. 'We know it is our Christian responsibility to care for my aged and sick mother,' says an ex-missionary. 'But at times it feels very strange.' Remember, though, that 'practicing godly devotion at home is acceptable in God's sight.' (1 Timothy 5:4) Remember, too, that "God is not unrighteous so as to forget your work and the love you showed for his name, in that you have ministered to the holy ones and continue ministering." (Hebrews 6:10) One couple who left behind many years of full-time service says: "The way we view it, it is just as important for us now to care for our folks as it was for us to be in full-time service."

¹⁰ Perhaps, though, some have left full-time service prematurely because their

---

8. (a) Are family members in full-time service exempt from sharing in their parents' care? (b) To what lengths have some in full-time service gone to meet obligations toward parents?

9. What encouragement can be given to those who have had no choice but to leave full-time service to care for parents?
10. (a) Why may some have left full-time service prematurely? (b) How should families view full-time service?

relatives reasoned: 'You are not tied down with jobs and families. Why cannot *you* take care of Dad and Mom?' However, is not the preaching work the most urgent work being done today? (Matthew 24:14; 28:19, 20) Those in full-time service are thus doing a vital work. (1 Timothy 4:16) Too, Jesus indicated that, in some circumstances, God's service might hold priority over family matters.

[11] For instance, when a man declined an invitation to be Jesus' follower, saying: "Permit me first to leave and bury my father," Jesus replied: "Let the [spiritually] dead bury their dead, but you go away and declare abroad the kingdom of God." (Luke 9:59, 60) Since the Jews buried their dead on the day they died, it is unlikely that the man's father was actually dead. Likely the man simply wanted to stay with his aging father till the father's death. However, since other relatives evidently were on hand to render this care, Jesus encouraged the man to "declare abroad the kingdom of God."

[12] Some families have similarly found that when all members cooperate, it can often be arranged for one in full-time service to share in his parent's care without his leaving full-time service. For example, some full-time ministers assist their parents on weekends or during vacation periods. Interestingly, quite a few elderly parents have insisted that their children remain in full-time service, even at considerable self-sacrifice on the part of the parents. Jehovah richly blesses those who put Kingdom interests first. —Matthew 6:33.

11, 12. (a) Why did Jesus advise a man to "let the dead bury their dead"? (b) What arrangements have some families made when one member is in full-time service?

"Wisdom" and "Discernment" When Parents Move In

[13] Jesus arranged for his widowed mother to live with her believing relatives. (John 19:25-27) Many Witnesses have similarly invited their parents to move in with them—and have experienced many joyful times and blessings as a result. However, incompatible life-styles, limited privacy, and the strain of providing daily care often make taking a parent into one's home frustrating for all concerned. "Caring for Mom has made me more tense," says Ann, whose mother-in-law suffers from Alzheimer's disease. "Sometimes I even lose patience and speak unkindly to Mom—and that makes me feel so guilty."

[14] Solomon said that "by wisdom a household will be built up, and by discernment it will prove firmly established." (Proverbs 24:3) Ann, for example, has tried to be more understanding of her mother-in-law's problem. "I keep in mind that she has an illness and is not acting up on purpose." Still, "we all stumble many times. If anyone does not stumble in word, this one is a perfect man." (James 3:2) But when conflicts arise, show wisdom by refusing to let resentment build or tempers flare. (Ephesians 4: 31, 32) Talk matters over as a family, and seek ways to make compromises or adjustments.

[15] Discernment also helps one communicate effectively. (Proverbs 20:5) Perhaps a parent has difficulty adjusting to the routine of the new home. Or maybe because of impaired judgment, he tends to be uncooperative. Under some circumstances, there may be no choice but to speak quite firmly. (Compare Genesis 43:6-11.) "If I

---

13. What problems can develop when a parent is invited to move in with his or her children?
14, 15. How can "wisdom" and "discernment" help 'build up' a family under these circumstances?

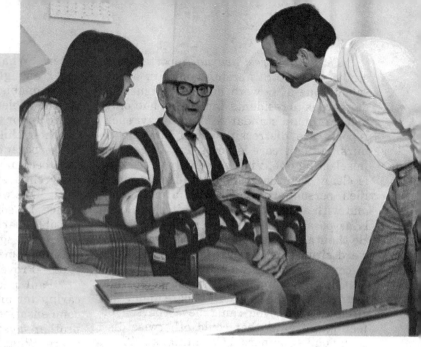

When nursing-home care is necessary, regular visits are essential to the emotional and spiritual well-being of older ones

didn't say no to my mother," says one sister, "she would spend all her money." One elder, though, finds at times that he can draw upon his mother's affection for him. "Many times when reasoning fails, I'll simply say, 'Mom, will you please just do it for me?' and she listens."

[16] Since the wife often carries most of the burden of care, a discerning husband will watch that she does not become worn out—emotionally, physically, or spiritually. Says Proverbs 24:10: "Have you shown yourself discouraged in the day of distress? Your power will be scanty." What can a husband do to renew his wife's enthusiasm? "My husband would come home," says one sister, "and put his arms around me and tell me how much he appreciated me. I couldn't have made it without him!" (Ephesians 5:25, 28, 29) He can also study the Bible with his mate and regularly pray with her. Yes, even under these difficult circumstances, a family can be "built up."

Nursing-Home Care

[17] Says one gerontologist: "There comes a point where the family has neither the expertise nor the money to keep the [parent] home." As one husband puts it: "It got to where my wife's health collapsed from trying to give Mom 24-hour-a-day care. We had no choice but to place Mom in a nursing home. But it tore at our hearts to have to do this."

[18] Nursing-home care may be the best care available under the circumstances. Yet, older ones placed in such facilities are often bewildered and upset, feeling that they have been abandoned. "We carefully explained to Mom why we had to do this," says a sister we will call Greta. "She has learned to adjust and now views the place as home." Regular visits also ease parents through the adjustment and prove the genuineness of your love for them. (Compare 2 Corinthians 8:8.) Where distance is a problem, keep in touch by telephone calls, letters, and periodic visits. (Compare 2 John 12.) Nevertheless, living amid worldlings has obvious drawbacks. Be 'conscious of their spiritual needs.' (Matthew 5:3) "We provide Mom with material to read, and we try to discuss spiritual things as much as possible," says Greta.

16. Why must a loving husband show "discernment" toward his wife? How can he do so?
17, 18. (a) What step have some families been forced to take? (b) In such cases, how can grown children help their parents to adjust?

¹⁹ *The Wall Street Journal* reported on a study of 406 U.S. nursing homes in which "about one-fifth were deemed potentially dangerous to residents and almost half only met minimum standards." Sad to say, such reports are distressingly common. So if nursing-home care is necessary, be careful in selecting one. Visit personally to see if it is clean, well maintained, staffed by qualified personnel, homelike in atmosphere, and with adequate meals. Monitor as closely as possible the care given your parents. Be their advocate, helping them avoid awkward situations that can develop, perhaps in connection with worldly holidays or recreation. By doing your utmost to provide your parents the very best of care under the circumstances, you can relieve yourself of feelings of guilt that could otherwise disturb you.—Compare 2 Corinthians 1:12.

Cheerful Givers, Cheerful Recipients

²⁰ "It's been difficult," says one Christian woman regarding looking after her parents. "I've had to cook for them, clean, deal with crying spells, change the sheets when they were incontinent." "But whatever we've done for them," says her husband, "we have done joyfully—cheerfully. We have tried hard never to let our folks feel that we resent having to care for them." (2 Corinthians 9:7) Older ones are often reluctant to accept help and do not want to be a burden on others. The attitude you display is thus critical.

²¹ At the same time, the attitude parents display is also important. Recalls one

---

sister: "Whatever I did for Mom, it was never enough." So, parents, avoid being unreasonable or overly demanding. After all, the Bible says "the children ought not to lay up for their parents, but the parents for their children." (2 Corinthians 12:14) Some parents squander their resources and become an unnecessary burden to their children. Proverbs 13:22, however, says: "One who is good will leave an inheritance to sons of sons." To the extent possible, parents can thus plan ahead for their old age, setting aside funds and making some arrangements for their own care.—Proverbs 21:5.

²² Paul put it well when he said that caring for one's parents amounts to "due compensation." (1 Timothy 5:4) As one brother says: "Mom took care of me for 20 years. What have I done in comparison to that?" May all Christians with elderly parents similarly be moved to 'practice godly devotion at home,' knowing that they will be richly rewarded by the God who promises to those honoring their parents: "You [will] endure a long time on the earth." —Ephesians 6:3.

22. How should a person view the efforts he puts forth to care for his aging parents?

---

19. (a) What care should be taken in selecting and monitoring nursing-home care? (b) How does it benefit a Christian to do his utmost to care for a parent?
20. Why is it important that children be cheerful givers?
21. (a) How can parents be cheerful recipients? (b) Why is it wise for a parent to plan ahead for his old age?

Points to Remember

□ How did some in Jesus' day seek to evade responsibility toward their parents?

□ Who should care for elderly parents, and why?

□ What problems can families experience when a parent moves in, and how can they be overcome?

□ Why may nursing-home care be necessary, and how can parents be helped to adjust to it?

Kingdom Proclaimers Report

A Happy Reunion in Brazil

Of the 67 Gilead-trained missionaries currently serving in Brazil, 63 got together at the branch office and posed for this historic picture. This happy reunion took place on November 18, 1986, during the visit of A. D. Schroeder, a member of the Governing Body of Jehovah's Witnesses in Brooklyn, New York.

It was 41 years earlier almost to the day—on November 17, 1945—that two graduates of the first class of the Watchtower Bible School of Gilead came to Brazil. For one of them, Charles Leathco (rear, left of center), this was a special reunion because he and visitor Charlotte Schroeder were classmates in Gilead, and Brother Schroeder was one of their instructors.

Since that first class, a total of 258 missionaries have come to Brazil. Among them were 16 native Brazilians. One of them, Augusto Machado (front left), learned the truth from an early missionary, went to Gilead and returned to Brazil. He has served at the branch office for the last 30 years and is now the coordinator of the Branch Committee. Even though many of the missionaries are no longer serving in the missionary field, the good work they have done remains. In 1945 there were only 394 Kingdom publishers in that land; now Brazil has passed the 200,000 mark, reporting a peak of 201,226 publishers in February 1987.

What a joy it was for the Brazilian missionaries, young and old, to reminisce at this happy reunion about all the marvelous activity of the last 41 years.

'My Cup Has Been Full'

As told by Tarissa P. Gott

"WHY did this have to happen?" My husband and I asked this question as we sat in a horse-drawn hack holding a little casket in our arms. My baby boy had suffered colic and died in a matter of weeks. Back in 1914, not much was known as to what to do with that illness. It was such a terrible thing to love a baby for six months, to see him smile at you, and then have death snatch him out of your arms. My heart was broken.

My mother visited us at this sad time and started comforting us with the Bible's message of the resurrection. It meant so much to us. What a relief for my husband Walter and me to learn that it would be possible to see little Stanley again.

That was not my first contact with Bible truth. Some time before, my grandfather had obtained the first three volumes of *Studies in the Scriptures,* by Charles Taze Russell. What Grandpa had read in them, along with his study of the Bible, moved him to go out and preach. This infuriated the local clergy, who put him out of the churches in Providence, Rhode Island. Mother never went to church after that either. She and Grandpa now attended the meetings of the Bible Students, but I did not do much with the truth at that time.

At age 16, I married a young man, Walter Skillings, and settled in Providence. We were both anxious to associate with people who loved God's Word. Although by 1914 we had a six-year-old daughter, Lillian, it was not until our baby boy died that what my mother had told us about the truth sank in. The next year, 1915, my husband and I were baptized by the Bible Students. Our baptism took place in the summertime at a nearby beach. I donned a long, black robe with high neck and long sleeves, quite different from the bathing suits worn now. Of course, this was not standard beachwear of those days but was specially provided for the baptism.

After our baptism, our lives were changed. Walter worked for the Lynn Gas and Electric Company, and on cold winter days, he was sometimes sent into various churches to thaw out their frozen water systems. He used to take advantage of the opportunity to write Scripture texts on the church's blackboard, scriptures that showed what the Bible had to say on immortality, Trinity, hell, and so forth. —Ezekiel 18:4; John 14:28; Ecclesiastes 9: 5, 10.

Kingdom School being conducted in our home during the 1930's

Where Were We to Go?

In 1916 Brother Russell, the first president of the Watch Tower Bible and Tract Society, died, and it seemed that everything fell apart. Now many of those who had seemed so strong, so devoted to the Lord, began to turn away. It became evident that some had been following a man rather than Jehovah and Christ Jesus.

Two elders who presided over our congregation went with an opposition group and thus became members of the "evil slave" class. (Matthew 24:48) All of this just did not seem right, yet it was happening and it upset us. But I said to myself: 'Was not this organization the one that Jehovah used to free us from the bonds of false religion? Have we not tasted of his goodness? If we were to leave now, where would we go? Would we not wind up following some man?' We could not see why we should go with the apostates, so we stayed.—John 6:68; Hebrews 6:4-6.

Tragedy Strikes Again

My husband contracted Spanish influenza, and on the 9th of January, 1919, he died while I, too, was confined to bed with the disease. I recovered from my illness, but I missed Walter very much.

With Walter gone, I had to go to work, so I sold my home and moved in with a spiritual sister. I put my furniture in storage at another sister's home in Saugus, Massachusetts. Her son, Fred A. Gott, later became my second husband. We were married in 1921, and within the next three years, we became parents to Fred and Shirley.

The Flag-Salute Issue

Later, when Fred and Shirley were in public school, the flag-salute issue arose. The issue centered on the Bible's teaching to "flee from idolatry." (1 Corinthians 10:14) A young brother in the Lynn Congregation had refused to salute and pledge allegiance to the flag. Within a month seven children in the congregation were expelled from school, among them Fred and Shirley.

I must confess that it came somewhat as a surprise to us that our children took a stand in school as they did. Of course, we had taught them respect for the country and the flag, and we had also taught them God's commandments about not bowing down to images and idols. As parents, we did not want our children expelled from school. Yet now that the issue had been forced, it seemed only proper that they take a stand for God's Kingdom. So in weighing things up, we appreciated that our children were doing the right thing and that if we trusted in Jehovah all would work out for a witness to his name.

Kingdom School Organized

The question now was, How will the children get their education? For a time we attempted to teach them at home with whatever textbooks we could muster. But my husband and I had a difficult time that first school year as we tried to educate our two children. My husband was working full-time, and I was taking in washing and ironing to supplement the weekly paycheck. In addition to that, I had a five-year-old son, Robert, to look after.

Just about then, in the spring of 1936, Cora Foster, a sister in the congregation and a teacher in the public schools of Lynn for 40 years, was dismissed from her job for not saluting the flag and not taking a teacher's oath that was in vogue at the time. It was therefore arranged that Cora would teach the children who had been expelled from school and that our home would be used as a Kingdom School. Cora had her piano shipped to our home along with some textbooks for the children to use, and some of the older boys fashioned desks out of orange crates and plywood. We started the school the following fall with ten children in attendance.

My younger son, Robert, commenced his education by attending the first grade at the Kingdom School. "Before we began our regular class work," recalls Robert, "Kingdom School opened with a Kingdom song every day, and then for a half hour we would study the *Watchtower* lesson for the coming week." In those days the Society did not print the questions for the paragraphs of the study article, so it became the responsibility of the children to come up with the questions for the paragraphs to be used at the congregation meeting.

Cora was a devoted teacher. "When I had whooping cough," reminisces Robert, and the school was closed till the contagious disease subsided, "Sister Foster visited the house of each student and gave homework." Despite her devotion, she must have felt frustrated at times, for she had to teach the students in all 12 grades in one room. At the end of the five-year period that we had the Kingdom School in our home, there were 22 children attending the school.

Prejudice and Kindness

The flag-salute issue brought not only a time of test and stress but also much publicity by newspaper and radio. It was quite a common thing to see photographers in front of our home taking pictures of the children as they arrived at the Kingdom School. Many of our neighbors, who had been quite friendly before, now became antagonistic. They thought it was a terrible thing for our children to refuse to salute the American flag. 'After all,' they would say, 'isn't this the country that gives you your bread and butter?' They did not appreciate that without Jehovah's watchcare, there would be neither bread nor butter.

On the other hand, there were others who understood the issues involved and gave us support. When people in the neighborhood boycotted a grocery store where our congregation's presiding overseer worked as manager, a well-to-do person interested in civil liberty bought up most of the groceries in the store and

distributed them free to the brothers in the congregation.

It was not until 1943, when the United States Supreme Court reversed its position on the flag-salute issue, that my son Robert was allowed to attend public school.

'My Cup Has Been Full'

How happy I was to see Robert dedicate his life to Jehovah and get baptized at the convention in St. Louis in 1941. It was at that convention, too, that all three of my youngsters were privileged to be among the many children who received a free personal copy of the book *Children* from Brother Rutherford, then president of the Watch Tower Society.

In 1943 my older son Fred took up the full-time pioneer ministry. This only lasted a few months, however, for World War II was being fought, and he was of draft age. When the local draft board refused to recognize his claims to ministerial exemption, he was subsequently sentenced to three years in the federal penitentiary at Danbury, Connecticut. In 1946 he was released, and by the end of that year, he was a full-time worker at the world headquarters of the Watch Tower Society in Brooklyn, New York, where he enjoyed several years of service. Now he is an overseer, serving with his family in Providence, Rhode Island.

In 1951 Robert, too, was invited to Bethel, and he remains there to this day with his wife Alice. He, too, is an overseer, in a New York City congregation.

Then there is my beloved daughter Shirley, who has remained at home. She looked after my husband and me until my husband died in 1972; since then she has been a great comfort to me. I really do not know how things would have gone without her, but I am grateful to Jehovah for her love and devotion.

I am 95 years old now, and yet the hope of Jehovah's new system is brighter than ever. At times I find myself saying, "If only I had the strength I had years ago." I can no longer go from house to house, but as long as I have a tongue, I will continue to praise Jehovah. I appreciate this privilege more today than I ever did in all my life. Yes, 'my cup has been full.' —Psalm 23:5.

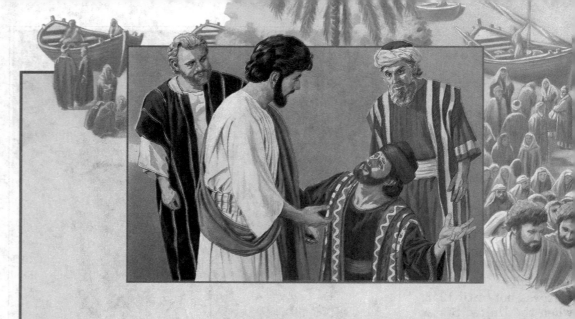

She Touched His Garment

NEWS of Jesus' return from the Decapolis reaches Capernaum, and a great crowd assembles by the sea to welcome him back. No doubt they have heard that he stilled the storm and cured the demon-possessed men. Now, as he steps ashore, they gather around him, eager and expectant.

One of those anxious to see Jesus is Jairus, a presiding officer of the synagogue. He falls at Jesus' feet and begs over and over: "My little daughter is in an extreme condition. Would you please come and put your hands upon her that she may get well and live." Since she is his only child and just 12 years old, she is especially precious to Jairus.

Jesus responds and, accompanied by the crowd, heads for the home of Jairus. We can imagine the excitement of the people as they anticipate another miracle. But the attention of one woman in the crowd is focused on her own severe problem.

For 12 long years this woman has suffered from a flow of blood. She has been to one doctor after another, spending all her money on treatments. But she has not been helped; rather, her problem has become worse.

As you can probably appreciate, besides weakening her very much, her ailment is also embarrassing and humiliating. One generally does not speak publicly about such an affliction. Moreover, under the Mosaic Law a running discharge of blood makes a woman unclean, and anyone touching her or her blood-stained garments is required to wash and be unclean until the evening.

The woman has heard of Jesus' miracles and has now sought him out. In view of her uncleanness, she makes her way through the crowd as inconspicuously as possible, saying to herself: "If I touch just his outer garments I shall get well." When she does so, immediately she senses that her flow of blood has dried up!

"Who was it that touched me?" How those words of Jesus must shock her!

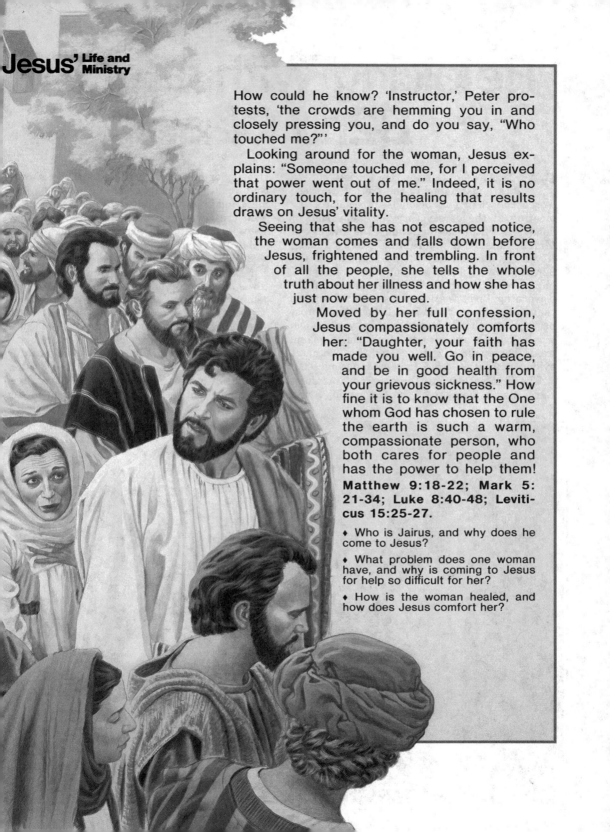

How could he know? 'Instructor,' Peter protests, 'the crowds are hemming you in and closely pressing you, and do you say, "Who touched me?"'

Looking around for the woman, Jesus explains: "Someone touched me, for I perceived that power went out of me." Indeed, it is no ordinary touch, for the healing that results draws on Jesus' vitality.

Seeing that she has not escaped notice, the woman comes and falls down before Jesus, frightened and trembling. In front of all the people, she tells the whole truth about her illness and how she has just now been cured.

Moved by her full confession, Jesus compassionately comforts her: "Daughter, your faith has made you well. Go in peace, and be in good health from your grievous sickness." How fine it is to know that the One whom God has chosen to rule the earth is such a warm, compassionate person, who both cares for people and has the power to help them! **Matthew 9:18-22; Mark 5: 21-34; Luke 8:40-48; Leviticus 15:25-27.**

♦ Who is Jairus, and why does he come to Jesus?

♦ What problem does one woman have, and why is coming to Jesus for help so difficult for her?

♦ How is the woman healed, and how does Jesus comfort her?

Rejoicing With Gilead's 82nd Class

"WE ARE not fair-weather Christians. We are just happy to be here." With these words the chairman opened a special all-day meeting at the Jersey City Assembly Hall of Jehovah's Witnesses on Sunday, the first day of March. Outside, it was raining heavily. Inside, it was graduation day for 24 students of the 82nd class of Gilead. Looking at the students' happy faces, chairman Theodore Jaracz of the Governing Body went on to say: "It's evident that they are eager and joyful about their prospects. Since the Bible says 'rejoice with people who rejoice,' I am sure all of us feel the same way!" The applause that greeted this comment evidenced that all 4,557 in attendance agreed.

The first speaker on the program was John Barr, also a member of the Governing Body.

Quoting extensively from Psalm 104, he showed that Jehovah not only created everything, animate and inanimate, but also created a place for each creation to occupy. He went on to say: "Now, as you go to your assignment, think: 'Jehovah has placed me here.' Never forget that."

Next to speak was a member of the Watchtower Farms Committee, John Stuefloten. He reminded the students: "The proverb tells us: 'Give to a wise person and he will become still wiser.'" (Proverbs 9:9) For five months the students had been given rich spiritual nourishment. Doubtless, on this graduation day they felt spiritually full. "But," said the speaker, "you have just barely started!" He encouraged the students to keep growing in wisdom and

82nd Class March 1987

mercy so as to be better able to help others. —Proverbs 3:27.

George Gangas of the Governing Body followed with some well-chosen words about happiness. He reminded the graduates that they serve the "happy God" and declared: "You will find happiness in your foreign assignments." Why? "Because Jehovah is sending you out to deliver people from bondage."

George Couch of the Brooklyn Bethel Committee spoke about anxiety. He recognized that the students were not strangers to anxiety. The challenges of coming to Gilead, living in Brooklyn Bethel, and preaching in New York City all caused some anxiety. Now the students were anxious about their missionary assignments. But reasonable anxiety is not an enemy. "Anxiety can help to spur us on to do our best," he explained, and he encouraged the students to trust in Jehovah and do their best in their assignments.

School instructor Jack Redford next came to the podium. He warned against unjustified criticism. Citing Biblical examples of hasty judgments that caused problems later, he quoted Jesus' words: "Stop judging that you may not be judged." (Matthew 7:1) The 82nd class represented a God of love. The students were being sent to their assignments to empathize, not to criticize.

Gilead instructor Ulysses Glass quoted the Bible proverb: "The swift do not have the race, nor the mighty ones the battle." (Ecclesiastes 9:11) The result of a matter does not always depend on our natural abilities. In missionary work, it is more often a matter of faith and willingness to accept a challenge. The speaker commended the 82nd class for being steady, dependable, and consistent. Such qualities would stand them in good stead.

The final speaker for the morning, Watch Tower Society president Frederick Franz, declared that the graduation of the 82nd class vindicated the faith of those who began the school back in the dark days of World War II. He spoke about the name Gilead, explaining that it is a Bible word meaning "Heap of Witness." (Compare Genesis 31:43-53.) Gilead missionaries who remain faithfully in their assignments serve as a heap of witness. They are a living testimony to the truth.

The students then received their diplomas, and the morning concluded with the reading of a letter of thanks from the 82nd class. The students noted that 'the blessing of Jehovah is what makes one rich.' In view of that, they said, "Jehovah has made us feel like the 24 richest people on earth!"—Proverbs 10:22.

In the afternoon, following an abbreviated *Watchtower* Study, the students presented a delightful program. It concluded with words of heartfelt appreciation to their parents, whose unselfishness and support allowed their children to go off and become missionaries.

The student program was followed by the presentation of a timely drama, after which the chairman, Theodore Jaracz, gave some final comments. And what a surprise the Society had stored up for these closing moments! The speaker announced that soon the Society will open a new school, the Ministerial Training School, for the training initially of single elders and ministerial servants. All took special note when the chairman announced one of the requirements for attending the new school: a willingness "to serve wherever there is a need in the worldwide field."

Enthusiastic applause greeted the news about this new school. (More details of this are given in the following article.) The program then concluded with song and a prayer of thanks to Jehovah. Everybody then went out into the cloudy New Jersey evening. There was still a little rain in the air, but few cared about it. All hearts were still rejoicing with the 82nd graduating class of Gilead.

Graduates of the 82nd Class of the Watchtower Bible School of Gilead

In the list below, rows are numbered from front to back, and names are listed from left to right in each row.

(1) Gish, L.; Evans, E.; Dean, S.; Hanson, R.; Suomalainen, A.; DuBose, D.

(2) Wallenberg, P.; Wallenberg, M.; Bauer, O.; Suomalainen, H.; Taylor, B.; DiStefano, G.

(3) Scott, K.; Evans, M.; Taylor, A., Jr.; Lindby, J.; Hanson, C.; Holmkvist, M.

(4) Sampson, T.; Gish, T.; Ball, D.; DuBose, J.; Dean, T.; Scott, D.

A New School to Open!

This article contains the substance of the chairman's concluding remarks at the graduation of the 82nd class of Gilead.

SINCE its beginning in February 1943, the Watchtower Bible School of Gilead has trained more than 6,000 dedicated ministers of Jehovah's Witnesses for missionary work. During the more than 40 years that these missionaries have been sent forth, scores of lands have been opened up to receive a thorough witness concerning the Kingdom. In looking back on what Jehovah has accomplished, God's people surely rejoice to see the fulfillment of a remarkable prophecy.

At Isaiah chapter 49, verses 9-12, the prophet foretold the release of righteously disposed people held as religious prisoners in "Babylon the Great." Through his anointed servant class on earth, Jehovah's commanding call has gone forth: "Say to the prisoners, 'Come out!' to those who are in the darkness, 'Reveal yourselves!' By the ways they will pasture . . . They will not go hungry, neither will they go thirsty, nor will parching heat or sun strike them. For the One who is having pity upon them will lead them, and by the springs of water he will conduct them . . . Look! These will come even from far away." Has there been a response? Indeed there has! Honesthearted ones by the hundreds of thousands have come, from all directions, revealing themselves to be hungering for truth, desiring to be fed and enlightened by God's Word, seeking to be liberated spiritually from "Babylon the Great." (Revelation 17:5) Now they are within the earthly realm of his Kingdom organization, feeding on an abundance of spiritual food.

Outstanding Increase

In the mid-1940's, lands in Latin America and the Caribbean area were among the first to benefit from Gilead missionaries. There were very few publishers in these places, which posed a real challenge to the giving of a thorough Kingdom witness. For example, Puerto Rico had only 25 publishers in 1944. Costa Rica had 181. Mexico had 2,431 publishers in 1944 when the first Gilead graduates arrived. But as truth-hungry individuals came out of religious darkness and revealed themselves to be seekers of God's Kingdom, they zealously preached, and some enrolled in the pioneer service. Men reached out for responsibility. The results? Today, Puerto Rico has reported 21,943 active ministers, four times as many as were active in the 12 lands reporting in the Caribbean area in 1947. Costa Rica has more publishers now than there were in all of Central America 40 years ago. In January of this year, Mexico reported a new peak of more than 206,000 publishers, which is about as many publishers as were preaching in the entire world 40 years ago.

In South America it has been similar. When missionaries were first sent to Argentina in 1947, there were 790 publishers. Today there are 63,613 active ministers, 26 times the number preaching in the 12 different countries in South America 40 years ago. And what about Brazil? When the first missionaries were sent there in 1945, only 394 publishers were carrying on the witness work. But they persevered, and Brazil has now surpassed 200,000 publishers. That is more than 80 times the number who were active in all of South America in 1947. Other countries on that continent have also recorded outstanding increases.

Turning to the Far East, we again see marvelous evidence of Jehovah's blessing as the liberating message of Kingdom truth enabled thousands to come out of darkness. When the first missionaries were assigned to Japan in 1949, a handful of eight publishers were reporting. In the eight Asiatic lands reporting activity 40 years ago, there was a total of 475 active ministers. Today, there are 116,272 in Japan alone.

In the South Pacific there were only two branches up until 1959. With the help of publishers from Australia who moved to serve where the need was greater, and the efforts of other congregation publishers and a few missionaries, thousands of people have been reached with the good news in various island territories. There are now six additional branches in that part of the field.

The history of Africa's development is also an exciting one. The 17 countries reporting in 1947 had a total of 24,896 publishers. But with missionaries helping to spread the good news rapidly, hundreds of thousands soon revealed themselves to be seeking Jehovah and his righteousness. Today, in Nigeria alone, about 130,000 Witnesses are zealously proclaiming the Kingdom message.

There is no question that Jehovah's liberating Word of truth is accomplishing that in which he delights. It is having certain success in that for which he has sent it. (Isaiah 55:10, 11) Now that such a great harvest is being gathered, that same Word assures us that Jehovah will raise up more trained shepherds. (Compare Jeremiah 23:4.) The Governing Body is keenly aware of the growing need for qualified men to care for responsibilities in the field as well as in the various branches of the Society. Steps have been taken to help meet this need.

The Ministerial Training School

You graduates of the 82nd class of Gilead, as well as all who have been present for this most upbuilding occasion, will be glad to know that in the fall of 1987 a new school will be opened. This Ministerial Training School, as it will be called, will be a part of the Watchtower Bible School of Gilead, thus enabling brothers from some other lands to attend. The first class is expected to commence around October 1 of this year in the city of Pittsburgh, Pennsylvania, U.S.A., the initial center of the Society's early development. Following the completion of the first class, other classes will be conducted at regular intervals in different parts of the United States.

Definite Scriptural requirements must be met by those to be enrolled. Training will be given initially to single elders and single ministerial servants who are in good health. If some are pioneers, so much the better. Those invited to the school must be willing to serve, following their training, wherever there is a need in the worldwide field. This will call for the spirit of Isaiah, who offered himself willingly, saying: "Here I am! Send me." (Isaiah 6:8) You graduates of this 82nd class, along with missionaries already serving in over a hundred lands, can look forward in due time to having other trained brothers working shoulder to shoulder with you.

An entirely new curriculum has been prepared for the Ministerial Training School. The school has been established for the purpose of training qualified brothers who have had some organizational experience as elders or ministerial servants in the congregation.

The Need for Progress

Following the festival day of Pentecost in 33 C.E., the Christian congregation was very active in spreading the good news in Jerusalem, in all Judea and Samaria, and then, later, to the more distant parts of the earth. (Acts 1:8) About the year 60 C.E. the apostle Paul, who had spearheaded evangelizing activities among the nations, wrote to the Colossians, saying: "This hope you heard of before by the telling of the truth of that good news which has presented itself to you, even as it is bearing fruit and increasing in all the world." Then, he added that those fellow believers 'should not be shifted away from the hope of that good news which

---

In Our Next Issue

- **The Supreme Being —One Person or Three?**

- **Family Care—How Far Does It Extend?**

- **'God Will Finish Your Training'**

they heard, and which was preached in all creation that is under heaven.'—Colossians 1: 5, 6, 23.

In a relatively short time, early Christians had spread the good news far and wide. Jehovah had given the increase, with the number of disciples multiplying very much. This called for more qualified men to teach in the congregation and to shepherd the flock. One of the young overseers charged with such responsibility was Timothy. What did the apostle Paul exhort Timothy to do? There was to be no letup in his training: "By giving these advices to the brothers you will be a fine minister of Christ Jesus, one nourished with the words of the faith and of the fine teaching which you have followed . . . Be training yourself with godly devotion as your aim." (1 Timothy 4:6-8) This would be far more important than concentrating on some personal interest or pursuit, including even bodily exercises and training. To accomplish his ministry fully, Timothy had to pay attention to himself and to his teaching.

You graduates of this class of Gilead have received training for your missionary activity. Fine spiritual gifts have been imparted to you by overseers qualified to teach. Now there is in store a further fine teaching program for qualified men with some experience in caring for congregational responsibility. They will be trained with godly devotion in view, which will help them maintain the right perspective and equip them to focus on what Paul further wrote to Timothy: "Let no man ever look down on your youth. On the contrary, become an example to the faithful ones in speaking, in conduct, in love, in faith, in chasteness. . . . Continue applying yourself to public reading, to exhortation, to teaching. Ponder over these things; be absorbed in them, that your advancement may be manifest to all persons."—1 Timothy 4:12, 13, 15.

As in the case of Timothy, those brothers appointed to congregational responsibility today, including younger men, should realize that this is an appropriate and urgent time for them to make their advancement manifest. By doing so, they will give evidence in a heartfelt way of measuring up to divine standards and of having a genuine disposition to care for spiritual interests, thus being qualified for further privileges of service.—Philippians 2:20, 21.

In view of the need that exists at this stage in the outworking of the divine purpose, it is a privilege to be used by Jehovah anywhere within his organization. How grateful we are to him as our Great Shepherd and to the Fine Shepherd, Jesus Christ, for this new, timely organizational provision, the Ministerial Training School!

Questions From Readers

■ Is it wise for a Christian whose mate has died to remain single in the hope of being reunited in the future?

How fine it is that a Christian should feel love for his or her mate even after that one has died! Some in this situation have remained single, not because of being content with singleness, but in hopes of resuming the marriage after the resurrection. While not being insensitive to the human feelings behind those hopes, we encourage such ones to consider some Biblical points.

For instance, bearing on the matter are the apostle Paul's words: "A wife is bound during all the time her husband is alive. But if her husband should fall asleep in death, she is free to be married to whom she wants, only in the Lord. But she is happier if she remains as she is." (1 Corinthians 7:39, 40) This shows that the marital bond ends when one's mate dies. It was a kindness for God to inform Christians of this, for thus widows and widowers can weigh their emotional and other needs in deciding whether to remarry; they are not bound to the deceased.—1 Corinthians 7: 8, 9.

Does the Bible, though, indicate whether resurrected ones will be able to marry or to resume a previous marriage that was ended by a death? One account seems to bear on this question. It involved Sadducees who, while not even believing in the resurrection, came to Jesus trying to entrap him. They presented this problem involving brother-in-law marriage: "There were seven brothers; and the first took a wife and died childless. So the second, and the third took her.* Likewise even the seven: they did not leave children behind, but died off. Lastly, the woman also died. Consequently, in the resurrection, of which one of them does she become the wife?"—Luke 20:27-33; Matthew 22:23-28.

Christians are not under the Law, but a similar difficulty could be raised concerning them. For example: Brother and Sister C—— were married and had two children. Then he died. Sister C—— loved and deeply missed him, but she felt a need for companionship, financial support, sexual expression, and help with the children. So she married Brother M——, which union was as Scriptural as the first. Later he became ill and died. If the former mates were resurrected and marriage were possible, whom might she marry?

Consider Jesus' response to the Sadducees: "The children of this system of things marry and are given in marriage, but those who have been counted worthy of gaining that system of things and the resurrection from the dead neither marry nor are given in marriage. In fact, neither can they die anymore, for they are like the angels, and they are God's children by being children of the resurrection. But that the

---
* If an Israelite died before his wife brought forth a son who could receive the inheritance, the man's brother had to marry the widow with the view of producing a son by her.—Deuteronomy 25:5-10.

dead are raised up even Moses disclosed . . . when he calls Jehovah 'the God of Abraham and God of Isaac and God of Jacob.' He is a God, not of the dead, but of the living, for they are all living to him."—Luke 20:34-38; Matthew 22:29-32.

Some have felt that Jesus was here referring to the heavenly resurrection, yet there are reasons to believe that his reply was about the earthly resurrection in the coming "system of things." What reasons underlie this view? Those questioning Jesus did not believe in him or know about a heavenly resurrection. They asked about a Jewish family under the Law. In reply Jesus referred to Abraham, Isaac, and Jacob, men who hoped for life again on earth. (Genesis 42:38; Job 14:13-15; compare Hebrews 11:19.) Those patriarchs, and millions of others, who are raised on earth and who prove faithful will be "like the angels." Though mortal, they will not die once God has declared them righteous for endless life.

Human emotions today might make this a difficult conclusion to accept. But it is to be noted that nowhere does the Bible say that God's resurrecting the faithful means restoring their marital status. Hence, no one believes that if Aquila and Priscilla have gained life in heaven, they have resumed their marriage. (Acts 18:2) And Joseph and Mary will evidently live in different realms —he on earth and she in heaven. (John 19:26; Acts 1:13, 14) Since none of us have lived in heaven, we cannot say what feelings Aquila, Priscilla, and Mary might have there, yet we can be sure of their finding full contentment in their heavenly service.

Similarly, we have never lived as perfect humans. Thus we can-

not be sure how we will feel about past relationships if and when we gain perfect human life in a paradise. It is good for us to remember that when Jesus made that statement he was a perfect human and therefore in a better position than we to appreciate the feelings of those who are "counted worthy of gaining that system of things." We can also trust that Jesus is able to 'sympathize with our present weaknesses.' (Hebrews 4:15) So if a Christian finds it hard to accept the conclusion that resurrected ones will not marry, he can be sure that God and Christ are understanding. And he can simply wait to see what occurs.

There is no reason now to overemphasize this matter. The psalmist wrote: "Know that Jehovah is God. It is he that has made us, and not we ourselves. We are his people and the sheep of his pasturage . . . Give thanks to him, bless his name. For Jehovah is good." (Psalm 100:3-5) Our good God will certainly provide amply for our true needs if we are "counted worthy of gaining that system of things."—Job 34:10-12; Psalm 104:28; 107:9.

God's goodness is reflected also in his informing us that the death of a mate concludes the marriage. (Romans 7:2) Thus anyone who has lost a mate can know that he or she is free to remarry now if that seems needed or best. Some have remarried, thereby helping to fill their own present needs and those of their family. (1 Corinthians 7:36-38; Ephesians 6:1-4) Consequently, a Christian whose mate has died should not feel obliged to remain mateless now out of an expectation that former marriage mates will be reunited in the resurrection to life here on earth in the coming system.

"Trust in Jehovah"
District Convention—Do Not Miss It!

Three full, rewarding days of Bible instruction and wholesome Christian association await you at the "Trust in Jehovah" District Convention of Jehovah's Witnesses. During June, July, and August, over 125 conventions are scheduled throughout the United States alone, so there will be one not far from your home. Plan to be present from the opening session beginning at 10:20 a.m. Friday, and stay until the concluding session Sunday afternoon.

The opening session will feature the informative talk "A People Set Apart From the World." In the afternoon, frank and pointed counsel will be directed to parents and then to youths. Youths will be helped to guard against living what could be called a double life. Then this matter will be highlighted in a heart-moving modern-day drama.

Saturday morning will feature the discourse on dedication and baptism, as well as instruction on the ways we can manifest our trust in Jehovah, in keeping with the convention theme. "Responsible Childbearing in This Time of the End" will be a principal address on the afternoon program, which will conclude with a symposium of talks on the theme "The Word of God Is Alive."

The Sunday program will feature the discourse "Detest Utterly the World's Disgraceful Course," as well as a full-costume Bible drama illustrating the urgency of our times. In the afternoon, the public talk "In Our Fearful Times, Whom Can You Really Trust?" will be another highlight of the convention.

Check with Jehovah's Witnesses locally for the time and place of the convention nearest to you.

The Watchtower

Announcing Jehovah's Kingdom

June 15, 1987

THE SUPREME BEING

ONE PERSON OR THREE?

The Watchtower®

Announcing Jehovah's Kingdom

June 15, 1987
Vol. 108, No. 12

In This Issue

THE PURPOSE OF "THE WATCHTOWER" is to exalt Jehovah God as the Sovereign of the universe. It keeps watch on world events as they fulfill Bible prophecy. It comforts all peoples with the good news that God's Kingdom will soon destroy those who oppress their fellowmen and that it will turn the earth into a paradise. It encourages faith in the now-reigning King, Jesus Christ, whose shed blood opens the way for mankind to gain eternal life. "The Watchtower," published by Jehovah's Witnesses continuously since 1879, is nonpolitical. It adheres to the Bible as its authority.

"WATCHTOWER" STUDIES FOR THE WEEKS

Average Printing Each Issue: 12,315,000

Now Published in 103 Languages

SEMIMONTHLY LANGUAGES AVAILABLE BY MAIL
Afrikaans, Arabic, Cebuano, Chichewa, Chinese, Cibemba, Danish,* Dutch,* Efik, English,* Finnish,* French,* German,* Greek,* Hiligaynon, Igbo, Iloko, Italian,* Japanese,* Korean, Lingala, Malagasy, Maltese, Norwegian, Portuguese,* Russian, Sepedi, Sesotho, Shona, Spanish,* Swahili, Swedish,* Tagalog, Thai, Tsonga, Tswana, Xhosa, Yoruba, Zulu

MONTHLY LANGUAGES AVAILABLE BY MAIL
Armenian, Bengali, Bicol, Bislama, Bulgarian, Croatian, Czech, Ewe, Fijian, Ga, Greenlandic, Gujarati, Gun, Hausa, Hebrew, Hindi, Hiri Motu, Hungarian, Icelandic, Kannada, Malayalam, Marathi, New Guinea Pidgin, Pangasinan, Papiamento, Polish, Rarotongan, Romanian, Samar-Leyte, Samoan, Sango, Serbian, Silozi, Sinhalese, Slovenian, Solomon Islands-Pidgin, Tahitian, Tamil, Telugu, Tongan, Tshiluba, Turkish, Twi, Ukrainian, Urdu, Venda, Vietnamese

* Study articles also available in large-print edition.

Watch Tower Society offices	Yearly subscription for the above:	
	Semimonthly Languages	Monthly Languages
America, U.S., Watchtower, Wallkill, N.Y. 12589	$4.00	$2.00
Australia, Box 280, Ingleburn, N.S.W. 2565	A$7.00	A$3.50
Canada, Box 4100, Halton Hills, Ontario L7G 4Y4	$5.50	$2.75
England, The Ridgeway, London NW7 1RN	£5.00	£2.50
Ireland, 29A Jamestown Road, Finglas, Dublin 11	IR£6.00	IR£3.00
New Zealand, P.O. Box 142, Manurewa	NZ$15.00	NZ$7.50
Nigeria, PMB 001, Shomolu, Lagos State	₦8.00	₦4.00
Philippines, P.O. Box 2044, Manila 2800	₱60.00	₱30.00
South Africa, Private Bag 2067, Krugersdorp, 1740	R9.00	R4.50

Remittances should be sent to the office in your country or to Watchtower, Wallkill, N.Y. 12589, U.S.A.

Changes of address should reach us 30 days before your moving date. Give us your old and new address (if possible, your old address label).

20 cents (U.S.) a copy

The Bible translation used is the "New World Translation of the Holy Scriptures," unless otherwise indicated.

The Watchtower (ISSN 0043-1087) is published semimonthly for $4.00 (U.S.) per year by Watch Tower Bible and Tract Society of Pennsylvania, 25 Columbia Heights, Brooklyn, N.Y. 11201. Second-class postage paid at Brooklyn, N.Y., and at additional mailing offices.

Postmaster: Send address changes to Watchtower, **Wallkill, N.Y. 12589.**

Published by
Watch Tower Bible and Tract Society of Pennsylvania

25 Columbia Heights, Brooklyn, N.Y. 11201, U.S.A.

Frederick W. Franz, President

THE SUPREME BEING IS UNIQUE

THE SUPREME BEING. Do you believe in him? Despite a widespread drift from the churches in many lands, millions still believe in an all-powerful, benevolent Being to whom they can turn, especially when they are in distress.

For example, in Africa there are many local, traditional religions that differ considerably from one another and that worship deities of many names. Yet, most of the people firmly believe in a Supreme Being who is "unique" and "the absolute controller of the universe."

As related in Dr. Peter Becker's book *Tribe to Township,* an elderly Sotho lay preacher of South Africa said: "My old father and his father . . . knew about God, the *Molimo,* long before the coming of the missionaries, God the Supreme Being who created all things . . . Does it matter that we [the Basuto] call God, *Molimo,* the Zulu, *Nkulunkulu,* the Xhosa, *Thixo* . . . ?"

Of course, a multiplicity of names is confusing. You would likely agree that a universal God should be the same for all people and should have a universal name. The inspired collection of ancient writings, the Bible, is respected around the globe. It declares: "That people may know that you, whose name is Jehovah, you alone are the Most High over all the earth." (Psalm 83:18) So, according to the Bible, the Supreme Being has a unique name.

What kind of Being is this one God, as revealed by the Bible? "All his ways are justice"; "a God merciful and gracious, slow to anger and abundant in loving-kindness and truth"; "very tender in affection and merciful"; "a God, not of disorder, but of peace"; "God is love."—Deuteronomy 32:4; Exodus 34:6; James 5:11; 1 Corinthians 14:33; 1 John 4:8.

The Bible also reveals that Jehovah is the only one who should be worshiped. Yes, being unique, he justly demands exclusive devotion. (Exodus 20:5) Jesus Christ said: "It is Jehovah your God you must worship, and it is to him alone you must render sacred service."—Matthew 4:10.

Nonetheless, most Africans, while claiming to believe in a Supreme Being, worship many deities. Would that not seem to you to suggest some confusion about the identity or nature of God? But even in most parts of Christendom, the clear, majestic, person of God is blurred by considering him to be a triune God. You may have heard of this as the Holy Trinity, a dogma that is mysterious and hard to understand. For example, the booklet *The Blessed Trinity* says: "The dogma of the Blessed Trinity . . . is a *mystery* . . . It cannot be proved by reason . . . It cannot even be proved to be *possible.*"* (Italics theirs.) The booklet adds: "Proof, therefore, of a mystery consists in showing that it is contained in revelation, in Holy Scripture."

But does Holy Scripture really teach this doctrine? Is the Supreme Being three persons in one God?

* Published by the Catholic Truth Society of London.

THE "BLESSED TRINITY" —IS IT IN THE BIBLE?

SHE was burned to death in England in 1550. Her name? Joan Bocher. Her crime? The *Encyclopædia Britannica* (1964) says: "She was condemned for open blasphemy in denying the Trinity, the one offense which all the church had regarded as unforgivable ever since the struggle with Arianism."

The Trinity is a fundamental doctrine of the vast majority of churches. But what exactly is the Trinity? *The Waverley Encyclopedia* defines it as "the mystery of one God in three persons—the Father, the Son, and the Holy Ghost, co-equal and co-eternal in all things." Yet *The New Encyclopædia Britannica* (1981) says: "Neither the word Trinity, nor the explicit doctrine as such, appears in the New Testament." This immediately raises questions about the doctrine.

Compounding the matter is a frank admission that the *New Catholic Encyclopedia* presents in terms of a question that seminary students often ask, "But how does one preach the Trinity?" This Catholic work continues: "If the question is symptomatic of confusion on the part of the students, perhaps it is no less symptomatic of similar confusion on the part of their professors. If 'the Trinity' here means Trinitarian theology, the best answer would be that one does not preach it at all . . . because the sermon, and especially the Biblical homily, is the place for the word of God, not its theological elaboration."

When did this "theological elaboration" begin? Answers *The New Encyclopædia Britannica* (1981): "The doctrine developed gradually over several centuries and through many controversies." Does that sound to you like a direct, clear revelation from God? So how can it be a revelation of Holy Scripture, as is claimed?

A Biblical statement that church teachers often use to support the Trinity is

Representation of the Trinity in 14th-century Catholic Church in Tagnon, France

Jesus' command that his followers make disciples, "baptizing them in the name of the Father and of the Son and of the holy spirit." (Matthew 28:19) This passage certainly mentions three entities, but it does *not* say that they are three persons or that they are all one. Furthermore, we know the name of the Father (Jehovah) and of the Son (Jesus), but what is the name of the holy spirit? This leads to the question . . .

Is the Holy Spirit a Person?

The fact that the Bible gives no indication of the holy spirit's having a personal name at least suggests that it may not be a person. You might ask also, 'Has the holy spirit ever been seen?' Well, at Jesus' baptism it was manifested as a dove and at Pentecost as tongues as if of fire. (Matthew 3:16; Acts 2:3, 4) If it is a person, why did it not appear as a person? And if the holy spirit is not a person, what is it? Undoubtedly, it is the active force from God that at Pentecost was 'poured out' on the disciples. (Acts 2:17, 18) By this active force, Jehovah performed his acts of creation—"God's active force was moving to and fro over the surface of the waters." (Genesis 1:2) The same active force inspired the writers of the Bible.—2 Timothy 3:16.

One of those inspired writers was the prophet Daniel. In Daniel chapter 7 he describes a wonderful vision Jehovah gave to him: "the Ancient of Days" on his heavenly throne, with a multitude of angels ministering to him. Daniel saw also "someone like a son of man [Jesus]," who was given "rulership and dignity and kingdom, that the peoples, national groups and languages should all serve even him." (Daniel 7:9, 10, 13, 14) What, though, about the holy spirit? It is not mentioned as a person in this celestial scene.

The final book of the Bible—Revelation—describes other remarkable heavenly visions. The Supreme Being, Jehovah, is depicted there on his throne, and the Lamb, Jesus Christ, is with him. But, again, the holy spirit is not mentioned as a distinct person. (Revelation, chapters

God's Finger

"It is the finger of God!" the magic-practicing priests of Egypt admitted when they failed to turn dust into gnats, as Moses had done. (Exodus 8:18, 19) On Mount Sinai, Jehovah gave Moses "tablets of stone written on by God's finger." (Exodus 31:18) Was this a literal finger? No. Jehovah obviously does not have literal fingers. What, then? Bible writers Luke and Matthew give us the key. One recorded that "by means of *God's finger*," Jesus expelled demons. The other explained that Jesus did this "by means of God's spirit." (Luke 11:20; Matthew 12:28) So the holy spirit is "God's finger," his instrument for accomplishing his will. It is not a person, but God's dynamic active force.

4–6) So even the final Bible book does not reveal that there are three persons in one god. This raises . . .

Another Important Question

The Trinity dogma has been described as "the central doctrine of the Christian religion." If this were true, why did Jesus not reveal it when he was on earth? His disciples, being Israelites, believed that Jehovah is unique. To this day, Jews continue to recite Deuteronomy 6:4: "Listen, O Israel: Jehovah our God is one Jehovah." There is no suggestion in the Hebrew Scriptures that the Supreme Being is in three persons. You may well wonder, 'If this were true, why did this "central doctrine" not become dogma until the fourth century—amid bitter controversy that caused widespread confusion?'

Some might argue: 'But Jesus did say, "I and the Father are one." ' (John 10:30) True. In what sense, though, are they one? Jesus himself clarified this later by saying in prayer: "Holy Father, watch over them [his disciples] . . . in order *that they may be one just as we are one.*" (John 17:11, 22) Hence, the unity of Father and Son is the same as the unity that exists among Christ's true followers—a harmony of purpose and cooperation.

Still, some may suggest that although Jesus did not spell out the Trinity doctrine, the apostle John did at 1 John 5:7, which, according to the *King James Version,* says: "For there are three that bear record in heaven, the Father, the Word, and the Holy Ghost: and these three are one." However, more modern versions omit this passage. Why? The Catholic *Jerusalem Bible* explains in a footnote that this text is not found in any of the early Greek or the best Latin manuscripts of the Bible. It is spurious. It was added, no doubt, to try to support the Trinity.

As you can check in your own Bible, the apostle Paul in the opening of his letters often used expressions like this: "May you have undeserved kindness and peace from God our Father and the Lord Jesus Christ." (Romans 1:7) Why did he not mention the holy spirit as a person? Because Paul knew nothing of the "Holy Trinity." James, Peter, and John used similar phrases in their letters where they likewise do not mention the holy spirit. Why? Because they were not Trinitarians either. The holy spirit is not a person as are God and his Son. But since the Son is a person, the question arises . . .

Is Jesus the Supreme Being?

Believers in the Trinity say yes. Yet you should be more interested in what Jesus said: "The Father is greater than I am." (John 14:28) "The Son cannot do a single thing of his own initiative, but only what he beholds the Father doing." (John 5:19) Paul added: "The head of the Christ is God."—1 Corinthians 11:3.

Consider carefully, too, these questions: Does Jehovah have a God? Obviously not, he is supreme, the Almighty. Does Jesus have a God? After his resurrection Jesus said to Mary Magdalene: "I am ascending to my Father and your Father and to my God and your God." The apostle Peter wrote: "Blessed be the God and Father of our Lord Jesus Christ."—John 20:17; 1 Peter 1:3.

Has God ever died? 'Of course not,' might be your correct response. God is immortal. The prophet Habakkuk said of Jehovah: "My Holy One, you do not die." (Habakkuk 1:12) In contrast, Jesus did die. Then who raised him from the dead? Said Peter: "God raised [Christ] up from the dead." It becomes evident, then, that Jesus is not the Supreme Being.—Acts 3:15; Romans 5:8.

You can go further. Has God ever been

The holy spirit appeared as a dove and as tongues of fire—never as a person

seen? "No man has seen God at any time." (John 1:18) Yet thousands saw Jesus on earth. Has God ever prayed to anyone? To whom could he pray? He is the great "Hearer of prayer." (Psalm 65:2) And Jesus? He frequently prayed to his Father, even spending a whole night in prayer. Is God a priest? Obviously not. Is Jesus? We read: "Consider the apostle and high priest whom we confess—Jesus."—Hebrews 3:1.

Is it not abundantly clear that Jesus is not the Supreme Being?

Is the Trinity Dogma Harmful?

Yes. This widespread dogma distorts the simple Bible truths that Jehovah alone is the Supreme Being, that Jesus is his Son, and that the holy spirit is God's active force. The doctrine causes confu-sion by presenting God in a haze of mystery, leading to spiritual darkness.

You, however, need not be in that darkness. You can fix clearly in mind some facts:

The Trinity dogma is not mentioned in the Bible. It is a "theological elaboration" that developed centuries after Jesus' day, and it was imposed under threat of death at the stake. It has downgraded the worship of the Supreme Being, teaching belief in a mystery.

If you have always believed the Trinity, what should you now do? We urge you to study God's Word and publications like this one that will help you to understand the Bible. Doing so is vital. Jesus said that *everlasting life* depends on taking in knowledge of him and of Jehovah—*"the only true God."*—John 17:3.

Tears Turned to Great Ecstasy

WHEN Jairus sees the woman with the flow of blood healed, his confidence in Jesus' miraculous powers no doubt increases. Earlier in the day, Jesus had been asked by Jairus to come and help his beloved 12-year-old daughter, who lay near death. But while they are en route to Jairus' home, which is in or near Capernaum, a woman who simply touches the fringe of Jesus' outer garment is healed.

In the meantime, however, what Jairus fears most occurs. While Jesus is still speaking with the woman, some men arrive and quietly tell Jairus: "Your daughter died! Why bother the teacher any longer?"

How devastating the news is! Just think: This man, who commands great respect in the community, is now totally helpless as he learns of his daughter's death. Jesus, however, overhears the conversation. So, turning to Jairus, he says encouragingly: "Have no fear, only exercise faith."

Jesus accompanies the grief-stricken man back to his home. When they arrive, they find a great commotion of weeping and wailing. A crowd of people have gathered, and they are beating themselves in grief. When Jesus steps inside, he asks: "Why are you causing noisy confusion and weeping? The young child has not died, but is sleeping."

On hearing this, the people begin to laugh scornfully at Jesus because they know that the girl is really dead. Jesus, however, says that she is only sleeping, in order to show that, with his God-given powers, people can be brought back from death as easily as they can be awakened from a deep sleep.

Jesus now has everyone sent outside except for Pe-

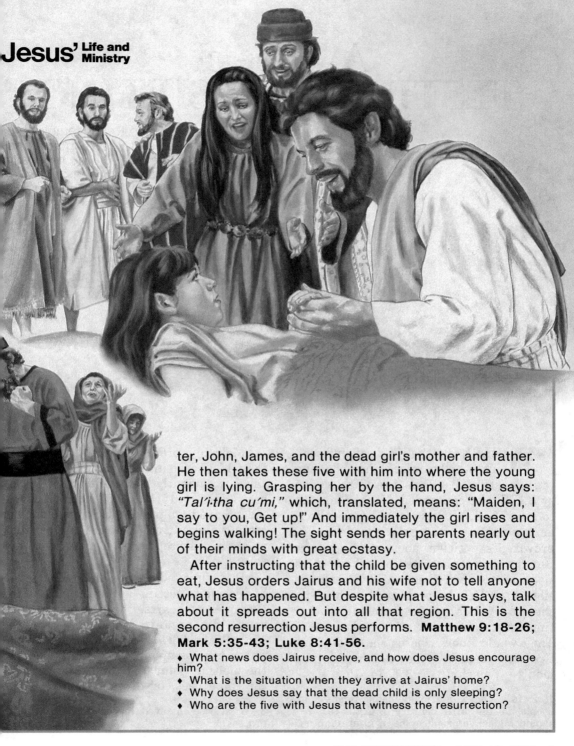

ter, John, James, and the dead girl's mother and father. He then takes these five with him into where the young girl is lying. Grasping her by the hand, Jesus says: *"Tal'i·tha cu'mi,"* which, translated, means: "Maiden, I say to you, Get up!" And immediately the girl rises and begins walking! The sight sends her parents nearly out of their minds with great ecstasy.

After instructing that the child be given something to eat, Jesus orders Jairus and his wife not to tell anyone what has happened. But despite what Jesus says, talk about it spreads out into all that region. This is the second resurrection Jesus performs. **Matthew 9:18-26; Mark 5:35-43; Luke 8:41-56.**

♦ What news does Jairus receive, and how does Jesus encourage him?
♦ What is the situation when they arrive at Jairus' home?
♦ Why does Jesus say that the dead child is only sleeping?
♦ Who are the five with Jesus that witness the resurrection?

A Time of
TESTING AND SIFTING

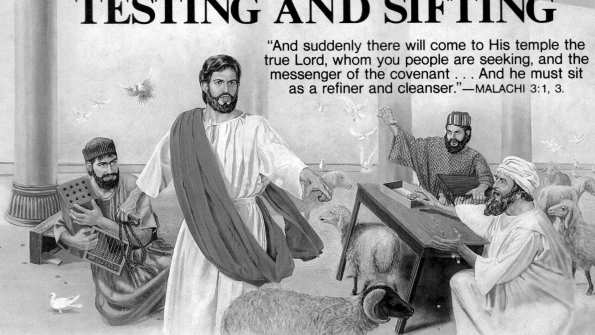

"And suddenly there will come to His temple the true Lord, whom you people are seeking, and the messenger of the covenant . . . And he must sit as a refiner and cleanser."—MALACHI 3:1, 3.

"WHERE is the God of justice?" Those who raised that challenging question back in the fifth century B.C.E. also contended: "It is of no value to serve God." Religious and moral decay among God's own people, the Jews, had provoked skepticism about divine justice. But the eyes of the true God, who does not sleep, were upon them. And he commissioned the Hebrew prophet Malachi to put them on notice that a cleansing work, a time of testing and sifting, lay ahead. They would know where "the God of justice" was when he came suddenly for judgment!—Malachi 2:17; 3:1, 14, 15.

² Malachi's prophecy should be of more than historical interest to us. Why? Because it evidently has a fulfillment in our day. (Romans 15:4) Yes, Jehovah's people today have been passing through a time of testing and sifting! How so? A close look at Malachi's prophecy will help us to answer.

³ But, first, why does Jehovah expose his people to testing and sifting? As "the examiner of hearts," he has purposed to refine his organized people. (Proverbs 17:3; Psalm 66:10) In Bible times the refining process involved heating a metal to the melting point and then skimming off the impurities, or dross. We read: "The

1, 2. (a) What conditions existed among God's people in the fifth century B.C.E.? (b) Why should Malachi's prophecy be of interest to us?

3. What was involved in the ancient refining process?

refiner watches the operation, either standing or sitting, with the greatest earnestness, until . . . the [liquid] metal has the appearance of a highly-polished mirror, reflecting every object around it; even the refiner, as he looks upon the mass of metal, may see himself as in a looking-glass, and thus he can form a very correct judgment respecting the purity of the metal. If he is satisfied, the fire is withdrawn, and the metal removed from the furnace; but if not considered pure, more lead is added and the process repeated." (*Cyclopedia of Biblical, Theological, and Ecclesiastical Literature,* by J. McClintock and J. Strong) Such refined gold or silver was more valuable.—Compare Revelation 3:18.

4 Jehovah allows testing and sifting so as to refine, or purify, his people, helping them to reflect more accurately his image. (Ephesians 5:1) In the refining process, he skims off the dross by clearing away unclean teachings and practices. (Isaiah 1:25) He also sifts out from among his people those who refuse to submit to the refining process and who "cause stumbling and persons who are doing lawlessness." This clears the way for "the sons of the kingdom," the spiritual Israelites, to shine with brightness so that an earthly class can also be gathered and cleave to them organizationally for survival.—Matthew 13:38, 41, 43; Philippians 2:15.

Malachi's Commission

5 Malachi prophesied after 443 B.C.E., almost a century after the Jewish exiles returned from Babylon. More than 70 years had passed since the inauguration of the temple rebuilt by Zerubbabel. The spiritual condition of the Israelites had deteriorated to a low level. Who, particularly, were responsible? The priests! How so? They were "despising" Jehovah's name by accepting sick and lame sacrifices. (Malachi 1:6-8) They "caused many to stumble in the law" by failing to instruct the people and by showing partiality in judgment.—Malachi 2:6-9; James 3:1.

6 As a result, Israelites in general began to question the value of serving God, even refusing to pay the tithe required by law. (Malachi 3:6-10, 14, 15; Leviticus 27:30) So far had they fallen from their devotion to God's Law that some had "dealt treacherously" with their wives, evidently by divorcing them in order to marry pagan women. Why, such detestable practices as sorcery, adultery, lying, and fraud were now prevalent among God's people!—Malachi 2:10-16; 3:5.

7 Malachi's commission was clear. In a forthright manner he exposed the negligent priests, and he made the people aware of their true spiritual state. Yet, he indicated that the God of merciful love was ready to forgive. "Return to me, and I will return to you," Jehovah pleaded. (Malachi 3:7) Malachi foretold that "the true Lord" was coming to his temple for judgment. The priests were in need of cleansing in order to "become to Jehovah people presenting a gift offering in righteousness." (Malachi 3:1-3) In addition, the people were put on notice that "the true Lord" would become "a speedy witness" against those who persisted in detestable practices.—Malachi 3:5.

8 Malachi was true to his commission; he sounded the warning. What he said was of benefit to the priests and the people

---

4. Why does Jehovah allow testing and sifting among his people?
5, 6. (a) Who, particularly, were responsible for the low spiritual level of the Israelites in Malachi's day? Why? (b) What bad effect did this have on the Israelites in general?

7, 8. What was the prophet Malachi's commission?

in his day. However, several centuries passed before his prophecy saw some of its features come true in a first fulfillment.

The First-Century Fulfillment

⁹ Speaking from his lofty throne in heaven, the Great Judge says: "Look! I am sending my messenger, and he must clear up a way before me." (Malachi 3:1a) Who was that "messenger"? Bible writer Mark combines the prophecies of Malachi 3:1 and Isaiah 40:3 and applies both of them to John the Baptizer. (Mark 1:1-4) Jesus Christ, too, later identified John as that "messenger." (Matthew 11:10-14) So it was that in the spring of 29 C.E., John the Baptizer began his work as a "messenger," a forerunner. He was to prepare the way for the coming of Jehovah in judgment by getting the Israelites ready for the coming of God's Chief Representative, Jesus Christ.

¹⁰ John's being sent ahead of time was an expression of God's loving-kindness toward the Jews. In a covenant relationship with Jehovah, they needed to repent of their sins against the Law. John set religious matters straight and exposed religious hypocrisy. (Matthew 3:1-3, 7-12) He aroused honesthearted Jews to expect the Christ that they might follow Him.—John 1:35-37.

¹¹ Malachi's prophecy continues: "'And suddenly there will come to His temple the true Lord, whom you people are seeking, and the messenger of the covenant in whom you are delighting. Look! He will certainly come,' Jehovah of armies has said." (Malachi 3:1b) Who was "the true

Lord" that would come to his temple "suddenly," or unexpectedly? The Hebrew expression used is *ha·'A·dhohn'*. The use of the definite article *ha* ("the") before the title *'A·dhohn'* ("Lord; Master") limits the application of this title exclusively to Jehovah God. Indeed, it was to "*His* temple" that Jehovah would come.—Habakkuk 2:20; Psalm 11:4.

¹² After having mentioned one messenger, Malachi indicated that "the true Lord" would come to "His temple" accompanied by another, a different, messenger, "the messenger of the covenant." Who would this be? Well, in view of how things worked out, it is reasonable to conclude that "the messenger of the covenant" is Jesus Christ, whom John the Baptizer introduced to his disciples as "the Lamb of God." (John 1:29-34) Of what "covenant" is the Messiah "the messenger"? The evidence of Luke 1:69-75 and Acts 3:12, 19-26 suggests that it is the Abrahamic covenant, on the basis of which the Jews were the first ones to be given the opportunity to become Kingdom heirs.

¹³ "The true Lord" Jehovah did not come personally to the literal temple in Jerusalem. (1 Kings 8:27) He came representatively, that is, by means of his "messenger of the covenant," Jesus Christ, who came in Jehovah's name and with the backing of God's holy spirit.*

¹⁴ In the spring of 30 C.E., Jesus came to Jehovah's temple in Jerusalem and

---

* On a number of occasions, angelic messengers spoke as though they were Jehovah God, for they were acting as Jehovah's representatives.—Genesis 31: 11-13; Judges 2:1-3; compare Genesis 16:11, 13.

---

9. In fulfillment of Malachi's prophecy, who was the "messenger"? Why do you so answer?
10. How did John the Baptizer serve "to get ready for Jehovah a prepared people"? (Luke 1:17)
11. How can we identify "the true Lord" that would come to the temple suddenly?

12. Who is "the messenger of the covenant," and of what "covenant" is he "the messenger"?
13. In what sense would "the true Lord" Jehovah come to the temple?
14. (a) Why was Jesus' cleansing of the temple in 30 C.E. evidently just a token of what was to come? (b) How and when was the temple cleansed in fulfillment of Malachi 3:1?

As a messenger, John the Baptizer prepared the people for the coming "messenger of the covenant"

drove out those who were making it "a house of merchandise." (John 2:13-16) But this was only a token of what was to come in fulfillment of Malachi's prophecy. Following this incident, John, as "the messenger," continued baptizing and directing his disciples to Jesus. (John 3: 23-30) However, on Nisan 9, 33 C.E., Jesus made his triumphal entry into Jerusalem, presenting himself as King. (Matthew 21:1-9; Zechariah 9:9) John had finished his work, having been beheaded by Herod about a year before. So when Jesus came to the temple on Nisan 10, he came officially as "the messenger of the covenant," the judicial representative of "the true Lord" Jehovah, in fulfillment of Malachi 3:1. Jesus cleansed the temple, throwing out those commercializing it, overturning the tables of the money changers. He kept saying: "Is it not written [at Isaiah 56:7], '[Jehovah's] house will be called a house of prayer for all the nations'? But you have made it a cave of robbers."—Mark 11:15-18.

[15] Notice was thus served upon Israel's religious leaders that their hour had come. As a class, they refused to accept Jehovah's "messenger of the covenant." They did not 'put up with the day of his coming,' for they refused to submit humbly to the refining process of the Great Refiner. (Malachi 3:2, 3) They deserved to be sifted out as worthy of destruction. Evidently, though, there were some "sons of Levi" with good hearts, for not long after Jesus' death "a great crowd of [Levite] priests began to be obedient to the faith."—Acts 6:7.

[16] On Nisan 11, the day after he cleansed the temple, Jesus forcefully exposed the religious hypocrites and foretold the destruction of the temple and the Jewish system of things. (Matthew, chapters 23, 24)

---

15. As a class, how did the Jewish religious leaders respond to the refining process, but what was true of some priests?
16. How and when did a "great and fear-inspiring day of Jehovah" overtake that Jewish nation?

Indeed, "the God of justice" came as "a speedy witness" upon that Jewish nation 37 years later in 70 C.E., when a "great and fear-inspiring day of Jehovah" overtook them. (Malachi 2:17; 3:5; 4:5, 6) At that time, Israel collectively, as a treelike organization that failed to produce fine fruit, was "cut down and thrown into the fire" by means of destruction at the hands of the Romans. (Luke 3:3-14) All of this 'because they did not discern the time of their being inspected.'—Luke 19:44.

Modern-Day Fulfillment

¹⁷ But what of a second, or modern-day, fulfillment of Malachi's prophecy? In the first century, the initial fulfillment followed Jesus' being anointed with holy spirit to become the King-Designate of God's Kingdom. Logically, there should be a further fulfillment of the prophecy after Jesus Christ was enthroned in the heavens in 1914. The prophecy itself indicated that it would find fulfillment "before the coming of the great and fear-inspiring day of Jehovah." (Malachi 4:5) While a "day of Jehovah" came upon the Jewish system in

17. What indicates that Malachi's prophecy would find a further fulfillment in modern times?

Can You Recall?

☐ Why does Jehovah allow his people to go through testing and sifting?

☐ How did John the Baptizer serve as a "messenger," a forerunner?

☐ In the first century, how did Jesus come to the temple as "the messenger of the covenant"?

☐ How do we know that Malachi's prophecy would have a modern-day fulfillment?

70 C.E., the Scriptures point forward to a future "day of Jehovah" during this time of Christ's "presence."—Matthew 24:3; 2 Thessalonians 2:1, 2; 2 Peter 3:10-13.

¹⁸ As early as 1922, Jehovah's people were made aware that they were in a time of judgment in fulfillment of Malachi's prophecy. The Watchtower of September 1 said: "But Malachi's prophecy looks beyond the partial fulfillment at our Lord's first advent, and forward to the time when Messiah should come in glory and strength, and when he should judge amongst his people . . . Now, once again, the time of judgment has come; again his professed people are tried as by fire, and the true-hearted sons of Levi are being gathered together for service."

¹⁹ As indicated at Malachi 3:1, a special messenger was sent ahead of time. This proved to be, not one individual, but a class serving like John the Baptizer. Since 1881 this class has used what is now the Watch Tower Bible and Tract Society in a remarkable Bible educational work. This resulted in restoring many basic truths to the hearts of Bible lovers. Some of these clarifications are: Man does not possess an immortal soul, but he is a soul; there is no burning hell; Jesus Christ would not return in the flesh; Jehovah is one God, not a Trinity. Indeed, it was a work that 'cleared up a way before Jehovah' for his judgment work.

²⁰ Suddenly, Jehovah, as "the true Lord," came to his spiritual temple. When? The pattern was set in the first-century fulfillment. Back there Jesus came and cleansed the temple three and a

18. In 1922, how were God's people made aware that they were in a time of judgment?
19. In the modern-day fulfillment, in what way was a "messenger" sent ahead of time?
20. (a) When, evidently, did Jehovah come to the temple? (b) What questions does this raise?

half years after he was *anointed* as King at the Jordan. True to that pattern, since Jesus was *enthroned* as King in the autumn of 1914, it seems reasonable that three and a half years later he would be expected to accompany "the true Lord" Jehovah to the spiritual temple. According to the prophecy, what was to happen from that time onward? Testing and sifting. But this raises some important questions: What evidences are there of this cleansing? Does it continue down to the present time? And how does all of this affect you personally? Let us see.

TESTING AND SIFTING in Modern Times

"Who will be putting up with the day of his coming, and who will be the one standing when he appears?"—MALACHI 3:2.

WHEN "the true Lord" came to the spiritual temple accompanied by his "messenger of the covenant," shortly after the Kingdom was set up in heaven in 1914, what did Jehovah find? His people were in need of refining and cleansing. Would they subject themselves to this and endure any needed cleaning of their organization, activity, doctrine, and conduct? As Malachi put it: "Who will be putting up with the day of his coming, and who will be the one standing when he appears?"—Malachi 3:1, 2.

² Jehovah accepts responsibility for cleansing and refining "the sons of Levi." (Malachi 3:3) In ancient Israel, the tribe of Levi furnished the priests and temple assistants. Such "sons of Levi" correspond to the collective body of anointed ones today serving as priests under Jesus, the High Priest. (1 Peter 2:7-9; Hebrews 3:1) They are the ones who first underwent testing when Jehovah came to the spiritual temple with his "messenger of the covenant." Now, what evidence is there that this refinement took place from the closing days of World War I onward?

A Time of Fiery Trials

³ When Jehovah accompanied his "messenger of the covenant" to the spiritual temple, He found the remnant in need of refining and cleansing. For example, *The Watch Tower* had encouraged its readers to set aside May 30, 1918, as a day of prayer for victory for the democratic powers, as requested by the U.S. congress and by President Wilson. This amounted to a violation of Christian neutrality.—John 17:14, 16.

⁴ The clergy and the governments brought great pressure to bear on

---

1. When Jehovah came to the spiritual temple in modern times, what did he find, raising what question?
2. In modern times, who are "the sons of Levi" of Malachi 3:3?

3. By the spring of 1918, what was the condition of God's witnesses?
4. What developed as to persecution of Jehovah's servants?

Jehovah's anointed servants. Falsely accused of sedition, the anointed remnant attempted to make their innocence clear publicly. However, on May 7, 1918, warrants were issued for the arrest of eight members of the management and editorial staff of the Watch Tower Bible and Tract Society, including the president, J. F. Rutherford. Their trial began Monday, June 3. On June 20 the jury returned a verdict of guilty on four counts. Then on July 4, 1918, these dedicated Christian men were taken by train to prison in Atlanta, Georgia, U.S.A.

⁵ By the summer of 1918, the once strong, organized voice of public preaching for Jehovah's Kingdom by the anointed was greatly reduced in volume. It was as if they were 'killed' respecting their public activity. (Revelation 11:3, 7) At the time of the Society's conventions that summer, some apostates turned away and formed their own opposing religious groups. Manifesting the traits of an "evil slave," they were 'winnowed' like "chaff" to be separated from Jehovah's faithful remnant. (Matthew 3:12; 24:48-51) The Memorial of Christ's death was celebrated on Sunday, April 13, 1919, with 17,961 attending in many lands. As compared to a partial report for 1917, the Memorial attendance had dropped by more than 3,000, indicating the effects of sifting.

⁶ However, Jehovah's permitting such fiery trials to befall his people was with their eventual blessing in view. He never left them entirely. On Tuesday, March 25, 1919, J. F. Rutherford and his seven associates were released from prison on bail and were later completely exonerated. Suddenly, for the cleansed survivors of this testing period, there had come freedom from bondage! Yes, "spirit of life from God entered into them, and they stood upon their feet," ready for action.—Revelation 11:11.

⁷ What would they do now? As a restored Christian community, the remnant scrutinized themselves. They prayed for Jehovah's forgiveness for any sins of compromise. (Compare Psalm 106:6; Isaiah 42:24.) They went forth as a cleansed people. As a result of being refined, the loyalhearted remnant 'became to Jehovah a people presenting a gift offering in righteousness.' (Malachi 3:3) The spiritual sacrifices of praise that they offered became pleasing to God. (Hebrews 13:15) They rejoiced that the brief interval of Jehovah's displeasure had ended. They were confident that their future service would be acceptable to him. (Isaiah 12:1) From September 1 to 8, 1919, a happy convention was held at Cedar Point, Ohio, with 7,000 attending and 200 being baptized. All of this indicated a restoration and a willingness to accomplish Jehovah's work of preaching.

⁸ How does all of this affect God's people living today? According to the proph-

5. How was it evident that there needed to be sifting among those serving God, and what shows that this occurred?

6. How did Jehovah's permitting such trials have the eventual blessing of his people in view?
7. (a) What did these restored witnesses now do? (b) What resulted from this refining and cleansing?
8. (a) How does the process of refining and cleansing affect us today? (b) In addition to the modern-day "sons of Levi," who else must pass through testing and sifting?

The ancient refiner skimmed off the impurities, or dross. Similarly, Jehovah allows testing and sifting to refine his people

ecy, Jehovah, accompanied by his messenger, would come and "sit as a refiner and cleanser." (Malachi 3:3) Yes, the process of refining and cleansing would continue, and he would "sit" and watch carefully. The fact that the loyal remnant came through a time of fiery trials early in this century did not mean that the Great Refiner had finished his cleansing of them. The testing and sifting has continued to our day. Jehovah is still at his temple, sitting in judgment. He has not been purifying just "the sons of Levi," the anointed remnant. Malachi's prophecy indicated His concern for "the alien resident," corresponding to the "great crowd," whose prospect is earthly life. (Malachi 3:5; Revelation 7: 9, 10) Yes, during the past 69 years, there has been a continuous purification of Jehovah's people in four general ways.

Organizational Refinements

9 First, cleansing occurred by progressive harmonizing of the worldwide congregation with newly understood Scriptural principles. There had to be a gradual putting away of democratic ways of conducting congregational affairs. Consider some of the progressive developments along this line.

---

9. What are some of the progressive developments in organizational structure since 1919?

1919: Appointments by the Governing Body began by the designating from the headquarters of the Watch Tower Society a permanent service director for each congregation to supervise field-service activities.

1932: The annual election of elders and deacons was terminated; congregational selection of men for these positions was replaced by selection of a service committee assisting (and including) the Society-appointed service director.

1937: It was recognized that "Jonadabs" [those with an earthly hope] may hold positions of responsibility in the congregation.

1938: All overseers and their assistants were to be appointed by the Society in a theocratic manner.

1972: It was made clear that the Scriptural method of governing each congregation was not by just one mature Christian man

A few have been 'winnowed' away as "chaff," but Jehovah's loyal servants joyfully accept progressive spiritual enlightenment

Pictorial Archive (Near Eastern History) Est.

by the spiritual and numerical growth of his worshipers. (Compare Acts 6:7; 16:5.) True, some overseers and others have been sifted out because they would not loyally submit to the God-directed way. By far the majority of Jehovah's people, though, have proved obedient and submissive to organizational improvements. (Hebrews 13:17) They appreciate that by means of such adjustments the Great Refiner has brought them into closer harmony with Scriptural methods for the congregations.

The Field Ministry

¹¹ Second, cleansing has

but by a body of elders, as appointed by the Society.

1975: Establishment of committees of the Governing Body to care for various responsibilities; no one man would direct matters, but all within a committee would have an equal voice and would look unitedly to the leadership of Christ Jesus.

¹⁰ What has been the result of such adjustments? Jehovah's blessing has undoubtedly been abundant, as evidenced

taken place through testings as to participation in field service.

1922: All associates of the congregations were urged to share in the house-to-house field service. Monthly **Bulletin** *(now* **Our Kingdom Ministry***) containing service directions became available.*

1927: Regular house-to-house preaching on Sundays began; books and booklets were distributed for a contribution.

1937: First **Model Study** *booklet for home Bible studies was received.*

---

10. (a) What has resulted from such refinements? (b) How do you feel about all such adjustments?

---

11. What progressive forms has the preaching work taken in recent decades?

1939: First annual Watchtower *subscription campaign took place; over 93,000 new subscriptions were obtained.*

1940: Magazine street work began.

This public preaching took on further progressive forms, including the making of return visits and the conducting of home Bible studies.

[12] What have been the results? Over the years some have been sifted out because they were unwilling to be fruit-bearing Christians. (John 15:5) Yet most of Jehovah's people have certainly responded to the call for Kingdom preachers. Why, that small band of fewer than 8,000 back in 1919 grew to a peak of 3,229,022 Kingdom publishers in 1986! What about the full-time ministry? Compared to 150 active colporteurs (pioneers) in the spring of 1919, last year saw an average of over 391,000 pioneer publishers active each month—the highest number in the history of Jehovah's modern-day Witnesses! By having an active share in preaching the good news, we demonstrate our loyal support of the way in which Jehovah has continued to cleanse his people.—1 Corinthians 9:16.

Increasing Light

[13] Third, cleansing occurred as God's people were tested as to acceptance of progressive spiritual enlightenment from the Bible. (Proverbs 4:18) From 1919 to the present a veritable flood of newly understood truths has flowed.

1925: It was clearly discerned that there

---

12. (a) What have been the results of such refinements of the field ministry? (b) How may we demonstrate our loyalty to the way Jehovah has refined his people?
13. What are some examples of how Jehovah has enlightened his people?

Year after year Jehovah continues to refine and cleanse his people

are two distinct and opposing organizations—Jehovah's and Satan's.

1931: The new name Jehovah's Witnesses was adopted.

1935: The "great crowd" of Revelation 7: 9-15 was identified as a class having an earthly destiny.

1941: The rightfulness of the universal sovereignty of Jehovah was shown to be the primary issue raised by Satan's challenge.

1962: The "superior authorities" of Romans 13:1 were properly identified as being the secular governmental authorities, to whom Christians are to be in relative subjection.

1986: It was appreciated that both the remnant and the "great crowd" must figuratively partake of Jesus' flesh and blood by accepting his sacrifice in order to be in harmony with him.—John 6:53-56.

Over the decades, as Jehovah enlightened his people, it became clear that there was a need for congregational attention to maintaining a clean, neutral organization that respected the sanctity of blood. —1 Corinthians 5:11-13; John 17:14, 16; Acts 15:28, 29.

[14] How have God's people responded to such progressive enlightenment? All along, there have been a few who could not accept certain adjustments. These were 'winnowed out.' (Matthew 3:12) On the other hand, how happy Jehovah's loyal servants are for such spiritual

---

14. (a) How have Jehovah's people responded to such progressive enlightenments? (b) What is your own determination as to Jehovah's channel of communication?

enlightenment! At a time when Christendom gropes in spiritual darkness, the path of Jehovah's people grows brighter and brighter. Should we not be determined to stick closely to the channel of communication that Jehovah is using, accepting all such progressive enlightenments as "food at the proper time"? —Matthew 24:45.

Putting Away Unclean Practices

¹⁵ Fourth, cleansing took place when it became mandatory to put away unclean or Babylonish practices. In the 1920's God's people ceased celebrating Christmas and other holidays that were shown to be of pagan origin. In 1945 the Christian stand on blood transfusions was explained. During the 1960's and 1970's, as the moral climate in the world continued to degenerate, *The Watchtower* continued to provide pointed counsel for God's people on such subjects as proper conduct between the sexes and the need to break free from tobacco and other drugs.

¹⁶ Of course, such adjustments as to unclean practices have often served as a test of loyalty for God's people. However, those who made the necessary adjustments looked upon such changes as assistance in putting away a filthy garment. (Colossians 3:9, 10) They realized that although the customs associated with some holidays may appear harmless, it is Jehovah's view that should concern us; he observed firsthand the pagan religious practices from which these originated. As to God's moral requirements, they viewed them as a protection rather than a restriction, so they were blessed by Jehovah for becoming clean. If an adjustment

15. How has Jehovah gradually refined his people as to unclean or Babylonish practices?
16. How should such adjustments as to unclean practices be viewed?

seemed difficult to understand, they trusted that Jehovah was 'teaching them to benefit themselves.'—Isaiah 48:17.

¹⁷ Year after year Jehovah continues to refine and cleanse his people. Collectively, they have subjected themselves to the refining process as to their organization, activity, doctrine, and moral cleanness. But what about us *individually?* Through his organization Jehovah continues to dispense "solid food" for guidance that refines the heart. Our motives are tested and examined. (Hebrews 4:12; 5:14) By responding to the refining, cleansing process of the Great Refiner, we keep clean as we await "the coming of the great and fear-inspiring day of Jehovah."—Malachi 4:5.

¹⁸ Thanks be to Jehovah, "the true Lord," and his "messenger of the covenant," Jesus Christ, who refine us and deliver us from uncleanness in this time of testing and sifting. May all of us be determined to continue walking in Jehovah's clean paths of peace under the "Prince of Peace," Christ Jesus, and thus keep our happy relationship with Jehovah.—Isaiah 9:6; Psalm 72:7.

17, 18. (a) How are we individually tested by the Great Refiner? (b) What should be our determination as we await Jehovah's day?

How Has Jehovah Refined His People As To—

☐ Organizational adjustments?

☐ Field service participation?

☐ Acceptance of progressive enlightenment?

☐ Putting away unclean practices?

Insight on the News

Who Are the Heretics?

"In the Bible we read that God is a Trinity," wrote Professor Johan Heyns, spiritual leader of South Africa's Dutch Reformed Church, in the November 15, 1986, edition of the South African newspaper *Naweek-Volksblad.* Of those who reason that God cannot be three and yet one, continues the professor, "the Christian Church said that these people were preaching a false doctrine, and therefore the church also denounced them as heretics."

But where is the word Trinity found in the Bible? Professor Heyns did not say. This is not surprising because, as *The New Encyclopædia Britannica* explains, "neither the word Trinity nor the explicit doctrine appears in the New Testament, nor did Jesus and his followers intend to contradict the Shema [Jewish confession of faith] in the Old Testament: 'Hear, O Israel: The Lord our God is one Lord' (Deut. 6:4)." If not taught by Jesus and his apostles nor specifically stated in the Bible, how did the Trinity doctrine become popular? Although the *Britannica* claims that the germ of the doctrine is in the "New Testament," it admits that "the doctrine developed gradually over several centuries and through many controversies" and that by the end of the fourth century "the doctrine of the Trinity took substantially the form it has maintained ever since."

If those who refuse to believe that God is three in one are heretics, then what about Jesus Christ himself? He repeated the above words of Deuteronomy 6:4: "The Lord our God is one Lord." (Mark 12:29, *King James Version*) Jesus also said: "The Father is greater than I am." (John 14:28) So who are the heretics? Those who stick to what Jesus taught or those who cling to a doctrine developed centuries after his death?—Compare 1 Corinthians 4:6 with 2 John 9.

"Fortress" City

"Sydney today is a city under siege," began an editorial in *The Sun-Herald,* a Sydney, Australia, newspaper. "Its residential suburbs are barred, double deadlocked and electronically-guarded fortresses. Its night trains are vandalised, graffiti-scarred and ominously empty. Its streets after dark are becoming increasingly unsafe."

Although the above could be a distressing portrait of many large cities around the world, it sets off alarms of deep concern for Australians. Yet, Bible students are not surprised to see lawlessness spreading. Why? Because they recall Jesus' prophetic words about conditions in our day. Jesus said that "because of the increasing of lawlessness the love of the greater number will cool off." (Matthew 24:12) And while the editorial in *The Sun-Herald* bewails the pall of fear affecting what has been called the Lucky Country's luckiest city, "luck" will not bring an end to wickedness. Only Jehovah, by means of his heavenly government, will. Psalm 5:4 assures us that Jehovah is "not a God taking delight in wickedness; no one bad may reside for any time with you."

Fatal Ironic Twist

The Bible commands Christians to 'abstain from blood.' (Acts 15:29) Jehovah's Witnesses believe that this Scriptural injunction applies to the eating of blood as well as to blood transfusions. AIDS, a fatal disease that attacks the body's immune system, can be contracted from blood transfusions. In a sad but ironic twist, a baby born with a rare and deadly immune-deficiency disease called reticular dysgenesis was given a bone-marrow transplant at the age of six months. The procedure involved blood transfusions. The transplant appeared to be a success until doctors discovered that the transfusions used gave the infant another deadly disease. "At 2 1/2 the patient is doing well except for one thing," reports *Physician's Weekly.* "The child was given posttransplant platelets before screening for (the AIDS virus) became mandatory and he now has AIDS."

Panama Rejoices
in Its Building Work

Panama
Panama City

BUILDING projects are not new to Panama. Toward the beginning of this century, work began on the huge canal that cuts through the center of this narrow isthmus country, joining the Atlantic and Pacific oceans. This prodigious building project earned tiny Panama the name "the crossroads of the world."

On January 18, 1986, a building work of another sort reached its culmination. On that day Jehovah's Witnesses held a dedication program for their newly constructed branch office facilities. While only 211 could attend the dedication program in person, thousands more listened by means of a telephone hookup. The new building houses the headquarters staff, missionaries, and a printery.

The construction of these facilities, however, is but a part of a spiritual building program that has been going on in Panama since the end of the 19th century. At that time seeds of Kingdom truth were sown here. By the year 1957, there were a thousand or so publishers of the "good news" in Panama. (Matthew 24:14) The small branch office and missionary home built in that year was sufficient. But in 20 years the number of Witnesses had tripled! So in September 1982 the Governing Body of Jehovah's Witnesses approved the construction of a new branch office.

The location? About 12 miles (19 km) outside Panama City in a beautiful spot overlooking a lake.

The Challenge of Building

But who would design the building? How would it be built and by whom? Bearing in mind the words of Psalm 127:1, the brothers moved ahead, knowing that Jehovah would help them overcome these seemingly insurmountable obstacles.

A drawing of tentative plans was made, showing the amount of space required for an office, a library, literature storage, a small printery, and housing for the headquarters staff. A spacious Kingdom Hall was included. The architectural staff at the Watch Tower Society's headquarters in Brooklyn, New York, followed through by designing a building to meet these needs.

Next came the challenge of doing the actual building. Hundreds of local Witnesses volunteered. Brothers in the United States also offered their skills and services. Within a period of just six weeks, a total of 230 helpers had arrived, including some from other Central American countries.

The local brothers were happy to open up their homes. One family even moved

into a tent temporarily so as to accommodate 11 volunteers. Some who owned small school buses provided transportation for these workers. Yet others shared in providing the 30,000 free meals that were served right on the construction site. Refreshing drinks made of pineapple, oranges, papaya, and mangoes, as well as coconut milk, were served frequently to quench the thirst of those toiling under the tropical sun.

No Tower of Babel

The work progressed rapidly. Within two weeks all the walls had been raised to the second-floor level, some of the steel beams were in place, and the floor of the Kingdom Hall on the second story was poured. Plumbing and electrical work proceeded simultaneously with the block laying, plastering, and installation of windows and doors. In less than a month the roof was put up, just in time to provide protection from a heavy downpour—unusual for this time of year.

There were some problems. At times, up to 800 volunteers were on hand, and a great deal of organization was needed to

keep all of them busy. Furthermore, most of the visiting brothers did not know Spanish. Rather than this causing the building work to stop, as at the infamous Tower of Babel, the brothers evinced the fruitage of the spirit—and got the assistance of some interpreters.—Galatians 5:22, 23.

Throughout the project, spiritual matters were emphasized. Regular congregation meetings were held at the building site, and time was set aside for sharing in the field ministry. There were also periods of recreation, sight-seeing, and social gatherings. But the brothers were primarily there to work, and the buildings were soon finished!

In his dedication talk, John Booth of the Governing Body summed matters up nicely, saying: "What's going to come from all this building we've been doing? Why, we're building for the eternal future. Not that the building will last forever, but the result of this building and the work of the brothers throughout the country and throughout the world will be people who will live forever." No wonder that the Witnesses in Panama rejoice over their ever-expanding building work!

Family Care
—How Far Does It Extend?

"AFRICAN culture tells me that I am my brother's keeper," said Nigerian writer S. A. Jegede. "African culture calls for respect and care for one's parents." Yes, in Africa and other parts of the world, helping out family members is a way of life.

Often, though, "family" is thought to include aunts, uncles, cousins, nieces, and nephews—even people who are simply from the same village! But as African families leave the rurals for city jobs, such extended family members have become a potential source of problems. Transplanted families often find themselves besieged by relatives requesting money or lodging. Because of the unique demands of city life, however, helping distant relatives or people from the same village is often difficult, if not impossible.

The Bible states: "Certainly if anyone does not provide for those who are his own, and especially for those who are members of his household, he has disowned the faith and is worse than a person without faith." (1 Timothy 5:8) How far, though, does the principle of family care extend? Is a Christian obliged to provide for extended family members in all circumstances? Or is it as the above-quoted Nigerian writer asserts: "The abuse of the extended family system has no room in African culture or in the Bible"?

Parents and Children

The extended family system existed in Bible times. Yet, in obligating a Christian to "provide for those who are his own," the Bible nowhere indicates that

Christian parents have a primary obligation toward their own children

this necessarily includes all the relatives and others of the extended family system.

The Bible particularly stresses the obligations of parents toward children. Regarding a congregation's helping him, the apostle Paul wrote: "For the children ought not to lay up for their parents, but the parents for their children." (2 Corinthians 12:14) H. B. Clark, a famous law authority, commented: "A natural and moral obligation rests upon a father to support his child." As the God-appointed head of the family unit, the father has the prime responsibility to be the breadwinner. Often the wife assists by caring for the home efficiently, spending wisely, even working outside the home when circumstances demand it.—Compare Proverbs 31:10-31.

Note, though, that parents are encouraged to do more than simply earn money. They are urged to "lay up" some earnings in behalf of their children. Parents that follow this wise counsel are often able to assist their children even after they have grown up and left home. Particularly is this appropriate when children pursue the full-time Christian ministry and occasionally need financial assistance to remain in that service. No mention is made of parents' having to "lay up" for innumerable extended family members.

"Due Compensation"

This loving care on the part of parents is not to go unrewarded. The apostle Paul says at 1 Timothy 5:4: "But if any widow has children or grandchildren, let these learn first to practice godly devotion in their own household and to keep paying a due compensation to their parents and grandparents, for this is acceptable in God's sight." Such support of an aging parent or grandparent would certainly harmonize with the Bible's command to

Christian responsibilities may extend to aged parents as well as to one's children

honor one's parents.—Ephesians 6:2; Exodus 20:12.

Again, note that Paul evidently laid no obligations upon distant relatives to care for such widows. Back then, in cases where no close relatives were on hand to care for a Christian widow with a record of faithful service, the congregation was to bear the burden of her support. —1 Timothy 5:3, 9, 10.

The Christian obligation to provide "for those who are his own" thus definitely includes a person's marriage mate and children, parents and grandparents. A responsibility of this sort exists even when such dependent ones are unbelievers or are physically disabled in some way. It continues as long as such ones are alive. And if one is married, it may even include helping one's mate to honor his or her parents. Serious marital difficulties have sometimes arisen when this principle has been overlooked or disregarded.

Provide What? When?

Nevertheless, parents should not conclude that they can squander their resources in the belief that they can, at any time, demand material support from their children. Nor does it mean that they should make unreasonable demands for attention from their offspring, who often have families of their own to whom their first obligation belongs. This view is in line with Paul's words: "Children ought not to lay up for their parents, but the parents for their children."—2 Corinthians 12:14.

In the normal course of events, parents may be able to acquire their own home, property, and source of income (including company or government retirement pay) that may sustain them in their old age. "Money is for a protection," and by 'laying up' for themselves prudently, parents can often avoid placing a great financial or emotional burden on their children later on in life.—Ecclesiastes 7:12.

Solomon's words at Ecclesiastes 9:11, however, remind us that even the best-laid plans are subject to "time and unforeseen occurrence." So, what if, in spite of careful planning, a couple's means of support fails or needs supplementing? Their God-fearing children would naturally be moved to help them in some reasonable way. This may mean providing financial assistance, inviting the parents to live with or near them, or, when necessary, arranging for institutional care. Of course, aged parents or grandparents certainly should be reasonable, not expecting their offspring to provide a lavish life-style, for the Bible's counsel is: "Having sustenance and covering, we shall be content with these things." —1 Timothy 6:8.

In many cases, government social-security programs, pensions, old-age benefits, and personal savings can provide adequate, albeit modest, support for aged parents or grandparents. It is wise to find out what provisions are available to those who qualify.—Romans 13:6.

Avoid Pharisaical Reasoning

Jesus chastised the scribes and the Pharisees because they said to needy parents: "Whatever I have by which you might get benefit from me is a gift dedicated to God." (Matthew 15:5) In Jesus' day, pious Jews could set aside money or property for eventual donation to the temple. The Pharisees fostered the view that once dedicated, such goods could under no circumstances be used for any other purpose—including caring for aged parents.

Christ condemned this Pharisaical thinking as being out of harmony with the spirit of God's Law. In his view, honoring one's parents took priority over a man-made rule. Similarly today, some

Christians have devoted their lives to the ministry, perhaps serving as missionaries, pioneers, or traveling overseers. Upon learning that their parents were in need, they tried hard to find ways to care for their folks while still continuing in their form of ministry. But when no such arrangements could in any way be worked out, they did not reason that their privileges in the ministry were more important than honoring their parents. Such ones are to be warmly commended for making adjustments in their lives—often at great personal sacrifice—so as to meet their family obligations.

Working What Is Good Toward All

Though the Bible obligates Christians to care for needy members of their immediate family, this does not rule out reasonably showing love to members of the extended family. At times certain aunts, cousins, or nephews seem as close as immediate family members! The Bible encourages us to "work what is good toward all." (Galatians 6:10) If a Christian has the means to help such a one, certainly he would not have to 'shut the door of his tender compassions.' Indeed, he may feel morally obligated to help.—1 John 3:17.

Nevertheless, a Christian's primary obligation is toward his immediate family —marriage mate, children, parents, and grandparents. He would therefore give serious thought before taking on a responsibility that could harm them—financially, emotionally, or spiritually.

The Bible's advice on family care is thus kind and reasonable. Applying it can relieve a Christian of much unnecessary anxiety, and it can help him to set his priorities. All of this is to the praise of Jehovah, "the Father, to whom every family in heaven and on earth owes its name."—Ephesians 3:14, 15.

'God Will Finish Your Training'

AN ATHLETE preparing for an important event has to train hard. He wants to get his body in shape so that on the big day, he will render his best possible performance. Christians, too, have to train hard but with a different goal. The apostle Paul said: "Be training yourself with godly devotion as your aim."—1 Timothy 4:7.

Thus, a Christian has to keep himself in shape spiritually. As an athlete builds his body, the Christian builds his spiritual strength and endurance. He does this by studying God's Word the Bible, by prayer, by regularly associating with fellow Christians, and by making public expressions of his faith.

An athlete often has a trainer, and Christians, too, have a trainer. Who? None other than Jehovah God himself! The apostle Peter pointed out Jehovah's concern for the Christian training program, writing: "The God of all undeserved kindness . . . will himself finish your training, he will make you firm, he will make you strong." (1 Peter 5:10) What training does Jehovah give us? Many kinds, and all are vital if we want to stay in shape as Christians.

Direct Discipline

Peter himself received training from Jehovah. We can learn a lot from his experience. Sometimes Peter's training was painful. Imagine how Peter must have felt when he tried to discourage Jesus from going through with God's purpose, and Jesus answered: "Get behind me, Satan! You are a stumbling block to me, because you think, not God's thoughts, but those of men." (Matthew 16:23) Imagine, too, how he felt many years later when fear of man led him to act unwisely. The apostle Paul administered Jehovah's discipline on that occasion: "When Cephas [Peter] came to Antioch, I resisted him face to face, because he stood condemned."—Galatians 2:11-14.

Nevertheless, on both occasions Jehovah was training Peter. He learned that "no discipline seems for the present to be joyous, but grievous; yet afterward to those who have been trained by it it yields peaceable fruit, namely, righteousness." (Hebrews 12:11) Accepting those strong reproofs as discipline from Jehovah helped Peter to get the right view of matters and trained him in the vital Christian qualities of meekness and humility.—Proverbs 3:34; 15:33.

Handling Situations

Jehovah can train us by permitting situations to arise that are difficult to handle —sometimes these are even within the Christian congregation. We grow as Christians as we pray for guidance, put into application the Bible principles we have learned, and see how applying those principles is *always* the best way.

Peter was involved in personality conflicts that arose among Jesus' apostles. When we read the accounts of this, it is interesting to see how Jesus used these conflicts—which were really the result of imperfection and inexperience—as opportunities to train his followers in the essential Christian qualities of love, humility, and forgiveness.—Matthew 18:15-17, 21, 22; Luke 22:24-27.

Paul also witnessed personality conflicts. (Acts 15:36-40; Philippians 4:2) He explained how such problems give Christians the opportunity to receive training: "Continue putting up with one another and forgiving one another freely if anyone has a cause for complaint against another. Even as Jehovah freely forgave you, so do you also. But, besides all these things, clothe yourselves with love, for it is a perfect bond of union."—Colossians 3: 13, 14.

In the first century, a more sinister danger appeared among Christians. Peter warned about it: "There will also be false teachers among you. These very ones will quietly bring in destructive sects and will disown even the owner that bought them, bringing speedy destruction upon themselves. Furthermore, many will follow their acts of loose conduct, and on account of these the way of the truth will be spoken of abusively." (2 Peter 2:1, 2) This experience would result in the destruction of the unrepentant "false teachers." (2 Peter 2:3) But what of those who remained faithful?

The experience would train them to 'rouse up their clear thinking faculties.' (2 Peter 3:1) Their alertness in guarding against the intrusion of false teachings would call for them to review the reasons for their faith. As they saw the bad results of the actions of the "false teachers," their confidence in Christian truth would be even stronger.—2 Peter 3:3-7.

For example, in one congregation the aged apostle John was opposed by a certain Diotrephes, an ambitious man who had little respect for John's authority and who not only refused to receive the messengers sent by John but may even have tried to disfellowship those who did. This must have been painful to all the sincere Christians who were in the same congregation as Diotrephes. But it did give them the opportunity to show that they were not 'imitators of what is bad' and thus to receive advanced training in loyalty to Jehovah and to apostolic authority.—3 John 9-12.

In Dealing With
Non-Christians

Jesus said that his followers were no part of the world. (John 17:16) A Christian's first loyalty is to Jehovah and his Kingdom. He tries to maintain God's moral standards, so his main interests and concerns are different from those of the world. However, a Christian has to live in the world, and this inevitably causes tensions.

Peter, during his long ministry, must have seen many occasions when Christians had to make difficult decisions, balancing the demands of the world with the dictates of their conscience. In Peter's first letter, he gave fine, practical counsel as to how to do this so that Christians could "hold a good conscience."—1 Peter 2:13-20; 3: 1-6, 16.

Of course, as Christians we look forward to the time when we no longer have to consider the demands of this system of things. But meanwhile we are being trained in endurance and allowed to demonstrate our loyalty in the face of temptation and ungodly influences. As we gain experience in applying Bible principles to different circumstances and courageously act the way we know Jehovah wants us to act, we are also trained in practical wisdom and courage. Think about how much more training we will have received because of having lived in this system and successfully handled so many difficult problems!

Under Persecution

When Peter spoke about God's training of us, he was particularly referring to persecution. He showed that Christians should expect persecution: "Keep your senses, be watchful. Your adversary, the Devil, walks about like a roaring lion, seeking to devour someone."—1 Peter 5:8; see also 2 Timothy 3:12.

Peter was qualified to speak about this because he had personally suffered persecution. In the early days of the Christian congregation, he and the other apostles were flogged and ordered to stop preaching. Their reaction? They "went their way from before the Sanhedrin, rejoicing because they had been counted worthy to be dishonored in behalf of his name."—Acts 5:41.

Hence, Peter spoke from experience, as well as under inspiration, when he said: "On the contrary, go on rejoicing forasmuch as you are sharers in the sufferings of the Christ, that you may rejoice and be overjoyed also during the revelation of his glory. If you are being reproached for the name of Christ, you are happy, because the spirit of glory, even the spirit of God, is resting upon you."—1 Peter 4:13, 14.

Yes, outright persecution can serve as a form of training. Under it, a Christian learns to rely even more on God's spirit. His faith develops a "tested quality." (1 Peter 1:7) He is trained in courage based on Jehovah's power. (2 Timothy 1:7) He develops patient endurance, and like Jesus, he 'learns obedience through the things he suffers.'—Hebrews 5:8; 1 Peter 2:23, 24.

Jehovah Finishes Our Training

Of course, the difficult problems, including persecution, that a Christian endures do not come from God. James counsels: "When under trial, let no one say: 'I am being tried by God.' For with evil things God cannot be tried nor does he himself try anyone." (James 1:13) Problems may arise from many causes, including when people make mistakes or do wrong of their own free will. However, since such things do happen, Jehovah uses them to train his servants in vital Christian qualities.

Job, Jeremiah, Peter, Paul, and all of God's servants in Bible times were trained in this way. We, too, as we face various difficult situations, should view them as a source of training permitted by Jehovah. By our facing up to them in Jehovah's strength, we will be trained in obedience,

In Our Next Issue

- **Controlling Anger in an Angry World**

- **Michael the Great Prince Stands Up**

- **Staying Close to Jehovah's Organization**

wisdom, humility, courage, love, tolerance, and many other qualities.—Compare James 1:2-4.

We are encouraged, too, by knowing that this stage of our training will one day be over. Hence, Peter comforted his fellow Christians, saying: "After you have suffered a little while, the God of all undeserved kindness, who called you to his everlasting glory in union with Christ, will himself finish your training, he will make you firm, he will make you strong." (1 Peter 5:10) These words apply with equal force to the "great crowd" that look forward to everlasting life in the Paradise earth.

That thought in itself should help us to submit patiently to these training experiences, to be determined not to compromise. Thus, we will experience the truthfulness of Paul's encouraging words: "So let us not give up in doing what is fine, for in due season we shall reap if we do not tire out."—Galatians 6:9.

Questions From Readers

■ When on the stake, Jesus cried: "My God, my God, why have you forsaken me?" Did he lack faith, believing that God had deserted him?

Upon reading these words at Matthew 27:46 or Mark 15:34, some have concluded that when Jesus faced a painful death, his confidence in God wavered. Others have said that this was merely Jesus' *human* response, an understandable cry of desperation by a flesh-and-blood man in agony. There is good reason, though, to look beyond such human evaluations based on surface appearances. While none of us today can know with certainty all that was involved in Jesus' crying out as he did, we can note two likely motives.

Jesus was well aware that he would have to "go to Jerusalem and suffer many things . . . , and be killed, and on the third day be raised up." (Matthew 16:21) In heaven the Son of God had observed even imperfect humans experience torturous deaths while maintaining their integrity. (Hebrews 11:36-38) So there just is no reason to believe that Jesus —a perfect human—would be seized with fear over what he faced; nor would death on a

stake suggest to him that his Father had rejected him. Jesus knew in advance "what sort of death he was about to die," that is, death by impalement. (John 12:32, 33) He was sure, too, that on the third day he would be raised up. How, then, could Jesus say that God had forsaken him?

First, he could have meant it in the qualified sense that Jehovah had taken away protection from his Son so that Jesus' integrity would be tested to the limit, a painful and shameful death. But God's releasing of Jesus to the wrath of enemies directed by Satan did not indicate total abandonment. Jehovah continued to show affection for Jesus, as proved on the third day when He raised his Son, which Jesus had known would occur.—Acts 2: 31-36; 10:40; 17:31.

Connected to the foregoing is a likely second reason for Jesus' utterance while on the stake, that by using these words he could fulfill a prophetic indication about the Messiah. Hours earlier Jesus told the apostles that things

would happen "just as it is written concerning him." (Matthew 26: 24; Mark 14:21) Yes, he wanted to carry out the things that were written, including things in Psalm 22. You may find it revealing to compare Psalm 22:7, 8 —Matthew 27:39, 43; Psalm 22:15—John 19:28, 29; Psalm 22:16—Mark 15:25 and John 20:27; Psalm 22:18—Matthew 27:35. Psalm 22, which gave so many prophetic indications of the Messiah's experiences, begins: "My God, my God, why have you left me?" Hence, when Jesus cried out as he did, he was adding to the record of prophecies that he fulfilled. —Luke 24:44.

The psalmist did not believe that his God had simply rejected or abandoned him, for David went on to say that he would 'declare God's name to his brothers,' and he urged others to praise Jehovah. (Psalm 22:22, 23) Similarly, Jesus, who knew Psalm 22 well, also had reason for confidence that his Father still approved of him and loved him, despite what God allowed him to experience on the stake.

She Met Her Goal

During a Bible talk, a minister said that Christians should set personal goals and then strive to meet them. A four-year-old girl who heard the talk announced to her parents the following morning that she had set the goal of listening to the entire 256-page *My Book of Bible Stories* that is recorded on tapes. Her mother writes:

"She arranged herself comfortably with pillow, recorder, tapes, and book, and requested that snacks be served throughout the day. Not really taking her seriously, I agreed, thinking that she would tire in just a short time. During the morning, I checked on her several times to see how she was doing. After about two hours, I suggested that perhaps it had been long enough and we could finish tomorrow. But she was determined. Later on in the afternoon, she came out of the room, stretching and a little stiff, but with a very proud smile. It had taken almost six hours, but she had reached her goal!

"Since this time she has started school, and her teacher says that she is the best oral reader they have ever heard."

the Watchtower

July 1, 1987

Announcing Jehovah's Kingdom

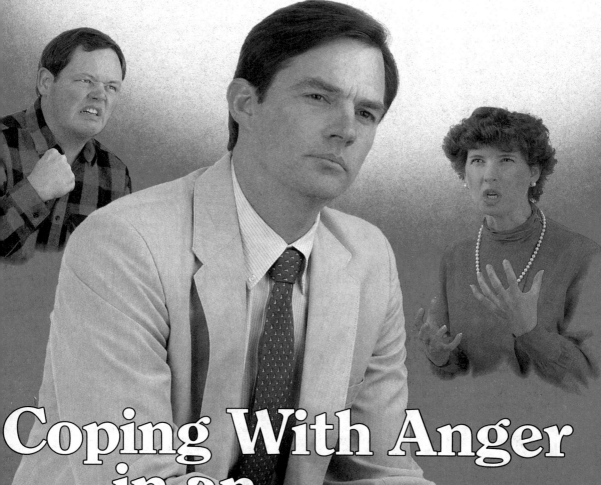

Coping With Anger in an Angry World

The Watchtower®
Announcing Jehovah's Kingdom

July 1, 1987
Vol. 108, No. 13

In This Issue

THE PURPOSE OF "THE WATCHTOWER" is to exalt Jehovah God as the Sovereign of the universe. It keeps watch on world events as they fulfill Bible prophecy. It comforts all peoples with the good news that God's Kingdom will soon destroy those who oppress their fellowmen and that it will turn the earth into a paradise. It encourages faith in the now-reigning King, Jesus Christ, whose shed blood opens the way for mankind to gain eternal life. "The Watchtower," published by Jehovah's Witnesses continuously since 1879, is nonpolitical. It adheres to the Bible as its authority.

"WATCHTOWER" STUDIES FOR THE WEEKS

August 2: 'No Peace for the Wicked Ones.' Page 10. Songs to Be Used: 113, 159.

August 9: Michael the Great Prince Stands Up. Page 15. Songs to Be Used: 112, 168.

August 16: Divine Blessings for "the Ones Having Insight." Page 21. Songs to Be Used: 185, 6.

Average Printing Each Issue: 12,315,000

Now Published in 103 Languages

SEMIMONTHLY LANGUAGES AVAILABLE BY MAIL
Afrikaans, Arabic, Cebuano, Chichewa, Chinese, Cibemba, Danish,* Dutch,* Efik, English,* Finnish,* French,* German,* Greek,* Hiligaynon, Igbo, Iloko, Italian,* Japanese,* Korean, Lingala, Malagasy, Maltese, Norwegian, Portuguese,* Russian, Sepedi, Sesotho, Shona, Spanish,* Swahili, Swedish,* Tagalog, Thai, Tsonga, Tswana, Xhosa, Yoruba, Zulu

MONTHLY LANGUAGES AVAILABLE BY MAIL
Armenian, Bengali, Bicol, Bislama, Bulgarian, Croatian, Czech, Ewe, Fijian, Ga, Greenlandic, Gujarati, Gun, Hausa, Hebrew, Hindi, Hiri Motu, Hungarian, Icelandic, Kannada, Malayalam, Marathi, New Guinea Pidgin, Pangasinan, Papiamento, Polish, Rarotongan, Romanian, Samar-Leyte, Samoan, Sango, Serbian, Silozi, Sinhalese, Slovenian, Solomon Islands-Pidgin, Tahitian, Tamil, Telugu, Tongan, Tshiluba, Turkish, Twi, Ukrainian, Urdu, Venda, Vietnamese

* Study articles also available in large-print edition.

Watch Tower Society offices	Yearly subscription for the above:	
	Semimonthly Languages	Monthly Languages
America, U.S., Watchtower, Wallkill, N.Y. 12589	$4.00	$2.00
Australia, Box 280, Ingleburn, N.S.W. 2565	A$7.00	A$3.50
Canada, Box 4100, Halton Hills, Ontario L7G 4Y4	$5.50	$2.75
England, The Ridgeway, London NW7 1RN	£5.00	£2.50
Ireland, 29A Jamestown Road, Finglas, Dublin 11	IR£6.00	IR£3.00
New Zealand, P.O. Box 142, Manurewa	NZ$15.00	NZ$7.50
Nigeria, PMB 001, Shomolu, Lagos State	N8.00	N4.00
Philippines, P.O. Box 2044, Manila 2800	P60.00	P30.00
South Africa, Private Bag 2067, Krugersdorp, 1740	R9.00	R4.50

Remittances should be sent to the office in your country or to Watchtower, Wallkill, N.Y. 12589, U.S.A.

Changes of address should reach us 30 days before your moving date. Give us your old and new address (if possible, your old address label).

20 cents (U.S.) a copy

The Bible translation used is the "New World Translation of the Holy Scriptures," unless otherwise indicated.

The Watchtower (ISSN 0043-1087) is published semimonthly for $4.00 (U.S.) per year by Watch Tower Bible and Tract Society of Pennsylvania, 25 Columbia Heights, Brooklyn, N.Y. 11201. Second-class postage paid at Brooklyn, N.Y., and at additional mailing offices.

Postmaster: Send address changes to Watchtower, *Wallkill, N.Y. 12589.*

Published by
Watch Tower Bible and Tract Society of Pennsylvania
25 Columbia Heights, Brooklyn, N.Y. 11201, U.S.A.
Frederick W. Franz, President

Anger
What Is It?

"**B**Y REPRESSING your God-given talent for anger, you're killing yourself." So warned an article quoted in the magazine *Newsweek*. For years, apparently, many psychologists have popularized the idea that unexpressed anger may cause such disorders as high blood pressure, heart disease, depression, anxiety, and alcoholism.

The Bible, on the other hand, has admonished for millenniums: "Let anger alone and leave rage." (Psalm 37:8) The Bible's diagnosis is to the point: "Be not hasty in thy spirit to be angry: for anger resteth in the bosom of fools."—Ecclesiastes 7:9, *King James Version.*

Who is right, the secular experts or the Bible? What really is anger? Is venting anger good for us?

Venting Anger

"Anger" is a general term describing a strong feeling or reaction of displeasure and antagonism. There are other words, too, that reveal the degree of anger or how it is expressed. Rage suggests a very intense anger. Fury can be destructive. Indignation may refer to anger for a righteous cause. And wrath often implies revenge or punishment.

Anger is usually specific: We are angry *about something.* But how we express anger or deal with it makes a big difference.

Interestingly, although some experts insist that the venting of anger is beneficial, recent psychological studies show that many people who allow themselves to express anger suffer from lower self-esteem, depression, guilt complex, escalated hostility, or anxiety. Moreover, "getting it off one's chest," or "blowing off steam," perhaps accompanied by angry outbursts, screaming, crying, or even physical assault, usually creates more problems than it solves. The angry person gets angrier, and hurt feelings build up in others.—Proverbs 30:33; Genesis 49:6, 7.

When we shout and yell in anger, we often do not get the results we hope for because the other person is usually provoked to strike back. For example, suppose that while you are driving your car, another driver does something to annoy you. In response, you shout and honk your horn. Your outburst could easily provoke the object of your rage to retaliate. At times, tragedy has resulted from such a situation. For example, a man in

Brooklyn, New York, was killed while arguing over a parking space on a street. The Bible highlights the problem when it says: "A man given to anger stirs up contention, and anyone disposed to rage has many a transgression." (Proverbs 29:22) How wise to follow the counsel: "Return evil for evil to no one. . . . If possible, as far as it depends upon you, be peaceable with all men"!—Romans 12:17, 18.

Hence, venting our anger does not help us socially. But is it good for us physically? A number of physicians have concluded that it is not. Studies have shown that persons who are prone to express anger have the highest levels of blood pressure. Some reported that anger produced cardiac sensations, headaches, nosebleed, dizziness, or inability to vocalize. On the other hand, the Giver of our life explains: "A calm heart is the life of the fleshly organism." (Proverbs 14:30) Jesus said: "Happy are the peaceable, since they will be called 'sons of God.'"—Matthew 5:9.

A number of physicians have concluded that venting anger is unhealthy

Causes of Anger

Some causes of anger are attacks on our self-esteem, personal criticism, insult, unfair treatment, and unjustified frustration. When people are angry, they are conveying an emphatic message: "You are threatening my happiness and security! You are hurting my pride! You are robbing me of my self-respect! You are taking advantage of me!"

Sometimes people use anger as a cover-up for something else. For example, a 14-year-old boy in New York City was constantly in an angry mood and always getting into fights. With the help of a doctor, the boy eventually admitted: "I would never say, okay, I need help, I want somebody to talk to . . . Your fear is that people are not going to like you." So, what he really wanted was attention and affection.

A married couple in California engaged in angry outbursts every time the wife visited her girlfriend. The husband's angry behavior triggered a similar reaction in the wife. At a counseling session, the husband eventually told her something he had never told anyone before. When his wife went away without him, even for a short while, deep inside he was afraid that she might leave him altogether because his father had abandoned him when he was young. When the wife understood the underlying reason for her husband's anger—a fear of abandonment—it helped her to dispel her own anger at him and to reassure him of her love.

Thus, anger may be a symptom. In such cases, by identifying its underlying cause, we can learn to deal with it properly.

Managing Anger

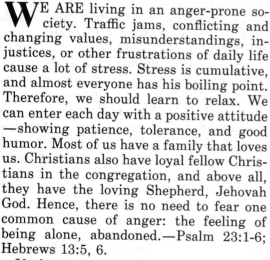

Yours and Others'

WE ARE living in an anger-prone society. Traffic jams, conflicting and changing values, misunderstandings, injustices, or other frustrations of daily life cause a lot of stress. Stress is cumulative, and almost everyone has his boiling point. Therefore, we should learn to relax. We can enter each day with a positive attitude —showing patience, tolerance, and good humor. Most of us have a family that loves us. Christians also have loyal fellow Christians in the congregation, and above all, they have the loving Shepherd, Jehovah God. Hence, there is no need to fear one common cause of anger: the feeling of being alone, abandoned.—Psalm 23:1-6; Hebrews 13:5, 6.

If, however, we feel anger or have to confront another person's anger, we should manage it properly so as to preserve our happiness and well-being. How? The Bible tells us: "He that is slow to anger is better than a mighty man, and he that is controlling his spirit than the one capturing a city." (Proverbs 16:32) Instead of hastily deciding to express anger, we should consider the possible outcome of our actions. Counting to ten may prevent us from doing something that we may later regret.—Proverbs 14:17.

In the case that we are angry and do not know why, we should humbly and honestly ask for help. To admit to others, especially those who love us, our fears or need for help is not weakness; it is a course of wisdom and courage. Then we can get to the root of the problem. The Bible says: "There is a frustrating of plans where there is no confidential talk, but in the multitude of counselors there is accomplishment."—Proverbs 15:22.

Trying to understand the reasons why others behave the way they do will help us to control our own emotional reactions. Furthermore, if we reply to an angry person, "I understand why you are angry," he may quickly cool down. The Bible counsels: "The insight of a man certainly slows down his anger, and it is beauty on his part to pass over transgression."—Proverbs 19:11.

Should we unintentionally injure someone, we owe him an apology. For example, if someone steps on your toe, you may tend to become angry. But when he apologizes, your anger fades. Your toe may still hurt, but your dignity is respected. Similarly, good manners on our part, along with common courtesy and healthy humor, can melt resentment and maintain respect toward us in our relationship with our spouse, children, friends, and members of the Christian congregation. —Proverbs 16:24; Colossians 4:6; 1 Peter 3:8.

In dealing with a situation that causes us to feel angry, it helps to know how to talk about our anger without attacking the other person. There is a marked distinction between verbal aggression ("You idiot!" or, "I'll punch you on the nose!") and reporting one's anger ("I am very upset" or, "I feel hurt"). Verbal aggression usually fails because it provokes the other person to retaliate, whereas reporting how you feel is less of an attack, and the other person may be moved to make amends. As the Bible says: "An answer, when mild, turns away rage, but a word causing pain makes anger to come up. An enraged man stirs up contention, but one that is slow to anger quiets down quarreling."—Proverbs 15:1, 18.

Righteous Anger

For most of us it is natural to feel angry from time to time. The Bible reports that even Jehovah feels anger. (Zephaniah 2: 2, 3; 3:8) So it is not surprising that man, made in His image, should experience a similar feeling. (Genesis 1:26) Hence, the *feeling* of anger is not in itself a sin.

However, when Jehovah is angry, it is always for a proper reason: Righteous principles have been violated. And his response is always exactly right and perfectly controlled. With imperfect humans it is different. We often feel angry because our pride has been hurt or because of some other human weakness. Hence the need for care in the way we handle our anger. As the apostle Paul warned: "Be wrathful,

and yet do not sin; let the sun not set with you in a provoked state, neither allow place for the Devil." (Ephesians 4:26, 27) Yes, Satan can take advantage of our uncontrolled anger. In fact, "fits of anger" are listed among "the works of the flesh" that keep a person from inheriting God's Kingdom.—Galatians 5:19-21.

That is why the disciple James counsels: "Know this, my beloved brothers. Every man must be . . . slow about wrath; for man's wrath does not work out God's righteousness." (James 1:19, 20) Even if our anger is for a justifiable reason, imperfection may lead us to react in an uncontrolled, wrong way. Hence, we should always be guided by the principle: "Do not avenge yourselves, beloved, but yield place to the wrath; for it is written: 'Vengeance is mine; I will repay, says Jehovah.'" (Romans 12:19) Remember, too, that as imperfect humans, we may be mistaken. It is, therefore, dangerous quickly to judge others in the name of righteous indignation.—James 2:13; 4:11, 12; 5:9.

According to the Scriptures, we are living in the time of the end. In these last days, "the nations became wrathful" against God's Kingdom, and the Devil has "great anger, knowing he has a short period of time." (Revelation 11:17, 18; 12: 10-12) Therefore, our living according to the Word of God is the only real safeguard for us. (Psalm 119:105) Soon God will render judgment among the nations, and the earth will be cleansed of all unrighteousness. (Isaiah 35:10; 65:23; Micah 4: 3, 4) In the meantime, we need to be sure not to imitate the ways of this angry world. Properly controlling our anger will help preserve marital love, Christian unity, and personal peace and happiness. And most important, it will help us to continue enjoying Jehovah God's favor and blessing.—Psalm 119:165.

Kingdom Proclaimers Report

Chile Prospers With Increased Enlightenment

LIKE brilliant sunlight shining forth over the Andes mountains at dawn, the light of Bible truth first came to Chile in 1930. In that year, one of Jehovah's dedicated servants came from Argentina with the good news. Today, the light of God's Word has shone forth and reached the far corners of the land.

While the first branch office in Chile was established in 1945, a new, larger branch building was constructed in 1970, when the number of Kingdom proclaimers had reached 7,000. In the next ten years, increased enlightenment from God's Word touched many responsive hearts. By the early 1980's further expansion of the branch office was urgently needed. Thus, in September 1982 a 17.5-acre (7 ha) piece of land on the outskirts of Santiago was purchased. And after much preliminary work, excavation began by June 1984.

It was heartwarming to see how the Chilean brothers, young and old, supported the project by their generous contributions. Thousands of others donated their time and talents. Some with technical training helped with the engineering. Others worked in carpentry, welding, curtain making, and landscaping, or offered plain labor of love by pulling weeds, pushing wheelbarrows, and digging ditches. Indeed, the progressive light of God's Word has touched the hearts of his people and moved them to offer themselves willingly.—Psalm 110:3.

The unity and willingness did not escape the notice of outsiders. Many salesmen and even university students and professors came to the construction site to observe and to learn. One builder wanted to hire the entire concrete crew to help with a supermarket he was building. A salesman comment-

ed on how different the work crew was—no swearing, no loitering. When being told that all were Jehovah's Witnesses and were there as volunteers, he responded: "One would not see this in any other place. You people are of another world."

Finally, in August 1986 the Chilean branch staff moved into the new building in Puente Alto. And on October 25, with A. D. Schroeder of the Governing Body of Jehovah's Witnesses present, an enthusiastic crowd of 933 voiced their wholehearted support in dedicating the new buildings to Jehovah's service. The next day, a special event was held at a nearby stadium, and 18,012 added their *sí* to the resolution.

Is this expansion really needed? Let the facts give the reply. When the property was purchased in 1982, there were 17,-500 Kingdom publishers in Chile. Now there are over 29,-000! And with almost 40,000 home Bible studies being conducted, there is no end in sight. So let the light from God's Word shine forth still more brightly in this fertile territory in the foothills of the Andes, to the praise of Jehovah and the blessing of his people.—Daniel 12:3.

Leaving Jairus' Home and Revisiting Nazareth

THE day has been busy for Jesus —a sea voyage from the Decapolis, healing the woman with the flow of blood, and resurrecting Jairus' daughter. But the day is not over. Evidently as Jesus leaves the home of Jairus, two blind men follow behind, shouting: "Have mercy on us, Son of David."

By addressing Jesus as "Son of David," these men are hereby expressing belief that Jesus is heir to the throne of David, hence that he is the promised Messiah. Jesus, however, seemingly ignores their cries for help, perhaps to test their persistence. But the men do not give up. They follow Jesus to where he is staying, and when he enters the house, they follow him inside.

There Jesus asks: "Do you have faith that I can do this?"

"Yes, Lord," they answer confidently.

So, touching their eyes, Jesus says: "According to your faith let it happen to you." Suddenly they can see! Jesus then sternly charges them: "See that nobody gets to know it." But filled with gladness, they ignore Jesus' command and talk about him all over the countryside.

Just as these men leave, people bring in a demon-possessed man whom the demon has robbed of his speech. Jesus expels the demon, and instantly the man begins to talk. The crowds marvel at these miracles, saying: "Never was anything like this seen in Israel."

Pharisees, too, are present. They cannot deny the miracles, but in their wicked unbelief they repeat their charge as to the source of Jesus' powerful works, saying: "It is by the ruler of the demons that he expels the demons."

Shortly after these events, Jesus returns to his hometown of Nazareth, this time accompanied by his disciples. About a year earlier, he had visited the synagogue and taught there. Although the people at first marveled at his pleasing words, they later took offense at his teaching and tried to kill him. Now, mercifully, Jesus makes another attempt to help his former neighbors.

While in other places people flock to Jesus, here they apparently do not. So, on the Sabbath, he goes to the synagogue to teach. Most of those hearing him are astounded. "Where did this man get this wisdom and these powerful works?" they ask. "Is this not the carpenter's son? Is not his mother called Mary, and his brothers James and Joseph and Simon and Judas? And his sisters, are they not all with us? Where, then, did this man get all these things?"

'Jesus is just a local man like us,' they reason. 'We saw him grow up, and we know his family. How can he be the Messiah?' So despite all the evidence —his great wisdom and miracles—they reject him. Even his own relatives, because of their intimate familiarity, stumble at him, causing Jesus to conclude: "A prophet is not unhonored except in his home territory and among his relatives and in his own house."

Indeed, Jesus wonders at their lack of faith. So he does not perform any miracles there apart from laying his hands on a few sick people and healing them. **Matthew 9:27-34; 13:54-58; Mark 6: 1-6; Isaiah 9:7.**

♦ By addressing Jesus as "Son of David," what do the blind men show they believe?
♦ What explanation for Jesus' miracles have the Pharisees settled upon?
♦ Why is it merciful for Jesus to return to help those in Nazareth?
♦ What reception does Jesus receive in Nazareth, and why?

'No Peace for the Wicked Ones'

"'There is no peace,' my God has said, 'for the wicked ones.'"—ISAIAH 57:21.

"**I** AM constantly aware that at any second the world might blow up in my face." This shocking statement, quoted in the magazine *Psychology Today,* was made by a North American high-school student. Sometime soon, the student feared, a nuclear war will likely destroy all mankind. A Russian schoolgirl describes the results of a nuclear war: "All living things will perish—no grass, no trees, no greenery." What a terrible prospect! Yet, people feel this could really happen. In a recent survey 40 percent of the adults interviewed felt that there was a "high chance" of nuclear war before the year 2000.—See Luke 21:26.

[2] World leaders also sense the danger. After the last world war, they set up the United Nations organization to try to bring peace and security to mankind —but in vain. Instead, the postwar years have seen the development of an intense rivalry between two nuclear-armed superpowers. From time to time, the leaders of these powers meet in an effort to defuse international tension but with few results. Despite the fact that religious leaders are praying for peace, the situation is much as Isaiah described: "Their very heroes have cried out in the street; the very messengers of peace will weep bitterly."—Isaiah 33:7.

[3] Informed Christians know why politicians will never bring lasting peace. They realize that as long as humans are full of selfishness, hatred, greed, pride, and ambition, there will be no peace. (Compare James 4:1.) Besides, human events are not fully controlled by humans. Rather, the Bible tells us: "The whole world is lying in the

1, 2. (a) How do many people feel about the future of mankind? (b) What is the result of human efforts to make peace?

U.S. National Archives

3. Why is there no possibility that men will succeed in their peace-making efforts?

power of the wicked one." (1 John 5:19; 2 Corinthians 4:4) The situation of mankind under this one's control was well described by Isaiah: "The wicked are like the sea that is being tossed, when it is unable to calm down . . . 'There is no peace,' my God has said, 'for the wicked ones.'"—Isaiah 57:20, 21.

"The God Who Gives Peace"

⁴ This does not mean that the human race cannot escape destruction in a future nuclear war. It simply means that if we are to see peace, it will have to come from an external source. Happily, that Source exists in the person of Jehovah God, "the God who gives peace." (Romans 16:20) He has the power to counter Satan's influence and has purposed to "bless his people with peace." (Psalm 29:11) Moreover, he has made the heartwarming promise: "The meek ones themselves will possess the earth, and they will indeed find their exquisite delight in the abundance of peace."—Psalm 37:11.

⁵ Many years ago, Jehovah revealed the historical development of events that would lead up to his bringing peace to the earth. Through an angel, he spoke to his faithful prophet Daniel about "the final part of the days," our own time. (Daniel 10:14) He foretold today's superpower rivalry and showed that it will soon end in a way that neither power suspects. And he promised that this unexpected development would usher in real peace. For Christians this prophecy is of vital interest. It gives a clear view of where we stand in the stream of time and strengthens our determination to remain neutral to the international rivalry while waiting patiently for God to act on our behalf. —Psalm 146:3, 5.

A Rivalry Begins

⁶ The truth is, today's superpower rivalry is not a new thing on the world scene. It is, rather, a continuation of something that began a long time ago. After the collapse of Alexander the Great's world empire toward the end of the fourth century B.C.E., two of his military leaders took power in Syria and Egypt. A lasting rivalry that ultimately led to the superpower rivalry of today sprang up between them and their successors—spoken of as the king of the north and the king of the south because they were situated to the north and south of the land of God's people. The historical development of this rivalry was revealed in advance to the prophet Daniel through an angel.

⁷ The angel first describes how he, supported by Michael, had been fighting against the spirit 'princes' of Persia and Greece. (Daniel 10:13, 20–11:1) This glimpse into the spirit realm confirms that national conflicts involve more than mere humans. There are demonic forces, or "princes," behind the visible human rulers. But from ancient times, God's people have had a "prince," Michael, to strengthen them against these demonic powers. (Ephesians 6:12) Then the angel focuses our attention on the rivalry between Syria and Egypt. He begins: "And the king of the south will become strong, even one of his princes." (Daniel 11:5a)

---

4. Who alone has the power to bring peace to the earth?
5. (a) How did Jehovah use Daniel to give us information about His purpose to bring peace? (b) Why should we be concerned with this prophecy recorded by Daniel?

6. Outline the historical background of today's superpower rivalry.
7. (a) How do we know that there is an unseen, spirit dimension to human affairs? (b) Who, originally, were the king of the north and the king of the south, and how did their rivalry get started?

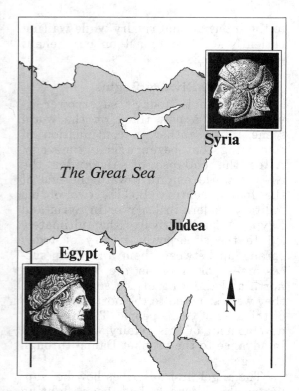

The Great Sea

Syria

Judea

Egypt

N

The king of the south here was Ptolemy I, ruler of Egypt, who captured Jerusalem about 312 B.C.E. The angel next refers to another king who "will prevail against him and will certainly rule with extensive dominion greater than that one's ruling power." (Daniel 11:5b) This is the king of the north in the person of Seleucus I Nicator, whose kingdom, Syria, became stronger than Egypt.

⁸ The angel goes on to prophesy many details of the continuing rivalry between successive rulers of Syria and Egypt. (Daniel 11:6-19) These prophecies were so accurate that some feel that the book of Daniel must have been written after the

8. What does the remarkable accuracy of the first part of the angel's prophecy about the king of the north and the king of the south mean for Christians today?

fact.* For Christians, though, the remarkable accuracy of these prophecies strengthens their faith in those parts of the prophecy yet to be fulfilled during "the final part of the days."

The Prince of the Covenant

⁹ It is not to be expected that the angel would cover every individual ruler from Ptolemy down to "the final part of the days." Rather, we understand that after verse 19 the prophecy jumps to the years immediately preceding our Common Era, when we read: "And there must stand up in his [the king of the north's] position one who is causing an exactor to pass through the splendid kingdom." (Daniel 11:20) By now, Syria is a province of Rome, and the king of the north is represented by the Roman emperor Augustus. He is the one who ordered the census that resulted in Jesus' being born in Bethlehem rather than in Nazareth.—Luke 2: 1-7; Micah 5:2.

¹⁰ After Augustus came Tiberius, a disgusting man described by the angel as "one who is to be despised." (Daniel 11:21) During his reign, a dangerous mutiny on the northern frontier of the Roman Empire was controlled and the frontier itself pacified, fulfilling the words of the prophecy: "The arms of the flood, they will be flooded over on account of him, and they will be broken." Furthermore, during his reign Jesus was killed by Roman soldiers in fulfillment of the angel's prophecy that "the Leader of the covenant" would be broken.—Daniel 11:22; 9:27.

---

* For more details, see the book "Your Will Be Done on Earth," chapter 10, published in 1958, by the Watchtower Bible and Tract Society of New York, Inc.

9. How did the action of the king of the north lead to Jesus' being born in Bethlehem?
10. What other connection between the king of the north and the Messiah did the angel draw to our attention?

At "the Time Appointed"

[11] Eventually, the prophecy brings us down to "the time appointed," in 1914. (Daniel 11:27; Luke 21:24) By now, there has been a change in the identity of God's people. Since fleshly Israel rejected the Messiah, Jehovah's chosen people has become spiritual Israel, the congregation of anointed Christians. (1 Peter 2:9, 10) The identity of the two kings has also changed. Britain, with its political partner the United States of America, has evidently become the king of the south, while the king of the north is now Germany. World War I was foretold in these words: "At the time appointed [the king of the north] will go back, and he will actually come against the south; but it will not prove to be at the last the same as at the first." (Daniel 11:29) The king of the south won that war. The situation was thus different from what was true "at the first," that is, when all-conquering Rome was king of the north.

[12] The angel goes on to tell of the competition between the two kings since 1914 and, particularly, of the way that both would oppose Jehovah's people. He also prophesies the appearance of "the disgusting thing that is causing desolation," which exists today as the United Nations organization. (Daniel 11:31) The setting up of the UN was a political effort in which both kings cooperated to bring peace. But it is doomed to fail because it is in opposition to God's Kingdom.* (Matthew 24:15; Revelation 17:3, 8) Finally, the angel directs our attention to "the time of the end."—Daniel 11:40.

"The Time of the End"

[13] What time is this? Sometimes the expression "time of the end" refers to the time of the end of this system of things, from 1914 to Armageddon. (Daniel 8:17, 19; 12:4) But events in the year 1914, "the time appointed," were foretold back in verse 29, and the angel's prophecy has brought us far beyond that.* Hence, "the time of the end" here in verse 40 must refer to the final stages of the 2,300-year-long struggle between the king of the north and the king of the south. We read on, then, with great interest, since we now learn of events to take place in the near future. By now, shifts in power on the world scene have led to further developments in the identity of the two kings. Since the collapse of the Nazi-Fascist powers at the end of World War II, we have witnessed rivalry between two superpowers, one represented as the king of the north, dominating a mostly socialistic bloc of nations, and the other represented as the king of the south, dominating a largely capitalistic bloc.

[14] The disposition of the latest king of the north is well described in verses 37, 38: "And to the God of his fathers he will give no consideration . . . But to the god of fortresses, in his position he will give glory; and to a god that his fathers did not know he will give glory by means

---

* For more information on this section of the prophecy, see *"Your Will Be Done on Earth,"* chapter 11.

* Notice, too, that in verse 35 "the time of the end" is said to be still in the future.

---

11. (a) In 1914, what was the identity of the king of the north and the king of the south? (b) What prophecy was fulfilled "at the time appointed"?
12. Describe features of world events since 1914 that were foretold in the angel's prophetic words to Daniel.

13. (a) To what does the expression "the time of the end" refer in this part of the prophecy? (b) Who have fulfilled the roles of the king of the north and the king of the south since the end of the second world war?
14. How does the angel describe the king of the north?

of gold and by means of silver and by means of precious stone and by means of desirable things." Can anyone fail to recognize this description? Today's king of the north officially promotes atheism, rejecting the religious gods of previous kings of the north. He prefers to trust in armaments, "the god of fortresses." This has contributed to a frantic arms race for which the two kings must share responsibility. Yearly defense spending by the king of the north alone reached almost 300 billion dollars in 1985. What a huge sacrifice of 'gold and silver and precious stone and desirable things' to the insatiable god of armaments!

15 So, what finally happens between these two kings? The angel says: "And in the time of the end [the end of the history of the two kings] the king of the south will engage with him in a pushing, and against him the king of the north will storm with chariots and with horsemen and with many ships." (Daniel 11:40; Matthew 24:3) Clearly, summit conferences are no solution to the superpower rivalry. The

_____
15, 16. (a) How will affairs develop between the king of the north and the king of the south? (b) What will this mean for God's people?

> **Can You Explain?**
>
> □ What spirit entities have been involved in human political affairs?
>
> □ Who were the king of the north and the king of the south in 1914?
>
> □ How does today's king of the north worship the god of fortresses?
>
> □ What pressure will be brought on God's people by the king of the north?
>
> □ What will finally happen to the king of the north?

---

tensions caused by the 'pushing' of the king of the south and the expansionism of the king of the north may go through more or less intense phases; but eventually, in some way, the king of the north will be provoked into the excessively violent action described by Daniel.*

16 These final days are especially difficult for God's people, who during this century have been persecuted by both kings. The angel warned that the king of the north "will also actually enter into the land of the Decoration, and there will be many lands that will be made to stumble." "The land of the Decoration" is symbolically the land of God's people. The angel's words must mean, then, that as well as conquering many nations, the king of the north attacks the spiritual estate of Jehovah's people. (Daniel 8:9; 11:41-44; Ezekiel 20:6) In verse 45, the prophecy adds: "And he will plant his palatial tents between the grand sea and the holy mountain of Decoration." In other words, he positions himself to make a final assault against their spiritual paradise.

"All the Way to His End"

17 But by then something will already have happened that neither the king of the north nor the king of the south foresaw. The angel prophesies: "But there will be reports that will disturb [the king of the north], out of the sunrising and out of the north, and he will certainly go forth in a great rage in order to annihilate and to devote many to destruction."—Daniel 11:44.

18 What will these reports be? The angel does not specify, but he does reveal their

_____
* See "Your Will Be Done on Earth," pages 298-303.

17. What unexpected development will provoke the king of the north?
18. (a) What is the source of the "reports" foretold by the angel? (b) What will be the final outcome for the king of the north?

source. They come "out of the sunrising," and Jehovah God and Jesus Christ are alluded to as "the kings from the rising of the sun." (Revelation 16:12) These reports also come "out of the north," and the Bible speaks symbolically of Mount Zion, the town of the grand King Jehovah, as being "on the remote sides of the north." (Psalm 48:2) Hence, it is "reports" from Jehovah God and Jesus Christ that send the king of the north on his last great campaign. But the results will be devastating to him. The end of verse 45 tells us: "He will have to come all the way to his end, and there will be no helper for him."

19 Indeed, there will be "no peace . . . for

---

19. (a) What will be the different outcomes for this world and for "upright" ones? (b) What questions remain to be answered?

the wicked ones." (Isaiah 57:21) Rather, the history of the king of the north will be marked by warfare right up to the end. But for His faithful servants, Jehovah promises: "The upright are the ones that will reside in the earth, and the blameless are the ones that will be left over in it. As regards the wicked, they will be cut off from the very earth." (Proverbs 2:21, 22) What, though, will happen to the king of the south when the king of the north 'comes all the way to his end'? What will happen to Christians when the king of the north 'plants his palatial tents' in a menacing position against them? (Daniel 11: 45) How will peace finally come to the earth? Jehovah, through his angel, has answered these questions, as we will see in the following articles.

Michael the Great Prince Stands Up

> "And during that time Michael will stand up, the great prince who is standing in behalf of the sons of your people."—DANIEL 12:1.

JEHOVAH has given fair warning: There will never be peace on earth as long as the rivalry between the king of the north and the king of the south continues. These two powers would always have conflicting interests. Moreover, at the climax of their enmity, the king of the north will threaten the spiritual estate of God's people before he 'comes all the way to his end.' (Daniel 11:44, 45) Will God's people

---

1. What future course of world events is foreseen in the Bible, and what question arises about God's people because of this?

survive the assault? And what happens to the king of the south when his great rival comes to his end?

2 A prophecy by Daniel's contemporary Ezekiel helps us to answer these questions. Ezekiel, too, was inspired to speak about "the final part of the days," and he

---

2, 3. (a) What prophecy do we find in the book of Ezekiel that helps us to understand the prophecy about the king of the north and the king of the south? (b) According to Ezekiel's prophecy, what will be the outcome of the great final attack on God's people?

A last desperate attempt to wipe out God's people will fail —but how?

warned of a coming attack of 'Gog of Magog' against the land of God's people. (Ezekiel 38:2, 14-16; Daniel 10:14) In that prophecy, Gog pictured Satan, and his armies pictured all of Satan's earthly agents who would make a last, desperate attempt to wipe out God's people. Since this attack, like that of the king of the north, takes place in the final part of the days, it is reasonable to conclude that the king of the north's 'planting of his palatial tents between the grand sea and the holy mountain of Decoration' is in support of Gog's attack. (Daniel 11:40, 45) Will the attack succeed?

[3] Ezekiel prophesied: "'It must occur in that day, in the day when Gog comes in upon the soil of Israel,' is the utterance of the Sovereign Lord Jehovah, 'that my rage will come up into my nose. And I will bring myself into judgment with him, with pestilence and with blood; and a flooding downpour and hailstones, fire and sulphur I shall rain down upon him and upon his bands and upon the many peoples that will be with him.'" (Ezekiel 38:18, 22) No, the attack will not succeed. True

Christians will be rescued, and Gog's crowd will be destroyed.—Ezekiel 39:11.

[4] Evidently, then, the time of the end of the king of the north is the time of the end for Gog and all his crowd, including the king of the south. This harmonizes with other prophecies in the book of Daniel. For example, we read that after God's Kingdom was established, it would "crush and put an end to *all* these kingdoms [including both the king of the north and the king of the south], and it itself will stand to times indefinite." (Daniel 2:44) Also, in Daniel's vision of the ram and the he-goat, the Anglo-American political power is represented by a little horn. This little horn, "in the final part of their kingdom," is destroyed by a superhuman agency, not by the king of the north: "It will be without [human] hand that he will be broken." —Daniel 7:24-27; 8:3-10, 20-25.

---

4. Will the king of the south survive the end of the king of the north? What other prophecies support this answer?

Michael the Great Prince

⁵ The angel next reveals the Agent that Jehovah will use to bring about the end of all these powers. He says: "And during that time Michael will stand up, the great prince who is standing in behalf of the sons of your people. And there will certainly occur a time of distress such as has not been made to occur since there came to be a nation until that time. And during that time your people will escape, every one who is found written down in the book." (Daniel 12:1) At the beginning of the angel's prophecy, Michael was reported as fighting for Israel against the princes of Persia and Greece. (Daniel 10: 20, 21) Now, as the prophecy draws to a close, this same Michael is "standing" for Daniel's people. Who is this champion of the people of God?

⁶ Back in the early 1800's, Bible scholar Joseph Benson stated that the description of Michael as found in the Bible "manifestly points out the Messiah." Nineteenth-century Lutheran E. W. Hengstenberg agreed that "Michael is no other than Christ." Similarly, theologian J. P. Lange, when commenting on Revelation 12:7, wrote: "We take it that Michael . . . is, from the outset, Christ in warlike array against Satan." Does the Bible support this identification? Yes, it does.*

⁷ For example, according to the angel, Michael is to "stand up." In the angel's prophecy, "to stand" or "to stand up" (He-

---

* Since Michael is called an archangel, some feel that identifying him as Jesus detracts in some way from Jesus' dignity or rank. (Jude 9) Yet, the evidence for such an identification led the above-mentioned scholars of Christendom to recognize Michael as Jesus despite the fact that they presumably believed in the Trinity.

---

5. Who will be Jehovah's Chief Agent for the salvation of His people, and why is this fitting?
6, 7. (a) According to some scholars of Christendom, who is Michael? (b) What Biblical evidence helps us to make a proper identification of Michael?

brew, 'a·madh') can mean "to give support." (Daniel 11:1) It can also variously imply "to prevail," "to rebel," "to oppose," or "to withstand." (Daniel 11:6, 11, 14, 15, 16a, 17, 25) But frequently, it refers to the action of a king, either taking up his royal power or acting effectively in his capacity as king. (Daniel 11:2-4, 7, 16b, 20, 21, 25) This is the meaning that fits best the angel's words in Daniel 12:1. And it certainly supports the fact that Michael is Jesus Christ, since Jesus is Jehovah's appointed King, commissioned to destroy all the nations at Armageddon. (Revelation 11:15; 16:14-16; 19:11-16) It also harmonizes with the other prophecies that point to the time when God's Kingdom, under Jesus Christ, acts against this world's nations.—Daniel 2:44; 7:13, 14, 26, 27.

⁸ Michael has long been associated with 'Daniel's people,' the Israelites. He was with them in the wilderness, and he supported them against the spirit "princes" of ancient empires. (Daniel 10:13, 21; Exodus 23:20, 21; Jude 9) And he was born on earth as the man Jesus to be the long-hoped-for Messiah, the "seed" promised to Daniel's ancestor Abraham. (Genesis 22: 16-18; Galatians 3:16; Acts 2:36) Sadly, natural Israel as a whole rejected Jesus; hence, Jehovah rejected them as his special nation. (Matthew 21:43; John 1:11) He determined to put his name on a new nation, a spiritual "Israel of God," made up of both natural Jews and non-Jews who put faith in Jesus.—Galatians 6:16; Acts 15:14; 1 Peter 2:9, 10.

⁹ This new nation, the anointed Christian congregation, began life in 33 C.E., and thereafter it served as the Israel of God. This would henceforth be 'Daniel's people.' (Romans 2:28, 29) Before his

---

8, 9. (a) Who were 'Daniel's people' originally, and who are they now? (b) How has Michael's keen interest in 'Daniel's people' been shown throughout the ages?

resurrection to heaven in 33 C.E., Jesus promised continued support for 'Daniel's people' when he told prospective members of that new Israel: "Look! I am with you all the days until the conclusion of the system of things."—Matthew 28: 20; Ephesians 5:23, 25-27.

"Standing" for Daniel's People

¹⁰ But now the angel says that Michael is going to act in a particular way. Using the word 'stand' twice, he says: "And during that time Michael will *stand* up, the great prince who *is standing* in behalf of the sons of your people." (Daniel 12:1) What does it mean that Jesus 'stands up'? And how can he "stand up" if he is already "standing in behalf of [Daniel's] people"? Before we answer these questions, consider some background information.

¹¹ After his resurrection in 33 C.E., Jesus

Salvation will come to God's people when Michael 'stands up' to end the rivalry of the two kings

told his followers: "All authority has been given me in heaven and on the earth." (Matthew 28:18) Jesus has long exercised such authority over his anointed servants on earth. (Colossians 1:13) However, the time had not yet come for Jesus to exercise authority as King of God's Kingdom. Rather, after his ascension he 'sat at God's right hand in heaven' until the time for the establishment of that Kingdom. (Psalm 110: 1, 2; Acts 2:34, 35) That time came in 1914, "the time appointed." (Daniel 11:29) In that year, Jesus was enthroned as reigning King of God's Kingdom and immediately, as Michael the archangel, he cast Satan out of heaven. (Revelation 11:15; 12:5-9) So since 1914 Jesus has been "standing" as King.—Psalm 2:6.

¹² Jesus' "standing" has been a great blessing for 'the sons of Daniel's people.' His taking up of royal power and casting Satan to the earth cleansed their fu-

---

10. According to the angel's words to Daniel, how is Michael going to act decisively, and what questions does this raise?

11. In what way would it be proper to say that Jesus has been "standing" since 1914?

12, 13. What outstanding blessings have God's people enjoyed in the years since 1914, showing that Jesus has been 'standing for Daniel's people'?

ture heavenly home. (John 14:2, 3) Thereafter, those who had already died faithful could be resurrected to their heavenly inheritance. (1 Thessalonians 4:16, 17) The remnant of them still on earth suffered considerable persecution during the first world war, which almost stopped their preaching work. But in 1919 they were resuscitated and brought forth on the world scene as a new nation.—Isaiah 66: 7, 8; Revelation 9:14; 11:11, 12.

13 After that, Jesus fulfilled his promise to "collect out from his kingdom all things that cause stumbling and persons who are doing lawlessness." (Matthew 13:41) In this way, he has maintained a clean congregation of anointed Christians who have 'known their God, prevailed, and acted effectively.' They have preached the good news of the Kingdom around the earth, thus 'imparting understanding to the many.' (Daniel 11:32, 33; Matthew 24:14) Since 1935 Jehovah has joined to this congregation a growing number of "other sheep," who entertain an earthly hope and who have faithfully shared in the work of preaching the good news of God's Kingdom.—John 10:16; Revelation 7:9, 14, 15.

14 The very existence of this group of Christians today is remarkable. In a politically divided world, they have maintained strict neutrality as subjects of God's Kingdom. (John 17:14) As a result, they have suffered persecution at the hands of both kings. False religion, too, has schemed and plotted to have them wiped out of existence. Instead of that happening, they have prospered and today are found in more than 200 lands and number well over three million faithful individuals. They enjoy a spiritual paradise under Christ's rule that is in stark contrast to the darkness and despondency of this world. (Isa-

iah 65:13, 14) Thus, Jesus has been "standing in behalf of the sons of [Daniel's] people" all throughout these last days.—Daniel 12:1.

Michael 'Stands Up'

15 So how is it that Jesus, who is already "standing," 'stands up' at that time? (Daniel 12:1) In that his rulership enters a new phase, as it were. It is time for him to act in an outstanding way to save 'Daniel's people' from annihilation at the hands of human governments. (Ezekiel 38:18, 19) The "time" referred to here is evidently "the time of the end" of the king of the north and the king of the south, when the king of the north threatens the spiritual estate of God's people. (Daniel 11:40-45) Before this time, Jesus' rulership has been taken seriously only by his faithful earthly subjects. (Psalm 2:2, 3) Now, though, it is time for "the revelation of the Lord Jesus," when everyone will be forced to recognize his kingship. (2 Thessalonians 1:7, 8) This will involve the destruction of all opposing forces, followed by the Thousand Year Reign of Jesus and his corulers, when the Kingdom will be the only government over mankind.—Revelation 19:19-21; 20:4.

16 In agreement with this, the angel says that when Michael stands up, "there will certainly occur a time of distress such as has not been made to occur since there came to be a nation until that time." (Daniel 12:1; compare Matthew 24:21.) It will be a time for the destruction of the wicked and salvation for the faithful. (Proverbs 2: 21, 22) Listen to the terrified reaction of unfaithful mankind at that time: "They keep saying to the mountains and to the rock-masses: 'Fall over us and hide us

14. What has been the result of Jesus' 'standing for Daniel's people' throughout the last days?

15. In what way does Jesus "stand up," and when does this occur?
16. What is the result of Jesus' 'standing up' to the ungodly nations?

from the face of the One seated on the throne and from the wrath of the Lamb, because the great day of their wrath has come, and who is able to stand?'"—Revelation 6:16, 17.

17 The result of this "time of distress" on Satan's earthly forces is described in Ezekiel's prophecy against Gog of Magog: "On the mountains of Israel you will fall, you and all your bands and the peoples that will be with you." (Ezekiel 39:4) Jeremiah, speaking of the same time of distress, said: "Those slain by Jehovah will certainly come to be in that day from one end of the earth clear to the other end of the earth." (Jeremiah 25:33) It will be a time of distress indeed. Jesus will end the long history of human warfare when he 'stands up' to remove the human powers that are responsible.—Psalm 46:9; 1 Corinthians 15:25.

Survivors of "a Time of Distress"

18 While God's people will feel the effects of enemy hostility, this will be "a time of distress" primarily for the wicked. (Psalm 37:20) The angel tells Daniel: "And during that time your people will escape, every one who is found written down in the book." (Daniel 12:1) Many of 'the sons of Daniel's people' will have died and received their heavenly reward by this time. These ones will undoubtedly share with Michael in this great military victory. (Revelation 2:26, 27; Psalm 2:8, 9) The ones remaining on earth will have no share in the fighting; but they will be integrity keepers, so they will be survivors. (Revelation 17:14; 19:7, 8) Their companions, the "great crowd," too, will

be survivors. (Revelation 7:9, 14) Both the anointed remnant and the "other sheep" will thus prove to be "found written down in the book," that is, their names will be on record as being in line to receive the gift of eternal life, either in heaven or on earth.—John 10:16; Exodus 32:32, 33; Malachi 3:16; Revelation 3:5.

19 These will be privileged to see the establishment of a genuine earth-wide peace. They will witness the fulfillment of Jehovah's promise: "For evildoers themselves will be cut off, but those hoping in Jehovah are the ones that will possess the earth." (Psalm 37:9) Because God's Kingdom will then be the sole government over the earth, every human alive will be a servant of Jehovah. (Isaiah 11:9) Thus, at "the time of the end" of the two kings, Michael "will stand up" to bring peace to mankind. No superpower arms buildup or other maneuvers can stop this development. Does that mean, though, that we have to wait until then to enjoy peace? No, there is a peace that Christians can enjoy even now—really, a better kind of peace than the mere absence of war. What is this peace? The angel's prophecy to Daniel goes on to shed light on this.

19. (a) How will Michael's 'standing up' bring peace to the earth? (b) What question remains to be answered?

17. What will then happen to Satan's earthly forces, including the king of the north and the king of the south?
18. (a) What will be the experience of true worshipers when Michael 'stands up'? (b) What does it mean to be "written down in the book"?

Do You Remember?

☐ Who is Michael the Great Prince?

☐ Who are Daniel's people today?

☐ How is Michael now standing for Daniel's people?

☐ How will Michael soon stand up in an outstanding way?

☐ Who will survive the time of Michael's standing up?

Divine Blessings for "the Ones Having Insight"

"The ones having insight will shine like the brightness of the expanse; and those who are bringing the many to righteousness, like the stars to time indefinite, even forever."—DANIEL 12:3.

THE angel's prophecy to Daniel has brought us all the way from the fourth century B.C.E. to Armageddon. It has shown that Michael will bring peace to the earth in the only possible way: by destroying the warmongers. Now, after such a remarkable survey of history in advance, the angel foretells some of the rich blessings enjoyed by God's people "in the final part of the days."—Daniel 10:14.

A Time of Resurrections

2 The angel tells Daniel: "And there will be many of those asleep in the ground of dust who will wake up, these to indefinitely lasting life and those to reproaches and to indefinitely lasting abhorrence." (Daniel 12:2) Evidently, "the final part of the days" is a time for resurrections, of raising those "asleep in the ground of dust." One such awakening began soon after Jesus became King in 1914. (Matthew 24:3) Looking forward to that time, the apostle Paul wrote: "We the living who survive to the presence of the Lord shall in no way precede those who have fallen asleep in death . . . Those who are dead in union with Christ will rise first." (1 Thessalonians 4:15, 16; Revelation 6:9-11) Evidently, then, soon after 1914 Jesus raised

to spirit life in the heavens those of "the Israel of God" who had already died faithful. (Galatians 6:16) For them, the awakening was to "indefinitely lasting life."

3 But the angel's words undoubtedly include another resurrection. For about 40 years preceding 1914, a small group of Christians had been warning that that year would mark the end of the Gentile Times as prophesied by Jesus. (Luke 21: 24) These Christians had Zion's Watch Tower Tract Society incorporated in 1884, and they published the results of their Bible research in a journal called *Zion's Watch Tower and Herald of Christ's Presence*.

4 In 1914 the truth of their message was dramatically confirmed when the first world war broke out, and the "pangs of distress" foretold by Jesus began. (Matthew 24:7, 8) Nevertheless, their religious enemies used the war hysteria to persecute them until finally, in 1918, their preaching work was virtually stopped, and principal servants of the Watch Tower Society were unjustly imprisoned. This caused great rejoicing in some quarters. It also fulfilled the prophecy recorded in the book of Revelation: "And when they have finished their witnessing, the wild beast that ascends out of the abyss will make war with them and conquer them and kill them."—Revelation 11:7.

---

1. After describing the time of distress on the warmongers, to what does the angel next turn his attention?
2. How did some dead ones "wake up" during "the final part of the days"?

3, 4. How did a group of faithful servants of God come to be 'dead' in 1918?

⁵ According to the prophecy, however, they were not to stay 'dead.' "And after the three and a half days spirit of life from God entered into them, and they stood upon their feet, and great fear fell upon those beholding them. . . . And they went up into heaven in the cloud, and their enemies beheld them." (Revelation 11: 11, 12; Ezekiel 37:1-14) Their resurrection was evidently a symbolical one, since a literal resurrection to spirit life in heaven would have been invisible to their enemies. Rather, they were resurrected from a deathlike state of inactivity to a vibrant state of zealous activity in full view of those who had schemed their end. In 1919 the representatives of the Watch Tower Society were released from prison, the preaching work was reorganized, and the world saw the beginning of the greatest Kingdom witnessing campaign in history. —Matthew 24:14.

⁶ In this symbolical sense, 'many of those asleep in the dust of the ground woke up.' Then, starting in 1919, that small, awakened body of Bible Students began to seek out and gather the remaining ones of Jesus' brothers so that the full number of the 144,000 could be sealed. (Matthew 24:31; Revelation 7:1-3) As individuals responded, they dedicated themselves to God through Christ and became members of Jehovah's visible organization on earth. Receiving the free gift of holy spirit, they were declared righteous on the basis of their faith in Jesus' ransom sacrifice and were adopted as sons of God in a spiritual way.—Romans 8:16; Galatians 2:17; 3:8.

⁷ Those of them who remain faithful to the end of their earthly lives have the firm prospect of taking their place in heaven alongside Jesus Christ. (1 Corinthians 15: 50-53) Thus, their spiritual awakening is to everlasting life. While still alive on earth, they experience peace among themselves even though living in a warring world. (Romans 14:19) But more importantly, they enjoy peace with Jehovah God himself, "the peace of God that excels all thought."—Philippians 4:7.

Awakening "to Reproaches"

⁸ Why, then, do some "wake up . . . to reproaches and to indefinitely lasting abhorrence"? The fact is, not all those who accept the invitation to be part of that Kingdom class stay faithful. Some let their faith weaken and they fail to endure. (Hebrews 2:1) A few even become apostate and have to be removed from the Christian congregation. (Matthew 13:41, 42) Such ones are described by Jesus as "that evil slave" whom the Master punishes "with the greatest severity," assigning him with the hypocrites. "There is where his weeping and the gnashing of his teeth will be."—Matthew 24:48-51; Ephesians 4:18; 5:6-8.

⁹ What a tragedy, to accept the highest privilege ever offered to imperfect humans and then to turn against it! Of those who act in this way, the apostle Paul said: "It is impossible as regards those who have once for all been enlightened, and who have tasted the heavenly free gift, and who have become partakers of holy spirit, and who have tasted the fine word of God and powers of the coming system of things, but who have fallen away, to revive them again to repentance, because they impale the Son of God afresh for themselves and expose him to public shame." (Hebrews 6:4-6) In this way, their

5, 6. How did this group's experiences in 1919 provide a fulfillment of the prophecy that "many of those asleep in the ground of dust . . . will wake up"?
7. For many of these, how will this prove to be an awakening "to indefinitely lasting life"?

8, 9. In what way could this spiritual awakening be "to reproaches and to indefinitely lasting abhorrence"?

awakening turns out to be "to reproaches and to indefinitely lasting abhorrence." They have no further prospect of everlasting life.

"Shining as Illuminators"

10 But for those who remain faithful, the prophecy says: "And the ones having insight will shine like the brightness of the expanse; and those who are bringing the many to righteousness, like the stars to time indefinite, even forever." (Daniel 12:3) "The ones having insight" are clearly the faithful remaining members of the anointed Christian congregation, who are 'filled with accurate knowledge of his will in all wisdom and spiritual comprehension.' Strengthened by Jehovah, they 'endure fully and are long-suffering with joy, thanking the Father who rendered them suitable for their participation in the inheritance of the holy ones in the light.' (Colossians 1:9, 11, 12) Ever since 1919, though 'darkness itself covers the earth, and thick gloom the national groups,' they have been "shining as illuminators" among mankind. (Isaiah 60:2; Philippians 2:15; Matthew 5:14-16) They "shine as brightly as the sun in the kingdom of their Father."—Matthew 13:43.

11 How do they prove to be "those who are bringing the many to righteousness"? (Daniel 12:3) Thanks to their faithful witnessing, the final ones of spiritual Israel have been gathered in and declared righteous for life in the heavens. Additionally, a great crowd of "other sheep" has manifested itself, flocking to the light from Jehovah as reflected by 'Daniel's people.' (John 10:16; Zechariah 8:23) These "other sheep" have willingly joined with the

Since 1919 those having insight have been shining forth life-giving truth

NASA photo

anointed in their work of preaching the "good news." (Matthew 24:14; Isaiah 61: 5, 6) They, too, exercise faith in the shed blood of Jesus Christ, so that they are declared righteous to enjoy friendship with God. (Revelation 7:9-15; compare James 2:23.) If they remain faithful to the end, their names will continue to be "found written down in the book." Thus, they may expect to survive the most calamitous time of distress ever to strike the nations.—Daniel 12:1; Matthew 24: 13, 21, 22.

"They Will Shine . . . Forever"

12 The angel told Daniel: "The ones having insight will shine like the brightness

10. Who are "the ones having insight," and how do they 'shine as illuminators'?
11. In what way have "the ones having insight" proved to be "those who are bringing the many to righteousness"?

12, 13. (a) How is it that "the ones having insight" are able to "shine . . . forever"? (b) How, in another way, will they prove to be "those who are bringing the many to righteousness"?

of the expanse . . . , like the stars to time indefinite, even forever." (Daniel 12:3) How can the anointed ones shine forever, since each one will eventually die? In that they will continue to "shine" even after death. Describing them in their heavenly position, Jesus tells us in the book of Revelation: "The throne of God and of the Lamb will be in the city, and his slaves will render him sacred service; and they will see his face, and his name will be on their foreheads. Also, night will be no more, and they have no need of lamplight nor do they have sunlight, because Jehovah God will shed light upon them, and they will rule as kings forever and ever." —Revelation 22:3-5.

13 Yes, these resurrected ones will rule as kings like stars in the heavens, "forever and ever." Their spiritual brilliance will bring great blessings to mankind. (Revelation 14:13) Describing them as the "New Jerusalem," the book of Revelation reports: "And the city has no need of the sun nor of the moon to shine upon it, for the glory of God lighted it up, and its lamp was the Lamb. And the nations will walk by means of its light, and the kings of the earth will bring their glory into it." (Revelation 21:2, 9, 23, 24) The resurrected ones will assist in applying the benefits of the ransom sacrifice "for the curing of the nations." (Revelation 22:2) When, by the end of the Thousand Year Reign, Jesus and his 144,000 associate kings and priests have restored faithful humans to perfection, they will indeed have brought "many to righteousness." After the final test at that time, restored mankind will form a perfect human society living on a paradise earth for eternity. (Revelation 20:7-10; Psalm 37:29) In this way, the visible results of the heavenly glory of 'Daniel's people' will also last "to time indefinite, even forever."

Another Resurrection

14 Thus, the angel's words take us beyond the time of Michael's 'standing up' and the unparalleled "time of distress" right into the new system of things. Moreover, the blessings channeled through these ones shining "like the stars" will not be limited to those who survive the "time of distress." Jesus, while still a man on earth, said: "The hour is coming in which all those in the memorial tombs will hear his voice and come out, those who did good things to a resurrection of life, those who practiced vile things to a resurrection of judgment." (John 5:28, 29) These words point to a literal resurrection of dead mankind, and doubtless this resurrection, too, is an extended fulfillment of the angel's words: "Many of those asleep in the ground of dust . . . will wake up."—Daniel 12:2.

15 Among those included in this particular awakening will be Daniel himself. He was told by the angel: "As for you yourself, go toward the end; and you will rest [fall asleep in death], but you will stand up for your lot at the end of the days." (Daniel 12:13) Those like Daniel who are resurrected then and who respond to the ministry of Jesus and his brothers from heaven will be raised to human perfection. When they pass the final test, they will have their names permanently inscribed in the book of life. (Revelation 20:5) For them, too, the awakening will be "to indefinitely lasting life."

16 Not all will so respond, however. Some will doubtless try to bring back the prac-

14. The prophecy that "many of those asleep in the ground of dust . . . will wake up" will come to include who else?
15. For those resurrected then, how can it prove to be an awakening "to indefinitely lasting life"?
16. For whom will the awakening in the new system of things prove to be "to indefinitely lasting abhorrence"?

tices that have robbed man of peace for so long. Such ones have fair warning in the Bible: "As for the cowards and those without faith and those who are disgusting in their filth and murderers and fornicators and those practicing spiritism and idolaters and all the liars, their portion will be in the lake that burns with fire and sulphur. This means the second death." (Revelation 21:8) This "second death" is a direct judgment from Jehovah from which there is no resurrection. It is eternal, unending oblivion. Those resurrected who prove to be unappreciative will suffer this second death; hence, their awakening will be "to reproaches and to indefinitely lasting abhorrence."—Daniel 12:2.

"True Knowledge Will Become Abundant"

17 The angel then offers words of counsel to Daniel: "And as for you, O Daniel, make secret the words and seal up the book, until the time of the end. Many will rove about, and the true knowledge will become abundant." (Daniel 12:4) These words arrest our attention. Although the angel's prophecy concerning the two kings began to be fulfilled some 2,300 years ago, the understanding of it has been opened up primarily during "the time of the end," particularly since 1919. In these days, "many . . . rove about" in the Bible, and true knowledge has indeed become abundant. Now is the time that Jehovah has given knowledge to understanding ones.

18 The fact that several features of the prophecy were fulfilled many centuries ago serves to strengthen our faith in the parts of the prophecy that have yet to take

place. (Joshua 23:14) The world today is engaged in a tug-of-war between the king of the north and the king of the south, just as the angel foretold. Moreover, the prophecy warns of even more dangerous times ahead. So we are helped to keep our balance and avoid being swayed by the propaganda of either king. This is the time to strengthen our trust in Jehovah. Never forget that "Michael . . . the great prince" is "standing" for God's people. Our only sure salvation is in submitting to God's Kingdom under Christ Jesus.—Acts 4:12; Philippians 2:9-11.

19 Stay close, then, to "the ones having insight," who are 'shining like the brightness of the expanse.' Stay active in working for God's Kingdom. (1 Corinthians 15:58; Romans 15:5, 6) Deepen your love of the truth of God's Word, and treasure deeply the peace that exists even now in God's organization. (Psalm 119:165; Ephesians 4:1-3; Philippians 2:1-5) Then, when Michael 'stands up' to crush Jehovah's enemies, may you escape, along with all of God's people whose names are "found written down in the book."

19. What significance do the angel's words to Daniel have for each one of us?

17. How do we know that the prophecy about the king of the north and the king of the south was recorded mainly for our benefit today?
18. (a) What major parts of the prophecy are now being fulfilled or about to be fulfilled? (b) What balanced attitude does this give us?

Can You Answer?

□ In what way has there been an awakening already of "many of those asleep in the ground"?

□ How could this 'waking up' turn out to be "to reproaches"?

□ How do "the ones having insight" shine as illuminators and bring many to righteousness?

□ What future fulfillment will there be as to the waking up of 'those asleep in the ground'?

□ How is Daniel 12:4 fulfilled?

Staying Close to Jehovah's Organization

As told by John Barr

I WAS on the last leg of a visit home a year ago last June, flying from Glasgow to Aberdeen. As our plane climbed steeply over the green Scottish countryside and on over the lazily flowing river Clyde, my thoughts raced back to the year 1906 and that little village of Bishopton, nestled somewhere down there to the south of the river.

You see, that was the year and place when my grandmother, Emily Jewell, started to read Charles T. Russell's book *The Divine Plan of the Ages.* Immediately her eyes were opened to the truth that the Bible does not teach the doctrine of hellfire. Soon her two grown daughters Bessie and Emily (the latter became my mother) also began to see the light of truth shining through the mists of false doctrine taught by the United Free Church of Scotland. In 1908 Granny was baptized in symbol of her dedication to do God's will, and her daughters were baptized shortly afterward.

My father was the session clerk in the same United Free Church in Bishopton. He had always found it difficult to accept the doctrine of the Trinity, so the church minister offered to preach a special sermon for his benefit one Sunday. That did it! On hearing the attempted explanation, my father was now convinced that the Trinity doctrine was false. He resigned from the church and was baptized in 1912 in symbol of his dedication to Jehovah. Shortly afterward my parents moved north to Aberdeen with their two children, Louie and James, and I was born there in 1913.

My thoughts about those early years and about my parents' efforts to bring us three children up "in the discipline and mental-regulating of Jehovah" stayed with me as the plane began its descent over the hills, rivers, and valleys that I had known from childhood. (Ephesians 6:4) On this beautiful sunny morning, how grateful I felt to Jehovah for that parental training! I knew that it had contributed toward my always remaining close to Jehovah's organization.

Value of Early Training

Our family was always a happily united one. If ever Father and Mother had some difference of viewpoint, they tried never to show this in front of us children. This created for us not only respect for our parents but also an environment of real peace and security within our home.

Some of my fondest memories center

around our family get-togethers in the evenings. We supplied our own entertainment, doing such things as singing to our own musical accompaniment and playing together board games such as Monopoly. Also, no matter how busy Father was, he never failed to spend some time with us practically every day, reading aloud from the Bible and the Watch Tower publications, as well as from other literature both of a light and of a more serious kind. All these things served to keep our family close together as we grew up.

We were the only "truth" family in that northern part of Scotland in those early years. As a result, our home became well known to many of the Watch Tower Society's traveling representatives (pilgrims, as they were then called), such as Albert Lloyd, Herbert Senior, and Fred Scott. Some even came from the Society's headquarters in Brooklyn, New York, including W. E. Van Amburgh and A. H. Macmillan. These visits were milestones in my early years.

To this day I feel thankful for the genuine spirit of hospitality shown by my parents. This enriched our family life, and although young I began to widen out in my appreciation for the whole association of brothers. Oh, how much parents can do toward cultivating a warm bond of love between their children and the worldwide association of their brothers!

Coping With a Personal Problem

As I entered my early teens, I became an increasingly shy and retiring boy. The older I grew, the more difficult I found it to meet people and make conversation with them. This shyness presented a big obstacle in many ways but especially so when it came to proving my faith by preaching the good news of the Kingdom.

Shortly after World War I, my grandmother and my mother became the first Witnesses in Aberdeen to take part in the house-to-house ministry. We children shared in distributing tracts, but now for me actually to talk to people at their homes —why, that was something different! That was a real challenge. But I finally met it. I shall never forget that Sunday afternoon in November 1927 when I told my father that I was going to accompany him in the door-to-door ministry. It was the first time ever that I saw tears on my father's cheeks —tears of joy in this case!

Family Tragedy Affected Me

The peaceful tranquillity of our family life was shattered on the evening of June 25, 1929, when I was 16. After a day in the ministry, my mother and my sister were hurrying home to prepare Father's supper. Suddenly, a speeding motorcycle hit Mother, dragging her along the street for about 40 yards (37 m). Her head injuries were so severe that she was not expected to live. But thanks to many months of loving care by my sister Louie, she survived. In time, Mother was able to lead a comparatively normal life until her death in 1952.

That traumatic experience did something very important for me—it made me take a serious look at my life and what I was doing with it. That summer I started to study the Bible far more deeply than previously—I made the truth my own. This was the big turning point for me, and I dedicated my life to Jehovah's service. However, it was not until some years later that I had the opportunity of symbolizing my dedication by water baptism.

Entering the Full-Time Service

On leaving school in 1932, I embarked on a course of training in mechanical and electrical engineering. In Britain in those days, there was not the encouragement that there is today for young ones to enter the full-time preaching work as pioneers.

John Barr (front left) about the year 1930, with his sister, brother, and parents

came by means of a surprise letter from the Society's headquarters in London, asking me to consider becoming a member of the Bethel family. I eagerly grasped the opportunity to go through that large door leading to greater privileges of service. Thus, in April 1939 I found myself working alongside Harold King, who later served as a missionary in China and, because of his preaching activity, spent years in a communist prison. We worked on assembling transcription machines and also phonographs used for playing recorded sermons at the doors of people's homes.

Harold and I would imagine all the different kinds of people who eventually would listen to the Kingdom message by means of the equipment we were making. In this way we never lost sight of the end result of our work. Since then, in all the different assignments I have received at Bethel, I have endeavored to keep this outlook. This has made my work a real joy and always meaningful in relation to the Kingdom-preaching work.

Privileges of Service

Shortly after arriving at London Bethel, I was appointed as company servant (now called presiding overseer) of a congregation with well over 200 publishers. Previously, I had been the overseer of a congregation of only ten publishers! Then I was put in charge of the Sound Department for a marvelous countrywide convention held in Leicester in 1941. Up to this time, I had had only limited experience in sound.

Later I was assigned to the traveling work as a servant to the brethren, now called circuit overseer. There were only six such servants in Britain when that work was started in January 1943. My assignment was to be only for a month, but it ended up with my visiting the congregations for more than three years. During those same difficult World War II years, I

Yet, as the years went on, I knew where I ought to be expending my energies—in the full-time ministry.

I vividly recall something we studied early in 1938 that emphasized to me the benefits of staying close to Jehovah's organization and personally applying its instructions. It was the *Watchtower* magazine issues regarding Jonah that explained the experiences he went through in running away from his assignment of service. I took this lesson very much to heart, making up my mind that I must never turn down any assignment that came to me through Jehovah's organization. Little did I realize then how many theocratic assignments lay ahead to test my resolve.

I prayed for guidance, and the answer

had the oversight of three large conventions—something I had never done previously.

The traveling work in those days was quite different from what it is today. We were always on the move, and travel throughout Britain during those war years was sometimes very difficult. On more than one occasion, I had to resort to a bicycle for part of the journey between congregations. Instead of visiting one congregation a week, as traveling overseers do today, if congregations were small, we would visit as many as six of them in one week!

Here was a typical day's schedule: Up at five-thirty; after breakfast, travel to the next congregation so as to start checking the congregation's records by eight o'clock. The afternoon was usually spent in the field ministry, this being followed in the evening by a one-hour meeting with the servants of the congregation and then a talk to the congregation. I was seldom in bed before 11, or even later if I wrote up the day's report on the congregation that same evening. Every Monday was set aside for completing the reports for the week, for personal study, and for any preparatory work for the following week.

'A very busy week's schedule,' you say? Yes, it was, but, oh, how rewarding to feel that we were strengthening the brothers during those war years when there was not always the same close contact with the organization! In a very literal sense, we had the satisfaction of feeling that we were helping the congregations "to be made firm in the faith."—Acts 16:5.

Back to Bethel Service

I was asked to return to Bethel service in April 1946. I was happy to do so, but I felt that my life had been enriched spiritually as a result of those three and a half years in the traveling work. The organization meant more to me now, and I felt as if I had been doing what is described at Psalm 48:12, 13: "March around Zion, you people, and go about it, count its towers. . . . Inspect its dwelling towers." Having moved about more among God's people had caused my love to grow for "the whole association of brothers."—1 Peter 2:17.

Following my return to Bethel, I was privileged to care for much of the printing done at our London printery and later was involved in the plate-making work as well. Then, in September 1977 I had the unique privilege extended to me of becoming a member of the Governing Body of Jehovah's Witnesses, located in Brooklyn, New York, U.S.A.

I must admit that at times I felt like 'running away' from some of the more difficult assignments given to me. But then I would recall Jonah and the mistake he made, and I would repeat to myself that wonderful promise found at Psalm 55:22: "Throw your burden upon Jehovah himself, and he himself will sustain you. Never will he allow the righteous one to totter." How true I have found these words to be!

Jehovah never asks any one of us to do something that he knows we cannot handle. However, it is only in his strength that we are able to do what he asks. And another thing—if you truly love your brothers

In Our Next Issue

- **Building Faith to Move Mountains**

- **How Meaningful Are Your Prayers?**

- **Does True Christianity Produce Fanatics?**

working alongside you, they will support you and back you up, working with you "shoulder to shoulder" in order to help you carry your assigned work load.—Zephaniah 3:9.

Precious Relationships

Of course, there are always some Christian brothers for whom you feel a special attachment. One of these was Alfred Pryce Hughes, who died in 1978. His life story appeared in the April 1, 1963, issue of *The Watchtower*. For many years he served as the branch servant, and later as a member of the Branch Committee. He was greatly loved by the brothers in the British field because of his great respect for Jehovah's organization and his loyalty to it and his love for all the brothers. Another thing was his love for the field ministry. This never diminished throughout his life, no matter what responsibility he had to shoulder. Working alongside faithful brothers like Pryce has meant so much to me, strengthening my determination to stay close to Jehovah's organization and remain active in the ministry.

On October 29, 1960, I entered an especially precious relationship with a long-time zealous pioneer and missionary of the 11th class of Gilead, who was at the time serving in Ireland. On that date Mildred Willett and I were married, and ever since she has been a faithful support to me in Bethel service.

Before Mildred's mother died in 1965, she advised her daughter never to be "jealous of Jehovah." Mildred has always remembered her mother's words, and this has helped prevent her from becoming discontented when I have often had to work overtime. This has greatly helped me to care happily for any added work assignments that have come my way. We have both especially enjoyed sharing many rewarding experiences in the ministry.

One young couple we studied the Bible with, for example, made rapid progress to the point of dedication and baptism and regularly shared in the ministry. We were so delighted! Then, suddenly, for no apparent reason, they stopped associating. Mildred and I shared the disappointment, and we kept wondering where we had gone wrong in our training of them. We constantly prayed to Jehovah that he would still open their hearts to prove their love for the truth. Can you imagine our happiness when we received a letter from this couple about ten years later telling us that they were again actively associated and that their home was now a Book Study center?

Husband Will wrote: "I wish to thank you for all the help and loving consideration you provided for us . . . My falling away was my fault, my heart appreciation was not right . . . We have found great joy being back in Jehovah's organization . . . It is with fond memories that I am writing you tonight, may Jehovah continue to bless you both in your service to him."

In another letter, a mother wrote us regarding her boy Mike: "I am so glad the angels sat him next to you." What did she mean? Well, Mike had come along to a convention with his mother and younger brother, but he was not really interested in the truth. Mildred noticed the lad sitting by himself and chatted with him. Then we both invited him and his brother to come to London Bethel and see the work we did.

Later, Mike came, and what he saw sparked his interest sufficiently to continue having a Bible study. The result? He's now an elder in the congregation, and his wife and two boys are all active in the ministry. Some time ago Mike's wife wrote: "[Mike] has often mentioned meeting you both . . . How impressed he was by your kindness and interest in him."

When my wife and I receive expressions

of appreciation from someone like Will or Mike that we have been privileged to help, our hearts simply overflow in gratefulness to Jehovah! What priceless rewards such living "letters of recommendation" are—all part of the joy received from staying close to Jehovah's organization.—2 Corinthians 3:1-3.

Serving at World Headquarters

"A nation unto itself." That is how the editor of a Brooklyn Heights newspaper described the big family of more than 3,500 Witnesses living at the world headquarters of Jehovah's Witnesses in Brooklyn, New York, and at Watchtower Farms, located about a hundred miles (160 km) away in upstate New York. Truly, Jehovah's anointed ones are a spiritual nation in Jehovah's eyes! Today, multitudes from many worldly nations are coming forward and saying to those of this nation: "We will go with you people, for we have heard that God is with you people."—Zechariah 8:23; 1 Peter 2:9.

Can you appreciate, then, how thrilling it was for my wife and me to become a permanent part of this big Bethel family? I would say without any hesitation that the last eight years of my life have been by far the most outstanding in all my theocratic experience. Here you feel the pulse of Jehovah's visible organization; here the spiritual food is prepared and then sent out to the four corners of the earth; here you see Jehovah's spirit at work guiding and directing momentous decisions that have to be made; and here you sense more than anywhere else the cumulative evidence of Jehovah's blessing upon the work of Kingdom preaching and disciple making. All these recent experiences and impressions have given me added incentive to stay ever closer to Jehovah's people.

I have recounted only a very few of my

John Barr today, with his wife Mildred

life's experiences. However, they may help you to understand why, as my plane finally touched down at Aberdeen Airport that sunny June morning, I felt so grateful to Jehovah that I was still a part of our loving worldwide association of brothers. I had spent the flight time reminiscing about my years in the truth, and this reminded me yet again how beneficial it is for us from time to time to recount our many blessings at Jehovah's hand.—Psalm 40:5.

My sister Louie was there to greet me —still faithful, zealous, and loyal after more than 60 years of dedicated service to Jehovah. I thanked Jehovah for that added blessing, for did not the apostle Paul say that it is faithfulness that Jehovah looks for in all of his "stewards"? (1 Corinthians 4:2) What great encouragement one member of a family can give to another by remaining faithful!

Moses once prayed: "Show us just how to count our days in such a way that we may bring a heart of wisdom in." (Psalm 90:12) As Mildred and I grow older, we appreciate the need always to lean on Jehovah's wisdom so as to use our life in a way that demonstrates our love for him and our brothers. Jehovah lovingly shows us that way if we stay close to his organization.

"Copies for Personal Friends"

Because they have enjoyed the book *Making Your Family Life Happy* so much, many have shared copies with others. For example, a person from Indiana, U.S.A., writes:

"I would like to compliment you on the wonderful book I have just read, *Making Your Family Life Happy*. It is a well-written and easily understood book, and our young people as well as old would benefit from reading it.

"I would like extra copies for personal friends, and I would also like to use the book as bridal-shower gifts.

"I am of the Nazarene faith . . . and would not appreciate materials, other than the book, sent my way . . . If it would be possible for me to purchase ten copies of the book at a reasonable price, I would appreciate hearing from you."

The Watchtower

Announcing Jehovah's Kingdom

July 15, 1987

FAITH CAN MOVE MOUNTAINS!

The Watchtower®

Announcing Jehovah's Kingdom

July 15, 1987
Vol. 108, No. 14

In This Issue

Cover photo: Pictorial Archive (Near Eastern History) Est.

THE PURPOSE OF "THE WATCHTOWER" is to exalt Jehovah God as the Sovereign of the universe. It keeps watch on world events as they fulfill Bible prophecy. It comforts all peoples with the good news that God's Kingdom will soon destroy those who oppress their fellowmen and that it will turn the earth into a paradise. It encourages faith in the now-reigning King, Jesus Christ, whose shed blood opens the way for mankind to gain eternal life. "The Watchtower," published by Jehovah's Witnesses continuously since 1879, is nonpolitical. It adheres to the Bible as its authority.

"WATCHTOWER" STUDIES FOR THE WEEKS

August 23: How Meaningful Are Your Prayers? Page 10. Songs to Be Used: 161, 88.

August 30: Prayers Require Works. Page 15. Songs to Be Used: 167, 160.

Average Printing Each Issue: 12,315,000

Now Published in 103 Languages

SEMIMONTHLY LANGUAGES AVAILABLE BY MAIL
Afrikaans, Arabic, Cebuano, Chichewa, Chinese, Cibemba, Danish,* Dutch,* Efik, English,* Finnish,* French,* German,* Greek,* Hiligaynon, Igbo, Iloko, Italian,* Japanese,* Korean, Lingala, Malagasy, Maltese, Norwegian, Portuguese,* Russian, Sepedi, Sesotho, Shona, Spanish,* Swahili, Swedish,* Tagalog, Thai, Tsonga, Tswana, Xhosa, Yoruba, Zulu

MONTHLY LANGUAGES AVAILABLE BY MAIL
Armenian, Bengali, Bicol, Bislama, Bulgarian, Croatian, Czech, Ewe, Fijian, Ga, Greenlandic, Gujarati, Gun, Hausa, Hebrew, Hindi, Hiri Motu, Hungarian, Icelandic, Kannada, Malayalam, Marathi, New Guinea Pidgin, Pangasinan, Papiamento, Polish, Rarotongan, Romanian, Samar-Leyte, Samoan, Sango, Serbian, Silozi, Sinhalese, Slovenian, Solomon Islands-Pidgin, Tahitian, Tamil, Telugu, Tongan, Tshiluba, Turkish, Twi, Ukrainian, Urdu, Venda, Vietnamese

* Study articles also available in large-print edition.

Watch Tower Society offices	Yearly subscription for the above:	
	Semimonthly Languages	Monthly Languages
America, U.S., Watchtower, Wallkill, N.Y. 12589	$4.00	$2.00
Australia, Box 280, Ingleburn, N.S.W. 2565	A$7.00	A$3.50
Canada, Box 4100, Halton Hills, Ontario L7G 4Y4	$5.50	$2.75
England, The Ridgeway, London NW7 1RN	£5.00	£2.50
Ireland, 29A Jamestown Road, Finglas, Dublin 11	IR£6.00	IR£3.00
New Zealand, P.O. Box 142, Manurewa	NZ$15.00	NZ$7.50
Nigeria, PMB 001, Shomolu, Lagos State	₦8.00	₦4.00
Philippines, P.O. Box 2044, Manila 2800	₱60.00	₱30.00
South Africa, Private Bag 2067, Krugersdorp, 1740	R9.00	R4.50

Remittances should be sent to the office in your country or to Watchtower, Wallkill, N.Y. 12589, U.S.A.

Changes of address should reach us 30 days before your moving date. Give us your old and new address (if possible, your old address label).

20 cents (U.S.) a copy

The Bible translation used is the "New World Translation of the Holy Scriptures," unless otherwise indicated.

The Watchtower (ISSN 0043-1087) is published semimonthly for $4.00 (U.S.) per year by Watch Tower Bible and Tract Society of Pennsylvania, 25 Columbia Heights, Brooklyn, N.Y. 11201. Second-class postage paid at Brooklyn, N.Y., and at additional mailing offices.

Postmaster: Send address changes to Watchtower, **Wallkill, N.Y. 12589.**

Published by
**Watch Tower Bible and Tract Society
of Pennsylvania**
25 Columbia Heights, Brooklyn, N.Y. 11201, U.S.A.
Frederick W. Franz, President

Faith Can Move Mountains!

T HE crowd was in suspense. A father had just brought his epileptic son to men considered capable of curing him. Eagerly, a cure was awaited. But nothing happened! Disappointed, the father turned away.

At that moment four other men appeared and among them their leader, Jesus of Nazareth. Running toward him, the father pleaded: "Have mercy on my son, because he is an epileptic and is ill, for he falls often into the fire and often into the water; and I brought him to your disciples, but they could not cure him."

"Bring him here to me," said Jesus. The result? "Then Jesus rebuked it, and the demon came out of him; and the boy was cured from that hour." Yes, another miracle! But why had Jesus' disciples failed?

Jesus explained why, saying: "Because of your little faith." Then he continued: "If you have faith the size of a mustard grain, you will say to this mountain, 'Transfer from here to there,' and it will transfer, and nothing will be impossible for you." —Matthew 17:14-20.

From this true-life experience, it is evident that faith is powerful. But just what is faith? Can it be built up and strengthened? Can it really move mountains?

What Is Faith?

The apostle Paul described faith as "the assured expectation of things hoped for, the evident demonstration [or, convincing evidence] of realities though not beheld." (Hebrews 11:1) In other words, faith is convincing evidence of something unseen. It is not based on mere hearsay but has a solid foundation. Hence, faith differs from credulity. One dictionary defines credulity as "belief or readiness of belief, esp[ecially] on slight or uncertain evidence." Contrariwise, the person with true faith has solid evidence for what he believes. Therefore, he can tell you why he is convinced that a certain thing will come to pass. The father mentioned at the outset had some evidence convincing him that Jesus could cure his son. What evidence? Well, Jesus had been performing miracles for more than two years, and his fame had spread throughout most of Palestine.—Luke 7:17; John 10:25.

Faith has also been described as "the *title-deed* of things hoped for." A man who purchases a distant property and has the title deed in his hand has convincing evidence that the property exists and that it really belongs to him, even though he may never have seen it. So, too, the person with faith can bring forth tangible evidence for what he believes. For example, suppose he has faith that Jehovah God will bring true peace to this earth through His

Kingdom. Then the individual must have at hand evidence that God exists and has the power, the will, and the wisdom needed to bring peace and that He has established the Kingdom for that purpose. Such evidence must be strong enough to convince not only the person having faith but also others who might 'demand of him the reason for his hope' for peace.—1 Peter 3:15.

Faith Can Move Mountains!

Someone may ask, however, 'Did Jesus mean that such faith could literally transfer mountains?' Jesus may have included that, but he often used illustrations. (Matthew 13:34) So he probably had in mind obstacles that could be like mountains to the believer. In fact, the word "mountain" is frequently used to mean a huge quantity, such as "a mountain of debts." That true faith can transfer or remove mountainlike obstacles is confirmed by many modern-day experiences.

For example, would you not agree that being paralyzed from the neck down would be such a mountain? Yet, a quadriplegic living in Vancouver, B.C., Canada, not only has learned to paint, with either a brush or a palette knife held in his mouth, but also supports himself by selling his paintings. Moreover, his faith moves him to talk to others about what he has learned from the Bible, doing so either in his wheelchair or by writing letters. He types his letters by striking the typewriter keys with a stick held in his mouth. He also attends Christian meetings regularly and gives talks in the Theocratic Ministry School conducted by Jehovah's Witnesses. His example of faith, coupled with hard work and determination, is a source of encouragement to those around him.

Faith in God's Word and his promises has similarly helped others. For example, it has helped many to overcome unchristian habits and customs, such as shady business practices, stealing, smoking, gambling, drunkenness, spiritism, sexual immorality, and false religious practices. The common factor in all such experiences was the obtaining of convincing evidence that Jehovah God exists, that the Bible is his written Word, and that his promises set forth in the Scriptures are trustworthy and will be fulfilled. Such faith *can* move mountains.

Building Faith to Move Mountains

"**I** *DO* have faith; oh, help me to have *more!*" These were the words of the distraught father of the epileptic boy mentioned in the preceding article. (Mark 9:24, *The Living Bible*) It may be that this statement also reflects your feelings. If so, be assured that you are not alone. World conditions today tend to weaken faith in God and his Word. Atheistic philosophy, materialism, crises in the churches, and the frightful increase in violence all tend to undermine true faith. Very appropriate, then, was Jesus Christ's question, "When the Son of man arrives, will he really find the faith on the earth?"—Luke 18:8.

On one occasion, even Jesus' apostles pleaded, "Give us more faith." Instead of miraculously giving them more faith, however, he said: "If you had faith the size of a mustard grain, you would say to this black mulberry tree, 'Be uprooted and planted in the sea!' and it would obey you." (Luke 17:5, 6) So, just how can we get more faith?

Building Faith

The apostle Paul wrote: "How . . . will they put faith in him of whom they have not heard? How, in turn, will they hear without someone to preach? . . . So faith follows the thing heard. In turn the thing heard is through the word about Christ." (Romans 10:14-17) It follows, then, that if we want more faith, we must hear and take in knowledge of the Scriptures. That is what the previously mentioned quadriplegic did. Jehovah's Witnesses studied the Bible with him, he gained faith, and then applied what he learned in his daily life. Thus he found faith so as to remove the mountainlike obstacle in his life.

It takes time to gather the convincing evidence as the basis for faith. (Hebrews 11:1) And it takes effort. Are you willing to spend time and put forth effort on a regular basis so as to gather the evidence needed to build faith?

"Blocks" for Building Faith

The process of building faith can be likened to the erecting of a structure. Even the largest buildings are made up of individual building blocks. Each block is put into place with hundreds of other blocks to give the building the stability needed to withstand violent storms as well as the ravages of time. Faith, too, is based on individual "blocks" of evidence carefully lined up in relation to others. Each "block" will add to the evidence that God exists, that he is the Creator of all things, and that he has a purpose involving his human creation. Just what are these building "blocks"?

In the first place, take a look at your own body. Do you not see convincing evidence of a Creator, for instance, in your fantastic brain—an organ that science cannot even dream of imitating? Can you say as did the psalmist, "In a fear-inspiring way I am wonderfully made"? (Psalm 139:14) If you can, then you have one "block" with which to build your faith.

Do you find further evidence of a loving Creator in the infinite variety and beauty of trees, plants, and flowers? Can you see such evidence in animal, bird, and marine creatures and in their interdependence as well as their importance to mankind? If we are willing to listen, we can "hear" all of them declare, 'God exists!'—Romans 1:20.

Nevertheless, belief in the existence of the Creator is not enough. To answer questions about him and his purposes, we need a revelation from this invisible, all-wise God. And we have it! Where? In the Bible. But many do not consider this source of information to be as reliable as the visible creation around us.

However, there is abundant proof, convincing evidence, that the Bible is a book inspired of God. For example, the harmony that exists among its writers—about 40 in all, writing during 16 centuries—is evidence of *one* Author, Jehovah God. Time and again the findings of true science and archaeology have also proved the Bible to be authentic and reliable. For instance, astronomer Robert Jastrow wrote: "The details differ, but the essential elements in the astronomical and biblical accounts of Genesis are the same: the chain of events leading to man commenced suddenly and sharply at a definite moment in time, in a flash of light and energy."

Consider just one example of how archaeology has confirmed the Bible record. At 2 Kings 18:13-15, we read: "In the fourteenth year of King Hezekiah, Sennacherib the king of Assyria came up against all the fortified cities of Judah and proceeded to seize them." At that time "the king of Assyria laid upon Hezekiah the king of Judah three hundred silver talents and thirty gold talents." In confirmation, during the 19th century archaeologist A. H. Layard discovered what is called King Sennacherib's Prism. Its cuneiform text reads: "As for Hezekiah the Jew, who did not submit to my yoke, 46 of his strong, walled cities, . . . I besieged and took. . . . I added to the former tribute, and laid upon him as their yearly payment, a tax . . . 30 talents of gold and 800 talents of silver." A remarkable corroboration of the Bible record, differing only in the amount of the silver tax!

Other "Blocks" for Building Faith

Outstanding among building "blocks" are those furnished by the fulfillment of Bible prophecies. A prophecy is a prediction of some future event. When that event occurs, it stamps the prediction as true. Such prophecies are beyond the ability of man, and the Bible correctly states: "Prophecy was at no time brought by man's will, but men spoke from God as they were borne along by holy spirit." (2 Peter 1:21) A look at a few of such Bible prophecies certainly is faith strengthening.

About 732 B.C.E., Isaiah foretold the downfall of Babylon at the hands of the Medes and the Persians, even giving the name of the conqueror, Cyrus. Remarkably, this prophecy was given some 200 years before Cyrus took Babylon! In part, the prophecy speaks of Jehovah as "the One saying to the watery deep, 'Be evaporated; and all your rivers I shall dry up.'" It was foretold that God would 'open before Cyrus the two-leaved doors, so that even the gates would not be shut.' "The copper doors I shall break in pieces, and the iron bars I shall cut down," said Jehovah, "and I will give you the treasures in the darkness." (Isaiah 44:24–45:3) How was this prophecy fulfilled?

It happened on a night of drunken revelry for Babylon and her princes. Unnoticed and under the cover of night, the army of Cyrus worked diligently to divert the waters of the Euphrates River, which passed through the center of the city. This allowed the soldiers to enter Babylon by the riverbed. The river gates had carelessly been left open during the feasting. Hence, the Medes and the Persians had no difficulty in taking Babylon and all its treasures. Isaiah's prophecy was fulfilled in all its details.

Jehovah God also saw fit to make Jesus Christ the focal point of many prophecies foretelling details of his birth, life, ministry, and death, some of them written centuries in advance. For example, it was foretold that he would be born in the tribe of Judah of David's family (Genesis 49:10; Isaiah 11:1, 2) and in the town of Bethlehem. (Micah 5:2) One close associate would be unfaithful and would betray him for 30 pieces of silver. (Psalm 41:9; Zechariah 11:12) Lots would be cast for his garments. (Psalm 22:18) He would be pierced, but none of his bones would be broken. (Zechariah 12:10; Psalm 34:20) Daniel 9:24-27 foretold the coming of Jesus as the Messiah, or Christ, after 69 weeks of years, a period of 483 years running from 455 B.C.E. until Jesus' baptism in 29 C.E. Half a "week" (3 1/2 years) later, in 33 C.E., Jesus was "cut off" in death as foretold. Other details of the prophecy were also fulfilled.

These are but a few "blocks" that can be used to build the faith that can move mountains. To gather all of them together

"BLOCKS" for Building Faith

Appreciate the things that Jehovah has made

Accept the Bible as God's Word

Note how archaeology and history confirm the Bible record

Examine the fulfillment of Bible prophecies

and put them in their place takes time, effort, and perseverance. But it has been done. John, living in Santos, Brazil, can testify that it can be done. Some years ago, he was indifferent toward religion, having no faith in the Bible, although he did believe that God exists. John agreed to visits by one of Jehovah's Witnesses. Weekly discussions finally convinced John that the Bible was not an ordinary book, and he finally "accepted it, not as the word of men, but, just as it truthfully is, as the word of God." (1 Thessalonians 2:13) It took time, but further Bible studies helped John to understand God's purpose toward mankind. Finally, in 1970 he was baptized as one of Jehovah's Witnesses. Now, as an appointed congregation elder, he helps others to build up and maintain their faith.

Do you want help in building up *your* faith? If so, remember that "faith follows the thing heard. In turn the thing heard is through the word about Christ." (Romans 10:17) More than 3,000,000 of Jehovah's Witnesses are diligently spreading "the word about Christ" and God's Kingdom in more than 200 lands. They will be glad to help you learn more about God's Word through free Bible discussions.

Rest assured that the time you devote to listening to "the thing heard" will be time well spent. It could help you to build faith that moves mountains. This, in turn, could lead to eternal life, "for God loved the world so much that he gave his only-begotten Son, in order that everyone exercising faith in him might not be destroyed but have everlasting life."—John 3:16.

Another Preaching Tour of Galilee

AFTER about two years of intensive preaching, will Jesus now begin to let up and take it easy? On the contrary, he expands his preaching activity by setting out on yet another tour, a third one of Galilee. He visits all the cities and villages in the territory, teaching in the synagogues and preaching the good news of the Kingdom. What he sees on this tour convinces him more than ever of the need to intensify the preaching work.

Wherever Jesus goes, he sees the crowds in need of spiritual healing and comfort. They are like sheep without a shepherd, skinned and thrown about, and he feels pity for them. He tells his disciples: "Yes, the harvest is great, but the workers are few. Therefore, beg the Master of the harvest to send out workers into his harvest."

Jesus has a plan of action. He summons the 12 apostles, whom he had chosen nearly a year earlier. He divides them into pairs, making six teams of preachers, and gives them instructions, saying: "Do not go off into the road of the nations, and do not enter into a Sa-

maritan city; but, instead, go continually to the lost sheep of the house of Israel. As you go, preach, saying, 'The kingdom of the heavens has drawn near.'"

This Kingdom that they are to preach about is the one Jesus taught them to pray for in the model prayer. The Kingdom had drawn near in the sense that God's designated King, Jesus Christ, was present. To establish his disciples' credentials as representatives of that superhuman government, Jesus empowers them to cure the sick and even raise the dead. He instructs them to perform these services free.

Next he tells his disciples not to make material preparations for their preaching tour. "Do not procure gold or silver or copper for your girdle purses, or a food pouch for the trip, or two undergarments, or sandals or a staff; for the worker deserves his food." Those who appreciate the message will respond and contribute food and housing. As Jesus says: "Into whatever city or village you enter, search out who in it is deserving, and stay there until you leave."

Jesus then gives instructions on how to approach householders with the Kingdom message. "When you are entering into the house," he instructs, "greet the household; and if the house is deserving, let the peace you wish it come upon it; but if it is not deserving, let the peace from you return upon you. Wherever anyone does not take you in or listen to your words, on going out of that house or that city shake the dust off your feet."

Of a city that rejects their message, Jesus says: "It will be more endurable for the land of Sodom and Gomorrah on Judgment Day than for that city." This shows that at least some unrighteous ones to whom his disciples would preach will be present during Judgment Day. When these former citizens are resurrected during Judgment Day, however, it will be even harder for them to humble themselves and accept Christ as King than it will be for resurrected persons from the ancient immoral cities of Sodom and Gomorrah. **Matthew 9: 35–10:15; Mark 6:6-12; Luke 9:1-5.**

♦ When does Jesus begin a third preaching tour of Galilee, and of what does it convince him?
♦ When sending his 12 apostles out to preach, what instructions does he give them?
♦ Why was it correct for the disciples to teach that the Kingdom had drawn near?
♦ How will it be more endurable for Sodom and Gomorrah than for those who rejected Jesus' disciples?

How Meaningful Are Your Prayers?

"I have called with my whole heart. Answer me, O Jehovah."
—PSALM 119:145.

WHAT kind of prayers does the Creator, Jehovah God, hear? A parable Jesus Christ told indicates one of the basic conditions for God to answer prayers. Jesus said that two men were praying at the temple in Jerusalem. One was a highly respected Pharisee, the other a despised tax collector. The Pharisee prayed: "O God, I thank you I am not as the rest of men, . . . or even as this tax collector. I fast twice a week, I give the tenth of all things I acquire." But the lowly tax collector "kept beating his breast, saying, 'O God, be gracious to me a sinner.'"—Luke 18:9-13.

[2] In commenting on these two prayers, Jesus said: "I tell you, This man [the tax collector] went down to his home proved more righteous than that man [the Pharisee]; because everyone that exalts himself will be humiliated, but he that humbles himself will be exalted." (Luke 18:14) Clearly, Jesus showed that merely praying to our heavenly Father is not enough. How we pray —our mental attitude—is also important.

[3] Prayer is indeed a precious, weighty, serious privilege, and all well-informed Christians are familiar with the basic rules that govern it. Prayers must be addressed to the one true God, Jehovah. They must be said in the name of his Son, Jesus Christ. To be acceptable, they must be

---

3. (a) Cite some basic rules governing prayer. (b) What forms may prayer take?

1, 2. (a) What parable of Jesus dealt with prayer? (b) What conclusion did Jesus draw from the two prayers, and what should this show us?

offered in faith. Yes, "he that approaches God must believe that he is." Moreover, one's prayers must be in line with God's will. (Hebrews 11:6; Psalm 65:2; Matthew 17:20; John 14:6, 14; 1 John 5:14) And from Scriptural examples, we learn that prayers can take the form of praise, thanksgiving, petition, and supplication. —Luke 10:21; Ephesians 5:20; Philippians 4:6; Hebrews 5:7.

Examples of Meaningful Prayers

[4] When weighty problems are to be faced, serious decisions are required, gross mistakes have been made, or our lives are threatened, our prayers especially take on earnestness and become meaningful. Because the Israelites rebelled after hearing the negative report of the ten unfaithful spies, Jehovah told Moses that the people deserved to be wiped out. In an earnest and meaningful prayer, Moses begged Jehovah not to take this action because His name was involved. (Numbers 14:11-19) When Israel was defeated at Ai because of Achan's greed, Joshua uttered a most impassioned plea also on the basis of Jehovah's name. (Joshua 7:6-9) Many of David's psalms are in the form of earnest prayers, a particularly striking example being Psalm 51. King Hezekiah's prayer at the time of Assyrian King Sennacherib's invasion of Judah is another fine example of a meaningful prayer, and again Jehovah's name was involved.—Isaiah 37: 14-20.

[5] The book of Lamentations might be said to be a long, earnest prayer by Jeremiah on behalf of his people, for Jehovah is repeatedly addressed therein. (Lamenta-tions 1:20; 2:20; 3:40-45, 55-66; 5:1-22) Ezra and Daniel also offered meaningful and earnest prayers on behalf of their people, confessing their nation's wrongs and pleading for forgiveness. (Ezra 9:5-15; Daniel 9:4-19) And we can be certain that the prayer Jonah said while he was in the belly of the huge fish was earnest and meaningful.—Jonah 2:1-9.

[6] Before choosing the 12 apostles, Jesus spent all night in prayer so that his Father's will might be done in making the choices. (Luke 6:12-16) There is also Jesus' meaningful prayer on the night of his betrayal, as recorded at John chapter 17. All these prayers give eloquent testimony to the fine relationship with Jehovah God that was enjoyed by those who uttered them. Without a doubt, this must be a basic factor in our prayers if they are to be meaningful. And earnest and meaningful they need to be if they are to be 'powerful' with Jehovah God.—James 5:16, *The Jerusalem Bible.*

Flaws Due to Human Imperfection

[7] As has been noted, under stressful conditions our prayers are likely to be especially earnest and meaningful. But what about our everyday prayers? Do they give evidence of the warm, close relationship we feel we have with our heavenly Father, Jehovah God? It has well been said: "Prayer must mean something to us if it is to mean anything to God." Do we give our prayers the thought they deserve and make sure that they really come from our figurative heart?

[8] It is easy to let our prayers deteriorate in these respects. Because of our inherited

---

4. (a) What examples of meaningful prayer did Moses and Joshua provide? (b) What examples did David and King Hezekiah give? (c) What common characteristic did several of these prayers have?
5. We have what other examples of meaningful prayers said by certain servants of Jehovah?

6. (a) Jesus gave us what examples of meaningful prayers? (b) What basic factor is needed to make our prayers meaningful?
7. What questions might we ask ourselves regarding our prayers?
8. Our prayers might have what flaws due to human imperfection?

imperfect inclinations, our hearts can easily deceive us, robbing our prayers of the qualities they should have. (Jeremiah 17:9) Unless, in most cases, we pause and think before we pray, we may find that the tendency is for our prayers to become mechanical, stereotyped, routine. Or they may become repetitious, which calls to mind what Jesus said about the improper way 'the people of the nations pray.' (Matthew 6:7, 8) Or our prayers may deal only with generalities rather than with specific matters or persons.

⁹ At times we may be inclined to hurry through our prayers. But noteworthy is the observation: "If you are too busy to pray, you *are* too busy." We should not want to memorize certain words and just repeat them each time we pray; neither should it be necessary for a witness of Jehovah to read his prayer, as at a public assembly. No doubt all these pitfalls arise, at least in part, from the fact that we cannot physically see Jehovah God, the One to whom we pray. However, we cannot expect him to be pleased with such prayers, nor do we benefit from saying them.

Overcoming the Flaws

¹⁰ We will be able to guard against the aforementioned pitfalls to the extent that we appreciate the importance of our daily prayers and have a good relationship with our heavenly Father. For one thing, such appreciation will help us to guard against hurrying through our prayers as if we needed to get to more important things. Nothing can be more important than talking to the Universal Sovereign, Jehovah God. True, there may be occasions when

time is limited. For example, when King Artaxerxes asked his cupbearer Nehemiah, "What is this that you are seeking to secure?" Nehemiah 'at once prayed to the God of the heavens.' (Nehemiah 2:4) Since the king was expecting an immediate reply, Nehemiah could not linger long in that prayer. But we may be sure that it was meaningful and came from his heart because Jehovah immediately answered it. (Nehemiah 2:5, 6) Except for such rare occasions, however, we should take time for our prayers and let other things wait. If our prayers tend to be hurried, we do not fully appreciate the importance of prayer.

¹¹ Another pitfall we may need to avoid is that of repeating generalities. Such prayers also fail to do justice to the precious privilege of prayer. In his model prayer, Jesus set a fine example for us in this regard. He mentioned seven distinct petitions: three dealing with the triumph of righteousness, one with our daily physical needs, and three with our spiritual welfare.—Matthew 6:9-13.

¹² The apostle Paul also set us a fine example along these lines. He asked that others pray for him 'that ability to speak with boldness might be given him.' (Ephesians 6:18-20) He was just as specific in his own prayers in behalf of others. "This is what I continue praying," said Paul, "that your love may abound yet more and more with accurate knowledge and full discernment; that you may make sure of the more important things, so that you may be flawless and not be stumbling others up to the day of Christ, and may be filled with righteous fruit, which is through Jesus Christ, to God's glory and praise."—Philippians 1: 9-11.

9. What other pitfalls may arise as regards our prayers, and what doubtless is one reason for these pitfalls?
10. (a) What attitude would betray a lack of appreciation for the importance of prayer? (b) What Scriptural instance is noted?

11. What is another pitfall we need to guard against, and what fine example did Jesus set in this regard?
12. Paul provides what fine examples as to being specific in our prayers?

¹³ Yes, our prayers should deal with specific things, and this requires that we give thought to our prayers. (Compare Proverbs 15:28.) While in the field ministry, we might ask God not only for his blessing on our efforts but also for wisdom, tact, largeheartedness, freeness of speech, or help for whatever weakness may tend to interfere with our effectiveness in witnessing. Moreover, could we not ask God to lead us to the ones hungering and thirsting for righteousness? Just before giving a public talk or having some part on a Service Meeting or in the Theocratic Ministry School, we can beg Jehovah to have his holy spirit dwell richly in us. Why? So that we may have confidence and poise, may speak with earnestness and conviction, so as to bring honor to God's name and build up our brothers. All such prayers are also conducive to our having the right frame of mind when speaking.

¹⁴ Do we have a fleshly weakness that wars against our spirituality and seems difficult to overcome? We should want to deal with it specifically in our prayers. And far from getting discouraged, we should never tire of humbly and earnestly asking God to help us and grant forgiveness. Yes, under such circumstances, we should want to go to Jehovah as a child goes to his father when in trouble, no matter how often we pray to God about the same weakness. If we are sincere, Jehovah will give us help and the realization that he has forgiven us. Under such circumstances, we can also draw comfort from the apostle Paul's confession that he had a problem.—Romans 7: 21-25.

Aids in Offering Meaningful Prayers

¹⁵ For our prayers to be truly meaningful, we must make an effort to dismiss all outside considerations and to concentrate on the fact that we are coming into the presence of the Great God, Jehovah. We need to approach him with deep respect, appreciating his awesomeness. As Jehovah told Moses, no man can see God and yet live. (Exodus 33:20) So we need to approach Jehovah with due humility and modesty, which is a point Jesus stressed in his parable of the Pharisee and the tax collector. (Micah 6:8; Luke 18:9-14) Jehovah must be very real to us. We must have the same mental attitude as Moses had. "He continued steadfast as seeing the One who is invisible." (Hebrews 11:27) Such traits bear testimony that we have a good relationship with our heavenly Father.

¹⁶ Our prayers will also be meaningful if we come to Jehovah with hearts full of love and affection for him. For instance, what appreciation of Jehovah God and love for him the psalmist David expressed in Psalms 23 and 103! There is no question about David's having had a fine relationship with his Great Shepherd, Jehovah God. In the Theocratic Ministry School, we are counseled to speak with warmth and feeling. This should especially be the case when we are reading scriptures and even more so when we are praying to our heavenly Father. Yes, we want to feel as did David when he prayed: "*Make* me know your own ways, O Jehovah; teach me your own paths. *Make* me walk in your truth and teach me, for you are my God of salvation." Also indicative of how we should feel are these words of another psalmist: "I have called with my whole

13. How may we say meaningful prayers as regards our various kinds of service to Jehovah?
14. What should be our attitude regarding fleshly weaknesses difficult to overcome?

15. With what mental attitude should we approach Jehovah God in prayer?
16. What part do our hearts play in saying meaningful prayers?

heart. Answer me, O Jehovah."—Psalm 25:4, 5; 119:145.

17 To keep our prayers meaningful and to avoid making them repetitious, we do well to vary their thought content. The Bible text for the day or some Christian publication we have been reading might furnish a thought. The theme of the *Watchtower* lesson, of the public talk, or of the assembly or the convention we are attending might serve such a purpose.

18 To help us to get more into the mood of prayer and make our prayers more meaningful, it is good to change our physical position. For public prayers, we naturally bow our heads. But for more personal prayers, some have found it good to kneel before Jehovah when praying individually or as a family because they find that position conducive to their having a humble mental attitude. At Psalm 95:6 we are urged: "O come in, let us worship and bow down; let us kneel before Jehovah our Maker." Solomon knelt when offering his prayer at the dedication of Jehovah's temple, and Daniel made it a habit to kneel when praying.—2 Chronicles 6:13; Daniel 6:10.

---

17. How can we keep our prayers from becoming repetitious?
18. To make our prayers more meaningful, what might we do in keeping with Biblical words and examples?

How Do You Respond?

☐ What are some meaningful prayers recorded in the Scriptures?

☐ Because of human imperfection, how might our prayers be flawed?

☐ How can we overcome certain flaws in our prayers?

☐ What are some aids in our offering meaningful prayers?

---

19 In view of the importance of prayer, appointed elders should use good judgment about whom they call upon to offer a public prayer on behalf of the congregation. The baptized man representing the congregation should be a mature Christian minister. His prayer should reveal that he has a fine relationship with God. And those privileged to offer such prayers should give thought to being heard, for they are praying not only in behalf of themselves but also in behalf of the entire congregation. Otherwise, how can the rest of the congregation join in saying "Amen" at the close of the prayer? (1 Corinthians 14:16) Of course, for the rest to be able to say a meaningful "Amen," they must listen attentively, not letting their minds wander but truly making the prayer their own. Another word of caution that might be added is that since such prayers are offered to Jehovah God, they should not be used as an excuse for preaching to the listeners or for presenting some purely personal ideas.

20 When our prayers that are spoken aloud are truly meaningful, they impart a blessing to the hearers. Because this is so, married couples and families would do well each day to have at least one common prayer. In it, one person, such as the family head, would speak for the other or for the rest.

21 For our prayers to be truly meaningful, there is yet another matter that merits our attention. This is the fact that we must be consistent as regards our prayers, this meaning what? That we live in harmony with our prayers and work at what we pray for. This aspect of our prayers will be considered in the succeeding article.

---

19. Those having the responsibility for public prayers would do well to have what facts in mind?
20. Because meaningful prayers spoken aloud impart a blessing to the hearers, what suggestion is made?
21. For our prayers to be meaningful, what is another matter that merits consideration?

Prayers Require Works

"Jehovah is far away from the wicked ones, but the prayer of the righteous ones he hears."—PROVERBS 15:29.

ALL of Jehovah's requirements are wise, just, and loving. By no means are they burdensome. (1 John 5:3) That includes his requirements regarding prayer, one of which is that we must lead lives in harmony with our prayers. Our course of action must please Jehovah God. Otherwise, how can we expect him to consider our petitions and supplications with favor?

2 This is an aspect of prayer that is overlooked by most of those in Christendom, even as it was overlooked by the apostate Israelites in Isaiah's day. That is why Jehovah had his prophet represent him as saying: "Even though you make many prayers, I am not listening . . . Wash yourselves; make yourselves clean; remove the badness of your dealings from in front of my eyes; cease to do bad. Learn to do good." (Isaiah 1:15-17) Yes, if those Israelites wanted God's favor, they had to act in a way that pleased him. As has well been said: "If you would have God hear you when you pray, you must hear Him when He speaks."

3 In fact, Jehovah God repeatedly found it necessary to remind his people Israel of these truths. Thus we read: "He that is turning his ear away from hearing the law —even his prayer is something detestable" to God. "Jehovah is far away from the wicked ones, but the prayer of the righteous ones he hears." (Proverbs 28:9; 15:29) Because of this situation, Jeremiah mourned: "You [Jehovah] have blocked approach to yourself with a cloud mass, that prayer may not pass through." (Lamentations 3:44) Truly, the warning that Micah was inspired to give was fulfilled: "They will call to Jehovah for aid, but he will not answer them. And he will conceal his face from them in that time, according as they committed badness in their dealings."—Micah 3:4; Proverbs 1:28-32.

4 So it is necessary to live in harmony with our prayers. Is it essential to stress this fact today? Indeed it is, not only because of the situation in Christendom but also because of the situation of some of Jehovah's dedicated people. Of the more than 3,000,000 publishers of the good news last year, upwards of 37,000 were disfellowshipped for conduct unbecoming a Christian. That amounts to a ratio of about one in 80. Quite likely, most of these individuals were praying at least now and then. But were they acting in harmony with their prayers? By no means! Even some elders who had been in the full-time service for decades were among those disciplined in one way or another. How sad! Truly, "Let him that thinks he is standing beware that he does not fall," that he does not act in a way that makes his prayers unacceptable to his Maker.—1 Corinthians 10:12.

---

1. What is one condition to be met if God is to answer our prayers?

2, 3. Why did Jehovah not answer the prayers of the Israelites, as seen by the words of Isaiah, Jeremiah, and Micah?

4. What indicates that even among Jehovah's people some do not appreciate the need for works harmonizing with their prayers?

Why Prayers Require Works

5 For our prayers to be heard by Jehovah God, not only must we be morally and spiritually clean but we must also prove the sincerity of our prayers by working at what we pray for. Prayer alone is not a substitute for honest, intelligent effort. Jehovah will not do for us what we can do for ourselves by earnestly applying the counsel of his Word and following the guidance of his holy spirit. We should be willing to do all we can in this regard so that he will have a basis for answering our prayers. Thus, we 'should not be asking for more than we are willing to work for,' as someone has well put it.

6 However, the question may be asked: 'Why pray if we have to work at what we pray for?' We should pray for at least two good reasons. First, by our prayers we acknowledge that all good things come from God. He is the Giver of every good and perfect present—the sunshine, the rain, the fruitful seasons, and so much more! (Matthew 5:45; Acts 14: 16, 17; James 1:17) Second, whether our efforts are successful or not depends upon Jehovah's blessing. As we read at Psalm 127:1: "Unless Jehovah himself builds the house, it is to no avail that its builders have worked hard on it. Unless Jehovah himself guards the city, it is to no avail that the guard has kept awake." Making the same point are these words of the apostle Paul at 1 Corinthians 3:6, 7: "I planted, Apollos watered, but God kept making it grow; so that neither is he that plants anything nor is he that waters, but God who makes it grow."

5. For Jehovah to answer our prayers, how must we prove our sincerity?
6. For what two reasons should we pray?

Some Ancient Examples

7 The Scriptures report many cases showing that Jehovah's faithful servants worked at what they prayed for. Let us consider a few representative examples. Because Abraham's grandson Jacob gained the birthright blessing, his older brother Esau bore him murderous hatred. (Genesis 27:41) Some 20 years later, when Jacob was returning from Paddan-aram to the land of his birth with a large household and much livestock, he heard that Esau was coming to meet him. Remembering Esau's animosity, Jacob prayed fervently to Jehovah for protection from his brother's wrath. But did he let it go at that? No, indeed. He sent generous gifts ahead of him, reasoning: "I may appease him by the gift going ahead of me." And so it turned out to be, for when the two brothers met, Esau embraced Jacob and kissed him.—Genesis, chapters 32, 33.

8 David furnished another example of working in behalf of what we pray for. When his son Absalom usurped his throne, David's counselor Ahithophel cast his lot with Absalom. So David made earnest supplication that Ahithophel's counsel might be frustrated. Did David merely pray to that effect? No, he instructed his loyal counselor Hushai to join Absalom so that he might frustrate Ahithophel's counsel. And that is the way things worked out. Absalom acted on the bad counsel given him by Hushai, rejecting the counsel of Ahithophel.—2 Samuel 15: 31-37; 17:1-14; 18:6-8.

9 Yet another example that might be cited for our admonition is that of Nehe-

7, 8. (a) What incident in Jacob's life shows that he appreciated that works must accompany prayers? (b) What example did King David provide in this regard?
9. How did Nehemiah show that he appreciated the principle that prayers require works?

Jesus urged his disciples to pray for more harvest workers. But he also sent them out into the preaching, or 'harvesting,' work

miah. He had a large project to carry out —rebuilding the walls of Jerusalem. However, many enemies were conspiring against him. Nehemiah both prayed and worked, even as we read: "We prayed to our God and kept a guard posted against them day and night." From then on, half of Nehemiah's young men stood ready to protect the other half, those building the wall.—Nehemiah 4:9, 16.

The Example of Jesus

¹⁰ Jesus Christ set us a fine example of working at what we pray for. He taught us to pray: "Let your name be sanctified." (Matthew 6:9) But Jesus also did all he could so that his listeners might sanctify

10, 11. What examples provided by Jesus show that he acted in harmony with his prayers?

his Father's name. Likewise, Jesus did not limit himself to praying: "Father, glorify your name." (John 12:28) No, he did what he could to glorify his Father's name and to get others to do so.—Luke 5:23-26; 17: 12-15; John 17:4.

¹¹ Seeing the great spiritual need that the people had, Jesus said to his disciples: "The harvest is great, but the workers are few. Therefore, beg the Master of the harvest [Jehovah God] to send out workers into his harvest." (Matthew 9:37, 38) Did Jesus let matters go at that? Not at all! Right after that, he sent out his 12 apostles in pairs on a preaching, or 'harvesting,' tour. Later, Jesus sent out the 70 evangelizers to do the same work.—Matthew 10:1-10; Luke 10:1-9.

Applying the Principle

[12] Clearly, Jehovah God expects us to be consistent, to act in harmony with our prayers, thereby proving our sincerity. Jesus told us to pray: "Give us today our bread for this day." (Matthew 6:11) Rightly, therefore, all his followers petition God to that effect. But do we expect our heavenly Father to answer that prayer without our doing anything about it? Of course not. That is why we read: "The lazy one is showing himself desirous"—perhaps even by praying—"but his soul has nothing." (Proverbs 13:4) The apostle Paul made the same point at 2 Thessalonians 3:10, saying: "If anyone does not want to work, neither let him eat." Praying for our daily bread must be accompanied by a willingness to work. Interestingly, Paul wisely said that those who did not "want to work" should not eat. Some who want to work may be unemployed, sick, or too old to work. They do want to work, but this is beyond their circumstances. Hence, they may rightly pray for their daily bread and hope to receive it.

[13] Jesus also counseled us to ask his heavenly Father for His holy spirit. As Jesus assures us, God is more willing to give us the holy spirit than earthly parents are to give good things to their children. (Luke 11:13) But can we expect Jehovah God to impart his holy spirit to us miraculously, without any effort on our part? By no means! We must do everything we can to receive holy spirit. In addition to praying for it, we need to feed

---

12. What bearing does work have on our prayers that God give us our daily bread?

13. For Jehovah to answer our prayers for his holy spirit, what must we do?

diligently on God's Word. Why? Because Jehovah God does not give his holy spirit apart from his Word, and we cannot hope to receive holy spirit if we ignore the earthly channel Jehovah is using today, "the faithful and discreet slave," represented by the Governing Body of Jehovah's Witnesses. Without help from this "slave," we would neither be able to understand the full import of what we read nor know how to apply what we learn.—Matthew 24:45-47.

¹⁴ The principle that prayers require works also applies to these words of the disciple James, the half brother of Jesus: "If any one of you is lacking in wisdom, let him keep on asking God, for he gives generously to all and without reproaching; and it will be given him." (James 1:5; Matthew 13:55) But does God impart this wisdom to us by some miracle? No. First of all, we must have the right attitude, as we read: "He will teach the meek ones his way." (Psalm 25:9) And how does God teach "the meek ones"? By means of his Word. Again, we must put forth an effort to understand it and apply it, as indicated at Proverbs 2:1-6: "My son, if you will receive my sayings and treasure up my own commandments with yourself, so as to pay attention to wisdom with your ear, that you may incline your heart to discernment; if, moreover, you call out for understanding itself and you give forth your voice for discernment itself, if you keep seeking for it as for silver, . . . in that case you will understand the fear of Jehovah, and you will find the very knowledge of God. For Jehovah himself gives wisdom."

¹⁵ When King Solomon prayed for wisdom and God miraculously answered his prayer, did the principle that prayers require works also apply? Yes, it did, for as king of Israel, Solomon was required to write his own copy of the Law, read in it daily, and apply it to his life. But when Solomon went contrary to its instructions, as by multiplying wives and horses, his works were no longer in harmony with his prayers. As a result, Solomon became an apostate and died as such a "senseless one."—Psalm 14:1; Deuteronomy 17:16-20; 1 Kings 10:26; 11:3, 4, 11.

¹⁶ The principle that works must accompany prayers also applies when we are requesting God's help to overcome some ingrained, selfish habit. Thus a pioneer sister admitted to being addicted to soap operas, watching them from 11:00 a.m. to 3:30 p.m. every day. Learning from a district convention talk how harmful these immoral programs are, she took the matter to God in prayer. But it took quite a while for her to overcome the habit. Why? Because, as she said: 'I would pray to overcome the habit and then would watch the programs anyway. So I decided to stay in the field service the whole day so that I would not have the temptation. At last I got to the point that I could turn off the

16. What illustration shows that our prayers to overcome fleshly weaknesses must be accompanied by works?

In Our Next Issue

■ Alcohol—What Is the Christian View of It?

■ Christ Actively Leads His Congregation

■ The Spirit That Jehovah Blesses

14, 15. (a) For Jehovah to answer our prayers for wisdom, how must we cooperate? (b) How is this borne out by King Solomon's example?

TV in the morning and keep it off all day.' Yes, in addition to praying to overcome her weakness, she had to work at overcoming it.

Prayer and Our Witnessing

[17] Nowhere is the principle that prayers require works more true than in the Kingdom-preaching work. Thus, all of Jehovah's Witnesses not only pray for an increase in harvest workers but also apply themselves to that work. As a result, they have seen phenomenal increases in one land after another. To note just one example: In 1930 there was only one witness of Jehovah preaching in Chile. Today, that one Witness has become not only a thousand but some 30,000. (Isaiah 60:22) Was this merely the result of prayers? No, work was also involved. Why, in 1986 alone, Jehovah's Witnesses in Chile devoted over 6,492,000 hours to the preaching work!

[18] The same is true when the preaching work is banned. Witnesses not only pray for increase but also go underground and keep on preaching. Despite official opposition, therefore, increases take place in these lands. Thus, in 33 lands where Jehovah's Witnesses meet with such official opposition, during the 1986 service year they devoted more than 32,600,000 hours to their preaching work and rejoiced in a 4.6-percent increase!

[19] Of course, the principle that prayers require works also applies individually. We may pray to Jehovah to get a home Bible study but may not be doing all we can to obtain one. That was the experience of one pioneer. Having only one Bible study, she prayed to have more. Did she let matters go at that? No, but she carefully took note of her ministry and found that on her return visits she was not bringing up the subject of having a home Bible study. Proceeding along this line, she soon had two more Bible studies.

[20] Many more examples could be given to prove that prayers require works. For instance, there are those relating to personal relationships in the family or the congregation. But the foregoing examples should suffice to make it fully clear that prayers do require works. This is most logical, for we cannot expect Jehovah God to give favorable consideration to our petitions if we offend him by our very conduct. It also follows that we must do all we can in harmony with our prayers if we are to expect Jehovah to do for us what we cannot do for ourselves. Truly, Jehovah's principles are wise and just. They make sense, and it is to our own benefit that we act in harmony with them.

20. How may the principle that prayers require works be summed up?

17-19. (a) What facts show that Jehovah's Witnesses have been acting in harmony with their prayers? (b) What example of an individual makes the same point?

Do You Recall?

□ What requirement regarding prayer was overlooked by many in ancient Israel?

□ Why is God not unreasonable in requiring that we work as well as pray for what we desire?

□ What ancient examples show that Jehovah's servants worked at what they prayed for?

□ For God to answer our prayers for his holy spirit and for wisdom, what must we be doing?

□ How does the principle that prayers require works apply to our field ministry?

William Tyndale's Bible for the People

From an old engraving in the Bibliothèque Nationale

IT WAS a day in May in the year 1530.* St. Paul's churchyard in London was crowded with people. Instead of milling around the booksellers' stalls and exchanging the latest news and gossip as usual, the crowd was visibly agitated. A fire was roaring at the center of the square. But it was no ordinary bonfire. Into the fire, some men were emptying basketfuls of books. It was a book burning!

Those were not ordinary books either. They were Bibles—William Tyndale's "New Testament" and Pentateuch—the first ever to be printed in English. Strangely, those Bibles were being burned at the order of the Bishop of London, Cuthbert Tunstall. In fact, he had spent a considerable sum buying all the copies he could find. What could possibly have been wrong with the Bibles? Why did Tyndale produce them? And why did the authorities go to such lengths to get rid of them?

The Bible—A Closed Book

In most parts of the world today, it is a relatively simple thing to purchase a Bible.

---

* Events similar to those described here had taken place in 1526 and at other times.

But this has not always been the case. Even in 15th- and early 16th-century England, the Bible was viewed as the property of the church, a book to be read only at public services and explained solely by the priests. What was read, however, was usually from the Latin Bible, which the common people could neither understand nor afford. Thus, what they knew of the Bible was no more than the stories and moral lessons drawn by the clergy.

But the common people were not the only ones ignorant of the Bible. Reportedly, during the reign of King Edward VI (1547-53), a bishop of Gloucester found that among 311 clergymen, 168 could not repeat the Ten Commandments and 31 did not know where to find them in the Bible. Forty could not recite the Lord's Prayer and about 40 did not know its originator. True, John Wycliffe had produced a Bible in English in 1384, and paraphrases of various parts of the Scriptures, such as the Gospels and the Psalms, existed in that tongue. Nevertheless, the Bible was in fact a closed book.

Conditions like these made Tyndale determine to make the Bible available to the English-speaking people. "I perceived how that it was impossible to establish the lay people in any truth," he wrote, "except the Scripture were plainly laid before their eyes in their mother tongue."

But by translating the Bible into English, Tyndale incurred the wrath of the authorities. Why? Because as early as 1408 a council of clergymen met at Oxford, England, to decide whether the common people should be allowed to have copies of the Bible in their own tongue for personal use. The decision read, in part: "We therefore decree and ordain, that from henceforward no unauthorised person shall translate any part of the holy Scripture into English or any other language . . . under the penalty of the greater excommunication, till the said translation shall be approved either by the bishop of the diocese, or a provincial council as occasion shall require."

More than a century later, Bishop Tunstall applied this decree in burning Tyndale's Bible, even though Tyndale had earlier sought the approval of Tunstall.* In the opinion of Tunstall, Tyndale's translation contained some 2,000 errors and was therefore "pestilent, scandalous, and seductive of simple minds." But was this an excuse on the part of the bishop to justify his burning of it? Was Tyndale really a poor translator, lacking the necessary scholarship in Hebrew, Greek, and English? How good a translator was Tyndale?

Tyndale—A Poor Translator?

Although the understanding of Hebrew and Greek then was not what it is today, Tyndale's grasp of these languages compared well with that of most scholars of his time. What makes Tyndale's work stand out is that he did not merely consult the Latin *Vulgate* and Luther's German translation. He went back to the original Greek text published for the first time in 1516 by Erasmus. Tyndale also did not forget his purpose: to make the Scriptures easy enough for the ordinary layman to read, right down to the "boy who plows the field." So his style and idiom are simple and clear, yet powerful. And his lively rhythm no doubt reflects the joy that he experienced in undertaking the task.

So it is true to say that "Tyndale was a

---

* For more details on Tyndale's life and work, see *The Watchtower* of January 1, 1982, pages 10-14.

translator whose judgment was unusually good. Working in extraordinarily adverse conditions, at his day's frontiers of knowledge of biblical languages, he produced translations which set the pattern for all the English translators who followed." —*The Making of the English Bible,* by Gerald Hammond, pages 42, 43.

An Accurate Translation

In matters of accuracy Tyndale also set a high standard. For example, in translating from Hebrew, he tried to be as literal as possible while maintaining an easy, flowing English style. He was careful even to reproduce the Hebrew fullness of description with its frequent repetition of the word "and" joining clause after clause in a sentence. (See Genesis chapter 33 in the *King James Version,* which retains Tyndale's wording almost entirely.) He paid close attention to the context and avoided additions to or omissions from the original text, even though paraphrasing was resorted to by most translators of the time.

Tyndale's word choice was also careful and accurate. For example, he used "love" instead of "charity," "congregation" for "church," and "elder" rather than "priest" where appropriate. This infuriated critics like Sir Thomas More because it changed words that had come to be venerated through tradition. Where the original demanded the repetition of a word, Tyndale was careful to reproduce it. To illustrate: At Genesis 3:15, his translation twice speaks of 'treading' done by the seed of the woman and by the serpent.*

Tyndale was also responsible for intro-

---

* Many modern translators fail to note the repeated Hebrew verb here with its reciprocal meaning. So instead of "bruise . . . bruise" (*New World Translation; Revised Standard Version*), they use "crush . . . strike" (*The Jerusalem Bible; New International Version*), "crush . . . bite" (*Today's English Version*), "tread . . . strike" (*Lamsa*), or "crush . . . lie in ambush" (*Knox*).

ducing God's personal name, *Jehovah,* into the English Bible. As writer J. F. Mozley observes, Tyndale used it "more than twenty times in his Old Testament" translations.

Looking back on the effect of Tyndale's efforts and their enduring qualities, this modern assessment well sums up his work: "Tindale's honesty, sincerity, and scrupulous integrity, his simple directness, his magical simplicity of phrase, his modest music, have given an authority to his wording that has imposed itself on all later versions. . . . Nine-tenths of the Authorized New Testament [*King James Version*] is still Tindale, and the best is still his."—*The Bible in Its Ancient and English Versions,* page 160.

Tyndale's Work Not in Vain

To escape the persecution of the authorities, Tyndale fled to mainland Europe to continue his work. But he was at last caught. Convicted of heresy, he was strangled and burned at the stake in October 1536. His final prayer was: "Lord, open the King of England's eyes." Little did he know how soon the situation would change. In August 1537, less than a year after Tyndale's death, King Henry VIII gave authorization to the Bible generally known as Matthew's Bible. He decreed that it should be freely sold and read within his realm.

What was Matthew's Bible? Professor F. F. Bruce explains: "On examination it is seen to be substantially Tyndale's Pentateuch, Tyndale's version of the historical books of the Old Testament as far as 2 Chronicles . . . Coverdale's version of the other Old Testament books and Apocrypha, and Tyndale's New Testament of 1535." Thus, the writer continues, "it was a signal act of justice . . . that the first English Bible to be published under royal licence should be Tyndale's Bible (so far as Tyndale's translation had reached), even if it was not yet advisable to associate Tyndale's name with it publicly."

In a few more years, the wheel was to turn full circle. When an edition of the translation known as the *Great Bible*—a revision of Matthew's Bible—was issued in 1541 and commanded to be placed in every church in England, the title page included this statement: "Oversene and perused at the comaundemet of the kynges hyghnes, by the ryghte reverende fathers in God Cuthbert bysshop of Duresme, and Nicholas bishop of Rochester." Yes, this 'Bishop of Durham' was none other than Cuthbert Tunstall, formerly Bishop of London. He who had so bitterly opposed the work of Tyndale was now giving approval to the issuing of the *Great Bible,* a work still essentially that of Tyndale.

Final Recognition

It may be surprising today to read of such controversy over the Bible and hatred for its translators. But perhaps more remarkable is the fact that, in spite of their efforts, opposers have been unable to prevent God's Word from reaching the common people. "The green grass has dried up, the blossom has withered," said the prophet Isaiah, "but as for the word of our God, it will last to time indefinite."—Isaiah 40:8.

Tyndale and others worked with the shadow of death looming over their heads. But by making the Bible available to many people in their native tongue, they opened before them the prospect, not of death, but of life eternal. As Jesus Christ said: "This means everlasting life, their taking in knowledge of you, the only true God, and of the one whom you sent forth, Jesus Christ." (John 17:3) May we, therefore, cherish and diligently study God's Word.

Insight on the News

Tolerance of Sin No Virtue

In a recent address to church leaders, religion columnist Michael J. McManus stated that the churches have contributed to a disintegration of the American family. So reports *The Fresno Bee,* a California newspaper. McManus noted that there were 1.2 million divorces and 750,000 illegitimate births in the United States during 1985 and that 2.2 million unmarried couples were living together.

McManus indicated that, instead of staunchly upholding Biblical standards on morality, which urge fidelity in marriage, the church has taken a more passive role on such issues in an effort to bolster attendance. As an example, he cited a recent proposal "that the Episcopal Church drop its opposition to couples who live together without being married."

Such modernistic views on sex and marriage stand in sharp conflict with the Bible. The Christian apostle Paul stated: "Let marriage be honorable among all, and the marriage bed be without defilement." (Hebrews 13:4) When the Pharisees confronted Jesus Christ on the matter of divorce, he said that "a man will leave his father and his mother and will stick to his wife, and the two will be one flesh." He added: "Whoever divorces his wife, except on the ground of fornication, and marries another commits adultery." —Matthew 19:4, 5, 9.

Responding to proposed leniency by the church on such moral issues, McManus said: "The Episcopal Church has gotten to the point where it says its highest virtue is tolerance. Nowhere does Jesus say to tolerate sin. He condemned sin." Well-informed Bible students agree.

Undeniable Evidence

"After years of proudly skeptical agnosticism, scientists are grudgingly beginning to give God a second look," observes columnist Pete McMartin of *The Vancouver Sun*, a British Columbia, Canada, newspaper. Although religion and science have been in conflict for centuries, "that's simply no longer true," says Wasley Krogdahl, a former University of Kentucky professor of astronomy and physics. He adds: "Cosmology has made it clear that the universe had a beginning, and that implies a creator."— *The State Journal-Register,* Springfield, Illinois.

At least some scientists are rethinking the origin of the universe. The reason? "The universe makes a lot more sense than it did 50 years ago," explains astronomer Krogdahl. During the last 25 years, the development of more sensitive equipment has resulted in the discovery of quasars, neutron stars, and pulsars. Krogdahl concedes that as the knowledge of the universe increases, so does the evidence that there *is* a God. Such evidence, he notes, "has simply knocked the props out from under the atheists."

Yet, what has taken scientific minds years to accept after exhaustive research and study, students of the Bible have known for centuries. "[The Creator's] invisible attributes, that is to say his everlasting power and deity, have been visible, ever since the world began, to the eye of reason, in the things he has made." (Romans 1: 20, *The New English Bible*) Simply put, the undeniable evidence has always been there.

Orion Nebula

U.S. Naval Observatory photo

'Fishing for Men' in the Arctic

Every summer many of Jehovah's Witnesses preach in "unassigned territories"—outlying areas with no established congregations. Many of them are working people and students who spend their vacation doing so. Others are full-time pioneers branching out in their ministry. They experience the joy of bringing the good news to isolated people and of being brought closer to their family and spiritual brothers. This is an account of such an expedition in the far north.

S LOWLY the fishing cutter *Skagstein* slid from the quay. It was an early summer's eve. A gentle easterly breeze rippled the sea and brought refreshing relief from the smell of fish and herring oil. Standing on deck, we waved good-bye to Båtsfjord, the largest fishing village in East Finnmark, Norway.

On board was a crew of eight. Øivind and Åshild had come to Båtsfjord 11 years earlier to help with the preaching work in this unassigned territory. Now, as they were moving to another area, a congregation of nearly 40 Kingdom publishers was flourishing here. The rest of the crew consisted of the skipper, Jarle (a professional fisherman and "seasonal" pioneer), two pioneer sisters, one excavator operator, one industrial worker, and one office clerk from the Norwegian Bethel Home. What had brought this group together? And on what kind of voyage were they embarking?

Going Island to Island

This time Jarle was not after codfish. The plan was for us to call from island to island and outpost to outpost on board *Skagstein* from Båtsfjord in the far north to Brønnøysund in the county of Nordland. We would be covering more than half the Norwegian coastline. Why? Well, many of these places can only be reached by private boat, and it is just once every several years that Jehovah's Witnesses call at these places with the Kingdom message. We had decided to go 'fishing for men' in these outposts.—Matthew 4:18, 19.

The boat headed out of Båtsfjorden and went westward along the coast all night. It was the first of July. The midnight sun, hidden by a smooth blanket of clouds, shone with a grayish, soft light. Thousands of sea gulls and kittiwakes were visible on the cliffs. The roll and swell of the open sea was just fine, according to the skipper. But for some of us landlubbers, it was a bit rough.

The next morning we drew up alongside the quay at Honningsvåg. This is where our "fishing"—preaching work—was to begin. The people in northern Norway have a reputation for being hospitable. When we had given a short account of our mission, we were generally offered a seat on a kitchen stool and were served coffee. Then we had to give a full account of who we were, where we had come from, our occupation, the name and size of our boat, whether we had caught any fish thus far, and the remainder of our itinerary. Only after that was out of the way could we get to the real point of the visit—the good news of God's Kingdom.

Warm Response in the Frozen Arctic

Would the message appeal to these people on an island 300 miles (480 km) north of the Arctic Circle? What were they really concerned about? Exactly what people everywhere else are concerned about: social injustice, unemployment, money, family and personal problems. They were also worried about the tense world situation —north-south relations and the east-west conflict.

It was easy for us to point to the Bible's solution—God's Kingdom. And how rewarding to see pessimism and skepticism melt away and be replaced by joy and hope!

Many people in these faraway places have prayed for the Kingdom since childhood, but they have never really understood the meaning of such a prayer. (Matthew 6:9-13) We left Bible literature with many of the islanders and arranged to correspond with them in order to keep up their interest.

Though it was summertime, the temperature was only in the mid-30's (2° C) in Rolvsøy, and a strong wind was blowing. Shivering and tightly bundled up in his coat, one of the brothers approached a man standing along the shore.

"Are you cold?" the man inquired.

"Eh . . . " the brother hesitated.

"Come along and have something hot to eat and drink!"

Inside the house, the brother was led to the kitchen, where the man's wife was busy.

"Have you got some coffee for this chap?" the man asked.

Hot coffee was served along with chunks of bread, homemade cloudberry jam, and salmon. After a pleasant conversation, the brother left some Bible literature and went on to the next call, warm and encouraged. Such were the experiences of witnessing to the friendly and hospitable people in these remote, isolated areas.

An Enriching Experience

As *Skagstein* plowed its way through the waves from island to island, the crew was thrown together in more ways than one. Eight people living closely together for days and weeks on a 38-foot (12 m) boat soon get to know one another's distinctive traits. We learned to get along with one another and to be considerate. The rough edges were smoothed out, and our Christian personality was polished. (Colossians 3:9, 10) So the experience proved to be most rewarding.

Together, we discussed the daily Bible

text and talked about the experiences of the day. We would review what had been said and done and what might have been said and done. This stimulated us to put forth greater effort to be effective in talking to the people. The younger and newer ones received sound advice and encouragement to widen out in their ministry.

"I have been thinking about the full-time ministry ever since I was baptized," said 27-year-old Bjørn. "During our trip, the desire and courage to 'test Jehovah out' grew in me little by little. I experienced what great confidence we can have in Jehovah. The trip made it easier for me to get into the pioneer work."—Malachi 3:10.

The trip also helped us to see more clearly the urgency of the times. Many of the communities we visited were slowly dying. Fishing mills were shutting down. Post offices and shops were closing. People were worried as they saw young people moving on for opportunities in faraway towns and cities, leaving behind fine new houses and the traditional way of life. Around the world, millions are homeless and starving. Here you find empty homes and plenty of food from the sea. Yet, comparatively few want them. All of this is silent proof of a world out of balance.

On With the Journey

The expedition went on along the north side of Sørøya to Kvænangen. At some of the stops, we had to get ashore by rowboat. But at other places, Skagstein could pull up right alongside the quay. Many of the local people crowded around to see who these strangers were because we surely did not look like fishermen to them. When they found out that we were Jehovah's Witnesses coming with good news from the Bible, lively conversations usually followed.

After covering this area, we headed for Tromsø, where some of us would attend the "Divine Peace" District Convention. This part of the journey was truly an outstanding experience. It was night, but the midnight sun shone brilliantly just over the horizon. To the right, darkened islands and islets stood in sharp silhouette. To the left, snow-covered mountains glistened in the sunlight. The weather was mild, and the sea was broken only by a slight ripple. All was calm and quiet, except for the rhythmic hum of the engine and a little soothing music from our radio. What a pleasant atmosphere!

After the convention in Tromsø, there was a slight change in the crew. Then the expedition went on, skirting Senja and going through the island group Vesterålen to Bodø and then down to Brønnøysund, our final destination. In many places along the way, such as Rødøy, we met people who had never spoken with Jehovah's Witnesses. It had been years since preaching visits had been made, and now a new generation had grown up.

An Unforgettable Voyage

By the time we reached Brønnøysund, it was the end of August. As we looked back on the weeks spent aboard Skagstein, we felt that it was truly an unforgettable voyage. On this trip we had spent a total of 880 hours preaching the good news and had placed 126 books and 1,026 magazines, also obtaining 12 subscriptions for The Watchtower and Awake! An abundance of Kingdom seed had been sown in these sparsely populated areas.

"It was the finest vacation I've ever had!" exclaimed one of the young publishers who went on the trip. Those of us who were privileged to share in this journey heartily agreed. We felt that it was not only a fine vacation but one of the most spiritually beneficial and rewarding things we had ever done.

Does True Christianity Produce Fanatics?

CHRISTENDOM has had its fanatics —from people who set themselves on fire in political protest to individuals acting intolerantly toward those holding different religious views. For example, the first Crusade was inspired by the Catholic Church to free Jerusalem from the hands of people she considered to be infidels. It began with three undisciplined mobs whose violent excesses included a pogrom of Jews in the Rhineland. When the military forces of this Crusade succeeded in taking Jerusalem, these so-called Christian soldiers turned the streets into rivers of blood.

In his book *The Outline of History,* H. G. Wells said of the first Crusade: "The slaughter was terrible; the blood of the conquered ran down the streets, until men splashed in blood as they rode. At nightfall, 'sobbing for excess of joy,' the crusaders came to the Sepulchre from their treading of the winepress, and put their blood-stained hands together in prayer."

In a later Crusade called by Pope Innocent III, the peaceful Albigenses and Waldenses, who objected to the doctrines of Rome and the excesses of the clergy, were massacred. Regarding the fanaticism expressed against them, Wells wrote: "This was enough for the Lateran, and so we have the spectacle of Innocent III preaching a crusade against these unfortunate sectaries, and permitting the enlistment of every wandering scoundrel . . . and every conceivable outrage among the most peaceful subjects of the King of France. The accounts of the cruelties and abominations of this crusade are far more terrible to read than any account of Christian martyrdoms by the pagans."

Christendom's history is full of accounts of fanatics, and they have usually produced fruits of violence. So we can conclude that fanaticism does not produce good fruitage. Funk and Wagnalls *New Standard Dictionary of the English Language* (1929 edition) defines fanaticism in the following way: "Extravagant or frenzied zeal." And it goes on to illustrate it with these words: "No period of history exhibits a larger amount of cruelty, licentiousness, and *fanaticism* than the Crusades."

It is also of interest to note the definition given to the word "fanatic" by *Webster's Third New International Dictionary,* 1961 edition. It says: 'Fanatic—Latin, inspired by a deity. 1. possessed by or as if by a demon; broadly: crazed, frantic, mad. 2. governed, produced, or characterized by too great zeal: extravagant, unreasonable; excessively enthusiastic, especially on religious subjects.' With these thoughts in mind, can it be said that true Christians are fanatics?

Identified by Fruits

As the fruit of a tree identifies it, so the results of human actions identify what kind of people are producing them. Jesus Christ, the Founder of Christianity, pointed this out. He said: "A good tree cannot bear worthless fruit, neither can a rotten tree produce fine fruit. Really, then, by their fruits you will recognize those men." —Matthew 7:18, 20.

Jesus founded true Christianity as a good tree. It could not, therefore, produce the bad fruits of fanaticism. At no time did Jesus urge his followers to do physical harm to themselves or to others. Instead, in quoting one of the two great commandments, he said: "You must love your neighbor as yourself." (Matthew 22:39) His followers were to be kind even to their enemies. Said Jesus: "Continue to love your enemies, to do good to those hating you, to bless those cursing you, to pray for those who are insulting you."—Luke 6: 27, 28.

Jesus' true followers went out among people of many different nations, not with fire and sword, but with God's written Word and peaceful persuasion. No military armies accompanied them to other lands in order to slaughter, torture, and rape those who rejected Christian baptism. Instead, Jesus' disciples followed his peaceful example of preaching the good news of God's Kingdom to all, encouraging them to reason on information presented from the Scriptures. The fruits of their work included the fruitage of God's spirit—"love, joy, peace, long-suffering, kindness, goodness, faith, mildness, self-control."—Galatians 5:22, 23.

It is not different today. True Christianity still produces good fruit. The tree, the Christian organization, that Jesus planted over 1,900 years ago was good, and it is still good. So it is incapable of producing the bad, intolerant, violent fruits of fanaticism. Why, then, has fanaticism been so common in Christendom?

The apostle Paul indicated that the time would come when imitation Christians would appear. They would bear the name Christian but not live up to it or produce its good fruits. He told elders from Ephesus: "I know that after my going away oppressive wolves will enter in among you and will not treat the flock with

There is no reason to view Jehovah's Witnesses as fanatics because of their zeal in the Christian ministry

tenderness, and from among you yourselves men will rise and speak twisted things to draw away the disciples after themselves." (Acts 20:29, 30) From these apostates arose Christendom with its hundreds of conflicting religious organizations teaching things that are merely represented as being Christian. Actually, they are "twisted things," ideas of men and not the truth of God's Word. It has been among these false Christians that the bad fruitage of fanaticism has manifested itself.

Is Christian Zeal Fanaticism?

It is true that fanaticism is a form of zeal. But fanaticism is an "extravagant or frenzied zeal," an "unreasonable" zeal. This cannot be said of true Christianity.

Repeatedly, the Bible admonishes Christians to be reasonable. For example, Philippians 4:5 says: "Let your reasonableness become known to all men." And Christians are counseled "to speak injuriously of no one, not to be belligerent, to be reasonable, exhibiting all mildness toward all men."—Titus 3:2.

Because Jehovah's Witnesses visit people in their homes to talk about the good news of God's Kingdom, they are different from the majority who claim to be Christians. This zeal in the Christian ministry is no basis for viewing them as fanatics. It is a reasonable zeal for a work that Jesus did and commanded his followers to do. (Matthew 24:14; 28:19, 20) A person who sets aside many time-consuming personal activities in order to devote as much time as possible to the Kingdom-preaching work is not a fanatic. Instead, he shows his appreciation for the urgency of helping others to learn about the life-giving truths of God's Word in the short time remaining for this work to be done. This is reasonable and beneficial.

Instead of being a fanatical work that injures others, this activity builds faith in God and his Word. It gives hope to those without hope, brings freedom from religious superstitions and ignorance, and transforms countless immoral and violent people into morally clean and peaceful Christians. These good fruits indicate a good organization.

In more than 200 lands, Jehovah's Witnesses maintain their loyalty to God's Kingdom, even though they are under official proscription in many places. Their loyalty to God, the Supreme Sovereign, can hardly be classed as fanaticism. He is the highest Authority, and when there is a conflict between his laws and those of a human government, a true Christian is obligated to obey him. Under human governments, local laws are sometimes nullified because they conflict with federal laws. Similarly, for true Christians human laws are nullified when in conflict with those of the Universal Sovereign, Jehovah God. Since a true Christian cannot obey two conflicting laws, he does what the apostles did. They said: "We must obey God as ruler rather than men." (Acts 5:29) This is reasonable.

The same reasonableness is shown by Jehovah's Witnesses with respect to national and religious celebrations that are in conflict with God's Word. It is not fanaticism to decline to participate in what the majority in a country are observing. Being different because of their religious conscience puts the Witnesses in the same category as the early Christians, who did not participate in the popular celebrations of their day. And Jehovah's Witnesses are glad to give a Scriptural reason for their nonparticipation.—1 Peter 3:15.

Some persons may class the Witnesses as fanatics because of their refusal to accept blood transfusions, a procedure that is popular with the majority of doctors. Here again it is a matter of obedience to the law of God. True followers of Jesus Christ are commanded to "keep abstaining . . . from blood."—Acts 15:28, 29.

Is a person fanatical because, for conscience' sake, he rejects a medical procedure that is currently popular? Some people who are not Jehovah's Witnesses reject blood transfusions out of fear of contracting AIDS or other diseases. So is it unreasonable for the Witnesses to request medical treatment that does not violate their conscience?

What, then, should be concluded from this? That Jehovah's Witnesses are not fanatics because they are different from the majority and insist on being obedient to God. Although they have a zeal for God, they do not have an "extravagant or frenzied zeal" as if possessed by a demon; nor do they appear to be "crazed, frantic," or "mad." At no time do they out of religious zeal do violent harm to others or to themselves. Rather, in harmony with what the Bible says about true Christians, they are "peaceable with all men."—Romans 12:18.

So the Christian organization that Jesus Christ began in the first century as a good tree continues today producing only good fruit. It is, therefore, impossible for true Christianity to produce fanatics.

Questions From Readers

■ **Are Jehovah and Jesus the ones meant at Proverbs 30:4, which asks: "What is his name and what the name of his son?"**

This verse makes it evident how limited man is compared to the Most High. Its rhetorical questions could be asked about any man, but these questions should lead a reasoning person to the Creator.

The writer Agur asked: "Who has ascended to heaven that he may descend? Who has gathered the wind in the hollow of both hands? Who has wrapped up the waters in a mantle? Who has made all the ends of the earth to rise? What is his name and what the name of his son, in case you know?"—Proverbs 30:1, 4.

No imperfect human has gone up to heaven and come back omniscient; nor has any human the ability to control the wind, the seas, or the geological forces shaping the earth. In effect, then, Agur asked: 'Do you know the name or family line of any man who has done these things?' We must answer no.—Compare Job 38:1–42:3; Isaiah 40:12-14; Jeremiah 23:18; 1 Corinthians 2:16.

Thus, we have to look outside the human sphere to find one who has the superhuman power to control natural forces. We are not, though, limited to learning about him by observing his accomplishments. (Romans 1:20) This is because he has, as it were, descended with information about himself and his dealings. He has provided specific information. He did this, for example, when he 'descended' to give the Law to Moses on Mount Sinai. (Exodus 19:20; Hebrews 2:2) He has also helped his servants to appreciate his meaningful name, Jehovah. (Exodus 3:13, 14; 6:3) Later, he identified his Son, who was named Jesus and who literally descended from heaven with additional information about the Creator.—John 1:1-3, 14, 18.

This should help all of us to reach certain conclusions: Like Agur, we cannot from our own resources gain true wisdom. (Proverbs 30:2, 3) And we cannot name any human who has superlative powers or knowledge. Hence, we should humbly look to the One who is able to provide the wisdom we need. This is the Most Holy One, whose name we can know and whose Son has died so that we might be ransomed and gain everlasting life. —Matthew 20:28.

"This book should receive an Oscar"

The following letter was received from East Orange, New Jersey, U.S.A.

"Dear Sir:

"I recently had the pleasure of reading the book *Life—How Did It Get Here? By Evolution or by Creation?* I picked it up by accident while working in the mail room on my job. And I thought the book was just fascinating. The people who composed this wonderful piece of work deserve to be complimented. I don't give out free compliments, but they certainly have my sincere compliments.

"I have two lovely daughters, eleven and seven years of age. I'm certain this book would prove to be a valuable instrument in the primary education they are now receiving. The book was very well written with large print—great for Dear Old Dad's eyes. This book should receive an Oscar [an award] because it is colorful, superbly illustrated and masterfully laid out. . . . Please tell me where and how to order. I want three copies, so please send some order forms and the price as soon as possible."

The Watchtower

Announcing Jehovah's Kingdom

August 1, 1987

Alcohol:
What the Bible Really Says

The Watchtower®

Announcing Jehovah's Kingdom

August 1, 1987
Vol. 108, No. 15

In This Issue

THE PURPOSE OF "THE WATCHTOWER" is to exalt Jehovah God as the Sovereign of the universe. It keeps watch on world events as they fulfill Bible prophecy. It comforts all peoples with the good news that God's Kingdom will soon destroy those who oppress their fellowmen and that it will turn the earth into a paradise. It encourages faith in the now-reigning King, Jesus Christ, whose shed blood opens the way for mankind to gain eternal life. "The Watchtower," published by Jehovah's Witnesses continuously since 1879, is nonpolitical. It adheres to the Bible as its authority.

"WATCHTOWER" STUDIES FOR THE WEEKS

September 6: Christ Actively Leads His Congregation. Page 10. Songs to Be Used: 18, 50.

September 13: Christ's Active Leadership Today. Page 15. Songs to Be Used: 11, 211.

Average Printing Each Issue: 12,315,000

Now Published in 103 Languages

SEMIMONTHLY LANGUAGES AVAILABLE BY MAIL
Afrikaans, Arabic, Cebuano, Chichewa, Chinese, Cibemba, Danish,* Dutch,* Efik, English,* Finnish,* French,* German,* Greek,* Hiligaynon, Igbo, Iloko, Italian,* Japanese,* Korean, Lingala, Malagasy, Maltese, Norwegian, Portuguese,* Russian, Sepedi, Sesotho, Shona, Spanish,* Swahili, Swedish,* Tagalog, Thai, Tsonga, Tswana, Xhosa, Yoruba, Zulu

MONTHLY LANGUAGES AVAILABLE BY MAIL
Armenian, Bengali, Bicol, Bislama, Bulgarian, Croatian, Czech, Ewe, Fijian, Ga, Greenlandic, Gujarati, Gun, Hausa, Hebrew, Hindi, Hiri Motu, Hungarian, Icelandic, Kannada, Malayalam, Marathi, New Guinea Pidgin, Pangasinan, Papiamento, Polish, Rarotongan, Romanian, Samar-Leyte, Samoan, Sango, Serbian, Silozi, Sinhalese, Slovenian, Solomon Islands-Pidgin, Tahitian, Tamil, Telugu, Tongan, Tshiluba, Turkish, Twi, Ukrainian, Urdu, Venda, Vietnamese

* Study articles also available in large-print edition.

Watch Tower Society offices	Yearly subscription for the above: Semimonthly Languages	Monthly Languages
America, U.S., Watchtower, Wallkill, N.Y. 12589	$4.00	$2.00
Australia, Box 280, Ingleburn, N.S.W. 2565	A$7.00	A$3.50
Canada, Box 4100, Halton Hills, Ontario L7G 4Y4	$5.50	$2.75
England, The Ridgeway, London NW7 1RN	£5.00	£2.50
Ireland, 29A Jamestown Road, Finglas, Dublin 11	IR£6.00	IR£3.00
New Zealand, P.O. Box 142, Manurewa	NZ$15.00	NZ$7.50
Nigeria, PMB 001, Shomolu, Lagos State	₦8.00	₦4.00
Philippines, P.O. Box 2044, Manila 2800	₱60.00	₱30.00
South Africa, Private Bag 2067, Krugersdorp, 1740	R9.00	R4.50

Remittances should be sent to the office in your country or to Watchtower, Wallkill, N.Y. 12589, U.S.A.

Changes of address should reach us 30 days before your moving date. Give us your old and new address (if possible, your old address label).

20 cents (U.S.) a copy

The Bible translation used is the "New World Translation of the Holy Scriptures," unless otherwise indicated.

The Watchtower (ISSN 0043-1087) is published semimonthly for $4.00 (U.S.) per year by Watch Tower Bible and Tract Society of Pennsylvania, 25 Columbia Heights, Brooklyn, N.Y. 11201. Second-class postage paid at Brooklyn, N.Y., and at additional mailing offices.

Postmaster: Send address changes to Watchtower, **Wallkill, N.Y. 12589.**

Published by
**Watch Tower Bible and Tract Society
of Pennsylvania**
25 Columbia Heights, Brooklyn, N.Y. 11201, U.S.A.
Frederick W. Franz, President

Questions People Are Asking About

Alcohol

"WISE men do not drink wine at all." So declared a Nigerian clergyman. Not long ago, such a statement would have been dismissed as intolerant and narrow-minded. Today, though, an anti-alcohol sentiment is growing in some parts of the world.

A recent *Reader's Digest*/Gallup survey (U.S.), for example, revealed that "Americans have started drinking less." *Time* magazine similarly reports that "America is tapering off [alcohol consumption], and doing so at a faster pace than at any time since Prohibition took effect in 1920." France reports a decrease in wine consumption.

The reason for this trend toward temperance? Some have raised a hue and cry over the terrible carnage on public highways due to drunken drivers. "In 1983," claimed *Reader's Digest,* "alcohol . . . cost the [United States] *$89.5* billion in lost employment and productivity, health care, property loss and crime, as well as immeasurable damage to the family lives of those involved." No wonder, then, that the UN's World Health Organization recently recommended that governments 'restrict the availability of alcohol in the interest of

the health and welfare of their populations.' —*New Nigerian,* March 16, 1983.

Some are even arguing for abstinence. The above-quoted Nigerian clergyman claims: "Proverbs 20:1 says specifically that those who drink wine are not wise." And asserts yet another preacher: "The Holy Scriptures condemn alcohol in the Book of Isaiah," referring to the texts at Isaiah 5:11, 12, and 22.

In view of such claims, people wonder: What do such Scripture texts mean? Does the Bible really categorically forbid the consumption of alcoholic beverages? Did not Jesus himself drink wine, or was nonalcoholic grape juice involved? In view of the obvious dangers involved, might it be best for Christians to abstain from the drinking of alcohol? The answers to these questions can be found by looking into the Bible itself.

Alcohol
What Is the Christian View of It?

"**W**HO has woe? Who has uneasiness? Who has contentions? Who has concern? Who has wounds for no reason? Who has dullness of eyes? Those staying a long time with the wine." (Proverbs 23: 29, 30) Yes, the Bible acknowledges that alcoholic drinks can produce some very evil effects: hallucinations, shameful conduct, psychotic behavior, health disorders, family problems, and even poverty.

Note that the above Bible text talks of those "staying a long time" with wine, habitual drunkards! For such ones, alcohol is like a poison, often causing adverse physical and mental effects. (Proverbs 23: 32-35) Heavy drinkers can lose self-control and begin to do things they would normally be ashamed of. The Bible thus warns: "Do not come to be among heavy drinkers of wine, among those who are gluttonous eaters of flesh. For a drunkard and a glutton will come to poverty, and drowsiness will clothe one with mere rags." (Proverbs 23:20, 21) Drunkenness is also classed among "the works of the flesh," which can debar one from entering God's Kingdom. —Galatians 5:19, 21; 1 Corinthians 6:10.

"Not Wise"—For Whom?

Does this mean that alcohol is absolutely forbidden to Christians? What of the clergyman's claim, mentioned in the preceding article, supposedly based on Proverbs 20:1, that "wise men do not drink wine at all." The *King James Version* renders this verse: "Wine is a mocker, strong drink is raging: and whosoever is deceived thereby is not wise." Again, the Bible does not chastise those who *drink* wine but, rather, those who are *deceived* by it! "Those staying a long time with the wine" and "heavy drinkers of wine"—these are the ones who are "not wise."

Consider, too, Isaiah 5:11, 22. These verses read: "Woe to those who are getting up early in the morning that they may seek just intoxicating liquor, who are lingering till late in the evening darkness so that wine itself inflames them! Woe to those who are mighty in drinking wine, and to the men with vital energy for mixing intoxicating liquor." What is Isaiah condemning? Is it not *excessive* drinking, that is, drinking from "early in the morning" till "late in the evening darkness"?

Faithful servants of God—like Abraham, Isaac, and Jesus—are reported as drinking wine, in moderation. (Genesis 14: 18; 27:25; Luke 7:34) The Bible also mentions wine among the blessings coming from Jehovah. (Genesis 27:37; Deuteronomy 11:14; Isaiah 25:6-8) The Bible even indicates that wine in moderation can have beneficial effects. Wine "makes the heart of mortal man rejoice," said the psalmist. (Psalm 104:15) The apostle Paul recommended to Timothy: "Do not drink [contaminated] water any longer, but use a little wine for the sake of your stomach and your frequent cases of sickness." —1 Timothy 5:23.

Wine or Grape Juice?

Some argue that the "wine" spoken of in such Bible texts was ordinary grape juice. McClintock and Strong's *Cyclopedia,* however, reminds us that "the Bible makes no distinction between intoxicating and non-intoxicating wines—never refers or alludes to such a distinction." Consistent with this, in the Bible "wine" is shown to be an intoxicating beverage and is associated with "strong drink."—Genesis 9:21; Luke 1:15; Deuteronomy 14:26; Proverbs 31:4, 6.

Interestingly, Jesus' first miracle was to convert water into wine. The Bible account says: "When, now, the director of the feast tasted the . . . wine but did not know what its source was, . . . [he] called the bridegroom and said to him: 'Every other man puts out the fine wine first, and when people are intoxicated, the inferior. You have reserved the fine wine until now.'" (John 2:9, 10) Yes, "the fine wine" Jesus produced was real wine.

Indeed, self-righteous religious leaders in Jesus' day criticized him for occasionally drinking wine. Said Jesus: "John the Baptist has come neither eating bread nor drinking wine, but you say, 'He has a demon.' The Son of man has come eating and drinking, but you say, 'Look! A man gluttonous and given to drinking wine!'" (Luke 7:33, 34) What would have been the point of contrast between Jesus' drinking and John's not drinking if Jesus had merely been drinking nonalcoholic grape juice?

Remember, it was said of John that he was to "drink no wine and strong drink at all." —Luke 1:15.

Obviously, Jesus did not condemn the drinking of alcoholic beverages in moderation. In his day the drinking of wine was a part of the celebration of the Passover.* And real wine continued to be a part of the Lord's Evening Meal, which replaced the Passover.

Judgment Is Required

So the Bible does not prohibit the drinking of alcoholic drinks. In most cases, whether to have strong drink or not is a matter for personal decision. Yet the Bible forcefully condemns *drunkenness,* along with gluttony: "Do not come to be among heavy drinkers of wine, . . . gluttonous eaters of flesh. For a drunkard and a glutton will come to poverty." (Proverbs 23: 20, 21) Thus, all should display moderation and self-control. "Do not be getting drunk with wine, in which there is debauchery, but keep getting filled with spirit." Remember, self-control is one of the fruits of God's spirit.—Ephesians 5:18; Galatians 5:19-23.

Indeed, one does not have to get drunk to run into problems with alcohol. A booklet produced by the U.S. National Institute on Drug Abuse reminds us: "When someone has a drink, the alcohol is absorbed through the digestive system into the bloodstream and reaches the brain quickly. It begins to slow down the parts of the brain that control thinking and emotion. The person feels less inhibited, freer." This "less inhibited" feeling can expose one to moral dangers.

Another danger exists when it comes to

* In Palestine, grapes were harvested in late summer. The Jewish Passover and the Lord's Evening Meal, however, took place in spring—six months later. Without means of preservation, grape juice would naturally ferment.

A Christian may decide to abstain from the drinking of alcoholic beverages on account of another's conscience

driving. According to some estimates, in the United States alone 25,000 people a year are killed in accidents caused by intoxicated drivers. Evidently, many greatly underestimate how severely alcohol impairs their reflexes. But Christians view life as a gift from Jehovah. (Psalm 36:9) Would it be consistent with this view for a person to risk his own life, and that of others, by driving while his reflexes are slowed down by alcohol? Thus, many Christians have decided not to touch alcohol at all when they have to drive.

A Christian is also concerned about the effect of his drinking on others. Doubtless this is why Christian overseers, ministerial servants, and older women all are exhorted not to give themselves "to a *lot* of wine." (1 Timothy 3:2, 3, 8; Titus 2:2, 3) While one person may have a seemingly high tolerance for intoxicating beverages, he is careful to be moderate in his drinking so as not to influence someone else wrongly; nor does he endeavor to force liquor on someone who does not wish to drink. The Bible further says: "It is well not to eat flesh or to drink wine or do anything over which your brother stumbles."—Romans 14:21.

Some circumstances may even call for abstaining from drinking. Consider pregnancy. The *International Herald Tribune* (Paris edition) cited a study done at the University of North Carolina (U.S.A.) and reported that "a single episode of heavy drinking early in pregnancy may result in serious physical and mental damage to the developing child." Women should seriously weigh such possible risks of drinking during pregnancy.

Those with a history of drunkenness or a tendency to be immoderate may also find it best to forsake drinking altogether.* It likewise might be best to avoid drinking in the presence of one who is an alcoholic or whose conscience condemns drinking. And drinking intoxicating beverages before Christian meetings or when engaged in the public preaching work would be improper. The ancient Levites set the pattern for this in abstaining when on duty in the temple.—Leviticus 10:8-10.

Finally, respect should be paid to the laws of the land. In some countries alcohol is absolutely forbidden. In others, it is restricted to adults above a certain age. A Christian obeys such policies of "the superior authorities."—Romans 13:1.

Of course, whether you will drink alcoholic beverages or not or how much or how little you will drink are personal decisions. God is glorified when we use discernment and willingly choose the course of moderation. Follow, then, this wise course so that "whether you are eating or drinking or doing anything else," you will "do all things for God's glory."—1 Corinthians 10:31.

---

* Doctors recommend that one diagnosed as an alcoholic *completely abstain* from alcohol. See *Awake!* of July 8, 1982.

Children's Unique Gift

THE sincere expressions of children often cause adults to stop and think. On one occasion, after seeing Jesus perform some of his miracles, boys began to cry out: "Save, we pray, the Son of David!" The religious leaders objected to this. Blinded by jealousy, they could not discern that Jesus was the Messianic descendant of King David. But Jesus answered them and said: "Did you never read this, 'Out of the mouth of babes and sucklings [God has] furnished praise'?" (Matthew 21:15, 16) Today, God still uses "the mouth of babes" to help those whose minds are blinded by false teaching.—2 Corinthians 4:4.

□ Daleen, aged 12, proved herself a responsible girl at school. One day she was assigned to keep the class busy while her teacher did other work. What would she do? "I decided to explain to my classmates that righteous people will live forever on earth and that everyone will not go to heaven," said Daleen. With the teacher's permission, Daleen presented her information to the class in the form of a conversation with a willing classmate. She read a number of scriptures, including Psalm 37:29: "The righteous themselves will possess the earth, and they will reside forever upon it." What was the response? "The teacher stopped her work and listened as attentively as the children," says Daleen. "Afterward she thanked me, and a few of the children asked questions."

□ Lillian, aged 5, and her parents lived 12 miles (19 km) from a small South African town where they frequently attended meetings and engaged in house-to-house preaching. One Sunday, because of some car trouble, her parents decided to stay home. "Why aren't we going out preaching?" asked Lillian. Not being satisfied with the reason, she said: "I'm not going to let that stop me." Later the mother noticed that Lillian and her witnessing bag were both missing. The little girl was busy visiting nearby homes, liberally giving out Bible literature—including her mother's personal Bible! One elderly lady was so impressed with Lillian's explanation of the coming Paradise that she later accepted the offer of a Bible study from Lillian's mother. This woman eventually became a dedicated worshiper of Jehovah.

Yes, God still uses "the mouth of babes" to furnish praise. Their sincerity can deeply touch adult hearts. Appropriately, then, children along with adults are included in the grand invitation: "Praise Jehovah from the earth, . . . you young men and also you virgins, you old men together with boys. Let them praise the name of Jehovah, for his name alone is unreachably high."—Psalm 148: 7, 12, 13.

Preparation to Face Persecution

AFTER instructing his apostles in methods of carrying out the preaching work, Jesus warns them about opposers. He says: "Look! I am sending you forth as sheep amidst wolves . . . Be on your guard against men; for they will deliver you up to local courts, and they will scourge you in their synagogues. Why, you will be haled before governors and kings for my sake."

Despite the severe persecution his followers will face, Jesus reassuringly promises: "When they deliver you up, do not become anxious about how or what you are to speak; for what you are to speak will be given you in that hour; for the ones speaking are not just you, but it is the spirit of your Father that speaks by you."

"Further," Jesus continues, "brother will deliver up brother to death, and a father his child, and children will rise up against parents and will have them put to death." He adds: "You will be objects of hatred by all people on account of my name; but he that has endured to the end is the one that will be saved."

The preaching is of primary importance, so Jesus emphasizes the need for discretion so as to remain free to carry out the work. "When they perse-

cute you in one city, flee to another," he says, "for truly I say to you, You will by no means complete the circuit of the cities of Israel until the Son of man arrives."

It is true that Jesus gave this instruction, warning, and encouragement to his 12 apostles, but it was also meant for those who would share in the worldwide preaching after his death and resurrection. This is shown by the fact that he said his disciples would be 'hated by all people,' not just by the Israelites to whom the apostles were sent to preach. Further, the apostles evidently were not haled before governors and kings when Jesus sent them out on their short preaching campaign. Moreover, believers were not then delivered up to death by family members.

So when saying that his disciples would not complete their circuit of preaching "until the Son of man arrives," Jesus was prophetically telling us that his disciples would not complete the circuit of the entire inhabited earth with the preaching about God's established Kingdom before the glorified King Jesus Christ would arrive as Jehovah's executional officer at Armageddon.

Continuing his preaching instructions, Jesus says: "A disciple is not above his teacher, nor a slave above his lord." So Jesus' followers must expect to receive the same ill-treatment and persecution as he did for preaching God's Kingdom. Yet he admonishes: "Do not become fearful of those who kill the body but cannot kill the soul; but rather be in fear of him that can destroy both soul and body in Gehenna."

Jesus set the example in this matter. He fearlessly endured death rather than compromise his loyalty to the One with all power, Jehovah God. Yes, it is Jehovah who not only can destroy one's "soul" (meaning in this instance one's future prospects as a living soul) but can even resurrect a person to enjoy everlasting life. What a loving, compassionate heavenly Father Jehovah is!

Jesus next encourages his disciples with an illustration that highlights Jehovah's loving care for them. "Do not two sparrows sell for a coin of small value?" he asks. "Yet not one of them will fall to the ground without your Father's knowledge. But the very hairs of your head are all numbered. Therefore have no fear: you are worth more than many sparrows."

The Kingdom message Jesus commissions his disciples to proclaim will divide households, as certain family members accept it and others reject it. "Do not think I came to put peace upon the earth," he explains. "I came to put, not peace, but a sword." Thus, for a family member to embrace Bible truth requires courage. "He that has greater affection for father or mother than for me is not worthy of me," Jesus observes, "and he that has greater affection for son or daughter than for me is not worthy of me."

Concluding his instructions, Jesus explains that those who receive his disciples receive him also. "And whoever gives one of these little ones only a cup of cold water to drink because he is a disciple, I tell you truly, he will by no means lose his reward." **Matthew 10:16-42.**

♦ What warnings did Jesus provide his disciples?
♦ What encouragement and comfort did he give them?
♦ Why do Jesus' instructions apply also to modern-day Christians?
♦ In what way is a disciple of Jesus not above his teacher?

Christ Actively Leads His Congregation

"The God of our Lord Jesus Christ . . . made him head over all things to the congregation."—EPHESIANS 1:17, 22.

JEHOVAH'S WITNESSES recognize no man as their leader. Their organizational structure has no equivalent of the pope of the Roman Catholic Church, the patriarchs of the Eastern Orthodox Churches, or the leaders of other churches and sects of Christendom. Their allegiance is to Jesus Christ, the Head of the Christian congregation, who stated: "Your Leader is one, the Christ."—Matthew 23:10.

1. How might some members of Christendom's churches answer the question, 'Who is your leader?' but how do Jehovah's Witnesses answer?

[2] At Pentecost the apostle Peter testified: "David did not ascend to the heavens, but he himself says, 'Jehovah said to my Lord: "Sit at my right hand, until I place your enemies as a stool for your feet."'' Therefore let all the house of Israel know for a certainty that God made him both Lord and Christ, this Jesus whom you impaled." (Acts 2:34-36) But while recognizing that in 33 C.E. Jesus was made Lord and Head of the congregation, are we inclined to think of him as having passively sat at Jehovah's right hand, awaiting his enthronement in 1914? Are we fully aware that right from the start Christ *actively* led his congregation?

2. Why do Jehovah's Witnesses recognize Christ as the Head of the Christian congregation, but what questions might be asked?

Christ also led his congregation by means of a visible governing body

Divine Means for Actively Governing

[3] The evening before his death, Jesus said to his faithful apostles: "It is for your benefit I am going away. For if I do not go away, the helper will by no means come to you; but if I do go my way, I will send him to you." (John 16:7) He was going to send not a person but an active force. He made this explicit just before ascending to heaven, saying to his assembled disciples: "I am sending forth upon you *that which is promised* by my Father. You, though, abide in the city until you become clothed with *power* from on high."—Luke 24:49.

[4] Jesus' faithful disciples stayed in the Jerusalem area until Pentecost. That day they "became filled with holy spirit," as promised. Peter testified: "Because he [Jesus] was exalted to the right hand of God and received the promised holy spirit from the Father, he has poured out this which you see and hear." (Acts 2:4, 33) By this means Jehovah begot these early Christians as his spiritual sons. (Galatians 4:6) Also, Jesus received the spirit from his Father as a means of actively governing his congregation on earth from his heavenly position at God's right hand.

[5] Furthermore, the apostle Peter wrote concerning Jesus: "He is at God's right hand, for he went his way to heaven; and angels and authorities and powers were made subject to him." (1 Peter 3:22) Angels are, therefore, another means that Jehovah put at Christ's disposal of actively leading the Christian congregation.

[6] Consequently, when we read in the book of Acts that "Jehovah's angel" or "an angel of God" acted in support of the Christian preaching work or intervened in behalf of members of the Christian congregation, there is every reason to believe that such angels acted under the supervision of Christ Jesus. (Acts 5:19; 8:26; 10:3-7, 22; 12:7-11; 27:23, 24) As "Michael the archangel," Christ has angels at his command, and he used them in actively leading the Christian congregation in the first century C.E.—Jude 9; 1 Thessalonians 4:16.

A Visible Governing Body

[7] The Scriptures also indicate that Jesus Christ used a group of men as a governing body to give direction to his congregation on earth. To start with, this governing body appears to have been made up of just the 11 apostles. When seeking Jehovah's will in the replacement of Judas Iscariot, Peter quoted Psalm 109:8, which states: "His office of oversight let someone else take." Then, in their prayer to Jehovah, Peter and his companions asked God to designate the man "to take the place of this ministry and apostleship, from which Judas deviated." Matthias was appointed to serve "along with the eleven apostles." —Acts 1:20, 24-26.

[8] The first recorded instance of the 12 apostles' performing in this "office of oversight" as a governing body was when they appointed spiritually qualified men to serve their brothers within the early congregation. (Acts 6:1-6) The second case was when Philip began to preach Christ to the Samaritans. As a result of this, "the apostles in Jerusalem . . . dispatched Peter and John to them." Only after these

---

3. What did Jesus promise to send to his disciples, and how do we know that he was not speaking of a person?
4. How was the holy spirit used from Pentecost on?
5, 6. (a) What is another means given to Christ to enable him to govern his congregation on earth? (b) Give specific examples of how Jesus used this means in behalf of his disciples and in support of the preaching work.

---

7. What other means did Christ use to give direction to his congregation, and what scriptures speak of this "office of oversight"?
8. What two early examples show how Christ used members of the visible governing body?

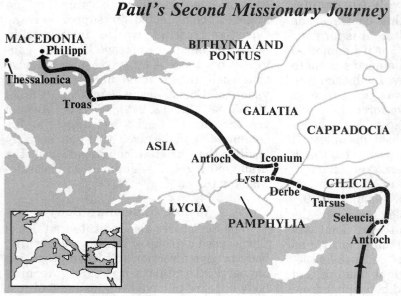

Paul's Second Missionary Journey

MACEDONIA
• Philippi
Thessalonica
Troas
BITHYNIA AND PONTUS
GALATIA
CAPPADOCIA
ASIA
Antioch   Iconium
Lystra•
Derbe
CILICIA
Tarsus
LYCIA
PAMPHYLIA
Seleucia
Antioch

apostle, or one sent forth, better known as the apostle Paul.

[10] Christ personally supervised the preaching work. By means of the holy spirit received from his Father Jehovah, he initiated Paul's missionary journeys and took a personal interest in them. We read: "The holy spirit said: 'Of all persons set Barnabas and Saul apart for me for the work to which I have called them.' . . . Accordingly these men, sent out by the holy spirit, went down to Seleucia, and from there they sailed away" on the first missionary trip. (Acts 13:2-4) Of course, the holy spirit, Jehovah's active force, could neither 'say' something nor 'send out' someone of itself. The one using the spirit to direct matters was obviously Christ, the Head of the congregation.

[11] This use of the spirit by Jesus as he actively led the early Christians is plainly shown in the account of Paul's second missionary journey. After having revisited congregations in Lycaonia (a region of Asia Minor) that had been founded during the first missionary tour, Paul and his traveling companions apparently intended to head west through the Roman province of Asia. Why did they not go through with their plan? "Because they were forbidden by the holy spirit to speak the word in the

representative members of the governing body had laid their hands upon the Samaritans did they 'begin to receive holy spirit.'—Acts 8:5, 14-17.

Christ's Personal Leadership

[9] Thus, right from the beginning of the Christian congregation, Christ had the holy spirit, angels, and a visible governing body at his disposal to enable him actively to lead his disciples on earth. On occasion he even acted personally. For example, Christ personally converted Saul of Tarsus. (Acts 9:3-6) Three days later Jesus spoke directly to "a certain disciple" named Ananias. Revealing to him the threefold mission he had in mind for Saul, Jesus stated: "This man is a chosen vessel to me to bear my name to the nations as well as to kings and the sons of Israel." (Acts 9:10-15) Christ called Saul for a particular work. Saul thus became an

9. Did Christ always act through angels or the governing body? Give an example.

10. How did Christ personally supervise the preaching work?
11. What happened during Paul's second missionary journey, and how does this clearly show that Jesus used the spirit in directing the preaching work?

district of Asia." (Acts 15:36, 40, 41; 16: 1-6) But who was using Jehovah's holy spirit to guide them? The following verse answers. It shows that when they headed north, intending to preach in Bithynia, "the spirit of Jesus did not permit them." (Acts 16:7) Yes, Jesus Christ was using the spirit he had received from his Father to direct the preaching work actively. He and his Father Jehovah wanted the good news to spread into Europe, so Paul received a vision to that effect.—Acts 16: 9, 10.

Christ Backed Up Members of the Governing Body

¹² At the time of the apostle Paul's first contact with the disciples in Jerusalem, they were understandably reluctant to meet him. "So Barnabas came to his aid and led him to the apostles." (Acts 9: 26, 27) Paul spent 15 days with the apostle Peter. He also met Jesus' half brother James, by then one of the elders of the Jerusalem congregation. (Galatians 1: 18, 19) Subsequent passages in Acts show that the Jerusalem elders became a part of the governing body of the early Christian congregation, along with the 12 apostles. —Acts 15:2; 21:18.

¹³ During his two-week stay in Jerusalem, Paul witnessed to Greek-speaking Jews, but "these made attempts to do away with him." Luke adds that "when the brothers detected this, they brought him down to Caesarea and sent him off to Tarsus." (Acts 9:28-30) But who was behind this wise decision? Years later, when relating the same episode in his life, Paul stated that Jesus had appeared to him and instructed him to leave Jerusalem quickly. When Paul objected, Jesus added: "Get on

your way, because I shall send you out to nations far off." (Acts 22:17-21) Christ was closely following matters from on high and acted both by means of the responsible brothers in Jerusalem and directly by speaking to Paul.

¹⁴ Similarly, an attentive reading of the Scriptures shows clearly that Christ was behind the important meeting of the governing body held to settle the question as to whether Gentile Christians should submit to circumcision and the Law of Moses or not. The book of Acts states that when the issue arose, "they [no doubt the responsible members, or elders, of the Antioch congregation] arranged for Paul and Barnabas and some others of them to go up to the apostles and older men in Jerusalem regarding this dispute." (Acts 15: 1, 2) But when Paul relates the circumstances that led to his going to Jerusalem to have the circumcision issue settled, he states: "I went up as a result of a revelation." (Galatians 2:1-3; compare 1:12.) As the active Head of the congregation, Christ wanted this important doctrinal matter to be settled by the entire visible governing body. By means of the holy spirit, he guided the minds of these devoted men in making their decision.—Acts 15:28, 29.

An Unusual Decision

¹⁵ Another interesting example of Christ's active direction of things from heaven is what took place after Paul's third missionary journey. Luke relates that upon returning to Jerusalem, Paul

---

12, 13. At the time of Paul's first visit to Jerusalem as a Christian, what occurred that showed how Christ backed up decisions made by the responsible brothers in that city?

14. What comparison between the accounts in Acts and Galatians shows that Christ was directing matters with regard to the meeting of the governing body dealing with circumcision?
15, 16. (a) What did the governing body require Paul to do after he returned from his third missionary journey? (b) Why might this instruction seem unusual, and why did Paul comply with it? (c) What question arises?

made a full report to the members of the governing body on hand. Luke wrote: "Paul went in with us to James; and all the older men were present. And he greeted them and began giving in detail an account of the things God did among the nations through his ministry." (Acts 21: 17-19) After hearing Paul, the assembled body gave him clear-cut instruction, stating: "Do this which we tell you." They ordered him to go to the temple and publicly demonstrate that he was not "teaching all the Jews among the nations an apostasy from Moses, telling them neither to circumcise their children nor to walk in the solemn customs."—Acts 21:20-24.

[16] One might question the wisdom of this instruction. As we have already seen, years earlier James, and perhaps other elders present on both occasions, had sent Paul away from Jerusalem because his life was threatened by "Greek-speaking Jews." (Acts 9:29) In spite of this, Paul complied with the order, in line with what he had already said at 1 Corinthians 9:20. But like causes produce like effects. "Jews from [the Roman province of] Asia" caused a riot and tried to kill Paul. Only quick action by Roman soldiers saved him from being lynched. (Acts 21:26-32) Since Christ is the active Head of the congregation, why did he cause the governing body to require Paul to go into the temple?

[17] The answer becomes apparent in what occurred the second night after Paul's arrest. He had given a fine witness to the mob that sought to kill him and, the following day, to the Sanhedrin. (Acts 22:1-21; 23: 1-6) For the second time he was nearly lynched. But that night, Jesus appeared to him and said: "Be of good courage! For as you have been giving a thorough witness on the things about me in Jerusalem, so you must also bear witness in Rome." (Acts 23:11) Remember the threefold mission Christ had foretold for Paul. (Acts 9:15) Paul had borne Christ's name to "the nations" and to "the sons of Israel," but the time had now come for him to witness "to kings." Because of that decision by the governing body, Paul was able to witness to Roman procurators Felix and Festus, to King Herod Agrippa II, and, finally, to Roman Emperor Nero. (Acts, chapters 24–26; 27:24) Who can doubt that Christ was behind all of this?

Christ Still Actively Leads His Congregation

[18] Before leaving his disciples and ascending to his Father's right hand, Jesus Christ stated: "All authority has been given me in heaven and on the earth. Go therefore and make disciples of people of all the nations, baptizing them in the name of the Father and of the Son and of the holy spirit, teaching them to observe all the things I have commanded you. And, look! I am with you all the days until the conclusion of the system of things." —Matthew 28:18-20.

Points to Remember

□ Why do Jehovah's Witnesses not recognize any man as their leader?

□ How did Christ use the holy spirit to lead the early Christian congregation?

□ How did Christ use angels in leading first-century Christians?

□ How did Christ use a visible governing body in directing his congregation on earth?

□ How did Christ personally direct matters at times?

---

17. How did this unusual decision turn out to be providential, and what does this indicate?
18. What did Jesus Christ state before ascending to heaven?

¹⁹ The book of Acts, relating the history of the early years of Christianity, shows beyond doubt that Christ used his authority by actively leading his congregation on earth. He did this by means of the holy spirit, the angels, and the governing body

19. How did Christ wield his God-given authority in the first century, and what will be considered in the next article?

made up of the 12 apostles and the elders of the Jerusalem congregation. Jesus stated that he would be with his disciples right up to the conclusion of the system of things, where we now are. In the following article, we will see how he is still the active Head of the Christian congregation and how he is leading his "sheep" today.

Christ's Active Leadership Today

"I am with you all the days until the conclusion of the system of things."—MATTHEW 28:20.

WHEN Christ was about to leave his disciples and return to heaven in 33 C.E., he "committed to them his belongings." This involved being "ambassadors substituting for Christ" and taking up the preaching work he had begun, extending it

1. In what way did Christ commit his "belongings" to his disciples?

to "the most distant part of the earth." Before leaving them, he had instructed them to "make disciples of people of all the nations." Do we have evidence that he was attentive as to how they carried out this commission? Indeed we do!—Matthew 25: 14; 2 Corinthians 5:20; Acts 1:8; Matthew 28:19.

² Over 60 years after Christ ascended to heaven, he showed that he had been following intently the activities of Christian congregations on earth. In the revelation given to the apostle John, a member of the first-century governing body, Jesus Christ sent messages to seven congregations located in Asia Minor. To five of them he said: "I know your deeds." And he showed that he was very familiar with what was going on within the other two, Smyrna and Pergamum. He gave specific encouragement and counsel to each congregation. There could be no doubt in their minds as to who was their active Leader.—Revelation 1:11; 2:1–3:22.

³ Actually, those seven messages were not limited in their scope to the seven congregations in Asia. The fine counsel and the warnings they contained applied to all congregations, from the first century down into "the Lord's day," where we now are.* Christ's eyes, likened to "a fiery flame," have continually watched what has been going on within "all the congregations."—Revelation 1:10; 2:18, 23.

The Master and His Slave

⁴ After having likened himself to "a man, about to travel abroad, [who] summoned slaves of his and committed to them his belongings," Christ added: "After a long time the master of those slaves came and settled accounts with them." (Matthew 25:14, 19) In 33 C.E. Christ "went his way to heaven," where he was seated "at God's right hand." (1 Peter

---

* For a full explanation of these seven messages and their application, see the book *"Then Is Finished the Mystery of God,"* chapters 7 to 14, published by the Watchtower Bible and Tract Society of New York, Inc.

2. What shows that Christ was closely following the activities of first-century congregations?
3. To whom were the seven messages really addressed, and what proves this?
4. How did Christ "travel abroad" and then come back "after a long time"?

3:22) "After a long time," following his enthronement in 1914, Christ began 'subduing in the midst of his enemies' by hurling Satan and his demons down to the earth. (Psalm 110:1, 2; Revelation 12:7-9) Then he turned his attention to his slaves. The time had come for settling accounts with them. More than ever, he was their active Leader.

⁵ The modern history of God's people shows that this time of accounting came in 1918-19. The parable of the talents illustrates how the Master would settle accounts with the remnant of his anointed slaves. They would have to account individually for the way they had used his belongings, "each one according to his own ability," or spiritual possibilities. Those who had been productive entered into the joy of their Master, who said to them: "You were faithful over a few things. I will appoint you over many things."—Matthew 25:15, 20-23.

⁶ Such individual anointed Christians were found to be faithful ambassadors of the now reigning King, willing to make disciples for their Master. They were collectively found to be the "slave" of whom their Master had said: "Who really is the faithful and discreet slave whom his master appointed over his domestics, to give them their food at the proper time? Happy is that slave if his master on arriving finds him doing so. Truly I say to you, He will appoint him over all his belongings."—Matthew 24:45-47.

⁷ Christ's "belongings" have become more numerous since 1914. He has been clothed with "kingly power," involving in-

---

5. When did the time of accounting come, and how were the faithful rewarded?
6. What did such faithful anointed Christians form collectively, and what did their Master commit to their care?
7. (a) How have Christ's "belongings" increased since 1914? (b) What shows that Christ is also the active Leader of the "other sheep"?

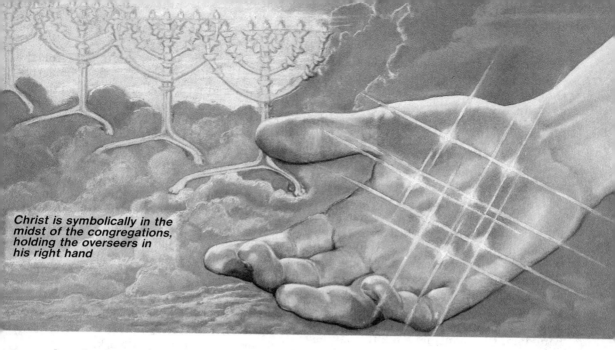

Christ is symbolically in the midst of the congregations, holding the overseers in his right hand

creased authority and larger responsibilities. (Luke 19:11, 12) He first proceeded to gather in the remainder of "the sons of the kingdom," the 144,000 anointed Christians "bought from among mankind" to become kings and priests with him in heaven. (Matthew 13:38; Revelation 14: 1-4; 5:9, 10) Then, as historically manifested since 1935, he has been gathering in "a great crowd" of "other sheep" of whom he said: "Those also I must bring." (Revelation 7:9, 10; John 10:16) Yes, he is the One who brings in these "sheep," and he becomes their active Leader. Interestingly, the Greek text means literally, "And those it is necessary [for] me to lead." How is he actively leading all his "sheep" today?

Overseers in Christ's Right Hand

8 The apostle John, a member of the governing body of the early Christian congregation, received a vision in which he "saw seven golden lampstands, and in the

8, 9. (a) What vision did the apostle John receive? (b) What was pictured by the seven lampstands and the seven stars?

midst of the lampstands someone like a son of man . . . And he had in his right hand seven stars." Jesus Christ explained to John: "As for the sacred secret of the seven stars that you saw upon my right hand, and of the seven golden lampstands: The seven stars mean the angels of the seven congregations, and the seven lampstands mean seven congregations."—Revelation 1:12-20.

9 Commenting on this passage, the book *"Then Is Finished the Mystery of God"* states: "Are such 'angels' invisible ones? No. The apostle John received the entire Revelation from Jesus Christ by means of a heavenly angel, and it would be unreasonable for him to be writing back to angels in heaven, in invisible realms. They do not need the messages written to the seven congregations in Asia. The basic meaning of the title 'angel' is 'messenger; message bearer.' . . . As these seven symbolic stars are seen to be upon Jesus' right hand, they are in his care and charge and under his direction, his 'right hand' of applied power being able to direct and protect them. . . .

As the 'seven lampstands' in the visionary 'Lord's day' pictured all the true Christian congregations in this present, real 'Lord's day' since 1914 C.E., so the 'seven stars' symbolize all the spirit-begotten, anointed angellike overseers of such congregations of today."*—Pages 102-4.

¹⁰ These anointed overseers in Christ's right hand are all a part of the collective "slave" whom He has appointed "over all his belongings." Because the slave's Master has himself been clothed with enlarged responsibilities since 1914, "all his belongings" must involve many more things for the slave than in the past. For one thing, as "ambassadors substituting for Christ," the remnant are now ambassadors of a reigning King ruling over an established Kingdom. (2 Corinthians 5:20) They have been put in charge of all the spiritual things that belong to the Master on earth. They must serve in fulfillment of the prophecies that apply since the establishment of the Kingdom. This includes preaching "this good news of the kingdom . . . in all the inhabited earth for a witness." (Matthew 24:14) More than ever, they must go on making "disciples of people of all the nations," thus gathering in the unnumbered "great crowd." (Matthew 28:19, 20; Revelation 7:9) Yes, these "desirable things of all the nations" are a part of Christ's increased "belongings" on earth.—Haggai 2:7.

---

* The December 15, 1971, issue of *The Watchtower* clarified this point still further, stating: "Doubtless, not one individual elder, presbyter, overseer or shepherd, but the entire 'body of elders' was what the glorified Lord, Jesus Christ, called the 'angel' that was symbolized by a heavenly star. . . . The 'body of elders' (or presbytery) there at Ephesus was to act like a star in shedding heavenly, spiritual light upon the congregation over which the holy spirit had made them shepherds."

---

10. What increased "belongings" have been committed to the slave's care?

¹¹ All of this means more work for the collective "slave," a larger field of activities, extending literally to "all the inhabited earth." It also requires larger headquarters and branch facilities for supervising the work and for printing and distributing literature for preaching and personal study. As in the first century, this work is carried out under the active leadership of Jesus Christ, who is figuratively "in the midst of the lampstands," or congregations. He directs them by means of anointed overseers, whom he holds symbolically "in his right hand." (Revelation 1:13, 16) As in early Christian times, a group of these anointed overseers makes up the visible Governing Body of Christ's congregation on earth. His "right hand" of applied power directs these faithful men as they supervise the Kingdom work.

By Means of the Spirit

¹² With the "other sheep" now numbering upwards of three million, organized into some 52,000 congregations, it is obvious that the anointed remnant need help in taking care of the Master's earthly belongings. Fewer than 9,000, including many sisters, partake of the Memorial emblems, so there is not even one anointed overseer per congregation. Does this mean that Jesus Christ is not in charge of congregations where there is no spirit-begotten "angel," or 'star'?

¹³ By no means! As we have seen in the previous article, in the first century Christ actively led his congregation by means of the holy spirit. Today he uses the spirit-begotten members of the Governing Body

---

11. (a) What do these increased "belongings" necessitate? (b) Who is directing the work, and how?
12, 13. (a) In view of the great increase, what question arises? (b) How does Christ use the spirit to fill the need for overseers among his disciples on earth?

to appoint overseers chosen from among the "other sheep." These must meet the same requirements as anointed elders, as outlined in such scriptures as 1 Timothy 3: 1-7 and Titus 1:5-9. These Scriptural qualifications were written under the direction of the holy spirit. Recommendations and appointments are made after prayer and under the guidance of the holy spirit. To such nonanointed elders Paul's counsel applies with equal force: "Pay attention to yourselves and to all the flock, among which the holy spirit has appointed you overseers."—Acts 20:28.

[14] Thus, in tens of thousands of congregations, the righteous reigning King Jesus Christ is using "other sheep" as "princes" to protect his "sheep" from spiritual wind, rainstorm, and drought. (Isaiah 32:1, 2) Like David of old, elders, whether of the anointed or the "other sheep," pray to Jehovah: "Your spirit is good; may it lead me in the land of uprightness." (Psalm 143: 10) And Jehovah hears their prayer. By means of his Son, He grants them His spirit, and Jesus uses this means actively to lead his disciples on earth. Naturally, all elders must submit to Christ's "right hand" of control, guidance, and direction, which he exercises by means of the spirit and the spirit-begotten members of the Governing Body.

By Means of Angels

[15] The previous article mentioned that angels were used in the first century to guide and deliver early Christians and help them in their preaching work. Would it be logical to think that our reigning King Jesus Christ no longer uses angels in actively leading his disciples today? Not only would it be illogical but it would also be unscriptural.

[16] According to Jesus' parable of the wheat and the weeds, harvesttime would come at "the conclusion of the system of things," which began in 1914. During the harvest, "the sons of the kingdom" would be separated from "the sons of the wicked one." Whom would the Master use to do the harvesting? "The reapers are angels." Christ added: "The Son of man will send forth his angels, and they will collect out from his kingdom all things that cause stumbling and persons who are doing lawlessness." (Matthew 13:37-41) Christ uses angels to protect his brothers on earth.

[17] But what about the "other sheep"? Does Christ use angels to gather them? Assuredly! His parable of the sheep and the goats says: "When the Son of man arrives in his glory, and all the angels with him, then he will sit down on his glorious throne. And all the nations will be gathered before him, and he will separate people one from another, just as a shepherd separates the sheep from the goats." (Matthew 25:31, 32) Christ uses his angels in this separating work. Just as an angel directed the steps of Philip toward the Ethiopian eunuch, so there is abundant evidence today that Christ uses his angels to direct the steps of his Witnesses toward sheeplike ones. Many people have attested to the fact that they had prayed for help just before a Witness knocked at their door.—Acts 8:26, 27.

Complete Confidence in Christ's Direction

[18] In the first century, circumstances

---

14. (a) How is the prophecy of Isaiah 32:1, 2 already being fulfilled? (b) How must all elders submit to Christ's "right hand"?
15. What other means does Christ have at his disposal to lead his disciples on earth actively?

16, 17. What proof do we have that Christ uses angels in harvesting "the sons of the kingdom" and in gathering the "other sheep"?
18, 19. On the basis of what occurred in the first century, of what are we confident?

Tests that come because of wars, revolutions or outright persecution and official bans may make it impossible for you to carry on Christian worship in a fully organized manner. Circumstances may develop making it impossible to hold large congregation meetings. Contact with the branch office may temporarily be broken off. Visits by circuit overseers may be interrupted. New publications may not arrive. If any of these things happen to you, what should you do?

The answer is: Under the circumstances, do whatever you can, and as much as you can, in the way of pure worship. Personal study should be possible. Usually small groups of brothers can meet for study in homes. Publications studied in the past and the Bible itself can be used as a basis for meetings. Do not become excited or worried. Generally, in a short time some form of communication with responsible brothers will be established. The Governing Body seeks to find ways of getting in touch with the brothers.

But even if you find yourself isolated from all your Christian brothers, keep in mind that you are not isolated from Jehovah and his Son Jesus Christ.—*Organized to Accomplish Our Ministry,* page 168.

did not always lend themselves to Christ's using the governing body in Jerusalem to solve a specific problem. When Paul was isolated up in northern Asia Minor and needed to know which territory to open up next, Christ acted through the spirit. (Acts 16:6-10) Today Jehovah's Witnesses are confident that any of their brothers who become temporarily isolated from the Governing Body because of persecution are still under Christ's active leadership, by means of the spirit and angelic support.

¹⁹ Back in early Christian times, some decisions made by the governing body may have been hard to understand at the time. This was doubtless the case when Paul was sent back to Tarsus or when he was sent to the temple after his third missionary journey. (Acts 9:30; 21:23-25) Yet, Christ was actually behind such decisions.

(Acts 22:17-21; 23:11) Today we can be confident that whatever Christ allows to occur among his disciples on earth has some lofty purpose behind it, even as in the first century.

²⁰ Thus, when we read in the Bible that Christ "is the head of the body, the congregation," we are convinced that he is not a mere titular Head. (Colossians 1:18) We know, from experience, that he is a real, active Head. When we read the book of Acts and see how Christ directed matters among the early Christians, we can observe that he is using the same means today. We see evidence of Christ's use of the holy spirit, angels, and "the faithful and discreet slave" and its Governing Body, to appoint spiritually qualified elders. Confident in Christ's active direction of things, we are determined to go on "speaking the truth" and growing up by love "in all things into him who is the head, Christ."—Ephesians 4:15.

20. Of what are we convinced, and what is our determination?

Main Points to Recall

□ What proof do we have that Christ closely followed the activities of first-century congregations?

□ Whom did Christ appoint over all his "belongings," and what do these include?

□ Who are symbolized by the seven stars in Christ's right hand?

□ How does Christ use the holy spirit, angels, and the anointed Governing Body in leading his congregation today?

□ Why can we have complete confidence in Christ's direction of things today?

My Generation —Unique and Highly Privileged!

As told by Melvin Sargent

MANY young people today have been born into a family of Jehovah's Witnesses. But in 1896 this was a rare privilege indeed. From infancy, I was taught by Mother to fear Jehovah properly and to appreciate the ransom sacrifice made by his Son. So I belong to a unique and highly privileged generation—old enough to have seen the beginning of the sign of Christ's presence in 1914 and yet possibly still young enough to live to see its completion at Armageddon.—Matthew 24:3, 33, 34.

Off to a Fine Start With TLC

As a child, I was given what is called the TLC treatment, Tender Loving Care. Yet at times that care could be displayed in ways some today might consider severe. I remember that once Mother overheard me playing with an older boy who suddenly began using words quite new to me. "Those are bad words that you must never use," she told me, impressing it upon me with more than just words! But I realized that her discipline was an expression of tender loving care, and I remember wondering why Jimmie's mother had not dis-

ciplined him. Did she not really love him enough?

We were the only Witness family in Jewell County, Kansas. Father was not a dedicated servant of Jehovah, but he obligingly conducted a Bible study with us children. My sister Eva was the oldest, and Walter was 16 months older than I. Every evening we were expected to share in washing the dishes. But Walter often found excuses and begged off. Eva and I, however, used this chore as a daily opportunity to talk about Bible truths, so it was a blessing in disguise. Later I came to appreciate that people who shirk responsibilities in life miss out on many blessings. This happened to Walter, who later turned away from the truth.

Our TLC treatment led to fine results on August 4, 1912. Eva and I got up before dawn and traveled ten miles (16 km) by horse and buggy to catch the early train to Jamestown, Kansas. A pilgrim, the designation of traveling Bible Students, was visiting there, and this was to be our first meeting with Bible Students outside our own home. It was also the day of our baptism.

Although only 16, I asked the pilgrim brother if I could take up the full-time ministry, then called colporteur work. He encouraged me to write the Watch Tower Society. Since I was still needed at home, however, this had to be delayed. Meanwhile, I used my spare time regularly helping the Jamestown Bible Students distribute tracts throughout some 75 surrounding cities and towns.

I also witnessed at other times. Once when our landlady came to town on business and stayed with us a few days, I gave her a tract. This must have impressed her. But after she returned home to Iowa, it was 30 years before I saw her again. She had become an Adventist and was not interested in 'my religion.' She had an estate that needed to be cared for, however, and knowing of no "truly Christian man" in her religion in whom she had confidence, she turned to me. The fee she paid me helped keep me in the full-time ministry for several years. What a confirmation of Ecclesiastes 11:1: "Send out your bread upon the surface of the waters, for in the course of many days you will find it again." Or of what Jesus once said: "Keep on, then, seeking first the kingdom and his righteousness, and all these other things will be added to you."—Matthew 6:33.

Unforgettable Impressions

I attended my first convention in 1913. I was impressed to see 41 new ones baptized, and I was also encouraged to think that with my head start (I had been baptized for ten months), I might have some hope of being able to develop a "Christlike character" by 1914, in order to make my 'calling and election' sure. I was also impressed at seeing so many red and yellow ribbons. Colporteurs who were looking for partners wore red ones, and anyone wanting to team up with them wore a yellow one.

For me, a highlight of the 1914 convention was seeing the *Photo-Drama of Creation* and getting a closer look at Brother Russell. He had a warm way about him and showed a real desire to impart encouraging information to his listeners. He was sympathetic and willing to listen to those who came to him with problems. But he was not too big for an occasional teenager's horseplay. One evening as I was handing out scenarios of the *Photo-Drama* program, he hurried past. I offered him a copy, pretending not to recognize him. At first he went by, but then he turned and with a laugh thanked me, letting me know he had caught the joke.

Finally in 1917, at 21, I was able to take up the colporteur work. World War I had already been in progress nearly three years. With a suitcase in hand, lots of books, and $30.00 in my pocket, I headed for Nebraska with my partner, Ernest Leuba, an older experienced colporteur. We had both positive and negative experiences. I remember, for example, when we once decided to use a hurry-up method of placing books. We had cards printed that offered people a free two-day examination of the book *The Finished Mystery,* with the privilege of obtaining it for 60 cents upon our return. One morning we each loaned out ten books in this fashion. Two days later, I was able to place seven of mine, whereas Brother Leuba, who had worked in an overwhelmingly Catholic neighborhood, placed only one. In order to retrieve one of the books he had loaned out, he had to go to the local Catholic priest to whom it had been passed. So we soon decided that our hurry-up method was really not as good as spending more time talking to the people.

Of course, we had very little money, which meant that we at times were quite ingenious in thinking up ways to be economical. So when we later moved to a new assignment in Boulder, Colorado, we bought a ticket to the nearest station beyond the state line. Then we got off the train and bought another ticket for the rest of the trip on the next train. Why? Because fares within a state were two cents a mile, but interstate rates were higher. Besides saving money, we were able to spend our time during the stopover doing informal witnessing.

Melvin and Lydia Sargent, colporteurs, 1921

Wartime Problems and a New Beginning

By now it was 1918, and the United States was well embroiled in the war. A storm of opposition openly began against the Bible Students, identifying those who were fearful and those who were not. Some brothers of draft age, although conscientious objectors, agreed to perform noncombatant military service.

When I registered, I claimed exemption as a minister. My arguments, I thought, were well based, and my induction was delayed while my case was sent to the appeal board. They thought otherwise and rejected my claim. This delay, however, helped keep me out of prison because by now it was harvesttime, and I was deferred until this essential work on my parents' farm could be finished. Finally my induction was set for November 15.

The war ended November 11. I had missed prison by only four days.

Others who fearlessly came out in support of Christian neutrality did not fare as well. At a convention in Denver, I met one of them. Explaining why he was bald, the brother told of being tied to a tree by a fanatical mob that had poured hot tar over him. "The women in the group," he said, "were the worst." He had shaved his hair off to get rid of the tar. Then he broke into a broad smile and said of his experience: "I wouldn't have missed it for anything."

Because of their uncompromising stand, some of the officials of the Watch Tower Society were wrongly imprisoned. But in 1919, while still in prison, they were reelected to their positions in the Society, despite an attempt by apostates to replace them. The faithful brothers accepted this as an indication of Jehovah's approval. Full of joy, encouraged by a fresh flow of holy spirit, they were now more determined than ever before to take up the Kingdom-preaching work anew and to expose the clergy for their hypocritical failure to support God's Kingdom. A complete break with Babylon had begun.

On February 24, 1918, in Los Angeles, California, after the United States got involved in World War I on April 6, 1917, Brother Rutherford delivered for the first time the thrilling talk "Millions Now Living Will Never Die."

Important Changes Over the Years

For seven years Lydia Tannahill and I had maintained a friendship mainly by correspondence. After prayerful consideration, we decided in 1921 it would be best for us to take advantage of Paul's concession when advising singleness, namely, that he who "gives his virginity in marriage does well." (1 Corinthians 7:38) Our marriage was a gift from Jehovah and caused our hearts to rejoice. Before long, however, we were faced with a crisis. Travel had caused an old back injury of Lydia's to become acute, and my heart, though loyal and loving, was slow, "a tired heart" the doctors called it. This gave way to anemia. Both of us were running out of strength. We were advised to change climate and to limit our daily travels. Our mobile home was ideal for helping us follow this counsel, and so we spent September 1923 on the road to California.

Belonging to the highly privileged generation that I do, I have been allowed to see how Jehovah's visible organization has developed over the years. I was there when Los Angeles was first laid out in individual preaching territories, when Sunday witnessing began, and when we received our new name, Jehovah's Witnesses, in 1931. What a thrill to see adjustments made in 1932 and 1938 that ensured the theocratic, rather than the democratic, appointment of elders. And it has been a joy to see unclear issues and questions, like those of neutrality and the sanctity of blood, clarified.

Although I had dropped out of the colpor-

Melvin and Evamae Sargent, 1976

teur work in 1923, I had always maintained a pioneer spirit. So in 1943 I was able to rejoin the fast-growing ranks of pioneers. In 1945 I was even privileged to become a special pioneer, serving nine years in that capacity until my "tired heart" once again caught up with me. Since 1954 I have served as a regular pioneer.

My marriage to Lydia lasted 48 years until in 1969 she moved on to a new assignment, an inheritance for her "reserved in the heavens," an assignment I, too, hope to receive in due time. (1 Peter 1:4) Although we were never blessed with children, we were blessed with what many considered to be an ideal marriage. Though my loss was great, keeping busy with theocratic interests helped me overcome it. Later I married an experienced pioneer I had known for many years, Evamae Bell. We enjoyed 13 years of companionship until she, too, passed away.

My Generation
—Unique in a Special Way

I have sometimes been asked: "What has been your greatest experience in the truth?" Without hesitation I answer:

"Seeing fulfilled within *my* generation the Bible prophecies set down by inspired and dedicated men centuries ago."

Members of my generation outside the theocratic organization, of course, have turned out to be exactly the way the *Photo-Drama of Creation* of 1914 said they would be: money-mad, pleasure-mad, and glory-mad. Those of us inside the Lord's organization have tried, in every way possible, to turn their attention to the message of life. We have used slogans, full-page advertisements, radio, sound cars, portable phonographs, gigantic conventions, parades of information-walkers carrying signs, and a growing army of house-to-house ministers. This activity has served to divide people—those in favor of God's established Kingdom on the one side, those against it on the other. This was the work foretold by Jesus for *my* generation!—Matthew 25:31-46.

Until this "tired heart" of mine beats its last, it will continue to beat in appreciation for the privilege I have enjoyed of belonging to a unique generation. It will continue to beat in excitement over the privilege I now have of seeing millions of smiling faces that are destined to keep on smiling forever.

A Young One Praises Jehovah

MANY opportunities for witnessing are open to young ones when they have a strong desire to serve Jehovah. This was seen in the experience of a five-year-old boy in western Kenya.—Ecclesiastes 12:1.

His mother asked him: "What do you want to be when you grow up?" The boy had observed a special pioneer in the congregation and replied: "I want to become a special pioneer like Brother F———." The mother answered: "But this is not possible; you cannot even be a regular pioneer because you do not have a Bible study." The boy asked: "What can I do then?" His mother suggested he try to teach his playmates from his copy of *My Book of Bible Stories.*

The five-year-old got his *Bible Stories* book and went calling on his friends, inviting them to study the Bible with him. The result?

He formed a group of ten that he could study with. He made good use of the pictures, raised many searching questions, and asked review questions at the end of the study. If they did not remember, he would go over the material with them again. The mother explained that it was really a joy to see all these children sitting on the ground in front of her house studying together! There was her five-year-old son asking questions, and then all the hands would go up to answer.

It was a further joy to the mother, as well as to the congregation, to see eight of these children attend congregation meetings. The other two were too small. All of this happened because a five-year-old wanted to praise Jehovah and help others.

The Spirit
That Jehovah Blesses

"THE Lord be with the spirit you show. His undeserved kindness be with you people." With these words, Paul concluded his second letter to Timothy. (2 Timothy 4:22) What joy this expression of commendation must have given Timothy and those with him—to know that they displayed the spirit that Jehovah blesses!

But just what is the spirit that Jehovah blesses? What really characterizes those who have this spirit? And how may we also display this spirit and receive Jehovah's blessing?

To help answer these questions, let us go back to the time of Moses. The Israelites are in the wilderness. Jehovah has recently concluded the Law covenant with them, and now he instructs them in the way that they should worship him. This includes the building of a portable tent of meeting that will require a great amount of gold, precious materials, and skilled workmanship to construct. The opportunity to make voluntary gift offerings to supply the needed materials and labor is presented to the nation in these words: "Let every willing-hearted one bring it as Jehovah's contribution, namely, gold and silver and copper and blue thread and wool dyed reddish purple . . . And let all the wisehearted ones among you come and make all that Jehovah has commanded, namely, the tabernacle with its tent and its covering."—Exodus 35:5-19.

How did the nation respond to this opportunity? The remainder of chapter 35 tells us that those 'whose heart impelled them' and 'whose spirit incited them' made contributions and set themselves to work with a diligence that showed that they treasured this opportunity that had been put before them. (Verses 21, 22, 26) Their response was such that chapter 36, verse 6, tells us that "Moses commanded that they should cause an announcement to pass through the camp, saying: 'Men and women, do not produce any more stuff for the holy contribution.' With that the people were restrained from bringing it in." Yes, they had to be restrained! Jehovah had used no pressure tactics when he had the announcement made: "Let every willing-hearted one . . . " The result was that the nation showed a *willing spirit,* and this brought blessings in the form of great joy, as well as Jehovah's protection and direction in all that they undertook.

Years later, the same spirit was once again manifested. This occurred when King Hezekiah was working to restore pure worship in Israel. The account tells us that, when given the opportunity, "the congregation began to bring sacrifices and thanksgiving sacrifices, and also every one willing of heart, burnt offerings." The result? "Consequently Hezekiah and all the people rejoiced over the fact that the true God had made preparation for the people, because it was all of a sudden that the thing had occurred."—2 Chronicles 29:31-36.

Christians Demonstrate the Right Spirit

Do we observe the same spirit of willing self-sacrifice in Christian times? Note what Paul wrote about the Philippian Christians at Philippians 1:3-5: "I thank my God always upon every remembrance of you in every supplication of mine for all of you, as I offer my supplication with joy, because of the contribution you have made to the good news from the first day until this moment." In what ways were the Philippian Christians outstanding in their 'contribution to the good news'? The succeeding verses make it apparent that not only were they willingly conforming their way of life to Bible principles so as to advance the good news but they were also zealous in their preaching and teaching of the good news to others.

That all Christians should willingly share in the preaching work in these ways is stressed at Hebrews 13:15: "Through him

let us always offer to God a sacrifice of praise, that is, the fruit of lips which make public declaration to his name." So the preaching of the good news by each and every Christian is a key way in which we can show the willing spirit that characterizes true worshipers of Jehovah today. Additionally, Christians are reminded that they should never "forget the doing of good and the sharing of things with others, for with such sacrifices God is well pleased."—Hebrews 13:16.

The Philippian brothers displayed this willing spirit in yet another way. In chapter 4 Paul mentions several occasions when they came to his aid in a financial way, so that the preaching of the good news was advanced. (Philippians 4:14-17) They thus imitated the fine example of those earlier worshipers of Jehovah. They obviously honored "Jehovah with [their] valuable things." (Proverbs 3:9) Do we show the same spirit when similar opportunities are set before us?

The Approved Spirit Evident Today

Psalm 110 shows that there would be many displaying this same fine spirit of willing self-sacrifice in the last days of this present system when the majority of people are interested only in "me." We are told in verse 3 that, after the Messiah took up rulership in the Kingdom in 1914, God's people would "offer themselves willingly" and that those doing so would be as numerous as "dewdrops." Has this proved true?

In April 1881 *The Watchtower* printed an appeal for 1,000 preachers to take up the full-time preaching work. The May 1881 issue stressed that those engaging in this work must be those who would be "working for heavenly wages." Within four years, over 300 had responded—outstanding in view of the small number of dedicated Christians associated with the Watch Tower Society at that time.

This same spirit continues to be evident

today. For example, in 1986 there were 391,-294 pioneers (full-time ministers) reporting, on the average, each month. That was a 21.2-percent increase, or 68,473 more than the previous year! However, this willing spirit is not limited to those who are able to spend their full time in the preaching work.*

Many with other Scriptural responsibilities—such as caring for a family, for incapacitated or aged parents—and those whose health will not permit them to share in the full-time Christian ministry also display this same spirit of willing self-sacrifice that is so pleasing to Jehovah. This becomes evident when one realizes that the bulk of the Kingdom preaching work in most lands is actually done by ministers who have to spend the greater part of their time working at some secular job or in caring for family obligations or other Scriptural responsibilities. Truly a commendable display of the spirit that Jehovah blesses.

Displaying the Right Spirit in Other Areas of Life

As in Moses' and Hezekiah's day, opportunities to show a willing spirit present themselves today when local congregations build a Kingdom Hall or other similar facilities. Is the same spirit evident in such cases? Yes, it most certainly is!

This has been especially manifest in a current method of Kingdom Hall construction often called quickly built Kingdom Hall projects. Many hundreds of Witnesses will gather and work from early Saturday morning on through to Sunday evening—some working all night—to accomplish what newspapers have called a "weekend mira-

* For some heartwarming and inspiring examples of those who have spent themselves willingly in the full-time preaching work, see the *Watchtower* articles of 5/15/55, pages 317-8; 6/15/62, pages 375-9; 7/15/63, pages 437-42; 11/1/70, pages 666-70; 3/15/71, pages 186-90; 8/15/76, pages 485-90; 6/15/80, pages 24-7. See *Watchtower Publications Index 1930-1985*, under the heading "Life Stories of Jehovah's Witnesses" for further examples.

cle." Where nothing but a concrete slab was on the lot on Friday, a finished Kingdom Hall is used for a meeting Sunday evening!*

Even greater opportunities to display a willing spirit present themselves in connection with the building of branch facilities in various lands. The amount of completely voluntary labor contributed to the work being done in these various projects staggers the imagination. In addition to the contributions of labor, there are, of course, the financial contributions that make it possible to purchase the necessary materials. Very often, Witnesses will spontaneously donate needed items that greatly reduce the cost of the building.

An example of this occurred during the construction of the new branch in Sydney, Australia. There, brothers living in the far north of Queensland prepared and sent to the construction site four semitrailer loads of timber having an estimated value of from $60,000 to $70,000! During the construction of the branch, Witnesses by the busload traveled from as far afield as Western Australia, 2,500 miles (4,000 km) away, to do volunteer work for four weeks at a time. Quite a few of the skilled tradesmen voluntarily worked at the site for months and several even for a year or more. This was

* See *The Watchtower* 8/1/82, pages 8-11 and *Awake!* 7/8/81, pages 16-19.

In Our Next Issue

■ **Women's Improved Role —A Mixed Blessing?**

■ **Youths—What Will You Do With Your Life?**

■ **Is the Cross for Christians?**

truly a manifestation of the same spirit that Jehovah has blessed so bountifully throughout the centuries past and that today is often repeated in other lands.

Additional opportunities to show a willing spirit present themselves when Witnesses are congregating at assemblies and conventions. Every such assembly requires many volunteers, often months in advance of the event, to ensure that everything will go smoothly and be well organized. And once under way, sometimes up to one in four of the Witnesses attending will volunteer to help do the many necessary jobs that make for a pleasant and successful convention. The work may involve serving food or cleaning. It may be a task that goes unnoticed by the majority of those in attendance. But it does not go unnoticed by Jehovah! He rewards those who willingly offer themselves to do what is needed. Do you also reap the reward that results when Christians "through love slave for one another" by voluntarily offering your services at assembly times? Have you thought of doing so as a family?—Galatians 5:13.

While these special projects give us fine opportunities to offer ourselves with this spirit of willingness, there are many other opportunities to display the same spirit day by day and week by week. For example, once the Kingdom Hall is built, do you share fully in cleaning and maintaining it? Do you support its operations by making financial contributions as Jehovah blesses you materially? Do you support the preaching work in your land by making contributions to the local branch office? And even more importantly, do you regularly engage in the work of preaching the good news and making disciples of people in your area? Nothing can really ever replace our personal share in this work that Jesus designated as the most important work to be done at the present time, before the end of this system.—Matthew 24:14; 28:19, 20; Acts 1:8.

All who cultivate this spirit that Jehovah so richly blesses have found it to be true that Jehovah "is not unrighteous so as to forget your work and the love you showed for his name." You too can, by displaying this spirit of willing self-sacrifice, prove that "the blessing of Jehovah—that is what makes rich, and he adds no pain with it."—Hebrews 6:10; Proverbs 10:22.

Annual Meeting
October 3, 1987

THE ANNUAL MEETING of the members of Watch Tower Bible and Tract Society of Pennsylvania will be held on October 3, 1987, at the Assembly Hall of Jehovah's Witnesses, 2932 Kennedy Boulevard, Jersey City, New Jersey. A preliminary meeting of the members only will convene at 9:30 a.m., followed by the general annual meeting at 10:00 a.m.

The members of the Corporation should inform the Secretary's Office *now* of any change in their mailing addresses during the past year so that the regular letters of notice and proxies can reach them shortly after August 15.

The proxies, which will be sent to the members along with the notice of the annual meeting, are to be returned so as to reach the Office of the Secretary of the Society not later than September 1. Each member should complete and return his proxy promptly, stating whether he is going to be at the meeting personally or not. The information given on each proxy should be definite on this point, since it will be relied upon in determining who will be personally present.

It is expected that the entire session, including the formal business meeting and reports, will be concluded by 1:00 p.m. or shortly thereafter. There will be no afternoon session. Because of limited space, admission will be by ticket only. No arrangements will be made for tying in the annual meeting by telephone lines to other locations.

Kingdom Proclaimers Report

In New Zealand—A Day to Remember

"WE ARE absolutely thrilled to be with you. We shall never forget it!"

"In all my theocratic associations, I have never experienced anything like this."

"It seemed as if we were enjoying a day in the new system of things."

These were some of the comments of delegates to the dedication program of the branch headquarters of the Watch Tower Bible and Tract Society in New Zealand, November 29, 1986. Why were these people so moved? Because it truly was a memorable day. Let us share with you some of the reasons why.

First, the beautiful facilities being dedicated made the day memorable. John E. Barr, of the Governing Body of Jehovah's Witnesses, described the newly built Kingdom Hall and associated branch facilities as "tasteful, elegant, charming . . . The finished work reflects very careful attention to detail, to beauty. It all seems to match."

A Christian Brotherhood

Then, it was memorable to see together so many old-timers, Witnesses who have been serving Jehovah faithfully for many, many years. In fact, these formed the majority among the 658 invited guests. When they met up with old friends, many of whom they had not seen for decades, they felt like Paul, when, after a long journey, he met up with the brothers from Rome: "Upon

catching sight of [his brothers], Paul thanked God and took courage." (Acts 28:15) To witness such examples of enduring loyalty—some present despite poor health—was a source of encouragement and gratitude.

The day was memorable, too, for the warm international brotherhood experienced. Jehovah's Witnesses belong to an earth-wide brotherhood, and this was evidenced by the guests who came from as far away as Australia, the United States, Canada, Britain, and Taiwan, as well as from Papua New Guinea, Samoa, and other islands of the South Pacific. Telegrams came from many who could not be present personally, including greetings from the Governing Body, members of the Brooklyn Bethel family, and the 82nd class of the missionary school of Gilead. Indeed, it was faith strengthening to be aware of the interest of so many brothers in so many lands in the dedication of the New Zealand branch facilities.

Foundations Laid by Loyal Witnesses

To be reminded of the long history of the preaching work in New Zealand that led up to the building of these latest branch facilities was thrilling and also made the day memorable. (Compare Hebrews 10:32.) As one speaker said: "As important as the physical foundations of the fine new Bethel complex are, the more significant ones are figurative foundations laid by loyal, self-sacrificing broth-

ers and sisters going right back to the beginning of the century."

This was followed by interviews of 11 faithful men and women who had a combined total of 680 years of dedicated service. They told of one of the earliest conventions in New Zealand, in 1913. They recalled the rigors of pioneering in the South Island in the 1930's, the hardships of the World War II years when the organization was banned, the formation of the New Zealand branch in 1947, the arrival of the first Gilead missionaries, and the building of the country's first Kingdom Hall in 1950. A common feeling of those interviewed was: "How grateful we are to be here and to see evidence of an increase that, in earlier days, we would never have dreamed possible!"

Jehovah's Blessing

Perhaps the main thing that made the day unforgettable was the awareness that Jehovah's blessing had guided the construction work and brought it to fruition. Appropriately, one section of the day's program was entitled: "The Good Hand of Our God Upon Us."—Nehemiah 2:8.

The good hand of Jehovah was seen in the helpfulness and cooperation of the local businessmen and authorities, as well as in the Christian qualities manifested by the workers themselves on the site. One businessman, visiting the building site, noted: "I have never

experienced anywhere else the feeling of peace and tranquillity that I have when I am here."

Jehovah's blessing was seen in the generosity of the ordinary Witnesses around the country who supported the project financially. It was also observed in the willingness of those who offered themselves to do the actual work. Altogether, 1,237 filled out applications volunteering their service, some traveling to the site from distant lands and at their own expense to spend a few weeks or months helping in construction work. Said one brother: "Helping out on the site was a turning point in my life."

As Brother Barr mentioned in the dedication talk, the new branch facilities should be viewed as "an outward, tangible evidence of God's Messianic Kingdom now established." Yes, it was truly a memorable day for New Zealand. At the end, there was a heartfelt response on the part of all in attendance to a resolution pledging "full support to Jehovah's organization as represented by our branch."

"The Drudgery Is Gone Forever!"

So commented one user of the *Watch Tower Publications Index 1930-1985*. She adds: "What a difference personal study is. . . . Can't get over how much I can look up in just a short period of time."

This new book has indexed every publication produced by the Watch Tower Bible and Tract Society since 1930. By using it with your library of Watch Tower publications, you can with ease find specific information on literally thousands of subjects, such as:

☐ the dos and don'ts of discipline in child training
☐ how to prepare for a job interview   ☐ the role of DNA in cell replication
☐ what a prayer should not include   ☐ the Christian view of birth control
☐ the secrets of attractive dress

The Watchtower

August 15, 1987

Announcing Jehovah's Kingdom

WOMAN'S
IMPROVED
ROLE

A Mixed Blessing?

The Watchtower®

Announcing Jehovah's Kingdom

August 15, 1987
Vol. 108, No. 16

In This Issue

THE PURPOSE OF "THE WATCHTOWER" is to exalt Jehovah God as the Sovereign of the universe. It keeps watch on world events as they fulfill Bible prophecy. It comforts all peoples with the good news that God's Kingdom will soon destroy those who oppress their fellowmen and that it will turn the earth into a paradise. It encourages faith in the now-reigning King, Jesus Christ, whose shed blood opens the way for mankind to gain eternal life. "The Watchtower," published by Jehovah's Witnesses continuously since 1879, is nonpolitical. It adheres to the Bible as its authority.

"WATCHTOWER" STUDIES FOR THE WEEKS

Average Printing Each Issue: 12,315,000

Now Published in 103 Languages

SEMIMONTHLY LANGUAGES AVAILABLE BY MAIL
Afrikaans, Arabic, Cebuano, Chichewa, Chinese, Cibemba, Danish,* Dutch,* Efik, English,* Finnish,* French,* German,* Greek,* Hiligaynon, Igbo, Iloko, Italian,* Japanese,* Korean, Lingala, Malagasy, Maltese, Norwegian, Portuguese,* Russian, Sepedi, Sesotho, Shona, Spanish,* Swahili, Swedish,* Tagalog, Thai, Tsonga, Tswana, Xhosa, Yoruba, Zulu

MONTHLY LANGUAGES AVAILABLE BY MAIL
Armenian, Bengali, Bicol, Bislama, Bulgarian, Croatian, Czech, Ewe, Fijian, Ga, Greenlandic, Gujarati, Gun, Hausa, Hebrew, Hindi, Hiri Motu, Hungarian, Icelandic, Kannada, Malayalam, Marathi, New Guinea Pidgin, Pangasinan, Papiamento, Polish, Rarotongan, Romanian, Samar-Leyte, Samoan, Sango, Serbian, Silozi, Sinhalese, Slovenian, Solomon Islands-Pidgin, Tahitian, Tamil, Telugu, Tongan, Tshiluba, Turkish, Twi, Ukrainian, Urdu, Venda, Vietnamese

* Study articles also available in large-print edition.

Watch Tower Society offices	Yearly subscription for the above: Semimonthly Languages	Monthly Languages
America, U.S., Watchtower, Wallkill, N.Y. 12589	$4.00	$2.00
Australia, Box 280, Ingleburn, N.S.W. 2565	A$7.00	A$3.50
Canada, Box 4100, Halton Hills, Ontario L7G 4Y4	$5.50	$2.75
England, The Ridgeway, London NW7 1RN	£5.00	£2.50
Ireland, 29A Jamestown Road, Finglas, Dublin 11	IR£6.00	IR£3.00
New Zealand, P.O. Box 142, Manurewa	NZ$15.00	NZ$7.50
Nigeria, PMB 001, Shomolu, Lagos State	₦8.00	₦4.00
Philippines, P.O. Box 2044, Manila 2800	₱60.00	₱30.00
South Africa, Private Bag 2067, Krugersdorp, 1740	R9,00	R4,50

Remittances should be sent to the office in your country or to Watchtower, Wallkill, N.Y. 12589, U.S.A.

Changes of address should reach us 30 days before your moving date. Give us your old and new address (if possible, your old address label).

20 cents (U.S.) a copy

The Bible translation used is the "New World Translation of the Holy Scriptures," unless otherwise indicated.

The Watchtower (ISSN 0043-1087) is published semimonthly for $4.00 (U.S.) per year by Watch Tower Bible and Tract Society of Pennsylvania, 25 Columbia Heights, Brooklyn, N.Y. 11201. Second-class postage paid at Brooklyn, N.Y., and at additional mailing offices.

Postmaster: Send address changes to Watchtower, **Wallkill, N.Y. 12589.**

Published by
**Watch Tower Bible and Tract Society
of Pennsylvania**
25 Columbia Heights, Brooklyn, N.Y. 11201, U.S.A.
Frederick W. Franz, President

Women's Improved Role
in Modern Times

BACK in 1906 Czar Nicholas of Russia received from some Russian peasant women a petition that, among other things, stated:

"For generations the women of the peasant class have lived without having any rights whatever. . . . We are not even considered human beings, but simply beasts of burden. We demand to be taught to read and write; we demand that our daughters be given the same facilities for learning as our sons. . . . We know that we are ignorant, but we are not to blame."

That sad situation is quite in contrast with the description that the Bible gives of a capable and respected woman, holding her out as an example worthy of imitation and praise. (Proverbs 31:10-31) Yet, the description from Russia reflects a truism stated long ago in the Bible by wise King Solomon: "Man has dominated man to his injury." (Ecclesiastes 8:9) That injury certainly has not been limited to males. The verse might be taken broadly to mean: 'Men have dominated other men *and women* to their injury.' But what a change in the lot of women, as the situation in Russia illustrates!

Today, "the majority of Soviet doctors and teachers are women. Women account for nearly two-thirds the total number of economists and three-quarters of cultural workers. Forty per cent of those

working in the sciences are women . . . Out of every thousand women engaged in the national economy, 862 have a higher or secondary (complete or incomplete) education."—*Women in the USSR.*

Women in Politics

What has developed in Russia has to a greater or lesser extent occurred in many other lands. The first nation to grant women the right to vote was New Zealand, back in 1893. Between 1917 and 1920, they were given that right in Russia, Great Britain, the United States, and Canada. In Switzerland they had to wait until 1971, although Swiss women could hold political office.

Today, women not only vote but compete with

men for political offices. Israel had a woman prime minister, Golda Meir, and so did India, Indira Gandhi. More recently, women have been chosen as prime ministers in Great Britain and Yugoslavia. Of Russia's Supreme Soviet, 492, or between 30 and 40 percent, are women. A woman is now a member of the U.S. Supreme Court, and in the 1984 presidential campaign, a woman was for the first time a vice-presidential candidate of a major political party. In France women hold some 15 percent of all cabinet posts.

Women in Employment

Instead of signs reading "Men at Work," many in the United States now read "People Working." Why? Because of a change in women's role in the economic sector. The number of women working outside the home has doubled in the past 25 years. Women held but 27 percent of office jobs back in 1970; 14 years later, women held 65 percent of them. For some, holding a job is an economic necessity; for others, it is by preference. In some places, wages for men and women doing identical jobs are gradually becoming more equal.

In Education, Arts, and Religion

Almost worldwide, women have made remarkable progress regarding education. The number of women in schools has increased from 95 million in 1950 to 390 million in 1985. In Spain 25 years ago,

there were twice as many illiterate women as men. By 1983 the situation had so improved that 30 percent of the college students were women. *Women in Britain* reports "a dramatic increase in the number of full-time women university students."

Over the years, women have figured prominently in the field of music as soloists, both vocal and instrumental. But in the United States before 1935, the only women playing in orchestras were the harpists, a role men seemed to avoid. In contrast, presently 40 percent of those playing in major, regional, and metropolitan orchestras are women.

There has been a similar increase in the field of religion. Many women have enrolled in seminaries, so that in the United States from 29 to 52 percent of such students are women. Women are appearing in pulpits, and there are also women rabbis. Some 11 percent of Swedish pastors are women, and there are Anglican women priests in the Orient. *The New York Times* (February 16, 1987) said "there are 968 ordained women in the Episcopal Church."

With What Effect?

So there is no denying that the situation of women has changed dramatically in recent times. You may have seen or personally felt these changes. But the question should be raised: Have all these changes been an unmixed blessing?

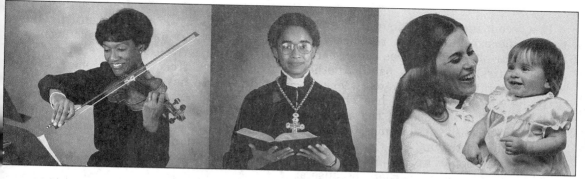

Women's Improved Role
A Mixed Blessing?

"IN SUM, women in the eighties are better educated, healthier, and live longer, fuller lives." With those words, a magazine concluded its article: "The Way We Were; the Way We Are Now." But could it be that women's improved role has actually been a mixed blessing because of its side effects?

Effect on Marriage and the Family

For example, there is the common clash between wholesome family life and pursuing a career. One report stated: "Women executives are far less likely to give their home life high priority than are their male peers, and they're twice as likely to be divorced." You might wonder why. A management professor at California State University explains: "Males look at their home environment as a support system, while women see it more as a burden. A guy comes home and he relaxes; that's what he's been working for. But to women it represents an added workload."

This does not apply just to executives. Russian women have been in the work force a generation longer than have women in Western lands. They still find caring for a job and a family to be a burden. A Russian editor of *Working Woman* says: "Women are the heart of the family and must be warmer to create the atmosphere of warmth and love." So they face a double load, while many husbands fail to share domestic duties.

Another cause of conflict is illustrated by one of Wall Street's most successful women. She boasts: "Work to me is recreation," and adds, "I like what I'm doing, and I make very few concessions"—even for her family. Its well-being depends upon the husband who looks after their two children, even though he is a businessman. Her associates describe her consuming interest as "clearly not good for family relationships."

It is similar with one of the modern prime ministers. Her family did not get much attention because of her political ambitions. While growing up, her children often stayed at the home of their uncle because, we are told, "one of the things [they] liked best was simply sitting down to meals as a family, something that was never easy to arrange" at home.

In a recent interview of four of Europe's top female executives, one revealed that her 12-year-old daughter was being reared almost entirely by her husband. Another executive stated that only on weekends was she able to care for her children. According to news reports, the audience noted that three of these women tended to lack the human touch.

Of course, some women hold secular jobs out of sheer need, perhaps because a husband died or left the family. So for such women, being able to find employment may be a partial blessing, but like it or not, they have to contend with the negative aspects.

Negative Effects

That women's changed role has been a mixed blessing is clear from the common effect when wives outdistance their husbands in earning power or professional status. According to therapists, this trend is "becoming a significant and recognized crisis point in more and more marriages." One husband's complaint is typical: "I know intellectually I applaud her success. But emotionally I feel badly. I feel I'm being abandoned. And I feel guilty because I am so upset." If both Christian mates presently have to work, loving discussion and consideration can help to minimize such negative feelings and effects. —1 Peter 4:8.

Another factor indicating that the progress made by women is a mixed blessing is the emphasis that many feminists put on what is primarily to their advantage. *The Coming Matriarchy* points to the time when the world will be run by women who are self-centered and who ask, "What's in it for *me?*" Interestingly, the successful woman financier previously described put it just about that way; she was not interested in helping others up the corporate ladder unless she stood to profit by it. She admitted: "I'm too profit-oriented." How wise is that, in view of Jesus' counsel? In the Sermon on the Mount he said: "You must always treat other people as you would like to have them treat you." "Do not worry about tomorrow, for tomorrow will have worries of its own." (Matthew 7:12; 6:34, *American Translation*) Certainly, Christian women strive to maintain Jesus' view on such matters.

Biblical Morality Expendable?

No doubt the most negative aspect of the changed role of women is the erosion of moral values. References by feminists to God and religion are rare and usually critical. Women who postpone marriage because of their careers often hold that marriage is not essential before having sex relations.

A negative trend of the feminist movement is its support of lesbianism. In 1971 the annual meeting of NOW (National Organization of Women) resolved: "That NOW recognizes the double oppression of women who are lesbians, That a woman's right to her own person includes the right to define and express her own sexuality and to choose her own lifestyle, That NOW acknowledges the oppression of lesbians as a legitimate concern of feminism." Compare, though, God's judgment at Romans 1:26, 27. Often going hand in hand with the feminist view on lesbianism is espousal of having abortions on demand. Tulane University law professor Billups Percy well stated: "To regard the destruction of the fetus as just another surgical procedure is to disregard centuries of criminology, theology and moral philosophy."

One report tells that in the past decade serious crimes on the part of women have increased far more rapidly than among men. Between 1974 and 1979, the number of women in the United States arrested

for fraud increased almost 50 percent, but the increase was only 13 percent among men. Embezzlement by women increased similarly about 50 percent but only 1.5 percent for men. Forgery and counterfeiting arrests among women rose 27.7 percent but less than 10 percent among men. Evidently the changed role of women has not resulted in full contentment.

Use of tobacco has also increased among women. Lung cancer due to smoking is replacing breast cancer as the number one cause of cancer deaths among women. In one recent year it accounted for 25 percent of all cancer deaths among women and is increasing at the rate of 7 percent each year.

A Satisfying Future—How?

Can a job or a career give most women complete satisfaction in life? Apparently not, as more and more are finding out. Hilary Cosell, author of *Woman on a Seesaw: The Ups and Downs of Making It,* addressed this problem in an article, asking: "If women had erred before on the side of marriage and motherhood and housewifery, might they be erring again on the side of professionalism, career and success?" She also asks: "Can we really do everything our mothers did, and everything our fathers did as well?"

Similarly, in *The Cost of Loving,* Megan Marshall revealed that "the facade of professional competence only thinly concealed the private wounds: disappointed loves, compulsive promiscuity, lesbian experimentation, abortions, divorce and just plain loneliness." She tells how the women's movement gave birth to the "Myth of Independence," but for most, this is not working.

Marshall concludes that "we must believe in the long-term love that a good marriage protects," that "the human self does not exist in isolation," and that "we must find others to care for, and who will care for us." This calls to mind the words of the greatest Teacher ever on earth, Jesus Christ. "There is more happiness in giving than there is in receiving."—Acts 20:35.

Truly, humans are prone to go from one extreme to another. That modern woman's improved role is not an unmixed blessing underscores the prophet Jeremiah's words: "It does not belong to man who is walking even to direct his step." (Jeremiah 10:23) Christian women, by knowing what changes have occurred (with attendant blessings and problems), can better appreciate the value of following God's counsel. Experience has shown that it is "more to be desired than gold." 'In the keeping of it there is a large reward.'—Psalm 19:7-11.

Murder During a Birthday Party

AFTER giving instructions to his apostles, Jesus sends them out into the territory in pairs. Probably the brothers Peter and Andrew went together, as did James and John, Philip and Bartholomew, Thomas and Matthew, James and Thaddaeus, and Simon and Judas Iscariot. The six pairs of evangelizers declare the good news of the Kingdom and perform miraculous cures everywhere they go.

Meanwhile, John the Baptizer is still in prison. He has been there almost two years now. You may recall that John had declared publicly that it was wrong for Herod Antipas to take Herodias, the wife of his brother Philip, as his own. Since Herod Antipas claimed to follow the Mosaic Law, John had properly exposed this adulterous union. It is for this that Herod had John thrown into prison, perhaps at the urging of Herodias.

Herod Antipas realizes that John is a righteous man and even listens to him with pleasure. So he is at a loss as to what to do with him. Herodias, on the other hand, hates John and keeps seeking to have him put to death. Finally, the opportunity she has been waiting for comes.

Shortly before the Passover of 32 C.E., Herod arranges a large celebration of his birthday. Assembled for the party are all Herod's top-ranking officials and army officers, as well as the leading citizens of Galilee. As the evening progresses, Salome, the young daughter of Herodias by her former husband Philip, is sent in to dance for the guests. The male audience is enthralled by her performance, which is no doubt most alluring.

Herod is highly pleased with Salome. "Ask me for whatever you want, and I will give it to you," he declares. He even swears: "Whatever you ask me for, I will give it to you, up to half my kingdom."

Before answering, Salome goes out to consult with her mother. "What should I ask for?" she inquires.

The opportunity at last! "The head of John the baptizer," Herodias answers without hesitation.

Quickly Salome returns to Herod and requests: "I want you to give me right away on a platter the head of John the Baptist."

Herod is greatly distressed. Yet because his guests have heard his oath, he is embarrassed not to grant it, even though this means murdering an innocent man. An executioner is immediately dispatched to the prison with his grisly instructions. Shortly he returns with John's head on a platter, and he gives it to Salome. She, in turn, takes it to her mother. When John's disciples hear what has happened, they come and remove his body and bury it, and then they report the matter to Jesus.

Later, when Herod hears of Jesus' healing people and casting out demons, he is frightened, fearing that Jesus is actually John who has been raised from the dead. Thereafter, he greatly desires to see Jesus, not to hear his preaching, but to confirm whether his fears are well founded or not. **Matthew 10:1-5; 11:1; 14:1-12; Mark 6:14-29; Luke 9: 7-9.**

♦ Why is John in prison, and why does Herod not want to put him to death?
♦ How is Herodias finally able to have John killed?
♦ After John's death, why does Herod want to see Jesus?

YOUTHS
What Will You Do With Your Life?

"That those who live might live no longer for themselves, but for him who died for them."
—2 CORINTHIANS 5:15.

'THANK you! I owe you my life!' People saved from a burning house or from drowning have said that to their rescuers. And appreciative Christian youths have made such an expression to their parents. They were referring not simply to the physical life received from their parents but especially to the loving care and instruction that put the youths on the way to receiving "the promised thing that he himself promised us, the life everlasting."—1 John 2:25.

² It was love that moved Jehovah God to make everlasting life, "the real life," available to each one of us. "He loved us and sent forth his Son as a propitiatory sacrifice for our sins." (1 Timothy 6:19; 1 John 4:10) Think, too, of the love that his Son Jesus showed in dying a painful death so that we might obtain everlasting life! (John 15:13) In light of the foregoing, What will you do with your life?

³ Youths are often asked this question, in one form or another, by student counselors at school or others interested in their future. What will determine your answer? Will it be determined simply by personal preference? Will the deciding factor be the advice of those wanting you to achieve a secure position in the secular world? Or will what you do with your life be determined by superior considerations? The inspired reminder says: "He died for all *that those who live might live no longer for themselves, but for him who died for them* and was raised up." (2 Corinthians 5:15) Yes, how fine it is when the way we use our lives reflects gratitude for what Jesus Christ and his heavenly Father have done for us!

Popular Role Models

⁴ Yet, who are the most popular figures today, the ones that young people generally adopt as role models? Is it not the rich

---

1. What expression of gratitude have people made, and why?
2. In the light of what information should you consider the question, What will you do with your life?

---

3. What often determines what people do with their lives?
4. Who are the most popular role models today?

and famous of the world, regardless of their moral standards? When you look in the rooms of many youths, whose pictures do you see hanging on the walls? Often it is those of musicians, movie stars, and athletes. Youths commonly dream of someday achieving similar worldly success or perhaps of marrying someone with the physical attributes of these persons. What about you? What do you want out of life?

[5] If you achieved the worldly success of admired celebrities, would you really be happy and satisfied? One of Hollywood's most successful actresses said: "I've had my taste of wealth and all the material things. They don't mean a thing. There's a psychiatrist that goes with every swimming pool out here, not to mention divorces and children who hate their parents."—Ecclesiastes 5:10; 1 Timothy 6:10.

[6] An outstanding student athlete, the 1981 winner of the women's division of a major 10-kilometer race in New York, became so disillusioned that she attempted suicide. "I have learned many truths about life in the past few months," she wrote afterward. "One is that true contentment is not attained in the ways that so many people strive for perfection and achievement. Contentment for me didn't come from having been a straight-A student, a state-championship runner or the possessor of an attractive figure." Yes, people need to learn that true contentment comes only with having a personal relationship with God, who alone can provide genuine peace and happiness.—Psalm 23: 1, 6; 16:11.

[7] Clearly, then, you should not want to imitate those who struggle merely to achieve prominence and wealth. Even sec- ular writers note the failure of worldly success to bring true satisfaction. Columnist Bill Reel wrote: "You graduate from college with dreams for the future. Sadly, most of your aspirations will turn to ashes. I don't want to demoralize you, but you might as well hear the truth: When you acquire the possessions you covet, if you acquire them, and when you achieve the successes you pursue, if you achieve them, they won't satisfy you. Instead, at those very moments when you would expect to be reveling in triumph, you will feel empty rather than fulfilled, depressed rather than elated, agitated rather than peaceful."—New York Daily News, May 26, 1983.

[8] But for us who are alert to the significance of world events in the light of Bible prophecy, there are much stronger reasons for not putting a worldly career foremost in life. (Matthew 24:3-14) We might compare ourselves to a person that sees a building with a sign: "This Company Going out of Business." Would we seek employment there? Of course not! And if we worked for such a company, we would wisely look for employment elsewhere. Well, the sign is evident everywhere on this world's institutions: "Going out of Business—End Near!" Yes, "The world is passing away," the Bible assures us. (1 John 2:17) So, wisely, we will not adopt as role models those who are deeply involved with it.

What Advice to Follow

[9] Your life is shaped not only by those you hold in esteem but often also by relatives and friends who, as they put it, 'want the best for you.' 'You have to earn a living,' they may say. So they may

---

5, 6. (a) Why can it be said that worldly success fails to bring true contentment? (b) What is the source of true contentment?
7. As to realizing true satisfaction, how important are a college education and worldly success?

8. What strong reason is there for not pursuing a worldly career?
9. What worldly advice may those give who seemingly want the best for you?

Luke, though a trained physician, put Christian pursuits first in life

advise you to get a college or university education to prepare yourself for a well-paying profession. 'The Bible writer Luke was a physician,' they may note, 'and the apostle Paul was instructed by the Law teacher Gamaliel.' (Colossians 4:14; Acts 5:34; 22:3) Yet, analyze carefully such advice.

¹⁰ The physician Luke never encouraged Christians to follow his former career example by becoming a doctor; rather, Luke held forth the lives of Jesus and his apostles for imitation. Evidently Luke became a physician *before* he learned about Christ but afterward put his Christian ministry first in life. The situation was similar with Paul. Rather than encouraging others to imitate him as he had imitated Gamaliel, Paul wrote: "Become imitators of me, *even as I am of Christ.*" So highly did Paul value the knowledge of Christ that he said that by comparison he considered his for-

mer pursuits "as a lot of refuse." —1 Corinthians 11:1; Philippians 3:8.

¹¹ Remember, sentiment can cause even those who love you to give poor advice. For example, when Jesus spoke of what awaited him during his ministry in Jerusalem, the apostle Peter replied: "Be kind to yourself, Lord; you will not have this destiny at all." Peter loved Jesus and did not want him to suffer. Yet Jesus rebuked Peter because He realized that to fulfill God's will would involve both suffering and being put to death by opposers.—Matthew 16:21-23.

¹² Similarly, some parents or friends may discourage you from a self-sacrificing course. Because of ill-advised sentiment, they may hesitate to encourage you to take an assignment in the full-time pioneer ministry, to serve as a missionary, or to do volunteer work at a branch office of Jehovah's Witnesses. They may say: 'Why not, rather, get married and settle down close to us?' Or, 'You know, the work is hard at Bethel. Maybe it's better you stay with us.' In other words, as Peter put it, "Be kind to yourself."

¹³ Even Jehovah's servants at times need to readjust their thinking. Peter needed to, and with a readjusted viewpoint, he wrote: "In fact, to this course you were called, because even Christ suffered for you, leaving you a model for you to follow his steps closely." (1 Peter 2:21)

---

10. What advice did Luke and Paul provide, and what can be said about their pre-Christian activity?

11. (a) What did Peter tell Jesus, and why? (b) How did Jesus respond?
12. What advice may well-meaning persons give youths, and why?
13. (a) What readjusted viewpoint did Peter express? (b) What is involved in being a true Christian?

Living a true Christian life involves self-sacrifice, yes, even suffering. It is not an easy course, but it is the one to which we were called as Christians. Accepting it involves 'no longer living for ourselves, but for him who died for us.' (2 Corinthians 5:15) Keeping in view good role models will help us to use our lives in this self-sacrificing way.

Role Models to Keep in View

14 The model you need particularly to keep in view is the one Jesus provided. As a perfect person, he could have become the greatest athlete, musician, physician, or lawyer that the world would ever know. But his attention was focused on pleasing his heavenly Father, even while Jesus was a youth. (Luke 2:42-49) He later said: "I must declare the good news of the kingdom of God, because for this I was sent forth." (Luke 4:43) Last summer a letter in the church magazine *Ministry* explained: "Our Saviour loved to get away from the multitude, and then He went from house to house—soul hunting. The one-soul audience was His delight. Then He could pour in the truth—the love of God."—Luke 10:1-16.

15 Granted, house-to-house preaching is not easy. It requires diligent study to understand the good news of the Kingdom and a lot of work to prepare meaningful presentations. Also, this service takes courage, since most householders are not interested, and some are even hostile. Yet, the house-to-house ministry of you young ones is having a marvelous effect, as noted in the Italian parish magazine *La Voce*. The writer said: "Personally, I like Jehovah's Witnesses," who, he explained, "come and visit you at home." He commented: "The ones I know are impeccably mannered, soft-spoken; beautiful people too and mostly young. Beauty and youth are, when on display, most persuasive."

16 Surely, you young ones who are accepting Christ as your model are to be commended! More than 12,000 youths, age 25 and under, are in the pioneer work in the United States, and tens of thousands more are pioneering elsewhere. (Psalm 110:3) Be assured that no other work you can do is more important! Even the writer in the above-mentioned church magazine said: "God says the most essential work is house-to-house visitation—soul hunting," yet he continued, "What do you say about this? How much visitation are you and I doing? I have not seen much mention of this kind of work in MINISTRY." Can we not be grateful that we are associated with an organization that emphasizes the requirement of imitating Jesus' example of preaching?

17 Since what you will do with your life will be largely influenced by those you admire, develop admiration also for the model provided by young Timothy. Born shortly before Jesus' death, Timothy as a young man left his family and joined the apostle Paul on his second missionary journey. A few months later a mob forced Paul and Silas to flee from Thessalonica, but not before they had made some disciples. (Acts 16:1-3; 17:1-10, 13-15) Soon afterward Paul sent Timothy into that dangerous territory to comfort these disciples in their trials. (1 Thessalonians 3: 1-3) Timothy was possibly in his late teens

14. What example did Jesus provide?
15. (a) Why is house-to-house preaching a challenge? (b) What shows that the house-to-house ministry of youths is effective?

16. (a) For what activity do youths deserve commendation? (b) How does the organization of Jehovah's Witnesses compare with the churches in performing the most important work on earth?
17. What had Timothy accomplished while possibly still a teenager, and what shows that he may have been that young at the time?

at the time, since some 12 to 14 years later Paul still spoke about his "youth." (1 Timothy 4:12) Do you not admire a courageous, self-sacrificing youth like that?

[18] Five years after Timothy's assignment to strengthen the brothers in Thessalonica, Paul wrote the Corinthians from Ephesus: "Become imitators of me. That is why I am sending Timothy to you, . . . and he will put you in mind of my methods in connection with Christ Jesus, just as I am teaching everywhere." (1 Corinthians 4: 16, 17) Young Timothy, having already worked five years with Paul, was well acquainted with Paul's teaching methods. He knew how Paul had presented the message to the Ephesians, including how he had taught them "publicly and from house to house." (Acts 20:20, 21) Having been trained well in such preaching methods, what a fine help Timothy could be to the congregations!

[19] Another five or six years pass, and Paul is in prison in Rome. Timothy, who himself was recently released from prison, is with him. (Hebrews 13:23) Imagine the scene: Possibly using Timothy as his sec-

retary, Paul is dictating a letter to the Philippians. Speaking deliberately, Paul proceeds: "I am hoping in the Lord Jesus to send Timothy to you shortly . . . For I have no one else of a disposition like his who will genuinely care for the things pertaining to you . . . You know the proof he gave of himself, that like a child with a father he slaved with me in furtherance of the good news."—Philippians 1:1; 2:19-22.

[20] Surely, young Timothy is an admirable example! He was such a reliable, faithful companion to Paul, sticking with him through thick and thin, supporting him in the preaching work, and being willing to serve wherever he was sent. He sacrificed a so-called normal life at home, yet what contentment and satisfaction his life in God's service brought him! Timothy was indeed 'living no longer for himself, but for Christ who had died for him.' (2 Corinthians 5:15) Are you moved to imitate his example?

Live for God's New World

[21] Timothy, in effect, was living for God's new world. He was not thinking simply of the here and now but of using his life to produce lasting benefits. (Matthew 6:19-21) Since Timothy's father was a Greek and apparently an unbeliever, he may have urged Timothy to pursue higher education and a worldly career. But as a result of the godly instruction from his mother and grandmother, Timothy's life was wrapped up with the Christian congregation. He pursued spiritual interests, apparently remained single at least for a time, and qualified to serve with the apostle Paul.—2 Timothy 1:5.

18. Why was Paul going to send Timothy to the Corinthians?
19. What did Paul say about Timothy more than ten years after they started serving together?

Questions for Review

□ Why should true Christians not put worldly careers first in life?

□ What faulty advice have some given, yet what can we learn from Jesus' answer to Peter?

□ In what ways did Jesus and Timothy provide fine role models for youths?

□ What is involved in being spiritually minded?

20. What makes Timothy such an admirable role model for youths?
21. Why can we say that Timothy was spiritually minded?

²² What about you? Will you use your youth in the way Timothy did? The brochure *School and Jehovah's Witnesses* was referring to such a life course when it explained regarding Witness youths: "Their main goal in life is to serve effectively as ministers of God, and they appreciate schooling as an aid to that end. So they generally choose courses that are useful for supporting themselves in the modern world. Thus, many may take vocational courses or attend a vocational school. When they leave school they desire to obtain work that will allow them to concentrate on their principal vocation, the Christian ministry."

²³ For you who really appreciate what Jehovah God and his Son have done for you, it should not be hard to answer the question, What will I do with my life? Rather than living for yourself and personal pleasure, you will use your life to do God's will. You will live, as did Timothy, as a spiritual person.

22. How does the *School* brochure highlight for youths today a life course similar to Timothy's?

23. Why should it not be hard for Christian youths to answer the question, What will I do with my life?

YOUTHS

Are You Spiritually Progressive?

"Ponder over these things; be absorbed in them, that your advancement may be manifest to all persons."—1 TIMOTHY 4:15.

WHAT does it mean to be spiritually progressive? It means being like young Jesus and Timothy, who put spiritual interests first in their lives. If you are spiritually progressive, you will know what you want to do with your life. You will not say: 'I'll begin to think seriously about serving Jehovah when I get older.' No, you will serve him *now!*

1, 2. What does it mean, and not mean, to be spiritually progressive?

² On the other hand, being spiritually progressive does not mean being monklike, putting on religious airs, or even becoming a bookworm; nor does it mean being sad, solemn, and never socializing. (John 2:1-10) Jehovah is a happy God, and he wants his earthly children to be happy. So moderate participation in sports and other recreational activities has God's approval.—1 Timothy 1:11; 4:8.

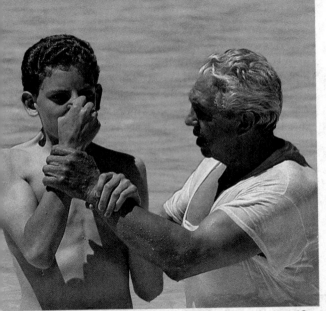

What prevents you from being baptized?

Baptism an Evidence

3 Preparing for and getting baptized are evidences that a youth is spiritually progressive. If, as has been suggested, Timothy was still a teenager when he became the apostle Paul's missionary companion, Timothy was probably baptized when he was in his mid or early teens. He had been instructed in the Scriptures from infancy, and once equipped with adequate knowledge and appreciation, he did not hesitate to get baptized.—2 Timothy 3:15.

4 What about you teenagers who have been instructed in the Scriptures? Have you considered the question: "What prevents me from getting baptized?" In the first century, that question was asked by a man who was well versed in the Scriptures but who had just then learned the identity of Christ. True, the man did not know all there is to know about God's purposes, yet he was moved with deep

appreciation for what he did know! Thus, the disciple Philip had no legitimate reason for not baptizing him.—Acts 8:26-39.

5 What prevents *you* from getting baptized? To qualify, of course, you must comprehend what is involved. You must truly want to serve Jehovah because you love him. You also need to make a personal dedication to him in prayer. In addition, you must be adhering to God's moral requirements and have sufficient experience in sharing your faith with others. When you thus qualify, it is vital to follow through and get baptized.—Matthew 28: 19, 20; Acts 2:38.

6 Though getting baptized is evidence that you are spiritually progressive, remember that baptism is just a beginning step. By making a dedication to Jehovah, you become an alien in this old world ruled by Satan. So dedication may be compared to applying for everlasting life in God's new system, and the formal ceremony of baptism is, in effect, a demonstration before witnesses confirming this fact. (John 12:31; Hebrews 11:13) Afterward you must faithfully live up to your dedication in order to receive God's gift of everlasting life.—Romans 6:23.

Evidenced by Conduct

7 Whether you are spiritually progressive or not will also be evidenced by your attitude toward things of the world. What things? They include a freewheeling lifestyle, drugs, sexual freedom, immoral movies, suggestive music, obscene talk, sensuous dancing, racial and national pride, and so forth. (1 John 2:16; Ephesians 5:3-5) Youths, in particular, need to be on guard. Remember, the way you be-

---

3. When was Timothy most likely baptized?
4. What question was Philip asked, and although the questioner had just learned about Christ, why did Philip grant his request?

5. What is required for you to be baptized?
6. What may baptism be compared to, and what must follow it?
7. How does your attitude toward things of the world relate to your spiritual progressiveness?

have regarding such things will reveal the state of your spiritual health.—Proverbs 20:11.

⁸ Satan sees to it that the world's immoral ways appear very attractive. In fact, a 15-year-old said: "The more we see sex and drugs on TV, the more it seems normal in society." Youths who do not participate in the ways of the world are made to feel that they are oddballs and that they are missing out on fun. Do you ever feel that way? Some associated with the congregation do, and they are indecisive. When asked about getting baptized, one youth said: 'I don't want to now because I may do something I would be disfellowshipped for.' Yet you cannot straddle the fence or be limping on two different opinions. God's prophet once said: "If Jehovah is the true God, go following him; but if Baal is, go following him." —1 Kings 18:21.

⁹ Really, by avoiding the immoral ways of the world, all that you are missing out on is a lot of trouble. "An enormous feeling of revulsion and remorse for the life I had been leading overwhelmed me," confessed one woman. "I had cheapened and cheated myself and the child I had conceived." Yes, the apparent glamour and glitter of the Devil's world is only a mirage, a deception. It holds nothing of value. Following the world's ways leads to out-of-wedlock pregnancies, broken homes, sexually transmitted disease, and untold frustration and misery. So listen to counsel, be spiritually progressive. "Turn away from what is bad and do what is good."—1 Peter 3:11.

¹⁰ A spiritually progressive youth will heed the admonition of the apostle Paul: "Be babes as to badness; yet become full-grown in powers of understanding." (1 Corinthians 14:20) Young Timothy certainly applied this counsel. Can you imagine his seeking the companionship of licentious, worldly youths of his day? Not at all! His companions were fellow servants of God. (Proverbs 13:20) Imitate his example. When about to engage in any questionable activity, ask yourself: Would Timothy or Jesus do this?

Evidenced by Bible Study

¹¹ An article from Italy published in *World Press Review* said: "The youths' delusion and desperation mount daily, and no one can offer them an encouraging future." The blinded eyes of those in Satan's world have no vision of God's promised new world and of the glorious future that awaits those who qualify for life there. (2 Corinthians 4:4; Proverbs 29:18; 2 Peter 3:13) But spiritually progressive youths have such a vision that is kept bright and clear through regular Bible study.

¹² Is God's new world real to you? It can be, but attaining it requires real effort on your part. You need to develop a keen appetite for Bible understanding so that "you keep seeking for it as for silver, and as for hid treasures you keep searching for it." (Proverbs 2:1-6) What keeps a treasure hunter searching and digging, sometimes for years? He passionately desires the riches that the treasure will bring him. Yet knowledge is so much more precious than material treasure. "This means everlasting life," Jesus said, "taking in knowledge of you, the only true God, and of the one whom you sent forth, Jesus Christ." (John 17:3) If you really believe

8. Why do some youths hesitate to get baptized?
9. What protection is realized by being spiritually progressive?
10. What admonition and whose examples will a spiritually progressive youth heed?

11. What vision do youths of the world lack, and how is it gained and maintained?
12. (a) How must we go about obtaining knowledge of God? (b) Why is this knowledge worth the effort?

what Jesus there said, Bible study will become an eager pursuit that will reward you with what is more precious than priceless gems.—Proverbs 3:13-18.

[13] You will find that the more you study, the greater your appetite will be for spiritual food. Learn good study methods. Do not simply underline answers, but look up cited Bible texts, and then pursue related texts through the Bible cross-references. You can also do additional research using indexes, such as the *Watch Tower Publications Index 1930-1985*. Analyze how the material applies and how it can be put to use. Talk to others about what you are studying. This will impress points on your mind and will serve to encourage others to do research as well. By really applying yourself, you will be heeding the counsel given to young Timothy: "Ponder over these things; be absorbed in them, that your advancement may be manifest to all persons."—1 Timothy 4:15; 2 Timothy 2:15.

13. What suggestions for study will spiritually progressive youths follow?

Shown at Meetings and in Service

[14] When you enjoy Bible study and have prepared well, Christian meetings become a greater pleasure. (Psalm 122:1; Hebrews 2:12) You then look forward even more to sharing in audience-participation parts and to giving talks in the Theocratic Ministry School. But when attending meetings, there are other ways to fulfill the instruction 'to encourage one another' and "to incite to love and fine works." (Hebrews 10:24, 25) Do you, for instance, take the initiative to speak to others? A friendly, "Hello, I'm glad to see you!" or a sincere inquiry, "How are you feeling?" can be so encouraging, especially when coming from a young person.

[15] A lot of work is involved in the operations of a congregation. Can you share? Likely, young Timothy performed many

14. What helps to make Christian meetings a greater pleasure, and in what ways can you encourage others while attending?
15. How can you make yourself available to perform needful services, and why is it good to keep Christ's example in mind?

helpful services for Paul—running errands, obtaining supplies, delivering messages, and so forth. If you have not done so, why not mention to the elders your willingness to be of help. Perhaps you will be asked to hand out meeting assignments, keep the hall clean, or perform some other needful service. Remember, Christ washed his disciples' feet, so no work is beneath the dignity of one who is spiritually progressive.—John 13:4, 5.

[16] When we look at other religions, we can indeed be grateful for the training we receive at our meetings for the all-important preaching work. Writing in *U.S. Catholic* last September, Kenneth Guentert said: "I grew up in the days when Catholics weren't supposed to read the Bible because they'd get strange ideas—like thinking Christians should go around knocking on doors trying to convert people. Then came Vatican II, and I started to read the Bible. Sure enough; now I think Christians should go around knocking on doors to try to convert people." He added: "It's not that I'm terribly comfortable with the idea, you understand; but if you read the New Testament, it is almost impossible to avoid this conclusion."—Matthew 10:11-13; Luke 10:1-6; Acts 20:20, 21.

[17] Yes, early Christians were active in house-to-house preaching, and evidently youngsters like Timothy were right out there in the ministry with older ones. Yet, admittedly, for some today this is not the most enjoyable work. Why not? Adeptness is a factor. For example, when you do well in a game or a sport, do you not enjoy it more? It is much the same with the ministry. As you become more proficient in using the Bible and discussing Bible topics, the ministry will become a source of pleasure, especially when you find someone with whom you can share life-giving knowledge. So be spiritually progressive! Practice your door-to-door presentations. Get suggestions from others. Petition Jehovah's help.—Luke 11:13.

By Relationships With Older Ones

[18] When he was just a youth of 12, Jesus enjoyed spending time with older ones, discussing spiritual things. His parents once "found him in the temple, sitting in the midst of the teachers and listening to them and questioning them." (Luke 2:46) It was similar with Timothy. When the apostle Paul and his companions visited Lystra, Timothy evidently enjoyed their company and paid earnest attention to their teachings. He had a rapport with the local brothers who highly recommended him.—Acts 16:1-3.

[19] Although Timothy willingly performed physical services for others, Paul chose him as a traveling companion particularly for his ability to minister to people's spiritual needs. In view of that, when a mob forced Paul to leave Thessalonica, he sent young Timothy to comfort and strengthen the new disciples. So not only was Timothy eager to learn from older ones and to enjoy their company; he was of real spiritual help to them as well.—Acts 17:1-10; 1 Thessalonians 3:1-3.

[20] You will be wise to imitate Jesus and Timothy and be eager to benefit from the experience and knowledge of older ones. Seek their company and ask them questions. But also show your spiritual

16. What activity did a Catholic periodical recognize to be a Christian responsibility?
17. How can the ministry become more pleasurable for you?

18. What kind of relationships did Jesus and Timothy enjoy with older ones?
19. Why particularly did Paul choose Timothy as a traveling companion, and how was Timothy of help?
20. What will you be wise to do, and what services can you perform in behalf of older ones?

progressiveness by being of assistance to them. Are there aged or infirm ones that would appreciate having you do some shopping or other needful services? Perhaps you could simply visit them, read to them, and share experiences you have enjoyed in the ministry.

Role of Parents and Others

[21] The spiritual health of youths is largely dependent upon the instruction and example provided by their parents. (Proverbs 22:6) Jesus surely benefited from the guidance given by his God-fearing earthly parents. (Luke 2:51, 52) And most certainly Timothy would not have been the spiritually progressive lad he was had it not been for the training of his mother and grandmother. (2 Timothy 1:5; 3:15) The importance of regular Bible instruction cannot be overemphasized! As parents, are you providing this? Or is it neglected?

[22] A young man at the world headquarters of Jehovah's Witnesses explains that through the years of growing up, an invariable feature of their family life was the weekly Bible study with the children. "Sometimes Dad would be so tired from work he could hardly keep awake, but the study was held regardless, and this helped us to appreciate the seriousness of it." Parents, it is unlikely that your children will highly value spiritual matters unless you do. So hold forth the goals of pioneering and of missionary and Bethel service. Help them to appreciate that the ministry is a career with a future and that there is no real future in worldly careers.—Compare 1 Samuel 1:26-28.

[23] Others, too, can help youths to progress spiritually. You can make a point of conversing with them at meetings. Also try to include them in some of your activities. With the parent's permission, an elder might arrange to take a youth on a speaking assignment or to include him on an outing. (Job 31:16-18) What may seem to be a little thing can mean a lot. A traveling overseer, noting that a boy who was listening to his talk did not have a Bible, afterward made a gift of one to him. The lad was impressed not only with the gift but also with the interest shown in him. Over 30 years later, the boy, now an elder himself, still remembers with fondness that brother's loving gesture.

[24] Is it not thrilling to realize that there are hundreds of thousands of "young men just like dewdrops" publishing the refreshing Kingdom message and that there is at least an equal number of young women forming 'a large army telling the good news'? May all of them apply themselves to being spiritually progressive, and may all of us help them to that end.—Psalm 110:3; 68:11.

---

24. What is it thrilling to realize, and what should be our determination?

---

21. How important is the role of parents, and what cannot be overemphasized?
22. (a) When parents consider family Bible study vital, how are children affected? (b) What direction should parents give to their children?
23. How can others in the congregation help youths to be spiritually progressive?

Questions for Review

☐ What can help a youth to decide when to be baptized?

☐ How is a youth's conduct a measure of his spiritual progressiveness?

☐ What can help youths to enjoy meetings and field service?

☐ What relationship should youths develop with older ones?

☐ How can parents and older ones help youths?

Is the *Cross* for Christians?

"MY MOTHER gave it to me." "It's manly." "I wear it as an ornament." "I'd feel uncomfortable without it." "It protects me from evil." "It's just something to hang on the chain."

Thus replied several people who were asked why they wore a cross. Though obviously not all do so out of religious devotion, wearing a cross is quite in vogue in some parts of the world. Even Soviet youths have been seen wearing one. Many attach deep religious significance to the cross, for, as one youth simply said, "It's sacred."

But is it really proper for a Christian to wear a cross? Does it accurately portray the way Christ died? And are there valid objections even to wearing it as an ornament? To see, let us first take a look at the origin of the cross.

A Christian Symbol?

You may assume that Christians were the first to use the cross. *The Encyclopedia Americana,* however, speaks of "its ancient usage by both Hindus and Buddhists in India and China, and by the Persians, Assyrians, and Babylonians." Similarly, *Chambers's Encyclopaedia,* (1969 edition) says that the cross "was an emblem to which religious and mystical meanings were attached long before the Christian era."

Indeed, there is no evidence that early Christians used the cross in their worship.

During the early days of Christianity, it was the pagan Romans who used the cross! Says *The Companion Bible:* "These crosses were used as symbols of the Babylonian sun-god . . . and are first seen on a coin of Julius Caesar, 100-44 B.C., and then on a coin struck by Caesar's heir (Augustus), 20 B.C." The Roman nature-god Bacchus was at times represented with a headband containing a number of crosses.

How, then, did the cross become the symbol of Christendom?

Constantine and the Cross

In 312 C.E., Constantine, ruling the area now known as France and Britain, headed out to war against his brother-in-law, Maxentius, of Italy. En route he reportedly saw a vision—a cross on which were the words *"Hoc vince,"* meaning, "By this conquer." After his victory, Constantine made the cross the standard of his armies. When Christianity later became the state religion of the Roman Empire, the cross became the symbol of the church.

But did such a vision actually take place? Accounts of this legend are, at best, secondhand and full of discrepancies. Frankly, it would be difficult to find a more unlikely candidate for a divine revelation than Constantine. At the time of this supposed event, he was an avid sun-god worshiper. Constantine even dedicated Sunday as the day for sun worship. His conduct after his so-called conversion also gave little evidence of real dedication to right principles. Murder, intrigue, and political ambition ruled his life. It seems that for Constantine, Christianity was little more than a political device to unite a fragmented empire.

There is also little evidence that the type

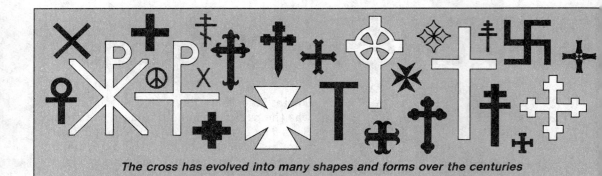

The cross has evolved into many shapes and forms over the centuries

of cross Constantine "saw" really represented the instrument used to put Christ to death. Stamped on many coins Constantine subsequently had minted are X-shaped crosses with a "P" superimposed. (See illustration.) *An Expository Dictionary of New Testament Words,* by W. E. Vine, says: "As for the Chi, or X, which Constantine declared he had seen in a vision leading him to champion the Christian faith, that letter was the initial of the word 'Christ' [in the Greek language] and had nothing to do with 'the Cross,'" that is, as an instrument of execution. In fact, this style of cross is nearly identical to the pagan symbol for the sun.

Why, then, was the cross so easily accepted by "Christians"? Vine's *Dictionary* continues: "By the middle of the 3rd cent. A.D. the churches had either departed from, or had travestied, certain doctrines of the Christian faith. In order to increase the prestige of the apostate ecclesiastical system pagans were received into the churches apart from regeneration by faith, and were permitted largely to retain their pagan signs and symbols. Hence the Tau or T, in its most frequent form, with the cross-piece lowered, was adopted to stand for the cross of Christ."

The Evolution of the Cross

Was it love for Christ that caused the cross, at this late time, to become such an object of veneration? The *Encyclopaedia of Religion and Ethics* says: "With the 4th cent[ury] magical belief began to take a firmer hold within the Church." As with a magic charm, simply making the sign of the cross was thought to be "the surest defence against demons, and the remedy for all diseases." Superstitious use of the cross continues to this day.

Over the years, some 400 different styles of crosses developed. At first, Christ himself was not portrayed. Rather, a youth holding a jeweled cross would be depicted. Later, a lamb was included. In 691 C.E., the council in Trullo made "official" a cross showing the bust of a young man, instead of a lamb, over the cross. In time this developed into the crucifix—a cross with a representation of the body of Christ.

Did Christ Die on a Cross?

'But does not the Bible teach that Christ actually died on a cross?' one may ask. To answer this, we must look into the meanings of the two Greek words that the Bible writers used to describe the instrument of Christ's death: *stau·ros'* and *xy'lon*.

The International Standard Bible Encyclopedia (1979) states under the heading "Cross": "Originally Gk. *staurós* designated a pointed, vertical wooden stake firmly fixed in the ground. . . . They were positioned side by side in rows to form fencing or defensive palisades around settlements, or singly they were set up as instruments of torture on which serious offenders of law were publicly suspended to die (or, if already killed, to have their corpses thoroughly dishonored)."

True, the Romans did use an instrument of execution known in Latin as the *crux*. And in translating the Bible into Latin, this word *crux* was used as a rendering of *stau·ros'*. Because the Latin word *crux* and the English word *cross* are similar, many mistakenly assume that a *crux* was necessarily a stake with a crossbeam. However, *The Imperial Bible-Dictionary* says: "Even amongst the Romans the *crux* (from which our *cross* is derived) appears to have been originally an upright pole, and this always remained the more prominent part."

The book *The Non-Christian Cross* adds: "There is not a single sentence in any of the numerous writings forming the New Testament, which, in the original Greek, bears even indirect evidence to the effect that the stauros used in the case of Jesus was other than an ordinary stauros [pole or stake]; much less to the effect that it consisted, not of one piece of timber, but of two pieces nailed together in the form of a cross." Christ could well have been impaled on a form of *crux* (*stau·ros'*) known as the *crux simplex*. That was how such a stake was illustrated by the Roman Catholic scholar Justus Lipsius of the 16th century.

What of the other Greek word, *xy'lon*? It was used in the Greek *Septuagint* translation of the Bible at Ezra 6:11. In the *New World Translation* this reads: "And by me an order has been put through that, as for anybody that violates this decree, a timber will be pulled out of his house and he will be impaled upon it, and his house will be turned into a public privy on this account." Clearly, a single beam, or "timber," was involved here.

Numerous translators of the Christian

Statue of the Greek god Marsyas flayed alive on a tree trunk —The Louvre, Paris

Greek Scriptures (New Testament) therefore translate Peter's words at Acts 5:30 to read: "The God of our forefathers raised up Jesus, whom you slew, hanging him upon *a stake* [or, "tree," according to the *King James Version, New International Version, The Jerusalem Bible,* and *Revised Standard Version*]." You might also wish to check how your Bible translates *xy'lon* at: Acts 10:39; 13:29; Galatians 3:13; and 1 Peter 2:24.

Walking by Faith, Not by Sight

Even after considering such evidence that Christ really died on a stake, some may still see nothing wrong with wearing a cross. 'It's just an ornament,' they may say.

Bear in mind, though, how the cross has been used down through history —as an object of pagan worship and of

ΙΗΣΟΥΣ Ο ΝΑΖΩΡΑΙΟΣ
Ο ΒΑΣΙΛΕΥΣ ΤΩΝ ΙΟΥΔΑΙΩΝ
ישוע הנוצרי מלך היהודים
IESVS NAZARENVS REX IVDAEORVM

superstitious awe. Could wearing a cross, even as just an ornament, be harmonized with the admonition of the apostle Paul at 1 Corinthians 10:14: "Therefore, my beloved ones, flee from idolatry"?

What about true Christians today? They, too, should be conscious of the need to 'guard themselves from idols,' as the Bible counsels. (1 John 5:21) So they do not find the cross to be an appropriate ornament. They recall Paul's statement: "Accursed is every man hanged upon a stake," and therefore prefer to think of Christ as a glorious enthroned King! —Galatians 3:13; Revelation 6:2.

Though such Christians do not wear crosses, they deeply appreciate the fact that Christ died for them. They know that Christ's sacrifice is a marvelous demonstration of "God's power" and eternal love. (1 Corinthians 1:18; John 3:16) But they need no material object like a cross to help them worship this God of love. For, as Paul exhorted, they "are walking by faith, not by sight."—2 Corinthians 5:7.

Christian Cross Before Constantine?

"THE sign of the cross has been a symbol of great antiquity, present in nearly every known culture. Its meaning has eluded anthropologists, though its use in funerary art could well point to a defense against evil. On the other hand, the famous *crux ansata* of Egypt, depicted coming from the mouth, must refer to life or breath. The universal use of the sign of the cross makes more poignant the striking lack of crosses in early Christian remains, especially any specific reference to the event on Golgotha. Most scholars now agree that the cross, as an artistic reference to the passion event, cannot be found prior to the time of Constantine."—*Ante Pacem —Archaeological Evidence of Church Life Before Constantine* (1985), by Professor Graydon F. Snyder, page 27.

NEW CALEDONIA

Lifou

LOYALTY ISLANDS

AUSTRALIA

Nouméa

Demonstrating Christian Loyalty in New Caledonia

ALL was not well in paradise. By early 1985, political unrest had claimed some 20 lives on the South Pacific island of New Caledonia. This led *Maclean's* magazine to comment: "The island is already beginning to resemble Northern Ireland, divided into two heavily armed and hostile camps."

The situation had become so serious in January 1985 that President François Mitterrand of France scurried half way around the world on an unscheduled Saturday visit to Nouméa, the island's capital. The islanders, divided in their loyalties, were anxious to express their feelings during his visit. The original inhabitants, pushed by religious leaders and feeling a strong sense of loyalty to their Melanesian roots, pressed hard for an end to over 130 years of French rule. On the other hand, many descendants of European Polynesians and Asian settlers, and even Melanesians, expressed their loyalty to the French government and advocated that its rule continue.

Meanwhile, on this same Saturday, 1,567 of Jehovah's Witnesses and their friends had also gathered in Nouméa to make a public display of loyalty. Their loyalty, however, was not to any particular ethnic group or to an earthly government; it was loyalty to God's established Kingdom. But how did it come about that they were in Nouméa on this particular day? For that matter, how did it come about that they were in New Caledonia at all?

The Beginnings of Christian Loyalty

New Caledonia has what you might expect of a South Pacific paradise—a pleasant climate the year round, luscious fruits to incite the palate, abundant vegetation to delight the eye, and a colorful mixture of over 150,000 Melanesians, Polynesians, Asians, and Europeans.

It was discovered in 1774 by Captain James Cook, the famous British navigator and explorer, but became a French colony in 1853. Half a step behind the first explorers and traders came Christendom's missionaries. The people they found obviously needed to be freed from certain wrong practices. The missionaries succeeded, for example, in wiping out cannibalism. They also introduced the people to the Bible and even translated it into four local languages. Commendably, they included God's name, rendered Iehova or Jehova in the vernacular. Yet, more was needed.

In the 1930's a group of Jehovah's Witnesses sailed through the Loyalty Islands distributing Bible literature. In the mid-1950's several Australian Witnesses moved to New Caledonia. Although they were later deported, the work prospered, and by 1967 the number of local

Witnesses had grown to over a hundred. In 1976 the Watch Tower Society established a branch office in Nouméa and oversaw the construction of the island's first Kingdom Hall.*

Especially since then, great strides have been made in gathering loyal subjects for Jehovah's established Kingdom from all the country's different ethnic groups. For example, some 17,000 people from Wallis and Futuna—tiny islands located north of Fiji—live in New Caledonia. Many of these Wallisians are Catholics and very devoted to their church. But their attitude has been changing as more and more of them have begun listening to the Kingdom message. A priest, upset about this, sent the lady in charge of church finances out to "save the sheep from going astray." However, she also listened. Then her daughter, who was studying in Rome to become a missionary, returned home and accepted the Bible truth taught by Jehovah's Witnesses. Now both she and her mother are dedicated, loyal Witnesses.

Today the Witnesses are well known everywhere in these islands; in certain areas, there is one Witness for every 80

* For a more complete report on the history of Jehovah's Witnesses in New Caledonia, see the 1984 Yearbook of Jehovah's Witnesses, pages 243-9.

persons. On the island of Lifou, a young carpenter became a Pentecostal. He went from village to village, announcing that Christ would return visibly to the island. To point up his conviction that material possessions are of no value, he publicly burned his clothes and money. But he became interested in what he read in a tract published by Jehovah's Witnesses. A regular Bible study helped him to an accurate knowledge of God's Word. Today, he is a balanced Christian, a full-time minister.

Loyalty to God's Kingdom Under Test

The political unrest and chaotic conditions that broke out in 1984 created problems for many New Caledonians, including the Witnesses. Some of these were mobbed and beaten while out preaching. Three men entered one Witness home, demanded the man's car keys at gunpoint, and then stole his car. A missionary discovered that his car had been set afire and destroyed while he was conducting a Bible study.

Whereas the islanders are divided in their loyalties, the Witnesses—regardless of which ethnic group—are united in their neutral stand. The clergy, themselves politically involved, have used the present state of unrest to stir up hatred of the

Witnesses. For example, Witnesses driving to pick up interested persons for a meeting were stopped. Their traveling overseer, who was visiting them that week, was dragged from one of the two cars and beaten, and his glasses were smashed. An interested person was shoved against a wall and beaten until his head was bloody, his pregnant wife being forced to watch.

Yet the Witnesses know that their loyalty has not been misplaced. They remember Paul's words: "All those desiring to live with godly devotion in association with Christ Jesus will also be persecuted." —2 Timothy 3:12; see also Matthew 10:16.

Loyally Expanding Despite Unrest

In mid-1984 the Witnesses saw the need for building an Assembly Hall. An appropriate piece of property was found on a hill overlooking Nouméa harbor, and work was started in September. But in November, because of the political unrest, the authorities imposed a curfew, and a state of emergency was declared. Despite these difficulties, Witnesses from the entire island responded to the need for help at the construction site. Up to 400 volunteers came at a time, much to the amazement of onlookers. Since the construction work took place during school holidays, many

---

In Our Next Issue

■ Spiritism—How Viewed by God?

■ "A Time to Speak"—When?

■ On Guard Against "Peace and Security" as Devised by Nations

---

youngsters assisted. One young girl said: "This was the best vacation I ever had." And seeing a 60-year-old female Witness shoveling cement and gravel into a concrete mixer was enough to surprise any professional builder!

After just four months the project was finished. Dedication plans were made, but it turned out to be the very weekend of Mitterrand's unexpected visit! Because of the possibly explosive political situation, the authorities asked the Witnesses to cancel their program. However, the man in charge of security, who had previously seen a Witness convention in France, told them: "I know you people. It will not be with you that we will be having our problems. Just take necessary security measures; we will not interfere with your meetings."

Over 1,500 persons showed up for the fine dedication program, climaxed by a dedication talk delivered by Lyman Swingle, a visiting member of the Governing Body of Jehovah's Witnesses. The attendance at this meeting, despite civil unrest, demonstrated loyalty to Jehovah's Kingdom, a loyalty that is bearing fruit in New Caledonia. A new peak of 889 Kingdom proclaimers has been reached, and prospects for further increase are excellent. Proof of this can be seen in the 2,145 who attended the Memorial of Christ's death in 1986.

The recent period of political unrest clearly shows that most New Caledonians are looking to human governments to solve their problems. Not so those loyal to God's Kingdom, who put their complete confidence in God-rule. During these difficulties, a sign was spotted on the east coast's main road reading: "Jehovah Out!" But Jehovah, as represented by his established Kingdom, is here to stay. So are "his loyal ones."—Psalm 37:28; see also verses 9-11, 22, 29, and 34.

Where Were His Legs?

"**V**ICTIM Twisted on Cross, Unearthed Remains Show." Did you see such a headline in January 1971? Quite possibly, for there were many newspaper articles on some new "evidence" about death on a cross.

After the above title, the article began: "Jerusalem, Jan. 3 (Reuter)—Israeli archaeologists, having unearthed the first material evidence of a crucifixion, said today it could indicate that Jesus Christ might have been crucified in a position different from that shown on the traditional cross."

Did this new evidence actually reveal how Jews in Jesus' time were executed on a cross or a stake? What did archaeologists determine as to the body position of the victim? Did this have a bearing on Jesus' death? And how solid, you may ask, was the evidence?

A Nail in the Heels

Back in 1968 some burial caves were accidentally discovered near Jerusalem. Inside, among the reburied bones, was what seemed to be an outstanding find —heel bones pierced by a rusty spike. Dr. Nico Haas, anatomist and anthropologist of Hebrew University-Hadassah Medical School, led an investigation of these particular bones. The respected *Israel Exploration Journal* (1970, Volume 20, pages 38-59) published his conclusions, which led to some sensational newspaper articles. What were those conclusions?

He reported that what was discovered was nothing less than the remains of a man executed on a cross in the first century. It seemed, basically, that the victim's two heels were nailed together to an upright stake, but the nail bent at the tip when it hit a knot in the wood. After the Jewish victim was dead, relatives had trouble pulling the nail free, so it was left in his heels at burial. Since one nail pierced both heel bones and

since it seemed that the leg bones had cut at an angle, Dr. Haas reported that the victim likely was executed in the position shown below. (Dr. Haas also felt that a scratch on an arm bone indicated that the man's arms were nailed to a crossbeam.) You may have seen such a drawing in a newspaper or magazine article. Many were excited about the implications as to how Jesus had died.

Again, though, you do well to ask: Was the evidence reliable, and did it really bear on the manner of Jesus' death?

Reappraising the Heels

In the next few years, some noted scholars, such as Professor Yigal Yadin, began to question conclusions that Haas had reached. Finally, *Israel Exploration Journal* (1985, Volume 35, pages 22-7) published "A Reappraisal," by anthropologist Joseph

Zias (Israel Department of Antiquities and Museums) and Eliezer Sekeles (Hebrew University-Hadassah Medical School). They had studied the original evidence, photographs, casts, and radiographs of the bones. You may be surprised at some of their findings:

The nail was shorter than Haas had reported and thus would not have been long enough to pierce two heel bones and the wood. Pieces of bone had been misidentified. There was no bone from a second heel; the nail pierced only *one* heel. Some bone fragments were from another individual altogether. The scratched arm bone "was not convincing" evidence of nailing to a crossbeam; 'in fact, two similar marks were observed on a leg bone; neither are connected with the crucifixion.'

What conclusions did this new analysis lead to? "Both the initial and final reconstruction of the crucifixion [by Haas] are technically and anatomically impossible when one considers the new evidence . . . We found no evidence of the left heel bone and calculated that the nail was sufficient

for affixing only one heel bone . . . The lack of traumatic injury to the forearm and metacarpals of the hand seems to suggest that the arms of the condemned were tied rather than nailed." You see on this page how Zias and Sekeles imagine the man was positioned for execution.

What About Jesus?

So, what does this indicate about how Jesus was executed? Really, not much at all! For instance, as we discussed on page 23, Jesus most likely was executed on an upright stake without any crossbeam. No man today can know with certainty even how many nails were used in Jesus' case. *The International Standard Bible Encyclopedia* (1979, Volume 1, page 826) comments: "The exact number of nails used . . . has been the subject of considerable speculation. In the earliest depictions of the crucifixion Jesus' feet are shown separately nailed, but in later ones they are crossed and affixed to the upright with one nail."

We do know that his hands or arms were not simply bound, for Thomas later said: "Unless I see in his hands the print of the nails." (John 20:25) That could have meant a nail through each hand, or the plural "nails" might have reference to nail prints in 'his hands and his feet.' (See Luke 24:39.) We cannot know precisely where the nails pierced him, though it obviously was in the area of his hands. The Scriptural account simply does not provide exact details, nor does it need to. And if scholars who have directly examined the bones found near Jerusalem in 1968 cannot even be sure how that corpse was positioned, it certainly does not prove how Jesus was positioned.

We thus recognize that depictions of Jesus' death in our publications, such as you see on page 24, are merely reasonable artistic renderings of the scene, not statements of anatomic absolutes. Such depictions need not reflect the changing and conflicting opinions of scholars, and the drawings definitely avoid religious symbols that stem from ancient paganism.

Insight on the News

Clergymen and AIDS

"AIDS Cases Rising Among Catholic Clergy" read the title of an article appearing in the *International Herald Tribune.* The report stated: "While it is impossible to document the scope of the problem, physicians, churchmen and social workers in several cities around the country said the number of Catholic clergymen affected by AIDS was on the rise, . . . The increasing awareness that [AIDS] victims include Catholic clergymen has posed a problem for the church because of the implication that some priests and brothers have not only broken their vows of celibacy but have also engaged in homosexual acts in violation of church laws."

Breaking vows of celibacy cannot, however, alone be blamed, for even churches whose ministers are allowed to marry have registered cases of AIDS among their clergy. The same report revealed that "AIDS has affected a broad range of Americans, including rabbis, Episcopal priests, Baptist ministers and other clergymen."

Of course, not all clergymen with AIDS are necessarily homosexuals. AIDS can also be contracted through normal sexual intercourse and by means of blood transfusions. Nevertheless, such cases among the clergy do illustrate what can happen when individuals fail to follow the clear ruling set down by the first-century council in Jerusalem, namely, "to abstain . . . from blood, from the meat of strangled animals, and from illicit sexual union."—Acts 15:29, *The New American Bible* (Catholic).

Wrong Channel

"Love yourself; you are God." A strange message, you say? Indeed, but among a growing number of persons searching for an alternative to traditional religion, the message is becoming a popular one. Those words, uttered by 27-year-old California housewife Penny Torres, are said to be spoken actually by Mafu, "a highly evolved 'entity from the seventh dimension' last incarnated as a leper in 1st Century Pompeii," for whom Torres serves as a "channel," reports the *Los Angeles Times.* Torres is one of a number of persons in the United States who "channel" for "dead spirits" that teach that everyone is his or her own God.

"Channels," according to the *Times,* are "mediums who purposefully enter a semi-conscious or unconscious trance state to communicate with the unseen 'spirit realm'" or "extraterrestrials." In this state, they may be called upon to offer counsel or provide answers to questions on personal matters. It is estimated that in Los Angeles alone there are as many as 1,000 persons who claim to be channels. Why the sudden interest in channels? In *The Miami Herald,* Ronald F. Thiemann, dean of Harvard Divinity School, says that "theology has become increasingly marginal in American intellectual life."

Centuries earlier, Moses warned Israel: "There should not be found in you anyone . . . who consults a spirit medium or a professional foreteller of events or anyone who inquires of the dead." The reason? "Everybody doing these things is something detestable to Jehovah."—Deuteronomy 18:10-12.

Groping in the Dark

Members of ISSOL (International Society for the Study of the Origin of Life) met last year in Berkeley, California, for their eighth conference. After acknowledging the need for a "self-critical stocktaking of achievements to date," ISSOL cofounder Professor Klaus Dose stated in *Naturwissenschaftliche Rundschau,* a German scientific magazine, that years of research have brought evolutionists no closer to understanding the origin of life.

Professor Dose writes: "Probably no discipline of natural science distinguishes itself by such a variety of contradictory ideas, hypotheses, and theories as does the whole field of the evolution of life. In 1986, more than 30 years after the initially promising start to the era of simulation experiments, we can hardly point to any more facts in explanation of the actual mechanism of the origin of life than Ernst Haeckel did 120 years ago. Unfortunately, it must be recognized that the products resulting from simulation experiments are, largely speaking, no closer to life than are the substances that make up coal tar." Similarly, New York University professor Irving Kristol wrote that "the gradual transformation of the population of one species into another is a biological hypothesis, not a biological fact."

While evolutionists continue to grope for answers, the Bible's explanation fits all known facts. As the Bible writer David recorded with conviction: "For with you [God] is the source of life."—Psalm 36:9.

Do You Remember?

Have you found the recent issues of *The Watchtower* to be of practical value? Then see if you can recall the following:

□ What does it mean to be marked for survival by the prophetic man with the secretary's inkhorn in Ezekiel's vision? (Ezekiel 9:2-6)

It means that one has dedicated oneself to God to do his will, has been baptized as a disciple of Jesus Christ, and has put on the Christlike personality.—4/15, pages 11, 12.

□ What purposes are served by Bible prophecy?

Prophecies make known the truth about God, his will, and his moral standards. They clarify man's relationship to Jehovah so as to bring mankind back into harmony with His purpose, leading up to its full accomplishment. (Isaiah 1: 18-20; 2:1-5; 55:8-11)—5/1, page 5.

□ What death-dealing famine pervades the whole earth today?

A spiritual famine, "for hearing the words of Jehovah." (Amos 8:11)—5/1, pages 10, 11.

□ What is "the fear of Jehovah"? (Proverbs 1:7)

It is a wholesome dread of displeasing Jehovah because we appreciate his loving-kindness and goodness. It also means acknowledging Jehovah as the Supreme Judge and the Almighty, trusting in him completely, and hating what is bad in his sight. (Psalm 2:11; 115:11; Proverbs 8:13)—5/15, page 28.

□ What guidelines are outlined in 1 Timothy 5 regarding caring for the elderly?

Though family members bear first responsibility, the problems of the elderly are the concern of the entire congregation; their care should be properly organized; such care should be limited to those truly in need.—6/1, pages 9, 10.

□ In what four general ways has Jehovah refined his people during the past 69 years?

(1) Organizationally; (2) sharing in the field ministry; (3) increasing light of truth; (4) discarding unclean practices.—6/15, pages 17-20.

□ In what two ways is the word "stand" used in relation to Michael in Daniel 12:1?

Michael is described as "standing in behalf of the sons of your people." Christ Jesus has been exercising authority in this regard on behalf of his people on earth since 1914 when he was enthroned as the reigning King of God's Kingdom. Daniel also says: "And during that time Michael will stand up." This refers to his rulership's entering a new phase in which he will yet act in an outstanding way to save Daniel's people. Thus, they will not be annihilated by the human governments at "the time of the end" for the king of the north and the king of the south. (Daniel 11: 40-45)—7/1, pages 18, 19.

'Children Just Love It'

Millions of families have enjoyed *My Book of Bible Stories*. Its 116 Bible accounts give the reader an idea of what the Bible is all about. Earlier this year a person in Western Australia illustrated how effective the book is, explaining:

"I am a teacher by profession and seek to inspire the children under my care to devote all their schoolwork to God and Jesus, as I do likewise in my work for the children. I have made it a point of duty to read to the class your 'Book of Bible Stories' that I purchased from one of your calling Witnesses. The children love the book, the stories in it, and beg for more when I put the book down."

September 1, 1987

The Watchtower

Announcing Jehovah's Kingdom

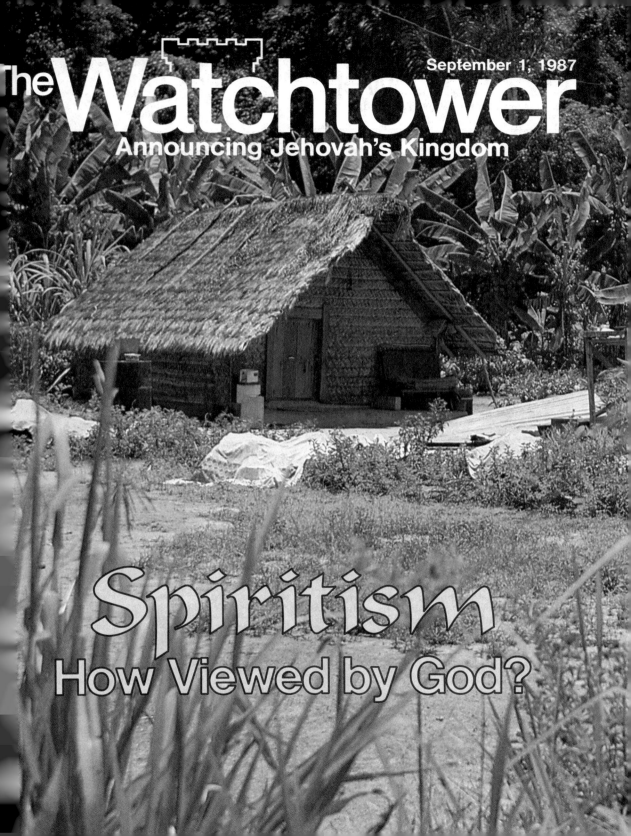

Spiritism
How Viewed by God?

The Watchtower ®

Announcing Jehovah's Kingdom

September 1, 1987
Vol. 108, No. 17

THE PURPOSE OF "THE WATCHTOWER" is to exalt Jehovah God as the Sovereign of the universe. It keeps watch on world events as they fulfill Bible prophecy. It comforts all peoples with the good news that God's Kingdom will soon destroy those who oppress their fellowmen and that it will turn the earth into a paradise. It encourages faith in the now-reigning King, Jesus Christ, whose shed blood opens the way for mankind to gain eternal life. "The Watchtower," published by Jehovah's Witnesses continuously since 1879, is nonpolitical. It adheres to the Bible as its authority.

"WATCHTOWER" STUDIES FOR THE WEEKS

October 4: On Guard Against "Peace and Security" as Devised by Nations. Page 18. Songs to Be Used: 33, 189.

October 11: Trust in Jehovah—Not in "a Conspiracy!" Page 23. Songs to Be Used: 85, 166.

Average Printing Each Issue: 12,315,000

Now Published in 103 Languages

SEMIMONTHLY LANGUAGES AVAILABLE BY MAIL
Afrikaans, Arabic, Cebuano, Chichewa, Chinese, Cibemba, Danish,* Dutch,* Efik, English,* Finnish,* French,* German,* Greek,* Hiligaynon, Igbo, Iloko, Italian,* Japanese,* Korean, Lingala, Malagasy, Maltese, Norwegian, Portuguese,* Russian, Sepedi, Sesotho, Shona, Spanish,* Swahili, Swedish,* Tagalog, Thai, Tsonga, Tswana, Xhosa, Yoruba, Zulu

MONTHLY LANGUAGES AVAILABLE BY MAIL
Armenian, Bengali, Bicol, Bislama, Bulgarian, Croatian, Czech, Ewe, Fijian, Ga, Greenlandic, Gujarati, Gun, Hausa, Hebrew, Hindi, Hiri Motu, Hungarian, Icelandic, Kannada, Malayalam, Marathi, New Guinea Pidgin, Pangasinan, Papiamento, Polish, Rarotongan, Romanian, Samar-Leyte, Samoan, Sango, Serbian, Silozi, Sinhalese, Slovenian, Solomon Islands-Pidgin, Tahitian, Tamil, Telugu, Tongan, Tshiluba, Turkish, Twi, Ukrainian, Urdu, Venda, Vietnamese

* Study articles also available in large-print edition.

Watch Tower Society offices	Yearly subscription for the above:	
	Semimonthly Languages	Monthly Languages
America, U.S., Watchtower, Wallkill, N.Y. 12589	$5.00	$2.50
Australia, Box 280, Ingleburn, N.S.W. 2565	A$7.00	A$3.50
Canada, Box 4100, Halton Hills, Ontario L7G 4Y4	$5.50	$2.75
England, The Ridgeway, London NW7 1RN	£5.00	£2.50
Ireland, 29A Jamestown Road, Finglas, Dublin 11	IR£6.00	IR£3.00
New Zealand, P.O. Box 142, Manurewa	NZ$15.00	NZ$7.50
Nigeria, PMB 001, Shomolu, Lagos State	₦8.00	₦4.00
Philippines, P.O. Box 2044, Manila 2800	₱60.00	₱30.00
South Africa, Private Bag 2067, Krugersdorp, 1740	R9.00	R4.50

Remittances should be sent to the office in your country or to Watchtower, Wallkill, N.Y. 12589, U.S.A.

Changes of address should reach us 30 days before your moving date. Give us your old and new address (if possible, your old address label).

25 cents (U.S.) a copy

The Bible translation used is the "New World Translation of the Holy Scriptures," unless otherwise indicated.

The Watchtower (ISSN 0043-1087) is published semimonthly for $5.00 (U.S.) per year by Watch Tower Bible and Tract Society of Pennsylvania, 25 Columbia Heights, Brooklyn, N.Y. 11201. Second-class postage paid at Brooklyn, N.Y., and at additional mailing offices.

Postmaster: Send address changes to Watchtower, **Wallkill, N.Y. 12589.**

Published by
**Watch Tower Bible and Tract Society
of Pennsylvania**
25 Columbia Heights, Brooklyn, N.Y. 11201, U.S.A.
Frederick W. Franz, President

Spiritism — Why the Growing Interest?

FRANS is a pillar of the local Protestant church. If there is church work to do, he is the first one to lend a helping hand. Wilhelmina is God fearing too. "You have to go to church," she says, and she goes. Esther likewise attends church regularly and does not let one day pass by without saying her prayers. All three have one more thing in common: They are also spirit mediums.

These three inhabitants of Suriname are not alone. Worldwide, there is a mushrooming interest in spiritism. Consider: In the United States alone, about 30 magazines with a combined circulation of over 10,000,000 are devoted to different fields of psychic phenomena. An estimated 2,000,000 people in England are interested in the same subject. A recent poll in the Netherlands showed that believers in supernatural occurrences are found among big-city dwellers, highly educated persons, and young people. Moreover, as inhabitants of Africa, Asia, and Latin America can testify, in numerous lands spiritism has become an integral part of daily life. No wonder authors John Weldon and Clifford Wilson conclude in their book *Occult Shock and Psychic Forces:* "A wide variety of commentators seem to feel we are in a time of unprecedented occult revival."

Yes, spiritism and the occult—in the forms of astrology, hypnotism, parapsychology, extrasensory perception, magic, interpretation of dreams, and so forth —are attracting people from all walks of life. Why?

For one thing, some of Christendom's churches condone and even sanction spiritism. They suggest that coming in touch with spirits is just another way of drawing closer to God.

As an example, take Izaak Amelo, a 70-year-old merchant in Suriname. For seven years he was a respected church-council member and a well-known spirit medium at the same time. He recalls: "Every Saturday our entire church council gathered outside the village to consult the spirits. We continued the whole night. When the next morning came, the deacon kept an eye on his watch, and about five o'clock, he signaled us to stop. We then took a bath, changed clothes, and headed for church—just in time for Sunday morning worship. All those years the pastor never said one disapproving word."

After studying the link between spiritism and the churches in Suriname, Dutch Professor R. van Lier confirms that many

Izaak Amelo recalls participation of an entire church council in spiritistic séances

view spiritism as a "supplementary religion." In a study recently published by Leiden University, he also notes that spiritism is recognized as "a part of a broad religious constitution in which it stands alongside Christianity."

But you may wonder, 'Is acceptance of spiritism by churches of Christendom an assurance that it is approved by God? Will coming in touch with spirits draw you closer to him? What does the Bible actually say about spiritism?'

Spiritism *How Viewed by God?*

"TO LIKE and dislike the same things, this is what makes a solid friendship," said the Roman historian Sallust. Indeed, a friend is one with whom you have the most in common, a person you can trust. Likewise, God looks at us as friends and allows us to draw closer to him if we like and dislike the same things he does. This means that we are attracted to such qualities of God as love, peace, kindness, and goodness, and that we are making earnest efforts to imitate these traits in our life.—Galatians 5:22, 23.

To find out if spiritism is approved by God, we might first examine its fruitage. (Matthew 7:17, 18) Does it help us to develop appealing godly qualities? To find out, let us look at two real-life examples.

Divination, Harassment, and Death

Asamaja Amelia, a middle-aged woman in Suriname, was 17 years old when she first became involved in divination, a form of spiritism. Since her predictions came true and inquirers benefited from her advice, she was highly esteemed in her community. (Compare Acts 16:16.) But one thing troubled her.

"The spirits that spoke through me were kind to those who sought their help," she says, "but at the same time they made my life miserable. After each sitting, I felt beaten up and could hardly move. When

night fell, I hoped for some rest, but the spirits did not leave me alone. They kept disturbing me, talking to me and keeping me awake. And the things they said!" She sighs and looks down, shaking her head in aversion. "They loved to talk about sex and insisted on having relations with me. It was shocking. I was married. I did not want to be unfaithful and told them so. It did not help. Once an invisible force overpowered me, touched and squeezed my body, and even bit me. I felt wretched."

'Spirits encouraging sexual immorality? That is farfetched!' you may exclaim. Are those spirits really that debased?

"It's even worse!" says Izaak, mentioned earlier. "One night we were called to help a sick woman troubled by a spirit. The leader of the group—the medium of a stronger spirit—tried to chase the spirit away. For a whole day we pleaded for his spirit's help. We danced and played the drums, and gradually the woman improved. He ordered her spirit out, and this worked. 'We gained the victory,' beamed the leader. Then we sat down and relaxed."

Izaak's gesticulating arms rest for a moment while he pauses meaningfully. Then he continues: "For a while all looked well, but then a scream broke the silence. We rushed to the house where it came from and saw the leader's wife. She was crying hysterically. Inside the house, we found her little daughter—her head facing backward! Some force had wrung and broken her neck, killing her like a chicken —apparently, the revenge of that ousted spirit. Sickening! Those spirits are sadistic murderers."

Spiritism and "the Works of the Flesh"

Uncleanness, sexual immorality, and murder—as encountered in these two experiences with spiritism—are traits squarely opposed to God's personality. And that helps to identify who those spirits truly are. They may pretend to be messengers of God, but their immoral and murderous works give them away as imitators of God's enemy and history's first murderer, Satan the Devil. (John 8:44) He is their leader. They are his helpers —wicked angels, or demons.—Luke 11: 15-20.

But you may ask: 'Do these satanic traits show up in spiritism only on rare occasions? Could spiritism as a rule put me in contact with good spirits that would help bring me closer to God?' No, the Bible lists the "practice of spiritism" with the other "works of the flesh" that are directly opposed to Christian qualities.—Galatians 5: 19-21.

At Revelation 21:8 "those practicing spiritism" ("those conversing with demons," *The Living Bible*) are put in the same category as "those without faith and those who are disgusting in their filth and murderers and fornicators . . . and idolaters and all the

liars." How does Jehovah regard willful liars, fornicators, murderers, and practicers of spiritism? He hates their deeds! —Proverbs 6:16-19.

Exploring spiritism, therefore, amounts to loving what Jehovah God hates. It is like rejecting Jehovah, being in Satan's camp, and siding with God's archenemy and his helpers. Now think of this: Would you want to be close to a person who takes sides with your enemies? Of course not. Rather, you would stay clear of that individual. Obviously, then, we can expect the same reaction from Jehovah God. Says Proverbs 15:29, "Jehovah is far away from the wicked ones."—See also Psalm 5:4.

Spiritism Leads to Death

Dabbling in spiritism is also life threatening. God viewed it as a reason for capital punishment among his people in ancient Israel. (Leviticus 20:27; Deuteronomy 18:9-12) So it should come as no surprise that practicers of spiritism "will not inherit God's kingdom." (Galatians 5: 20, 21) Instead, "their portion will be in the lake that burns with fire," which denotes "the second death," or eternal destruction. (Revelation 21:8) True, today some of Christendom's churches may

Asamaja Amelia relates: "The spirits . . . made my life miserable. . . . And the things they said!"

tolerate spiritism, but the Bible's viewpoint has not changed.

What if you have already taken the first steps on the road to spiritism? Then you will do well to stop immediately and make a turnabout. Follow the divinely inspired advice that God's prophet Isaiah gave to the Israelites of old. Their situation resembles that of people today who engage in unclean practices but think they are worshiping God at the same time. Hence, there are vital lessons in their experience. What lessons?

Heed Isaiah's Warning

A look at the first chapter of Isaiah shows that the Israelites had "left Jehovah" and had "turned backwards." (Verse 4) Although they had gone astray, they continued presenting sacrifices, holding religious observances, and offering prayers. But to no avail! Since they lacked an inward desire to please their Creator, Jehovah said: "I hide my eyes from you. Even though you make many prayers, I am not listening." Those Israelites had revolted against him by taking up unclean practices, even to the point of 'filling their hands with bloodshed.'—Verses 11-15.

Under what circumstances would Jehovah accept them back? Note the requirements spelled out at Isaiah 1:16. He says: "Wash yourselves; make yourselves clean." So if we take that counsel seriously, we will quit or refrain from unclean practices, including spiritism, one of "the works of the flesh." Since we know that the evil mind behind spiritism is that of Satan the Devil, we will develop a hatred for it.

Then we should remove all objects connected with spiritism. Izaak did so. He says: "One day I gathered all my spiritistic belongings in front of my house, grabbed an ax, and chopped them to pieces. My neighbor screamed that I would regret what I had done. While she was screaming, I poured gasoline over the pieces and burned every single item. Nothing was left."

That was 28 years ago. Did Izaak regret his action? On the contrary. Today, he is serving Jehovah happily as a Christian minister in one of the congregations of Jehovah's Witnesses.

Isaiah 1:17 gives this further counsel: "Learn to do good." That requires studying Jehovah's Word, the Bible, so as to find out what is "the good and acceptable and perfect will of God." (Romans 12:2) And applying that newly found knowledge will lead to refreshing blessings. That is what Asamaja found out.

Despite bitter opposition from relatives and neighbors, Asamaja courageously studied the Bible with Jehovah's Witnesses and shortly thereafter broke with spiritism. Then she dedicated her life to Jehovah God and was baptized during an assembly. Now, some 12 years later, she says gratefully: "Since my baptism, I have not been troubled by spirits." And she recalls with a smile: "The night following my baptism, my sleep was so deep and undisturbed that I was late for the next morning's assembly program."

Lasting Benefits

Today, both Izaak and Asamaja can heartily say with the psalmist Asaph: "The drawing near to God is good for me." (Psalm 73:28) Indeed, drawing near to Jehovah has brought them physical and emotional benefits. But most of all, it has given them an inner peace and a close relationship with Jehovah.

Such blessings far outweigh the pain and struggle required to shake off the yoke of spiritism. Breaking away, though, can be an ordeal. Lintina van Geenen, a woman in Suriname, had that experience. Next, we will see how she wrestled for years but finally succeeded.

Shaking Off the Yoke of Spiritism

CALAMITY struck my family when I was a girl of 14. At that time, a vicious murderer began to eliminate my relatives. His first victims were my sister's children—all nine of them. Then he turned against her husband. Shortly thereafter, he killed one of my sisters too. Four more of my brothers and sisters followed, until only my mother and I were left. Oh, was I frightened!

During the years that followed, I ate, worked, and slept in daily dread. I wondered: 'When will he strike? And who will be next—Mother or I?'

My Background

To help you understand what happened afterward, let me tell you about my background. In 1917, I was born as a member of the Paramaccaner Bush-Negroe tribe on an island in the Maroni River in Suriname. My forefathers were *den lowenengre,* or runaway slaves, who had fled into the jungle to eke out a hard but free life. Well, actually it was a life free from slavery to men but not free from the demons.

Everyday life in our village was ruled by demon and ancestor worship. To bind others with a spell and bring sickness and death upon their fellowman, some people

used *wisi,* black magic, or they enlisted the help of a *koenoe* (pronounced koo noo), a teaser. These teasers are believed to be persons who were mistreated by a family member. After their death, they supposedly return to the family to wreak vengeance. Actually, however, these teasers are debased demons that force people to worship them.

As a member of the Evangelical Brother Community, a Protestant church, I also learned something about God. Although I was left in the dark about how to worship him, the rain forest around me gave abundant proof that he is a good Provider. 'I want to worship a good God but not an evil spirit that causes suffering,' I reasoned. I knew that teasers enjoy torturing their unwilling victims until death.

Imagine how shocked I was to find out

In breaking free from spiritism, Lintina van Geenen learned that "the name of Jehovah is a strong tower"

that enemies of our family had sent a *koenoe* to us. I was 14 years old when he set out on his deadly mission. Twenty-six years later, only Mother and I were left.

The First Encounter

Mother was a hard worker. One day, while walking to her farm, she was knocked down and could not get up. The *koenoe* had chosen my mother. Her health weakened and she became paralyzed. She needed help—my help. But I was torn between love for her and fear of the demon that possessed her. During the attacks of the *koenoe,* however, poor Mother cried out in so much pain that I could not bear it any longer and laid her head in my lap for comfort. She then calmed down, but I felt "hands" squeezing my body.

When I wanted to flee, Mother cried again. So for her sake I stayed and endured my first shivering encounter with this killer. I was 40 years old.

Intensified Attacks

Mother died. Only three days later, I heard a friendly voice saying: "Lintina, Lintina, don't you hear me? I'm calling you." That was the beginning of a misery so great that I wished for a quick death.

First the demon troubled me only when I was going to sleep. As I was about to doze off, the voice would awaken me, talking about burial places and death. Losing sleep made me feel weak, although I continued caring for my children.

Later the demon stepped up his attacks. Several times I felt as if he were strangling me. Though I tried to run away, I could not because a heavy weight seemed to press on my body. I wanted to scream but could not produce a sound. Still, I refused to worship my attacker.

Upon recuperating after each attack, I resumed farming, growing cassava and sugarcane and selling them at the market in a small coastal town. It became easier to make a living, but my worst sufferings were ahead.

Searching for a Cure

One day I heard the foreboding voice of the demon say, "I will make your belly swell like a ball." Some time later, there was a hard lump in my belly that grew bigger until I looked pregnant. Really frightened, I wondered: 'Can God, the Creator, help me to get rid of the *koenoe?* Can He send a good and stronger spirit to chase him away?' To find out, I went to a *bonoeman,* a witch doctor.

The first witch doctor gave me *tapoes,* or amulets, but the swelling remained. Determined to find a cure, I traveled from one *bonoeman* to another—all to no avail. Between those visits, I continued farming to get funds to buy the beer, wine, champagne, and loincloths to pay the witch doctors. Many times they advised: "Kneel down for the *koenoe.* Beg him as your master. Worship him, and he will leave you." But how could I kneel for a spirit that tortured me and wanted to kill me? I could not.

However, in desperation I did everything else that the witch doctors told me to do. One of them treated me for five months. He bathed me with herbs and pressed the juice of 11 different plants into my eyes—"to purify them," he said as I screamed from pain. But at the end of the treatment, I went home penniless, abused, and sicker than ever.

"This Is Your End"

One of my sons, who lives in the Netherlands, sent me money to continue the search for help. So I went to a medical doctor in the capital. After an examination, he said: "I cannot help you. Go and see a *bonoeman.*" So I tried a spirit medium of East Indian origin—but again no

Suriname hinterland where many people are captive to spiritism

help. I headed home but got only as far as the capital, where I reached the house of one of my daughters. There I collapsed —broke and sick. In vain, I had spent 17 years and 15,000 guilders ($8,300, U.S.) searching for a cure. I was 57 years old.

Next, the demon threatened: "I'm finished with you. This is your end."

"But you are not God, you are not Jesus," I cried.

"Even God cannot stop me," the demon answered. "Your days are numbered."

The Final Struggle

Some weeks passed. Meena, a neighbor lady who was a full-time minister of Jehovah's Witnesses, asked my daughter about my condition and said: "Your mother can be helped but only with the Bible." Overhearing the conversation, I walked toward them. Before I reached them, however, I was thrown to the ground. Meena hurriedly came and said: "That demon will not leave you alone. The only one that can help you is Jehovah, no one else." Then she prayed with me to Jehovah God and began to visit me. But the more she visited me,

the fiercer were the demon's attacks. During the night, my body shook so violently that no one in the house could sleep. I stopped eating and had moments when I completely lost my mind.

My condition became so serious that my sons came from the interior to take me back to my village to die. Being too weak to travel, I refused. But feeling death approaching, I called the Witness to say farewell. Meena explained from the Bible that even if I died, there is the resurrection hope.

"Resurrection? What do you mean?"

"God can raise you to life in Paradise," she answered. A ray of hope!

But that very night the demon possessed me. In a trance, I seemed to see the *koenoe* followed by a crowd of people. He ridiculed: "She thinks she is going to get a resurrection." Then the crowd laughed and laughed. But then I did something I had never done before. I called: "Jehovah! Jehovah!" That is all I knew to say. And the demon left!

My sons came again and begged: "Mama, don't die in the city. Let us take you to your village." I refused, for I wanted to learn more about Jehovah. "All right, perhaps I will still die," I told them, "but I will at least have served the Creator."

Like a Strong Tower

Meena and other Witnesses continued visiting me. They taught me to pray to Jehovah. Among other things, they told me about the issue between Jehovah and Satan and how the Devil brought suffering upon Job to get him to renounce God. Learning these things strengthened my conviction never to worship the demon. The Witnesses read a scripture that became dear to me: "The name of Jehovah is a strong tower. Into it the righteous runs and is given protection."—Proverbs 18:10.

Slowly my strength came back. When my son returned, I told him to wait outside. I dressed and tucked a blouse into my skirt to show that the swelling was almost gone. Then I walked outside.

"Is this Mama Lintina?" my son blurted out.

"Yes, it is—thanks to Jehovah, my God!"

Taking My Stand

From the moment I could walk a bit, I went to the Kingdom Hall of Jehovah's Witnesses. There I received so much encouragement from the friends that I never stopped attending meetings. A few months later, I accompanied the Witnesses in the public preaching work. Shortly thereafter, I was baptized and became a servant of Jehovah, my loving Rescuer. I was 58 years old.

However, something remained to be done. Years earlier, back in my hut in the village, I had built an altar on which to offer sacrifices to my ancestors. To be spiritually clean, I had to destroy it. I asked Jehovah for help, since my action could cause an uproar among the villagers.

When I reached my hut and opened the door, someone yelled: "Pingos!" (Wild hogs!) A herd was crossing the island and jumping into the river to swim across. Immediately, both young and old deserted the village for this easy catch. Thrilled, I knelt and thanked Jehovah for this development. Quickly, I dragged the altar outside, poured kerosene over it and set it on fire. The altar was gone before the crowd returned. Of course, they found out, but nothing could be done about it anymore. Thus, with peace of mind, I returned to the capital.

From Misery to Happiness

More blessings came my way. My son in the Netherlands did not believe the stories he had heard about me and boarded a plane for Suriname to see for himself. He was so happy to see me healthy that he bought a fine house for me in the capital, where I now live. What a change I have experienced—from a penniless slave of demons to a well-cared-for servant of Jehovah!

Eleven years after my baptism, I have even more reason to be grateful. Moved by the many blessings I received, three of my children and one son-in-law also became interested in Bible truth and eventually dedicated their lives to Jehovah God. And time and again, I have related my experience with demonism when brothers and sisters have taken me along to see their Bible students who lack the courage to break free from the demons. In that way, even those dreadful years have been of some use in the Kingdom-preaching activity.

I lack sufficient words to express my gratitude to Jehovah, my God. Surely, I have seen his almighty hand in my behalf. Indeed, Jehovah has been good to me! —Compare Psalm 18:17-19.

Kingdom Proclaimers Report

Bible Truth Frees From Spiritism

JEHOVAH'S view of spiritism was well expressed to Israel in these words: "You must not look for omens, and you must not practice magic." (Leviticus 19:26) But how can one who is involved in magic and spiritism be liberated from the power of the demons? Jesus said: "You will know the truth, and the truth will set you free." (John 8:32) This was proved true, as seen in the following experience of a Witness in France.

"When I moved to my new home, I had just settled in when a friendly neighbor came around and offered to cast my horoscope. I immediately decided to have nothing more to do with her, which was no small undertaking, for she really was of a very sociable nature.

"In November 1980 I fell sick,

and around she came to offer help. I came to appreciate her kindheartedness. I was all the more drawn to her when she confided that she would often wake up choking from anguish. I then realized that she was not as happy as I had imagined. But how could this problem of spiritism be tackled? Feeling that I could wait no longer, I resolved to talk to her about the truth.

"We started out discussing the financial problems peculiar to us single women. She then said: 'I have a solution. I make money reading tarot cards.' So I took out my Bible and showed her how dangerous it was to get involved with powerful evil forces.

"This set off a serious discussion on spiritism. She explained

that everything she foretold came to pass. I tried to help her reason things out. I went on to show her Moses' words at Deuteronomy 18:10, 11: 'There should not be found in you anyone who . . . employs divination, a practicer of magic or anyone who looks for omens . . . or anyone who consults a spirit medium or a professional foreteller of events or anyone who inquires of the dead.' As I was leaving, she said: 'To think I believed I'd found the solution to my problems.' How these words encouraged me, for here she was, after just one discussion, talking about spiritism in the past tense! To me it meant that deep down she had really grasped the point.

"Having an insatiable appetite for spiritual food, she would read the Bible until three or four o'clock in the morning. To start with, we had two studies a week. She attended meetings and made rapid progress. Of course, we thoroughly delved into the subject of spiritism, using the Bible and the Watch Tower publications, and she made a personal decision to burn everything she possessed pertaining to demonism.

"The lady persevered and was soon out preaching the 'good news' to others. From time to time she received telephone calls from ex-customers, and after explaining that she had given up her spiritistic activities, she invited them over to hear about something much more interesting. She was baptized and now is our sister."

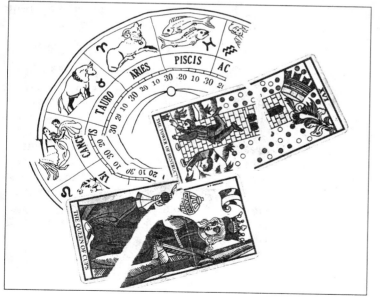

"A Time to Speak"
—When?

MARY works as a medical assistant at a hospital. One requirement she has to abide by in her work is confidentiality. She must keep documents and information pertaining to her work from going to unauthorized persons. Law codes in her state also regulate the disclosure of confidential information on patients.

One day Mary faced a dilemma. In processing medical records, she came upon information indicating that a patient, a fellow Christian, had submitted to an abortion. Did she have a Scriptural responsibility to expose this information to elders in the congregation, even though it might lead to her losing her job, to her being sued, or to her employer's having legal problems? Or would Proverbs 11:13 justify keeping the matter concealed? This reads: "The one walking about as a slanderer is uncovering confidential talk, but the one faithful in spirit is covering over a matter."—Compare Proverbs 25:9, 10.

Situations like this are faced by Jehovah's Witnesses from time to time. Like Mary, they become acutely aware of what King Solomon observed: "For everything there is an appointed time, even a time for every affair under the heavens: . . . a time to keep quiet and a time to speak." (Ecclesiastes 3:1, 7) Was this the time for Mary to keep quiet, or was it the time to speak about what she had learned?*

---

* Mary is a hypothetical person facing a situation that some Christians have faced. The way she handles the situation represents how some have applied Bible principles in similar circumstances.

Circumstances can vary greatly. Hence, it would be impossible to set forth a standard procedure to be followed in every case, as if everyone should handle matters the way Mary did. Indeed, each Christian, if ever faced with a situation of this nature, must be prepared to weigh all the factors involved and reach a decision that takes into consideration Bible principles as well as any legal implications and that will leave him or her with a clear conscience before Jehovah. (1 Timothy 1:5, 19) When sins are minor and due to human imperfection, the principle applies: "Love covers a multitude of sins." (1 Peter 4:8) But when there seems to be serious wrongdoing, should a loyal Christian out of love of God and his fellow Christian reveal what he knows so that the apparent sinner can receive help and the congregation's purity be preserved?

Applying Bible Principles

What are some basic Bible principles that apply? First, anyone committing serious wrongdoing should not try to conceal it. "He that is covering over his transgressions will not succeed, but he that is confessing and leaving them will be shown mercy." (Proverbs 28:13) Nothing escapes the notice of Jehovah. Hidden transgressions must eventually be accounted for. (Proverbs 15:3; 1 Timothy 5:24, 25) At times Jehovah brings concealed wrongdoing to the attention of a member of the congregation that this might be given proper attention.—Joshua 7:1-26.

Another Bible guideline appears at Leviticus 5:1: "Now in case a soul sins in that he has heard public cursing and he is a witness or he has seen it or has come to know of it, if he does not report it, then he must answer for his error." This "public cursing" was not profanity or blasphemy. Rather, it often occurred when someone who had been wronged demanded that any potential witnesses help him to get justice, while calling down curses—likely from Jehovah—on the one, perhaps not yet identified, who had wronged him. It was a form of putting others under oath. Any witnesses of the wrong would know who had suffered an injustice and would have a responsibility to come forward to establish guilt. Otherwise, they would have to 'answer for their error' before Jehovah.*

This command from the Highest Level of authority in the universe put the responsibility upon each Israelite to report to the judges any serious wrongdoing that he observed so that the matter might be handled. While Christians are not strictly under the Mosaic Law, its principles still apply in the Christian congregation. Hence, there may be times when a Christian is obligated to bring a matter to the attention of the elders. True, it is illegal in many countries to disclose to unauthorized ones what is found in private records. But if a Christian feels, after prayerful consideration, that he is facing a situation where the law of God required

him to report what he knew despite the demands of lesser authorities, then that is a responsibility he accepts before Jehovah. There are times when a Christian "must obey God as ruler rather than men." —Acts 5:29.

While oaths or solemn promises should never be taken lightly, there may be times when promises required by men are in conflict with the requirement that we render exclusive devotion to our God. When someone commits a serious sin, he, in effect, comes under a 'public curse' from the One wronged, Jehovah God. (Deuteronomy 27:26; Proverbs 3:33) All who become part of the Christian congregation put themselves under "oath" to keep the congregation clean, both by what they do personally and by the way they help others to remain clean.

Personal Responsibility

These are some of the Bible principles Mary likely considered in making her personal decision. Wisdom dictated that she should not act quickly, without weighing matters very carefully. The Bible counsels: "Do not become a witness against your fellowman without grounds. Then you would have to be foolish with your lips." (Proverbs 24:28) To establish a matter conclusively, the testimony of at least two eyewitnesses is needed. (Deuteronomy 19:15) If Mary had seen only a brief mention of abortion, she might have decided conscientiously that the evidence of any guilt was so inconclusive that she should not proceed further. There could have been a mistake in billing, or in some other way the records may not have properly reflected the situation.

In this instance, however, Mary had some other significant information. For example, she knew that the sister had paid the bill, apparently acknowledging that she had received the service specified.

---

* In their *Commentary on the Old Testament*, Keil and Delitzsch state that a person would be guilty of error or sin if he "knew of another's crime, whether he had seen it, or had come to the certain knowledge of it in any other way, and was therefore qualified to appear in court as a witness for the conviction of the criminal, neglected to do so, and did not state what he had seen or learned, when he heard the solemn adjuration of the judge at the public investigation of the crime, by which all persons present, who knew anything of the matter, were urged to come forward as witnesses."

Also, she knew personally that the sister was single, thus raising the possibility of fornication. Mary felt a desire lovingly to help one who may have erred and to protect the cleanness of Jehovah's organization, remembering Proverbs 14:25: "A true witness is delivering souls, but a deceitful one launches forth mere lies."

Mary was somewhat apprehensive about the legal aspects but felt that in this situation Bible principles should carry more weight than the requirement that she protect the privacy of the medical records. Surely the sister would not want to become resentful and try to retaliate by making trouble for her, she reasoned. So when Mary analyzed all the facts available to her, she decided conscientiously that this was a time to "speak," not to "keep quiet."

Now Mary faced an additional question: To whom should she speak, and how could she do so discreetly? She could go directly to the elders, but she decided to go first privately to the sister. This was a loving approach. Mary reasoned that this one under some suspicion might welcome the opportunity to clarify matters or, if guilty, confirm the suspicion. If the sister had already spoken to the elders about the matter, likely she would say so, and Mary would not need to pursue matters further. Mary reasoned that if the sister had submitted to an abortion and had not confessed to this serious transgression of God's law, she would encourage her to do this. Then the elders could help her in accord with James 5:13-20. Happily, this is how matters worked out. Mary found that the sister had submitted to an abortion under much pressure and because of being spiritually weak. Shame and fear had moved her to conceal her sin, but she was glad to get help from the elders toward spiritual recovery.

If Mary had reported first to the body of elders, they would have been faced with a similar decision. How would they handle confidential information coming into their possession? They would have had to make a decision based on what they felt Jehovah and his Word required of them as shepherds of the flock. If the report involved a baptized Christian who was actively associated with the congregation, they would have had to weigh the evidence as did Mary in determining if they should proceed further. If they decided that there was a strong possibility that a condition of "leaven" existed in the congregation, they might have chosen to assign a judicial committee to look into the matter. (Galatians 5:9, 10) If the one under suspicion had, in effect, resigned from being a member, not having attended any meetings for some time and not identifying herself as one of Jehovah's Witnesses, they might choose to let the matter rest until such time as she did begin to identify herself again as a Witness.

Thinking Ahead

Employers have a right to expect that their Christian employees will 'exhibit good fidelity to the full,' including observing rules on confidentiality. (Titus 2:9, 10) If an oath is taken, it should not be taken lightly. An oath makes a promise more solemn and binding. (Psalm 24:4) And where the law reinforces a requirement on confidentiality, the matter becomes still more serious. Hence, before a Christian takes an oath or puts himself under a confidentiality restriction, whether in connection with employment or otherwise, it would be wise to determine to the extent possible what problems this may produce because of any conflict with Bible requirements. How will one handle matters if a brother or a sister becomes a client? Usually such jobs as working with doctors,

It is the right and loving course to encourage an erring Witness to speak with the elders, confident that they will handle the problem in a kind and understanding way

hospitals, courts, and lawyers are the type of employment in which a problem could develop. We cannot ignore Caesar's law or the seriousness of an oath, but Jehovah's law is supreme.

Anticipating the problem, some brothers who are lawyers, doctors, accountants, and so forth, have prepared guidelines in writing and have asked brothers who may consult them to read these over before revealing anything confidential. Thus an understanding is required in advance that if serious wrongdoing comes to light, the wrongdoer would be encouraged to go to the elders in his congregation about the matter. It would be understood that if he did not do so, the counselor would feel an obligation to go to the elders himself.

There may be occasions when a faithful servant of God is motivated by his personal convictions, based on his knowledge of God's Word, to strain or even breach the requirements of confidentiality because of the superior demands of divine law. Courage and discretion would be needed. The objective would not be to spy on another's freedom but to help erring ones and to keep the Christian congregation clean. Minor transgressions due to sin should be overlooked. Here, "love covers a multitude of sins," and we should forgive "up to seventy-seven times." (Matthew 18: 21, 22) This is the "time to keep quiet." But when there is an attempt to conceal major sins, this may be the "time to speak."

Jesus Miraculously Feeds Thousands

THE 12 apostles have enjoyed a remarkable preaching tour throughout Galilee. Now, shortly after John's execution, they return to Jesus and relate their wonderful experiences. Seeing that they are tired and that so many people are coming and going that they don't even have time to eat, Jesus says: 'Let us go off by ourselves to a lonely place where you can rest up.'

Boarding their boat, probably near Capernaum, they head for an out-of-the-way place, evidently east of the Jordan beyond Bethsaida. Many people, however, see them leave, and others learn about it. These all run ahead along the shore, and when the boat lands, they are there to meet them.

Getting out of the boat and seeing the great crowd, Jesus is moved with pity because the people are as sheep without a shepherd. So he heals their sick and begins teaching them many things.

Quickly the time passes, and Jesus' disciples come to him and say: "The place is isolated, and the hour is already late. Send them away, that they may go off into the countryside and villages round about and buy themselves something to eat."

However, in reply Jesus says: "You give them something to eat." Then, since Jesus already knew what he was going to do, he tested Philip by asking him: "Where shall we buy loaves for these to eat?"

From Philip's viewpoint the situation is impossible. Why, there are about 5,000 men, and probably well over 10,000 people counting also women and children! "Two hundred denarii [a denarius was then a day's wage] worth of loaves is not enough for them, so that each one may get a little," Philip responds.

Perhaps to show the impossibility of feeding so many, Andrew volunteers: "Here is a little boy that has five barley loaves and two small fishes," adding: "But what are these among so many?"

Since it is springtime, just before the Passover of 32 C.E., there is a lot of green grass. So Jesus has his disciples tell the people to recline on the grass in groups of 50 and of a 100. He takes the five loaves and two fishes, looks to heaven, and says a blessing. Then he begins breaking the loaves and dividing up the fishes. He gives these to his disciples, who, in turn, distribute them to the people. Amazingly, all the people eat until they have had enough!

Afterward Jesus tells his disciples: "Gather together the fragments that remain over, so that nothing is wasted." When they do, they fill 12 baskets with the leftovers from what they have eaten! **Matthew 14:13-21; Mark 6:30-44; Luke 9:10-17; John 6:1-13.**

♦ Why does Jesus seek a place of privacy for his apostles?

♦ Where does Jesus take his disciples, and why does their need for rest go unfulfilled?

♦ When it becomes late, what do the disciples urge, but how does Jesus care for the people?

On Guard Against
"Peace and Security"
as Devised by Nations

"Whenever it is that they are saying:
'Peace and security!'"—1 THESSALONIANS 5:3.

NEVER has the whole world of mankind been as insecure as it is today. There is a feeling of dread of a third world war involving highly militarized nations possessing what now appears to be the ultimate of weapons—the nuclear bomb. The nations' ability to put the very nucleus of atoms to work in the pursuit of war has carried them about as far as they can go in mass human slaughter. Hence, peace has become the better part of wisdom.

[2] Yes, indeed, for in our era a third world war using such weapons would signify nothing less than world suicide, with people exploded into virtual nothingness or perishing from the aftereffects of a nu-

clear holocaust. Keen-sighted politicians and military commanders painfully sense that fact. They do not want to become responsible for such a global disaster. Thus, diametrically opposed political systems will find it convenient to come to an accord, yes, to follow the worldly-wise philosophy of "live and let live."

[3] Nevertheless, the nations do not fully trust one another. As a precaution, they maintain their military establishments at full strength. Hence, will it be because of a sincere, genuine love for one another as members of the same human family that rulers will unite in making the proclama-

---

1, 2. (a) Why has peace become the better part of wisdom? (b) Thus, what will opposed political systems agree upon?

3. For what reason will the nations proclaim "Peace and security"?

No doubt the UN will be in the forefront of the coming proclamation of "Peace and security!"

tion of "Peace and security" for all the world of humankind? No, but it will be to allay the justifiable fears of the people. —1 Thessalonians 5:3.

Clergy and Public Reaction to the Coming Proclamation

4 When this proclamation is finally made, the public reaction to it should be favorable all around the earth. No doubt the world's religious leaders, including the clergymen of Christendom, Catholic and Protestant, will hail this international gesture. In whichever way the wind blows, the clergy go in order to remain in popular favor and to have political assistance and consideration.

5 However, the clergy's backing of the loudly proclaimed political arrangement does not mean that the God of the universe, including our earth, will support it. In their religious edifices, the clergy may offer up long and loud prayers in the hearing of their religious patronizers and ask the divine blessing upon the measures taken by the political element for international peace and security. But are all such solemn prayers, to which listening congregations append a vigorous "Amen," acceptable to the God of this universe? Can he be at peace with a religiously divided world, the prayers of which for peace and security are modeled according to the disagreeing religious sects and denominations?

6 Nowhere are the claims for God's backing louder than in the nations of Christendom. But the God of the universe is not the One reigning over Christendom. She has taken a course of action similar to that of the ancient Israelites. When they became discontented with Jehovah's arrangement for their government and got to thinking that the political setup of the pagan nations around them was preferable, they went to Jehovah's prophet Samuel and asked him to set up a king over them. Samuel was highly displeased and grieved at this. No less so was the God of whom he was the prophet.

7 Jehovah rightly felt hurt at this request for a departure from his theocratic setup over Israel. As he said to his prophet Samuel: "It is not you whom they have rejected, but it is I whom they have rejected from being king over them." (1 Samuel 8:4-9) This prefigured the course that Christendom has taken in this 20th century. So the clergy's future hailing of the proclamation of "Peace and security" will have no favorable result, no divine blessing.

Throwing Mankind Off Guard

8 The United Nations may boast of 159 members today, embracing virtually all nations. No doubt in due time the United Nations will be at the forefront with regard to the coming proclamation of "Peace and security!" Sad to say, that world organization is throwing the billions of mankind off guard. Why so? Because such peace, even though backed by all the religious organizations of this world, including those of Christendom, does not mean peace with the Creator of the universe, who has the power to give life and to take it away according to his determination of vital matters in the heavens and on the earth.

4, 5. (a) What public reaction to the coming proclamation may we expect? (b) Despite the clergy's backing of the coming proclamation, what questions arise as to whether God will support it?
6, 7. (a) Like the Jews of ancient times, what course of action has Christendom taken? (b) What will result from clergy support of the proclamation of "Peace and security"?

8. What role will the United Nations likely play in the coming proclamation, and why is this organization throwing mankind off guard?

⁹ In the prophecy of Isaiah, the Creator explicitly says: "The heavens are my throne, and the earth is my footstool." (Isaiah 66:1) The nations down here on his footstool are not adorning it by their United Nations organization. They are striving politically to maintain global peace and security and thereby keep the United Nations in existence. Jehovah's dedicated Witnesses on earth cannot join with the world in depending upon the man-made measures that are being undertaken for the peace and security of the worldly nations. They take to heart the words of James 4:4: "Adulteresses, do you not know that the friendship with the world is enmity with God? Whoever, therefore, wants to be a friend of the world is constituting himself an enemy of God."

¹⁰ Although not actively opposing the peace and security devised by nations, Jehovah's Witnesses cannot recommend it to the millions of people who are seeking a place of safety when the world's greatest trouble erupts and puts an end to this system of things. (Matthew 24:21) For it is God's new system of things that will bring in worldwide security under the "Prince of Peace," Jesus Christ.—Isaiah 9:6, 7.

¹¹ History bears testimony to the failure of man-made schemes for peace. We recall that at the close of World War I in 1918, the League of Nations was proposed as a preventive of world war. The Federal Council of the Churches of Christ in America hailed the proposal and said: "Such a League is not a mere political expedient; it is rather the political expression of the Kingdom of God on earth." But did that so-called political expression of God's earthly kingdom bring lasting peace and security for the earth?

¹² Like the symbolic "scarlet-colored wild beast" of Revelation chapter 17, upon which the old harlot, "Babylon the Great," has seated herself, the League of Nations went into "the abyss" at the outbreak of World War II in 1939. This obliged its harlot rider to hop off. After the close of World War II in 1945, the United Nations was set up as the successor to the ill-fated League of Nations. It has far more members than the League had, so it should be a stronger organization and deserving of more confidence on the part of the world of mankind. Thus it was in 1945 that the symbolic "scarlet-colored wild beast" ascended "out of the abyss," and the symbolic harlot, "Babylon the Great," again climbed onto its back, where she shamelessly sits to this day. (Revelation 17:3, 5, 8) But not for long now, according to what Revelation 17:16–18:24 foretells. Why not?

¹³ The United Nations is actually a worldly confederacy against Jehovah God and his dedicated Witnesses on earth. It is really a conspiracy, with the worldly nations getting their heads together and scheming up what they may do against the visible organization of Jehovah God on earth. During this "conclusion of the system of things," it was foreshadowed by the conspiracy referred to at Isaiah 8:12.—Matthew 24:3.

Look to Jehovah for Peace and Security

¹⁴ Before Isaiah's time the nation of the

9, 10. What is the stand of Jehovah's Witnesses regarding the "Peace and security" as devised by nations, and why so?
11. How did the clergy view the proposal to set up the League of Nations after World War I?

12. (a) How has Revelation 17:8 been fulfilled? (b) Who continues her ride on the back of the "scarlet-colored wild beast," and for how long?
13. (a) What is the United Nations? (b) How was it long ago foreshadowed?
14. Why did the ten-tribe kingdom of Israel enter into a confederacy with Syria, and what question confronted the kingdom of Judah?

Assyrian official Rabshakeh belittled Israel's God, but the outcome showed that true peace and security comes only from Jehovah God

12 tribes of Israel had split up over the issue of kingship. This was after the glorious reign of King Solomon. The seceding ten tribes to the north established what came to be called the kingdom of Israel, with its capital at Samaria. The two remaining tribes, the tribes of Judah and Benjamin, remained loyal to the royal dynasty of King David at the capital city of Jerusalem. The ten-tribe kingdom of Israel turned in hostility against the two-tribe kingdom of Judah. In time, the kingdom of Israel leagued up with the kingdom of Syria, which had its capital at Damascus. The idea was to overthrow the kingdom of Judah and bring it into subjection. Should the kingdom of Judah therefore enter into a confederacy with another strong nation in order to withstand the onslaught of the nation of Israel confederated with the pagan nation of Syria?—Isaiah 7:3-6.

15 There were those in the small kingdom of Judah that lost faith in the national God Jehovah. These favored a confederacy, or conspiracy, with a mighty pagan kingdom of this world. Advocating such an unfaithful yoking of Jehovah's kingdom of Judah with a kingdom of the ungodly world, some were saying, "A conspiracy!" to undecided ones in the kingdom of Judah. Thus they betrayed their lack of faith and confidence in the God whose temple was in Jerusalem. The prophet Isaiah was inspired to speak against such a conspiracy, saying in chapter 8, verse 12: "You men must not say, 'A conspiracy!' respecting all that of which this people keep saying, 'A conspiracy!' and the object of their fear you men

15. (a) What did some people in the kingdom of Judah favor, and what did this attitude betray? (b) How did the prophet Isaiah speak out against such an attitude?

must not fear, nor must you tremble at it."

16 Jehovah's being with the people in covenant relationship with him meant peace and security for them. This was demonstrated when the Assyrian monarch Sennacherib sent a committee of three high officers to call upon King Hezekiah and the people of Jerusalem to make a capitulation to Sennacherib. The Assyrian official and spokesman, Rabshakeh, stood before the walls of Jerusalem and blatantly belittled Jehovah God so as to weaken or destroy the confidence of the Jews in Him. Sorely grieved at this downgrading of the one living and true God Jehovah and rightly feeling the peril of Jerusalem before this overwhelming horde of Assyrians, King Hezekiah went to the temple and laid the matter before Jehovah God. Pleased with this expression of sublime faith in him and with this resort to him for a demonstration of his universal sovereignty, Jehovah gave a favorable reply. His prophet Isaiah joined in with confirmatory remarks. No response at all was given to the intimidating Assyrian Rabshakeh, just as King Hezekiah had ordered.—2 Kings 18:17-36; 19: 14-34.

17 Doubtless greatly amazed at this, Rabshakeh returned to the camp of Sennacherib, who was then fighting against Libnah. (2 Kings 19:8) After hearing Rabshakeh's report, Sennacherib sent threatening letters to Hezekiah, warning: "Do not let your God in whom you are trusting deceive you, saying: 'Jerusalem will not be given into the hand of the king of Assyria.'" (2 Kings 19:9, 10) After nightfall, Jehovah God did his own talking back to the Assyrian mouthpiece, Rabshakeh, and He himself answered Sennacherib's threatening letters to prove

that He was superior to the imperial god of the Assyrians. The ending up of the account of this episode, as given at 2 Kings 19:35, says: "And it came about on that night that the angel of Jehovah proceeded to go out and strike down a hundred and eighty-five thousand in the camp of the Assyrians. When people rose up early in the morning, why, there all of them were dead carcasses." At dawn when the surviving Assyrians, including King Sennacherib and possibly Rabshakeh, arose, they saw the horrifying spectacle round about of casualties of war with Jehovah God.

18 Defeated in his ambitious designs against Jehovah's organization and tremendously humiliated, Sennacherib hurried back "with shame of face" to his national capital, Nineveh, only to be assassinated by two of his sons. (2 Chronicles 32:21; 2 Kings 19:36, 37) Never again did the Assyrian empire menace Jehovah's visible organization. Here, indeed, was a top-ranking vindication of the universal sovereignty of the Most High God. Moreover, Jerusalem's safekeeping is an excellent example showing to whom Jehovah's Witnesses of today should in full confi-

18. (a) What was the outcome with regard to the ambitious Sennacherib? (b) What example should this historical account furnish to Jehovah's Witnesses of today?

How Would You Answer?
□ What will likely be the public reaction to the proclamation of "Peace and security"?
□ What was foreshadowed by the "conspiracy" of Isaiah 8:12?
□ How is the UN throwing mankind off guard?
□ Why will Jehovah's Witnesses not be caught off guard?

16, 17. What meant true peace and security for Jehovah's ancient people, and how was this demonstrated when Assyrian King Sennacherib threatened Jerusalem?

dence look for continual, imperturbable peace and security—not a political conspiracy but Jehovah God.

Keeping on Guard

[19] To help you keep on guard, the Watch Tower Society will continue issuing in its publications timely warnings to the reading public, so that you will not be caught off guard by the coming pretentious proclamation "Peace and security," as devised by the nations of this old system of things.

[20] Jehovah's dedicated Witnesses can by no means promote reliance on the "Peace and security" confidently to be proclaimed

---

19. What will the Watch Tower Society keep on doing?
20. Why will Jehovah's Witnesses by no means promote reliance on the coming "Peace and security," and so now is the time for what?

by the worldly nations; nor can they congratulate the devisers of such international "Peace and security" and, at the same time, have Jehovah God with them. They guard against leaguing up with the nations of this old system of things. They unfailingly remind themselves that a new "nation," separate and distinct from the League of Nations, was brought to birth in the postwar year of 1919. This new "nation" continues to grow and expand in all the earth, just as foretold at Isaiah 60:22: "The little one himself will become a thousand, and the small one a mighty nation. I myself, Jehovah, shall speed it up in its own time." Yes, now is the time for all to be on guard against the forthcoming "Peace and security" as devised by nations.

Trust in Jehovah
—Not in "a Conspiracy!"

DURING World War I, the ranks of Jehovah's people had been considerably reduced by outright apostasies. Persecution incited by religious enemies also raged against them. Their Brooklyn, New York, headquarters was shut down. Furthermore, they were without the assistance of the Society's president, the secretary-treasurer, the office manager, an editorial staff writer, and four other representatives of the Society—all of whom were imprisoned in the federal penitentiary in Atlanta, Georgia. It appeared as if the end had come for the spirit-begotten Bible Students and

---

1. What was the state of Jehovah's visible organization during World War I?

that their heavenly glorification was at hand. But not so!

[2] In fact, in the spring of 1919 the questions posed by the prophet Isaiah could be voiced again in a modern application of Isaiah 66:6-8: "There is a sound of uproar out of the city, a sound out of the temple! It is the sound of Jehovah repaying what is deserved to his enemies. Before she began to come into labor pains she gave birth. Before birth pangs could come to her, she even gave deliverance to a male child. Who has heard of a thing like this? Who has seen things like these?

---

2. What prophecy of Isaiah had a modern application in 1919?

Will a land [condition of glorious spiritual prosperity] be brought forth with labor pains in one day? Or will a nation be born at one time? For Zion has come into labor pains as well as given birth to her sons."

³ As if resurrected from the dead, the International Bible Students held their first postwar convention at Cedar Point, Ohio, on September 1-8, 1919. The Society's president, the secretary-treasurer, the office manager, and the other former prisoners, exonerated from all charges, were present for this gladsome occasion. To the joy of the conventioners, President Rutherford announced the publication of a new magazine, *The Golden Age* —known today as *Awake!* Also, a baptism of over 200 newly dedicated persons was performed. Jehovah's theocratic organization brought forth her sons to an active life in the postwar era. That called for new, yes, daring, pioneering procedures on the part of the "nation" born, as it were, at one stroke and settled down on "a land" brought forth at once.

⁴ The situation was a challenging one. It caught "Babylon the Great," the world empire of false religion, by surprise. Her membership, particularly Christendom, became highly disturbed. She felt that her peace was being trespassed upon. Her security as an incontestable claimant to the field of religious activity was now put in jeopardy. She was going to be exposed as to her real relationship with superhuman heavenly powers, not with the God of the Holy Bible, but with "the god of this system of things"—Satan,

the promoter of the Antichrist foretold in Bible prophecy. (2 Corinthians 4:4; 1 John 2:18) This exposure was merely the precursor of her death throes. Then the Supreme Judge of the universe will take her directly in hand and execute her, granting her no escape from the now highly incensed former lovers of hers, her political paramours.

⁵ Even Christendom, which possesses the Bible that foretells all of this, will be caught off guard. She will trust in the coming cry of "peace and security" as devised by the nations in which she has carried on her religious formalism. At the same time, her churches pass the collection plate, enriching themselves by the contributions deposited therein. To the God of the Holy Scriptures, however, she is "poor and blind and naked." She does not trust in Jehovah, nor does she avail herself of the real spiritual values that he provides. (Revelation 3:17, 18) She does not see the handwriting on the wall. What do we mean by this?

Handwriting on the Wall Appears

⁶ To understand, we must look back at the last hours of the third world power of Bible history, Babylon, on the banks of the Euphrates River. Belshazzar was the last ruler over Babylon, which included the site of the Tower of Babel, where almighty God confused the one language of the builders, scattering them. (Genesis 11:1-9) At the time of Babylon's last hours, Jehovah's typical people, the Jews, were captive exiles in that pagan land. But their 70 years of captivity were about to come to a close.

---

3. What evidence was there in 1919 that Zion had brought forth her sons and that a new "nation" had been born "at one time"?
4. (a) What effect was all of this to have on "Babylon the Great"? (b) Exposure of the real status of "Babylon the Great" with superhuman heavenly powers is the precursor of what?

5. (a) Why will Christendom be caught off guard, and how is she viewed by the God of the Bible? (b) What does "Babylon the Great" not see?
6. What ancient world power now comes to mind, and how were Jehovah's typical people then faring?

Daniel interprets the mysterious writing as a message of doom for the Babylonian empire

⁷ The united Medes and Persians, who were to make up the fourth world power of Bible history, came against the highly fortified, seemingly impregnable, walled city of Babylon. The Euphrates River flowed through the midst of the city, with quays along its banks onto which two-leaved copper doors of the city walls opened. With full confidence in the security of the city, King Belshazzar held "a big feast for a thousand of his grandees"—a feast that proved to be his last one. Suddenly, within Belshazzar's line of vision, there appeared at the wall a moving hand. And it wrote upon the wall the fateful words "MENE, MENE, TEKEL and PARSIN." (Daniel 5:1, 5, 25) That was on the night of October 5, 539 B.C.E. The words had a stunning impact. King Bel-

shazzar shook with fear. Wait now! Get the wise men—the magicians and astrologers who had a reputation for being able to explain signs and omens. But the deciphering of the miraculous words, which they were not even able to read, was beyond them. What now was to be done?

⁸ Send for a Jew. What? A Jew? Yes, one of those princes and nobles who had been taken away from Jerusalem in his native land and brought by Emperor Nebuchadnezzar to Babylon to be trained for governmental service. Well, as a last resort, that was the best thing that could be done. Daniel was recommended by the queen mother as being a man of wisdom—a man who was able to decipher things and to

7. (a) Why did King Belshazzar hold a feast for his grandees with full confidence? (b) What took place during the feast, and with what effect on the king?

8, 9. (a) As a last resort, what course of action was recommended to the king? (b) How did Daniel interpret the handwriting on the wall? (c) Why did King Belshazzar's big feast result in such a dire prophecy?

interpret them. (Daniel 5:10-12) We can feel the hush that permeated the banqueting room as Daniel, in compliance with the request of King Belshazzar, proceeded to interpret those mystifying words to the emperor of the third world power of Bible history and his grandees.

⁹ Daniel proceeds to say: "Consequently from before him there was being sent the back of a hand, and this very writing was inscribed. And this is the writing that was inscribed: MENE, MENE, TEKEL and PARSIN. This is the interpretation of the word: MENE, God has numbered the days of your kingdom and has finished it. TEKEL, you have been weighed in the balances and have been found deficient. PERES,* your kingdom has been divided and given to the Medes and the Persians." (Daniel 5:24-28) King Belshazzar and his grandees and their women companions had been showing deliberate, profane contempt for the worship of Daniel's God. How? By drinking wine from the gold vessels that had been taken from the temple of Jehovah in Jerusalem at the time of the destruction of that holy city in the year 607 B.C.E. That was like adding contemptuous insult to injury.—Daniel 5:3, 4, 23.

The Foretold Cyrus Takes Over

¹⁰ At Isaiah 45:1-3 the Most High God had foretold: "This is

---

* "Parsin" is the plural number of the word "Peres" and means "divisions."

10, 11. (a) Whom had Jehovah foretold to be the conqueror of Babylon, and how did Isaiah describe the coming conquest? (b) How did Jehovah fulfill this prophecy and bring about condign punishment for King Belshazzar and his grandees?

what Jehovah has said to his anointed one, to Cyrus, whose right hand I have taken hold of, to subdue before him nations, so that I may ungird even the hips of kings; to open before him the two-leaved doors, so that even the gates will not be shut: 'Before you I myself shall go, and the swells of land I shall straighten out. The copper doors I shall break in pieces, and the iron bars I shall cut down. And I will give you the treasures in the darkness and the hidden treasures in the concealment places, in order that you may know that I am Jehovah, the One calling you by your name.'"

¹¹ To fulfill this prophecy, Jehovah put it into the mind of Cyrus the Persian to turn aside the waters of the Euphrates River and divert them into a local lake. Then, after the riverbed had been emptied, under cover of night, Cyrus' troops marched down the bed of the river and right on into the middle of the city. Since the two-leaved

doors along the waterfront had been left open, they climbed up the riverbank and entered into the banqueting chamber, overpowering the guards. So the feast of King Belshazzar came to a tragic end as a condign punishment for him and his grandees—because of their holding up "the Lord of the heavens" to shame, contempt, and indignity by misuse of the temple vessels stolen from Jehovah's sacred dwelling place in Jerusalem.

[12] The last verse of Daniel chapter 5 says that after the putting of King Belshazzar to death, Darius the Mede "received the kingdom, being about sixty-two years old." Since Darius was the elder of Cyrus the Persian, Daniel attributed the capture of Babylon to this Median king. He reigned from 539 to 537 B.C.E. as the royal ruler over the Medo-Persian empire. He well pictures Jehovah God. Darius' associate, Cyrus the Persian, prefigured Jesus Christ, who will be most prominently used by Jehovah to overthrow and destroy "Babylon the Great," the world empire of false religion.

[13] On the accession of Cyrus to the throne over Medo-Persia in 537 B.C.E., doubtless the prophet Daniel pointed out to him Jehovah's prophecy concerning him as found at Isaiah 45. The postexilic book of Ezra opens up with these words:

[14] "And in the first year of Cyrus the king of Persia, that Jehovah's word from the mouth of Jeremiah [regarding the exile's being 70 years in length (Jeremiah 25:12; 29:10, 14)] might be accomplished, Jehovah roused the spirit of Cyrus the king of Persia so that he caused a cry to pass

through all his realm, and also in writing, saying: 'This is what Cyrus the king of Persia has said, "All the kingdoms of the earth Jehovah the God of the heavens has given me, and he himself has commissioned me to build him a house in Jerusalem, which is in Judah. Whoever there is among you of all his people, may his God prove to be with him. So let him go up to Jerusalem, which is in Judah, and rebuild the house of Jehovah the God of Israel—he is the true God—which was in Jerusalem."'"—Ezra 1:1-3.

The Greater Cyrus Conquers "Babylon the Great"

[15] The present-day antitypical Cyrus the Great began to reign in 1914 at the end of "the appointed times of the nations," as foretold by Jesus himself at Luke 21:24. In total disregard of this world-important fact, the nations inside the United Nations settled upon the year 1986 as their International Year of Peace. But Jehovah's Witnesses are by no means caught off guard in this connection. When the foretold proclamation of "peace and security" is finally made, they will not join political adherents and friendly associates of "Babylon the

---

15. (a) When did the antitypical Cyrus begin to reign? (b) What immovable position do Jehovah's Witnesses take regarding a conspiracy with the United Nations, and why?

12. (a) Since Isaiah had foretold that Cyrus would conquer Babylon, why does Daniel attribute Babylon's capture to Darius the Mede? (b) Whom did Darius and his associate, Cyrus the Persian, prefigure?
13, 14. What did Daniel doubtless point out to Cyrus the Persian, and how does the postexilic book of Ezra open up?

In Our Next Issue

■ How You Can Make True Friends

■ Breathing This World's "Air" Is Death-Dealing!

■ Is Religious History of Any Benefit to You?

Great" in the feasting over such a phenomenal feat at this late date in the history of the worldly nations. They advocate no conspiracy with the United Nations or other peace media. (Isaiah 8:12) As a countermeasure, they say in the words of Isaiah 8:20: "To the law and to the testimony! If they do not speak according to this word, they have no light of dawn." (*New International Version*) And giving the reason for their immovable position, they say: "For God is with us!" (Isaiah 8:10) Bluntly, that means that Jehovah God is taking no part in the political measures adopted by the nations in behalf of "peace and security" but, rather, is unequivocally against them.

¹⁶ By adroit maneuvering, Jehovah, by means of his Greater Cyrus, will put it into the heart and mind of the political leaders of the world to turn against "Babylon the Great," the world empire of false religion. As with the horns of a vicious wild beast, they will gore her to death. The prophetic word at Revelation 17 will be vindicated to the full, and over this Jehovah's Witnesses on earth will jubilate.—Revelation 17: 16, 17; 19:1-3.

Keeping Up Our Proper Association With Jehovah

¹⁷ Then, although Jehovah's Witnesses are no part of "Babylon the Great" but are her avowed exposers, and although they have taken no part in the political affairs of this world, those irreligious political elements will turn against the surviving Witnesses. Determined to be dictators with totalitarian control over all segments of human society on earth, they will make

---

16. How will the prophetic word at Revelation 17:16, 17 be vindicated to the full, and with what effect on Jehovah's people?
17. Though Jehovah's Witnesses are no part of "Babylon the Great," what will the world's rulers do?

a full-scale lunge at the integrity-keeping Witnesses of the Supreme One, who is the Source of all righteous government.

¹⁸ Here now is where the Almighty Sovereign of heaven and earth must step in and must make those destroyers of "Babylon the Great" know and understand that the One of whom there have been 20th-century Witnesses is a real God, an almighty God—a God entitled to wholehearted, undivided worship by creatures down here on his footstool, the earth. He will do this in an awe-inspiring manner that will simply make the lower jaw of the mouths of his observing Witnesses on the sidelines drop for sheer amazement. He will perform his unprecedented, glorious maneuvers of warfare to divine victory. (Revelation 16: 14, 16; 19:19-21) That will spell the end of this wicked, Devil-controlled system of things with a flourish that will outdo the world-destroying Flood of Noah's day.

¹⁹ Just as Jehovah had witnesses to

---

18. What awe-inspiring feat will Jehovah perform, eclipsing the Flood of Noah's day?
19. What witnesses will Jehovah have as to his vindicating of himself as the Universal Sovereign, and what will this demonstrate?

Do You Recall?

☐ What does "Babylon the Great" not see?

☐ What does the tragic outcome of Belshazzar's feast prefigure?

☐ Who will conquer "Babylon the Great"?

☐ What stand do Jehovah's Witnesses take regarding a conspiracy with the United Nations?

☐ Why will all who put their trust in Jehovah for peace and security be happy?

testify to the end of the old world in a Flood that drowned all humankind outside the ark, he will, on a far grander scale, have witnesses right down here on earth regarding his unrepeatable act of vindicating himself as the Universal Sovereign. (2 Peter 3:6, 7, 13, 14) These will be those who trust in *him* for peace and security amid this doomed world. Happy will you be at being counted among those miraculously favored Witnesses. Your peace and security will have been demonstrated as coming from Jehovah God and not from any confederacy, or conspiracy, with political powers of this Devil-controlled system of things.

[20] Jehovah God will emerge gloriously as the rightful One to be worshiped and served as the supreme Divine Being—the God of gods, the exclusive One to whom the words of the inspired psalmist were directed: "Even from time indefinite to time indefinite you are God." (Psalm 90:2) With ever-growing appreciation, let us keep up our trust in Jehovah God and our association with him through the Greater Cyrus, Jesus Christ.

20. How will Jehovah emerge, and what are we determined to do?

Questions From Readers

■ What is God's "book of life," and how can my name be written in it and kept there?

Various Bible texts indicate that Jehovah God has a "book," or "scroll," listing faithful persons who are in line to receive everlasting life, whether in heaven or on earth.

From the heavens the true God notes humans who manifest faith, meriting his approval and remembrance. We read concerning some Jews in Malachi's day: "At that time those in fear of Jehovah spoke with one another, . . . and Jehovah kept paying attention and listening. And a book of remembrance began to be written up before him for those in fear of Jehovah and for those thinking upon his name." —Malachi 3:16.

Evidently, from the time of Abel forward, God has been noting, as if writing down in a book, those in the world of savable mankind who should be remembered as to everlasting life. (Matthew 23:35; Luke 11:50, 51) Anointed Chris-

tians, too, have their 'names in this book of life,' or book of remembrance for receiving everlasting life, and for them it will be heavenly life. (Philippians 3: 14, 20; 4:3) In contrast, Revelation 17:8 says of those who "wonder admiringly" over "the wild beast": "Their names have not been written upon the scroll of life from the founding of the world."

A person's being noted with remembrance and approval (having his name "in the book of life") does not mean that he is guaranteed eternal life, as if this were predestined or unchangeable. Concerning the Israelites, Moses asked Jehovah: "Now if you will pardon their sin,—and if not, wipe me out, please, from your book that you have written." God replied: "Whoever has sinned against me, I shall wipe him out of my book." (Exodus 32:32, 33) Yes, even after God listed someone with approval in his "book," the individual could become disobedient or abandon his faith. If that developed, God would "blot out his name from the book of life."—Revelation 3:5.

On the other hand, if our names are now in God's "book of life," or "book of remembrance," we ought to continue exercising faith. In that way we will keep our names there. Similarly, as persons are raised in the coming 'resurrection of the unrighteous,' they will have the opportunity to exercise faith and hence qualify to have their names recorded in that book. (Acts 24:15) Finally, individuals so written down will be able to keep their names there permanently. That is true of the anointed as they prove themselves "faithful even to death." (Revelation 2:10; 3:5) As to those with earthly prospects, by proving faithful now, down through Christ's Millennial Reign, and then through the decisive test to follow, their names will become permanently "written in the book of life."—Revelation 20:5-15.

A Remarkable Accomplishment for Costa Rica

"YOU are doing what we've only studied about!" remarked an architectural engineer who had come to see the new branch being put up seven miles (11 km) outside of San José, Costa Rica.

What was so remarkable about these buildings? They were built with the tilt-up method—a first in Costa Rica. The foundation and pillars were built first. Then, right on the site, concrete sections of the walls were cast one on top of another in stacks. These precast wall sections were then tilted up and lifted by a crane and welded into their proper places. Finally, the roof went on, and all that remained to be done was the finishing details.

This project was also the Watch Tower Society's first attempt to construct a building by the tilt-up method outside the United States. For this reason, personnel from other branches that are planning to build or expand were on hand to observe how the process worked. Present, too, were engineers and architects from other concerns. All were impressed by what they saw.

The buildings were done in the handsome Spanish-colonial style, with red tile roof and arching windows. The driveway around a circular garden leads to the main entrance and lobby. To the right is the two-story, 24-room residence building with a large family room that contains the library, study areas, and an attractive fireplace. Connected to this is a 100-seat dining room, and a modern kitchen and laundry. Across the courtyard is the office building with 13 individual offices and a conference room laid out around an open-air tropical garden under a skylight. The large building to the left is the warehouse for storing literature and other supplies.

Everyone who had come to visit marveled at what he saw. Heard over and over again were comments like: "What quality work!" "Never have I seen anything as beautiful as this!" "This is obviously a labor of love."

Indeed, all of this was made possible by "a labor of love." Over 4,700 brothers and sisters, including 295 from other lands, labored for 24 months on the project. Much of the equipment and material was made on site. For example, at an early stage a two-story hoist, affectionately known by the brothers as Julio, was built. Cement mixers known as Bertha and Martha were purchased and overhauled for the project. Lamps, lighting fixtures, wrought-iron grillwork, Palladian marble steps and landings, and so on, were all made by brothers who have had no particular experience in these areas. "The enthusiasm for the project on the part of the brothers from this country was remarkable," declared the project supervisor.

The height of enthusiasm was manifested on January 4, 1987, when a crowd of 13,111 came for the dedication. The balcony on the north side of the family room was used as a stage and the crowd gathered on the spacious grounds below. Brothers M. G. Henschel and L. A. Swingle of the Governing Body of Jehovah's Witnesses were the principal speakers on the program. Brother Swingle's enthusias-

A precast wall section being tilted up . . . and set in place

Circular driveway leads up to Spanish-colonial-style building

Part of the enthusiastic crowd on dedication day

tic talk was on the theme "Jehovah Keeps Making It Grow," and in the dedication talk, Brother Henschel helped all to appreciate that a beautiful building is useful to Jehovah's people only if they continue to produce the fruitage of his spirit.

Brought together for this special occasion were members of the first Gilead missionary family in Costa Rica. Now well along in years, they were deeply moved by this reunion and by the visible evidence of Jehovah's rich blessing on the Kingdom-preaching work in Costa Rica over the years. With the marvelous provision of such a spacious, comfortable, and efficient home, all present were confident that Jehovah's name will be further magnified in this tropical land.

'One of the Most Outstanding Books in History'

What publication could the writer from New Zealand have in mind? His letter explains: "We were all overjoyed to receive what must be one of the most outstanding works in the history of modern publishing, the book *Life—How Did It Get Here? By Evolution or by Creation?*

"The research that has preceded this outstanding and scholarly work is evident from the very start, and the clear and concise way in which each subject is dealt with has at least one scientist at our local Horticultural research centre of the Ministry of Agriculture and Fisheries eager to read the book through."

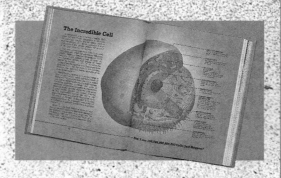

The Watchtower

Announcing Jehovah's Kingdom

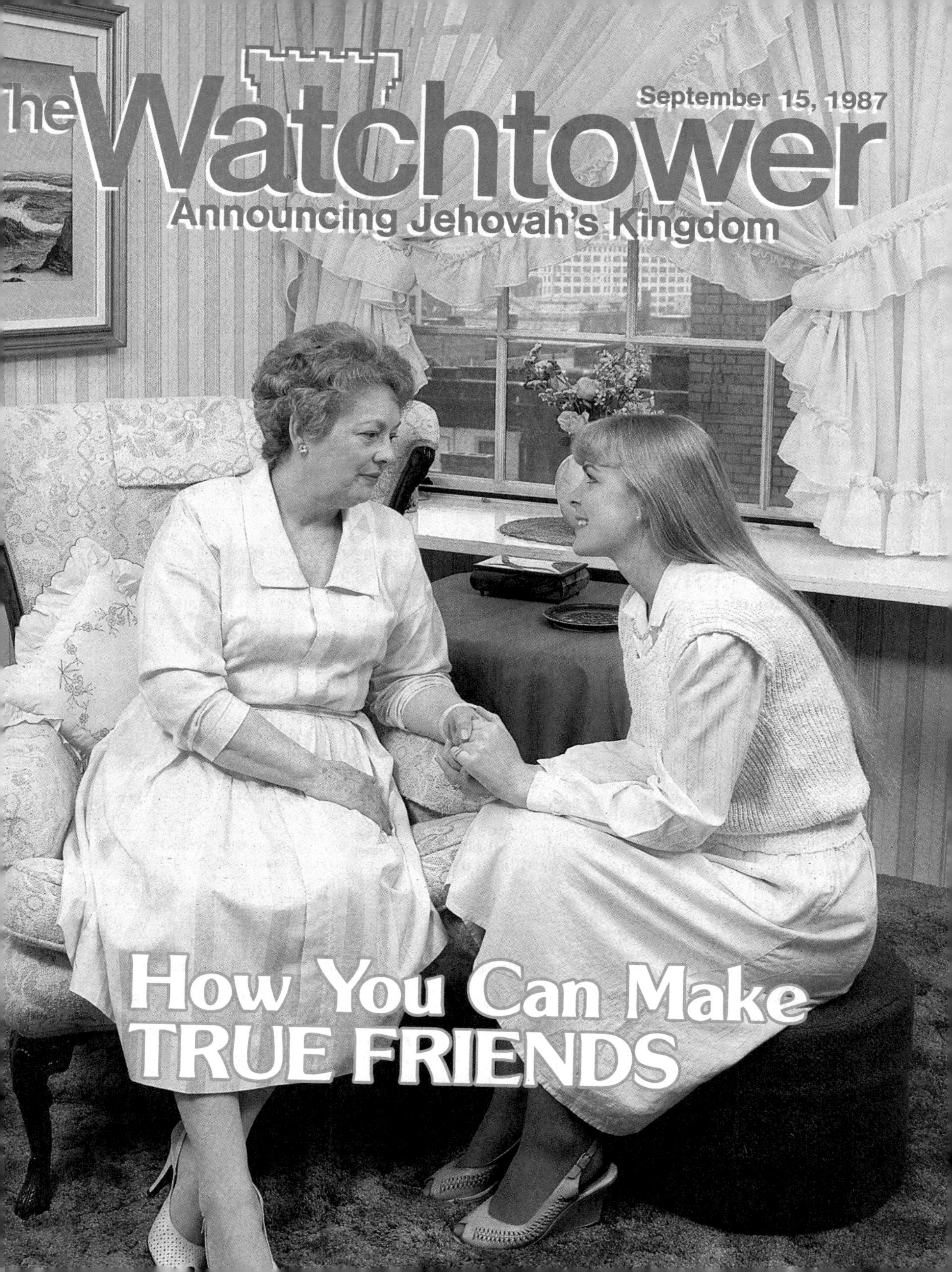

September 15, 1987

How You Can Make
TRUE FRIENDS

The Watchtower®
Announcing Jehovah's Kingdom

September 15, 1987
Vol. 108, No. 18

In This Issue

THE PURPOSE OF *THE WATCHTOWER* is to exalt Jehovah God as the Sovereign of the universe. It keeps watch on world events as they fulfill Bible prophecy. It comforts all peoples with the good news that God's Kingdom will soon destroy those who oppress their fellowmen and that it will turn the earth into a paradise. It encourages faith in the now-reigning King, Jesus Christ, whose shed blood opens the way for mankind to gain eternal life. *The Watchtower,* published by Jehovah's Witnesses continuously since 1879, is nonpolitical. It adheres to the Bible as its authority.

WATCHTOWER STUDIES FOR THE WEEKS

October 18: Breathing This World's "Air" Is Death-Dealing! Page 10. Songs to Be Used: 29, 3.

October 25: Keep Submitting to "the Spirit That Is Life-Giving." Page 15. Songs to Be Used: 41, 191.

Average Printing Each Issue: 12,315,000

Now Published in 103 Languages

SEMIMONTHLY LANGUAGES AVAILABLE BY MAIL
Afrikaans, Arabic, Cebuano, Chichewa, Chinese, Cibemba, Danish,* Dutch,* Efik, English,* Finnish,* French,* German,* Greek,* Hiligaynon, Igbo, Iloko, Italian,* Japanese,* Korean, Lingala, Malagasy, Maltese, Norwegian, Portuguese,* Russian, Sepedi, Sesotho, Shona, Spanish,* Swahili, Swedish,* Tagalog, Thai, Tsonga, Tswana, Xhosa, Yoruba, Zulu

MONTHLY LANGUAGES AVAILABLE BY MAIL
Armenian, Bengali, Bicol, Bislama, Bulgarian, Croatian, Czech, Ewe, Fijian, Ga, Greenlandic, Gujarati, Gun, Hausa, Hebrew, Hindi, Hiri Motu, Hungarian, Icelandic, Kannada, Malayalam, Marathi, New Guinea Pidgin, Pangasinan, Papiamento, Polish, Rarotongan, Romanian, Samar-Leyte, Samoan, Sango, Serbian, Silozi, Sinhalese, Slovenian, Solomon Islands-Pidgin, Tahitian, Tamil, Telugu, Tongan, Tshiluba, Turkish, Twi, Ukrainian, Urdu, Venda, Vietnamese

* Study articles also available in large-print edition.

	Yearly subscription for the above:	
Watch Tower Society offices	Semimonthly Languages	Monthly Languages
America, U.S., Watchtower, Wallkill, N.Y. 12589	$5.00	$2.50
Australia, Box 280, Ingleburn, N.S.W. 2565	A$7.00	A$3.50
Canada, Box 4100, Halton Hills, Ontario L7G 4Y4	$5.50	$2.75
England, The Ridgeway, London NW7 1RN	£5.00	£2.50
Ireland, 29A Jamestown Road, Finglas, Dublin 11	IR£6.00	IR£3.00
New Zealand, P.O. Box 142, Manurewa	NZ$15.00	NZ$7.50
Nigeria, PMB 001, Shomolu, Lagos State	₦8.00	₦4.00
Philippines, P.O. Box 2044, Manila 2800	₱60.00	₱30.00
South Africa, Private Bag 2067, Krugersdorp, 1740	R9,00	R4,50

Remittances should be sent to the office in your country or to Watchtower, Wallkill, N.Y. 12589, U.S.A.

Changes of address should reach us 30 days before your moving date. Give us your old and new address (if possible, your old address label).

25 cents (U.S.) a copy

The Bible translation used is the *New World Translation of the Holy Scriptures,* unless otherwise indicated.

The Watchtower (ISSN 0043-1087) is published semimonthly for $5.00 (U.S.) per year by Watch Tower Bible and Tract Society of Pennsylvania, 25 Columbia Heights, Brooklyn, N.Y. 11201. Second-class postage paid at Brooklyn, N.Y., and at additional mailing offices.

Postmaster: Send address changes to Watchtower, *Wallkill, N.Y. 12589.*

Published by
Watch Tower Bible and Tract Society of Pennsylvania
25 Columbia Heights, Brooklyn, N.Y. 11201, U.S.A.
Frederick W. Franz, President

The Quest for *True Friends*

A YOUNG man was badly hurt in a motorcycle accident. For weeks he was in a coma and then began to recover slowly. "If I had as many good friends as I do acquaintances I would recover at a much faster rate," he said. 'A lot of the friends I had before the accident have left me. But good friends can be very curative.'

This situation is typical of today's unfriendly world. So-called friends can be many when all goes well. But when misfortune strikes, they disappear. True friends are usually hard to find.

Yet, having just one or two true, warm friends makes a vast difference in life. Experts on the subject say: "The yearning for closer personal ties is a major theme of our times." And as an old saying puts it: 'Friends in need are friends indeed.'

At one time, people were more concerned about others and were willing to help their friends or neighbors. But the pivotal period of World War I brought a general worsening of human relations. An ungrateful, callous, me-first attitude is now the norm.

This sad state of affairs was foretold 19 centuries ago in these words: "In the last days it is going to be very difficult to be a Christian. For people will love only themselves and their money; they will be proud and boastful, sneering at God, disobedient to their parents, ungrateful to them, and thoroughly bad. They will be hardheaded and never give in to others; they will be constant liars and troublemakers and will think nothing of immorality. They will be rough and cruel, and sneer at those who try to be good. They will betray their friends."—2 Timothy 3:1-4, *The Living Bible.*

What a gloomy yet accurate picture of the world today! And it apparently gives us little hope of finding true friends. Nevertheless, even now it is possible to make true friends. And how precious they are! You can always turn to them for help, advice, comfort, and warm companionship. But it is vital to distinguish between true and false friends.

Not All "Friends" Are True Friends

The young man hurt in the accident mentioned at the outset was a member of a football team and had many "friends." Members of clubs or small communities often form relationships that are pleasant. But such "friendships" may not be very stable. And to have many "friends" and then lose all of them is very discouraging, as the young man discovered. To acquire acquaintances is easy; to make true friends is not.

Wealthy people or those in high station can easily make many "friends." As the Bible says: "The rich have many friends." "Everyone tries to gain the favor of important people; everyone claims the friendship of those who give out favors." (Proverbs 14:20; 19:6, *Today's English Version*)

Your companions can powerfully influence you

But how many of them have ulterior motives? And if the much-befriended persons lose wealth or status, they may soon be completely friendless.

Physically attractive people often have lots of "friends" too—many of them influenced by physical factors. But such "friendships" can be very harmful and can vanish amid adversity like mist in the heat. So there is a real need to . . .

Be Selective

Yes, there is wisdom in being selective about friends. False friends are often great flatterers who curry favor with some ulterior motive. "The man who flatters his neighbour spreads a net for his feet." —Proverbs 29:5, *The Jerusalem Bible*.

Therefore, think carefully about your present circle of friends. Do they influence you for good or for bad? Are they self-centered, opinionated, or conceited? Do they act rashly and delight in taking risks? What is their attitude toward those of the opposite sex? Are they courteous and respectful or overly familiar, perhaps actually immoral? Have your regular companions proved to be dishonest, unreliable people? Are they drug takers? Heavy drinkers? If so, you are in danger. You may be honest, clean, and humble, but remember: "Bad associations spoil useful habits."—1 Corinthians 15:33.

The great danger in having bad companions is that you will imitate them. Slowly, maybe imperceptibly, their ways and attitudes will rub off on you. As the Bible says: "Keep company with the wise and you will become wise. If you make friends with stupid people, you will be ruined."—Proverbs 13:20, *TEV*.

It is easy to take a false step when acquiring friends. But do not be discouraged. There are still millions of fine, friendly people in the world. So how can you find such true friends?

How You Can Make
True Friends

"THE only way to have a friend is to be one," wrote Emerson, the American poet. Friendship is a two-way street involving the spirit of giving. Introverts and those with selfish tendencies find it difficult to make true friends. Nevertheless, they can succeed, as we shall see.

True friendship grows out of love because love draws people. Yet some have difficulty making friends. How can a person overcome this?

"Be a good listener. Encourage others to talk about themselves," advised Dale Carnegie. When strangers meet, perhaps at a social gathering, who are the ones that make friends? Not the big talkers but those who take a warm interest in others, drawing them out and really listening to them. Remembering names and interesting facts about new acquaintances can also help to develop friendships.

In *Fundamentals of Interpersonal Communication*, Kim Giffin and Bobby R. Patton recommend self-disclosure and genuineness. "For someone to be important to you," they say, "you must know something about him/her that matters to you . . . [Be] open and frank at all times . . . Your responses to the other person must be sincere."

True friends are not only honest but also considerate, never imposing on each other or being overly possessive. They understand each other, can sense the other person's view of things, and can thus show empathy. As the relationship grows, they open their hearts to each other, becoming not only true friends but also close friends. Not all true friends are *close* friends. Jesus Christ, the friendliest person ever on earth, made many friends, but only a few were really close friends. —Mark 9:1-10; Luke 8:51.

The Book of True Friendship

The Bible, by far the best book on the subject of friendship, says: "A true companion is loving all the time, and is a brother that is born for when there is distress." (Proverbs 17:17) True friends are compassionate and ready to provide help when problems arise. Here is a fine example of this—a story from the days of ancient Israel.

Because of famine, a man of Judah moved to Moab with his wife, Naomi. In time he died. Later, his two sons married the Moabite girls Ruth and Orpah. Then the sons died, leaving three widows alone. Naomi, the mother, decided to return to Judah, and her two daughters-in-law set off with her. However, along the way Naomi urged the young women to go back and seek new husbands among their own people. Orpah did so, but Ruth insisted on going with Naomi. Why? Because she was much more than a daughter-in-law; she was also a true friend. For one thing, her compassionate nature would not permit her to let the elderly widow, bereft of her family, go on alone.—Ruth 1:1-17.

Ruth showed real empathy, kindness, loyalty, and love. Those qualities form the solid basis of true friendship. There was, however, another factor involved in Ruth's relationship with Naomi.

Friendship on a Higher Plane

When Naomi urged her to go back, Ruth said: "Do not plead with me to abandon you, . . . for where you go I shall go . . . Your people will be my people, and *your God my God.*" (Ruth 1:16) Naomi had helped Ruth, formerly a pagan, to know and love the true God, Jehovah. Their shared belief became a powerful spiritual bond drawing the two women together as true friends. And Jehovah blessed them with a new family. In time, Ruth married Boaz, a prosperous landowner in Judah, and had a son named Obed, who became the grandfather of King David.—Ruth 4: 13-22; Matthew 1:5, 6.

This spiritual factor puts friendship on a higher plane. How? In the case of Ruth and Naomi, both worshiped Jehovah, "a God merciful and gracious, slow to anger and abundant in loving-kindness and truth." (Exodus 34:6) "God is love," and if we sincerely worship him with spirit and truth, we are sure to grow in love for him and fellow creatures. (1 John 4:8; John 4:24) Thus, we change. We develop a friendly interest in others, especially the meek, suffering people of all races. Introverts thus become less self-centered. Selfish people develop concern for others. We begin to display the fruitage of God's spirit—"love, joy, peace, long-suffering, kindness, goodness, faith, mildness, self-control."—Galatians 5:22, 23.

These qualities help us to develop the vital ability to forgive weaknesses and mistakes in others—"not, Up to seven times, but, Up to seventy-seven times," as Jesus said. (Matthew 18:21, 22) Many friendships founder on this point. But Jesus Christ both preached and practiced this. How often he forgave his imperfect, fallible disciples for their errors, including even Peter's shameful denial of the Lord! —Matthew 26:69-75.

As a result of all this spiritual development, our circle of friends grows. Eventually, we find that we belong to a vast, global family of friends! We also find that the general standard of our friends is much higher. For example, Brian, a fairly new worshiper of Jehovah, recalls that former friends got him involved in drinking and neglecting his wife and children. But now he is very devoted to his family. Concerning his many new friends with the same faith in Jehovah, he says: "If I have a problem, I know that I can pick up a phone and call any one of them, and they would be happy to help."

Alan had friends whose conversation usually centered around cars and girls. But he found those topics "flat and empty" when he made many new friends, fellow lovers of Jehovah. They overwhelmed Alan by their "spontaneous, genuine, loving interest" in him.

Some Guidelines for True Friendship

Be selective about those with whom you associate.

Take a warm interest in others, and be a good listener.

Do things together—shared experiences strengthen friendship.

Be frank, open, and sincere at all times.

Show empathy and compassion when others are in trouble.

When friends make mistakes or upset you, be ready to forgive—even "up to seventy-seven times."—Matthew 18:22.

When friends are slandered or unfairly criticized, be loyal and defend them.

Shared worship of Jehovah immeasurably strengthens friendship.

Our Best Friends

All these individuals and millions more form a worldwide, nonpolitical family of

Ruth would not abandon Naomi because their friendship had a solid spiritual basis. Do you have such true friends?

friends that transcends national, racial, and social barriers—a true brotherhood of mankind, just like that of the early Christians. (3 John 14) The same bond that drew Ruth and Naomi together also unites this family, namely, pure worship of Jehovah God. All of them humbly and gratefully recognize that Jehovah and Jesus Christ are their best friends.

'Almighty God and his Son as friends?' you may wonder. 'How is that possible? Is that not presumptuous?' Well, the Bible says: "Abraham put faith in Jehovah, . . . and he came to be called 'Jehovah's friend.'" That certainly was undeserved kindness. Yet Jehovah's Word says: "God opposes the haughty ones, but he gives undeserved kindness to the humble ones." —James 2:23; 4:6.

Perhaps some feel too sinful for such a privilege. But James goes on to say: "Draw close to God, and he will draw close to you. Cleanse your hands, you sinners, and purify your hearts, you indecisive ones. Humble yourselves in the eyes of Jehovah, and he will exalt you."—James 4:8, 10.

Jesus said: "You are my friends if you do what I am commanding you." He also pointed out that the greatest commandments are to 'love Jehovah God with all our heart, soul, and mind, and our neighbor as ourselves.' (John 15:14; Matthew 22:37-40) If we do that, we will have many true friends. Moreover, we will thus qualify for another great privilege—everlasting life on a cleansed earth under God's Kingdom. (Matthew 6:9, 10) As Jesus said: "His [Jehovah's] commandment means everlasting life."—John 12:50.

Will you allow Jehovah's Witnesses to help you? As genuinely friendly people, they are willing to visit you and discuss this vital matter with you free of charge. They can assist you to make many true friends.

A Desired Superhuman Ruler

WHEN Jesus miraculously feeds the thousands, the people are amazed. "This is for a certainty the prophet that was to come into the world," they say. They conclude not only that Jesus must be that prophet greater than Moses but also that he would make a most desirable ruler. So they plan to seize him and make him king.

Jesus, however, is aware of what they are planning. So he quickly moves to avoid being forcibly drafted by them. He dismisses the crowds, compels his disciples to get in their boat and head back toward Capernaum, and then withdraws into the mountain to pray. That night Jesus is there all alone.

Shortly before dawn Jesus looks out from his elevated vantage point and observes waves being whipped up on the sea by a strong wind. In the light of the almost full moon, since it is near Passover, Jesus sees the boat with his disciples struggling to make headway against the waves. The men are rowing with all their might.

At seeing this, Jesus descends from the mountain and begins walking toward the boat across the waves. Covering a distance of about three or four miles, he reaches his disciples. However, he continues on as though he is going to pass them by. When they see him, they cry: "It is an apparition!"

Jesus comfortingly responds: "It is I; have no fear."

But Peter says: "Lord, if it is you, command me to come to you over the waters."

"Come!" Jesus answers.

Thereupon, Peter, getting out of the boat, walks over the waters toward Jesus. But looking at the windstorm, Peter becomes afraid, and starting to sink, he cries: "Lord, save me!"

Immediately stretching out his hand, Jesus catches him, saying: "You with little faith, why did you give way to doubt?"

After Peter and Jesus get back into the boat, the wind stops, and the disciples are amazed. But should they be? If they had grasped "the meaning of the loaves" by appreciating the great miracle Jesus performed a few hours earlier of feeding thousands with only five loaves and two little fishes, then it should not have seemed so amazing that he could walk on water and cause the wind to abate. Now, however, the disciples do obeisance to Jesus and say: "You are really God's Son."

In a short time they reach Gennesaret, a beautiful, fruitful plain near Capernaum. There they anchor the boat. But when they go ashore, people recognize Jesus and go into the surrounding country, finding those who are sick. When these are brought on their cots and just touch the fringe of Jesus' outer garment, they are made completely well.

The next day the crowd that witnessed the miraculous feeding of the thousands discover that Jesus has left. So when little boats from Tiberias arrive, they board these and sail to Capernaum to look for Jesus. When they find him, they ask: "Rabbi, when did you get here?" Jesus' answer will be quite revealing. **John 6:14-25; Matthew 14: 22-36; Mark 6:45-56.**

♦ After Jesus miraculously fed the thousands, what do the people want to do to him?

♦ What does Jesus see from the mountain to which he has withdrawn, and what does he then do?

♦ Why should the disciples not be so amazed by these things?

♦ What happens after they reach the shore?

Breathing This World's "Air" Is Death-Dealing!

"It is you God made alive though you were dead in your trespasses and sins, in which you at one time walked . . . according to the ruler of the authority of the air."—EPHESIANS 2:1, 2.

A BREATH of fresh air! How refreshing after one's being in a stuffy room! But even in the wide open spaces, pollution is a major problem today. Poisons spewed into the atmosphere are at alarming levels in many countries. Toxic fumes, radioactive dust, disease-causing germs, and certain viruses all travel by air. Life-sustaining air, so generously provided by our loving Creator, is becoming more and more death-dealing due to man's greed and carelessness.

1. How has air pollution come to be death-dealing to humans?

[2] As dangerous as air pollution is, however, there is an even more deadly form of polluted "air." It is not contaminated air from the nuclear accident at Chernobyl (U.S.S.R.) or smog-filled air of Los Angeles, California (U.S.A.). No, we are in danger of breathing much more lethal "air." The apostle Paul mentioned it when he told fellow Christians: "It is you God made alive though you were dead in your trespasses and sins, in which you at one

2. What contaminated "air" is more dangerous than the polluted air we may breathe?

Are you refusing to breathe this world's death-dealing "air"?

time walked according to the system of things of this world, according to the ruler of the authority of the air, the spirit that now operates in the sons of disobedience." —Ephesians 2:1, 2.

[3] What is this "air"? Paul shows that it has "authority," or power, and there is a "ruler" over it. There is no doubt who this ruler is. He is Satan the Devil, the one Jesus Christ called "the ruler of this world." (John 12:31) Realizing this, some Bible scholars feel that Paul here borrowed from Jewish or pagan sources and spoke of the air as being the abode of the demons over which the Devil has control. Many Bible translations reflect this view. But this "air" is not the same as "the heavenly places" in which "the wicked spirit forces" dwell.—Ephesians 6:11, 12.

[4] When Paul wrote to Christians at Ephesus, Satan and the demons were still in heaven, although being outside God's favor. They were yet to be cast down to the vicinity of the earth. (Revelation 12: 7-10) Moreover, air relates more to humans than to spirit creatures. Accordingly, human society was to feel the effects when the last bowl of God's anger was poured out upon "the air."—Revelation 16:17-21.

[5] Hence, it appears that Paul uses the literal air, or atmosphere, to illustrate the general spirit, or dominant attitude of selfishness and disobedience, reflected by people alienated from God. It is the same as "the spirit that now operates in the sons of disobedience" and "the spirit of the world." (Ephesians 2:2; 1 Corinthians 2:12) Just as the literal air is everywhere, ready to be breathed in, so "the

spirit of the world" is always present. From infancy to the grave, it permeates, influences, and shapes the way people think and act as they seek to fulfill their desires, hopes, and ambitions.

[6] This spirit of sinfulness and rebellion predominates in imperfect human society. As this "air" is breathed in, its lethal potency is intensified by peer pressure and an ever-increasing appetite for sensual pleasure. Thus, it has pronounced "authority" over people. (Compare Romans 6: 12-14.) The Devil, of course, is the originator of all that is wicked. (John 8:44) So he influences humans to imitate his own rebellious course and thereby inspires, shapes, and controls this community spirit, or "air." As the "ruler" over this sinister power, or "authority," Satan uses it to control the thinking of people. Its elements are formulated to keep people so occupied with satisfying fleshly desires and pursuing worldly interests that they have no time or inclination to get to know God and submit to his holy spirit, "the spirit that is life-giving." (John 6:63) Spiritually speaking, they are dead.

[7] Christians too were under the "authority," or control, of this polluted "air" before they learned the truth of God's Word and began to conform to his righteous standards. "Yes, among them [worldly people] we all at one time conducted ourselves in harmony with the desires of our flesh, doing the things willed by the flesh and the thoughts, and we were naturally children of wrath even as the rest." But upon becoming Christians, we stopped breathing in the death-dealing "air" of

3, 4. (a) Who is "the ruler of the authority of the air"? (b) Why is the "air" of Ephesians 2:1, 2 not the abode of the demons?
5. What is the "air" here under discussion, and what effect does it have upon people?

6. (a) How is the potency of this world's "air" intensified, and how does it exercise "authority"? (b) How can breathing this "air" induce one to imitate the Devil's rebellious course?
7. (a) In what way were Christians "children of wrath" at one time? (b) Upon our becoming Christians, what transformation took place?

this world. We 'put away the old personality which conformed to our former course of conduct and put on the new personality which was created according to God's will in true righteousness and loyalty.'—Ephesians 2:3; 4:22-24.

8 The danger now is that after escaping from this world's polluted atmosphere we may be enticed to go back into it. Here we are, deep into "the time of the end" and on the very threshold of the new world. (Daniel 12:4) Surely, we do not want to lose out because of falling into the same traps as did the Israelites. After they had been miraculously delivered from Egypt and had arrived at the border of the Promised Land, thousands "were laid low in the wilderness." Why? Because some became idolaters, others committed fornication, and still others put Jehovah to the test by their murmuring and complaining. Paul makes a powerful point in saying: "Now these things went on befalling them as examples, and they were written for a warning to us upon whom the ends of the systems of things have arrived."—1 Corinthians 10:1-11.

9 Regarding his disciples, Jesus prayed: "They are no part of the world, just as I am no part of the world. I request you, not to take them out of the world, but to watch over them because of the wicked one." (John 17:14, 15) Jehovah will safeguard us, but he does not place "a hedge" around us, nor does he miraculously shield us from this world's "air." (Job 1:9, 10) So our challenge is to be in Satan's world, yet being no part of it, to be surrounded by its contaminated "air," yet not breathing it in. When we read secular publications,

watch television, or go to places of entertainment, we are likely to be exposed to the world's "air." While some contact with worldly people is unavoidable—at work, at school, and otherwise—we must be vigilant so as to keep from being sucked back into the death-dealing atmosphere of this world.—1 Corinthians 15:33, 34.

10 We might compare our situation to sitting in a restaurant having "smoking" and "no smoking" areas. As Christians in Jehovah's spiritual paradise, we are properly in the "no smoking" section, away from the spirit of this world. Surely, we would not deliberately sit in the "smoking" section. That would be foolish. But what often happens when we are in the "no smoking" section of a restaurant? Why, the smoke-saturated, filthy air drifts over, and we get whiffs of it! When this happens, do we find the polluted air enticing? Or do we not rather get away from it as quickly as we can?

11 But what do you do when whiffs of this world's "air" come your way? Do you take immediate action to get away from this foul influence? If you stay there and breathe it in, you can be sure that your thinking will be affected. The longer you breathe in this "air," the more tolerance you build up for it. Moreover, in time the smell is not so repulsive but is alluring, intoxicating, desirable to the flesh. It may intensify some secret desire you have been fighting to control.

12 Some death-dealing pollutants of this world's "air" are not easily detected, even as such contaminants of the literal air as carbon monoxide are odorless and taste-

---

8. How is our situation today similar to that of the nation of Israel in the wilderness?
9. (a) How can we be in the world and yet be no part of it? (b) What must we be to keep from being sucked back into the death-dealing atmosphere of the world?

10, 11. (a) How might our being in Jehovah's spiritual paradise be compared to occupying a "no smoking" area? (b) What steps should be taken if whiffs of this world's "air" are detected? 12. What is required to avoid being affected by those aspects of this world's "air" that are not easily detected?

less. The danger, then, is that we may not detect the 'deadly fumes' until they have overcome us. Thus, we need to be alert that we may not be led into a death trap by this world's permissive attitudes or its disobedience to God's standards of righteousness. Paul encouraged his fellow Christians to "keep on exhorting one another each day . . . for fear any one of you should become hardened by the deceptive power of sin."—Hebrews 3:13; Romans 12:2.

What Makes Up This World's "Air"?

¹³ What common attitudes might we begin to adopt, even before we realize it, because of the strong influence of this world's "air"? One is the inclination to *toy with things immoral*. This world's ideas on sex and morality are all around us. Many say: 'It's all right to commit fornication, bear children out of wedlock, and practice homosexuality. We're just doing what's normal, natural.' Has this "air," or worldly spirit, affected Jehovah's people? Unfortunately, during the 1986 service year, 37,426 had to be disfellowshipped from the Christian congregation, the greater number of them for practicing sexual immorality. And this does not include the even higher number reproved for immorality but not disfellowshipped because they were sincerely repentant.—Proverbs 28:13.

What do you do when whiffs of this world's "air" drift your way?

¹⁴ What happens in the case of those who succumb to sexual immorality? When the facts become known, often it is found that they have resumed breathing in the death-dealing "air" of this world. They have let worldly attitudes cause them to lower their standards. For example, they may start watching movies that they would have walked out on years earlier. Worse still, on home video equipment they may watch movies clearly unfit for a Christian. Such toying with things immoral is in direct opposition to the Scriptural injunction: "Let fornication and uncleanness of every sort or greediness not even be mentioned among you, just as it befits holy people; neither shameful conduct nor foolish talking nor obscene jesting."—Ephesians 5:3, 4.

¹⁵ True, you may quickly reject any outright proposal to commit fornication. But

---

13. (a) What is one form of this world's "air" that we should guard against? (b) How is it apparent that this "air" has affected some of Jehovah's people?

14. Why do some Christians go astray morally, rejecting what Scriptural counsel?
15. How might temptation to toy with sexual immorality begin casually?

how do you act when someone on the job or at school attempts to flirt with you, tries to get overly familiar in a physical way, or invites you to go out on a date? Whiffs of this world's "air" have thus drifted your way. Do you allow yourself to enjoy the attention, to encourage it? According to reports received from elders, wrongdoing often starts in such casual ways. A worldly man may say to a Christian woman: "How nice you look today!" That may be pleasant to hear, especially if the woman feels somewhat lonely. More seriously, some have not reacted wisely to attempts at improper touching. They have given the appearance of objecting but in such a halfhearted way that the worldly person was encouraged to continue what he was doing. What if such immoral advances toward a Christian woman persist, like strong puffs of polluted air blown her way? In a firm way, she should tell him that she does not want and will not accept his attentions. If she continues to breathe in this "air," her resistance will likely break down. She could be led into immorality, if not into an unwise marriage.

—Compare Proverbs 5:3-14; 1 Corinthians 7:39.

16 Be quick, therefore, to reject the immoral, death-dealing "air" of this world. Instead of submitting to its alluring smell and bringing reproach upon Jehovah's name and organization, become a pleasant odor to God by your godly attitude and conduct. Paul put it this way: "For to God we are a sweet odor of Christ among those who are being saved and among those who are perishing; to the latter ones an odor issuing from death to death, to the former ones an odor issuing from life to life." (2 Corinthians 2:15, 16) What does it matter if many turn up their noses at the Christian course? (1 Peter 4:1-5) Let the world go along in its way, reaping its bad fruitage in the form of broken homes, illegitimate births, sexually transmitted diseases, such as AIDS, and countless other emotional and physical woes. Not only will you be spared many pains but you will also have the favor of God. Moreover, at least some will be impressed by your good conduct and the Kingdom message you preach, thereby being attracted by the "odor issuing from life to life."

The "Air" of Worldly Styles

17 Another aspect of this world's "air" pertains to styles of clothing and grooming. Many in the world dress in order to make themselves sexually alluring. Even preteens want to make themselves up to appear older, accentuating sex. Are you affected by this widespread "air," or attitude? Do you dress to thrill, to tease, to arouse improperly the interest of those of the opposite sex? If so, you are playing with fire. Breathing this "air" will choke

---

How Would You Answer?

☐ What is this world's "air," and who dominates it?

☐ The world's "air" has what "authority" over people?

☐ Why may it be said that Christians are in a "no smoking" area?

☐ As to toying with things immoral, how can this world's "air" affect Jehovah's people?

☐ How can modesty help us to avoid being influenced by this world's "air" as regards dress and grooming?

---

16. What is required in order to be "a sweet odor of Christ"?
17. How may styles of clothing and grooming reveal that one has been influenced by the spirit of this world?

your spirit of modesty, your desire to be chaste. (Micah 6:8) Those who have a worldly spirit will be drawn to you. From your actions, they will get the message that you are ready to join them in immorality. But why start in this direction by letting such "air" entice you to do what is bad in God's sight?

¹⁸ To be modest, we do not have to dress or groom ourselves shoddily or unattractively. Consider the way the vast majority of Jehovah's Witnesses dress and groom themselves. They avoid the extreme styles of this world but present themselves attractively, keeping in mind that they are ministers representing the Sovereign of the universe, Jehovah. Let the old world be critical of their modest styles. They dare not let this world's attitudes cause them to lower their Christian standards. "This, therefore, I say and bear witness to in the Lord," wrote the apostle Paul, "that you no longer go on walking just as the nations also walk in the unprofitableness of their minds . . . Having come to be past all moral sense, they gave themselves over to loose conduct to work uncleanness of every sort." (Ephesians 4:17-19) The mature Christian will dress modestly, not walking just as the nations do.—1 Timothy 2:9, 10.

¹⁹ So far, we have considered only two aspects of the "air" of this world. But already we have seen that this "air" is very harmful to spiritual health. In the next article, we will take up other features of this deadly "air" that the Devil and his system continually blow toward Christians, hoping that they will succumb to it. How important that we avoid such "air," for absorbing the spirit of this world is like breathing the vapors of death!

18. How will always remembering that we represent Jehovah help us in selecting styles of dress and grooming?

19. Having considered two major aspects of this world's "air," what is already apparent as to the danger of breathing it in?

Keep Submitting to
"the Spirit That Is Life-Giving"

"It is the spirit that is life-giving; the flesh is of no use at all."—JOHN 6:63.

JEHOVAH GOD'S holy spirit is vitally needed if we are to resist the influence of this world's "air," or its attitudes. (Ephesians 2:1, 2) We also need the Bible, which contains God's thoughts recorded under the guidance of the holy spirit. And we need to have a humble Christian attitude, produced by cultivating the fruits of God's spirit—"love, joy, peace, longsuffering, kindness, goodness, faith, mildness, self-control." The apostle Paul urged: "Keep walking by spirit and you will carry out no fleshly desire at all. For the flesh is against the spirit in its desire, and the spirit against the flesh; for these are opposed to each other, so that the very things that you would like to do you do not do."—Galatians 5:16, 17, 22, 23.

1. (a) How does Jehovah help his people to resist the influence of this world's "air"? (b) How will cultivating the fruitage of God's spirit assist us to have the right mental inclination?

Is your family strong
enough spiritually to
resist this world's "air"?

improper styles of clothing and grooming. But there are many other aspects. For example, this world's atmosphere is saturated with *greed,* by an intense selfish desire for material advantages or material things. 'The ruler of the air' has seen to it that this world's propaganda and advertising make you feel unfulfilled if you do not have an abundance of material possessions. This aspect of the world's "air" can intoxicate you with the idea that these are the big things in life. Have you been affected by this materialistic "air"?

4 The Bible says: "No fornicator or unclean person or *greedy person—which means being an idolater*—has any inheritance in the kingdom of the Christ and of God." (Ephesians 5:5) Note that a greedy person is really an idolater. You may think, 'Surely, I will not go that far, becoming an idolater.' But what is idolatry? Is it not putting something else in the place of Jehovah and his worship, giving attention to it rather than to God and his service? Greed may involve the virtual worshiping of money and its power and influence. If you put the getting of a new automobile, a video cassette recorder, or any other material thing ahead of increasing your opportunities in Jeho-

2 Paul also wrote: "We received, not the spirit of the world, but the spirit which is from God, that we might know the things that have been kindly given us by God." (1 Corinthians 2:12) The "air," or mental attitude, of this world kills, but what God gives by holy spirit brings everlasting life to those who accept it. Jesus said: "It is the spirit that is life-giving; the flesh is of no use at all. The sayings that I have spoken to you are spirit and are life." (John 6:63) Since "the flesh is of no use at all," we need divine help to conquer sin and resist the world's spirit.

3 In the previous article, we discussed two dangerous aspects of this world's "air"—toying with things immoral and

---

2. How does what is produced by God's spirit contrast with the results of adopting "the spirit of the world"?
3, 4. (a) What is greed, and how does 'the ruler of the air' play upon fleshly desire for material things? (b) How is a greedy person an idolater?

If we do things "as to Jehovah," we will not be affected by the selfish, lazy "air" of this world

vah's service, is that not evidence that this world's "air" is affecting you detrimentally? Are not material things becoming like idols to you?

⁵ If you are seeking advanced education or a lucrative job, are you doing so to get rich and have more material advantages than you need? Are you intrigued by get-rich-quick schemes, wanting to get involved in them? This world's "air" is filled with selfish desire for wealth and cheating as regards the paying of government-imposed taxes. In this atmosphere gambling and similar activities flourish. Do not be tempted. Those who avoid the influence of this world's greed-laden "air" find that genuine happiness comes from being content with necessities and putting Kingdom interests first.—Matthew 6:25-34; 1 John 2:15-17.

Proper Use of the Tongue

⁶ What about our *speech habits?* Obscenities, angry words, lying—this world's "air" is thoroughly polluted with such foul speech. Yet, even the speech of a few

associated with the Christian congregation at times reflects coarseness, even vulgarity. The disciple James forcefully tells us: "Out of the same mouth come forth blessing and cursing. It is not proper, my brothers, for these things to go on occurring this way. A fountain does not cause the sweet and the bitter to bubble out of the same opening, does it?" (James 3: 10, 11) Have you picked up some of the jargon or slang of this world? Do you have two vocabularies, one for use among Christians, the other for use elsewhere? Paul wrote: "Let a rotten saying not proceed out of your mouth, but whatever saying is good for building up as the need may be, that it may impart what is favorable to the hearers." (Ephesians 4:29) How important it is to use proper, clean speech all the time!

⁷ We also need to be careful that we

5. In what ways is this world's "air" filled with selfish desire for riches?
6. What effect can this world's speech habits have on us as Christians?

7. What is included in 'putting away falsehood and speaking the truth'?

always tell the truth. Being devious or deliberately misleading others in order to avoid responsibility really amounts to lying. So be sure to heed Paul's counsel: "Now that you have put away falsehood, speak truth each one of you with his neighbor, because we are members belonging to one another."—Ephesians 4:25; Proverbs 3:32.

8 Unrestrained *venting of anger* is another feature of this world's spirit. Many worldly people lose self-control easily. They blow up, then excuse themselves by saying that they were just letting off steam. But this is not what Paul advised, for he wrote: "Let all malicious bitterness and anger and wrath and screaming and abusive speech be taken away from you along with all badness." (Ephesians 4:31) But what if anger builds up despite our developing self-control and other fruits of God's spirit? "Be wrathful, and yet do not sin," wrote Paul. "Let the sun not set with you in a provoked state, neither allow place for the Devil." (Ephesians 4:26, 27) So if we are provoked to anger, we should settle the matter quickly, before the day ends. Otherwise, bitterness and resentment begin to take root in the heart, and they are hard to uproot. Do not allow yourself to breathe in the angry, vengeful "air" of this world!—Psalm 37:8.

9 What about your *work habits?* Loafing on the job and stealing items from an employer are common today. Have you absorbed some of this "air"? Has the attitude that 'everybody does it' rubbed off on you? Never forget that the way we do our work as Christians reflects on Jehovah and his true worship. Would you want

someone to reject the truth spoken by one of Jehovah's Witnesses at his door because of the way you act on the job? "Let the stealer steal no more," said Paul, "but rather let him do hard work . . . that he may have something to distribute to someone in need."—Ephesians 4:28.

10 Although the master-slave relationship that existed in the first century is rare today, Christian employees can learn from what Paul wrote to Christian slaves at Ephesians 6:5-8. There workers were told to 'be obedient to those for whom they worked, not simply as men pleasers, but as Christ's slaves.' So a Christian should never maneuver things to avoid giving a full day's work or providing promised goods or services. If we do things "as to Jehovah," we will have the right attitude and will not be affected by the selfish, lazy "air" of this world.

Food, Drink, and Entertainment

11 Has the world's *immoderate use of food and drink* affected you? Its attitude is 'eat, drink, and be merry, for tomorrow we may die.' (1 Corinthians 15:32) And this spirit has affected some of God's servants, even since ancient times. Recall the occasion in the wilderness when the Israelites "sat down to eat and drink. Then they got up to have a good time." (Exodus 32:6) That "good time" led to unrestrained loose conduct and idolatry, so that God's anger blazed against them. Let us never follow that course.—1 Peter 4:3-6.

12 Jehovah has given us a huge variety of tasty, colorful, and nutritious foods and drinks, but he wants us to use these

8. (a) How do many worldly people act when provoked? (b) If we are provoked to anger, what should we do?
9. What are some common attitudes of employees, and why should we examine our work habits?

10. In doing secular work, how can we show that we are not being affected by the selfish "air" of this world?
11. How did a worldly attitude toward food and drink affect some of Jehovah's people in Bible times?
12. If our eating and drinking habits need some attention, what should we do?

things in moderation. Gluttony and drunkenness are condemned in the Bible. (Proverbs 23:20, 21) So be honest and ask yourself: Is there room for improvement in my eating and drinking habits? If you need to exercise greater self-control, recognize this and work in harmony with your prayers for God's spirit to help you overcome this problem. "Do not be getting drunk with wine, in which there is debauchery, but keep getting filled with spirit," said Paul. (Ephesians 5:18) Yes, become filled with God's spirit, and do not succumb to the unrestrained spirit of this world! "Whether you are eating or drinking or doing anything else, do all things for God's glory." (1 Corinthians 10:31) If you have persistent problems along these lines, however, seek the help of spiritually mature men in the congregation.—Galatians 6:1; James 5:14, 15.

¹³ This world is strongly addicted to *sports, music, and various forms of entertainment.* Unless they violate Scriptural principles, enjoying such things is not necessarily wrong. But the problem is that Satan, "the ruler who governs the air," has corrupted much of the entertainment available today. (Ephesians 2:2, *The Jerusalem Bible*) Often, immorality is promoted, violence is condoned, and success through deceit, fraud, and even murder is portrayed. When we watch such entertainment, we breathe these attitudes deeply into our system, and their toxic effects are bound to harm us. Moreover, even where some forms of entertainment are not Scripturally objectionable, there is a danger of becoming addicted to them, so that little time is left for spiritual things. Hence, we need to be selective. Take time to enjoy some healthful and beneficial re-

laxation in moderation, but avoid imitating the excesses of the world. Whether this world's "air" smells good or acrid, it is polluted and deadly!—Proverbs 11:19.

Pride of Race—An Evil Wind

¹⁴ A rather subtle aspect of this world's "air" is *pride of race and nationality.* Some promote the erroneous idea that certain races are superior and others inferior. Nationalism encourages people to view their native land as superior to all others. In fact, many suffer needlessly and are deprived of basic human rights and necessities because of the selfishness and prejudice of others. Resentment, even violence, results. Many rise up in revolt, taking the law into their own hands, confident of solving social problems their own way. We, too, might get caught up in these ideas. When we observe or suffer injustices and then hear those who are pressing for social change, we could be influenced if we are not careful. We could begin to abandon our neutral position and take sides. (John 15:19) Even more serious, we might feel tempted to join in picketing, campaigning, or resorting to violence in order to force changes.

¹⁵ A congregation's spirit can be affected detrimentally by racial or nationalistic feelings. (Compare Acts 6:1-7.) But we will have the right spirit if we heed the counsel: "If possible, as far as it depends upon you, be peaceable with all men. Do not avenge yourselves, beloved, but yield place to the wrath; for it is written: 'Vengeance is mine; I will repay, says Jehovah.'" (Romans 12:18, 19) Since all races came from the first human pair, and God is not partial, there is no room for pride of race or nationality in the Christian

---

13. (a) How is it evident that the Devil has corrupted much of the entertainment available today? (b) How can we avoid this world's attitude toward entertainment?

14. With regard to social problems, how could we be affected by this world's "air"?
15. What course does the Bible recommend when we feel inclined to 'avenge ourselves'?

congregation.—Acts 10:34, 35; 17:26; Romans 10:12; Ephesians 4:1-3.

Keep Breathing Life-Giving "Air"

¹⁶ We have discussed the main death-dealing features of this world's "air," or spirit. It surrounds us and exerts such pressure that if we allow a vacuum to develop in our spirituality, this foul "air" will rush in to fill it. Success in resisting it depends greatly on how much we love what is pure, clean, and righteous, and hate what is impure, unclean, and wicked. We will keep breathing the right "air" if we keep cultivating the right mental attitude in response to the leading of Jehovah's holy spirit.—Romans 12:9; 2 Timothy 1:7; Galatians 6:7, 8.

¹⁷ By all means, do not let any of this world's foul "air" begin to smell pleasant to you. The ruler of this "air" knows just what is needed to appeal to the senses and to set up a craving that often leads to sin. (James 1:14, 15) Keep in the "no smoking" section, Jehovah's spiritual paradise. When you detect a whiff of this world's "air" coming your way, shun it. Turn aside from it just as you would shun death-dealing poison. "Keep strict watch that how you walk is not as unwise but as wise persons, buying out the opportune time for yourselves, because the days are wicked. On this account cease becoming unreasonable, but go on perceiving what the will of Jehovah is."—Ephesians 5:15-17.

¹⁸ It is God's will that we serve him as integrity keepers. Doing so will mean life in his new system, now very near. When we take in a breath of air then, how refreshing it will be! No death-dealing pollutants, just pure life-sustaining air. That will be true of the physical air and, more importantly, of the spirit of those privileged to live on the cleansed earth. They will have an obedient, humble, responsive attitude. The "air" of this old world, filled with rebellious, corrupt, and ungodly influences, will be gone.—Revelation 21:5-8.

¹⁹ Surely, we do not want to be among those breathing the "air" of this system when Jehovah clears away both pollution and polluters at Armageddon. When the old world is gone and 'the ruler of the air' has been abyssed, what relief there will be! Everyone who loves Jehovah and keeps loving what is clean, decent, and righteous will be there. Jehovah wants them there and will help them by his spirit. He will give them eternal life in a clean, healthy new system. Let us not lose out on that privilege because of breathing in the death-dealing "air" of this old system!

19. Who will survive into Jehovah's new system?

16. What will help to prevent our being affected by the spirit of this world?
17. What should be done immediately if we detect some of this world's "air" blowing our way?
18. What will be the spirit of those privileged to live on the cleansed earth?

How Would You Respond?

☐ In what way does a greedy person become an idolater?

☐ How might this world's "air" affect your speech habits?

☐ What spirit should Christian employees reflect while doing secular work?

☐ How can you avoid being affected by this world's attitude toward food, drink, and entertainment?

☐ What spirit as to race and nationalism must not come into the Christian congregation?

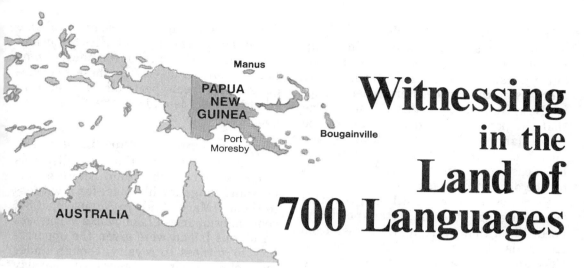

Manus

PAPUA
NEW
GUINEA

Port
Moresby

Bougainville

AUSTRALIA

Witnessing in the Land of 700 Languages

DO YOU know of a country with a land area smaller than that of Spain, yet whose population of well under four million speak almost a quarter of the world's languages? Can you name the country that occupies roughly half of the second-largest island in the world? The island is New Guinea, the country is Papua New Guinea, and the number of languages spoken by its inhabitants is over 700! How did this linguistic melting pot come about?

A Vast Melting Pot

Papua New Guinea is an island country situated just to the north of Australia and only a few degrees south of the equator. It is made up of some 600 tropical islands sprawled out over a distance of 1,000 miles (1,600 km). However, over four fifths of the total land area of Papua New Guinea is on the huge island of New Guinea, which the nation shares with Indonesia, to the west.

Papua New Guinea's earliest inhabitants are said to have migrated from Asia through Indonesia. These were later joined by Melanesians and Polynesians. The people range in skin color from light brown to jet black and in stature from short and heavyset to tall and thin. Because of the rugged nature of much of the interior, with its thick forests and high mountains, the many tribes lived virtually isolated from one another and developed their own languages. Most of these Papuan languages have extremely complex grammar. Yes, Papua New Guinea is the land of some 700 *languages,* not dialects!

In 1975 Papua New Guinea became an independent nation within the British Commonwealth. It is a parliamentary democracy with the British monarch as head of state but with a local prime minister. Although English is the official language today, large numbers of those within the 700 linguistic groups speak either of two common languages, Hiri Motu or New Guinea Pidgin.

Another Language Added

Yet, believe it or not, some years ago one "language" was still missing in this land of 700 languages. Which one was that? It was the "pure language"—Bible truth about God and his Kingdom. (Zephaniah 3:9) This new tongue was not introduced into Papua New Guinea until the mid-1930's.

It all started in 1935 when the *Lightbearer*, a small motorized sailing ship manned by a crew of Jehovah's Witnesses, left Australia and eventually put into Port Moresby on the southeastern coast of Papua New Guinea. This was the first time that the populace heard the sound of the "pure language"—literally hearing the message of God's Kingdom as it was broadcast by means of sound equipment on the deck of the *Lightbearer*.

However, it was not until 1951 that this "pure language" became better known and used. From that year on, Witnesses from Australia, Canada, the United States, Germany, England, and New Zealand volunteered to go to the Territory of Papua and New Guinea, as it was then called. After witnessing to Europeans there, they soon found ways and means of talking to the native Papuans about God's Kingdom. This involved going from house to house, which took extra effort because some houses were built on stilts above water or on land.

Of course, in order to teach the "pure language" to this multilingual population, the Witnesses from abroad had to learn at least one of the two common, or trade, languages. This did not solve all their problems because neither of these two languages was the mother tongue of the inhabitants but merely linguistic mixtures that enabled people speaking different languages to communicate. And even these two were not spoken by everyone on the islands. So witnessing often involved a laborious process of speaking to a person in one of the trade languages and then having him translate the message for the benefit of others present.

The Witnesses also resorted to using original teaching methods, such as drawing simple pictures on a blackboard or any other material available. In time, Bible literature and magazines became available in the trade languages of Hiri Motu and New Guinea Pidgin. The brochure *Enjoy Life on Earth Forever!* in these two languages has been particularly useful in teaching the islanders the "pure language."

Royalty Hears the "Pure Language"

Jesus Christ said that his disciples would be 'put on the stand before governors and kings for his sake, for a witness to them.' (Mark 13:9) On August 9, 1984, some missionaries of Jehovah's Witnesses on Manus Island were given the opportunity to witness to royalty, though under more pleasant circumstances. On that day Prince Charles, heir to the throne of Great Britain, visited the island.

In their decorated canoes, members of the Titan tribe escorted Prince Charles from his ship to the beach, just across the road from the missionary home. After he was greeted by a hundred dancers and was crowned as a "chieftain," he attended a luncheon to which the Premier of Manus Island had invited the missionaries. When the Prince asked them what they were doing on the island, they gladly gave him a brief explanation of their work. They were delighted to have an opportunity to inform him that Jehovah God has Witnesses also on distant Manus Island.

Incidentally, the official who introduced the missionaries to Prince Charles has herself read the book *You Can Live Forever in Paradise on Earth*. On occasion, she has also dropped by the missionary home for a chat over coffee and cake.

A New Language for a Politician

A New Guinea businessman was involved in politics and in the Lutheran Church. However, the local church he attended was so divided that the two opposing pastors formed two clans that fought each other for nearly a year with bows, arrows, spears, and war shields. The fighting left nine people dead and many injured. The man decided to leave the Lutheran Church but did not know where to look for truly united Christians. 'Not Jehovah's Witnesses, for they are false prophets,' he thought.

He was still of this frame of mind when a local group of Jehovah's Witnesses applied to hire his bus in order to attend a district convention. For business reasons, he accepted and actually drove the bus himself. He attended the Sunday program and was greatly impressed with the peace and quiet, the rapt attention of the audience—adults and children—who followed the speakers by consulting their Bibles. He was even more impressed during the lunch hour, when he saw the happy Witnesses patiently line up for their meal, the whites and the speakers awaiting their turn like the others and eating the same food. During the six-hour return trip, he heard the Witnesses happily singing Kingdom songs. 'What a contrast with the warring Lutherans!' he thought.

This man agreed to study the Bible with a local Witness, but secretly, so as not to offend his fellow Lutherans. However, he quickly acquired the spiritual strength to resign both from the church and from his political functions. He and his wife underwent "the change to a pure language" and began "to call upon the name of Jehovah, in order to serve him shoulder to shoulder" with His united witnesses.—Zephaniah 3:9.

Still Much Teaching to Be Done

What a marvelous work has been done by the missionaries and other Witnesses who have volunteered to come from other countries to teach the "pure language" in Papua New Guinea! From just two publishers in 1951, the number of Witness preachers and teachers has grown to over 1,800, most of whom are now from the local population.

These local Witnesses are a source of encouragement to those who have come from other lands to serve here. An English brother living on the island of Bougainville writes: "One of the most encouraging things that motivates us to continue serving Jehovah here is to see how our Papua New Guinean brothers continue to serve Jehovah faithfully, often under very difficult conditions. Many of them do not have homes of their own but have to live with relatives. Often they have to walk long distances in very hot weather or in heavy rain to come to meetings or go out in the field service. One of our local sisters lives out in the bush. In order to save time when she meets us for street witnessing, her husband ferries her, along with her small daughter and baby, across a river on a large inner tube."

There is still much teaching work to be done among the local population. The interest is there. This is evident from the fact that 10,235 persons attended the Memorial of Christ's death in 1987. But more help is needed to take care of all this interest in the "pure language." As a foreign Witness, who came here to serve where the need was greater, expressed it: "It makes my heart sad to think of the many interested people in these way-out bush villages of Papua New Guinea. We just don't have enough workers in the field here. There is certainly a great need in this part of the world. We know that Jehovah is aware of this and that he will make provisions to care for these truth-hungry people."

What about you? Would you like to share in teaching the "pure language" in this land of 700 languages?

"Fear the True God and Keep His Commandments"

In this day and age, fearing and obeying God is, at best, considered impractical. But the book of Ecclesiastes (Hebrew, *Qohe'leth,* congregator), written some 3,000 years ago by King Solomon (1:1), describes the futility of human endeavors that ignore God's purpose.

What makes this book so fascinating is the wide range of subjects the writer delves into—human wisdom and rule, material wealth and pleasures, formalistic religion, and so forth. All these things are vanity, for they are not lasting. On the other hand, meditating on them leads the perceptive mind to one conclusion: "Fear the true God and keep his commandments. For this is the whole obligation of man."—Ecclesiastes 12:13.

"Everything Is Vanity!"

Please read chapters 1 and 2. Compared with the never-ending cycles of nature, all human striving is fleeting and temporary (1:4-7). Even the great accomplishments of the congregator must be passed on to someone perhaps less worthy (2:18, 19). "Vanity," in Hebrew, means "vapor" or "breath."

♦ 1:9—In what way is there "nothing new under the sun"?

In the natural cycles of day-to-day living upon which the sun shines, there is nothing altogether new. Even "new" inventions are mostly applications of principles Jehovah had already applied in creation. But "under the sun" Jehovah has brought about new spiritual developments affecting mankind. —See *The Watchtower,* March 1, 1987, pages 27-9.

♦ 2:2—Is it wrong to have a good time?

No, it is not. Laughter, or having a good time, may help take the mind off one's problems temporarily, but the problems do not go away. So trying to find true happiness by merrymaking is "insanity"; it makes no sense. Similarly, "rejoicing" does not solve life's problems. Merriment and pleasures are thus contrasted with the happiness that results from having Jehovah's blessing upon one's work.—2:24.

Lesson for Us: We should heed Solomon's counsel and not make the pursuit of material advantages and thrilling new experiences life's sole objective. Rather, we should be 'good before Jehovah' by obeying him. Then we will enjoy his blessing of "wisdom and knowledge and rejoicing."—2:26.

A Time for Everything

Read chapters 3 and 4. Solomon was not promoting a fatalistic view of life (3:1-9). Rather, he was pointing out that man simply cannot alter what God has set in motion (3:14). In this regard, humans are not better than the beasts (3:19-21). So a cooperative attitude (4:9-12) is far more rewarding than a competitive spirit (4:4).

♦ 3:11—How has God made everything "pretty in its time"?

The word "pretty" also has the meaning of "good, proper, appropriate." In its own time, the proper place in which each work of God fits into his purpose will be revealed. God has made many things "pretty" for mankind. For example, he gave humans a perfect start in Eden. He foretold the coming of a redeeming Seed when man fell in sin. At the proper time, God sent the Seed. And, 'prettiest' of all, Jehovah made the Seed the King of His Kingdom.

♦ 4:6—Was Solomon advocating an easy life?

No. But Solomon observed that hard work and proficiency for profit's sake often lead to competition and rivalry (4:4). In turn, this can result in problems and even an early grave. (1 Timothy 6:9, 10) So, what is the balanced view? Be content with less gain coupled with peace, rather than double the gain along with toil and strife.

Lesson for Us: Now is the time to seek first God's Kingdom rather than ambitious personal interests (3:1). We should work in cooperation with fellow Christians rather than in isolation (4:9-12). In that way, we can receive the needed help and encouragement in spite of hardship and opposition.

True Worship Satisfies

Read chapters 5 and 6. Since Jehovah is almighty, we must take our relationship with him seriously, not acting foolishly and expecting him to accept our "sacrifice" (5:1, 2). One who fears God receives satisfaction from using his material wealth, but one who hoards it gets no enjoyment. —Compare 5:18-20 with 6:2, 3.

♦ 5:2—How does this advice apply?

We should pour out our hearts to God, but we must guard against impulsive, thoughtless words because of his greatness and majesty. (Psalm 62:8) Rather than rambling on, we should use simple, heartfelt expressions. (Matthew 6:7) In only five short Hebrew words, Moses pleaded for Miriam and received a favorable reply.—Numbers 12:13.

♦ 6:9—What is "the walking about of the soul"?

"Soul" here has the meaning of "soulful desire." So this expression refers to the endless search to satisfy desires that cannot be fulfilled. This is contrasted with "seeing by the eyes," that is, facing reality. Thus, knowing that only God's Kingdom can bring about real change, we should be content and not allow unrealistic or unattainable desires to deprive us of peace.

Lesson for Us: At our place of worship, we must conduct ourselves with proper dignity and should be attentive (5:1). We must also be quick to fulfill our obligations before Jehovah. If we are married, this includes fulfilling our marriage vow.—5:4.

Words of Wisdom

Read chapters 7 and 8. The congregator considers the sobering effect of death (7:1-4) and the value of wisdom (7:11, 12, 16-19); he also warns against the bad woman (7:26). Advice is given on such matters as acting wisely toward rulers (8:2-4) and not getting heated up over injustices.—8:11-14.

♦ 7:28—Are these words downgrading womankind?

It appears that the prevailing moral standard was very low. Thus, Solomon was speaking about the rarity of righteous men or women *at the time.* Among a thousand people, it was hard to find one righteous man, and it was even harder to find one righteous woman. The Bible, however, speaks about the "excellent woman" and the "capable wife." (Ruth 3:11; Proverbs 31:10) This verse may also be prophetic, for never has a woman given Jehovah perfect obedience, whereas there has been such a man—Jesus Christ.

♦ 8:8—Of what was the congregator here speaking?

He was speaking of death. No one can prevent the life-force from departing from his cells in order to postpone the day of death. In the war waged with our common enemy death, no one can get a discharge or send a substitute. (Psalm 49:7-9) Even the wicked ones with their devious schemes will not escape death.

Lesson for Us: Though material riches have become the life goal of many, only godly wisdom can lead to everlasting life. (7:12; Luke 12:15) Longing for 'the good old days' will not make things better for us (7:10). Rather, matters will "turn out well" for us only if we continue to fear God.—8:5, 12.

Life's Eventualities

Read chapters 9 and 10. Life is precious, and God wants us to enjoy it (9:4, 7). Since we have no control of life's outcome (9:11, 12), it is better to heed godly wisdom, even though most people do not appreciate it (9:17). Because of life's uncertainties, we should guard our heart (10:2), exercise caution in all we do, and act with practical wisdom.—10:8-10.

♦ 9:1—How are the works of the righteous in God's hand?

Though calamity besets the wise and the righteous, this happens only by God's permission, and he will never abandon them. By God's "hand," or applied power, righteous ones can either be delivered from a trial or be strengthened to endure it. (1 Corinthians 10:13) Remembering this fact can be of comfort to a servant of Jehovah when difficulties occur.

♦ 10:2—How is the heart at the right hand?

The "right hand" often denotes a position of favor. (Matthew 25:33) So the fact that the heart of the wise person is "at his right hand" indicates that it motivates him to pursue a good, favorable course. But the stupid individual lacks good motive and acts foolishly and improperly. His heart's being at his "left hand" indicates that he is motivated to follow a wrong path.

Lesson for Us: Since sudden death can befall any one of us (9:12), we should be using our life

in Jehovah's service in case our demise should bring everything to a halt (9:10). We also need to become skillful in our service because incompetence, even in such simple things as digging a hole or chopping wood, can be damaging to ourselves and others.—10:8, 9.

Youth and Life's Purpose

Read chapters 11 and 12. All of us should practice generosity and take decisive action (11:1-6). Youths who use their time and energy well in serving the Creator will have no regrets later in life (11:9, 10). Rather, they will have the satisfaction of pleasing God before they lose their health and vigor.—12:1-7; see *The Watchtower,* December 15, 1977, page 746.

♦ 11:1—What is meant by thus 'sending out bread'?

Bread is the staff of life. To send it out on "waters" is to part with something valuable. Yet, "you will find it again," for in an unexpected way the generous one will be repaid.—Luke 6:38.

♦ 12:12—Why such a negative view regarding books?

Compared with the Word of Jehovah, the 'endless' volumes of the world contain mere human reasoning. Much of this thinking reflects the mind of Satan. (2 Corinthians 4:4) Accordingly, "much devotion" to such secular material produces little of lasting value.

Lesson for Us: Like Solomon, we should meditate on what God's Word says about life. Then our resolve to fear and obey God will be strengthened. Knowing that Jehovah is intimately concerned about us (12:13, 14) draws us closer to him.

———————

May we, therefore, "fear the true God and keep his commandments." This is our obligation and will bring us lasting happiness.

Is Religious History of Any Benefit to You?

"AT SCHOOL, I didn't like history at all," Barbara openly admits. But now she appreciates knowledge about World War I, for example. Along with her Bible, this information helps her to explain more effectively why the world since 1914 has been without peace. (Revelation 6:4) Similarly, religious history can assist us to understand the world we live in.

Why have nations, communities, and even families been split between Catholic and Protestant faiths since the 16th century? "In the struggle for the pure teaching of the Gospel, then initiated mainly by German, Swiss, and French teachers of the church, Rome was unwilling to give in," comments historian Friedrich Oehninger. This led to the formation of denominational churches.

But was "the pure teaching of the Gospel" truly reestablished? A look at religious history will help us to discover what really happened.

What the Sale of Indulgences Revealed

"The Reformation started off with Luther's fight against abuse in the sale of indulgences, seemingly a matter of practical significance only to the church," remarks historian Gottfried Fitzer. "But in reality it revealed that ecclesiastical matters had become closely entwined with finance, economics, and politics." Let us take a closer look.

Prince Albert of Brandenburg acquired several influential positions in the church. He had to pay the Vatican the equivalent of about a quarter of a million dollars, financed by a bank loan. The pope appointed Archbishop Albert as his commissioner for indulgences for central Germany and allowed him half of the profits to repay his debts.

Albert's indulgence preachers canvassed effectively, assuring "total remission of all sins" and immediate release from purgatory. Strictly speaking, the church offered only remission from church penalties, but people believed that the indulgence letters would free them from all sin. Martin Luther was indignant and, in 1517, published his famous 95 theses, "out of love for truth," as he wrote in the introduction.*

---

* In modern times, Roman Catholic Church historians have asserted that Luther's nailing of the theses to the door of the castle church in Wittenberg on October 31, 1517, is "a legend of history by the Protestant churches." Uncontested, however, is the fact that he wrote a respectful letter to Archbishop Albert that day and enclosed a copy of the theses. Luther asked him to reprove his indulgence preachers and to cancel the instructions. The original letter still exists in the Swedish State Archives in Stockholm.

Since Luther merely sought discussion among scholars, to which he as a professor had the right, the theses were written in Latin. But they created "a startling sensation," according to Friedrich Oehninger. "Within 14 days they [the printed German translations] were known all over Germany, within 4 weeks in all Christendom. Some rejoiced that finally one man had taken a stand against the Roman oppression; for others, Luther became an object of hatred." The effect of his theses surprised Luther himself. What did they reveal?

What Luther's 95 Theses Revealed

According to his first thesis, "the believers' whole life should be penance." The sinner could attain peace with God not through letters of indulgence but through genuine repentance and Christian conduct. One of the last theses read: "Away, therefore, with all those prophets who preach to Christians: 'Peace, peace,' and yet there is no peace."—92nd.

Not tradition but the gospel must be "the highest" and the "real treasure," Luther wrote. (55th, 62nd, 65th) True. Jesus set the pattern by teaching with the inspired Scriptures, saying of God's Word: "Your word is truth." (John 17:17; Luke 24:44) By deviating from this pattern, the clergy rejected the Bible as the highest authority and were caught in the trap of human teachings. Luther reproached them, saying: "Teachings of men are preached by those who say that the soul flies (out of purgatory) as soon as money jingles in the box."—27th.

Luther warned that "profit and greed increase" through such preaching. (28th) Religious history proves that the clergy neglected Scriptural warnings and became victims of the love of money. (Hebrews 13:5) A Catholic history book admits: "The root cause of decay in the church of that period was the fiscal policy of the Curia, which was thoroughly blemished by simony."

When Luther raised his voice against "the 'sanctified' church tradition" and "bluntly denounced the church's decline into the realms of money and power," as one Protestant historian expressed it, he touched the heart of the problem: the general abandonment of early Christian teachings.

How Desertion of True Faith Started

The 11th thesis described one unscriptural doctrine as "a weed that obviously was sown when the bishops were sleeping." This reminds us of Jesus' parable of the wheat and the weeds, in which he prophesied the planting of imitation Christians. (Matthew 13:36-43) After the death of the apostles, these false Christians, together with apostate teachers, mixed pure Bible teachings with Greek philosophy and introduced unscriptural doctrines such as immortality of the soul, hellfire, and the Trinity.*—Acts 20:29, 30.

For example, the early Christians had no pictorial art, and the so-called Church Fathers viewed the veneration of an image as an "aberration and offense." By the end of the fourth century, however, the churches were already full of portrait images of Jesus, Mary, the apostles, angels, and the prophets. According to Epiphanius of Salamis, the ones portrayed received improper veneration when persons curtsied before them. Gradually, the warning "guard yourselves from idols" began to be ignored.—1 John 5:21; compare Acts 10:25, 26.

Professed Christians rejected Jesus' command when they started to "lord it

---

* See "A Field Producing Wheat and Weeds" in *The Watchtower* of August 1, 1981, pages 16-20, and "Quietly Bringing in Destructive Sects" in *The Watchtower* of September 15, 1983, pages 10-15.

The Indulgence—A Special Catholic Doctrine

The confessor imposes upon the repentant Catholic a penance (such as prayer, fasting, alms, or pilgrimage). The pope can remit these penalties because, according to Roman Catholic theory, he is lord over all temporal punishments (including purgatory) and grants indulgence from the so-called treasury of the merits of Christ and the saints. In the Middle Ages, this privilege lent itself to serious abuse and was described as "a commercial business of great dimensions, carried out at the expense of moral standards and in contradiction to the teachings of the Holy Scriptures."

The church does not equate penance with the pardoning of sins. However, even in medieval times, people retained "the simple belief that through payment the [sin] debt was canceled," and preachers of indulgences supported this notion. Luther's theses were directed against those "fables" and were thus summarized: "Indulgences are works of men and have nothing in common with the pure gospel."

Pope Clement VI established the doctrine in 1343 but did not clearly define it. Thus, Luther could appeal to its noncommittal nature. The church quickly made up for this by issuing an official definition of indulgence in 1518. But the papal bull of Leo X offered no "biblical proof for making the merit of Christ and the saints equal to the treasury of indulgences." This prompted in Catholic Luther a momentous decision. His rejection of the unscriptural indulgence system unleashed the Reformation, and the dismissal of his critique led to the great church division.

In modern times, severe criticism from within the ranks of the Roman Catholic Church "did not lead to a change of the system but only led to reforms of the practice." In 1967 Pope Paul VI decided in favor of the old indulgence theory. For Catholics, the decisive question still is: Do I follow God's Word, or do I believe doctrines of men?

The 16th century saw more changes. "The mood of the time was in his [Luther's] favor," Oehninger says, adding that "opponents attacked him, threatening him with death as a heretic, but they only drove him to make more and newer investigations on the basis of the Holy Scriptures, until the whole Roman system, as a mere human creation, began to crumble before his eyes." But were the newborn churches truly free, as they claimed, from "awful abuses and false doctrines"?

The Reformation—No Restoration

The call for reform in the 16th century led to a restoration of neither the "universal" church nor early Christian teachings but caused only a splitting of apostate Christendom into apostate parts that separated again. Today's bishops, including Luther's heirs, still seem to be "sleeping," as the 11th thesis mentioned.

The Protestants rejected the doctrine of indulgences but adopted many other false teachings. "From Greek philosophy, Christian theology also accepted the doctrine of the *immortality of the soul*," says *Evangelischer Erwachsenenkatechismus* (Protestant Catechism for Adults). It was "combined . . . with the biblical witness about the resurrection of the body."

By using doctrines of men and mixing their ministry with worldly things, including politics, Christendom's leaders, as in the days of Luther, undermine the Bible's authority. Therefore, their mere "form of godly devotion" proves to be without power and is unable to reverse shrinking attendance at church services, indifference of church members, the politicizing of church discussions, and the increasing withdrawals of membership.—2 Timothy 3:5.

Just as information concerning a patient's past can help a doctor to diagnose the person's illness, so religious history

over" their brothers by organizing a clerical hierarchy. (Matthew 20:25-27; 23: 8-11) Later, bishops of Rome claimed preeminence. While the "decay of ecclesiastical life under the reign of the secularized papacy proceeded unchecked," the church made attempts "to reform itself but was incapable of doing so," comments historian Oehninger.

can assist us in understanding why Christendom remains terminally ill in our day. Is there, then, no hope for pure Christianity? On the contrary! Jesus' parable indicated that his wheatlike followers, the true "sons of the kingdom," would be identified at the harvest in "the time of the end." (Matthew 13:38, 39; Daniel 12:4) How would this come about?

A Lesson From Modern Religious History

In 1891 a group of Bible Students visited Luther's former home in Wittenberg. "How vividly it brought to mind those stormy times," one traveler reported. Among those who entered Luther's "study and sat in his old chair" was Charles Taze Russell. The report continues: "[We] have great cause for rejoicing today that, although the beginners of the great reformation stopped short in the work and went about organizing other systems of error, nevertheless, under divine providence, the cleansing of the sanctuary progressed to completion, and the golden vessels of divine truth are now being replaced in order." What Luther failed to achieve, this visitor helped to accomplish.

It was an event of historical dimensions when Russell—together with other truth-loving men and women—started an independent Bible study in the 1870's. Be-

tween 1870 and 1875, however, they were "merely getting the outlines of God's Plan and unlearning many cherished errors, the time for the clear discernment of the minutia not having fully come," as Russell later wrote. But the following years became milestones in restoration of original Christian standards.

Through the magazine *Zion's Watch Tower,* the Bible Students announced that the name of the Most High is Jehovah, that the soul is mortal (1881), that the Trinity is unscriptural (1882), and that the Bible hell is the grave (1883). Just as false doctrines entered gradually, so now the light of truth gradually got lighter and lighter. (Proverbs 4:18, 19) From the beginning, these Christians understood the basic truth regarding Jesus, who gave his life as a ransom, and they made his invisible return and God's Kingdom the heart of their activity.—1 Timothy 2:6.

For better organized "dissemination of Bible truths in various languages" by means of publications, the Bible Students in 1884 legally incorporated in the United States the already established Zion's Watch Tower Tract Society. The previous year had already seen publications in Swedish, and then in 1885, the first German literature. In 1892 missionary work in foreign countries was considered. Today, the Bible Students—well known as Jehovah's Witnesses—preach "this good news of the kingdom" in 208 countries and territories and in some 200 languages. —Matthew 24:14.

Most of the Witnesses were members of Christendom's churches or of other religions and believed God-dishonoring doctrines. After taking in accurate knowledge about God and exercising faith, they repented of their wrong course, turned around, and became dedicated, baptized servants of Jehovah. Their "doing works

In Our Next Issue

- How Practical Is Modern-Day Religion?

- Discipline Yields Peaceable Fruit

- The Reformation Waters Burst Forth

that befit repentance" resulted in a clean conscience and in peace with God.—Acts 26:20; John 17:3.

Is Religious History of Any Benefit?

Indeed it is. Large parts of the Bible contain beneficial religious history. (Romans 15:4) The Gospels show how Jesus taught the truth about God and His purpose for the earth. Jesus' followers were to wait for the heavenly Kingdom that would solve earthly problems. "Keep on the watch, therefore, because you know neither the day nor the hour," Jesus said. —Matthew 6:9, 10; 25:1-13.

Religious history confirms the coming of the predicted imitation Christians, who established their own earthly reign. The Reformation changed the face of the world but did not restore pure Bible teachings. History also points to the existence of modern Christians who "keep on the watch," are "no part of the world," and put God's Kingdom first. (John 17:16) This information has helped many people to identify Jesus' true followers today.

Barbara, mentioned at the beginning of this article, is one of the more than 3,000,-000 active Witnesses worldwide who try to reach honest people with "the pure teaching of the Gospel." A certain amount of knowledge about religious history has been of benefit to these Kingdom proclaimers too.

Dangers of Wealth and of Poverty

DOES the Bible disparage wealth and encourage poverty? Many people think so. But two related proverbs help to clarify this.

Proverbs 10:15 states: "The valuable things of a rich man are his strong town. The ruin of the lowly ones is their poverty." Then verse 16 adds: "The activity of the righteous one results in life; the produce of the wicked one results in sin." Note how these two complement each other.

Verse 15 testifies that wealth has its advantages, poverty its disadvantages. Riches may help to protect a person from *some* of the uncertainties of life. The poor person, though, may have added problems because of being financially unable to cope with unexpected developments. In this the Bible is realistic.—Ecclesiastes 7:12.

However, verse 15 can also be understood as hinting at a danger involving wealth or poverty. Many a rich man puts his complete trust in his money; he views it as all the protection he needs. (Proverbs 18: 11) Yet, riches cannot help him to get a good name with God or ensure his lasting happiness. In fact, riches can make that more difficult. Jesus' illustration of the rich man who built bigger storehouses but was not rich toward God bears this out. (Luke 12: 16-21; 18:24, 25) On the other hand, many poor people mistakenly take the view that their poverty makes their future hopeless.

Notice how verse 16 rounds out the matter. Whether a righteous person has much or little financially, his work can bring him pleasure. He does not let the financial gain from his labor interfere with his good standing before God. Rather, a righteous man's efforts in life bring him, in addition to happiness now, assurance of everlasting life in the future. (Job 42:10-13) The wicked one, though, does not benefit even if he gains much money. Instead of appreciating money's protective value and living in accord with God's will, he uses his riches to promote a life of sin.

Questions From Readers

■ What is "the seed of God" mentioned at Malachi 2:15?

This intricate verse reads, in part: "And there was one who did not do it, as he had what was remaining of the spirit. And what was that one seeking? The seed of God." "The seed" evidently refers to the nation of ancient Israel, which at the time the verse was written was in danger of religious contamination.

Malachi prophesied during a period of national moral decay. Some Israelite men were not only taking 'the daughters of a foreign god as brides' but also divorcing their original Jewish wives, the 'wives of their youth,' to take on perhaps younger heathen wives. Yet, not all Israelite men did this "detestable thing." (Malachi 2:11, 13, 14; Deuteronomy 7:3, 4) Evidently referring to individuals who refused to break their marriage covenant with a fellow worshiper of Jehovah, Malachi wrote: "And there was one who did not do it, as he had what was remaining of the spirit."

The "spirit" is God's holy spirit, which he had poured out on the nation. The disobedient Israelites, however, were resisting, and hence grieving, that spirit. (Isaiah 63:10; Acts 7:51-53; compare Ephesians 4:30.) Some individual Jews were loyal to God's laws, and by their obedience they had retained what "was remaining of the spirit." These faithful worshipers did not seek their own selfish pleasure. Of such an individual, Malachi wrote: "What was that one seeking? The seed of God." This "seed" was the nation of ancient Israel, which Malachi said was 'created by God.' This 'creation' occurred when Jehovah drew the Israelites into a covenant with him at Mount Sinai, making them his "special property" and "a holy nation." The true "seed" of Abraham that would bless people of all the earth was to come through this nation. —Malachi 2:10; Exodus 19:5, 6; Genesis 22:18.

However, the Israelites had to keep religiously pure by not intermarrying with people of the nations who did not worship Jehovah. The ungodliness of such persons would be corrupting, as can be seen from the situation in Ezra's time. The Israelites then "accepted some of [the surrounding nations'] daughters for themselves and for their sons; and they, the holy seed, [became] mingled with the peoples of the lands." (Ezra 9:2) This same "great badness" occurred during the days of Nehemiah, a contemporary of Malachi. Jewish men loyal to God saw the clear spiritual peril to themselves and to the children born of such a union.

There was the danger of being drawn away from Jehovah's worship by a wife who was not devoted to Him. Nehemiah even reported that among those Jews who had intermarried, 'none of their children knew how to speak Jewish.'—Nehemiah 13:23-27.

The disloyal Jews were seeking their own pleasure regardless of the detrimental religious impact on their nation, "the seed of God." No wonder Malachi admonished: "And you people must guard yourselves respecting your spirit, and with the wife of your youth may no one deal treacherously"! (Malachi 2:15) The faithful Jews guarded their spirit, or attitude, so as to stay loyal to their Jewish wives. These men highly valued the religious purity of their "holy nation." They desired that their children read God's Word and grow up to love Jehovah, contributing to the religious strength of the nation.

Dedicated Christians today need to exercise the same diligence over their spirit, or dominant attitude. If married, these individuals need to avoid treacherously divorcing their mates. And a single Christian should heed the counsel of the apostle Paul to marry "only in the Lord," entering wedlock only with another dedicated, baptized witness of Jehovah.—1 Corinthians 7:39.

'Rhythms That Calm the Heart'

Surely, these are most desirable in these hectic times. In this connection, a young mother from Japan wrote regarding the meetings of Jehovah's Witnesses:

"When I first went to the Kingdom Hall and heard the songs of praise, I thought, 'What beautiful music, . . . rhythms that calm the heart!' . . . I had been wondering for some time whether there were cassette tapes or records of these songs of praise. If there are any, I would like to buy them. . . . I consider the songs of praise to be exactly right. If we had the cassette tapes, I could listen to them while I do my housework and when playing with my child, and that would be wonderful."

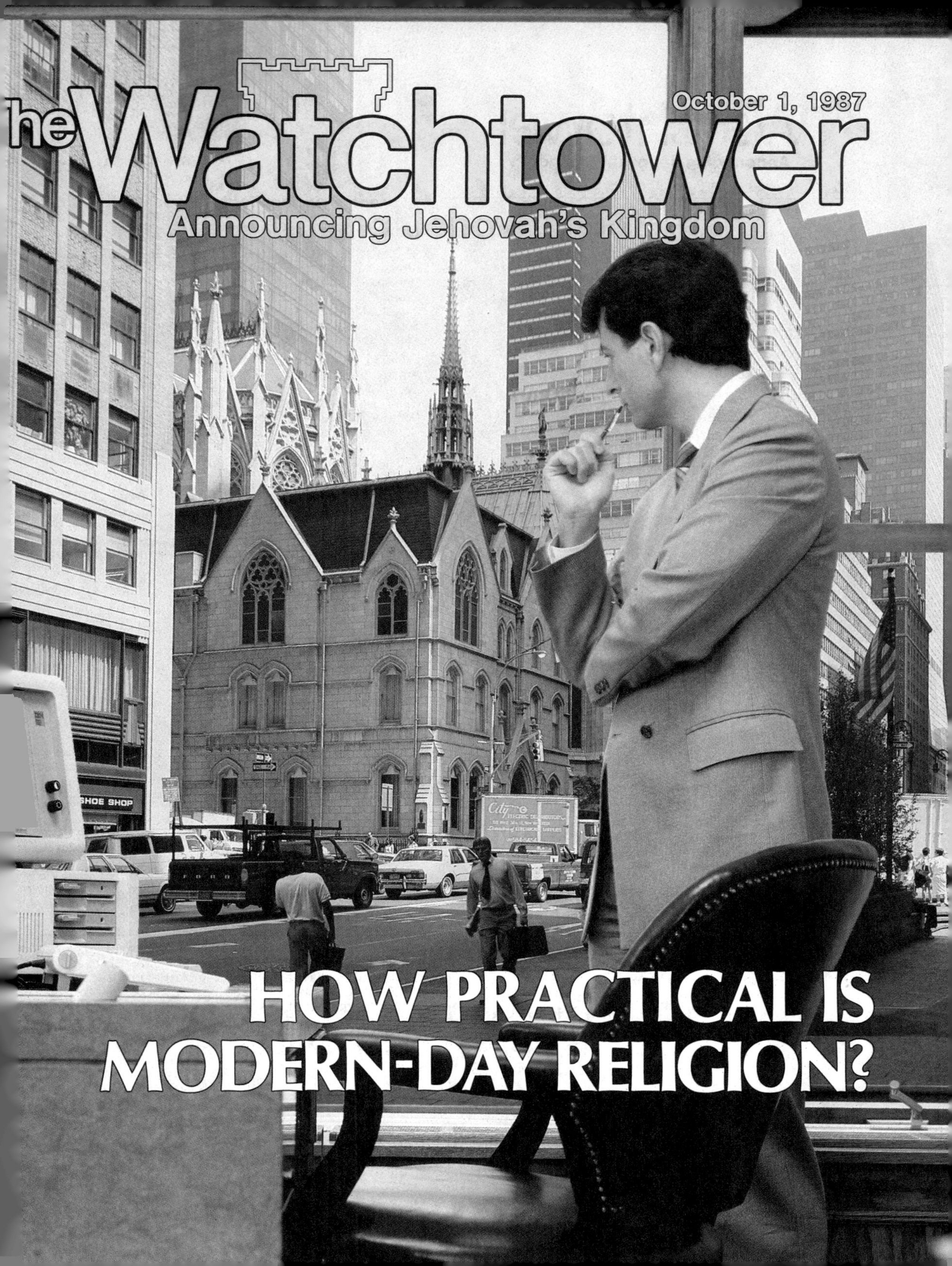
The Watchtower
October 1, 1987
Announcing Jehovah's Kingdom
HOW PRACTICAL IS MODERN-DAY RELIGION?
SHOE SHOP

The Watchtower®

Announcing Jehovah's Kingdom

October 1, 1987
Vol. 108, No. 19

In This Issue

THE PURPOSE OF *THE WATCHTOWER* is to exalt Jehovah God as the Sovereign of the universe. It keeps watch on world events as they fulfill Bible prophecy. It comforts all peoples with the good news that God's Kingdom will soon destroy those who oppress their fellowmen and that it will turn the earth into a paradise. It encourages faith in the now-reigning King, Jesus Christ, whose shed blood opens the way for mankind to gain eternal life. *The Watchtower,* published by Jehovah's Witnesses continuously since 1879, is nonpolitical. It adheres to the Bible as its authority.

WATCHTOWER STUDIES FOR THE WEEKS

Average Printing Each Issue: 12,315,000

Now Published in 103 Languages

SEMIMONTHLY LANGUAGES AVAILABLE BY MAIL
Afrikaans, Arabic, Cebuano, Chichewa, Chinese, Cibemba, Danish,* Dutch,* Efik, English,* Finnish,* French,* German,* Greek,* Hiligaynon, Igbo, Iloko, Italian,* Japanese,* Korean, Lingala, Malagasy, Maltese, Norwegian, Portuguese,* Russian, Sepedi, Sesotho, Shona, Spanish,* Swahili, Swedish,* Tagalog, Thai, Tsonga, Tswana, Xhosa, Yoruba, Zulu

MONTHLY LANGUAGES AVAILABLE BY MAIL
Armenian, Bengali, Bicol, Bislama, Bulgarian, Croatian, Czech, Ewe, Fijian, Ga, Greenlandic, Gujarati, Gun, Hausa, Hebrew, Hindi, Hiri Motu, Hungarian, Icelandic, Kannada, Malayalam, Marathi, New Guinea Pidgin, Pangasinan, Papiamento, Polish, Rarotongan, Romanian, Samar-Leyte, Samoan, Sango, Serbian, Silozi, Sinhalese, Slovenian, Solomon Islands-Pidgin, Tahitian, Tamil, Telugu, Tongan, Tshiluba, Turkish, Twi, Ukrainian, Urdu, Venda, Vietnamese

* Study articles also available in large-print edition.

	Yearly subscription for the above:	
	Semimonthly	Monthly
Watch Tower Society offices	Languages	Languages
America, U.S., Watchtower, Wallkill, N.Y. 12589	$5.00	$2.50
Australia, Box 280, Ingleburn, N.S.W. 2565	A$7.00	A$3.50
Canada, Box 4100, Halton Hills, Ontario L7G 4Y4	$7.00	$3.50
England, The Ridgeway, London NW7 1RN	£5.00	£2.50
Ireland, 29A Jamestown Road, Finglas, Dublin 11	IR£6.00	IR£3.00
New Zealand, P.O. Box 142, Manurewa	NZ$15.00	NZ$7.50
Nigeria, PMB 001, Shomolu, Lagos State	₦8.00	₦4.00
Philippines, P.O. Box 2044, Manila 2800	₱60.00	₱30.00
South Africa, Private Bag 2067, Krugersdorp, 1740	R9.00	R4.50

Remittances should be sent to the office in your country or to Watchtower, Wallkill, N.Y. 12589, U.S.A.

Changes of address should reach us 30 days before your moving date. Give us your old and new address (if possible, your old address label).

25 cents (U.S.) a copy

The Bible translation used is the *New World Translation of the Holy Scriptures,* unless otherwise indicated.

The Watchtower (ISSN 0043-1087) is published semimonthly for $5.00 (U.S.) per year by Watch Tower Bible and Tract Society of Pennsylvania, 25 Columbia Heights, Brooklyn, N.Y. 11201. Second-class postage paid at Brooklyn, N.Y., and at additional mailing offices.

Postmaster: Send address changes to Watchtower, **Wallkill, N.Y. 12589.**

Published by
**Watch Tower Bible and Tract Society
of Pennsylvania**
25 Columbia Heights, Brooklyn, N.Y. 11201, U.S.A.
Frederick W. Franz, President

How Practical Is Modern-Day Religion?

"I THREW the Bible in the den on my way to my bedroom. I thought I would never pick it up again or attend another church. I had been searching for about six years. Still I found no help."

Ronald, a 26-year-old computer operator, had gone through some hardships and feared his life would fall apart. Religion seemed to be of no practical value to him. "I am through with it," he said.

Many people, like Ronald, are disappointed with religion. How about you? Do you think religion has given people practical help and guidance to become better workmates, neighbors, husbands, wives, parents, or children? Has religion been a force for peace and unity among people? Has it helped them understand the purpose of life? Has it instilled in their minds and hearts a sure hope for the future?

Practical Guidance Lacking

In this complex world, people need wise, clear guidance. Can they expect this from spiritual leaders? In a letter to a magazine columnist, a woman complained:

"All we ever hear now in our church . . . for quite awhile now is love, love, love. . . . What ever happened to the 'Thou shalt nots'—'Thou shalt not kill. Thou shalt not steal,' and all the rest? We need to be reminded often that some things are No-No's. . . . But we don't even hear the word 'Sin' any more. It's like they shun it as if it were a dirty three letter word."

Evidently, some feel that their religious counselors have become too lax, too permissive. Such spiritual guides are weak. They are like a doctor who glosses over his patient's problem and prescribes diluted medicine. What are some reasons for such failure?

Profession in Crisis

A person who is weighed down with his own problems is not going to be able to spend much time and effort helping others. Media reports show that an increasing number of clergymen are deeply encumbered with their own professional and personal problems. Here are some examples:

"While stress and burnout are common in many professions today, nowhere are they more critical than among the Jewish clergy," says clinical psychologist Dr. Leslie R. Freedman after a four-year university study of the Jewish clergy.

"If I had a son, would I want him to become a priest? Regrettably, my answer has to be no," contends a priest, William Wells, in a report on clergymen's problems. Why not? He says he cannot encourage a young man to consider a profession so plagued by "conflict, turbulence, and uncertainties as the Roman Catholic priesthood is today."

Priests in the Swedish State-supported Lutheran Church are also in trouble. A Swedish daily says: "Priests have psychological problems, which in severe cases lead to suicide. . . . The clerical profession is in crisis."

Distracting Disunity

In those countries where the religious leaders are involved in exhausting and divisive wars, they are diverted from giving proper attention to people's spiritual needs. They also have to share the responsibility for the loss of manpower and money that could have been used for people's material welfare.

There are those in all parts of the world who have lost their trust in religion and become religiously indifferent. Loss of members and decline in churchgoing are reported from such places as Sweden, Finland, Germany, Britain, Italy, Canada, and the United States.

Are you among those who, like Ronald, think they are through with religion? And yet, could there be a religion that has proved to be of practical value to many? The following article will discuss this.

Can You Find the Right Religion?

RONALD—mentioned in the preceding article—thought he should give up his search for a religion that could give him practical help and guidance. But he decided to give himself a last chance. "If there really was a God, I wanted him to know that I was honestly searching for him," he said. So one night Ronald prayed: "If you really are a loving God, you find me because for years I have looked for you and found nothing."

A few days later at his job, Ronald was assigned to work on a shift with one of Jehovah's Witnesses. He began to ask her questions about the Bible. The answers triggered his curiosity. Soon he began to study the Bible regularly. He also went to meetings of the local congregation of Jehovah's Witnesses.

Six months later Ronald was convinced that he had found a religion that gave him the incentive to adjust his life in a most practical way. After three years of association with Jehovah's Witnesses, he explained in a letter to the *Watchtower* magazine some benefits he had derived from this association.

"Killer Instinct" Done Away With

Ronald writes: "The first benefit from learning the truth [the Bible's teaching] was being better able to control my temper. For a long time I was involved in the martial arts. . . . I used to train from six to eight hours a day, and it was always instilled in me to develop a killer instinct."

Fighting and killing are not effective ways to solve conflicts with one's fellowman. Therefore, a useful religion is a force for peace. The Bible says at Romans 12:18: "Be peaceable with all men." Jehovah's Witnesses do not train their bodies for fighting, nor do they seek to protect themselves by learning to handle guns. They are known around the globe for their peaceful, neutral stand in time of war.

Seeing the practical force or potential of such a religion, a Roman Catholic nun wrote in an Italian church magazine: "How different the world would be if we all woke up one morning firmly decided not to take up arms again, . . . just like Jehovah's Witnesses!"

This peaceable attitude among the Witnesses has contributed to the forming of a worldwide brotherhood of more than three million people in 208 lands. They treat one another as true friends, whatever their nationality, race, or social rank. This is most practical in a hostile world, especially when help is needed. Eva, a young Swedish woman who is one of Jehovah's Witnesses, experienced this.

While visiting Greece, Eva contracted meningitis. Unconscious, and with blood poisoning and internal bleeding, she was rushed to a hospital in Athens, where she knew no one. Her father in Sweden was informed by phone. He called an elder in the local congregation of Jehovah's Witnesses. This elder called Witnesses he knew in Athens. Eva was quickly contacted by Greek fellow believers she had never met before.

This calls to mind an illustration that the apostle Paul used, showing how oneness and compassion belong together. He said at 1 Corinthians 12:25, 26: "There should be no division in the body, but . . . its members should have the same care for one another. And if one member suffers, all the other members suffer with it."

This is what Eva experienced in Greece. For almost three weeks her new friends did not leave her unattended. She recovered and returned to her home. She says: "I really experienced the benefits of a loving brotherhood."

Not Desiring "That Extra Dollar"

Let us go back to Ronald's letter. After telling

Real Christians treat one another as true friends

how his new belief helped him to control his temper, get rid of that "killer instinct," and become more peaceable, he says that the Bible's teaching gave him a balanced view of work and money. "I was my employer's number one computer operator," Ronald says, "and I used to skip being with my family and friends just to work overtime. I worked nights for over seven years. I always wanted that extra dollar."

Such desire for "that extra dollar" can, in the long run, be harmful, fatally harmful. "To some, money means security. To some it means power. To others it means they're going to be able to buy love, and to a fourth group it means competition and winning the game," says psychiatrist Jay Rohrlich, whose clients are mostly financial executives from New York's Wall Street district.

Commenting on this statement, a report in the magazine *Science Digest* says: "The belief that money can produce these things . . . often leads to impotence, insomnia, heart attacks and problems with a spouse or children." The Bible's advice is: "Let your manner of life be free of the love of money." Ronald learned that and applied it. He found it most beneficial. —Hebrews 13:5.

Proper View of Work

The quest for money often induces people to force themselves up the career ladder. This can cause the healthiest people severe stress and emotional conflict—even to the point of suicide. "One man, who came into work one morning to find that his desk had been moved, climbed up to the top of the building and jumped off." Dr. Douglas LaBier related that in a *U.S.News & World Report* interview dealing with the link between careers and emotional problems.

"What is needed," says Dr. LaBier, "is a more developed life, one that is not so centered around a career. In addition to such things as adequate diet, rest and exercise, people who want more balanced lives need to think about doing more with their families and developing noncareer competencies that give them pleasure."

Jehovah's Witnesses learn from the Bible to be balanced as to work and money. Ecclesiastes 4:4, 6 speaks about hard work that involves "rivalry of one toward another" and says: "Better is a handful of rest than a double handful of hard work and striving after the wind." Ronald found this to be practical wisdom. He cut down on his secular work so as to have more time for his spiritual interests and for his family and friends.

A Happier Family Life

Ronald then says in his letter that the Bible's counsel on marriage and family life has helped him to deal more wisely with family situations. This is essential now when family life seems to be on the way out in many places. Industrialized countries report fewer marriages, more divorces, and a falling birth rate.

This trend is alarming because the family circle is where some of the most basic human needs are satisfied. In a survey, the Australian *Sydney Morning Herald* asked 2,000 people which of the following gave them greatest satisfaction: work, family, friends, leisure activities, possessions, or religion. The overwhelming majority gave "family" the first place.

Jehovah's Witnesses are interested in keeping their families strong. For example, over just the last five years, their two magazines *The Watchtower* and *Awake!* (combined circulation of some 22 million copies in over 100 languages) have carried some 60 practical articles about handling different situations in family life. Without a doubt, a Bible-based religion that helps

people to take care of their families in a wise and loving way is practical.

The Big "Why?" Answered

Ronald concludes his letter by saying: "There is one thing that often comes to mind when I read the newspaper, watch the news, converse with workmates, or tell others about my faith. It is that being one of Jehovah's Witnesses gives me the answer to one of the most widely asked questions in the world—'Why?' Why all the crime, violence, war, immorality, disease, turmoil, besides all the everyday problems? Knowing that this system and its problems are only temporary has lifted a heavy weight from my shoulders."

The Bible reveals what is behind today's perplexing world situation. It explains why the Creator's original purpose to make this earth a paradise home for mankind has not yet become a reality. It explains how God will remove all disturbing influences from the earth and establish a permanent paradise for people to enjoy forever.—2 Peter 3:9-13.

For a religion to be of practical value, it must bear good fruit. It must produce better people. It must be able to explain why things are as they are on earth today. And it should instill a sure hope for the future in people's minds and hearts. Ronald searched for such a religion, and he found it. The same opportunity is still open for you.—Matthew 7:17-20.

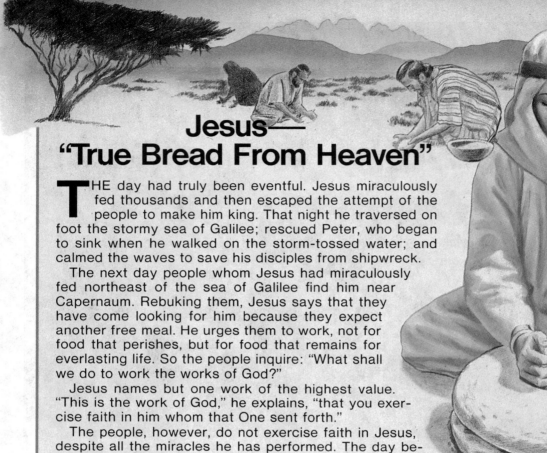

Jesus—
"True Bread From Heaven"

THE day had truly been eventful. Jesus miraculously fed thousands and then escaped the attempt of the people to make him king. That night he traversed on foot the stormy sea of Galilee; rescued Peter, who began to sink when he walked on the storm-tossed water; and calmed the waves to save his disciples from shipwreck.

The next day people whom Jesus had miraculously fed northeast of the sea of Galilee find him near Capernaum. Rebuking them, Jesus says that they have come looking for him because they expect another free meal. He urges them to work, not for food that perishes, but for food that remains for everlasting life. So the people inquire: "What shall we do to work the works of God?"

Jesus names but one work of the highest value. "This is the work of God," he explains, "that you exercise faith in him whom that One sent forth."

The people, however, do not exercise faith in Jesus, despite all the miracles he has performed. The day before, he miraculously fed 5,000 men, as well as women and children, and yet now, unbelievably, they ask: "What, then, are you performing as a sign, in order for us to see it and believe you? What work are you doing? Our forefathers ate the manna in the wilderness, just as it is written, 'He gave them bread from heaven to eat.'"

In response to their request for a sign, Jesus makes clear the Source of miraculous provisions, saying: "Moses did not give you the bread from heaven, but my Father does give you the true bread from heaven. For the bread of God is the one who comes down from heaven and gives life to the world."

"Lord," the people say, "always give us this bread."

"I am the bread of life," Jesus explains. "He that comes to me will not get hungry at all, and he that exercises faith in me will never get thirsty at all. But I have said to you, You have even seen me and yet do not believe. Everything the Father gives me will come to me, and the one that comes to me I will by no means drive away; because I have come down from heaven to do, not my will, but the will of him that sent me. This is the will of him that sent me, that I should lose nothing out of all that he has given me but that I should resurrect it at the last day. For this is the will of my Father, that everyone that beholds the Son and exercises faith in him should have everlasting life."

At this the Jews begin murmuring at Jesus because he said, "I am the bread that came down from heaven." They see in him nothing more than a son of human parents and so object in the same manner as did the people of Nazareth: "Is this not Jesus the son of Joseph, whose father and mother we know? How is it that now he says, 'I have come down from heaven'?"

"Stop murmuring among yourselves," Jesus responds. "No man can come to me unless the Father, who sent me, draws him; and I will resurrect him in the last day. It is written in the Prophets, 'And they will all be taught by Jehovah.' Everyone that has heard from the Father and has learned comes to me. Not that any man has seen the Father, except he who is from God; this one has seen the

Father. Most truly I say to you, He that believes has everlasting life."

Continuing, Jesus repeats: "I am the bread of life. Your forefathers ate the manna in the wilderness and yet died. This is the bread that comes down from heaven, so that anyone may eat of it and not die. I am the living bread that came down from heaven; if anyone eats of this bread he will live forever." Yes, by exercising faith in Jesus, the one God sent forth, people can have everlasting life. No manna, or any other such bread, can provide that!

The discussion regarding the bread from heaven apparently began shortly after the people found Jesus near Capernaum. But it continued, reaching a climax later while Jesus was teaching in a synagogue in Capernaum. **John 6: 26-51, 59; Psalm 78:24; Isaiah 54:13; Matthew 13:55-57.**

♦ What events preceded Jesus' discussion regarding the bread from heaven?
♦ In view of what Jesus has just done, why is the request for a sign so inappropriate?
♦ Why do the Jews murmur at Jesus' claim that he is the true bread from heaven?
♦ Where did the discussion about the bread from heaven take place?

Are You Satisfied With
Jehovah's Spiritual Provisions?

IF YOU stop breathing air, you will die in a few minutes. If you stop drinking water, you will die in a few days. If you stop eating food, you will die in a few weeks. If you stop feeding on Jehovah's spiritual provisions, then when you die you will be dead forever. Jehovah provides the air, water, and food that all living creatures need. Hence, to Jehovah the psalmist says: "You are opening your hand and satisfying the desire of every living thing." (Psalm 145:16) The desire of most living things is fulfilled by the material provisions. But this is not true of human creatures.

² Jesus pointed this out when he said: "Man must live, not on bread alone, but on every utterance coming forth through Jehovah's mouth." (Matthew 4:4)

1. With what provisions are most living creatures satisfied?
2. What is the desire of man's heart, and what provision is necessary for its fulfillment?

"'Test me out, please, in this respect,' Jehovah of armies has said, 'whether I shall not open to you people the floodgates of the heavens and actually empty out upon you a blessing until there is no more want.'"
—MALACHI 3:10.

The lower creations have n[o] concept of eternity, but ma[n] does, as Ecclesiastes 3:1[1] says: "Even time indefinit[e] he has put in their heart." O[r,] as the *Revised Standard Ver[-]sion* renders it: "He has pu[t] eternity into man's mind.[']

Hence, man's heartfel[t] desire is to live t[o] time indefinite, eve[n] forever. Air, water[,] and bread alone ar[e] not enough for that[.]

To live forever requires spiritual provisions based on "every utterance coming forth through Jehovah's mouth." Today, they are found in one book, the Bible, and the supply is inexhaustible—all that you need, more than you can hold. This cupboard is never bare.

³ Jesus taught us to pray for the needed material food: "Give us today our bread for this day." But soon thereafter he put spiritual matters in first place when he said: "Keep on, then, seeking first the kingdom and his righteousness." (Matthew 6:11, 33) Material food keeps us alive a day at a time; continued spiritual feeding can do it for a lifetime, and even for eternity. So do not be anxious about material things. Paul was not. He spoke of spiritual resources that enabled him to be content regardless of material circumstances, saying: "I have learned the secret of both how to be full and how to hunger, both how to have an abundance and how to suffer want. For all things I have the strength by virtue of him who imparts power to me."—Philippians 4:12, 13.

Calamity Comes to Dissatisfied Ones

⁴ Many, however, are not satisfied with Jehovah's provisions. Our first parents were not. They lived in a paradise garden—beautiful scenery delighted their eyes, fragrant flowers perfumed the air they breathed, delicious foods stimulated their taste buds, the songs of birds serenaded their ears. Moreover, they had the interesting work of caring for this garden, plus the blessing of filling the earth with perfect offspring. But they were selfish. What God had given was not enough. They wanted more. They wanted to decide for themselves what was right and what was

wrong. So they did, and the very first decision they made was calamitous, resulting in the loss of everything, for themselves and for their offspring.—Genesis 3: 1-7, 16-19.

⁵ The Israelites copied their bad example. God delivered them from slavery in Egypt, made them a nation, gave them a perfect Law, guided them in their wilderness journeyings, provided them with clothes that never wore out, and miraculously sustained them with manna that fell from heaven and water that gushed out of a rock. But they were not satisfied with Jehovah's provisions. (1 Corinthians 10:1-5) As they traveled through the wilderness, they complained time and time again.—Exodus 13:21, 22; Numbers 11: 1-6; Deuteronomy 29:5.

⁶ They still grumbled after they were established in the Promised Land—a fertile, well-watered land "flowing with milk and honey." Still ungrateful, still dissatisfied with Jehovah's provisions, they abandoned worship of him, turned to idolatrous sex worship, sacrificed their children to Molech, and brought destruction upon themselves as a nation. Restored from Babylonian captivity, they followed oral traditions that made void God's Word. They ended up killing their promised Messiah, Christ Jesus.—Deuteronomy 6:3; 8: 7-9; Judges 10:6; 1 Kings 14:22-24; 2 Kings 21:1-16; Isaiah 24:1-6; Matthew 15:3-9; 27:17-26.

⁷ Down to this day mankind generally has continued to prefer false religious creeds. The clergy despise Jehovah's name, not even using it. They dishonor

3. What did Jesus single out as most important, and what secret did Paul learn?
4. What provisions were not enough for the first human pair, and what more did they want?

5. With what did Jehovah bless the Israelites, and what was their reaction?
6. What course brought destruction upon the Israelites as a nation?
7. How have Christendom's clergy of today continued in the same course as the unfaithful priests of Malachi's time?

him with such unscriptural teachings as the Trinity, the immortal soul, and eternal torment in hellfire. Their doctrines are not only polluted with falsehoods taken from ancient Babylon and Egypt but also, in many cases, poisoned by the denial of Christ's ransom and the acceptance of evolution. They rob Jehovah of his deserved praise, just as did the priests in Malachi's day.—Malachi 1:6-8; 3:7-9.

8 Israelites back then were encouraged to cleanse themselves and return to Jehovah. "Return to me, and I will return to you," Jehovah said. He further invited them: "'Test me out, please, in this respect,' Jehovah of armies has said, 'whether I shall not open to you people the floodgates of the heavens and actually empty out upon you a blessing until there is no more want.'" (Malachi 3:7, 10) Only a remnant of the Jewish nation returned; today, a faithful remnant of spiritual Israel have come out of this world's false religions. They, together with a growing great crowd of other sheeplike worshipers, praise Jehovah as his Witnesses. (John 10:16) To them, Jehovah has kept his promise and has 'opened the floodgates of heaven and emptied out upon them blessings until there is no more want'—a veritable banquet of spiritual food!—Isaiah 25:6.

Spiritual Food in Abundance

9 "The faithful and discreet slave" Jesus foretold for our day is busily providing spiritual food in abundance. (Matthew 24: 45) Last year alone, in 208 lands and islands of the sea, and in some 200 languages, over three million of Jehovah's Witnesses made these spiritual provisions available through house-to-house visits and the distribution of hundreds of millions of books, magazines, and Bibles. Many partook of this spiritual food and were satisfied: Over 225,000 new ones were baptized in one year!

10 Jehovah's spiritual provisions have also been made available by means of district conventions, circuit assemblies, and the five weekly meetings regularly held in some 52,000 congregations of Jehovah's Witnesses—all in obedience to Paul's admonition at Hebrews 10:25 'not to forsake our gathering together.'

11 When a woman invites guests to a meal, she does not just boil a piece of meat and plop it on a plate. She uses spices and sauces to add tantalizing flavors and some decorative touches to give it eye appeal. Just its appearance and aroma are enough to make the mouth water and the gastric juices flow. That is the way Jehovah's spiritual provisions have been prepared —not in a dry, encyclopedic style, but in a tasty way to delight the mind and touch the heart. Each individual Christian should follow that example. "Does not the ear itself test out words as the palate tastes food?"—Job 12:11.

12 The Theocratic Ministry School Guidebook in its first lesson stresses using delightful words. Solomon used not only correct words but also delightful ones. (Ecclesiastes 12:10) Psalm 45:2 foretold of the Messiah, Jesus Christ: "Charm has been poured out upon your lips." It proved to be so. His hearers marveled "at the winsome words proceeding out of his mouth." They kept hanging onto him to

8. (a) What invitation did the priests of Malachi's day and the religious leaders of today reject? (b) Who did respond to the invitation, and with what result?
9. What spiritual provisions are available today, by what means, and with what result?

10. What provisions are available for heeding Paul's admonition to assemble together?
11. What illustrates the desirable way for spiritual food to be prepared?
12. What examples do we have of spiritual food being appetizingly prepared?

hear him, came early to the temple to hear him, listened to him with pleasure, were astounded at his way of teaching. Officers sent to arrest him declared: "Never has another man spoken like this." (Luke 4:22; 19:48; 21:38; Mark 12:37; Matthew 7:28; John 7:46) The *Guidebook* was provided to help us speak delightful words of truth. Do you use it to the full?

¹³ Ephesians 5:15-17 admonishes us: "Keep strict watch that how you walk is not as unwise but as wise persons, buying out the opportune time for yourselves, because the days are wicked. On this account cease becoming unreasonable, but go on perceiving what the will of Jehovah is." The Greek word here translated "time" does not mean time in just a general sense but signifies an appointed time, a seasonable time for a specific purpose. The Greek verb translated "buying out" is in the intensive form, and "in this context it probably means to 'buy up intensively'; i.e., to snap up every opportunity that comes."* Do you snap up time from your schedule to make yourself wise by partaking of Jehovah's spiritual provisions? You should. All of us should. Why? "Because the days are wicked."

From Spiritual Desert to Spiritual Paradise

¹⁴ An outstanding spiritual provision is our *New World Translation of the Holy Scriptures—With References,* released in 1984. It has many features that make it possible to use 'bought-out time' to in-

---

* See *The New International Dictionary of New Testament Theology,* Volume 1, page 268, by Colin Brown.

13. How emphatic is Ephesians 5:15-17 about 'buying out time,' and why is this stressed?
14. What Bible verse serves as an example of what feature of our English-language *New World Translation Reference Bible?*

crease our knowledge.* One example is its cross-references. Take Psalm 1:3, which deals with the condition of the man that meditates on God's law day and night. That verse reads: "He will certainly become like a tree planted by streams of water, that gives its own fruit in its season and the foliage of which does not wither, and everything he does will succeed." There is more, much more, to this verse than meets the eye of the reader who merely reads quickly and passes on.

¹⁵ Please take note: The tree is planted. Who planted it? It is by streams, plural. Does one tree grow on the banks of several streams? No. So be curious. What is this tree all about? The cross-references open the eyes of our mind. They are Isaiah 44:4, 61:3, and Jeremiah 17:8. Isaiah 44:4 says that his people will be like trees "by the water ditches." Many water ditches? Why, yes! The streams are irrigation ditches that water the trees in an orchard!

¹⁶ Isaiah 61:3 calls some of these trees "big trees of righteousness, the planting of Jehovah, for him to be beautified." Jehovah is the one who plants and irrigates these, and he is the one beautified by the fruits the trees bear! Jeremiah 17:8 likens the man who meditates on God's law day and night to "a tree planted by the waters, that sends out its roots right by the watercourse; and he will not see when heat comes, but his foliage will actually prove to be luxuriant. And in the year of drought he will not become anxious, nor will he leave off from producing fruit." Its

---

* You may not have it in your language as yet but will no doubt find interest in the above example of its use.

15. What questions are raised about the tree of Psalm 1:3, and what enlightenment does Isaiah 44:4 give?
16. What further clarification is given by Isaiah 61:3 and Jeremiah 17:8?

foliage does not wither; everything it does succeeds!

¹⁷ Now the scales fall from our eyes! Psalm 1:3 is painting a beautiful picture. Those who meditate on Jehovah's law day and night are like trees planted by an unfailing source of water. They are no longer any part of spiritually arid worldly organizations but are now associated with God's organization that is abundantly supplied with the refreshing waters of truth. Indeed, they are in a spiritual paradise, are refreshed spiritually, and are bearing spiritual fruitage to Jehovah's praise. And just think! God is using his Witnesses to direct people away from the arid, parched, worldly organizations to this refreshing, well-watered spiritual paradise.

¹⁸ To accomplish this work effectively, we must discipline our minds and hearts so as to make use of all of Jehovah's spiritual provisions. Some hear others explain Bible texts and then say: "I wish I

17. What picture now emerges concerning Psalm 1:3, and what role do we play in it?
18. How do some react when they see others excelling in witnessing, and why may they fall short?

Do You Recall?
□ How did the nation of Israel show its dissatisfaction with Jehovah's provisions?
□ How has Malachi 3:10 been fulfilled upon Jehovah's Witnesses?
□ What is the underlying meaning of Psalm 1:3?
□ Why is it essential to make use of the things learned through Jehovah's spiritual provisions?

knew the Bible as he does!" But if such ones discipline themselves to study the Bible, they too can increase in Bible knowledge. Some hear others witness at the doors and then say: "I wish I could witness at the doors the way she does!" But if they discipline themselves to share frequently in the field service, using the book *Reasoning From the Scriptures,* they too can become more skilled Witnesses. Some hear others give Bible lectures and then say: "I wish I could give talks the way he does." But, again, if these ones discipline themselves to prepare their speaking assignments well, absorbing the lessons of the *Theocratic Ministry School Guidebook,* they too will progress in speaking ability.

¹⁹ Now, to wish is fine, but wishing without working does not get the job done. It is work that makes the wish come true. Discipline yourself to buy out the time, and do the work that makes the wish come true. If you do not use a muscle, it will atrophy. If you do not use a skill, it will fade away. If you do not use your mind, thinking ability will wither. If you do not use knowledge, you will lose what you have. In each and every case, the rule is, "Use it or lose it." It is 'through use that the perceptive powers are trained.' Then "thinking ability itself will keep guard over you, discernment itself will safeguard you."—Hebrews 5:14; Proverbs 2:11.

²⁰ So use Jehovah's spiritual provisions. Rejoice with his satisfied ones. Escape the famine that Amos foretold: " 'Look! There are days coming,' is the utterance of the Sovereign Lord Jehovah, 'and I will send a famine into the land, a famine, not for bread, and a thirst, not for water, but for hearing the words of Jehovah.' " (Amos

19. What is the key to developing our potentials for witnessing?
20. By taking advantage of Jehovah's spiritual provisions, what will we avoid, and what will we gain?

Those who meditate on Jehovah's law are like trees planted by an unfailing source of water

8:11) Share with those who eat and rejoice, not with those who reject the food and suffer shame: "This is what the Sovereign Lord Jehovah has said: 'Look! My own servants will eat, but you yourselves will go hungry. Look! My own servants will drink, but you yourselves will go thirsty. Look! My own servants will rejoice, but you yourselves will suffer shame."—Isaiah 65:13.

Discipline Yields Peaceable Fruit

"No discipline seems for the present to be joyous, but grievous; yet afterward to those who have been trained by it it yields peaceable fruit, namely, righteousness."—HEBREWS 12:11.

JEHOVAH'S Word says that "it does not belong to man who is walking even to direct his step." (Jeremiah 10:23) Man says it is in him to do so, and from the outbreak

of rebellion in Eden, he has done so. From then until now, with many people it has been as it was in the days of the Judges in Israel: "What was right in his own eyes was what each one was accustomed to do." (Judges 21:25) But the words of Jehovah at Proverbs 14:12 have proved true: "There exists a way that is upright before a man,

---

1. (a) What does Jehovah's Word say about man's ability to direct his life's course, yet what does man say? (b) Who has been proved true, and who false?

but the ways of death are the end of it afterward." For 6,000 years, men have taken the way that seemed right to them, and all that time it has led to war, famine, sickness, crime, and death. History has proved Jehovah's words true and man's ways false.

[2] Imperfect people need discipline. They need it from childhood onward. God's Word says: "The one holding back his rod is hating his son, but the one loving him is he that does look for him with discipline." (Proverbs 13:24) Many child psychologists dispute this divine wisdom. Years ago one asked: "Do you mothers realize that every time you spank your child you show that you are hating your child?" Yet their permissiveness produced such a deluge of juvenile delinquents that a Brooklyn court judge made this caustic comment: "I think we need the woodshed for some young folks. But that is not considered fashionable now. Now we are told you must not strike a child; you may be stunting a genius." But their permissiveness produced no crop of geniuses—only a lawless wave of teenage criminals.

[3] Now winds of change are in the air. Burton L. White, authority on child development, says that your strictness will not cause your child to "love you less than if you were lenient. . . . Even if you spank them regularly, you will find they keep coming back to you." He stresses the child's primary need for overflowing "irrational love." Dr. Joyce Brothers reported on a study of hundreds of strictly disciplined fifth and sixth graders who believed that the strict rules "were an expression of parental love." The *Journal of Lifetime Living* said: "The child psychologists, wrangling over scheduled versus demand feeding, spanking versus non-spanking, have found that none of it makes much difference *so long as the child is loved*." Even Dr. Benjamin Spock, author of *Baby and Child Care,* took part of the blame for the lack of parental firmness and the resulting delinquency. He said blame rested on the experts, "the child psychiatrists, psychologists, teachers, social workers and pediatricians like myself."

The Rod of Discipline

[4] "Rod" as used above does not necessarily mean spanking; it represents the means of correction, whatever form it may take. *The New International Version* says on this verse: "*rod.* Probably a figure of speech for discipline of any kind." A rod is a symbol of rule or authority—in this case parental authority. A parent gets no thanks later for his permissiveness and spoiling: "If one is pampering one's servant [or child] from youth on, in his later life he will even become a thankless one." (Proverbs 29:21) To abdicate parental authority by permissiveness brings shame and shows not love but indifference; to use the rod of discipline kindly but firmly reflects loving concern. "The rod and reproof are what give wisdom; but a boy let on the loose will be causing his mother shame."—Proverbs 29:15.

[5] Referring to Proverbs 13:24, the Keil-Delitzsch *Commentary on the Old Testament* explains: "A father who truly wishes well to his son keeps him betimes under strict discipline, to give him while he is yet capable of being influenced the right direction, and to allow no errors to

2. What position do child psychologists take on spanking, but what fruitage has their permissiveness produced?
3. Based on the statements of several authorities, what trend is becoming evident?

4. Of what is the rod of discipline a symbol, and what is shown by its proper use in contrast with permissiveness?
5. (a) What does one commentary say on Proverbs 13:24, and with what other Bible text is it in agreement? (b) Who are the ones that Jesus and Jehovah discipline?

Do you wisely "listen to discipline"?

root themselves in him; but he who is indulgent toward his child when he ought to be strict, acts as if he really wished his ruin." Moffatt's *New Translation of the Bible* at Proverbs 19:18 concurs: "Chastise your son, while there is still hope of him, and do not let him run to ruin." Kind but firm discipline from early childhood reflects parental love. Jesus said: "All those for whom I have affection I reprove and discipline." As for Jehovah, "whom Jehovah loves he disciplines."—Revelation 3:19; Hebrews 12:6.

6 Discipline may at times involve spanking, but often it does not. Proverbs 8:33 does not say, "feel" discipline but, "listen to discipline and become wise." Many times discipline comes in the form of words, not spankings: "The reproofs of discipline are the way of life." "Take hold on discipline; do not let go. Safeguard it, for it itself is your life." (Proverbs 4:13; 6:23) When Jehovah's servant Job needed to be disciplined, it was accomplished by reproving words, first by Elihu and then by Jehovah himself. (Job, chapters 32-41) Job accepted the reproof and said to Jehovah: "I make a retraction, and I do repent in dust and ashes."—Job 42:6.

7 *Pai·dei'a* is the Greek word translated "discipline." In its various forms it means to train, to educate, to be "instructing with mildness." (2 Timothy 2:25) It relates more to training in conduct than to acquiring knowledge. This disciplining is to be "with all long-suffering and art of teaching." (2 Timothy 4:2) It is well exemplified in the admonition to fathers: "And you, fathers, do not be irritating your children, but go on bringing them up in the discipline and mental-regulating of Jehovah." (Ephesians 6:4) Kindly but firmly, this discipline is to regulate youth in Jehovah's way of thinking.

The Source of Discipline

8 The principles involved in disciplining children also apply to adults. The Bible is the source of information about what we

___

6. What form does discipline often take, and what examples support your answer?

7. What is the meaning of the Greek word translated "discipline," how is it to be administered, and what does it accomplish?

8. From what source and in what ways can we discipline ourselves?

The principles involved in disciplining children also apply to adults

crushed Peter: "Get behind me, Satan!" (Matthew 16: 23) Reading Watch Tower publications, attending meetings, talking with others, enduring hard experiences—all such activities may open our eyes to areas where we need to make changes. The all-important source and guide for disciplining, however, is God's Word itself.—Psalm 119: 105.

¹⁰ The proverbs of Solomon were given for people of all ages, for them "to know wisdom and discipline, to discern the sayings of understanding, to receive the discipline that gives insight, righteousness and judgment and uprightness, to give to the inexperienced ones shrewdness, to a young man knowledge and thinking ability." But perhaps a person "will not let himself be corrected by mere words, for he understands but he is paying no heed." (Proverbs 1:2-4; 29:19) Some inexperienced ones insist on learning in life's "school of hard knocks," as did the prodigal son before "he came to his senses." —Luke 15:11-17.

¹¹ Commenting on a letter that he had

should and should not be. As we read it, we can test ourselves and apply correction where needed. (2 Corinthians 13:5) As we ponder Jehovah's precepts, feelings of guilt may be stirred up in us, helping to identify needed changes for us. It did this for the psalmist: "I shall bless Jehovah, who has given me advice. Really, during the nights my kidneys ["my deepest emotions"] have corrected me." (Psalm 16:7) We may discipline ourselves as Paul did: "I pummel my body and lead it as a slave, that, after I have preached to others, I myself should not become disapproved somehow."—1 Corinthians 9:27.

⁹ Discipline may come from someone else. It may come as a look, a frown, a word, a gesture, a verbal reproof. Jesus gave Peter a look that reminded him of the prediction of his grave sin, and he went out and wept bitterly. (Luke 22:61, 62) Another time it was a rebuke in four words that

---

9. What other means are there for beneficial disciplining?

---

10. Of what value are the proverbs of Solomon for disciplining, yet what course do some insist on following?
11. (a) How were the Corinthian congregation and Jonah disciplined? (b) What disciplinary punishments were visited upon David for his adultery and cover-up efforts? (c) What words of Psalm 51 written by David show the depth of his repentance?

previously written to the Christian congregation at Corinth, Paul said: "You were saddened into repenting; for you were saddened in a godly way, . . . [and it resulted in the] righting of the wrong." (2 Corinthians 7:9-11) Jonah was disciplined by means of an ocean storm and a big fish. (Jonah 1:2, 3, 12, 17; 2:10; 3:1-4) David's adultery and attempts at a cover-up brought disciplinary punishments upon him, as shown at 2 Samuel 12:9-14. His repentance was movingly expressed in these words from the 51st Psalm: 'Wash me from my error, cleanse me from my sin. My sin is in front of me constantly. Wipe out all my errors, create in me a pure heart, put within me a new spirit. Do not throw me away from before your face. A heart broken and crushed, O God, you will not despise.'—Verses 2, 3, 9-11, 17.

¹² With some persons more drastic measures may be necessary, as Proverbs 26:3 indicates: "A whip is for the horse, a bridle is for the ass, and the rod is for the back of stupid people." At times Jehovah let his nation of Israel be subdued by the troubles they brought upon themselves: "They had behaved rebelliously against the sayings of God; and the counsel of the Most High they had disrespected. So with trouble he proceeded to subdue their heart; they stumbled, and there was no one helping. And they began calling to Jehovah for help in their distress; out of the stresses upon them he as usual saved them." (Psalm 107:11-13) Some stupid ones, however, harden themselves beyond the reach of any kind of healing discipline: "A man repeatedly reproved but making his neck hard will suddenly be broken, and that without healing." —Proverbs 29:1.

12. What more drastic measures are needed for some, and what is the outcome for those who reject repeated reproofs?

Giving and Receiving Reproof

¹³ Whatever form the discipline may take, it should never be given in anger. In fact, rather than helping, "anger stirs up contention." We are also advised: "He that is slow to anger is abundant in discernment, but one that is impatient is exalting foolishness." Moreover, "the insight of a man certainly slows down his anger, and it is beauty on his part to pass over transgression." (Proverbs 29:22; 14:29; 19:11) When needed, discipline should never be excessive. Give it at the proper time and to the proper degree—not too soon, not too late, not too little, not too much.

¹⁴ Here are some guidelines for those giving reproof: "Do not severely criticize an older man. To the contrary, entreat him as a father, younger men as brothers, older women as mothers, younger women as sisters with all chasteness." (1 Timothy 5:1, 2) Do you entreat, not browbeat? "Brothers, even though a man takes some false step before he is aware of it, you who have spiritual qualifications try to readjust such a man in a spirit of mildness, as you each keep an eye on yourself, for fear you also may be tempted." (Galatians 6:1) Do we counsel in mildness, always aware of our own frailties? "Always treat others as you would like them to treat you." (Matthew 7:12, *The New English Bible*) Do you put yourself in the other one's place, showing empathy?

¹⁵ Receiving reproof requires humility. Does it seem picky, unfair, unjust? Do not be hasty. Think about it. Do not be negative. Reflect on it positively. If not all seems valid, is part of it? Open your mind to be receptive; evaluate it objectively. Are

13. What should we avoid in giving reproof, and how should it be given?
14. What other guidelines are given for those offering reproof?
15. What does receiving reproof require, and what additional counsel is given to those being reproved?

you being overly sensitive, too quickly offended? It may take time to see it in a positive light, after any initial hurt or offense has subsided. So wait. Hold your tongue. Calmly evaluate what was said. Is it possible that you are prejudiced against the one giving the counsel, and you rejected it on that basis? Nevertheless, see it as well meant and not to be summarily rejected.

¹⁶ Here are some scriptures to reflect on when you are reproved: "Anyone holding back his sayings is possessed of knowledge, and a man of discernment is cool of spirit." (Proverbs 17:27) Do you listen and remain cool? "The way of the foolish one is right in his own eyes, but the one listening to counsel is wise." (Proverbs 12:15) Do you quickly decide that you are right, or do you listen receptively? "Be swift about hearing, slow about speaking, slow about wrath." (James 1:19) Do you follow these words when counseled? "Do not hurry yourself in your spirit to become offended, for the taking of offense is what rests in the bosom of the stupid ones." (Ecclesiastes 7:9) Are you quick to take offense? How lovely if we can feel as the psalmist did: "Should the righteous one strike me, it would be a loving-kindness; and should he reprove me, it would be oil upon the head, which my head would not want to refuse."—Psalm 141:5.

Endure Discipline and Reap Peaceable Fruit

¹⁷ Discipline is not always easy to take. It may involve some embarrassment and bring some restrictions. It may even cause you some grief. But endure all of this. It will

16. (a) What scriptures and related questions should we consider when receiving counsel? (b) What feeling expressed by the psalmist might we imitate?
17. Why is discipline not always easy to take, yet how will keeping Hebrews 12:7, 11 in mind help us endure it?

pass; joy comes afterward. Remember: "It is for discipline you are enduring. God is dealing with you as with sons. For what son is he that a father does not discipline? True, no discipline seems for the present to be joyous, but grievous; yet afterward to those who have been trained by it it yields peaceable fruit, namely, righteousness."—Hebrews 12:7, 11.

¹⁸ So if the discipline is grievous and hard to endure, wait for the peaceable fruit that comes afterward. Wait for Jehovah, as did Jeremiah: "Without fail your soul will remember and bow low over me. This is what I shall bring back to my heart. That is why I shall show a waiting attitude." (Lamentations 3:20, 21) Remember what the psalmist in distress said to himself: "Why are you in despair, O my soul, and why are you boisterous within me? Wait for God, for I shall yet laud him as the grand salvation of my person."—Psalm 42:5, 11; 43:5.

¹⁹ So when disciplined, let each one of us wait for God. After we have been trained by it, we will reap the harvest of peaceable fruit, namely, righteousness.

18, 19. What strong feelings did both Jeremiah and the psalmist express that set a proper course for us when we are undergoing discipline?

Do You Recall?

□ What is the value of using the rod of discipline?

□ What is the main source of discipline? What are other sources of discipline?

□ In addition to words of reproof, what stronger measures may be needed?

□ What are some guidelines for giving reproof?

□ What counsel will help us to accept reproof?

Kingdom Proclaimers Report

A Chief Speaks Up

IT IS encouraging to know that there are still men in high station in this world who love honesty and justice and who speak out to uphold these qualities. An example is a chief in an African country where the work of Jehovah's Witnesses is restricted. Let the report tell us:

"Recently different religious groups held an interdenominational convention in our town, and this included Catholics, Presbyterians, Pentecostals, and so forth. The Paramount Chief was invited to address the convention toward the closing sessions. To the surprise of the whole gathering, he told them, among other things, to imitate the honesty and high moral standards of Jehovah's Witnesses, adding that if all were like Jehovah's Witnesses, there would be peace in the nation.

"The next day leading members of the churches represented at the convention came to the Chief's palace and protested vehemently against the part of his address that praised the Witnesses and asked him if he was not aware that the Witnesses had been banned in the country. The Chief replied in the affirmative but told them that he found no fault in Jehovah's Witnesses. He went on to say: 'For all my years as Paramount Chief, not once has one of Jehovah's Witnesses been brought to my court for gross wrongdoing. On the other hand, if cassava is stolen from a farm, it often turns out that a Catholic is the thief. If yam is stolen, it is a Presbyterian who is responsible. Members of your church have polluted my land with abortions, and yet not one of Jehovah's Witnesses has been brought to my court for such offenses. Do not God's laws forbid such evils, or are the churches no longer bound by God's law?' The clergymen had no answer.

"Later, the Paramount Chief called representatives of Jehovah's Witnesses and exhorted them to take good care of themselves so that no reproach is brought upon the name of their God and upon his own name as the Paramount Chief who has spoken up for Jehovah's Witnesses."

The report states that now many new ones are taking their stand for the truth. One Witness states that he has recently been able to start Bible studies with three chiefs in the area, one of them being the Paramount Chief, and all three are attending meetings of Jehovah's Witnesses!

Jehovah God takes note of those who love truth and righteousness and speak up in behalf of his servants.—Matthew 10:42.

The Reformation Waters Burst Forth

"**S**UDDENLY I heard another sound, as if of thunder, rushing toward us. Our family . . . started to run frantically to a nearby hill. The foaming waters overtook us. We swam as never before. Though gulping down a quantity of seawater . . . , we made it."

This is how one Filipino recounted a terrifying experience that changed his world. You have probably never been hit by a natural disaster—of water or any other kind. But a look at history reveals that millions of lives have been reshaped by cataclysms of one form or another.

Religion has also witnessed a number of tremendous upheavals, turning upside down the daily lot of countless people. These have included Hindus, Buddhists, Muslims, Jews, and Christians. Has your life been affected by such turmoil? Almost certainly it has, wherever you happen to live. Let us illustrate this by journeying back some 400 years in time to the 16th century. First of all we focus our attention on Europe, which was then churning with dissent, like a whirlpool gathering speed.

A Growing Swell

For centuries, leading up to what we call the Reformation, the Roman Catholic Church and European monarchs had vied with one another, each claiming authority over the other and over the populace. A body of people on the continent raised their voices in objection to what they saw as abuses by the church.

What sort of abuses did they see? Greed, flagrant immorality, and interference in politics. Common folk were indignant at men and women who on the one hand claimed special privileges by reason of their vows of poverty and chastity but at the same time flouted the law by being openly corrupt and immoral. Noblemen in England were incensed at the rather strange situation of having to pay tribute to a pope who was then living in and allied with France, England's enemy at war.

The corruption within the Catholic Church seeped down from the top. Historian Barbara W. Tuchman writes in her book *The March of Folly* that the six popes who were in office from 1471 onward carried on "an excess of venality, amorality, avarice, and spectacularly calamitous power politics." Barbara Tuchman further describes how Pope Sixtus IV, in order to elevate and enrich his hitherto poor family, appointed five nephews and a grandnephew as cardinals, another grandnephew as bishop, and married six of his other relatives into ruling families. Alexander VI, when he became pope, was known to have had several mistresses and seven children. In his determination to be elected to office, he bribed his two main rivals, one of them receiving "four muleloads of bullion," writes Barbara Tuchman. He later presided over a Vatican banquet that became "famous in the annals of pornography." The same work then outlines how famous sculptor Michelangelo was commissioned by Pope Julius II to model a statue of him. When asked by the

craftsman if the statue should show him holding a book, the warrior pope replied: "Put a sword there. I know nothing of letters."

Breach in the Dam

Ordinary Europeans still desired spiritual guidance. Observing the various echelons of power locked in a frenzy of self-gratification, these more lowly ones turned to an alternative source of authority, one they considered superior to all others—the Bible. According to author Joel Hurstfield, the Reformation was "in the profoundest sense a crisis of authority." Appalled at the corruption in the church, preachers and friars in Italy took to speaking publicly on the need for reform. But nowhere were the waters of discontent gathering more ominously than in Germany.

In pagan times, Germanic tribes had a tradition whereby money could be paid to effect release from punishment for crimes. With the expansion of the Roman faith, the custom found accommodation within the church in the form of indulgences. This allowed a sinner to buy from the pope the value of dead "saints'" merits and apply these against temporal penalties for sins committed. Under financial pressure, caused by wars against France and by extensive building works in Rome, Pope Leo X authorized the sale of indulgences, offering total remission of temporal penalties for sin. An indignant Martin Luther expounded his now famous 95 theses on the false teachings of the church. The movement toward reform, which had started as a trickle some generations before, became a torrent as more and more people gave their support.

In the 16th century, individuals such as Luther in Germany, Zwingli and Calvin in Switzerland, and Knox in Scotland became rallying points for many who saw the chance to purify Christianity and return to the original values and standards of the Bible. A term was coined in Germany to describe those who refused to acknowledge restrictions placed on faith by Roman Catholic princes, and who avowed allegiance to God above anyone else. This term later came to include all who lent support to the Reformation movement. The term was "Protestant."

Protestantism swept through Europe with breathtaking speed, reshaping the religious landscape, sketching new theological boundaries. Germany and Switzerland led the way, quickly followed by Scotland, Sweden, Norway, and Denmark.

There were reformation movements in Austria, Bohemia, Poland, Transylvania, the Netherlands, and France.

In England discontent had been surfacing for more than a century, since the days of John Wycliffe and the Lollards. But when the break from the Catholic Church finally came, it was for more mundane reasons. The king resolved to change not his religion but his wife. In 1534 Henry VIII declared himself head of the new Church of England. His motives were different from those of the continental dissenters, but his action nonetheless opened the floodgates for the waters of religious change to flow into Britain. All over Europe, these waters swiftly turned red with the blood of thousands who were stretched on the rack of religious polarization.

Wherever the urge for reform took hold, church properties and estates caught the eye. Within just four years, the English Crown confiscated 560 monasteries, some having huge incomes. Other countries saw kings as well as laymen taking over church lands. When Rome itself was sacked, cruelty knew no bounds. "The ferocity and bloodthirstiness of the attackers 'would have moved a stone to compassion,'" is how Barbara Tuchman describes it. "Screams and groans filled every quarter; the Tiber floated with dead bodies." Minorities, both Catholic and Protestant, were brutally persecuted. In Bohemia, Protestants were expropriated, whereas in Ireland it was the Catholics' turn. Protestant French Huguenots were hounded, as were Scottish Presbyterians and English Puritans. It seemed as if a senseless merry-go-round of slaughter had been set in motion, and religion was the chief lubricant. Would the atrocities never stop?

The church had no olive branch to offer. But the monarchs, tired of the drain of civil war, reached agreements that formalized the boundaries between opposing faiths. The Peace of Augsburg in 1555 and the Peace of Westphalia in 1648 brought religious and national frontiers into unison, allowing the local prince to decide which faith his populace was to follow. Europe thus embarked upon a new epoch, one which was to last some 300 years. Not until the end of World War II was influence in Europe to be totally redefined by the then victorious Allies.

The yearning for religious freedom and reform had built up pressure behind the dam of church restraint. After centuries of unyielding constraint, the waters finally burst forth, cascading through the valleys of Europe, leaving a devastated landscape in their wake. When the swell settled, guidance in matters of faith in Protestant lands had been swept away from the clergy and lay beached on the shores of secular powers. Europe was still drenched in religious intolerance, though, and refugees fled from one country to another. The continent could no longer embrace the loosened waters. They soon began to spill abroad. The 17th century offered a channel for the overflow. The New World was being colonized.

Spillover Funneled Abroad

"One of the prime causes for early migration to America," writes A. P. Stokes in *Church and State in the United States,* "was the desire for religious freedom." People were tired of the harassment. Baptists, Quakers, Roman Catholics, Huguenots, Puritans, Mennonites, and others all were willing to put up with the rigors of the voyage and to take a plunge into the unknown. Stokes quotes one as saying: "I yearned for a country where I could be free to worship God according to what the Bible taught me." The measure of intolerance these emigrants left behind can be judged by the hardships they were willing to endure. According to historian David Hawke in *The Colonial Experience,* a heartbreaking departure from the home country was likely to be followed by "two, three, or four months spent with daily expectation of swallowing waves and cruel pirates." Thereafter, the weather-beaten traveler would be "landed among barbarous Indians, famous for nothing but cruelty . . . [and would remain] in a famishing condition for a long space."

Individuals reached out for freedom, the colonial powers for wealth. Regardless of motive, settlers took with them their own religion. Germany, Holland, and Britain made North America a Protestant stronghold. Particularly the British government wanted "to prevent Roman Catholicism . . . from getting the upper hand in North America." Canada came under the influence of both France and Britain. The policy of the French government was that of "keeping New France in the Roman Catholic faith," even refusing to allow Huguenots to immigrate to Quebec. Southern Africa and parts of West Africa came under Protestant influence. This influence increased with the passage of time as Australia, New Zealand, and many Pacific islands were added to the Protestant fold.

Spain and Portugal were already Catholicizing South and Central America. French and Portuguese hoisted the Catholic banner in Central Africa. In India, Goa was under Portuguese influence, so Catholicism took root there.

The Society of Jesus (Jesuits) was formed in the 16th century to advance the Catholic cause. By the middle of the 18th century, there were over 22,000 Jesuits working all over the globe, and they even solidified Catholic influence in China and Japan.

The New Panorama

Unleashed water has tremendous power, as the witness quoted at the beginning of this article testified. It flattens landscapes, carves new valleys and ravines, smashes obstacles in its path. A raging torrent knows no master, cannot be controlled or directed. It was just so with the Reformation deluge.

"What happened . . . was, therefore, not so much the triumph of a new separatist faith," states G. R. Elton in *The Reformation Crisis,* "as the general and gradual acceptance of a divided Christendom which no one had wanted." Christendom was split, storm tossed, sapped of its strength. Allegiance became more closely tied to local monarchs and to smaller national churches. The long-established rule from Rome had been undermined. Nationalism took root in the sodden landscape of Protestantism. Britain and the United States, firmly in the hands of Protestant secular leaders, together formed the seventh world power of Bible history, taking hold of the rudder in the 18th century.

However, the Reformation movement did not do the very thing that it had been hoped it would accomplish. What was that? With the passage of time, basic doctrines of Protestant churches, whether national churches or otherwise, fell largely into line with those of Rome. Early reformers had dreamed of returning to Bible standards, to pure Christianity. As the wave of support grew in size and momentum, confusion in direction simply poured cold water on those dreams.

The ground swell of the Reformation waters has left trenches even in our 20th century. Can you identify some of them? Still more important, we stand on the brink of a final worldwide religious upheaval. Religion's past is catching up with it. Will you then survive to peruse the new horizon? These questions will be answered in a November issue of this magazine.

I Have Seen That Jehovah Is Good

As told by Lennart Johnson

ON SUNDAY, July 26, 1931, the second president of the Watch Tower Bible and Tract Society, J. F. Rutherford, delivered the talk "The Kingdom, the Hope of the World" at the Columbus, Ohio, coliseum. Our family in Rockford, Illinois, listened to it on the radio. I was only 14 years old, but this program lifted, as it were, a thick curtain from my eyes.

Though my father was interested in the Kingdom message, and later my brother too, my mother was always indifferent. Father died the following year, in 1932. Other Watch Tower broadcasts kept feeding me spiritually, but it was not until April 1933 that I found the place where Jehovah's Witnesses met, miles away on the other side of the river.

What a surprise it was for the small group there to see a slim teenager bicycle up to their meeting for a study in *Vindication* Book Two! At each meeting, I kept learning more and was glad two months later to start going from door to door with the Kingdom message. I was baptized at a regional (now circuit) assembly that same year.

After school each day, I would spend an hour or so visiting the neighbors in the area around our home with the Kingdom message. I also had opportunity to witness in school. For example, one course echoed the hellfire and torment theory. This prompted me to provide Scriptural proof that the dead are not suffering but, rather, are not conscious and are in their graves with the prospect of the resurrection. The teacher allowed me to read my extensive composition before the entire class.

The Full-Time Ministry

In May 1935, I attended the Washington, D.C., convention, where pioneering (the full-time ministry) was emphasized. On returning home, I wrote to the Watch Tower Society, and they not only sent back a list of available territories but also, to my surprise, included several plans for building a house trailer. In those days pioneering often meant going to new areas, and a trailer provided one a place in which to live. So I decided to work toward getting a car and a trailer so that I might pursue the full-time ministry.

In the meantime, I became involved in using a sound car that our congregation had acquired to advertise the Kingdom message. When another brother and I were invited up to Monroe, Wisconsin, to use it, I met and soon afterward married Virginia Ellis. Now we could work together to get that car and trailer to use in the pioneer work!

In the fall of 1938 my mother died, and about then Harold Woodworth wrote us from New Mexico: "Come on out here; the need is great." So we set out for New Mexico, which was an overland trip of about a thousand miles. At one address along the way, a telegram reached us. "Come back home," it urged. I was offered a well-paying job with excellent chances for advancement. I tore the telegram up. If Jehovah had helped us to prepare for pioneering, I was not going to let anything interfere!

In March 1939 we began our pioneer service around Hobbs, New Mexico. This was cattle country; there were also many new oil-field settlements to visit in this area. The small congregation had meetings on Friday and Sunday, so we would take along literature, water, food, a small stove, and a folding cot and spend Monday through Friday afternoon preaching in the rurals. When night came, we slept in the wilds with the sky as a roof and an oil-field "torch" nearby to scare away the rattlesnakes. We spent the weekends in town working with the congregation.

After several months of this schedule, the Society sent us on to Roswell and then to Albuquerque, New Mexico. Here we again used the sound car, which was particularly effective in witnessing to Indian villages in the area. When the new work of street witnessing with our magazines began early in 1940, we were glad to share in it with the brothers in Albuquerque.

Opposition During War Hysteria

The second world war had begun in Europe the previous September, and a period of vicious opposition followed because of our neutral stand toward participation in the war. Once my shirt was literally torn off my back while I was sharing in the ministry.

It was Jehovah who gave his servants the victory!

In the summer of 1940, brothers were working with the magazines near El Paso, Texas, and a number of them were arrested. The following Monday, Harold Woodworth and I went to help them during their trial. By questioning the brothers before the court, I was able to bring out pertinent points in their defense. After all of them were declared innocent, the newspaper report referred to me as a "promising young lawyer from Albuquerque." But really, it was Jehovah who gave his servants the victory that day!

Similarly, our brothers were jailed for preaching in another city. After I appeared in court in their defense, Brother David Gray and I took a letter to each city official. The letter noted the legal right of Jehovah's Witnesses to do their work, and it warned that if the Witnesses continued to be harassed, the officials would be held responsible for any damages that might result.

The mayor received the letter and read it without comment, but the chief of police told us: 'Out here in the West, people take a trip out of town, and . . . well . . . others look for them later, and they can never be found.' The threat was not carried out, however; rather, things quieted down, and the court action against the brothers was dropped.

About this time I was appointed by the Watch Tower Society as a zone servant (now called circuit overseer). My assignment covered much of New Mexico and a portion of Texas.

Gilead and a Foreign Assignment

In 1943 Virginia and I received an invitation to attend the second class of the Watchtower Bible School of Gilead. After graduation in January 1944, we were at first assigned to work with the Flatbush Congregation in Brooklyn, New York. We lived behind the Society's factory in an old building that was later demolished to enlarge the Adams Street factory facility.

All the loyal ones greatly cherished the spiritual strength that Jehovah kept giving them

---

In time, however, we received our assignment to the Dominican Republic, where Rafael Leónidas Trujillo Molina was the absolute dictator. When we arrived on Sunday, April 1, 1945, Virginia and I were the only Witnesses in the country. We went to the Victoria Hotel and acquired accommodations—$5 a day for the two of us, including meals. That very afternoon we started our first home Bible study.

It happened this way: Two Dominican women with whom we had studied the Bible in Brooklyn had given us the names of relatives and acquaintances, one of whom was a Dr. Green. When we visited him, we also met his neighbor Moses Rollins. After telling them how we got their names and addresses, they listened intently to the Kingdom message and agreed to a Bible study. Soon Moses became the first local Kingdom publisher.

That very evening Dr. Green took us house hunting from the upper deck of a two-story bus. We finally rented a small concrete home there in the capital, Ciudad Trujillo (now Santo Domingo). In June four more missionaries joined us. A second missionary home was opened, and then more missionaries arrived. By August 1946 we had a peak of 28 publishers. Soon many more missionaries arrived, and homes were opened for them too. The increase was on!

Serving Under Ban

By 1950 we had grown to well over 200 publishers. However, because Jehovah's Witnesses maintain a position of strict neutrality, Trujillo's government began putting our young brothers in prison. Then, to top it all off, a total ban was placed on the work of Jehovah's Witnesses on June 21, 1950.

Unable to meet in Kingdom Halls, the brothers began meeting quietly in small groups in private homes. There we studied *Watchtower* articles that were produced by mimeograph. All the loyal ones greatly cherished the spiritual strength that Jehovah kept giving them in these small study groups.

In Our Next Issue

- Is Religion a Force for Moral Good?

- Setting Matters Straight Between God and You

- Opening the Way to Increase in Gibraltar

Virginia and I worked with many faithful brothers from all parts of Puerto Rico

Sunday was our day to visit the many Dominican brothers in Trujillo's prisons. We would be frisked on entry, with our full identification being duly noted. Sometimes soldiers would surround us when we were with these brothers, watching us carefully. On one occasion we were joined by Stanley Aniol from Chicago, who was visiting his missionary daughter Mary (now Mary Adams, serving at Brooklyn Bethel). Moved by the integrity of the young Dominican brothers, Brother Aniol tenderly kissed all of them before the eyes of the onlooking soldiers.

At the end of the visit, as we were walking down the main business street, a car full of Trujillo's men followed us at a snail's pace. This was one of Trujillo's well-known methods of trying to instill fear in people. When we told Brother Aniol what they were up to, it did not shake him in the least. Indeed, it was necessary to ignore Trujillo's efforts to intimidate and to put full confidence in Jehovah.

At times impostors, Trujillo's spies, would call at our door, claiming to be brothers. So we had to be "cautious as serpents and yet innocent as doves." (Matthew 10:16) We would test such persons with searching questions to determine whether they were really our brothers or not.

During the ban several speakers would each give Memorial talks at three different study groups, traveling as unobtrusively as possible from one location to the other. Often we had torrential rains on Memorial night, and since Trujillo's army of spies were as afraid of a heavy rain as people in other places are of a severe blizzard, it was a blessing to us.

Since reentry into the country would have been refused by Trujillo's government, most of the missionaries did not attend the international conventions in New York City in 1950 and 1953. We had to be content with the convention coverage in *The New York Times,* which provided beautiful convention pictures and detailed day-by-day descriptions of the program. Also, a local theater gave a lengthy showing of the large baptism at the 1953 convention.

In 1956 Roy Brandt and I were called in for official questioning. Officials of the Trujillo government had earlier invited Brother Manuel Hierrezuelo to come and see them. But later Manuel was returned to his family as a corpse. So now, how would things work out for us?

Upon arriving, we were questioned

separately, our answers evidently being recorded. Nothing more took place then, but two months later the newspapers announced that the Trujillo government was removing the ban on Jehovah's Witnesses and that we could resume our activities publicly. Kingdom Halls were again located, and Jehovah's work kept on progressing.

However, in June 1957 a violent new wave of persecution began, and all the missionaries were expelled from the country. Our departure was indeed a sad day for us. Virginia and I had served 12 years in the Dominican Republic and had seen the number of Witnesses grow from just the two of us to well over 600. In 1960 the second ban was removed, and the number of publishers continued to grow until now it is about 10,000!

Serving in Puerto Rico

When we arrived in Puerto Rico in August 1957, our Christian brothers as well as newspaper reporters were on hand to receive us. The resulting press accounts gave a wide witness. At the time, there were fewer than 1,200 Kingdom publishers in Puerto Rico; now there are nearly 22,000!

In 1958 the Society invited me to become a traveling overseer. Thus, over the years we came to know and work with many faithful brothers from all parts of Puerto Rico and the Virgin Islands. In due course, my wife and I became members of the local Bethel family. And since the formation of the Branch Committee here, Jehovah has favored me with being a member of it.

It fills me with happiness to have received personally from Jehovah the foretold "hundredfold now . . . brothers and sisters and mothers and children." (Mark 10:30) I never have wanted to spend my life in any other way than in his service. And so, as I look back on the some 48 years since I began to pioneer, I rejoice to say that, indeed, I have seen that Jehovah is good!—Psalm 34:8.

> While the above life story of Lennart Johnson was in final preparation, Virginia Johnson died peacefully in her sleep on January 31, 1987

Questions From Readers

■ Why did Jesus say that a proselyte of the Pharisees was "a subject for Gehenna twice as much so" as the Pharisees?

Evidently, Gentiles who converted to the Pharisaic sect of Judaism were very reprehensible. Some of them may previously have had God's disapproval, but on becoming Pharisees, they became doubly disapproved, certainly headed for destruction in Gehenna.

The Valley of Hinnom was south/southwest of Jerusalem's walls. It had at times been used for idolatry and human sacrifices. (2 Chronicles 28:1-3; 33:1-6; Jeremiah 32:35) So it became a place for waste disposal, including bodies of criminals viewed as unfit for burial with the prospect of a resurrection.—Compare Matthew 5:22.

The New Bible Dictionary (edited by J. D. Douglas, 1962) says that the 'valley of Hinnom was situated outside Jerusalem, where children had been sacrificed by fire to Molech. It became a prophetic symbol for judgment and later for final punishment.' Jesuit John L. McKenzie, in his Dictionary of the Bible (1965), adds: "Because of this [cultic shrine for human sacrifice] Jeremiah cursed the place and predicted that it would be a place of death and corruption (7:32; 19:6 ff). This valley is referred to, not by name in Is[aiah] 66:24, as a place where the dead bodies of the rebels against Yahweh shall lie . . . In rabbinical literature, however, the eternal fire is not surely eternal punishment . . . [Gehenna] is a place where the wicked are destroyed body and soul, which perhaps echoes the idea of annihilation (Mt 10:28)."

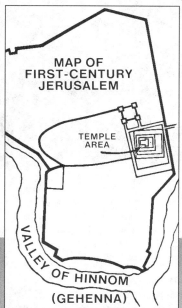

MAP OF
FIRST-CENTURY
JERUSALEM

TEMPLE
AREA

VALLEY OF HINNOM
(GEHENNA)

When we read accounts such as Matthew 15:1-8; John 8: 12-19, 31-41; 9:13-34; 11:45-53, we can understand why Jesus said that the Pharisees merited annihilation, symbolized by Gehenna. True, some might repent and win God's approval, but as a class, they were worthy of permanent destruction. Christ said: "Woe to you, scribes and Pharisees, hypocrites! because you traverse sea and dry land to make one proselyte, and when he becomes one you make him a subject for Gehenna twice as much so as yourselves."—Matthew 23:15.

So much for the Jewish Pharisees, but how would those who became proselytes be 'subjects for Gehenna twice as much' as the Pharisees? These proselytes were not Gentiles who were simply sympathetic toward the Jews or even those who converted and were circumcised. (Luke 7:2-10; Mark 7:24-30; Acts 8:26-34; 10: 1, 2) No, Jesus was not speaking

of proselytes to Judaism but of proselytes to hypocritical Pharisaism. What had their state become?

Some of these may formerly have been gross sinners or fanatical worshipers of demon gods, thus having God's serious disapproval. Perhaps some were even in line for Gehenna because they had somehow sinned against God's spirit. (Matthew 12:32) If their situation before Jehovah had not yet reached that stage, they took a step for the worse. They converted to follow the extremism of the Pharisees. These proselytes immersed themselves in hypocritical ritual and extreme views that overruled any moral goodness and truth that other converts to Judaism might have gained. Evidently, these proselyte Pharisees became more extreme than their condemned teachers. So if the Jewish Pharisees were 'subjects for Gehenna,' these proselytes were more so or, as Jesus expressed it, doubly so.

Pictorial Archive (Near Eastern History) Est.

◀ *A portion of the Valley of Hinnom today*

TO CULTIVATE in their youngsters a desire to learn, wise parents make fine literature readily available to them. Many, for example, see to it that their children have a personal subscription for the Bible journal *The Watchtower*, which is used as the basis for weekly Bible discussions at meetings of Jehovah's Witnesses. But at what age should a child be provided a personal subscription?

Earlier this year, the following letter was received from a mother: "This subscription is for our two-year-old son. During the *Watchtower* Study, he must have his own copy. I've tried to give him another one when we didn't have an extra copy, but he would notice that the pictures didn't match, and he wanted the issue we were using. I'm sure the beautiful color pictures impress even a young child and will help his early appreciation of the spiritual food he can't understand as yet."

the Watchtower

October 15, 1987

Announcing Jehovah's Kingdom

Is Religion
a Force for Moral Good?

The Watchtower

Announcing Jehovah's Kingdom

October 15, 1987
Vol. 108, No. 20

In This Issue

Photos, pages 10, 31: Pictorial Archive (Near Eastern History) Est.

THE PURPOSE OF *THE WATCHTOWER* is to exalt Jehovah God as the Sovereign of the universe. It keeps watch on world events as they fulfill Bible prophecy. It comforts all peoples with the good news that God's Kingdom will soon destroy those who oppress their fellowmen and that it will turn the earth into a paradise. It encourages faith in the now-reigning King, Jesus Christ, whose shed blood opens the way for mankind to gain eternal life. *The Watchtower*, published by Jehovah's Witnesses continuously since 1879, is nonpolitical. It adheres to the Bible as its authority.

WATCHTOWER STUDIES FOR THE WEEKS

November 15: Setting Matters Straight Between God and You. Page 10. Songs to Be Used: 10, 45.

November 22: Will You Say, "Here I Am! Send Me"? Page 15. Songs to Be Used: 204, 57.

November 29: Talk About the Glory of God's Kingship. Page 22. Songs to Be Used: 162, 56.

Average Printing Each Issue: 12,315,000

Now Published in 103 Languages

SEMIMONTHLY LANGUAGES AVAILABLE BY MAIL
Afrikaans, Arabic, Cebuano, Chichewa, Chinese, Cibemba, Danish,* Dutch,* Efik, English,* Finnish,* French,* German,* Greek,* Hiligaynon, Igbo, Iloko, Italian,* Japanese,* Korean, Lingala, Malagasy, Maltese, Norwegian, Portuguese,* Russian, Sepedi, Sesotho, Shona, Spanish,* Swahili, Swedish,* Tagalog, Thai, Tsonga, Tswana, Xhosa, Yoruba, Zulu

MONTHLY LANGUAGES AVAILABLE BY MAIL
Armenian, Bengali, Bicol, Bislama, Bulgarian, Croatian, Czech, Ewe, Fijian, Ga, Greenlandic, Gujarati, Gun, Hausa, Hebrew, Hindi, Hiri Motu, Hungarian, Icelandic, Kannada, Malayalam, Marathi, New Guinea Pidgin, Pangasinan, Papiamento, Polish, Rarotongan, Romanian, Samar-Leyte, Samoan, Sango, Serbian, Silozi, Sinhalese, Slovenian, Solomon Islands-Pidgin, Tahitian, Tamil, Telugu, Tongan, Tshiluba, Turkish, Twi, Ukrainian, Urdu, Venda, Vietnamese

* Study articles also available in large-print edition.

	Yearly subscription for the above:	
	Semimonthly	Monthly
Watch Tower Society offices	Languages	Languages
America, U.S., Watchtower, Wallkill, N.Y. 12589	$5.00	$2.50
Australia, Box 280, Ingleburn, N.S.W. 2565	A$7.00	A$3.50
Canada, Box 4100, Halton Hills, Ontario L7G 4Y4	$7.00	$3.50
England, The Ridgeway, London NW7 1RN	£5.00	£2.50
Ireland, 29A Jamestown Road, Finglas, Dublin 11	IR£6.00	IR£3.00
New Zealand, P.O. Box 142, Manurewa	NZ$15.00	NZ$7.50
Nigeria, PMB 001, Shomolu, Lagos State	₦8.00	₦4.00
Philippines, P.O. Box 2044, Manila 2800	₱60.00	₱30.00
South Africa, Private Bag 2067, Krugersdorp, 1740	R9.00	R4.50

Remittances should be sent to the office in your country or to Watchtower, Wallkill, N.Y. 12589, U.S.A.

Changes of address should reach us 30 days before your moving date. Give us your old and new address (if possible, your old address label).

25 cents (U.S.) a copy

The Bible translation used is the *New World Translation of the Holy Scriptures,* unless otherwise indicated.

The Watchtower (ISSN 0043-1087) is published semimonthly for $5.00 (U.S.) per year by Watch Tower Bible and Tract Society of Pennsylvania, 25 Columbia Heights, Brooklyn, N.Y. 11201. Second-class postage paid at Brooklyn, N.Y., and at additional mailing offices.

Postmaster: Send address changes to Watchtower, **Wallkill, N.Y. 12589.**

Published by
**Watch Tower Bible and Tract Society
of Pennsylvania**
25 Columbia Heights, Brooklyn, N.Y. 11201, U.S.A.
Frederick W. Franz, President

Is Religion / *a Force for Moral Good?*

IN ANSWER to this question, millions would agree with George Bernard Shaw, who wrote: "Religion is a great force —the only real motive force in the world." Contrariwise, 19th-century English author John Ruskin, writing on the basis for honesty, satirized: *"A knave's religion is* always *the rottenest thing about him."* Which view do you think is closer to the truth?

As evidence for religion's moral force, someone might point to an individual who became a "changed man" when he 'dedicated his life to Jesus Christ.' That is how an international magazine described the "conversion" of Charles Colson, who had been involved in the Watergate scandal. Someone else might point to those who claim that their religion saved them from a life of prostitution or alcoholism. In non-Christian lands, millions of Bibles have been distributed, which undoubtedly has helped many people to improve their lives morally. Evidently, religion has exerted a good moral influence on such persons.

The Negative Side

On the other hand, Hitler's religion was not much of a deterrent to him. This led sincere persons to wonder why an appeal made to Pope Pius XII to excommunicate Hitler was never answered. The *Catholic Telegraph-Register* of Cincinnati, Ohio, under the heading "Reared as Catholic but Violates Faith Says Cable to Pope," reported: "An appeal has been made to Pius XII that Reichsfuehrer Adolph Hitler be excommunicated." If this action had been taken, might it have affected the outcome of the war and helped spare mankind much suffering? Sad to say, the pope never responded.

Concubinage is very common in some Catholic countries in South America. And in North America a monsignor wrote the editorial: "Legalize Prostitution—It's the Saintly Solution." (*Philadelphia Daily News*) Take a look also at the conditions in some Protestant countries where wife swapping, premarital sex, and sex without marriage are quite common. We find a reason for this suggested in the newspaper caption: "Pastors Silent on Premarital Sex." The article said: "The pastors of America have been sinfully silent in preaching on premarital sex . . . They are afraid they will lose some of their parishioners." (*Telegraph,* North Platte, Nebraska) So is all religion a force for moral good?

In Christendom, religion's lack of moral force is most evident during wartime. See what you think of these nice-sounding claims. In 1934 Walter W. Van Kirk, then secretary of a department of the Federal Council of the Churches of Christ in America, wrote: "Preachers and laymen have taken a solemn stand against war . . . This peace crusade of the churches emerges from the conviction that war is absolutely contrary to the preaching and practice of Jesus." (*Religion Renounces War*) After citing several churches and clergymen, the book concluded: "The churches, in the main, have clearly stated that they are no longer to be regarded as allies in the business of killing and maiming humans. The preachers are . . . washing their hands of the blood of their fellows, they are parting company with Caesar."

However, those optimistic predictions regrettably did not come true. When World War II broke out, not one of the main religions of Christendom took a firm stand to 'renounce war.' Did the church in your area do so?

Broken Moral Fences

Having considered some evidence on both sides, would you not agree that in all too many cases, the popular religions of the world have not been a strong force for moral good? *Look* magazine declared: "The churches . . . have failed to supply moral leadership, and because their responsibility is the greatest, their failure is the worst." *The Courier-Mail* of Brisbane, Australia, commented on the failure of Christendom's religion to provide a restraint on sexual immorality: "When it comes to Bishops and Canons . . . writing that extramarital intercourse may be an act of charity that 'proclaims the Glory of God,' . . . that fornication is not bad in itself nor adultery necessarily wrong; then the ordinary man and woman, and particularly the adolescent boy and girl, become confused between right and wrong. The result of all this propaganda for the New Morality has been a breaking down of moral fences."

No, in the main, the world's religions are not a real force for moral good. On the contrary, they must take some responsibility for the sad state of morals today. However, since religion is supposed to mean "service and worship of God or the supernatural," should it not be a force for good in all countries where it prevails? What is lacking? How can your religion exert such a force today?

Love for God / *The Force for Moral Good*

R EASONABLE people will readily admit that immorality needs to be restrained. As a minister of the United Church of Canada put it: "The consequences, when individuals and society ignore the moral law, are frightening; wars, inflation, Watergate, and anarchy." As shown in the previous article, the major religions of this world have not proved to be a strong force for moral good. So if we individually want to live moral lives, we must look to another authority to provide such a force and then be willing to abide by that authority.

The influence of such a superior authority was evident in an incident in the life of Joseph, a Hebrew administrator for a court official in Egypt. When enticed by the official's wife to have sexual relations with her, Joseph resisted, saying: "How could I commit this great badness and actually sin against God?" (Genesis 39:7-9) Recognizing God's authority and desiring to please him gave Joseph the moral strength to resist her advances.

Two hundred years later, the nation of Israel, descendants of Joseph's father, Jacob, received the Ten Commandments as part of the Law given through Moses. Whereas disobedience incurred Jehovah God's displeasure, obedience to this Law brought divine blessings. So these commandments served as a moral guide for the nation.

The Ten Commandments —A Force for Good

How strong a force were the Ten Commandments? Their influence is still felt even in this 20th century. In 1962 the then governor-general of New Zealand said: "I suppose some people think the Ten Commandments are out of date. But it may not be without significance that if we all faithfully observed them today, the ordinary law of the land would be superfluous."

Nevertheless, in a conversation with a young Jewish ruler, Jesus Christ showed that something more than keeping the Ten Commandments was needed. The young man had asked: "What good must I do in order to get everlasting life?" When Jesus said that he should "observe the commandments continually," listing some of the Ten, the ruler answered: "I have kept all these; what yet am I lacking?" Jesus replied: "Go sell your belongings and give to the poor and you will have treasure in heaven, and come be my follower." The account continues: "When the young man heard this saying, he went away grieved, for he was holding many possessions."—Matthew 19:16-22.

A comparison of this account with a similar one in Luke 10:25-28 helps us to discern the young ruler's basic problem. We read: "A certain man versed in the Law rose up, to test him [Jesus] out, and said: 'Teacher, by doing what shall I inherit everlasting life?'" Jesus helped him to reason on the matter, and as a result, the man was able to answer his own question, saying in substance: 'Love Jehovah God with your whole heart, soul, strength, and mind, and your neighbor as yourself.' Jesus then concluded: "Keep on doing this and you will get life."

Can you now see the problem of the young ruler mentioned previously? His love for God and for neighbor was eclipsed by his love for material possessions. How sad! In spite of his attempting to keep the Ten Commandments, he was in danger of losing everlasting life.

What Does Love for God Mean?

We live in a time when love for God and neighbor has been supplanted by love of self, material possessions, and sex. Why, even belief in God as a Creator has been replaced in many minds by belief in the unproved theory of evolution. What has brought all of this about?

For centuries, Christendom's clergy used the non-Biblical doctrine of a fearful hellfire in an attempt to dominate the morals of the people. The *Encyclopedia International* states: "The strongest force for good with ordinary men through the Middle Ages was undoubtedly the fear of hell, which made even Kings and Emperors subservient to the Church, and was probably the only restraint upon their unbridled passions." This hellfire doctrine created the impression that God was unloving, unmerciful, and vindictive. Even though the doctrine may have acted as a restraint to some people, it turned many others away from God, leaving them easy prey to unscriptural teachings and theories, such as that of evolution.

The Bible, however, does not teach that God tortures souls in hellfire. Instead, the apostle John tells us: "God is love." "He is faithful and righteous so as to forgive us our sins." Moses wrote: "Jehovah, a God merciful and gracious, slow to anger and abundant in loving-kindness and truth." (1 John 4:8; 1:9; Exodus 34:6) These are just a few of God's wonderful qualities. They draw us to him. These qualities, especially his love, are what make us want to love him. "As for us, we love, because he first loved us." (1 John 4:19) It is this love for God that is the greatest force for moral good; it can lead to everlasting life!

Genuine love for God is not just an abstract quality. It moves a person to act in another's interest. The apostle Paul listed many ways that this love can be shown. To mention just a few: "Love is long-suffering and kind. Love is not jealous, it does not brag, does not get puffed up, does not behave indecently, does not look for its own interests, does not become provoked." (1 Corinthians 13:4, 5) Our displaying this love is an attempt to imitate our heavenly Father. Jesus said: "These two commands [loving God and neighbor] sum up the whole of the Law and the Prophets." (Matthew 22:40, *An American Translation*) In other words, if we show this love, we will not steal from our neighbor or murder him or commit adultery with his wife. The apostle John agreed, saying: "This is what the love of God means, that we observe his commandments."—1 John 5:3.

Love of God a Force for Good

Note the effect that love for God had on early Christians, as shown by Tertullian, of the second century. He challenged his opponents to point out one Christian among their criminals. When they could not, he added: "We, then, alone are without crime." The book *The Old Roman*

Concerning early Christians, the book "The Old Roman World" states: "We have testimony to their blameless lives, to their irreproachable morals." What was the force behind their "irreproachable morals"?

World supports this view, saying: "We have testimony to their blameless lives, to their irreproachable morals." Also, *Christianity Today* quotes church historian Roland Bainton: "From the end of the New Testament period to the decade 170-180 there is no evidence whatever of Christians in the army." Love for God moved them to obey him by living moral lives. You may wonder, though, 'Is there evidence of this beneficial moral force today?'

Indeed there is! Newspaper columnist Mike McManus wrote in the *Herald & Review* that he had never heard a sermon against premarital sex. A month later he reported that among the letters received in response was one from a 14-year-old, one of Jehovah's Witnesses, who wrote: "Just the thought of contracting these diseases should be enough to deter most people [from premarital sex]. But the reason Witnesses refrain is that *Jehovah commands us to flee from fornication*." (Italics ours.) Commenting on the letter, McManus asked: "How many 14-year-olds in your congregation could quote St. Paul so clearly (1 Cor. 6:18)?"

The same principle of obeying Jehovah's commands, cited by that young girl, is applied by the Witnesses in other areas. The essence of some of God's commands recorded in the Scriptures is: 'Be honest in all things,' 'Avoid idols,' 'Abstain from blood and fornication,' 'Be truthful,' 'Train your children in God's ways.' (Hebrews 13:18; 1 John 5:21; Acts 15:29; Ephesians 4:25; 6:4) Have you noted Jehovah's Witnesses in your neighborhood or place of work trying to obey these commands? Have you ever wondered why they do so, why they reject blood transfusions, why they refuse to go to war, why they visit you at your home, in short, why they are different? Their love for God is the answer.

Love for God can help you to resist being tempted into wrongdoing

Love Never Fails

Wanting to please God, Jehovah's Witnesses take to heart the counsel: "Be transformed by making your mind over, that you may prove to yourselves the good and acceptable and perfect will of God." (Romans 12:2) When they learn what is the "will of God" for them, they want to *do* it. Their love for God is the force behind this desire. Do you feel that this is fanciful, impractical for our time? Ponder a moment on the following actual accounts.

Back in 1963, José, of São Paulo, Brazil, began living with Eugênia, who was already married. Two years later, they began to study the Bible with Jehovah's Witnesses. From this study the couple learned that God requires that "marriage be honorable among all." (Hebrews 13:4) They realized that they should get married, but Brazil had no divorce law by which Eugênia could be freed to marry José. However, in 1977, when a divorce law went into effect, she applied for divorce, and in 1980 they were able to marry, fulfilling God's requirements. Their love for God had its reward.

Inire had tried all types of drugs in New York. He lived with his girlfriend, Ann. In need of money, he had her send pictures of herself to a well-known men's maga-

zine. She was offered a large sum of money to pose in the nude at a photo session. Meanwhile, Inire began to study the Bible with Jehovah's Witnesses, and later Ann joined in. Inire stopped using drugs. After three weeks they, on their own accord, decided to get married. Then, learning from the Bible that a Christian must dress modestly, Ann decided that she could not conscientiously agree to the photo session, no matter how much money was offered. (1 Timothy 2:9) What do you think prompted such changes? Ann says that when she realized that being one of Jehovah's Witnesses was not just a matter of joining a religion but involved living a life devoted to God, she knew she had to make changes fast. Truly, love for God is a strong force for good.

Someone may feel, 'Well, these are isolated cases.' But they are not. Similar changes have occurred many times in places where Jehovah's Witnesses are active. Why not look into this further? Prove for yourself that love for God as expressed in true religion is still *the* force for moral good.

Many Disciples Quit Following Jesus

JESUS is teaching in a synagogue in Capernaum about his part as the true bread from heaven. His talk is evidently an extension of the discussion that began with the people when they found him on their return from the eastern side of the Sea of Galilee, where they had eaten from the miraculously provided loaves and fishes.

Jesus continues his remarks, saying: "The bread that I shall give is my flesh in behalf of the life of the world." Just two years before, in the spring of 30 C.E., Jesus told Nicodemus that God loved the world so much that he provided his Son as a Savior. Thus, Jesus is now showing that anyone of the world of mankind who eats symbolically of his flesh, by exercising faith in the sacrifice he is soon to make, may receive everlasting life.

The people, however, stumble over Jesus' words. "How can this man give us his flesh to eat?" they ask. Jesus wants his listeners to understand that the eating of his flesh would be done in a figurative way. So, to emphasize this, he says something still more objectionable if taken in a literal way.

"Unless you eat the flesh of the Son of man and drink his blood," Jesus declares, "you have no life in yourselves. He that feeds on my flesh and drinks my blood has everlasting life, and I shall resurrect him at the last day; for

my flesh is true food, and my blood is true drink. He that feeds on my flesh and drinks my blood remains in union with me, and I in union with him."

True, if Jesus were here suggesting cannibalism, his teaching would sound most offensive. But, of course, Jesus is not advocating literally eating flesh or drinking blood. He is simply emphasizing that all who receive everlasting life must exercise faith in the sacrifice that he is to make when he offers up his perfect human body and pours out his lifeblood. Yet, even many of his disciples make no attempt to understand his teaching

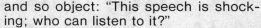

and so object: "This speech is shocking; who can listen to it?"

Knowing that many of his disciples are murmuring, Jesus says: "Does this stumble you? What, therefore, if you should behold the Son of man ascending to where he was before? . . . The sayings that I have spoken to you are spirit and are life. But there are some of you that do not believe."

Jesus continues: "This is why I have said to you, No one can come to me unless it is granted him by the Father." With that, many of his disciples leave and no longer follow him. So Jesus turns to his 12 apostles and asks: "You do not want to go also, do you?"

Peter responds: "Lord, whom shall we go away to? You have sayings of everlasting life; and we have believed and come to know that you are the Holy One of God." What a fine expression of loyalty, even though Peter and the other apostles may not have fully understood Jesus' teaching on this matter!

Although pleased by Peter's response, Jesus observes: "I chose you twelve, did I not? Yet one of you is a slanderer." He is speaking about Judas Iscariot. Possibly at this point Jesus detects in Judas a "beginning," or an outset, of a wrongful course.

Jesus has just disappointed the people by resisting their attempts to make him king, and they may reason, 'How can this be the Messiah if he will not assume the Messiah's rightful position?' This, too, would be a matter fresh in the people's minds. **John 6:51-71; 3:16.**

♦ For whom does Jesus give his flesh, and how do these 'eat his flesh'?
♦ What further words of Jesus shock the people, yet what is he emphasizing?
♦ When many quit following Jesus, what is Peter's response?

Setting Matters Straight Between God and You

"Though the sins of you people should prove to be as scarlet, they will be made white just like snow."—ISAIAH 1:18.

IF, BECAUSE of some past error or unkindness, strained relations existed between you and another, how would you respond to these words: "Come now, and let us reason together"? That could be an invitation to sit down for a give-and-take, with mutual concessions and compromise. Each could present his view, and each

1, 2. (a) What might you imagine if someone said: "Come now, and let us reason together"? (b) Why ought we not expect to have a give-and-take with God?

might then concede some measure of fault or misunderstanding.

² But could you imagine that the Creator would in that sense plead, "Come now, and let us reason together," as Isaiah 1:18 reads in many Bibles? Not at all. None of us could expect to "argue it out" (*The New English Bible*) or to have a give-and-take with Jehovah, as if he might need to concede fault and to compromise. If, though, we want peace with God, what does Isaiah 1:18 require?

Snowy slopes of Mount Hermon, looking southwest across the upper Jordan Valley to the hills of Galilee

³ The Hebrew word rendered "reason together" basically means "decide, adjudge, prove." It has a legal flavor, implying more than two persons just reasoning together. A decision was involved.* (Genesis 31: 37, 42; Job 9:33; Psalm 50:21; Isaiah 2:4) *Wilson's Old Testament Word Studies* offers the meaning "to be right; to reason, to demonstrate what is right and true." God was commanding: "Come now, let us set things right" (*The New American Bible*) or, "Let us set matters straight."

⁴ Jehovah God used the prophet Isaiah to deliver this potent message. Who was Isaiah, and why was his message appropriate in his time? Moreover, how can we benefit from it?

⁵ At the mention of "prophet," many today might conjure up thoughts of some ascetic young man who was proclaiming his distorted view of reality. Others might think of an old eccentric who styles himself a judge of prevailing conditions. How different from such was the balanced and rational man Isaiah, whom Jehovah God used to write the Bible book bearing his name!

⁶ "Isaiah the son of Amoz" lived in Judah and actively served Jehovah "in the days of Uzziah, Jotham, Ahaz and Hezekiah, kings of Judah"—over 40 years. Modestly, Isaiah did not provide much information about himself. Tradition says that he was related to Judah's royal family. We know for sure that he was a family man whose wife bore him two sons. He may have remarried after she died, becoming father to another son, prophetically named Immanuel.—Isaiah 1:1; 7:3, 14; 8: 3, 18.

⁷ There are similarities between Isaiah's time and ours. You have seen that we live in a time of international tension, of wars or threats thereof. While religious and political leaders who claim to worship God project themselves as examples to be followed, we regularly see press reports of their financial and moral scandals. How does God view such leaders, especially those linked with Christendom? What lies ahead for them and for those following them? In the book of Isaiah, we find divine comments that are most relevant to such current matters. We also find lessons for each of us as we personally strive to serve God.

Prophet to a Guilty Nation

⁸ Reading the book of Isaiah, you will find messages about the guilt of Judah and Jerusalem, historical details of enemy invasions, pronouncements of desolation for surrounding nations, and encouraging predictions of restoration and salvation for Israel. This is written in a vivid, gripping style. Dr. I. Slotki says: "Scholars pay wholehearted tribute to Isaiah's brilliance of imagination and his picturesque and graphic descriptions, his command of powerful metaphor, alliteration, assonance, and the fine balance and rhythmic flow of his sentences." Let us examine in particular the opening message of Isaiah —that found in chapter 1.

⁹ The prophet does not state exactly when he wrote this chapter. Isaiah 6:1-13

---

* Dr. E. H. Plumptre explains: "The [rendering in the *King James Version*] suggests the thought of a discussion between equals. The Hebrew implies rather the tone of one who gives an authoritative *ultimatum*, as from a judge to the accused."

---

3. What is the proper sense of the Hebrew word sometimes translated "reason together" at Isaiah 1:18?
4-6. Who was Isaiah, and when did he serve as a prophet?

---

7. Why should we be interested in Isaiah's prophecy?
8. What does the book of Isaiah contain, and in what style was it written?
9. What do we know about the time and circumstances of the writing of Isaiah chapter 1?

dates from the year that King Uzziah died. So if it was earlier that Isaiah recorded his opening chapters, they may reflect the situation below the surface during Uzziah's kingship. Basically, Uzziah (829-777 B.C.E.) "kept doing what was right in Jehovah's eyes," so God blessed his reign with prosperity. Yet, we know that all was not well, for "the people were still sacrificing and making sacrificial smoke on the high places" before God struck Uzziah (or, Azariah) with leprosy for presumptuously offering incense in the temple. (2 Chronicles 26:1-5, 16-23; 2 Kings 15:1-5) The underlying badness in Uzziah's time may have led to the crop of wickedness we read about involving his grandson King Ahaz (762-745 B.C.E.), which also might be what Isaiah was describing. But more important than a specific date for chapter 1 is what moved God to say: "Let us set matters straight between us."

10 Isaiah frankly proclaimed: "Woe to the sinful nation, the people heavy with error, an evildoing seed, ruinous sons! They have left Jehovah, they have treated the Holy One of Israel with disrespect, they have turned backwards. . . . The whole head is in a sick condition, and the whole heart is feeble. From the sole of the foot even to the head there is no sound spot in it." (Isaiah 1:4-6) King Ahaz' 16-year rule was marked by rank idolatry. He burned "his sons [as sacrifices] in the fire, according to the detestable things of the nations . . . And he regularly . . . made sacrificial smoke on the high places and upon the hills and under every sort of luxuriant tree." (2 Chronicles 28:1-4; 2 Kings 16:3, 4) Injustice, bribery, and immorality were rife among the princes, who were more fit to be rulers in ancient

Sodom. (Isaiah 1:10, 21-23; Genesis 18: 20, 21) Certainly, God could not approve of them. And with such leaders, how would the people fare?

11 The prophet Isaiah illustrated the deplorable situation of the people by mentioning the sacred trees and gardens where they offered idolatrous sacrifices and burned incense to pagan deities. These "mighty trees" would become a cause for shame. (Isaiah 1:29; 65:3) Transferring the imagery to the idolaters themselves, Isaiah wrote: "You will become like a big tree the foliage of which is withering, and like a garden that has no water." (Isaiah 1:30) Yes, people leaving Jehovah would "come to their finish." They would become like tow (combustible pieces of flax), and their idols would become a spark—both to be consumed.—Isaiah 1:28, 31.

12 Now compare that with the situation today. Within a month's time, the press in the United States reported: A leading presidential candidate withdrew in a scandal over reports of his "womanizing"; a prominent clergyman was replaced after confessing to adultery and being accused of homosexuality, wife swapping, and misusing funds to pay hush money. (He "reportedly had drawn an astounding $4.6 million in compensation since 1984." *Time*, May 11, 1987) In Austria last year, the Abbot of Rein 'was dismissed and charged with squandering $6 million on a hunting lodge and parties for members of the former ruling family and for young women of less noble background.' You probably could give other examples of such leaders. What do you think God's view of them is?

13 As to the people in general, there is

---

10. During King Ahaz' reign, what situation prevailed in Judah, especially among the leaders?

11. How should we understand Isaiah 1:29, 30?
12, 13. What similarities can be drawn between our time and Isaiah's?

Isaiah said that 'an ass knows its owner's manger.'
What lesson is there in this?

increasing religious polarization. Some turn from religion in disgust or apathy. For instance, merely 3 percent of England's population attend the established church. At the other pole, we find extreme religiousness. This is evident in the growing charismatic churches, with their emotional appeal of being "saved," speaking in tongues, or seeing the sick "healed." Crowds flock to shrines hoping for miracles. Others make sacrifices as acts of "faith," such as crawling on bleeding knees to see the Virgin of Guadalupe [Mexico City]. A newspaper said: "While to outsiders her existence and the fervor with which she is worshiped might seem a blatant mixing of Christianity and paganism, the Virgin is arguably the most important figure in Mexican Catholicism."

How Can You Gain His Favor?

¹⁴ Jehovah God leaves no confusion as to his view of those who claim to be on his side but who will not "worship the Father with spirit and truth." (John 4:23) If a nation, a religious group, or a person is not acting in accord with God's revealed standards, any religious displays are pointless. For instance, religious festivals and sacrifices were a required part of true worship in ancient Israel. (Leviticus, chapters 1–7, 23) Yet, Isaiah set out God's view—displeasure with the unfaithful Jews keeping those observances. God said: "When you spread out your palms, I hide my eyes from you. Even though you make many prayers, I am not listening." (Isaiah 1:11-15) That is just as true today. Rather than mere religious ceremonies or memorized creeds and prayers, God wants prayers and right deeds that come from the heart.

¹⁵ Our knowing that provides the basis for hope. Humans can win God's favor. How? Isaiah urged: "Wash yourselves; make yourselves clean; remove the badness of your dealings from in front of my eyes; cease to do bad. Learn to do good; search for justice." At this point Isaiah presented God's command: "Come, now, you people, and let us set matters straight between us." So Jehovah was not asking for a session between equals who would sit down for a give-and-take. God knew what was right, or straight. His judgment was:

---

14. Through Isaiah, how did Jehovah make it clear that He does not accept all who claim to worship Him?

15. Why does Isaiah 1:18 give us reason for hope, and what is the meaning of the words, 'Come and let us set matters straight'?

Any changes that are needed are to be on the part of humans, who needed to conform to his just and righteous standards. That is so today too. Change is possible, with resulting favor. Even someone whose course has been unquestionably bad can change. Isaiah wrote: "Though the sins of you people should prove to be as scarlet, they will be made white just like snow." —Isaiah 1:16-18.

16 There is a tendency, however, to note such counsel but to think that it applies to others. Evidently, many in Isaiah's day did that. Actually, each individual should examine himself. If a Christian is guilty of serious sin, be it lying, fraud, sexual immorality, or other grave wrongs, repentance and works befitting repentance are vital. (Acts 26:20) Commendably, some have acted to 'set matters straight between them and Jehovah.' For example, *The Watchtower* of April 15, 1985, discussed the matter of rectifying faults that might be secret to outsiders but are observed by God. (Matthew 6:6; Philippians 4:13) Three areas for attention were mentioned: secretly accepting a blood transfusion, masturbation, and alcohol abuse. Af-

---

16. How have some responded to Bible-based advice concerning wrongdoing?

Points for Review

☐ What was meant by the command to 'come and set matters straight' with God?

☐ How was Isaiah's time similar to ours?

☐ What did Isaiah show was needed for individuals to gain God's favor?

☐ Aside from gross sin, in what areas might we need to set matters straight between us and God?

ter considering that material, quite a number of readers wrote letters of appreciation; they admitted that they had had those faults, but they had been moved to repent and change.

17 Of course, most Christians who are considering this matter are not guilty of gross misconduct. Nevertheless, Isaiah's message still ought to move us to a heart-searching examination. Might we need to set some matter straight with God? An essential element of Isaiah's message was right heart motive. Regarding prayer, one might ask: 'Do my prayers come from my heart, and to the best of my ability, are my actions consistent with my prayers?' Some making such an examination have seen room for improvement. They had been praying for increased knowledge of God's will, yet they spent little time studying the Bible and Christian publications. Others had been praying to have a greater share in the ministry, but they pursued a life-style that allowed for no cutback in their income by reducing their secular work. Or have you prayed that God bless your disciple making? To what extent, then, do you work at being a more effective teacher? Have you conscientiously increased your making of return visits and been willing to commit time to conducting a regular Bible study with another? Exerting yourself in line with your prayers will show that you sincerely want God to listen.

18 It is altogether proper that each of us strive to have all aspects of our life 'set straight' with God, our Creator. Note how Isaiah reasoned along this line: "A bull well knows its buyer, and the ass the manger of its owner; Israel itself has not

---

17. Even if we are not committing gross wrongs, how can Isaiah 1:18 apply to us and help us?
18. Why should we give attention to setting things straight between us and God?

known, my own people have not behaved understandingly." (Isaiah 1:3) None of us would like to be depicted as less knowing or appreciative than a bull or an ass. That description would apply, though, if we felt that we did not need to work at learning about our Life-Giver and his requirements and then earnestly trying to live accordingly.

[19] Isaiah offered his people reason for optimism. He said that their standing before Jehovah could be transformed into a pure one. It could be like a crimson-red cloth that would become as white as wool

19. What prospect did Isaiah outline for those setting matters straight with God, and what meaning does this have for us?

or as the snow blanketing Mount Hermon's peak. (Isaiah 1:18; Psalm 51:7; Daniel 7:9; Revelation 19:8) Even if the majority did not respond, and thus the nation was given to the sword and into captivity, a faithful remnant could return. Likewise, we can gain Jehovah's favor, perhaps with the assistance of conscientious overseers, who serve in the congregation as loving 'judges and counselors.' (Isaiah 1:20, 24-27; 1 Peter 5:2-4; Galatians 6:1, 2) So be assured, you can set matters straight between God and you. Or, if you already have God's favor, you can strengthen your relationship with him. That truly is worth your every effort.

Will You Say, "Here I Am! Send Me"?

"Jehovah [said]: 'Whom shall I send, and who will go for us?' And I proceeded to say: 'Here I am! Send me.'"—ISAIAH 6:8.

"WE ARE happy to send our letter of acceptance to go to Colombia. We have enjoyed our privilege of service here in Ecuador much more than this typewriter can describe." Thus began a letter from two of Jehovah's Witnesses who had gone to Ecuador where a new branch office for the Watch Tower Society was being built.

[2] These ministers went to Ecuador to do more than help on the building; they could also help as Christian teachers. They write: "We have found that the field service is one of the most important things. Just three weeks ago, eight of us went out

1, 2. What special reason for happiness did one couple have?

to an open market and placed 73 books and over 40 magazines. The week before, we started two new Bible studies. We can truly see the need for the new branch. My wife and I would like to thank you for the privilege to continue in this special form of full-time service" now in Colombia.

[3] This couple, and hundreds of others who have offered to be sent to a foreign country, reflect a spirit similar to the prophet Isaiah's. When he heard Jehovah say: "Whom shall I send, and who will go for us?" Isaiah replied: "Here I am! Send me." God then commanded: "Go, and you

3. How have many reflected a spirit similar to that which Isaiah showed?

must say to this people, 'Hear again and again, O men, but do not understand.'" (Isaiah 6:8, 9) For what was Isaiah volunteering to be sent, and what resulted therefrom? And what can we learn from this account in terms of modern parallels and of any personal lessons for us?

Isaiah's Commission to Preach

⁴ Jehovah God asked Isaiah, "Whom shall I send?" in the year that King Uzziah died. (Isaiah 6:1) That was 777 B.C.E., or about a century and three quarters before the Babylonians destroyed Jerusalem and desolated the land of Judah. Jehovah could see that sad development coming, and he commissioned Isaiah to deliver a message about it. What can we learn from his preaching commission?

⁵ As we would have been, so Isaiah must have been profoundly impressed by the setting in which he received his commission. He wrote: "I . . . got to see Jehovah, sitting on a throne lofty and lifted up, and his skirts were filling the temple. Seraphs were standing above him. Each one had six wings. With two he kept his face covered, and with two he kept his feet covered, and with two he would fly about. And this one called to that one and said: 'Holy, holy, holy is Jehovah of armies. The fullness of all the earth is his glory.'"—Isaiah 6:1-3.

⁶ Isaiah knew that Uzziah had been struck with leprosy when he, not being of the priestly tribe, presumptuously invaded the Holy of the temple to offer incense. So, what a privilege for Isaiah to view the very presence of God! Isaiah, an imperfect human, did not literally see Jehovah, but he was permitted to see Him in a vision. (Exodus 33:20-23) The grandness of this

was highlighted by angels of high rank (seraphs) who attended at Jehovah's throne. They, sensing God's holiness, respectfully covered their 'faces.' Beyond this self-effacing act, they emphatically proclaimed God's holiness. What effect do you imagine that all of this would have on a human?

⁷ Let Isaiah answer. "I proceeded to say: 'Woe to me! For I am as good as brought to silence, because a man unclean in lips I am, and in among a people unclean in lips I am dwelling; for my eyes have seen the King, Jehovah of armies, himself!'" (Isaiah 6:5) Isaiah knew that he was a spokesman for God, yet this vision impressed on him that he was unclean, not having the pure lips that would befit a spokesman of this glorious and holy King. Some of us, too, may at times have been struck by our sinfulness, not feeling worthy to approach God in prayer, much less to have his name called upon us. Isaiah's further experience should, then, be encouraging.

⁸ One of the attending seraphs flew to him with a fiery coal from the altar of animal sacrifice. Touching the coal to Isaiah's mouth, the angel said: "Look! This has touched your lips, and your error has departed and your sin itself is atoned for." (Isaiah 6:6, 7) In the days of Solomon, fire from heaven evidenced that Jehovah had accepted the altar of sacrifice, even though the offerings could not make even the priests completely clean before God. (2 Chronicles 7:1-3; Hebrews 10:1-4, 11) Still, when Isaiah had his uncleanness cauterized away by the fiery coal, he could accept Jehovah's judgment that his sinfulness was atoned for to the extent needed to receive a special preaching commission. What interesting portents

4, 5. (a) What situation prevailed when Isaiah received the vision recorded in chapter 6? (b) What did Isaiah see in this vision?
6. Why was it a privilege for Isaiah to see what he did?

7. How did Isaiah react, and why might we have felt similarly?
8. An angel performed what service, with what effect?

Isaiah was cleansed and sent to preach

does this suggest regarding the future?

⁹ This amazing experience led up to the prophet's receiving the preaching commission mentioned. (Isaiah 6:8, 9) But why was Isaiah to say that the people would repeatedly hear but still not get any knowledge? God's voice added: "Make the heart of this people unreceptive, and make their very ears unresponsive, and paste their very eyes together, that they may not see . . . and that they may not actually turn back and get healing." (Isaiah 6:10) Does that mean that Isaiah, by bluntness or tactlessness, should repel the Jews so that they would remain at odds with Jeho-

vah? No. This was simply an indication of how most Jews would respond no matter how faithfully and thoroughly Isaiah fulfilled the preaching task for which he had volunteered by saying, "Here I am! Send me."

¹⁰ The fault lay with the people. Despite Isaiah's allowing them to "hear again and again," they would not take in knowledge or gain understanding. God stated beforehand that most, because of their stubborn and unspiritual attitude, would not respond. A minority might. But the majority

---

9. What was the tenor of Isaiah's message?

10. (a) Where did the fault lie as to the people's being as if blind and deaf? (b) What did Isaiah mean by asking, "How long?"

would be as blind as if their eyes were pasted shut with the strongest glue, if you can imagine that. How long would this bad state continue? That, rather than how many years he would have to serve, is what Isaiah asked with the words: "How long, O Jehovah?" God replied: "Until the cities actually crash in ruins, to be without an inhabitant." And so it happened, though after Isaiah's lifetime. The Babylonians removed earthling men, leaving Judah "ruined into a desolation."—Isaiah 6: 11, 12; 2 Kings 25:1-26.

[11] Finally, though, Jehovah assured Isaiah that all was not hopeless. "There will still be in [the land] a tenth." Yes, it was 'like a massive tree in which, when there is a cutting down of it, there would be a stump, a holy seed.' (Isaiah 6:13) After 70 years of Babylonian exile, a seed, or remnant, returned to the land, as if a new sprout emerging from the stump of a massive tree. (2 Chronicles 36: 22, 23; Ezra 1:1-4; compare Job 14:7-9; Daniel 4: 10, 13-15, 26.) Hence, while Isaiah's message was somber, it contained a consoling element. There is Scriptural reason, though, for us to view Isaiah as a pattern for future developments. How so?

Greater Fulfillments

[12] Centuries after Isaiah's death, one came whom we might call the Greater Isaiah—Jesus Christ. In his prehuman existence, he had volunteered to be sent by his Father to earth, where he would include in his preaching things that Isaiah had written. (Proverbs 8:30, 31; John 3:17, 34; 5:36-38; 7:28; 8:42; Luke 4:16-19; Isaiah 61:1) More pointedly, Jesus tied himself in with Isaiah chapter 6 when explaining why He taught as He did. (Matthew 13: 10-15; Mark 4:10-12; Luke 8:9, 10) That was fitting, for most Jews who heard Jesus were no more willing to accept his message and act on it than those who heard the prophet Isaiah were willing to accept his. (John 12: 36-43) Also, in 70 C.E. the Jews who had made themselves 'blind and deaf' to Jesus' message met a destruction like that of 607 B.C.E. This development in the first century was a tribulation on Jerusalem 'such as had not occurred since the world's beginning nor would occur again.' (Mat-

Many have responded, saying, "Here I am! Send me"

11. How did Isaiah's preaching offer consolation?
12. What Scriptural basis is there for calling Jesus the Greater Isaiah?

thew 24:21) Yet, as Isaiah prophesied, a remnant, or "holy seed," exercised faith. These were formed into a spiritual nation, the anointed "Israel of God."—Galatians 6:16.

¹³ We now come to another Bible-based fulfillment of Isaiah chapter 6. As a key to understanding this, consider the words of the apostle Paul around the year 60 C.E. He explained why many Jews who heard him in Rome would not accept his "witness concerning the kingdom of God." The reason was that Isaiah 6:9, 10 was again being fulfilled. (Acts 28:17-27) Does this mean that after Jesus left the earthly scene, his anointed disciples were to carry out a commission comparable to Isaiah's? Yes, indeed!

¹⁴ Before the Greater Isaiah ascended to heaven, he said that his disciples would receive holy spirit and would thereafter "be witnesses of [him] both in Jerusalem and in all Judea and Samaria and to the most distant part of the earth." (Acts 1:8) Just as the sacrificial altar supplied what was needed for Isaiah's error to depart, so Jesus' sacrifice was the basis for his disciples' having their 'sin itself atoned for.' (Leviticus 6:12, 13; Hebrews 10:5-10; 13:10-15) Thus, God could anoint them with holy spirit, which would also empower them to be 'witnesses to the most distant part of the earth.' Both the prophet Isaiah and the Greater Isaiah had been sent to proclaim God's message. Similarly, Jesus' anointed followers were "sent from God . . . in company with Christ."—2 Corinthians 2:17.

¹⁵ In modern times, particularly since the close of World War I, anointed Chris-

tians have seen the need to declare God's message. This includes the sobering fact that "the day of vengeance on the part of our God" is near. (Isaiah 61:2) Its devastation will be a blow especially to Christendom, which has long professed to be God's people, as did Israel of old. Despite decades of loyal preaching by God's anointed witnesses, most in Christendom have 'made their heart unreceptive and their ears unresponsive; their eyes are pasted together.' Isaiah's prophecy indicates that this will continue to be the case "until the cities actually crash in ruins, to be without an inhabitant, and the houses be without earthling man, and the ground itself is ruined into a desolation." This will mark the end of this wicked system of things. —Isaiah 6:10-12.

"Send Me"

¹⁶ Today, there are millions of devoted Christians who have the Biblical hope of living everlastingly on a paradise earth. On the basis of Jesus' sacrificial blood, this "great crowd" can have their sins forgiven to the extent now necessary. They also receive power and support through God's spirit as they join with the remaining number of anointed Christians in saying, "Here I am! Send me." Send them to do what? Paul says at Romans 10:13-15: "'Everyone who calls on the name of Jehovah will be saved.' However, how will they call on him in whom they have not put faith? How, in turn, will they put faith in him of whom they have not heard? How, in turn, will they hear without someone to preach? How, in turn, will they preach unless they have been sent forth? Just as it is written [at Isaiah 52:7]: 'How comely are the feet of those who declare good news of good things!'"—Revelation 7:9-15.

13. Why can we expect yet another fulfillment of Isaiah 6?
14. How were Jesus' disciples to do a work like Isaiah's?
15. What has been the general response to the preaching like that of Isaiah in our time, pointing to what future?

16. Why can it be said that the "great crowd" are sharing in a work like that of Isaiah?

¹⁷ Recall that it was before he knew the full content of the message that Isaiah said, "Here I am! Send me." In contrast, we know what God wants declared now by those responding to his invitation: "Whom shall I send, and who will go for us?" It includes forewarning about "the day of vengeance on the part of our God." Yet, the message also includes "good news of good things." For instance, those who are "sent forth" share in proclaiming "liberty to those taken captive and the wide opening of the eyes even to the prisoners." Should not doing that be a source of great satisfaction?—Isaiah 61:1, 2.

¹⁸ If you already are declaring "good news of good things," this review of Isaiah chapter 6 might prompt you to ask: How might I respond more fully in the spirit of Isaiah 6:8? As with the couple mentioned at the outset, hundreds have shared in the International Volunteer Construction Workers program. Many others, who lack construction skills, have moved to lands where the need for Kingdom preachers is greater. This is best done after seeking advice from the branch office of the Watch Tower Society. Of course, planning is vital, for language, living standards, job prospects, and other things may be vastly different in a foreign land. Yet, do not dismiss the possibility out of hand just because major adjustments might be required. Many who have the attitude "Here I am! Send me" have made such moves and have been richly blessed by God for so doing.—Compare Proverbs 24:27; Luke 14:28-30.

¹⁹ Still others—single brothers or sisters, married couples, even whole families—have moved elsewhere within their own land or area where there is a greater need for Kingdom preachers or for Christian overseers. (Acts 16:9, 10) Doing this may have required making sacrifices, such as obtaining another kind of secular work, perhaps one that paid less. Some have taken early retirement with a limited pension and found part-time work so as to have more time for the ministry. How fine it is when entire families say, "Here we are! Send us." This, too, reflects Isaiah's situation. His wife actively shared in doing God's will as a prophetess, and his sons were involved in prophetic messages. —Isaiah 7:3, 14-17; 8:3, 4.

²⁰ Even if your present circumstances do not permit such major changes, you can consider, 'Am I doing all I can where I am, imitating Isaiah's responsiveness?' Exert yourself in declaring God's message, even in inclement weather or in the face of public indifference; certainly, Isaiah did the same. Be zealous in speaking to others about the "good news of good things!" Jehovah has said, "Whom shall I send?" Prove that, like Isaiah of old, your response is, "Here I am! Send me" to proclaim His message.

---

20. With Isaiah 6:8 in mind, what should you consider?

---

17. Comparable to Isaiah's prophecy, what is the content of our message?
18, 19. In what special ways are many saying, "Send me"?

Points for Review

□ In what circumstances did Isaiah receive the vision of chapter 6, and what did he see?

□ What kind of commission did Isaiah receive?

□ Why can Jesus be called the Greater Isaiah, and how are his disciples involved in a work like Isaiah's?

□ How can you display a spirit like that of Isaiah?

Insight on the News

Recipe for Disaster

"During the early days of television, violence was depicted less frequently and less realistically than it is today," notes Dr. Paul Wilson of the Australian Institute of Criminology. However, in describing what he considers to be the recipe for social disaster and anarchy, Wilson adds: "Now, blood gushes from body gashes and the death agony is captured in its lingering harshness. . . . Teenagers are axed to death and choke slowly from slashed necks and their death gurgles are lovingly captured by the camera."

In his article appearing in *The Sydney Morning Herald,* Dr. Wilson commented on the difficulty news reporters experienced in capturing Australian public interest over the recent bloodless coup d'etat in nearby Fiji. The reason? "Violence is the benchmark of modern entertainment," says Wilson. The news coverage by TV and press was accurate, carefully analyzed, and factual, but there were no "pulsating television images of violence and newspaper paragraphs describing riots," he explained.

How well this escalating lust to be entertained by violence fits the Bible's description of those living in "the last days" of the present system of things! In this critical final generation, men are described as being "without self-control, fierce, without love of goodness."—2 Timothy 3:1, 3.

Monogamy or Polygamy?

Should the church accept members who have more than one marriage mate? To resolve this question, the Anglican Church in Uganda has appointed a group to study "polygamy and the Christian family." The Ecumenical Press Service reports that, according to one study-group member, Bishop Christopher Senyonjo, having more mates is not only acceptable but also beneficial. Why does he feel that way? Polygamous marriages, he claims, can help to curb the spread of the disease AIDS. On top of that, he asserts that polygamy is optional for Christians, saying that Christ will "transform our stale and tasteless marriages into sweet wine, be they monogamous or polygamous."

Yet, the Bible clearly shows that Jehovah God, the Originator of monogamous marriage, disagrees. He inspired the apostle Paul to write: "Let each man have his own wife and each woman have her own husband." (1 Corinthians 7:2) Significantly, Paul later wrote regarding the qualifications of those who shepherd the flock: "A bishop then must be blameless, the husband of *one* wife."—1 Timothy 3:2, *King James Version.*

Hence, true Christians in Africa, as elsewhere, view polygamy for what it is—a violation of God's law.

Preaching for a Price

Priests of the Lutheran Church of Sweden have been unhappy with their paychecks because, as reported, their salaries are "low in comparison with those paid to other professions with much shorter studies or training behind them." However, according to the news service of the World Council of Churches, things are now looking up. After "a long and partly bitter campaign," the priests have recently gained a 40-hour workweek. But what if the Swedes need priestly help after working hours? The new labor agreement also guarantees overtime payment for each extra hour of pastoral care. Such overtime wages are expected to increase their yearly salaries by 10 to 12 percent.

In contrast with the concern among Swedish priests for better wages for their services, when Jesus sent his disciples out to preach, he told them: "You received free, give free. Do not procure gold or silver or copper for your girdle purses." (Matthew 10: 8, 9) What did he mean? The Kingdom good news was not to be commercialized, nor was it to be used for selfish personal advantage. The disciples adhered to Jesus' direction, and their ministry was accomplished. Why? Because *God* sustained them in the ministry.

Talk About the Glory of God's Kingship

"About the glory of your kingship they will talk, and about your mightiness they will speak." —PSALM 145:11.

JEHOVAH had a purpose in endowing us with speech. (Exodus 4:11) Chiefly, it was that our lips might "bubble forth praise" to him. (Psalm 119:171, 172) As the psalmist David said: "All your works will laud you, O Jehovah, and your loyal ones will bless you. About the glory of your kingship they will talk, and about your mightiness they will speak, to make known to the sons of men his mighty acts and the glory of the splendor of his kingship. Your kingship is a kingship for all times indefinite, and your dominion is throughout all successive generations." —Psalm 145:10-13.

2 Anointed followers of Jesus Christ and their companions of the "great crowd" are eager to praise Jehovah, the "King of eternity." (Revelation 7:9; 15:3) Through diligent study of the Bible with *The Watchtower* and other Christian publications as aids, we can acquire accurate knowledge about God that is like a spring of pure, refreshing, life-giving water. Thus, in our case 'the well of wisdom becomes a torrent bubbling forth.' (Proverbs 18:4) We are impelled to "bubble forth praise" in house-to-house witnessing and other forms of the field ministry. But there is also a Scriptural reason for informal witnessing.

Scriptural Precedents

3 The first preaching Jesus did after being anointed with holy spirit was at his lodging place, to which he invited John, Andrew, and apparently Peter. They spent the day there, obviously receiving quite a witness in that informal setting. (John 1:35-42) It was also under informal circumstances—"while passing along"—that Jesus saw Matthew at the tax office and got positive results when He said: "Be my follower."—Matthew 9:9.

4 Jesus was the best example of 'a torrent of wisdom bubbling forth.' Although he sat hungry and weary by Jacob's fountain near Sychar, he witnessed to a Samaritan woman who came along to draw water. "Whoever drinks from the water that I will give him will never get thirsty at all," said Jesus, "but the water that I will give him will become in him a fountain of water bubbling up to impart everlasting life." This informal witnessing led to Jesus' preaching to a group that the woman stirred up to come together and hear what he had to say.—John 4:6-42.

5 Philip the evangelizer hailed a passing chariot and witnessed informally to its occupant, who was reading Isaiah's prophecy. Invited up into the chariot, Philip explained "the good news about Jesus" to

---

1. Chiefly, why has Jehovah endowed us with speech?
2. We are impelled to "bubble forth praise" to God in what ways?
3. Please cite an example of informal witnessing on the part of Jesus Christ.

4. What did Jesus say when witnessing to a Samaritan woman, and this led to what?
5. Philip the evangelizer and the apostle Paul furnish what examples of informal witnessing?

that Ethiopian eunuch, whose appreciative response resulted in his baptism. (Acts 8:26-38) When the apostle Paul's prison bonds were loosed in a great earthquake at Philippi, he witnessed informally to the jailer. The result? "One and all, he and his were baptized without delay."—Acts 16:19-34.

⁶ Today, informal witnessing is one means of declaring the good news where our Christian work is under restrictions. Even though we are persecuted, however, our hearts impel us to talk about the glory of God's kingship. After Stephen was stoned to death, most of the persecuted disciples were dispersed. Yet, they kept on declaring the good news, and doubtless informal witnessing was included in their Kingdom-preaching endeavors. —Acts 8:4-8; 11:19-21.

⁷ Informal witnessing is one way to talk about the glory of God's kingship if we are imprisoned or are confined to our homes because of illness or infirmity. Paul was confined for two years under Roman guard. But instead of pining away, he sent for an audience and "would kindly receive all those who came in to him, preaching the kingdom of God to them and teaching the things concerning the Lord Jesus Christ with the greatest freeness of speech." (Acts 28:16-31) What a fine example! If you are a shut-in witness of Jehovah, could you do something similar?

⁸ As Paul's guards shifted from time to time, different ones heard him talk to others about the glory of God's kingship. We can be sure, though, that he also witnessed directly to those guards. So effective was this informal witnessing that Paul could write: "My affairs have turned out for the advancement of the good news rather than otherwise, so that my bonds have become public knowledge in association with Christ among all the Praetorian Guard and all the rest; and most of the

If you are a shut-in, do you witness as Paul did while in confinement?

6. Informal witnessing likely played a part in what activities of Jesus' disciples after Stephen was stoned?

7. When confined, what did Paul do, this raising what question?

8. How effective was Paul's informal witnessing?

brothers in the Lord, feeling confidence by reason of my prison bonds, are showing all the more courage to speak the word of God fearlessly." (Philippians 1:12-14) Like Paul, if we should be imprisoned and deprived of opportunities for formal witnessing, we can still talk about God's kingship. And what courage this will instill in our brothers!

9 Informal witnessing was so common among early Christians that even of later years it could be said: "From a Christian writer, probably in Carthage about 200, we get a picture . . . [that] concerns people who were highly educated. Three young lawyers, close friends, spend a day's holiday at the seaside. Two are Christians, the third pagan. Their talk soon turns to religion . . . The account of the long argument ends, 'We went home happy, all three. One was happy because he had come to the Christian faith, the others because they had led him to it.' The writing does not pretend to be actual history; it is an Apology, by Minucius Felix. But it does represent the sort of thing that happened among the more privileged people." (*Church History 1—The First Advance: AD 29—500,* by John Foster, pages 46, 48) Yes, and this account shows that informal witnessing had not died out among professing Christians of that time.

10 Concerning the early Christians, it has also been stated: "There was simply a constantly increasing number of individual Christian believers, who, wherever they went, whether on their regular business or driven by persecution, preached Christ . . . Of those who made their trade, their profession, their every-day occupation, of whatever sort, the means of extending their faith, there was a multitude." (*The Missionary Enterprise,* by Edwin Munsell

9, 10. What secular evidence is there that early Christians witnessed informally?

Bliss, page 14) Yes, early Kingdom proclaimers witnessed formally and informally.

Forethought and Preparation

11 Like Jesus and his early followers, we should witness both formally and informally. Doing so effectively requires forethought and preparation. To witness informally or give instruction, Jesus referred to children, food, clothing, birds, flowers, weather conditions, and occupations. (Matthew 4:18, 19; 6:25-34; 11:16-19; 13:3-8; 16:1-4) We too can use nearly any subject as a basis for focusing attention on God's truth.

12 We can witness informally to people sitting in parks, standing in lines at shopping centers, and so forth. In Athens, Paul reasoned "every day in the marketplace with those who happened to be on hand." (Acts 17:17) But we need to prepare for informal witnessing. For instance, are you planning a trip by plane, train, or bus? Then take along a Bible and some tracts, magazines, or brochures. Reading Christian publications on public transportation or elsewhere often sparks a conversation.

13 A friendly introduction obviously comes first. The handbook *Reasoning From the Scriptures* suggests introductions for use in the field ministry, but some of these can be modified for use when witnessing informally. For example, if while traveling you are seated next to an elderly person, you might say: "My name is ———. I've been thinking quite a lot about the purpose of life. Many people are so busy making a living that they hardly have time to think about life's pur-

11. What can we learn from Jesus about focusing attention on God's truth?
12. When planning a trip, how can one prepare for informal witnessing?
13. Illustrate how you might start witnessing to an elderly person while traveling.

pose. As we get up in years, though, we realize that life is rather short and may wonder: 'Is this all that life is meant to be?' Do you think that God has a purpose for our existence?" Allow for a response. Then you might speak about God's purpose for mankind and comment on the grand things promised at Revelation 21:3, 4. For effective informal witnessing, you can also apply other fine points learned at congregation meetings and in Christian publications.

Advance preparation will enable us to witness informally in an effective way

Good Results Can Be Expected

[14] Like Jesus and his early followers, we can have success when witnessing informally. To illustrate: During a plane trip, one Witness spoke to a military officer who had been married for 20 years. That man's wife was on drugs, had attempted suicide several times, and was about to leave him for a younger man. When the Witness spoke of the Scriptural help that he was receiving from *The Watchtower* and its companion journal *Awake!,* the officer subscribed and wanted to have the magazines sent to his wife. Other passengers heard what the Witness said. The result? Why, because of witnessing on that occasion, he obtained 22 subscriptions and placed 45 magazines and 21 books!

[15] What about witnessing informally to fellow workers? One brother left copies of our journals in the washroom at his place

of employment. A workmate read the magazines, contacted the brother, and subscribed for them. The man also accepted a Bible study and abandoned his debauched life, but his wife left the house every time God's name was mentioned. When the man wanted to resign from the local church, the minister came to discuss this, finding only the man's wife home. The minister's lack of faith and his lies about Jehovah's Witnesses shocked her, for she had seen her husband change for the better. She told the minister: "You can write a certificate of resignation for me and the children too!" In time, this man and his wife became baptized Witnesses.

[16] Years ago, a brother now living in the United States witnessed informally to a coworker in England and took the young man to a film showing arranged by Jehovah's Witnesses. Thirty-one years later,

---

14. What success did one brother have in witnessing informally during a trip?
15, 16. (a) Give examples of successful informal witnessing to fellow workers. (b) What do these results suggest to you?

the brother received this letter: "I would like to tell you now that the witness you gave [the young man] paid off, for about two years later another brother spoke to him, placed magazines, and took him along to the local Kingdom Hall . . . He became a Witness, was baptized in 1959, and now is an elder in his congregation . . . After some 14 years his wife became a Witness and was baptized also. Two years later his daughter was baptized and is now a regular pioneer in North Derbyshire . . . From that bit of witnessing you did way back there in Ashford, that chap, his wife and daughter, a cousin and her daughter, husband and five children, and one child of the cousin's other daughter all became Witnesses. . . . I would like to thank you, Ted, very much indeed, for I am the steel erector, and the story I have just related is my own story of your witness to me and how it all turned out."

17 You younger servants of Jehovah also have a fine witnessing territory—your schoolmates and teachers. Do you give an informal witness in essays, oral reviews, and so forth? As source material for an essay, an Ecuadorean high school student with whom a Bible study was being conducted used the August 22, 1985, *Awake!*

---

17. What opportunities for informal witnessing do younger servants of Jehovah have?

What Are Your Answers?

□ Informal witnessing has what Scriptural basis?

□ What are some ways to prepare for informal witnessing?

□ If we witness informally, what results may we expect?

□ How should we view informal witnessing in relation to regular field ministry?

cover series "Hiroshima—Has Its Lesson Been Lost?" Her composition won the commendation of judges in an international contest and resulted in a free trip to Japan. Of course, the winning of contests is not the purpose of Christian publications. But this illustrates the value of such literature and the effectiveness of giving a witness to God's praise in school.

18 For financial reasons, a sister had to rent out a room. Upon receiving a telephone inquiry about it, she told the female caller that she was one of Jehovah's Witnesses and could not permit promiscuity in her home. Visitors would have to leave at an early hour, and male visitors would have to be visible at all times. The caller hesitated, then said: "I studied when I was a teenager, but it didn't impress me. So I went to college." Asked if she wished to resume her Bible study, she replied, "Yes." In time, the caller, her mother, and her sister became dedicated servants of Jehovah—all because a sister witnessed informally.

19 In the Bahamas a certain Catholic woman's conscience bothered her because she had not been to church for five years. So one rainy Sunday morning, she set out on the road to church. Along came three Witnesses, who gave her a car ride—and a witness. When they got to the church, she wanted to hear more and remained with them as they drove on to pick up a Bible student. They again passed the church, yet she wanted to hear more and so went on to the Kingdom Hall. The public talk was on the very subject discussed in the car. A Bible study was started with the woman, who dismissed the man with whom she was living (the father of her four children), and she was baptized

---

18. What resulted from giving a brief witness to a person seeking to rent a room?
19. How did informal witnessing turn out in the case of a woman in the Bahamas?

during a convention in Nassau in 1986. How happy she was that someone witnessed to her informally!

Keep Talking About God's Kingship!

20 Witnessing informally is no substitute for the regular field ministry of Jehovah's Witnesses. Preaching from house to house clearly is both Scriptural and effective. (Acts 5:42; 20:20, 21) Nevertheless, informal witnessing is fruitful, and Jehovah's servants should share in it. Wherever there are people—relatives, fellow students, workmates, others—there are opportunities to talk about the glory of God's kingship. So let neither fear nor timidity hinder you. (Proverbs 29:25;

20. (a) How should informal witnessing be viewed in relation to the field ministry? (b) What is suggested if one is reluctant to witness informally?

2 Timothy 1:6-8) If you are reluctant to witness informally, why not pray as did Jesus' persecuted disciples? They pleaded: "Jehovah, . . . grant your slaves to keep speaking your word with all boldness." Was their prayer answered? Yes, for "the place in which they were gathered together was shaken; and they were one and all filled with the holy spirit and were speaking the word of God with boldness."—Acts 4:23-31.

21 So, then, cultivate a positive attitude toward informal witnessing. Let love for God move you to give a witness under all kinds of circumstances. Be enthusiastic, virtually bubbling with the truth at every opportunity. Indeed, keep talking about the glory of God's kingship.

21. What will motivate a person to give a witness under all circumstances?

Opening the Way to Increase in Gibraltar

THE stadium is in full view of Gibraltar—only about a mile away. Yet, for more than 13 years, the Gibraltarians had to make a journey of at least ten hours to get there. It involved a voyage by sea first to North Africa, then back to Spain, and finally a ride by bus. Why so long a journey to get to a point so close?

In 1969 Spain's Franco regime closed the border at the narrow isthmus connecting Spain and Gibraltar. It was the result of a dispute between Spain and Britain over territorial sovereignty regarding the Rock, as Gibraltar is often called. Such an inconvenience, however, was not new for the Gibraltarians. Because of its unique strategic importance, Gibraltar has been a fortress often isolated from neighboring countries.

Early in the eighth century, Moorish invaders under Ṭārik captured this piece of land and named it "Jabal Ṭāriq" (Ṭārik's mountain), which has since been corrupted to "Gibraltar." The Moors strongly fortified the Rock, which rises about 1,400 feet above sea level. Over the centuries, it was the scene of numerous sieges by the Moors and the Spaniards. The Spaniards finally took over Gibraltar in 1462, holding it till 1704, when the British captured it and built a naval base there.

In addition to the garrison, people from many countries settled in the town that lies at the foot of the Rock, giving rise to a mixed population descended largely from Moorish, Spanish, British, Hebrew, and Genoese settlers. The majority of the population now speak Spanish and English.

Bible Truth Reaches Gibraltar

In modern times, seeds of Bible truth were first planted in Gibraltar in the summer of 1958. Jehovah's Witnesses traveling to attend a convention in London, England, took advantage of their port of call at Gibraltar to preach the good news of the Kingdom. Some residents accepted subscriptions to *The Watchtower*.

A missionary couple arrived in Gibraltar the following year to water these "seeds." But the authorities yielded to the pressure from religious leaders and expelled the couple after two years. Yet, a small group of some 25 Witnesses had been formed, and their faithful work over the years has been rewarded by a steady increase, reaching 132 Kingdom proclaimers in March 1987. Certainly, this growth testifies to the endurance of the congregation in the face of problems peculiar to Gibraltar.

Isolation—A Unique Problem

Apart from the economic and social problems that subsequently arose from the border closing, Jehovah's Witnesses were severely hampered in associating with others of their faith in neighboring congregations in Spain. During the 13 years of the land blockade, however, they did not miss out on the rich spiritual food offered at both the circuit assemblies and district conventions. The program was always repeated later at the local Kingdom Hall in Gibraltar.

The forced isolation posed a special test for the younger ones of the congregation. Restricted to the 2.25-square-mile area of Gibraltar, they had to act wisely to face the issues of nationalism, materialism, and marriage.

Marriage? Yes, for being restricted to just their small congregation limited their opportunity of finding a suitable marriage mate. Female members of the congregation were besieged by invitations from worldly youths who wanted to date them. The young Witnesses in Gibraltar had to take to heart the wise counsel of the Bible to marry "only in the Lord."—1 Corinthians 7:39; compare Genesis 24:1-4.

In one case a young Witness, ignoring the counsel from the Author of marriage, started dating a local girl who was not a member of the congregation. But the patient help of the elders in the congregation made him think more seriously about the dangers involved. Finally, he approached his girlfriend and told her that although he felt strong affection for her, his Bible knowledge obligated him to terminate their relationship. 'I want to marry a girl with whom I can live forever, not just for a few years,' he explained.

Though surprised and upset, she was intrigued over just what it was that could interest him more than her companionship. Eventually she started to study the Bible. What began as curiosity blossomed into genuine interest, and she made rapid progress in the truth and was baptized. After this clear indication of her desire to serve Jehovah, the brother renewed the courtship. Some time later they were happily married, reaping the blessing of following Jehovah's wise counsel on marriage.

Border Opening Leads to Theocratic Increase

December 14, 1982, saw the opening of a pedestrian gate on the border. Then on February 6, 1985, free passage was completely restored. The populace fell into a more relaxed atmosphere. Capitalizing on this development, the local congregation stepped up their witnessing work and utilized the occasions to meet together in larger gatherings. Favorably disposed persons now had greater opportunities to come to know the love and harmony that exists among Jehovah's congregated throngs.

For example, a man whose wife had been a Witness for some 20 years decided to accept the invitation to accompany his wife and children as they attended a circuit assembly in Spain. He enjoyed the program and association so much that he decided to stay for the second day. When the assembly concluded, he was offered a home Bible study. "Why not?" he replied, adding, "How about starting this week?" His wife, after long years of praying for such an outcome, was overjoyed.

To make full use of the additional opportunities for preaching, the number of Witnesses serving as auxiliary pioneers (those who devote 60 hours a month to the public ministry) increased. Such zealous activity has brought about a 35-percent increase in the congregation since 1982.

Informal witnessing has also played a large part in the growth of the congregation. Two Witnesses making an inspection at the port during their secular work noticed a New World Translation Bible that was just barely visible through the porthole of a yacht. Immediately, they looked up the owner. He turned out to be the pier master, who had studied with Jehovah's Witnesses in Britain before recently settling in Gibraltar. He readily renewed his study and made rapid progress together with his lady companion. Soon they legalized their marital status

In Our Next Issue

- Religion and Superstition —Friends or Foes?

- Are You Remaining Clean in Every Respect?

- Religion's Tidal Wave —The Final Reckoning

and were baptized. This British couple now devote much of the time they spend in the ministry working among the English-speaking community and have been instrumental in the formation of a study group there.

One Bible study they started was with Tim and Tracy, a young married couple living in a military barracks. Although Tim played the trombone in the regiment's band, he became determined to devote himself wholly to the peaceful Kingdom interests of Jehovah. Relatives brought pressure on the couple, urging them to stop associating with the Witnesses. However, they continued their Bible study and became firmer in their faith.

Tim requested a discharge, though he had originally enlisted for a six-year term. When the review of his case seemed to delay unnecessarily, Tim took the initiative to speak to the military doctor, explaining that the uncertainty of their future was adversely affecting his wife.

The doctor concurred and used his influence to speed up the review. Soon Tim was transferred back to England with his regiment, where he finally won his discharge. Now both are serving as dedicated Witnesses.

Future Prospects

With the border opened, the Witnesses in Gibraltar also have been able to give a helping hand to nearby Spanish congregations. They preach along the renowned Costa del Sol (Sun Coast), where many English-speaking people are found.

Although the "Gibraltar question" still remains unresolved from a political point of view, Jehovah's Witnesses in Gibraltar and Spain are completely united spiritually, as is true earth wide. They put their trust in the "Rock" whose strength is eternal, echoing the words of the psalmist: "O come let us cry out joyfully to Jehovah! Let us shout in triumph to our Rock of salvation."—Psalm 95:1.

Questions From Readers

■ What was Moses' error that cost him the privilege of entering the Promised Land? Was it that he *hit* the rock instead of just *speaking* to it or that he failed to glorify Jehovah God?

It seems that Moses' error was more than just that he hit the rock instead of speaking to it, as God had directed.

Near the end of 40 years of wandering, the Israelites camped at Kadesh-barnea in the wilderness of Zin (or, Paran). They had camped there decades earlier, likely because three springs in the area produce a verdant oasis, such as seen in the accompanying photograph. On this occasion, though, water was scarce, which may have meant that the people could not find much food.

So they quarreled with Moses, Jehovah's representative, saying: "Why have you conducted us up out of Egypt to bring us into this evil place? It is no place of seed and figs and vines and pomegranates, and there is no water to drink."—Numbers 20:5.

Then God told Moses and Aaron: "Take the rod and call the assembly together, . . . and you *must speak to the crag* before their eyes that it may indeed give its water; and you must bring out water for them from the crag and give the assembly and their beasts of burden drink." (Numbers 20:8) What happened next?

"Moses and Aaron called the congregation together before the crag, and he proceeded to say to them: 'Hear, now, you rebels! Is it from this crag that *we* shall bring out water for you?' With that Moses lifted his hand up and *struck the crag* with his rod twice; and much water began to come out."—Numbers 20:10, 11.

Some have noted that God directed Moses and Aaron to "speak to the crag," but they "struck the crag." Did this difference so displease Jehovah that he told Moses and Aaron that He would not permit them to lead Israel into the Promised Land?

Springtime at oasis around one of the springs in the area of Kadesh-barnea

It does not seem so. The fact is that just months after the Exodus, the people had first complained over lack of water. This was near Mount Sinai (Horeb), at a place that came to be called Meribah (in the area seen below). Note what God told Moses on that occasion: "I am standing before you there on the rock in Horeb. And *you must strike on the rock,* and water must come out of it, and the people must drink it." (Exodus 17:2-7; 33:6) So when, at Kadesh, Moses was told to speak to the rock, he might have been inclined to do what he had earlier done at God's direction, even if God meant that *speaking* to the rock would be sufficient.

It seems that something more led to God's judgment of Moses and Aaron. What might that have been? Moses said to the quarrelsome people: "Is it from this crag that we shall bring out water for you?" Psalm 106:33 gives us insight into this, for it shows that Moses acted out of a bitter spirit and that he 'spoke rashly with his lips.' With angry words, he called attention to himself and Aaron rather than to the One who really could miraculously provide water. Thus, just before Moses died at the border of the Promised Land, God referred to the incident at Kadesh-barnea and indicated that Moses' error was that he failed to 'sanctify God before the eyes of the people.'—Numbers 27:12-14.

We can take a lesson from this. While it certainly is important to restrain ourselves from angry acts, it is equally vital to control our spirit, particularly when others fall short. If we let ourselves become overly disturbed, we might begin to view God's servants on a human basis, rather than recognizing that they still are God's "sheep." True, they are imperfect and may do irritating things, but they are "his people and the sheep of his pasturage." (Psalm 100:3) God let his Son die for such ones, so should we not strive to be patient with them, focusing less on how we feel or are affected and more on their standing with God?

She Missed the Bus

ONE day James saw his daughter Rebecca walking with unusual slowness to meet the school bus. Though Rebecca could see the bus coming, she walked even slower and deliberately missed the bus.

That same evening James and his wife, Veronica, discussed the matter by reviewing the story of "Jonah and the Big Fish" from *My Book of Bible Stories*. It was one of Rebecca's favorites. After finishing the story, the parents tied it in with their daughter's problem. She really got the point and said: "Even though Jonah ran away and got into trouble in the sea, and he was swallowed by the fish and was vomited out —his work for Jehovah was still waiting for him to do."

The next day Rebecca went to school with a new attitude and *My Book of Bible Stories* under her arm.

the Watchtower

November 1, 1987

Announcing Jehovah's Kingdom

Does Superstition Affect Your Life?

The Watchtower®
Announcing Jehovah's Kingdom

November 1, 1987
Vol. 108, No. 21

In This Issue

THE PURPOSE OF *THE WATCHTOWER* is to exalt Jehovah God as the Sovereign of the universe. It keeps watch on world events as they fulfill Bible prophecy. It comforts all peoples with the good news that God's Kingdom will soon destroy those who oppress their fellowmen and that it will turn the earth into a paradise. It encourages faith in the now-reigning King, Jesus Christ, whose shed blood opens the way for mankind to gain eternal life. *The Watchtower,* published by Jehovah's Witnesses continuously since 1879, is nonpolitical. It adheres to the Bible as its authority.

WATCHTOWER STUDIES FOR THE WEEKS

Average Printing Each Issue: 12,315,000

Now Published in 103 Languages

SEMIMONTHLY LANGUAGES AVAILABLE BY MAIL
Afrikaans, Arabic, Cebuano, Chichewa, Chinese, Cibemba, Danish,* Dutch,* Efik, English,* Finnish,* French,* German,* Greek,* Hiligaynon, Igbo, Iloko, Italian,* Japanese,* Korean, Lingala, Malagasy, Maltese, Norwegian, Portuguese,* Russian, Sepedi, Sesotho, Shona, Spanish,* Swahili, Swedish,* Tagalog, Thai, Tsonga, Tswana, Xhosa, Yoruba, Zulu

MONTHLY LANGUAGES AVAILABLE BY MAIL
Armenian, Bengali, Bicol, Bislama, Bulgarian, Croatian, Czech, Ewe, Fijian, Ga, Greenlandic, Gujarati, Gun, Hausa, Hebrew, Hindi, Hiri Motu, Hungarian, Icelandic, Kannada, Malayalam, Marathi, New Guinea Pidgin, Pangasinan, Papiamento, Polish, Rarotongan, Romanian, Samar-Leyte, Samoan, Sango, Serbian, Silozi, Sinhalese, Slovenian, Solomon Islands-Pidgin, Tahitian, Tamil, Telugu, Tongan, Tshiluba, Turkish, Twi, Ukrainian, Urdu, Venda, Vietnamese

* Study articles also available in large-print edition.

Watch Tower Society offices	Yearly subscription for the above: Semimonthly Languages	Monthly Languages
America, U.S., Watchtower, Wallkill, N.Y. 12589	$5.00	$2.50
Australia, Box 280, Ingleburn, N.S.W. 2565	A$7.00	A$3.50
Canada, Box 4100, Halton Hills, Ontario L7G 4Y4	$7.00	$3.50
England, The Ridgeway, London NW7 1RN	£5.00	£2.50
Ireland, 29A Jamestown Road, Finglas, Dublin 11	IR£6.00	IR£3.00
New Zealand, P.O. Box 142, Manurewa	NZ$15.00	NZ$7.50
Nigeria, PMB 001, Shomolu, Lagos State	₦8.00	₦4.00
Philippines, P.O. Box 2044, Manila 2800	₱60.00	₱30.00
South Africa, Private Bag 2067, Krugersdorp, 1740	R9.00	R4.50

Remittances should be sent to the office in your country or to Watchtower, Wallkill, N.Y. 12589, U.S.A.

Changes of address should reach us 30 days before your moving date. Give us your old and new address (if possible, your old address label).

25 cents (U.S.) a copy

The Bible translation used is the *New World Translation of the Holy Scriptures,* unless otherwise indicated.

The Watchtower (ISSN 0043-1087) is published semimonthly for $5.00 (U.S.) per year by Watch Tower Bible and Tract Society of Pennsylvania, 25 Columbia Heights, Brooklyn, N.Y. 11201. Second-class postage paid at Brooklyn, N.Y., and at additional mailing offices.

Postmaster: Send address changes to Watchtower, **Wallkill, N.Y. 12589.**

Published by
Watch Tower Bible and Tract Society of Pennsylvania
25 Columbia Heights, Brooklyn, N.Y. 11201, U.S.A.

Frederick W. Franz, President

Religion and Superstition

Friends or Foes?

ON Saturday, June 11, 1983, villagers on the Indonesian island of Java could be seen rushing to their houses, frantically sealing all cracks in ceilings, windows, and doors. Why the panic? A solar eclipse had begun, and the villagers feared that the shadow of the eclipse would enter their houses and cause calamity.

Inhabitants of the so-called developing world often follow such beliefs with religious fervor. Thus, in some parts of Africa, people avoid walking in the sun at noontime because they "may become insane." Children are forbidden to eat eggs for fear "they will become thieves." Parents will not tell the exact number of their children, for "witches may hear you bragging and take one of them."—*African Primal Religions.*

Westerners tend to laugh at such practices as a display of superstitious fear, the product of 'pagan ignorance.' Yet, such beliefs are not limited to non-Christians. They "are found among people all over the world," says Dr. Wayland Hand, professor of folklore and Germanic languages. He and his colleague Dr. Tally have already col-

lected nearly a million examples of superstitions in the United States alone.

Yearning to know their fate, many so-called Christians look to astrology—one of the oldest forms of superstition. And curiously, superstitious beliefs sometimes receive the open support and backing of religious leaders. For example, on a cold day in New York, January 10, 1982, Eastern Greek Orthodox patriarch Vasilios presided over an open-air Mass to celebrate the Feast of the Epiphany. After that, reports the *New York Post,* he hurled a golden cross into the East River and told bystanders that the first person to retrieve the cross would have good luck for the rest of his life.

But are Christian beliefs and superstition compatible? A writer once observed: "On the grave of faith there blooms the flower of superstition." Therefore, would you not expect Christian religion to counteract and dispel superstitious fear?

Religion —Does It Dispel Superstitious Fear?

True religion should, and in the first century it did. Although the early

Christians were living in the midst of the superstitious Roman world, they rejected superstitions. But after the death of Christ's apostles, false religious teachings, including superstitions, began to filter into the congregation. (1 Timothy 4:1, 7; Acts 20:30) A clergy class began to emerge that, according to the book *A History of the Christian Church,* went along with the practice of using horoscopes and following other superstitions. In time such popular practices were labeled "Christian."

And today? Religion still tolerates superstitious customs. Consider Suriname, where so-called Christians of African descent can often be seen wearing amulets for supposed protection against evil spirits. Says one observer: "Daily these people live, eat, work and sleep in dread." Millions throughout the world have a similar fear of the "spirits" of the dead. Ironically, religion has often promoted such superstitious beliefs.

Take as an example what happened on the African island of Madagascar. When Christendom's missionaries began to spread their beliefs, the Madagascans were responsive but unwilling to let go of traditional beliefs. The reaction of the churches? Says the *Daily Nation,* a newspaper from Kenya: "The early missionaries were tolerant and flexible and came to accept this situation." The result? Today, half the people of Madagascar are listed as Christian. Yet, they also fear the "spirits" of dead ancestors! Thus, they commonly invite the priest or pastor to bless the bones of an ancestor before they are put back in the family sepulcher. Yes, religious leaders have perpetuated the lie that God, the Devil, and dead ancestors can be cajoled, flattered, and bribed by observing superstitious habits.

The same is true in South Africa, where 77 percent of the population claims to be Christian and church attendance is high. Yet, traditional African religion, with its superstitious fear of dead ancestors, lingers on among millions of those churchgoers. Thus, in many so-called Christian countries, religion is merely a veneer. Scratch the surface, and the old superstitions can be seen to have survived and thrived.

True religion, however, dispels superstitious fear. How? The key is knowledge. Knowledge of what? And how can you get it?

True Religion Dispels Fear How?

BRITISH authors Edwin and Mona Radford were puzzled. After collecting over two thousand superstitions, they found the same superstitious fears in Scotland, India, and Uganda, and in Central America as well. They wondered, 'What could account for this?' Writer Robertson Davies correctly observes: "Superstition seems to have a link with some body of belief that far antedates the religions we know." Then, what pre-Christian "body of belief" is the root of superstition?

Superstition's Root and Branches

The Bible points to the land of Shinar (the area between the Tigris and Euphrates rivers, later called Babylonia) as the birthplace of false religious concepts, including superstitions. There, "a mighty hunter" named Nimrod began the building of the infamous Tower of Babel. It was to be used for false worship. Jehovah God, though, frustrated the plans of the builders by confusing their language. Gradually, the building work halted, and they were scattered. (Genesis 10:8-10; 11:2-9) But wherever they settled, they carried the same beliefs, ideas, and myths with them. Babel, however, remained a center of false religion, in time also expanding its role as mother and wet nurse to magic, sorcery, and superstitious beliefs, such as astrology. (Compare Isaiah 47:12, 13; Daniel 2:27; 4:7.) Thus, the book *Great Cities of the Ancient World* notes: "Astrology was based upon two Babylonic ideas: the zodiac, and the divinity of the heavenly bodies. . . . The Babylonians credited the planets with the influences that one would expect of their respective deities."

How have these ancient events affected us? The Bible book of Revelation indicates that a worldwide, false religious system has developed from the ideas of ancient Babylon. It exists down to our day and is called "Babylon the Great." (Revelation 17:5) Of course, the passing of time and local developments have influenced those original Babylonian ideas. The great diversity of religion seen today is the result. But just

Superstitions spread worldwide from their fountainhead at Babylon

as diverse trees often grow in the same soil, so diverse religions and superstitions around the world have their roots in common ground —Babylon. To illustrate, let us see how one of Babylon's superstitious beliefs has filtered into nearly all religions of the world today.

Fear of the Dead —Based on What?

The Babylonians believed that a spiritual part of man survived the death of the fleshly body and could come back to affect the living for good or for bad. They thus invented religious rites designed to appease the dead and avoid their vengeance. This belief is still alive in many lands today. In Africa, for example, it "plays a vital role in the everyday life of almost every . . . society."—*African Religions—Symbol, Ritual, and Community.*

Even professed Christians in such lands are affected. For example, Henriette, a 63-year-old woman of African descent, admits: "Although I was an active member of the local Protestant church, I feared the 'spirits' of the dead. We lived close to a cemetery, and whenever a funeral procession approached our house, I woke up my child and held it close until the procession had passed. Otherwise, the 'spirit' of the dead would enter my house and possess the sleeping child."

Such superstition survives because the

teaching of the immortal soul prevails in Christendom. History shows that Greek philosophers—especially Plato—elaborated on the Babylonian idea of immortality. Under their influence, writes John Dunnett, a British senior lecturer in theology, "the concept of the immortality of the soul came largely to permeate the Christian Church." This Babylonian teaching has kept millions in slavery to superstitious fear.

True religion, however, dispels such fear. Why? Because true religion is not based on beliefs rooted in Babylon but on teachings found in the Bible.

The Soul According to the Bible

The first book of the Bible tells us that man *became* a soul, a living person. (Genesis 2:7) So when a person dies, the soul dies. Confirms the prophet Ezekiel: "The soul that is sinning—it itself will die." (Ezekiel 18:4; Romans 3:23) The soul is mortal and does not live on after death. Instead, as Psalm 146:4 says: "His spirit goes out, he goes back to his ground; in that day his thoughts do perish." Hence, lecturer John Dunnett concludes, the immortality of the soul "remains a non-Biblical belief."

If there is no immortal soul, there can be no "spirits" of the dead to terrify persons on earth. The foundation for superstitious fear of the dead thus crumbles.

Fear Based on Deception

Superstitious fear of the dead dies hard. Why? Because eerie things do happen —like that night when a middle-aged woman in Suriname heard someone calling her name. She ignored it, but invisible "hands" then began to touch her, and when she objected to that, she was nearly strangled by an invisible force. Perhaps you wonder, 'If the "spirits" of the dead are not alive, then who was responsible?'

Again, Bible knowledge dissolves superstitious fear.

It explains that wicked spirit forces, called demons, do exist. Those demons, however, are not departed souls. They are angels of God who rebelled and sided with Satan, "who is misleading the entire inhabited earth." (Revelation 12:9; James 2:19; Ephesians 6:12; 2 Peter 2:4) The Bible shows that the demons find delight in misleading, frightening, and harassing humans. The account at Luke 9:37-43 relates that a demon threw a boy "into convulsions with foam" and afflicted him with bruises. Even when the boy was led to Jesus, "the demon dashed him to the ground and violently convulsed him. However," the account continues, "Jesus rebuked the unclean spirit and healed the boy and delivered him to his father."

Interestingly, the *Cyclopedia of Biblical, Theological, and Ecclesiastical Literature* defines superstition as "the worship of false gods." Thus, if you perform such superstitious acts, you are, perhaps unwittingly, appeasing "false gods," or the demons! Such false worship is a serious offense against Jehovah God.—Compare 1 Corinthians 10:20 and Deuteronomy 18: 10-12.*

'Subject Yourselves to God'—Do You?

Would you have the courage to turn your back on those demons by rejecting superstition? True, demons are powerful. But after showing that we have to choose to serve either Jehovah God or the demons, the apostle Paul asked: "We are not stronger than [Jehovah] is, are we?" (1 Corinthians 10:21, 22) No, we are not —but remember, neither are Satan and

---

* Some Bible versions (for example, the *King James Version, Douay, The Comprehensive Bible*) use the word "superstition" at Acts 25:19 to translate the Greek word *dei·si·dai·mo·ni´as,* meaning "dread of demons." See also *New World Translation Reference Bible* footnote.

his demons! Instead, those demons "shudder" out of dread of Jehovah. (James 2:19) But the Almighty God offers you his protection if you ask for it. Bible writer James further says: "Subject yourselves, therefore, to God; but oppose the Devil, and he will flee from you." (James 4:7) Your superstitious fear will likewise flee.

Thousands around the globe who once lived in fear and slavery to superstitious customs can now testify to that. The Devil fled from them! In what way? Remember, the enemy of superstitious fear is knowledge. Says Professor Rudolph Brasch, an expert on the origin of superstitions: "It's a matter of education—that the more educated people get, the less superstitious they get."

Thus, when Henriette, mentioned before, accepted the invitation of Jehovah's Witnesses to begin a free study of the Bible, she soon saw through the demonic ruse. The tentacles of superstition lost their grip. She, and thousands like her, have experienced the truthfulness of the words at Hebrews 2:15. There, the apostle Paul says that Jesus will "free those who all their lives were held in slavery by their fear of death." (*New International Version*) Just as the tropical morning sun evaporates the heavy dew of the rain forest, the light of Bible truth dispels all superstitious fear.

Today, numerous former 'fearful slaves' have removed the amulets from their necks and the protective strings from their children. Now they feel as does Isaac, a 68-year-old former South African witch doctor. After studying the Bible with Jehovah's Witnesses, he said: "I feel very happy and free because I am no longer burdened by the fear of spirits." How true Jesus' words prove to be: "You will know the truth, and the truth will set you free"! —John 8:32.

Yes, true religion does dispel fear!

What Defiles a Man?

OPPOSITION to Jesus becomes stronger. Not only do many of his disciples leave but Jews in Judea are seeking to kill him, even as they did when he was in Jerusalem during the Passover of 31 C.E.

It is now the Passover of 32 C.E. Likely, in accordance with God's requirement to attend, Jesus goes up to the Passover in Jerusalem. However, he does so cautiously because his life is in danger. Afterward he returns to Galilee.

Jesus is perhaps in Capernaum when Pharisees and scribes from Jerusalem come to him. They are looking for grounds on which to accuse him of religious lawbreaking. "Why is it your disciples overstep the tradition of the men of former times?" they inquire. "For example, they do not wash their hands when about to eat a meal." This is not something required by God, yet the Pharisees consider it a serious offense not to perform this traditional ritual, which included washing up to the elbows.

Rather than answering their accusation, Jesus points to their wicked and willful breaking of God's Law. "Why is it you also overstep the commandment of God because of your tradition?" he wants to know. "For example, God said, 'Honor your father and your mother'; and, 'Let him that reviles father or mother end up in death.' But you say, 'Whoever says to his father or mother: "Whatever I have by which you might get benefit from me is a gift dedicated to God," he must not honor his father at all.'"

Indeed, the Pharisees teach that money, property, or anything dedicated as a gift to God belongs to the temple, and it cannot be used for some other purpose. Yet, actually, the dedicated gift is kept by the person who dedicated it. In this way a son, by simply saying that his money or property is "corban" —a gift dedicated to God or to the temple—evades his responsibility to help his aged parents, who may be in desperate straits.

Properly indignant at the Pharisees' wicked twisting of God's Law, Jesus says: "You have made the word of God invalid because of your tradition. You hypocrites, Isaiah aptly prophesied about you, when he said, 'This people honors me with their lips, yet their heart is far removed from me. It is in vain that they keep worshiping me, because they teach commands of men as doctrines.'"

Perhaps the crowd had backed away to allow the Pharisees to question Jesus. Now, when the Pharisees have no

answer to Jesus' strong censure of them, he calls the crowd near. "Listen to me," he says, "and get the meaning. There is nothing from outside a man that passes into him that can defile him; but the things that issue forth out of a man are the things that defile a man."

Later, when they enter a house, his disciples ask: "Do you know that the Pharisees stumbled at hearing what you said?"

"Every plant that my heavenly Father did not plant will be uprooted," Jesus answers. "Let them be. Blind guides is what they are. If, then, a blind man guides a blind man, both will fall into a pit."

Jesus seems surprised when, in behalf of the disciples, Peter asks for clarification regarding what defiles a man.

"Are you also yet without understanding?" Jesus responds. "Are you not aware that everything entering into the mouth passes along into the intestines and is discharged into the sewer? However, the things proceeding out of the mouth come out of the heart, and those things defile a man. For example, out of the heart come wicked reasonings, murders, adulteries, fornications, thieveries, false testimonies, blasphemies. These are the things defiling a man; but to take a meal with unwashed hands does not defile a man."

Jesus is not here discouraging normal hygiene. He is not arguing that a person need not wash his hands before preparing food or eating a meal. Rather, Jesus is condemning the hypocrisy of religious leaders who deviously try to circumvent God's righteous laws by insisting on unscriptural traditions. Yes, it is wicked deeds that defile a man, and Jesus shows that these originate in a person's heart. **John 7:1; Deuteronomy 16: 16; Matthew 15:1-20; Mark 7:1-23; Exodus 20:12; 21:17; Isaiah 29:13.**

♦ What opposition does Jesus now face?

♦ What accusation do the Pharisees make, but according to Jesus, how do the Pharisees willfully break God's Law?

♦ What does Jesus reveal are the things that defile a man?

"You Must Be Holy . . ."

"In accord with the Holy One who called you, do you also become holy yourselves in all your conduct, because it is written: 'You must be holy, because I am holy.'"
—1 PETER 1:15, 16.

"HOLINESS belongs to Jehovah." These stirring words were displayed for all to see, engraved upon a pure gold plate tied upon the turban worn by the high priest of Israel. (Exodus 28: 36-38) They served as a shining reminder that unlike the heathen nations who rendered homage to unclean deities, Israel worshiped a clean, holy God.

² If you are already one of Jehovah's Witnesses, do you appreciate just how pure, clean, holy, and righteous is the God whom you worship? A reminder of such an elementary truth may hardly seem necessary. After all, as Jehovah's people, we have been blessed with an insight into "the deep things of God"—intricate Bible prophecies, the application of Bible principles, Bible doctrine. (1 Corinthians 2:10; compare Daniel 12:4.) Yet, it is evident that a heartfelt appreciation of Jehovah's holiness is lacking on the part of some. Why? Because thousands each year lapse into forms of immorality. Thousands more invite calamity by engaging in actions that are just short of being violations of Bible law. Clearly, some do not grasp the seriousness of the words at 1 Peter 1: 15, 16: "In accord with the Holy One who called you, do you also become holy yourselves in all your conduct, because it is written: 'You must be holy, because I am holy.'"

Holy God, Holy Worshipers

³ 'An imperfect person—holy? Impossible!' you might say. However, consider the background of Peter's admonition. The apostle here quoted words that were first addressed to Israel shortly after the Exodus from Egypt. Through this miraculous

1, 2. (a) What reminder was displayed on the turban of the high priest, and what purpose did it serve? (b) Why is a reminder of Jehovah's holiness appropriate today? (c) What admonition does Peter give regarding holiness?

3. What does Moses' song indicate as to Jehovah?

deliverance, Jehovah had been revealed as a Deliverer, a Fulfiller of promises, "a manly person of war." (Exodus 3:14-17; 15:3) In a song celebrating the Egyptian debacle at the Red Sea, Moses now revealed yet another facet of Jehovah: "Who among the gods is like you, O Jehovah? Who is like you, proving yourself *mighty in holiness?*" (Exodus 15:11) This is the first recorded occasion on which holiness was ascribed to Jehovah.

⁴ The Hebrew and Greek words rendered "holy" in the Bible convey the idea of being 'bright, new, fresh, untarnished, and clean.' Moses thus portrayed Jehovah as clean in the superlative degree, devoid of impurity, beyond corruption, unrelentingly intolerant of uncleanness. (Habakkuk 1:13) Jehovah stood in radiant contrast to the gods of the land the Israelites would soon inhabit—Canaan. Documents unearthed at Ras Shamra, a town on the north Syrian coast, give a limited, but nonetheless illuminating, glimpse of the Canaanite pantheon. These texts describe gods that were, according to John Gray's book *The Canaanites,* "contentious, jealous, vindictive, lustful."

⁵ Predictably, Canaanite culture reflected the dissolute gods they worshiped. Explains *The Religion of the People of Israel:* "Acts in imitation of the deity were regarded as service to the god. . . . [The sex goddess] Ashtart had a number of men and women ministrants who were described as consecrated persons . . . They consecrated themselves in her service to prostitution." Adds scholar William F. Albright: "At its worst, however, the erotic aspect of their cult must have sunk to

The worship of dissolute gods led to the degradation of the Canaanites

extremely sordid depths of social degradation." The worship of phallic "sacred poles," child sacrifices, magic, binding with spells, incest, sodomy, and bestiality —all of these became 'the way of the land' in Canaan.—Exodus 34:13; Leviticus 18: 2-25; Deuteronomy 18:9-12.

⁶ Jehovah, on the other hand, is "mighty in holiness." He could not tolerate such degradation in his worshipers. (Psalm 15) So, unlike the degrading Canaanite gods, Jehovah elevated his people. Uttering the words Peter would later quote, Jehovah repeatedly exhorted: "You should prove yourselves holy, because I Jehovah your God am holy."—Leviticus 11:44; 19:2; 20:26.

'The Law Is Holy, Righteous, and Good'

⁷ 'Proving themselves holy' meant neither perfection nor an assumed air of false

---

4. (a) In what way is Jehovah "mighty in holiness"? (b) How did Jehovah thus contrast with the gods of Canaan?
5, 6. (a) How did worshiping dissolute gods affect the Canaanites? (b) How did worshiping the holy God affect the Israelites?

7, 8. (a) How could the Israelites 'prove themselves holy'? (b) Contrast Jehovah's Law with the Babylonian Code of Hammurabi.

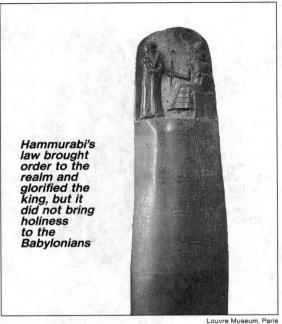

Hammurabi's law brought order to the realm and glorified the king, but it did not bring holiness to the Babylonians

piety; it meant obedience to an extensive law code given to Israel through Moses. (Exodus 19:5, 6) Unlike any other national law, God's Law could be described as "holy and righteous and good."—Romans 7:12.

⁸ True, the Babylonian Code of Hammurabi, which is said to predate the Mosaic Law, covered a similar span of subjects. Some of its statutes, such as the law of 'eye for eye,' or talion, are similar to Mosaic principles. Critics thus claim that Moses merely borrowed his laws from Hammurabi's code. Hammurabi's code, however, did little more than glorify Hammurabi and serve his political interests. God's Law was given to Israel 'for their good always, that they might keep alive.' (Deuteronomy 6:24) There is also little evidence that Hammurabi's law was ever legally binding in Babylon, serving as little more than "legal aid for persons in search of advice." (*The New Encyclopœdia Britannica*, 1985 edition, Volume 21, page 921) The Mosaic Law, though, was binding and carried just penalties for dis-

obedience. Finally, Hammurabi's code focuses on how to deal with wrongdoers; only 5 out of its 280 laws are direct prohibitions. The thrust of God's Law, however, was toward preventing, not punishing, wrongdoing.

⁹ Because it was 'holy, righteous, and good,' the Mosaic Law had a powerful impact upon the personal lives of the Jews. It regulated their worship, provided for Sabbaths of desisting from work, controlled the nation's economic structure, outlined some requirements as to clothing, and gave beneficial guidance in matters of diet, sexual activity, and hygienic habits. Even normal body functions came under the scrutiny of the Mosaic Law.

"The Commandment of Jehovah Is Clean"

¹⁰ Such detailed regulations covering day-to-day living had a lofty purpose: to make the Israelites clean—physically, spiritually, mentally, and morally. For example, laws requiring them to bathe themselves, bury their excreta, quarantine the contagiously ill, and avoid certain foods all promoted health and physical cleanness.*
—Exodus 30:18-20; Leviticus, chapter 11; 13:4, 5, 21, 26; 15:16-18, 21-23; Deuteronomy 23:12-14.

---

* Hammurabi's law had no such provisions; nor has a comparable hygienic code been discovered among the ancient Egyptians, although they practiced a relatively advanced form of medicine. Says the book *Ancient Egypt:* "Magical spells and formulae are freely interspersed [in Egyptian medicine texts] with rational prescriptions." God's Law, however, had no demonic overtones but was scientifically sound. Only in modern times, for example, have doctors seen the need to wash after touching corpses, something the Mosaic Law required millenniums ago!—Numbers, chapter 19.

---

9. What impact did the Mosaic Law have on the lives of the Jews?
10. (a) Why did the Law concern itself with so many areas of life? (b) How did the Law promote physical cleanness and good health? (Include footnote.)

¹¹ Yet, good health and sanitation were really secondary to spiritual cleanness. That is why one who perhaps ate one of the prohibited foods, engaged in sexual relations, or touched a dead body was also declared unclean in a ceremonial way. (Leviticus, chapters 11, 15; Numbers, chapter 19) Such an unclean one was thus barred from participation in worship—in some cases under the pain of death! (Leviticus 15:31; 22:3-8) But what did such prohibitions have to do with spiritual cleanness?

¹² Pagan worship was characterized by prostitution, the worship of the dead, and revelry. But *The International Standard Bible Encyclopedia* points out: "No sexual act was permitted as a means of worshiping Yahweh. All such activity in this regard, therefore, rendered one unclean. . . . In Israel the dead received their proper honor, but in no way were they given undue veneration nor did they become objects of worship . . . Further fellowship at the festivals of pagan neighbors, which would include banqueting, was impossible for an Israelite, because their food was unclean." The regulations of the Law thus constituted a "wall" of separation from unclean religious elements.—Ephesians 2:14.

¹³ The Law also worked for the mental cleanness of the Israelites. Its statutes regarding marital intimacies, for example, served to elevate man's thinking. (Leviticus 15:16-33) Israelites learned self-control in sexual matters, not giving in to unrestrained passion like the Canaanites. The Law even taught its adherents to control their feelings and desires, condemning covetous thinking.—Exodus 20:17.

¹⁴ Most remarkable of all, though, was the Law's stress on moral cleanness. True, Hammurabi's code also condemned such wrongs as adultery. However, an article in *The Biblical Archaeologist* observed: "Unlike the Babylonians and the Assyrians who viewed adultery only as a crime against the proprietary rights of the husband, the Old Testament legislation considers adultery also as a grave offense against morality."

¹⁵ How true, then, the psalmist's words: "The commandment of Jehovah is clean, making the eyes shine." (Psalm 19:8) Granted, at times remaining clean required considerable effort. New mothers, just weeks after the birth of their children, had to go up to Jerusalem so as to engage in purification procedures. (Leviticus 12:1-8; Luke 2:22-24) Both men and women were required to cleanse themselves ceremonially following marital relations, as well as in other related situations. (Leviticus 15:16, 18; Deuteronomy 23:9-14; 2 Samuel 11:11-13) If they conscientiously followed the Law and remained clean, they would 'benefit themselves'—physically, mentally, morally, and spiritually. (Isaiah 48:17) Furthermore, the importance and seriousness of remaining clean would be indelibly impressed upon them. Best of all, such sincere efforts to maintain holiness would win them God's approval.

Clean in an Unclean World

¹⁶ We can now better appreciate Peter's

---

11. What did it mean to be ceremonially unclean?
12. How did the laws of ceremonial cleanness promote spiritual cleanness?
13. How did the Law promote mental cleanness?

14. How was God's Law unique as to promoting moral cleanness?
15. (a) Illustrate how an Israelite might have had to put forth considerable effort to remain clean. (b) How did the Israelites benefit from such efforts?
16, 17. (a) To what extent are Christians today required to remain clean? (b) Why is remaining clean so difficult today? (c) How have prominent individuals failed as role models?

words to Christians: "As obedient children, quit being fashioned according to the desires you formerly had in your ignorance, but, in accord with the Holy One who called you, do you also become holy yourselves in all your conduct, because it is written: 'You must be holy, because I am holy.'"—1 Peter 1:14-16.

[17] Admittedly, this is not easy. Everywhere we look, we see people practicing deceitfulness, dishonesty, sexual immorality. *The New York Times* reported: "Americans are increasingly choosing to live together before marrying." Even prominent people set poor examples. Some of the most popular people in the world today in the fields of sports, politics, and entertainment openly practice forms of uncleanness. "It's terribly disappointing," bemoaned a sports fan, "to have faith in someone as a role model and have them turn out to be tainted." The problem? Several popular athletes had confessed to drug abuse. How often it is that individuals held up as idols lead unclean lives, yes, even sordid lives, as adulterers, fornicators, homosexuals, Lesbians, thieves, extortioners, and drug addicts! They might appear clean physically, but their mouths are filled with foul gutter language. They may even take delight in flouting public decency, boasting about their immoral escapades.

[18] Yet, the Bible's words are not easily brushed aside: "God is not one to be mocked. ["There is no thumbing your nose at God."—*Byington*] For whatever a man is sowing, this he will also reap; because he who is sowing with a view to his flesh will reap corruption from his flesh." (Galatians 6:7, 8) Lewd behavior often results in sickness, or even untimely death, from diseases such as syphilis, gonorrhea, and AIDS, to name the outstanding ones. Mental and emotional imbalance, depression, and even suicide are also at times the result of promiscuous life-styles. So while those sharing in immoral practices may laugh in scorn at those trying to keep themselves clean, the laughter stops as the mockers begin 'reaping what they have sown.'—Compare Romans 1:24-27.

[19] We also live in a religiously defiled world. The clergy may wear beautiful, clean garments, but they teach impure Babylonish practices and doctrines, such as idolatry, the Trinity, hellfire, immortality of the human soul, and purgatory. They are like the religious leaders of whom Jesus said: "Woe to you, scribes and Pharisees, hypocrites! because you resemble whitewashed graves, which outwardly indeed appear beautiful but inside are full of dead men's bones and of every sort of uncleanness. In that way you also, outwardly indeed, appear righteous to men, but inside you are full of hypocrisy and lawlessness."—Matthew 23:27, 28.

[20] The clergy even condone uncleanness in their flock. Individuals who are known as immoral and unclean—practicers of fornication, adulterers, homosexuals—are

---

Questions for Review

☐ How is Jehovah "mighty in holiness," and what does this mean for his worshipers?

☐ How did the Law of Moses differ from the laws of all other nations?

☐ How did the Mosaic Law promote physical, spiritual, mental, and moral cleanness?

☐ How are many who lead unclean lives 'reaping what they have sown'?

---

18. How are many who lead unclean lives 'reaping what they have sown'?
19, 20. How have Christendom's clergy proved themselves religiously and morally contaminated?

permitted to remain in good standing. On this point, *Newsweek* reports: "Maryland psychologist Richard Sipe, a former priest, concludes that about 20 percent of the 57,000 U.S. Catholic priests are homosexual . . . Other therapists think the true figure today may be closer to 40 percent." Catholic theologian John J. McNeill (an admitted homosexual) openly justifies homosexuality: "The love between two lesbians or two homosexuals, assuming that it is a constructive human love, is not sinful nor does it alienate the lovers from God's plan, but can be a holy love."—*The Christian Century.*

[21] The reminder displayed on the high priest's turban is thus more apropos than ever: "Holiness belongs to Jehovah." (Exodus 28:36) Jehovah requires, yes, demands, that we remain clean in all respects! But just how can one do so? What areas might need particular attention? The following article will discuss these questions.

21. How is the reminder "Holiness belongs to Jehovah" appropriate for us today?

Are You Remaining Clean in Every Respect?

"Turn away, turn away, get out of there, touch nothing unclean; get out from the midst of her, keep yourselves clean, you who are carrying the utensils of Jehovah."—ISAIAH 52:11.

SUDDENLY they were free—after 70 years of slavery! A royal decree of about 538 B.C.E. allowed the Jewish nation to return "and rebuild the house of Jehovah the God of Israel." (Ezra 1:2, 3) Next, another startling development: "King Cyrus [of Persia] himself brought forth the utensils of the house of Jehovah, which Nebuchadnezzar had brought out from Jerusalem." (Ezra 1:7, 8) Among these were the sacred vessels Belshazzar and his grandees had defiled on the night of Babylon's fall by brazenly using them to praise false gods! (Daniel 5:3, 4) Now the former exiles could return these utensils to Jerusalem and use them in praise of Jehovah!

[2] As they excitedly prepared for departure, the returning Jews doubtless recalled the words of the prophet Isaiah: "Turn away, turn away, get out of there, touch nothing unclean; get out from the midst of her, keep yourselves clean, you who are carrying the utensils of Jehovah." (Isaiah 52:11) The Levites, of course, did the actual transporting of the utensils. (Numbers 1:50, 51; 4:15) However, Isaiah had foretold that all returnees would be honorary vessel bearers. All were thus

1. (a) How did a royal decree permit the utensils of Jehovah to be returned to Jerusalem? (b) How had some of those vessels been defiled?

2. (a) What prophecy of Isaiah would the returnees call to mind? To whom would it apply? (b) Why were they exhorted not to touch anything unclean?

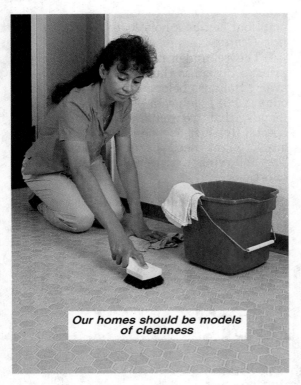

Our homes should be models of cleanness

tians of his day, saying: "Let us cleanse ourselves of every defilement of flesh and spirit, perfecting holiness in God's fear." (2 Corinthians 6:17–7:1) Besides living in an unclean world, we have to grapple with our inherited fallen tendencies. (Genesis 8:21) Jeremiah 17:9 reminds us: "The heart is more treacherous than anything else and is desperate. Who can know it?" Some deceive themselves and others into believing that their lives are clean and acceptable to God, when in reality such is not the case. They practice a form of hypocrisy. Each of us must therefore ask, 'Am I putting forth every effort to be clean before Jehovah in every respect?' To assist us in doing so, let us now focus on four aspects of cleanness.

Physical Cleanness: A Priority

4 Physical cleanness is a priority among Jehovah's people today as it was in ancient times. (Exodus 30:17-21; 40:30-32) After all, would we be treating the "utensils of Jehovah" with respect if our hair, hands, face, teeth, or fingernails were dirty, or if we emitted unpleasant body odors? It is easy, though, to let the world's low standards influence us.—Romans 12:2.

5 How can we stand out as different from the world if we settle for the world's low standards? Would not a dirty home or a slovenly place of worship cause 'the word of God to be spoken of abusively'? (Titus 2:5) But when we practice good personal hygiene, pick up litter at convention sites, assist in Kingdom Hall maintenance, and keep our homes—even the humblest

obliged to be clean. They were not to strip the Babylonians of valuables as did the Israelites when leaving Egypt. (Compare Exodus 12:34-38.) They had to be free of any materialistic or selfish motive in returning. As for Babylon's "dungy idols," just touching one would be defiling.* (Jeremiah 50:1, 2) Only by being clean in every way could the Jews walk "the Way of Holiness" back to Jerusalem.—Isaiah 35:8, 9.

3 Jehovah's Witnesses today must similarly be clean as bearers of Jehovah's "utensils." The apostle Paul quoted Isaiah's words and applied them to Chris-

---

* The Hebrew word for dungy idols, gil·lu·lim′, was a term of contempt that originally meant "dung pellets" —something detestable to the Jews.—Deuteronomy 23:12-14; 1 Kings 14:10; Ezekiel 4:12-17.

---

3. Who today bear Jehovah's "utensils"? Why is it such a challenge for them to remain clean?

---

4. (a) Why is physical cleanness a priority among Jehovah's people? (b) Why may it be difficult sometimes to maintain a high standard of cleanliness?
5. (a) Why is it so important that we keep our standard of cleanness high? Give local examples of how this counsel could be applied. (b) How can elders assist?

abode—neat and clean, we bring glory to God! (Compare 1 Peter 2:12.) Elders, set a good personal example in cleanliness. Do not "hold back" from giving appropriate counsel where necessary.—Acts 20:20.

⁶ What about the clothing we wear when worshiping at meetings and when in field service? Should it not be 'modest and well arranged'? (1 Timothy 2:9; Hebrews 10: 23-25) Do not reason that we are obliged to dress up only if we have a part on the meeting. Overly casual attire is immodest and inappropriate for worship. Worn-out book bags and dog-eared or soiled Bibles also detract from the Kingdom message.

Avoiding Mental Contamination

⁷ At Philippians 4:8 Paul counseled: "Finally, brothers, whatever things are true, whatever things are of serious concern, whatever things are righteous, whatever things are chaste, whatever things are lovable, whatever things are well spoken of, whatever virtue there is and whatever praiseworthy thing there is, continue considering these things." Nevertheless, everywhere we are assailed with temptations to peer into "the 'deep things of Satan.'"—Revelation 2:24.

⁸ For example, the easy availability of pornographic and excessively violent material has resulted in serious problems for some users of videocassette recorders. In Europe, a married brother would watch unclean tapes after his wife had gone to bed. The seed of wrongdoing was firmly planted, resulting in adultery. (Compare James 1:14, 15.) In one African land, a group of Witness youths borrowed un-

Christians must use good judgment in avoiding video tapes and TV programs that could contaminate the mind

clean tapes from school friends and watched them while their parents were away. An elder in Nigeria, however, observes: 'Greater danger often lies in regular TV programs that similarly depict violence, crime, war, lovemaking scenes, and contempt for marital integrity.' Cheap tabloid newspapers, pornographic magazines, sexually arousing novels, movies, and debasing music are also prevalent dangers.

⁹ We cannot afford to dirty our minds with things "shameful even to relate." (Ephesians 5:12) So be selective about what you listen to, watch, and read. Be on guard and react quickly to reject objectionable material. (Psalm 119:37) This will require real self-control, perhaps

6. What should be our standard of dress for meetings and field service?
7. What is the key to mental cleanness, according to Philippians 4:8?
8. How may the dangers posed by various forms of entertainment be illustrated? Give local examples.

9. (a) Why must we be selective about what we listen to, watch, and read? (b) How should we react if confronted with objectionable material?

Small gatherings can be morally upbuilding

figuratively 'pummeling your body and leading it as a slave.' (1 Corinthians 9:27) Always remember, though, that what we watch in secrecy is observed by "the One who is invisible." (Hebrews 11:27) So shun what is questionable. "Keep on making sure of what is acceptable to the Lord." —Ephesians 5:10.

"Keeping on Guard" to Stay Morally Clean

¹⁰ At Ephesians 5:5 Paul warned: "For you know this, recognizing it for yourselves, that no fornicator or unclean person or greedy person—which means being an idolater—has any inheritance in the kingdom of the Christ and of God." Yet,

10. (a) What is one reason so many are reproved or disfellowshipped each year? (b) What Bible principle should guide our conduct on vacations and at work?

thousands each year are reproved or disfellowshipped because of sexual immorality—'sinning against the body.' (1 Corinthians 6:18) Often, it is simply a result of not "keeping on guard according to [God's] word." (Psalm 119:9) Many brothers, for example, drop their moral guard during vacation periods. Neglecting theocratic association, they strike up friendships with worldly vacationers. Reasoning that these are 'really nice people,' some Christians have joined them in questionable activities. Similarly, others have become overly friendly with their workmates. One Christian elder became so involved with a female employee that he abandoned his family and took up living with her! Disfellowshipping resulted. How true the Bible's words, "Bad associations spoil useful habits"!—1 Corinthians 15:33.

¹¹ From South Africa comes this report: "Another danger that threatens the moral uprightness of many is large parties . . . some of which were held after sessions of the district convention." However, smaller Christian gatherings that are well supervised seldom deteriorate into "revelries." (Galatians 5:21) If alcoholic beverages are to be served, do so under supervision and in moderation. "Wine is a ridiculer," and under its influence, some brothers have dropped their moral guard or awakened slumbering weaknesses. (Proverbs 20:1) Thus, two young ministers engaged in homosexual acts after overindulging in alcohol.

¹² When tempted to err, call to mind that, no matter how clean we may appear outwardly, it is what we are inside that counts. (Proverbs 21:2) Some evidently

11. Why should Christian gatherings be properly supervised?
12, 13. (a) How have some justified immoral conduct? Why is such reasoning fallacious? (b) How can we stay on guard against threats to good morals?

feel that God will forgive repeated excursions into immoral conduct because they are weak. But is this not "turning the undeserved kindness of our God into an excuse for loose conduct"? (Jude 4) Some even imagine that "Jehovah is not seeing us." (Ezekiel 8:12) Remember, though, that "there is not a creation that is not manifest to his sight, but all things are naked and openly exposed to the eyes of him with whom we have an accounting."—Hebrews 4:13.

¹³ So be on guard against threats to good morals! "Let fornication and uncleanness of every sort or greediness not even be mentioned among you, just as it befits holy people; neither shameful conduct nor foolish talking nor obscene jesting, things which are not becoming." (Ephesians 5:3, 4) "Abhor what is wicked," no matter how pleasurable it might be to the flesh.—Romans 12:9.

Keeping Spiritually Clean

¹⁴ Some have exposed themselves to possible spiritual contamination by tuning in to religious radio and television broadcasts. In one African land, some have watched TV dramas that portray the superstitions of traditional animist religions in a favorable light. The apostle Paul, though, warned of a more lethal danger —apostate men who were "subverting the faith of some." (2 Timothy 2:16-18) Individuals like that still exist! (2 Peter 2:1-3) And at times they have succeeded in sullying the thinking of others. As Proverbs 11:9 says: "By his mouth the one who is an apostate brings his fellowman to ruin."

¹⁵ Apostates often appeal to the ego, claiming that we have been deprived of

---

14, 15. (a) How have some exposed themselves to spiritual contamination? (b) How do apostates use their 'mouths to bring their fellowman to ruin'? (c) In what ways are apostates really unclean, and what have they forgotten?

our freedoms, including the freedom to interpret the Bible for ourselves. (Compare Genesis 3:1-5.) In reality, these would-be defilers offer nothing more than a return to the nauseating teachings of "Babylon the Great." (Revelation 17:5; 2 Peter 2:19-22) Others appeal to the flesh, urging former associates to "take it easy" because the humble work of witnessing from house to house is "unnecessary" or "unscriptural." (Compare Matthew 16: 22, 23.) True, such smooth talkers may look outwardly clean in a physical and moral way. But inside they are spiritually unclean, having given in to prideful, independent thinking. They have forgotten all that they learned about Jehovah, his holy name and attributes. They no longer acknowledge that all they learned about Bible truth—the glorious hope of the Kingdom and a paradise earth and the

Zealous Witnesses keep spiritually clean and find protection and joy through diligent Bible study

overturning of false doctrines, such as the Trinity, the immortal human soul, eternal torment, and purgatory—yes, all of this came to them through "the faithful and discreet slave."—Matthew 24:45-47.

[16] Interestingly, a circuit overseer in France observes: "Some brothers are deceived because they lack accurate knowledge." That is why Proverbs 11:9 states: "By knowledge are the righteous rescued." This does not mean giving apostates a hearing ear or delving into their writings. Rather, it means coming to "an accurate knowledge of the sacred secret of God" through diligent personal study of the Bible and the Society's Bible-based publications. Having this accurate knowledge, who would become so curious as to pay any attention to apostate mouthings? May no man "delude you with persuasive arguments"! (Colossians 2:2-4) False religious propaganda from any source should be avoided like poison! Really, since our Lord has used "the faithful and discreet slave" to convey to us "sayings of everlasting life," why should we ever want to look anywhere else?—John 6:68.

Will You Remain Clean?

[17] Much is therefore involved in remaining clean before Jehovah God. Keeping our bodies, our homes, our clothing, and our Kingdom Halls physically clean adorns our Kingdom message. Keeping mentally clean helps us stay clean morally and spiritually. This calls for our heeding Paul's admonition at Philippians 4:8, to keep our minds on things that are true, chaste, and praiseworthy.

[18] We can also appreciate more than ever that we must stay morally clean in both word and deed. Jehovah explicitly warns us that those who engage in any form of immorality will not inherit God's Kingdom. (1 Corinthians 6:9-11) No matter how pleasant such unclean things may seem, if we sow to the flesh, we will reap corruption from the flesh. (Galatians 6:8) Finally, there is the matter of remaining spiritually clean, doctrinally clean. Such cleanness helps us maintain the purity of our hearts and minds. We are thus moved always to seek God's thoughts on matters —not our own.

[19] Soon the main promoter of uncleanness—Satan the Devil—will, along with his demons, be cast into the deep abyss. Until then, may all of Jehovah's servants—of the anointed and of the "great crowd"—remain clean as bearers of Jehovah's vessels. (Revelation 7:9, 13-15; 19: 7, 8; 20:1-3) The fight is unrelenting and hard. Remember, though, that Jehovah gives freely of his "spirit of holiness." (Romans 1:4) His clean organization, with its elders, also stands ready to assist us by offering sound, Scriptural advice. With such help and our own determination, we can remain clean in every respect!

19. What can aid both the anointed and the "great crowd" in remaining clean in all respects?

16. How are the righteous rescued "by knowledge"?
17, 18. Why is it vital to cultivate (a) physical cleanness, (b) mental cleanness, (c) moral cleanness, and (d) spiritual cleanness?

Questions for Review

□ Why did the Jews returning from Babylon have to be clean?

□ How can we give attention to physical cleanness?

□ How can we protect our minds from contamination?

□ How can we stay on guard against moral dangers?

□ How can we maintain our spiritual cleanness?

Religious Freedom Upheld in India

THE August 11, 1986, Supreme Court verdict in New Delhi took millions by surprise. At a time when nationalism was running strong, few expected that the religious freedom of a mostly unknown religious minority would be respected. But after a close examination of the facts, India's highest court decreed that the children of Jehovah's Witnesses cannot be compelled to sing the national anthem. In a landmark decision the court said:

"We are satisfied, in the present case, that the expulsion of the three children from the school for the reason that because of their conscientiously held religious faith, they do not join the singing of the national anthem in the morning assembly though they do stand up respectfully when the anthem is sung, is a violation of their fundamental right 'to freedom of conscience and freely to profess, practice and propagate religion.'"

Justice O. Chinnappa Reddy and Justice M. M. Dutt of the Supreme Court of India were the judges who heard the now famous anthem case of Jehovah's Witnesses.

How the Issue Arose

Nearly half of the 8,000 Jehovah's Witnesses in India are found in the small state of Kerala in the southernmost part of this vast nation. In most schools there, the national anthem is sung daily. The custom in the particular school in question was for all the students to sing the anthem in chorus. The children of Jehovah's Witnesses, however, merely stood while the others sang. As the Supreme Court judgment said: "No one bothered. No one worried. No one thought it disrespectful or unpatriotic. The children were left in peace and to their beliefs." This was the situation for years.

Then came July 1985. A member of the State Legislative Assembly objected that he thought it was unpatriotic for anyone to refuse to sing the national anthem. A discussion followed, and what was discussed was published in many prominent newspapers in the country.

The authorities of most schools in Kerala, who until then were sympathetic to the children of Jehovah's Witnesses, became afraid because of the objection in the Legislative Assembly and the negative publicity. As a result, the children of Jehovah's Witnesses were dismissed from one school after another.

Children Versus the State

V. J. Emmanuel, whose three minor children, Bijoe, Binu Mol, and Bindu, were expelled from school, sought legal remedy. Mr. Emmanuel was firmly convinced that the law was on his side. He knew that, according to Article 25 (1) of the Constitution of India, "all persons are equally entitled to freedom of conscience and the right freely to profess, practise and propagate religion."

Eventually a Division Bench of the High Court of Kerala heard the case, but it rejected the appeal of V. J. Emmanuel. This was a great shock because the Constitution of India does not say that the national anthem must be sung to show respect for it. It only says that citizens should "abide by the Constitution and respect its ideals and institutions, the National Flag and the National Anthem." Neither is there any other law requiring all citizens of India to sing the national anthem.

The case was appealed to the Supreme Court of India. In overruling the Kerala High Court, the Supreme Court judgment said: "The High Court misdirected itself and went off at a tangent. They considered, in minute detail, each and every word and thought of the National Anthem and concluded that there was no word or thought in the National Anthem which could offend anyone's religious susceptibilities." Yet, as the Supreme Court correctly noted, "that is not the question at all."

The question is a religious one, namely, the right of individuals to maintain their freedom of worship. The fact is, Jehovah's Witnesses do not sing the national anthem of *any* country. Such anthems are, in effect, hymns or prayers set to music, and Jehovah's Witnesses conscientiously object to singing them. "They desist from actual singing," the Indian Supreme Court judgment understandingly explained, "because of their honest belief and conviction that their religion does not permit them to join any rituals except it be in their prayers to Jehovah their God."

Significantly, the Constitution of India guarantees "freedom of speech and expression," which includes the freedom to be silent. That was what the children were doing when the anthem was sung during the morning assembly at school—they remained silent. Yet, the Kerala educational authorities had, in effect, imposed a ban

on silence. So the question arose whether such a ban was consistent with the rights guaranteed by the Constitution.

The Supreme Court concluded on this matter: "We may at once say that there is no provision of law which obliges anyone to sing the National Anthem nor do we think that it is disrespectful to the National Anthem if a person who stands up respectfully when the National Anthem is sung does not join the singing."

As noted earlier, the duty of every citizen, according to the Constitution, is to 'respect the National Anthem.' Regarding such respect, the Prevention of Insults to National Honor Act of 1971 says: "Whoever intentionally prevents the singing of the National Anthem or causes disturbance to any assembly engaged in such singing shall be punished with imprisonment for a term which may extend to three years, or with fines, or with both." The children of Jehovah's Witnesses, however, had never prevented anyone from singing the national anthem. They had never caused any disturbance to any assembly engaged in such singing.

A Threat to National Unity?

One of the State's arguments was that singing the national anthem was essential for the unity and integrity of the country. Yet, does the forced singing of a national anthem really contribute to a country's unity or to the integrity of its citizens?

Interestingly, the Indian national anthem is only in the language of one state, and so it is not understood by the majority of Indians who sing it. Thus, for the majority, singing the national anthem is probably meaningless and constitutes, basically, an empty ritual. Jehovah's Witnesses do not join in such rituals. They pray only to their God, Jehovah.

It was also argued that if the Supreme Court judgment went in favor of Jeho-

The three children who respectfully declined to share in a patriotic ceremony

The dedicated family of the three children

These four persons read of the court case, studied the Bible, and were baptized

vah's Witnesses, it could threaten the security of the country. But Jehovah's Witnesses in India are a small minority, numbering only some 8,000 persons. Would such a small group be a threat to a nation of over 800 million people? Besides, Jehovah's Witnesses are noted worldwide for their honesty and obedience to the laws of the governments under which they reside.

In Nigeria a lawyer said: 'Witnesses are tax-paying and law-abiding citizens. Any Witness who can be honest with his religion to the extent of obeying it at the risk of losing certain privileges will be equally honest in most other things. The reason he refuses to steal government money while his other colleagues sing the national anthem and yet embezzle funds is that his Bible which asks him not to sing the national anthem also said he should not steal.'

The last sentence of the landmark Supreme Court judgment is noteworthy. It said: "We only wish to add: our tradition teaches tolerance; our philosophy teaches tolerance; our constitution practices tolerance; let us not dilute it." Will the government and the leaders appreciate this fine thought? Will the decision by the Supreme Court remain final? Only time will tell.

Kingdom Proclaimers Report

Guinea Welcomes "Divine Peace" Conventioners

THE first four days of 1987 saw the first district convention of Jehovah's Witnesses ever held in the Republic of Guinea, West Africa. Though Guinea is a predominantly Muslim country where the work of Jehovah's Witnesses is not yet officially recognized, the Witnesses there have earned a reputation as good, kind, peaceable people. It was because of this reputation that the government opened the doors wide to receive the "Divine Peace" conventioners.

Among the delegates were nine missionaries who traveled from Freetown, Sierra Leone, in a van and on two motorcycles. At the border, they had to cross a river on a ferry that consisted of three dugout canoes with planks laid across them. Once they had safely crossed with the vehicles, the missionaries asked: "How much do we have to pay?" "You people are Jehovah's Witnesses," was the reply. "No charge."

What about customs and immigrations? "Don't worry about it," they were told. "Everything has been taken care of. Just wear your lapel cards." Hundreds of other delegates were having similar experiences. Not only had the government of Guinea allowed free passage across the river separating Guinea from Sierra Leone and Liberia; they had waived customs and immigration formalities for anyone possessing a "Divine Peace" lapel badge! One circuit overseer, who came from Liberia, said: "The lapel badge was far better than a passport."

The Guinean government was helpful in other ways. They provided a vehicle to transport Witnesses from the capital, Conakry, to the convention city of Guéckédou, over 400 miles away. They authorized the purchase of gasoline for the vehicles that had come from Freetown. They directed the hotel nearest the convention site to reserve all their rooms for the Witnesses. They also sanctioned the use of the city hall for the convention, providing it free of charge.

The district governor, who is the highest official in that part of the country, hosted 11 delegates at his own residence. He was also among the 1,132 who listened to the public talk on Sunday.

Jehovah God will not forget such kindness shown to his servants.—Matthew 10:42; 25:40.

U.S. Postal Service
STATEMENT OF OWNERSHIP, MANAGEMENT AND CIRCULATION
Required by 39 U.S.C. 3685

1A. TITLE OF PUBLICATION: THE WATCHTOWER
1B. PUBLICATION NO.: 6 6 8 5 8 0
2. DATE OF FILING: Sept. 1, 1987

3. FREQUENCY OF ISSUE: Semimonthly
3A. NO. OF ISSUES PUBLISHED ANNUALLY: 24
3B. ANNUAL SUBSCRIPTION PRICE: $5.00

4. COMPLETE MAILING ADDRESS OF KNOWN OFFICE OF PUBLICATION (Street, City, County, State and ZIP+4 Code) (Not printers): 117 Adams Street, Brooklyn, Kings, New York 11201

5. COMPLETE MAILING ADDRESS OF THE HEADQUARTERS OF GENERAL BUSINESS OFFICES OF THE PUBLISHER (Not printers): 25 Columbia Heights, Brooklyn, New York 11201

6. FULL NAMES AND COMPLETE MAILING ADDRESS OF PUBLISHER, EDITOR, AND MANAGING EDITOR (This item MUST NOT be blank):
PUBLISHER (Name and Complete Mailing Address): Watch Tower Bible and Tract Society of Pennsylvania, 117 Adams Street, Brooklyn, New York 11201
EDITOR (Name and Complete Mailing Address): Same as "Publisher"
MANAGING EDITOR (Name and Complete Mailing Address): By corporation - Same as "Publisher"

7. OWNER (If owned by a corporation, its name and address must be stated and also immediately thereunder the names and addresses of stockholders owning or holding 1 percent or more of total amount of stock. If not owned by a corporation, the names and addresses of the individual owners must be given. If owned by a partnership or other unincorporated firm, its name and address, as well as that of each individual must be given. If the publication is published by a nonprofit organization, its name and address must be stated.) (Item must be completed.)

FULL NAME	COMPLETE MAILING ADDRESS
Watch Tower Bible and Tract Society of Pennsylvania	25 Columbia Heights Brooklyn, New York 11201
No stockholders	

8. KNOWN BONDHOLDERS, MORTGAGEES, AND OTHER SECURITY HOLDERS OWNING OR HOLDING 1 PERCENT OR MORE OF TOTAL AMOUNT OF BONDS, MORTGAGES OR OTHER SECURITIES (If there are none, so state)

FULL NAME	COMPLETE MAILING ADDRESS
None	

9. FOR COMPLETION BY NONPROFIT ORGANIZATIONS AUTHORIZED TO MAIL AT SPECIAL RATES (Section 423.12 DMM only)
The purpose, function, and nonprofit status of this organization and the exempt status for Federal income tax purposes (Check one)
[X] (1) HAS NOT CHANGED DURING PRECEDING 12 MONTHS
[ ] (2) HAS CHANGED DURING PRECEDING 12 MONTHS (If changed, publisher must submit explanation of change with this statement.)

10. EXTENT AND NATURE OF CIRCULATION (See instructions on reverse side)	AVERAGE NO. COPIES EACH ISSUE DURING PRECEDING 12 MONTHS	ACTUAL NO. COPIES OF SINGLE ISSUE PUBLISHED NEAREST TO FILING DATE
A. TOTAL NO. COPIES (Net Press Run)	4,532,679	4,657,573
B. PAID AND/OR REQUESTED CIRCULATION 1. Sales through dealers and carriers, street vendors and counter sales	3,631,839	3,696,696
2. Mail Subscription (Paid and/or requested)	889,662	949,944
C. TOTAL PAID AND/OR REQUESTED CIRCULATION (Sum of 1081 and 1082)	4,521,501	4,646,640
D. FREE DISTRIBUTION BY MAIL, CARRIER OR OTHER MEANS SAMPLES, COMPLIMENTARY, AND OTHER FREE COPIES	1	4
E. TOTAL DISTRIBUTION (Sum of C and D)	4,521,502	4,646,644
F. COPIES NOT DISTRIBUTED 1. Office use, left over, unaccounted, spoiled after printing	11,177	10,929
2. Return from News Agents	None	None
G. TOTAL (Sum of E, F1 and 2—should equal net press run shown in A)	4,532,679	4,657,573

11. I certify that the statements made by me above are correct and complete
SIGNATURE AND TITLE OF EDITOR, PUBLISHER, BUSINESS MANAGER, OR OWNER: *[signature]* Director

PS Form 3526, July 1984
(See instruction on reverse)

Religion's Tidal Wave
—The Final Reckoning

BONFIRES crackle, sparklers flash, rockets rush to color the sky red, blue, yellow, and green. Potatoes in their jackets. Peals of laughter, shrieks of delight. Bonfire Night in England.

WORKERS found the 25 corpses by accident. The skeletons had been carefully buried, arms folded. Historians thus stumbled onto a trail of mystery going back some 200 years. Quebec, Canada.

The above are two unconnected events with a common root—the Reformation.

AN ARTICLE in our October 1 issue showed that Europe witnessed tremendous religious upheaval in the 16th century. The results spread to other parts of the world. Many aspects of life today are nothing more than gullies left by the Reformation waters. Perhaps they even influence your daily routine. Still more important, we stand on the brink of a final religious catastrophe that will definitely affect your life. Do you know how?

Trace the Reformation tracks in the following countries:

Germany: Some say that Luther's influence on German culture is unequaled by that of any individual in the English-speaking world. His translation of the Scriptures is one of the most widely accepted German Bibles. Luther did much to set the tone of the language and to lay the framework for German domestic relations. He made the State recognize the need for schooling for all, elevating the status of the teaching profession.

Canada: The colonial past saw Britain and France engaged in a tug-of-war that left its mark on one province in particular—Quebec. Originally settled by French Catholic immigrants, Quebec came under British, and hence Protestant, control in 1763. It was shortly before then that the corpses mentioned at the start of this article were secretly buried near the fortified walls of the city. Why secretly? Because they seem to have been Protestants, who at that time were denied burial in Catholic cemeteries. Quebec still stands as an island of French-speaking Catholicism, and this gives rise to modern separatist movements.

Ireland: Unimpressed by the Reformation, the Emerald Isle kept its distance. In time, Protestant influence seeped across the Irish Sea from England into the northern provinces. The legacy today is a partitioned Ireland. Annual summer marches in Ulster commemorate Protestant victories of the past. Celebrations commonly leave a trail of barricades, bombs, and plastic bullets. The Orange Day Parade in July 1986 left 160 injured. It memorialized the day some 300 years ago when King William of Orange, who made Protestantism in Britain secure, defeated England's last Catholic monarch, James II.

United States: "[The] variety of sects with differing European backgrounds was a potent factor in bringing about religious freedom in America," writes A. P. Stokes in *Church and State in the United States.* Colonial days saw the United States draped in Protestant colors.

Martin Luther and John Calvin—leaders in the Reformation

Calvinist values gave direction in religion, politics, and commerce. The fundamental belief was that each man stood directly accountable to his Creator without priestly mediation. This ideal bred a character intent on working out its own destiny, on reaping the rewards of its own labor.

T. H. White recalls in his book *In Search of History* that at the turn of this century, 13 percent of the U.S. population was Catholic. This proportion rose to over 25 percent by 1960. Even so, few Catholics attained to the upper reaches of politics. White continues: "At the higher level of the Senate, where war and peace were made, where treaties and foreign policy were decided, where Supreme Court Justices were confirmed, Americans still preferred Protestants of the old tradition as custodians of national purpose." The custom was broken when John F. Kennedy became the first Catholic president of the United States.

For further examples from other countries, please see box on page 29.

A Swamped Landscape

Under Protestantism, theological debate swelled, and Bible translations and commentaries came to float on the tide of liberty and individual expression. However, as time passed, freedom dredged Bible criticism to the surface. New ideas were accommodated; self-determination became the order of the day. Progress was no longer the gentle lapping of waves but the thunderous roar of breakers. The powerful current of reform swept away the very foundations of traditional Christian doctrine. Modern alternatives like evolution, women's liberation, and the 'new morality' have been washed up like driftwood, silent witnesses to the storm. Personalized religion in some Protestant lands left each individual stranded, a castaway on his own lonely island of faith.

Terrain in Protestant areas is molded by a penchant for questioning established norms. People are raised on a credo of progress, freedom, and human rights. Max Weber, German sociologist and economist, published an essay in 1904 on Protestantism and capitalism. He stated that capitalism was not simply a result of the Reformation. But he did discover that in successful capitalist areas of mixed religious backgrounds, it was outstandingly the Protestants who were the owners, the leaders, the skilled, and the trained. According to *Der Fischer Weltalmanach,* of the 540 Nobel prizes awarded up until 1985, two thirds went to citizens from Protestant cultures. Inhabitants of Catholic environments won only 20 percent. Of the top 20 nations, in terms of gross national product per person, nine were Protestant, two Catholic. On the other hand, of the ten indebted developing countries listed, five were Catholic, none Protestant.

German newsweekly *Der Spiegel* wrote that Calvinist ideals spurred the British on to becoming a major world power. From the 19th century, the growing political strength of the United States, Germany, and Great Britain became a force for social renewal. Equality of opportunity for all was emphasized. Eddies within the mainstream of the Reformation are regarded by some as being precursors of modern socialism. A political awareness of social responsibility paved the way for the welfare state. Especially in Protestant surroundings, civil authorities gradually took over control of the legal aspects of birth, death, marriage, divorce, and inheritance. The availability of divorce and legal abortion in Catholic countries is now often quite different from that in Protestant lands.

Two bulwarks of Protestantism, the United States and Great Britain, grew together into the two-horned beast of Bible prophecy. (Revelation 13:11) A 20th-century giant of politics, the United Nations organization, first called the League of Nations, blossomed out of Protestant initiatives.

The Flood Will Return

A receding tide leaves a tidemark on the beach that reminds us of its pending return. Similarly, the Reformation of the 16th century left visible traces that we can see today. And there is strong evidence that we are standing on the threshold of an ultimate wave of religious change that will surpass all previous upheavals, sweep away false religion forever, and affect everyone alive. Will you survive it? Worldwide, there is a broad-based dissatisfaction with organized religion, among individuals and governments. Why the dissatisfaction?

Religion often goes beyond its spiritual mandate, confusing the cloak of office with the cloth of ordination, the crown with the miter, the scepter with the cross. Some years ago the *Observer* Sunday newspaper raised the question as to whether politicians in Ireland were prepared to take over from the priests the running of the country. Former West German chancellor Helmut Schmidt commented on religious interference in politics by saying, "I do not believe that this can be permitted indefinitely." And *Le Figaro* of Paris accused the church of "meddling in politics" so much that "it is in danger of seeing politics meddle with religion." From India to Egypt to the United States, from Poland to Nicaragua, from Malaysia to Chile, the weary struggle between politics and religion goes on.

This is no surprise, nothing new. Revelation chapter 17 describes the whole of false religion as a harlot, "Babylon the Great," which commits fornication with the politicians of the earth. Verse 4 further pictures her as being "adorned with gold and precious stone and pearls." The religious empire is insatiate, wallowing in luxury, oozing wealth. In the 16th century, the glittering coffers of the Catholic Church attracted longing glances. The same is true of the jewel-studded lucre of all religion in our 20th century.

Governments already cast covetous eyes toward such opulence. Albania saw the more than 2,000 mosques, churches, and other religious buildings, and either secularized or razed them. The *Sunday Times* reported in 1984 that the government of Malta "began eyeing the church's wealth," cutting subsidies of church schools. Asked how the church should make up the loss, a government minister replied: "If need be, they can melt down their gold crosses and silver altars." The Greek Orthodox Church has strongly fought legislation approved earlier this year by the Greek Parliament that would enable the government to take over huge church land holdings (about 10 percent of the area of the country).

Worldwide, religion is a great disappointment. Instead of unifying, it splits asunder. One German daily newspaper noted the "rivalry between Catholics and Protestants that amounts to hatred." The *Frankfurter Allgemeine Zeitung* wrote that even ecumenical movements, designed to bridge the gap, started out from a position of "mutual distrust, irreconcilable enmity between Catholics and Protestants." Elie Wiesel, 1986 Nobel Peace

Prize winner, was quoted in another German daily as saying: "I often think we have failed. If someone had told us in 1945 that we would yet again see religiously motivated wars raging on practically every continent . . . we would not have believed it." Religion that foments trouble, incites or condones war, is false religion. And the Creator decided long ago to do away with it.

Chapter 17 of Revelation leaves no doubt as to the fate of all false religion. In verse 16 we read: "The ten horns [governmental powers within the United Nations organization] that you saw, and the wild beast [United Nations], these will hate the harlot [false religion] and will make her devastated and naked, and will eat up her fleshy parts and will completely burn her with fire."

Where Do You Stand?

Remarkable as it may seem, false religion has had its day. Its practices, customs, traditions, and privileges will soon

---

In Our Next Issue

- **Can Religion Satisfy Our Needs?**

- **Singleness—A Rewarding Way of Life**

- **Anabaptists and "the Pattern of Healthful Words"**

disappear. That may seem as unlikely to you as the swamping of the Catholic Church did to people in the 16th century. But the Reformation waters were overwhelming. Church wealth went to the people, its power to the monarchs. Even so in our day, the nations will preside over the final dissolution of false religion.

What does that mean for you personally? Examine the religious institution to which you belong. Does what it stands for agree with the Bible in every way? If not, then your organization is part of "Babylon the Great," or the world empire of false religion. Follow the command found at Revelation 18:4, which is: "Get out of her, my people, . . . if you do not want to receive part of her plagues."

Remember, the tidal wave bringing conclusive destruction to false religion is on its way. It can be seen on the horizon. Where will you be standing when it brings thunderous destruction? In the valley of indifference? On the hill of some secular authority? Or on the mountain of Jehovah? There is only one safe place to be.

South Africa: Calvinist belief in predestination offered apartheid a theological foundation. The German daily *Frankfurter Allgemeine Zeitung* called the theologians of the Nederduitse Gereformeerde Kerk (as the Dutch Reformed Church in South Africa became known) "architects of the politics of apartheid."

Switzerland: As the center of the Calvinist movement, Geneva attracted many thousands of refugees, who brought with them wealth and know-how. As a result, this is still a major banking city and has a thriving industry producing watches and clocks.

India: The Society of Jesus (Jesuits) grew as part of the Counter-Reformation, a movement to revive Catholicism following Reformation reverses. Society members came to the province of Goa in the 16th century, shortly after its colonization by Portugal. The influence of the church is reflected in the population today: In Goa, 3 persons out of 10 are Catholic, whereas in India overall, only 1 person in 25 is a professed Christian.

England: The year 1605 saw James I, a Protestant, on the throne. As oppression of Catholics in the country grew, a plot was conceived to blow up Parliament, King and all. The conspirators, a group of Catholics led by Guy Fawkes, were discovered and executed. November 5 marks the celebration of Bonfire Night. Families and friends still gather to warm up the damp evening with fireworks and to burn a "guy," or model, of the plotter.

Fine Increase
"Beyond the Mountains"

HAITI was the first black republic in the West to gain independence. Its name comes from the Arawak Indian language and means "mountains." Indeed, there is an old Creole proverb that says: "Beyond the mountains are mountains." This is a good description of the Haitian countryside.

In recent years something remarkable has been happening here "beyond the mountains." Increasing numbers have responded to the preaching of the good news of the Kingdom and taken their stand for Jehovah and his appointed King. (Isaiah 60:22) By 1980 an average of almost 3,000 publishers were reporting field service each month, and the branch office in the capital city of Port-au-Prince was too small to care for their needs. New premises were needed. So in November 1984 construction of a brand-new facility was begun in Santo, a delightful location on the outskirts of Port-au-Prince.

First the property had to be enclosed by a 4,000-foot-long wall. A local company made the concrete panels for this wall, but local Witnesses were hired, and many volunteers worked weekends, to accomplish the project. Then the building construction work was begun, and over a period of three years, as many as a hundred volunteers from the Port-au-Prince congregations helped out on weekends. Members of the International Volunteer Construction Worker Program came from the United States, Canada, and other countries—many at their own expense—to lend a hand.

As construction progressed, an unforeseen problem developed. On one side of the property, there is a ravine. During the rainy season, river waters flood down the ravine, causing considerable erosion. This would eventually have caused the collapse of the fence around that part of the property. So a retaining wall was built right in the riverbed, and the property is now well protected from the rampaging waters that run by during the rainy season.

With Jehovah's help, a fine facility was eventually completed. The branch is a U-shaped structure made of concrete and block. Its left wing has eight bedrooms, a laundry, and a library. The right wing is the literature depot. In the front part of the building, a spacious lobby comfortably accommodates the brothers who arrive from different parts of the country at various times during the month in order to pick up magazines and literature for their respective congregations. The front also houses the offices, dining room, and kitchen.

Along with the branch office, a new Assembly Hall seating about 3,000 was also built on the property. Two sides of the hall are open, so that those seated inside are constantly cooled by the prevailing winds—a welcome relief from the hot Haitian sun. There is also a modern, fully equipped kitchen and facilities to serve refreshments, as well as a baptismal pool and a carpenter shop. The grounds are tastefully landscaped with tropical shrubs and flowers.

By the beginning of 1987, the number

Views of the Assembly Hall (top right) and of the new branch

of Witnesses "beyond the mountains" had increased to more than 4,700. What a grand event it was for all of these to come together on January 25, 1987, for the dedication of these two fine buildings! Some foreign brothers who had worked on the site earlier returned with their families to share the occasion.

The dedication program began in the early afternoon with the various members of the Branch Committee explaining the great need that existed for the new buildings because of the fine increase that was taking place in Haiti. After a short intermission, the 5,384 in attendance were treated to a slide program showing the various stages of the construction work.

Finally, the dedication talk was given by Charles Molohan, a visiting zone overseer from Brooklyn, New York. Brother Molohan spoke of the importance of build-

ing for true Christian worship. He discussed how Noah and his family were among the earliest construction workers, and their faithfully completing their work assignment meant survival for the human family, as well as the continuation of true worship on earth. Another ancient building project was Herod's temple, but this was eventually destroyed because it was not used to promote true worship. (Matthew 23:38) Today, we must be busy building faith and other Christian qualities if we are to avoid a similar eventuality.

It was truly a stimulating and joyful occasion. When it was over, all present returned to their respective homes knowing that this new construction in the land "beyond the mountains" will continue to play a vital role in the gathering of true worshipers in this part of the Caribbean.

Make Bible Reading More Meaningful

THE *New World Translation of the Holy Scriptures—With References* really does this.

An appreciative reader recently wrote regarding the *New World Translation Reference Bible:* "It is the answer to my prayers. When I do my Bible reading, I check many of the references. They help me see other important principles that are related to the account. It surely broadens my understanding, and I can make better personal application."

he Watchtower

November 15, 1987

Announcing Jehovah's Kingdom

Can Religion Satisfy Our Needs?

The Watchtower®

Announcing Jehovah's Kingdom

November 15, 1987
Vol. 108, No. 22

In This Issue

Photos, pages 30, 31: Pictorial Archive (Near Eastern History) Est.

THE PURPOSE OF *THE WATCHTOWER* is to exalt Jehovah God as the Sovereign of the universe. It keeps watch on world events as they fulfill Bible prophecy. It comforts all peoples with the good news that God's Kingdom will soon destroy those who oppress their fellowmen and that it will turn the earth into a paradise. It encourages faith in the now-reigning King, Jesus Christ, whose shed blood opens the way for mankind to gain eternal life. *The Watchtower,* published by Jehovah's Witnesses continuously since 1879, is nonpolitical. It adheres to the Bible as its authority.

WATCHTOWER STUDIES FOR THE WEEKS

December 20: Unmarried but Complete for God's Service. Page 10. Songs to Be Used: 69, 172.

December 27: Singleness—A Rewarding Way of Life. Page 15. Songs to Be Used: 124, 138.

Average Printing Each Issue: 12,315,000

Now Published in 103 Languages

SEMIMONTHLY LANGUAGES AVAILABLE BY MAIL
Afrikaans, Arabic, Cebuano, Chichewa, Chinese, Cibemba, Danish,* Dutch,* Efik, English,* Finnish,* French,* German,* Greek,* Hiligaynon, Igbo, Iloko, Italian,* Japanese,* Korean, Lingala, Malagasy, Maltese, Norwegian, Portuguese,* Russian, Sepedi, Sesotho, Shona, Spanish,* Swahili, Swedish,* Tagalog, Thai, Tsonga, Tswana, Xhosa, Yoruba, Zulu

MONTHLY LANGUAGES AVAILABLE BY MAIL
Armenian, Bengali, Bicol, Bislama, Bulgarian, Croatian, Czech, Ewe, Fijian, Ga, Greenlandic, Gujarati, Gun, Hausa, Hebrew, Hindi, Hiri Motu, Hungarian, Icelandic, Kannada, Malayalam, Marathi, New Guinea Pidgin, Pangasinan, Papiamento, Polish, Rarotongan, Romanian, Samar-Leyte, Samoan, Sango, Serbian, Silozi, Sinhalese, Slovenian, Solomon Islands-Pidgin, Tahitian, Tamil, Telugu, Tongan, Tshiluba, Turkish, Twi, Ukrainian, Urdu, Venda, Vietnamese

* Study articles also available in large-print edition.

	Yearly subscription for the above:	
Watch Tower Society offices	Semimonthly Languages	Monthly Languages
America, U.S., Watchtower, Wallkill, N.Y. 12589	$5.00	$2.50
Australia, Box 280, Ingleburn, N.S.W. 2565	A$7.00	A$3.50
Canada, Box 4100, Halton Hills, Ontario L7G 4Y4	$7.00	$3.50
England, The Ridgeway, London NW7 1RN	£5.00	£2.50
Ireland, 29A Jamestown Road, Finglas, Dublin 11	IR£6.00	IR£3.00
New Zealand, P.O. Box 142, Manurewa	NZ$15.00	NZ$7.50
Nigeria, PMB 001, Shomolu, Lagos State	₦8.00	₦4.00
Philippines, P.O. Box 2044, Manila 2800	₱60.00	₱30.00
South Africa, Private Bag 2067, Krugersdorp, 1740	R9.00	R4.50

Remittances should be sent to the office in your country or to Watchtower, Wallkill, N.Y. 12589, U.S.A.

Changes of address should reach us 30 days before your moving date. Give us your old and new address (if possible, your old address label).

25 cents (U.S.) a copy

The Bible translation used is the *New World Translation of the Holy Scriptures,* unless otherwise indicated.

The Watchtower (ISSN 0043-1087) is published semimonthly for $5.00 (U.S.) per year by Watch Tower Bible and Tract Society of Pennsylvania, 25 Columbia Heights, Brooklyn, N.Y. 11201. Second-class postage paid at Brooklyn, N.Y., and at additional mailing offices.

Postmaster: Send address changes to Watchtower, *Wallkill, N.Y. 12589.*

Published by
Watch Tower Bible and Tract Society of Pennsylvania
25 Columbia Heights, Brooklyn, N.Y. 11201, U.S.A.
Frederick W. Franz, President

Has Religion *Satisfied Our Needs?*

MARIA was a Roman Catholic nun for 21 years. She grew up in a very religious environment. Why, even as a child, she would get up at night to pray for others! Eventually, however, the poverty, suffering, and injustice that persisted despite thousands of years of religious influence made her wonder: 'Has religion really satisfied our needs?'

Most religions advocate high ideals and moral principles. But religion is often viewed as causing problems, adding to our difficulties, rather than satisfying our needs. For instance, consider these comments by observers of the religious scene: "The innermost reason for inhuman savagery is religious." (*National Review*) "The chief motivation for war is no longer greed but religion." (*Toronto Star*) "The Holocaust 'was all done by baptized Christians.'"—*The Tampa Tribune.*

Is it any wonder that people dismiss religion's claims that it is the satisfier of our needs? They have seen its fruitage. For example, "it was Shinto, the native religion of Japan, that had not only given its wholehearted support to the war machine but had provided its very rationale," said *The Christian Century.* How many religions have done just that—'given wholehearted support to the war machine'! Think of the massacres and reprisals perpetrated by Buddhists and Hindus in Sri Lanka, the murders and atrocities involving Catholics and Protestants in Ireland—why, the list seems endless! "Hindus, Moslems, Sikhs and other sects have been bloodying each other for centuries in India," lamented *U.S.News & World Report.*

Others may not see religion as a force for bad, but they surely do not look upon it as a powerful force for good. The *National Catholic Reporter* spoke of "the traditional church's failure to adequately address human wants and needs." And the journal *Liberty* said that society seems to view the clergyman as a "blessersanctifier-benedictor" brought out only on ceremonial occasions. It added: "In the minds of many people he is the *minister of the status quo.*" Have you viewed religion in that light—not likely to do us harm but also unlikely to do us much good?

Religion today is much as it was when Jesus Christ was on the earth. He said that the religious leaders of his day honored God only with their lips. The result of their practices was that they added to people's burdens instead of satisfying their needs. "They bind up heavy loads and put them upon the shoulders of men," he said. (Matthew 23:4) Today, religion promises much but seems to deliver very little. So is there any reason to believe that religion can satisfy our needs?

Can Religion *Satisfy Our Needs?*

WHAT are we to eat? What are we to drink? What are we to put on? There is an urgency about these questions, especially when it is difficult to get the basic necessities of life. Yet, notice what Jesus Christ said: "Stop being anxious about your souls as to what you will eat or what you will drink, or about your bodies as to what you will wear." (Matthew 6:25) Does that seem strange? After all, if someone lacks food, clothing, and shelter, what he needs is practical help, not what some might view as a religious platitude.

Jesus was not unsympathetic, nor was he trying to dodge the issue. He was well aware of people's needs. Nevertheless, he also knew of a very real danger. When it comes to satisfying our needs, it is so easy to center our lives around material things and to feel that God is unimportant. Therefore, we need to get our priorities straight.

We will be getting our priorities straight if we follow Jesus' advice: "Keep on, then, seeking first the kingdom and [God's] righteousness, and all these other things will be added to you." (Matthew 6:33) If we follow this advice, religion —true religion based on Bible truths— *can* satisfy our needs.

Jesus was not so unrealistic as to suggest, however, that merely becoming one of his disciples and following his religious teachings would immediately solve all our problems; neither did he mean that his disciples should just sit back and wait for God to provide for them miraculously. Why, everyone might become a Christian if that meant instantaneous freedom from all life's difficulties! What Jesus did mean was that his Father, Jehovah God, provides everything necessary to satisfy all our needs. That is why Jesus also said: "Your heavenly Father knows you need all these things."—Matthew 6:32.

Jehovah also satisfies our vitally important spiritual needs. By means of the Holy Scriptures, he has given us inspired guidance to direct our lives in the best possible manner. (Isaiah 48:17) God has established an association of worshipers who give support when required. (Acts 4:34) He also steps in to help his servants by means of his holy spirit, or active force. (Luke 11:13; Galatians 5:22-25) Moreover, God has made provision to restore Paradise to the earth.—Luke 23:43; Revelation 21:1-4.

Satisfying Our Material Needs

Consider now some Bible principles that have helped people to satisfy their material needs. The Christian apostle Paul wrote:

"Let us cleanse ourselves of every defilement of flesh and spirit."
(2 Corinthians 7:1)

Think of all the problems we can escape if we avoid defilement by tobacco, illegal drugs, and other things that pollute the body. And how much better off we are if we do not squander money, time, and thought on immoral literature and entertainment that can defile our spirit!

The Scriptures also say:

"Do not come to be among heavy drinkers of wine, among those who are gluttonous eaters of flesh. For a drunkard and a glutton will come to poverty, and drowsiness will clothe one with mere rags."
(Proverbs 23:20, 21)

Notice the final result of drunkenness and gluttony—poverty and rags. Many today—even very religious people—remain in poverty because they overindulge in alcoholic beverages or are addicted to things that defile the flesh. Avoiding such things so as to conform to Bible standards can do much to help us satisfy our needs for food, clothing, and shelter.

Another principle that has helped Christians to satisfy their needs is seen in the apostle Paul's words:

"We trust we have an honest conscience, as we wish to conduct ourselves honestly in all things."
(Hebrews 13:18)

Honesty in all their dealings has enabled many Christians to provide well for themselves and their families. It has won them a good reputation, and others are then more likely to do business with them. An honest person may not always have the most in a material way, but he usually has the basic necessities of life and preserves his self-respect.

Closely related to this is the counsel:

"Let the stealer steal no more, but rather let him do hard work, doing with his hands what is good work."
(Ephesians 4:28)

Applying this principle has assisted many to obtain and hold on to employment because they are trustworthy. Consequently, they are able to provide for themselves and their families. Rather than being infected by the spirit of this world, which turns a blind eye to many dishonest practices, Christians are honest, and this brings good results.

To illustrate: One of Jehovah's Witnesses in Japan wanted to work fewer hours each week so as to have more time for spiritual pursuits. When he made this request, however, his employer dismissed him from his job. At that, the employer's mother asked: "Did you fire the most reliable man?" Things got worse for the Witness when he injured his back doing other work. Soon thereafter, he met his former employer, who was upset because he had just learned that one of his employees had been stealing gold, platinum, and rings from his jewelry company. The employer immediately asked the Witness to return to work, this time on his own conditions. The man wanted an honest worker.

According to the apostle Paul, a Christian should "do hard work" not only to provide for himself but also to "have something to distribute to someone in need." (Ephesians 4:28) In times of need, true Christians are always willing to help others. A certain family in Fiji experienced this when their home was severely damaged by cyclones while they were at a Christian convention. Upon returning home, they found a scene of devastation. But they also found fellow believers who gladly used their resources to provide the family with shelter and assistance to rebuild their home. "It is comforting," said the father, "when you know there are Christians who really care about you."

Jesus Christ felt great sympathy for the needy. On many occasions, he personally assisted the disadvantaged in one way or another. Of course, Jesus knew that as long as this corrupt system of things is allowed to exist, poverty and other social problems will remain. (John 12:8) Therefore, although he did much to help people materially, the real thrust of his ministry was to satisfy their spiritual needs.

When a crowd whose hunger had been satisfied followed Jesus to Capernaum, he made this significant comment: "You are looking for me, not because you saw signs, but because you ate from the loaves and were satisfied. Work, not for the food that perishes, but for the food that remains for life everlasting, which the Son of man will give you." (John 6:26, 27) What did Jesus mean?

Jesus meant that there was a danger that people would associate with him and his disciples solely for material advantage. But he knew that this would not bring lasting benefits. So he said: "Happy are those conscious of their spiritual need, since the kingdom of the heavens belongs to them. Happy are those hungering and thirsting for righteousness, since they will be filled."—Matthew 5:3, 6.

Besides a hunger for material food, there is a hunger for truth and spiritual fulfillment. True happiness results when this spiritual hunger is satisfied. Christendom has produced a materialistically minded society. Eastern religions have left people in spiritual darkness. But true worship—the religion of Jesus Christ—has satisfied people's spiritual needs. It can do the same for you. These provisions can be yours if you will avail yourself of them.

For example, from a Christian engaged in street witnessing, one young man in Mauritius accepted copies of *The Watchtower* and its companion journal *Awake!* The following week, he came back for more magazines. He explained that he had been contemplating suicide because of his financial problems, but the magazines had helped him to realize that there is a God who cares for us. The young man's spiritual hunger was beginning to be satisfied.

True religion will satisfy all our needs

Will we ever see a time when all our needs are fully satisfied? The Bible promises that we will. True, people are weary of hearing promise after promise of better things to come. They have been disappointed so often. But we can have confidence in the promises of the Bible. Its Author, Jehovah God, fulfills every promise he makes. Joshua expressed this well when he reminded his fellow Israelites: "You well know with all your hearts and with all your souls that not one word out of all the good words that Jehovah your God has spoken to you has failed. They have all come true for you. Not one word of them has failed."—Joshua 23:14.

The real solution to all our problems lies in the fulfillment of God's marvelous promises to cleanse the whole earth. (Revelation 11:18) All our needs will be satisfied when his Kingdom restores Paradise on the earth,

fulfilling his original purpose for mankind. (Matthew 6:9, 10) Then we will not hear 'the sound of weeping or a plaintive cry' from people whose needs cannot be satisfied. Through honest work and by applying godly principles, they will enjoy a full, satisfying life.—Isaiah 65:17-25.

Maria, the former Catholic nun mentioned earlier, gained this confidence. She realized that she had lived in spiritual darkness for years, plagued by fears about the future and unable to see real meaning in life. But learning Bible truth changed all of that. "I came from the dark into an ever-brighter shining light," she said. (Psalm 43:3; Proverbs 4:18) This not only helped her to meet her immediate material needs but also satisfied her spiritual hunger and thirst. Yes, religion—true religion—can satisfy our needs.

Compassion for the Afflicted

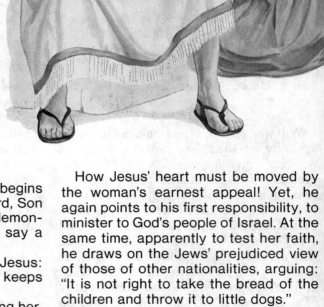

AFTER denouncing the Pharisees for their self-serving traditions, Jesus leaves with his disciples. Not long before, you may recall, his attempt to get away with them to rest up a bit was interrupted when crowds found them. Now, with his disciples, he departs for the regions of Tyre and Sidon, many miles to the north. This apparently is the only trip Jesus makes with his disciples beyond Israel's borders.

After finding a house to stay in, Jesus lets it be known that he does not want anyone to learn of their whereabouts. Yet, even in this non-Israelite territory, he cannot escape notice. A Greek woman, born here in Phoenicia of Syria, finds him and begins begging: "Have mercy on me, Lord, Son of David. My daughter is badly demonized." Jesus, however, does not say a word in reply.

Eventually, his disciples tell Jesus: "Send her away; because she keeps crying out after us."

Explaining his reason for ignoring her, Jesus says: "I was not sent forth to any but to the lost sheep of the house of Israel."

However, the woman does not give up. She approaches Jesus, prostrates herself before him, and pleads, "Lord, help me!"

How Jesus' heart must be moved by the woman's earnest appeal! Yet, he again points to his first responsibility, to minister to God's people of Israel. At the same time, apparently to test her faith, he draws on the Jews' prejudiced view of those of other nationalities, arguing: "It is not right to take the bread of the children and throw it to little dogs."

By his compassionate tone of voice and facial expression, Jesus surely reveals his own tender feelings toward non-Jews. He even softens the prejudiced comparison of Gentiles to dogs by referring to them as *"little* dogs," or puppies. Rather than taking offense, the

Jesus' Life and Ministry

woman picks up on Jesus' reference to Jewish prejudices and makes the humble observation: "Yes, Lord; but really the little dogs do eat of the crumbs falling from the table of their masters."

"O woman, great is your faith," Jesus replies. "Let it happen to you as you wish." And it does! When she returns to her home, she finds her daughter on the bed, completely healed.

From the coastal region of Sidon, Jesus and his disciples head across country toward the headwaters of the Jordan River. They apparently ford the Jordan somewhere above the Sea of Galilee and enter the region of the Decapolis, east of the sea. There they climb a mountain, but the crowds find them and bring to Jesus their lame, crippled, blind, and dumb, and many that are otherwise sick and deformed. They fairly throw them at Jesus' feet,

and he cures them. The people are amazed as they see the dumb speaking, the lame walking, and the blind seeing, and they praise the God of Israel.

One man who is deaf and hardly able to talk is given Jesus' special attention. The deaf are often easily embarrassed, especially in a crowd. Jesus may note this man's particular nervousness. So Jesus compassionately takes him away from the crowd privately. When alone, Jesus indicates what he is going to do for him. He puts his fingers into the man's ears and, after spitting, touches his tongue. Then, looking toward heaven, Jesus sighs deeply and says: "Be opened." At that, the man's hearing powers are restored, and he is able to speak normally.

When Jesus has performed these many cures, the crowds respond with appreciation: "He has done all things well. He even makes the deaf hear and the speechless speak." Matthew 15:21-31; Mark 7:24-37.

□ Why does Jesus not immediately heal the Greek woman's child?

□ Afterward, where does Jesus take his disciples?

□ How does Jesus compassionately treat the deaf man who can hardly speak?

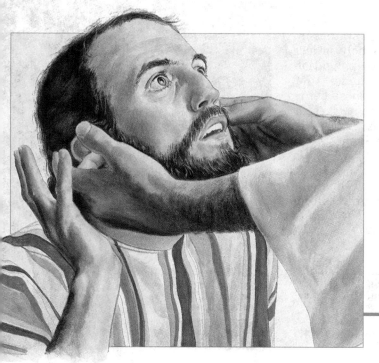

Unmarried but Complete for God's Service

"He also that gives his virginity in marriage does well, but he that does not give it in marriage will do better."—1 CORINTHIANS 7:38.

JEHOVAH never expected the first man to remain single. Rather, God created a marriage mate for Adam, the progenitor of the human race. (Genesis 2:20-24; Acts 17:26) And what a blessing marriage proved to be! It supplied companionship, made mutual assistance possible, was an honorable arrangement for producing offspring, and contributed greatly to human happiness. Why, even the poor and downtrodden can enjoy what no amount of money can buy—marital love!—Song of Solomon 8:6, 7.

² Some, however, view marriage in a different way. Says one religious publication: "Celibacy is the ecclesiastical law in the Western Church imposed on clerics forbidding those in the married state from being ordained and those in holy orders from marrying. It includes the obligation of observing perfect chastity under vow. The reasons for this are: that those being ordained may serve God with a greater singleness of purpose (1 Cor. 7:32), and that so living a life of continence they observe the state of virginity, which is holier and higher than that of marriage. In the NT [New Testament] the celibate or virginal state is raised to a higher calling than that of the married."—*The Catholic Encyclopedia,* compiled by Robert C. Broderick.

1. How has marriage proved to be a blessing?
2, 3. (a) What view did one religious publication take of celibacy and marriage? (b) Scripturally, how should marriage be viewed?

³ Is it really possible that enforced celibacy is 'holier and higher than marriage'? Not according to the "New Testament," which says in the Catholic *Jerusalem Bible:* "The Spirit has explicitly said that during the last times there will be some who will desert the faith and choose to listen to deceitful spirits and doctrines that come from the devils; and the cause of this is the lies told by hypocrites whose consciences are branded as though with a red-hot iron: they will say marriage is forbidden, and lay down rules about ab-

Though unmarried, the apostle Paul was complete

staining from foods which God created to be accepted with thanksgiving by all who believe and who know the truth." (1 Timothy 4:1-3) Actually, marriage is a gift from God, and it is good.—Ruth 1:9.

⁴ Although marriage is a gift from God, the apostle Paul wrote: "He also that gives his virginity in marriage does well, but he that does not give it in marriage will do better." (1 Corinthians 7:38) Why did Paul indicate that it would be better to remain unmarried? Should a single person feel incomplete? And can singleness be rewarding?

The Centerpiece of Christian Life

⁵ Serving Jehovah should be the very centerpiece of our Christian life, whether we are single or married. Sacred service joyfully rendered to God gives evidence of our attachment to him as the Universal Sovereign. Wholehearted obedience and zealous participation in the Christian ministry are ways to demonstrate that attachment. (1 John 5:2, 3; 1 Corinthians 9:16) Both the ministry and other obedient actions in harmony with the divine will can be accomplished if a person is unmarried.

⁶ Evangelizers are now carrying out the Kingdom-preaching work to Jehovah's praise. And whether we are married or single, a zealous ministry affords us opportunity to focus at least some of our personal resources and endowments on God's service. But we must develop and control our circumstances so that the ministry is never relegated to a place that is less than central to our life. We must 'seek the Kingdom first.' (Matthew 6:33) There

is joy in concentrating on divine interests rather than merely on personal interests.

Complete for the Ministry

⁷ Christians can be complete for the ministry whether they are single or married. So the unmarried state is a foundation not necessarily requiring a change. (Compare 1 Corinthians 7:24, 27.) God's Word does not take the view of some tribes that a man does not reach his full estate unless he is married. Jesus Christ died unmarried, and a spiritual bride in heaven is the only wife Jehovah has authorized Jesus to have. (Revelation 21:2, 9) Yet, God's Son, though unmarried as a human, was the foremost example of a person complete for the ministry.

⁸ Actually, being unmarried allows greater personal freedom and time for the ministry. Recommending singleness, Paul said: "I want you to be free from anxiety. The unmarried man is anxious for the things of the Lord, how he may gain the Lord's approval. . . . Further, the unmarried woman, and the virgin, is anxious for the things of the Lord." (1 Corinthians 7:32-34) This applies to single Christians and to those once married but whose circumstances have changed, returning them to an unmarried state.—Matthew 19:9; Romans 7:2, 3.

⁹ Attaining physical, mental, and spiritual maturity brings completeness for God's service. Jesus Christ needed no marriage mate to be complete for the role of God's Chief Minister and the one through whom the ransom would be provided. (Matthew 20:28) Being unmarried,

4. In view of 1 Corinthians 7:38, what questions arise?
5. What should be the centerpiece of Christian life?
6. Whether we are married or single, a zealous ministry enables us to do what?

7. What example is there to show that an unmarried Christian can be complete for the ministry?
8. As Paul shows, being unmarried allows for what?
9. How does Jesus' example show that being unmarried does not make a person incomplete for the Christian ministry?

Jesus was the foremost example of a person complete for the ministry

free from anxiety. The unmarried man is anxious for the things of the Lord, how he may gain the Lord's approval. But the married man is anxious for the things of the world, how he may gain the approval of his wife, and he is divided. Further, the unmarried woman, and the virgin, is anxious for the things of the Lord, that she may be holy both in her body and in her spirit. However, the married woman is anxious for the things of the world, how she may gain the approval of her husband. But this I am saying for your personal advantage, not that I may cast a noose upon you, but to move you to that which is becoming and that which means constant attendance upon the Lord without distraction."—1 Corinthians 7:32-35.

¹¹ Clearly, for a more undistracted life, Paul recommended singleness. He himself may have been a widower who did not choose to remarry. (1 Corinthians 9:5) In any case, he knew that there are anxieties associated with married life in this world. He was showing the comparative freedom that unmarried Christians can enjoy and how the interests of married believers necessarily are divided between fleshly and spiritual matters. The married person does not exercise full authority over his body, for his mate is one flesh with him and therefore has a claim upon his body. (1 Corinthians 7:3-5) In view of this, Paul correctly said that the unmarried Christian is able to be holy, that is, fully set apart and reserved for Jehovah God's direct use, both in body and in spirit.

Jesus was free to focus his full powers on his ministry. His unmarried state differed sharply from the Jewish norm, under which marriage and children were emphasized. Nevertheless, Jesus was fully capable of finishing his God-given work. (Luke 3:23; John 17:3, 4) Hence, being unmarried does not make a person incomplete for the Christian ministry.

Married Persons "Divided"

¹⁰ In contrast with single people, married Christians should pursue the ministry with recognition of their "one flesh" bond. (Matthew 19:5, 6) Because of that bond and its various responsibilities, Paul said that married individuals are "divided." He wrote: "I want you to be

---

10. Because of the "one flesh" bond, what did Paul say about those married as compared with those unmarried?

11. What was Paul showing at 1 Corinthians 7: 32-35?

¹² The single Christian's spirit, or mental inclination, moves him to the active, undistracted service of God's Kingdom. Having no spouse claiming partial control of his body, he can follow the spirit, or inclination, of his mind and heart. He can specialize on Jehovah's service with concentration of body and mind. So the unmarried man or woman can best look to pleasing only the Lord with the greatest personal liberty. We cannot rightly take exception to what Paul said, for Jehovah saw fit to have it recorded for our instruction.

A Married Person Incomplete?

¹³ With the mistaken idea that they could do more in God's service, some married Christians might relegate their marriage to a rather insignificant place in life. For instance, the wife might start acting independently of her husband in consequential ways. The husband might become preoccupied with congregational activities. Under such circumstances, they might conclude that they are doing quite well in Jehovah's service. Actually, however, they might be taking a course that slights the "one flesh" bond. If so, that would not please Jehovah.

¹⁴ In fact, slighting the "one flesh" bond would make a married person incomplete for the Christian ministry. Marriage does not add to ministerial completeness but reduces personal attention that can be given to the ministry. (Compare Luke 14: 16, 17, 20.) Yet, if married people are to please God and be complete as his ministers, they must live up to their marital obligations.

12. Having no spouse, what can an unmarried person do?
13, 14. What mistaken course slights the "one flesh" bond and would make a married person incomplete for the Christian ministry?

Unmarried for the Kingdom's Sake

¹⁵ While married servants of Jehovah should live up to their marital obligations, single Christians should cultivate contentment in their unmarried completeness. As Paul said: "Now I say to the unmarried persons and the widows, it is well for them that they remain even as I am [unmarried]. Are you bound to a wife? Stop seeking a release. Are you loosed from a wife? Stop seeking a wife." (1 Corinthians 7: 8, 27) With Jehovah's help, as a single person, cultivate the settled state that God makes possible. Any change of status should not be a foregone conclusion, just a matter of custom or a reaction to peer pressure. Rather, it should arise from Scriptural necessity, for Paul said: "If anyone thinks he is behaving improperly toward his virginity, if that is past the bloom of youth, and this is the way it should take place, let him do what he wants; he does not sin. Let them marry. But if anyone stands settled in his heart, having no necessity, but has authority over his own will and has made this decision in his own heart, to keep his own virginity, he will do well."—1 Corinthians 7:36, 37.

¹⁶ Thus Paul showed that it would not be wrong to marry if a person was behaving in some unseemly way toward his virginity, although the apostle doubtless was not alluding to gross sin. As he said earlier, "It is better to marry than to be inflamed with passion." (1 Corinthians 7:9) Of course, he was referring to marriage under those circumstances if a person was

15. (a) Unmarried Christians should cultivate what quality? (b) What basic point about marriage and singleness did Paul make at 1 Corinthians 7:36, 37?
16. (a) What does it mean to be "past the bloom of youth"? (b) Of what should the Christian remaining unmarried be convinced?

"past the bloom of youth," beyond the time when sexual interest first became strong. If a mature individual had "authority over his own will" and had firmly decided in his heart to make room for singleness, he would do well. Successful singleness does not mean suppressing a nagging and nearly overpowering desire for marriage and family life. Rather, the Christian choosing to remain unmarried should be fully convinced at heart that maintaining singleness is right in his or her case and should be willing to put forth whatever effort is required to maintain that state in chastity. The Christian doing so would have fewer distractions and greater freedom to serve the Lord.

[17] Unmarried Christians will be helped to maintain the single state if they cultivate the mind of Jesus Christ. Though he was unmarried in a culture that stressed marriage, he concentrated his time and gifts on his unrepeatable ministry. Like Jesus, an unmarried Christian can rejoice in the gift of singleness that God grants to those who make room for it. Concerning this, Jesus said: "Not all men make room for the saying, but only those who have the gift. For there are eunuchs that were born such from their mother's womb, and there are eunuchs that were made eunuchs by men, and there are eunuchs that have made themselves eunuchs on account of the kingdom of the heavens. Let him that can make room for it make room for it."—Matthew 19:11, 12.

[18] Jesus did not say that a single person is superior to a married person. He did not urge singleness simply to have a carefree life, and he surely did not recommend it so that the unmarried person could spread his or her attentions to a number of the opposite sex. No, but those who make themselves "eunuchs" for the Kingdom's sake are morally upright persons who make room for this in their hearts. What keeps them from getting married? Not some physical disability but an overpowering desire to apply themselves as fully as possible to God's service. This service is especially important now since the Kingdom was established in heaven in 1914 and "this good news of the kingdom" must be preached earth wide for a witness before the rapidly approaching end of this doomed system of things.—Matthew 24:14.

Commend Unmarried Christians

[19] All Christians should commend and encourage those who remain unmarried for the Kingdom's sake. After all, being single "means constant attendance upon the Lord without distraction." (1 Corinthians 7:35) Parents will do well to teach their children what the Bible says about the unmarried state and its advantages for the service of Jehovah. All of us can encourage unmarried fellow believers and should never weaken

17. According to Jesus, why do some remain unmarried?
18. What keeps "eunuchs" for the Kingdom's sake from getting married?

19. As regards those remaining single for the Kingdom's sake, what should all Christians do?

What Are Your Answers?

☐ What should be the centerpiece of Christian life?

☐ Why can unmarried servants of Jehovah be complete for the Christian ministry?

☐ In what way could a married person be incomplete?

☐ What does it mean to be a "eunuch" for the Kingdom's sake?

☐ Why should we encourage unmarried Christians?

their resolve to remain unmarried for the sake of the Kingdom.

[20] Unmarried Christians can rejoice as complete ministers of God. In these climactic times, they are delighted to share in the urgent work of Kingdom preaching. Therefore, if you are single, rejoice in being used by Jehovah as a complete unmarried Christian minister. 'Work out your salvation with fear and trembling, while you shine as an illuminator in the world, keeping a tight grip on the word of life.' (Philippians 2:12-16) Concentrate on Kingdom interests as you remain united with the international brotherhood of Jehovah's Witnesses and fulfill the Christian ministry. Doing so as a single person is a rewarding way of life, as we shall see.

Do you commend those who remain unmarried for the Kingdom's sake?

20. If you are an unmarried Christian, what should you do?

Singleness

A Rewarding Way of Life

"She is free to be married to whom she wants, only in the Lord. But she is happier if she remains as she is."
—1 CORINTHIANS 7:39, 40.

JEHOVAH deserves the whole-souled worship of all those dedicated to him. Whether married or single, we should love God with our whole heart, soul, mind, and strength. (Mark 12:30) True, the single Christian has fewer distractions than do those united in wedlock. But can the unmarried servant of Jehovah be truly happy?

1. Whether we are single or married, what do we owe Jehovah?

[2] The apostle Paul answers yes. Concerning those once married but whose circumstances had changed, he wrote: "A wife is bound during all the time her husband is alive. But if her husband should fall asleep in death, she is free to be married to whom she wants, only in the Lord. But she is happier if she remains as

2, 3. (a) In essence, what did Paul say at 1 Corinthians 7:39, 40? (b) What questions merit consideration?

she is, according to my opinion. I certainly think I also have God's spirit."—1 Corinthians 7:39, 40.

3 Since Paul indicates that unmarried people can be happy, who might reasonably consider remaining single, at least for some time? What contributes to the happiness of unmarried Christians? Indeed, how can singleness be a rewarding way of life?

Rewarding Years of Singleness

4 Wise King Solomon urged: "Remember, now, your Grand Creator in the days of your young manhood, before the calamitous days [of old age] proceed to come, or the years have arrived when you will say: 'I have no delight in them.'" (Ecclesiastes 12:1) The years of young manhood and womanhood generally are a time of at least comparative vitality and good health. How appropriate, then, that these assets be used in Jehovah's service without distraction! Moreover, these earlier years are a time to gain experience in life, to develop stability. But this is also a period when young people of the world experience infatuation. For instance, consider the results of a survey involving 1,079 persons between the ages of 18 and 24. They had had an average of seven "romantic experiences" each and invariably said that their current experience was true love, not infatuation.

5 Statistics for separation, divorce, and otherwise broken families spell out the inadvisability of early marriage. Rather than rushing into dating, courtship, and wedlock, young Christians are wise to think positively about how they can use at least their earlier years in undistracted service to Jehovah. In evaluating your circumstances as a young person, you may well ask yourself such questions as these: Am I now emotionally mature and ready to think seriously of wedlock? Do I have enough experience in life to be a good marriage mate? Could I properly shoulder the responsibilities of marriage and possibly of a family with children? In view of my dedication to Jehovah, should I not give him the energy and strength of youth without the distractions related to marriage?

Rewards of Chaste Singleness

6 Unmarried Christians enjoy freedom from distraction and can find "plenty to do in the work of the Lord." (1 Corinthians 7: 32-34; 15:58) Instead of focusing attention on one individual of the opposite sex, the single person has more opportunities to widen out in Christian love for many in the congregation, including the elderly and others who are in need of loving assistance. (Psalm 41:1) Generally, single persons have more time for study and meditation on God's Word. (Proverbs 15: 28) They have a greater opportunity to cultivate a close relationship with Jehovah, learning to rely heavily on him and seek his direction. (Psalm 37:5; Philippians 4:6, 7; James 4:8) An unmarried man who has served Jehovah for years as a missionary in Africa said:

7 "Life in the African villages has been simple over these years, with not too many distractions of modern civilization. Without these distractions, I have had ample opportunity to study and meditate on God's Word. This has kept me strong. Yes, missionary life has been a real blessing and protection against materialism. During the pleasant tropical evenings

4. What is true of the years of young manhood and womanhood?
5. Regarding marriage, what personal questions is it appropriate for a young person to consider?

6, 7. (a) What are some advantages generally enjoyed by unmarried Christians? (b) In this regard, what did an unmarried missionary in Africa say?

there has been ample time to meditate and reflect on Jehovah's creation and draw near to him. My greatest happiness comes each evening when my mind is still awake, and while alone I can spend some time under the starry heavens walking and talking with Jehovah. This has drawn me closer to Jehovah."

[8] Noteworthy, too, is this comment of a single sister with many years of service at the Watch Tower Society's headquarters: "I have chosen to lead a single life in my service to Jehovah. Do I ever get lonely? Not at all. Really, my moments alone are among some of the most precious. I can commune with Jehovah in prayer. I can enjoy meditation and personal study without distraction. . . . Singleness has contributed not a little to my joy."

[9] A single person can also accept privileges of service that may not be open to married persons having family responsibilities. For instance, there may be opportunities to engage in the full-time ministry as a pioneer in an area where the need for Kingdom proclaimers is great. Or a single young man may be privileged to

---

8. Regarding singleness, what was said by an unmarried sister with many years of service at the Society's headquarters?
9. What are some privileges of service that a single Christian may be able to enjoy?

In Our Next Issue

■ Faith Healing—Is it From God?

■ Maintain Your Fear of Jehovah

■ The Value of Singing in True Worship

---

serve as a member of the Bethel family at the Watch Tower Society's headquarters or a branch office. A young unmarried woman may be able to join a somewhat older single sister in pioneer service in their home congregation or another having territory that needs to be covered. Why not discuss such possibilities with the circuit overseer? As an unmarried Christian, make yourself available for increased service to Jehovah's praise, and he will bless you abundantly.—Malachi 3:10.

Examples From the Past

[10] The prime example of an unmarried servant of Jehovah was Jesus Christ. He was totally absorbed in doing God's will. "My food is for me to do the will of him that sent me and to finish his work," said Jesus. (John 4:34) How busy he was —preaching, healing the sick, and so forth! (Matthew 14:14) Jesus had genuine interest in people and was comfortable in the presence of men, women, and children. Indeed, he traveled about in his ministry, with others accompanying him on certain occasions. (Luke 8:1-3) But how difficult that activity would have been if he had been accompanied by a wife and small children! Unquestionably, singleness was an advantage in Jesus' case. Today, a single Christian may enjoy similar advantages, especially if called upon to declare the Kingdom message in remote or dangerous areas.

[11] But others also found singleness practical and rewarding. Jephthah's daughter voluntarily fulfilled her father's vow by remaining single in a society that placed great stress on marriage and children. She found joy in her service to Jehovah, and it

---

10. Who provided the prime example of an unmarried servant of Jehovah, and why do you think that his singleness was advantageous?
11, 12. What fine examples are cited for single women serving Jehovah today?

is noteworthy that others regularly encouraged her. Why, "from year to year the daughters of Israel would go to give commendation to the daughter of Jephthah the Gileadite, four days in the year"! (Judges 11:34-40) Similarly, married Christians and others should commend and encourage single women valiantly serving Jehovah today.

¹² Philip's four virgin daughters "prophesied." (Acts 21:8, 9) These unmarried women must have drawn much satisfaction from their active service to Jehovah's praise. Comparably, many young single women today have the rewarding privilege of serving as pioneers, or full-time Kingdom proclaimers. Surely, they deserve commendation as part of the 'large army of women declaring the good news.' —Psalm 68:11.

¹³ The apostle Paul found singleness to be advantageous. He traveled thousands

of miles in his ministry and faced great hardships, many dangers, sleepless nights, gnawing hunger. (2 Corinthians 11:23-27) Undoubtedly, all of this would have been much more difficult and distressing if Paul had been married. Moreover, it is not at all likely that he would ever have had his privileges as "an apostle to the nations" if he had been raising a family. (Romans 11:13) Despite the trials he faced, Paul had firsthand evidence that singleness can be a rewarding way of life.

Modern-Day Examples

¹⁴ Like Paul and other unmarried early Christians, a number of God's people who shared in colporteur work (from 1881 onward) were single persons without dependent families. They willingly went into unfamiliar cities, towns, and rural areas, seeking those with good hearts and plac-

---

13. How does Paul's case illustrate that singleness can be a rewarding way of life?

14. What experiences were enjoyed by colporteurs, most of whom were unmarried?

Jephthah's daughter, the apostle Paul, and other servants of Jehovah found singleness to be a rewarding way of life. Can you?

ing Bible literature with them. Travel might be by train, bicycle, horse-drawn buggy, or automobile. Mostly, they happily walked from house to house. (Acts 20: 20, 21) "Sometimes they would trade [Bible literature] for farm produce, chickens, soap and what-not, which they would use or sell to others," recalled one witness of Jehovah, adding: "At times, in a sparsely settled area, they stayed with farmers and ranchers overnight, and at times even slept in haystacks . . . These faithful ones [most of whom were unmarried] kept on for years and years until age overtook them." Surely, one of them spoke for those old-time colporteurs in general when she wrote: "We were young and happy in the service, delighted to expend our strength in serving Jah."

¹⁵ Many pioneers, or full-time Kingdom proclaimers, of later times were also unmarried. They often witnessed in isolated areas, helped to start new congregations, and enjoyed other blessings in Jehovah's service. For some of them, an exciting door leading to greater activity swung open when the Watchtower Bible School of Gilead began to function in 1943 while World War II was still raging. (1 Corinthians 16:9) Yes, many of those unmarried pioneers received missionary training at Gilead School and were soon spreading the Kingdom message in new territories. Unencumbered by marital responsibilities, they made themselves available for Jehovah's service, and some of those early graduates are still single and active in the missionary field or some other avenue of full-time service.

¹⁶ Many unmarried Christians have

---

15. For many unmarried pioneers, what door leading to greater activity swung open some 45 years ago?
16. What evidence is there that unmarried members of the Bethel family have found singleness to be a rewarding way of life?

Aids in Maintaining Chaste Singleness

◆ Pray regularly for God's spirit and his help in displaying its fruitage
◆ Ponder over and always apply the counsel of God's Word
◆ Avoid pornography and immoral entertainment
◆ Guard your associations
◆ Shun unclean speech and obscene jesting

---

served for years as members of the Bethel family at the Watch Tower Society's headquarters or at its branches elsewhere in the world. Have they found singleness to be a rewarding way of life? Yes, indeed. For instance, a single brother who had served at Brooklyn Bethel for many years remarked: "The joy of seeing millions of magazines and other publications bearing the message of God's Word spreading to the ends of the earth has been a marvelous reward in itself." After some 45 years of Bethel service, another unmarried brother said: "Every day I ask our dear heavenly Father in prayer for help and wisdom to keep myself spiritually as well as physically healthy and strong so that I can keep on doing his holy will. . . . I have indeed enjoyed a happy, rewarding and blessed way of life."

Maintaining Chaste Singleness

¹⁷ That a life of singleness can be rewarding is evident from Biblical and modern-day examples. Of course, during whatever period of your life is spent in the

---

17. What are two aids in maintaining chaste singleness?

single state, you need to 'stand settled in your heart.' (1 Corinthians 7:37) But what can help you to maintain chastity while unmarried? The greatest Source of help is Jehovah, the "Hearer of prayer." (Psalm 65:2) So make it a habit to petition him often. "Persevere in prayer," asking for God's spirit and his help in displaying its fruitage, which includes peace and self-control. (Romans 12:12; Luke 11:13; Galatians 5:22, 23) Then, too, with a prayerful attitude, regularly ponder over and always apply the counsel of God's Word.

¹⁸ Another aid in maintaining chaste singleness is avoiding anything that arouses sexual passion. Obviously, this includes pornography and immoral entertainment. Paul said: "Be babes as to badness; yet become full-grown in powers of understanding." (1 Corinthians 14:20) Do not seek knowledge or experience regarding evil, but with God's help wisely remain inexperienced and innocent as a baby in this regard. At the same time, remember that sexual immorality and wrongdoing are improper in Jehovah's sight.

¹⁹ You will also be helped to remain chaste as an unmarried person by guarding your associations. (1 Corinthians 15: 33) Avoid associating with those who make sex and marriage big features in their lives and conversations. By all means shun obscene jesting! Paul counseled: "Let fornication and uncleanness of every sort or greediness not even be mentioned among you, just as it befits holy people; neither shameful conduct nor foolish talking nor obscene jesting, things which are not becoming, but rather the giving of thanks."—Ephesians 5:3, 4.

18. How does 1 Corinthians 14:20 relate to one's remaining chaste as an unmarried person?
19. What scriptures point to other ways to remain chaste as a single person?

A Rewarding Future

²⁰ Putting your years as an unmarried Christian to the best possible use in Jehovah's service will bring present satisfaction and peace of mind. Doing so will also contribute to your spiritual maturity and stability. If you remain single for the Kingdom's sake until the end of this wicked system of things, Jehovah will not forget your self-sacrificing efforts in his sacred service.

²¹ If you diligently pursue Kingdom interests as an unmarried man or woman, you will enjoy many blessings. (Proverbs 10:22) Then if you should get married later in life, you will enter wedlock with greater experience and a rich spiritual background. Moreover, by following the counsel of the Scriptures, you will choose a dedicated integrity-keeping mate who will help you to serve God faithfully. In the meantime, you can find singleness to be a rewarding way of life in the service of our loving God, Jehovah.

20. Putting one's years of singleness to the best use in Jehovah's service will result in what?
21. If you should get married after a period of chaste and rewarding singleness, with what are you likely to enter wedlock?

How Would You Respond?

□ Among Jehovah's servants, what are some rewards of chaste singleness?

□ What Scriptural examples are there to show that singleness can be rewarding?

□ In modern times, what examples of rewarding singleness do we have?

□ What can help a Christian to remain chaste while unmarried?

Anabaptists and
"the Pattern of Healthful Words"

THE apostle Paul warned that after his death, apostate Christians, like "oppressive wolves," would enter in among the flock of God and would seek to "draw away the disciples after themselves." How would they do this? By bringing in traditions and false teachings to distort the truth of the Scriptures.—Acts 20:29, 30; 1 Timothy 4:1.

For this reason, Paul exhorted the young man Timothy: "Keep holding the pattern of healthful words that you heard from me with the faith and love that are in connection with Christ Jesus. This fine trust guard through the holy spirit which is dwelling in us." What was this "pattern of healthful words"?—2 Timothy 1: 13, 14.

"The Pattern" Established

All the books of the Christian Greek Scriptures were completed in the first century of our Common Era. Although they were penned by different writers, God's holy spirit, or active force, ensured that they were harmonious not just within themselves but also with the earlier Hebrew Scriptures. In this way, a "pattern" of sound Scriptural teaching was formed and had to be adhered to by Christians, even as Jesus Christ had become "a model" for them to follow.—1 Peter 2:21; John 16:12, 13.

During the spiritually dark centuries following the death of the apostles, what happened to "the pattern of healthful words"? Many sincere people tried to rediscover it, although a full restoration would have to wait until "the time of the end." (Daniel 12:4) Sometimes it was a lone voice, and at other times it was a small group of people who were searching for "the pattern."

The Waldenses appear to have been such a minority.* They lived in France, Italy, and other areas of Europe during the 12th to the 14th centuries. From this movement the Anabaptists later emerged. Who were they, and what did they believe?

Basic Teachings

The Anabaptists first became prominent about the year 1525, in Zurich, Switzerland. From that city their beliefs spread rapidly to many parts of Europe. The early 16th-century Reformation had made some changes, but in the eyes of the Anabaptists, it had not gone far enough.

In their desire to get back to the Christian teachings of the first century, they rejected more of the Roman Catholic dogma than did Martin Luther and other reformers. For example, the Anabaptists maintained that there could only be an *adult* dedication to Christ. On account of their practice of adult baptism, even for a person who had been baptized as an infant, they were given the name "Anabaptists," which means "rebaptizers."—Matthew 28:19; Acts 2:41; 8:12; 10:44-48.

"To the Anabaptists the real Church was an association of believing people," writes Dr. R. J. Smithson in his book *The Anabaptists—Their Contribution to Our Protestant Heritage.* As such, they

---

* See *The Watchtower* of August 1, 1981, pages 12-15.

considered themselves to be a society of believers within the community at large and at the outset did not have a specially trained, or paid, ministry. Like the disciples of Jesus, they were itinerant preachers who visited towns and villages, talking to people in marketplaces, workshops, and homes.—Matthew 9:35; 10:5-7, 11-13; Luke 10:1-3.

Each individual Anabaptist was considered personally accountable to God, enjoying freedom of will and showing his faith by his works, yet recognizing that salvation did not come from works alone. If somebody transgressed the faith, he could be expelled from the congregation. Reinstatement followed only upon evidence of proper repentance.—1 Corinthians 5: 11-13; compare 2 Corinthians 12:21.

Their View of the World

The Anabaptists realized that they could not reform the world. Although the Church had become allied with the State since the time of Roman emperor Constantine in the fourth century C.E., to them this did not mean that the State had become Christian. From what Jesus had said, they knew that a Christian had to be "no part of the world," even if this resulted in persecution.—John 17:15, 16; 18:36.

Where there was no conflict between the Christian conscience and secular interests, the Anabaptists acknowledged that the State should rightly be respected and obeyed. But an Anabaptist would not get involved in politics, hold a civil office, be a magistrate, or swear oaths. Rejecting all forms of violence and force, he would also take no part in warfare or military service.—Mark 12:17; Acts 5:29; Romans 13:1-7; 2 Corinthians 10:3, 4.

The Anabaptists maintained a high moral standard in a sober simplicity of life, basically free from materialistic goods and desires. Because of their love for one another, they often established settlements, although most of them rejected communal living as a way of life. On the basis that everything belongs to God, however, they were always ready to make use of their material possessions for the good of the poor.—Acts 2:42-45.

Through a close study of the Bible, especially of the Christian Greek Scriptures, some Anabaptists refused to accept the Trinity doctrine of three persons in one God, as some of their writings testify. Their way of worship was usually quite simple, with the Lord's Supper holding a special place. Rejecting the traditional Roman Catholic, Lutheran, and Calvinistic views, they saw this act of commemoration as a memorial of Jesus' death. "To them," writes R. J. Smithson, "it was the most solemn act in which a Christian can participate, involving the renewal of the believer's covenant to devote his life unreservedly to Christ's service."

Persecution—And After

The Anabaptists were misunderstood, as were the early Christians. Like them, they were viewed as upsetting the established order of society, 'overturning the inhabited earth.' (Acts 17:6) In Zurich, Switzerland, the authorities, linked with reformer Huldrych Zwingli, especially took issue with the Anabaptists over their refusal to baptize infants. In 1527 they cruelly drowned Felix Manz, one of the Anabaptist leaders, and so bitterly persecuted the Swiss Anabaptists that they were almost wiped out.

In Germany the Anabaptists were bitterly persecuted by both Catholics and Protestants. An imperial mandate, passed in the year 1528, imposed the death penalty on any who became Anabaptists—and that without any form of trial. Persecution in Austria caused most Anabaptists there to seek refuge in Moravia, Bohemia, and Poland, and later on in Hungary and Russia.

With the death of so many of the original leaders, it was inevitable that extremists should come to the fore. They brought with them an imbalance that led to much confusion and a subsequent falling away from the standards that had marked earlier days. This was tragically evident in the year 1534, when such extremists forcibly took over the municipal government of Münster, Westphalia. The following year the city was recaptured amid much bloodshed and torture. This episode was out of harmony with true Anabaptist teaching and did much to discredit them. Some followers sought to disown the name Anabaptists in favor of the title "Baptists." But whatever name they chose, they still became the victims of opposition and of the Catholic Inquisition in particular.

Eventually, groups of Anabaptists emigrated in search of greater freedom and peace. Today, we find them in North and South America, as well as in Europe. Many denominations have been influenced by their early teachings, including the Quakers, the modern-day Baptists, and the Plymouth Brethren. The Quakers share the Anabaptist hatred of war and the idea of guidance by an 'inner light.'

The survival of the Anabaptists is most clearly seen today in two particular groups. The first is the Hutterian Brethren, named after their 16th-century leader, Jacob Hutter. They founded community settlements in England, Western Canada, Paraguay, and South Dakota in the United States. The Mennonites are the other group. They take their name from Menno Simons, who did much to obliterate the bad record left in the Netherlands following the Münster affair. Simons died in 1561. Today, Mennonites are found in Europe and North America, along with the Amish Mennonites.

Jehovah's Witnesses help many to understand "the pattern of healthful words"

"The Pattern" Today

Although the Anabaptists may have sought "the pattern of healthful words," they did not succeed in discovering it. Moreover, in his book *A History of Christianity,* K. S. Latourette observes: "Originally vigorously missionary, persecution caused them largely to withdraw within themselves and to perpetuate themselves by birth rather than conversion." And the same is true even now of those small groups traceable to the Anabaptist movement. Their desire to stand apart from the world and its ways has led them to keep distinctive modes of dress, encouraged by their often separate community life.

So, then, can "the pattern of healthful words" really be found today? Yes, but it does take time and a love of truth to find it. Why not check to see if what you believe measures up to the divinely revealed "pattern"? It is not difficult to determine what is man-made tradition and what is Scriptural fact. Jehovah's Witnesses in your locality will gladly help you, for they themselves appreciate the way they have been helped to understand "the pattern of healthful words."

True Love Is Triumphant!

There is love that never fails. It is constant, enduring, triumphant. Such unswerving love exists between Jesus Christ and his "bride," or spirit-begotten congregation. (Revelation 21:2, 9; Ephesians 5: 21-33) And how beautifully this love is portrayed in The Song of Solomon!

Composed some 3,000 years ago by wise King Solomon of Israel, this "superlative song" (1:1) tells of the love existing between a shepherd and a country girl from the village of Shunem (Shulem). With all his wealth and splendor, the king was unable to win the Shulammite's love, for she was loyal to her beloved shepherd.

When this poetic book is read with due care and appreciation, it gives single and married servants of Jehovah much food for thought regarding the purity, tenderness, loyalty, and abiding love that should be hallmarks of Christian wedlock. Indeed, all of us can benefit from this song about the triumph of true love.

The Shulammite in Solomon's Camp

Please read The Song of Solomon 1:1-14. In the royal tents, the Shulammite spoke as if her beloved shepherd were present. Solomon extolled her beauty and promised to adorn her with articles of gold and silver. But the maiden resisted his advances and let him know that she had true love only for the shepherd.

♦ 1:2, 3—Why were these comparisons with wine and oil apropos?

Wine gladdens the heart and strengthens the depressed soul. (Psalm 104:15; Proverbs 31:6) Oil was poured out on favored guests for its soothing properties. (Psalm 23:5; Luke 7:38) Thus the distressed Shulammite was strengthened and comforted by recalling the shepherd's "expressions of endearment" and his "name." Similarly, the remnant of Christ's anointed followers are encouraged by meditating on the love and assurances of their Shepherd, Jesus Christ, although they are yet in the world and separated from him.

Lesson for Us: Solomon would have decked the Shulammite with "circlets of gold" and "studs of silver," but she resisted these material temptations and affirmed her unfailing love for the shepherd. (1: 11-14) Reflecting on her attitude can strengthen the resolve of the "bride" class to spurn the world's seductive materialism and remain faithful to their heavenly Bridegroom. If our hopes are earthly and we are contemplating matrimony, may this maiden's example move us to make spiritual, not material, interests our prime concern.

Mutual Longing

Read 1:15–3:5. The shepherd entered the royal camp and voiced his love for the modest Shulammite, who esteemed him above all others. When they were separated, the maiden recalled joyful times with her beloved and pleaded that he hasten to her side. At night, she longed for him.

♦ 2:1-3—What is meant by these figures of speech?

The Shulammite called herself "a mere saffron of the coastal plain" because she was a humble, modest young woman who viewed herself as only one of many common flowers. The shepherd, however, realized that she was "a lily among thorny weeds," for she was comely, capable, and faithful to Jehovah. To the maiden, the shepherd was "like an apple tree among the trees of the forest" because he was a spiritually inclined young man similarly devoted to God and having very desirable traits and abilities. An unmarried Christian seeking a partner in life should be looking only for a faithful fellow believer having qualities like those of the Shulammite or her beloved shepherd.

♦ 3:5—Why was this oath associated with these animals?

Gazelles and hinds are gentle, graceful, and beautiful animals that are also swift and surefooted. In essence, then, the maiden was binding the "daughters of Jerusalem" in an oath by all that is graceful and beautiful. By these creatures, she was obligating these women to refrain from trying to arouse love in her for anyone other than her beloved shepherd.

Lesson for Us: The maiden put the "daughters of Jerusalem," or court women who waited on the king, under oath 'not to arouse love in her until it felt inclined.' (2:7; 3:5) This indicates that it is not possible to have romantic love for just anyone. The maiden herself felt no attraction for Solomon. How wise it is, then, for an unmarried Christian contemplating wedlock to consider only an eligible and faithful worshiper of Jehovah who can truly be loved!—1 Corinthians 7:39.

The Maiden in Jerusalem

Read 3:6–6:3. Solomon returned to Jerusalem in splendor. The shepherd got in touch with the maiden there and strengthened her with expressions of endearment. In a dream, she belatedly responded to the knock of her beloved and was mistreated by watchmen as she made a desperate search for him. Asked what made her dear one outstanding, she gave the "daughters of Jerusalem" a glowing description of him.

♦ 5:12—How were the shepherd's eyes 'like doves bathing in milk'?

Earlier, the Shulammite's eyes had been likened to those of a dove because of being soft, gentle. (1:15; 4:1) For that matter, the shepherd had called the maiden herself his "dove." (5:2) Here the lovesick young woman likened the shepherd's eyes to blue-gray doves bathing in pools of milk. (5:8, 12) Likely, this simile referred to the shepherd's dark iris surrounded by the gleaming white of his eyes.

Lesson for Us: The Shulammite was like "a garden barred in." (4:12) Often a garden in ancient Israel was park-like, a veritable paradise with a good water source and a variety of vegetables, flowers, and trees. Usually, it was enclosed by a hedge or a wall and could be entered only through a locked gate. (Isaiah 5:5) To the shepherd, the Shulammite's moral purity and loveliness were like a garden of rare beauty, fine fruitage, delightful fragrances, and exhilarating pleasantness. Her affections were not available to just any man, for she was chaste, like "a garden barred" to unwelcome intruders and open only to its lawful owner. In moral rectitude and loyalty the Shulammite thus set a fine example for yet unmarried Christian women today.

"The Flame of Jah"

Read 6:4–8:14. Solomon praised the maiden's beauty, but she rejected him and declared her devotion to the shepherd. Unable to gain her love, Solomon let her go home. With her "dear one" at her side, she returned to Shunem as a mature woman of proved stability. The love between her and the shepherd was as strong as death, and its blazings were as "the flame of Jah."

♦ 6:4—What was "Pleasant City"?

This expression can be rendered "Tirzah," meaning "Pleasantness, Delightfulness." Tirzah was a city of renowned beauty that became the first capital of the northern kingdom of Israel. —1 Kings 14:17; 16:5, 6, 8, 15.

♦ 7:4—How was the maiden's neck "like an ivory tower"?

Apparently it had the smoothness of ivory and the slenderness of a tower. Earlier, her neck had been likened to "the tower of David," perhaps the tower of the King's House along Jerusalem's east wall. Upon it 'were hung a thousand circular shields of mighty men,' suggesting that the Shulammite's stately neck was graced with a necklace strung with round ornaments or jewels. —4:4; Nehemiah 3:25-27.

♦ 8:6, 7—How is love "as strong as death"?

Death has unfailingly claimed the lives of sinful humans, and true love is that strong. In its insistence on exclusive devotion, such love is just as unyielding as Sheol (gravedom) is in demanding the bodies of the deceased. Since Jehovah God put the capacity for love within humans, this quality emanates from him and is fittingly termed "the flame of Jah." Not even rich King Solomon could buy such love.

Lesson for Us: The Shulammite's experience with King Solomon was a searching test that she passed successfully. She was not unsteady in love and virtue, like a door easily turning on its hinges and needing to be barred with a cedar plank to prevent its swinging open to someone unwelcome or unwholesome. No, the maiden triumphed over the enticements of the king, standing like a wall against all the material attractions of this world. With reliance on God and by recalling the Shulammite's fine example, Christian women today can similarly prove their stature as individuals firm in virtuous principles to Jehovah's praise.—8:8-10.

Surely, this "superlative song," having love as its theme, heightens our appreciation for the bond existing between Jesus and those chosen to be his heavenly "bride." But all young men and women as well as husbands and wives devoted to Jehovah can benefit from seeking to imitate the integrity of the Shulammite and the shepherd in the face of trials and temptations. And this splendid portion of God's Word should move all of us to remain ever loyal to Jehovah, the Source of triumphant love.

Answering the Call of the Micronesian Islands

NAMES like Truk, Yap, Ponape, Guam, and Saipan may sound somewhat familiar to you. But what about Belau, Rota, Kosrae, Nauru, or Kiribati? These and others are all part of the more than 2,000 islands and atolls scattered over some three million square miles of the Western Pacific and known collectively as Micronesia, or small islands.

Within this vast expanse, approximately the size of Australia or the continental United States, Jehovah's Witnesses are busy proclaiming the Kingdom good news. (Mark 13:10) Currently, this work is being done by about 740 Kingdom publishers in 13 congregations. Indeed, there is a great need for more workers to bring in the harvest in these faraway islands of the sea.—Compare Jeremiah 31:10.

Over the last 20 years or so, individuals from Hawaii, the Philippines, Canada, the United States, and Australia have answered the call and taken up missionary service in the Micronesian islands. When the first of them arrived in 1965, there were only 76 Kingdom publishers in all of this vast territory. In 1987, however, a total of 4,510 persons attended the Memorial of Jesus Christ's death. Clearly, Christian labors of love over the years had been richly blessed.

Today, there are 49 missionaries serving out of 14 missionary homes scattered among the islands, all working under the supervision of the Watch Tower Society's Guam branch. Their love for Jehovah and for their Micronesian neighbors has moved them to answer the missionary call. What experiences have they had while serving in these remote islands? In terms of new languages and customs, what challenges have they had to overcome? And what has helped them to stay in their assignments? Let us hear from some of them about their work in these islands.

The Challenge of New Languages

There are eight or nine major languages in Micronesia. But because these are not considered written languages, it is difficult for the new missionaries to find books to use in learning them. Still, they work hard at it. One effective method, they were told, was to try to use what had been learned immediately in the preaching work. Well, they still remember the many hilarious—and embarrassing—situations that developed when they tried to do that.

Roger, a native of Hawaii, recalls one such situation when he first came to Belau 13 years ago. "When one householder said, 'I'm a Catholic,' the only Palauan word I knew to answer with was 'Why?'" The householder then went into a long explanation. "I did not understand a word she said. At her conclusion, I said the only other word I knew, 'Thank you,' and left!"

Salvador, who came to Truk with his wife, Helen, ten years ago, remembers trying to ask a Trukese lady if she wanted to be happy (*pwapwa*). Instead, he asked if she wanted to be pregnant (*pwopwo*). And Zenette, who came from Canada with her husband, David, recalls the time when she tried to say "Thank you" (*kilisou*) but wound up saying "Horsefly" (*kiliso*). Needless to say, they know those words well now.

When James was transferred to the island of Kosrae after serving four years in Ponape, he had to start all over again. He especially remembers trying to befriend one householder. But instead of asking, "How are you?" he told him, "You are a freak"! Now, after ten years, he confesses: "At first, it was hard to say some of the Kosraean words because they sounded so much like swear words in English."

Such experiences, however, never discourage these missionaries from pressing on with their language studies. "There is little one can do to help the people without learning the language," said one missionary. "This provides real incentive to study diligently."

Customs and Superstitions

To the newcomers, many of the local customs seemed amusing. For instance, David met a man who had named his three sons Sardine, Tuna, and Spam. Later, he was introduced to three men named Desire, Sin, and Repent. Zenette found it strange that people call their grandparents Papa and Mama and their parents by their first names. When Sheri first came from Hawaii, she thought it was most amusing that people use their nose to point out directions. And it took some time to get used to this custom: When a woman enters a public gathering, she "walks" on her knees to her "seat" on the floor to show respect for the men.

Many, too, are the superstitious beliefs. In the Marshall Islands, for example, when someone dies the family will put food, cigarettes, and flowers on the grave for the deceased. Or when a bird flies around the house singing, this is taken to mean danger and imminent death for someone in the family.

Some in the islands are also deeply involved in spiritism. Jon was one of them. Once an elder in a Protestant church, he was able to expel demons by prayers and by using medicine prepared from coconut oil.

"One day an ugly face of a demon as wide as a door appeared at the entrance of my room," Jon related. At first Jon thought he was dreaming but soon realized that he was fully awake.

"The demon told me that he was the source of my magical powers. This shocked me and caused me to wonder why the demons would work through me, a deacon in the church, and why the minister himself sought my demonistic services." Jon was soon contacted by the

Witness missionaries and started to study the Bible.

"It brought me great joy to learn the truth about the demons and about how to identify the true religion," Jon recalled. He withdrew from his church and discontinued his practice of demonism. Today he warns others to avoid all demonistic practices.—Deuteronomy 18:9-13; Revelation 21:8.

Reaching the Smaller Islands

Taking the good news to people on the small outer islands is a real challenge. Often the only way to reach them is to book passage on a copra ship. As the ship stops at each islet for a few hours or days to pick up cargo, the missionaries and other Kingdom publishers busy themselves in witnessing to the islanders. Weekly radio broadcasts are another way of bringing the good news to them.

Residents of the outer islands often travel to the main island centers for food, medical attention, and schooling. While there, they may be contacted by Jehovah's Witnesses and may obtain Bible literature. Interest is followed up by mail or when publishers visit their island. One couple was contacted this way in Majuro in the Marshall Islands and then returned to their home island of Ailuk, 250 miles away. They began making progress in their understanding of the Bible. Soon they severed ties with their church, legalized their marriage, and got baptized. Now both preach zealously on their isolated island, frequently serving as auxiliary pioneers.

Missionaries in Ponape, Truk, and Belau use their own boats for island witnessing. Since there are no docking facilities at most places, they often have to wade ashore in mud up to their knees. Most residents are friendly and welcome the visitors by spreading out woven floor mats for them and serving them cool coconut water. The entire family is summoned and will listen attentively. Because many do not have money, it is not uncommon to see publishers returning after two or three days with their boat loaded with fruit received in exchange for Bible literature.

Sacrifices and Rewards

For the missionaries, life in the islands is not what it was back home. They have to get used to frequent power failures and water shortages, depending on rainwater for their supply. On some islands, there are no power, water, or sewage systems, no paved roads, and no automobiles. But the missionaries have learned to be adaptable. "When I see the local brothers living in houses built out of discarded lumber and flooring, we feel empathy for them, and this tends to keep us balanced in our needs and wants," observes Julian, who has served faithfully for 17 years in Guam and the Marshall Islands.

Rodney and Sheri came to Truk from Hawaii. He admits: "Frankly, I experienced a culture shock." Now, ten years later, he writes: "We have a very satisfying work to do here. We have our ups and downs; at times we feel discouraged and lonely. But we want to continue to pursue our purpose in life in missionary work here." And Sheri cheerfully adds: "Self-sacrificing people are happy people."

Indeed, their sacrifices are richly rewarded. Clemente and his wife, Eunice, who came to the Marshall Islands ten years ago, now conduct 34 weekly home Bible studies. "Fourteen of the students have symbolized their dedication to Jehovah by water immersion," he reports, "and others are progressing toward baptism. Such lifesaving work is of great value in our eyes." James, a missionary for more than ten years, states: "To see the endurance of our Kosraean brothers year after year is a real blessing." Over in Belau, Roger comments: "We have been blessed with a new Kingdom Hall and a loyal group of publishers." And looking back over the years, Placido says: "Jehovah's direction and holy spirit have been evident in our lives. This has helped us to draw very close to him."

Such experiences have encouraged the missionaries to remain in their assignments. Many of them can look back and remember the formation of the first congregation in their area. Like the apostle Paul, they have the unique joy of 'not building on another man's foundation.'

(Romans 15:20) Their feeling is well expressed by this comment: "There is still much work to be done. I believe Jehovah will yet open up many opportunities to bring in more sheeplike ones in the islands, and we are privileged to share in it."

"The blessing of Jehovah—that is what makes rich, and he adds no pain with it," says the Bible at Proverbs 10:22. Those who have answered the missionary call of the Micronesian islands have truly experienced this blessing along with the joy and satisfaction that come from serving Jehovah.

Questions From Readers

■ Was Paul referring to Jehovah or to Jesus when he wrote: 'The Lord said to me: "My power is being made perfect in weakness"'?

It seems that the apostle Paul was referring to the Lord Jehovah. By noting Paul's words in context, not only can we see why this is so but we can also deepen our appreciation for the relationship between God and his Son. Paul wrote:

"That I might not feel overly exalted, there was given me a thorn in the flesh, an angel of Satan, to keep slapping me, that I might not be overly exalted. In this behalf I three times entreated the Lord that it might depart from me; and yet he really said to me: 'My undeserved kindness is sufficient for you; for my power is being made perfect in weakness.' Most gladly, therefore, will I rather boast as respects my weaknesses, that the power of the Christ may like a tent remain over me."—2 Corinthians 12:7-9.

The thorn in Paul's flesh may have been either some eye affliction or false apostles who challenged his apostleship. (Galatians 4:15; 6:11; 2 Corinthians 11:5, 12-15) Whichever it was, it tended to discourage Paul or keep him from exulting over his ministry. So he thrice asked that it be removed. But whom did he ask, and who responded by speaking of "my power"?

Since the passage mentions "the power of the Christ," it might seem that Paul had asked the Lord Jesus. Unquestionably, he has power and can impart it to his disciples. (Mark 5:30; 13:26; 1 Timothy 1:12) In fact, the Son of God "sustains all things by the word of his power."—Hebrews 1:3; Colossians 1:17, 29.

However, the Lord God is the ultimate source of power, which he can and does supply to his worshipers. (Psalm 147:5; Isaiah 40:26, 29-31) Such power from God enabled Jesus to perform miracles and will yet enable him to act. (Luke 5:17; Acts 10:38) Similarly, Jesus' apostles and other disciples received power from Jehovah. (Luke 24:49; Ephesians 3:14-16; 2 Timothy 1:7, 8) This included Paul, who ministered "according to the free gift of the undeserved kindness of God that was given [the apostle] according to the way his power operates."—Ephesians 3:7.

Since Paul asked for the removal of the 'thorn in his flesh, an angel of Satan,' it is logical that he looked to the Lord God to do this, Jehovah being the one to whom prayers are directed. (Philippians 4:6; Psalm 145:18) Furthermore, Jehovah's somehow encouraging Paul with the words, "My power is being made perfect in weakness," does not leave out Christ. Power from the Lord God could be described as "the power of the Christ [that was] like a tent" over Paul, for 'Christ is the power of God and the wisdom of God.' (1 Corinthians 1:24) Thus, 2 Corinthians 12:7-9 helps us to appreciate better the pivotal way in which Jehovah uses his Son in the outworking of the divine will.

From Brickmaking Slavery
to Freedom!

DO THE pyramids of Giza (near modern Cairo) bring to mind abused slaves toiling under a hot sun to drag huge stones into place? And do you imagine Hebrew slaves among them?

Actually, the Egyptian pyramids seen on the next page date from before the time when the family of Joseph's father Jacob (or, Israel) moved to Egypt. But more common than building with huge stones was the use of bricks, produced by the millions under the same blazing sun.

The Hebrews who were welcome in Egypt during Joseph's time were blessed by God with increase, bringing dread to the Egyptians. We read: "So they set over [the Hebrews] chiefs of forced labor for the purpose of oppressing them in their burden-bearing; and they went building cities . . . The Egyptians made the sons of Israel slave under tyranny. And they kept making their life bitter with hard slavery at clay mortar and bricks."—Exodus 1:7-14.

On the right, you can see that bricks are still made in Egypt, some being baked in kilns such as the one seen here. (Compare Genesis 11:1-3; 19:

28.) Evidently, however, most ancient Egyptian bricks were sun dried. What persists is the use of straw in making bricks. Straw is visible in bricks found in the unearthed ruins of ancient Beer-sheba (inset).

Adding straw strengthened the bricks. To make them, mud (or clay), water, and straw were slowly trampled by foot, then pressed in molds, and finally set out to dry. Imagine toiling at such work one long day after another. Surely, you can understand why the Israelites 'sighed because of the slavery and cried out in complaint, so that their cry for help kept going up to the true God.'—Exodus 2:23.

Jehovah heard them and sent Moses to Pharaoh to gain the Israelites' freedom. Instead, haughty Pharaoh increased their burden. Now they would have to gather their own straw, still maintaining their quota of bricks as before. Why, this was like a death sentence! God said: "Now you will see what I shall do to Pharaoh, because on account of a strong hand he will send them away."—Exodus 5:1–6:1.

You probably know the rest. Jehovah was capable of defeating tyrannical Pharaoh. After the tenth plague, God 'brought the sons of Israel out of the land of Egypt.' (Exodus 12:37-51) Leaving behind the pyramids, the bricks, and the harsh slavery, Israel marched toward the Promised Land. Such historical facts should reassure us of Jehovah God's ability to provide true freedom for Christians in the coming new world, with its earthly Paradise.—Compare Romans 8:20, 21.

'It Helped Me a Great Deal'

Youths surely need help today, what with an epidemic of teenage suicides, pregnancies, alcoholism, drug abuse, and other problems. But where can they receive it? A youth from Buffalo, New York, wrote the Watchtower Society:

"I have read your book . . . *Your Youth—Getting the Best Out of It.* I must say that you have written a good book. It has helped me a great deal, and I know that it can do the same for someone else. . . . I have passed my book to a friend, and he has made some progress. Thank you, Sir, a million times, for writing such a good, good book."

the Watchtower

Announcing Jehovah's Kingdom

December 1, 1987

FAITH HEALING
—IS IT FROM GOD?

The Watchtower®

Announcing Jehovah's Kingdom

December 1, 1987
Vol. 108, No. 23

In This Issue

THE PURPOSE OF *THE WATCHTOWER* is to exalt Jehovah God as the Sovereign of the universe. It keeps watch on world events as they fulfill Bible prophecy. It comforts all peoples with the good news that God's Kingdom will soon destroy those who oppress their fellowmen and that it will turn the earth into a paradise. It encourages faith in the now-reigning King, Jesus Christ, whose shed blood opens the way for mankind to gain eternal life. *The Watchtower*, published by Jehovah's Witnesses continuously since 1879, is nonpolitical. It adheres to the Bible as its authority.

WATCHTOWER STUDIES FOR THE WEEKS

January 3: Fear of God—Can It Benefit You?
    Page 10. Songs to Be Used: 84, 175.

January 10: Maintain Your Fear of Jehovah.
    Page 16. Songs to Be Used: 37, 79.

Average Printing Each Issue: 12,315,000

Now Published in 103 Languages

SEMIMONTHLY LANGUAGES AVAILABLE BY MAIL
Afrikaans, Arabic, Cebuano, Chichewa, Chinese, Cibemba, Danish,* Dutch,* Efik, English,* Finnish,* French,* German,* Greek,* Hiligaynon, Igbo, Iloko, Italian,* Japanese,* Korean, Lingala, Malagasy, Maltese, Norwegian,* Portuguese,* Russian, Sepedi, Sesotho, Shona, Spanish,* Swahili, Swedish,* Tagalog, Thai, Tsonga, Tswana, Xhosa, Yoruba, Zulu

MONTHLY LANGUAGES AVAILABLE BY MAIL
Armenian, Bengali, Bicol, Bislama, Bulgarian, Croatian, Czech, Ewe, Fijian, Ga, Greenlandic, Gujarati, Gun, Hausa, Hebrew, Hindi, Hiri Motu, Hungarian, Icelandic, Kannada, Malayalam, Marathi, New Guinea Pidgin, Pangasinan, Papiamento, Polish, Rarotongan, Romanian, Samar-Leyte, Samoan, Sango, Serbian, Silozi, Sinhalese, Slovenian, Solomon Islands-Pidgin, Tahitian, Tamil, Telugu, Tongan, Tshiluba, Turkish, Twi, Ukrainian, Urdu, Venda, Vietnamese

* Study articles also available in large-print edition.

	Yearly subscription for the above:	
Watch Tower Society offices	*Semimonthly Languages*	*Monthly Languages*
America, U.S., Watchtower, Wallkill, N.Y. 12589	$5.00	$2.50
Australia, Box 280, Ingleburn, N.S.W. 2565	A$7.00	A$3.50
Canada, Box 4100, Halton Hills, Ontario L7G 4Y4	$7.00	$3.50
England, The Ridgeway, London NW7 1RN	£5.00	£2.50
Ireland, 29A Jamestown Road, Finglas, Dublin 11	IR£6.00	IR£3.00
New Zealand, P.O. Box 142, Manurewa	NZ$15.00	NZ$7.50
Nigeria, PMB 001, Shomolu, Lagos State	₦8.00	₦4.00
Philippines, P.O. Box 2044, Manila 2800	₱60.00	₱30.00
South Africa, Private Bag 2067, Krugersdorp, 1740	R9.00	R4.50

Remittances should be sent to the office in your country or to Watchtower, Wallkill, N.Y. 12589, U.S.A.

Changes of address should reach us 30 days before your moving date. Give us your old and new address (if possible, your old address label).

25 cents (U.S.) a copy

The Bible translation used is the *New World Translation of the Holy Scriptures,* unless otherwise indicated.

The Watchtower (ISSN 0043-1087) is published semimonthly for $5.00 (U.S.) per year by Watch Tower Bible and Tract Society of Pennsylvania, 25 Columbia Heights, Brooklyn, N.Y. 11201. Second-class postage paid at Brooklyn, N.Y., and at additional mailing offices.

Postmaster: Send address changes to Watchtower, **Wallkill, N.Y. 12589.**

Published by
**Watch Tower Bible and Tract Society
of Pennsylvania**
25 Columbia Heights, Brooklyn, N.Y. 11201, U.S.A.
Frederick W. Franz, President

Faith Healing
What Is Its Appeal?

The church reverberates with the sound of the guitar, trumpet, drums, tambourines, and clashing cymbals. Men, women, and children dance and sing in a frenzied state of ecstasy. The mood is right for the healings to begin.

The faith healer, clad in flowing white robes, begins by laying his hands upon a crippled man who goes about on all fours. Next, a blind man, whose dark glasses cover his unseeing eyes. "It's a miracle!" onlookers cry as the lame begin to walk and the blind begin to see . . .

SCENES like this are common in many African faith-healing churches. Indeed, faith healers have large followings in Africa and other lands due to their claims that they can solve all manner of problems through prayer and faith in God. Some thus come to faith healers with financial problems. And since in African society childlessness is often a stigma, some come to faith healers hoping for a cure for barrenness.

Health problems, however, engage the attention of faith healers more than anything else. Though medicinal drugs flood the world market and laudable efforts are being made in the medical field to bring relief to the sick, man is still a long way from finding an answer to the problem of sickness. Some victims of illness have spent large sums of money searching for cures, only to meet with failure. No wonder, then, that in desperation, many turn to faith healers!

Some feel that faith healing has worked for them and can see no conflict between it and Christianity. Indeed, since the healers often claim that they work in the name of Jesus, it is not unusual for their followers to be members of both a mainstream religion and a faith-healing church. But can a true worshiper of God appropriately avail himself of a faith healer? (John 4:23) And can any cures effected by such a one really be attributed to God?

Faith Healing
Is It From God?

THE man had been sick for 38 years. "Do you want to become sound in health?" asked Jesus. If you were this man, would you not have eagerly answered yes? Jesus told him: "Get up, pick up your cot and walk." The effect of those words? "The man *immediately* became sound in health, and he picked up his cot and began to walk."—John 5:5-9.

This feat of divine healing was but one of many that Jesus performed during his earthly ministry. (Matthew 11:4, 5) Faith healers today claim that God still performs such healings, and they are backed by the testimonials of thousands who claim to have been healed by them.

Crucial Differences

A study of the Bible reveals several crucial differences between the cures reported in the Bible and those reported by faith healers today. Jesus and his disci-

ples, for example, never charged for their cures. "You received free, give free," taught Jesus. (Matthew 10:8) Thus they followed the example set by Elisha, who refused a gift from a man named Naaman whom Elisha cured of leprosy. (2 Kings 5: 1, 14-16) Therefore, when faith healers charge for their services, they violate this Scriptural precedent.

It is also noteworthy that healings performed in Bible times were either instantaneous or accomplished within a short period of time. When the apostle Peter saw a man "that was lame from his mother's womb," he told the man: "In the name of Jesus Christ the Nazarene, walk!" The account reveals: "*Instantly* the soles of [the lame man's] feet and his anklebones were made firm; and, leaping up, he stood up and began walking." (Acts 3:1-8) Read for yourself other examples at Acts 5: 15, 16 and 14:8-10.

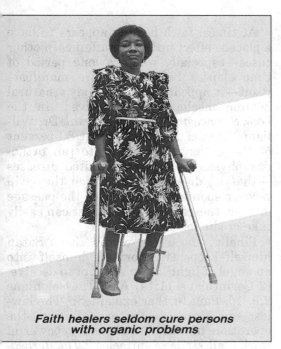
Faith healers seldom cure persons with organic problems

Today's faith-healing cures, however, often take days, weeks, or even months to work! Noteworthy, too, is the fact that faith healers tend to focus on functional illnesses, such as blindness, paralysis, or deafness—maladies that at times have a psychological basis. Observes surgeon Paul Brand: "Once an organic fact has become incontrovertible—missing legs, eyes, or hair follicles—miracles rarely occur." Jesus, however, cured "every sort of disease and every sort of infirmity," including defects obviously organic in nature, such as a shriveled hand.—Matthew 9:35; Mark 3:3-5.

'You Lack Faith!'

Tragically, many grievously ill people attend 'healing crusades' only to return home as sick as ever. Faith healers explain away such failures by claiming, 'They lack faith!' This, however, smacks of fraud. As Dr. William Nolen observes: "Unlike the orthodox physician, a psychic healer never

has to take the responsibility when his healing fails. I must confess that I would like the option of resorting to such an excuse when I encounter a patient whom I cannot cure."

Neither God's prophets, Jesus, nor Jesus' disciples ever had need to offer the excuse that the infirm one was not cured because he lacked faith. True, a lack of faith may have limited the number of people who came forward to be healed. But for those who did come forward, a complete cure always took place!—Mark 6:5, 6.

Indeed, in some cases people obviously lacking faith were cured. Naaman, the chief of the Syrian army, for example, did not fully believe he could be cured of his leprosy in the way the prophet Elisha directed. It was only after his cure that he admitted: "Here, now, I certainly know that there is no God anywhere in the earth but in Israel." (2 Kings 5:11-13, 15) The flimsy excuses of faith healers thus fall flat.

Healing—A Gift That Passed Away

But is it not true that miraculous gifts of healing were common among early Christians? (1 Corinthians 12:9) Yes, but there was good reason for the miracles that took place back then. For a millennium and a half, the nation of fleshly Israel was God's chosen people; but in the first century of our Common Era, Israel was rejected because of its lack of faith and replaced by the new Christian congregation. Those early Christians needed extraordinary help to strengthen their faith and to give evidence to the outside world that they had Jehovah God's backing.

Thus, miraculous gifts, including healing, were given the infant Christian congregation. These served as "a sign" to unbelievers and as a means of building up the faith of believers. (1 Corinthians 14:

22) However, nearly two thousand years later, Christianity is no longer in its infancy. (Compare 1 Corinthians 13:9-13.) The Bible has long been completed and is in circulation by the millions of copies. So true Christians today can easily direct unbelievers to its pages in support of what they teach. Miraculous manifestations are no longer needed.

Paul further indicated that supernatural gifts would "be done away with." (1 Corinthians 13:8) Such gifts were passed on only directly by or in the presence of Christ Jesus' apostles. (Acts 8:18-20; 10: 44-46; 19:6) After the death of the apostles, miraculous manifestations ceased.

The *Cyclopedia of Biblical, Theological, and Ecclesiastical Literature* by McClintock and Strong (Volume VI, page 320) observes that it is "an uncontested statement that during the first hundred years after the death of the apostles we hear little or nothing of the working of miracles by the early Christians."

Reason to Beware

Jesus Christ warned that a time would come when many would say to him: "Lord, Lord, did we not prophesy in your name, and expel demons in your name, and perform many powerful works in your name?" And yet Jesus would tell them: "I never knew you! Get away from me, you workers of lawlessness." (Matthew 7: 22, 23) What, then, accounts for their seeming success in performing "powerful works" if it is not the spirit of God?

In some cases, outright fraud appears to be involved. For example, *The Herald,* a newspaper of Zimbabwe, reported on three individuals whom a famous faith healer heralded as having been cured. The paper exposed this as a fraud: "One child can still neither hear nor speak; one child was never deaf or dumb; and a woman, who was just deaf, still cannot hear."

At times, faith healing appears to have a placebo effect upon the sufferer. In other cases—especially where a long period of time elapses before the cure manifests itself—it appears that the body's natural healing mechanism is involved. In the book *Science and the Paranormal,* Dr. William Nolen claims that "about 80 percent of the patients who come to [an orthodox physician] have self-limited diseases —that is, diseases from which they will recover spontaneously." With the passage of time, therefore, a faith healer can easily take credit for the cure.

Finally, the Bible warns that "Satan himself keeps transforming himself into an angel of light" in an attempt to deceive. (2 Corinthians 11:14) At 2 Thessalonians 2:9, 10, Paul further explained: "The lawless one's presence is according to the operation of Satan with every powerful work ["all kinds of miracles," *The Jerusalem Bible*] and lying signs and portents and with every unrighteous deception for those who are perishing." So beware! Faith healing often involves demonic powers! "I do not want you to become sharers with the demons," warned Paul. "You cannot be drinking the cup of Jehovah and the cup of demons."—1 Corinthians 10: 20, 21.

When a Christian Is Sick

True, when one is ill, a miraculous cure may seem an attractive possibility. Notice, though, that the apostle Paul's fellow worker Epaphroditus became sick nearly to the point of death. (Philippians 2:25-27) Paul's close companion Timothy likewise suffered "frequent cases of sickness." (1 Timothy 5:23) Yet, Paul did not cure either of these men miraculously. And when Paul needed medical attention himself, he may have used the services of Luke, "the beloved physician," who traveled with him.—Colossians 4:14.

A Christian who is sick prays for strength to endure.

He also looks forward to the new world, where "no resident will say: 'I am sick'"

Likewise today, a Christian who is ill can seek the aid of a qualified physician or therapist, avoiding any dabbling in demon-inspired cures or in the quackery that is so common in many lands today. He can also pray, not for a miraculous cure, but for wisdom to deal with the illness. (James 1:5) He can also implore that Jehovah "sustain him upon a divan of illness."—Psalm 41:3.

Granted, it can be most discouraging when medical science is unable to cure a particular ailment. Nevertheless, even when ill a Christian must strive to "make sure of the more important things," not allowing concern over health to overshadow spiritual concerns completely. (Philippians 1:10) He can sustain himself with the hope of living under God's Kingdom when "no resident will say: 'I am sick.'"—Isaiah 33:24; 65:17-19.

Really, this hope of a righteous new world is of far more value than the empty promises of faith healers. Consider Peter, a blind man living in Akumadan, Ghana. He spent a total of 26 years in different faith-healing churches in hopes that his blindness would be cured. But no faith healer opened his eyes. Then, while still attending a faith-healing church, he was contacted by Jehovah's Witnesses.

The Witnesses explained from the Bible that under God's Kingdom a total healing of all infirmities would take place. This opened Peter's eyes of understanding. Full of appreciation for the Bible's wonderful truths, he became a full-time proclaimer of God's Kingdom and has served as such for over three years! He looks forward to the time when, in a literal way, "the eyes of the blind ones will be opened, and the very ears of the deaf ones will be unstopped."—Isaiah 35:5, 6.

With the help of God's Word, thousands of others have similarly freed themselves from mistaken trust in faith healers.

The Loaves and the Leaven

GREAT crowds have flocked to Jesus in the Decapolis. Many came a long way to this largely Gentile-populated region to listen to him and to be healed of their infirmities. They have brought with them large baskets, or hampers, that they customarily use to carry provisions when traveling through Gentile areas.

Eventually, however, Jesus calls his disciples and says: "I feel pity for the crowd, because it is already three days that they have remained near me and they have nothing to eat; and if I should send them off to their homes fasting, they will give out on the road. Indeed, some of them are from far away."

"From where will anybody here in an isolated place be able to satisfy these people with loaves?" the disciples ask.

Jesus inquires: "How many loaves have you?"

"Seven," they answer, "and a few little fishes."

Instructing the people to recline on the ground, Jesus takes the loaves and the fishes, prays to God, breaks them, and begins giving them to his disciples. They, in turn, serve the people, who all eat to satisfaction. Afterward, when the leftovers are picked up, there are seven provision baskets full, even though about 4,000 men, as well as women and children, have eaten!

Jesus sends the crowds away, boards a boat with his disciples, and crosses to the western shore of the Sea of Galilee. Here the Pharisees, this time accompanied by members of the religious sect of the Sadducees, try to tempt Jesus by asking him to display a sign from heaven.

Aware of their efforts to tempt him, Jesus replies: "When evening falls you are accustomed to say, 'It will be fair weather, for the sky is fire-red'; and at morning, 'It will be wintry, rainy weather today, for the sky is fire-red, but gloomy-looking.' You know how to interpret the appearance of the sky, but the signs of the times you cannot interpret."

With that, Jesus calls them wicked and adulterous and warns them that, as he told the Pharisees earlier, no sign will be given them except the sign of Jonah. Departing, he and his disciples get in a boat and head toward Bethsaida on the northeast shore of the Sea of Galilee. En route the disciples discover that they have forgotten to bring bread, there being but one loaf among them.

Having in mind his encounter with the Pharisees and the Sadducean supporters of Herod, Jesus admonishes: "Keep your eyes open, look out for the leaven of the Pharisees and the leaven of Her-

od." Since the disciples believe that Jesus is referring to their forgetting to bring bread, leaven evidently suggesting to their minds the idea of bread, they begin to argue about the matter. Noting their misunderstanding, Jesus says: "Why do you argue over your having no loaves?"

Recently, Jesus had miraculously provided bread for thousands of people, performing this last miracle perhaps only a day or two before. They should know that he is not concerned about a lack of literal loaves. "Do you not remember," he reminds them, "when I broke the five loaves for the five thousand men, how many baskets full of fragments you took up?"

"Twelve," they reply.

"When I broke the seven for the four thousand men, how many provision baskets full of fragments did you take up?"

"Seven," they answer.

"Do you not yet get the meaning?" Jesus asks. "How is it you do not discern that I did not talk to you about loaves? But watch out for the leaven of the Pharisees and Sadducees."

The disciples finally get the point. Leaven, a substance to cause fermentation and make bread rise, was a word often used to denote corruption. So now the disciples understand that Jesus is using a symbolism, that he is warning them to be on guard against "the *teaching* of the Pharisees and Sadducees," which teaching has a corrupting effect.　**Mark 8:1-21; Matthew 15: 32–16:12.**

♦ Why do people have large provision baskets with them?

♦ After leaving the Decapolis, what boat trips does Jesus take?

♦ What misunderstanding did the disciples have regarding Jesus' comment about leaven?

♦ What did Jesus mean by "the leaven of the Pharisees and Sadducees"?

Fear of God
Can It Benefit You?

"Fear the true God
and keep his
commandments. For
this is the whole
obligation of man."
—ECCLESIASTES 12:13.

DOES the expression "fear of God" sound strange to you? Many may feel that if they really love God, they should not have to fear him too. Do we really have to do both? If so, how does the fear of God benefit us?

² The Scriptures show that our worship and service of God must be based on love. Jesus made this clear when he told us to love Jehovah with our whole heart, soul, mind, and strength. (Mark 12:30) But the importance of fearing God is also stressed in his Word. Very pointedly, we are told at Ecclesiastes 12:13: "Fear the true God and keep his commandments. For this is the whole obligation of man." Is Jehovah inconsistent in asking us to fear him and to love him at the same time?

³ Not really—if we keep in mind that there are different kinds of fear. When

people think of fear, they usually have in mind a morbid feeling that destroys hope and makes us discouraged. Obviously, Jehovah would not want us to feel that way about him! Our heavenly Father wants us to come to him just as a child would come to his father, confident of his father's love and yet at the same time fearing to displease him. Such fear will help us remain obedient to our heavenly Father when tempted to do wrong. This is a proper "godly fear" that Christians must have.—Hebrews 5:7; 11:7.

⁴ Jehovah is not like an unfeeling judge who simply punishes his servants each time they slip. Rather, he loves them and wants them to succeed. So if we make a mistake or commit a sin, fear of Jehovah should not restrain us from speaking to him about it. (1 John 1:9; 2:1) Our respectful fear of Jehovah is not a fear of being rebuffed or rejected. As we read at 1 John

---

1, 2. (a) On what should our worship of God be based? (b) What else, however, does God require? (Deuteronomy 10:12)
3. Concerning fear, what must be kept in mind?

4. What type of fear would love eliminate?

4:18: "There is no fear in love, but perfect love throws fear outside, because fear exercises a restraint." "Perfect love," however, would not eliminate the deep respect and proper fear that we should have for Jehovah as our Creator and Life-giver. —Psalm 25:14.

Consider the Benefits

5 Let us consider some of the benefits that flow from "the fear of Jehovah." For example, it leads to our gaining true wisdom. Men have tried in many ways, they have spared no effort, to gain such wisdom, but they have failed because they ignore a basic principle: "The fear of Jehovah is the beginning of wisdom." (Psalm 111:10; Proverbs 9:10) Consider how such fear helped a former drug addict to act wisely. He explains: "As I took in knowledge of God, I also developed a fear of hurting or displeasing him. I knew he was watching, and I had a longing to be approved in his sight. It moved me to destroy the drugs that were in my possession by flushing them down the toilet." This man overcame his bad practices, dedicated his life to Jehovah, and is now a minister in Johannesburg, South Africa.

6 Would you like to avoid what is bad? "The fear of Jehovah means the hating of bad." (Proverbs 8:13) Yes, this proper fear can keep you from many bad habits that God condemns, such as smoking, drug abuse, drunkenness, and sexual immorality. Besides pleasing Jehovah, you are protecting yourself against the horrible things that happen to people, including the fearsome diseases to which they expose themselves. (Romans 1:26, 27; 12:1, 2; 1 Corinthians 6:9, 10; 1 Thessalonians 4:3-8) Fear of God not only will help you to guard against what is bad and perverse but will lead you to what is pure and wholesome, for we are told that "the fear of Jehovah is pure."—Psalm 19:9.

7 Happiness is another goal sought by most people. How can you gain it? Says God's Word: "Happy is the man in fear of Jehovah." (Psalm 112:1; 128:1) The experience of a teenage girl verifies this. She had become involved in all types of illicit sex, as well as spiritism and stealing. She then began to study the Bible and saw the need to listen to and fear Jehovah. She says: "Knowing Jehovah is the best thing that has happened to me. Jehovah helped me so much in finding the truth and happiness. I feel I owe so much to him because he opened my eyes and gave me the chance really to think and find him. I now want to help other people find this happiness."

8 Jehovah also promises that he will reward 'those fearing his name.' (Revelation 11:18) Furthermore, "the fear of Jehovah tends toward life, and one will spend the night satisfied; one will not be visited with what is bad." (Proverbs 19:23) Really, it is "the fear of Jehovah" that will bring to us all that we would ever need. When linked with humility, the result is "riches and glory and life."—Proverbs 22:4; 10:27.

9 Does this not give us every encouragement to fear the true God? Indeed, "the fear of Jehovah" is most appealing. It leads to all the things that will bring us true satisfaction—a rare experience today. How encouraging these inspired words are: "Although a sinner may be doing bad a hundred times and continuing

5. (a) How only can wisdom be gained? (b) What prompted a former drug addict to change his unwise course in life?
6. How will "the fear of Jehovah" protect us against bad things, and to what will it lead us?

7, 8. (a) How did one young girl experience that "the fear of Jehovah" leads to happiness? (b) Mention further benefits that come to those who fear Jehovah.
9. Why does "the fear of Jehovah" lead to the only course in life that shows wisdom? (Job 28:28; Micah 6:9)

Fear of Jehovah will help youths reject temptations to do what is bad

he has shown to us. Everything we have has come from him. (Revelation 4:11) Moreover, he is the Supreme Judge, the Almighty, with power to put to death those who disobey him. "Keep working out your own salvation with fear and trembling," urges the apostle Paul. —Philippians 2:12; Hosea 3:5; Luke 12:4, 5.

¹¹ There is no indication here that we can gain salvation by adopting a lackadaisical attitude, doing as little as possible and hoping that somehow things will turn out well. This is not the attitude to be displayed by Christians who in these last days are striving to maintain a relationship with the One who can see right into their hearts and who knows their innermost thoughts and intentions. (Jeremiah 17:10) Only those who have a proper recognition of Jehovah will be acknowledged by him. He says: "To this one, then, I shall look, to the one afflicted and contrite in spirit and trembling at my word." —Isaiah 66:2.

a long time as he pleases, yet I am also aware that it will turn out well with those fearing the true God, because they were in fear of him. But it will not turn out well at all with the wicked one, neither will he prolong his days that are like a shadow, because he is not in fear of God"! (Ecclesiastes 8:12, 13) Who is the man that does not desire matters to "turn out well" for him? This happy experience will be enjoyed only by those who fear God.—Psalm 145:19.

¹⁰ Should this not make us determined to have a profound reverence for our heavenly Father Jehovah, yes, an awe of him? Really, we should have a wholesome dread of displeasing him. We deeply appreciate all the loving-kindness and goodness that

We Must Learn to Fear Jehovah

¹² Considering Jehovah's dealings with Israel can further impress on our minds the need to fear him. No other nation

10. What are some vital reasons that should move us to fear God?

11. (a) What attitude should be avoided by Christians in these last days? (b) What spirit should be developed?
12. (a) In what ways was the nation of Israel favored above other nations? (b) What did Jehovah expect in return?

experienced such care and attention from the Sovereign of the universe. (Deuteronomy 4:7, 8, 32-36; 1 Samuel 12:24) With their own eyes the Israelites saw what Jehovah did to the Egyptians, who, having no fear of him, enslaved and oppressed his people. What did he expect in return? "Congregate the people, the men and the women and the little ones and your alien resident who is within your gates, in order that they may listen and in order that they may learn, as they must fear Jehovah your God and take care to carry out all the words of this law. And their sons who have not known should listen, and they must learn to fear Jehovah your God all the days that you are living upon the soil to which you are crossing the Jordan to take possession of it."—Deuteronomy 31: 12, 13; 14:23.

¹³ As with the Israelites, God's modern-day servants "must learn to fear Jehovah." What a responsibility this places on all of us—parents especially! Parents, ask yourselves: 'How can I assist my children to gain a heart that fears Jehovah?' One day when they grow up and leave home, what will provide better protection for your children, spiritually, mentally, or materially, than that? Jehovah himself stresses the importance of this when he pleads: "If only they would develop this heart of theirs to fear me and to keep all my commandments always, in order that it might go well with them and their sons to time indefinite!"—Deuteronomy 5:29; 4:10.

¹⁴ Any Christian who has raised a family will readily agree that this is not an easy task. Nevertheless, God's inspired Word brings several vital factors to the atten-

tion of parents. One is to *start when the children are young.* How young? When the Israelites met to receive instruction from Jehovah, the "little ones" were included. (Deuteronomy 29:10-13; 31:12, 13) Obviously, Israelite women came with their babies on such occasions, since all were required to be in attendance. Right "from infancy," their sons and daughters would learn the need to be quiet and listen at such gatherings. (2 Timothy 3:15) So bring your "little ones" with you to the meetings. Also, involve them in field service as soon as they are able to have a share. Many youths have learned to present a magazine or a tract even before they begin attending school. Start early to teach your "little ones," in little ways, "the fear of Jehovah."

¹⁵ Another factor is to *be consistent.* This can be done if we always stick to God's Word in the training, discipline, and instruction we give to our children. Even when it comes to relaxation or recreation, be consistent in allowing Bible principles to dictate what will be allowed on such occasions. (Ephesians 6:4) This will require effort, as God's Word so clearly indicates when it says: "And these words that I am commanding you today must prove to be on your heart; and you must inculcate them in your son and speak of them when you sit in your house and when you walk on the road and when you lie down and when you get up." (Deuteronomy 6:4-9; 4:9; 11:18-21) Such consistency over the years will do much to help your children to develop a heart that fears Jehovah.

¹⁶ Parents must also strive to impress on the minds and hearts of their children

13. What should be of primary concern to parents regarding their children?
14. Name one factor that parents should keep in mind in training their children to be fearers of Jehovah, and explain how this should be applied.

15. What is a second factor, and how can parents accomplish it?
16. (a) What is the third factor, and why is this so important? (b) What questions could parents ask themselves?

that they themselves, as parents, are "fearers of Jehovah." (Psalm 22:23) One way in which they can do this is by *applying theocratic counsel* when training and disciplining their children. This is the third factor to be considered. Ask yourself: 'Am I regularly having a Bible study with my children?' 'Do I put to full use for my younger children such aids as *My Book of Bible Stories* and *Listening to the Great Teacher?*' 'As they grow older, am I using the book *Your Youth—Getting the Best out of It* and the "Young People Ask" articles in *Awake!?*' 'Do I arrange for wholesome recreation and entertainment that will not have a detrimental effect on my children?' 'Have I accepted what has been said by Jehovah's organization about higher education?' 'Am I instructing my children accordingly?' 'Are the goals that I have set for my children ones that will help them to have "godly fear"?'—Hebrews 5:7.

¹⁷ The benefits and joys will come not only to your children but also to you for doing all you can to instruct them in "the fear of Jehovah." For example, a Witness who at the end of a day feels, as she says, "battle-scarred" considers everything worthwhile when she hears her seven-year-old daughter pray to Jehovah. Tears come to her eyes and a lump to her throat as she listens to her daughter's prayer: "Loving Jehovah, thank you for all the good things you've done for me today. And thank you for my food. Help all the brothers in prison and the concentration camps to get food, Jehovah, and all the thin brothers and sisters in other lands. Help them also to get enough food, Jehovah. And those who are sick, help them get better so they can go to the meetings. Let the angels

17. Who benefit when children learn to fear Jehovah? Illustrate.

Points to Ponder

☐ How can we both love and fear Jehovah?

☐ What are some of the benefits of fearing Jehovah?

☐ What three factors can help parents to assist their children to develop a heart that fears Jehovah?

☐ How do we affect one another in the matter of fearing Jehovah?

By courtesy of Hartebeespoort Snake and Animal Park

"It will turn out well with those fearing the true God."
—Ecclesiastes 8:12

please look after me while I sleep in the night, Jehovah, and my mommy and daddy, and my brother, and my granny and grandpa, and all the brothers and sisters in the truth. Through your Son Jesus, Amen."

¹⁸ In this matter of fearing Jehovah, we must remember that we affect one another by the example we set. Parents affect their children. Elders and ministerial servants affect their congregations. Traveling overseers affect those whom they serve. Obviously, this is why the kings in Israel were instructed to read God's Law all the days of their life so that they "may learn to fear Jehovah." (Deuteronomy 17:18-20) The example that the king would set in fearing Jehovah could affect the entire nation.

¹⁹ History testifies to the fact that Israel, as a nation, lost their fear of Jehovah. They thought that having the temple in Jerusalem would serve as a protection for them, like some sort of "lucky" charm, regardless of whether they obeyed his laws or not. (Jeremiah 7:1-4; Micah 3:11, 12) But they were wrong. Jerusalem and its temple were destroyed. Later, when they were reestablished as a nation, they again failed to show proper fear of Jehovah.

(Malachi 1:6) There is much we can learn from this experience, which will be covered in the next article.

²⁰ Remember, then, that fear of Jehovah does not weaken our love for him; rather, it strengthens and reinforces it. Obedience to all his commands will prove not only that we fear Jehovah but that we love him. Both are vital. It is impossible to have the one without the other. How important it is for parents to inculcate this godly fear of Jehovah and love for him into their children! And what great joy this brings to both old and young! May we, therefore, feel the same way as the psalmist did when he said: "Unify my heart to fear your name." —Psalm 86:11.

18. How do we affect one another in this matter of fearing Jehovah?
19. To what does history testify regarding the Israelites?

20. How could we sum up why we should fear Jehovah?

Maintain Your
Fear of Jehovah

"'I am a great King,' Jehovah of armies has said, 'and
my name will be fear-inspiring among the nations.'"
—MALACHI 1:14.

"A PRONOUNCEMENT: The word of Jehovah concerning Israel by means of Malachi." (Malachi 1:1) This brief, stirring statement begins the Bible book of Malachi. In the Bible a pronouncement is usually a denunciation of wickedness. This is certainly true in the case of the book of Malachi with its direct and forceful message to the nation of Israel. Our considering it will highlight the need to maintain our fear of Jehovah and our love for him.

² The first two verses of the book provide a lesson in giving counsel. Jehovah assures his listeners of his desire to help them: "'I have loved you people,' Jehovah has said." What a reassuring, heartwarming introduction for honesthearted ones of delinquent Israel. The message continues: "And you have said: 'In what way have you loved us?' 'Was not Esau the brother of Jacob?' is the utterance of Jehovah. 'But I loved Jacob, and Esau I have hated; and I finally made his mountains a desolated waste and his inheritance for the jackals of the wilderness.'"—Malachi 1:2, 3.

³ Why did Jehovah love Jacob and, later, the descendants of Jacob, the Israelites? It

---

was because Jacob was God-fearing and he respected his God-fearing parents. Esau, on the other hand, was a selfish person, lacking fear of God. Also, he lacked respect for his parents, who had the God-given, natural right to expect his obedience. Rightly, Jehovah loved Jacob but hated Esau. This is a warning to us. We must avoid ever losing the fear of God and becoming a materialist like Esau, who sought only to satisfy his fleshly desires. —Genesis 26:34, 35; 27:41; Hebrews 12:16.

⁴ Just as Jacob's course proved to be a blessing for his descendants, the Israelites, so Esau's course proved to be the exact opposite for his descendants, the Edomites. The Edomites did not enjoy Jehovah's blessing. Instead, by their vicious opposition to his covenant people, they incurred Jehovah's hatred. They were overrun by Nebuchadnezzar's armies and later by the Arabians. Eventually, as prophesied by Jehovah, the Edomites vanished as a nation.—Obadiah 18.

⁵ God's judgments upon Edom started before Malachi's day. How should this have affected the Israelites? Jehovah tells them: "Your own eyes will see it, and you yourselves will say: 'May Jehovah be magnified over the territory of

---

1, 2. (a) What powerful message is contained in the book of Malachi? (b) What lesson is provided by the opening words of Jehovah's message?
3. What were the reasons for Jehovah's feelings toward Jacob and Esau?

4, 5. (a) The course in life of Jacob and Esau had what effect upon their descendants? (b) How should this have affected the Israelites?

Israelites despised Jehovah by offering blind, lame, or sick animals as sacrifices

Israel.'" (Malachi 1:5) Down through the centuries, Israel had seen with its "own eyes" the love Jehovah had for it as a nation.

Our Actions Will Show Whether We Fear God

⁶ The pronouncement continues: "'A son, for his part, honors a father; and a servant, his grand master. So if I am a father, where is the honor to me? And if I am a grand master, where is the fear of me?' Jehovah of armies has said to you, O priests who are despising my name." (Malachi 1:6; Exodus 4:22, 23; Deuteronomy 32:6) Jehovah had corrected the Israelites, provided for them, and protected them, just as a father would his son. What did he rightly expect in return? To be honored and feared. The nation, including the priests, failed to do this but, rather, showed a disrespect for Jehovah's name, and a despising of it. They became "renegade sons."—Jeremiah 3:14, 22; Deuteronomy 32:18-20; Isaiah 1:2, 3.

6. What accusation did Jehovah make against the Israelites?

⁷ The Israelites asked: "In what way have we despised your name?" Jehovah forcefully replied: "'By presenting upon my altar polluted bread.' And you have said: 'In what way have we polluted you?' By your saying: 'The table of Jehovah is something to be despised.' And when you present a blind animal for sacrificing: 'It is nothing bad.' And when you present a lame animal or a sick one: 'It is nothing bad.' 'Bring it near, please, to your governor. Will he find pleasure in you, or will he receive you kindly?' Jehovah of armies has said."—Malachi 1:6-8.

⁸ One can imagine an Israelite looking over his flock and slyly selecting a blind or

7. How did the Israelites feel about this accusation, and what was Jehovah's reply to them?
8. What were the Israelites indicating by their actions?

a lame animal to offer to Jehovah. In this way he could go through the motions of making a sacrifice and yet selfishly keep the best of the flock for himself. He would not dare to do such a thing to the governor! But the Israelites did it to Jehovah —as if he could not see their scheming and cheating. Rightly, Jehovah asked them, "Where is the fear of me?" By their words, they may have claimed to fear Jehovah, but their actions clearly indicated otherwise.—Deuteronomy 15:21.

9 What was the reaction of the priests to these contemptible sacrifices? They said: "It is nothing bad." They justified the wicked course of the Israelites. So even though the exiles who returned from Babylon made a zealous start in restoring true worship, they later became careless, proud, and self-righteous. They lost their fear of Jehovah. Hence, their temple service became a mockery, and they kept the festivals in a formalistic way.—Malachi 2: 1-3; 3:8-10.

10 Some may object: 'This does not apply to us; we no longer offer animal sacrifices.' But we have another type of sacrifice to offer. Note Paul's urgent appeal: "I entreat you by the compassions of God, brothers, to present your bodies a sacrifice living, holy, acceptable to God, a sacred service with your power of reason." (Romans 12:1) The sacrifice Jehovah wants today is you! That is, your energies, as-

sets, and abilities. Our sacrifice will meet with his approval only if it is our best. Offering Jehovah the leftovers, like a lame, sick sacrifice, is sure to affect our relationship with him.

11 Even though some may say, in effect, "It is nothing bad," we know how Jehovah feels about it. Let us, therefore, carefully scrutinize the "sacrifice" of "sacred service" we are offering, which includes the share we have in preaching, personal study, prayer, and attending the meetings. Are you satisfied that you are offering Jehovah your best, or is it just leftovers? There is a danger of getting so involved in entertainment or recreation on the weekend that one does not have time or energy to preach the Kingdom good news and attend meetings. Our whole way of life, our day-to-day living, including attitudes and motives, should be tied in with the sacrifice that we make to Jehovah. Let it be nothing but the best!

Identifying True Fearers of God

12 "And now," says the prophecy, "please, soften the face of God, that he may show us favor." (Malachi 1:9) Jehovah urges the Israelites to do what is right, show proper fear of God, and offer him what he deserves. We must do the same today. Only by living up to Jehovah's requirements can we gain and maintain his favor.

---

9. How did the priests react to what the people were doing?
10. (a) What sacrifice does Jehovah want today? (b) How only can our sacrifice meet with Jehovah's approval?

11. What scrutinizing should each dedicated servant of Jehovah do?
12. What counsel is now given?

¹³ Without proper fear of God, our service to him may be done merely out of formalism and for selfish gain. Note how Jehovah questions the Israelite priests regarding their temple service: " 'Who also is there among you that will shut the doors? And you men will not light my altar—for nothing. No delight do I have in you,' Jehovah of armies has said, 'and in the gift offering from your hand I take no pleasure.' " (Malachi 1:10) Oh, yes, the priests were there performing temple duty, locking the doors of the sanctuary, lighting the altars. But they did not do this for nothing. They were looking for handouts and bribes from the Israelites who came to make sacrifices at the temple. Jehovah found no pleasure then, and he finds no pleasure now, in service that is done merely for selfish gain. It is disgusting to him.

¹⁴ The need to be on guard against selfishness and greed has not diminished in our day. Repeatedly the Scriptures warn us against greed, stating that greedy people are not favored by Jehovah. (1 Corinthians 6:10; Ephesians 5:5) In fulfilling our ministry, may our love and fear of Jehovah keep us free from ever performing it for selfish gain. We should be quick to root out any such tendencies that may arise in our heart. Elders and ministerial servants are particularly cautioned not to be "greedy of dishonest gain." (Titus 1:7; 1 Timothy 3:8; 1 Peter 5:2) Some may purposely cultivate relationships only with brothers who can help them materially, resulting in favoritism and a reluctance to counsel such ones. Never do we want to become like the greedy priests of Israel who were looking for handouts and bribes from their fellow Israelites.

13. (a) Without fear of God, into what trap could we fall? (b) How did greed affect the Israelite priests?
14. Why is there an ever-present need for guarding against greed?

¹⁵ Today, if Jehovah asked the question, "Where is the fear of me?" could any people reply, 'Here we are, the ones who fear you'? Most definitely! Who? Jehovah's faithful witnesses, who are found in all parts of the earth. This international group of people and the work they would do was foretold at Malachi 1:11: " 'For from the sun's rising even to its setting my name will be great among the nations, and . . . a presentation will be made to my name, even a clean gift; because my name will be great among the nations,' Jehovah of armies has said."—See also Psalm 67:7; Isaiah 33:5, 6; 41:5; 59:19; Jeremiah 32:39, 40.

¹⁶ How aptly Malachi here tells of the great work being done in our day with the preaching of the good news in all the earth. (Matthew 24:14; Revelation 14:6, 7) From sunrise to sunset, in a geographical sense, means from east to west. No matter where we look in the earth today, we find fearers of Jehovah doing his will. From sunrise to sunset also means all day long. Yes, praise is constantly being offered up by God-fearing servants. As Jehovah promised, his name is being declared in all the earth by those who truly fear him. —Exodus 9:16; 1 Chronicles 16:23, 24; Psalm 113:3.

Maintain Proper Fear of God

¹⁷ For those who fail to respect and fear Jehovah, worship and service become a burden. Jehovah said to the Israelites: "You men are profaning me by your saying, 'The table of Jehovah is something

15. (a) How did Malachi indicate that there would be fearers of Jehovah in all parts of the earth? (b) What other scriptures support this?
16. From sunrise to sunset could have what different meanings, and how is this being fulfilled?
17. What may be the result of losing our respect for Jehovah and our fear of him?

polluted, and its fruit is something to be despised, its food.' And you have said, 'Look! What a weariness!'" (Malachi 1:12, 13) The same can be true in modern times. For those who lose the fear of Jehovah, meetings, field service, and other Christian activities could become a burden.

[18] Notice how such ones were described in *The Watchtower* of January 1, 1937: "To those unfaithful ones the privilege of serving God by bringing the fruits of the kingdom before others, as the Lord has commanded, has become only a tiresome ceremony and formality, which offers them no opportunity to shine in the eyes of men. The carrying of the kingdom message from house to house in printed form, and presenting this to the people, is too humiliating for such self-important ones. They find no joy in it . . . Therefore they have said, and continue to say: 'This carrying books about is merely a book-selling scheme. What a wearisome task that is!'" Even today there are those who, from time to time, find the field service a drudgery and attending meetings tedious. This is what can happen when we lose our fear of Jehovah and, along with it, our love for him.

[19] Maintaining fear of Jehovah will keep us humble before him and ever appreciative of all that he is doing for us. Whether we are at a small gathering in a home or at a large gathering of tens of thousands in a stadium, we are thankful to Jehovah for the privilege of being with our Christian brothers. We will show our thankfulness by being present there and by inciting others present to "love and fine works" by our upbuilding conversation and by the comments we make during meetings. (He-brews 10:24, 25) If it should be our privilege to care for parts at meetings, we will avoid putting off preparation to the last minute, hastily gathering some ideas together. Never treat such assignments as something commonplace. They are sacred privileges, and the way we care for them is another indication of how we respect and fear Jehovah.

[20] How sad the outcome is for those who lose the fear of God! They lack appreciation for the undeserved privilege of having a relationship with the Sovereign of the universe. "'I am a great King,' Jehovah of armies has said, 'and my name will be fear-inspiring among the nations.'" (Malachi 1:14; Revelation 15:4) May we never forget that. May each of us be like the psalmist who said: "A partner I am of all those who do fear you." (Psalm 119:63) After considering this matter, we come to the same conclusion that Solomon did when he said: "Fear the true God and keep his commandments. For this is the whole obligation of man. For the true God himself will bring every sort of work into the judgment in relation to every hidden thing, as to whether it is good or bad." —Ecclesiastes 12:13, 14.

20. (a) What must we never forget? (b) To what conclusion do we come?

Lessons From the Book of Malachi—

□ Why did the Israelites owe Jehovah their fear?

□ How do our actions show whether we truly fear Jehovah?

□ What proves that there are fearers of Jehovah earth wide today?

□ Why must we maintain proper fear of God?

---

18. From time to time, what has happened to some of God's modern-day servants?
19. How may we continue to demonstrate our appreciation for Jehovah's provisions?

Kingdom Proclaimers Report

Young Ones in Italy Make Opportunities to Witness

THOSE who appreciate God's wonderful purposes are delighted to help others learn of the marvelous Kingdom hope. This often involves taking advantage of opportunities that arise, as the following report from Sardinia shows.

□ "A 12-year-old publisher was traveling back from field service by bus. Also on the bus were two young boys and a girl, all about 18 years of age. The young publisher sat near the girl and began reading the *Awake!* magazine, hoping to arouse her curiosity. She noticed the magazine and asked what he was reading. He explained he was reading an article dealing with the solution to problems young people have to face. He said that he had greatly benefited from this material and that it could help her also. She gladly accepted the magazines.

"Having listened in on the conversation, the other two youths asked for magazines. While they were getting the contribution, the driver told them not to waste their money on such useless things. The youths answered that they were intelligent, and the magazines were interesting. At this the bus driver pulled over to the side of the road, stopped the bus, and wanted to see what was so interesting in these

magazines. He also accepted copies.

"The young Witness who related this experience said: 'I am really glad I began witnessing on the bus.'"

□ Another young Witness took advantage of a situation in school. This youth relates: "Our schoolteacher taught us a study method that was quite different from the traditional one. After considering the material, we were to work up an outline including main points and secondary points and then give an extemporaneous talk on the subject.

"'I am very familiar with this method,' stated the Witness. 'It is the one suggested by the *Theocratic Ministry School Guidebook.*' The teacher soon noticed I was the only one who was successful in applying this method. He asked why there was such a difference between my work and that of the others. I explained that I had learned this method in the Theocratic Ministry School. He was very pleased and invited me to illustrate it to the class, using the *Theocratic Ministry School Guidebook.* This I did.

"When I went home, I told my family what had happened. My father, who is not a Witness, had always said that being one of Jehovah's Witnesses was a handicap at school, but after listening to my experience, he was forced to change his mind."

What a grand privilege you young ones, as well as you older ones, have to uphold and make known Jehovah's name! —Psalm 148:12, 13.

Graduation of the 83rd Gilead Class
Truly a Festive Occasion

"**G**IVE thanks to Jehovah, O you people, for he is good: for his lovingkindness is to time indefinite." (Psalm 136:1) That was the heartfelt sentiment of all 4,391 who attended the graduation exercises of the 83rd class of the Watchtower Bible School of Gilead this fall. The talks, the experiences, and the Bible drama presented during the exercises caused all to leave in high spirits. The graduation took place September 6, 1987, at the beautiful Jersey City Assembly Hall, formerly known as the Stanley Theater.

After the opening song, and prayer by John Booth of the Governing Body, the chairman, Albert Schroeder, another member of the Governing Body, welcomed one and all to this festive occasion. The 24 students had come from five countries, and they were now being sent to eight different lands. Brother Schroeder highlighted the confidence Jehovah's people have because their faith is based on absolutes. They know, for example, that Jehovah is the Universal Sovereign and that his Word, the Holy Bible, is absolute truth. This is in striking contrast with human philosophies based on uncertainties and speculations.

The first speaker was Martin Poetzinger, also a member of the Governing Body, who spent nine years in Nazi concentration camps. His theme was "In Whom Do You Trust?" based on Proverbs 3:5, 6. He stressed to the students the need of trusting fully in Jehovah and his visible organization, as well as individually proving trustworthy. The students' Gilead training was only a foundation; now they had to build on it by following Paul's advice at Ephesians 5:15, 16. 'Do not stand still,' urged the speaker. 'You will have your problems in your missionary assignment as to language, climate, food, and so forth; but by trusting in Jehovah, you can solve all those problems. Love for people is your key to success. Every encouragement is from God; every discouragement is from Satan.'

The next speaker was Eldor Timm, a member of the Factory Committee, who based his remarks on 2 Corinthians 13: 5: "Keep testing whether you are in the faith." The students were finished with written tests, he said, but they will keep facing many other tests in their missionary assignments. How they meet those tests will determine their success as missionaries. They need to guard against overconfidence by heeding the counsel: "Let him that thinks he is standing beware that he does not fall." (1 Corinthians 10: 12) They will keep making improvements if they keep a good mental attitude.

A member of the Service Department Committee, Joel Adams, followed. He spoke on the subject: "Think Like Jesus, Show a Personal Interest in Others." What a fine example Jesus set in this regard! His example of unselfishness and humility is highlighted for us at Philippians 2:3-5. If some are a trial to us by reason of their shortcomings or lack of tact, let us go out of our way to show kindness to them. During the Gilead School course, many showed an interest in the students; now it was up to them to do the same toward others. The most successful missionaries are those who show an interest in others' customs, language, needs, and so forth.

Next, the students were encouraged by one who had been a missionary for many years, Lloyd Barry, also a member of the Governing Body. He spoke on the theme "Sing to Jehovah," based on Psalm 96:1. Jehovah's people enjoy singing. Singing goes with joy, and so he encouraged the students never to lose the joy of bringing the truth to others. 'If you have to learn a new language,' he urged, 'put your heart into it from the start. The Devil will try to discourage you, make you homesick, cause disunity in your ranks. Never allow him one inch!' Brother Barry referred to the "dean of missionaries," Edwin Skinner, who has been in his foreign assignment in India for 60 years, and who now at the age of 93 still does a full day's work. According

83rd Graduating Class of the Watchtower Bible School of Gilead
In the list below, rows are numbered from front to back and names are listed from left to right in each row.
(1) Melin, D.; Goode, M.; Ramos, M.; Chow, N.; Hermanson, A.; Dagostini, D. (2) David, E.; DiPaolo, A.; Neiman, D.; Shephard, J.; Foster, M.; Ramos, R. (3) Foster, W.; Melin, D.; Fristad, D.; Fristad, R.; White, L.; Dagostini, F. (4) Neiman, D.; Ness, S.; Shephard, D.; Goode, J.; White, K.; Hermanson, L.

to Brother Skinner, the key to success as a missionary consists of four words: "Humility is the keynote!"

Following these remarks, the chairman read a number of telegrams congratulating the students and extending a welcome to them. Messages were received from Bolivia, Canada, Ecuador, Honduras, Spain, Sweden, and Trinidad.

Jack Redford, one of the instructors of the Gilead School, spoke on the subject "Continue to Be Jehovah's Friend." He began by noting that there are many commercial institutions that offer training on achieving success in business by winning friends and influencing people. The students, as future missionaries, have also been taught how to win friends and influence people, not for selfish gain, however, but so that such people can become friends of God. 'Yours is a life of self-sacrifice,' said the speaker. 'You received free, give free. There is no satisfaction or joy greater than succeeding in helping people to become friends of God. Friendship with God is the greatest honor any creature can have. James 2:23 tells that Abraham became Jehovah's friend because of exercising faith in God. He went to a foreign land and did not look back; neither should you missionaries look back, but, instead, look forward to the blessings in God's new world.'

Ulysses Glass, a Gilead instructor and registrar of the school, now spoke on the subject "The Final Lesson." He noted that the students had learned how far-reaching and exacting Jehovah's laws really are. By way of example, he pointed to the many details associated with sacrifices offered on the Day of Atonement and the many animals that were involved. (Leviticus, chapter 16) He commended the students for their manifest deephearted appreciation and said that Psalm 145:7 well describes their mental attitude: "With the mention of the abundance of your goodness they will bubble over, and because of your righteousness they will cry out joyfully." In his conclusion, he also quoted Proverbs 3:5-7, stressing their need to 'trust in Jehovah with all their heart.'

Brother F. W. Franz, the 94-year-old president of Gilead School as well as president of the Watch Tower Bible and Tract Society, gave the concluding talk of the morning. In it he recounted the history of the Society from the time of the first president, C. T. Russell, until the establishing of the Gilead School. His vigorous and enthusiastic presentation was greatly appreciated by all. After his talk, the 24 students received their diplomas together with some gifts, and then one of the students read a fine letter expressing the students' appreciation for all the help they had received from the Governing Body and also from the Bethel family.

After an intermission of approximately two hours, Phil Wilcox, a member of the Watchtower Farms Committee, conducted an abbreviated study of the current *Watchtower* lesson in which the study questions were answered by the students. That was followed by the students' program in which they reenacted experiences they had enjoyed while witnessing during Wednesday afternoons in New York City. This was part of their Gilead training. They also vividly demonstrated the various problems they could expect to meet up with when they reached their foreign assignments.

As a fitting conclusion to the whole program, the students presented a costumed Bible drama in two parts, highlighting the seriousness of the times we are living in. The drama did this by comparing our days with past judgment periods. At 4:15 p.m., with the singing of the song "Theocracy's Increase" and a prayer by Governing Body member Milton Henschel, the most delightful program came to an end.

The Value of Singing in True Worship

CAN you picture a world without song? Never again to hear the happy singing of children or the sweet voice of the nightingale or the bellbird? No more to hear the magpie's infectious chuckle or the throaty laughter of a kookaburra? Happily, this will never be. But such contemplation highlights one of God's many gifts to man: the gift of song.

Jehovah a God of Song

Why does singing bring pleasure and joy to us? For one thing, Jehovah himself enjoys and is pleased with songs of praise by his creatures. Can you picture the occasion when all the angels shouted for joy at the magnificence of Jehovah's earthly creation? Or can you imagine standing spellbound among the shepherds on the autumn night of Jesus' human birth, thrilling to the sound of a vast host of angels singing: "Glory in the heights above to God"?—Luke 2:13, 14; Job 38:7.

One way that Jehovah indicated he is a God of song was by making singing part of true worship in Israel. Later, God again revealed the close tie between singing and true worship in the Revelation vision given to the apostle John. In one prophetic scene a tremendous choir—144,000 strong—sings a magnificent new song before the throne of God.—Revelation 14:3.

Singing in Pre-Christian Times

God's majesty and awesome acts also inspired his earthly servants to break out in song. Feel the stirring effects that singing had on the Israelites soon after their miraculous deliverance from Egyptian slavery. The hearts of Moses and his fellow Israelites were moved emotionally as they sang the victory song recounting what Jehovah had done to Pharaoh and his hosts.—Exodus 15:1-21.

Later in Israel's history, the momentous day came when, under King David's direction, the ark of the covenant was to be placed inside its specially erected tent. What a historic event! Not only outstanding singing but soul-stirring orchestral accompaniment added to the grandeur of the day.—1 Chronicles 16:4-36.

David's love for music and his skillfulness on the harp accentuated his keenness to promote music and singing in true worship. At Psalm 33:1, 3, we hear his passionate plea for worshipers of Jehovah to sing aloud to God with all their heart: "Cry out joyfully, O you righteous ones, because of Jehovah. . . . Do your best at playing on the strings along with joyful shouting."

Singing in Christian Times

In early Christian times, singing also played a prominent role in true worship. Jesus and his apostles sang together after the evening meal just before Jesus' death. (Mark 14:26) In prison Paul and Silas sang aloud so that all could hear. (Acts 16:25) Like David the apostle Paul was enthusiastic about the use of song. More than once, he encouraged fellow believers to sing songs of praise to Jehovah. —Ephesians 5:18, 19; Colossians 3:16.

In present-day Christian worship, singing also features prominently. In 1905 the book *Hymns of the Millennial Dawn* was published. The title page describes its 333 songs as "A Choice Collection of Psalms and Hymns and Spiritual Songs to Aid God's People in Singing and Making Melody in their Hearts unto the Lord."

Then in 1928 a revised songbook with 337 songs was provided. It was called *Songs of Praise to Jehovah,* and its preface said: "These Songs will be found to be in harmony with the divine truths now due to be understood." However, as years passed and the light of truth increased, it became clear that some of these songs were influenced by thinking carried over from false religion. Additionally, Kingdom songs to encourage preaching the good news were needed, as public declaration came more to the fore.—Matthew 24:14; Hebrews 13:15.

In 1944 *Kingdom Service Songbook* was provided, with 62 songs. Two decades later, in 1966, the book *Singing and Accompanying Yourselves With Music in Your Hearts* was released. This contained 119 Kingdom songs that covered every aspect of Christian living and worship, including witnessing to others and praising Jehovah God and Christ Jesus.

Almost another two decades passed, during which the light of truth kept on increasing. (Proverbs 4:18) The need was seen for yet another songbook. So in 1984 came the release of the songbook entitled *Sing Praises to Jehovah*. It has 225 Kingdom songs, with words and melodies composed entirely by dedicated servants of Jehovah from all parts of the earth.

Use Theocratic Singing to the Full

The illustration shown on the double-spread endsheet at the back of this latest songbook stimulates us to use theocratic singing to the full at Christian meetings. Trained temple singers there depicted are clearly raising their hearts and their voices in song to God.—1 Chronicles 25:7.

We can likewise sing at our Christian meetings, opening our mouths and singing from our hearts. However, not all of us do that. Perhaps pride causes us to miss out on the joy of singing to Jehovah without embarrassment, no matter what sort of voice we have. We may be overly concerned with the impression being

In Our Next Issue

- Angels—Do They Affect Your Life?

- Honoring the God of Hope

- Who Really Is Jesus?

made on those standing nearby. Moses had a similar problem—not with singing but with speaking. The answer Jehovah gave him might assist us if we tend to hold back from singing because of lack of ability. Jehovah asked Moses: "Who appointed a mouth for man? . . . Is it not I, Jehovah?" (Exodus 4:11) Surely, Jehovah will gladly listen as we use whatever ability he has given us to sing his praises out loud!

Think, too, how Paul and Silas sang aloud while in prison. No embarrassment there, and they had no musical accompaniment, not even a songbook to follow. Picture the occasion: "But about the middle of the night Paul and Silas were praying and praising God with song; yes, the prisoners were hearing them." (Acts 16:25) Was this because either Paul or Silas had trained singing voices? Not necessarily. Their chief concern was to sing aloud and from the heart! What is *our* chief concern when singing songs of praise?

All of Us Can Improve

Musician David's advice is appropriate here: "Do your best at playing on the strings along with joyful shouting." (Psalm 33:3) That is what Jehovah expects of all his servants—nothing more, nothing less than that we 'do our best.' If we do just that, we can expect Jehovah to bless our efforts, and to our delight—and sometimes to our surprise—we will likely make improvement.*

Here are some practical suggestions that may help to improve the quality of your singing: Try listening frequently to the newer Kingdom melodies, using recorded musical tapes or records where possible. For some, singing the songs at home or at small gatherings with fellow believers has proved beneficial as well as pleasant. At congregation meetings it is important that musical accompaniment be played loud enough to be heard by all those singing. This makes it easier to follow the tune and increases confidence on the part of those singing. The one announcing a song should state its theme, perhaps even noting its appropriateness, not just the number.

Parents, do you encourage your children to sing Kingdom songs with enthusiasm and from their hearts? Families that have encouraged their young ones to sing from the heart, and with understanding, have many times found such singing to be a fine aid to spiritual growth.

Benefits Are Many

There are many benefits from singing aloud and from the heart. Our personal involvement in public worship becomes stronger. Those standing nearby are encouraged to sing louder when they hear our unembarrassed singing. The entire congregation also benefits, for increased volume is contagious!

Additionally, strong singing gives a good witness to those attending meetings for the first time. Those passing by our Kingdom Halls, as well as neighbors living nearby, are impressed by our fine singing, just as doubtless were those other prisoners who heard Paul and Silas. This has even resulted in some hearers' wanting to know more about the truth.

Most importantly, our improved singing will bring greater praise to Jehovah, the Originator of music and singing, the one deserving to be praised in song above all others.

---

* Some of the latest songs may be a little difficult for us to sing at first, but after we become familiar with them, they may well prove to be our favorites. For example, when the previous songbook came out, song 88, "Walking in Integrity," was not liked in one country, but later on it became the favorite.

Is Your Giving a Sacrifice?

A Balanced View of Contributions

AFTER teaching the people many things in the temple, Jesus "sat down with the treasury chests in view and began observing how the crowd was dropping money into the treasury chests." (Mark 12:41) What followed was the well-known account of the widow's mite. But why did Jesus sit there and watch the people make their offering? Did he not tell his disciples that they should not even let their left hand know what their right hand was doing when they made their gifts of mercy? —Matthew 6:3.

Earlier, Jesus had strongly denounced the religious leaders for using unscrupulous methods to devour "the houses of the widows." He said that these religionists "will receive a heavier judgment." (Mark 12:40) In order to teach a lesson, he then turned his attention to what the people were doing there at the treasury chests. Today, when we hear so much about the big money involved in church organizations, the misuse of such funds, and the lavish life-styles of those in charge, we would do well to listen closely to what Jesus had to say.—Please read Mark 12:41-44.

The Treasury Chests

The account relates that Jesus "sat down with the treasury chests in view." This was evidently in the Court of Women, where a number of chests, or boxes, were placed along the walls for the people to drop in their offerings. Jewish tradition tells us that there were 13 boxes in all. In Hebrew they were called trumpets, because they had a small opening at the top in the shape of the bell of a trumpet. It is said that 'no one entered the temple without putting something in.'

The French professor Edmond Stapfer, in his book *Palestine in the Time of Christ* (1885), gave a rather detailed description of these treasury chests. His account gives us some insight into the religious life of the people of the time, especially with respect to their contributions toward the services at the temple.

"Each chest was for a different object, indicated by an inscription in the Hebrew tongue. The first was inscribed: *New shekels;* that is, shekels set apart for the expenses of the current year. The second: *Old shekels;* that is, shekels dedicated to the expenses of the previous year. Third: *Turtle doves and young pigeons;* the money placed in this chest was the price to be paid by those who had to offer two turtle doves or two young pigeons, the one as a burnt offering, the other as a sacrifice for sin. Above the fourth chest was written: *Burnt offerings;* this money covered the expense of the other burnt offerings. The fifth had the inscription: *Wood,* and held the gifts of the faithful for the purchase of wood for the altar. The sixth: *Incense* (money for buying incense). The seventh: *For the sanctuary* (money for the mercy-seat). The six remaining chests bore the inscription: *Freewill offerings.*"

The designation on the first two chests had reference to the half-shekel (two drachmas in Grecian money) head tax each adult male was required by law to pay for the maintenance of the temple, the services performed there, and the daily sacrifices offered on behalf of the entire nation. This tax was often collected in local communities and then brought to the temple.—Matthew 17:24.

The people were also required by the Law to make various offerings on their own behalf. Some were for sins committed, others for ceremonial reasons, and still others out of their devotion and thanksgiving. The boxes marked "Turtle doves and young pigeons" and "Burnt offerings" would be for such purposes. "Into Trumpet III," says the book *The Temple, Its Ministry and Services,* "those women who had to bring turtledoves for a burnt- and a sin-offering dropped their equivalent in money, which was daily taken out and a corresponding number of turtledoves offered." Likely this was what the parents of the infant Jesus did.—See Luke 2:22-24; Leviticus 12:6-8.

Then there were offerings for the wood and incense used at the altar and for the voluntary offerings. Again, according to Professor Stapfer, "if any one gave money for *wood* or *incense,* there was a minimum fixed, and less than this might not be offered. It was necessary to give at least the price of a handful of incense, or two logs of wood a cubit long and large in proportion."

What do we learn from all of this? It is quite evident that the Israelites had numerous responsibilities toward the maintenance of the tabernacle and later the temple in Jerusalem, the center of true worship. Sacrifices and offerings were an integral part of their worship. In fact, the Law commanded that "none should appear before Jehovah empty-handed." (Deuteronomy 16:16) But what was their view of these obligations?

Differing Views

The Bible record shows that the people were most liberal and generous in the time of Moses and David and later during the reign of Jehoash and Josiah. (Exodus 36:

3-7; 1 Chronicles 29:1-9; 2 Chronicles 24: 4-14; 34:9, 10) They were happy to have a share in building the house of Jehovah and maintaining it as well as in advancing true worship. Their sentiment was well expressed by the words of David when he said: "I rejoiced when they were saying to me: 'To the house of Jehovah let us go.'" —Psalm 122:1.

This generous spirit, however, was not shared by all. For instance, we read that in the days of Malachi, the priests were offering to Jehovah "something torn away, and the lame one, and the sick one." Rather than rejoicing at their privilege of service, they said: "Look! What a weariness!" —Malachi 1:13.

Similarly, in Jesus' time some took advantage of the situation to advance their own interests. The notorious money changers at the temple, for example, were not there just to make change. Rather, they capitalized on the fact that only Hebrew shekels were acceptable as offerings, and all those with Roman or Greek money would have to exchange it. According to Alfred Edersheim, an authority on Jewish history, "the bankers were allowed to charge a silver *meah,* or about one-fourth of a denar [or denarius, a laborer's wage for a day's work] on every half-shekel." If this is correct, it is not hard to see what a lucrative business this must have become and why the religious leaders were so incensed when Jesus drove out the money changers.

"Out of Her Want"

All of this only emphasizes Jesus' illustration about the poor widow's small contribution, which she no doubt dropped into one of the boxes marked "Freewill offerings." As a widow, she was not required to give the head tax, and with limited means, she was probably not able to meet the minimum requirements for the burnt offerings or the wood or incense offerings. Yet, she wanted to do something to show her love for Jehovah. She did not want to be counted out or just leave it to those who could 'afford it.' Jesus said: "She, out of her want, dropped in all of what she had, her whole living."—Mark 12:44.

There are many valuable lessons we can learn from this account. The most outstanding one, perhaps, is that while all of us have the privilege of lending support to true worship by means of our material possessions, what is truly precious in God's sight is, not our giving what we can do without anyway, but our giving what is valuable to us. In other words, are we giving something we will not really miss? Or is our giving a real sacrifice?

Advancing True Worship Today

Today, Jehovah's Witnesses advance true worship by zealously preaching "this good news of the kingdom . . . in all the inhabited earth." (Matthew 24:14) To accomplish this global task involves not only dedicated effort, time, and energy but also considerable expense. The *1987 Yearbook of Jehovah's Witnesses* reports that "during 1986, a total of $23,545,801.70 was spent in financial support of . . . the 2,762 missionaries, 13,351 special pioneers, and overseers and their wives for the world's 3,353 circuits and districts." This was in addition to "much expense in purchasing, constructing, and renovating properties; in equipping factories and offices at headquarters and in the Society's 93 branches; and in providing for the material needs of the 8,920 volunteers who serve in the Bethel families."

'Where do such funds come from?' is an often-asked question. Unlike the churches of Christendom, Jehovah's Witnesses do not take up collections or send out envelopes to solicit donations. Rather, contribution boxes—like the treasury chests of Biblical times—are set up at their Kingdom Halls. At times, other boxes may be set up for designated purposes, such as construction of Kingdom Halls or Assembly Halls or to assist missionaries to attend conventions in their homeland. Contributions may

HOW SOME CONTRIBUTE TO THE KINGDOM WORK

☐ GIFTS: Voluntary donations of money may be sent directly to the Watch Tower Bible and Tract Society of Pennsylvania, 25 Columbia Heights, Brooklyn, New York 11201, or to the Society's local branch office. Property such as real estate, as well as jewelry or other valuables, can also be donated. A brief letter stating that such is an outright donation should accompany these contributions.

☐ CONDITIONAL-DONATION ARRANGEMENT: Money may be given to the Watch Tower Society to be held in trust, with the provision that in case of personal need, it will be returned to the donor.

☐ INSURANCE: The Watch Tower Society may be named as the beneficiary of a life-insurance policy or in a retirement/pension plan. The Society should be informed of any such arrangements.

☐ TRUSTS: Bank savings accounts can be placed *in trust for* the Society. If this is done, please inform the Society. Stocks, bonds, and property can also be donated under an arrangement to benefit the donor during his or her lifetime. This method eliminates the expense and uncertainties of probate of will, while ensuring that the Society receives the property in the event of death.

☐ WILLS: Property or money may be bequeathed to the Watch Tower Society by means of a legally executed will. A copy should be sent to the Society.

For more information and advice regarding such matters, write to the Treasurer's Office, Watch Tower Bible and Tract Society of Pennsylvania, 25 Columbia Heights, Brooklyn, New York 11201, or to the Society's local branch office.

also be sent directly to the Watch Tower Society at 25 Columbia Heights, Brooklyn, New York 11201, or to the Society's branch office in your country, for advancing the preaching work worldwide.

How do you view these many and varied ways contributions are made? Do you, like some in Malachi's day, view them as a tiresome burden, perhaps saying in your heart: "Look! What a weariness!"? Or do you, like the "poor widow," view them as opportunities to demonstrate your zeal and concern for true worship and your desire to honor Jehovah with your valuable things? Do not forget the pertinent question: Is your giving a sacrifice?

"'Test me out, please, in this respect,' Jehovah of armies has said, 'whether I shall not open to you people the floodgates of the heavens and actually empty out upon you a blessing until there is no more want.'" (Malachi 3:10) The spiritual prosperity and the worldwide expansion among Jehovah's people prove that Jehovah is already doing that. May we continue to give to Jehovah an offering that is truly a sacrifice.

Questions From Readers

■ Some scholars contend that "rope" should replace "camel" at Matthew 19:24, which reads: "It is easier for a camel to get through a needle's eye." Which word is correct?

Certain Bible scholars mistakenly conclude that Jesus' words here were originally recorded in Aramaic. The Aramaic word used in such versions (*gam·la'*) can mean "camel." Depending on the context, however, it can also be rendered "a large rope and a beam." But according to Papias of Hierapolis, perhaps a contemporary of the apostle John, Matthew wrote his Gospel account originally in Hebrew, not Aramaic, thereafter translating it into Greek. The Hebrew word for camel (*ga·mal'*) is quite different from the words translated rope (*che'vel*) or cord (*'avoth'*), and it is certain that Matthew would have selected the correct Greek term.

The oldest and most reliable Greek manuscripts (Sinaiticus and Vatican No. 1209) have the word *ka'me·los,* which means camel. This same word is used at Matthew 23:24, where there is little doubt that "camel" is intended.

Through the centuries some have tried to soften Jesus' biting hyperbole. Some even took liberties with the sacred text. From about the fifth century, a similar word *ka'mi·los* is found at this text in some Greek manuscripts. This rare word means "rope, ship's cable." According to *A Greek-English Lexicon of the New Testament* by Arndt and Gingrich, it "has no place in the NT [New Testament]." Greek scholars Westcott and Hort blame this substitution on fifth-century professed Christian Cyril of Alexandria, who asserted that the word used by Matthew (*ka'me·los*) could mean a cable, saying: "It is the custom of those well versed in navigation to call the thicker cables 'camels.'" Yet, of this idea Westcott and Hort state: "It is certainly wrong."

The idea of a huge camel trying to fit through the eye of a tiny sewing needle "savours of Eastern exaggeration," according to one reference work. In fact, in discussing some individuals renowned for such shrewdness that they seemed to do the impossible, *The Babylonian Talmud* states: "They draw an elephant through the eye of a needle." So Jesus was using a typical Oriental image to emphasize the impossibility of something by way of a vivid contrast. Indeed, it would be impossible to thread any large object through a needle's eye—whether rope, camel, or elephant.

Jesus was not saying that it was impossible for a rich person to gain life, for some wealthy individuals became his followers. (Matthew 27:57; Luke 19:2, 9; John 19:38, 39) But just before Jesus gave this 'hard saying,' a rich young man had turned down great spiritual opportunities because of a greater love for his "many possessions." (Matthew 19:16-22) It would be impossible for any rich man with this attitude to inherit everlasting life. Only with God's extreme help could such a person change and receive the salvation that must come through God's power. —Matthew 19:25, 26.

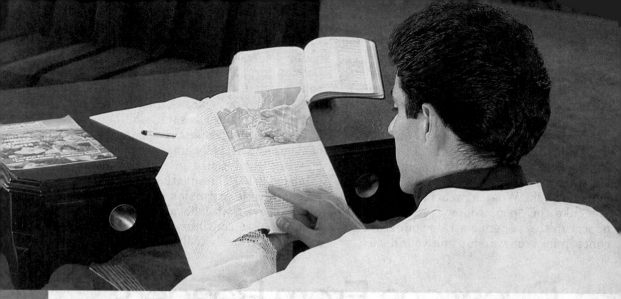

'Like Bread and Water to the Heart'

That is what a Protestant minister from Málaga, Spain, said the *Watchtower* and *Awake!* magazines were like to him. He explained:

"I have been a Protestant pastor for several years, and I can assure you that in all my theological studies, I have not found the simplicity and clarity that your publications have. To me, Jehovah's Witnesses are admirable people; in a hypocritical world,

they live according to what they believe. . . .

"At the moment, due to personal problems, I can't study with you as I would like to, but thanks to God, I do receive your magazines, and they are 'bread' and 'water' to my heart, which hungers and thirsts for the living God."

the **Watchtower**

December 15, 1987

Announcing Jehovah's Kingdom

ANGELS—Do They Affect Your Life?

December 15, 1987
Vol. 108, No. 24

In This Issue

THE PURPOSE OF *THE WATCHTOWER* is to exalt Jehovah God as the Sovereign of the universe. It keeps watch on world events as they fulfill Bible prophecy. It comforts all peoples with the good news that God's Kingdom will soon destroy those who oppress their fellowmen and that it will turn the earth into a paradise. It encourages faith in the now-reigning King, Jesus Christ, whose shed blood opens the way for mankind to gain eternal life. *The Watchtower,* published by Jehovah's Witnesses continuously since 1879, is nonpolitical. It adheres to the Bible as its authority.

WATCHTOWER STUDIES FOR THE WEEKS

January 17: Hope in Jehovah. Page 10. Songs to Be Used: 206, 23.

January 24: Honoring the God of Hope. Page 15. Songs to Be Used: 148, 125.

Average Printing Each Issue: 12,315,000

Now Published in 103 Languages

SEMIMONTHLY LANGUAGES AVAILABLE BY MAIL
Afrikaans, Arabic, Cebuano, Chichewa, Chinese, Cibemba, Danish,* Dutch,* Efik, English,* Finnish,* French,* German,* Greek,* Hiligaynon, Igbo, Iloko, Italian,* Japanese,* Korean, Lingala, Malagasy, Maltese, Norwegian, Portuguese,* Russian, Sepedi, Sesotho, Shona, Spanish,* Swahili, Swedish,* Tagalog, Thai, Tsonga, Tswana, Xhosa, Yoruba, Zulu

MONTHLY LANGUAGES AVAILABLE BY MAIL
Armenian, Bengali, Bicol, Bislama, Bulgarian, Croatian, Czech, Ewe, Fijian, Ga, Greenlandic, Gujarati, Gun, Hausa, Hebrew, Hindi, Hiri Motu, Hungarian, Icelandic, Kannada, Malayalam, Marathi, New Guinea Pidgin, Pangasinan, Papiamento, Polish, Rarotongan, Romanian, Samar-Leyte, Samoan, Sango, Serbian, Silozi, Sinhalese, Slovenian, Solomon Islands-Pidgin, Tahitian, Tamil, Telugu, Tongan, Tshiluba, Turkish, Twi, Ukrainian, Urdu, Venda, Vietnamese

* Study articles also available in large-print edition.

	Yearly subscription for the above:	
	Semimonthly	Monthly
Watch Tower Society offices	Languages	Languages
America, U.S., Watchtower, Wallkill, N.Y. 12589	$5.00	$2.50
Australia, Box 280, Ingleburn, N.S.W. 2565	A$7.00	A$3.50
Canada, Box 4100, Halton Hills, Ontario L7G 4Y4	$7.00	$3.50
England, The Ridgeway, London NW7 1RN	£5.00	£2.50
Ireland, 29A Jamestown Road, Finglas, Dublin 11	IR£6.00	IR£3.00
New Zealand, P.O. Box 142, Manurewa	NZ$15.00	NZ$7.50
Nigeria, PMB 001, Shomolu, Lagos State	₦8.00	₦4.00
Philippines, P.O. Box 2044, Manila 2800	₱60.00	₱30.00
South Africa, Private Bag 2067, Krugersdorp, 1740	R9,00	R4,50

Remittances should be sent to the office in your country or to Watchtower, Wallkill, N.Y. 12589, U.S.A.

Changes of address should reach us 30 days before your moving date. Give us your old and new address (if possible, your old address label).

25 cents (U.S.) a copy

The Bible translation used is the *New World Translation of the Holy Scriptures,* unless otherwise indicated.

The Watchtower (ISSN 0043-1087) is published semimonthly for $5.00 (U.S.) per year by Watch Tower Bible and Tract Society of Pennsylvania, 25 Columbia Heights, Brooklyn, N.Y. 11201. Second-class postage paid at Brooklyn, N.Y., and at additional mailing offices.

Postmaster: Send address changes to Watchtower, **Wallkill, N.Y. 12589.**

Published by
**Watch Tower Bible and Tract Society
of Pennsylvania**
25 Columbia Heights, Brooklyn, N.Y. 11201, U.S.A.
Frederick W. Franz, President

Angels
Past and Present

"They are exemplified at Christmas in the decorations we hang on the tree, or view on Christmas cards—golden dolls with pretty faces, playing the harp or the church organ or carrying candles. They have stubby wings like those of small birds. In a word, they are cute."—*The Sunday Denver Post.*

"ANGELS are generally ignored in schools of theology, slighted in Sunday school, and aren't even mentioned in the index of the National Catechetical Directory, the guidebook for Catholic religious education in America."

So declared Charles W. Bell, religion editor. He noted that some theologians, especially from mainline Protestant churches, feel "uneasy and uncertain about angels." The *New Catholic Encyclopedia* observes that some modern thinkers say that "all belief in the existence of angels should be repudiated."

This has not always been the case. For example, in the 13th century, scholars who studied angelology, a branch of theology dealing with angels, were said to be intrigued with thoughts regarding the "nature, intelligence, and will" of angels. For several centuries, prayers were even made to "guardian angels." But, as noted above, attitudes have changed since then.

According to the *New Catholic Encyclopedia,* "in the modern mind angels . . . are more and more being relegated to the sphere of legend, fairy tale, and child's fancy." Indeed, by the middle of the 19th century, in the minds of many people angels had become less linked to religion and more associated with secular romantic notions. Today, even more people consider them to be products of the imagination; hence, such people deny the existence of angels.

Angels in Some Religions

However, angels still hold a place in some religions. For example, the Roman Catholic Church "encourages the faithful to love, respect, and invoke the angels." In fact, Catholicism has exalted three whom it considers to be angels—Michael, Gabriel, and Raphael—to sainthood. Raphael appears only in the Apocryphal books and not in the Bible canon.

In Eastern Orthodox churches, angels are important in the litany, a form of prayer in which invocations or petitions are made, with responses by the congregation. Angels also have a place in Islam, belief in angels being one of the articles of faith in Muslim theology.

Still, there is no doubt that in our day belief in the existence of angels is diminishing.

Do You Believe in Angels?

Regarding belief in angels, the *New Catholic Encyclopedia* says: "Gradually . . . in the course of a long development and refinement . . . through *speculative elaboration* of the concepts contained in Holy Scripture, there evolved an angelology that, with varying degrees of certitude, has become the doctrine of the Church." [Italics ours.] How firm a belief in angels would you have if you knew that your faith was based on "speculative elaboration"?

Interestingly, divisions of thought on this matter exist even within the Catholic Church. As to when angels were created, the *Enciclopedia de la Religión Católica* states: "In the opinion of the Greek fathers, angels were created before the visible world, but the general opinion of the Latin fathers is that they were created afterwards. Nevertheless, the opinion that has the majority of supporters is that they were created at the same time as the world." Such uncertainty creates confusion in the minds of people and helps to influence the trend toward disbelief today.

A Jewish philosopher, Philo, contended that angels were simply "manifestations and powers of the universe." Over the years, theologians have debated pointless issues regarding the nature and characteristics of angels, such as the frivolous question, How many angels could stand on the point of a needle? Is it any wonder that many people in our modern age have preferred not to believe in angels?

In view of all these contrasting concepts, why not examine what the Bible itself has to say about angels? This will help us get firm answers about questions such as: Are angels real? If so, have they ever intervened in man's affairs? And, more importantly, can angels affect your life?

Angels
Do They Affect Your Life?

DO ANGELS really exist? Or are they just a product of the imagination? If they do exist, can they affect *your* life?

There is only one reliable source for the answers to such questions. That is the inspired Record that God has given to mankind—his Word, the Holy Bible. Of it the apostle Paul wrote: "All Scripture is inspired of God and beneficial . . . for setting things straight."—2 Timothy 3:16.

Thus, we can have confidence that the Bible will give us straight answers as to the existence of angels and whether they affect us. Surely the Creator of the universe can tell us if angels were among his creations.

Are Angels Real?

The Bible clearly states: "He [God] makes his angels spirits." (Hebrews 1:7)

So the Creator has spirit creatures in the heavenly realm. These are invisible to us, and they are powerful.—Psalm 104:4; 2 Peter 2:11.

Did God intend for the angels to be just impersonal, vague entities? If that were the case, why does the Bible portray angels as having feelings? For example, it tells us that when the foundation of the earth was laid, the angels "joyfully cried out together, and all the sons of God [the angels] began shouting in applause." —Job 38:4-7.

It appears that, like God's intelligent earthly creatures, the intelligent spirit creatures, the angels, have their own personality. Although the Bible states the names of only two angels (Michael and Gabriel), the fact that angels do have names adds to their individuality. (Luke 1:

11, 19, 26; Jude 9) The Bible strongly condemns the worshiping of angels, and that includes praying to them. Rather than our praying to angels, the apostle Paul advises us: "In everything by prayer and supplication along with thanksgiving let your petitions be made known to *God*."—Philippians 4:6; Revelation 19:10; 22:8, 9.

But were angels programmed to be without the power of personal choice between right and wrong like mindless robots? No, angels are free moral agents, just as humans are. For example, when certain angels broke God's laws in the days of Noah, God rejected them, and they have been expelled from God's heavenly courts. Their disobedient behavior was an obvious display of angelic individuality. —Genesis 6:1, 2; 2 Peter 2:4; Matthew 25:41.

Thus, the Bible provides us with helpful information about the origin, existence, and nature of angels. To go beyond what God's Word says about them could cause an individual to ponder needlessly over questions that the Bible does not answer. It could even lead to giving undue attention or worship to angels. (Colossians 2:18) The Bible reminds us to "make sure of the more important things" and not to go 'beyond what has already been declared as good news.'—Philippians 1:10; Galatians 1:8.

Angels in God's Purpose

Although many may agree on the origin and characteristics of angels, few are really aware of the reason for their existence and how angels affect our lives today.

In the Bible, the two words used for "angel" are *mal·'akh'* (Hebrew) and *ag'ge·los* (Greek). These both mean "messenger." They tell us something about one of the functions of angels. The angels serve as messengers, or couriers, between God and man.

For example, an angel was sent to deliver a message to Abraham regarding his son Isaac and the blessing that would come through him, a blessing that we can receive. (Genesis 22:11-17) An angel was sent to communicate with Moses. (Acts 7: 37, 38) God also sent an angel with instructions to the prophet Elijah. (2 Kings 1:3) And an angel appeared to Joseph, Jesus' adoptive father, with special instructions regarding the infant.—Matthew 2:13.

Angels have also been sent to protect God's people: "The angel of Jehovah is camping all around those fearing him, and he rescues them." (Psalm 34:7) For instance, an angel released the apostle Peter from prison. (Acts 12:6-11) Two angels helped Lot and his daughters to survive the destruction of Sodom and Gomorrah by escorting them out of that area. Lot's wife, however, did not act in full accord with the angels, so she went down in destruction with those cities.—Genesis 19:1-26.

The Bible mentions many other instances of angelic help, reinforcing what Hebrews 1:7 and 14 states: "With reference to the angels he says: 'And he makes his angels spirits, and his public servants a flame of fire.' Are they not all spirits for public service, sent forth to minister for those who are going to inherit salvation?"

An angel brought great comfort to Jesus. The night before his death, Jesus knew what lay before him—that he would be betrayed, beaten, and cruelly executed. He needed strength to endure this test of his integrity. At that crucial time, an angel appeared to him 'to strengthen him.' What a blessing that angelic comfort must have been for Jesus! As a result, although he experienced such anguish that "his sweat became as drops of blood falling to the ground," he was able to endure faithfully to death.—Luke 22:43, 44.

God has also used angels to annihilate the enemies of his people. When the Assyrian World Power threatened God's ancient worshipers, the following took place: "It came about on that night that the angel of Jehovah proceeded to go out and strike down a hundred and eighty-five thousand in the camp of the Assyrians. When people rose up early in the morning, why, there all of them were dead carcasses." (2 Kings 19:35) You can see the awesome power of angels—it took only *one* angel to execute 185,000 opposers of God and his people!

Blasphemous Herod too was confronted with the power of an angel. When Herod began to think of himself as being godlike, "instantly the angel of Jehovah struck him, because he did not give the glory to God; and he became eaten up with worms and expired."—Acts 12:21-23.

We are informed that soon, when God brings this entire wicked system of things to its end, angels will again be used as executioners. "The Son of man will send forth his angels, and they will collect out from his kingdom all things that cause stumbling and persons who are doing lawlessness, and they will pitch them into the fiery furnace."—Matthew 13:41, 42.

Thus, angels are far from what many people may imagine. The German religion author Dr. Manfred Barthel stated: "If we want to imagine the angels of the Lord as the authors of the Old Testament saw them, first we will have to forget the dimpled cherubs . . . that decorate our greeting cards."—*What the Bible Really Says.*

How Do Angels Affect You?

However, the question remains: What are the angels doing today? Are they affecting us right now? Yes, they certainly are!

Recall that in his prophecy concerning "the conclusion of the system of things" Jesus foretold: "When the Son of man arrives in his glory [assuming Kingdom power], and *all the angels with him,* then he will sit down on his glorious throne. And all the nations will be gathered before him, and he will separate people one from another."—Matthew 24:3; 25:31, 32.

How will this separation of people be accomplished? Jesus foretold: "This good news of the kingdom will be preached in all the inhabited earth for a witness to all the nations; and then the end will come." (Matthew 24:14) Yes, God uses his people on earth to do this global preaching work.

God's Kingdom is the government that will bring the only solution to mankind's problems. Today, the message about it is being proclaimed throughout the world by more than three million of Jehovah's Witnesses, who have angels backing them up. "That is how it will be in the conclusion of the system of things: the angels will go out and separate the wicked from among the righteous."—Matthew 13:49.

This angel-directed preaching work today receives a mixed reaction from the people. Some say they are too busy to listen or simply refuse to do so. Others are hesitant or indecisive. Yet, many honesthearted ones, concerned about their future, have willingly responded. How?

In 208 lands, Jehovah's Witnesses are conducting home Bible studies with millions of people who are "conscious of their spiritual need" and who are 'hungering for righteousness.' (Matthew 5:3, 6) Many experiences show that angels often direct God's servants to contact such honesthearted persons with the message of salvation. Revelation 14:6 symbolically describes an "angel flying in midheaven" having "everlasting good news to declare as glad tidings to those who dwell on the earth." That is certainly happening right now! How will this affect your future?

Angels in Your Future

The Bible clearly identifies our times as "the last days" of this present system. (2 Timothy 3:1-5) The Bible also informs us that angels are now "standing upon the four corners of the earth, holding tight the four winds." (Revelation 7:1) What does this symbolism mean?

Angels are now 'holding back the four winds.' Why?

Being at the "corners" of the earth, the angels are in position to loose destructive "winds" from all directions. No area of the earth will be spared, which will mean "harm," or destruction, for this wicked system and all its supporters. God's angels are thus described as ready to go into action when the signal is given!—Revelation 7:3; 19:11-21.

The destructive "harm," though, is to be on only those who do not respond to the angelically backed message now being preached earth wide. It will not harm those who are searching for God and who listen to the Kingdom message. They will be preserved, as God's Word says: "Seek Jehovah, all you meek ones of the earth . . . Seek righteousness, seek meekness. Probably you may be concealed in the day of Jehovah's anger."—Zephaniah 2:3.

What will then be the lot of such "meek ones"? Psalm 37:11 says: "The meek ones themselves will possess the earth, and they will indeed find their exquisite delight in the abundance of peace." For how long? "The righteous themselves will possess the earth, and they will reside *forever* upon it." (Psalm 37:29) That means that everlasting life will be possible on an earth that is to be transformed into a paradise, as Jesus indicated.—Luke 23:43.

So, then, the question you need to ask is: 'What will be my future?' The answer depends on how you react to angelic direction. Will you listen and respond when you are presented with the message that they are backing? If you do, you will be among those who can look forward with confidence to the future, having God's sure promise: "The world is passing away and so is its desire, but he that does the will of God remains forever."—1 John 2:17.

Who Really Is Jesus?

WHEN the boat carrying Jesus and his disciples puts in at Bethsaida, the people bring a blind man to him and beg that he touch the man and heal him. Jesus leads the man by the hand outside the village and, after spitting on his eyes, asks: "Do you see anything?"

"I see men," the man answers, "because I observe what seem to be trees, but they are walking about." Laying his hands on the man's eyes, Jesus restores his sight so that he sees clearly. Jesus then sends the man home with the instruction not to enter into the city.

Jesus now leaves with his disciples for the village of Caesarea Philippi, in the extreme north of Palestine. It is a long ascent covering about 30 miles to the beautiful location of Caesarea Philippi, some 1,150 feet above sea level. The trip probably takes a couple of days.

On the way, Jesus goes off by himself to pray. Only about nine or ten months remain before his death, and he is concerned about his disciples. Many have already left off following him. Others are apparently confused and disappointed because he rejected the people's efforts to make him king and because he did not, when challenged by his enemies, provide a sign from heaven to prove his kingship. What do his apostles believe about his identity? When they come over to where he is praying, Jesus inquires: "Who are the crowds saying that I am?"

"Some say John the Baptist," they answer, "others Elijah, still others Jeremiah or one of the prophets." Yes, they think Jesus is one of these men raised from the dead!

"You, though, who do you say I am?" Jesus asks.

Peter quickly responds: "You are the Christ, the Son of the living God."

After expressing approval of Peter's response, Jesus says: "I say to you, You are Peter, and on this rock-mass I will build my congregation, and the gates of Hades will not overpower it." Here Jesus first announces that he will build a congregation and that even death will not hold its members captive after their faithful course on earth. Then he tells Peter: "I will give you the keys of the kingdom of the heavens."

Jesus thus reveals that Peter is to receive special privileges. No, Peter is not given first place among the apostles, nor is he made the foundation of the congregation. Jesus himself is the Rock-mass upon which his congregation will be built. But Peter is to be given three keys with which to open, as it were, the opportunity for groups of people to enter the Kingdom of the heavens.

Peter used the first key at Pentecost 33 C.E. when he showed repentant Jews what they must do to be saved. He used the second shortly afterward when he opened to believing Samaritans the opportunity to enter God's Kingdom. Then, in 36 C.E. he used the third key by opening to uncircumcised Gentiles, Cornelius and his friends, the same opportunity.

Jesus continues his discussion with his apostles. He disappoints them by telling of the sufferings and death that he will soon face in Jerusalem. Failing to understand that Jesus will be resurrected to heavenly life, Peter takes Jesus aside. "Be kind to yourself, Lord," he says. "You will not have this destiny at all." Turning his back, Jesus answers: "Get behind me, Satan! You are a stum-

bling block to me, because you think, not God's thoughts, but those of men."

Evidently, others besides the apostles are traveling with Jesus, so he now calls them to explain that it will not be easy to be his follower. "If anyone wants to come after me," he says, "let him disown himself and pick up his torture stake and follow me continually. For whoever wants to save his soul will lose it; but whoever loses his soul for the sake of me and the good news will save it."

Yes, Jesus' followers must be courageous and self-sacrificing if they would prove worthy of his favor, as he relates: "For whoever becomes ashamed of me and my words in this adulterous and sinful generation, the Son of man will also be ashamed of him when he arrives in the glory of his Father with the holy angels." **Mark 8: 22-38; Matthew 16:13-28; Luke 9: 18-27.**

♦ Why is Jesus concerned about his disciples?
♦ What views as to Jesus' identity do people have?
♦ What keys were given to Peter, and how were they used?
♦ What correction did Peter receive, and why?

Hope in Jehovah

"Hope in Jehovah and keep his way, and he will exalt you to take possession of the earth. When the wicked ones are cut off, you will see it."—PSALM 37:34.

INTELLECTUALLY, the human family has attained to its most advanced stage of development. Because of its effort, it has finally reached the nuclear age. Atomic power appears able to provide abundant energy and thus to open up grand things globally. Ironically, it has also paved the way for extreme hurt to the human race.

[2] What stands in the way of the human family's destroying itself in a nuclear holocaust? It could appear to be the United Nations, which boasts of some 159 member nations with many forms of governments. Politically, these governments do not agree with one another, each believing that its own form of rule is superior, yes, the best. Within itself, therefore, the UN is a discordant body. National pride and desire for independence pervade. Moreover, a number of nations have renounced belief in God, becoming atheistic.

[3] The name Christendom still applies to nations that do not want to be classed as godless but profess faith in Jesus Christ in conjunction with "God the Father" in triune connection with Jesus and with a personified "holy ghost," or holy spirit. The members of the Trinity are asserted to be coequal. But Jesus' Father had the prophet Isaiah pen these words of identifi-

---

1, 2. Where does mankind appear to stand, and how is the United Nations involved?

3. How is Christendom's view of God different from the one God himself has?

As sheep follow their shepherd, so David looked to and hoped in Jehovah

cation: "I am Jehovah. That is my name; and to no one else shall I give my own glory, neither my praise to graven images." (Isaiah 42:8) This Jehovah, or Yahweh (*The Jerusalem Bible*), has made an incomparable historical record for himself.

⁴ In no way to its credit, the United Nations has abstained from rendering to God's name due honor and recognition. It does not encourage mankind, now facing its most desperate plight, to hope in the bearer of that name. Yet, that One is rightly styled "the God of hope," seeing that he has laid the basis for the only valid hope that humankind may now entertain. (Romans 15:13, *King James Version*) The hope that he gives has strengthened and sustained many men and women.

Early On—Hope!

⁵ The basis for entertaining that hope was laid early in the history of the human family. Yes, it was laid immediately prior to the ejection of our first parents from their Edenic garden home in the Middle East. The record written in the Hebrew language about that garden, or Paradise, is no fable, no myth of peoples who veered away from worshiping their Creator.—Genesis 2:7–3:24.

⁶ More than 4,000 years later, the Christian apostle Paul was inspired to write: "Through one man sin entered into the world and death through sin, and thus death spread to all men because they had all sinned." (Romans 5:12) In another of his writings, he identified the one guilty man: "As in Adam all are dying, so also in the Christ all will be made alive." (1 Corinthians 15:22) A physician named Luke, in the 3rd chapter of his Gospel, traced Jesus' lineage all the way back to Adam, who, before being expelled from Eden, heard Jehovah's message of hope.—Luke 3: 23-38.

⁷ Naturally, you should want to know the content of that message. But before reading it, take note of the fact that for a long time Jehovah has been a hope giver. In the beginning Adam was God's earthly son, and God permitted him to produce offspring. If you foresaw a grim situation, you might want to encourage or give hope to your offspring. God did something similar. After Adam heard God's words of condemnation pronounced upon him personally, he heard words of hope for his descendants.

⁸ What were those words from this hope-instilling God? To a "serpent" involved in Adam's sin, God said: "I shall put enmity between you and the woman and between your seed and her seed [offspring]. He will bruise you in the head and you will bruise him in the heel." (Genesis 3:14, 15) You might wonder how those words could be said to raise up hope. First, we learn that "the serpent" was to have his head bruised.

⁹ In Revelation 12:9 it is written: "So down the great dragon was hurled, *the original serpent, the one called Devil and Satan,* who is misleading the entire inhabited earth; he was hurled down to the earth, and his angels were hurled down with him." Yes, "the serpent" involved in Eden was none other than the wicked spirit creature known as Satan the Devil. Not only did that symbolic serpent come to have angels in heaven but he has had a "seed" down here on earth, a "seed" that in due time will be crushed out of existence with him.

---

4. The United Nations is diverting mankind from what?
5. When was the basis for hope laid?
6. How did mankind come to need hope?

7. What encouraging thing did God do while Adam was yet alive?
8. How did Genesis 3:15 provide a basis for hope?
9. Who was "the serpent" referred to at Genesis 3:14, 15?

¹⁰ Confirming this identification of the Devil as being "the serpent" behind the downfall of our original parents, Jesus Christ said to Jewish religious leaders in the first century: "You are from your father the Devil, and you wish to do the desires of your father. That one was a manslayer when he began, and he did not stand fast in the truth . . . When he speaks the lie, he speaks according to his own disposition, because he is a liar and the father of the lie." (John 8:44) Jesus also called those religious opposers "offspring of vipers."—Matthew 12:34; 23:33.

Hope Kept Alive

¹¹ The divine promise of the bruising of the head of the symbolic serpent actually set a heartwarming hope before all the human family that was yet to come into existence. We can see why by examining other aspects of Genesis 3:15. The "seed" of the woman is mentioned. The identity of that "seed" was long left shrouded in mystery. But it was clear that Jehovah God would put that yet unidentified "seed" at enmity with the symbolic serpent and its anti-God "seed." Victory was promised, yes, guaranteed, for the "seed" of "the woman"! Its victory was set as a hope before mankind. So the members of the human family could hope for the coming of that "seed" of "the woman."

¹² Over the centuries, God revealed that this "seed" was his only-begotten Son, who was sent to earth to become the Messiah and to offer his life as a ransom sacrifice. (Genesis 22:17, 18; Galatians 3:16; 1 John 2:2; Revelation 5:9, 10) For this reason the hope of Jehovah's Witnesses does not rest

upon the United Nations. It rests on a living Jesus Christ, Chief Spokesman of Jehovah God. We can be confident that Christ is living, since he rose from the dead to be seated at the right hand of Jehovah in heaven. As Paul says: "If in this life only [which life includes our 20th century] we have hoped in Christ, we are of all men most to be pitied. However, now Christ has been raised up from the dead, the firstfruits of those who have fallen asleep in death." (1 Corinthians 15:19, 20) As has often been Biblically established in the pages of this magazine, Jesus Christ is today installed as heavenly King.—Revelation 11:15.

¹³ Of course, Jesus has not replaced Jehovah as the hope of mankind. Psalm 37:34 still remains applicable: "Hope in Jehovah and keep his way, and he will exalt you to take possession of the earth. When the wicked ones are cut off, you will see it." It is still necessary to keep hoping

10. How did Jesus confirm the identification of "the serpent"?
11. What additional reason for hope did Genesis 3:15 provide?
12. In time, what more was revealed about the "seed" of "the woman"?

13, 14. Where do Jehovah's Witnesses place their hope, and what do they do about it?

in Jehovah and to encourage all peoples to leave off from hoping in man-made institutions.

14 In harmony with this fact, Jehovah's Witnesses are active in 208 lands, preaching the Kingdom good news. They cannot be stopped from doing so. Political institutions, aided and abetted by religious organizations, are without divine right in trying to stop them. We can continue to be witnesses of Jehovah and to hope in him, as did David of Bethlehem, who wrote:

15 "Jehovah is my shepherd; I shall not want. He maketh me to lie down in green pastures; he leadeth me beside still waters. He restoreth my soul: He guideth me in the paths of righteousness for his name's sake. Yea, though I walk through the valley of the shadow of death, I will fear no evil; for thou art with me; thy rod and thy staff, they comfort me. Thou preparest a table before me in the presence of mine enemies: Thou hast anointed my head with oil; my cup runneth over. Surely goodness and lovingkindness shall follow me all the days of my life; and I shall dwell in the house of Jehovah for ever."—Psalm 23, *American Standard Version.*

16 King David was Jehovah's spiritual shepherd for the tribes of ancient Israel, and he paved the way for Jerusalem to be the nation's capital, where his son Solomon reigned for 40 years. With good reason, Jesus Christ was spoken of as the "son of David." (Luke 1:31; 18:39; 20:41) If David hoped in Jehovah God, his earthly descendant Jesus Christ would do similarly. And he did.

17 As evidence that David's most famous earthly descendant, Jesus Christ, followed

the counsel of Psalm 37:34 when breathing his last on the torture stake, Jesus said: "Father, into your hands I entrust my spirit." (Luke 23:46) He was quoting and fulfilling David's words at Psalm 31:5, addressed to God: "Into your hand I entrust my spirit." Jesus' hope was not disappointed, any more than was that of King David. Christ was resurrected from the dead on the third day. Forty days later he returned to his heavenly Father. At the end of the Gentile Times in 1914, Jehovah exalted his Son to become Ruler of the earth.

A Time for Hope Now

18 Today, as the new year 6014 A.M. (in the Year of the World) carries the human family forward into the future, what hope can be entertained for the human family? That question is now most appropriate because we are nearly 1,900 years into the post-Bible era. It has been a long time since David wrote Psalm 37:34.

19 Jehovah God, the Almighty God who resurrected Jesus from the dead, has a far grander role for him than that conjured up by shortsighted men. By resurrecting and exalting his only-begotten Son to his right hand in the heavens, Jehovah God has added reason for us to look to Him with

18. Why is today an appropriate time for hope?
19. Jehovah did what for Jesus, giving us hope?

15. What sort of hope did King David have in Jehovah?
16. Why can it be said that Jesus had the same outlook as David had?
17. What evidence is there that Jesus hoped in Jehovah?

In Our Next Issue

- **Who Are the True Evangelizers?**

- **The Last Days —A Time of Harvest**

- **Ancient Coins Testify to Prophetic Truth**

unfailing hope, our ultimate hope. It can mean our everlasting life in happiness, just as the inspired writer Paul says: "We [are] saved in this hope."—Romans 8:24.

²⁰ The apostle goes on to say: "But hope that is seen is not hope, for when a man sees a thing, does he hope for it? But if we hope for what we do not see, we keep on waiting for it with endurance." (Romans 8: 24, 25) And so that original hope still lives on, yes, nears a glorious fulfillment upon the human race. (2 Peter 3:13; Revelation 21:4, 5) For the very reason that it is a hope for all mankind, it deserves to be made known to all. This is the idea of our "God of hope."

²¹ Now of all times is his time for this idea to be carried out. Even in our era when some nations of the UN have achieved scientific mastery of the very nucleus of all matter, the leaders of these governments do not feel the need to leave the solving of problems to some higher intelligence.—Compare Genesis 11:6.

²² As never before, popular religion is on the defensive, with its back against the wall. Its divisive influence must be done away with. The Bible shows that the ruling

20. Why can we say that Jehovah is still "the God of hope"?
21, 22. What can we expect the nations to do in the near future?

How Would You Answer?

☐ Why is the hope of the nations deceptive?

☐ How did God provide a basis for hope in Genesis 3:15?

☐ What was Jesus' position regarding Psalm 37:34?

☐ Why do we now have reason for hope?

---

elements will assert their superiority and divorce themselves from the parasitical religions that have been trying for so long a time to suck the worldly system of things for all that they can get. It is no surprise, then, that the political element will take this course. Their getting away safely with this attack on religion will indicate, from their point of view, that there is no God who deserves to be worshiped and served. The prophetic indication is that they will then turn against the witnesses of God, who remain. They will look for the easiest of victories over Jehovah's Witnesses as the finale of their anti-God campaign.—Revelation 17:12-17; Ezekiel 38: 10-23.

²³ However, they will finally get to know the shameful defeat that must come to one who dares to enter into conflict with Jehovah of armies, who has never lost a battle. That will make it unmistakably clear that they have been serving the ends of the chief opponent of the one true God, namely, "the serpent," Satan, "the god of this system of things."—2 Corinthians 4:4.

²⁴ What a humiliation this will mean for them! What they had hoped to demonstrate will prove to be the height of effrontery, provoking the very God of heaven and earth to righteous indignation. To puny mankind he could say: "'For the thoughts of you people are not my thoughts, nor are my ways your ways,' is the utterance of Jehovah. 'For as the heavens are higher than the earth, so my ways are higher than your ways, and my thoughts than your thoughts. For just as the pouring rain descends, and the snow, from the heavens and does not return to that place, unless it actually saturates the earth and makes it produce and sprout, and seed is actually given to the sower and

23, 24. How will Jehovah react to the nations' attack on his people?

bread to the eater, so my word that goes forth from my mouth will prove to be. It will not return to me without results, but it will certainly do that in which I have delighted, and it will have certain success in that for which I have sent it.'"—Isaiah 55:8-11.

²⁵ This Creator of man has put into the human heart keen sensitiveness, such as he himself has. "For this is what Jehovah of armies has said, 'Following after the

---

25. Why, then, do we now have good reason to look to Jehovah as our "God of hope"?

glory he has sent me to the nations that were despoiling you people; for he that is touching you is touching my eyeball.'" (Zechariah 2:8) So, then, Jehovah's Witnesses will have to hope in Jehovah. He will measure up to that hope to the most beauteous embellishment of his universal sovereignty. He will prove beyond all further dispute that he is the most high, almighty, eternal God, who has lived up to the highest hopes of his creatures in all heaven and earth. Hallelujah!—Psalm 150:6.

Honoring the God of Hope

"The utterance of Jehovah is: . . . 'Those honoring me I shall honor, and those despising me will be of little account.'"—1 SAMUEL 2:30.

IN VIEW of the prospects that we can have, based on the Bible, it is altogether fitting and reasonable for us to honor "the God of hope," "the God who gives hope." (Romans 15:13, *King James Version; New World Translation*) Why is that? How can we, who are but tiny, imperfect humans, honor the Grand Creator of the entire universe? And will he honor us in return?

² We can learn from what occurred with Jesus. None of us would deny that Jesus always wanted his Father to be honored,

---

1. What reason do we have for wanting to honor Jehovah? (1 Timothy 1:17; Revelation 4:11)
2. How did Jesus feel about honor being given to God?

glorified. (John 5:23; 12:28; 15:8) In fact, Jesus criticized Pharisees and scribes who 'honored God with their lips but whose hearts were far removed from him.' Please note, their not honoring God involved inappropriate motives and actions. (Matthew 15:7-9) Can we, though, say that in Christ's honoring God, his hope was involved? And how did Jehovah respond to being thus honored?

³ Jesus took to heart David's words at Psalm 16:10: "You will not leave my soul in Sheol. You will not allow your loyal one to

---

3. How do we know that Jesus hoped in Jehovah?

see the pit." Because he had this hope of being resurrected, Jesus Christ could say electrifying words to an evildoer impaled beside him: "Truly I tell you today, You will be with me in Paradise." (Luke 23:39-43) That evildoer soon died, so he was not able three days later to witness the confirmation of Jesus' hope of being raised. But an eyewitness reported: "This Jesus God resurrected, of which fact we are all witnesses." (Acts 2:31, 32) It was a fact.

4 Many of the common people to whom Jesus ministered knew that he merited esteem, or honor. (Luke 4:15; 19:36-38; 2 Peter 1:17, 18) Then he died like a criminal. Did that change things? No, for Jesus had the approval of the God in whom he hoped. Thus, Jehovah brought him back to life. The fact that "the God of hope" raised his Son to life and clothed him with immortality in the spirit realm proves that the Father was continuing to honor his Son. Paul says: "We behold Jesus . . . crowned with glory and honor for having suffered death, that he by God's undeserved kindness might taste death for every man." —Hebrews 2:7, 9; Philippians 2:9-11.

5 Jesus, who had honored Jehovah, mentioned one special way in which the Father honored him. In an appearance to his faithful apostles, he said: "All authority has been given me in heaven and on the earth. Go therefore and make disciples of people of all the nations, baptizing them in the name of the Father and of the Son and of the holy spirit . . . Look! I am with you all the days until the conclusion of the system of things." (Matthew 28:18-20) So the Father additionally honored the Son by giving him unique authority. This was to be used in behalf of humans who would do a work that brings honor to the One whom

Jesus strives to honor. Does this mean, then, that we imperfect humans can in some way honor the Father and be honored by him in return?

Humans Honor God

6 Most humans hardly think of honoring God first, for they are more interested in gaining honor for themselves. Some might even say that it is normal for us to want to be honored. There is a measure of truth in this, as it is normal to desire a good reputation, with a measure of honor from this. (1 Timothy 3:2, 13; 5:17; Acts 28:10) Yet, the desire for honor from men can easily be exaggerated. This is evident by the many who will chase fame at any cost or who will do anything to save face.

7 When you think about it, even the greatest honor from men is fleeting, for all soon die. Oh, the memory of a few heroes may be honored for a while, but most of the dead are forgotten. How many people know their great-grandparents' names or know who were the leaders of their nation a hundred years ago? Actually, whether someone lived or did not live does not change matters. He is but a minute speck of dust on the scales of time, a tiny drop in the stream of life. And even if he is honored briefly after death, he is unaware of it. (Job 14:21; 2 Chronicles 32:33; Ecclesiastes 9:5; Psalm 49:12, 20) The only thing that can make a difference is having the hope that God provides, honoring him, and being honored in return. We can see this in the lives of two contemporaries in ancient Israel.

8 Eli was one. He served God in the unique position of high priest for 40 years

---

4. What honor did Jesus merit and receive? (Revelation 5:12)
5. In what special way was Jesus honored, resulting in what added honor to God?

6. Is it appropriate to desire to be honored, but what danger exists in this? (Luke 14:10)
7. Why is being honored by men of such limited value?
8. Eli fell into what trap involving the giving of honor?

and was also privileged to judge Israel. (1 Samuel 1:3, 9; 4:18) Nonetheless, in time he showed weakness concerning his sons Hophni and Phinehas. Though being priests, they abused their office by stealing parts of the sacrifices and by engaging in immoral sex. When their father did little more than mildly criticize them, God declared that Eli 'kept honoring his sons more than me.' Jehovah had promised to continue the Aaronic priesthood, but he would cut off the house of Eli from the high-priestly office. Why? God explained: "Those honoring me I shall honor, and those despising me will be of little account."—1 Samuel 2:12-17, 29-36; 3: 12-14.

⁹ In contrast there was Samuel. You likely know that his parents brought him at a young age to serve at the tabernacle in Shiloh. One night Jehovah spoke to the lad. You may enjoy reading this account at 1 Samuel 3:1-14, imagining this boy's being awakened, not by a thunderous roar, but by a low voice that he mistook for elderly Eli's. Then think how intimidating it must have been for young Samuel to have to tell the aged high priest of God's determination to punish the house of Eli. Yet Samuel did it; he honored God by obedience.—1 Samuel 3:18, 19.

¹⁰ Samuel honored Jehovah for years as a prophet, and God honored him. Note this at 1 Samuel 7:7-13. Jehovah quickly responded to Samuel's prayer for help to defeat the Philistines. Would you not feel honored to have such divine recognition? When Samuel's sons did not follow his lead, God did not reject him as he had rejected Eli. This evidently was because Samuel did all he could to honor God. Further showing this, Samuel disapproved of the people's request for a human king. (1 Samuel 8:6, 7) God used Samuel to anoint both Saul and David. At Samuel's death, Israel honored him by mourning. More importantly, however, God honored him by mentioning him in the Bible among men of faith who will be blessed with a resurrection and the good

9. How was Samuel given the opportunity to honor Jehovah?

10. In response to being honored, how did God honor Samuel?

things God has in store for them. (Psalm 99:6; Jeremiah 15:1; Hebrews 11:6, 16, 32, 39, 40) Does this not show that honoring "the God of hope" is of great value?

Will You Honor "the God of Hope"?

[11] The cases of Jesus and Samuel, to give just two Bible examples, establish that humans can put honoring their "God of hope" as the highest priority in life. And those two cases show that by our doing so we can fittingly seek and receive honor from God. But how can you do this with reasonable assurance that you will please God, will be honored by him, and will attain your Bible-based hope?

[12] Having a genuine, respectful fear of displeasing God is one way. (Malachi 1:6) Likely we readily agree with that statement. Yet, remember Eli's sons. If you had asked them whether they wanted to honor God by respectfully fearing him, most likely they would have said yes. The problem comes in translating into the reality of actions in everyday life our desire to honor God by fearing him.

[13] If we are faced with a tempting situation in which we could steal or engage in some sexual impropriety without its becoming general knowledge, would our desire to honor God affect our actions? We ought to cultivate the feeling, 'Even if the wrongdoing could remain hidden, my very giving in to such sin is a dishonor to "the God of hope" whose name I bear.' And the fact is that the wrong will not permanently remain hidden, any more than did the things that Eli's sons committed. This is borne out by Paul's words concerning "God's righteous judgment": "He will render to each one according to his works:

everlasting life to those who are seeking glory and honor and incorruptibleness by endurance in work that is good; however, for those who are contentious and who disobey the truth but obey unrighteousness there will be wrath and anger."—Romans 2:5-8.

[14] On the other hand, Paul mentions participation "in work that is good," which honors God and results in "glory and honor" from him. A primary work of this kind today is what Jesus mentioned at Matthew 28:19, 20: 'Make disciples of people of all the nations, baptizing them and teaching them to observe all the things that I have commanded you.' Earth wide, millions of Jehovah's Witnesses are active in this God-honoring preaching and teaching work. Many are even exerting themselves to be full-time ministers as pioneers, either on a permanent basis or during vacation from secular work or school. With this in mind, each one of us can beneficially consider how he stands as to this work. You might ask, for example, 'Am I honoring "the God of hope" by having a full share in the preaching work?'

[15] Some Christians who for years were active preachers have gradually slowed down. They have settled into a pattern of having only a small or infrequent share in the important disciple-making work. We do not mean individuals who have physical limitations and slow down because of the effects of old age. Quite aside from such, a slowing down is seen among certain Witnesses of various ages. Interestingly, Paul was not referring to a certain age group when he warned Christians against 'tiring out.' Rather, no matter what a person's age, the crux of the matter is that regular

---

11, 12. What do we need to consider about honoring Jehovah, and what is one way for us to do that?
13. Illustrate how a desire to honor God by fearing him can help us.

14. What is another way in which we can honor God, and what might we ask ourselves?
15. What has happened to some Christians in regard to honoring Jehovah through the public ministry?

participation in the ministry requires effort. As evidently occurred in Paul's day, some today are reasoning, 'I've done my share over the years, so now newer Christians can exert themselves.'—Galatians 6:9; Hebrews 12:3.

16 Those who have been affected in this way are certainly in the minority, but you might ask, 'Do I frankly recognize any such tendency in my case? How does my share in the ministry compare with that in the past?' Whether any slowing down has occurred or not, we all should bear in mind that our "God of hope" promises to provide "glory and honor and peace for everyone who *works* what is good." (Romans 2:10) Paul used a Greek word that means "to work something, produce, perform." How vital it is that we avoid what befell the Pharisees and scribes, who simply honored God by a form of lip service! (Mark 7:6; Revelation 2:10) Conversely, when from the heart we actively share in the public ministry, we confirm to ourselves and to others that we do have a real hope. We honor our Creator and Life-giver. And we come in line to be honored by him, now and endlessly.—Luke 10:1, 2, 17-20.

With Our Valuable Things

17 As to one other way in which we can honor our "God of hope," Proverbs 3:9 says: "Honor Jehovah with your valuable things and with the firstfruits of all your produce." Spurrell renders this verse: "Glorify Jehovah with thy wealth, and with the best of all thine increase."—*A Translation of the Old Testament Scriptures from the Original Hebrew.*

18 Since various clergymen have become notorious for their boundless greed and opulent life-style, many individuals hesitate to give to churches and religious organizations whose aim clearly seems to be just the gaining of wealth. (Revelation 18: 4-8) Such abuses, however, do not alter the validity of Proverbs 3:9. In accord with that inspired counsel, how can we use our "valuable things" to "honor Jehovah," our "God of hope"?

19 Jehovah's Witnesses find that the growing number of people responding to the Kingdom message requires the expanding of Kingdom Halls or the building of new ones. Here, then, is one way to "glorify Jehovah with thy wealth." Young and old have shared in doing this, such as by personally resolving to contribute toward the building funds. To hold to such secret resolves may take personal discipline or even some sacrifice, particularly if the planning and completing of a building project extends over a long period of time. (2 Corinthians 9:6, 7) Still, using funds in this way truly honors Jehovah, for the Kingdom Halls are places where Christians worship him and where they and their associates gain knowledge of God. Jesus' words at Matthew 6:3, 4 give us good reason to trust that God will honor those who have thus honored him.

20 A word of caution, though: The Pharisees and scribes, who Jesus said were not putting foremost the honoring of God, made sure that they were the first ones to benefit from their wealth. So the counsel at Matthew 15:4-8 recommends that we submit to self-scrutiny as to 'honoring Jehovah with our valuable things.' (Jeremiah 17:9, 10) For example, a Christian who has become somewhat wealthy through his

16. Why might we benefit from self-examination in this regard?
17, 18. What is another way in which we can honor God, and why is reluctance to do so not valid?

19. Illustrate how some have applied Proverbs 3:9.
20. (a) Why is self-scrutiny in order in applying Proverbs 3:9? (b) What questions might we ask ourselves?

business might rationalize his continuing to work full-time so as to earn still more. He might reason, 'Others enter the pioneer ministry or move to serve where preachers are especially needed, but my special way to serve God is by earning more and then having plenty to donate.' His contributions may do much good. But he could well ask, 'Does my personal life-style reflect that using money in honoring God is my *primary* motive for earning more and more?' (Luke 12:16-19; compare Mark 12:41-44.) And, 'Could I arrange my affairs to have a greater personal share in the most important work for our day—declaring the good news?' In fact, no matter what our circumstances in life are, we can examine our motives and actions and ask, 'How can I more fully honor my Life-giver and "God of hope"?'

21 Jehovah will not disappoint us. What a delightful prospect it is that he might, now and on into the future, say about us

_____
21. What prospect do we have if we honor Jehovah now?

How Would You Answer?

□ As to humans honoring Jehovah, what can we learn from Jesus' example?

□ How did Eli and Samuel differ regarding honoring God?

□ What are some ways in which you can increase the honor you bring to God, and what response may you receive?

□ What future awaits those who put first the honoring of our "God of hope"?

what he said of faithful Israel: "Owing to the fact that you have been precious in my eyes, you have been considered honorable, and I myself have loved you"! (Isaiah 43:4) That same One promises "everlasting life to those who are seeking glory and honor." This promise he directs to those who endure "in work that is good." What a "God of hope"!

LETTERS ABOUT CONTRIBUTIONS

Here are some excerpts from letters received by the Brooklyn, New York, office of the Watch Tower Society:

"My name is Abijah. I am nine years old. I want to give you $4 for the brothers working on the Kingdom Halls. They can use it for lumber or for a candy bar, I don't mind."—Oregon.

'You will find enclosed my personal check. I am past 96 years old and very hard of hearing, but I really enjoy saving my money for this. Yes, I know, I am driving a secondhand car, and I do not spend my winters in Florida or California. I can do such a little toward getting the good news of the Kingdom preached by knocking on doors. But by saving my money and sending some to you, I feel that I am still having a part in it.'—Ohio.

'Thank you for everything you did for the Kingdom Hall. This money [$5] is to help you with books and *The Watchtowers* for us to read. The money is from my piggybank. Thanks for the *School* brochure to tell us about drugs.'

"Enclosed please find a check. Two hundred dollars of it is for the Kingdom Hall Building Fund. The rest is to be used any way you see fit to promote the preaching work."—Missouri.

Ignoring Warnings and Testing God

"Not even with the water up to their ankles did they want to escape."—*El País,* Colombia.

THAT headline from a Colombian daily newspaper highlighted one of the reasons for the terrible loss of life in the Armero avalanche disaster of November 1985. Dora Elisa Rada Esguerra, a telephone operator in Armero, alerted by the falling ash and overflowing river, decided to flee. Then she warned her fellow workers at the telephone exchange of the oncoming tragedy. She later explained: "They saw the water, that was . . . flowing strongly, very strongly, but even then they did not move." Dora escaped from the doomed city.

The other telephone operators died along with some 21,000 other victims in a torrent of volcanic mud, ice, and boulders that roared down from the volcano Nevado del Ruiz. Among those swept away were the mayor of the town and most of the local police force, which indicates that hardly anybody took the threat seriously—until it was too late.

Why Did They Not Flee?

There were signs and warnings of the impending disaster. Why did so many people in Armero ignore them? In the first place, official warnings came late, when disaster was already striking the city. Prior to this, the people had been told to be calm, that there might be flooding but that it would be nothing serious. Instead, the city was wiped off the map by a vast wall of death that poured down the river Lagunilla.

Likely, some did not want to abandon their homes and their possessions, knowing that pillagers would soon sneak in and steal. This turned out to be a real threat. A few looters were shot by the army. Some who survived the disaster came back to their flooded homes to find that locks had been shot off the doors and valuables had been stolen. But the majority of the townspeople never lived long enough to come back to their homes. And in most cases, there were no homes to come back to.

Perhaps others felt that God or the Virgin Mary would intervene in their behalf. Yet, is it reasonable to expect God to intervene today in behalf of certain persons when natural disasters occur? Why should some be saved by divine intervention and others, in similar conditions, be allowed to perish?

Is there a solid basis for a person to believe that he can lead a charmed life with special protection from God? For example, can a car driver trust in

A diploma found in the ruins of Armero is a grim reminder that thousands did not heed warnings

Do your driving habits reflect Christian soundness of mind?

apostles. King Herod, out to gain favor with the Jews, had Peter imprisoned under heavy guard. The congregation in Jerusalem prayed intensely in his behalf. What happened? Jehovah's angel came and released Peter from jail. Even Peter was astonished by what was happening. Eventually he realized what was going on and said: "Now I actually know that Jehovah sent his angel forth and delivered me out of Herod's hand." —Acts 12:1-11.

The same account tells us that Herod had already done away with the apostle James, the brother of John. Jehovah allowed that martyrdom to take place. Therefore, it is evident that while Jehovah can give protection and deliverance, he may permit events to take their course, and so allow some of his devoted servants to prove their integrity even to death. The words of James, the half brother of Jesus, are appropriate: "You do not know what your life will be tomorrow. For you are a mist appearing for a little while and then disappearing. Instead, you ought to say: 'If Jehovah wills, we shall live and also do this or that.'"—James 4:14, 15; compare Job 2:3-5.

One thing is sure, in times of natural disasters and accidents, the Bible principle applies equally to all people: "Time and unforeseen occurrence befall them all." (Ecclesiastes 9:11) And while it is appropriate to pray for help and protection in times of persecution, we have to recognize that "persecution is inevitable for those who are determined to live really Chris-

his "guardian angel" or favorite "saint"? Too many sincere Catholics with "Saint" Christopher medallions have died in car accidents for that to be credible. Or should a Christian believe that he has God's special protection when traveling in an airplane? What about special protection when sharing in some dangerous sport? Is it reasonable to test God in those circumstances?

Jehovah's Hand Not Short

The Scriptures help us to see that there are situations in which Jehovah God might intervene in behalf of his people when the preaching of the Kingdom good news is affected or when his congregation is threatened. The prophet Isaiah assures us: "Look! The hand of Jehovah has not become too short that it cannot save, nor has his ear become too heavy that it cannot hear."—Isaiah 59:1.

The Bible gives clear examples of Jehovah's protecting hand in relation to the

tian lives."—2 Timothy 3:12, *Phillips*.

A Spirit of a Sound Mind

While it is true that in times past Jehovah has acted to protect his people, as when he saved Israel from Egypt and from Pharaoh's armies, it would be presumptuous to think that God must protect each Christian from the results of 'time and unforeseen circumstance' or from the consequences of his own imprudence. Paul's letter to the Christians in Rome, some of whom perhaps died later in the arena as martyrs, has a bearing on this: "I tell everyone there among you not to think more of himself than it is necessary to think; but to think so as to have a sound mind, each one as God has distributed to him a measure of faith." (Romans 12:3) J. B. Phillips' translation states: "Try to have a sane estimate of your capabilities."

The counsel expressed here has equal application today, although in a different context. If a Christian imagines that he can drive carelessly or under the influence of alcohol and get away with it because he has God's protection, does that display "a sound mind"? Does the Christian have 'a sane estimate of his capabilities'? Also, if he puts his fellowman in jeopardy, does he really 'love his neighbor as himself'?
—Matthew 22:39.

Now let us apply the spirit of a sound mind to the situation where man has established communities in earthquake-prone areas or where active volcanoes represent a latent but real threat. A good

The now-desolated site where Armero stood. Over 20,000 persons perished here

example is the already cited area around the Nevado del Ruiz volcano in Colombia. According to the Colombian daily *El País,* architect César Zárate prepared a study in 1982 that indicated that the Lagunilla River had flooded Armero in the past and that the city was still without adequate defenses. It was also known that the Nevado del Ruiz volcano had erupted six times since 1570. According to historical sources, the volcano has a regular cycle of

This demolished automobile epitomizes the disaster that struck Armero

activity that alternates between 140 years 9 months and 110 years 2 months.

This information was sent to the Sunday edition of the Colombian newspaper *El Tiempo* some weeks prior to the Armero disaster. It stated categorically: "The next flood . . . will take place about the middle of November of this year. The characteristic signs have already been observed: smoke from the 'Arenas' crater. A rain of ashes and gases. Contamination of the water and the crops. Nauseous smells. . . . A roaring sound originating in the volcano on September 11. Progressive thawing of the snowcap . . . Consequently, it is time to act."

However, the article was not published. Perhaps it was viewed as unnecessary calamity howling. *El Tiempo's* editors later put it down to "a lack of foresight, a lack of intuition, or the naive belief that nothing would happen."

Right on schedule, though, Nevado del Ruiz blew its top on the night of November 13, 1985. More than 20,000 people lost their lives in Armero, and there were thousands of victims from Chinchiná and other nearby towns. Among those who died in Armero were 41 of Jehovah's Witnesses and their associates. Some inadvisably had fled to the Kingdom Hall, which was on lower ground. They were swept away and entombed with it. Happily, other Witnesses were able to flee to higher ground and were saved.

Obviously, wisdom after the fact is easy. But at least lessons can be learned from those terrible events.

Ancient Warnings Ignored

The Bible offers examples of some who ignored timely warnings or thought 'it couldn't happen in their time' or in their area of the earth. One clear case is when Lot was warned to flee from Sodom and Gomorrah. He alerted his sons-in-law,

saying: "Get up! Get out of this place, because Jehovah is bringing the city to ruin!" How did they react? "In the eyes of his sons-in-law [Lot] seemed like a man who was joking." The "joke" was short-lived. Jehovah made it rain sulfur and fire upon the doomed, perverse cities. The sons-in-law died along with the immoral inhabitants of that region. Lot's wife evidently fled from Sodom with doubts and misgivings. She "began to look around from behind [Lot], and she became a pillar of salt."—Genesis 19:12-26.

Over 1,900 years ago, Jesus prophesied that ancient Jerusalem would undergo a terrible destruction. He gave specific details of events that would take place before the city's desolation, saying: "When you see Jerusalem surrounded by encamped armies, then know that the desolating of her has drawn near." He added the warning: "Then let those in Judea begin fleeing to the mountains, and let those in the midst of her withdraw, and let those in the country places not enter into her."—Luke 21:20-24.

When the Roman armies surrounded Jerusalem in the year 66 C.E., the Christians in that city recognized the sign that Jesus had given. Then, with total conquest within his grasp, General Cestius Gallus inexplicably withdrew his troops. That was the opportunity the Christians were waiting for, and they fled to the other side of the Jordan. In 70 C.E. the Romans returned under General Titus and destroyed Jerusalem. Hundreds of thousands of Jews who stayed on in the doomed city died during the siege and the fighting.

True, in these cases divine warning was given. But the point is that only a few heeded the message and escaped. The majority took no note. They refused to take God's warning seriously.

In What Way Can We Rightly Test God?

Even with natural disasters, there are often warnings—the previous history of the area, recent signs, or scientific data—that indicate a strong possibility of danger within a certain time period. Perhaps an area is prone to flooding. Then a reasonable person must weigh all the factors to decide if a move to another district is necessary and viable. Of course, it is impossible to predict the time and place of every natural disaster. Still, the law of averages can be taken into account and also the margin for safety if the worst happens. But it is not reasonable to expect special protection from God. To do so would be to put God to the test in a way that is not licit or balanced.

However, in a different sense, Jehovah does invite us to test him. Back in the time of the prophet Malachi, Israel was wrongly testing God by presenting shoddy sacrifices on the altar. By their polluted bread and lame animal offerings, they showed that they despised Jehovah's table. Through Malachi, Jehovah invited them to turn around and rectify their course of action. "'Bring all the tenth parts into the storehouse, that there may come to be food in my house; and test me out, please, in this respect,' Jehovah of armies has said, 'whether I shall not open to you people the floodgates of the heavens and actually empty out upon you a blessing until there is no more want.'"—Malachi 3:10.

Yes, in regard to spiritual blessings, we can "test," or prove, Jehovah's faithfulness. If we seek first his Kingdom and his righteousness, then, as Jesus said, all 'other necessary things will be added to us.' Jesus also said: "Keep on asking, and it will be given you; keep on seeking, and you will find; keep on knocking, and it will be opened to you." If imperfect men give kind gifts to their children, "how much more so will your Father who is in the heavens give good things to those asking him [in accordance with his will]?"—Matthew 6:33; 7:7-11; 1 John 5:14.

At this very time, a warning is being given to the nations to the effect that soon Jehovah will initiate his act of retribution against all parts of Satan's system of things. (Revelation 16:14, 16; 18:20) Millions of prudent people are heeding this message preached by Jehovah's Witnesses and are separating themselves to the side of God's Kingdom rule. They are getting out of the corrupt political and religious alliance before it is too late. (Revelation 18:4) By so doing, they are preparing for everlasting life under Christ's rulership of our earth, which will be transformed into a paradise of justice and equity. Are you heeding this warning? —2 Peter 3:13; Titus 1:2.

Search for the Truth Rewarded

FINDING little satisfaction as a lay preacher in the Presbyterian Church, a gentleman started looking for God's true church. He drew up ten requirements that he felt the true church should have. He already had an accurate understanding of the unscripturalness of hellfire, immortality of the soul, and so forth. For 30 years he conducted this search. When contacted by one of Jehovah's Witnesses, he began firing his questions, such as: "Who is the little flock? Who are the 144,000 and the other sheep?" Getting satisfying answers, he agreed to a Bible study. After three months he said to the Witness: "Well, Brother, the true church of God is Jehovah's Witnesses." He is now 71 years of age and happy that he has found the true church after a 30-year search!

Jehovah Builds a House

SATURDAY, March 21, 1987, was a day that the staff of the Watch Tower Society's South Africa branch will never forget. It was a historic occasion. The new complex at Roodekrans was dedicated—the culmination of six years of hard work. But the honor goes to Jehovah. As Solomon expressed it: "Unless Jehovah himself builds the house, it is to no avail that its builders have worked hard on it." —Psalm 127:1.

Let us briefly trace the growth of Jehovah's Witnesses in South Africa. In 1902 the first two local individuals started studying the Society's publications and preaching to others. In 1910 Will Johnston was directed by Brother Russell to open a one-man branch office in Durban. The next year one of the first African congregations was organized in nearby Ndwedwe. During the crucial year of 1914, the first convention was held in Durban and had an attendance of 50. The branch was moved to Cape Town in 1923, and the following year a simple press was put in use. The branch was moved to larger premises in 1933, but there was no Bethel Home.

Still another important move took place in 1952, to Elandsfontein—some 1,500 kilometers north of Cape Town and about 20 kilometers east of Johannesburg. It was the first of the buildings in South Africa that was actually designed by the Society, so it included ample space for printing as well as a Bethel Home, or residence. Meanwhile, the Kingdom work was opening up in several countries cared for by the South Africa branch. So the branch needed to be expanded in 1959, again in 1971, and yet again in 1978. Then there was no room for further expansion at that site.

The original two publishers in South Africa had increased to about 28,000. It was time to look for a new place, which involved a long search. At last a fine farm of 87 hectares was found at Roodekrans, which is some 60 kilometers from Elandsfontein. Jehovah's guidance and help were very evident in the finding and purchasing of this lovely place.

Overcoming Problems

However, serious problems had to be overcome. The initial cost seemed huge, and special permits were needed to build a factory, offices, and a residence in a municipal area. An added complication was the desirability of having black Witnesses who were translators live there. It seemed miraculous how these obstacles were overcome, giving evidence that Jehovah was building the house. Another problem was a serious lack of artisans. But volunteer workers were quick to learn the various trades. This included sisters. One overseer remarked: "Refined young girls who don't fit on a building site became expert tilers. I've never seen better."

Construction work went slowly at first. Then volunteers flocked to Roodekrans —blacks, whites, Colored, and Indians. Brothers even came from other countries, such as New Zealand and the United States. This was very unusual in South Africa. "It's beautiful to see brothers and sisters working together, different nationalities and races from different backgrounds," said one volunteer. Many gave up good jobs or took long leaves to help with the construction at Roodekrans. They included experienced mechanics, an architect, an engineer, qualified draftsmen, and construction overseers. Much expensive machinery was donated or loaned.

How about the enormous cost involved? The Governing Body of Jehovah's Witnesses made provision for a very substantial loan, and local Witnesses of all races and all ages contributed generously. A girl

near an attractive suburb, there is still wildlife present, such as guinea fowl and hares. Black eagles and jackals often pay a visit too. The residence building, strung along the lower slopes of the hills for some 360 meters, is of red brick. It has three stories, with beautiful views. In the center is a service area with a dining room, a kitchen, a laundry, and an infirmary. Nearby are the office block and a huge printery, which is roughly the size of Noah's ark. It houses the large four-color TKS offset press.

of six wrote: "I was saving this money to buy a doll, but I am sending it to you. I hope you can finish Roodekrans with this money. When I am big, I also want to go to Roodekrans and work there." A five-year-old Indian boy contributed his pocket money from the previous six months!

On weekends hundreds of additional Witnesses came to share in this vital project. Other volunteers came on a daily basis, often making real sacrifices and putting forth great effort to do so. Non-Witness visitors shook their heads in disbelief at seeing the massive, enthusiastic support. Many people living in the vicinity were deeply impressed. Local commercial firms vied for business at Roodekrans, and their representatives often commented on the atmosphere of peace and unity.

A Majestic Building in a Beautiful Setting

Rocky hills on the southern side of the construction site overlook a pleasant valley and stream. Although the property is

To the west of the residence building is a farming area and a large barn, which was used as the dining room and kitchen during the construction. Fields of grass and alfalfa provide fodder for a herd of milk cows. There are hundreds of protea shrubs on the hills behind the residence. In addition to existing tall eucalyptus trees, many new trees, colorful flower beds, and spacious lawns have been planted.

The Dedication Program

A crowd of about 4,000 gathered in an open space near the residence building for the dedication on Saturday afternoon, March 21, 1987. A temporary platform faced the hills, giving the effect of an amphitheater. The chairman, Brother R. F. Stow, read supportive messages from 17 countries. The most moving of these was from Maud Johnston, the wife of the first branch overseer in Durban. At 92 years of age, she is still serving in the Australia Bethel.

P. J. Wentzel, overseer of the Service

Department, was the first speaker, and he gave a brief summary of the history of Kingdom work in South Africa. He compared the attendance of 50 at the first assembly in 1914 with the attendance of 99,000 at the 1986 conventions. Next, J. R. Kikot, factory overseer, described the printing of literature in many languages and the work of over 50 translators. He mentioned also that in 1979 a large TKS press, a gift from the Japan branch, was installed, but it printed in only two colors. Recently, two more units, also a gift from Japan, were added to the press. As a result, *The Watchtower* of April 1, 1987, was printed in full color, to the delight of all.

C. F. Muller, the coordinator of the Branch Committee, described how Jehovah helped to provide the site, the funds, the experts, and the skilled workers. God's spirit also produced fine harmony among the various races. Though at one stage it seemed impossible to build a factory in a prime residential area and for blacks to live there, Jehovah opened the way, so he was the real Master Builder!

The next speaker was Carey Barber, a member of the Governing Body of Jehovah's Witnesses. His fine talk was based on Isaiah 65:17-19, which foretells how Jehovah's people will "exult . . . and be joyful forever." The speaker explained that "exult" means "to leap for joy" and that it is the supreme form of happiness. It certainly was a very happy day for those present. The dedication talk was given by Milton Henschel, also of the Governing Body. He offered a special prayer to Jehovah, giving thanks for providing the building, which was now dedicated to Him.

The next day 28,250 Witnesses and interested persons gathered in the Rand Stadium, Johannesburg, where they heard a brief summary of the program at Roodekrans. In a talk translated into Zulu, Henschel showed how Jehovah's Witnesses, led by Jehovah and Jesus, are triumphant everywhere and spreading "a sweet odor of Christ" and other Bible knowledge. (2 Corinthians 2:14-17) He concluded with many encouraging experiences that delighted the vast audience.

During the next few days, similar gatherings were held in Durban and Cape Town. These were occasions that will never be forgotten by Jehovah's Witnesses in South Africa. The Bethel family at Roodekrans will certainly long remember the dedication of their new home. With over 40,000 Witnesses currently active in South Africa instead of the 28,000 when work began at Roodekrans, the 'house that Jehovah built' fills an urgent and vital need.

Do You Remember?

Have you found the recent issues of *The Watchtower* of practical value to you? Then why not test your memory with the following:

□ Why was Timothy such a fine example for youths to follow?

Timothy sacrificed a so-called normal life at home to become a reliable, faithful companion of Paul. He stuck with Paul through thick and thin, supporting him in the preaching work and being willing to serve wherever assigned. (Philippians 2:19, 20) —8/15, page 14.

□ What are the qualifications for baptism?

The baptismal candidate must comprehend what is involved. He must truly want to serve Jehovah because he loves Him. He shows this by adhering to God's moral requirements and sharing his faith with others. He also needs to make a personal dedication to Jehovah in prayer. —8/15, page 16.

□ Why is it wrong to explore spiritism?

Exploring spiritism amounts to loving what Jehovah hates. (Proverbs 6:16-19) Actually, it is like rejecting Jehovah and siding with God's archenemy and his supporters. —9/1, page 5.

□ What is the "book of remembrance" spoken of in Malachi 3:16?

From the time of Abel forward, God has been noting, as if writing down in a book, those of redeemable mankind who are worthy of being remembered as to everlasting life. This "book of remembrance" is the same as "the

book of life" and "the scroll of life." (Revelation 3:5; 17:8; Matthew 23:35)—9/1, page 29.

□ What makes a true friend so precious?

You can always turn to a true friend for help, advice, comfort, and warm companionship. —9/15, pages 3, 4.

□ What is the death-dealing "air" of this world?

It is the general spirit, or dominant attitude of selfishness and disobedience, reflected by people alienated from God. (Ephesians 2:2; 1 Corinthians 2:12) —9/15, page 11.

□ For a religion to be of practical value, what must it do?

It must bear good fruit. It must produce better people. It must be able to explain why things are as they are on earth today. And it should instill in people's minds and hearts a sure hope for the future. (Matthew 7:17-20) —10/1, page 7.

□ What did the Reformation fail to accomplish?

Some early reformers dreamed of returning to Bible standards, to pure Christianity. This dream was never realized. With the passage of time, basic doctrines of Protestant churches, whether national or otherwise, fell largely into line with those of the Roman Catholic Church. —10/1, page 25.

□ What led to God's adverse judgment of Moses and Aaron following the incident at Kadesh-barnea?

Psalm 106:32, 33 gives an insight into this incident, showing that Moses acted out of a bitter

spirit and 'spoke rashly with his lips.' With angry words, he called attention to himself and Aaron rather than to Jehovah, who really could miraculously provide water. In this way Moses failed to 'sanctify God before the eyes of the people.' (Numbers 27:12-14) —10/15, page 31.

□ What lofty purpose was served by God's Law given to Israel?

The Law was given to Israel in order to keep the nation clean physically, spiritually, mentally, and morally. —11/1, page 12.

□ What are some aids to maintaining chaste singleness?

Pray regularly for God's spirit and his help to display its fruitage. Ponder over and apply the counsel in God's Word. Avoid pornography and immoral entertainment. Guard your associations. Shun all unclean speech and obscene jesting. —11/15, page 20.

□ What crucial differences are there between the cures reported in the Bible and those reported by faith healers today?

Jesus and his disciples never charged fees for their cures. Healings performed in Bible times either were instantaneous or were accomplished within a short period of time. —12/1, pages 4, 5.

□ What are some of the benefits of singing aloud in true worship?

Our personal involvement in public worship becomes stronger. Singing gives a good witness to newcomers. Most importantly, greater praise is brought to Jehovah. —12/1, page 27.

SUBJECT INDEX FOR *THE WATCHTOWER* 1987

Indicating date of issue in which article appears

Advertising
—What It Can Accomplish

FOR years the back page of *The Watchtower* has carried an advertisement for Bible literature. Recently, a letter from Georgia, U.S.A., praised these advertisements. The writer explained that the married couple with whom she and her husband study the Bible have responded to these ads and have obtained, among other publications, cassette tapes of *My Book of Bible Stories*. Later, they purchased the *Bible Stories* book itself. The writer explains the effect that this book has had upon that couple:

"They have been given a historical background from Adam forward that just this week resulted in their being able to see the different races of men in the proper light. After reading a few scriptures, such as Acts 17:26 and Genesis chapter 10, and referring to man's history from the *Bible Stories* book, Jim observed: 'I said I wasn't prejudiced before, but for the first time, tonight I can say it and really mean it.'"

The writer concluded: "Truly, your advertisements have led to much spiritual growth in a short time."

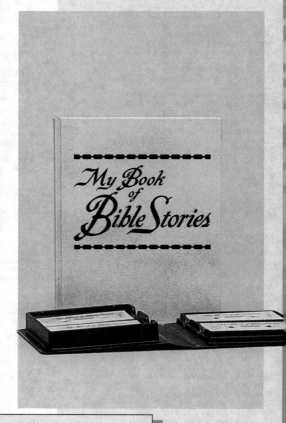